I0763283

LUCY MAUD MONTGOMERY

—

THE COMPLETE SHORT STORIES COLLECTION

Cover Photograph: twm1340

ISBN: 978-1-78139-239-3

Contents

LUCY MAUD MONTGOMERY SHORT STORIES, 1896 TO 1901

LUCY MAUD MONTGOMERY SHORT STORIES, 1902 TO 1903

LUCY MAUD MONTGOMERY SHORT STORIES, 1904

LUCY MAUD MONTGOMERY SHORT STORIES, 1905 TO 1906

LUCY MAUD MONTGOMERY SHORT STORIES, 1907 TO 1908

LUCY MAUD MONTGOMERY SHORT STORIES, 1909 TO 1922

LUCY MAUD MONTGOMERY SHORT STORIES, 1896 TO 1901

A Case of Trespass

It was the forenoon of a hazy, breathless day, and Dan Phillips was trouting up one of the back creeks of the Carleton pond. It was somewhat cooler up the creek than out on the main body of water, for the tall birches and willows, crowding down to the brim, threw cool, green shadows across it and shut out the scorching glare, while a stray breeze now and then rippled down the wooded slopes, rustling the beech leaves with an airy, pleasant sound.

Out in the pond the glassy water creamed and shimmered in the hot sun, unrippled by the faintest breath of air. Across the soft, pearly tints of the horizon blurred the smoke of the big factory chimneys that were owned by Mr. Walters, to whom the pond and adjacent property also belonged.

Mr. Walters was a comparative stranger in Carleton, having but recently purchased the factories from the heirs of the previous owner; but he had been in charge long enough to establish a reputation for sternness and inflexibility in all his business dealings.

One or two of his employees, who had been discharged by him on what they deemed insufficient grounds, helped to deepen the impression that he was an unjust and arbitrary man, merciless to all offenders, and intolerant of the slightest infringement of his cast-iron rules.

Dan Phillips had been on the pond ever since sunrise. The trout had risen well in the early morning, but as the day wore on, growing hotter and hotter, they refused to bite, and for half an hour Dan had not caught one.

He had a goodly string of them already, however, and he surveyed them with satisfaction as he rowed his leaky little skiff to the shore of the creek.

"Pretty good catch," he soliloquized. "Best I've had this summer, so far. That big spotted one must weigh near a pound. He's a beauty. They're a good price over at the hotels now, too. I'll go home and get my dinner and go straight over with them. That'll leave me time for another try at them about sunset. Whew, how hot it is! I must take Ella May home a bunch of them blue flags. They're real handsome!"

He tied his skiff under the crowding alders, gathered a big bunch of the purple flag lilies with their silky petals, and started homeward, whistling cheerily as he stepped briskly along the fern-carpeted wood path that wound up the hill under the beeches and firs.

He was a freckled, sunburned lad of thirteen years. His neighbours all said that Danny was "as smart as a steel trap," and immediately added that they wondered where he got his smartness from—certainly not from his father!

The elder Phillips had been denominated "shiftless and slack-twisted" by all who ever had any dealings with him in his unlucky, aimless life—one of those improvident, easygoing souls who sit contentedly down to breakfast with a very faint idea where their dinner is to come from.

When he had died, no one had missed him, unless it were his patient, sad-eyed wife, who bravely faced her hard lot, and toiled unremittingly to keep a home for her two children—Dan and a girl two years younger, who was a helpless cripple, suffering from some form of spinal disease.

Dan, who was old and steady for his years, had gone manfully to work to assist his mother. Though he had been disappointed in all his efforts to obtain steady employment, he was active and obliging, and earned many a small amount by odd jobs around the village, and by helping the Carleton farmers in planting and harvest.

For the last two years, however, his most profitable source of summer income had been the trout pond. The former owner had allowed anyone who wished to fish in his pond, and Dan made a regular business of it, selling his trout at the big hotels over at Mosquito Lake. This, in spite of its unattractive name, was a popular summer resort, and Dan always found a ready market for his catch.

When Mr. Walters purchased the property it somehow never occurred to Dan that the new owner might not be so complaisant as his predecessor in the matter of the best trouting pond in the country.

To be sure, Dan often wondered why it was the pond was so deserted this summer. He could not recall having seen a single person on it save himself. Still, it did not cross his mind that there could be any particular reason for this.

He always fished up in the cool, dim creeks, which long experience had taught him were best for trout, and came and went by a convenient wood path; but he had no thought of concealment in so doing. He would not have cared had all Carleton seen him.

He had done very well with his fish so far, and prices for trout at the Lake went up every day. Dan was an enterprising boy, and a general favourite with the hotel owners. They knew that he could always be depended on.

Mrs. Phillips met him at the door when he reached home.

"See, Mother," said Dan exultantly, as he held up his fish. "Just look at that fellow, will you? A pound if he's an ounce! I ought to get a good price for these, I can tell you. Let me have my dinner now, and I'll go right over to the Lake with them."

"It's a long walk for you, Danny," replied his mother pityingly, "and it's too hot to go so far. I'm afraid you'll get sun-struck or something. You'd better wait till the cool of the evening. You're looking real pale and thin this while back."

"Oh, I'm all right, Mother," assured Dan cheerfully. "I don't mind the heat a bit. A fellow must put up with some inconveniences. Wait till I bring home the money for these fish. And I mean to have another catch tonight. It's you that's looking tired. I wish you didn't have to work so hard, Mother. If I could only get a good place you could take it easier. Sam French says that Mr. Walters wants a boy up there at the factory, but I know I wouldn't do. I ain't big enough. Perhaps something will turn up soon though. When our ship comes in, Mother, we'll have our good times."

He picked up his flags and went into the little room where his sister lay.

"See what I've brought you, Ella May!" he said, as he thrust the cool, moist clusters into her thin, eager hands. "Did you ever see such beauties?"

"Oh, Dan, how lovely they are! Thank you ever so much! If you are going over to the Lake this afternoon, will you please call at Mrs. Henny's and get those nutmeg geranium slips she promised me? Just look how nice my others are growing. The pink one is going to bloom."

"I'll bring you all the geranium slips at the Lake, if you like. When I get rich, Ella May, I'll build you a big conservatory, and I'll get every flower in the world in it for you. You shall just live and sleep among posies. Is dinner ready, Mother? Trouting's hungry work, I tell you. What paper is this?"

He picked up a folded newspaper from the table.

"Oh, that's only an old Lake *Advertiser*," answered Mrs. Phillips, as she placed the potatoes on the table and wiped her moist, hot face with the corner of her gingham apron. "Letty Mills brought it in around a parcel this morning. It's four weeks old, but I kept it to read if I ever get time. It's so seldom we see a paper of any kind nowadays. But I haven't looked at it yet. Why, Danny, what on earth is the matter?"

For Dan, who had opened the paper and glanced over the first page, suddenly gave a choked exclamation and turned pale, staring stupidly at the sheet before him.

"See, Mother," he gasped, as she came up in alarm and looked over his shoulder. This is what they read:

Notice

> Anyone found fishing on my pond at Carleton after date will be prosecuted according to law, without respect of persons.
>
> June First.
>
> H.C. Walters.

"Oh, Danny, what does it mean?"

Dan went and carefully closed the door of Ella May's room before he replied. His face was pale and his voice shaky.

"Mean? Well, Mother, it just means that I've been stealing Mr. Walters's trout all summer—*stealing* them. That's what it means."

"Oh, Danny! But you didn't know."

"No, but I ought to have remembered that he was the new owner, and have asked him. I never thought. Mother, what does 'prosecuted according to law' mean?"

"I don't know, I'm sure, Danny. But if this is so, there's only one thing to be done. You must go straight to Mr. Walters and tell him all about it."

"Mother, I don't dare to. He is a dreadfully hard man. Sam French's father says—"

"I wouldn't believe a word Sam French's father says about Mr. Walters!" said Mrs. Phillips firmly. "He's got a spite against him because he was dismissed. Besides, Danny, it's the only right thing to do. You know that. We're poor, but we have never done anything underhand yet."

"Yes, Mother, I know," said Dan, gulping his fear bravely down. "I'll go, of course, right after dinner. I was only scared at first. I'll tell you what I'll do. I'll clean these trout nicely and take them to Mr. Walters, and tell him that, if he'll only give me time, I'll pay him back every cent of money I got for all I sold this summer. Then maybe he'll let me off, seeing as I didn't know about the notice."

"I'll go with you, Danny."

"No, I'll go alone, Mother. You needn't go with me," said Dan heroically. To himself he said that his mother had troubles enough. He would never subject her to the added ordeal of an interview with the stern factory owner. He would beard the lion in his den himself, if it had to be done.

"Don't tell Ella May anything about it. It would worry her. And don't cry, Mother, I guess it'll be all right. Let me have my dinner now and I'll go straight off."

Dan ate his dinner rapidly; then he carefully cleaned his trout, put them in a long basket, with rhubarb leaves over them, and started with an assumed cheerfulness very far from his real feelings.

He had barely passed the gate when another boy came shuffling along—a tall, raw-boned lad, with an insinuating smile and shifty, cunning eyes. The newcomer nodded familiarly to Dan.

"Hello, sonny. Going over to the Lake with your catch, are you? You'll fry up before you get there. There'll be nothing left of you but a crisp."

"No, I'm not going to the Lake. I'm going up to the factory to see Mr. Walters."

Sam French gave a long whistle of surprise.

"Why, Dan, what's taking you there? You surely ain't thinking of trying for that place, are you? Walters wouldn't look at you. Why, he wouldn't take *me*! You haven't the ghost of a chance."

"No, I'm not going for that. Sam, did you know that Mr. Walters had a notice in the Lake *Advertiser* that nobody could fish in his pond this summer?"

"Course I did—the old skinflint! He's too mean to live, that's what. He never goes near the pond himself. Regular dog in the manger, he is. Dad says—"

"Sam, why didn't you tell me about that notice?"

"Gracious, didn't you know? I s'posed everybody did, and here I've been taking you for the cutest chap this side of sunset—fishing away up in that creek where no one could see you, and cutting home through the woods on the sly. You don't mean to tell me you never saw that notice?"

"No, I didn't. Do you think I'd have gone near the pond if I had? I never saw it till today, and I'm going straight to Mr. Walters now to tell him about it."

Sam French stopped short in the dusty road and stared at Dan in undisguised amazement.

"Dan Phillips," he ejaculated, "have you plum gone out of your mind? Boy alive, you needn't be afraid that I'd peach on you. I'm too blamed glad to see any-one get the better of that old Walters, smart as he thinks himself. Gee! To dream of going to him and telling him you've been fishing in his pond! Why, he'll put you in jail. You don't know what sort of a man he is. Dad says—"

"Never mind what your dad says, Sam. My mind's made up."

"Dan, you chump, listen to me. That notice says 'prosecuted according to law.' Why, Danny, he'll put you in prison, or fine you, or something dreadful."

"I can't help it if he does," said Danny stoutly. "You get out of here, Sam French, and don't be trying to scare me. I mean to be honest, and how can I be if I don't own up to Mr. Walters that I've been stealing his trout all summer?"

"Stealing, fiddlesticks! Dan, I used to think you were a chap with some sense, but I see I was mistaken. You ain't done no harm. Walters will never miss them trout. If you're so dreadful squeamish that you won't fish no more, why, you needn't. But just let the matter drop and hold your tongue about it. That's *my* ad-vice."

"Well, it isn't my mother's, then. I mean to go by *hers*. You needn't argue no more, Sam. I'm going."

"Go, then!" said Sam, stopping short in disgust. "You're a big fool, Dan, and serve you right if Walters lands you off to jail; but I don't wish you no ill. If I can do anything for your family after you're gone, I will, and I'll try and give your remains Christian burial—if there are any remains. So long, Danny! Give my love to old Walters!"

Dan was not greatly encouraged by this interview. He shrank more than ever from the thought of facing the stern factory owner. His courage had almost evapo-rated when he entered the office at the factory and asked shakily for Mr. Walters.

"He's in his office there," replied the clerk, "but he's very busy. Better leave your message with me."

"I must see Mr. Walters himself, please," said Dan firmly, but with inward trepidation.

The clerk swung himself impatiently from his stool and ushered Dan into Mr. Walters's private office.

"Boy to see you, sir," he said briefly, as he closed the ground-glass door be-hind him.

Dan, dizzy and trembling, stood in the dreaded presence. Mr. Walters was writing at a table covered with a businesslike litter of papers. He laid down his pen and looked up with a frown as the clerk vanished. He was a stern-looking man with deep-set grey eyes and a square, clean-shaven chin. There was not an ounce of superfluous flesh on his frame, and his voice and manner were those of the decided, resolute, masterful man of business.

He pointed to a capacious leather chair and said concisely, "What is your business with me, boy?"

Dan had carefully thought out a statement of facts beforehand, but every word had vanished from his memory. He had only a confused, desperate consciousness that he had a theft to confess and that it must be done as soon as possible. He did not sit down.

"Please, Mr. Walters," he began desperately, "I came to tell you—your notice—I never saw it before—and I've been fishing on your pond all summer—but I didn't know—honest—I've brought you all I caught today—and I'll pay back for them all—some time."

An amused, puzzled expression crossed Mr. Walters's noncommittal face. He pushed the leather chair forward.

"Sit down, my boy," he said kindly. "I don't quite understand this somewhat mixed-up statement of yours. You've been fishing on my pond, you say. Didn't you see my notice in the *Advertiser*?"

Dan sat down more composedly. The revelation was over and he was still alive.

"No, sir. We hardly ever see an *Advertiser*, and nobody told me. I'd always been used to fishing there, and I never thought but what it was all right to keep on. I know I ought to have remembered and asked you, but truly, sir, I didn't mean to steal your fish. I used to sell them over at the hotels. We saw the notice today, Mother and me, and I came right up. I've brought you the trout I caught this morning, and—if only you won't prosecute me, sir, I'll pay back every cent I got for the others—every cent, sir—if you'll give me time."

Mr. Walters passed his hand across his mouth to conceal something like a smile.

"Your name is Dan Phillips, isn't it?" he said irrelevantly, "and you live with your mother, the Widow Phillips, down there at Carleton Corners, I understand."

"Yes, sir," said Dan, wondering how Mr. Walters knew so much about him, and if these were the preliminaries of prosecution.

Mr. Walters took up his pen and drew a blank sheet towards him.

"Well, Dan, I put that notice in because I found that many people who used to fish on my pond, irrespective of leave or licence, were accustomed to lunch or camp on my property, and did not a little damage. I don't care for trouting myself; I've no time for it. However, I hardly think you'll do much damage. You can keep on fishing there. I'll give you a written permission, so that if any of my men see you they won't interfere with you. As for these trout here, I'll buy them from you at Mosquito Lake prices, and will say no more about the matter. How will that do?"

"Thank you, sir," stammered Dan. He could hardly believe his ears. He took the slip of paper Mr. Walters handed to him and rose to his feet.

"Wait a minute, Dan. How was it you came to tell me this? You might have stopped your depredations, and I should not have been any the wiser."

"That wouldn't have been honest, sir," said Dan, looking squarely at him.

There was a brief silence. Mr. Walters thrummed meditatively on the table. Dan waited wonderingly.

Finally the factory owner said abruptly, "There's a vacant place for a boy down here. I want it filled as soon as possible. Will you take it?"

"Mr. Walters! *Me!*" Dan thought the world must be turning upside down.

"Yes, you. You are rather young, but the duties are not hard or difficult to learn. I think you'll do. I was resolved not to fill that place until I could find a perfectly honest and trustworthy boy for it. I believe I have found him. I discharged the last boy because he lied to me about some trifling offence for which I would have forgiven him if he had told the truth. I can bear with incompetency, but falsehood and deceit I cannot and will not tolerate," he said, so sternly that Dan's face paled. "I am convinced that you are incapable of either. Will you take the place, Dan?"

"I will if you think I can fill it, sir. I will do my best."

"Yes, I believe you will. Perhaps I know more about you than you think. Businessmen must keep their eyes open. We'll regard this matter as settled then. Come up tomorrow at eight o'clock. And one word more, Dan. You have perhaps heard that I am an unjust and hard master. I am not the former, and you will never have occasion to find me the latter if you are always as truthful and straightforward as you have been today. You might easily have deceived me in this matter. That you did not do so is the best and only recommendation I require. Take those trout up to my house and leave them. That will do. Good afternoon."

Dan somehow got his dazed self through the glass door and out of the building. The whole interview had been such a surprise to him that he was hardly sure whether or not he had dreamed it all.

"I feel as if I were some person else," he said to himself, as he started down the hot white road. "But Mother was right. I'll stick to her motto. I wonder what Sam will say to this."

A Christmas Inspiration

"Well, I really think Santa Claus has been very good to us all," said Jean Lawrence, pulling the pins out of her heavy coil of fair hair and letting it ripple over her shoulders.

"So do I," said Nellie Preston as well as she could with a mouthful of chocolates. "Those blessed home folks of mine seem to have divined by instinct the very things I most wanted."

It was the dusk of Christmas Eve and they were all in Jean Lawrence's room at No. 16 Chestnut Terrace. No. 16 was a boarding-house, and boarding-houses are not proverbially cheerful places in which to spend Christmas, but Jean's room, at least, was a pleasant spot, and all the girls had brought their Christmas presents in to show each other. Christmas came on Sunday that year and the Saturday evening mail at Chestnut Terrace had been an exciting one.

Jean had lighted the pink-globed lamp on her table and the mellow light fell over merry faces as the girls chatted about their gifts. On the table was a big white box heaped with roses that betokened a bit of Christmas extravagance on somebody's part. Jean's brother had sent them to her from Montreal, and all the girls were enjoying them in common.

No. 16 Chestnut Terrace was overrun with girls generally. But just now only five were left; all the others had gone home for Christmas, but these five could not go and were bent on making the best of it.

Belle and Olive Reynolds, who were sitting on the bed—Jean could never keep them off it—were High School girls; they were said to be always laughing, and even the fact that they could not go home for Christmas because a young brother had measles did not dampen their spirits.

Beth Hamilton, who was hovering over the roses, and Nellie Preston, who was eating candy, were art students, and their homes were too far away to visit. As for Jean Lawrence, she was an orphan, and had no home of her own. She worked on the staff of one of the big city newspapers and the other girls were a little in awe of her cleverness, but her nature was a "chummy" one and her room was a favourite rendezvous. Everybody liked frank, open-handed and hearted Jean.

"It was so funny to see the postman when he came this evening," said Olive. "He just bulged with parcels. They were sticking out in every direction."

"We all got our share of them," said Jean with a sigh of content.

"Even the cook got six—I counted."

"Miss Allen didn't get a thing—not even a letter," said Beth quickly. Beth had a trick of seeing things that other girls didn't.

"I forgot Miss Allen. No, I don't believe she did," answered Jean thoughtfully as she twisted up her pretty hair. "How dismal it must be to be so forlorn as that on Christmas Eve of all times. Ugh! I'm glad I have friends."

"I saw Miss Allen watching us as we opened our parcels and letters," Beth went on. "I happened to look up once, and such an expression as was on her face, girls! It was pathetic and sad and envious all at once. It really made me feel bad—for five minutes," she concluded honestly.

"Hasn't Miss Allen any friends at all?" asked Beth.

"No, I don't think she has," answered Jean. "She has lived here for fourteen years, so Mrs. Pickrell says. Think of that, girls! Fourteen years at Chestnut Terrace! Is it any wonder that she is thin and dried-up and snappy?"

"Nobody ever comes to see her and she never goes anywhere," said Beth. "Dear me! She must feel lonely now when everybody else is being remembered by their friends. I can't forget her face tonight; it actually haunts me. Girls, how would you feel if you hadn't anyone belonging to you, and if nobody thought about you at Christmas?"

"Ow!" said Olive, as if the mere idea made her shiver.

A little silence followed. To tell the truth, none of them liked Miss Allen. They knew that she did not like them either, but considered them frivolous and pert, and complained when they made a racket.

"The skeleton at the feast," Jean called her, and certainly the presence of the pale, silent, discontented-looking woman at the No. 16 table did not tend to heighten its festivity.

Presently Jean said with a dramatic flourish, "Girls, I have an inspiration—a Christmas inspiration!"

"What is it?" cried four voices.

"Just this. Let us give Miss Allen a Christmas surprise. She has not received a single present and I'm sure she feels lonely. Just think how we would feel if we were in her place."

"That is true," said Olive thoughtfully. "Do you know, girls, this evening I went to her room with a message from Mrs. Pickrell, and I do believe she had been crying. Her room looked dreadfully bare and cheerless, too. I think she is very poor. What are we to do, Jean?"

"Let us each give her something nice. We can put the things just outside of her door so that she will see them whenever she opens it. I'll give her some of Fred's roses too, and I'll write a Christmassy letter in my very best style to go with them," said Jean, warming up to her ideas as she talked.

The other girls caught her spirit and entered into the plan with enthusiasm.

"Splendid!" cried Beth. "Jean, it is an inspiration, sure enough. Haven't we been horribly selfish—thinking of nothing but our own gifts and fun and pleasure? I really feel ashamed."

"Let us do the thing up the very best way we can," said Nellie, forgetting even her beloved chocolates in her eagerness. "The shops are open yet. Let us go up town and invest."

Five minutes later five capped and jacketed figures were scurrying up the street in the frosty, starlit December dusk. Miss Allen in her cold little room heard their gay voices and sighed. She was crying by herself in the dark. It was Christmas for everybody but her, she thought drearily.

In an hour the girls came back with their purchases.

"Now, let's hold a council of war," said Jean jubilantly. "I hadn't the faintest idea what Miss Allen would like so I just guessed wildly. I got her a lace handkerchief and a big bottle of perfume and a painted photograph frame—and I'll stick my own photo in it for fun. That was really all I could afford. Christmas purchases have left my purse dreadfully lean."

"I got her a glove-box and a pin tray," said Belle, "and Olive got her a calendar and Whittier's poems. And besides we are going to give her half of that big plummy fruit cake Mother sent us from home. I'm sure she hasn't tasted anything so delicious for years, for fruit cakes don't grow on Chestnut Terrace and she never goes anywhere else for a meal."

Beth had bought a pretty cup and saucer and said she meant to give one of her pretty water-colours too. Nellie, true to her reputation, had invested in a big box of chocolate creams, a gorgeously striped candy cane, a bag of oranges, and a brilliant lampshade of rose-coloured crepe paper to top off with.

"It makes such a lot of show for the money," she explained. "I am bankrupt, like Jean."

"Well, we've got a lot of pretty things," said Jean in a tone of satisfaction. "Now we must do them up nicely. Will you wrap them in tissue paper, girls, and tie them with baby ribbon—here's a box of it—while I write that letter?"

While the others chatted over their parcels Jean wrote her letter, and Jean could write delightful letters. She had a decided talent in that respect, and her correspondents all declared her letters to be things of beauty and joy forever. She put her best into Miss Allen's Christmas letter. Since then she has written many bright and clever things, but I do not believe she ever in her life wrote anything more genuinely original and delightful than that letter. Besides, it breathed the very spirit of Christmas, and all the girls declared that it was splendid.

"You must all sign it now," said Jean, "and I'll put it in one of those big envelopes; and, Nellie, won't you write her name on it in fancy letters?"

Which Nellie proceeded to do, and furthermore embellished the envelope by a border of chubby cherubs, dancing hand in hand around it and a sketch of No. 16 Chestnut Terrace in the corner in lieu of a stamp. Not content with this she hunted out a huge sheet of drawing paper and drew upon it an original pen-and-ink design after her own heart. A dudish cat—Miss Allen was fond of the No. 16 cat if she could be said to be fond of anything—was portrayed seated on a rocker arrayed in smoking jacket and cap with a cigar waved airily aloft in one paw while the other held out a placard bearing the legend "Merry Christmas." A second cat in full street costume bowed politely, hat in paw, and waved a banner inscribed with "Happy New Year," while faintly suggested kittens gambolled around the border. The girls laughed until they cried over it and voted it to be the best thing Nellie had yet done in original work.

All this had taken time and it was past eleven o'clock. Miss Allen had cried herself to sleep long ago and everybody else in Chestnut Terrace was abed when five figures cautiously crept down the hall, headed by Jean with a dim lamp. Outside of Miss Allen's door the procession halted and the girls silently arranged their gifts on the floor.

"That's done," whispered Jean in a tone of satisfaction as they tiptoed back. "And now let us go to bed or Mrs. Pickrell, bless her heart, will be down on us for burning so much midnight oil. Oil has gone up, you know, girls."

It was in the early morning that Miss Allen opened her door. But early as it was, another door down the hall was half open too and five rosy faces were peering cautiously out. The girls had been up for an hour for fear they would miss the sight and were all in Nellie's room, which commanded a view of Miss Allen's door.

That lady's face was a study. Amazement, incredulity, wonder, chased each other over it, succeeded by a glow of pleasure. On the floor before her was a snug little pyramid of parcels topped by Jean's letter. On a chair behind it was a bowl of delicious hot-house roses and Nellie's placard.

Miss Allen looked down the hall but saw nothing, for Jean had slammed the door just in time. Half an hour later when they were going down to breakfast Miss Allen came along the hall with outstretched hands to meet them. She had been crying again, but I think her tears were happy ones; and she was smiling now. A cluster of Jean's roses were pinned on her breast.

"Oh, girls, girls," she said, with a little tremble in her voice, "I can never thank you enough. It was so kind and sweet of you. You don't know how much good you have done me."

Breakfast was an unusually cheerful affair at No. 16 that morning. There was no skeleton at the feast and everybody was beaming. Miss Allen laughed and talked like a girl herself.

"Oh, how surprised I was!" she said. "The roses were like a bit of summer, and those cats of Nellie's were so funny and delightful. And your letter too, Jean! I cried and laughed over it. I shall read it every day for a year."

After breakfast everyone went to Christmas service. The girls went uptown to the church they attended. The city was very beautiful in the morning sunshine. There had been a white frost in the night and the tree-lined avenues and public squares seemed like glimpses of fairyland.

"How lovely the world is," said Jean.

"This is really the very happiest Christmas morning I have ever known," declared Nellie. "I never felt so really Christmassy in my inmost soul before."

"I suppose," said Beth thoughtfully, "that it is because we have discovered for ourselves the old truth that it is more blessed to give than to receive. I've always known it, in a way, but I never realized it before."

"Blessing on Jean's Christmas inspiration," said Nellie. "But, girls, let us try to make it an all-the-year-round inspiration, I say. We can bring a little of our own sunshine into Miss Allen's life as long as we live with her."

"Amen to that!" said Jean heartily. "Oh, listen, girls—the Christmas chimes!"

And over all the beautiful city was wafted the grand old message of peace on earth and good will to all the world.

A Christmas Mistake

"Tomorrow is Christmas," announced Teddy Grant exultantly, as he sat on the floor struggling manfully with a refractory bootlace that was knotted and tagless and stubbornly refused to go into the eyelets of Teddy's patched boots. "Ain't I glad, though. Hurrah!"

His mother was washing the breakfast dishes in a dreary, listless sort of way. She looked tired and broken-spirited. Ted's enthusiasm seemed to grate on her, for she answered sharply:

"Christmas, indeed. I can't see that it is anything for us to rejoice over. Other people may be glad enough, but what with winter coming on I'd sooner it was spring than Christmas. Mary Alice, do lift that child out of the ashes and put its shoes and stockings on. Everything seems to be at sixes and sevens here this morning."

Keith, the oldest boy, was coiled up on the sofa calmly working out some algebra problems, quite oblivious to the noise around him. But he looked up from his slate, with his pencil suspended above an obstinate equation, to declaim with a flourish:

"Christmas comes but once a year,
And then Mother wishes it wasn't here."

"I don't, then," said Gordon, son number two, who was preparing his own noon lunch of bread and molasses at the table, and making an atrocious mess of crumbs and sugary syrup over everything. "I know one thing to be thankful for, and that is that there'll be no school. We'll have a whole week of holidays."

Gordon was noted for his aversion to school and his affection for holidays.

"And we're going to have turkey for dinner," declared Teddy, getting up off the floor and rushing to secure his share of bread and molasses, "and cranb'ry sauce and—and—pound cake! Ain't we, Ma?"

"No, you are not," said Mrs. Grant desperately, dropping the dishcloth and snatching the baby on her knee to wipe the crust of cinders and molasses from the chubby pink-and-white face. "You may as well know it now, children, I've kept it from you so far in hopes that something would turn up, but nothing has. We can't have any Christmas dinner tomorrow—we can't afford it. I've pinched and saved every way I could for the last month, hoping that I'd be able to get a turkey for you anyhow, but you'll have to do without it. There's that doctor's bill to pay and a dozen other bills coming in—and people say they can't wait. I suppose they can't, but it's kind of hard, I must say."

The little Grants stood with open mouths and horrified eyes. No turkey for Christmas! Was the world coming to an end? Wouldn't the government interfere if anyone ventured to dispense with a Christmas celebration?

The gluttonous Teddy stuffed his fists into his eyes and lifted up his voice. Keith, who understood better than the others the look on his mother's face, took his blubbering young brother by the collar and marched him into the porch. The twins, seeing the summary proceeding, swallowed the outcries they had intended to make, although they couldn't keep a few big tears from running down their fat cheeks.

Mrs. Grant looked pityingly at the disappointed faces about her.

"Don't cry, children, you make me feel worse. We are not the only ones who will have to do without a Christmas turkey. We ought to be very thankful that we have anything to eat at all. I hate to disappoint you, but it can't be helped."

"Never mind, Mother," said Keith, comfortingly, relaxing his hold upon the porch door, whereupon it suddenly flew open and precipitated Teddy, who had been tugging at the handle, heels over head backwards. "We know you've done your best. It's been a hard year for you. Just wait, though. I'll soon be grown up, and then you and these greedy youngsters shall feast on turkey every day of the year. Hello, Teddy, have you got on your feet again? Mind, sir, no more blubbering!"

"When I'm a man," announced Teddy with dignity, "I'd just like to see you put me in the porch. And I mean to have turkey all the time and I won't give you any, either."

"All right, you greedy small boy. Only take yourself off to school now, and let us hear no more squeaks out of you. Tramp, all of you, and give Mother a chance to get her work done."

Mrs. Grant got up and fell to work at her dishes with a brighter face.

"Well, we mustn't give in; perhaps things will be better after a while. I'll make a famous bread pudding, and you can boil some molasses taffy and ask those little Smithsons next door to help you pull it. They won't whine for turkey, I'll be bound. I don't suppose they ever tasted such a thing in all their lives. If I could afford it, I'd have had them all in to dinner with us. That sermon Mr. Evans preached last Sunday kind of stirred me up. He said we ought always to try and share our Christmas joy with some poor souls who had never learned the meaning of the word. I can't do as much as I'd like to. It was different when your father was alive."

The noisy group grew silent as they always did when their father was spoken of. He had died the year before, and since his death the little family had had a hard time. Keith, to hide his feelings, began to hector the rest.

"Mary Alice, do hurry up. Here, you twin nuisances, get off to school. If you don't you'll be late and then the master will give you a whipping."

"He won't," answered the irrepressible Teddy. "He never whips us, he doesn't. He stands us on the floor sometimes, though," he added, remembering the many times his own chubby legs had been seen to better advantage on the school platform.

"That man," said Mrs. Grant, alluding to the teacher, "makes me nervous. He is the most abstracted creature I ever saw in my life. It is a wonder to me he doesn't walk straight into the river some day. You'll meet him meandering along the street, gazing into vacancy, and he'll never see you nor hear a word you say half the time."

"Yesterday," said Gordon, chuckling over the remembrance, "he came in with a big piece of paper he'd picked up on the entry floor in one hand and his hat in the other—and he stuffed his hat into the coal-scuttle and hung up the paper on a nail as grave as you please. Never knew the difference till Ned Slocum went and told him. He's always doing things like that."

Keith had collected his books and now marched his brothers and sisters off to school. Left alone with the baby, Mrs. Grant betook herself to her work with a heavy heart. But a second interruption broke the progress of her dish-washing.

"I declare," she said, with a surprised glance through the window, "if there isn't that absent-minded schoolteacher coming through the yard! What can he want? Dear me, I do hope Teddy hasn't been cutting capers in school again."

For the teacher's last call had been in October and had been occasioned by the fact that the irrepressible Teddy would persist in going to school with his pockets filled with live crickets and in driving them harnessed to strings up and down the aisle when the teacher's back was turned. All mild methods of punishment having failed, the teacher had called to talk it over with Mrs. Grant, with the happy result that Teddy's behaviour had improved—in the matter of crickets at least.

But it was about time for another outbreak. Teddy had been unnaturally good for too long a time. Poor Mrs. Grant feared that it was the calm before a storm, and it was with nervous haste that she went to the door and greeted the young teacher.

He was a slight, pale, boyish-looking fellow, with an abstracted, musing look in his large dark eyes. Mrs. Grant noticed with amusement that he wore a white straw hat in spite of the season. His eyes were directed to her face with his usual unseeing gaze.

"Just as though he was looking through me at something a thousand miles away," said Mrs. Grant afterwards. "I believe he was, too. His body was right there on the step before me, but where his soul was is more than you or I or anybody can tell."

"Good morning," he said absently. "I have just called on my way to school with a message from Miss Millar. She wants you all to come up and have Christmas dinner with her tomorrow."

"For the land's sake!" said Mrs. Grant blankly. "I don't understand." To herself she thought, "I wish I dared take him and shake him to find if he's walking in his sleep or not."

"You and all the children—every one," went on the teacher dreamily, as if he were reciting a lesson learned beforehand. "She told me to tell you to be sure and come. Shall I say that you will?"

"Oh, yes, that is—I suppose—I don't know," said Mrs. Grant incoherently. "I never expected—yes, you may tell her we'll come," she concluded abruptly.

"Thank you," said the abstracted messenger, gravely lifting his hat and looking squarely through Mrs. Grant into unknown regions. When he had gone Mrs. Grant went in and sat down, laughing in a sort of hysterical way.

"I wonder if it is all right. Could Cornelia really have told him? She must, I suppose, but it is enough to take one's breath."

Mrs. Grant and Cornelia Millar were cousins, and had once been the closest of friends, but that was years ago, before some spiteful reports and ill-natured gossip had come between them, making only a little rift at first that soon widened into a chasm of coldness and alienation. Therefore this invitation surprised Mrs. Grant greatly.

Miss Cornelia was a maiden lady of certain years, with a comfortable bank account and a handsome, old-fashioned house on the hill behind the village. She always boarded the schoolteachers and looked after them maternally; she was an active church worker and a tower of strength to struggling ministers and their families.

"If Cornelia has seen fit at last to hold out the hand of reconciliation I'm glad enough to take it. Dear knows, I've wanted to make up often enough, but I didn't think she ever would. We've both of us got too much pride and stubbornness. It's the Turner blood in us that does it. The Turners were all so set. But I mean to do my part now she has done hers."

And Mrs. Grant made a final attack on the dishes with a beaming face.

When the little Grants came home and heard the news, Teddy stood on his head to express his delight, the twins kissed each other, and Mary Alice and Gordon danced around the kitchen.

Keith thought himself too big to betray any joy over a Christmas dinner, but he whistled while doing the chores until the bare welkin in the yard rang, and Teddy, in spite of unheard of misdemeanours, was not collared off into the porch once.

When the young teacher got home from school that evening he found the yellow house full of all sorts of delectable odours. Miss Cornelia herself was concocting mince pies after the famous family recipe, while her ancient and faithful handmaiden, Hannah, was straining into moulds the cranberry jelly. The open pantry door revealed a tempting array of Christmas delicacies.

"Did you call and invite the Smithsons up to dinner as I told you?" asked Miss Cornelia anxiously.

"Yes," was the dreamy response as he glided through the kitchen and vanished into the hall.

Miss Cornelia crimped the edges of her pies delicately with a relieved air. "I made certain he'd forget it," she said. "You just have to watch him as if he were a mere child. Didn't I catch him yesterday starting off to school in his carpet slippers? And in spite of me he got away today in that ridiculous summer hat. You'd better set that jelly in the out-pantry to cool, Hannah; it looks good. We'll give those poor little Smithsons a feast for once in their lives if they never get another."

At this juncture the hall door flew open and Mr. Palmer appeared on the threshold. He seemed considerably agitated and for once his eyes had lost their look of space-searching.

"Miss Millar, I am afraid I did make a mistake this morning—it has just dawned on me. I am almost sure that I called at Mrs. Grant's and invited her and her family instead of the Smithsons. And she said they would come."

Miss Cornelia's face was a study.

"Mr. Palmer," she said, flourishing her crimping fork tragically, "do you mean to say you went and invited Linda Grant here tomorrow? Linda Grant, of all women in this world!"

"I did," said the teacher with penitent wretchedness. "It was very careless of me—I am very sorry. What can I do? I'll go down and tell them I made a mistake if you like."

"You can't do that," groaned Miss Cornelia, sitting down and wrinkling up her forehead in dire perplexity. "It would never do in the world. For pity's sake, let me think for a minute."

Miss Cornelia did think—to good purpose evidently, for her forehead smoothed out as her meditations proceeded and her face brightened. Then she got up briskly. "Well, you've done it and no mistake. I don't know that I'm sorry, either. Anyhow, we'll leave it as it is. But you must go straight down now and invite the Smithsons too. And for pity's sake, don't make any more mistakes."

When he had gone Miss Cornelia opened her heart to Hannah. "I never could have done it myself—never; the Turner is too strong in me. But I'm glad it is done. I've been wanting for years to make up with Linda. And now the chance has come, thanks to that blessed blundering boy, I mean to make the most of it. Mind, Hannah, you never whisper a word about its being a mistake. Linda must never know. Poor Linda! She's had a hard time. Hannah, we must make some more pies, and I must go straight down to the store and get some more Santa Claus stuff; I've only got enough to go around the Smithsons."

When Mrs. Grant and her family arrived at the yellow house next morning Miss Cornelia herself ran out bareheaded to meet them. The two women shook hands a little stiffly and then a rill of long-repressed affection trickled out from some secret spring in Miss Cornelia's heart and she kissed her new-found old friend tenderly. Linda returned the kiss warmly, and both felt that the old-time friendship was theirs again.

The little Smithsons all came and they and the little Grants sat down on the long bright dining room to a dinner that made history in their small lives, and was eaten over again in happy dreams for months.

How those children did eat! And how beaming Miss Cornelia and grim-faced, soft-hearted Hannah and even the absent-minded teacher himself enjoyed watching them!

After dinner Miss Cornelia distributed among the delighted little souls the presents she had bought for them, and then turned them loose in the big shining kitchen to have a taffy pull—and they had it to their hearts' content! And as for the shocking, taffyfied state into which they got their own rosy faces and that once immaculate domain—well, as Miss Cornelia and Hannah never said one word about it, neither will I.

The four women enjoyed the afternoon in their own way, and the schoolteacher buried himself in algebra to his own great satisfaction.

When her guests went home in the starlit December dusk, Miss Cornelia walked part of the way with them and had a long confidential talk with Mrs. Grant. When she returned it was to find Hannah groaning in and over the kitchen and the schoolteacher dreamily trying to clean some molasses off his boots with the kitchen hairbrush. Long-suffering Miss Cornelia rescued her property and despatched Mr. Palmer into the woodshed to find the shoe-brush. Then she sat down and laughed.

"Hannah, what will become of that boy yet? There's no counting on what he'll do next. I don't know how he'll ever get through the world, I'm sure, but I'll look after him while he's here at least. I owe him a huge debt of gratitude for this Christmas blunder. What an awful mess this place is in! But, Hannah, did you ever in the world see anything so delightful as that little Tommy Smithson stuffing himself with plum cake, not to mention Teddy Grant? It did me good just to see them."

A Strayed Allegiance

"Will you go to the Cove with me this afternoon?"

It was Marian Lesley who asked the question.

Esterbrook Elliott unpinned with a masterful touch the delicate cluster of Noisette rosebuds she wore at her throat and transferred them to his buttonhole as he answered courteously: "Certainly. My time, as you know, is entirely at your disposal."

They were standing in the garden under the creamy bloom of drooping acacia trees. One long plume of blossoms touched lightly the soft, golden-brown coils of the girl's hair and cast a wavering shadow over the beautiful, flower-like face beneath it.

Esterbrook Elliott, standing before her, thought proudly that he had never seen a woman who might compare with her. In every detail she satisfied his critical, fastidious taste. There was not a discordant touch about her.

Esterbrook Elliott had always loved Marian Lesley—or thought he had. They had grown up together from childhood. He was an only son and she an only daughter. It had always been an understood thing between the two families that the boy and girl should marry. But Marian's father had decreed that no positive pledge should pass between them until Marian was twenty-one.

Esterbrook accepted his mapped-out destiny and selected bride with the conviction that he was an exceptionally lucky fellow. Out of all the women in the world Marian was the very one whom he would have chosen as mistress of his fine, old home. She had been his boyhood's ideal. He believed that he loved her sincerely, but he was not too much in love to be blind to the worldly advantages of his marriage with his cousin.

His father had died two years previously, leaving him wealthy and independent. Marian had lost her mother in childhood; her father died when she was eighteen. Since then she had lived alone with her aunt. Her life was quiet and lonely. Esterbrook's companionship was all that brightened it, but it was enough. Marian lavished on him all the rich, womanly love of her heart. On her twenty-first birthday they were formally betrothed. They were to be married in the following autumn.

No shadow had drifted across the heaven of her happiness. She believed herself secure in her lover's unfaltering devotion. True, at times she thought his manner lacked a lover's passionate ardour. He was always attentive and courteous. She had only to utter a wish to find that it had been anticipated; he spent every spare minute at her side.

Yet sometimes she half wished he would betray more lover-like impatience and intensity. Were all lovers as calm and undemonstrative?

She reproached herself for this incipient disloyalty as often as it vexingly intruded its unwelcome presence across her inner consciousness. Surely Esterbrook was fond and devoted enough to satisfy the most exacting demands of affection. Marian herself was somewhat undemonstrative and reserved. Passing acquaintances called her cold and proud. Only the privileged few knew the rich depths of womanly tenderness in her nature.

Esterbrook thought that he fully appreciated her. As he had walked homeward the night of their betrothal, he had reviewed with unconscious criticism his mental catalogue of Marian's graces and good qualities, admitting, with supreme satisfaction, that there was not one thing about her that he could wish changed.

This afternoon, under the acacias, they had been planning about their wedding. There was no one to consult but themselves.

They were to be married early in September and then go abroad. Esterbrook mapped out the details of their bridal tour with careful thoughtfulness. They would visit all the old-world places that Marian wished to see. Afterwards they would come back home. He discussed certain changes he wished to make in the old Elliott mansion to fit it for a young and beautiful mistress.

He did most of the planning. Marian was content to listen in happy silence. Afterwards she had proposed this walk to the Cove.

"What particular object of charity have you found at the Cove now?" asked Esterbrook, with lazy interest, as they walked along.

"Mrs. Barrett's little Bessie is very ill with fever," answered Marian. Then, catching his anxious look, she hastened to add, "It is nothing infectious—some kind of a slow, sapping variety. There is no danger, Esterbrook."

"I was not afraid for myself," he replied quietly. "My alarm was for you. You are too precious to me, Marian, for me to permit you to risk health and life, if it were dangerous. What a Lady Bountiful you are to those people at the Cove. When we are married you must take me in hand and teach me your creed of charity. I'm afraid I've lived a rather selfish life. You will change all that, dear. You will make a good man of me."

"You are that now, Esterbrook," she said softly. "If you were not, I could not love you."

"It is a negative sort of goodness, I fear. I have never been tried or tempted severely. Perhaps I should fail under the test."

"I am sure you would not," answered Marian proudly.

Esterbrook laughed; her faith in him was pleasant. He had no thought but that he would prove worthy of it.

The Cove, so-called, was a little fishing hamlet situated on the low, sandy shore of a small bay. The houses, clustered in one spot, seemed like nothing so much as larger shells washed up by the sea, so grey and bleached were they from long exposure to sea winds and spray.

Dozens of ragged children were playing about them, mingled with several disreputable yellow curs that yapped noisily at the strangers.

Down on the sandy strip of beach below the houses groups of men were lounging about. The mackerel, season had not yet set in; the spring herring netting was past. It was holiday time among the sea folks. They were enjoying it to the full, a happy, ragged colony, careless of what the morrows might bring forth.

Out beyond, the boats were at anchor, floating as gracefully on the twinkling water as sea birds, their tall masts bowing landward on the swell. A lazy, dreamful calm had fallen over the distant seas; the horizon blues were pale and dim; faint purple hazes blurred the outlines of far-off headlands and cliffs; the yellow sands sparkled in the sunshine as if powdered with jewels.

A murmurous babble of life buzzed about the hamlet, pierced through by the shrill undertones of the wrangling children, most of whom had paused in their play to scan the visitors with covert curiosity.

Marian led the way to a house apart from the others at the very edge of the shelving rock. The dooryard was scrupulously clean and unlittered; the little footpath through it was neatly bordered by white clam shells; several thrifty geraniums in bloom looked out from the muslin-curtained windows.

A weary-faced woman came forward to meet them.

"Bessie's much the same, Miss Lesley," she said, in answer to Marian's inquiry. "The doctor you sent was here today and did all he could for her. He seemed quite hopeful. She don't complain or nothing—just lies there and moans. Sometimes she gets restless. It's very kind of you to come so often, Miss Lesley. Here, Magdalen, will you put this basket the lady's brought up there on the shelf?"

A girl, who had been sitting unnoticed with her back to the visitors, at the head of the child's cot in one corner of the room, stood up and slowly turned around. Marian and Esterbrook Elliott both started with involuntary surprise. Esterbrook caught his breath like a man suddenly awakened from sleep. In the name of all that was wonderful, who or what could this girl be, so little in harmony with her surroundings?

Standing in the crepuscular light of the corner, her marvellous beauty shone out with the vivid richness of some rare painting. She was tall, and the magnificent proportions of her figure were enhanced rather than marred by the severely plain dress of dark print that she wore. The heavy masses of her hair, a shining auburn dashed with golden foam, were coiled in a rich, glossy knot at the back of the classically modelled head and rippled back from a low brow whose waxen fairness even the breezes of the ocean had spared.

The girl's face was a full, perfect oval, with features of faultless regularity, and the large, full eyes were of tawny hazel, darkened into inscrutable gloom in the dimness of the corner.

Not even Marian Lesley's face was more delicately tinted, but not a trace of colour appeared in the smooth, marble-like cheeks; yet the waxen pallor bore no trace of disease or weakness, and the large, curving mouth was of an intense crimson.

She stood quite motionless. There was no trace of embarrassment or self-consciousness in her pose. When Mrs. Barrett said, "This is my niece, Magdalen Crawford," she merely inclined her head in grave, silent acknowledgement. As she moved forward to take Marian's basket, she seemed oddly out of place in the low, crowded room. Her presence seemed to throw a strange restraint over the group.

Marian rose and went over to the cot, laying her slender hand on the hot forehead of the little sufferer. The child opened its brown eyes questioningly.

"How are you today, Bessie?"

"Mad'len—I want Mad'len," moaned the little plaintive voice.

Magdalen came over and stood beside Marian Lesley.

"She wants me," she said in a low, thrilling voice; free from all harsh accent or intonation. "I am the only one she seems to know always. Yes, darling, Mad'len is here—right beside you. She will not leave you."

She knelt by the little cot and passed her arm under the child's neck, drawing the curly head close to her throat with a tender, soothing motion.

Esterbrook Elliott watched the two women intently—the one standing by the cot, arrayed in simple yet costly apparel, with her beautiful, high-bred face, and the other, kneeling on the bare, sanded floor in her print dress, with her splendid head bent low over the child and the long fringe of burnished lashes sweeping the cold pallor of the oval cheek.

From the moment that Magdalen Crawford's haunting eyes had looked straight into his for one fleeting second, an unnamable thrill of pain and pleasure stirred his heart, a thrill so strong and sudden and passionate that his face paled with emotion; the room seemed to swim before his eyes in a mist out of which gleamed that wonderful face with its mesmeric, darkly radiant eyes, burning their way into deeps and abysses of his soul hitherto unknown to him.

When the mist cleared away and his head grew steadier, he wondered at himself. Yet he trembled in every limb and the only clear idea that struggled out of his confused thoughts was an overmastering desire to take that cold face between his hands and kiss it until its passionless marble glowed into warm and throbbing life.

"Who is that girl?" he said abruptly, when they had left the cottage. "She is the most beautiful woman I have ever seen—present company always excepted," he concluded, with a depreciatory laugh.

The delicate bloom on Marian's face deepened slightly.

"You had much better to have omitted that last sentence," she said quietly, "it was so palpably an afterthought. Yes, she is wonderfully lovely—a strange beauty, I fancied. There seemed something odd and uncanny about it to me. She must be Mrs. Barrett's niece. I remember that when I was down here about a month ago Mrs. Barrett told me she expected a niece of hers to live with her—for a time at least. Her parents were both dead, the father having died recently. Mrs. Barrett seemed troubled about her. She said that the girl had been well brought up and used to better things than the Cove could give her, and she feared that she would be very discontented and unhappy. I had forgotten all about it until I saw the girl today. She certainly seems to be a very superior person; she will find the Cove very lonely, I am sure. It is not probable she will stay there long. I must see what I can do for her, but her manner seemed rather repellent, don't you think?"

"Hardly," responded Esterbrook curtly. "She seemed surprisingly dignified and self-possessed, I fancied, for a girl in her position. A princess could not have looked and bowed more royally. There was not a shadow of embarrassment in her manner, in spite of the incongruity of her surroundings. You had much better leave her alone, Marian. In all probability she would resent any condescension on your part. What wonderful, deep, lovely eyes she has."

Again the sensitive colour flushed Marian's cheek as his voice lapsed unconsciously into a dreamy, retrospective tone, and a slight restraint came over her manner, which did not depart. Esterbrook went away at sunset. Marian asked him to remain for the evening, but he pleaded some excuse.

"I shall come tomorrow afternoon," he said, as he stooped to drop a careless good-bye kiss on her face.

Marian watched him wistfully as he rode away, with an unaccountable pain in her heart. She felt more acutely than ever that there were depths in her lover's nature that she was powerless to stir into responsive life.

Had any other that power? She thought of the girl at the Cove, with her deep eyes and wonderful face. A chill of premonitory fear seized upon her.

"I feel exactly as if Esterbrook had gone away from me forever," she said slowly to herself, stooping to brush her cheek against a dew-cold, milk-white acacia bloom, "and would never come back to me again. If that could happen, I wonder what there would be left to live for?"

Esterbrook Elliott meant, or honestly thought he meant, to go home when he left Marian. Nevertheless, when he reached the road branching off to the Cove he turned his horse down it with a flush on his dark cheek. He realized that the motive of the action was disloyal to Marian and he felt ashamed of his weakness.

But the desire to see Magdalen Crawford once more and to look into the depths of her eyes was stronger than all else, and overpowered every throb of duty and resistance.

He saw nothing of her when he reached the Cove. He could think of no excuse for calling at the Barrett cottage, so he rode slowly past the hamlet and along the shore.

The sun, red as a smouldering ember, was half buried in the silken violet rim of the sea; the west was a vast lake of saffron and rose and ethereal green, through which floated the curved shallop of a thin new moon, slowly deepening from lustreless white, through gleaming silver, into burnished gold, and attended by one solitary, pearl-white star. The vast concave of sky above was of violet, infinite and flawless. Far out dusky amethystine islets clustered like gems on the shining breast of the bay. The little pools of water along the low shores glowed like mirrors of polished jacinth. The small, pine-fringed headlands ran out into the water, cutting its lustrous blue expanse like purple wedges.

As Esterbrook turned one of them he saw Magdalen standing out on the point of the next, a short distance away. Her back was towards him, and her splendid figure was outlined darkly against the vivid sky.

Esterbrook sprang from his horse and left the animal standing by itself while he walked swiftly out to her. His heart throbbed suffocatingly. He was conscious of no direct purpose save merely to see her.

She turned when he reached her with a slight start of surprise. His footsteps had made no sound on the tide-rippled sand.

For a few moments they faced each other so, eyes burning into eyes with mute soul-probing and questioning. The sun had disappeared, leaving a stain of fiery red to mark his grave; the weird, radiant light was startlingly vivid and clear. Little crisp puffs and flakes of foam scurried over the point like elfin things. The fresh wind, blowing up the bay, tossed the lustrous rings of hair about Magdalen's pale face; all the routed shadows of the hour had found refuge in her eyes.

Not a trace of colour appeared in her face under Esterbrook Elliott's burning gaze. But when he said "Magdalen!" a single, hot scorch of crimson flamed up into her cheeks protestingly. She lifted her hand with a splendid gesture, but no word passed her lips.

"Magdalen, have you nothing to say to me?" he asked, coming closer to her with an imploring passion in his face never seen by Marian Lesley's eyes. He reached out his hand, but she stepped back from his touch.

"What should I have to say to you?"

"Say that you are glad to see me."

"I am not glad to see you. You have no right to come here. But I knew you would come."

"You knew it? How?"

"Your eyes told me so today. I am not blind—I can see further than those dull fisher folks. Yes, I knew you would come. That is why I came here tonight—so that you would find me alone and I could tell you that you were not to come again."

"Why must you tell me that, Magdalen?"

"Because, as I have told you, you have no right to come."

"But if I will not obey you? If I will come in defiance of your prohibition?"

She turned her steady luminous eyes on his pale, set face.

"You would stamp yourself as a madman, then," she said coldly. "I know that you are Miss Lesley's promised husband. Therefore, you are either false to her or insulting to me. In either case the companionship of Magdalen Crawford is not what you must seek. Go!"

She turned away from him with an imperious gesture of dismissal. Esterbrook Elliott stepped forward and caught one firm, white wrist.

"I shall not obey you," he said in a low, intense tone; his fine eyes burned into hers. "You may send me away, but I will come back, again and yet again until you have learned to welcome me. Why should you meet me like an enemy? Why can we not be friends?"

The girl faced him once more.

"Because," she said proudly, "I am not your equal. There can be no friendship between us. There ought not to be. Magdalen Crawford, the fisherman's niece, is no companion for you. You will be foolish, as well as disloyal, if you ever try to see me again. Go back to the beautiful, high-bred woman you love and forget me. Perhaps you think I am talking strangely. Perhaps you think me bold and unwomanly to speak so plainly to you, a stranger. But there are some circumstances in life when plain-speaking is best. I do not want to see you again. Now, go back to your own world."

Esterbrook Elliott slowly turned from her and walked in silence back to the shore. In the shadows of the point he stopped to look back at her, standing out like some inspired prophetess against the fiery background of the sunset sky and silver-blue water. The sky overhead was thick-sown with stars; the night breeze was blowing up from its lair in distant, echoing sea caves. On his right the lights of the Cove twinkled out through the dusk.

"I feel like a coward and a traitor," he said slowly. "Good God, what is this madness that has come over me? Is this my boasted strength of manhood?"

A moment later the hoof beats of his horse died away up the shore.

Magdalen Crawford lingered on the point until the last dull red faded out into the violet gloom of the June sea dusk, than which nothing can be rarer or diviner, and listened to the moan and murmur of the sea far out over the bay with sorrowful eyes and sternly set lips.

The next day, when the afternoon sun hung hot and heavy over the water, Esterbrook Elliott came again to the Cove. He found it deserted. A rumour of mackerel had come, and every boat had sailed out in the rose-red dawn to the fishing grounds. But down on a strip of sparkling yellow sand he saw Magdalen Crawford standing, her hand on the rope that fastened a small white dory to the fragment of a half-embedded wreck.

She was watching a huddle of gulls clustered on the tip of a narrow, sandy spit running out to the left. She turned at the sound of his hurried foot-fall behind her. Her face paled slightly, and into the depths of her eyes leapt a passionate, mesmeric glow that faded as quickly as it came.

"You see I have come back in spite of your command, Magdalen."

"I do see it," she answered in a gravely troubled voice. "You are a madman who refuses to be warned."

"Where are you going, Magdalen?" She had loosened the rope from the wreck.

"I am going to row over to Chapel Point for salt. They think the boats will come in tonight loaded with mackerel—look at them away out there by the score—and salt will be needed."

"Can you row so far alone?"

"Easily. I learned to row long ago—for a pastime then. Since coming here I find it of great service to me."

She stepped lightly into the tiny shallop and picked up an oar. The brilliant sunshine streamed about her, burnishing the rich tints of her hair into ruddy gold. She balanced herself to the swaying of the dory with the grace of a sea bird. The man looking at her felt his brain reel.

"Good-bye, Mr. Elliott."

For answer he sprang into the dory and, snatching an oar, pushed against the old wreck with such energy that the dory shot out from the shore like a foam bell. His sudden spring had set it rocking violently. Magdalen almost lost her footing and caught blindly at his arm. As her fingers closed on his wrist a thrill as of fire shot through his every vein.

"Why have you done this, Mr. Elliott? You must go back."

"But I will not," he said masterfully, looking straight into her eyes with an imperiousness that sat well upon him. "I am going to row you over to Chapel Point. I have the oars—I will be master this once, at least."

For an instant her eyes flashed defiant protest, then drooped before his. A sudden, hot blush crimsoned her pale face. His will had mastered hers; the girl trembled from head to foot, and the proud, sensitive, mouth quivered.

Into the face of the man watching her breathlessly flashed a triumphant, passionate joy. He put out his hand and gently pushed her down into the seat. Sitting opposite, he took up the oars and pulled out over the sheet of sparkling blue water, through which at first the bottom of white sand glimmered wavily but afterwards deepened to translucent, dim depths of greenness.

His heart throbbed tumultuously. Once the thought of Marian drifted across his mind like a chill breath of wind, but it was forgotten when his eyes met Magdalen's.

"Tell me about yourself, Magdalen," he said at last, breaking the tremulous, charmed, sparkling silence.

"There is nothing to tell," she answered with characteristic straightforwardness. "My life has been a very uneventful one. I have never been rich, or very well educated, but—it used to be different from now. I had some chance before—before Father died."

"You must have found it very lonely and strange when you came here first."

"Yes. At first I thought I should die—but I do not mind it now. I have made friends with the sea; it has taught me a great deal. There is a kind of inspiration in the sea. When one listens to its never-ceasing murmur afar out there, always sounding at midnight and midday, one's soul goes out to meet Eternity. Sometimes it gives me so much pleasure that it is almost pain."

She stopped abruptly.

"I don't know why I am talking to you like this."

"You are a strange girl, Magdalen. Have you no other companion than the sea?"

"No. Why should I wish to have? I shall not be here long."

Elliott's face contracted with a spasm of pain.

"You are not going away, Magdalen?"

"Yes—in the fall. I have my own living to earn, you know. I am very poor. Uncle and Aunt are very kind, but I cannot consent to burden them any longer than I can help."

A sigh that was almost a moan broke from Esterbrook Elliott's lips.

"You must not go away, Magdalen. You must stay here—with me!"

"You forget yourself," she said proudly. "How dare you speak to me so? Have you forgotten Miss Lesley? Or are you a traitor to us both?"

Esterbrook made no answer. He bowed his pale, miserable face before her, self-condemned.

The breast of the bay sparkled with its countless gems like the breast of a fair woman. The shores were purple and amethystine in the distance. Far out, bluish, phantom-like sails clustered against the pallid horizon. The dory danced like a feather over the ripples. They were close under the shadow of Chapel Point.

Marian Lesley waited in vain for her lover that afternoon. When he came at last in the odorous dusk of the June night she met him on the acacia-shadowed verandah with cold sweetness. Perhaps some subtle woman-instinct whispered to her where and how he had spent the afternoon, for she offered him no kiss, nor did she ask him why he had failed to come sooner.

His eyes lingered on her in the dim light, taking in every detail of her sweet womanly refinement and loveliness, and with difficulty he choked back a groan. Again he asked himself what madness had come over him, and again for an answer rose up the vision of Magdalen Crawford's face as he had seen it that day, crimsoning beneath his gaze.

It was late when he left. Marian watched him out of sight, standing under the acacias. She shivered as with a sudden chill. "I feel as I think Vashti must have felt," she murmured aloud, "when, discrowned and unqueened, she crept out of the gates of Shushan to hide her broken heart. I wonder if Esther has already usurped my sceptre. Has that girl at the Cove, with her pale, priestess-like face and mysterious eyes, stolen his heart from me? Perhaps not, for it may never have been mine. I know that Esterbrook Elliott will be true to the letter of his vows to me, no matter what it may cost him. But I want no pallid shadow of the love that belongs to another. The hour of abdication is at hand, I fear. And what will be left for throneless Vashti then?"

Esterbrook Elliott, walking home through the mocking calm of the night, fought a hard battle with himself.

He was face to face with the truth at last—the bitter knowledge that he had never loved Marian Lesley, save with a fond, brotherly affection, and that he did love Magdalen Crawford with a passion that threatened to sweep before it every vestige of his honour and loyalty.

He had seen her but three times—and his throbbing heart lay in the hollow of her cold white hand.

He shut his eyes and groaned. What madness. What unutterable folly! He was not free—he was bound to another by every cord of honour and self-respect. And, even were he free, Magdalen Crawford would be no fit wife for him—in the eyes of the world, at least. A girl from the Cove—a girl with little education and no social standing—aye! but he loved her.

He groaned again and again in his misery. Afar down the slope the bay waters lay like an inky strip and the distant, murmurous plaint of the sea came out of the stillness of the night; the lights at the Cove glimmered faintly.

In the week that followed he went to the Cove every day. Sometimes he did not see Magdalen; at other times he did. But at the end of the week he had conquered in the bitter, heart-crushing struggle with himself. If he had weakly given way to the first mad sweep of a new passion, the strength of his manhood reasserted itself at last. Faltering and wavering were over, though there was passionate pain in his voice when he said at last, "I am not coming back again, Magdalen."

They were standing in the shadow of the pine-fringed point that ran out to the left of the Cove. They had been walking together along the shore, watching the splendour of the sea sunset that flamed and glowed in the west, where there was a sea of mackerel clouds, crimson and amber tinted, with long, ribbon-like strips of apple-green sky between. They had walked in silence, hand in hand, as children might have done, yet with the stir and throb of a mighty passion seething in their hearts.

Magdalen turned as Esterbrook spoke, and looked at him in a long silence. The bay stretched out before them, tranced and shimmering; a few stars shone down through the gloom of dusk. Right across the translucent greens and roses and blues of the west hung a dark, unsightly cloud, like the blurred outline of a monstrous bat. In the dim, reflected light the girl's mournful face took on a weird, unearthly beauty. She turned her eyes from Esterbrook Elliott's set white face to the radiant gloom of the sea.

"That is best," she answered at last, slowly.

"Best—yes! Better that we had never met! I love you—you know it—words are idle between us. I never loved before—I thought I did. I made a mistake and I must pay the penalty of that mistake. You understand me?"

"I understand," she answered simply.

"I do not excuse myself—I have been weak and cowardly and disloyal. But I have conquered myself—I will be true to the woman to whom I am pledged. You and I must not meet again. I will crush this madness to death. I think I have been delirious ever since that day I saw you first, Magdalen. My brain is clearer now. I see my duty and I mean to do it at any cost. I dare not trust myself to say more. Magdalen, I have much for which to ask your forgiveness."

"There is nothing to forgive," she said steadily. "I have been as much to blame as you. If I had been as resolute as I ought to have been—if I had sent you away the second time as I did the first—this would not have come to pass. I have been weak too, and I deserve to atone for my weakness by suffering. There is only one path open to us. Esterbrook, good-bye." Her voice quivered with an uncontrollable spasm of pain, but the misty, mournful eyes did not swerve from his. The man stepped forward and caught her in his arms.

"Magdalen, good-bye, my darling. Kiss me once—only once—before I go."

She loosened his arms and stepped back proudly.

"No! No man kisses my lips unless he is to be my husband. Good-bye, dear."

He bowed his head silently and went away, looking back not once, else he might have seen her kneeling on the damp sand weeping noiselessly and passionately.

Marian Lesley looked at his pale, determined face the next evening and read it like an open book.

She had grown paler herself; there were purple shadows under the sweet violet eyes that might have hinted of her own sleepless nights.

She greeted him calmly, holding out a steady, white hand of welcome. She saw the traces of the struggle through which he had passed and knew that he had come off victor.

The knowledge made her task a little harder. It would have been easier to let slip the straining cable than to cast it from her when it lay unresistingly in her hand.

For an instant her heart thrilled with an unutterably sweet hope. Might he not forget in time? Need she snap in twain the weakened bond between them after all? Perhaps she might win back her lost sceptre, yet if—

Womanly pride throttled the struggling hope. No divided allegiance, no hollow semblance of queenship for her!

Her opportunity came when Esterbrook asked with grave earnestness if their marriage might not be hastened a little—could he not have his bride in August? For a fleeting second Marian closed her eyes and the slender hands, lying among the laces in her lap, clasped each other convulsively.

Then she said quietly, "Sometimes I have thought, Esterbrook, that it might be better—if we were never married at all."

Esterbrook turned a startled face upon her.

"Not married at all! Marian, what do you mean?"

"Just what I say. I do not think we are as well suited to each other after all as we have fancied. We have loved each other as brother and sister might—that is all. I think it will be best to be brother and sister forever—nothing more."

Esterbrook sprang to his feet.

"Marian, do you know what you are saying? You surely cannot have heard—no one could have told you—"

"I have heard nothing," she interrupted hurriedly. "No one has told me anything. I have only said what I have been thinking of late. I am sure we have made a mistake. It is not too late to remedy it. You will not refuse my request, Esterbrook? You will set me free?"

"Good heavens, Marian!" he said hoarsely. "I cannot realize that you are in earnest. Have you ceased to care for me?" The rigidly locked hands were clasped a little tighter.

"No—I shall always care for you as my friend if you will let me. But I know we could not make each other happy—the time for that has gone by. I would never be satisfied, nor would you. Esterbrook, will you release me from a promise which has become an irksome fetter?"

He looked down on her upturned face mistily. A great joy was surging up in his heart—yet it was mingled with great regret.

He knew—none better—what was passing out of his life, what he was losing when he lost that pure, womanly nature.

"If you really mean this, Marian," he said slowly, "if you really have come to feel that your truest love is not and never can be mine—that I cannot make you happy—then there is nothing for me to do but to grant your request. You are free."

"Thank you, dear," she said gently, as she stood up.

She slipped his ring from her finger and held it out to him. He took it mechanically. He still felt dazed and unreal.

Marian held out her hand.

"Good-night, Esterbrook," she said, a little wearily. "I feel tired. I am glad you see it all in the same light as I do."

"Marian," he said earnestly, clasping the outstretched hand, "are you sure that you will be happy—are you sure that you are doing a wise thing?"

"Quite sure," she answered, with a faint smile. "I am not acting rashly. I have thought it all over carefully. Things are much better so, dear. We will always be friends. Your joys and sorrows will be to me as my own. When another love comes to bless your life, Esterbrook, I will be glad. And now, good-night. I want to be alone now."

At the doorway he turned to look back at her, standing in all her sweet stateliness in the twilight duskness, and the keen realization of all he had lost made him bow his head with a quick pang of regret.

Then he went out into the darkness of the summer night.

An hour later he stood alone on the little point where he had parted with Magdalen the night before. A restless night wind was moaning through the pines that fringed the bank behind him; the moon shone down radiantly, turning the calm expanse of the bay into a milk-white sheen.

He took Marian's ring from his pocket and kissed it reverently. Then he threw it from him far out over the water. For a second the diamond flashed in the moonlight; then, with a tiny splash, it fell among the ripples.

Esterbrook turned his face to the Cove, lying dark and silent in the curve between the crescent headlands. A solitary light glimmered from the low eaves of the Barrett cottage.

Tomorrow, was his unspoken thought, I will be free; to go back to Magdalen.

An Invitation Given on Impulse

It was a gloomy Saturday morning. The trees in the Oaklawn grounds were tossing wildly in the gusts of wind, and sodden brown leaves were blown up against the windows of the library, where a score of girls were waiting for the principal to bring the mail in.

The big room echoed with the pleasant sound of girlish voices and low laughter, for in a fortnight school would close for the holidays, and they were all talking about their plans and anticipations.

Only Ruth Mannering was, as usual, sitting by herself near one of the windows, looking out on the misty lawn. She was a pale, slender girl, with a sad face, and was dressed in rather shabby black. She had no special friend at Oaklawn, and the other girls did not know much about her. If they had thought about it at all, they would probably have decided that they did not like her; but for the most part they simply overlooked her.

This was not altogether their fault. Ruth was poor and apparently friendless, but it was not her poverty that was against her. Lou Scott, who was "as poor as a church mouse," to quote her own frank admission, was the most popular girl in the seminary, the boon companion of the richest girls, and in demand with everybody. But Lou was jolly and frank and offhanded, while Ruth was painfully shy and reserved, and that was the secret of the whole matter.

There was "no fun in her," the girls said, and so it came about that she was left out of their social life, and was almost as solitary at Oaklawn as if she had been the only girl there. She was there for the special purpose of studying music, and expected to earn her own living by teaching it when she left. She believed that the girls looked down on her on this account; this was unjust, of course, but Ruth had no idea how much her own coldness and reserve had worked against her.

Across the room Carol Golden was, as usual, the centre of an animated group; Golden Carol as her particular friends sometimes called her, partly because of her beautiful voice, and partly because of her wonderful fleece of golden hair. Carol was one of the seminary pets, and seemed to Ruth Mannering to have everything that she had not.

Presently the mail was brought in, and there was a rush to the table, followed by exclamations of satisfaction or disappointment. In a few minutes the room was almost deserted. Only two girls remained: Carol Golden, who had dropped into a big chair to read her many letters; and Ruth Mannering, who had not received any and had gone silently back to her part of the window.

Presently Carol gave a little cry of delight. Her mother had written that she might invite any friend she wished home with her to spend the holidays. Carol had asked for this permission, and now that it had come was ready to dance for joy. As to whom she would ask, there could be only one answer to that. Of course it must be her particular friend, Maud Russell, who was the cleverest and prettiest girl at Oaklawn, at least so her admirers said. She was undoubtedly the richest, and was the acknowledged "leader." The girls affectionately called her "Princess," and Carol adored her with that romantic affection that is found only among school girls. She knew, too, that Maud would surely accept her invitation because she did not intend to go home. Her parents were travelling in Europe, and she expected to spend her holidays with some cousins, who were almost strangers to her.

Carol was so much pleased that she felt as if she must talk to somebody, so she turned to Ruth.

"Isn't it delightful to think that we'll all be going home in a fortnight?"

"Yes, very—for those that have homes to go to," said Ruth drearily.

Carol felt a quick pang of pity and self-reproach. "Haven't you?" she asked.

Ruth shook her head. In spite of herself, the kindness of Carol's tone brought the tears to her eyes.

"My mother died a year ago," she said in a trembling voice, "and since then I have had no real home. We were quite alone in the world, Mother and I, and now I have nobody."

"Oh, I'm so sorry for you," cried Carol impulsively. She leaned forward and took Ruth's hand in a gentle way. "And do you mean to say that you'll have to stay here all through the holidays? Why, it will be horrid."

"Oh, I shall not mind it much," said Ruth quickly, "with study and practice most of the time. Only now, when everyone is talking about it, it makes me wish that I had some place to go."

Carol dropped Ruth's hand suddenly in the shock of a sudden idea that darted into her mind.

A stray girl passing through the hall called out, "Ruth, Miss Siviter wishes to see you about something in Room C."

Ruth got up quickly. She was glad to get away, for it seemed to her that in another minute she would break down altogether.

Carol Golden hardly noticed her departure. She gathered up her letters and went abstractedly to her room, unheeding a gay call for "Golden Carol" from a group of girls in the corridor. Maud Russell was not in and Carol was glad. She wanted to be alone and fight down that sudden idea.

"It is ridiculous to think of it," she said aloud, with a petulance very unusual in Golden Carol, whose disposition was as sunny as her looks. "Why, I simply cannot. I have always been longing to ask Maud to visit me, and now that the chance has come I am not going to throw it away. I am very sorry for Ruth, of course. It must be dreadful to be all alone like that. But it isn't my fault. And she is so fearfully quiet and dowdy—what would they all think of her at home? Frank and Jack would make such fun of her. I shall ask Maud just as soon as she comes in."

Maud did come in presently, but Carol did not give her the invitation. Instead, she was almost snappish to her idol, and the Princess soon went out again in something of a huff.

"Oh, dear," cried Carol, "now I've offended her. What has got into me? What a disagreeable thing a conscience is, although I'm sure I don't know why mine should be prodding me so! I don't want to invite Ruth Mannering home with me for the holidays, but I feel exactly as if I should not have a minute's peace of mind all the time if I didn't. Mother would think it all right, of course. She would not mind if Ruth dressed in calico and never said anything but yes and no. But how the boys would laugh! I simply won't do it, conscience or no conscience."

In view of this decision it was rather strange that the next morning, Carol Golden went down to Ruth Mannering's lonely little room on Corridor Two and said, "Ruth, will you go home with me for the holidays? Mother wrote me to invite anyone I wished to. Don't say you can't come, dear, because you must."

Carol never, as long as she lived, forgot Ruth's face at that moment.

"It was absolutely transfigured," she said afterwards. "I never saw anyone look so happy in my life."

A fortnight later unwonted silence reigned at Oaklawn. The girls were scattered far and wide, and Ruth Mannering and Carol Golden were at the latter's home.

Carol was a very much surprised girl. Under the influence of kindness and pleasure Ruth seemed transformed into a different person. Her shyness and reserve melted away in the sunny atmosphere of the Golden home. Mrs. Golden took her into her motherly heart at once; and as for Frank and Jack, whose verdict Carol had so dreaded, they voted Ruth "splendid." She certainly got along very well with them; and if she did not make the social sensation that pretty Maud Russell might have made, the Goldens all liked her and Carol was content.

"Just four days more," sighed Carol one afternoon, "and then we must go back to Oaklawn. Can you realize it, Ruth?"

Ruth looked up from her book with a smile. Even in appearance she had changed. There was a faint pink in her cheeks and a merry light in her eyes.

"I shall not be sorry to go back to work," she said. "I feel just like it because I have had so pleasant a time here that it has heartened me up for next term. I think it will be very different from last. I begin to see that I kept to myself too much and brooded over fancied slights."

"And then you are to room with me since Maud is not coming back," said Carol. "What fun we shall have. Did you ever toast marshmallows over the gas? Why, I declare, there is Mr. Swift coming up the walk. Look, Ruth! He is the richest man in Westleigh."

Ruth peeped out of the window over Carol's shoulder.

"He reminds me of somebody," she said absently, "but I can't think who it is. Of course, I have never seen him before. What a good face he has!"

"He is as good as he looks," said Carol, enthusiastically. "Next to Father, Mr. Swift is the nicest man in the world. I have always been quite a pet of his. His wife is dead, and so is his only daughter. She was a lovely girl and died only two years ago. It nearly broke Mr. Swift's heart. And he has lived alone ever since in that great big house up at the head of Warner Street, the one you admired so, Ruth, the last time we were uptown. There's the bell for the second time, Mary can't have heard it. I'll go myself."

As Carol showed the caller into the room, Ruth rose to leave and thus came face to face with him. Mr. Swift started perceptibly.

"Mr. Swift, this is my school friend, Miss Mannering," said Carol.

Mr. Swift seemed strangely agitated as he took Ruth's timidly offered hand.

"My dear young lady," he said hurriedly, "I am going to ask you what may seem a very strange question. What was your mother's name?"

"Agnes Hastings," answered Ruth in surprise. And then Carol really thought that Mr. Swift had gone crazy, for he drew Ruth into his arms and kissed her.

"I knew it," he said. "I was sure you were Agnes' daughter, for you are the living image of what she was when I last saw her. Child, you don't know me, but I am your Uncle Robert. Your mother was my half-sister."

"Oh, Mr. Swift!" cried Carol, and then she ran for her mother.

Ruth turned pale and dropped into a chair, and Mr. Swift sat down beside her.

"To think that I have found you at last, child. How puzzled you look. Did your mother never speak of me? How is she? Where is she?"

"Mother died last year," said Ruth.

"Poor Agnes! And I never knew! Don't cry, little girl. I want you to tell me all about it. She was much younger than I was, and when our mother died my stepfather went away and took her with him. I remained with my father's people and eventually lost all trace of my sister. I was a poor boy then, but things have looked up with me and I have often tried to find her."

By this time Carol had returned with her father and mother, and there was a scene—laughing, crying, explaining—and I don't really know which of the two girls was the more excited, Carol or Ruth. As for Mr. Swift, he was overjoyed to find his niece and wanted to carry her off with him then and there, but Mrs. Golden insisted on her finishing her visit. When the question of returning to Oaklawn came up, Mr. Swift would not hear of it at first, but finally yielded to Carol's entreaties and Ruth's own desire.

"I shall graduate next year, Uncle, and then I can come back to you for good."

That evening when Ruth was alone in her room, trying to collect her thoughts and realize that the home and love that she had so craved were really to be hers at last, Golden Carol was with her mother in the room below, talking it all over.

"Just think, Mother, if I had not asked Ruth to come here, this would not have happened. And I didn't want to, I wanted to ask Maud so much, and I was dreadfully disappointed when I couldn't—for I really couldn't. I could not help remembering the look in Ruth's eyes when she said that she had no home to go to, and so I asked her instead of Maud. How dreadful it would have been if I hadn't."

Detected by the Camera

One summer I was attacked by the craze for amateur photography. It became chronic afterwards, and I and my camera have never since been parted. We have had some odd adventures together, and one of the most novel of our experiences was that in which we played the part of chief witness against Ned Brooke.

I may say that my name is Amy Clarke, and that I believe I am considered the best amateur photographer in our part of the country. That is all I need tell you about myself.

Mr. Carroll had asked me to photograph his place for him when the apple orchards were in bloom. He has a picturesque old-fashioned country house behind a lawn of the most delightful old trees and flanked on each side by the orchards. So I went one June afternoon, with all my accoutrements, prepared to "take" the Carroll establishment in my best style.

Mr. Carroll was away but was expected home soon, so we waited for him, as all the family wished to be photographed under the big maple at the front door. I prowled around among the shrubbery at the lower end of the lawn and, after a great deal of squinting from various angles, I at last fixed upon the spot from which I thought the best view of the house might be obtained. Then Gertie and Lilian Carroll and I got into the hammocks and swung at our leisure, enjoying the cool breeze sweeping through the maples.

Ned Brooke was hanging around as usual, watching us furtively. Ned was one of the hopeful members of a family that lived in a tumble-down shanty just across the road from the Carrolls. They were wretchedly poor, and old Brooke, as he was called, and Ned were employed a good deal by Mr. Carroll—more out of charity than anything else, I fancy.

The Brookes had a rather shady reputation. They were notoriously lazy, and it was suspected that their line of distinction between their own and their neighbours' goods was not very clearly drawn. Many people censured Mr. Carroll for encouraging them at all, but he was too kind-hearted to let them suffer actual want and, as a consequence, one or the other of them was always dodging about his place.

Ned was a lank, tow-headed youth of about fourteen, with shifty, twinkling eyes that could never look you straight in the face. His appearance was anything but prepossessing, and I always felt, when I looked at him, that if anyone wanted to do a piece of shady work by proxy, Ned Brooke would be the very lad for the business.

Mr. Carroll came at last, and we all went down to meet him at the gate. Ned Brooke also came shuffling along to take the horse, and Mr. Carroll tossed the reins to him and at the same time handed a pocketbook to his wife.

"Just as well to be careful where you put that," he said laughingly. "There's a sum in it not to be picked up on every gooseberry bush. Gilman Harris paid me this morning for that bit of woodland I sold him last fall—five hundred dollars. I promised that you and the girls should have it to get a new piano, so there it is for you."

"Thank you," said Mrs. Carroll delightedly. "However, you'd better put it back in your pocket till we go in. Amy is in a hurry."

Mr. Carroll took back the pocketbook and dropped it carelessly into the inside pocket of the light overcoat that he wore.

I happened to glance at Ned Brooke just then, and I could not help noticing the sudden crafty, eager expression that flashed over his face. He eyed the pocketbook in Mr. Carroll's hands furtively, after which he went off with the horse in a great hurry.

The girls were exclaiming and thanking their father, and nobody noticed Ned Brooke's behaviour but myself, and it soon passed out of my mind.

"Come to take the place, are you, Amy?" said Mr. Carroll. "Well, everything is ready, I think. I suppose we'd better proceed. Where shall we stand? You had better group us as you think best."

Whereupon I proceeded to arrange them in due order under the maple. Mrs. Carroll sat in a chair, while her husband stood behind her. Gertie stood on the steps with a basket of flowers in her hand, and Lilian was at one side. The two little boys, Teddy and Jack, climbed up into the maple, and little Dora, the dimpled six-year-old, stood gravely in the foreground with an enormous grey cat hugged in her chubby arms.

It was a pretty group in a pretty setting, and I thrilled with professional pride as I stepped back for a final, knowing squint at it all. Then I went to my camera, slipped in the plate, gave them due warning and took off the cap.

I took two plates to make sure and then the thing was over, but as I had another plate left I thought I might as well take a view of the house by itself, so I carried my camera to a new place and had just got everything ready to lift the cap when Mr. Carroll came down and said:

"If you girls want to see something pretty, come to the back field with me. That will wait till you come back, won't it, Amy?"

So we all betook ourselves to the back field, a short distance away, where Mr. Carroll proudly displayed two of the prettiest little Jersey cows I had ever seen.

We returned to the house by way of the back lane and, as we came in sight of the main road, my brother Cecil drove up and said that if I were ready, I had better go home with him and save myself a hot, dusty walk.

The Carrolls all went down to the fence to speak to Cecil, but I dashed hurriedly down through the orchard, leaped over the fence into the lawn and ran to the somewhat remote corner where I had left my camera. I was in a desperate hurry, for I knew Cecil's horse did not like to be kept waiting, so I never even glanced at the house, but snatched off the cap, counted two and replaced it.

Then I took out my plate, put it in the holder and gathered up my traps. I suppose I was about five minutes at it all and I had my back to the house the whole time, and when I laid all my things ready and emerged from my retreat, there was nobody to be seen about the place.

As I hurried up through the lawn, I noticed Ned Brooke walking at a smart pace down the lane, but the fact did not make any particular impression on me at the time, and was not recalled until afterwards.

Cecil was waiting for me, so I got in the buggy and we drove off. On arriving home I shut myself up in my dark room and proceeded to develop the first two negatives of the Carroll housestead. They were both excellent, the first one being a trifle the better, so that I decided to finish from it. I intended also to develop the third, but just as I finished the others, a half-dozen city cousins swooped down upon us and I had to put away my paraphernalia, emerge from my dark retreat and fly around to entertain them.

The next day Cecil came in and said:

"Did you hear, Amy, that Mr. Carroll has lost a pocketbook with five hundred dollars in it?"

"No!" I exclaimed. "How? When? Where?"

"Don't overwhelm a fellow. I can answer only one question—last night. As to the 'how,' they don't know, and as to the 'where'—well, if they knew that, there might be some hope of finding it. The girls are in a bad way. The money was to get them their longed-for piano, it seems, and now it's gone."

"But how did it happen, Cecil?"

"Well, Mr. Carroll says that Mrs. Carroll handed the pocketbook back to him at the gate yesterday, and he dropped it in the inside pocket of his over-coat—"

"I saw him do it," I cried.

"Yes, and then, before he went to be photographed, he hung his coat up in the hall. It hung there until the evening, and nobody seems to have thought about the money, each supposing that someone else had put it carefully away. After tea Mr. Carroll put on the coat and went to see somebody over at Netherby. He says the thought of the pocketbook never crossed his mind; he had forgotten all about putting it in that coat pocket. He came home across the fields about eleven o'clock and found that the cows had broken into the clover hay, and he had a great chase before he got them out. When he went in, just as he entered the door, the remembrance of the money flashed over him. He felt in his pocket, but there was no pocketbook there; he asked his wife if she had taken it out. She had not, and nobody else had. There was a hole in the pocket, but Mr. Carroll says it was too small for the pocketbook to have worked through. However, it must have done so—unless someone took it out of his pocket at Netherby, and that is not possible, because he never had his coat off, and it was in an inside pocket. It's not likely that they will ever see it again. Someone may pick it up, of course, but the chances are slim. Mr. Carroll doesn't know his exact path across the fields, and if he lost it while he was after the cows, it's a bluer show still. They've been searching all day, of course. The girls are awfully disappointed."

A sudden recollection came to me of Ned Brooke's face as I had seen it the day before at the gate, coupled with the remembrance of seeing him walking down the lane at a quick pace, so unlike his usual shambling gait, while I ran through the lawn.

"How do they know it was lost?" I said. "Perhaps it was stolen before Mr. Carroll went to Netherby."

"They think not," said Cecil. "Who would have stolen it?"

"Ned Brooke. I saw him hanging around. And you never saw such a look as came over his face when he heard Mr. Carroll say there was five hundred dollars in that pocketbook."

"Well, I did suggest to them that Ned might know something about it, for I remembered having seen him go down the lane while I was waiting for you, but they won't hear of such a thing. The Brookes are kind of protégés of theirs, you know, and they won't believe anything bad of them. If Ned did take it, however, there's not a shadow of evidence against him."

"No, I suppose not," I answered thoughtfully, "but the more I think it over, the more I'm convinced that he took it. You know, we all went to the back field to look at the Jerseys, and all that time the coat was hanging there in the hall, and not a soul in the house. And it was just after we came back that I saw Ned scuttling down the lane so fast."

I mentioned my suspicions to the Carrolls a few days afterwards, when I went down with the photographs, and found that they had discovered no trace of the lost pocketbook. But they seemed positively angry when I hinted that Ned Brooke might know more about its whereabouts than anyone else. They declared that they would as soon think of suspecting one of themselves as Ned, and altogether they seemed so offended at my suggestion that I held my peace and didn't irritate them by any more suppositions.

Afterwards, in the excitement of our cousins' visit, the matter passed out of my mind completely. They stayed two weeks, and I was so busy the whole time that I never got a chance to develop that third plate and, in fact, I had forgotten all about it.

One morning soon after they went away, I remembered the plate and decided to go and develop it. Cecil went with me, and we shut ourselves up in our den, lit our ruby lantern and began operations. I did not expect much of the plate, because it had been exposed and handled carelessly, and I thought that it might prove to be underexposed or light-struck. So I left Cecil to develop it while I prepared the fixing bath. Cecil was whistling away when suddenly he gave a tremendous "whew" of astonishment and sprang to his feet.

"Amy, Amy, look here!" he cried.

I rushed to his side and looked at the plate as he held it up in the rosy light. It was a splendid one, and the Carroll house came out clear, with the front door and the steps in full view.

And there, just in the act of stepping from the threshold, was the figure of a boy with an old straw hat on his head and—in his hand—the pocketbook!

He was standing with his head turned towards the corner of the house as if listening, with one hand holding his ragged coat open and the other poised in mid-air with the pocketbook, as if he were just going to put it in his inside pocket. The whole scene was as clear as noonday, and nobody with eyes in his head could have failed to recognize Ned Brooke.

"Goodness!" I gasped. "In with it—quick!"

And we doused the thing into the fixing bath and then sat down breathlessly and looked at each other.

"I say, Amy," said Cecil, "what a sell this will be on the Carrolls! Ned Brooke couldn't do such a thing—oh, no! The poor injured boy at whom everyone has such an unlawful pick! I wonder if this will convince them."

"Do you think they can get it all back?" I asked. "It's not likely he would have dared to use any of it yet."

"I don't know. We'll have a try, anyhow. How long before this plate will be dry enough to carry down to the Carrolls as circumstantial evidence?"

"Three hours or thereabouts," I answered, "but perhaps sooner. I'll take two prints off when it is ready. I wonder what the Carrolls will say."

"It's a piece of pure luck that the plate should have turned out so well after the slap-dash way in which it was taken and used. I say, Amy, isn't this quite an adventure?"

At last the plate was dry, and I printed two proofs. We wrapped them up carefully and marched down to Mr. Carroll's.

You never saw people so overcome with astonishment as the Carrolls were when Cecil, with the air of a statesman unfolding the evidence of some dreadful conspiracy against the peace and welfare of the nation, produced the plate and the proofs, and held them out before them.

Mr. Carroll and Cecil took the proofs and went over to the Brooke shanty. They found only Ned and his mother at home. At first Ned, when taxed with his guilt, denied it, but when Mr. Carroll confronted him with the proofs, he broke down in a spasm of terror and confessed all. His mother produced the pocketbook and the money—they had not dared to spend a single cent of it—and Mr. Carroll went home in triumph.

Perhaps Ned Brooke ought not to have been let off so easily as he was, but his mother cried and pleaded, and Mr. Carroll was too kind-hearted to resist. So he did not punish them at all, save by utterly discarding the whole family and their concerns. The place got too hot for them after the story came out, and in less than a month all moved away—much to the benefit of Mapleton.

In Spite of Myself

My trunk was packed and I had arranged with my senior partner—I was the junior member of a law firm—for a month's vacation. Aunt Lucy had written that her husband had gone on a sea trip and she wished me to superintend the business of his farm and mills in his absence, if I could arrange to do so. She added that "Gussie" thought it was a pity to trouble me, and wanted to do the overseeing herself, but that she—Aunt Lucy—preferred to have a man at the head of affairs.

I had never seen my step-cousin, Augusta Ashley, but I knew, from Aunt Lucy's remarks concerning her, pretty much what sort of person she was—just the precise kind I disliked immeasurably. I had no idea what her age was, but doubtless she was over thirty, tall, determined, aggressive, with a "faculty" for managing, a sharp, probing nose, and a y-formation between her eyebrows. I knew the type, and I was assured that the period of sojourn with my respected aunt would be one of strife between Miss Ashley and myself.

I wrote to Aunt Lucy to expect me, made all necessary arrangements, and went to bid Nellie goodbye. I had made up my mind to marry Nellie. I had never openly avowed myself her suitor, but we were cousins, and had grown up together, so that I knew her well enough to be sure of my ground. I liked her so well that it was easy to persuade myself that I was in love with her. She more nearly fulfilled the requirements of my ideal wife than anyone I knew. She was pleasant to look upon, without being distractingly pretty; small and fair and womanly. She dressed nicely, sang and played agreeably, danced well, and had a cheerful, affectionate disposition. She was not alarmingly clever, had no "hobbies," and looked up to me as heir to all the wisdom of the ages—what man does not like to be thought clever and brilliant? I had no formidable rival, and our families were anxious for the match. I considered myself a lucky fellow. I felt that I would be very lonely without Nellie when I was away, and she admitted frankly that she would miss me awfully. She looked so sweet that I was on the point of asking her then and there to marry me. Well, fate interfered in the guise of a small brother, so I said goodbye and left, mentally comparing her to my idea of Miss Augusta Ashley, much to the latter's disadvantage.

When I stepped from the train at a sleepy country station next day I was promptly waylaid by a black-eyed urchin who informed me that Mrs. Ashley had sent him with an express wagon for my luggage, and that "Miss Gussie" was waiting with the carriage at the store, pointing down to a small building before whose door a girl was trying to soothe her frightened horse.

As I went down the slope towards her I noticed she was tall—quite too tall for my taste. I dislike women who can look into my eyes on a level—but I had to admit that her form was remarkably symmetrical and graceful. She put out her hand—it was ungloved and large, but white and firm, with a cool, pleasant touch—and said, with a composure akin to indifference, "Mr. Carslake, I presume. Mother could not come to meet you, so she sent me. Will you be kind enough to hold my horse for a few minutes? I want to get something in the store." Whereupon she calmly transferred the reins to me and disappeared.

At the time she certainly did not impress me as pretty, yet neither could I call her plain. Taken separately, her features were good. Her nose was large and straight, the mouth also a trifle large but firm and red, the brow wide and white, shadowed by a straying dash of brown curl or two. She had a certain cool, statuesque paleness, accentuated by straight, fine, black brows, and her eyes were a bluish grey; but the pupils, as I afterward found out, had a trick of dilating into wells of blackness which, added to a long fringe of very dark lashes, made her eyes quite the most striking feature of her face. Her expression was open and frank, and her voice clear and musical without being sweet. She looked about twenty-two.

At the time I did not fancy her appearance and made a mental note to the effect that I would never like Miss Ashley. I had no use for cool, businesslike women—women should have no concern with business. Nellie would never have troubled her dear, curly head over it.

Miss Ashley came out with her arms full of packages, stowed them away in the carriage, got in, told me which road to take, and did not again speak till we were out of the village and driving along a pretty country lane, arched over with crimson maples and golden-brown beeches. The purplish haze of a sunny autumn day mellowed over the fields, and the bunch of golden rod at my companion's belt was akin to the plumed ranks along the fences. I hazarded the remark that it was a fine day; Miss Ashley gravely admitted that it was. Then a deep smile seemed to rise somewhere in her eyes and creep over her face, discovering a dimple here and there as it proceeded.

"Don't let's talk about the weather—the subject is rather stale," she said. "I suppose you are wondering why on earth Mother had to drag you away out here. I tried to show her how foolish it was, but I didn't succeed. Mother thinks there must be a man at the head of affairs or they'll never go right. I could have taken full charge easily enough; I haven't been Father's 'boy' all my life for nothing. There was no need to take you away from your business."

I protested. I said I was going to take a vacation anyway, and business was not pressing just then. I also hinted that, while I had no doubt of her capacity, she might have found the duties of superintendent rather arduous.

"Not at all," she said, with a serenity that made me groan inwardly. "I like it. Father always said I was a born business manager. You'll find Ashley's Mills very quiet, I'm afraid. It's a sort of charmed Sleepy Hollow. See, there's home," as we turned a maple-blazoned corner and looked from the crest of one hill across to that of another. "Home" was a big, white, green-shuttered house buried amid a riot of autumn colour, with a big grove of dark green spruces at the back. Below them was a glimpse of a dark blue mill pond and beyond it long sweeps of golden-brown meadow land, sloping up till they dimmed in horizon mists of pearl and purple.

"How pretty," I exclaimed admiringly.

"Isn't it?" said Gussie proudly. "I love it." Her pupils dilated into dark pools, and I rather unwillingly admitted that Miss Ashley was a fine-looking girl.

As we drove up Aunt Lucy was standing on the steps of the verandah, over whose white roof trailed a luxuriant creeper, its leaves tinged by October frosts into lovely wine reds and tawny yellows. Gussie sprang out, barely touching my offered hand with her fingertips.

"There's Mother waiting to pounce on you and hear all the family news," she said, "so go and greet her like a dutiful nephew."

"I must take out your horse for you first," I said politely.

"Not at all," said Miss Ashley, taking the reins from my hands in a way not to be disputed. "I always unharness Charley myself. No one understands him half so well. Besides, I'm used to it. Didn't I tell you I'd always been Father's boy?"

"I well believe it," I thought in disgust, as she led the horse over to the well and I went up to Aunt Lucy. Through the sitting-room windows I kept a watchful eye on Miss Ashley as she watered and deftly unharnessed Charley and led him into his stable with sundry pats on his nose. Then I saw no more of her till she came in to tell us tea was ready, and led the way out to the dining room.

It was evident Miss Gussie held the reins of household government, and no doubt worthily. Those firm, capable white hands of hers looked as though they might be equal to a good many emergencies. She talked little, leaving the conversation to Aunt Lucy and myself, though she occasionally dropped in an apt word. Toward the end of the meal, however, she caught hold of an unfortunate opinion I had incautiously advanced and tore it into tatters. The result was a spirited argument, in which Miss Gussie held her own with such ability that I was utterly routed and found another grievance against her. It was very humiliating to be worsted by a girl—a country girl at that, who had passed most of her life on a farm! No doubt she was strong-minded and wanted to vote. I was quite prepared to believe anything of her.

After tea Miss Ashley proposed a walk around the premises, in order to initiate me into my duties. Apart from his farm, Mr. Ashley owned large grist-and saw-mills and did a flourishing business, with the details of which Miss Gussie seemed so conversant that I lost all doubt of her ability to run the whole thing as she had claimed. I felt quite ignorant in the light of her superior knowledge, and our walk was enlivened by some rather too lively discussions between us. We walked about together, however, till the shadows of the firs by the mills stretched nearly across the pond and the white moon began to put on a silvery burnish.

Then we wound up by a bitter dispute, during which Gussie's eyes were very black and each cheek had a round, red stain on it. She had a little air of triumph at having defeated me.

"I have to go now and see about putting away the milk, and I dare say you're not sorry to be rid of me," she said, with a demureness I had not credited her with, "but if you come to the verandah in half an hour I'll bring you out a glass of new milk and some pound cake I made today by a recipe that's been in the family for one hundred years, and I hope it will choke you for all the snubs you've been giving me." She walked away after this amiable wish, and I stood by the pond till the salmon tints faded from its waters and stars began to mirror themselves brokenly in its ripples. The mellow air was full of sweet, mingled eventide sounds as I walked back to the house. Aunt Lucy was knitting on the verandah. Gussie brought out cake and milk and chatted to us while we ate, in an inconsequent girlish way, or fed bits of cake to a green-eyed goblin in the likeness of a black cat.

She appeared in such an amiable light that I was half inclined to reconsider my opinion of her. When I went to my room the vase full of crimson leaves on my table suggested Gussie, and I repented of my unfriendliness for a moment—and only for a moment. Gussie and her mother passed through the hall below, and Aunt Lucy's soft voice floated up through my half-open door.

"Well, how do you like your cousin, my dear?"

Whereat that decided young lady promptly answered, "I think he is the most conceited youth I've met for some time."

Pleasant, wasn't it? I thought of Nellie's meek admiration of all my words and ways, and got her photo out to soothe my vanity. For the first time it struck me that her features were somewhat insipid. The thought seemed like disloyalty, so I banished it and went to bed.

I expected to dream of that disagreeable Gussie, but I did not, and I slept so soundly that it was ten o'clock the next morning before I woke. I sprang out of bed in dismay, dressed hastily, and ran down, not a little provoked at myself. Through the window I saw Gussie in the garden digging up some geraniums. She was enveloped in a clay-stained brown apron, a big flapping straw hat half hid her face, and she wore a pair of muddy old kid gloves. Her whole appearance was disreputable, and the face she turned to me as I said "Good morning" had a diagonal streak of clay across it. I added slovenliness to my already long list of her demerits.

"Good afternoon, rather. Don't you know what time it is? The men were here three hours ago for their orders. I thought it a pity to disturb your peaceful dreams, so I gave them myself and sent them off."

I was angrier than ever. A nice beginning I had made. And was that girl laughing at me?

"I expected to be called in time, certainly," I said stiffly. "I am not accustomed to oversleep myself. I promise it will not occur again."

My dignity was quite lost on Gussie. She peeled off her gloves cheerfully and said, "I suppose you'd like some breakfast. Just wait till I wash my hands and I'll get you some. Then if you're pining to be useful you can help me take up these geraniums."

There was no help for it. After I had breakfasted I went, with many misgivings. We got on fairly well, however. Gussie was particularly lively and kept me too busy for argument. I quite enjoyed the time and we did not quarrel until nearly the last, when we fell out bitterly over some horticultural problem and went in to dinner in sulky silence. Gussie disappeared after dinner and I saw no more of her. I was glad of this, but after a time I began to find it a little dull. Even a dispute would have been livelier. I visited the mills, looked over the farm, and then carelessly asked Aunt Lucy where Miss Ashley was. Aunt Lucy replied that she had gone to visit a friend and would not be back till the next day.

This was satisfactory, of course, highly so. What a relief it was to be rid of that girl with her self-assertiveness and independence. I said to myself that I hoped her friend would keep her for a week. I forgot to be disappointed that she had not when, next afternoon, I saw Gussie coming in at the gate with a tolerably large satchel and an armful of golden rod. I sauntered down to relieve her, and we had a sharp argument under way before we were halfway up the lane. As usual Gussie refused to give in that she was wrong.

Her walk had brought a faint, clear tint to her cheeks and her rippling dusky hair had half slipped down on her neck. She said she had to make some cookies for tea and if I had nothing better to do I might go and talk to her while she mixed them. It was not a gracious invitation but I went, rather than be left to my own company.

By the end of the week I was as much at home at Ashley Mills as if I had lived there all my life. Gussie and I were thrown together a good deal, for lack of other companions, and I saw no reason to change my opinion of her. She could be lively and entertaining when she chose, and at times she might be called beautiful. Still, I did not approve of her—at least I thought so, most of the time. Once in a while came a state of feeling which I did not quite understand.

One evening I went to prayer meeting with Aunt Lucy and Gussie. I had not seen the minister of Ashley Mills before, though Gussie and her mother seemed to know him intimately. I had an idea that he was old and silvery-haired and benevolent-looking. So I was rather surprised to find him as young as myself—a tall, pale, intellectual-looking man, with a high, white brow and dark, earnest eyes—decidedly attractive.

I was still more surprised when, after the service, he joined Gussie at the door and went down the steps with her. I felt distinctly ill-treated as I fell back with Aunt Lucy. There was no reason why I should—none; it ought to have been a relief. Rev. Carroll Martin had every right to see Miss Ashley home if he chose. Doubtless a girl who knew all there was to be known about business, farming, and milling, to say nothing of housekeeping and gardening, could discuss theology also. It was none of my business.

I don't know what kept me awake so late that night. As a consequence I overslept myself. I had managed to redeem my reputation on this point, but here it was lost again. I felt cross and foolish and cantankerous when I went out.

There was some unusual commotion at the well. It was an old-fashioned open one, with a chain and windlass. Aunt Lucy was peering anxiously down its mouth, from which a ladder was sticking. Just as I got there Gussie emerged from its depths with a triumphant face. Her skirt was muddy and draggled, her hair had tumbled down, and she held a dripping black cat.

"Coco must have fallen into the well last night," she explained, as I helped her to the ground. "I missed him at milking-time, and when I came to the well this morning I heard the most ear-splitting yowls coming up from it. I couldn't think where he could possibly be, for the water was quite calm, until I saw he had crept into a little crevice in the stones on the side. So I got a ladder and went down after him."

"You should have called me," I said sourly. "You might have killed yourself, going down there."

"And Coco might have tumbled in and drowned while you were getting up," retorted Gussie. "Besides, what was the need? I could go down as well as you."

"No doubt," I said, more sharply than I had any business to. "I don't dream of disputing your ability to do anything you may take it into your head to do. Most young ladies are not in the habit of going down wells, however."

"Perhaps not," she rejoined, with freezing calmness. "But, as you may have discovered, I am not 'most young ladies.' I am myself, Augusta Ashley, and accountable to nobody but myself if I choose to go down the well every day for pure love of it."

She walked off in her wet dress with her muddy cat. Gussie Ashley was the only girl I ever saw who could be dignified under such circumstances.

I was in a very bad humour with myself as I went off to see about having the well cleaned out. I had offended Gussie and I knew she would not be easily appeased. Nor was she. For a week she kept me politely, studiously, at a distance, in spite of my most humble advances. Rev. Carroll was a frequent caller, ostensibly to make arrangements about a Sunday school they were organizing in a poor part of the community. Gussie and he held long conversations on this enthralling subject. Then Gussie went on another visit to her friend, and when she came back so did Rev. Carroll.

One calm, hazy afternoon I was coming slowly up from the mills. Happening to glance at the kitchen roof, I gasped. It was on fire in one place. Evidently the dry shingles had caught fire from a spark. There was not a soul about save Gussie, Aunt Lucy, and myself. I dashed wildly into the kitchen, where Gussie was peeling apples.

"The house is on fire," I exclaimed. Gussie dropped her knife and turned pale.

"Don't wake Mother," was all she said, as she snatched a bucket of water from the table. The ladder was still lying by the well. In a second I had raised it to the roof and, while Gussie went up it like a squirrel and dashed the water on the flames, I had two more buckets ready for her.

Fortunately the fire had made little headway, though a few minutes more would have given it a dangerous start. The flames hissed and died out as Gussie threw on the water, and in a few seconds only a small black hole in the shingles remained. Gussie slid down the ladder. She trembled in every limb, but she put out her wet hand to me with a faint, triumphant smile. We shook hands across the ladder with a cordiality never before expressed.

For the next week, in spite of Rev. Carroll, I was happy when I thought of Gussie and miserable when I thought of Nellie. I held myself in some way bound to her and—was she not my ideal? Undoubtedly!

One day I got a letter from my sister. It was long and newsy, and the eighth page was most interesting.

"If you don't come home and look after Nellie," wrote Kate, "you'll soon not have her to look after. You remember that old lover of hers, Rod Allen? Well, he's home from the west now, immensely rich, they say, and his attentions to Nellie are the town talk. I think she likes him too. If you bury yourself any longer at Ashley Mills I won't be responsible for the consequences."

This lifted an immense weight from my mind, but the ninth page hurled it back again.

"You never say anything of Miss Ashley in your letters. What is she like—young or old, ugly or pretty, clever or dull? I met a lady recently who knows her and thinks she is charming. She also said Miss Ashley was to be married soon to Rev. Something-or-Other. Is it true?"

Aye, was it? Quite likely. Kate's letter made a very miserable man of me. Gussie found me a dull companion that day. After several vain attempts to rouse me to interest she gave it up.

"There's no use talking to you," she said impatiently. "I believe you are homesick. That letter you got this morning looked suspicious. Anyhow, I hope you'll get over it before I get back."

"Are you going away again?" I asked.

"Yes. I am going to stay a few days with Flossie." Flossie was that inseparable chum of hers.

"You seem to spend a good deal of your time with her," I remarked discontentedly.

Gussie opened her eyes at my tone.

"Why, of course," she said. "Flossie and I have always been chums. And she needs me more than ever just now, for she is awfully busy. She is to be married next month."

"Oh, I see—and you—"

"I'm to be bridesmaid, of course, and we've heaps to do. Flossie wanted to wait until Christmas, but Mr. Martin is in a—"

"Mr. Martin," I interrupted. "Is Mr. Martin going to marry your friend?"

"Why, yes. Didn't you know? They just suit each other. There he comes now. He's going to drive me over, and I'm not ready. Talk to him, for pity's sake, while I go and dress."

I never enjoyed a conversation more. Rev. Carroll Martin was a remarkably interesting man.

Nellie married Rod Allen at Christmas and I was best man. Nellie made a charming little bride, and Rod fairly worshipped her. My own wedding did not come off until spring, as Gussie said she could not get ready before that.

Kismet

The fifth heat in the free-for-all was just over. "Lu-Lu" had won, and the crowd on the grand stand and the hangers-on around the track were cheering themselves hoarse. Clear through the noisy clamour shrilled a woman's cry.

"Ah—I have dropped my scorecard."

A man in front of her turned.

"I have an extra one, madame. Will you accept it?"

Her small, modishly-gloved hand closed eagerly on it before she lifted her eyes to his face. Both started convulsively. The man turned very pale, but the woman's ripe-tinted face coloured darkly.

"You?" she faltered.

His lips parted in the coldly-grave smile she remembered and hated.

"You are not glad to see me," he said calmly, "but that, I suppose, was not to be expected. I did not come here to annoy you. This meeting is as unexpected to me as to you. I had no suspicion that for the last half-hour I had been standing next to my—"

She interrupted him by an imperious gesture. Still clutching the scorecard she half-turned from him. Again he smiled, this time with a tinge of scorn, and shifted his eyes to the track.

None of the people around them had noticed the little by-play. All eyes were on the track, which was being cleared for the first heat of another race. The free-for-all horses were being led away blanketed. The crowd cheered "Lu-Lu" as she went past, a shapeless oddity. The backers of "Mascot", the rival favourite, looked gloomy.

The woman noticed nothing of all this. She was small, very pretty, still young, and gowned in a quite unmistakable way. She studied the man's profile furtively. He looked older than when she had seen him last—there were some silver threads gleaming in his close-clipped dark hair and short, pointed beard. Otherwise there was little change in the quiet features and somewhat stern grey eyes. She wondered if he had cared at all.

They had not met for five years. She shut her eyes and looked in on her past. It all came back very vividly. She had been eighteen when they were married—a gay, high-spirited girl and the season's beauty. He was much older and a quiet, serious student. Her friends had wondered why she married him—sometimes she wondered herself, but she had loved him, or thought so.

The marriage had been an unhappy one. She was fond of society and gaiety, he wanted quiet and seclusion. She Was impulsive and impatient, he deliberate and grave. The strong wills clashed. After two years of an unbearable sort of life they had separated—quietly, and without scandal of any sort. She had wanted a divorce, but he would not agree to that, so she had taken her own independent fortune and gone back to her own way of life. In the following five years she had succeeded in burying all remembrance well out of sight. No one knew if she were satisfied or not; her world was charitable to her and she lived a gay and quite irreproachable life. She wished that she had not come to the races. It was such an irritating encounter. She opened her eyes wearily; the dusty track, the flying horses, the gay dresses of the women on the grandstand, the cloudless blue sky, the brilliant September sunshine, the purple distances all commingled in a glare that made her head ache. Before it all she saw the tall figure by her side, his face turned from her, watching the track intently.

She wondered with a vague curiosity what induced him to come to the races. Such things were not greatly in his line. Evidently their chance meeting had not disturbed him. It was a sign that he did not care. She sighed a little wearily and closed her eyes. When the heat was over he turned to her.

"May I ask how you have been since—since we met last? You are looking extremely well. Has Vanity Fair palled in any degree?"

She was angry at herself and him. Where had her careless society manner and well-bred composure gone? She felt weak and hysterical. What if she should burst into tears before the whole crowd—before those coldly critical grey eyes? She almost hated him.

"No—why should it? I have found it very pleasant—and I have been well—very well. And you?"

He jotted down the score carefully before he replied.

"I? Oh, a book-worm and recluse always leads a placid life. I never cared for excitement, you know. I came down here to attend a sale of some rare editions, and a well-meaning friend dragged me out to see the races. I find it rather interesting, I must confess, much more so than I should have fancied. Sorry I can't stay until the end. I must go as soon as the free-for-all is over, if not before. I have backed 'Mascot'; you?"

"'Lu-Lu'" she answered quickly—it almost seemed defiantly. How horribly unreal it was—this carrying on of small talk, as if they were the merest of chance-met acquaintances! "She belongs to a friend of mine, so I am naturally interested."

"She and 'Mascot' are ties now—both have won two heats. One more for either will decide it. This is a good day for the races. Excuse me."

He leaned over and brushed a scrap of paper from her grey cloak. She shivered slightly.

"You are cold! This stand is draughty."

"I am not at all cold, thank you. What race is this?—oh! the three-minute one."

She bent forward with assumed interest to watch the scoring. She was breathing heavily. There were tears in her eyes—she bit her lips savagely and glared at the track until they were gone.

Presently he spoke again, in the low, even tone demanded by circumstances.

"This is a curious meeting, is it not?—quite a flavor of romance! By-the-way, do you read as many novels as ever?"

She fancied there was mockery in his tone. She remembered how very frivolous he used to consider her novel-reading. Besides, she resented the personal tinge. What right had he?

"Almost as many," she answered carelessly.

"I was very intolerant, wasn't I?" he said after a pause. "You thought so—you were right. You have been happier since you—left me?"

"Yes," she said defiantly, looking straight into his eyes.

"And you do not regret it?"

He bent down a little. His sleeve brushed against her shoulder. Something in his face arrested the answer she meant to make.

"I—I—did not say that," she murmured faintly.

There was a burst of cheering. The free-for-all horses were being brought out for the sixth heat. She turned away to watch them. The scoring began, and seemed likely to have no end. She was tired of it all. It didn't matter a pin to her whether "Lu-Lu" or "Mascot" won. What *did* matter! Had Vanity Fair after all been a satisfying exchange for love? He *had* loved her once, and they had been happy at first. She had never before said, even in her own heart: "I am sorry," but—suddenly, she felt his hand on her shoulder, and looked up. Their eyes met. He stooped and said almost in a whisper:

"Will you come back to me?"

"I don't know," she whispered breathlessly, as one half-fascinated.

"We were both to blame—but I the most. I was too hard on you—I ought to have made more allowance. We are wiser now both of us. Come back to me—my wife."

His tone was cold and his face expressionless. It was on her lips to cry out "No," passionately.

But the slender, scholarly hand on her shoulder was trembling with the intensity of his repressed emotion. He *did* care, then. A wild caprice flashed into her brain. She sprang up.

"See," she cried, "they're off now. This heat will probably decide the race. If 'Lu-Lu' wins I will not go back to you, if 'Mascot' does I will. That is my decision."

He turned paler, but bowed in assent. He knew by bitter experience how unchangeable her whims were, how obstinately she clung to even the most absurd.

She leaned forward breathlessly. The crowd hung silently on the track. "Lu-Lu" and "Mascot" were neck and neck, getting in splendid work. Half-way round the course "Lu-Lu" forged half a neck ahead, and her backers went mad. But one woman dropped her head in her hands and dared look no more. One man with white face and set lips watched the track unswervingly.

Again "Mascot" crawled up, inch by inch. They were on the home stretch, they were equal, the cheering broke out, then silence, then another terrific burst, shouts, yells and clappings—"Mascot" had won the free-for-all. In the front row a woman stood up, swayed and shaken as a leaf in the wind. She straightened her scarlet hat and readjusted her veil unsteadily. There was a smile on her lips and tears in her eyes. No one noticed her. A man beside her drew her hand through his arm in a quiet proprietary fashion. They left the grand stand together.

Lilian's Business Venture

Lilian Mitchell turned into the dry-goods store on Randall Street, just as Esther Miller and Ella Taylor came out. They responded coldly to her greeting and exchanged significant glances as they walked away.

Lilian's pale face crimsoned. She was a tall, slender girl of about seventeen, and dressed in mourning. These girls had been her close friends once. But that was before the Mitchells had lost their money. Since then Lilian had been cut by many of her old chums and she felt it keenly.

The clerks in the store were busy and Lilian sat down to wait her turn. Near to her two ladies were also waiting and chatting.

"Helen wants me to let her have a birthday party," Mrs. Saunders was saying wearily. "She has been promised it so long and I hate to disappoint the child, but our girl left last week, and I cannot possibly make all the cakes and things myself. I haven't the time or strength, so Helen must do without her party."

"Talking of girls," said Mrs. Reeves impatiently, "I am almost discouraged. It is so hard to get a good all-round one. The last one I had was so saucy I had to discharge her, and the one I have now cannot make decent bread. I never had good luck with bread myself either."

"That is Mrs. Porter's great grievance too. It is no light task to bake bread for all those boarders. Have you made your jelly yet?"

"No. Maria cannot make it, she says, and I detest messing with jelly. But I really must see to it soon."

At this point a saleswoman came up to Lilian, who made her small purchases and went out.

"There goes Lilian Mitchell," said Mrs. Reeves in an undertone. "She looks very pale. They say they are dreadfully poor since Henry Mitchell died. His affairs were in a bad condition, I am told."

"I am sorry for Mrs. Mitchell," responded Mrs. Saunders. "She is such a sweet woman. Lilian will have to do something, I suppose, and there is so little chance for a girl here."

Lilian, walking down the street, was wearily turning over in her mind the problems of her young existence. Her father had died the preceding spring. He had been a supposedly prosperous merchant; the Mitchells had always lived well, and Lilian was a petted and only child. Then came the shock of Henry Mitchell's sudden death and of financial ruin. His affairs were found to be hopelessly involved; when all the debts were paid there was left only the merest pittance—barely enough for house-rent—for Lilian and her mother to live upon. They had moved into a tiny cottage in an unfashionable locality, and during the summer Lilian had tried hard to think of something to do. Mrs. Mitchell was a delicate woman, and the burden of their situation fell on Lilian's young shoulders.

There seemed to be no place for her. She could not teach and had no particular talent in any line. There was no opening for her in Willington, which was a rather sleepy little place, and Lilian was almost in despair.

"There really doesn't seem to be any real place in the world for me, Mother," she said rather dolefully at the supper table. "I've no talent at all; it is dreadful to have been born without one. And yet I *must* do something, and do it soon."

And Lilian, after she had washed up the tea dishes, went upstairs and had a good cry.

But the darkest hour, so the proverb goes, is just before the dawn, and after Lilian had had her cry out and was sitting at her window in the dusk, watching a thin new moon shining over the trees down the street, her inspiration came to her. A minute later she whirled into the tiny sitting-room where her mother was sewing.

"Mother, our fortune is made! I have an idea!"

"Don't lose it, then," said Mrs. Mitchell with a smile. "What is it, my dear?"

Lilian sobered herself, sat down by her mother's side, and proceeded to recount the conversation she had heard in the store that afternoon.

"Now, Mother, this is where my brilliant idea comes in. You have often told me I am a born cook and I always have good luck. Now, tomorrow morning I shall go to Mrs. Saunders and offer to furnish all the good things for Helen's birthday party, and then I'll ask Mrs. Reeves and Mrs. Porter if I may make their bread for them. That will do for a beginning, I like cooking, you know, and I believe that in time I can work up a good business."

"It seems to be a good idea," said Mrs. Mitchell thoughtfully, "and I am willing that you should try. But have you thought it all out carefully? There will be many difficulties."

"I know. I don't expect smooth sailing right along, and perhaps I'll fail altogether; but somehow I don't believe I will."

"A great many of your old friends will think—"

"Oh, yes; I know *that* too, but I am not going to mind it, Mother. I don't think there is any disgrace in working for my living. I'm going to do my best and not care what people say."

Early next morning Lilian started out. She had carefully thought over the details of her small venture, considered ways and means, and decided on the most advisable course. She would not attempt too much, and she felt sure of success.

To secure competent servants was one of the problems of Willington people. At Drayton, a large neighbouring town, were several factories, and into these all the working girls from Willington had crowded, leaving very few who were willing to go out to service. Many of those who did were poor cooks, and Lilian shrewdly suspected that many a harassed housekeeper in the village would be glad to avail herself of the new enterprise.

Lilian was, as she had said of herself, "a born cook." This was her capital, and she meant to make the most of it. Mrs. Saunders listened to her businesslike details with surprise and delight.

"It is the very thing," she said. "Helen is so eager for that party, but I could not undertake it myself. Her birthday is Friday. Can you have everything ready by then?"

"Yes, I think so," said Lilian briskly, producing her notebook. "Please give me the list of what you want and I will do my best."

From Mrs. Saunders she went to Mrs. Reeves and found a customer as soon as she had told the reason of her call. "I'll furnish all the bread and rolls you need," she said, "and they will be good, too. Now, about your jelly. I can make good jelly, and I'll be very glad to make yours."

When she left, Lilian had an order for two dozen glasses of apple jelly, as well as a standing one for bread and rolls. Mrs. Porter was next visited and grasped eagerly at the opportunity.

"I know your bread will be good," she said, "and you may count on me as a regular customer."

Lilian thought she had enough on hand for a first attempt and went home satisfied. On her way she called at the grocery store with an order that surprised Mr. Hooper. When she told him of her plan he opened his eyes.

"I must tell my wife about that. She isn't strong and she doesn't like cooking."

After dinner Lilian went to work, enveloped in a big apron, and whipped eggs, stoned raisins, stirred, concocted, and baked until dark. When bedtime came she was so tired that she could hardly crawl upstairs; but she felt happy too, for the day had been a successful one.

And so also were the days and weeks and months that followed. It was hard and constant work, but it brought its reward. Lilian had not promised more than she could perform, and her customers were satisfied. In a short time she found herself with a regular and growing business on her hands, for new customers were gradually added and always came to stay.

People who gave parties found it very convenient to follow Mrs. Saunders's example and order their supplies from Lilian. She had a very busy winter and, of course, it was not all plain sailing. She had many difficulties to contend with. Sometimes days came on which everything seemed to go wrong—when the stove smoked or the oven wouldn't heat properly, when cakes fell flat and bread was sour and pies behaved as only totally depraved pies can, when she burned her fingers and felt like giving up in despair.

Then, again, she found herself cut by several of her old acquaintances. But she was too sensible to worry much over this. The friends really worth having were still hers, her mother's face had lost its look of care, and her business was prospering. She was hopeful and wide awake, kept her wits about her and looked out for hints, and learned to laugh over her failures.

During the winter she and her mother had managed to do most of the work themselves, hiring little Mary Robinson next door on especially busy days, and now and then calling in the assistance of Jimmy Bowen and his hand sled to carry orders to customers. But when spring came Lilian prepared to open up her summer campaign on a much larger scale. Mary Robinson was hired for the season, and John Perkins was engaged to act as carrier with his express wagon. A summer kitchen was boarded in in the backyard, and a new range bought; Lilian began operations with a striking advertisement in the Willington *News* and an attractive circular sent around to all her patrons. Picnics and summer weddings were frequent. In bread and rolls her trade was brisk and constant. She also took orders for pickles, preserves, and jellies, and this became such a flourishing branch that a second assistant had to be hired.

It was a cardinal rule with Lilian never to send out any article that was not up to her standard. She bore the loss of her failures, and sometimes stayed up half of the night to fill an order on time. "Prompt and perfect" was her motto.

The long hot summer days were very trying, and sometimes she got very tired of it all. But when on the anniversary of her first venture she made up her accounts she was well pleased. To be sure, she had not made a fortune; but she had paid all their expenses, had a hundred dollars clear, and had laid the solid foundations of a profitable business.

"Mother," she said jubilantly, as she wiped a dab of flour from her nose and proceeded to concoct the icing for Blanche Remington's wedding cake, "don't you think my business venture has been a decided success?"

Mrs. Mitchell surveyed her busy daughter with a motherly smile. "Yes, I think it has," she said.

Miriam's Lover

I had been reading a ghost story to Mrs. Sefton, and I laid it down at the end with a little shrug of contempt.

"What utter nonsense!" I said.

Mrs. Sefton nodded abstractedly above her fancywork.

"That is. It is a very commonplace story indeed. I don't believe the spirits of the departed trouble themselves to revisit the glimpses of the moon for the purpose of frightening honest mortals—or even for the sake of hanging around the favourite haunts of their existence in the flesh. If they ever appear, it must be for a better reason than that."

"You don't surely think that they ever do appear?" I said incredulously.

"We have no proof that they do not, my dear."

"Surely, Mary," I exclaimed, "you don't mean to say that you believe people ever do or can see spirits—ghosts, as the word goes?"

"I didn't say I believed it. I never saw anything of the sort. I neither believe nor disbelieve. But you know queer things do happen at times—things you can't account for. At least, people who you know wouldn't lie say so. Of course, they may be mistaken. And I don't think that everybody can see spirits either, provided they are to be seen. It requires people of a certain organization—with a spiritual eye, as it were. We haven't all got that—in fact, I think very few of us have. I dare say you think I'm talking nonsense."

"Well, yes, I think you are. You really surprise me, Mary. I always thought you the least likely person in the world to take up with such ideas. Something must have come under your observation to develop such theories in your practical head. Tell me what it was."

"To what purpose? You would remain as sceptical as ever."

"Possibly not. Try me; I may be convinced."

"No," returned Mrs. Sefton calmly. "Nobody ever is convinced by hearsay. When a person has once seen a spirit—or thinks he has—he thenceforth believes it. And when somebody else is intimately associated with that person and knows all the circumstances—well, he admits the possibility, at least. That is my position. But by the time it gets to the third person—the outsider—it loses power. Besides, in this particular instance the story isn't very exciting. But then—it's true."

"You have excited my curiosity. You must tell me the story."

"Well, first tell me what you think of this. Suppose two people, both sensitively organized individuals, loved each other with a love stronger than life. If they were apart, do you think it might be possible for their souls to communicate with each other in some inexplicable way? And if anything happened to one, don't you think that that one could and would let the spirit of the other know?"

"You're getting into too deep waters for me, Mary," I said, shaking my head. "I'm not an authority on telepathy, or whatever you call it. But I've no belief in such theories. In fact, I think they are all nonsense. I'm sure you must think so too in your rational moments."

"I dare say it is all nonsense," said Mrs. Sefton slowly, "but if you had lived a whole year in the same house with Miriam Gordon, you would have been tainted too. Not that she had 'theories'—at least, she never aired them if she had. But there was simply something about the girl herself that gave a person strange impressions. When I first met her I had the most uncanny feeling that she was all spirit—soul—what you will! no flesh, anyhow. That feeling wore off after a while, but she never seemed like other people to me.

"She was Mr. Sefton's niece. Her father had died when she was a child. When Miriam was twenty her mother had married a second time and went to Europe with her husband. Miriam came to live with us while they were away. Upon their return she was herself to be married.

"I had never seen Miriam before. Her arrival was unexpected, and I was absent from home when she came. I returned in the evening, and when I saw her first she was standing under the chandelier in the drawing room. Talk about spirits! For five seconds I thought I had seen one.

"Miriam was a beauty. I had known that before, though I think I hardly expected to see such wonderful loveliness. She was tall and extremely graceful, dark—at least her hair was dark, but her skin was wonderfully fair and clear. Her hair was gathered away from her face, and she had a high, pure, white forehead, and the straightest, finest, blackest brows. Her face was oval, with very large and dark eyes.

"I soon realized that Miriam was in some mysterious fashion different from other people. I think everyone who met her felt the same way. Yet it was a feeling hard to define. For my own part I simply felt as if she belonged to another world, and that part of the time she—her soul, you know—was back there again.

"You must not suppose that Miriam was a disagreeable person to have in the house. On the contrary, it was the very reverse. Everybody liked her. She was one of the sweetest, most winsome girls I ever knew, and I soon grew to love her dearly. As for what Dick called her 'little queernesses'—well, we got used to them in time.

"Miriam was engaged, as I have told you, to a young Harvard man named Sidney Claxton. I knew she loved him very deeply. When she showed me his photograph, I liked his appearance and said so. Then I made some teasing remark about her love-letters—just for a joke, you know. Miriam looked at me with an odd little smile and said quickly:

"'Sidney and I never write to each other.'

"'Why, Miriam!' I exclaimed in astonishment. 'Do you mean to tell me you never hear from him at all?'

"'No, I did not say that. I hear from him every day—every hour. We do not need to write letters. There are better means of communication between two souls that are in perfect accord with each other.'

"'Miriam, you uncanny creature, what do you mean?' I asked.

"But Miriam only gave another queer smile and made no answer at all. Whatever her beliefs or theories were, she would never discuss them.

"She had a habit of dropping into abstracted reveries at any time or place. No matter where she was, this, whatever it was, would come over her. She would sit there, perhaps in the centre of a gay crowd, and gaze right out into space, not hearing or seeing a single thing that went on around her.

"I remember one day in particular; we were sewing in my room. I looked up and saw that Miriam's work had dropped on her knee and she was leaning forward, her lips apart, her eyes gazing upward with an unearthly expression.

"'Don't look like that, Miriam!' I said, with a little shiver. 'You seem to be looking at something a thousand miles away!'

"Miriam came out of her trance or reverie and said, with a little laugh:

"'How do you know but that I was?'

"She bent her head for a minute or two. Then she lifted it again and looked at me with a sudden contraction of her level brows that betokened vexation.

"'I wish you hadn't spoken to me just then,' she said. 'You interrupted the message I was receiving. I shall not get it at all now.'

"'Miriam,' I implored. 'I so wish my dear girl, that you wouldn't talk so. It makes people think there is something queer about you. Who in the world was sending you a message, as you call it?'

"'Sidney,' said Miriam simply.

"'Nonsense!'

"'You think it is nonsense because you don't understand it,' was her calm response.

"I recall another event was when some caller dropped in and we had drifted into a discussion about ghosts and the like—and I've no doubt we all talked some delicious nonsense. Miriam said nothing at the time, but when we were alone I asked her what she thought of it.

"'I thought you were all merely talking against time,' she retorted evasively.

"'But, Miriam, do you really think it is possible for ghosts—'

"'I detest that word!'

"'Well, spirits then—to return after death, or to appear to anyone apart from the flesh?'

"'I will tell you what I know. If anything were to happen to Sidney—if he were to die or be killed—he would come to me himself and tell me.'

"One day Miriam came down to lunch looking pale and worried. After Dick went out, I asked her if anything were wrong.

"'Something has happened to Sidney,' she replied, 'some painful accident—I don't know what.'

"'How do you know?' I cried. Then, as she looked at me strangely, I added hastily, 'You haven't been receiving any more unearthly messages, have you? Surely, Miriam, you are not so foolish as to really believe in that!'

"'I know,' she answered quickly. 'Belief or disbelief has nothing to do with it. Yes, I have had a message. I know that some accident has happened to Sidney—painful and inconvenient but not particularly dangerous. I do not know what it is. Sidney will write me that. He writes when it is absolutely necessary.'

"'Aerial communication isn't perfected yet then?' I said mischievously. But, observing how really worried she seemed, I added, 'Don't fret, Miriam. You may be mistaken.'

"Well, two days afterwards she got a note from her lover—the first I had ever known her to receive—in which he said he had been thrown from his horse and had broken his left arm. It had happened the very morning Miriam received her message.

"Miriam had been with us about eight months when one day she came into my room hurriedly. She was very pale.

"'Sidney is ill—dangerously ill. What shall I do?'

"I knew she must have had another of those abominable messages—or thought she had—and really, remembering the incident of the broken arm, I couldn't feel as sceptical as I pretended to. I tried to cheer her, but did not succeed. Two hours later she had a telegram from her lover's college chum, saying that Mr. Claxton was dangerously ill with typhoid fever.

"I was quite alarmed about Miriam in the days that followed. She grieved and fretted continually. One of her troubles was that she received no more messages; she said it was because Sidney was too ill to send them. Anyhow, she had to content herself with the means of communication used by ordinary mortals.

"Sidney's mother, who had gone to nurse him, wrote every day, and at last good news came. The crisis was over and the doctor in attendance thought Sidney would recover. Miriam seemed like a new creature then, and rapidly recovered her spirits.

"For a week reports continued favourable. One night we went to the opera to hear a celebrated prima donna. When we returned home Miriam and I were sitting in her room, chatting over the events of the evening.

"Suddenly she sat straight up with a sort of convulsive shudder, and at the same time—you may laugh if you like—the most horrible feeling came over me. I didn't see anything, but I just felt that there was something or someone in the room besides ourselves.

"Miriam was gazing straight before her. She rose to her feet and held out her hands.

"'Sidney!' she said.

"Then she fell to the floor in a dead faint.

"I screamed for Dick, rang the bell and rushed to her.

"In a few minutes the whole household was aroused, and Dick was off post-haste for the doctor, for we could not revive Miriam from her death-like swoon. She seemed as one dead. We worked over her for hours. She would come out of her faint for a moment, give us an unknowing stare and go shudderingly off again.

"The doctor talked of some fearful shock, but I kept my own counsel. At dawn Miriam came back to life at last. When she and I were left alone, she turned to me.

"'Sidney is dead,' she said quietly. 'I saw him—just before I fainted. I looked up, and he was standing between me and you. He had come to say farewell.'

"What could I say? Almost while we were talking a telegram came. He was dead—he had died at the very hour at which Miriam had seen him."

Mrs. Sefton paused, and the lunch bell rang.

"What do you think of it?" she queried as we rose.

"Honestly, I don't know what I think of it," I answered frankly.

Miss Calista's Peppermint Bottle

Miss Calista was perplexed. Her nephew, Caleb Cramp, who had been her right-hand man for years and whom she had got well broken into her ways, had gone to the Klondike, leaving her to fill his place with the next best man; but the next best man was slow to appear, and meanwhile Miss Calista was looking about her warily. She could afford to wait a while, for the crop was all in and the fall ploughing done, so that the need of a successor to Caleb was not as pressing as it might otherwise have been. There was no lack of applicants, such as they were. Miss Calista was known to be a kind and generous mistress, although she had her "ways," and insisted calmly and immovably upon wholehearted compliance with them. She had a small, well-cultivated farm and a comfortable house, and her hired men lived in clover. Caleb Cramp had been perfection after his kind, and Miss Calista did not expect to find his equal. Nevertheless, she set up a certain standard of requirements; and although three weeks, during which Miss Calista had been obliged to put up with the immature services of a neighbour's boy, had elapsed since Caleb's departure, no one had as yet stepped into his vacant and coveted shoes.

Certainly Miss Calista was somewhat hard to please, but she was not thinking of herself as she sat by her front window in the chilly November twilight. Instead, she was musing on the degeneration of hired men, and reflecting that it was high time the wheat was thrashed, the house banked, and sundry other duties attended to.

Ches Maybin had been up that afternoon to negotiate for the vacant place, and had offered to give satisfaction for smaller wages than Miss Calista had ever paid. But he had met with a brusque refusal, scarcely as civil as Miss Calista had bestowed on drunken Jake Stinson from the Morrisvale Road.

Not that Miss Calista had any particular prejudice against Ches Maybin, or knew anything positively to his discredit. She was simply unconsciously following the example of a world that exerts itself to keep a man down when he is down and prevent all chance of his rising. Nothing succeeds like success, and the converse of this is likewise true—that nothing fails like failure. There was not a person in Cooperstown who would not have heartily endorsed Miss Calista's refusal.

Ches Maybin was only eighteen, although he looked several years older, and although no flagrant misdoing had ever been proved against him, suspicion of such was not wanting. He came of a bad stock, people said sagely, adding that what was bred in the bone was bound to come out in the flesh. His father, old Sam Maybin, had been a shiftless and tricky rascal, as everybody knew, and had ended his days in the poorhouse. Ches's mother had died when he was a baby, and he had come up somehow, in a hand-to-mouth fashion, with all the cloud of heredity hanging over him. He was always looked at askance, and when any mischief came to light in the village, it was generally fastened on him as a convenient and handy scapegoat. He was considered sulky and lazy, and the local prophets united in predicting a bad end for him sooner or later; and, moreover, diligently endeavoured by their general treatment of him to put him in a fair way to fulfil their predictions. Miss Calista, when she had shut Chester Maybin out into the chill gloom of the November dusk, dismissed him from her thoughts. There were other things of more moment to her just then than old Sam Maybin's hopeful son.

There was nobody in the house but herself, and although this was neither alarming nor unusual, it was unusual—and Miss Calista considered it alarming—that the sum of five hundred dollars should at that very moment be in the upper right-hand drawer of the sideboard, which sum had been up to the previous day safe in the coffers of the Millageville bank. But certain unfavourable rumours were in course of circulation about that same institution, and Miss Calista, who was nothing if not prudent, had gone to the bank that very morning and withdrawn her deposit. She intended to go over to Kerrytown the very next day and deposit it in the Savings Bank there. Not another day would she keep it in the house, and, indeed, it worried her to think she must keep it even for the night, as she had told Mrs. Galloway that afternoon during a neighbourly back-yard chat.

"Not but what it's safe enough," she said, "for not a soul but you knows I've got it. But I'm not used to have so much by me, and there are always tramps going round. It worries me somehow. I wouldn't give it a thought if Caleb was here. I s'pose being all alone makes me nervous."

Miss Calista was still rather nervous when she went to bed that night, but she was a woman of sound sense and was determined not to give way to foolish fears. She locked doors and windows carefully, as was her habit, and saw that the fastenings were good and secure. The one on the dining-room window, looking out on the back yard, wasn't; in fact, it was broken altogether; but, as Miss Calista told herself, it had been broken just so for the last six years, and nobody had ever tried to get in at it yet, and it wasn't likely anyone would begin tonight.

Miss Calista went to bed and, despite her worry, slept soon and soundly. It was well on past midnight when she suddenly wakened and sat bolt upright in bed. She was not accustomed to waken in the night, and she had the impression of having been awakened by some noise. She listened breathlessly. Her room was directly over the dining-room, and an empty stovepipe hole opened up through the ceiling of the latter at the head of her bed.

There was no mistake about it. Something or some person was moving about stealthily in the room below. It wasn't the cat—Miss Calista had shut him in the woodshed before she went to bed, and he couldn't possibly get out. It must certainly be a beggar or tramp of some description.

Miss Calista might be given over to nervousness in regard to imaginary thieves, but in the presence of real danger she was cool and self-reliant. As noiselessly and swiftly as any burglar himself, Miss Calista slipped out of bed and into her clothes. Then she tip-toed out into the hall. The late moonlight, streaming in through the hall windows, was quite enough illumination for her purpose, and she got downstairs and was fairly in the open doorway of the dining-room before a sound betrayed her presence.

Standing at the sideboard, hastily ransacking the neat contents of an open drawer, stood a man's figure, dimly visible in the moonlight gloom. As Miss Calista's grim form appeared in the doorway, the midnight marauder turned with a start and then, with an inarticulate cry, sprang, not at the courageous lady, but at the open window behind him.

Miss Calista, realizing with a flash of comprehension that he was escaping her, had a woman-like impulse to get a blow in anyhow; she grasped and hurled at her unceremonious caller the first thing that came to hand—a bottle of peppermint essence that was standing on the sideboard.

The missile hit the escaping thief squarely on the shoulder as he sprang out of the window, and the fragments of glass came clattering down on the sill. The next moment Miss Calista found herself alone, standing by the sideboard in a half-dazed fashion, for the whole thing had passed with such lightning-like rapidity that it almost seemed as if it were the dissolving end of a bad dream. But the open drawer and the window, where the bits of glass were glistening in the moonlight, were no dream. Miss Calista recovered herself speedily, closed the window, lit the lamp, gathered up the broken glass, and set up the chairs which the would-be thief had upset in his exit. An examination of the sideboard showed the precious five hundred safe and sound in an undisturbed drawer.

Miss Calista kept grim watch and ward there until morning, and thought the matter over exhaustively. In the end she resolved to keep her own counsel. She had no clue whatever to the thief's whereabouts or identity, and no good would come of making a fuss, which might only end in throwing suspicion on someone who might be quite innocent.

When the morning came Miss Calista lost no time in setting out for Kerrytown, where the money was soon safely deposited in the bank. She heaved a sigh of relief when she left the building.

I feel as if I could enjoy life once more, she said to herself. Goodness me, if I'd had to keep that money by me for a week itself, I'd have been a raving lunatic by the end of it.

Miss Calista had shopping to do and friends to visit in town, so that the dull autumn day was well nigh spent when she finally got back to Cooperstown and paused at the corner store to get a bundle of matches.

The store was full of men, smoking and chatting around the fire, and Miss Calista, whose pet abomination was tobacco smoke, was not at all minded to wait any longer than she could help. But Abiram Fell was attending to a previous customer, and Miss Calista sat grimly down by the counter to wait her turn.

The door opened, letting in a swirl of raw November evening wind and Ches Maybin. He nodded sullenly to Mr. Fell and passed down the store to mutter a message to a man at the further end.

Miss Calista lifted her head as he passed and sniffed the air as a charger who scents battle. The smell of tobacco was strong, and so was that of the open boxes of dried herring on the counter, but plainly, above all the commingled odours of a country grocery, Miss Calista caught a whiff of peppermint, so strong as to leave no doubt of its origin. There had been no hint of it before Ches Maybin's entrance.

The latter did not wait long. He was out and striding along the shadowy road when Miss Calista left the store and drove smartly after him. It never took Miss Calista long to make up her mind about anything, and she had weighed and passed judgement on Ches Maybin's case while Mr. Fell was doing up her matches.

The lad glanced up furtively as she checked her fat grey pony beside him.

"Good evening, Chester," she said with brisk kindness. "I can give you a lift, if you are going my way. Jump in, quick—Dapple is a little restless."

A wave of crimson, duskily perceptible under his sunburned skin, surged over Ches Maybin's face. It almost seemed as if he were going to blurt out a blunt refusal. But Miss Calista's face was so guileless and her tone so friendly, that he thought better of it and sprang in beside her, and Dapple broke into an impatient trot down the long hill lined with its bare, wind-writhen maples.

After a few minutes' silence Miss Calista turned to her moody companion.

"Chester," she said, as tranquilly as if about to ask him the most ordinary question in the world, "why did you climb into my house last night and try to steal my money?"

Ches Maybin started convulsively, as if he meant to spring from the buggy at once, but Miss Calista's hand was on his arm in a grasp none the less firm because of its gentleness, and there was a warning gleam in her grey eyes.

"It won't mend matters trying to get clear of me, Chester. I know it was you and I want an answer—a truthful one, mind you—to my question. I am your friend, and I am not going to harm you if you tell me the truth."

Her clear and incisive gaze met and held irresistibly the boy's wavering one. The sullen obstinacy of his face relaxed.

"Well," he muttered finally, "I was just desperate, that's why. I've never done anything real bad in my life before, but people have always been down on me. I'm blamed for everything, and nobody wants anything to do with me. I'm willing to work, but I can't get a thing to do. I'm in rags and I haven't a cent, and winter's coming on. I heard you telling Mrs. Galloway yesterday about the money. I was behind the fir hedge and you didn't see me. I went away and planned it all out. I'd get in some way—and I meant to use the money to get away out west as far from here as I could, and begin life there, where nobody knew me, and where I'd have some sort of a chance. I've never had any here. You can put me in jail now, if you like—they'll feed and clothe me there, anyhow, and I'll be on a level with the rest."

The boy had blurted it all out sullenly and half-chokingly. A world of rebellion and protest against the fate that had always dragged him down was couched in his voice.

Miss Calista drew Dapple to a standstill before her gate.

"I'm not going to send you to jail, Chester. I believe you've told me the truth. Yesterday you wanted me to give you Caleb's place and I refused. Well, I offer it to you now. If you'll come, I'll hire you, and give you as good wages as I gave him."

Ches Maybin looked incredulous.

"Miss Calista, you can't mean it."

"I do mean it, every word. You say you have never had a chance. Well, I am going to give you one—a chance to get on the right road and make a man of yourself. Nobody shall ever know about last night's doings from me, and I'll make it my business to forget them if you deserve it. What do you say?"

Ches lifted his head and looked her squarely in the face.

"I'll come," he said huskily. "It ain't no use to try and thank you, Miss Calista. But I'll live my thanks."

And he did. The good people of Cooperstown held up their hands in horror when they heard that Miss Calista had hired Ches Maybin, and prophesied that the deluded woman would live to repent her rash step. But not all prophecies come true. Miss Calista smiled serenely and kept on her own misguided way. And Ches Maybin proved so efficient and steady that the arrangement was continued, and in due time people outlived their old suspicions and came to regard him as a thoroughly smart and trustworthy young man.

"Miss Calista has made a man of Ches Maybin," said the oracles. "He ought to be very grateful to her."

And he was. But only he and Miss Calista and the peppermint bottle ever knew the precise extent of his gratitude, and they never told.

The Jest That Failed

"I think it is simply a disgrace to have a person like that in our class," said Edna Hayden in an injured tone.

"And she doesn't seem a bit ashamed of it, either," said Agnes Walters.

"Rather proud of it, I should say," returned her roommate, spitefully. "It seems to me that if I were so poor that I had to 'room' myself and dress as dowdily as she does that I really couldn't look anybody in the face. What must the boys think of her? And if it wasn't for her being in it, our class would be the smartest and dressiest in the college—even those top-lofty senior girls admit that."

"It's a shame," said Agnes, conclusively. "But she needn't expect to associate with our set. I, for one, won't have anything to do with her."

"Nor I. I think it is time she should be taught her place. If we could only manage to inflict some decided snub on her, she might take the hint and give up trying to poke herself in where she doesn't belong. The idea of her consenting to be elected on the freshmen executive! But she seems impervious to snubs."

"Edna, let's play a joke on her. It will serve her right. Let us send an invitation in somebody's name to the senior 'prom.'"

"The very thing! And sign Sidney Hill's name to it. He's the handsomest and richest fellows at Payzant, and belongs to one of the best families in town, and he's awfully fastidious besides. No doubt she will feel immensely flattered and, of course, she'll accept. Just think how silly she'll feel when she finds out he never sent it. Let's write it now, and send it at once. There is no time to lose, for the 'prom' is on Thursday night."

The freshmen co-eds at Payzant College did not like Grace Seeley—that is to say, the majority of them. They were a decidedly snobbish class that year. No one could deny that Grace was clever, but she was poor, dressed very plainly—"dowdily," the girls said—and "roomed" herself, that phrase meaning that she rented a little unfurnished room and cooked her own meals over an oil stove.

The "senior prom," as it was called, was the annual reception which the senior class gave in the middle of every autumn term. It was the smartest and gayest of all the college functions, and a Payzant co-ed who received an invitation to it counted herself fortunate. The senior girls were included as a matter of course, but a junior, soph, or freshie could not go unless one of the senior boys invited her.

Grace Seeley was studying Greek in her tiny room that afternoon when the invitation was brought to her. It was scrupulously orthodox in appearance and form, and Grace never doubted that it was genuine, although she felt much surprised that Sidney Hill, the leader of his class and the foremost figure in all college sports and societies, should have asked her to go with him to the senior prom.

But she was girlishly pleased at the prospect. She was as fond of a good time as any other girl, and she had secretly wished very much that she could go to the brilliant and much talked about senior prom.

Grace was quite unaware of her own unpopularity among her class co-eds, although she thought it was very hard to get acquainted with them. Without any false pride herself, and of a frank, independent nature, it never occurred to her that the other Payzant freshies could look down on her because she was poor, or resent her presence among them because she dressed plainly.

She straightway wrote a note of acceptance to Sidney Hill, and that young man naturally felt much mystified when he opened and read it in the college library next morning.

"Grace Seeley," he pondered. "That's the jolly girl with the brown eyes that I met at the philomathic the other night. She thanks me for my invitation to the senior prom, and accepts with pleasure. Why, I certainly never invited her or anyone else to go with me to the senior prom. There must be some mistake."

Grace passed him at this moment on her way to the Latin classroom. She bowed and smiled in a friendly fashion and Sidney Hill felt decidedly uncomfortable. What was he to do? He did not like to think of putting Miss Seeley in a false position because somebody had sent her an invitation in his name.

"I suppose it is some cad who has a spite at me that has done it," he reflected, "but if so I'll spoil his game. I'll take Miss Seeley to the prom as if I had never intended doing anything else. She shan't be humiliated just because there is someone at Payzant who would stoop to that sort of thing."

So he walked up the hall with Grace and expressed his pleasure at her acceptance, and on the evening of the prom he sent her a bouquet of white carnations, whose spicy fragrance reminded her of her own little garden at home. Grace thought it extremely nice of him, and dressed in a flutter of pleasant anticipation.

Her gown was a very simple one of sheer white organdie, and was the only evening dress she had. She knew there would be many smarter dresses at the reception, but the knowledge did not disturb her sensible head in the least.

She fingered the dainty white frills lovingly as she remembered the sunny summer days at home in the little sewing-room, where cherry boughs poked their blossoms in at the window, when her mother and sisters had helped her to make it, with laughing prophesies and speculations as to its first appearance. Into seam and puff and frill many girlish hopes and dreams had been sewn, and they all came back to Grace as she put it on, and helped to surround her with an atmosphere of happiness.

When she was ready she picked up her bouquet and looked herself over in the mirror, from the top of her curly head to the tips of her white shoes, with a little nod of satisfaction. Grace was not exactly pretty, but she had such a bright, happy face and such merry brown eyes and such a friendly smile that she was very pleasant to look upon, and a great many people thought so that night.

Grace had never in all her life before had so good a time as she had at that senior prom. The seniors were quick to discover her unaffected originality and charm, and everywhere she went she was the centre of a merry group. In short, Grace, as much to her own surprise as anyone's, found herself a social success.

Presently Sidney brought his brother up to be introduced, and the latter said:

"Miss Seeley, will you excuse my asking if you have a brother or any relative named Max Seeley?"

Grace nodded. "Oh, yes, my brother Max. He is a doctor out west."

"I was sure of it," said Murray Hill triumphantly. "You resemble him so strongly. Please don't consider me as a stranger a minute longer, for Max and I are like brothers. Indeed, I owe my life to him. Last summer I was out there on a surveying expedition, and I took typhoid in a little out-of-the-way place where good nursing was not to be had for love or money. Your brother attended me and he managed to pull me through. He never left me day or night until I was out of danger, and he worked like a Trojan for me."

"Dear old Max," said Grace, her brown eyes shining with pride and pleasure. "That is so like him. He is such a dear brother and I haven't seen him for four years. To see somebody who knows him so well is next best thing to seeing himself."

"He is an awfully fine fellow," said Mr. Hill heartily, "and I'm delighted to have met the 'little sister' he used to talk so much about. I want you to come ever and meet my mother and sister. They have heard me talk so much about Max that they think almost as much of him as I do, and they will be glad to meet his sister."

Mrs. Hill, a handsome, dignified lady who was one of the chaperones of the prom, received Grace warmly, while Beatrice Hill, an extremely pretty, smartly gowned girl, made her feel at home immediately.

"You came with Sid, didn't you?" she whispered. "Sid is so sly—he never tells us whom he is going to take anywhere. But when I saw you come in with him I knew I was going to like you, you looked so jolly. And you're really the sister of that splendid Dr. Seeley who saved Murray's life last summer? And to think you've been at Payzant nearly a whole term and we never knew it!"

"Well, how have you enjoyed our prom, Miss Seeley?" asked Sid, as they walked home together under the arching elms of the college campus.

"Oh! it was splendid," said Grace enthusiastically. "Everybody was so nice. And then to meet someone who could tell me so much about Max! I must write them home all about it before I sleep, just to calm my head a bit. Mother and the girls will be so interested, and I must send Lou and Mab a carnation apiece for their scrapbooks."

"Give me one back, please," said Sid. And Grace with a little blush, did so.

That night, while Grace was slipping the stems of her carnations and putting them into water, three little bits of conversation were being carried on which it is necessary to report in order to round up this story neatly and properly, as all stories should be rounded up.

In the first place, Beatrice Hill was saying to Sidney, "Oh, Sid, that Miss Seeley you had at the prom is a lovely girl. I don't know when I've met anyone I liked so much. She was so jolly and friendly and she didn't put on learned airs at all, as so many of those Payzant girls do. I asked her all about herself and she told me, and all about her mother and sisters and home and the lovely times they had together, and how hard they worked to send her to college too, and how she taught school in vacations and 'roomed' herself to help along. Isn't it so brave and plucky of her! I know we are going to be great friends."

"I hope so," said Sidney briefly, "because I have an idea that she and I are going to be very good friends too."

And Sidney went upstairs and put away a single white carnation very carefully.

In the second place, Mrs. Hill was saying to her eldest son, "I liked that Miss Seeley very much. She seemed a very sweet girl."

And, finally, Agnes Walters and Edna Hayden were discussing the matter in great mystification in their room.

"I can't understand it at all," said Agnes slowly. "Sid Hill took her to the prom and he must have sent her those carnations too. She could never have afforded them herself. And did you see the fuss his people made over her? I heard Beatrice telling her that she was coming to call on her tomorrow, and Mrs. Hill said she must look upon 'Beechlawn' as her second home while she was at Payzant. If the Hills are going to take her up we'll have to be nice to her."

"I suppose," said Edna conclusively, "the truth of the matter is that Sid Hill meant to ask her anyway. I dare say he asked her long ago, and she would know our invitation was a fraud. So the joke is on ourselves, after all."

But, as you and I know, that, with the exception of the last sentence, was not the truth of the matter at all.

The Penningtons' Girl

Winslow had been fishing—or pretending to—all the morning, and he was desperately thirsty. He boarded with the Beckwiths on the Riverside East Shore, but he was nearer Riverside West, and he knew the Penningtons well. He had often been there for bait and milk and had listened times out of mind to Mrs. Pennington's dismal tales of her tribulations with hired girls. She never could get along with them, and they left, on an average, after a fortnight's trial. She was on the lookout for one now, he knew, and would likely be cross, but he thought she would give him a drink.

He rowed his skiff into the shore and tied it to a fir that hung out from the bank. A winding little footpath led up to the Pennington farmhouse, which crested the hill about three hundred yards from the shore. Winslow made for the kitchen door and came face to face with a girl carrying a pail of water—Mrs. Pennington's latest thing in hired girls, of course.

Winslow's first bewildered thought was "What a goddess!" and he wondered, as he politely asked for a drink, where on earth Mrs. Pennington had picked her up. She handed him a shining dipper half full and stood, pail in hand, while he drank it.

She was rather tall, and wore a somewhat limp, faded print gown, and a big sunhat, beneath which a glossy knot of chestnut showed itself. Her skin was very fair, somewhat freckled, and her mouth was delicious. As for her eyes, they were grey, but beyond that simply defied description.

"Will you have some more?" she asked in a soft, drawling voice.

"No, thank you. That was delicious. Is Mrs. Pennington home?"

"No. She has gone away for the day."

"Well, I suppose I can sit down here and rest a while. You've no serious objections, have you?"

"Oh, no."

She carried her pail into the kitchen and came out again presently with a knife and a pan of apples. Sitting down on a bench under the poplars she proceeded to peel them with a disregard of his presence that piqued Winslow, who was not used to being ignored in this fashion. Besides, as a general rule, he had been quite good friends with Mrs. Pennington's hired girls. She had had three strapping damsels during his sojourn in Riverside, and he used to sit on this very doorstep and chaff them. They had all been saucy and talkative. This girl was evidently a new species.

"Do you think you'll get along with Mrs. Pennington?" he asked finally. "As a rule she fights with her help, although she is a most estimable woman."

The girl smiled quite broadly.

"I guess p'r'aps she's rather hard to suit," was the answer, "but I like her pretty well so far. I think we'll get along with each other. If we don't I can leave—like the others did."

"What is your name?"

"Nelly Ray."

"Well, Nelly, I hope you'll be able to keep your place. Let me give you a bit of friendly advice. Don't let the cats get into the pantry. That is what Mrs. Pennington has quarrelled with nearly every one of her girls about."

"It is quite a bother to keep them out, ain't it?" said Nelly calmly. "There's dozens of cats about the place. What on earth makes them keep so many?"

"Mr. Pennington has a mania for cats. He and Mrs. Pennington have a standing disagreement about it. The last girl left here because she couldn't stand the cats; they affected her nerves, she said. I hope you don't mind them."

"Oh, no; I kind of like cats. I've been tryin' to count them. Has anyone ever done that?"

"Not that I know of. I tried but I had to give up in despair—never could tell when I was counting the same cat over again. Look at that black goblin sunning himself on the woodpile. I say, Nelly, you're not going, are you?"

"I must. It's time to get dinner. Mr. Pennington will be in from the fields soon."

The next minute he heard her stepping briskly about the kitchen, shooing out intruding cats, and humming a darky air to herself. He went reluctantly back to the shore and rowed across the river in a brown study.

I don't know whether Winslow was afflicted with chronic thirst or not, or whether the East side water wasn't so good as that of the West side; but I do know that he fairly haunted the Pennington farmhouse after that. Mrs. Pennington was home the next time he went, and he asked her about her new girl. To his surprise the good lady was unusually reticent. She couldn't really say very much about Nelly. No, she didn't belong anywhere near Riverside. In fact, she—Mrs. Pennington—didn't think she had any settled home at present. Her father was travelling over the country somewhere. Nelly was a good little girl, and very obliging. Beyond this Winslow could get no more information, so he went around and talked to Nelly, who was sitting on the bench under the poplars and seemed absorbed in watching the sunset.

She dropped her g's badly and made some grammatical errors that caused Winslow's flesh to creep on his bones. But any man could have forgiven mistakes from such dimpled lips in such a sweet voice.

He asked her to go for a row up the river in the twilight and she assented; she handled an oar very well, he found out, and the exercise became her. Winslow tried to get her to talk about herself, but failed signally and had to content himself with Mrs. Pennington's meagre information. He told her about himself frankly enough—how he had had fever in the spring and had been ordered to spend the summer in the country and do nothing useful until his health was fully restored, and how lonesome it was in Riverside in general and at the Beckwith farm in particular. He made out quite a dismal case for himself and if Nelly wasn't sorry for him, she should have been.

At the end of a fortnight Riverside folks began to talk about Winslow and the Penningtons' hired girl. He was reported to be "dead gone" on her; he took her out rowing every evening, drove her to preaching up the Bend on Sunday nights, and haunted the Pennington farmhouse. Wise folks shook their heads over it and wondered that Mrs. Pennington allowed it. Winslow was a gentleman, and that Nelly Ray, whom nobody knew anything about, not even where she came from, was only a common hired girl, and he had no business to be hanging about her. She was pretty, to be sure; but she was absurdly stuck-up and wouldn't associate with other Riverside "help" at all. Well, pride must have a fall; there must be something queer about her when she was so awful sly as to her past life.

Winslow and Nelly did not trouble themselves in the least over all this gossip; in fact, they never even heard it. Winslow was hopelessly in love, when he found this out he was aghast. He thought of his father, the ambitious railroad magnate; of his mother, the brilliant society leader; of his sisters, the beautiful and proud; he was honestly frightened. It would never do; he must not go to see Nelly again. He kept this prudent resolution for twenty-four hours and then rowed over to the West shore. He found Nelly sitting on the bank in her old faded print dress and he straightway forgot everything he ought to have remembered.

Nelly herself never seemed to be conscious of the social gulf between them. At least she never alluded to it in any way, and accepted Winslow's attentions as if she had a perfect right to them. She had broken the record by staying with Mrs. Pennington four weeks, and even the cats were in subjection.

Winslow was well enough to have gone back to the city and, in fact, his father was writing for him. But he couldn't leave Beckwiths', apparently. At any rate he stayed on and met Nelly every day and cursed himself for a cad and a cur and a weak-brained idiot.

One day he took Nelly for a row up the river. They went further than usual around the Bend. Winslow didn't want to go too far, for he knew that a party of his city friends, chaperoned by Mrs. Keyton-Wells, were having a picnic somewhere up along the river shore that day. But Nelly insisted on going on and on, and of course she had her way. When they reached a little pine-fringed headland they came upon the picnickers, within a stone's throw. Everybody recognized Winslow. "Why, there is Burton!" he heard Mrs. Keyton-Wells exclaim, and he knew she was putting up her glasses. Will Evans, who was an especial chum of his, ran down to the water's edge. "Bless me, Win, where did you come from? Come right in. We haven't had tea yet. Bring your friend too," he added, becoming conscious that Winslow's friend was a mighty pretty girl. Winslow's face was crimson. He avoided Nelly's eye.

"Are them people friends of yours?" she asked in a low tone.

"Yes," he muttered.

"Well, let us go ashore if they want us to," she said calmly. "I don't mind."

For three seconds Winslow hesitated. Then he pulled ashore and helped Nelly to alight on a jutting rock. There was a curious, set expression about his fine mouth as he marched Nelly up to Mrs. Keyton-Wells and introduced her. Mrs. Keyton-Wells's greeting was slightly cool, but very polite. She supposed Miss Ray was some little country girl with whom Burton Winslow was carrying on a summer flirtation; respectable enough, no doubt, and must be treated civilly, but of course wouldn't expect to be made an equal of exactly. The other women took their cue from her, but the men were more cordial. Miss Ray might be shabby, but she was distinctly fetching, and Winslow looked savage.

Nelly was not a whit abashed, seemingly, by the fashionable circle in which she found herself, and she talked away to Will Evans and the others in her soft drawl as if she had known them all her life. All might have gone passably well, had not a little Riverside imp, by name of Rufus Hent, who had been picked up by the picnickers to run their errands, come up just then with a pail of water.

"Golly!" he ejaculated in very audible tones. "If there ain't Mrs. Pennington's hired girl!"

Mrs. Keyton-Wells stiffened with horror. Winslow darted a furious glance at the tell-tale that would have annihilated anything except a small boy. Will Evans grinned and went on talking to Nelly, who had failed to hear, or at least to heed, the exclamation.

The mischief was done, the social thermometer went down to zero in Nelly's neighbourhood. The women ignored her altogether. Winslow set his teeth together and registered a mental vow to wring Rufus Hent's sunburned neck at the first opportunity. He escorted Nelly to the table and waited on her with ostentatious deference, while Mrs. Keyton-Wells glanced at him stonily and made up her mind to tell his mother when she went home.

Nelly's social ostracism did not affect her appetite. But after lunch was over, she walked down to the skiff. Winslow followed her.

"Do you want to go home?" he asked.

"Yes, it's time I went, for the cats may be raidin' the pantry. But you must not come; your friends here want you."

"Nonsense!" said Winslow sulkily. "If you are going I am too."

But Nelly was too quick for him; she sprang into the skiff, unwound the rope, and pushed off before he guessed her intention.

"I can row myself home and I mean to," she announced, taking up the oars defiantly.

"Nelly," he implored.

Nelly looked at him wickedly.

"You'd better go back to your friends. That old woman with the eyeglasses is watchin' you."

Winslow said something strong under his breath as he went back to the others. Will Evans and his chums began to chaff him about Nelly, but he looked so dangerous that they concluded to stop. There is no denying that Winslow was in a fearful temper just then with Mrs. Keyton-Wells, Evans, himself, Nelly—in fact, with all the world.

His friends drove him home in the evening on their way to the station and dropped him at the Beckwith farm. At dusk he went moodily down to the shore. Far up the Bend was dim and shadowy and stars were shining above the wooded shores. Over the river the Pennington farmhouse lights twinkled out alluringly. Winslow watched them until he could stand it no longer. Nelly had made off with his skiff, but Perry Beckwith's dory was ready to hand. In five minutes, Winslow was grounding her on the West shore. Nelly was sitting on a rock at the landing place. He went over and sat down silently beside her. A full moon was rising above the dark hills up the Bend and in the faint light the girl was wonderfully lovely.

"I thought you weren't comin' over at all tonight," she said, smiling up at him, "and I was sorry, because I wanted to say goodbye to you."

"Goodbye? Nelly, you're not going away?"

"Yes. The cats were in the pantry when I got home."

"Nelly!"

"Well, to be serious. I'm not goin' for that, but I really am goin'. I had a letter from Dad this evenin'. Did you have a good time after I left this afternoon? Did Mrs. Keyton-Wells thaw out?"

"Hang Mrs. Keyton-Wells! Nelly, where are you going?"

"To Dad, of course. We used to live down south together, but two months ago we broke up housekeepin' and come north. We thought we could do better up here, you know. Dad started out to look for a place to settle down and I came here while he was prospectin'. He's got a house now, he says, and wants me to go right off. I'm goin' tomorrow."

"Nelly, you mustn't go—you mustn't, I tell you," exclaimed Winslow in despair. "I love you—I love you—you must stay with me forever."

"You don't know what you're sayin', Mr. Winslow," said Nelly coldly. "Why, you can't marry me—a common servant girl."

"I can and I will, if you'll have me," answered Winslow recklessly. "I can't ever let you go. I've loved you ever since I first saw you. Nelly, won't you be my wife? Don't you love me?"

"Well, yes, I do," confessed Nelly suddenly; and then it was fully five minutes before Winslow gave her a chance to say anything else.

"Oh, what will your people say?" she contrived to ask at last. "Won't they be in a dreadful state? Oh, it will never do for you to marry me."

"Won't it?" said Winslow in a tone of satisfaction. "I rather think it will. Of course, my family will rampage a bit at first. I daresay Father'll turn me out. Don't worry over that, Nelly. I'm not afraid of work. I'm not afraid of anything except losing you."

"You'll have to see what Dad says," remarked Nelly, after another eloquent interlude.

"He won't object, will he? I'll write to him or go and see him. Where is he?"

"He is in town at the Arlington."

"The Arlington!" Winslow was amazed. The Arlington was the most exclusive and expensive hotel in town.

"What is he doing there?"

"Transacting a real estate or railroad deal with your father, I believe, or something of that sort."

"Nelly!"

"Well?"

"What do you mean?"

"Just what I say."

Winslow got up and looked at her.

"Nelly, who are you?"

"Helen Ray Scott, at your service, sir."

"Not Helen Ray Scott, the daughter of the railroad king?"

"The same. Are you sorry that you're engaged to her? If you are, she'll stay Nelly Ray."

Winslow dropped back on the seat with a long breath.

"Nelly, I don't understand. Why did you deceive me? I feel stunned."

"Oh, do forgive me," she said merrily. "I shouldn't have, I suppose—but you know you took me for the hired girl the very first time you saw me, and you patronized me and called me Nelly; so I let you think so just for fun. I never thought it would come to this. When Father and I came north I took a fancy to come here and stay with Mrs. Pennington—who is an old nurse of mine—until Father decided where to take up our abode. I got here the night before we met. My trunk was delayed so I put on an old cotton dress her niece had left here—and you came and saw me. I made Mrs. Pennington keep the secret—she thought it great fun; and I really was a great hand to do little chores and keep the cats in subjection too. I made mistakes in grammar and dropped my g's on purpose—it was such fun to see you wince when I did it. It was cruel to tease you so, I suppose, but it was so sweet just to be loved for myself—not because I was an heiress and a belle—I couldn't bear to tell you the truth. Did you think I couldn't read your thoughts this afternoon, when I insisted on going ashore? You were a little ashamed of me—you know you were. I didn't blame you for that, but if you hadn't gone ashore and taken me as you did I would never have spoken to you again. Mrs. Keyton-Wells won't snub me next time we meet. And some way I don't think your father will turn you out, either. Have you forgiven me yet, Burton?"

"I shall never call you anything but Nelly," said Winslow irrelevantly.

The Red Room

You would have me tell you the story, Grandchild? 'Tis a sad one and best forgotten—few remember it now. There are always sad and dark stories in old families such as ours.

Yet I have promised and must keep my word. So sit down here at my feet and rest your bright head on my lap, that I may not see in your young eyes the shadows my story will bring across their bonny blue.

I was a mere child when it all happened, yet I remember it but too well, and I can recall how pleased I was when my father's stepmother, Mrs. Montressor—she not liking to be called grandmother, seeing she was but turned of fifty and a handsome woman still—wrote to my mother that she must send little Beatrice up to Montressor Place for the Christmas holidays. So I went joyfully though my mother grieved to part with me; she had little to love save me, my father, Conrad Montressor, having been lost at sea when but three months wed.

My aunts were wont to tell me how much I resembled him, being, so they said, a Montressor to the backbone; and this I took to mean commendation, for the Montressors were a well-descended and well-thought-of family, and the women were noted for their beauty. This I could well believe, since of all my aunts there was not one but was counted a pretty woman. Therefore I took heart of grace when I thought of my dark face and spindling shape, hoping that when I should be grown up I might be counted not unworthy of my race.

The Place was an old-fashioned, mysterious house, such as I delighted in, and Mrs. Montressor was ever kind to me, albeit a little stern, for she was a proud woman and cared but little for children, having none of her own.

But there were books there to pore over without let or hindrance—for nobody questioned of my whereabouts if I but kept out of the way—and strange, dim family portraits on the walls to gaze upon, until I knew each proud old face well, and had visioned a history for it in my own mind—for I was given to dreaming and was older and wiser than my years, having no childish companions to keep me still a child.

There were always some of my aunts at the Place to kiss and make much of me for my father's sake—for he had been their favourite brother. My aunts—there were eight of them—had all married well, so said people who knew, and lived not far away, coming home often to take tea with Mrs. Montressor, who had always gotten on well with her step-daughters, or to help prepare for some festivity or other—for they were notable housekeepers, every one.

They were all at Montressor Place for Christmas, and I got more petting than I deserved, albeit they looked after me somewhat more strictly than did Mrs. Montressor, and saw to it that I did not read too many fairy tales or sit up later at nights than became my years.

But it was not for fairy tales and sugarplums nor yet for petting that I rejoiced to be at the Place at that time. Though I spoke not of it to anyone, I had a great longing to see my Uncle Hugh's wife, concerning whom I had heard much, both good and bad.

My Uncle Hugh, albeit the oldest of the family, had never married until now, and all the countryside rang with talk of his young wife. I did not hear as much as I wished, for the gossips took heed to my presence when I drew anear and turned to other matters. Yet, being somewhat keener of comprehension than they knew, I heard and understood not a little of their talk.

And so I came to know that neither proud Mrs. Montressor nor my good aunts, nor even my gentle mother, looked with overmuch favour on what my Uncle Hugh had done. And I did hear that Mrs. Montressor had chosen a wife for her stepson, of good family and some beauty, but that my Uncle Hugh would have none of her—a thing Mrs. Montressor found hard to pardon, yet might so have done had not my uncle, on his last voyage to the Indies—for he went often in his own vessels—married and brought home a foreign bride, of whom no one knew aught save that her beauty was a thing to dazzle the day and that she was of some strange alien blood such as ran not in the blue veins of the Montressors.

Some had much to say of her pride and insolence, and wondered if Mrs. Montressor would tamely yield her mistress-ship to the stranger. But others, who were taken with her loveliness and grace, said that the tales told were born of envy and malice, and that Alicia Montressor was well worthy of her name and station.

So I halted between two opinions and thought to judge for myself, but when I went to the Place my Uncle Hugh and his bride were gone for a time, and I had even to swallow my disappointment and bide their return with all my small patience.

But my aunts and their stepmother talked much of Alicia, and they spoke slightingly of her, saying that she was but a light woman and that no good would come of my Uncle Hugh's having wed her, with other things of a like nature. Also they spoke of the company she gathered around her, thinking her to have strange and unbecoming companions for a Montressor. All this I heard and pondered much over, although my good aunts supposed that such a chit as I would take no heed to their whisperings.

When I was not with them, helping to whip eggs and stone raisins, and being watched to see that I ate not more than one out of five, I was surely to be found in the wing hall, poring over my book and grieving that I was no more allowed to go into the Red Room.

The wing hall was a narrow one and dim, connecting the main rooms of the Place with an older wing, built in a curious way. The hall was lighted by small, square-paned windows, and at its end a little flight of steps led up to the Red Room.

Whenever I had been at the Place before—and this was often—I had passed much of my time in this same Red Room. It was Mrs. Montressor's sitting-room then, where she wrote her letters and examined household accounts, and sometimes had an old gossip in to tea. The room was low-ceilinged and dim, hung with red damask, and with odd, square windows high up under the eaves and a dark wainscoting all around it. And there I loved to sit quietly on the red sofa and read my fairy tales, or talk dreamily to the swallows fluttering crazily against the tiny panes.

When I had gone this Christmas to the Place I soon bethought myself of the Red Room—for I had a great love for it. But I had got no further than the steps when Mrs. Montressor came sweeping down the hall in haste and, catching me by the arm, pulled me back as roughly as if it had been Bluebeard's chamber itself into which I was venturing.

Then, seeing my face, which I doubt not was startled enough, she seemed to repent of her haste and patted me gently on the head.

"There, there, little Beatrice! Did I frighten you, child? Forgive an old woman's thoughtlessness. But be not too ready to go where you are not bidden, and never venture foot in the Red Room now, for it belongs to your Uncle Hugh's wife, and let me tell you she is not over fond of intruders."

I felt sorry overmuch to hear this, nor could I see why my new aunt should care if I went in once in a while, as had been my habit, to talk to the swallows and misplace nothing. But Mrs. Montressor saw to it that I obeyed her, and I went no more to the Red Room, but busied myself with other matters.

For there were great doings at the Place and much coming and going. My aunts were never idle; there was to be much festivity Christmas week and a ball on Christmas Eve. And my aunts had promised me—though not till I had wearied them of my coaxing—that I should stay up that night and see as much of the gaiety as was good for me. So I did their errands and went early to bed every night without complaint—though I did this the more readily for that, when they thought me safely asleep, they would come in and talk around my bedroom fire, saying that of Alicia which I should not have heard.

At last came the day when my Uncle Hugh and his wife were expected home—though not until my scanty patience was well nigh wearied out—and we were all assembled to meet them in the great hall, where a ruddy firelight was gleaming.

My Aunt Frances had dressed me in my best white frock and my crimson sash, with much lamenting over my skinny neck and arms, and bade me behave prettily, as became my bringing up. So I slipped in a corner, my hands and feet cold with excitement, for I think every drop of blood in my body had gone to my head, and my heart beat so hardly that it even pained me.

Then the door opened and Alicia—for so I was used to hearing her called, nor did I ever think of her as my aunt in my own mind—came in, and a little in the rear my tall, dark uncle.

She came proudly forward to the fire and stood there superbly while she loosened her cloak, nor did she see me at all at first, but nodded, a little disdainfully, it seemed, to Mrs. Montressor and my aunts, who were grouped about the drawing-room door, very ladylike and quiet.

But I neither saw nor heard aught at the time save her only, for her beauty, when she came forth from her crimson cloak and hood, was something so wonderful that I forgot my manners and stared at her as one fascinated—as indeed I was, for never had I seen such loveliness and hardly dreamed it.

Pretty women I had seen in plenty, for my aunts and my mother were counted fair, but my uncle's wife was as little like to them as a sunset glow to pale moonshine or a crimson rose to white day-lilies.

Nor can I paint her to you in words as I saw her then, with the long tongues of firelight licking her white neck and wavering over the rich masses of her red-gold hair.

She was tall—so tall that my aunts looked but insignificant beside her, and they were of no mean height, as became their race; yet no queen could have carried herself more royally, and all the passion and fire of her foreign nature burned in her splendid eyes, that might have been dark or light for aught that I could ever tell, but which seemed always like pools of warm flame, now tender, now fierce.

Her skin was like a delicate white rose leaf, and when she spoke I told my foolish self that never had I heard music before; nor do I ever again think to hear a voice so sweet, so liquid, as that which rippled over her ripe lips.

I had often in my own mind pictured this, my first meeting with Alicia, now in one way, now in another, but never had I dreamed of her speaking to me at all, so that it came to me as a great surprise when she turned and, holding out her lovely hands, said very graciously:

"And is this the little Beatrice? I have heard much of you—come, kiss me, child."

And I went, despite my Aunt Elizabeth's black frown, for the glamour of her loveliness was upon me, and I no longer wondered that my Uncle Hugh should have loved her.

Very proud of her was he too; yet I felt, rather than saw—for I was sensitive and quick of perception, as old-young children ever are—that there was something other than pride and love in his face when he looked on her, and more in his manner than the fond lover—as it were, a sort of lurking mistrust.

Nor could I think, though to me the thought seemed as treason, that she loved her husband overmuch, for she seemed half condescending and half disdainful to him; yet one thought not of this in her presence, but only remembered it when she had gone.

When she went out it seemed to me that nothing was left, so I crept lonesomely away to the wing hall and sat down by a window to dream of her; and she filled my thoughts so fully that it was no surprise when I raised my eyes and saw her coming down the hall alone, her bright head shining against the dark old walls.

When she paused by me and asked me lightly of what I was dreaming, since I had such a sober face, I answered her truly that it was of her—whereat she laughed, as one not ill pleased, and said half mockingly:

"Waste not your thoughts so, little Beatrice. But come with me, child, if you will, for I have taken a strange fancy to your solemn eyes. Perchance the warmth of your young life may thaw out the ice that has frozen around my heart ever since I came among these cold Montressors."

And, though I understood not her meaning, I went, glad to see the Red Room once more. So she made me sit down and talk to her, which I did, for shyness was no failing of mine; and she asked me many questions, and some that I thought she should not have asked, but I could not answer them, so 'twere little harm.

After that I spent a part of every day with her in the Red Room. And my Uncle Hugh was there often, and he would kiss her and praise her loveliness, not heeding my presence—for I was but a child.

Yet it ever seemed to me that she endured rather than welcomed his caresses, and at times the ever-burning flame in her eyes glowed so luridly that a chill dread would creep over me, and I would remember what my Aunt Elizabeth had said, she being a bitter-tongued woman, though kind at heart—that this strange creature would bring on us all some evil fortune yet.

Then would I strive to banish such thoughts and chide myself for doubting one so kind to me.

When Christmas Eve drew nigh my silly head was full of the ball day and night. But a grievous disappointment befell me, for I awakened that day very ill with a most severe cold; and though I bore me bravely, my aunts discovered it soon, when, despite my piteous pleadings, I was put to bed, where I cried bitterly and would not be comforted. For I thought I should not see the fine folk and, more than all, Alicia.

But that disappointment, at least, was spared me, for at night she came into my room, knowing of my longing—she was ever indulgent to my little wishes. And when I saw her I forgot my aching limbs and burning brow, and even the ball I was not to see, for never was mortal creature so lovely as she, standing there by my bed.

Her gown was of white, and there was nothing I could liken the stuff to save moonshine falling athwart a frosted pane, and out from it swelled her gleaming breast and arms, so bare that it seemed to me a shame to look upon them. Yet it could not be denied they were of wondrous beauty, white as polished marble.

And all about her snowy throat and rounded arms, and in the masses of her splendid hair, were sparkling, gleaming stones, with hearts of pure light, which I know now to have been diamonds, but knew not then, for never had I seen aught of their like.

And I gazed at her, drinking in her beauty until my soul was filled, as she stood like some goddess before her worshipper. I think she read my thought in my face and liked it—for she was a vain woman, and to such even the admiration of a child is sweet.

Then she leaned down to me until her splendid eyes looked straight into my dazzled ones.

"Tell me, little Beatrice—for they say the word of a child is to be believed—tell me, do you think me beautiful?"

I found my voice and told her truly that I thought her beautiful beyond my dreams of angels—as indeed she was. Whereat she smiled as one well pleased.

Then my Uncle Hugh came in, and though I thought that his face darkened as he looked on the naked splendour of her breast and arms, as if he liked not that the eyes of other men should gloat on it, yet he kissed her with all a lover's fond pride, while she looked at him half mockingly.

Then said he, "Sweet, will you grant me a favour?"

And she answered, "It may be that I will."

And he said, "Do not dance with that man tonight, Alicia. I mistrust him much."

His voice had more of a husband's command than a lover's entreaty. She looked at him with some scorn, but when she saw his face grow black—for the Montressors brooked scant disregard of their authority, as I had good reason to know—she seemed to change, and a smile came to her lips, though her eyes glowed balefully.

Then she laid her arms about his neck and—though it seemed to me that she had as soon strangled as embraced him—her voice was wondrous sweet and caressing as she murmured in his ear.

He laughed and his brow cleared, though he said still sternly, "Do not try me too far, Alicia."

Then they went out, she a little in advance and very stately.

After that my aunts also came in, very beautifully and modestly dressed, but they seemed to me as nothing after Alicia. For I was caught in the snare of her beauty, and the longing to see her again so grew upon me that after a time I did an undutiful and disobedient thing.

I had been straitly charged to stay in bed, which I did not, but got up and put on a gown. For it was in my mind to go quietly down, if by chance I might again see Alicia, myself unseen.

But when I reached the great hall I heard steps approaching and, having a guilty conscience, I slipped aside into the blue parlour and hid me behind the curtains lest my aunts should see me.

Then Alicia came in, and with her a man whom I had never before seen. Yet I instantly bethought myself of a lean black snake, with a glittering and evil eye, which I had seen in Mrs. Montressor's garden two summers agone, and which was like to have bitten me. John, the gardener, had killed it, and I verily thought that if it had a soul, it must have gotten into this man.

Alicia sat down and he beside her, and when he had put his arms about her, he kissed her face and lips. Nor did she shrink from his embrace, but even smiled and leaned nearer to him with a little smooth motion, as they talked to each other in some strange, foreign tongue.

I was but a child and innocent, nor knew I aught of honour and dishonour. Yet it seemed to me that no man should kiss her save only my Uncle Hugh, and from that hour I mistrusted Alicia, though I understood not then what I afterwards did.

And as I watched them—not thinking of playing the spy—I saw her face grow suddenly cold, and she straightened herself up and pushed away her lover's arms.

Then I followed her guilty eyes to the door, where stood my Uncle Hugh, and all the pride and passion of the Montressors sat on his lowering brow. Yet he came forward quietly as Alicia and the snake drew apart and stood up.

At first he looked not at his guilty wife but at her lover, and smote him heavily in the face. Whereat he, being a coward at heart, as are all villains, turned white and slunk from the room with a muttered oath, nor was he stayed.

My uncle turned to Alicia, and very calmly and terribly he said, "From this hour you are no longer wife of mine!"

And there was that in his tone which told that his forgiveness and love should be hers nevermore.

Then he motioned her out and she went, like a proud queen, with her glorious head erect and no shame on her brow.

As for me, when they were gone I crept away, dazed and bewildered enough, and went back to my bed, having seen and heard more than I had a mind for, as disobedient people and eavesdroppers ever do.

But my Uncle Hugh kept his word, and Alicia was no more wife to him, save only in name. Yet of gossip or scandal there was none, for the pride of his race kept secret his dishonour, nor did he ever seem other than a courteous and respectful husband.

Nor did Mrs. Montressor and my aunts, though they wondered much among themselves, learn aught, for they dared question neither their brother nor Alicia, who carried herself as loftily as ever, and seemed to pine for neither lover nor husband. As for me, no one dreamed I knew aught of it, and I kept my own counsel as to what I had seen in the blue parlour on the night of the Christmas ball.

After the New Year I went home, but ere long Mrs. Montressor sent for me again, saying that the house was lonely without little Beatrice. So I went again and found all unchanged, though the Place was very quiet, and Alicia went out but little from the Red Room.

Of my Uncle Hugh I saw little, save when he went and came on the business of his estate, somewhat more gravely and silently than of yore, or brought to me books and sweetmeats from town.

But every day I was with Alicia in the Red Room, where she would talk to me, oftentimes wildly and strangely, but always kindly. And though I think Mrs. Montressor liked our intimacy none too well, she said no word, and I came and went as I listed with Alicia, though never quite liking her strange ways and the restless fire in her eyes.

Nor would I ever kiss her, after I had seen her lips pressed by the snake's, though she sometimes coaxed me, and grew pettish and vexed when I would not; but she guessed not my reason.

March came in that year like a lion, exceedingly hungry and fierce, and my Uncle Hugh had ridden away through the storm nor thought to be back for some days.

In the afternoon I was sitting in the wing hall, dreaming wondrous day-dreams, when Alicia called me to the Red Room. And as I went, I marvelled anew at her loveliness, for the blood was leaping in her face and her jewels were dim before the lustre of her eyes. Her hand, when she took mine, was burning hot, and her voice had a strange ring.

"Come, little Beatrice," she said, "come talk to me, for I know not what to do with my lone self today. Time hangs heavily in this gloomy house. I do verily think this Red Room has an evil influence over me. See if your childish prattle can drive away the ghosts that riot in these dark old corners—ghosts of a ruined and shamed life! Nay, shrink not—do I talk wildly? I mean not all I say—my brain seems on fire, little Beatrice. Come; it may be you know some grim old legend of this room—it must surely have one. Never was place fitter for a dark deed! Tush! never be so frightened, child—forget my vagaries. Tell me now and I will listen."

Whereat she cast herself lithely on the satin couch and turned her lovely face on me. So I gathered up my small wits and told her what I was not supposed to know—how that, generations agone, a Montressor had disgraced himself and his name, and that, when he came home to his mother, she had met him in that same Red Room and flung at him taunts and reproaches, forgetting whose breast had nourished him; and that he, frantic with shame and despair, turned his sword against his own heart and so died. But his mother went mad with her remorse, and was kept a prisoner in the Red Room until her death.

So lamely told I the tale, as I had heard my Aunt Elizabeth tell it, when she knew not I listened or understood. Alicia heard me through and said nothing, save that it was a tale worthy of the Montressors. Whereat I bridled, for I too was a Montressor, and proud of it.

But she took my hand soothingly in hers and said, "Little Beatrice, if tomorrow or the next day they should tell you, those cold, proud women, that Alicia was unworthy of your love, tell me, would you believe them?"

And I, remembering what I had seen in the blue parlour, was silent—for I could not lie. So she flung my hand away with a bitter laugh, and picked lightly from the table anear a small dagger with a jewelled handle.

It seemed to me a cruel-looking toy and I said so—whereat she smiled and drew her white fingers down the thin, shining blade in a fashion that made me cold.

"Such a little blow with this," she said, "such a little blow—and the heart beats no longer, the weary brain rests, the lips and eyes smile never again! 'Twere a short path out of all difficulties, my Beatrice."

And I, understanding her not, yet shivering, begged her to cast it aside, which she did carelessly and, putting a hand under my chin, she turned up my face to hers.

"Little, grave-eyed Beatrice, tell me truly, would it grieve you much if you were never again to sit here with Alicia in this same Red Room?"

And I made answer earnestly that it would, glad that I could say so much truly. Then her face grew tender and she sighed deeply.

Presently she opened a quaint, inlaid box and took from it a shining gold chain of rare workmanship and exquisite design, and this she hung around my neck, nor would suffer me to thank her but laid her hand gently on my lips.

"Now go," she said. "But ere you leave me, little Beatrice, grant me but the one favour—it may be that I shall never ask another of you. Your people, I know—those cold Montressors—care little for me, but with all my faults, I have ever been kind to you. So, when the morrow's come, and they tell you that Alicia is as one worse than dead, think not of me with scorn only but grant me a little pity—for I was not always what I am now, and might never have become so had a little child like you been always anear me, to keep me pure and innocent. And I would have you but the once lay your arms about my neck and kiss me."

And I did so, wondering much at her manner—for it had in it a strange tenderness and some sort of hopeless longing. Then she gently put me from the room, and I sat musing by the hall window until night fell darkly—and a fearsome night it was, of storm and blackness. And I thought how well it was that my Uncle Hugh had not to return in such a tempest. Yet, ere the thought had grown cold, the door opened and he strode down the hall, his cloak drenched and wind-twisted, in one hand a whip, as though he had but then sprung from his horse, in the other what seemed like a crumpled letter.

Nor was the night blacker than his face, and he took no heed of me as I ran after him, thinking selfishly of the sweetmeats he had promised to bring me—but I thought no more of them when I got to the door of the Red Room.

Alicia stood by the table, hooded and cloaked as for a journey, but her hood had slipped back, and her face rose from it marble-white, save where her wrathful eyes burned out, with dread and guilt and hatred in their depths, while she had one arm raised as if to thrust him back.

As for my uncle, he stood before her and I saw not his face, but his voice was low and terrible, speaking words I understood not then, though long afterwards I came to know their meaning.

And he cast foul scorn at her that she should have thought to fly with her lover, and swore that naught should again thwart his vengeance, with other threats, wild and dreadful enough.

Yet she said no word until he had done, and then she spoke, but what she said I know not, save that it was full of hatred and defiance and wild accusation, such as a mad woman might have uttered.

And she defied him even then to stop her flight, though he told her to cross that threshold would mean her death; for he was a wronged and desperate man and thought of nothing save his own dishonour.

Then she made as if to pass him, but he caught her by her white wrist; she turned on him with fury, and I saw her right hand reach stealthily out over the table behind her, where lay the dagger.

"Let me go!" she hissed.

And he said, "I will not."

Then she turned herself about and struck at him with the dagger—and never saw I such a face as was hers at the moment.

He fell heavily, yet held her even in death, so that she had to wrench herself free, with a shriek that rings yet in my ears on a night when the wind wails over the rainy moors. She rushed past me unheeding, and fled down the hall like a hunted creature, and I heard the heavy door clang hollowly behind her.

As for me, I stood there looking at the dead man, for I could neither move nor speak and was like to have died of horror. And presently I knew nothing, nor did I come to my recollection for many a day, when I lay abed, sick of a fever and more like to die than live.

So that when at last I came out from the shadow of death, my Uncle Hugh had been long cold in his grave, and the hue and cry for his guilty wife was well nigh over, since naught had been seen or heard of her since she fled the country with her foreign lover.

When I came rightly to my remembrance, they questioned me as to what I had seen and heard in the Red Room. And I told them as best I could, though much aggrieved that to my questions they would answer nothing save to bid me to stay still and think not of the matter.

Then my mother, sorely vexed over my adventures—which in truth were but sorry ones for a child—took me home. Nor would she let me keep Alicia's chain, but made away with it, how I knew not and little cared, for the sight of it was loathsome to me.

It was many years ere I went again to Montressor Place, and I never saw the Red Room more, for Mrs. Montressor had the old wing torn down, deeming its sorrowful memories dark heritage enough for the next Montressor.

So, Grandchild, the sad tale is ended, and you will not see the Red Room when you go next month to Montressor Place. The swallows still build under the eaves, though—I know not if you will understand their speech as I did.

The Setness of Theodosia

When Theodosia Ford married Wesley Brooke after a courtship of three years, everybody concerned was satisfied. There was nothing particularly romantic in either the courtship or marriage. Wesley was a steady, well-meaning, rather slow fellow, comfortably off. He was not at all handsome. But Theodosia was a very pretty girl with the milky colouring of an auburn blonde and large china-blue eyes. She looked mild and Madonna-like and was known to be sweet-tempered. Wesley's older brother, Irving Brooke, had married a woman who kept him in hot water all the time, so Heatherton folks said, but they thought there was no fear of that with Wesley and Theodosia. They would get along together all right.

Only old Jim Parmelee shook his head and said, "They might, and then again they mightn't"; he knew the stock they came of and it was a kind you could never predict about.

Wesley and Theodosia were third cousins; this meant that old Henry Ford had been the great-great-grandfather of them both. Jim Parmelee, who was ninety, had been a small boy when this remote ancestor was still alive.

"I mind him well," said old Jim on the morning of Theodosia's wedding day. There was a little group about the blacksmith's forge. Old Jim was in the centre. He was a fat, twinkling-eyed old man, fresh and ruddy in spite of his ninety years. "And," he went on, "he was about the settest man you'd ever see or want to see. When old Henry Ford made up his mind on any p'int a cyclone wouldn't turn him a hairsbreadth—no, nor an earthquake neither. Didn't matter a mite how much he suffered for it—he'd stick to it if it broke his heart. There was always some story or other going round about old Henry's setness. The family weren't quite so bad—only Tom. He was Dosia's great-grandfather, and a regular chip of the old block. Since then it's cropped out now and again all through the different branches of the family. I mistrust if Dosia hasn't got a spice of it, and Wes Brooke too, but mebbe not."

Old Jim was the only croaker. Wesley and Theodosia were married, in the golden prime of the Indian summer, and settled down on their snug little farm. Dosia was a beautiful bride, and Wesley's pride in her was amusingly apparent. He thought nothing too good for her, the Heatherton people said. It was a sight to make an old heart young to see him march up the aisle of the church on Sunday in all the glossy splendour of his wedding suit, his curly black head held high and his round boyish face shining with happiness, stopping and turning proudly at his pew to show Theodosia in.

They always sat alone together in the big pew, and Alma Spencer, who sat behind them, declared that they held each other's hands all through the service. This lasted until spring; then came a sensation and scandal, such as decorous Heatherton had not known since the time Isaac Allen got drunk at Centreville Fair and came home and kicked his wife.

One evening in early April Wesley came home from the store at "the Corner," where he had lingered to talk over politics and farming methods with his cronies. This evening he was later than usual, and Theodosia had his supper kept warm for him. She met him on the porch and kissed him. He kissed her in return, and held her to him for a minute, with her bright head on his shoulder. The frogs were singing down in the south meadow swamp, and there was a splendour of silvery moonrise over the wooded Heatherton hills. Theodosia always remembered that moment.

When they went in, Wesley, full of excitement, began to talk of what he had heard at the store. Ogden Greene and Tom Cary were going to sell out and go to Manitoba. There were better chances for a man out there, he said; in Heatherton he might slave all his life and never make more than a bare living. Out west he might make a fortune.

Wesley talked on in this strain for some time, rehashing all the arguments he had heard Greene and Cary use. He had always been rather disposed to grumble at his limited chances in Heatherton, and now the great West seemed to stretch before him, full of alluring prospects and visions. Ogden and Tom wanted him to go too, he said. He had half a notion to. Heatherton was a stick-in-the-mud sort of place anyhow.

"What say, Dosia?"

He looked across the table at her, his eyes bright and questioning. Theodosia had listened in silence, as she poured his tea and passed him her hot, flaky biscuits. There was a little perpendicular wrinkle between her straight eyebrows.

"I think Ogden and Tom are fools," she said crisply. "They have good farms here. What do they want to go west for, or you, either? Don't get silly notions in your head, Wes."

Wesley flushed.

"Wouldn't you go with me, Dosia?" he said, trying to speak lightly.

"No, I wouldn't," said Theodosia, in her calm, sweet voice. Her face was serene, but the little wrinkle had grown deeper. Old Jim Parmelee would have known what it meant. He had seen the same expression on old Henry Ford's face many a time.

Wesley laughed good-humouredly, as if at a child. His heart was suddenly set on going west, and he was sure he could soon bring Theodosia around. He did not say anything more about it just then. Wesley thought he knew how to manage women.

When he broached the subject again, two days later, Theodosia told him plainly that it was no use. She would never consent to leave Heatherton and all her friends and go out to the prairies. The idea was just rank foolishness, and he would soon see that himself.

All this Theodosia said calmly and sweetly, without any trace of temper or irritation. Wesley still believed that he could persuade her and he tried perseveringly for a fortnight. By the end of that time he discovered that Theodosia was not a great-great-granddaughter of old Henry Ford for nothing.

Not that Theodosia ever got angry. Neither did she laugh at him. She met his arguments and pleadings seriously enough, but she never wavered.

"If you go to Manitoba, Wes, you'll go alone," she said. "I'll never go, so there is no use in any more talking."

Wesley was a descendant of old Henry Ford too. Theodosia's unexpected opposition roused all the latent stubbornness of his nature. He went over to Centreville oftener, and kept his blood at fever heat talking to Greene and Cary, who wanted him to go with them and spared no pains at inducement.

The matter was gossiped about in Heatherton, of course. People knew that Wesley Brooke had caught "the western fever," and wanted to sell out and go to Manitoba, while Theodosia was opposed to it. They thought Dosia would have to give in in the end, but said it was a pity Wes Brooke couldn't be contented to stay where he was well off.

Theodosia's family naturally sided with her and tried to dissuade Wesley. But he was mastered by that resentful irritation, roused in a man by opposition where he thinks he should be master, which will drive him into any cause.

One day he told Theodosia that he was going. She was working her butter in her little, snowy-clean dairy under the great willows by the well. Wesley was standing in the doorway, his stout, broad-shouldered figure filling up the sunlit space. He was frowning and sullen.

"I'm going west in two weeks' time with the boys, Dosia," he said stubbornly. "You can come with me or stay here—just exactly as you please. But I'm going."

Theodosia went on spatting her balls of golden butter on the print in silence. She was looking very neat and pretty in her big white apron, her sleeves rolled up high above her plump, dimpled elbows, and her ruddy hair curling about her face and her white throat. She looked as pliable as her butter.

Her silence angered her husband. He shuffled impatiently.

"Well, what have you to say, Dosia?"

"Nothing," said Theodosia. "If you have made up your mind to go, go you will, I suppose. But I will not. There is no use in talking. We've been over the ground often enough, Wes. The matter is settled."

Up to that moment Wesley had always believed that his wife would yield at last, when she saw that he was determined. Now he realized that she never would. Under that exterior of milky, dimpled flesh and calm blue eyes was all the iron will of old dead and forgotten Henry Ford. This mildest and meekest of girls and wives was not to be moved a hairsbreadth by all argument or entreaty, or insistence on a husband's rights.

A great, sudden anger came over the man. He lifted his hand and for one moment it seemed to Theodosia as if he meant to strike her. Then he dropped it with the first oath that had ever crossed his lips.

"You listen to me," he said thickly. "If you won't go with me I'll never come back here—never. When you want to do your duty as a wife you can come to me. But I'll never come back."

He turned on his heel and strode away. Theodosia kept on spatting her butter. The little perpendicular wrinkle had come between her brows again. At that moment an odd, almost uncanny resemblance to the old portrait of her great-great-grandfather, which hung on the parlour wall at home, came out on her girlish face.

The fortnight passed by. Wesley was silent and sullen, never speaking to his wife when he could avoid it. Theodosia was as sweet and serene as ever. She made an extra supply of shirts and socks for him, put up his lunch basket, and packed his trunk carefully. But she never spoke of his journey.

He did not sell his farm. Irving Brooke rented it. Theodosia was to live in the house. The business arrangements were simple and soon concluded.

Heatherton folks gossiped a great deal. They all condemned Theodosia. Even her own people sided against her now. They hated to be mixed up in a local scandal, and since Wes was bound to go they told Theodosia that it was her duty to go with him, no matter how much she disliked it. It would be disgraceful not to. They might as well have talked to the four winds. Theodosia was immoveable. They coaxed and argued and blamed—it all came to the same thing. Even those of them who could be "set" enough themselves on occasion could not understand Theodosia, who had always been so tractable. They finally gave up, as Wesley had done, baffled. Time would bring her to her senses, they said; you just had to leave that still, stubborn kind alone.

On the morning of Wesley's departure Theodosia arose at sunrise and prepared a tempting breakfast. Irving Brooke's oldest son, Stanley, who was to drive Wesley to the station, came over early with his express wagon. Wesley's trunk, corded and labelled, stood on the back platform. The breakfast was a very silent meal. When it was over Wesley put on his hat and overcoat and went to the door, around which Theodosia's morning-glory vines were beginning to twine. The sun was not yet above the trees and the long shadows lay on the dewy grass. The wet leaves were flickering on the old maples that grew along the fence between the yard and the clover field beyond. The skies were all pearly blue, cleanswept of clouds. From the little farmhouse the green meadows sloped down to the valley, where a blue haze wound in and out like a glistening ribbon.

Theodosia went out and stood looking inscrutably on, while Wesley and Irving hoisted the trunk into the wagon and tied it. Then Wesley came up the porch steps and looked at her.

"Dosia," he said a little huskily, "I said I wouldn't ask you to go again, but I will. Will you come with me yet?"

"No," said Theodosia gently.

He held out his hand. He did not offer to kiss her.

"Goodbye, Dosia."

"Goodbye, Wes."

There was no tremor of an eyelash with her. Wesley smiled bitterly and turned away. When the wagon reached the end of the little lane he turned and looked back for the last time. Through all the years that followed he carried with him the picture of his wife as he saw her then, standing amid the airy shadows and wavering golden lights of the morning, the wind blowing the skirt of her pale blue wrapper about her feet and ruffling the locks of her bright hair into a delicate golden cloud. Then the wagon disappeared around a curve in the road, and Theodosia turned and went back into her desolate home.

For a time there was a great buzz of gossip over the affair. People wondered over it. Old Jim Parmelee understood better than the others. When he met Theodosia he looked at her with a curious twinkle in his keen old eyes.

"Looks as if a man could bend her any way he'd a mind to, doesn't she?" he said. "Looks is deceiving. It'll come out in her face by and by—she's too young yet, but it's there. It does seem unnatteral to see a woman so stubborn—you'd kinder look for it more in a man."

Wesley wrote a brief letter to Theodosia when he reached his destination. He said he was well and was looking about for the best place to settle. He liked the country fine. He was at a place called Red Butte and guessed he'd locate there.

Two weeks later he wrote again. He had taken up a claim of three hundred acres. Greene and Cary had done the same. They were his nearest neighbours and were three miles away. He had knocked up a little shack, was learning to cook his own meals, and was very busy. He thought the country was a grand one and the prospects good.

Theodosia answered his letter and told him all the Heatherton news. She signed herself "Theodosia Brooke," but otherwise there was nothing in the letter to indicate that it was written by a wife to her husband.

At the end of a year Wesley wrote and once more asked her to go out to him. He was getting on well, and was sure she would like the place. It was a little rough, to be sure, but time would improve that.

"Won't you let bygones be bygones, Dosia?" he wrote, "and come out to me. Do, my dear wife."

Theodosia wrote back, refusing to go. She never got any reply, nor did she write again.

People had given up talking about the matter and asking Theodosia when she was going out to Wes. Heatherton had grown used to the chronic scandal within its decorous borders. Theodosia never spoke of her husband to anyone, and it was known that they did not correspond. She took her youngest sister to live with her. She had her garden and hens and a cow. The farm brought her enough to live on, and she was always busy.

When fifteen years had gone by there were naturally some changes in Heatherton, sleepy and; unprogressive as it was. Most of the old people were in the little hillside burying-ground that fronted the sunrise. Old Jim Parmelee was there with his recollections of four generations. Men and women who had been in their prime when Wesley went away were old now and the children were grown up and married.

Theodosia was thirty-five and was nothing like! the slim, dimpled girl who had stood on the porch steps and watched her husband drive away that morning fifteen years ago. She was stout and comely; the auburn hair was darker and arched away from her face in smooth, shining waves instead of the old-time curls. Her face was unlined and fresh-coloured, but no woman could live in subjection to her own unbending will for so many years and not show it. Nobody, looking at Theodosia now, would have found it hard to believe that a woman with such a determined, immoveable face could stick to a course of conduct in defiance of circumstances.

Wesley Brooke was almost forgotten. People knew, through correspondents of Greene and Cary, that he had prospered and grown rich. The curious old story had crystallized into accepted history.

A life may go on without ripple or disturbance for so many years that it may seem to have settled into a lasting calm; then a sudden wind of passion may sweep over it and leave behind a wake of tempestuous waters. Such a time came at last to Theodosia.

One day in August Mrs. Emory Merritt dropped in. Emory Merritt's sister was Ogden Greene's wife, and the Merritts kept up an occasional correspondence with her. Hence, Cecilia Merritt always knew what was to be known about Wesley Brooke, and always told Theodosia because she had never been expressly forbidden to do so.

Today she looked slightly excited. Secretly she was wondering if the news she brought would have any effect whatever on Theodosia's impassive calm.

"Do you know, Dosia, Wesley's real sick? In fact, Phoebe Greene says they have very poor hopes of him. He was kind of ailing all the spring, it seems, and about a month ago he was took down with some kind of slow fever they have out there. Phoebe says they have a hired nurse from the nearest town and a good doctor, but she reckons he won't get over it. That fever goes awful hard with a man of his years."

Cecilia Merritt, who was the fastest talker in Heatherton, had got this out before she was brought up by a queer sound, half gasp, half cry, from Theodosia. The latter looked as if someone had struck her a physical blow.

"Mercy, Dosia, you ain't going to faint! I didn't suppose you'd care. You never seemed to care."

"Did you say," asked Theodosia thickly, "that Wesley was sick—dying?"

"Well, that's what Phoebe said. She may be mistaken. Dosia Brooke, you're a queer woman. I never could make you out and I never expect to. I guess only the Lord who made you can translate you."

Theodosia stood up. The sun was getting low, and the valley beneath them, ripening to harvest, was like a river of gold. She folded up her sewing with a steady hand.

"It's five o'clock, so I'll ask you to excuse me, Cecilia. I have a good deal to attend to. You can ask Emory if he'll drive me to the station in the morning. I'm going out to Wes."

"Well, for the land's sake," said Cecilia Merritt feebly, as she tied on her gingham sunbonnet. She got up and went home in a daze.

Theodosia packed her trunk and worked all night, dry-eyed, with agony and fear tearing at her heart. The iron will had snapped at last, like a broken reed, and fierce self-condemnation seized on her. "I've been a wicked woman," she moaned.

A week from that day Theodosia climbed down from the dusty stage that had brought her from the station over the prairies to the unpretentious little house where Wesley Brooke lived. A young girl, so like what Ogden Greene's wife had been fifteen years before that Theodosia involuntarily exclaimed, "Phoebe," came to the door. Beyond her, Theodosia saw the white-capped nurse.

Her voice trembled.

"Does—does Wesley Brooke live here?" she asked.

The girl nodded.

"Yes. But he is very ill at present. Nobody is allowed to see him."

Theodosia put up her hand and loosened her bonnet strings as if they were choking her. She had been sick with the fear that Wesley would be dead before she got to him. The relief was almost overwhelming.

"But I must see him," she cried hysterically—she, the calm, easy-going Dosia, hysterical—"I am his wife—and oh, if he had died before I got here!"

The nurse came forward.

"In that case I suppose you must," she conceded. "But he does not expect you. I must prepare him for the surprise."

She turned to the door of a room opening off the kitchen, but Theodosia, who had hardly heard her, was before her. She was inside the room before the nurse could prevent her. Then she stood, afraid and trembling, her eyes searching the dim apartment hungrily.

When they fell on the occupant of the bed Theodosia started in bitter surprise. All unconsciously she had been expecting to find Wesley as he had been when they parted. Could this gaunt, haggard creature, with the unkempt beard and prematurely grey hair and the hollow, beseeching eyes, be the ruddy, boyish-faced husband of her youth? She gave a choking cry of pain and shame, and the sick man turned his head. Their eyes met.

Amazement, incredulity, hope, dread, all flashed in succession over Wesley Brooke's lined face. He raised himself feebly up.

"Dosia," he murmured.

Theodosia staggered across the room and fell on her knees by the bed. She clasped his head to her breast and kissed him again and again.

"Oh, Wes, Wes, can you forgive me? I've been a wicked, stubborn woman—and I've spoiled our lives. Forgive me."

He held his thin trembling arms around her and devoured her face with his eyes.

"Dosia, when did you come? Did you know I was sick?"

"Wes, I can't talk till you say you've forgiven me."

"Oh, Dosia, you have just as much to forgive. We were both too set. I should have been more considerate."

"Just say, I forgive you, Dosia,'" she entreated.

"I forgive you, Dosia," he said gently, "and oh, it's so good to see you once more, darling. There hasn't been an hour since I left you that I haven't longed for your sweet face. If I had thought you really cared I'd have gone back. But I thought you didn't. It broke my heart. You did though, didn't you?"

"Oh, yes, yes, yes," she said, holding him more closely, with her tears falling.

When the young doctor from Red Butte came that evening he found a great improvement in his patient. Joy and happiness, those world-old physicians, had done what drugs and medicines had failed to do.

"I'm going to get better, Doc," said Wesley. "My wife has come and she's going to stay. You didn't know I was married, did you? I'll tell you the story some day. I proposed going back east, but Dosia says she'd rather stay here. I'm the happiest man in Red Butte, Doc."

He squeezed Theodosia's hand as he had used to do long ago in Heatherton church, and Dosia smiled down at him. There were no dimples now, but her smile was very sweet. The ghostly finger of old Henry Ford, pointing down through the generations, had lost its power to brand with its malediction the life of these, his descendants. Wesley and Theodosia had joined hands with their long-lost happiness.

The Story of an Invitation

Bertha Sutherland hurried home from the post office and climbed the stairs of her boarding-house to her room on the third floor. Her roommate, Grace Maxwell, was sitting on the divan by the window, looking out into the twilight.

A year ago Bertha and Grace had come to Dartmouth to attend the Academy, and found themselves roommates. Bertha was bright, pretty and popular, the favourite of her classmates and teachers; Grace was a grave, quiet girl, dressed in mourning. She was quite alone in the world, the aunt who had brought her up having recently died. At first she had felt shy with bright and brilliant Bertha; but they soon became friends, and the year that followed was a very pleasant one. It was almost ended now, for the terminal exams had begun, and in a week's time the school would close for the holidays.

"Have some chocolates, Grace," said Bertha gaily. "I got such good news in my letter tonight that I felt I must celebrate it fittingly. So I went into Carter's and invested all my spare cash in caramels. It's really fortunate the term is almost out, for I'm nearly bankrupt. I have just enough left to furnish a 'tuck-out' for commencement night, and no more."

"What is your good news, may I ask?" said Grace.

"You know I have an Aunt Margaret—commonly called Aunt Meg—out at Riversdale, don't you? There never was such a dear, sweet, jolly aunty in the world. I had a letter from her tonight. Listen, I'll read you what she says."

I want you to spend your holidays with me, my dear. Mary Fairweather and Louise Fyshe and Lily Dennis are coming, too. So there is just room for one more, and that one must be yourself. Come to Riversdale when school closes, and I'll feed you on strawberries and cream and pound cake and doughnuts and mince pies, and all the delicious, indigestible things that school girls love and careful mothers condemn. Mary and Lou and Lil are girls after your own heart, I know, and you shall all do just as you like, and we'll have picnics and parties and merry doings galore.

"There," said Bertha, looking up with a laugh. "Isn't that lovely?"

"How delightful it must be to have friends like that to love you and plan for you," said Grace wistfully. "I am sure you will have a pleasant vacation, Bertie. As for me, I am going into Clarkman's bookstore until school reopens. I saw Mr. Clarkman today and he agreed to take me."

Bertha looked surprised. She had not known what Grace's vacation plans were.

"I don't think you ought to do that, Grace," she said thoughtfully. "You are not strong, and you need a good rest. It will be awfully trying to work at Clarkman's all summer."

"There is nothing else for me to do," said Grace, trying to speak cheerfully. "You know I'm as poor as the proverbial church mouse, Bertie, and the simple truth is that I can't afford to pay my board all summer and get my winter outfit unless I do something to earn it. I shall be too busy to be lonesome, and I shall expect long, newsy letters from you, telling me all your fun—passing your vacation on to me at second-hand, you see. Well, I must set to work at those algebra problems. I tried them before dark, but I couldn't solve them. My head ached and I felt so stupid. How glad I shall be when exams are over."

"I suppose I must revise that senior English this evening," said Bertha absently.

But she made no move to do so. She was studying her friend's face. How very pale and thin Grace looked—surely much paler and thinner than when she had come to the Academy, and she had not by any means been plump and rosy then.

I believe she could not stand two months at Clarkman's, thought Bertha. If I were not going to Aunt Meg's, I would ask her to go home with me. Or even if Aunt Meg had room for another guest, I'd just write her all about Grace and ask if I could bring her with me. Aunt Meg would understand—she always understands. But she hasn't, so it can't be.

Just then a thought darted into Bertha's brain.

"What nonsense!" she said aloud so suddenly and forcibly that Grace fairly jumped.

"What is?"

"Oh, nothing much," said Bertha, getting up briskly. "See here, I'm going to get to work. I've wasted enough time."

She curled herself up on the divan and tried to study her senior English. But her thoughts wandered hopelessly, and finally she gave it up in despair and went to bed. There she could not sleep; she lay awake and wrestled with herself. It was after midnight when she sat up in bed and said solemnly, "I will do it."

Next day Bertha wrote a confidential letter to Aunt Meg. She thanked her for her invitation and then told her all about Grace.

"And what I want to ask, Aunt Meg, is that you will let me transfer my invitation to Grace, and ask her to go to Riversdale this summer in my place. Don't think me ungrateful. No, I'm sure you won't, you always understand things. But you can't have us both, and I'd rather Grace should go. It will do her so much good, and I have a lovely home of my own to go to, and she has none."

Aunt Meg understood, as usual, and was perfectly willing. So she wrote to Bertha and enclosed a note of invitation for Grace.

I shall have to manage this affair very carefully, reflected Bertha. Grace must never suspect that I did it on purpose. I will tell her that circumstances have prevented me from accepting Aunt Meg's invitation. That is true enough—no need to say that the circumstances are hers, not mine. And I'll say I just asked Aunt Meg to invite her in my place and that she has done so.

When Grace came home from her history examination that day, Bertha told her story and gave her Aunt Meg's cordial note.

"You must come to me in Bertha's place," wrote the latter. "I feel as if I knew you from her letters, and I will consider you as a sort of honorary niece, and I'll treat you as if you were Bertha herself."

"Isn't it splendid of Aunt Meg?" said Bertha diplomatically. "Of course you'll go, Gracie."

"Oh, I don't know," said Grace in bewilderment. "Are you sure you don't want to go, Bertha?"

"Indeed, I do want to go, dreadfully," said Bertha frankly. "But as I've told you, it is impossible. But if I am disappointed, Aunt Meg musn't be. You must go, Grace, and that is all there is about it."

In the end, Grace did go, a little puzzled and doubtful still, but thankful beyond words to escape the drudgery of the counter and the noise and heat of the city. Bertha went home, feeling a little bit blue in secret, it cannot be denied, but also feeling quite sure that if she had to do it all over again, she would do just the same.

The summer slipped quickly by, and finally two letters came to Bertha, one from Aunt Meg and one from Grace.

"I've had a lovely time," wrote the latter, "and, oh, Bertie, what do you think? I am to stay here always. Oh, of course I am going back to school next month, but this is to be my home after this. Aunt Meg—she makes me call her that—says I must stay with her for good."

In Aunt Meg's letter was this paragraph:

Grace is writing to you, and will have told you that I intend to keep her here. You know I have always wanted a daughter of my own, but my greedy brothers and sisters would never give me one of theirs. So I intend to adopt Grace. She is the sweetest girl in the world, and I am very grateful to you for sending her here. You will not know her when you see her. She has grown plump and rosy.

Bertha folded her letters up with a smile. "I have a vague, delightful feeling that I am the good angel in a storybook," she said.

The Touch of Fate

Mrs. Major Hill was in her element. This did not often happen, for in the remote prairie town of the Canadian Northwest, where her husband was stationed, there were few opportunities for match-making. And Mrs. Hill was—or believed herself to be—a born matchmaker.

Major Hill was in command of the detachment of Northwest Mounted Police at Dufferin Bluff. Mrs. Hill was wont to declare that it was the most forsaken place to be found in Canada or out of it; but she did her very best to brighten it up, and it is only fair to say that the N.W.M.P., officers and men, seconded her efforts.

When Violet Thayer came west to pay a long-promised visit to her old schoolfellow, Mrs. Hill's cup of happiness bubbled over. In her secret soul she vowed that Violet should never go back east unless it were post-haste to prepare a wedding trousseau. There were at least half a dozen eligibles among the M.P.s, and Mrs. Hill, after some reflection, settled on Ned Madison as the flower of the flock.

"He and Violet are simply made for each other," she told Major Hill the evening before Miss Thayer's arrival. "He has enough money and he is handsome and fascinating. And Violet is a beauty and a clever woman into the bargain. They can't help falling in love, I'm sure; it's fate!"

"Perhaps Miss Thayer may be booked elsewhere already," suggested Major Hill. He had seen more than one of his wife's card castles fall into heartbreaking ruin.

"Oh, no; Violet would have told me if that were the case. It's really quite time for her to think of settling down. She is twenty-five, you know. The men all go crazy over her, but she's dreadfully hard to please. However, she can't help liking Ned. He hasn't a single fault. I firmly believe it is foreordained."

And in this belief Mrs. Hill rested securely, but nevertheless did not fail to concoct several feminine artifices for the helping on of foreordination. It was a working belief with her that it was always well to have the gods in your debt.

Violet Thayer came, saw, and conquered. Within thirty-six hours of her arrival at Dufferin Bluff she had every one of the half-dozen eligibles at her feet, not to mention a score or more ineligibles. She would have been surprised indeed had it been otherwise. Miss Thayer knew her power, and was somewhat unduly fond of exercising it. But she was a very nice girl into the bargain, and so thought one and all of the young men who frequented Mrs. Hill's drawing-room and counted it richly worth while merely to look at Miss Thayer after having seen nothing for weeks except flabby half-breed girls and blue-haired squaws.

Madison was foremost in the field, of course. Madison was really a nice fellow, and quite deserved all Mrs. Hill's encomiums. He was good-looking and well groomed—could sing and dance divinely and play the violin to perfection. The other M.P.s were all jealous of him, and more so than ever when Violet Thayer came. They did not consider that any one of them had the ghost of a chance if Madison entered the lists against them.

Violet liked Madison, and was very chummy with him after her own fashion. She thought all the M.P.s were nice boys, and they amused her, for which she was grateful. She had expected Dufferin Bluff to be very dull, and doubtless it would pall after a time, but for a change it was delightful.

The sixth evening after her arrival found Mrs. Hill's room crowded, as usual, with M.P.s. Violet was looking her best in a distracting new gown—Sergeant Fox afterwards described it to a brother officer as a "stunning sort of rig between a cream and a blue and a brown"; she flirted impartially with all the members of her circle at first, but gradually narrowed down to Ned Madison, much to the delight of Mrs. Hill, who was hovering around like a small, brilliant butterfly.

Violet was talking to Madison and watching John Spencer out of the tail of her eye. Spencer was not an M.P. He had some government post at Dufferin Bluff, and this was his first call at Lone Poplar Villa since Miss Thayer's arrival. He did not seem to be dazzled by her at all, and after his introduction had promptly retired to a corner with Major Hill, where they talked the whole evening about the trouble on the Indian reservation at Loon Lake.

Possibly this indifference piqued Miss Thayer. Possibly she considered it refreshing after the servile adulation of the M.P.s. At any rate, when all the latter were gathered about the piano singing a chorus with gusto, she shook Madison off and went over to the corner where Spencer, deserted by the Major, whose bass was wanted, was sitting in solitary state.

He looked up indifferently as Violet shimmered down on the divan beside him. Sergeant Robinson, who was watching them jealously from the corner beyond the palms, and would have given his eyes, or at least one of them, for such a favour, mentally vowed that Spencer was the dullest fellow he had ever put those useful members on.

"Don't you sing, Mr. Spencer?" asked Violet by way of beginning a conversation, as she turned her splendid eyes full upon him. Robinson would have lost his head under them, but Spencer kept his heroically.

"No," was his calmly brief reply, given without any bluntness, but with no evident intention of saying anything more.

In spite of her social experience Violet felt disconcerted.

"If he doesn't want to talk to me I won't try to make him," she thought crossly. No man had ever snubbed her so before.

Spencer listened immovably to the music for a time. Then he turned to his companion with a palpable effort to be civilly sociable.

"How do you like the west, Miss Thayer?" he said.

Violet smiled—the smile most men found dangerous.

"Very much, so far as I have seen it. There is a flavour about the life here that I like, but I dare say it would soon pall. It must be horribly lonesome here most of the time, especially in winter."

"The M.P.s are always growling that it is," returned Spencer with a slight smile. "For my own part I never find it so."

Violet decided that his smile was very becoming to him and that she liked the way his dark hair grew over his forehead.

"I don't think I've seen you at Lone Poplar Villa before?" she said.

"No. I haven't been here for some time. I came up tonight to see the Major about the Loon Lake trouble."

"Otherwise you wouldn't have come," thought Violet. "Flattering—very!" Aloud she said, "Is it serious?"

"Oh, no. A mere squabble among the Indians. Have you ever visited the Reservation, Miss Thayer? No? Well, you should get some of your M.P. friends to take you out. It would be worth while."

"Why don't you ask me to go yourself?" said Violet audaciously.

Spencer smiled again. "Have I failed in politeness by not doing so? I fear you would find me an insufferably dull companion."

So he was not going to ask her after all. Violet felt piqued. She was also conscious of a sensation very near akin to disappointment. She looked across at Madison. How trim and dapper he was!

"I hate a bandbox man," she said to herself.

Spencer meanwhile had picked up one of Mrs. Hill's novels from the stand beside him.

"*Fools of Habit*," he said, glancing at the cover. "I see it is making quite a sensation down east. I suppose you've read it?"

"Yes. It is very frivolous and clever—all froth but delightful froth. Did you like it?"

Spencer balanced the novel reflectively on his slender brown hand.

"Well, yes, rather. But I don't care for novels as a rule. I don't understand them. The hero of this book, now—do you believe that a man in love would act as he did?"

"I don't know," said Violet amusedly. "You ought to be a better judge than I. You are a man."

"I have never loved anybody, so I am in no position to decide," said Spencer.

There was as little self-consciousness in his voice as if he were telling her a fact concerning the Loon Lake trouble. Violet rose to the occasion.

"You have an interesting experience to look forward to," she said.

Spencer turned his deep-set grey eyes squarely upon her.

"I don't know that. When I said I had never loved, I meant more than the love of a man for some particular woman. I meant love in every sense. I do not know what it is to have an affection for any human being. My parents died before I can remember. My only living relative was a penurious old uncle who brought me up for shame's sake and kicked me out on the world as soon as he could. I don't make friends easily. I have a few acquaintances whom I like, but there is not a soul on earth for whom I care, or who cares for me."

"What a revelation love will be to you when it comes," said Violet softly. Again he looked into her eyes.

"Do you think it will come?" he asked.

Before she could reply Mrs. Hill pounced upon them. Violet was wanted to sing. Mr. Spencer would excuse her, wouldn't he? Mr. Spencer did so obligingly. Moreover, he got up and bade his hostess good night. Violet gave him her hand.

"You will call again?" she said.

Spencer looked across at Madison—perhaps it was accidental.

"I think not," he said. "If, as you say, love will come some time, it would be a very unpleasant revelation if it came in hopeless guise, and one never knows what may happen."

Miss Thayer was conscious of a distinct fluttering of her heart as she went across to the piano. This was a new sensation for her, and worthy of being analyzed. After the M.P.s had gone she asked Mrs. Hill who Mr. Spencer was.

"Oh, John Spencer," said Mrs. Hill carelessly. "He's at the head of the Land Office here. That's really all I know about him. Jack says he is a downright good fellow and all that, you know. But he's no earthly good in a social way; he can't talk or he won't. He's flat. So different from Mr. Madison, isn't he?"

"Very," said Violet emphatically.

After Mrs. Hill had gone out Violet walked to the nearest mirror and looked at herself with her forefinger in the dimple of her chin.

"It is very odd," she said. She did not mean the dimple.

Spencer had told her he was not coming back. She did not believe this, but she did not expect him for a few days. Consequently, when he appeared the very next evening she was surprised. Madison, to whom she was talking when Spencer entered, does not know to this day what she had started to say to him, for she never finished her sentence.

"I wonder if it is the Loon Lake affair again?" she thought nervously.

Mrs. Hill came up at this point and whisked Madison off for a waltz. Spencer, seeing his chance, came straight across the room to her. Sergeant Robinson, who was watching them as usual, is willing to make affidavit that Miss Thayer changed colour.

After his greeting Spencer said nothing. He sat beside her, and they watched Mrs. Hill and Madison dancing. Violet wondered why she did not feel bored. When she saw Madison coming back to her she was conscious of an unreasonable anger with him. She got up abruptly.

"Let us go out on the verandah," she said imperiously. "It is absolutely stifling in here."

They went out. It was very cool and dusky. The lights of the town twinkled out below them, and the prairie bluffs behind them were dark and sibilant.

"I am going to drive over to Loon Lake tomorrow afternoon to look into affairs there," said Spencer. "Will you go with me?"

Violet reflected a moment. "You didn't ask me as if you really wanted me to go," she said.

Spencer put his hand over the white fingers that rested on the railing. He bent forward until his breath stirred the tendrils of hair on her forehead.

"Yes, I do," he said distinctly. "I want you to go with me to Loon Lake tomorrow more than I ever wanted any thing in my life before."

Later on, when everybody had gone, Violet had her bad quarter of an hour with Mrs. Hill. That lady felt herself aggrieved.

"I think you treated poor Ned very badly tonight, Vi. He felt really blue over it. And it was awfully bad form to go out with Spencer as you did and stay there so long. And you oughtn't to flirt with him—he doesn't understand the game."

"I'm not going to flirt with him," said Miss Thayer calmly.

"Oh, I suppose it's just your way. Only don't turn the poor fellow's head. By the way, Ned is coming up with his camera tomorrow afternoon to take us all."

"I'm afraid he won't find me at home," said Violet sweetly. "I am going out to Loon Lake with Mr. Spencer."

Mrs. Hill flounced off to bed in a pet. She was disgusted with everything, she declared to the Major. Things had been going so nicely, and now they were all muddled.

"Isn't Madison coming up to time?" queried the Major sleepily.

"Madison! It's Violet. She is behaving abominably. She treated poor Ned shamefully tonight. You saw yourself how she acted with Spencer, and she's going to Loon Lake with him tomorrow, she says. I'm sure I don't know what she can see in him. He's the dullest, pokiest fellow alive—so different from her in every way."

"Perhaps that is why she likes him," suggested the Major. "The attraction of opposites and all that, you know."

But Mrs. Hill crossly told him he didn't know anything about it, so, being a wise man, he held his tongue.

During the next two weeks Mrs. Hill was the most dissatisfied woman in the four districts, and every M.P. down to the rawest recruit anathemized Spencer in secret a dozen times a day. Violet simply dropped everyone else, including Madison, in the coolest, most unmistakable way.

One night Spencer did not come to Lone Poplar Villa. Violet looked for him to the last. When she realized that he was not coming she went to the verandah to have it out with herself. As she sat huddled up in a dim corner beneath a silkily rustling western maple two M.P.s came out and, not seeing her, went on with their conversation.

"Heard about Spencer?" questioned one.

"No. What of him?"

"Well, they say Miss Thayer's thrown him over. Yesterday I was passing here about four in the afternoon and I saw Spencer coming in. I went down to the Land Office and was chatting to Cribson when the door opened about half an hour later and Spencer burst in. He was pale as the dead, and looked wild. 'Has Fyshe gone to Rainy River about those Crown Lands yet?' he jerked out. Cribson said, 'No.' Then tell him he needn't; I'm going myself,' said Spencer and out he bolted. He posted off to Rainy River today, and won't be back for a fortnight. She'll be gone then."

"Rather rough on Spencer after the way she encouraged him," returned the other as they passed out of earshot.

Violet got up. All the callers were gone, and she swept in to Mrs. Hill dramatically.

"Edith," she said in the cold, steady voice that, to those who knew her, meant breakers ahead for somebody, "Mr. Spencer was here yesterday when I was riding with the Major, was he not? What did you tell him about me?"

Mrs. Hill looked at Violet's blazing eyes and wilted.

"I—didn't tell him anything—much."

"What was it?"

Mrs. Hill began to sob.

"Don't look at me like that, Violet! He just dropped in and we were talking about you—at least I was—and I had heard that Harry St. Maur was paying you marked attention before you came west—and—and that some people thought you were engaged—and so—and so—"

"You told Mr. Spencer that I was engaged to Harry St. Maur?"

"No-o-o—I just hinted. I didn't mean an-any harm. I never dreamed you'd really c-care. I thought you were just amusing yourself—and so did everybody—and I wanted Ned Madison—"

Violet had turned very pale.

"I love him," she said hoarsely, "and you've sent him away. He's gone to Rainy River. I shall never see him again!"

"Oh, yes, you will," gasped Mrs. Hill faintly. "He'll come back when he knows—you c-can write and tell him—"

"Do you suppose I am going to write and ask him to come back?" said Violet wildly. "I've enough pride left yet to keep me from doing that for a man at whose head I've thrown myself openly—yes, openly, and who has never, in words at least, told me he cared anything about me. I will never forgive you, Edith!"

Then Mrs. Hill found herself alone with her lacerated feelings. After soothing them with a good cry, she set to work thinking seriously. There was no doubt she had muddled things badly, but there was no use leaving them in a muddle when a word or two fitly spoken might set them straight.

Mrs. Hill sat down and wrote a very diplomatic letter before she went to bed, and the next morning she waylaid Sergeant Fox and asked him if he would ride down to Rainy River with a very important message for Mr. Spencer. Sergeant Fox wondered what it could be, but it was not his to reason why; it was his only to mount and ride with all due speed, for Mrs. Hill's whims and wishes were as stringent and binding as the rules of the force.

That evening when Mrs. Hill and Violet—the latter very silent and regal—were sitting on the verandah, a horseman came galloping up the Rainy River trail. Mrs. Hill excused herself and went in. Five minutes later John Spencer, covered with the alkali dust of his twenty miles' ride, dismounted at Violet's side.

The M.P.s gave a concert at the barracks that night and Mrs. Hill and her Major went to it, as well as everyone else of any importance in town except Violet and Spencer. They sat on Major Hill's verandah and watched the moon rising over the bluffs and making milk-white reflections in the prairie lakes.

"It seems a year of misery since last night," sighed Violet happily.

"You couldn't have been quite as miserable as I was," said Spencer earnestly. "You were everything—absolutely everything to me. Other men have little rills and driblets of affection for sisters and cousins and aunts, but everything in me went out to you. Do you remember you told me the first time we met that love would be a revelation to me? It has been more. It has been a new gospel. I hardly dared hope you could care for me. Even yet I don't know why you do."

"I love you," said Violet gravely, "because you are you."

Than which, of course, there could be no better reason.

The Waking of Helen

Robert Reeves looked somewhat curiously at the girl who was waiting on him at his solitary breakfast. He had not seen her before, arriving at his summer boarding house only the preceding night.

It was a shabby farmhouse on the inland shore of a large bay that was noted for its tides, and had wonderful possibilities of light and shade for an impressionist. Reeves was an enthusiastic artist. It mattered little to him that the boarding accommodations were most primitive, the people uncultured and dull, the place itself utterly isolated, as long as he could revel in those transcendent sunsets and sunrises, those marvellous moonlights, those wonderful purple shores and sweeps of shimmering blue water.

The owner of the farm was Angus Fraser, and he and his wife seemed to be a reserved, uncouth pair, with no apparent interest in life save to scratch a bare living out of their few stony acres. He had an impression that they were childless and was at a loss to place this girl who poured his tea and brought in his toast. She did not resemble either Fraser or his wife. She was certainly not beautiful, being very tall and rather awkward, and dressed in a particularly unbecoming dark print wrapper. Her luxuriant hair was thick and black, and was coiled in a heavy knot at the nape of her neck. Her features were delicate but irregular, and her skin was very brown. Her eyes attracted Reeves's notice especially; they were large and dark and full of a half-unconscious, wistful longing, as if a prisoned soul behind them were vainly trying to reveal itself.

Reeves could find out nothing of her from herself, for she responded to his tentative questions about the place in the briefest fashion. Afterwards he interviewed Mrs. Fraser cautiously, and ascertained that the girl's name was Helen Fraser, and that she was Angus's niece.

"Her father and mother are dead and we've brought her up. Helen's a good girl in most ways—a little obstinate and sulky now and then—but generally she's steady enough, and as for work, there ain't a girl in Bay Beach can come up to her in house or field. Angus calculates she saves him a man's wages clear. No, I ain't got nothing to say against Helen."

Nevertheless, Reeves felt somehow that Mrs. Fraser did not like her husband's niece. He often heard her scolding or nagging Helen at her work, and noticed that the latter never answered back. But once, after Mrs. Angus's tongue had been especially bitter, he met the girl hurrying along the hall from the kitchen with her eyes full of tears. Reeves felt as if someone had struck him a blow. He went to Angus and his wife that afternoon. He wished to paint a shore picture, he said, and wanted a model. Would they allow Miss Fraser to pose for him? He would pay liberally for her time.

Angus and his wife had no objection. They would pocket the money, and Helen could be spared a spell every day as well as not. Reeves told Helen of his plan himself, meeting her in the evening as she was bringing the cows home from the low shore pastures beyond the marsh. He was surprised at the sudden illumination of her face. It almost transfigured her from a plain, sulky-looking girl into a beautiful woman.

But the glow passed quickly. She assented to his plan quietly, almost lifelessly. He walked home with her behind the cows and talked of the sunset and the mysterious beauty of the bay and the purple splendour of the distant coasts. She listened in silence. Only once, when he spoke of the distant murmur of the open sea, she lifted her head and looked at him.

"What does it say to you?" she asked.

"It speaks of eternity. And to you?"

"It calls me," she answered simply, "and then I want to go out and meet it—and it hurts me too. I can't tell how or why. Sometimes it makes me feel as if I were asleep and wanted to wake and didn't know how."

She turned and looked out over the bay. A dying gleam of sunset broke through a cloud and fell across her hair. For a moment she seemed the spirit of the shore personified—all its mystery, all its uncertainty, all its elusive charm.

She has possibilities, thought Reeves.

Next day he began his picture. At first he had thought of painting her as the incarnation of a sea spirit, but decided that her moods were too fitful. So he began to sketch her as "Waiting"—a woman looking out across the bay with a world of hopeless longing in her eyes. The subject suited her well, and the picture grew apace.

When he was tired of work he made her walk around the shore with him, or row up the head of the bay in her own boat. He tried to draw her out, at first with indifferent success. She seemed to be frightened of him. He talked to her of many things—the far outer world whose echoes never reached her, foreign lands where he had travelled, famous men and women whom he had met, music, art and books. When he spoke of books he touched the right chord. One of those transfiguring flashes he delighted to evoke now passed over her plain face.

"That is what I've always wanted," she said hungrily, "and I never get them. Aunt hates to see me reading. She says it is a waste of time. And I love it so. I read every scrap of paper I can get hold of, but I hardly ever see a book."

The next day Reeves took his Tennyson to the shore and began to read the *Idylls of the King* to her.

"It is beautiful," was her sole verbal comment, but her rapt eyes said everything.

After that he never went out with her without a book—now one of the poets, now some prose classic. He was surprised by her quick appreciation of and sympathy with the finest passages. Gradually, too, she forgot her shyness and began to talk. She knew nothing of his world, but her own world she knew and knew well. She was a mine of traditional history about the bay. She knew the rocky coast by heart, and every old legend that clung to it. They drifted into making excursions along the shore and explored its wildest retreats. The girl had an artist's eye for scenery and colour effect.

"You should have been an artist," Reeves told her one day when she had pointed out to him the exquisite loveliness of a shaft of light falling through a cleft in the rocks across a dark-green pool at their base.

"I would rather be a writer," she said slowly, "if I could only write something like those books you have read to me. What a glorious destiny it must be to have something to say that the whole world is listening for, and to be able to say it in words that will live forever! It must be the noblest human lot."

"Yet some of those men and women were neither good nor noble," said Reeves gently, "and many of them were unhappy."

Helen dismissed the subject as abruptly as she always did when the conversation touched too nearly on the sensitive edge of her soul dreams.

"Do you know where I am taking you today?" she said.

"No—where?"

"To what the people here call the Kelpy's Cave. I hate to go there. I believe there is something uncanny about it, but I think you will like to see it. It is a dark little cave in the curve of a small cove, and on each side the headlands of rock run far out. At low tide we can walk right around, but when the tide comes in it fills the Kelpy's Cave. If you were there and let the tide come past the points, you would be drowned unless you could swim, for the rocks are so steep and high it is impossible to climb them."

Reeves was interested.

"Was anyone ever caught by the tide?"

"Yes," returned Helen, with a shudder. "Once, long ago, before I was born, a girl went around the shore to the cave and fell asleep there—and the tide came in and she was drowned. She was young and very pretty, and was to have been married the next week. I've been afraid of the place ever since."

The treacherous cave proved to be a picturesque and innocent-looking spot, with the beach of glittering sand before it and the high gloomy walls of rock on either hand.

"I must come here some day and sketch it," said Reeves enthusiastically, "and you must be the Kelpy, Helen, and sit in the cave with your hair wrapped about you and seaweed clinging to it."

"Do you think a kelpy would look like that?" said the girl dreamily. "I don't. I think it is a wild, wicked little sea imp, malicious and mocking and cruel, and it sits here and watches for victims."

"Well, never mind your sea kelpies," Reeves said, fishing out his Longfellow. "They are a tricky folk, if all tales be true, and it is supposed to be a very rash thing to talk about them in their own haunts. I want to read you 'The Building of the Ship.' You will like it, I'm sure."

When the tide turned they went home.

"We haven't seen the kelpy, after all," said Reeves.

"I think I shall see him some day," said Helen gravely. "I think he is waiting for me there in that gloomy cave of his, and some time or other he will get me."

Reeves smiled at the gloomy fancy, and Helen smiled back at him with one of her sudden radiances. The tide was creeping swiftly up over the white sands. The sun was low and the bay was swimming in a pale blue glory. They parted at Clam Point, Helen to go for the cows and Reeves to wander on up the shore. He thought of Helen at first, and the wonderful change that had come over her of late; then he began to think of another face—a marvellously lovely one with blue eyes as tender as the waters before him. Then Helen was forgotten.

The summer waned swiftly. One afternoon Reeves took a fancy to revisit the Kelpy's Cave. Helen could not go. It was harvest time, and she was needed in the field.

"Don't let the kelpy catch you," she said to him half seriously. "The tide will turn early this afternoon, and you are given to day-dreaming."

"I'll be careful," he promised laughingly, and he meant to be careful. But somehow when he reached the cave its unwholesome charm overcame him, and he sat down on the boulder at its mouth.

"An hour yet before tide time," he said. "Just enough time to read that article on impressionists in my review and then stroll home by the sandshore."

From reading he passed to day-dreaming, and day-dreaming drifted into sleep, with his head pillowed on the rocky walls of the cave.

How long he had slept he did not know, but he woke with a start of horror. He sprang to his feet, realizing his position instantly. The tide was in—far in past the headlands already. Above and beyond him towered the pitiless unscalable rocks. There was no way of escape.

Reeves was no coward, but life was sweet to him, and to die like that—like a drowned rat in a hole—to be able to do nothing but wait for that swift and sure oncoming death! He reeled against the damp rock wall, and for a moment sea and sky and prisoning headlands and white-lined tide whirled before his eyes.

Then his head grew clearer. He tried to think. How long had he? Not more than twenty minutes at the outside. Well, death was sure and he would meet it bravely. But to wait—to wait helplessly! He should go; mad with the horror of it before those endless minutes would have passed!

He took something from his pocket and bent his, head over it, pressing his lips to it repeatedly. And then, when he raised his face again, a dory was coming around the headland on his right, and Helen Fraser was in it.

Reeves was dizzy again with the shock of joy and thankfulness. He ran down over the little stretch of sand still uncovered by the tide and around to the rocks of the headlands against which the dory was already grating. He sprang forward impulsively and caught the girl's cold hands in his as she dropped the oars and stood up.

"Helen, you have saved me! How can I ever thank you? I—"

He broke off abruptly, for she was looking up at him, breathlessly and voicelessly, with her whole soul in her eyes. He saw in them a revelation that amazed him; he dropped her hands and stepped back as if she had struck him in the face.

Helen did not notice the change in him. She clasped her hands together and her voice trembled.

"Oh, I was afraid I should be too late! When I came in from the field Aunt Hannah said you had not come back—and I knew it was tide time—and I felt somehow that it had caught you in the cave. I ran down over the marsh and took Joe Simmon's dory. If I had not got here in time—"

She broke off shiveringly. Reeves stepped into the dory and took up the oars.

"The kelpy would have been sure of its victim then," he said, trying to speak lightly. "It would have almost served me right for neglecting your warning. I was very careless. You must let me row back. I am afraid you have overtasked your strength trying to cheat the kelpy."

Reeves rowed homeward in an absolute silence. Helen did not speak and he could not. When they reached the dory anchorage he helped her out.

"I think I'll go out to the Point for a walk," he said. "I want to steady my nerves. You must go right home and rest. Don't be anxious—I won't take any more chances with sea kelpies."

Helen went away without a word, and Reeves walked slowly out to the Point. He was grieved beyond measure at the discovery he believed he had made. He had never dreamed of such a thing. He was not a vain man, and was utterly free from all tendency to flirtation. It had never occurred to him that the waking of the girl's deep nature might be attended with disastrous consequences. He had honestly meant to help her, and what had he done?

He felt very uncomfortable; he could not conscientiously blame himself, but he saw that he had acted foolishly. And of course he must go away at once. And he must also tell her something she ought to know. He wished he had told her long ago.

The following afternoon was a perfect one. Reeves was sketching on the sandshore when Helen came. She sat down on a camp stool a little to one side and did not speak. After a few moments Reeves pushed away his paraphernalia impatiently.

"I don't feel in a mood for work," he said. "It is too dreamy a day—one ought to do nothing to be in keeping. Besides, I'm getting lazy now that my vacation is nearly over. I must go in a few days."

He avoided looking at her, so he did not see the sudden pallor of her face.

"So soon?" she said in a voice expressive of no particular feeling.

"Yes. I ought not to have lingered so long. My world will be forgetting me and that will not do. It has been a very pleasant summer and I shall be sorry to leave Bay Beach."

"But you will come back next summer?" asked Helen quickly. "You said you would."

Reeves nerved himself for his very distasteful task.

"Perhaps," he said, with an attempt at carelessness, "but if I do so, I shall not come alone. Somebody who is very dear to me will come with me—as my wife. I have never told you about her, Helen, but you and I are such good friends that I do not mind doing so now. I am engaged to a very sweet girl, and we expect to be married next spring."

There was a brief silence. Reeves had been vaguely afraid of a scene and was immensely relieved to find his fear unrealized. Helen sat very still. He could not see her face. Did she care, after all? Was he mistaken?

When she spoke her voice was perfectly calm.

"Thank you, it is very kind of you to tell me about her. I suppose she is very beautiful."

"Yes, here is her picture. You can judge for yourself."

Helen took the portrait from his hand and looked at it steadily. It was a miniature painted on ivory, and the face looking out from it was certainly lovely.

"It is no wonder you love her," said the girl in a low tone as she handed it back. "It must be strange to be so beautiful as that."

Reeves picked up his Tennyson.

"Shall I read you something? What will you have?"

"Read 'Elaine,' please. I want to hear that once more."

Reeves felt a sudden dislike to her choice.

"Wouldn't you prefer something else?" he asked, hurriedly turning over the leaves. "'Elaine' is rather sad. Shan't I read 'Guinevere' instead?"

"No," said Helen in the same lifeless tone. "I have no sympathy for Guinevere. She suffered and her love was unlawful, but she was loved in return—she did not waste her love on someone who did not want or care for it. Elaine did, and her life went with it. Read me the story."

Reeves obeyed. When he had finished he held the book out to her.

"Helen, will you take this Tennyson from me in remembrance of our friendship and of the Kelpy's Cave? I shall never forget that I owe my life to you."

"Thank you."

She took the book and placed a little thread of crimson seaweed that had been caught in the sand between the pages of "Elaine." Then she rose.

"I must go back now. Aunt will need me. Thank you again for the book, Mr. Reeves, and for all your kindness to me."

Reeves was relieved when the interview was over. Her calmness had reassured him. She did not care very much, after all; it was only a passing fancy, and when he was gone she would soon forget him.

He went away a few days later, and Helen bade him an impassive good-bye. When the afternoon was far spent she stole away from the house to the shore, with her Tennyson in her hand, and took her way to the Kelpy's Cave.

The tide was just beginning to come in. She sat down on the big boulder where Reeves had fallen asleep. Beyond stretched the gleaming blue waters, mellowing into a hundred fairy shades horizonward.

The shadows of the rocks were around her. In front was the white line of the incoming tide; it had almost reached the headlands. A few minutes more and escape would be cut off—yet she did not move.

When the dark green water reached her, and the lapping wavelets swished up over the hem of her dress, she lifted her head and a sudden strange smile flashed over her face.

Perhaps the kelpy understood it.

The Way of the Winning of Anne

Jerome Irving had been courting Anne Stockard for fifteen years. He had begun when she was twenty and he was twenty-five, and now that Jerome was forty, and Anne, in a village where everybody knew everybody else's age, had to own to being thirty-five, the courtship did not seem any nearer a climax than it had at the beginning. But that was not Jerome's fault, poor fellow!

At the end of the first year he had asked Anne to marry him, and Anne had refused. Jerome was disappointed, but he kept his head and went on courting Anne just the same; that is he went over to Esek Stockard's house every Saturday night and spent the evening, he walked home with Anne from prayer meeting and singing school and parties when she would let him, and asked her to go to all the concerts and socials and quilting frolics that came off. Anne never would go, of course, but Jerome faithfully gave her the chance. Old Esek rather favoured Jerome's suit, for Anne was the plainest of his many daughters, and no other fellow seemed at all anxious to run Jerome off the track; but she took her own way with true Stockard firmness, and matters were allowed to drift on at the will of time or chance.

Three years later Jerome tried his luck again, with precisely the same result, and after that he had asked Anne regularly once a year to marry him, and just as regularly Anne said no a little more brusquely and a little more decidedly every year. Now, in the mellowness of a fifteen-year-old courtship, Jerome did not mind it at all. He knew that everything comes to the man who has patience to wait.

Time, of course, had not stood still with Anne and Jerome, or with the history of Deep Meadows. At the Stockard homestead the changes had been many and marked. Every year or two there had been a wedding in the big brick farmhouse, and one of old Esek's girls had been the bride each time. Julia and Grace and Celia and Betty and Theodosia and Clementina Stockard were all married and gone. But Anne had never had another lover. There had to be an old maid in every big family she said, and she was not going to marry Jerome Irving just for the sake of having Mrs. on her tombstone.

Old Esek and his wife had been put away in the Deep Meadows burying-ground. The broad, fertile Stockard acres passed into Anne's possession. She was a good business-woman, and the farm continued to be the best in the district. She kept two hired men and a servant girl, and the sixteen-year-old of her oldest sister lived with her. There were few visitors at the Stockard place now, but Jerome "dropped in" every Saturday night with clockwork regularity and talked to Anne about her stock and advised her regarding the rotation of her crops and the setting out of her orchards. And at ten o'clock he would take his hat and cane and tell Anne to be good to herself, and go home.

Anne had long since given up trying to discourage him; she even accepted attentions from him now that she had used to refuse. He always walked home with her from evening meetings and was her partner in the games at quilting parties. It was great fun for the young folks. "Old Jerome and Anne" were a standing joke in Deep Meadows. But the older people had ceased to expect anything to come of it.

Anne laughed at Jerome as she had always done, and would not have owned for the world that she could have missed him. Jerome was useful, she admitted, and a comfortable friend; and she would have liked him well enough if he would only omit that ridiculous yearly ceremony of proposal.

It was Jerome's fortieth birthday when Anne refused him again. He realized this as he went down the road in the moonlight, and doubt and dismay began to creep into his heart. Anne and he were both getting old—there was no disputing that fact. It was high time that he brought her to terms if he was ever going to. Jerome was an easy-going mortal and always took things placidly, but he did not mean to have all those fifteen years of patient courting go for nothing He had thought Anne would get tired of saying no, sooner or later, and say yes, if for no other reason than to have a change; but getting tired did not seem to run in the Stockard blood. She had said no that night just as coolly and decidedly and unsentimentally as she said it fifteen years before. Jerome had the sensation of going around in a circle and never getting any further on. He made up his mind that something must be done, and just as he got to the brook that divides Deep Meadows West from Deep Meadows Central an idea struck him; it was a good idea and amused him. He laughed aloud and slapped his thigh, much to the amusement of two boys who were sitting unnoticed on the railing of the bridge.

"There's old Jerome going home from seeing Anne Stockard," said one. "Wonder what on earth he's laughing at. Seems to me if I couldn't get a wife without hoeing a fifteen-year row, I'd give up trying."

But, then, the speaker was a Hamilton, and the Hamiltons never had any perseverance.

Jerome, although a well-to-do man, owning a good farm, had, so to speak, no home of his own. The old Irving homestead belonged to his older brother, who had a wife and family. Jerome lived with them and was so used to it he didn't mind.

At forty a lover must not waste time. Jerome thought out the details that night, and next day he opened the campaign. But it was not until the evening after that that Anne Stockard heard the news. It was her niece, Octavia, who told her. The latter had been having a chat up the lane with Sam Mitchell, and came in with a broad smile on her round, rosy face and a twinkle in her eyes.

"I guess you've lost your beau this time, Aunt Anne. It looks as if he meant to take you at your word at last."

"What on earth do you mean?" asked Anne, a little sharply. She was in the pantry counting eggs, and Octavia's interruption made her lose her count. "Now I can't remember whether it was six or seven dozen I said last. I shall have to count them all over again. I wish, Octavia, that you could think of something besides beaus all the time."

"Well, but listen," persisted Octavia wickedly. "Jerome Irving was at the social at the Cherry Valley parsonage last night, and he had Harriet Warren there—took her there, and drove her home again."

"I don't believe it," cried Anne, before she thought. She dropped an egg into the basket so abruptly that the shell broke.

"Oh, it's true enough. Sam Mitchell told me; he was there and saw him. Sam says he looked quite beaming, and was dressed to kill, and followed Harriet around like her shadow. I guess you won't have any more bother with him, Aunt Anne."

In the process of picking the broken egg out of the whole ones Anne had recovered her equanimity. She gave a careful little laugh.

"Well, it's to be hoped so. Goodness knows it's time he tried somebody else. Go and change your dress for milking, Octavia, and don't spend quite so much time gossiping up the lane with Sam Mitchell. He always was a fetch-and-carry. Young girls oughtn't to be so pert."

When the subdued Octavia had gone, Anne tossed the broken eggshell out of the pantry window viciously enough.

"There's no fool like an old fool. Jerome Irving always was an idiot. The idea of his going after Harriet Warren! He's old enough to be her father. And a Warren, too! I've seen the time an Irving wouldn't be seen on the same side of the road with a Warren. Well, anyhow, I don't care, and he needn't suppose I will. It will be a relief not to have him hanging around any longer."

It might have been a relief, but Anne felt strangely lonely as she walked home alone from prayer meeting the next night. Jerome had not been there. The Warrens were Methodists and Anne rightly guessed that he had gone to the Methodist prayer meeting at Cherry Valley.

"Dancing attendance on Harriet," she said to herself scornfully.

When she got home she looked at her face in the glass more critically than she had done for years. Anne Stockard at her best had never been pretty. When young she had been called "gawky." She was very tall and her figure was lank and angular. She had a long, pale face and dusky hair. Her eyes had been good—a glimmering hazel, large and long-lashed. They were pretty yet, but the crow's feet about them were plainly visible. There were brackets around her mouth too, and her cheeks were hollow. Anne suddenly realized, as she had never realized before, that she had grown old—that her youth was left far behind. She was an old maid, and Harriet Warren was young, and pretty. Anne's long, thin lips suddenly quivered.

"I declare, I'm a worse fool than Jerome," she said angrily.

When Saturday night came Jerome did not. The corner of the big, old-fashioned porch where he usually sat looked bare and lonely. Anne was short with Octavia and boxed the cat's ears and raged at herself. What did she care if Jerome Irving never came again? She could have married him years ago if she had wanted to—everybody knew that!

At sunset she saw a buggy drive past her gate. Even at that distance she recognized Harriet Warren's handsome, high-coloured profile. It was Jerome's new buggy and Jerome was driving. The wheel spokes flashed in the sunlight as they crept up the hill. Perhaps they dazzled Anne's eyes a little; at least, for that or some other reason she dabbed her hand viciously over them as she turned sharply about and went upstairs. Octavia was practising her music lesson in the parlour below and singing in a sweet shrill voice. The hired men were laughing and talking in the yard. Anne slammed down her window and banged her door and then lay down on her bed; she said her head ached.

The Deep Meadows people were amused and made joking remarks to Anne, which she had to take amiably because she had no excuse for resenting them. In reality they stung her pride unendurably. When Jerome had gone she realized that she had no other intimate friend and that she was a very lonely woman whom nobody cared about. One night—it was three weeks afterward—she met Jerome and Harriet squarely. She was walking to church with Octavia, and they were driving in the opposite direction. Jerome had his new buggy and crimson lap robe. His horse's coat shone like satin and had rosettes of crimson on his bridle. Jerome was dressed extremely well and looked quite young, with his round, ruddy, clean-shaven face and clear blue eyes.

Harriet was sitting primly and consciously by his side; she was a very handsome girl with bold eyes and was somewhat overdressed. She wore a big flowery hat and a white lace veil and looked at Anne with a supercilious smile.

Anne felt dowdy and old; she was very pale. Jerome lifted his hat and bowed pleasantly as they drove past. Suddenly Harriet laughed out. Anne did not look back, but her face crimsoned darkly. Was that girl laughing at her? She trembled with anger and a sharp, hurt feeling. When she got home that night she sat a long while by her window.

Jerome was gone—and he let Harriet Warren laugh at her and he would never come back to her. Well, it did not matter, but she had been a fool. Only it had never occurred to her that Jerome could act so.

"If I'd thought he would I mightn't have been so sharp with him," was as far as she would let herself go even in thought.

When four weeks had elapsed Jerome came over one Saturday night. He was fluttered and anxious, but hid it in a masterly manner.

Anne was taken by surprise. She had not thought he would ever come again, and was off her guard. He had come around the porch corner abruptly as she stood there in the dusk, and she started very perceptibly.

"Good evening, Anne," he said, easily and unblushingly.

Anne choked up. She was very angry, or thought she was. Jerome appeared not to notice her lack of welcome. He sat coolly down in his old place. His heart was beating like a hammer, but Anne did not know that.

"I suppose," she said cuttingly, "that you're on your way down to the bridge. It's almost a pity for you to waste time stopping here at all, any more than you have of late. No doubt Harriet'll be expecting you."

A gleam of satisfaction flashed over Jerome's face. He looked shrewdly at Anne, who was not looking at him, but was staring uncompromisingly out over the poppy beds. A jealous woman always gives herself away. If Anne had been indifferent she would not have given him that slap in the face.

"I dunno's she will," he replied coolly. "I didn't say for sure whether I'd be down tonight or not. It's so long since I had a chat with you I thought I'd drop in for a spell. But of course if I'm not wanted I can go where I will be."

Anne could not get back her self-control. Her nerves were "all strung up," as she would have said. She had a feeling that she was right on the brink of a "scene," but she could not help herself.

"I guess it doesn't matter much what I want," she said stonily. "At any rate, it hasn't seemed that way lately. You don't care, of course. Oh, no! Harriet Warren is all you care about. Well, I wish you joy of her."

Jerome looked puzzled, or pretended to. In reality he was hugging himself with delight.

"I don't just understand you, Anne," he said hesitatingly "You appear to be vexed about something."

"I? Oh, no, I'm not, Mr. Irving. Of course old friends don't count now. Well, I've no doubt new ones will wear just as well."

"If it's about my going to see Harriet," said Jerome easily "I don't see as how it can matter much to you. Goodness knows, you took enough pains to show me you didn't want me. I don't blame you. A woman has a right to please herself, and a man ought to have sense to take his answer and go. I hadn't, and that's where I made my mistake. I don't mean to pester you any more, but we can be real good friends, can't we? I'm sure I'm as much your friend as ever I was."

Now, I hold that this speech of Jerome's, delivered in a cool, matter-of-fact tone, as of a man stating a case with dispassionate fairness, was a masterpiece. It was the last cleverly executed movement of the campaign. If it failed to effect a capitulation, he was a defeated man. But it did not fail.

Anne had got to that point where an excited woman must go mad or cry. Anne cried. She sat flatly down on a chair and burst into tears.

Jerome's hat went one way and his cane another. Jerome himself sprang across the intervening space and dropped into the chair beside Anne. He caught her hand in his and threw his arm boldly around her waist.

"Goodness gracious, Anne! Do you care after all? Tell me that!"

"I don't suppose it matters to you if I do," sobbed Anne. "It hasn't seemed to matter, anyhow."

"Anne, look here! Didn't I come after you for fifteen years? It's you I always have wanted and want yet, if I can get you. I don't care a rap for Harriet Warren or anyone but you. Now that's the truth right out, Anne."

No doubt it was, and Anne was convinced of it. But she had to have her cry out—on Jerome's shoulder—and it soothed her nerves wonderfully. Later on Octavia, slipping noiselessly up the steps in the dusk, saw a sight that transfixed her with astonishment. When she recovered herself she turned and fled wildly around the house, running bump into Sam Mitchell, who was coming across the yard from a twilight conference with the hired men.

"Goodness, Tavy, what's the matter? Y' look 'sif y'd seen a ghost."

Octavia leaned up against the wall in spasms of mirth.

"Oh, Sam," she gasped, "old Jerome Irving and Aunt Anne are sitting round there in the dark on the front porch and he had his arms around her, kissing her! And they never saw nor heard me, no more'n if they were deaf and blind!"

Sam gave a tremendous whistle and then went off into a shout of laughter whose echoes reached even to the gloom of the front porch and the ears of the lovers. But they did not know he was laughing at them and would not have cared if they had. They were too happy for that.

There was a wedding that fall and Anne Stockard was the bride. When she was safely his, Jerome confessed all and was graciously forgiven.

"But it was kind of mean to Harriet," said Anne rebukingly, "to go with her and get her talked about and then drop her as you did. Don't you think so yourself, Jerome?"

Her husband's eyes twinkled.

"Well, hardly that. You see, Harriet's engaged to that Johnson fellow out west. 'Tain't generally known, but I knew it and that's why I picked on her. I thought it probable that she'd be willing enough to flirt with me for a little diversion, even if I was old. Harriet's that sort of a girl. And I made up my mind that if that didn't fetch it nothing would and I'd give up for good and all. But it did, didn't it, Anne?"

"I should say so. It was horrid of you, Jerome—but I daresay it's just as well you did or I'd likely never have found out that I couldn't get along without you. I did feel dreadful. Poor Octavia could tell you I was as cross as X. How did you come to think of it, Jerome?"

"A fellow had to do something," said Jerome oracularly, "and I'd have done most anything to get you, Anne, that's a fact. And there it was—courting fifteen years and nothing to show for it. I dunno, though, how I did come to think of it. Guess it was a sort of inspiration. Anyhow, I've got you and that's what I set out to do in the beginning."

Young Si

Mr. Bentley had just driven into the yard with the new summer boarder. Mrs. Bentley and Agnes were peeping at her from behind the parlour curtains with the keen interest that they—shut in by their restricted farm life—always felt in any visitor from the outside world lying beyond their boundary of purple misted hills.

Mrs. Bentley was a plump, rosy-cheeked woman with a motherly smile. Agnes was a fair, slim schoolgirl, as tall as her mother, with a sweet face and a promise of peach blossom prettiness in the years to come. The arrival of a summer boarder was a great event in her quiet life.

"Ain't she pretty?" whispered Mrs. Bentley admiringly, as the girl came slowly up the green slope before the house. "I do hope she's nice. You can generally calculate on men boarders, but girls are doubtful. Preserve me from a cranky boarder! I've had enough of them. I kinder like her looks, though."

Ethel Lennox had paused at the front door as Mrs. Bentley and Agnes came into the hall. Agnes gazed at the stranger with shy, unenvious admiration; the latter stood on the stone step just where the big chestnut by the door cast flickering gleams and shadows over her dress and shining hair.

She was tall, and gowned in some simple white material that fell about her in graceful folds. She wore a cluster of pale pink roses at her belt, and a big, picturesque white hat shaded her face and the glossy, clinging masses of her red hair—hair that was neither auburn nor chestnut but simply red. Nor would anyone have wished it otherwise, having once seen that glorious mass, with all its wonderful possibilities of rippling luxuriance.

Her complexion was of that perfect, waxen whiteness that goes with burnished red hair and the darkest of dilated violet eyes. Her delicately chiselled features wore what might have been a somewhat too decided impress of spirit and independence, had it not been for the sweet mouth, red and dimpled and curving, that parted in a slow, charming smile as Mrs. Bentley came forward with her kindly welcome.

"You must be real tired, Miss Lennox. It's a long drive from the train down here. Agnes, show Miss Lennox up to her room, and tea will be ready when you come down."

Agnes came forward with the shy grace that always won friends for her, and the two girls went slowly up the broad, old-fashioned staircase, while Mrs. Bentley bustled away to bring in the tea and put a goblet of damask roses on the table.

"She looks like a picture, doesn't she, John?" she said to her husband. "I never saw such a face—and that hair too. Would you have believed red hair could be so handsome? She seems real friendly—none of your stuck-up fine ladies! I've had all I want of them, I can tell you!"

"Sh—sh—sh!" said Mr. Bentley warningly, as Ethel Lennox came in with her arm about Agnes.

She looked even more lovely without her hat, with the soft red tendrils of hair lying on her forehead. Mrs. Bentley sent a telegraphic message of admiration across the table to her husband, who was helping the cold tongue and feeling his way to a conversation.

"You'll find it pretty quiet here, Miss Lennox. We're plain folks and there ain't much going and coming. Maybe you don't mind that, though?"

"I like it. When one has been teaching school all the year in a noisy city, quiet seems the one thing to be desired. Besides, I like to fancy myself something of an artist. I paint and sketch a little when I have time, and Miss Courtland, who was here last summer, said I could not find a more suitable spot. So I came because I knew that mackerel fishing was carried on along the shore, and I would have a chance to study character among the fishermen."

"Well, the shore ain't far away, and it's pretty—though maybe us folks here don't appreciate it rightly, being as we're so used to it. Strangers are always going crazy over its 'picturesqueness,' as they call it. As for 'character,' I reckon you'll find all you want of that among the Pointers; anyway, I never seed such critters as they be. When you get tired of painting, maybe you can amuse yourself trying to get to the bottom of our mystery."

"Oh, have you a mystery? How interesting!"

"Yes, a mystery—a mystery," repeated Mr. Bentley solemnly, "that nobody hain't been able to solve so far. I've give it up—so has everyone else. Maybe you'll have better luck."

"But what is it?"

"The mystery," said Mr. Bentley dramatically, "is—Young Si. He's the mystery. Last spring, just when the herring struck in, a young chap suddenly appeared at the Point. He appeared—from what corner of the globe nobody hain't ever been able to make out. He bought a boat and a shanty down at my shore and went into a sort of mackerel partnership with Snuffy Curtis—Snuffy supplying the experience and this young fellow the cash, I reckon. Snuffy's as poor as Job's turkey; it was a windfall for him. And there he's fished all summer."

"But his name—Young Si?"

"Well, of course, that isn't it. He did give himself out as Brown, but nobody believes that's his handle—sounds unnatteral here. He bought his establishment from 'old Si,' who used to fish down there and was a mysterious old critter in a way too. So when this young fellow stepped in from goodness knows where, some of the Pointers christened him Young Si for a joke, and he never gets anything else. Doesn't seem to mind it. He's a moody, keep-to-himself sort of chap. Yet he ain't unpopular along shore, I believe. Snuffy was telling me they like him real well, considering his unsociableness. Anyways, he's as handsome a chap as I ever seed, and well eddicated too. He ain't none of your ordinary fishermen. Some of us kind of think he's a runaway—got into some scrape or another, maybe, and is skulking around here to keep out of jail. But wife here won't give in to that."

"No, I never will," said Mrs. Bentley firmly. "Young Si comes here often for milk and butter, and he's a perfect gentleman. Nobody'll ever convince me that he has done anything to be ashamed of, whatever's his reason for wasting his life down there at that shore."

"He ain't wasting his life," chuckled Mr. Bentley. "He's making money, Young Si is, though he don't seem to care about that a mite. This has been a big year for mackerel, and he's smart. If he didn't know much when he begun, he's ahead of Snuffy now. And as for work, I never saw his beat. He seems possessed. Up afore sunrise every blessed morning and never in bed till midnight, and just slaving away all between time. I said to him t'other day, says I: 'Young Si, you'll have to let up on this sort of thing and take a rest. You can't stand it. You're not a Pointer. Pointers can stand anything, but it'll kill you.'

"He give one of them bitter laughs of his. Says he: 'It's no difference if it does. Nobody'll care,' and off he walks, sulky like. There's something about Young Si I can't understand," concluded Mr. Bentley.

Ethel Lennox was interested. A melancholy, mysterious hero in a setting of silver-rimmed sand hills and wide blue sweeps of ocean was something that ought to lend piquancy to her vacation.

"I should like to see this prince in disguise," she said. "It all sounds very romantic."

"I'll take you to the shore after tea if you'd like," said Agnes eagerly. "Si's just splendid," she continued in a confidential aside as they rose from the table. "Pa doesn't half like him because he thinks there's something queer about him. But I do. He's a gentleman, as Ma says. I don't believe he's done anything wrong."

Ethel Lennox sauntered out into the orchard to wait for Agnes. She sat down under an apple tree and began to read, but soon the book slipped from her hands and the beautiful head leaned back against the grey, lichened trunk of the old tree. The sweet mouth drooped wistfully. There was a sad, far-away look in the violet eyes. The face was not that of a happy girl, so thought Agnes as she came down the apple tree avenue.

But how pretty she is! she thought. Won't the folks around here stare at her! They always do at our boarders, but we've never had one like her.

Ethel sprang up. "I had no idea you would be here so soon," she said brightly. "Just wait till I get my hat."

When she came out they started off, and presently found themselves walking down a grassy, deep-rutted lane that ran through mown hay fields, green with their rich aftergrowth, and sheets of pale ripening oats and golden-green wheat, until it lost itself in the rolling sand hills at the foot of the slope.

Beyond the sand hills stretched the shining expanse of the ocean, of the faint, bleached blue of hot August seas, and reaching out into a horizon laced with long trails of pinkish cloud. Numberless fishing boats dotted the shimmering reaches.

"That furthest-off boat is Young Si's," said Agnes. "He always goes to that particular spot."

"Is he really all your father says?" asked Miss Lennox curiously.

"Indeed, he is. He isn't any more like the rest of the shore men than you are. He's queer, of course. I don't believe he's happy. It seems to me he's worrying over something, but I'm sure it is nothing wrong. Here we are," she added, as they passed the sand hills and came out on the long, level beach.

To their left the shore curved around in a semi-circle of dazzling whiteness; at their right stood a small grey fish-house.

"That's Young Si's place," said Agnes. "He lives there night and day. Wouldn't it make anyone melancholy? No wonder he's mysterious. I'm going to get his spy-glass. He told me I might always use it."

She pushed open the door and entered, followed by Ethel. The interior was rough but clean. It was a small room, lighted by one tiny window looking out on the water. In one corner a rough ladder led up to the loft above. The bare lathed walls were hung with fishing jackets, nets, mackerel lines and other shore appurtenances. A little stove bore a kettle and a frying pan. A low board table was strewn with dishes and the cold remnants of a hasty repast; benches were placed along the walls. A fat, bewhiskered kitten, looking as if it were cut out of black velvet, was dozing on the window sill.

"This is Young Si's cat," explained Agnes, patting the creature, which purred joyously and opened its sleepy green eyes. "It's the only thing he cares for, I believe. Witch! Witch! How are you, Witch? Well, here's the spyglass. Let's go out and have a look. Si's catching mackerel," announced Agnes a few minutes later, after she had scrutinized each boat in turn, "and he won't be in for an hour yet. If you like, we have time for a walk up the shore."

The sun slipped lower and lower in the creamy sky, leaving a trail of sparkles that ran across the water and lost itself in the west. Sea gulls soared and dipped, and tiny "sand peeps" flitted along the beach. Just as the red rim of the sun dipped in the purpling sea, the boats began to come in.

"Most of them will go around to the Point," explained Agnes, with a contemptuous sweep of her hand towards a long headland running out before them. "They belong there and they're a rough crowd. You don't catch Young Si associating with the Pointers. There, he's getting up sail. We'll just have time to get back before he comes in."

They hurried back across the dampening sand as the sun disappeared, leaving a fiery spot behind him. The shore was no longer quiet and deserted. The little spot where the fishing house stood had suddenly started into life. Roughly clad boys were running hither and thither, carrying fish or water. The boats were hauled up on the skids. A couple of shaggy old tars, who had strolled over from the Point to hear about Young Si's catch, were smoking their pipes at the corner of his shanty. A mellow afterlight was shining over sea and shore. The whole scene delighted Ethel's artist eyes.

Agnes nudged her companion.

"There! If you want to see Young Si," she whispered, pointing to the skids, where a busy figure was discernible in a large boat, "that's him, with his back to us, in the cream-coloured boat. He's counting out mackerel. If you go over to that platform behind him, you'll get a good look when he turns around. I'm going to coax a mackerel out of that stingy old Snuffy, if I can."

She tripped off, and Ethel walked slowly over to the boats. The men stared at her in open-mouthed admiration as she passed them and walked out on the platform behind Young Si. There was no one near the two. The others were all assembled around Snuffy's boat. Young Si was throwing out the mackerel with marvellous rapidity, but at the sound of a footstep behind him he turned and straightened up his tall form. They stood face to face.

"Miles!"

"Ethel!"

Young Si staggered back against the mast, letting two silvery bloaters slip through his hands overboard. His handsome, sunburned face was very white.

Ethel Lennox turned abruptly and silently and walked swiftly across the sand. Agnes felt her arm touched, and turned to see Ethel standing, pale and erect, beside her.

"Let us go home," said the latter unsteadily. "It is very damp here—I feel chilled."

"Oh, dear!" exclaimed Agnes penitently. "I ought to have told you to bring a shawl. It is always damp on the shore after sunset. Here, Snuffy, give me my mackerel. Thank you. I'm ready now, Miss Lennox."

They reached the lane before Agnes remembered to ask the question Ethel dreaded.

"Oh, did you see Young Si? And what do you think of him?"

Ethel turned her face away and answered with studied carelessness. "He seems to be quite a superior fisherman so far as I could see in the dim light. It was very dusky there, you know. Let us walk a little faster. My shoes are quite wet."

When they reached home, Miss Lennox excused herself on the plea of weariness and went straight to her room.

Back at the shore Young Si had recovered himself and stooped again to his work. His face was set and expressionless. A dull red burned in each bronzed cheek. He threw out the mackerel mechanically, but his hands trembled.

Snuffy strolled over to the boat. "See that handsome girl, Si?" he asked lazily. "One of the Bentleys' boarders, I hear. Looks as if she might have stepped out of a picture frame, don't she?"

"We've no time to waste, Curtis," said Young Si harshly, "with all these fish to clean before bedtime. Stop talking and get to work."

Snuffy shrugged his shoulders and obeyed in silence. Young Si was not a person to be trifled with. The catch was large and it was late before they finished. Snuffy surveyed the full barrels complacently.

"Good day's work," he muttered, "but hard—I'm dead beat out. 'Low I'll go to bed. In the name o' goodness, Si, whar be you a-goin' to?"

Young Si had got into a dory and untied it. He made no answer, but rowed out from the shore. Snuffy stared at the dory blankly until it was lost in the gloom.

"Ef that don't beat all!" he ejaculated. "I wonder if Si is in his right senses? He's been actin' quar right along, and now to start off, Lord knows whar, at this hour o' night! I really don't believe it's safe to stay here alone with him."

Snuffy shook his unkempt head dubiously.

Young Si rowed steadily out over the dark waves. An eastern breeze was bringing in a damp sea fog that blurred darkly over the outlines of horizon and shore. The young fisherman found himself alone in a world of water and grey mist. He stopped rowing and leaned forward on his oars.

"To see her here, of all places!" he muttered. "Not a word, scarcely a look, after all this long heartbreak! Well, perhaps it is better so. And yet to know she is so near! How beautiful she is! And I love her more than ever. That is where the sting lies. I thought that in this rough life, amid all these rude associations, where nothing could remind me of her, I might forget. And now—"

He clenched his hands. The mist was all around and about him, creeping, impalpable, phantom-like. The dory rocked gently on the swell. From afar came the low persistent murmur of the ocean.

The next day Ethel Lennox declined to visit Si's shore. Instead she went to the Point and sketched all day. She went again the next day and the next. The Point was the most picturesque part of the shore, she averred, and the "types" among its inhabitants most interesting. Agnes Bentley ceased to suggest another visit to Si's shore. She had a vague perception that her companion did not care to discuss the subject.

At the end of a week Mrs. Bentley remarked: "What in the world can have happened to Young Si? It's a whole week since he was here for milk or butter. He ain't sick, is he?"

Mr. Bentley chuckled amusedly.

"I 'low I can tell you the reason of that. Si's getting his stuff at Walden's now. I saw him going there twice this week. 'Liza Walden's got ahead of you at last, Mary."

"Well, I never did!" said Mrs. Bentley. "Well, Young Si is the first that ever preferred 'Liza Walden's butter to mine. Everyone knows what hers is like. She never works her salt half in. Well, Young Si's welcome to it, I'm sure; I wish him joy of his exchange."

Mrs. Bentley rattled her dishes ominously. It was plain her faith in Young Si had received a severe shock.

Upstairs in her room, Ethel Lennox, with a few undried tears glistening on her cheeks, was writing a letter. Her lips were compressed and her hand trembled:

"I have discovered that it is no use to run away from fate," she wrote. "No matter how hard we try to elude it, and how sure we are that we have succeeded, it will rise and meet us where we least expect it. I came down here tired and worn out, looking for peace and rest—and lo! the most disquieting element of my life is here to confront me.

"I'm going to confess, Helen. 'Open confession is good for the soul,' you know, and I shall treat myself to a good dose while the mood is on.

"You know, of course, that I was once engaged to Miles Lesley. You also know that that engagement was broken last autumn for unexplained reasons. Well, I will tell you all about it and then mail this letter speedily, before I change my mind.

"It is over a year now since Miles and I first became engaged. As you are aware, his family is wealthy, and noted for its exclusiveness. I was a poor school teacher, and you may imagine with what horror his relatives received the news of Miles's attentions to one whom they considered his inferior. Now that I have thought the whole matter over calmly, I scarcely blame them. It must be hard for aristocratic parents who have lavished every care upon a son, and cherished for him the highest hopes, when he turns from the women of his own order to one considered beneath him in station. But I did not view the subject in this light then; and instead of declining his attentions, as I perhaps should have done, I encouraged them—I loved him so dearly, Nell!—and in spite of family opposition, Miles soon openly declared his attachment.

"When his parents found they could not change his purpose, their affection for him forced them into outward acquiescence, but their reluctant condescension was gall and wormwood to me. I saw things only from my own point of view, and was keenly sensitive to their politely concealed disapprobation, and my offended vanity found its victim in Miles. I belonged to the class who admit and resent slights, instead of ignoring them, as do the higher bred, and I thought he would not see those offered to me. I grew cold and formal to him. He was very patient, but his ways were not mine, and my manner puzzled and annoyed him. Our relations soon became strained, and the trifle necessary for an open quarrel was easily supplied.

"One evening I went to a large At Home given by his mother. I knew but few and, as Miles was necessarily busy with his social duties to her guests, I was, after the first hurried greeting, left unattended for a time. Not being accustomed to such functions, I resented this as a covert insult and, in a fit of jealous pique, I blush to own that I took the revenge of a peasant maid and entered into a marked flirtation with Fred Currie, who had paid me some attention before my engagement. When Miles was at liberty to seek me, he found me, to all appearances, quite absorbed in my companion and oblivious of his approach. He turned on his heel and went away, nor did he come near me the rest of the evening.

"I went home angry enough, but so miserable and repentant that if Miles had been his usual patient self when he called the following evening I would have begged his forgiveness. But I had gone too far; his mother was shocked by my gaucherie, and he was humiliated and justly exasperated. We had a short, bitter quarrel. I said a great many foolish, unpardonable things, and finally I threw his ring at him. He gave me a startled look then, in which there was something of contempt, and went away without another word.

"After my anger had passed, I was wretchedly unhappy. I realized how unworthily I had acted, how deeply I loved Miles, and how lonely and empty my life would be without him. But he did not come back, and soon after I learned he had gone away—whither no one knew, but it was supposed abroad. Well, I buried my hopes and tears in secret and went on with my life as people have to do—a life in which I have learned to think, and which, I hope, has made me nobler and better.

"This summer I came here. I heard much about a certain mysterious stranger known as 'Young Si' who was fishing mackerel at this shore. I was very curious. The story sounded romantic, and one evening I went down to see him. I met him face to face and, Helen, it was Miles Lesley!

"For one minute earth, sky and sea reeled around me. The next, I remembered all, and turned and walked away. He did not follow.

"You may be sure that I now religiously avoid that part of the shore. We have never met since, and he has made no effort to see me. He clearly shows that he despises me. Well, I despise myself. I am very unhappy, Nell, and not only on my own account, for I feel that if Miles had never met me, his mother would not now be breaking her heart for her absent boy. My sorrow has taught me to understand hers, and I no longer resent her pride.

"You need hardly be told after this that I leave here in another week. I cannot fabricate a decent excuse to go sooner, or I would."

In the cool twilight Ethel went with Agnes Bentley to mail her letter. As they stopped at the door of the little country store, a young man came around the corner. It was Young Si. He was in his rough fishing suit, with a big herring net trailing over his shoulder, but no disguise could effectually conceal his splendid figure. Agnes sprang forward eagerly.

"Si, where have you been? Why have you never I been up to see us for so long?"

Young Si made no verbal reply. He merely lifted his cap with formal politeness and turned on his heel.

"Well, I never!" exclaimed Agnes, as soon as she recovered her powers of speech. "If that is how Young Si is going to treat his friends! He must have got offended at something. I wonder what it is," she added, her curiosity getting the better of her indignation.

When they came out they saw the solitary figure of Young Si far adown, crossing the dim, lonely shore fields. In the dusk Agnes failed to notice the pallor of her companion's face and the unshed tears in her eyes.

"I've just been down to the Point," said Agnes, coming in one sultry afternoon about a week later, "and Little Ev said as there was no fishing today he'd take us out for that sail tonight if you wanted to go."

Ethel Lennox put her drawing away listlessly. She looked pale and tired. She was going away the next day, and this was to be her last visit to the shore.

About an hour before sunset a boat glided out from the shadow of the Point. In it were Ethel Lennox and Agnes, together with Little Ev, the sandy-haired, undersized Pointer who owned the boat.

The evening was fine, and an off-shore breeze was freshening up rapidly. They did not notice the long, dark bank of livid cloud low in the northwest.

"Isn't this glorious!" exclaimed Ethel. Her hat was straining back from her head and the red rings of her hair were blowing about her face.

Agnes looked about her more anxiously. Wiser in matters of sea and shore than her companion, there were some indications she did not like.

Young Si, who was standing with Snuffy their skids, lowered his spyglass with a start.

"It is Agnes Bentley and—and—that boarder of theirs," he said anxiously, "and they've gone out with Little Ev in that wretched, leaky tub of his. Where are their eyes that they can't see a squall coming up?"

"An' Little Ev don't know as much about managing a boat as a cat!" exclaimed Snuffy excitedly. "Sign 'em to come back."

Si shook his head. "They're too far out. I don't know that the squall will amount to very much. In a good boat, with someone who knew how to manage it, they'd be all right. But with Little Ev—" He began walking restlessly up and down the narrow platform.

The boat was now some distance out. The breeze had stiffened to a slow strong wind and the dull-grey level of the sea was whipped into white-caps.

Agnes bent towards Ethel. "It's getting too rough. I think we'd better go back. I'm afraid we're in for a thunder squall. Look at the clouds."

A long, sullen muttering verified her words.

"Little Ev," she shouted, "we want to go in."

Little Ev, thus recalled to things about him, looked around in alarm. The girls questioned each other with glances of dismay. The sky had grown very black, and the peals of thunder came louder and more continuously. A jagged bolt of lightning hurtled over the horizon. Over land and sea was "the green, malignant light of coming storm."

Little Ev brought the boat's head abruptly round as a few heavy drops of rain fell.

"Ev, the boat is leaking!" shrieked Agnes, above the wind. "The water's coming in!"

"Bail her out then," shouted Ev, struggling with the sail. "There's two cans under the seat. I've got to lower this sail. Bail her out."

"I'll help you," said Ethel.

She was very pale, but her manner was calm. Both girls bailed energetically.

Young Si, watching through the glass, saw them. He dropped it and ran to his boat, white and resolute.

"They've sprung a leak. Here, Curtis, launch the boat. We've got to go out or Ev will drown them."

They shot out from the shore just as the downpour came, blotting out sea and land in one driving sheet of white rain.

"Young Si is coming off for us," said Agnes. "We'll be all right if he gets here in time. This boat is going to sink, sure."

Little Ev was completely demoralized by fear. The girls bailed unceasingly, but the water gained every minute. Young Si was none too soon.

"Jump, Ev!" he shouted as his boat shot alongside. "Jump for your life!"

He dragged Ethel Lennox in as he spoke. Agnes sprang from one boat to the other like a cat, and Little Ev jumped just as a thunderous crash seemed to burst above them and air and sky were filled with blue flame.

The danger was past, for the squall had few difficulties for Si and Snuffy. When they reached the shore, Agnes, who had quite recovered from her fright, tucked her dripping skirts about her and announced her determination to go straight home with Snuffy.

"I can't get any wetter than I am," she said cheerfully. "I'll send Pa down in the buggy for Miss Lennox. Light the fire in your shanty, Si, and let her get dry. I'll be as quick as I can."

Si picked Ethel up in his strong arms and carried her into the fish-house. He placed her on one of the low benches and hurriedly began to kindle a fire. Ethel sat up dazedly and pushed back the dripping masses of her bright hair. Young Si turned and looked down at her with a passionate light in his eyes. She put out her cold, wet hands wistfully.

"Oh, Miles!" she whispered.

Outside, the wind shook the frail building and tore the shuddering sea to pieces. The rain poured down. It was already settling in for a night of storm. But, inside, Young Si's fire was casting cheery flames over the rude room, and Young Si himself was kneeling by Ethel Lennox with his arm about her and her head on his broad shoulder. There were happy tears in her eyes and her voice quivered as she said, "Miles, can you forgive me? If you knew how bitterly I have repented—"

"Never speak of the past again, my sweet. In my lonely days and nights down here by the sea, I have forgotten all but my love."

"Miles, how did you come here? I thought you were in Europe."

"I did travel at first. I came down here by chance, and resolved to cut myself utterly adrift from my old life and see if I could not forget you. I was not very successful." He smiled down into her eyes. "And you were going away tomorrow. How perilously near we have been to not meeting! But how are we going to explain all this to our friends along shore?"

"I think we had better not explain it at all. I will go away tomorrow, as I intended, and you can quietly follow soon. Let 'Young Si' remain the mystery he has always been."

"That will be best—decidedly so. They would never understand if we did tell them. And I daresay they would be very much disappointed to find I was not a murderer or a forger or something of that sort. They have always credited me with an evil past. And you and I will go back to our own world, Ethel. You will be welcome there now, sweet—my family, too, have learned a lesson, and will do anything to promote my happiness."

Agnes drove Ethel Lennox to the station next day. The fierce wind that had swept over land and sea seemed to have blown away all the hazy vapours and oppressive heats in the air, and the morning dawned as clear and fresh as if the sad old earth with all her passionate tears had cleansed herself from sin and stain and come forth radiantly pure and sweet. Ethel bubbled over with joyousness. Agnes wondered at the change in her.

"Good-bye, Miss Lennox," she said wistfully. "You'll come back to see us some time again, won't you?"

"Perhaps," smiled Ethel, "and if not, Agnes, you must come and see me. Some day I may tell you a secret."

About a week later Young Si suddenly vanished, and his disappearance was a nine-day's talk along shore. His departure was as mysterious as his advent. It leaked out that he had quietly disposed of his boat and shanty to Snuffy Curtis, sent his mackerel off and, that done, slipped from the Pointers' lives, never more to re-enter them.

Little Ev was the last of the Pointers to see him tramping along the road to the station in the dusk of the autumn twilight. And the next morning Agnes Bentley, going out of doors before the others, found on the doorstep a basket containing a small, vociferous black kitten with a card attached to its neck. On it was written: "Will Agnes please befriend Witch in memory of Young Si?"

LUCY MAUD MONTGOMERY SHORT STORIES, 1902 TO 1903

A Patent Medicine Testimonial

"You might as well try to move the rock of Gibraltar as attempt to change Uncle Abimelech's mind when it is once made up," said Murray gloomily.

Murray is like dear old Dad; he gets discouraged rather easily. Now, I'm not like that; I'm more like Mother's folks. As Uncle Abimelech has never failed to tell me when I have annoyed him, I'm "all Foster." Uncle Abimelech doesn't like the Fosters. But I'm glad I take after them. If I had folded my hands and sat down meekly when Uncle Abimelech made known his good will and pleasure regarding Murray and me after Father's death, Murray would never have got to college—nor I either, for that matter. Only I wouldn't have minded that very much. I just wanted to go to college because Murray did. I couldn't be separated from him. We were twins and had always been together.

As for Uncle Abimelech's mind, I knew that he never had been known to change it. But, as he himself was fond of saying, there has to be a first time for everything, and I had determined that this was to be the first time for him. I hadn't any idea how I was going to bring it about; but it just had to be done, and I'm not "all Foster" for nothing.

I knew I would have to depend on my own thinkers. Murray is clever at books and dissecting dead things, but he couldn't help me out in this, even if he hadn't settled beforehand that there was no use in opposing Uncle Abimelech.

"I'm going up to the garret to think this out, Murray," I said solemnly. "Don't let anybody disturb me, and if Uncle Abimelech comes over don't tell him where I am. If I don't come down in time to get tea, get it yourself. I shall not leave the garret until I have thought of some way to change Uncle Abimelech's mind."

"Then you'll be a prisoner there for the term of your natural life, dear sis," said Murray sceptically. "You're a clever girl, Prue—and you've got enough decision for two—but you'll never get the better of Uncle Abimelech."

"We'll see," I said resolutely, and up to the garret I went. I shut the door and bolted it good and fast to make sure. Then I piled some old cushions in the window seat—for one might as well be comfortable when one is thinking as not—and went over the whole ground from the beginning.

Outside the wind was thrashing the broad, leafy top of the maple whose tallest twigs reached to the funny grey eaves of our old house. One roly-poly little sparrow blew or flew to the sill and sat there for a minute, looking at me with knowing eyes. Down below I could see Murray in a corner of the yard, pottering over a sick duck. He had set its broken leg and was nursing it back to health. Anyone except Uncle Abimelech could see that Murray was simply born to be a doctor and that it was flying in the face of Providence to think of making him anything else.

From the garret windows I could see all over the farm, for the house is on the hill end of it. I could see all the dear old fields and the spring meadow and the beech woods in the southwest corner. And beyond the orchard were the two grey barns and down below at the right-hand corner was the garden with all my sweet peas fluttering over the fences and trellises like a horde of butterflies. It was a dear old place and both Murray and I loved every stick and stone on it, but there was no reason why we should go on living there when Murray didn't like farming. And it wasn't our own, anyhow. It all belonged to Uncle Abimelech.

Father and Murray and I had always lived here together. Father's health broke down during his college course. That was one reason why Uncle Abimelech was set against Murray going to college, although Murray is as chubby and sturdy a fellow as you could wish to see. Anybody with Foster in him would be that.

To go back to Father. The doctors told him that his only chance of recovering his strength was an open-air life, so Father rented one of Uncle Abimelech's farms and there he lived for the rest of his days. He did not get strong again until it was too late for college, and he was a square peg in a round hole all his life, as he used to tell us. Mother died before we could remember, so Murray and Dad and I were everything to each other. We were very happy too, although we were bossed by Uncle Abimelech more or less. But he meant it well and Father didn't mind.

Then Father died—oh, that was a dreadful time! I hurried over it in my thinking-out. Of course when Murray and I came to look our position squarely in the face we found that we were dependent on Uncle Abimelech for everything, even the roof over our heads. We were literally as poor as church mice and even poorer, for at least they get churches rent-free.

Murray's heart was set on going to college and studying medicine. He asked Uncle Abimelech to lend him enough money to get a start with and then he could work his own way along and pay back the loan in due time. Uncle Abimelech is rich, and Murray and I are his nearest relatives. But he simply wouldn't listen to Murray's plan.

"I put my foot firmly down on such nonsense," he said. "And you know that when I put my foot down something squashes."

It was not that Uncle Abimelech was miserly or that he grudged us assistance. Not at all. He was ready to deal generously by us, but it must be in his own way. His way was this. Murray and I were to stay on the farm, and when Murray was twenty-one Uncle Abimelech said he would deed the farm to him—make him a present of it out and out.

"It's a good farm, Murray," he said. "Your father never made more than a bare living out of it because he wasn't strong enough to work it properly—that's what *he* got out of a college course, by the way. But you are strong enough and ambitious enough to do well."

But Murray couldn't be a farmer, that was all there was to it. I told Uncle Abimelech so, firmly, and I talked to him for days about it, but Uncle Abimelech never wavered. He sat and listened to me with a quizzical smile on that handsome, clean-shaven, ruddy old face of his, with its cut-granite features. And in the end he said,

"You ought to be the one to go to college if either of you did, Prue. You would make a capital lawyer, if I believed in the higher education of women, but I don't. Murray can take or leave the farm as he chooses. If he prefers the latter alternative, well and good. But he gets no help from me. You're a foolish little girl, Prue, to back him up in this nonsense of his."

It makes me angry to be called a little girl when I put up my hair a year ago, and Uncle Abimelech knows it. I gave up arguing with him. I knew it was no use anyway.

I thought it all over in the garret. But no way out of the dilemma could I see. I had eaten up all the apples I had brought with me and I felt flabby and disconsolate. The sight of Uncle Abimelech stalking up the lane, as erect and lordly as usual, served to deepen my gloom.

I picked up the paper my apples had been wrapped in and looked it over gloomily. Then I saw something, and Uncle Abimelech was delivered into my hand.

The whole plan of campaign unrolled itself before me, and I fairly laughed in glee, looking out of the garret window right down on the little bald spot on the top of Uncle Abimelech's head, as he stood laying down the law to Murray about something.

When Uncle Abimelech had gone I went down to Murray.

"Buddy," I said, "I've thought of a plan. I'm not going to tell you what it is, but you are to consent to it without knowing. I think it will quench Uncle Abimelech, but you must have perfect confidence in me. You must back me up no matter what I do and let me have my own way in it all."

"All right, sis," said Murray.

"That isn't solemn enough," I protested. "I'm serious. Promise solemnly."

"I promise solemnly, 'cross my heart,'" said Murray, looking like an owl.

"Very well. Remember that your role is to lie low and say nothing, like Brer Rabbit. Alloway's Anodyne Liniment is pretty good stuff, isn't it, Murray? It cured your sprain after you had tried everything else, didn't it?"

"Yes. But I don't see the connection."

"It isn't necessary that you should. Well, what with your sprain and my rheumatics I think I can manage it."

"Look here, Prue. Are you sure that long brooding over our troubles up in the garret hasn't turned your brain?"

"My brain is all right. Now leave me, minion. There is that which I would do."

Murray grinned and went. I wrote a letter, took it down to the office, and mailed it. For a week there was nothing more to do.

There is just one trait of Uncle Abimelech's disposition more marked than his fondness for having his own way and that one thing is family pride. The Melvilles are a very old family. The name dates back to the Norman conquest when a certain Roger de Melville, who was an ancestor of ours, went over to England with William the Conqueror. I don't think the Melvilles ever did anything worth recording in history since. To be sure, as far back as we can trace, none of them has ever done anything bad either. They have been honest, respectable folks and I think that is something worth being proud of.

But Uncle Abimelech pinned his family pride to Roger de Melville. He had the Melville coat of arms and our family tree, made out by an eminent genealogist, framed and hung up in his library, and he would not have done anything that would not have chimed in with that coat of arms and a conquering ancestor for the world.

At the end of a week I got an answer to my letter. It was what I wanted. I wrote again and sent a parcel. In three weeks' time the storm burst.

One day I saw Uncle Abimelech striding up the lane. He had a big newspaper clutched in his hand. I turned to Murray, who was poring over a book of anatomy in the corner.

"Murray, Uncle Abimelech is coming. There is going to be a battle royal between us. Allow me to remind you of your promise."

"To lie low and say nothing? That's the cue, isn't it, sis?"

"Unless Uncle Abimelech appeals to you. In that case you are to back me up."

Then Uncle Abimelech stalked in. He was purple with rage. Old Roger de Melville himself never could have looked fiercer. I *did* feel a quake or two, but I faced Uncle Abimelech undauntedly. No use in having your name on the roll of Battle Abbey if you can't stand your ground.

"Prudence, what does this mean?" thundered Uncle Abimelech, as he flung the newspaper down on the table. Murray got up and peered over. Then he whistled. He started to say something but remembered just in time and stopped. But he did give me a black look. Murray has a sneaking pride of name too, although he won't own up to it and laughs at Uncle Abimelech.

I looked at the paper and began to laugh. We did look so funny, Murray and I, in that advertisement. It took up the whole page. At the top were our photos, half life-size, and underneath our names and addresses printed out in full. Below was the letter I had written to the Alloway Anodyne Liniment folks. It was a florid testimonial to the virtues of their liniment. I said that it had cured Murray's sprain after all other remedies had failed and that, when I had been left a partial wreck from a very bad attack of rheumatic fever, the only thing that restored my joints and muscles to working order was Alloway's Anodyne Liniment, and so on.

It was all true enough, although I dare say old Aunt Sarah-from-the-Hollow's rubbing had as much to do with the cures as the liniment. But that is neither here nor there.

"What does this mean, Prudence?" said Uncle Abimelech again. He was quivering with wrath, but I was as cool as a cucumber, and Murray stood like a graven image.

"Why, that, Uncle Abimelech," I said calmly, "well, it just means one of my ways of making money. That liniment company pays for those testimonials and photos, you know. They gave me fifty dollars for the privilege of publishing them. Fifty dollars will pay for books and tuition for Murray and me at Kentville Academy next winter, and Mrs. Tredgold is kind enough to say she will board me for what help I can give her around the house, and wait for Murray's until he can earn it by teaching."

I rattled all this off glibly before Uncle Abimelech could get in a word.

"It's disgraceful!" he stormed. "Disgraceful! Think of Sir Roger de Melville—and a patent medicine advertisement! Murray Melville, what were you about, sir, to let your sister disgrace herself and her family name by such an outrageous transaction?"

I quaked a bit. If Murray should fail me! But Murray was true-blue.

"I gave Prue a free hand, sir. It's an honest business transaction enough—and the family name alone won't send us to college, you know, sir."

Uncle Abimelech glared at us.

"This must be put an end to," he said. "This advertisement must not appear again. I won't have it!"

"But I've signed a contract that it is to run for six months," I said sturdily. "And I've others in view. You remember the Herb Cure you recommended one spring and that it did me so much good! I'm negotiating with the makers of that and—"

"The girl's mad!" said Uncle Abimelech. "Stark, staring mad!"

"Oh, no, I'm not, Uncle Abimelech. I'm merely a pretty good businesswoman. You won't help Murray to go to college, so I must. This is the only way I have, and I'm going to see it through."

After Uncle Abimelech had gone, still in a towering rage, Murray remonstrated. But I reminded him of his promise and he had to succumb.

Next day Uncle Abimelech returned—a subdued and chastened Uncle Abimelech.

"See here, Prue," he said sternly. "This thing must be stopped. I say it *must*. I am not going to have the name of Melville dragged all over the country in a patent medicine advertisement. You've played your game and won it—take what comfort you can out of the confession: If you will agree to cancel this notorious contract of yours I'll settle it with the company—and I'll put Murray through college—and you too if you want to go! Something will have to be done with you, that's certain. Is this satisfactory?"

"Perfectly," I said promptly. "If you will add thereto your promise that you will forget and forgive, Uncle Abimelech. There are to be no hard feelings."

Uncle Abimelech shrugged his shoulders.

"In for a penny, in for a pound," he said. "Very well, Prue. We wipe off all scores and begin afresh. But there must be no more such doings. You've worked your little scheme through—trust a Foster for that! But in future you've got to remember that in law you're a Melville whatever you are in fact."

I nodded dutifully. "I'll remember, Uncle Abimelech," I promised.

After everything had been arranged and Uncle Abimelech had gone I looked at Murray. "Well?" I said.

Murray twinkled. "You've accomplished the impossible, sis. But, as Uncle Abimelech intimated—don't you try it again."

A Sandshore Wooing

Fir Cottage, Plover Sands.
July Sixth.

We arrived here late last night, and all day Aunt Martha has kept her room to rest. So I had to keep mine also, although I felt as fresh as a morning lark, and just in the mood for enjoyment.

My name is Marguerite Forrester—an absurdly long name for so small a girl. Aunt Martha always calls me Marguer*ite*, with an accent of strong disapproval. She does not like my name, but she gives me the full benefit of it. Connie Shelmardine used to call me Rita. Connie was my roommate last year at the Seminary. We correspond occasionally, but Aunt Martha frowns on it.

I have always lived with Aunt Martha—my parents died when I was a baby. Aunt Martha says I am to be her heiress if I please her—which means—but, oh, you do not know what "pleasing" Aunt Martha means.

Aunt is a determined and inveterate man-hater. She has no particular love for women, indeed, and trusts nobody but Mrs. Saxby, her maid. I rather like Mrs. Saxby. She is not quite so far gone in petrifaction as Aunt, although she gets a little stonier every year. I expect the process will soon begin on me, but it hasn't yet. My flesh and blood are still unreasonably warm and pulsing and rebellious.

Aunt Martha would be in danger of taking a fit if she ever saw me talking to a man. She watches me jealously, firmly determined to guard me from any possible attack of a roaring and ravening lion in the disguise of nineteenth-century masculine attire. So I have to walk demurely and assume a virtue, if I have it not, while I pine after the untested flesh-pots of Egypt in secret.

We have come down to spend a few weeks at Fir Cottage. Our good landlady is a capacious, kindly-souled creature, and I think she has rather a liking for me. I have been chattering to her all day, for there are times when I absolutely must talk to someone or go mad.

July Tenth.

This sort of life is decidedly dull. The program of every day is the same. I go to the sandshore with Aunt Martha and Mrs. Saxby in the morning, read to Aunt in the afternoons, and mope around by my disconsolate self in the evenings. Mrs.

Blake has lent me, for shore use, a very fine spyglass which she owns. She says her "man" brought it home from "furrin' parts" before he died. While Aunt and Mrs. Saxby meander up and down the shore, leaving me free to a certain extent, I amuse myself by examining distant seas and coasts through it, thus getting a few peeps into a forbidden world. We see few people, although there is a large summer hotel about a mile up the beach. Our shore haunts do not seem to be popular with its guests. They prefer the rocks. This suits Aunt Martha admirably. I may also add that it doesn't suit her niece—but that is a matter of small importance.

The first morning I noticed a white object on the rocks, about half a mile away, and turned my glass on it. There—apparently within a stone's throw of me—was a young man. He was lounging on a rock, looking dreamily out to sea. There was something about his face that reminded me of someone I know, but I cannot remember whom.

Every morning he has reappeared on the same spot. He seems to be a solitary individual, given to prowling by himself. I wonder what Aunt would say if she knew what I am so earnestly watching through my glass at times.

July Eleventh.

I shall have to cease looking at the Unknown, I am afraid.

This morning I turned my glass, as usual, on his pet haunt. I nearly fell over in my astonishment, for he was also looking through a spyglass straight at me, too, it seemed. How foolish I felt! And yet my curiosity was so strong that a few minutes afterward I peeped back again, just to see what he was doing. Then he coolly laid down his glass, rose, lifted his cap and bowed politely to me—or, at least, in my direction. I dropped my glass and smiled in a mixture of dismay and amusement. Then I remembered that he was probably watching me again, and might imagine my smile was meant for him. I banished it immediately, shut my glass up and did not touch it again. Soon after we came home.

July Twelfth.

Something has happened at last. Today I went to the shore as usual, fully resolved not even to glance in the forbidden direction. But in the end I had to take a peep, and saw him on the rocks with his glass levelled at me. When he saw that I was looking he laid down the glass, held up his hands, and began to spell out something in the deaf-mute alphabet. Now, I know that same alphabet. Connie taught it to me last year, so that we might hold communication across the schoolroom. I gave one frantic glance at Aunt Martha's rigid back, and then watched him while he deftly spelled: "I am Francis Shelmardine. Are you not Miss Forrester, my sister's friend?"

Francis Shelmardine! Now I knew whom he resembled. And have I not heard endless dissertations from Connie on this wonderful brother of hers, Francis the clever, the handsome, the charming, until he has become the only hero of dreams I have ever had? It was too wonderful. I could only stare dazedly back through my glass.

"May we know each other?" he went on. "May I come over and introduce myself? Right hand, yes; left, no."

I gasped! Suppose he were to come? *What* would happen? I waved my left hand sorrowfully. He looked quite crestfallen and disappointed as he spelled out: "Why not? Would your friends disapprove?"

I signalled: "Yes."

"Are you displeased at my boldness?" was his next question.

Where had all Aunt Martha's precepts flown to then? I blush to record that I lifted my left hand shyly and had just time to catch his pleased expression when Aunt Martha came up and said it was time to go home. So I picked myself meekly up, shook the sand from my dress, and followed my good aunt dutifully home.

July Thirteenth.

When we went to the shore this morning I had to wait in spasms of remorse and anxiety until Aunt got tired of reading and set off along the shore with Mrs. Saxby. Then I reached for my glass.

Mr. Shelmardine and I had quite a conversation. Under the circumstances there could be no useless circumlocution in our exchange of ideas. It was religiously "boiled down," and ran something like this:

"You are not displeased with me?"

"No—but I should be."

"Why?"

"It is wrong to deceive Aunt."

"I am quite respectable."

"That is not the question."

"Cannot her prejudices be overcome?"

"Absolutely no."

"Mrs. Allardyce, who is staying at the hotel, knows her well. Shall I bring her over to vouch for my character?"

"It would not do a bit of good."

"Then it is hopeless."

"Yes."

"Would you object to knowing me on your own account?"

"No."

"Do you ever come to the shore alone?"

"No. Aunt would not permit me."

"Must she know?"

"Yes. I would not come without her permission."

"You will not refuse to chat with me thus now and then?"

"I don't know. Perhaps not."

I had to go home then. As we went Mrs. Saxby complimented me on my good colour. Aunt Martha looked her disapproval. If I were really ill Aunt would spend her last cent in my behalf, but she would be just as well pleased to see me properly pale and subdued at all times, and not looking as if I were too well contented in this vale of tears.

July Seventeenth.

I have "talked" a good deal with Mr. Shelmardine these past four days. He is to be at the beach for some weeks longer. This morning he signalled across from the rocks: "I mean to see you at last. Tomorrow I will walk over and pass you."

"You must not. Aunt will suspect."

"No danger. Don't be alarmed. I will do nothing rash."

I suppose he will. He seems to be very determined. Of course, I cannot prevent him from promenading on our beach all day if he chooses. But then if he did, Aunt would speedily leave him in sole possession of it.

I wonder what I had better wear tomorrow.

July Nineteenth.

Yesterday morning Aunt Martha was serene and unsuspicious. It is dreadful of me to be deceiving her and I do feel guilty. I sat down on the sand and pretended to read the "Memoirs of a Missionary"—Aunt likes cheerful books like that—in an agony of anticipation. Presently Aunt said, majestically: "Marguer*ite*, there is a man coming this way. We will move further down."

And we moved. Poor Aunt!

Mr. Shelmardine came bravely on. I felt my heart beating to my very finger tips. He halted by the fragment of an old stranded boat. Aunt had turned her back on him.

I ventured on a look. He lifted his hat with a twinkle in his eye. Just then Aunt said, icily: "We will go home, Marguer*ite*. That creature evidently intends to persist in his intrusion."

Home we came accordingly.

This morning he signalled across: "Letter from Connie. Message for you. I mean to deliver it personally. Do you ever go to church?"

Now, I *do* go regularly to church at home. But Aunt Martha and Mrs. Saxby are both such rigid church people that they would not darken the doors of the Methodist church at Plover Sands for any consideration. Needless to say, I am not allowed to go either. But it was impossible to make this long explanation, so I merely replied: "Not here."

"Will you not go tomorrow morning?"

"Aunt will not let me."

"Coax her."

"Coaxing never has any effect on her."

"Would she relent if Mrs. Allardyce were to call for you?"

Now, I have been cautiously sounding Aunt about Mrs. Allardyce, and I have discovered that she disapproves of her. So I said: "It would be useless. I will ask Aunt if I may go, but I feel almost sure that she will not consent."

This evening, when Aunt was in an unusually genial mood, I plucked up heart of grace and asked her.

"Marguer*ite*," she said impressively, "you know that I do not attend church here."

"But, Aunt," I persisted, quakingly, "couldn't I go alone? It is not very far—and I will be very careful."

Aunt merely gave me a look that said about forty distinct and separate things, and I was turning away in despair when Mrs. Saxby—bless her heart—said: "I really think it would be no harm to let the child go."

As Aunt attaches great importance to Mrs. Saxby's opinion, she looked at me relentingly and said: "Well, I will think it over and let you know in the morning, Marguer*ite*."

Now, everything depends on the sort of humour Aunt is in in the morning.

July Twentieth.

This morning was perfect, and after breakfast Aunt said, condescendingly: "I think you may attend church if you wish, Marguer*ite*. Remember that I expect you to conduct yourself with becoming prudence and modesty."

I flew upstairs and pulled my prettiest dress out of my trunk. It is a delicate, shimmering grey stuff with pearly tints about it. Every time I get anything new, Aunt Martha and I have a battle royal over it. I verily believe that Aunt would like me to dress in the fashions in vogue in her youth. There is always a certain flavour of old-fashionedness about my gowns and hats. Connie used to say that it was delicious and gave me a piquant uniqueness—a certain unlikeness to other people that possessed a positive charm. That is only Connie's view of it, however.

But I had had my own way about this dress and it is really very becoming. I wore a little silvery-grey chip hat, trimmed with pale pink flowers, and I pinned at my belt the sweetest cluster of old-fashioned blush rosebuds from the garden. Then I borrowed a hymn book from Mrs. Blake and ran down to undergo Aunt Martha's scrutiny.

"Dear me, child," she said discontentedly, "you have gotten yourself up very frivolously, it seems to me."

"Why, Aunty," I protested, "I'm all in grey—every bit."

Aunt Martha sniffed. You don't know how much Aunt can express in a sniff. But I tripped to church like a bird.

The first person I saw there was Mr. Shelmardine. He was sitting right across from me and a smile glimmered in his eyes. I did not look at him again. Through the service I was subdued enough to have satisfied even Aunt Martha.

When church came out, he waited for me at the entrance to his pew. I pretended not to see him until he said "Good morning," in a voice vibrating and deep, which sounded as though it might become infinitely tender if its owner chose. When we went down the steps he took my hymnal, and we walked up the long, bowery country road.

"Thank you so much for coming today," he said—as if I went to oblige him.

"I had a hard time to get Aunt Martha's consent," I declared frankly. "I wouldn't have succeeded if Mrs. Saxby hadn't taken my part."

"Heaven bless Mrs. Saxby," he remarked fervently. "But is there any known way of overcoming your aunt's scruples? If so, I am ready to risk it."

"There is none. Aunt Martha is very good and kind to me, but she will never stop trying to bring me up. The process will be going on when I am fifty. And she hates men! I don't know what she would do if she saw me now."

Mr. Shelmardine frowned and switched the unoffending daisies viciously with his cane.

"Then there is no hope of my seeing you openly and above-board?"

"Not at present," I said faintly.

After a brief silence we began to talk of other things. He told me how he happened to see me first.

"I was curious to know who the people were who were always in the same place at the same time, so one day I took my telescope. I could see you plainly. You were reading and had your hat off. When I went back to the hotel I asked Mrs. Allardyce if she knew who the boarders at Fir Cottage were and she told me. I had heard Connie speak of you, and I determined to make your acquaintance."

When we reached the lane I held out my hand for the hymnal.

"You mustn't come any further, Mr. Shelmardine," I said hurriedly. "Aunt—Aunt might see you."

He took my hand and held it, looking at me seriously.

"Suppose I were to walk up to the cottage tomorrow and ask for you?"

I gasped. He looked so capable of doing anything he took it into his head to do.

"Oh, you wouldn't," I said piteously. "Aunt Martha would—you are not in earnest."

"I suppose not," he said regretfully. "Of course I would not do anything that would cause you unpleasantness. But this must not—shall not be our last meeting."

"Aunt will not let me come to church again," I said.

"Does she ever take a nap in the afternoon?" he queried.

I wriggled my parasol about in the dust uneasily.

"Sometimes."

"I shall be at the old boat tomorrow afternoon at two-thirty," he said.

I pulled my hand away.

"I couldn't—you know I couldn't," I cried—and then I blushed to my ears.

"Are you sure you couldn't?" bending a little nearer.

"Quite sure," I murmured.

He surrendered my hymnal at last.

"Will you give me a rose?"

I unpinned the whole cluster and handed it to him. He lifted it until it touched his lips. As for me, I scuttled up the lane in the most undignified fashion. At the turn I looked back. He was still standing there with his hat off.

July Twenty-fourth.

On Monday afternoon I slipped away to the shore while Aunt Martha and Mrs. Saxby were taking their regular nap and I was supposed to be reading sermons in my room.

Mr. Shelmardine was leaning against the old boat, but he came swiftly across the sand to meet me.

"This is very kind of you," he said.

"I ought not to have come," I said repentantly. "But it is so lonely there—and one can't be interested in sermons and memoirs *all* the time."

Mr. Shelmardine laughed.

"Mr. and Mrs. Allardyce are on the other side of the boat. Will you come and meet them?"

How nice of him to bring them! I knew I should like Mrs. Allardyce, just because Aunt Martha didn't. We had a delightful stroll. I never thought of the time until Mr. Shelmardine said it was four o'clock.

"Oh, is it so late as that?" I cried. "I must go at once."

"I'm sorry we have kept you so long," remarked Mr. Shelmardine in a tone of concern. "If she should be awake, what will the consequences be?"

"Too terrible to think of," I answered seriously. "I'm sorry, Mr. Shelmardine, but you mustn't come any further."

"*We* will be here tomorrow afternoon," he said.

"Mr. Shelmardine!" I protested. "I wish you wouldn't put such ideas into my head. They won't come out—no, not if I read a whole volume of sermons right through."

We looked at each other for a second. Then he began to smile, and we both went off into a peal of laughter.

"At least let me know if Miss Fiske rampages," he called after me as I fled.

But Aunt Martha was not awake—and I have been to the shore three afternoons since then. I was there today, and I'm going tomorrow for a boat sail with Mr. Shelmardine and the Allardyces. But I am afraid the former will do something rash soon. This afternoon he said: "I don't think I can stand this much longer."

"Stand what?" I asked.

"You know very well," he answered recklessly. "Meeting you in this clandestine manner, and thereby causing that poor little conscience of yours such misery. If your aunt were not so—unreasonable, I should never have stooped to it."

"It is all my fault," I said contritely.

"Well, I hardly meant that," he said grimly. "But hadn't I better go frankly to your aunt and lay the whole case before her?"

"You would never see me again if you did that," I said hastily—and then wished I hadn't.

"That is the worst threat you could make," he said.

July Twenty-fifth.

It is all over, and I am the most miserable girl in the world. Of course this means that Aunt Martha has discovered everything and the deserved punishment of my sins has overtaken me.

I slipped away again this afternoon and went for that boat sail. We had a lovely time but were rather late getting in, and I hurried home with many misgivings. Aunt Martha met me at the door.

My dress was draggled, my hat had slipped back, and the kinks and curls of my obstreperous hair were something awful. I know I looked very disreputable and also, no doubt, very guilty and conscience-stricken. Aunt gave me an unutterable look and then followed me up to my room in grim silence.

"Marguer*ite*, what does this mean?"

I have lots of faults, but untruthfulness isn't one of them. I confessed everything—at least, almost everything. I didn't tell about the telescopes and deaf-mute alphabet, and Aunt was too horror-stricken to think of asking how I first made Mr. Shelmardine's acquaintance. She listened in stony silence. I had expected a terrible scolding, but I suppose my crimes simply seemed to her too enormous for words.

When I had sobbed out my last word she rose, swept me one glance of withering contempt, and left the room. Presently Mrs. Saxby came up, looking concerned.

"My dear child, what have you been doing? Your aunt says that we are to go home on the afternoon train tomorrow. She is terribly upset."

I just curled up on the bed and cried, while Mrs. Saxby packed my trunk. I will have no chance to explain matters to Mr. Shelmardine. And I will never see him again, for Aunt is quite capable of whisking me off to Africa. He will just think me a feather-brained flirt. Oh, I am so unhappy!

July Twenty-sixth.

I am the happiest girl in the world! That is quite a different strain from yesterday. We leave Fir Cottage in an hour, but that doesn't matter now.

I did not sleep a wink last night and crawled miserably down to breakfast. Aunt took not the slightest notice of me, but to my surprise she told Mrs. Saxby that she intended taking a farewell walk to the shore. I knew I would be taken, too, to be kept out of mischief, and my heart gave a great bound of hope. Perhaps I would have a chance to send word to Francis, since Aunt did not know of the part my spyglass had played in my bad behaviour.

I meekly followed my grim guardians to the shore and sat dejectedly on my rug while they paced the sand. Francis was on the rocks. As soon as Aunt Martha and Mrs. Saxby were at a safe distance, I began my message: "All discovered. Aunt is very angry. We go home today."

Then I snatched my glass. His face expressed the direst consternation and dismay. He signalled: "I must see you before you go."

"Impossible. Aunt will never forgive me. Good-bye."

I saw a look of desperate determination cross his face. If forty Aunt Marthas had swooped down upon me, I could not have torn my eyes from that glass.

"I love you. You know it. Do you care for me? I must have my answer now."

What a situation! No time or chance for any maidenly hesitation or softening aureole of words. Aunt and Mrs. Saxby had almost reached the point where they invariably turned. I had barely time to spell out a plain, blunt "yes" and read his answer.

"I shall go home at once, get Mother and Connie, follow you, and demand possession of my property. I shall win the day. Have no fear. Till then, good-bye, my darling."

"Marguerite," said Mrs. Saxby at my elbow, "it is time to go."

I got up obediently. Aunt Martha was as grim and uncompromising as ever, and Mrs. Saxby looked like a chief mourner, but do you suppose I cared? I dropped behind them just once before we left the shore. I knew he was watching me and I waved my hand.

I suppose I am really engaged to Francis Shelmardine. But was there ever such a funny wooing? And *what* will Aunt Martha say?

After Many Days

The square, bare front room of the Baxter Station Hotel—so called because there was no other house in the place to dispute the title—was filled with men. Some of them were putting up at the hotel while they worked at the new branch line, and some of them had dropped in to exchange news and banter while waiting for the mail train.

Gabe Foley, the proprietor, was playing at checkers with one of the railroad men, but was not too deeply absorbed in the game to take in all that was said around him. The air was dim with tobacco smoke, and the brilliant, scarlet geraniums which Mrs. Foley kept in the bay window looked oddly out of place. Gabe knew all those present except one man—a stranger who had landed at Baxter Station from the afternoon freight. Foley's hotel did not boast of a register, and the stranger did not volunteer any information regarding his name or business. He had put in the afternoon and early evening strolling about the village and talking to the men on the branch line. Now he had come in and ensconced himself in the corner behind the stove, where he preserved a complete silence.

He had a rather rough face and was flashily dressed. Altogether, Gabe hardly liked his looks, put as long as a man paid his bill and did not stir up a row Gabe Foley did not interfere with him.

Three or four farmers from "out Greenvale way" were drawn up by the stove, discussing the cheese factory sales and various Greenvale happenings. The stranger appeared to be listening to them intently, although he took no part in their conversation.

Presently he brought his tilted chair down with a sharp thud. Gabe Foley had paused in his manipulation of a king to hurl a question at the Greenvale men.

"Is it true that old man Strong is to be turned out next week?"

"True enough," answered William Jeffers. "Joe Moore is going to foreclose. Stephen Strong has got three years behind with the interest and Moore is out of patience. It seems hard on old Stephen, but Moore ain't the man to hesitate for that. He'll have his own out of it."

"What will the Strongs do?" asked Gabe.

"That's the question everyone in Greenvale is asking. Lizzie Strong has always been a delicate little girl, but maybe she'll manage to scare up a living. Old Stephen is to be the most pitied. I don't see anything for him but the poorhouse."

"How did Stephen Strong come to get into such a tight place?" the stranger asked suddenly. "When I was in these parts a good many years ago he was considered a well-to-do man."

"Well, so he was," replied William Jeffers. "But he began to get in debt when his wife took sick. He spent no end of money on doctors and medicines for her. And then he seemed to have a streak of bad luck besides—crops failed and cows died and all that sort of thing. He's been going behind ever since. He kind of lost heart when his wife died. And now Moore is going to foreclose. It's my opinion poor old Stephen won't live any time if he's turned out of his home."

"Do you know what the mortgage comes to?"

"Near three thousand, counting overdue interest."

"Well, I'm sorry for old Stephen," said Gabe, returning to his game. "If anybody deserves a peaceful old age he does. He's helped more people than you could count, and he was the best Christian in Greenvale, or out of it."

"He was too good," said a Greenvale man crustily. "He just let himself be imposed upon all his life. There's dozens of people owes him and he's never asked for a cent from them. And he's always had some shiftless critter or other hanging round and devouring his substance."

"D'ye mind that Ben Butler who used to be in Greenvale twenty years ago?" asked a third man. "If ever there was an imp of Satan 'twas him—old Ezra Butler's son from the valley. Old Stephen kept him for three or four years and was as good to him as if he'd been his own son."

"Most people out our way do mind Ben Butler," returned William Jeffers grimly, "even if he ain't been heard tell of for twenty years. He wasn't the kind you could forget in a hurry. Where'd he go? Out to the Kootenay, wasn't it?"

"Somewhere there. He was a reg'lar young villain—up to every kind of mischief. Old Stephen caught him stealing his oats one time and 'stead of giving him a taste of jail for it, as he ought to have done, he just took him right into his family and kept him there for three years. I used to tell him he'd be sorry for it, but he always persisted that Ben wasn't bad at heart and would come out all right some day. No matter what the young varmint did old Stephen would make excuses for him—'his ma was dead,' or he 'hadn't had no bringing-up.' I was thankful when he did finally clear out without doing some penitentiary work."

"If poor old Stephen hadn't been so open-handed to every unfortunate critter he came across," said Gabe, "he'd have had more for himself today."

The whistle of the mail train cut short the discussion of Stephen Strong's case. In a minute the room was vacant, except for the stranger. When left to himself he also rose and walked out. Turning away from the station, he struck briskly into the Greenvale road.

About three miles from the station he halted before a house built close to the road. It was old-fashioned, but large and comfortable-looking, with big barns in the rear and an orchard on the left slope. The house itself was in the shadow of the firs, but the yard lay out in the moonlight and the strange visitor did not elect to cross it. Instead, he turned aside into the shadow of the trees around the garden and, leaning against the old rail fence, gave himself up to contemplation of some kind.

There was a light in the kitchen. The window-blind was not down and he had a fairly good view of the room. The only visible occupant was a grey-haired old man sitting by the table, reading from a large open volume before him. The stranger whistled softly.

"That's old Stephen—reading the Bible same as ever, by all that's holy! He hasn't changed much except that he's got mighty grey. He must be close on to seventy. It's a shame to turn an old man like him out of house and home. But Joe Moore always was a genuine skinflint."

He drew himself softly up and sat on the fence. He saw old Stephen Strong close his book, place his spectacles on it, and kneel down by his chair. The old man remained on his knees for some time and then, taking up his candle, left the kitchen. The man on the fence still sat there. Truth to tell, he was chuckling to himself as he recalled all the mischief he had done in the old days—the doubtful jokes, tricks, and escapades he had gone through with.

He could not help remembering at the same time how patient old Stephen Strong had always been with him. He recalled the time he had been caught stealing the oats. How frightened and sullen he had been! And how gently the old man had talked to him and pointed out the sin of which he had been guilty!

He had never stolen again, but in other respects he had not mended his ways much. Behind old Stephen's back he laughed at him and his "preaching." But Stephen Strong had never lost faith in him. He had always asserted mildly that "Ben would come out all right by and by." Ben Butler remembered this too, as he sat on the fence.

He had "always liked old Stephen," he told himself. He was sorry he had fallen on such evil times.

"Preaching and praying don't seem to have brought him out clear after all," he said with a chuckle that quickly died away. Somehow, even in his worst days, Ben Butler had never felt easy when he mocked old Stephen. "Three thousand dollars! I could do it but I reckon I'd be a blamed fool. I ain't a-going to do it. Three thousand ain't picked up every day, even in the Kootenay—'specially by chaps like me."

He patted his pocket knowingly. Fifteen years previously he had gone to the Kootenay district with visions of making a fortune that were quickly dispelled by reality. He had squandered his wages as soon as paid, and it was only of late years that he had "pulled up a bit," as he expressed it, and saved his three thousand dollars.

He had brought the money home with him, having some vague notion of buying a farm and "settling down to do the respectable." But he had already given up the idea. This country was too blamed quiet for him, he said. He would go back to the Kootenay, and he knew what he would do with his money. Jake Perkins and Wade Brown, two "pals" of his, were running a flourishing grocery and saloon combined. They would be glad of another partner with some cash. It would suit him to a T.

"I'll clear out tomorrow," he mused as he walked back. "As long as I stay here old Stephen will haunt me, sure as fate. Wonder what he was praying for tonight. He always used to say the Lord would provide, but He don't appear to have done it. Well, I ain't His deputy."

The next afternoon Ben Butler went over to Greenvale and called at Stephen Strong's. He found only the old man at home. Old Stephen did not recognize him at first, but made him heartily welcome when he did.

"Ben, I do declare! Ben Butler! How are you? How are you? Sit down, Ben—here, take this chair. Where on earth did you come from?"

"Baxter just now—Kootenay on the large scale," answered Ben. "Thought I'd come over and see you again. Didn't expect you'd remember me at all."

"Remember you! Why, of course I do. I haven't ever forgot you, Ben. Many's the time I've wondered where you was and how you was getting on. And you tell me you've been in the Kootenay! Well, well, you have seen a good bit more of the world than I ever have. You've changed a lot, Ben. You ain't a boy no longer. D'ye mind all the pranks you used to play?"

Ben laughed sheepishly.

"I reckon I do. But it ain't myself I come here to talk about—not much to say if I did. It's just been up and down with me. How are you yourself, sir? They were telling me over at Baxter that you were kind of in trouble."

The old man's face clouded over; all the sparkle went out of his kind blue eyes.

"Yes, Ben, yes," he said, with a heavy sigh. "I've kind of gone downhill, that's a fact. The old farm has to go, Ben—I'm sorry for that—I'd have liked to have ended my days here, but it's not to be. I don't want to complain. The Lord does all things well. I haven't a doubt but that it all fits into His wise purposes—not a doubt, Ben, although it may be kind of hard to see it."

Ben was always skittish of "pious talk." He veered around adroitly.

"I dunno as the Lord has had much to do with this, sir. Seems to me as if 'twas the other one as was running it, with Joe Moore for deputy. The main thing, as I look at it, is to get a cinch on him. How much does the mortgage amount to, sir?"

"About three thousand dollars, interest and all."

Old Stephen's voice trembled. The future looked very dark to him in his old age.

Ben put his hand inside his coat and brought out a brand-new, plump pocket-book. He opened it, laid it on his knee, and counted out a number of crisp notes.

"Here, sir," he said, pushing them along the table. "I reckon that'll keep you out of Joe Moore's clutches. There's three thousand there if I ain't made a mistake. That'll set you clear, won't it?"

"Ben!" Old Stephen's voice trembled with amazement. "Ben, I can't take it. It wouldn't be fair—or right. I could never pay you back."

Ben slipped the rubber band around his wallet and replaced it airily.

"I don't want it paid back, sir. It's a little gift, so to speak, just to let you know I ain't ungrateful for all you did for me. If it hadn't been for you I might have been in the penitentiary by now. As for the money, it may seem a pile to you, but we don't think anything more of a thousand or so in the Kootenay than you Greenvale folks do of a fiver—not a bit more. We do things on a big scale out there."

"But, Ben, are you sure you can afford it—that you won't miss it?"

"Pop sure. Don't you worry, I'm all right."

"Bless you—bless you!" The tears were running down old Stephen's face as he gathered up the money with a shaking hand. "I always knew you would do well, Ben—always said it. I knew you'd a good heart. I just can't realize this yet—it seems too good to be true. The old place saved—I can die in peace. Of course, I'll pay you back some of it anyhow if I'm spared a while longer. Bless you, Ben."

Ben would not stay long after that. He said he had to leave on the 4:30 train. He was relieved when he got away from the old man's thanks and questions. Ben did not find it easy to answer some of the latter. When he was out of sight of the house he sat on a fence and counted up his remaining funds.

"Just enough to take me back to the Kootenay—and then begin over again, I s'pose. But 'twas worth the money to see the old fellow's face. He'd thank the Lord and me, he said. How Jake and Wade'd roar to hear them two names in partnership! But I'm going to pull up a bit after this, see if I don't, just to justify the old man's faith in me. 'Twould be too bad to disappoint him if he's believed for so long that I was going to turn out all right yet."

When the 4:30 train went out Ben Butler stood on the rear platform. Gabe Foley watched him abstractedly as he receded.

"Blamed if I know who that fellow was," he remarked to a crony. "He never told his name, but seems to me I've seen him before. He has a kind of hang-dog look, I think. But he paid up square and it is none of my business."

An Unconventional Confidence

The Girl in Black-and-Yellow ran frantically down the grey road under the pines. There was nobody to see her, but she would have run if all Halifax had been looking on. For had she not on the loveliest new hat—a "creation" in yellow chiffon with big black *choux*—and a dress to match? And was there not a shower coming straight from the hills across the harbour?

Down at the end of the long resinous avenue the Girl saw the shore road, with the pavilion shutting out the view of the harbour's mouth. Below the pavilion, clean-shaven George's Island guarded the town like a sturdy bulldog, and beyond it were the wooded hills, already lost in a mist of rain.

"Oh, I shall be too late," moaned the Girl. But she held her hat steady with one hand and ran on. If she could only reach the pavilion in time! It was a neck-and-neck race between the rain and the Girl, but the Girl won. Just as she flew out upon the shore road, a tall Young Man came pelting down the latter, and they both dashed up the steps of the pavilion together as the rain swooped down upon them and blotted George's Island and the smoky town and the purple banks of the Eastern Passage from view.

The pavilion was small at the best of times, and just now the rain was beating into it on two sides, leaving only one dry corner. Into this the Girl moved. She was flushed and triumphant. The Young Man thought that in all his life he had never seen anyone so pretty.

"I'm so glad I didn't get my hat wet," said the Girl breathlessly, as she straightened it with a careful hand and wondered if she looked very blown and blowsy.

"It would have been a pity," admitted the Young Man. "It is a very pretty hat."

"Pretty!" The Girl looked the scorn her voice expressed. "Anyone can have a *pretty* hat. Our cook has one. This is a *creation*."

"Of course," said the Young Man humbly. "I ought to have known. But I am very stupid."

"Well, I suppose a mere man couldn't be expected to understand exactly," said the Girl graciously.

She smiled at him in a friendly fashion, and he smiled back. The Girl thought that she had never seen such lovely brown eyes before. He could not be a Haligonian. She was sure she knew all the nice young men with brown eyes in Halifax.

"Please sit down," she said plaintively. "I'm tired."

The Young Man smiled again at the idea of his sitting down because the Girl was tired. But he sat down, and so did she, on the only dry seat to be found.

"Goodness knows how long this rain will last," said the Girl, making herself comfortable and picturesque, "but I shall stay here until it clears up, if it rains for a week. I will *not* have my hat spoiled. I suppose I shouldn't have put it on. Beatrix said it was going to rain. Beatrix is such a horribly good prophet. I detest people who are good prophets, don't you?"

"I think that they are responsible for all the evils that they predict," said the Young Man solemnly.

"That is just what I told Beatrix. And I was determined to put on this hat and come out to the park today. I simply *had* to be alone, and I knew I'd be alone out here. Everybody else would be at the football game. By the way, why aren't you there?"

"I wasn't even aware that there was a football game on hand," said the Young Man, as if he knew he ought to be ashamed of his ignorance, and was.

"Dear me," said the Girl pityingly. "Where can you have been not to have heard of it? It's between the Dalhousie team and the Wanderers. Almost everybody here is on the Wanderers' side, because they are Haligonians, but I am not. I like the college boys best. Beatrix says that it is just because of my innate contrariness. Last year I simply screamed myself hoarse with enthusiasm. The Dalhousie team won the trophy."

"If you are so interested in the game, it is a wonder you didn't go to see it yourself," said the Young Man boldly.

"Well, I just couldn't," said the Girl with a sigh. "If anybody had ever told me that there would be a football game in Halifax, and that I would elect to prowl about by myself in the park instead of going to it, I'd have laughed them to scorn. Even Beatrix would never have dared to prophesy *that*. But you see it has happened. I was too crumpled up in my mind to care about football today. I had to come here and have it out with myself. That is why I put on my hat. I thought, perhaps, I might get through with my mental gymnastics in time to go to the game afterwards. But I didn't. It is just maddening, too. I got this hat and dress on purpose to wear to it. They're black and yellow, you see—the Dalhousie colours. It was my own idea. I was sure it would make a sensation. But I couldn't go to the game and take any interest in it, feeling as I do, could I, now?"

The Young Man said, of course, she couldn't. It was utterly out of the question.

The Girl smiled. Without a smile, she was charming. With a smile, she was adorable.

"I like to have my opinions bolstered up. Do you know, I want to tell you something? May I?"

"You may. I'll never tell anyone as long as I live," said the Young Man solemnly.

"I don't know you and you don't know me. That is why I want to tell you about it. I *must* tell somebody, and if I told anybody I knew, they'd tell it all over Halifax. It is dreadful to be talking to you like this. Beatrix would have three fits, one after the other, if she saw me. But Beatrix is a slave to conventionality. I glory in discarding it at times. You don't mind, do you?"

"Not at all," said the Young Man sincerely.

The Girl sighed.

"I have reached that point where I must have a confidant, or go crazy. Once I could tell things to Beatrix. That was before she got engaged. Now she tells everything to *him*. There is no earthly way of preventing her. I've tried them all. So, nowadays, when I get into trouble, I tell it out loud to myself in the glass. It's a relief, you know. But that is no good now. I want to tell it to somebody who can say things back. Will you promise to say things back?"

The Young Man assured her that he would when the proper time came.

"Very well. But please don't look at me while I'm telling you. I'll be sure to blush in places. When Beatrix wants to be particularly aggravating she says I have lost the art of blushing. But that is only her way of putting it, you know. Sometimes I blush dreadfully."

The Young Man dragged his eyes from the face under the black-and-yellow hat, and fastened them on a crooked pine tree that hung out over the bank.

"Well," began the Girl, "the root of the whole trouble is simply this. There is a young man in England. I always think of him as the Creature. He is the son of a man who was Father's especial crony in boyhood, before Father emigrated to Canada. Worse than that, he comes of a family which has contracted a vile habit of marrying into our family. It has come down through the ages so long that it has become chronic. Father left most of his musty traditions in England, but he brought this pet one with him. He and this friend agreed that the latter's son should marry one of Father's daughters. It ought to have been Beatrix—she is the oldest. But Beatrix had a pug nose. So Father settled on me. From my earliest recollection I have been given to understand that just as soon as I grew up there would be a ready-made husband imported from England for me. I was doomed to it from my cradle. Now," said the Girl, with a tragic gesture, "I ask you, could *anything* be more hopelessly, appallingly stupid and devoid of romance than that?"

The Young Man shook his head, but did not look at her.

"It's pretty bad," he admitted.

"You see," said the Girl pathetically, "the shadow of it has been over my whole life. Of course, when I was a very little girl I didn't mind it so much. It was such a long way off and lots of things might happen. The Creature might run away with some other girl—or I might have the smallpox—or Beatrix's nose might be straight when she grew up. And if Beatrix's nose were straight she'd be a great deal prettier than I am. But nothing did happen—and her nose is puggier than ever. Then when I grew up things were horrid. I never could have a single little bit of fun. And Beatrix had such a good time! She had scores of lovers in spite of her nose. To be sure, she's engaged now—and he's a horrid, faddy little creature. But he is her own choice. She wasn't told that there was a man in England whom she must marry by and by, when he got sufficiently reconciled to the idea to come and ask her. Oh, it makes me furious!"

"Is—is there—anyone else?" asked the Young Man hesitatingly.

"Oh, dear, no. How could there be? Why, you know, I couldn't have the tiniest flirtation with another man when I was as good as engaged to the Creature. That is one of my grievances. Just think how much fun I've missed! I used to rage to Beatrix about it, but she would tell me that I ought to be thankful to have the chance of making such a good match—the Creature is rich, you know, and clever. As if I cared how clever or rich he is! Beatrix made me so cross that I gave up saying anything and sulked by myself. So they think I'm quite reconciled to it, but I'm not."

"He might be very nice after all," suggested the Young Man.

"*Nice*! That isn't the point. Oh, don't you see? But no, you're a man—you *can't* understand. You must just take my word for it. The whole thing makes me furious. But I haven't told you the worst. The Creature is on his way out to Canada now. He may arrive here at any minute. And they are all so aggravatingly delighted over it."

"What do you suppose *he* feels like?" asked the Young Man reflectively.

"Well," said the Girl frankly, "I've been too much taken up with my own feelings to worry about his. But I daresay they are pretty much like mine. He must loathe and detest the very thought of me."

"Oh, I don't think he does," said the Young Man gravely.

"Don't you? Well, what do you suppose he *does* think of it all? You ought to understand the man's part of it better than I can."

"There's as much difference in men as in women," said the Young Man in an impersonal tone. "I may be right or wrong, you see, but I imagine he would feel something like this: From boyhood he has understood that away out in Canada there is a little girl growing up who is some day to be his wife. She becomes his boyish ideal of all that is good and true. He pictures her as beautiful and winsome and sweet. She is his heart's lady, and the thought of her abides with him as a safeguard and an inspiration. For her sake he resolves to make the most of himself, and live a clean, loyal life. When she comes to him she must find his heart fit to receive her. There is never a time in all his life when the dream of her does not gleam before him as of a star to which he may aspire with all reverence and love."

The Young Man stopped abruptly, and looked at the Girl. She bent forward with shining eyes, and touched his hand.

"You are splendid," she said softly. "If he thought so—but no—I am sure he doesn't. He's just coming out here like a martyr going to the stake. He knows he will be expected to propose to me when he gets here. And he knows that I know it too. And *he* knows and *I* know that I will be expected to say my very prettiest 'yes.'"

"But are you going to say it?" asked the Young Man anxiously.

The Girl leaned forward. "No. That is my secret. I am going to say a most emphatic 'no.'"

"But won't your family make an awful row?"

"Of course. But I rather enjoy a row now and then. It stirs up one's grey matter so nicely. I came out here this afternoon and thought the whole affair over from beginning to end. And I have determined to say 'no.'"

"Oh, I wouldn't make it so irreconcilable as that," said the Young Man lightly. "I'd leave a loophole of escape. You see, if you were to like him a little better than you expect, it would be awkward to have committed yourself by a rash vow to saying 'no,' wouldn't it?"

"I suppose it would," said the Girl thoughtfully, "but then, you know, I won't change my mind."

"It's just as well to be on the safe side," said the Young Man.

The Girl got up. The rain was over and the sun was coming out through the mists.

"Perhaps you are right," she said. "So I'll just resolve that I will say 'no' if I don't want to say 'yes.' That really amounts to the same thing, you know. Thank you so much for letting me tell you all about it. It must have bored you terribly, but it has done me so much good. I feel quite calm and rational now, and can go home and behave myself. Goodbye."

"Goodbye," said the Young Man gravely. He stood on the pavilion and watched the Girl out of sight beyond the pines.

When the Girl got home she was told that the Dalhousie team had won the game, eight to four. The Girl dragged her hat off and waved it joyously.

"What a shame I wasn't there! They'd have gone mad over my dress."

But the next item of information crushed her. The Creature had arrived. He had called that afternoon, and was coming to dinner that night.

"How fortunate," said the Girl, as she went to her room, "that I relieved my mind to that Young Man out in the park today. If I had come back with all that pent-up feeling seething within me and heard this news right on top of it all, I might have flown into a thousand pieces. What lovely brown eyes he had! I do dote on brown eyes. The Creature will be sure to have fishy blue ones."

When the Girl went down to meet the Creature she found herself confronted by the Young Man. For the first, last, and only time in her life, the Girl had not a word to say. But her family thought her confusion very natural and pretty. They really had not expected her to behave so well. As for the Young Man, his manner was flawless.

Toward the end of the dinner, when the Girl was beginning to recover herself, he turned to her.

"You know I promised never to tell," he said.

"Be sure you don't, then," said the Girl meekly.

"But aren't you glad you left the loophole?" he persisted.

The Girl smiled down into her lap.

"Perhaps," she said.

Aunt Cyrilla's Christmas Basket

When Lucy Rose met Aunt Cyrilla coming downstairs, somewhat flushed and breathless from her ascent to the garret, with a big, flat-covered basket hanging over her plump arm, she gave a little sigh of despair. Lucy Rose had done her brave best for some years—in fact, ever since she had put up her hair and lengthened her skirts—to break Aunt Cyrilla of the habit of carrying that basket with her every time she went to Pembroke; but Aunt Cyrilla still insisted on taking it, and only laughed at what she called Lucy Rose's "finicky notions." Lucy Rose had a horrible, haunting idea that it was extremely provincial for her aunt always to take the big basket, packed full of country good things, whenever she went to visit Edward and Geraldine. Geraldine was so stylish, and might think it queer; and then Aunt Cyrilla always would carry it on her arm and give cookies and apples and molasses taffy out of it to every child she encountered and, just as often as not, to older folks too. Lucy Rose, when she went to town with Aunt Cyrilla, felt chagrined over this—all of which goes to prove that Lucy was as yet very young and had a great deal to learn in this world.

That troublesome worry over what Geraldine would think nerved her to make a protest in this instance.

"Now, Aunt C'rilla," she pleaded, "you're surely not going to take that funny old basket to Pembroke this time—Christmas Day and all."

"'Deed and 'deed I am," returned Aunt Cyrilla briskly, as she put it on the table and proceeded to dust it out. "I never went to see Edward and Geraldine since they were married that I didn't take a basket of good things along with me for them, and I'm not going to stop now. As for it's being Christmas, all the more reason. Edward is always real glad to get some of the old farmhouse goodies. He says they beat city cooking all hollow, and so they do."

"But it's so countrified," moaned Lucy Rose.

"Well, I am countrified," said Aunt Cyrilla firmly, "and so are you. And what's more, I don't see that it's anything to be ashamed of. You've got some real silly pride about you, Lucy Rose. You'll grow out of it in time, but just now it is giving you a lot of trouble."

"The basket is a lot of trouble," said Lucy Rose crossly. "You're always mislaying it or afraid you will. And it does look so funny to be walking through the streets with that big, bulgy basket hanging on your arm."

"I'm not a mite worried about its looks," returned Aunt Cyrilla calmly. "As for its being a trouble, why, maybe it is, but I have that, and other people have the pleasure of it. Edward and Geraldine don't need it—I know that—but there may be those that will. And if it hurts your feelings to walk 'longside of a countrified old lady with a countrified basket, why, you can just fall behind, as it were."

Aunt Cyrilla nodded and smiled good-humouredly, and Lucy Rose, though she privately held to her own opinion, had to smile too.

"Now, let me see," said Aunt Cyrilla reflectively, tapping the snowy kitchen table with the point of her plump, dimpled forefinger, "what shall I take? That big fruit cake for one thing—Edward does like my fruit cake; and that cold boiled tongue for another. Those three mince pies too, they'd spoil before we got back or your uncle'd make himself sick eating them—mince pie is his besetting sin. And that little stone bottle full of cream—Geraldine may carry any amount of style, but I've yet to see her look down on real good country cream, Lucy Rose; and another bottle of my raspberry vinegar. That plate of jelly cookies and doughnuts will please the children and fill up the chinks, and you can bring me that box of ice-cream candy out of the pantry, and that bag of striped candy sticks your uncle brought home from the corner last night. And apples, of course—three or four dozen of those good eaters—and a little pot of my greengage preserves—Edward'll like that. And some sandwiches and pound cake for a snack for ourselves. Now, I guess that will do for eatables. The presents for the children can go in on top. There's a doll for Daisy and the little boat your uncle made for Ray and a tatted lace handkerchief apiece for the twins, and the crochet hood for the baby. Now, is that all?"

"There's a cold roast chicken in the pantry," said Lucy Rose wickedly, "and the pig Uncle Leo killed is hanging up in the porch. Couldn't you put them in too?"

Aunt Cyrilla smiled broadly. "Well, I guess we'll leave the pig alone; but since you have reminded me of it, the chicken may as well go in. I can make room."

Lucy Rose, in spite of her prejudices, helped with the packing and, not having been trained under Aunt Cyrilla's eye for nothing, did it very well too, with much clever economy of space. But when Aunt Cyrilla had put in as a finishing touch a big bouquet of pink and white everlastings, and tied the bulging covers down with a firm hand, Lucy Rose stood over the basket and whispered vindictively:

"Some day I'm going to burn this basket—when I get courage enough. Then there'll be an end of lugging it everywhere we go like a—like an old market-woman."

Uncle Leopold came in just then, shaking his head dubiously. He was not going to spend Christmas with Edward and Geraldine, and perhaps the prospect of having to cook and eat his Christmas dinner all alone made him pessimistic.

"I mistrust you folks won't get to Pembroke tomorrow," he said sagely. "It's going to storm."

Aunt Cyrilla did not worry over this. She believed matters of this kind were fore-ordained, and she slept calmly. But Lucy Rose got up three times in the night to see if it were storming, and when she did sleep had horrible nightmares of struggling through blinding snowstorms dragging Aunt Cyrilla's Christmas basket along with her.

It was not snowing in the early morning, and Uncle Leopold drove Aunt Cyrilla and Lucy Rose and the basket to the station, four miles off. When they reached there the air was thick with flying flakes. The stationmaster sold them their tickets with a grim face.

"If there's any more snow comes, the trains might as well keep Christmas too," he said. "There's been so much snow already that traffic is blocked half the time, and now there ain't no place to shovel the snow off onto."

Aunt Cyrilla said that if the train were to get to Pembroke in time for Christmas, it would get there; and she opened her basket and gave the stationmaster and three small boys an apple apiece.

"That's the beginning," groaned Lucy Rose to herself.

When their train came along Aunt Cyrilla established herself in one seat and her basket in another, and looked beamingly around her at her fellow travellers.

These were few in number—a delicate little woman at the end of the car, with a baby and four other children, a young girl across the aisle with a pale, pretty face, a sunburned lad three seats ahead in a khaki uniform, a very handsome, imposing old lady in a sealskin coat ahead of him, and a thin young man with spectacles opposite.

"A minister," reflected Aunt Cyrilla, beginning to classify, "who takes better care of other folks' souls than of his own body; and that woman in the sealskin is discontented and cross at something—got up too early to catch the train, maybe; and that young chap must be one of the boys not long out of the hospital. That woman's children look as if they hadn't enjoyed a square meal since they were born; and if that girl across from me has a mother, I'd like to know what the woman means, letting her daughter go from home in this weather in clothes like that."

Lucy Rose merely wondered uncomfortably what the others thought of Aunt Cyrilla's basket.

They expected to reach Pembroke that night, but as the day wore on the storm grew worse. Twice the train had to stop while the train hands dug it out. The third time it could not go on. It was dusk when the conductor came through the train, replying brusquely to the questions of the anxious passengers.

"A nice lookout for Christmas—no, impossible to go on or back—track blocked for miles—what's that, madam?—no, no station near—woods for miles. We're here for the night. These storms of late have played the mischief with everything."

"Oh, dear," groaned Lucy Rose.

Aunt Cyrilla looked at her basket complacently. "At any rate, we won't starve," she said.

The pale, pretty girl seemed indifferent. The sealskin lady looked crosser than ever. The khaki boy said, "Just my luck," and two of the children began to cry. Aunt Cyrilla took some apples and striped candy sticks from her basket and carried them to them. She lifted the oldest into her ample lap and soon had them all around her, laughing and contented.

The rest of the travellers straggled over to the corner and drifted into conversation. The khaki boy said it was hard lines not to get home for Christmas, after all.

"I was invalided from South Africa three months ago, and I've been in the hospital at Netley ever since. Reached Halifax three days ago and telegraphed the old folks I'd eat my Christmas dinner with them, and to have an extra-big turkey because I didn't have any last year. They'll be badly disappointed."

He looked disappointed too. One khaki sleeve hung empty by his side. Aunt Cyrilla passed him an apple.

"We were all going down to Grandpa's for Christmas," said the little mother's oldest boy dolefully. "We've never been there before, and it's just too bad."

He looked as if he wanted to cry but thought better of it and bit off a mouthful of candy.

"Will there be any Santa Claus on the train?" demanded his small sister tearfully. "Jack says there won't."

"I guess he'll find you out," said Aunt Cyrilla reassuringly.

The pale, pretty girl came up and took the baby from the tired mother. "What a dear little fellow," she said softly.

"Are you going home for Christmas too?" asked Aunt Cyrilla.

The girl shook her head. "I haven't any home. I'm just a shop girl out of work at present, and I'm going to Pembroke to look for some."

Aunt Cyrilla went to her basket and took out her box of cream candy. "I guess we might as well enjoy ourselves. Let's eat it all up and have a good time. Maybe we'll get down to Pembroke in the morning."

The little group grew cheerful as they nibbled, and even the pale girl brightened up. The little mother told Aunt Cyrilla her story aside. She had been long estranged from her family, who had disapproved of her marriage. Her husband had died the previous summer, leaving her in poor circumstances.

"Father wrote to me last week and asked me to let bygones be bygones and come home for Christmas. I was so glad. And the children's hearts were set on it. It seems too bad that we are not to get there. I have to be back at work the morning after Christmas."

The khaki boy came up again and shared the candy. He told amusing stories of campaigning in South Africa. The minister came too, and listened, and even the sealskin lady turned her head over her shoulder.

By and by the children fell asleep, one on Aunt Cyrilla's lap and one on Lucy Rose's, and two on the seat. Aunt Cyrilla and the pale girl helped the mother make up beds for them. The minister gave his overcoat and the sealskin lady came forward with a shawl.

"This will do for the baby," she said.

"We must get up some Santa Claus for these youngsters," said the khaki boy. "Let's hang their stockings on the wall and fill 'em up as best we can. I've nothing about me but some hard cash and a jack-knife. I'll give each of 'em a quarter and the boy can have the knife."

"I've nothing but money either," said the sealskin lady regretfully.

Aunt Cyrilla glanced at the little mother. She had fallen asleep with her head against the seat-back.

"I've got a basket over there," said Aunt Cyrilla firmly, "and I've some presents in it that I was taking to my nephew's children. I'm going to give 'em to these. As for the money, I think the mother is the one for it to go to. She's been telling me her story, and a pitiful one it is. Let's make up a little purse among us for a Christmas present."

The idea met with favour. The khaki boy passed his cap and everybody contributed. The sealskin lady put in a crumpled note. When Aunt Cyrilla straightened it out she saw that it was for twenty dollars.

Meanwhile, Lucy Rose had brought the basket. She smiled at Aunt Cyrilla as she lugged it down the aisle and Aunt Cyrilla smiled back. Lucy Rose had never touched that basket of her own accord before.

Ray's boat went to Jacky, and Daisy's doll to his oldest sister, the twins' lace handkerchiefs to the two smaller girls and the hood to the baby. Then the stockings were filled up with doughnuts and jelly cookies and the money was put in an envelope and pinned to the little mother's jacket.

"That baby is such a dear little fellow," said the sealskin lady gently. "He looks something like my little son. He died eighteen Christmases ago."

Aunt Cyrilla put her hand over the lady's kid glove. "So did mine," she said. Then the two women smiled tenderly at each other. Afterwards they rested from their labours and all had what Aunt Cyrilla called a "snack" of sandwiches and pound cake. The khaki boy said he hadn't tasted anything half so good since he left home.

"They didn't give us pound cake in South Africa," he said.

When morning came the storm was still raging. The children wakened and went wild with delight over their stockings. The little mother found her envelope and tried to utter thanks and broke down; and nobody knew what to say or do, when the conductor fortunately came in and made a diversion by telling them they might as well resign themselves to spending Christmas on the train.

"This is serious," said the khaki boy, "when you consider that we've no provisions. Don't mind for myself, used to half rations or no rations at all. But these kiddies will have tremendous appetites."

Then Aunt Cyrilla rose to the occasion.

"I've got some emergency rations here," she announced. "There's plenty for all and we'll have our Christmas dinner, although a cold one. Breakfast first thing. There's a sandwich apiece left and we must fill up on what is left of the cookies and doughnuts and save the rest for a real good spread at dinner time. The only thing is, I haven't any bread."

"I've a box of soda crackers," said the little mother eagerly.

Nobody in that car will ever forget that Christmas. To begin with, after breakfast they had a concert. The khaki boy gave two recitations, sang three songs, and gave a whistling solo. Lucy Rose gave three recitations and the minister a comic reading. The pale shop girl sang two songs. It was agreed that the khaki boy's whistling solo was the best number, and Aunt Cyrilla gave him the bouquet of everlastings as a reward of merit.

Then the conductor came in with the cheerful news that the storm was almost over and he thought the track would be cleared in a few hours.

"If we can get to the next station we'll be all right," he said. "The branch joins the main line there and the tracks will be clear."

At noon they had dinner. The train hands were invited in to share it. The minister carved the chicken with the brakeman's jack-knife and the khaki boy cut up the tongue and the mince pies, while the sealskin lady mixed the raspberry vinegar with its due proportion of water. Bits of paper served as plates. The train furnished a couple of glasses, a tin pint cup was discovered and given to the children, Aunt Cyrilla and Lucy Rose and the sealskin lady drank, turn about, from the latter's graduated medicine glass, the shop girl and the little mother shared one of the empty bottles, and the khaki boy, the minister, and the train men drank out of the other bottle.

Everybody declared they had never enjoyed a meal more in their lives. Certainly it was a merry one, and Aunt Cyrilla's cooking was never more appreciated; indeed, the bones of the chicken and the pot of preserves were all that was left. They could not eat the preserves because they had no spoons, so Aunt Cyrilla gave them to the little mother.

When all was over, a hearty vote of thanks was passed to Aunt Cyrilla and her basket. The sealskin lady wanted to know how she made her pound cake, and the khaki boy asked for her receipt for jelly cookies. And when two hours later the conductor came in and said the snowploughs had got along and they'd soon be starting, they all wondered if it could really be less than twenty-four hours since they met.

"I feel as if I'd been campaigning with you all my life," said the khaki boy.

At the next station they all parted. The little mother and the children had to take the next train back home. The minister stayed there, and the khaki boy and the sealskin lady changed trains. The sealskin lady shook Aunt Cyrilla's hand. She no longer looked discontented or cross.

"This has been the pleasantest Christmas I have ever spent," she said heartily. "I shall never forget that wonderful basket of yours. The little shop girl is going home with me. I've promised her a place in my husband's store."

When Aunt Cyrilla and Lucy Rose reached Pembroke there was nobody to meet them because everyone had given up expecting them. It was not far from the station to Edward's house and Aunt Cyrilla elected to walk.

"I'll carry the basket," said Lucy Rose.

Aunt Cyrilla relinquished it with a smile. Lucy Rose smiled too.

"It's a blessed old basket," said the latter, "and I love it. Please forget all the silly things I ever said about it, Aunt C'rilla."

Davenport's Story

It was a rainy afternoon, and we had been passing the time by telling ghost stories. That is a very good sort of thing for a rainy afternoon, and it is a much better time than after night. If you tell ghost stories after dark they are apt to make you nervous, whether you own up to it or not, and you sneak home and dodge upstairs in mortal terror, and undress with your back to the wall, so that you can't fancy there is anything behind you.

We had each told a story, and had had the usual assortment of mysterious noises and death warnings and sheeted spectres and so on, down through the whole catalogue of horrors—enough to satisfy any reasonable ghost-taster. But Jack, as usual, was dissatisfied. He said our stories were all second-hand stuff. There wasn't a man in the crowd who had ever seen or heard a ghost; all our so-called authentic stories had been told us by persons who had the story from other persons who saw the ghosts.

"One doesn't get any information from that," said Jack. "I never expect to get so far along as to see a real ghost myself, but I would like to see and talk to one who had."

Some persons appear to have the knack of getting their wishes granted. Jack is one of that ilk. Just as he made the remark, Davenport sauntered in and, finding out what was going on, volunteered to tell a ghost story himself—something that had happened to his grandmother, or maybe it was his great-aunt; I forget which. It was a very good ghost story as ghost stories go, and Davenport told it well. Even Jack admitted that, but he said:

"It's only second-hand too. Did you ever have a ghostly experience yourself, old man?"

Davenport put his finger tips critically together.

"Would you believe me if I said I had?" he asked.

"No," said Jack unblushingly.

"Then there would be no use in my saying it."

"But you don't mean that you ever really had, of course?"

"I don't know. Something queer happened once. I've never been able to explain it—from a practical point of view, that is. Want to hear about it?"

Of course we did. This was exciting. Nobody would ever have suspected Davenport of seeing ghosts.

"It's conventional enough," he began. "Ghosts don't seem to have much originality. But it's firsthand, Jack, if that's what you want. I don't suppose any of you have ever heard me speak of my brother, Charles. He was my senior by two years, and was a quiet, reserved sort of fellow—not at all demonstrative, but with very strong and deep affections.

"When he left college he became engaged to Dorothy Chester. She was very beautiful, and my brother idolized her. She died a short time before the date set for their marriage, and Charles never recovered from the blow.

"I married Dorothy's sister, Virginia. Virginia did not in the least resemble her sister, but our eldest daughter was strikingly like her dead aunt. We called her Dorothy, and Charles was devoted to her. Dolly, as we called her, was always 'Uncle Charley's girl.'

"When Dolly was twelve years old Charles went to New Orleans on business, and while there took yellow fever and died. He was buried there, and Dolly half broke her childish heart over his death.

"One day, five years later, when Dolly was seventeen, I was writing letters in my library. That very morning my wife and Dolly had gone to New York en route for Europe. Dolly was going to school in Paris for a year. Business prevented my accompanying them even as far as New York, but Gilbert Chester, my wife's brother, was going with them. They were to sail on the *Aragon* the next morning.

"I had written steadily for about an hour. At last, growing tired, I threw down my pen and, leaning back in my chair, was on the point of lighting a cigar when an unaccountable impulse made me turn round. I dropped my cigar and sprang to my feet in amazement. There was only one door in the room and I had all along been facing it. I could have sworn nobody had entered, yet there, standing between me and the bookcase, was a man—and that man was my brother Charles!

"There was no mistaking him; I saw him as plainly as I see you. He was a tall, rather stout man, with curly hair and a fair, close-clipped beard. He wore the same light-grey suit which he had worn when bidding us good-bye on the morning of his departure for New Orleans. He had no hat on, but wore spectacles, and was standing in his old favourite attitude, with his hands behind him.

"I want you to understand that at this precise moment, although I was surprised beyond measure, I was not in the least frightened, because I did not for a moment suppose that what I saw was—well, a ghost or apparition of any sort. The thought that flashed across my bewildered brain was simply that there had been some absurd mistake somewhere, and that my brother had never died at all, but was here, alive and well. I took a hasty step towards him.

"'Good heavens, old fellow!' I exclaimed. 'Where on earth have you come from? Why, we all thought you were dead!'

"I was quite close to him when I stopped abruptly. Somehow I couldn't move another step. He made no motion, but his eyes looked straight into mine.

"'Do not let Dolly sail on the *Aragon* tomorrow,' he said in slow, clear tones that I heard distinctly.

"And then he was gone—yes, Jack, I know it is a very conventional way of ending up a ghost story,| but I have to tell you just what occurred, or at least what I thought occurred. One moment he was there and the next moment he wasn't. He did not pass me or go out of the door.

"For a few moments I felt dazed. I was wide awake and in my right and proper senses so far as I could judge, and yet the whole thing seemed incredible. Scared? No, I wasn't conscious of being scared. I was simply bewildered.

"In my mental confusion one thought stood out sharply—Dolly was in danger of some kind, and if the warning was really from a supernatural source, it must not be disregarded. I rushed to the station and, having first wired to my wife not to sail on the *Aragon*, I found that I could connect with the five-fifteen train for New York. I took it with the comfortable consciousness that my friends would certainly think I had gone out of my mind.

"I arrived in New York at eight o'clock the next morning and at once drove to the hotel where my wife, daughter and brother-in-law were staying. I found them greatly mystified by my telegram. I suppose my explanation was a very lame one. I know I felt decidedly like a fool. Gilbert laughed at me and said I had dreamed the whole thing. Virginia was perplexed, but Dolly accepted the warning unhesitatingly.

"'Of course it was Uncle Charley,' she said confidently. 'We will not sail on the *Aragon* now.'

"Gilbert had to give in to this decision with a very bad grace, and the *Aragon* sailed that day minus three of her intended passengers.

"Well, you've all heard of the historic collision between the *Aragon* and the *Astarte* in a fog, and the fearful loss of life it involved. Gilbert didn't laugh when the news came, I assure you. Virginia and Dolly sailed a month later on the *Marseilles*, and reached the other side in safety. That's all the story, boys—the only experience of the kind I ever had," concluded Davenport.

We had many questions to ask and several theories to advance. Jack said Davenport had dreamed it and that the collision of the *Aragon* and the *Astarte* was simply a striking coincidence. But Davenport merely smiled at all our suggestions and, as it cleared up just about three, we told no more ghost stories.

Emily's Husband

Emily Fair got out of Hiram Jameson's waggon at the gate. She took her satchel and parasol and, in her clear, musical tones, thanked him for bringing her home. Emily had a very distinctive voice. It was very sweet always and very cold generally; sometimes it softened to tenderness with those she loved, but in it there was always an undertone of inflexibility and reserve. Nobody had ever heard Emily Fair's voice tremble.

"You are more than welcome, Mrs. Fair," said Hiram Jameson, with a glance of bold admiration. Emily met it with an unflinching indifference. She disliked Hiram Jameson. She had been furious under all her external composure because he had been at the station when she left the train.

Jameson perceived her scorn, but chose to disregard it.

"Proud as Lucifer," he thought as he drove away. "Well, she's none the worse of that. I don't like your weak women—they're always sly. If Stephen Fair don't get better she'll be free and then—"

He did not round out the thought, but he gloated over the memory of Emily, standing by the gate in the harsh, crude light of the autumn sunset, with her tawny, brown hair curling about her pale, oval face and the scornful glint in her large, dark-grey eyes.

Emily stood at the gate for some time after Jameson's waggon had disappeared. When the brief burst of sunset splendour had faded out she turned and went into the garden where late asters and chrysanthemums still bloomed. She gathered some of the more perfect ones here and there. She loved flowers, but tonight the asters seemed to hurt her, for she presently dropped those she had gathered and deliberately set her foot on them.

A sudden gust of wind came over the brown, sodden fields and the ragged maples around the garden writhed and wailed. The air was raw and chill. The rain that had threatened all day was very near. Emily shivered and went into the house.

Amelia Phillips was bending over the fire. She came forward and took Emily's parcels and wraps with a certain gentleness that sat oddly on her grim personality.

"Are you tired? I'm glad you're back. Did you walk from the station?"

"No. Hiram Jameson was there and offered to drive me home. I'd rather have walked. It's going to be a storm, I think. Where is John?"

"He went to the village after supper," answered Amelia, lighting a lamp. "We needed some things from the store."

The light flared up as she spoke and brought out her strong, almost harsh features and deep-set black eyes. Amelia Phillips looked like an overdone sketch in charcoal.

"Has anything happened in Woodford while I've been away?" asked Emily indifferently. Plainly she did not expect an affirmative answer. Woodford life was not eventful.

Amelia glanced at her sharply. So she had not heard! Amelia had expected that Hiram Jameson would have told her. She wished that he had, for she never felt sure of Emily. The older sister knew that beneath that surface reserve was a passionate nature, brooking no restraint when once it overleaped the bounds of her Puritan self-control. Amelia Phillips, with all her naturally keen insight and her acquired knowledge of Emily's character, had never been able to fathom the latter's attitude of mind towards her husband. From the time that Emily had come back to her girlhood's home, five years before, Stephen Fair's name had never crossed her lips.

"I suppose you haven't heard that Stephen is very ill," said Amelia slowly.

Not a feature of Emily's face changed. Only in her voice when she spoke was a curious jarring, as if a false note had been struck in a silver melody.

"What is the matter with him?"

"Typhoid," answered Amelia briefly. She felt relieved that Emily had taken it so calmly. Amelia hated Stephen Fair with all the intensity of her nature because she believed that he had treated Emily ill, but she had always been distrustful that Emily in her heart of hearts loved her husband still. That, in Amelia Phillips' opinion, would have betrayed a weakness not to be tolerated.

Emily looked at the lamp unwinkingly.

"That wick needs trimming," she said. Then, with a sudden recurrence of the untuneful note:

"Is he dangerously ill?"

"We haven't heard for three days. The doctors were not anxious about him Monday, though they said it was a pretty severe case."

A faint, wraith-like change of expression drifted over Emily's beautiful face and was gone in a moment. What was it—relief? Regret? It would have been impossible to say. When she next spoke her vibrant voice was as perfectly melodious as usual.

"I think I will go to bed, Amelia. John will not be back until late I suppose, and I am very tired. There comes the rain. I suppose it will spoil all the flowers. They will be beaten to pieces."

In the dark hall Emily paused for a moment and opened the front door to be cut in the face with a whip-like dash of rain. She peered out into the thickly gathering gloom. Beyond, in the garden, she saw the asters tossed about, phantom-like. The wind around the many-cornered old farmhouse was full of wails and sobs.

The clock in the sitting-room struck eight. Emily shivered and shut the door. She remembered that she had been married at eight o'clock that very morning seven years ago. She thought she could see herself coming down the stairs in her white dress with her bouquet of asters. For a moment she was glad that those mocking flowers in the garden would be all beaten to death before morning by the lash of wind and rain.

Then she recovered her mental poise and put the hateful memories away from her as she went steadily up the narrow stairs and along the hall with its curious slant as the house had settled, to her own room under the north-western eaves.

When she had put out her light and gone to bed she found that she could not sleep. She pretended to believe that it was the noise of the storm that kept her awake. Not even to herself would Emily confess that she was waiting and listening nervously for John's return home. That would have been to admit a weakness, and Emily Fair, like Amelia, despised weakness.

Every few minutes a gust of wind smote the house, with a roar as of a wild beast, and bombarded Emily's window with a volley of rattling drops. In the silences that came between the gusts she heard the soft, steady pouring of the rain on the garden paths below, mingled with a faint murmur that came up from the creek beyond the barns where the pine boughs were thrashing in the storm. Emily suddenly thought of a weird story she had once read years before and long forgotten—a story of a soul that went out in a night of storm and blackness and lost its way between earth and heaven. She shuddered and drew the counterpane over her face.

"Of all things I hate a fall storm most," she muttered. "It frightens me."

Somewhat to her surprise—for even her thoughts were generally well under the control of her unbending will—she could not help thinking of Stephen—thinking of him not tenderly or remorsefully, but impersonally, as of a man who counted for nothing in her life. It was so strange to think of Stephen being ill. She had never known him to have a day's sickness in his life before. She looked back over her life much as if she were glancing with a chill interest at a series of pictures which in no way concerned her. Scene after scene, face after face, flashed out on the background of the darkness.

Emily's mother had died at her birth, but Amelia Phillips, twenty years older than the baby sister, had filled the vacant place so well and with such intuitive tenderness that Emily had never been conscious of missing a mother. John Phillips, too, the grave, silent, elder brother, loved and petted the child. Woodford people were fond of saying that John and Amelia spoiled Emily shamefully.

Emily Phillips had never been like the other Woodford girls and had no friends of her own age among them. Her uncommon beauty won her many lovers, but she had never cared for any of them until Stephen Fair, fifteen years her senior, had come a-wooing to the old, gray, willow-girdled Phillips homestead.

Amelia and John Phillips never liked him. There was an ancient feud between the families that had died out among the younger generation, but was still potent with the older.

From the first Emily had loved Stephen. Indeed, deep down in her strange, wayward heart, she had cared for him long before the memorable day when he had first looked at her with seeing eyes and realized that the quiet, unthought-of child who had been growing up at the old Phillips place had blossomed out into a woman of strange, seraph-like beauty and deep grey eyes whose expression was nevermore to go out of Stephen Fair's remembrance from then till the day of his death.

John and Amelia Phillips put their own unjustifiable dislike of Stephen aside when they found that Emily's heart was set on him. The two were married after a brief courtship and Emily went out from her girlhood's home to the Fair homestead, two miles away.

Stephen's mother lived with them. Janet Fair had never liked Emily. She had not been willing for Stephen to marry her. But, apart from this, the woman had a natural, ineradicable love of making mischief and took a keen pleasure in it. She loved her son and she had loved her husband, but nevertheless, when Thomas Fair had been alive she had fomented continual strife and discontent between him and Stephen. Now it became her pleasure to make what trouble she could between Stephen and his wife.

She had the advantage of Emily in that she was always sweet-spoken and, on the surface, sweet-tempered. Emily, hurt and galled in a score of petty ways, so subtle that they were beyond a man's courser comprehension, astonished her husband by her fierce outbursts of anger that seemed to him for the most part without reason or excuse. He tried his best to preserve the peace between his wife and mother; and when he failed, not understanding all that Emily really endured at the elder woman's merciless hands, he grew to think her capricious and easily irritated—a spoiled child whose whims must not be taken too seriously.

To a certain extent he was right. Emily had been spoiled. The unbroken indulgence which her brother and sister had always accorded her had fitted her but poorly to cope with the trials of her new life. True, Mrs. Fair was an unpleasant woman to live with, but if Emily had chosen to be more patient under petty insults, and less resentful of her husband's well-meant though clumsy efforts for harmony, the older woman could have effected real little mischief. But this Emily refused to be, and the breach between husband and wife widened insidiously.

The final rupture came two years after their marriage. Emily, in rebellious anger, told her husband that she would no longer live in the same house with his mother.

"You must choose between us," she said, her splendid voice vibrating with all the unleashed emotion of her being, yet with no faltering in it. "If she stays I go."

Stephen Fair, harassed and bewildered, was angry with the relentless anger of a patient man roused at last.

"Go, then," he said sternly, "I'll never turn my mother from my door for any woman's whim."

The stormy red went out of Emily's face, leaving it like a marble wash.

"You mean that!" she said calmly. "Think well. If I go I'll never return."

"I do mean it," said Stephen. "Leave my house if you will—if you hold your marriage vow so lightly. When your senses return you are welcome to come back to me. I will never ask you to."

Without another word Emily turned away. That night she went back to John and Amelia. They, on their part, welcomed her back gladly, believing her to be a wronged and ill-used woman. They hated Stephen Fair with a new and personal rancour. The one thing they could hardly have forgiven Emily would have been the fact of her relenting towards him.

But she did not relent. In her soul she knew that, with all her just grievances, she had been in the wrong, and for that she could not forgive him!

Two years after she had left Stephen Mrs. Fair died, and his widowed sister-in-law went to keep house for him. If he thought of Emily he made no sign. Stephen Fair never broke a word once passed.

Since their separation no greeting or look had ever passed between husband and wife. When they met, as they occasionally did, neither impassive face changed. Emily Fair had buried her love deeply. In her pride and anger she would not let herself remember even where she had dug its grave.

And now Stephen was ill. The strange woman felt a certain pride in her own inflexibility because the fact did not affect her. She told herself that she could not have felt more unconcerned had he been the merest stranger. Nevertheless she waited and watched for John Phillips' homecoming.

At ten o'clock she heard his voice in the kitchen. She leaned out of the bed and pulled open her door. She heard voices below, but could not distinguish the words, so she rose and went noiselessly out into the hall, knelt down by the stair railing and listened. The door of the kitchen was open below her and a narrow shaft of light struck on her white, intent face. She looked like a woman waiting for the decree of doom.

At first John and Amelia talked of trivial matters. Then the latter said abruptly:

"Did you hear how Stephen Fair was?"

"He's dying," was the brief response.

Emily heard Amelia's startled exclamation. She gripped the square rails with her hands until the sharp edges dinted deep into her fingers. John's voice came up to her again, harsh and expressionless:

"He took a bad turn the day before yesterday and has been getting worse ever since. The doctors don't expect him to live till morning."

Amelia began to talk rapidly in low tones. Emily heard nothing further. She got up and went blindly back into her room with such agony tearing at her heart-strings that she dully wondered why she could not shriek aloud.

Stephen—her husband—dying! In the burning anguish of that moment her own soul was as an open book before her. The love she had buried rose from the deeps of her being in an awful, accusing resurrection.

Out of her stupor and pain a purpose formed itself clearly. She must go to Stephen—she must beg and win his forgiveness before it was too late. She dared not go down to John and ask him to take her to her husband. He might refuse. The

Phillipses had been known to do even harder things than that. At the best there would be a storm of protest and objection on her brother's and sister's part, and Emily felt that she could not encounter that in her present mood. It would drive her mad.

She lit a lamp and dressed herself noiselessly, but with feverish haste. Then she listened. The house was very still. Amelia and John had gone to bed. She wrapped herself in a heavy woollen shawl hanging in the hall and crept downstairs. With numbed fingers she fumbled at the key of the hall door, turned it and slipped out into the night.

The storm seemed to reach out and clutch her and swallow her up. She went through the garden, where the flowers already were crushed to earth; she crossed the long field beyond, where the rain cut her face like a whip and the wind almost twisted her in its grasp like a broken reed. Somehow or other, more by blind instinct than anything else, she found the path that led through commons and woods and waste valleys to her lost home.

In after years that frenzied walk through the storm and blackness seemed as an unbroken nightmare to Emily Fair's recollection. Often she fell. Once as she did so a jagged, dead limb of fir struck her forehead and cut in it a gash that marked her for life. As she struggled to her feet and found her way again the blood trickled down over her face.

"Oh God, don't let him die before I get to him—don't—don't—don't!" she prayed desperately with more of defiance than entreaty in her voice. Then, realizing this, she cried out in horror. Surely some fearsome punishment would come upon her for her wickedness—she would find her husband lying dead.

When Emily opened the kitchen door of the Fair homestead Almira Sentner cried out in her alarm, who or what was this creature with the white face and wild eyes, with her torn and dripping garments and dishevelled, wind-writhen hair and the big drops of blood slowly trickling from her brow?

The next moment she recognized Emily and her face hardened. This woman, Stephen's sister-in-law, had always hated Emily Fair.

"What do you want here?" she said harshly.

"Where is my husband?" asked Emily.

"You can't see him," said Mrs. Sentner defiantly. "The doctors won't allow anyone in the room but those he's used to. Strangers excite him."

The insolence and cruelty of her speech fell on unheeding ears. Emily, understanding only that her husband yet lived, turned to the hall door.

"Stand back!" she said in a voice that was little more than a thrilling whisper, but which yet had in it something that cowed Almira Sentner's malice. Sullenly she stood aside and Emily went unhindered up the stairs to the room where the sick man lay.

The two doctors in attendance were there, together with the trained nurse from the city. Emily pushed them aside and fell on her knees by the bed. One of the doctors made a hasty motion as if to draw her back, but the other checked him.

"It doesn't matter now," he said significantly.

Stephen Fair turned his languid, unshorn head on the pillow. His dull, fevered eyes met Emily's. He had not recognized anyone all day, but he knew his wife.

"Emily!" he whispered.

Emily drew his head close to her face and kissed his lips passionately.

"Stephen, I've come back to you. Forgive me—forgive me—say that you forgive me."

"It's all right, my girl," he said feebly.

She buried her face in the pillow beside his with a sob.

In the wan, grey light of the autumn dawn the old doctor came to the bedside and lifted Emily to her feet. She had not stirred the whole night. Now she raised her white face with dumb pleading in her eyes. The doctor glanced at the sleeping form on the bed.

"Your husband will live, Mrs. Fair," he said gently. "I think your coming saved him. His joy turned the ebbing tide in favour of life."

"Thank God!" said Emily.

And for the first time in her life her beautiful voice trembled.

Min

The morning sun hung, a red, lustreless ball, in the dull grey sky. A light snow had fallen in the night and the landscape, crossed by spider-like trails of fences, was as white and lifeless as if wrapped in a shroud.

A young man was driving down the road to Rykman's Corner; the youthful face visible above the greatcoat was thoughtful and refined, the eyes deep blue and peculiarly beautiful, the mouth firm yet sensitive. It was not a handsome face, but there was a strangely subtle charm about it.

The chill breathlessness of the air seemed prophetic of more snow. The Reverend Allan Telford looked across the bare wastes and cold white hills and shivered, as if the icy lifelessness about him were slowly and relentlessly creeping into his own heart and life.

He felt utterly discouraged. In his soul he was asking bitterly what good had come of all his prayerful labours among the people of this pinched, narrow world, as rugged and unbeautiful in form and life as the barren hills that shut them in.

He had been two years among them and he counted it two years of failure. He had been too outspoken for them; they resented sullenly his direct and incisive tirades against their pet sins. They viewed his small innovations on their traditional ways of worship with disfavour and distrust and shut him out of their lives with an ever-increasing coldness. He had meant well and worked hard and he felt his failure keenly.

His thoughts reverted to a letter received the preceding day from a former classmate, stating that the pastorate of a certain desirable town church had become vacant and hinting that a call was to be moderated for him unless he signified his unwillingness to accept.

Two years before, Allan Telford, fresh from college and full of vigorous enthusiasm and high ideas, would have said:

"No, that is not for me. My work must lie among the poor and lowly of earth as did my Master's. Shall I shrink from it because, to worldly eyes, the way looks dreary and uninviting?"

Now, looking back on his two years' ministry, he said wearily:

"I can remain here no longer. If I do, I fear I shall sink down into something almost as pitiful as one of these canting, gossiping people myself. I can do them no good—they do not like or trust me. I will accept this call and go back to my own world."

Perhaps the keynote of his failure was sounded in his last words, "my own world." He had never felt, or tried to feel, that this narrow sphere was his own world. It was some lower level to which he had come with good tidings and honest intentions but, unconsciously, he had held himself above it, and his people felt and resented this. They expressed it by saying he was "stuck-up."

Rykman's Corner came into view as he drove over the brow of a long hill. He hated the place, knowing it well for what it was—a festering hotbed of gossip and malice, the habitat of all the slanderous rumours and innuendoes that permeated the social tissue of the community. The newest scandal, the worst-flavoured joke, the latest details of the most recent quarrel, were always to be had at Rykman's store.

As the minister drove down the hill, a man came out of a small house at the foot and waited on the road. Had it been possible Telford would have pretended not to see him, but it was not possible, for Isaac Galletly meant to be seen and hailed the minister cheerfully.

"Good mornin', Mr. Telford. Ye won't mind giving me a lift down to the Corner, I dessay?"

Telford checked his horse reluctantly and Galletly crawled into the cutter. He was that most despicable of created beings, a male gossip, and he spent most of his time travelling from house to house in the village, smoking his pipe in neighbourly kitchens and fanning into an active blaze all the smouldering feuds of the place. He had been nicknamed "The Morning Chronicle" by a sarcastic schoolteacher who had sojourned a winter at the Corner. The name was an apt one and clung. Telford had heard it.

I suppose he is starting out on his rounds now, he thought.

Galletly plunged undauntedly into the conversational gap.

"Quite a fall of snow last night. Reckon we'll have more 'fore long. That was a grand sermon ye gave us last Sunday, Mr. Telford. Reckon it went home to some folks, judgin' from all I've heard. It was needed and that's a fact. 'Live peaceably with all men'—that's what I lay out to do. There ain't a house in the district but what I can drop into and welcome. 'Tain't everybody in Rykman's Corner can say the same."

Galletly squinted out of the corner of his eye to see if the minister would open on the trail of this hint. Telford's passive face was discouraging but Galletly was not to be baffled.

"I s'pose ye haven't heard about the row down at Palmers' last night?"

"No."

The monosyllable was curt. Telford was vainly seeking to nip Galletly's gossip in the bud. The name of Palmer conveyed no especial meaning to his ear. He knew where the Palmer homestead was, and that the plaintive-faced, fair-haired woman, whose name was Mrs. Fuller and who came to church occasionally, lived there. His knowledge went no further. He had called three times and found nobody at home—at least, to all appearances. Now he was fated to have the whole budget of some vulgar quarrel forced on him by Galletly.

"No? Everyone's talkin' of it. The long and short of it is that Min Palmer has had a regular up-and-down row with Rose Fuller and turned her and her little gal out of doors. I believe the two women had an awful time. Min's a Tartar when her temper's up—and that's pretty often. Nobody knows how Rose managed to put up with her so long. But she has had to go at last. Goodness knows what the poor critter'll do. She hasn't a cent nor a relation—she was just an orphan girl that Palmer brought up. She is at Rawlingses now. Maybe when Min cools off, she'll let her go back but it's doubtful. Min hates her like p'isen."

To Telford this was all very unintelligible. But he understood that Mrs. Fuller was in trouble of some kind and that it was his duty to help her if possible, although he had an odd and unaccountable aversion to the woman, for which he had often reproached himself.

"Who is this woman you call Min Palmer?" he said coldly. "What are the family circumstances? I ought to know, perhaps, if I am to be of any service—but I have no wish to hear idle gossip."

His concluding sentence was quite unheeded by Galletly.

"Min Palmer's the worst woman in Rykman's Corner—or out of it. She always was an odd one. I mind her when she was a girl—a saucy, black-eyed baggage she was! Handsome, some folks called her. I never c'd see it. Her people were a queer crowd and Min was never brung up right—jest let run wild all her life. Well, Rod Palmer took to dancin' attendance on her. Rod was a worthless scamp. Old Palmer was well off and Rod was his only child, but this Rose lived there and kept house for them after Mis' Palmer died. She was a quiet, well-behaved little creetur. Folks said the old man wanted Rod to marry her—dunno if 'twas so or not. In the end, howsomever, he had to marry Min. Her brother got after him with a horse-whip, ye understand. Old Palmer was furious but he had to give in and Rod brought her home. She was a bit sobered down by her trouble and lived quiet and sullen-like at first. Her and Rod fought like cat and dog. Rose married Osh Fuller, a worthless, drunken fellow. He died in a year or so and left Rose and her baby without a roof over their heads. Then old Palmer went and brought her home. He set great store by Rose and he c'dn't bear Min. Min had to be civil to Rose as long as old Palmer lived. Fin'lly Rod up and died and 'twasn't long before his father went too. Then the queer part came in. Everyone expected that he'd purvide well for Rose and Min'd come in second best. But no will was to be found. I don't say but what it was all right, mind you. I may have my own secret opinion, of course. Old Palmer had a regular mania, as ye might say, for makin' wills. He'd have a lawyer out from town every year and have a new will made and the old one burnt. Lawyer Bell was there and made one 'bout eight months 'fore he died. It was s'posed he'd destroyed it and then died 'fore he'd time to make another. He went off awful sudden. Anyway, everything went to Min's child—to Min as ye might say. She's been boss. Rose still stayed on there and Min let her, which was more than folks expected of her. But she's turned her out at last. Min's in one of her tantrums now and 'tain't safe to cross her path."

"What is Mrs. Fuller to do?" asked Telford anxiously.

"That's the question. She's sickly—can't work much—and then she has her leetle gal. Min was always jealous of that child. It's a real purty, smart leetle creetur and old Palmer made a lot of it. Min's own is an awful-looking thing—a cripple from the time 'twas born. There's no doubt 'twas a jedgement on her. As for Rose, no doubt the god of the widow and fatherless will purvide for her."

In spite of his disgust, Telford could not repress a smile at the tone, half-whine, half-snuffle, with which Galletly ended up.

"I think I had better call and see this Mrs. Palmer," he said slowly.

"'Twould be no airthly use, Mr. Telford. Min'd slam the door in your face if she did nothing worse. She hates ministers and everything that's good. She hasn't darkened a church door for years. She never had any religious tendency to begin with, and when there was such a scandal about her, old Mr. Dinwoodie, our pastor then—a godly man, Mr. Telford—he didn't hold no truck with evildoers—he went right to her to reprove and rebuke her for her sins. Min, she flew at him. She vowed then she'd never go to church again, and she never has. People hereabouts has talked to her and tried to do her good, but it ain't no use. Why, I've heard that woman say there was no God. It's a fact, Mr. Telford—I have. Some of our ministers has tried to visit her. They didn't try it more than once. The last one—he was about your heft—he got a scare, I tell you. Min just caught him by the shoulder and shook him like a rat! Didn't see it myself but Mrs. Rawlings did. Ye ought to hear her describin' of it."

Galletly chuckled over the recollection, his wicked little eyes glistening with delight. Telford was thankful when they reached the store. He felt that he could not endure this man's society any longer.

Nevertheless, he felt strangely interested. This Min Palmer must at least be different from the rest of the Cornerites, if only in the greater force of her wickedness. He almost felt as if her sins on the grand scale were less blameworthy than the petty vices of her censorious neighbours.

Galletly eagerly joined the group of loungers on the dirty wet platform, and Telford passed into the store. A couple of slatternly women were talking to Mrs. Rykman about "the Palmer row." Telford made his small purchases hastily. As he turned from the counter, he came face to face with a woman who had paused in the doorway to survey the scene with an air of sullen scorn. By some subtle intuition Telford knew that this was Min Palmer.

The young man's first feeling was one of admiration for the woman before him, who, in spite of her grotesque attire and defiant, unwomanly air, was strikingly beautiful. She was tall, and not even the man's ragged overcoat which she wore could conceal the grace of her figure. Her abundant black hair was twisted into a sagging knot at her neck, and from beneath the old fur cap looked out a pair of large and brilliant black eyes, heavily lashed, and full of a smouldering fire. Her skin was tanned and coarsened, but the warm crimson blood glowed in her cheeks with a dusky richness, and her face was a perfect oval, with features chiselled in almost classic regularity of outline.

Telford had a curious experience at that moment. He seemed to see, looking out from behind this external mask of degraded beauty, the semblance of what this woman might have been under more favouring circumstance of birth and environment, wherein her rich, passionate nature, potent for either good or evil, might have been trained and swayed aright until it had developed grandly out into the glorious womanhood the Creator must have planned for her. He knew, as if by revelation, that this woman had nothing in common with the narrow, self-righteous souls of Rykman's Corner. Warped and perverted though her nature might be, she was yet far nobler than those who sat in judgement upon her.

Min made some scanty purchases and left the store quickly, brushing unheedingly past the minister as she did so. He saw her step on a rough wood-sleigh and drive down the river road. The platform loungers had been silent during her call, but now the talk bubbled forth anew. Telford was sick at heart as he drove swiftly away. He felt for Min Palmer a pity he could not understand or analyze. The attempt to measure the gulf between what she was and what she might have been hurt him like the stab of a knife.

He made several calls at various houses along the river during the forenoon. After dinner he suddenly turned his horse towards the Palmer place. Isaac Galletly, comfortably curled up in a neighbour's chimney corner, saw him drive past.

"Ef the minister ain't goin' to Palmers' after all!" he chuckled. "He's a set one when he does take a notion. Well, I warned him what to expect. If Min claws his eyes out, he'll only have himself to blame."

Telford was not without his own misgivings as he drove into the Palmer yard. He tied his horse to the fence and looked doubtfully about him. Untrodden snowdrifts were heaped about the front door, so he turned towards the kitchen and walked slowly past the bare lilac trees along the fence. There was no sign of life about the place. It was beginning to snow again, softly and thickly, and the hills and river were hidden behind a misty white veil.

He lifted his hand to knock, but before he could do so, the door was flung open and Min herself confronted him on the threshold.

She did not now have on the man's overcoat which she had worn at the store, and her neat, close-fitting home-spun dress revealed to perfection the full, magnificent curves of her figure. Her splendid hair was braided about her head in a glossy coronet, and her dark eyes were ablaze with ill-suppressed anger. Again Telford was overcome by a sense of her wonderful loveliness. Not all the years of bondage to ill-temper and misguided will had been able to blot out the beauty of that proud, dark face.

She lifted one large but shapely brown hand and pointed to the gate.

"Go!" she said threateningly.

"Mrs. Palmer," began Telford, but she silenced him with an imperious gesture.

"I don't want any of your kind here. I hate all you ministers. Did you come here to lecture me? I suppose some of the Corner saints set you on me. You'll never cross my threshold."

Telford returned her defiant gaze unflinchingly. His dark-blue eyes, magnetic in their power and sweetness, looked gravely, questioningly, into Min's stormy orbs. Slowly the fire and anger faded out of her face and her head drooped.

"I ain't fit for you to talk to anyway," she said with a sort of sullen humility. "Maybe you mean well but you can't do me any good. I'm past that now. The Corner saints say I'm possessed of the devil. Perhaps I am—if there is one."

"I do mean well," said Telford slowly. "I did not come here to reprove you. I came to help you if I could—if you needed help, Mrs. Palmer—"

"Don't call me that," she interrupted passionately. She flung out her hands as if pushing some loathly, invisible thing from her. "I hate the name—as I hated all who ever bore it. I never had anything but wrong and dog-usage from them all. Call me Min—that's the only name that belongs to me now. Go—why don't you go? Don't stand there looking at me like that. I'm not going to change my mind. I don't want any praying and whining round me. I've been well sickened of that. Go!"

Telford threw back his head and looked once more into her eyes. A long look passed between them. Then he silently lifted his cap and, with no word of farewell, he turned and went down to the gate. A bitter sense of defeat and disappointment filled his heart as he drove away.

Min stood in the doorway and watched the sleigh out of sight down the river road. Then she gave a long, shivering sigh that was almost a moan.

"If I had met that man long ago," she said slowly, as if groping vaguely in some hitherto unsounded depth of consciousness, "I would never have become what I am. I felt that as I looked at him—it all came over me with an awful sickening feeling—just as if we were standing alone somewhere out of the world where there was no need of words to say things. He doesn't despise me—he wouldn't sneer at me, bad as I am, like those creatures up there. He could have helped me if we had met in time, but it's too late now."

She locked her hands over her eyes and groaned, swaying her body to and fro as one in mortal agony. Presently she looked out again with hard, dry eyes.

"What a fool I am!" she said bitterly. "How the Corner saints would stare if they saw me! I suppose some of them do—" with a glance at the windows of a neighbouring house. "Yes, there's Mrs. Rawlings staring out and Rose peeking over her shoulder."

Her face hardened. The old sway of evil passion reasserted itself.

"She shall never come back here—never. Oh, she was a sweet-spoken cat of a thing—but she had claws. I've been blamed for all the trouble. But if ever I had a chance, I'd tell that minister how she used to twit and taunt me in that sugary way of hers—how she schemed and plotted against me as long as she could. More fool I to care what he thinks either! I wish I were dead. If 'twasn't for the child, I'd go and drown myself at that black spring-hole down there—I'd be well out of the way."

It was a dull grey afternoon a week afterwards when Allan Telford again walked up the river road to the Palmer place. The wind was bitter and he walked with bent head to avoid its fury. His face was pale and worn and he looked years older.

He paused at the rough gate and leaned over it while he scanned the house and its surroundings eagerly. As he looked, the kitchen door opened and Min, clad in the old overcoat, came out and walked swiftly across the yard.

Telford's eyes followed her with pitiful absorption. He saw her lead a horse from the stable and harness it into a wood-sleigh loaded with bags of grain. Once she paused to fling her arms about the animal's neck, laying her face against it with a caressing motion.

The pale minister groaned aloud. He longed to snatch her forever from that hard, unwomanly toil and fold her safely away from jeers and scorn in the shelter of his love. He knew it was madness—he had told himself so every hour in which Min's dark, rebellious face had haunted him—yet none the less was he under its control.

Min led the horse across the yard and left it standing before the kitchen door; she had not seen the bowed figure at the gate. When she reappeared, he saw her dark eyes and the rose-red lustre of her face gleam out from under the old crimson shawl wrapped about her head.

As she caught the horse by the bridle, the kitchen door swung heavily to with a sharp, sudden bang. The horse, a great, powerful, nervous brute, started wildly and then reared in terror.

The ice underfoot was glib and treacherous. Min lost her foothold and fell directly under the horse's hoofs as they came heavily down. The animal, freed from her detaining hand, sprang forward, dragging the laden sleigh over the prostrate woman.

It had all passed in a moment. The moveless figure lay where it had fallen, one outstretched hand still grasping the whip. Telford sprang over the gate and rushed up the slope like a madman. He flung himself on his knees beside her.

"Min! Min!" he called wildly.

There was no answer. He lifted her in his arms and staggered into the house with his burden, his heart stilling with a horrible fear as he laid her gently down on the old lounge in one corner of the kitchen.

The room was a large one and everything was neat and clean. The fire burned brightly, and a few green plants were in blossom by the south window. Beside them sat a child of about seven years who turned a startled face at Telford's reckless entrance.

The boy had Min's dark eyes and perfectly chiselled features, refined by suffering into cameo-like delicacy, and the silken hair fell in soft, waving masses about the spiritual little face. By his side nestled a tiny dog, with satin ears and paws fringed as with ravelled silk.

Telford paid heed to nothing, not even the frightened child. He was as one distraught.

"Min," he wailed again, striving tremblingly to feel her pulse while cold drops came out on his forehead.

Min's face was as pallid as marble, save for one heavy bruise across the cheek and a cruel cut at the edge of the dark hair, from which the blood trickled down on the pillow.

She opened her eyes wonderingly at his call, looking up with a dazed, appealing expression of pain and dread. A low moan broke from her white lips. Telford sprang to his feet in a tumult of quivering joy.

"Min, dear," he said gently, "you have been hurt—not seriously, I hope. I must leave you for a minute while I run for help—I will not be long."

"Come back," said Min in a low but distinct tone.

He paused impatiently.

"It is of no use to get help," Min went on calmly. "I'm dying—I know it. Oh, my God!"

She pressed her hand to her side and writhed. Telford turned desperately to the door. Min raised her arm.

"Come here," she said resolutely.

He obeyed mutely. She looked up at him with bright, unquailing eyes.

"Don't you go one step—don't leave me here to die alone. I'm past help—and I've something to say to you. I must say it and I haven't much time."

Telford hardly heeded her in his misery.

"Min, let me go for help—let me do something," he implored. "You must not die—you must not!"

Min had fallen back, gasping, on the blood-stained pillow.

He knelt beside her and put his arm about the poor, crushed body.

"I must hurry," she said faintly. "I can't die with it on my mind. Rose—it's all hers—all. There was a will—he made it—old Gran'ther Palmer. He always hated me. I found it before he died—and read it. He left everything to her—not a cent to me nor his son's child—we were to starve—beg. I was like a madwoman. When he died—I hid the will. I meant—to burn it—but I never could. It's tortured me—night and day—I've had no peace. You'll find it in a box—in my room. Tell her—tell Rose—how wicked I've been. And my boy—what will become of him? Rose hates him—she'll turn him out—or ill-treat him—"

Telford lifted his white, drawn face.

"I will take your child, Min. He shall be to me as my own son."

An expression of unspeakable relief came into the dying woman's face.

"It is good—of you. I can die—in peace—now. I'm glad to die—to get clear of it all. I'm tired—of living so. Perhaps—I'll have a chance—somewhere else. I've never—had any—here."

The dark eyes drooped—closed. Telford moaned shudderingly.

Once again Min opened her eyes and looked straight into his.

"If I had met you—long ago—you would have—loved me—and I would have been—a good woman. It is well for us—for you—that I am—dying. Your path will be clear—you will be good and successful—but you will always—remember me."

Telford bent and pressed his lips to Min's pain-blanched mouth.

"Do you think—we will—ever meet again?" she said faintly. "Out there—it's so dark—God can never—forgive me—I've been so—wicked."

"Min, the all-loving Father is more merciful than man. He will forgive you, if you ask Him, and you will wait for me till I come. I will stay here and do my duty—I will try hard—"

His voice broke. Min's great black eyes beamed out on him with passionate tenderness. The strong, deep, erring nature yielded at last. An exceeding bitter cry rose to her lips.

"Oh, God—forgive me—forgive me!"

And with the cry, the soul of poor suffering, sinning, sinned-against Min Palmer fled—who shall say whither? Who shall say that her remorseful cry was not heard, even at that late hour, by a Judge more merciful than her fellow creatures?

Telford still knelt on the bare floor, holding in his arms the dead form of the woman he loved—his, all his, in death, as she could never have been in life. Death had bridged the gulf between them.

The room was very silent. To Min's face had returned something of its girlhood's innocence. The hard, unlovely lines were all smoothed out. The little cripple crept timidly up to Telford, with the silky head of the dog pressed against his cheek. Telford gathered the distorted little body to his side and looked earnestly into the small face—Min's face, purified and spiritualized. He would have it near him always. He bent and reverently kissed the cold face, the closed eyelids and the blood-stained brow of the dead woman. Then he stood up.

"Come with me, dear," he said gently to the child.

The day after the funeral, Allan Telford sat in the study of his little manse among the encircling wintry hills. Close to the window sat Min's child, his small, beautiful face pressed against the panes, and the bright-eyed dog beside him.

Telford was writing in his journal.

"I shall stay here—close to her grave. I shall see it every time I look from my study window—every time I stand in my pulpit—every time I go in and out among my people. I begin to see wherein I have failed. I shall begin again patiently and humbly. I wrote today to decline the C—— church call. My heart and my work are here."

He closed the book and bowed his head on it. Outside the snow fell softly; he knew that it was wrapping that new-made grave on the cold, fir-sentinelled hillside with a stainless shroud of infinite purity and peace.

Miss Cordelia's Accommodation

"Poor little creatures!" said Miss Cordelia compassionately.

She meant the factory children. In her car ride from the school where she taught to the bridge that spanned the river between Pottstown, the sooty little manufacturing village on one side, and Point Pleasant, which was merely a hamlet, on the other, she had seen dozens of them, playing and quarrelling on the streets or peering wistfully out of dingy tenement windows.

"Tomorrow is Saturday," she reflected, "and they've no better place to play in than the back streets and yards. It's a shame. There's work for our philanthropists here, but they don't seem to see it. Well, I'm so sorry for them it hurts me to look at them, but I can't do anything."

Miss Cordelia sighed and then brightened up, because she realized that she was turning her back upon Pottstown for two blissful days and going to Point Pleasant, which had just one straggling, elm-shaded street hedging on old-fashioned gardens and cosy little houses and trailing off into the real country in a half-hour's walk.

Miss Cordelia lived alone in a tiny house at Point Pleasant. It was so tiny that you would have wondered how anyone could live in it.

"But it's plenty big for a little old maid like me," Miss Cordelia would have told you. "And it's my own—I'm queen there. There's solid comfort in having one spot for your own self. To be sure, if I had less land and more house it would be better."

Miss Cordelia always laughed here. It was one of her jokes. There was a four-acre field behind the house. Both had been left to her by an uncle. The field was of no use to Miss Cordelia; she didn't keep a cow and she hadn't time to make a garden. But she liked her field; when people asked her why she didn't sell it she said:

"I'm fond of it. I like to walk around in it when the grass grows long. And it may come in handy some time. Mother used to say if you kept anything seven years it would come to use. I've had my field a good bit longer than that, but maybe the time will come yet. Meanwhile I rejoice in the fact that I am a landed proprietor to the extent of four acres."

Miss Cordelia had thought of converting her field into a playground for the factory children and asking detachments of them over on Saturday afternoon. But she knew that her Point Pleasant neighbours would object to this, so that project was dropped.

When Miss Cordelia pushed open her little gate, hung crookedly in a very compact and prim spruce hedge, she stopped in amazement and said, "Well, for pity's sake!"

Cynthia Ann Flemming, who lived on the other side of the spruce hedge, now came hurrying over.

"Good evening, Cordelia. I have a letter that was left with me for you."

"But—that—horse," said Miss Cordelia, with a long breath between every word. "Where did he come from? Tied at my front door—and he's eaten the tops off every one of my geraniums! Where's his owner or rider or something?"

The horse in question was a mild-eyed, rather good-looking quadruped, tied by a halter to the elm at Miss Cordelia's door and contentedly munching a mouthful of geranium stalks. Cynthia Ann came through the hedge with the letter.

"Maybe this will explain," she said. "Same boy brought it as brought the horse—a little freckly chap mostly all grin and shirtsleeves. Said he was told to take the letter and horse to Miss Cordelia Herry, Elm Street, Point Pleasant, and he couldn't wait. So he tied the creature in there and left the letter with me. He came half an hour ago. Well, he has played havoc with your geraniums and no mistake."

Miss Cordelia opened and read her letter. When she finished it she looked at the curious Cynthia Ann solemnly.

"Well, if that isn't John Drew all over! I suspected he was at the bottom of it as soon as I laid my eyes on that animal. John Drew is a cousin of mine. He's been living out at Poplar Valley and he writes me that he has gone out west, and wants me to take 'old Nap.' I suppose that is the horse. He says that Nap is getting old and not much use for work and he couldn't bear the thought of shooting him or selling him to someone who might ill-treat him, so he wants me to take him and be kind to him for old times' sake. John and I were just like brother and sister when we were children. If this isn't like him nothing ever was. He was always doing odd things and thinking they were all right. And now he's off west and here is the horse. If it were a cat or a dog—but a horse!"

"Your four-acre field will come in handy now," said Cynthia Ann jestingly.

"So it will." Miss Cordelia spoke absently. "The very thing! Yes, I'll put him in there."

"But you don't really mean that you're going to keep the horse, are you?" protested Cynthia Ann. "Why, he is no good to you—and think of the expense of feeding him!"

"I'll keep him for a while," said Miss Cordelia briskly. "As you say, there is the four-acre field. It will keep him in eating for a while. I always knew that field had a mission. Poor John Drew! I'd like to oblige him for old times' sake, as he says, although this is as crazy as anything he ever did. But I have a plan. Meanwhile, I can't feed Nap on geraniums."

Miss Cordelia always adapted herself quickly and calmly to new circumstances. "It is never any use to get in a stew about things," she was wont to say. So now she untied Nap gingerly, with many rueful glances at her geraniums, and led him away to the field behind the house, where she tied him safely to a post with such an abundance of knots that there was small fear of his getting away.

When the mystified Cynthia Ann had returned home Miss Cordelia set about getting her tea and thinking over the plan that had come to her concerning her white elephant.

"I can keep him for the summer," she said. "I'll have to dispose of him in the fall for I've no place to keep him in, and anyway I couldn't afford to feed him. I'll see if I can borrow Mr. Griggs's express wagon for Saturday afternoons, and if I can those poor factory children in my grade shall have a weekly treat or my name is not Cordelia Herry. I'm not so sure but that John Drew has done a good thing after all. Poor John! He always did take things so for granted."

All the point pleasant people soon knew about Miss Cordelia's questionable windfall, and she was overwhelmed with advice and suggestions. She listened to all tranquilly and then placidly followed her own way. Mr. Griggs was very obliging in regard to his old express wagon, and the next Saturday Point Pleasant was treated to a mild sensation—nothing less than Miss Cordelia rattling through the village, enthroned on the high seat of Mr. Griggs's yellow express wagon, drawn by old Nap who, after a week of browsing idleness in the four-acre field, was quite frisky and went at a decided amble down Elm Street and across the bridge. The long wagon had been filled up with board seats, and when Miss Cordelia came back over the bridge the boards were crowded with factory children—pale-faced little creatures whose eyes were aglow with pleasure at this unexpected outing.

Miss Cordelia drove straight out to the big pine-clad hills of Deepdale, six miles from Pottstown. Then she tied Nap in a convenient lane and turned the children loose to revel in the woods and fields. How they did enjoy themselves! And how Miss Cordelia enjoyed seeing them enjoy themselves!

When dinner time came she gathered them all around her and went to the wagon. In it she had a basket of bread and butter.

"I can't afford anything more," she told Cynthia Ann, "but they must have something to stay their little stomachs. And I can get some water at a farmhouse."

Miss Cordelia had had her eye on a certain farmhouse all the morning. She did not know anything about the people who lived there, but she liked the looks of the place. It was a big, white, green-shuttered house, throned in wide-spreading orchards, with a green sweep of velvety lawn in front.

To this Miss Cordelia took her way, surrounded by her small passengers, and they all trooped into the great farmhouse yard just as a big man stepped out of a nearby barn. As he approached, Miss Cordelia thought she had never seen anybody so much like an incarnate smile before. Smiles of all kinds seemed literally to riot over his ruddy face and in and out of his eyes and around the corners of his mouth.

"Well, well, well!" he said, when he came near enough to be heard. "Is this a runaway school, ma'am?"

"I'm the runaway schoolma'am," responded Miss Cordelia with a twinkle. "And these are a lot of factory children I've brought out for a Saturday treat. I thought I might get some water from your well, and maybe you will lend us a tin dipper or two?"

"Water? Tut, tut!" said the big man, with three distinct smiles on his face. "Milk's the thing, ma'am—milk. I'll tell my housekeeper to bring some out. And all of you come over to the lawn and make yourselves at home. Bless you, ma'am, I'm fond of children. My name is Smiles, ma'am—Abraham Smiles."

"It suits you," said Miss Cordelia emphatically, before she thought, and then blushed rosy-red over her bluntness.

Mr. Smiles laughed. "Yes, I guess I always have an everlasting grin on. Had to live up to my name, you see, in spite of my naturally cantankerous disposition; But come this way, ma'am, I can see the hunger sticking out of those youngsters' eyes. We'll have a sort of impromptu picnic here and now, I'll tell my housekeeper to send out some jam too."

While the children devoured their lunch Miss Cordelia found herself telling Mr. Smiles all about old Nap and her little project.

"I'm going to bring out a load every fine Saturday all summer," she said. "It's all I can do. They enjoy it so, the little creatures. It's terrible to think how cramped their lives are. They just exist in soot. Some of them here never saw green fields before today."

Mr. Smiles listened and beamed and twinkled until Miss Cordelia felt almost as dazzled as if she were looking at the sun.

"Look here, ma'am, I like this plan of yours and I want to have a hand in helping it along. Bring your loads of children out here every Saturday, right here to Beechwood Farm, and turn them loose in my beech woods and upland pastures. I'll put up some swings for them and have some games, and I'll provide the refreshments also. Trouble, ma'am? No, trouble and I ain't on speaking terms. It'll be a pleasure, ma'am. I'm fond of children even if I am a grumpy cross-grained old bachelor. If you can give up your own holiday to give them a good time, surely I can do something too."

When Miss Cordelia and her brood of tired, happy little lads and lasses ambled back to town in the golden dusk she felt that the expedition had been an emphatic success. Even old Nap seemed to jog along eye-deep in satisfaction. Probably he was ruminating on the glorious afternoon he had spent in Mr. Smiles's clover pasture.

Every fine Saturday that summer Miss Cordelia took some of the factory children to the country. The Point Pleasant people nicknamed her equipage "Miss Cordelia's accommodation," and it became a mild standing joke.

As for Mr. Smiles, he proved a valuable assistant. Like Miss Cordelia, he gave his Saturdays over to the children, and high weekly revel was held at Beechwood Farm.

But when the big bronze and golden leaves began to fall in the beech woods, Miss Cordelia sorrowfully realized that the summer was over and that the weekly outings which she had enjoyed as much as the children must soon be discontinued.

"I feel so sorry," she told Mr. Smiles, "but it can't be helped. It will soon be too cold for our jaunts and of course I can't keep Nap through the winter. I hate to part with him, I've grown so fond of him, but I must."

She looked regretfully at Nap, who was nibbling Mr. Smiles's clover aftermath. He was sleek and glossy. It had been the golden summer of Nap's life.

Mr. Smiles coughed in an embarrassed fashion. Miss Cordelia looked at him and was amazed to see that not a smile was on or about his face. He looked absurdly serious.

"I want to buy Nap," he said in a sepulchral tone, "but that is not the only thing I want. I want you too, ma'am. I'm tired of being a cross old bachelor. I think I'd like to be a cross old husband, for a change. Do you think you could put up with me in that capacity, Miss Cordelia, my dear?"

Miss Cordelia gave a half gasp and then she had to laugh. "Oh, Mr. Smiles, I'll agree to anything if you'll only smile again. It seems unnatural to see you look so solemn."

The smiles at once broke loose and revelled over her wooer's face.

"Then you will come?" he said eagerly.

Half an hour later they had their plans made. At New Year's Miss Cordelia was to leave her school and sooty Pottstown and come to be mistress of Beechwood Farm.

"And look here," said Mr. Smiles. "Every fine Saturday you shall have a big, roomy sleigh and Nap, and drive into town for some children and bring them out here for their weekly treat as usual. The house is large enough to hold them, goodness knows, and if it isn't there are the barns for the overflow. This is going to be our particular pet charity all our lives, ma'am—I mean Cordelia, my dear."

"Blessings on old Nap," said Miss Cordelia with a happy light in her eyes.

"He shall live in clover for the rest of his days," added Mr. Smiles smilingly.

Ned's Stroke of Business

"Jump in, Ned; I can give you a lift if you're going my way." Mr. Rogers reined up his prancing grey horse, and Ned Allen sprang lightly into the comfortable cutter. The next minute they were flying down the long, glistening road, rosy-white in the sunset splendour. The first snow of the season had come, and the sleighing was, as Ned said, "dandy."

"Going over to Windsor, I suppose," said Mr. Rogers, with a glance at the skates that were hanging over Ned's shoulder.

"Yes, sir; all the Carleton boys are going over tonight. The moon is out, and the ice is good. We have to go in a body, or the Windsor fellows won't leave us alone. There's safety in numbers."

"Pretty hard lines when boys have to go six miles for a skate," commented Mr. Rogers.

"Well, it's that or nothing," laughed Ned. "There isn't a saucerful of ice any nearer, except that small pond in Old Dutcher's field, behind his barn. And you know Old Dutcher won't allow a boy to set foot there. He says they would knock down his fences climbing over them, and like as not set fire to his barn."

"Old Dutcher was always a crank," said Mr. Rogers, "and doubtless will be to the end. By the way, I heard a rumour to the effect that you are soon going to take a course at the business college in Trenton. I hope it's true."

Ned's frank face clouded over. "I'm afraid not, sir. The truth is, I guess Mother can't afford it. Of course, Aunt Ella has very kindly offered to board me free for the term, but fees, books, and so on would require at least fifty dollars. I don't expect to go."

"That's a pity. Can't you earn the necessary money yourself?"

Ned shook his head. "Not much chance for that in Carleton, Mr. Rogers. I've cudgelled my brains for the past month trying to think of some way, but in vain. Well, here is the crossroad, so I must get off. Thank you for the drive, sir."

"Keep on thinking, Ned," advised Mr. Rogers, as the lad jumped out. "Perhaps you'll hit on some plan yet to earn that money, and if you do—well, it will prove that you have good stuff in you."

"I think it would," laughed Ned to himself, as he trudged away. "A quiet little farming village in winter isn't exactly a promising field for financial operations."

At Winterby Corners Ned found a crowd of boys waiting for him, and soon paired off with his chum, Jim Slocum. Jim, as usual, was grumbling because they had to go all the way to Windsor to skate.

"Like as not we'll get into a free fight with the Windsorites when we get there, and be chevied off the ice," he complained.

The rivalry which existed between the Carleton and the Windsor boys was bitter and of long standing.

"We ought to be able to hold our own tonight," said Ned. "There'll be thirty of us there."

"If we could only get Old Dutcher to let us skate on his pond!" said Jim. "It wouldn't hurt his old pond! And the ice is always splendid on it. I'd give a lot if we could only go there."

Ned was silent. A sudden idea had come to him. He wondered if it were feasible. "Anyhow, I'll try it," he said to himself. "I'll interview Old Dutcher tomorrow."

The skating that night was not particularly successful. The small pond at Windsor was crowded, the Windsor boys being out in force and, although no positive disturbance arose, they contrived to make matters unpleasant for the Carletonites, who tramped moodily homeward in no very good humour, most of them declaring that, skating or no skating, they would not go to Windsor again.

The next day Ned Allen went down to see Mr. Dutcher, or Old Dutcher, as he was universally called in Carleton. Ned did not exactly look forward to the interview with pleasure. Old Dutcher was a crank—there was no getting around that fact. He had "good days" occasionally when, for him, he was fairly affable, but they were few and far between, and Ned had no reason to hope that this would be one. Old Dutcher was unmarried, and his widowed sister kept house for him. This poor lady had a decidedly lonely life of it, for Old Dutcher studiously discouraged visitors. His passion for solitude was surpassed only by his eagerness to make and save money. Although he was well-to-do, he would wrangle over a cent, and was the terror of all who had ever had dealings with him.

Fortunately for Ned and his project, this did turn out to be one of Old Dutcher's good days. He had just concluded an advantageous bargain with a Windsor cattle-dealer, and hence he received Ned with what, for Old Dutcher, might be called absolute cordiality. Besides, although Old Dutcher disliked all boys on principle, he disliked Ned less than the rest because the boy had always treated him respectfully and had never played any tricks on him on Hallowe'en or April Fool's Day.

"I've come down to see you on a little matter of business, Mr. Dutcher," said Ned, boldly and promptly. It never did to beat about the bush with Old Dutcher; you had to come straight to the point. "I want to know if you will rent your pond behind the barn to me for a skating-rink."

Old Dutcher's aspect was certainly not encouraging. "No, I won't. You ought to know that. I never allow anyone to skate there. I ain't going to have a parcel of whooping, yelling youngsters tearing over my fences, disturbing my sleep at nights, and like as not setting fire to my barns. No, sir! I ain't going to rent that pond for no skating-rink."

Ned smothered a smile. "Just wait a moment, Mr. Dutcher," he said respectfully. "I want you to hear my proposition before you refuse definitely. First, I'll give you ten dollars for the rent of the pond; then I'll see that there will be no running over your fields and climbing your fences, no lighting of fire or matches about it, and no 'whooping and yelling' at nights. My rink will be open only from two to six in the afternoon and from seven to ten in the evening. During that time I shall always be at the pond to keep everything in order. The skaters will come and go by the lane leading from the barn to the road. I think that if you agree to my proposition, Mr. Dutcher, you will not regret it."

"What's to prevent my running such a rink myself?" asked Old Dutcher gruffly.

"It wouldn't pay you, Mr. Dutcher," answered Ned promptly. "The Carleton boys wouldn't patronize a rink run by you."

Old Dutcher's eyes twinkled. It did not displease him to know that the Carleton boys hated him. In fact, it seemed as if he rather liked it.

"Besides," went on Ned, "you couldn't afford the time. You couldn't be on the pond for eight hours a day and until ten o'clock at night. I can, as I've nothing else to do just now. If I had, I wouldn't have to be trying to make money by a skating-rink."

Old Dutcher scowled. Ten dollars was ten dollars and, as Ned had said, he knew very well that he could not run a rink by himself. "Well," he said, half reluctantly, "I suppose I'll let you go ahead. Only remember I'll hold you responsible if anything happens."

Ned went home in high spirits. By the next day he had placards out in conspicuous places—on the schoolhouse, at the forge, at Mr. Rogers's store, and at Winterby Corners—announcing that he had rented Mr. Dutcher's pond for a skating-rink, and that tickets for the same at twenty-five cents a week for each skater could be had upon application to him.

Ned was not long left in doubt as to the success of his enterprise. It was popular from the start. There were about fifty boys in Carleton and Winterby, and they all patronized the rink freely. At first Ned had some trouble with two or three rowdies, who tried to evade his rules. He was backed up, however, by Old Dutcher's reputation and by the public opinion of the other boys, as well as by his own undoubted muscle, and soon had everything going smoothly. The rink flourished amain, and everybody, even Old Dutcher, was highly pleased.

At the end of the season Ned paid Old Dutcher his ten dollars, and had plenty left to pay for books and tuition at the business college in Trenton. On the eve of his departure Mr. Rogers, who had kept a keen eye on Ned's enterprise, again picked him up on the road.

"So you found a way after all, Ned," he said genially. "I had an idea you would. My bookkeeper will be leaving me about the time you will be through at the college. I will be wanting in his place a young man with a good nose for business, and I rather think that you will be that young man. What do you say?"

"Thank you, sir," stammered Ned, scarcely believing his ears. A position in Mr. Rogers's store meant good salary and promotion. He had never dared to hope for such good fortune. "If you—think I can give satisfaction—"

"You manipulated Old Dutcher, and you've earned enough in a very slow-going place to put you through your business-college term, so I am sure you are the man I'm looking for. I believe in helping those who have 'gumption' enough to help themselves, so we'll call it a bargain, Ned."

Our Runaway Kite

Of course there was nobody for us to play with on the Big Half Moon, but then, as Claude says, you can't have everything. We just had to make the most of each other, and we did.

The Big Half Moon is miles from anywhere, except the Little Half Moon. But nobody lives there, so that doesn't count.

We live on the Big Half Moon. "We" are Father and Claude and I and Aunt Esther and Mimi and Dick. It used to be only Father and Claude and I. It is all on account of the kite that there are more of us. This is what I want to tell you about.

Father is the keeper of the Big Half Moon lighthouse. He has always been the keeper ever since I can remember, although that isn't very long. I am only eleven years old. Claude is twelve.

In winter, when the harbour is frozen over, there isn't any need of a light on the Big Half Moon, and we all move over to the mainland, and Claude and Mimi and Dick and I go to school. But as soon as spring comes, back we sail to our own dear island, so glad that we don't know what to do with ourselves.

The funny part used to be that people always pitied us when the time came for us to return. They said we must be so lonesome over there, with no other children near us, and not even a woman to look after us.

Why, Claude and I were never lonesome. There was always so much to do, and Claude is splendid at making believe. He makes the very best pirate chief I ever saw. Dick is pretty good, but he can never roar out his orders in the blood-curdling tones that Claude can.

Of course Claude and I would have liked to have someone to play with us, because it is hard to run pirate caves and things like that with only two. But we used to quarrel a good deal with the mainland children in winter, so perhaps it was just as well that there were none of them on the Big Half Moon. Claude and I never quarrelled. We used to argue sometimes and get excited, but that was as far as it ever went. When I saw Claude getting too excited I gave in to him. He is a boy, you know, and they have to be humoured; they are not like girls.

As for having a woman to look after us, I thought that just too silly, and so did Claude. What did we need with a woman when we had Father? He could cook all we wanted to eat and make molasses taffy that was just like a dream. He kept our clothes all mended, and everything about the lighthouse was neat as wax. Of course I helped him lots. I like pottering round.

He used to hear our lessons and tell us splendid stories and saw that we always said our prayers. Claude and I wouldn't have done anything to make him feel bad for the world. Father is just lovely.

To be sure, he didn't seem to have any relations except us. This used to puzzle Claude and me. Everybody on the mainland had relations; why hadn't we? Was it because we lived on an island? We thought it would be so jolly to have an uncle and aunt and some cousins. Once we asked Father about it, but he looked so sorrowful all of a sudden that we wished we hadn't. He said it was all his fault. I did-didn't see how that could be, but I never said anything more about it to Father. Still, I did wish we had some relations.

It is always lovely out here on the Big Half Moon in summer. When it is fine the harbour is blue and calm, with little winds and ripples purring over it, and the mainland shores look like long blue lands where fairies dwell. Away out over the bar, where the big ships go, it is always hazy and pearl-tinted, like the inside of the mussel shells. Claude says he is going to sail out there when he grows up. I would like to too, but Claude says I can't because I'm a girl. It is dreadfully inconvenient to be a girl at times.

When it storms it is grand to see the great waves come crashing up against the Big Half Moon as if they meant to swallow it right down. You can't see the Little Half Moon at all then; it is hidden by the mist and spume.

We had our pirate cave away up among the rocks, where we kept an old pistol with the lock broken, a rusty cutlass, a pair of knee boots, and Claude's jute beard and wig. Down on the shore, around one of the horns of the Half Moon, was the Mermaid's Pool, where we sailed our toy boats and watched for sea kelpies. We never saw any. Dick says there is no such thing as a kelpy. But then Dick has no imagination. It is no argument against a thing that you've never seen it. I have never seen the pyramids, either, but I know that there are pyramids.

Every summer we had some hobby. The last summer before Dick and Mimi came we were crazy about kites. A winter boy on the mainland showed Claude how to make them, and when we went back to the Big Half Moon we made kites galore. Even pirating wasn't such good fun. Claude would go around to the other side of the Big Half Moon and we would play shipwrecked mariners signalling to each other with kites. Oh, it was very exciting.

We had one kite that was a dandy. It was as big as we could make it and covered with lovely red paper; we had pasted gold tinsel stars all over it and written our names out in full on it—Claude Martin Leete and Philippa Brewster Leete, Big Half Moon Lighthouse. That kite had the most magnificent tail, too.

It used to scare the gulls nearly to death when we sent up our kites. They didn't know what to make of them. And the Big Half Moon is such a place for gulls—there are hundreds of them here.

One day there was a grand wind for kite-flying, and Claude and I were having a splendid time. We used our smaller kites for signalling, and when we got tired of that Claude sent me to the house for the big one. I'm sure I don't know how it happened, but when I was coming back over the rocks I tripped and fell, and my elbow went clear through that lovely kite. You would never have believed that one small elbow could make such a big hole. Claude said it was just like a girl to fall and stick her elbow through a kite, but I don't see why it should be any more like a girl than a boy. Do you?

We had to hurry to fix the kite if we wanted to send it up before the wind fell, so we rushed into the lighthouse to get some paper. We knew there was no more red paper, and the looks of the kite were spoiled, anyhow, so we just took the first thing that came handy—an old letter that was lying on the bookcase in the sitting-room. I suppose we shouldn't have taken it, although, as matters turned out, it was the best thing we could have done; but Father was away to the mainland to buy things, and we never thought it could make any difference about an old yellow letter. It was one Father had taken from a drawer in the bookcase which he had cleaned out the night before. We patched the kite up with the letter, a sheet on each side, and dried it by the fire. Then we started out, and up went the kite like a bird. The wind was glorious, and it soared and strained like something alive. All at once—snap! And there was Claude, standing with a bit of cord in his hand, looking as foolish as a flatfish, and our kite sailing along at a fearful rate of speed over to the mainland.

I might have said to Claude, So like a boy! but I didn't. Instead, I sympathized with him, and pointed out that it really didn't matter because I had spoiled it by jabbing my elbow through it. By this time the kite was out of sight, and we never expected to see or hear of it again.

A month later a letter came to the Big Half Moon for Father. Jake Wiggins brought it over in his sloop. Father went off by himself to read it, and such a queer-looking face as he had when he came back! His eyes looked as if he had been crying, but that couldn't be, I suppose, because Claude says men never cry. Anyhow, his face was all glad and soft and smiley.

"Do you two young pirates and freebooters want to know what has become of your kite?" he said.

Then he sat down beside us on the rocks at the Mermaid's Pool and told us the whole story, and read his letter to us. It was the most amazing thing.

It seems Father had had relations after all—a brother and a sister in particular. But when he was a young man he quarrelled with his brother, who didn't treat him very well—but he's been dead for years, so I won't say a word against him—and had gone away from home. He never went back, and he never even let them know he was living.

Father says that this was very wrong of him, and I suppose it was, since he says so; but I don't see how Father could do anything wrong.

Anyway, he had a sister Esther whom he loved very much; but he felt bitter against her too, because he thought she took his brother's part too much. So, though a letter of hers, asking him to go back, did reach him, he never answered it, and he never heard anything more. Years afterward he felt sorry and went back, but his brother was dead and his sister had gone away, and he couldn't find out a single thing about her.

So much for that; and now about the kite. The letter Father had just received was from his sister, our Aunt Esther and the mother of Dick and Mimi. She was living at a place hundreds of miles inland. Her husband was dead and, as we found out later, although she did not say a word about it in the letter, she was very poor. One day when Dick and Mimi were out in the woods looking for botany specimens they saw something funny in the top of a tree. Dick climbed up and got it. It was a big red kite with a patch on each side and names written on it. They carried it home to their mother. Dick has since told us that she turned as pale as the dead when she saw our names on it. You see, Philippa was her mother's name and Claude was her father's. And when she read the letter that was pasted over the hole in the kite she knew who we must be, for it was the very letter she had written to her brother so long ago. So she sat right down and wrote again, and this was the letter Jake Wiggins brought to the Big Half Moon. It was a beautiful letter. I loved Aunt Esther before I ever saw her, just from that letter.

Next day Father got Jake to take his place for a few days, and he left Claude and me over on the mainland while he went to see Aunt Esther. When he came back he brought Aunt Esther and Dick and Mimi with him, and they have been here ever since.

You don't know how splendid it is! Aunt Esther is such a dear, and Dick and Mimi are too jolly for words. They love the Big Half Moon as well as Claude and I do, and Dick makes a perfectly elegant shipwrecked mariner.

But the best of it all is that we have relations now!

The Bride Roses

Miss Corona awoke that June morning with a sigh, the cause of which she was at first too sleepy to understand. Then it all came over her with a little sickening rush; she had fallen asleep with tear-wet lashes the night before on account of it.

This was Juliet Gordon's wedding day, and she, Miss Corona, could not go to the wedding and was not even invited, all because of the Quarrel, a generation old, and so chronic and bitter and terrible that it always presented itself to Miss Corona's mental vision as spelled with a capital. Well might Miss Corona hate it. It had shut her up into a lonely life for long years. Juliet Gordon and Juliet's father, Meredith Gordon, were the only relations Miss Corona had in the world, and the old family feud divided them by a gulf which now seemed impassable.

Miss Corona turned over on her pillows, lifted one corner of the white window-blind and peeped out. Below her a river of early sunshine was flowing through the garden, and the far-away slopes were translucent green in their splendour of young day, with gauzy, uncertain mists lingering, spiritlike, in their intervales. A bird, his sleek plumage iridescent in the sunlight, was perched on the big chestnut bough that ran squarely across the window, singing as if his heart would burst with melody and the joy of his tiny life. No bride could have wished anything fairer for her day of days, and Miss Corona dropped back on her pillows with another gentle sigh.

"I'm so glad that the dear child has a fine day to be married," she said.

Juliet Gordon was always "dear child" to Miss Corona, although the two had never spoken to each other in their lives.

Miss Corona was a brisk and early riser as a rule, with a genuine horror of lazy people who lay late abed or took over-long to get their eyes well opened, but this morning she made no hurry about rising, even though scurrying footsteps, banging doors, and over-loud tinkling of dishes in the room below betokened that Charlotta was already up and about. And Charlotta, as poor Miss Corona knew only too well, was fatally sure to do something unfortunate if she were not under some careful, overseeing eye. To be sure, Charlotta's intentions were always good.

But Miss Corona was not thinking about Charlotta this morning, and she felt so strong a distaste for her lonely, purposeless life that she was in no haste to go forth to meet another day of it.

Miss Corona felt just the least little bit tired of living, although she feared it was very wicked of her to feel so. She lay there listlessly for half an hour longer, looking through a mist of tears at the portrait of her stern old father hanging on the wall at the foot of the bed, and thinking over the Quarrel.

It had happened thirty years ago, when Miss Corona had been a girl of twenty, living alone with her father at the old Gordon homestead on the hill, with the big black spruce grove behind it on the north and far-reaching slopes of green fields before it on the south. Down in the little northern valley below the spruce grove lived her uncle, Alexis Gordon. His son, Meredith, had seemed to Corona as her own brother. The mothers of both were dead; neither had any other brother or sister. The two children had grown up together, playmates and devoted friends. There had never been any sentiment or lovemaking between them to mar a perfect comradeship. They were only the best of friends, whatever plans the fathers might have cherished for the union of their estates and children, putting the property consideration first, as the Gordons were always prone to do.

But, if Roderick and Alexis Gordon had any such plans, all went by the board when they quarreled. Corona shivered yet over the bitterness of that time. The Gordons never did anything half-heartedly. The strife between the two brothers was determined and irreconcilable.

Corona's father forbade her to speak to her uncle and cousin or to hold any communication with them. Corona wept and obeyed him. She had always obeyed her father; it had never entered into her mind to do anything else. Meredith had resented her attitude hotly, and from that day they had never spoken or met, while the years came and went, each making a little wider and more hopeless the gulf of coldness and anger and distrust.

Ten years later Roderick Gordon died, and in five months Alexis Gordon followed him to the grave. The two brothers who had hated each other so unyieldingly in life slept very peaceably side by side in the old Gordon plot of the country graveyard, but their rancour still served to embitter the lives of their descendants.

Corona, with a half-guilty sense of disloyalty to her father, hoped that she and Meredith might now be friends again. He was married, and had one little daughter. In her new and intolerable loneliness Corona's heart yearned after her own people. But she was too timid to make any advances, and Meredith never made any. Corona believed that he hated her, and let slip her last fluttering hope that the old breach would ever be healed.

"Oh, dear! oh, dear!" she sobbed softly into her pillows. It seemed a terrible thing to her that one of her race and kin was to be married and she could not be present at the ceremony, she who had never seen a Gordon bride.

When Miss Corona went downstairs at last, she found Charlotta sobbing in the kitchen porch. The small handmaiden was doubled up on the floor, with her face muffled in her gingham apron and her long braids of red hair hanging with limp straightness down her back. When Charlotta was in good spirits, they always hung perkily over each shoulder, tied up with enormous bows of sky-blue ribbon.

"What have you done this time?" asked Miss Corona, without the slightest intention of being humorous or sarcastic.

"I've—I've bruk your green and yaller bowl," sniffed Charlotta. "Didn't mean to, Miss C'rona. It jest slipped out so fashion 'fore I c'd grab holt on it. And it's bruk into forty millyun pieces. Ain't I the onluckiest girl?"

"You certainly are," sighed Miss Corona. At any other time she would have been filled with dismay over the untoward fate of her green and yellow bowl, which had belonged to her great-grandmother and had stood on the hall table to hold flowers as long as she could remember. But just now her heart was so sore over the Quarrel that there was no room for other regrets. "Well, well, crying won't mend it. I suppose it is a judgment on me for staying abed so late. Go and sweep up the pieces, and do try and be a little more careful, Charlotte."

"Yes'm," said Charlotta meekly. She dared not resent being called Charlotte just then. "And I'll tell you what I'll do, ma'am, to make up, I'll go and weed the garden. Yes'm, I'll do it beautiful."

"And pull up more flowers than weeds," Miss Corona reflected mournfully. But it did not matter; nothing mattered. She saw Charlotta sally forth into the garden with a determined, do-or-die expression surmounting her freckles, without feeling interest enough to go and make sure that she did not root out all the late asters in her tardy and wilfully postponed warfare on weeds.

This mood lasted until the afternoon. Then Miss Corona, whose heart and thoughts were still down in the festive house in the valley, roused herself enough to go out and see what Charlotta was doing. After finding out, she wandered idly about the rambling, old-fashioned place, which was full of nooks and surprises. At every turn you might stumble on some clump or tangle of sweetness, showering elusive fragrance on the air, that you would never have suspected. Nothing in the garden was planted quite where it should be, yet withal it was the most delightful spot imaginable.

Miss Corona pushed her way into the cherry-tree copse, and followed a tiny, overgrown path to a sunshiny corner beyond. She had not been there since last summer; the little path was getting almost impassable. When she emerged from the cherry trees, somewhat rumpled and pulled about in hair and attire, but attended, as if by a benediction, by the aromatic breath of the mint she had trodden on, she gave a little cry and stood quite still, gazing at the rosebush that grew in the corner. It was so large and woody that it seemed more like a tree than a bush, and it was snowed over with a splendour of large, pure white roses.

"Dear life," whispered Miss Corona tremulously, as she tiptoed towards it. "The bride roses have bloomed again! How very strange! Why, there has not been a rose on that tree for twenty years."

The rosebush had been planted there by Corona's great-grandmother, the lady of the green and yellow bowl. It was a new variety, brought out from Scotland by Mary Gordon, and it bore large white roses which three generations of Gordon brides had worn on their wedding day. It had come to be a family tradition among the Gordons that no luck would attend the bride who did not carry a white rose from Mary Gordon's rose-tree.

Long years ago the tree had given up blooming, nor could all the pruning and care given it coax a single blossom from it. Miss Corona, tinctured with the superstition apt to wait on a lonely womanhood, believed in her heart that the rosebush had a secret sympathy with the fortunes of the Gordon women. She, the last of them on the old homestead, would never need the bride roses. Wherefore, then, should the old tree bloom? And now, after all these years, it had flung all its long-hoarded sweetness into blossom again. Miss Corona thrilled at the thought. The rosebush had bloomed again for a Gordon bride, but Miss Corona was sure there was another meaning in it too; she believed it foretokened some change in her own life, some rejuvenescence of love and beauty like to that of the ancient rose-tree. She bent over its foam of loveliness almost reverently.

"They have bloomed for Juliet's wedding," she murmured. "A Gordon bride must wear the bride roses, indeed she must. And this—why, it is almost a miracle."

She ran, light-footedly as a girl, to the house for scissors and a basket. She would send Juliet Gordon the bride roses. Her cheeks were pink from excitement as she snipped them off. How lovely they were! How very large and fragrant! It was as if all the grace and perfume and beauty and glory of those twenty lost summers were found here at once in them. When Miss Corona had them ready, she went to the door and called, "Charlotte! Charlotte!"

Now Charlotta, having atoned to her conscience for the destruction of the green and yellow bowl by faithfully weeding the garden, a task which she hated above all else, was singing a hymn among the sweet peas, and her red braids were over her shoulders. This ought to have warned Miss Corona, but Miss Corona was thinking of other things, and kept on calling patiently, while Charlotta weeded away for dear life, and seemed smitten with treble deafness.

After a time Miss Corona remembered and sighed. She did hate to call the child that foolish name with its foreign sound. Just as if plain "Charlotte" were not good enough for her, and much more suitable to "Smith" too! Ordinarily Miss Corona would not have given in. But the case was urgent; she could not stand upon her dignity just now.

"Charlotta!" she called entreatingly.

Instantly Charlotta flew to the garden gate and raced up to the door.

"Yes'm," she said meekly. "You want me, Miss C'rona?"

"Take this box down to Miss Juliet Gordon, and ask that it be given to her at once," said Miss Corona, "Don't loiter, Charlotta. Don't stop to pick gum in the grove, or eat sours in the dike, or poke sticks through the bridge, or—"

But Charlotta had gone.

Down in the valley, the other Gordon house was in a hum of excitement. Upstairs Juliet had gone to her invalid mother's room to show herself in her wedding dress to the pale little lady lying on the sofa. She was a tall, stately young girl with the dark grey Gordon eyes and the pure creaminess of colouring, flawless as a lily petal. Her face was a very sweet one, and the simple white dress she wore became her dainty, flowerlike beauty as nothing elaborate could have done.

"I'm not going to put on my veil until the last moment," she said laughingly. "I would feel married right away if I did. And oh, Mother dear, isn't it too bad? My roses haven't come. Father is back from the station, and they were not there. I am so disappointed. Romney ordered pure white roses because I said a Gordon bride must carry nothing else. Come in"—as a knock sounded at the door.

Laura Burton, Juliet's cousin and bridesmaid, entered with a box.

"Juliet dear, the funniest little red-headed girl with the most enormous freckles has just brought this for you. I haven't an idea where she came from; she looked like a messenger from pixy-land."

Juliet opened the box and gave a cry.

"Oh, Mother, look—look! What perfect roses! Who could have sent them? Oh, here's a note from—from—why, Mother, it's from Cousin Corona."

> "My dear child," ran the letter in Miss Corona's fine, old-fashioned script. "I am sending you the Gordon bride roses. The rose-tree has bloomed for the first time in twenty years, my dear, and it must surely be in honour of your wedding day. I hope you will wear them for, although I have never known you, I love you very much. I was once a dear friend of your father's. Tell him to let you wear the roses I send for old times' sake. I wish you every happiness, my dear.
>
> "Your affectionate cousin,
> "Corona Gordon."

"Oh, how sweet and lovely of her!" said Juliet gently, as she laid the letter down. "And to think she was not even invited! I wanted to send her an invitation, but Father said it would be better not to—she was so hard and bitter against us that she would probably regard it as an insult."

"He must have been mistaken about her attitude," said Mrs. Gordon. "It certainly is a great pity she was not invited, but it is too late now. An invitation sent two hours before the ceremony would be an insult indeed."

"Not if the bride herself took it!" exclaimed Juliet impulsively. "I'll go myself to Cousin Corona, and ask her to come to my wedding."

"Go yourself! Child, you can't do such a thing! In that dress...."

"Go I must, Momsie. Why, it's only a three minutes' walk. I'll go up the hill by the old field-path, and no one will see me. Oh, don't say a word—there, I'm gone!"

"That child!" sighed the mother protestingly, as she heard Juliet's flying feet on the stairs. "What a thing for a bride to do!"

Juliet, with her white silken skirts caught up above grasses and dust, ran light-footedly through the green lowland fields and up the hill, treading for the first time the faint old field-path between the two homes, so long disused that it was now barely visible in its fringing grasses and star-dust of buttercups. Where it ran into the spruce grove was a tiny gate which Miss Corona had always kept in good repair, albeit it was never used. Juliet pushed up the rusty hasp and ran through.

Miss Corona was sitting alone in her shadowy parlour, hanging over a few of the bride roses with falling tears, when something tall and beautiful and white, came in like a blessing and knelt by her chair.

"Cousin Corona," said a somewhat breathless bride, "I have come to thank you for your roses and ask you to forgive us all for the old quarrel."

"Dear child," said Miss Corona out of her amazement, "there is nothing to forgive. I've loved you all and longed for you. Dear child, you have brought me great happiness."

"And you must come to my wedding," cried Juliet. "Oh, you must—or I shall think you have not really forgiven us. You would never refuse the request of a bride, Cousin Corona. We are queens on our wedding day, you know."

"Oh, it's not that, dear child—but I'm not dressed—I—"

"I'll help you dress. And I won't go back without you. The guests and the minister must wait if necessary—yes, even Romney must wait. Oh, I want you to meet Romney. Come, dear."

And Miss Corona went. Charlotta and the bride got her into her grey silk and did her hair, and in a very short time she and Juliet were hurrying down the old field-path. In the hollow Meredith Gordon met them.

"Cousin Meredith," said Miss Corona tremulously.

"Dear Corona."

He took both her hands in his, and kissed her heartily. "Forgive me for misunderstanding you so long. I thought you hated us all."

Turning to Juliet, he said with a fatherly smile,

"What a terrible girl it is for having its own way! Who ever heard of a Gordon bride doing such an unconventional thing? There, scamper off to the house before your guests come. Laura has made your roses up into what she calls 'a dream of a bouquet,' I'll take Cousin Corona up more leisurely."

"Oh, I knew that something beautiful was going to happen when the old rose-tree bloomed," murmured Miss Corona happily.

The Josephs' Christmas

The month before Christmas was always the most exciting and mysterious time in the Joseph household. Such scheming and planning, such putting of curly heads together in corners, such counting of small hoards, such hiding and smuggling of things out of sight, as went on among the little Josephs!

There were a good many of them, and very few of the pennies; hence the reason for so much contriving and consulting. From fourteen-year-old Mollie down to four-year-old Lennie there were eight small Josephs in all in the little log house on the prairie; so that when each little Joseph wanted to give a Christmas box to each of the other little Josephs, and something to Father and Mother Joseph besides, it is no wonder that they had to cudgel their small brains for ways and means thereof.

Father and Mother were always discreetly blind and silent through December. No questions were asked no matter what queer things were done. Many secret trips to the little store at the railway station two miles away were ignored, and no little Joseph was called to account because he or she looked terribly guilty when somebody suddenly came into the room. The air was simply charged with secrets.

Sister Mollie was the grand repository of these; all the little Josephs came to her for advice and assistance. It was Mollie who for troubled small brothers and sisters did such sums in division as this: How can I get a ten-cent present for Emmy and a fifteen-cent one for Jimmy out of eighteen cents? Or, how can seven sticks of candy be divided among eight people so that each shall have one? It was Mollie who advised regarding the purchase of ribbon and crepe paper. It was Mollie who put the finishing touches to most of the little gifts. In short, all through December Mollie was weighed down under an avalanche of responsibility. It speaks volumes for her sagacity and skill that she never got things mixed up or made any such terrible mistake as letting one little Joseph find out what another was going to give him. "Dead" secrecy was the keystone of all plans and confidences.

During this particular December the planning and contriving had been more difficult and the results less satisfactory than usual. The Josephs were poor at any time, but this winter they were poorer than ever. The crops had failed in the summer, and as a consequence the family were, as Jimmy said, "on short commons." But they made the brave best of their small resources, and on Christmas Eve every little Joseph went to bed with a clear conscience, for was there not on the corner table in the kitchen a small mountain of tiny—sometimes very tiny—gifts labelled with the names of recipients and givers, and worth their weight in gold if love and good wishes count for anything?

It was beginning to snow when the small small Josephs went to bed, and when the big small Josephs climbed the stairs it was snowing thickly. Mr. and Mrs. Joseph sat before the fire and listened to the wind howling about the house.

"I'm glad I'm not driving over the prairie tonight," said Mr. Joseph. "It's quite a storm. I hope it will be fine tomorrow, for the children's sake. They've set their hearts on having a sleigh ride, and it will be too bad if they can't have it when it's about all the Christmas they'll have this year. Mary, this is the first Christmas since we came west that we couldn't afford some little extras for them, even if 'twas only a box of nuts and candy."

Mrs. Joseph sighed over Jimmy's worn jacket which she was mending. Then she smiled.

"Never mind, John. Things will be better next Christmas, we'll hope. The children will not mind, bless their hearts. Look at all the little knick-knacks they've made for each other. Last week when I was over at Taunton, Mr. Fisher had his store all gayified up,' as Jim says, with Christmas presents. I did feel that I'd ask nothing better than to go in and buy all the lovely things I wanted, just for once, and give them to the children tomorrow morning. They've never had anything really nice for Christmas. But there! We've all got each other and good health and spirits, and a Christmas wouldn't be much without those if we had all the presents in the world."

Mr. Joseph nodded.

"That's so. I don't want to grumble; but I tell you I did want to get Maggie a 'real live doll,' as she calls it. She never has had anything but homemade dolls, and that small heart of hers is set on a real one. There was one at Fisher's store today—a big beauty with real hair, and eyes that opened and shut. Just fancy Maggie's face if she saw such a Christmas box as that tomorrow morning."

"Don't let's fancy it," laughed Mrs. Joseph, "it is only aggravating. Talking of candy reminds me that I made a big plateful of taffy for the children today. It's all the 'Christmassy' I could give them. I'll get it out and put it on the table along with the children's presents. That can't be someone at the door!"

"It is, though," said Mr. Joseph as he strode to the door and flung it open.

Two snowed-up figures were standing on the porch. As they stepped in, the Josephs recognized one of them as Mr. Ralston, a wealthy merchant in a small town fifteen miles away.

"Late hour for callers, isn't it?" said Mr. Ralston. "The fact is, our horse has about given out, and the storm is so bad that we can't proceed. This is my wife, and we are on our way to spend Christmas with my brother's family at Lindsay. Can you take us in for the night, Mr. Joseph?"

"Certainly, and welcome!" exclaimed Mr. Joseph heartily, "if you don't mind a shakedown by the kitchen fire for the night. My, Mrs. Ralston," as his wife helped her off with her things, "but you are snowed up! I'll see to putting your horse away, Mr. Ralston. This way, if you please."

When the two men came stamping into the house again Mrs. Ralston and Mrs. Joseph were sitting at the fire, the former with a steaming hot cup of tea in her hand. Mr. Ralston put the big basket he was carrying down on a bench in the corner.

"Thought I'd better bring our Christmas flummery in," he said. "You see, Mrs. Joseph, my brother has a big family, so we are taking them a lot of Santa Claus stuff. Mrs. Ralston packed this basket, and goodness knows what she put in it, but she half cleaned out my store. The eyes of the Lindsay youngsters will dance tomorrow—that is, if we ever get there."

Mrs. Joseph gave a little sigh in spite of herself, and looked wistfully at the heap of gifts on the corner table. How meagre and small they did look, to be sure, beside that bulgy basket with its cover suggestively tied down.

Mrs. Ralston looked too.

"Santa Claus seems to have visited you already," she said with a smile.

The Josephs laughed.

"Our Santa Claus is somewhat out of pocket this year," said Mr. Joseph frankly. "Those are the little things the small folks here have made for each other. They've been a month at it, and I'm always kind of relieved when Christmas is over and there are no more mysterious doings. We're in such cramped quarters here that you can't move without stepping on somebody's secret."

A shakedown was spread in the kitchen for the unexpected guests, and presently the Ralstons found themselves alone. Mrs. Ralston went over to the Christmas table and looked at the little gifts half tenderly and half pityingly.

"They're not much like the contents of our basket, are they?" she said, as she touched the calendar Jimmie had made for Mollie out of cardboard and autumn leaves and grasses.

"Just what I was thinking," returned her husband, "and I was thinking of something else, too. I've a notion that I'd like to see some of the things in our basket right here on this table."

"I'd like to see them all," said Mrs. Ralston promptly. "Let's just leave them here, Edward. Roger's family will have plenty of presents without them, and for that matter we can send them ours when we go back home."

"Just as you say," agreed Mr. Ralston. "I like the idea of giving the small folk of this household a rousing good Christmas for once. They're poor I know, and I dare say pretty well pinched this year like most of the farmers hereabout after the crop failure."

Mrs. Ralston untied the cover of the big basket. Then the two of them, moving as stealthily as if engaged in a burglary, transferred the contents to the table. Mr. Ralston got out a small pencil and a note book, and by dint of comparing the names attached to the gifts on the table they managed to divide theirs up pretty evenly among the little Josephs.

When all was done Mrs. Ralston said, "Now, I'm going to spread that tablecloth carelessly over the table. We will be going before daylight, probably, and in the hurry of getting off I hope that Mr. and Mrs. Joseph will not notice the difference till we're gone."

It fell out as Mrs. Ralston had planned. The dawn broke fine and clear over a vast white world. Mr. and Mrs. Joseph were early astir; breakfast for the storm-stayed travellers was cooked and eaten by lamplight; then the horse and sleigh were brought to the door and Mr. Ralston carried out his empty basket.

"I expect the trail will be heavy," he said, "but I guess we'd get to Lindsay in time for dinner, anyway. Much obliged for your kindness, Mr. Joseph. When you and Mrs. Joseph come to town we shall hope to have a chance to return it. Good-bye and a merry Christmas to you all."

When Mrs. Joseph went back to the kitchen her eyes fell on the heaped-up table in the corner.

"Why-y!" she said, and snatched off the cover.

One look she gave, and then this funny little mother began to cry; but they were happy tears. Mr. Joseph came too, and looked and whistled.

There really seemed to be everything on that table that the hearts of children could desire—three pairs of skates, a fur cap and collar, a dainty workbasket, half a dozen gleaming new books, a writing desk, a roll of stuff that looked like a new dress, a pair of fur-topped kid gloves just Mollie's size, and a china cup and saucer. All these were to be seen at the first glance; and in one corner of the table was a big box filled with candies and nuts and raisins, and in the other a doll with curling golden hair and brown eyes, dressed in "real" clothes and with all her wardrobe in a trunk beside her. Pinned to her dress was a leaf from Mr. Ralston's notebook with Maggie's name written on it.

"Well, this is Christmas with a vengeance," said Mr. Joseph.

"The children will go wild with delight," said his wife happily.

They pretty nearly did when they all came scrambling down the stairs a little later. Such a Christmas had never been known in the Joseph household before. Maggie clasped her doll with shining eyes, Mollie looked at the workbasket that her housewifely little heart had always longed for, studious Jimmy beamed over the books, and Ted and Hal whooped with delight over the skates. And as for the big box of good things, why, everybody appreciated that. That Christmas was one to date from in that family.

I'm glad to be able to say, too, that even in the heyday of their delight and surprise over their wonderful presents, the little Josephs did not forget to appreciate the gifts they had prepared for each other. Mollie thought her calendar just too pretty for anything, and Jimmy was sure the new red mittens which Maggie had knitted for him with her own chubby wee fingers, were the very nicest, gayest mittens a boy had ever worn.

Mrs. Joseph's taffy was eaten too. Not a scrap of it was left. As Ted said loyally, "It was just as good as the candy in the box and had more 'chew' to it besides."

The Magical Bond of the Sea

A late September wind from the northwest was sweeping over the waters of Racicot Harbour. It blew in, strong with the tang of the salt seas, past the grim lighthouse rock on the one hand and the sandbars on the other, up the long, narrow funnel of darkly blue water, until it whistled among the masts of the boats at anchor and among the stovepipe chimneys of the fishing village. It was a wind that sang and piped and keened of many things—but what it sang to each listener was only what was in that listener's heart. And Nora Shelley, standing at the door of her father's bleached cottage on the grey sands, heard a new strain in it. The wind had sung often to her of the outer world she longed for, but there had never been the note of fulfilment in it before.

There's a new life beyond, Nora, whistled the wind. A good life—and it's yours for the taking. You have but to put out your hand and all you've wished for will be in your grasp.

Nora leaned out from the door to meet the wind. She loved that northwest gale; it was a staunch old friend of hers. Very slim and straight was Nora, with a skin as white as the foam flakes crisping over the sands, and eyes of the tremulous, haunting blue that deepens on the water after a fair sunset. But her hair was as black as midnight, and her lips blossomed out with a ripe redness against the uncoloured purity of her face. She was far and away the most beautiful of the harbour girls, but hardly the most popular. Men and women alike thought her proud. Even her friends felt themselves called upon to make excuses for her unlikeness to themselves.

Nora had dosed the door behind her to shut in the voices. She wanted to be alone with the wind while she made her decision. Before her the sandy shingle, made firm by a straggling growth of some pale sea-ivy, sloped down to the sapphire cup of the harbour. Around her were the small, uncouth houses of the village—no smaller or more uncouth than the one which was her home—with children playing noisily on the paths between them. The mackerel boats curtsied and nodded outside; beyond them the sharp tip of Sandy Point was curdled white with seagulls. Down at the curve of the cove a group of men were laughing and talking loudly in front of French Joe's fish-house. This was the life that she had always known.

Across the harbour, on a fir-fringed headland, stood Dalveigh. John Cameron, childless millionaire, had built a summer cottage on that point two years ago, and given it the name of the old ancestral estate in Scotland. To the Racicot fishing folk the house and grounds were as a dream of enchantment made real. Few of them had ever seen anything like it.

Nora Shelley knew Dalveigh well. She had been the Camerons' guest many times that summer, finding in the luxury and beauty of their surroundings something that entered with a strange aptness into her own nature. It was as if it were hers by right of fitness. And this was the life that might be hers, did she so choose.

In reality, her choice was already made, and she knew it. But it pleased her to pretend for a little time that it was not, and to dally tenderly with-the old loves and emotions that tugged at her heart and clamoured to be remembered.

Within, in the low-ceilinged living room, with its worn, uneven floor and its blackened walls hung with fish nets and oilskins, four people were sitting. John Cameron and his wife were given the seats of honour in the middle of the room. Mrs. Cameron was a handsome, well-dressed woman, with an expression that was discontented and, at times, petulant. Yet her face had a good deal of plain common sense in it, and not even the most critical of the Racicot folks could say that she "put on airs." Her husband was a small, white-haired man, with a fresh, young-looking face. He was popular in Racicot, for he mingled freely with the sailors and fishermen. Moreover, Dalveigh was an excellent market for fresh mackerel.

Nathan Shelley, in his favourite corner behind the stove, sat lurching forward with his hands on his knees. He had laid aside his pipe out of deference to Mrs. Cameron, and it was hard for him to think without it. He wished his wife would go to work; it seemed uncanny to see her idle. She had sat idle only once that he remembered—the day they had brought Ned Shelley in, dank and dripping, after the August storm ten years before. Mrs. Shelley sat by the crooked, small-paned window and looked out down the harbour. The coat she had been patching for her husband when the Camerons came still lay in her lap, and she had folded her hands upon it. She was a big woman, slow of speech and manner, with a placid, handsome face—a face that had not visibly stirred even when she had heard the Camerons' proposition.

They wanted Nora—these rich people who had so much in life wanted the blossom of girlhood that had never bloomed for them. John Cameron pleaded his cause well.

"We will look on her as our own," he said at last. "We have grown to love her this summer. She is beautiful and clever—she has a right to more than Racicot can give her. You have other children—we are childless. And we do not take her from you utterly. You will see her every summer when we come to Dalveigh."

"It won't be the same thing quite," said Nathan Shelley drily. "She'll belong to your life then—not ours. And no matter how many young ones folks has, they don't want to lose none of 'em. But I dunno as we ought to let our feelings stand in

Nora's light. She's clever, and she's been hankering for more'n we can ever give her. I was the same way once. Lord, how I raged at Racicot! I broke away finally—went to a city and got work. But it wasn't no use. I'd left it too long. The sea had got into my blood. I toughed it out for two years, and then I had to come back. I didn't want to, mark you, but I had to come. Been here ever since. But maybe 'twill be different with the girl. She's younger than I was; if the hankering for the sea and the life of the shore hasn't got into her too deep, maybe she'll be able to cut loose for good. But you don't know how the sea calls to one of its own."

Cameron smiled. He thought that this dry old salt was a bit of a poet in his own way. Very likely Nora got her ability and originality from him. There did not seem to be a great deal in the phlegmatic, good-looking mother.

"What say, wife?" asked Shelley at last.

His wife had said in her slow way, "Leave it to Nora," and to Nora it was left.

When she came in at last, her face stung to radiant beauty by the northwest wind, she found it hard to tell them after all. She looked at her mother appealingly.

"Is it go or stay, girl," demanded her father brusquely.

"I think I'll go," said Nora slowly. Then, catching sight of her mother's face, she ran to her and flung her arms about her. "But I'll never forget you, Mother," she cried. "I'll love you always—you and Father."

Her mother loosened the clinging arms and pushed her gently towards the Camerons.

"Go to them," she said calmly. "You belong to them now."

The news spread quickly over Racicot. Before night everyone on the harbour shore knew that the Camerons were going to adopt Nora Shelley and take her away with them. There was much surprise and more envy. The shore women tossed their heads.

"Reckon Nora is in great feather," they said. "She always did think herself better than anyone else. Nate Shelley and his wife spoiled her ridiculous. Wonder what Rob Fletcher thinks of it?"

Nora asked her brother to tell the news to Rob Fletcher himself, but Merran Andrews was before him. She was at Rob before he had fairly landed, when the fishing boats came in at sunset.

"Have you heard the news, Rob? Nora's going away to be a fine lady. The Camerons have been daft about her all summer, and now they are going to adopt her."

Merran wanted Rob herself. He was a big, handsome fellow, and well-off—the pick of the harbour men in every way. He had slighted her for Nora, and it pleased her to stab him now, though she meant to be nice to him later on.

He turned white under his tan, but he did not choose to make a book of his heart for Merran's bold black eyes to read. "It's a great thing for her," he answered calmly. "She was meant for better things than can be found at Racicot."

"She was always too good for common folks, if that is what you mean," said Merran spitefully.

Nora and Rob did not meet until the next evening, when she rowed herself home from Dalveigh. He was at the shore to tie up her boat and help her out. They walked up the sands together in the heart of the autumn sunset, with the northwest wind whistling in their ears and the great star of the lighthouse gleaming wanly out against the golden sky. Nora felt uncomfortable, and resented it. Rob Fletcher was nothing to her; he never had been anything but the good friend to whom she told her strange thoughts and longings. Why should her heart ache over him? She wished he would talk, but he strode along in silence, with his fine head drooping a little.

"I suppose you have heard that I am going away, Rob?" she said at last.

He nodded. "Yes, I've heard it from a hundred mouths, more or less," he answered, not looking at her.

"It's a splendid thing for me, isn't it?" dared Nora.

"Well, I don't know," he said slowly. "Looking at it from the outside, it seems so. But from the inside it mayn't look the same. Do you think you'll be able to cut twenty years of a life out of your heart without any pain?"

"Oh, I'll be homesick, if that is what you mean," said Nora petulantly. "Of course I'll be that at first. I expect it—but people get over that. And it is not as if I were going away for good. I'll be back next summer—every summer."

"It'll be different," said Rob stubbornly, thinking as old Nathan Shelley had thought. "You'll be a fine lady—oh, all the better for that perhaps—but you'll not be the same. No, no, the new life will change you; not all at once, maybe, but in the end. You'll be one of them, not one of us. But will you be happy? That's the question I'm asking."

In anyone else Nora would have resented this. But she never felt angry with Rob.

"I think I shall be," she said thoughtfully. "And, anyway, I must go. It doesn't seem as if I could help myself if I wanted to. Something—out beyond there—is calling me, always has been calling me ever since I was a tiny girl and found out there was a big world far away from Racicot. And it always seemed to me that I would find a way to it some day. That was why I kept going to school long after the other girls stopped. Mother thought I'd better stop home; she said too much book learning would make me discontented and too different from the people I had to live along. But Father let me go; he understood; he said I was like him when he was young. I learned everything and read everything I could. It seems to me as if I had been walking along a narrow pathway all my life. And now it seems as if a gate were opened before me and I can pass through into a wider world. It isn't the luxury and the pleasure or the fine house and dresses that tempt me, though the people here think so—even Mother thinks so. But it is not. It's just that something seems to be in my grasp that I've always longed for, and I must go—Rob, I must go."

"Yes, if you feel like that you must go," he answered, looking down at her troubled face gently. "And it's best for you to go, Nora. I believe that, and I'm not so selfish as not to be able to hope that you'll find all you long for. But it will change you all the more if it is so. Nora! Nora! Whatever am I going to do without you!"

The sudden passion bursting out in his tone frightened her.

"Don't, Rob, don't! And you won't miss me long. There's many another."

"No, there isn't. Don't fling me that dry bone of comfort. There's no other, and never has been any other—none but you, Nora, and well you know it."

"I'm sorry," she said faintly.

"You needn't be," said Rob grimly. "After all, I'd rather love you than not, hurt as it will. I never had much hope of getting you to listen to me, so there's no great disappointment there. You're too good for me—I've always known that. A girl that is fit to mate with the Camerons is far above Rob Fletcher, fisherman."

"I never had such a thought," protested Nora.

"I know it," he said, casing himself up in his quietness again. "But it's so—and now I've got to lose you. But there'll never be any other for me, Nora."

He left her at her father's door. She watched his stalwart figure out of sight around the point, and raged to find tears in her eyes and a bitter yearning in her heart. For a moment she repented—she would stay—she could not go. Then over the harbour flashed out the lights of Dalveigh. The life behind them glittered, allured, beckoned. Nay, she must go on—she had made her choice. There was no turning back now.

Nora Shelley went away with the Camerons, and Dalveigh was deserted. Winter came down on Racicot Harbour, and the colony of fisher folk at its head gave themselves over to the idleness of the season—a time for lounging and gossipping and long hours of lazy contentment smoking in the neighbours' chimney corners, when tales were told of the sea and the fishing. The Harbour laid itself out to be sociable in winter. There was no time for that in summer. People had to work eighteen hours out of the twenty-four then. In the winter there was spare time to laugh and quarrel, woo and wed and—were a man so minded—dream, as did Rob Fletcher in his loneliness.

In a Racicot winter much was made of small things. The arrival of Nora Shelley's weekly letter to her father and mother was an event in the village. The post-mistress in the Cove store spread the news that it had come, and that night the Shelley kitchen would be crowded. Isobel Shelley, Nora's younger sister, read the letter aloud by virtue of having gone to school long enough to be able to pronounce the words and tell where the places named were situated.

The Camerons had spent the autumn in New York and had then gone south for the winter. Nora wrote freely of her new life. In the beginning she admitted great homesickness, but after the first few letters she made no further mention of that. She wrote little of herself, but she described fully the places she had visited, the people she had met, the wonderful things she had seen. She sent affectionate messages to all her old friends and asked after all her old interests. But the letters came to be more and more like those of a stranger and one apart from the Racicot life, and the father and mother felt it.

"She's changing," muttered old Nathan. "It had to be so—it's well for her that it is so—but it hurts. She ain't ours any more. We've lost the girl, wife, lost her forever."

Rob Fletcher always came and listened to the letters in silence while the others buzzed and commented. Rob, so the Harbour folk said, was much changed. He had grown unsociable and preferred to stay home and read books rather than go a-visiting as did others. The Harbour folk shook their heads over this. There was something wrong with a man who read books when there was a plenty of other amusements. Jacob Radnor had read books all one winter and had drowned himself in the spring—jumped overboard from his dory at the herring nets. And that was what came of books, mark you.

The Camerons came later to Dalveigh the next summer, on account of John Cameron's health, which was not good. It was the first of August before a host of servants came to put Dalveigh in habitable order, and a week later the family came. They brought a houseful of guests with them.

At sunset on the day of her arrival Nora Shelley looked out cross the harbour to the fishing village. She was tired after her journey, and she had not meant to go over until the morning, but now she knew she must go at once. Her mother was over there; the old life called to her; the northwest wind swept up the channel and whistled alluringly to her at the window of her luxurious room. It brought to her the tang of the salt wastes and filled her heart with a great, bitter-sweet yearning.

She was more beautiful than ever. In the year that had passed she had blossomed out to a gracious fulfilment of womanhood. Even the Camerons had wondered at her swift adaptation to her new surroundings. She seemed to have put Racicot behind her as one puts by an old garment. In everything she had held her own royally. Her adopted parents were proud of her beauty and her nameless, untamed charm. They had lavished every indulgence upon her. In those few short months she had lived more keenly and fully than in all her life before. The Nora Shelley who went away was not, so it would seem, the Nora Shelley who came back.

But when she looked from her window to the waves and saw the star of the lighthouse and the blaze of the sunset in the window of the fishing-houses and heard the summons of the wind, something broke loose in her soul and overwhelmed her, like a wave of the sea. She must go at once—at once—at once. Not a moment could she wait.

She was dressed for dinner, but with tingling fingers she threw off her costly gown and put on her dark travelling suit again. She left her hair as it was and knotted a crimson scarf about her head. She would slip away quietly to the boat-house, get Davy to launch the little sailboat for her—and then for a fleet skim over the harbour before that glorious wind! She hoped not to be seen, but Mrs. Cameron met her in the hall.

"Nora!" she said in astonishment.

"Oh, I must go, Aunty! I must go!" the girl cried feverishly. She was afraid Mrs. Cameron would try to prevent her going, and all at once she knew that she could not bear that.

"Must go? Where? Dinner is almost ready, and—"

"Oh, I don't want any dinner. I'm going home—I will sail over."

"My dear child, don't be foolish. It's too late to go over the harbour tonight. They won't be expecting you. Wait until the morning."

"No—oh, you don't understand. I must go—I must! My mother is over there."

Something in the girl's last sentence or the tone in which it was uttered brought a look of pain to Mrs. Cameron's face. But she made no further attempt to dissuade her.

"Well, if you must. But you cannot go alone—no, Nora, I cannot allow it. The wind is too high and it is too late for you to go over by yourself. Clark Bryant will take you."

Nora would have protested but she knew it would be in vain. She submitted somewhat sullenly and walked down to the shore in silence. Clark Bryant strode beside her, humouring her mood. He was a tall, stout man, with an ugly, clever, sarcastic face. He was as clever as he looked, and was one of the younger millionaires whom John Cameron drew around him in the development of his huge financial schemes. Bryant was in love with Nora. This was why the Camerons had asked him to join their August house party at Dalveigh, and why he had accepted. It had occurred to Nora that this was the case, but as yet she had never troubled to think the situation over seriously.

She liked Clark Bryant well enough, but just at the moment he was in the way. She did not want to take him over to Racicot—just why she could not have explained. There was in her no snobbish shame of her humble home. But he did not belong there; he was an alien, and she wished to go back to it for the first time alone.

At the boathouse Davy launched the small sailboat and Nora took the tiller. She knew every inch of the harbour. As the sail filled before the wind and the boat sprang across the upcurling waves, her brief sullenness fell away from her. She no longer resented Clark Bryant's presence—she forgot it. He was no more to her than the mast by which he stood. The spell of the sea and the wind surged into her heart and filled it with wild happiness and measureless content. Over yonder, where the lights gleamed on the darkening shore under the high-sprung arch of pale golden sky, was home. How the wind whistled to welcome her back! The lash of it against her face—the flick of salt spray on her lips—the swing of the boat as it cut through the racing crests—how glorious it all was!

Clark Bryant watched her, understanding all at once that he was nothing to her, that he had no part or lot in her heart. He was as one forgotten and left behind. And how lovely, how desirable she was! He had never seen her look so beautiful. The shawl had slipped down to her shoulders and her head rose out of it like some magnificent flower out of a crimson calyx. The masses of her black hair lifted from her face in the rush of the wind and swayed back again like rich shadows.

Her lips were stung scarlet with the sea's sharp caresses, and her eyes, large and splendid, looked past him unseeing to the harbour lights of Racicot.

When they swung in by the wharf Nora sprang from the boat before Bryant had time to moor it. Pausing for an instant, she called down to him, carelessly, "Don't wait for me. I shall not go back tonight."

Then she caught her shawl around her head and almost ran up the wharf and along the shore. No one was abroad, for it was supper hour in Racicot. In the Shelley kitchen the family was gathered around the table, when the door was flung open and Nora stood on the threshold. For a moment they gazed at her as at an apparition. They had not known the precise day of her coming and were not aware of the Camerons' arrival at Dalveigh.

"It's the girl herself. It's Nora," said old Nathan, rising from his bench.

"Mother!" cried Nora. She ran across the room and buried her face in her mother's breast, sobbing.

When the news spread, the Racicot people crowded in to see Nora until the house was full. They spent a noisy, merry, whole-hearted evening of the old sort. The men smoked and most of the women knitted while they talked. They were pleased to find that Nora did not put on any airs. Old Jonas Myers bluntly told her that he didn't see as her year among rich folks had done her much good, after all.

"You're just the same as when you went away," he said. "They haven't made a fine lady of you. Folks here thought you'd be something wonderful."

Nora laughed. She was glad that they did not find her changed. Old Nathan chuckled in his dry way. There was a difference in the girl, and he saw it, though the neighbours did not, but it was not the difference he had feared. His daughter was not utterly taken from him yet.

Nora sat by her mother and was happy. But as the evening wore away she grew very quiet, and watched the door with something piteous in her eyes. Old Nathan noticed it and thought she was tired. He gave the curious neighbours a good-natured hint, and they presently withdrew. When they had all gone Nora went out to the door alone.

The wind had died down and the shore, gemmed with its twinkling lights, was very still, for it was too late an hour for Racicot folk to be abroad in the mackerel season. The moon was rising and the harbour was a tossing expanse of silver waves. The mellow light fell on a tall figure lurking at the angle of the road that led past the Shelley cottage. Nora saw and recognized it. She flew down the sandy slope with outstretched hands.

"Rob—Rob!"

"Nora!" he said huskily, holding out his hand. But she flung herself on his breast and clung to him, half laughing, half crying.

"Oh, Rob! I've been looking for you all the evening. Every time there was a step I said to myself, 'That is Rob, now.' And when the door opened to let in another, my heart died within me. I dared not even ask after you for fear of what they might tell me. Why didn't you come?"

"I didn't know that I'd be welcome," he whispered, holding her closer to him. "I've been hanging about thinking to get a glimpse of you unbeknown. I thought maybe you wouldn't want to see me tonight."

"Not want to see you! Oh, Rob, this evening at Dalveigh, when I looked across to Racicot, it was you I thought of before all—even before Mother."

She drew back and looked at him with her soul in her eyes.

"What a splendid fellow you are—how handsome you are, Rob!" she cried. All the reserve of womanhood fell away from her in the inrush of emotions. For the moment she was a child again, telling out her thoughts with all a child's frankness. "I've been in a dream this past year—a lovely dream—a fair dream, but only a dream, after all. And now I've wakened. And you are part of the wakening—the best part! Oh, to think I never knew before!"

"Knew what, my girl?"

He had her close against his heart now; the breath of her lips mingled with his, but he would not kiss her yet.

"That I loved you," she whispered back. "Oh, Rob, you are all the world to me. I belong to you and the sea. But I never knew it until I crossed the harbour tonight. Then I knew—it came to me all at once, like a flood of understanding. I knew I could never go away again—that I must stay here forever where I could hear that call of wind and waves. The new life was good—good—but it could not go deep enough. And when you did not come I knew what was in my heart for you as well."

That night Nora lay beside her sisters in the tiny room that looked out on the harbour. The younger girls slept soundly, but Nora kept awake to listen to the laughter of the wind outside, and con over what she and Rob had said to each other. There was no blot on her happiness save a sorry wonder what the Camerons would say when they knew.

"They will think me ungrateful and fickle," she sighed. "They don't know that I can't help it even if I would. They will never understand."

Nor did they. When Nora told them that she was going back to Racicot, they laughed at her kindly at first, treating it as the passing whim of a homesick girl. Later, when they came to understand that she meant it, they were grieved and angry. There were scenes of pleading and tears and reproaches. Nora cried bitterly in Mrs. Cameron's arms, but stood rock-firm. She could never go back to them—never.

They appealed to Nathan Shelley finally, but he refused to say anything.

"It can't be altered," he told them. "The sea has called her and she'll listen to naught else. I'm sorry enough for the girl's own sake. It would have been better for her if she could have cut loose from it all and lived your life, I dare say. But you've made a fair trial and it's of no use. I know what's in her heart—it was in mine once—and I'll say no word of rebuke to her. She's free to go or stay as she chooses—just as free as she was last year."

Mrs. Cameron made one more appeal to Nora. She told the girl bitterly that she was ungrateful.

"I'm not that," said Nora with quivering lips. "I love you, and I'm grateful to you. But your life isn't for me, after all. I thought it was—I longed so for it. And I loved it, too—I love it yet. But there's something stronger in me that holds me here."

"I don't think you realize what you are doing, Nora. You have been a little homesick and you are glad to be back. But after we have gone and you must settle into the old Racicot life again, you will not be contented. You will find that your life with us will have unfitted you for this. There will be no real place for you here—nothing for you to do. You will be as a stranger here."

"Oh, no. I am going to marry Rob Fletcher," said Nora proudly.

"Marry Rob Fletcher! And you might have married Clark Bryant, Nora!"

Nora shook her head. "That could never have been. I thought it might once—but I know better now. You see, I love Rob."

There did not seem to be anything more to say after that. Mrs. Cameron did not try to say anything. She went away in sorrow.

Nora cried bitterly after she had gone. But there were no tears in her eyes that night when she walked on the shore with Rob Fletcher. The wind whistled around them, and the stars came out in the great ebony dome of the sky over the harbour. Laughter and song of the fishing folk were behind them, and the deep, solemn call of the sea before. Over the harbour gleamed the score of lights at Dalveigh. Rob looked from them to Nora.

"Do you think you'll ever regret yon life, my girl?"

"Never, Rob. It seems to me now like a beautiful garment put on for a holiday and worn easily and pleasantly for a time. But I've put it off now, and put on workaday clothes again. It is only a week since I left Dalveigh, but it seems long ago. Listen to the wind, Rob! It is singing of the good days to be for you and me."

He bent over and kissed her.

"My own dear lass!" he said softly.

The Martyrdom of Estella

Estella was waiting under the poplars at the gate for Spencer Morgan. She was engaged to him, and he always came to see her on Saturday and Wednesday evenings. It was after sunset, and the air was mellow and warm-hued. The willow trees along the walk and the tall birches in the background stood out darkly distinct against the lemon-tinted sky. The breath of mint floated out from the garden, and the dew was falling heavily.

Estella leaned against the gate, listening for the sound of wheels and dreamily watching the light shining out from the window of Vivienne LeMar's room. The blind was up and she could see Miss LeMar writing at her table. Her profile was clear and distinct against the lamplight.

Estella reflected without the least envy that Miss LeMar was very beautiful. She had never seen anyone who was really beautiful before—beautiful with the loveliness of the heroines in the novels she sometimes read or the pictures she had seen.

Estella Bowes was not pretty. She was a nice-looking girl, with clear eyes, rosy cheeks, and a pervading air of the content and happiness her life had always known. She was an orphan and lived with her uncle and aunt. In the summer they sometimes took a boarder for a month or two, and this summer Miss LeMar had come. She had been with them about a week. She was an actress from the city and had around her all the glamour of a strange, unknown life. Nothing was known about her. The Boweses liked her well enough as a boarder. Estella admired and held her in awe. She wondered what Spencer would think of this beautiful woman. He had not yet seen her.

It was quite dark when he came. Estella opened the gate for him, but he got out of his buggy and walked up the lane beside her with his arm about her. Miss LeMar's light had removed to the parlour where she was singing, accompanying herself on the cottage organ. Estella felt annoyed. The parlour was considered her private domain on Wednesday and Saturday night, but Miss LeMar did not know that.

"Who is singing?" asked Spencer. "What a voice she has!"

"That's our new boarder, Miss LeMar," answered Estella. "She's an actress and sings and does everything. She is awfully pretty, Spencer."

"Yes?" said the young man indifferently.

He was not in the least interested in the Boweses' new boarder. Indeed, he considered her advent a nuisance. He pressed Estella closer to him, and when they reached the garden gate he kissed her. Estella always remembered that moment afterwards. She was so supremely happy.

Spencer went off to put up his horse, and Estella waited for him on the porch steps, wondering if any other girl in the world could be quite so happy as she was, or love anyone as much as she loved Spencer. She did not see how it could be possible, because there was only one Spencer.

When Spencer came back she took him into the parlour, half shyly, half proudly. He was a handsome fellow, with a magnificent physique. Miss LeMar stopped singing and turned around on the organ stool as they entered. The little room was flooded with a mellow light from the pink-globed lamp on the table, and in the soft, shadowy radiance she was as beautiful as a dream. She wore a dress of crepe, cut low in the neck. Estella had never seen anyone dressed so before. To her it seemed immodest.

She introduced Spencer. He bowed awkwardly and sat stiffly down by the window with his eyes riveted on Miss LeMar's face. Estella, catching a glimpse of herself in the old-fashioned mirror above the mantel, suddenly felt a cold chill of dissatisfaction. Her figure had never seemed to her so stout and stiff, her brown hair so dull and prim, her complexion so muddy, her features so commonplace. She wished Miss LeMar would go out of the room.

Vivienne LeMar watched the two faces before her; a hard gleam, half mockery, half malice, flashed into her eyes and a smile crept about her lips. She looked straight in Spencer Morgan's honest blue eyes and read there the young man's dazzled admiration. There was contempt in the look she turned on Estella.

"You were singing when we came in," said Spencer. "Won't you go on, please? I am very fond of music."

Miss LeMar turned again to the organ. The gleaming curves of her neck and shoulders rose out of their filmy sheathings of lace. Spencer, sitting where he could see her face with its rose-leaf bloom and the ringlets of golden hair clustering about it, gazed at her, unheeding of aught else. Estella saw his look. She suddenly began to hate the black-eyed witch at the organ—and to fear her as well. Why did Spencer look at her like that? She wished she had not brought him in at all. She felt commonplace and angry, and wanted to cry.

Vivienne LeMar went on singing, drifting from one sweet love song into another. Once she looked up at Spencer Morgan. He rose quickly and went to her side, looking down at her with a strange fire in his eyes.

Estella got up abruptly and left the room. She was angry and jealous, but she thought Spencer would follow her. When he did not, she could not believe it. She waited on the porch for him, not knowing whether she were more angry or miserable. She would not go back into the room. Vivienne LeMar had stopped singing. She could hear a low murmur of voices. When she had waited there an hour, she went in and upstairs to her room with ostentatious footsteps. She was too angry to cry or to realize what had happened, and still kept hoping all sorts of impossible things as she sat by her window.

It was ten o'clock when Spencer went away and Vivienne LeMar passed up the hall to her room. Estella clenched her hands in an access of helpless rage. She was very angry, but under her fury was a horrible ache of pain. It could not be only three hours since she had been so happy! It must be more than that! What had happened? Had she made a fool of herself? Ought she to have behaved in any other way? Perhaps Spencer had come out to look for her after she had gone upstairs and, not finding her, had gone back to Miss LeMar to show her he was angry. This poor hope was a small comfort. She wished she had not acted as she had. It looked spiteful and jealous, and Spencer did not like people who were spiteful and jealous. She would show him she was sorry when he came back, and it would be all right.

She lay awake most of the night, thinking out plausible reasons and excuses for Spencer's behaviour, and trying to convince herself that she had exaggerated everything absurdly. Towards morning she fell asleep and awoke hardly remembering what had happened. Then it rolled back upon her crushingly.

But she rose and dressed in better spirits. It had been hardest to lie there and do nothing. Now the day was before her and something pleasant might happen. Spencer might come back in the evening. She would be doubly nice to him to make up.

Mrs. Bowes looked sharply at her niece's dull eyes and pale cheeks at the breakfast table. She had her own thoughts of things. She was a large, handsome woman with a rather harsh face.

"Did you go upstairs last night and leave Spencer Morgan with Miss LeMar?" she asked bluntly.

"Yes," muttered Estella.

"Did you have a quarrel with him?"

"No."

"What made you act so queer?"

"I couldn't help it," faltered the girl.

The food she was eating seemed to choke her. She wished she were a hundred miles away from everyone she ever knew.

Mrs. Bowes gave a grunt of dissatisfaction.

"Well, I think it is a pretty queer piece of business. But if you are satisfied, it isn't anyone else's concern, I suppose. He stayed with her till ten o'clock and when he left she did everything but kiss him—and she asked him to come back too. I heard."

"Aunt!" protested the girl.

She felt as if her aunt were striking her blow after blow on a sensitive, quivering spot. It was bad enough to know it all, but to hear it put into such cold, brutal words was more than she could endure. It seemed to make everything so horribly sure.

"I guess I had a right to listen, hadn't I, with such goings on in my own house? You're a little fool, Estella Bowes! I don't believe that LeMar girl is a bit better than she ought to be. I wish I'd never taken her to board, and if you say so, I'll send her packing right off and not give her a chance to make mischief atween folks."

Estella's suffering found vent in a burst of anger.

"You needn't do anything of the sort!" she cried.

"It's all nonsense about Spencer—it was my fault—and anyhow, if he is so easily led away as that, I am sure I don't want him! I wish to goodness, Aunt, you'd leave me alone!"

"Oh, very well!" returned Mrs. Bowes in an offended tone. "It was for your own good I spoke. You know best, I suppose. If you don't care, I don't know that anyone else need."

Estella went about her work like one in a dream. A great hatred had sprung up in her heart against Vivienne LeMar. The simple-hearted country girl felt almost murderous. The whole day seemed like a nightmare to her. When night came she dressed herself with feverish care, for she could not quell the hope that Spencer would surely come again. But he did not; and when she went up to bed, it did not seem as if she could live through the night. She lay staring wide-eyed through the darkness until dawn. She wished that she might cry, but no tears came to her relief.

Next day she went to work with furious energy. When her usual tasks were done, she ransacked the house for other employment. She was afraid if she stopped work for a moment she would go mad. Mrs. Bowes watched her with a grim pity.

At night she walked to prayer meeting in the schoolhouse a mile away. She always went, and Spencer was generally on hand to see her home. He was not there tonight. She wished she had not come. It was dreadful to have to sit still and think. She did not hear a word the minister said.

She had to walk home with a crowd of girls and nerve herself to answer their merry sallies that no one might suspect. She was tortured by the fear that everyone knew her shame and humiliation and was pitying her. She got hysterically gay, but underneath all she was constantly trying to assign a satisfactory reason for Spencer's nonappearance. He was often kept away, and of course he was a little cross at her yet, as was natural. If he had come before her then, she could have gone down in the very dust at his feet and implored his forgiveness.

When she reached home she went into the garden and sat down. The calm of the night soothed her. She felt happier and more hopeful. She thought over all that had passed between her and Spencer and all his loving assurances, and the recollection comforted her. She was almost happy when she went in.

Tomorrow is Sunday, she thought when she wakened in the morning. Her step was lighter and her face brighter. Mrs. Bowes seemed to be in a bad humour. Presently she said bluntly:

"Do you know that Spencer Morgan was here last night?"

Estella felt the cold tighten round her heart. Yet underneath it sprang up a wild, sweet hope.

"Spencer here! I suppose he forgot it was prayer meeting night. What did he say? Why didn't you tell him where I was?"

"I don't know that he forgot it was prayer meeting night," returned Mrs. Bowes with measured emphasis. "'Tisn't likely his memory has failed so all at once. He didn't ask where you was. He took good care to go before you got home too. Miss LeMar entertained him. I guess she was quite capable of it."

Estella bent over her dishes in silence. Her face was deadly white.

"I'll send her away," said Mrs. Bowes pityingly. "When she's gone, Spencer will soon come back to you."

"No, you won't!" said Estella fiercely. "If you do, she'll only go over to Barstows', and it would be worse than ever. I don't care—I'll show them both I don't care! As for Spencer coming back to me, do you think I want her leavings? He's welcome to go."

"He's only just fooled by her pretty face," persisted Mrs. Bowes in a clumsy effort at consolation. "She's just turning his head, the hussy, and he isn't really in his proper senses. You'll see, he'll be ashamed of himself when he comes to them again. He knows very well in his heart that you're worth ten girls like her."

Estella faced around.

"Aunt," she said desperately, "you mean well, I know, but you're killing me! I can't stand it. For pity's sake, don't say another word to me about this, no matter what happens. And don't keep looking at me as if I were a martyr! She watches us and it would please her to think I cared. I don't—and I mean she shall see I don't. I guess I'm well rid of a fellow as fickle as he is, and I've sense enough to know it."

She went upstairs then, tearing off her turquoise engagement ring as she climbed the steps. All sorts of wild ideas flashed through her head. She would go down and confront Vivienne LeMar—she would rush off and find Spencer and throw his ring at him, no matter where he was—she would go away where no one would ever see her again. Why couldn't she die? Was it possible people could suffer like this and yet go on living?

"I don't care—I don't care!" she moaned, telling the lie aloud to herself, as if she hoped that by this means she would come to believe it.

When twilight came she went out to the front steps and leaned her aching head against the honeysuckle trellis. The sun had just set and the whole world swam in dusky golden light. The wonderful beauty frightened her. She felt like a blot on it.

While she stood there, a buggy came driving up the lane and wheeled about at the steps. In it was Spencer Morgan.

Estella saw him and, in spite of the maddening throb of hope that seemed suddenly to transfigure the world for her, her pride rose in arms. Had Spencer come the night before, he would have found her loving and humble. Even now, had she but been sure that he had come to see her, she would have unbent. But was it the other? The torturing doubt stung her to the quick.

She waited, stubbornly resolved that she would not speak first. It was not in her place. Spencer Morgan flicked his horse sharply with his whip. He dared not look at Estella, but he felt her uncompromising attitude. He was miserably ashamed of himself, and he felt angry at Estella for his shame.

"Do you care to come for a drive?" he asked awkwardly, with a covert glance at the parlour windows.

Estella caught the glance and her jealous perception instantly divined its true significance. Her heart died within her. She did not care what she said.

"Oh," she cried with a toss of her head, "it's not me you want—it's Miss LeMar, isn't it? She's away at the shore. You'll find her there, I dare say."

Still, in spite of all, she perversely hoped. If he would only make any sign, the least in the world, that he was sorry—that he still loved her—she could forgive him everything. When he drove away without another word, she could not believe it again. Surely he would not go—surely he knew she did not mean it—he would turn back before he got to the gate.

But he did not. She saw him disappear around the turn of the road. She could not see if he took the shore lane further on, but she was sure he would. She was furious at herself for acting as she had done. It was all her fault again! Oh, if he would only give her another chance!

She was in her room when she heard the buggy drive up again. She knew it was Spencer and that he had brought Vivienne LeMar home. Acting on a sudden wild impulse, the girl stepped out on the landing and confronted her rival as she came up the stairs.

The latter paused at sight of the white face and anguished eyes. There was a little mocking smile on her lovely face.

"Miss LeMar," said Estella in a quivering voice, "what do you mean by all this? You know I'm engaged to Spencer Morgan!"

Miss LeMar laughed softly.

"Really? If you are engaged to the young man, my dear Miss Bowes, I would advise you to look after him more sharply. He seems very willing to flirt, I should say."

She passed on to her room with a malicious smile. Estella shrank back against the wall, humiliated and baffled. When she found herself alone, she crawled back to her room and threw herself face downward on the bed, praying that she might die.

But she had to live through the horrible month that followed—a month so full of agony that she seemed to draw every breath in pain. Spencer never sought her again; he went everywhere with Miss LeMar. His infatuation was the talk of the settlement. Estella knew that her story was in everyone's mouth, and her pride smarted; but she carried a brave front outwardly. No one should say she cared.

She believed that the actress was merely deluding Spencer for her own amusement and would never dream of marrying him. But one day the idea occurred to her that she might. Estella had always told herself that even if Spencer wanted to come back to her she would never take him back, but now, by the half-sick horror that came over her, she knew how strong the hope had really been and despised herself more than ever.

One evening she was alone in the parlour. She had lit the lamp and was listlessly arranging the little room. She looked old and worn. Her colour was gone and her eyes were dull. As she worked, the door opened and Vivienne LeMar walked or, rather, reeled into the room.

Estella dropped the book she held and gazed at her as one in a dream. The actress's face was flushed and her hair was wildly disordered. Her eyes glittered with an unearthly light. She was talking incoherently. The air was heavy with the fumes of brandy.

Estella laughed hysterically. Vivienne LeMar was grossly intoxicated. This woman whom Spencer Morgan worshipped, for whom he had forsaken her, was reeling about the room, laughing idiotically, talking wildly in a thick voice. If he could but see her now!

Estella turned white with the passion of the wild idea that had come to her. Spencer Morgan should see this woman in her true colours.

She lost no time. Swiftly she left the room and locked the door behind her on the maudlin, babbling creature inside. Then she flung a shawl over her head and ran from the house. It was not far to the Morgan homestead. She ran all the way, hardly knowing what she was doing. Mrs. Morgan answered her knock. She gazed in bewilderment at Estella's wild face.

"I want Spencer," said the girl through her white lips.

The elder woman stepped back in dumb amazement. She knew and rued her son's folly. What could Estella want with him?

The young man appeared in the doorway. Estella caught him by the arm and pulled him outside.

"Miss LeMar wants you at once," she said hoarsely. "At once—you are to come at once!"

"Has anything happened to her?" cried Spencer savagely. "Is she ill—is she—what is the matter?"

"No, she is not ill. But she wants you. Come at once."

He started off bareheaded. Estella followed him up the road breathlessly. Surely it was the strangest walk ever a girl had, she told herself with mirthless laughter. She pushed the key into his hand at the porch.

"She's in the parlour," she said wildly. "Go in and look at her, Spencer."

Spencer snatched the key and fitted it into the door. He was full of fear. Had Estella gone out of her mind? Had she done anything to Vivienne? Had she—

As he entered, the actress reeled to her feet and came to meet him. He stood and gazed at her stupidly. This could not be Vivienne, this creature reeking with brandy, uttering such foolish words! What fiend was this in her likeness?

He grew sick at heart and brain; she had her arms about him. He tried to push her away, but she clung closer, and her senseless laughter echoed through the room. He flung her from him with an effort and rushed out through the hall and down the road like a madman. Estella, watching him, felt that she was avenged. She was glad with a joy more pitiful than grief.

Vivienne LeMar left the cottage the next day. Mrs. Bowes, suspecting some mystery, questioned Estella sharply, but could find out nothing. The girl kept her own counsel stubbornly. The interest and curiosity of the village centred around Spencer Morgan, and his case was well discussed. Gossip said that the actress had jilted him and that he was breaking his heart about it. Then came the rumour that he was going West.

Estella heard it apathetically. Life seemed ended for her. There was nothing to look forward to. She could not even look back. All the past was embittered. She had never met Spencer since the night she went after him. She sometimes wondered what he must think of her for what she had done. Did he think her unwomanly and revengeful? She did not care. It was rather a relief to hear that he was going away. She would not be tortured by the fear of meeting him then. She was sure he would never come back to her. If he did, she would never forgive him.

One evening in early harvest Estella was lingering by the lane gate at twilight. She had worked slavishly all day and was very tired, but she was loath to go into the house, where her trouble always seemed to weigh on her more heavily. The dusk, sweet night seemed to soothe her as it always did.

She leaned her head against the poplar by the gate. How long Spencer Morgan had been standing by her she did not know, but when she looked up he was there. In the dim light she could see how haggard and hollow-eyed he had grown. He had changed almost as much as herself.

The girl's first proud impulse was to turn coldly away and leave him. But some strange tumult in her heart kept her still. What had he come to say?

There was a moment's fateful silence. Then Spencer spoke in a muffled voice.

"I couldn't go away without seeing you once more, Estella, to say good-bye. Perhaps you won't speak to me. You must hate me. I deserve it."

He paused, but she said no word. She could not. After a space, he went wistfully on.

"I know you can never forgive me—no girl could. I've behaved like a fool. There isn't any excuse to be made for me. I don't think I could have been in my right senses, Estella. It all seems like some bad dream now. When I saw her that night, I came to my right mind, and I've been the most miserable man alive ever since. Not for her—but because I'd lost you. I can't bear to live here any longer, so I am going away. Will you say good-bye, Estella?"

Still she did not speak. There were a hundred things she wanted to say but she could not say them. Did he mean that he loved her still? If she were sure of that, she could forgive him anything, but her doubt rendered her mute.

The young man turned away despairingly from her rigid attitude. So be it—he had brought his fate on himself.

He had gone but a few steps when Estella suddenly found her voice with a gasp.

"Spencer!" He came swiftly back. "Oh, Spencer—do—you—do you love me still?"

He caught her hands in his.

"Love you—oh, Estella, yes, yes! I always have. That other wasn't love—it was just madness. When it passed I hated life because I'd lost you. I know you can't forgive me, but, oh—"

He broke down. Estella flung her arms around his neck and put her face up to his. She felt as if her heart must break with its great happiness. He understood her mute pardon. In their kiss the past was put aside. Estella's martyrdom was ended.

The Old Chest at Wyther Grange

When I was a child I always thought a visit to Wyther Grange was a great treat. It was a big, quiet, old-fashioned house where Grandmother Laurance and Mrs. DeLisle, my Aunt Winnifred, lived. I was a favourite with them, yet I could never overcome a certain awe of them both. Grandmother was a tall, dignified old lady with keen black eyes that seemed veritably to bore through one. She always wore stiffly-rustling gowns of rich silk made in the fashion of her youth. I suppose she must have changed her dress occasionally, but the impression on my mind was always the same, as she went trailing about the house with a big bunch of keys at her belt—keys that opened a score of wonderful old chests and boxes and drawers. It was one of my dearest delights to attend Grandmother in her peregrinations and watch the unfolding and examining of all those old treasures and heirlooms of bygone Laurances.

Of Aunt Winnifred I was less in awe, possibly because she dressed in a modern way and so looked to my small eyes more human and natural. As Winnifred Laurance she had been the beauty of the family and was a handsome woman still, with brilliant dark eyes and cameo-like features. She always looked very sad, spoke in a low sweet voice, and was my childish ideal of all that was high-bred and graceful.

I had many beloved haunts at the Grange, but I liked the garret best. It was a roomy old place, big enough to have comfortably housed a family in itself, and was filled with cast-off furniture and old trunks and boxes of discarded finery. I was never tired of playing there, dressing up in the old-fashioned gowns and hats and practising old-time dance steps before the high, cracked mirror that hung at one end. That old garret was a veritable fairyland to me.

There was one old chest which I could not explore and, like all forbidden things, it possessed a great attraction for me. It stood away back in a dusty, cobwebbed corner, a strong, high wooden box, painted blue. From some words which I had heard Grandmother let fall I was sure it had a history; it was the one thing she never explored in her periodical overhaulings. When I grew tired of playing I liked to creep up on it and sit there, picturing out my own fancies concerning it—of which my favourite one was that some day I should solve the riddle and open the chest to find it full of gold and jewels with which I might restore the fortune of the Laurances and all the traditionary splendours of the old Grange.

I was sitting there one day when Aunt Winnifred and Grandmother Laurance came up the narrow dark staircase, the latter jingling her keys and peering into the dusty corners as she came along the room. When they came to the old chest, Grandmother rapped the top smartly with her keys.

"I wonder what is in this old chest," she said. "I believe it really should be opened. The moths may have got into it through that crack in the lid."

"Why don't you open it, Mother?" said Mrs. DeLisle. "I am sure that key of Robert's would fit the lock."

"No," said Grandmother in the tone that nobody, not even Aunt Winnifred, ever dreamed of disputing. "I will not open that chest without Eliza's permission. She confided it to my care when she went away, and I promised that it should never be opened until she came for it."

"Poor Eliza," said Mrs. DeLisle thoughtfully. "I wonder what she is like now. Very much changed, like all the rest of us, I suppose. It is almost thirty years since she was here. How pretty she was!"

"I never approved of her," said Grandmother brusquely. "She was a sentimental, fanciful creature. She might have married well but she preferred to waste her life pining over the memory of a man who was not worthy to untie the shoelace of a Laurance."

Mrs. DeLisle sighed softly and made no reply. People said that she had had her own romance in her youth and that her mother had sternly repressed it. I had heard that her marriage with Mr. DeLisle was loveless on her part and proved very unhappy. But he had been dead many years, and Aunt Winnifred never spoke of him.

"I have made up my mind what to do," said Grandmother decidedly. "I will write to Eliza and ask her if I may open the chest to see if the moths have got into it. If she refuses, well and good. I have no doubt that she *will* refuse. She will cling to her old sentimental ideas as long as the breath is in her body."

I rather avoided the old chest after this. It took on a new significance in my eyes and seemed to me like the tomb of something—possibly some dead and buried romance of the past.

Later on a letter came to Grandmother; she passed it over the table to Mrs. DeLisle.

"That is from Eliza," she said. "I would know her writing anywhere—none of your modern sprawly, untidy hands, but a fine lady-like script, as regular as copperplate. Read the letter, Winnifred; I haven't my glasses and I dare say Eliza's rhapsodies would tire me very much. You need not read them aloud—I can imagine them all. Let me know what she says about the chest."

Aunt Winnifred opened and read the letter and laid it down with a brief sigh.

"This is all she says about the chest. 'If it were not for one thing that is in it, I would ask you to open the chest and burn all its contents. But I cannot bear that anyone but myself should see or touch that one thing. So please leave the chest as it is, dear Aunt. It is no matter if the moths do get in.' That is all," continued Mrs. DeLisle, "and I must confess that I am disappointed. I have always had an almost childish curiosity about that old chest, but I seem fated not to have it gratified. That 'one thing' must be her wedding dress. I have always thought that she locked it away there."

"Her answer is just what I expected of her," said Grandmother impatiently. "Evidently the years have not made her more sensible. Well, I wash my hands of her belongings, moths or no moths."

It was not until ten years afterwards that I heard anything more of the old chest. Grandmother Laurance had died, but Aunt Winnifred still lived at the Grange. She was very lonely, and the winter after Grandmother's death she sent me an invitation to make her a long visit.

When I revisited the garret and saw the old blue chest in the same dusty corner, my childish curiosity revived and I begged Aunt Winnifred to tell me its history.

"I am glad you have reminded me of it," said Mrs. DeLisle. "I have intended to open the chest ever since Mother's death but I kept putting it off. You know, Amy, poor Eliza Laurance died five years ago, but even then Mother would not have the chest opened. There is no reason why it should not be examined now. If you like, we will go and open it at once and afterwards I will tell you the story."

We went eagerly up the garret stairs. Aunt knelt down before the old chest and selected a key from the bunch at her belt.

"Would it not be too provoking, Amy, if this key should not fit after all? Well, I do not believe you would be any more disappointed than I."

She turned the key and lifted the heavy lid. I bent forward eagerly. A layer of tissue paper revealed itself, with a fine tracing of sifted dust in its crinkles.

"Lift it up, child," said my aunt gently. "There are no ghosts for you, at least, in this old chest."

I lifted the paper up and saw that the chest was divided into two compartments. Lying on the top of one was a small, square, inlaid box. This Mrs. DeLisle took up and carried to the window. Lifting up the cover she laid it in my lap.

"There, Amy, look through it and let us see what old treasures have lain hidden there these forty years."

The first thing I took out was a small square case covered with dark purple velvet. The tiny clasp was almost rusted away and yielded easily. I gave a little cry of admiration. Aunt Winnifred bent over my shoulder.

"That is Eliza's portrait at the age of twenty, and that is Willis Starr's. Was she not lovely, Amy?"

Lovely indeed was the face looking out at me from its border of tarnished gilt. It was the face of a young girl, in shape a perfect oval, with delicate features and large dark-blue eyes. Her hair, caught high on the crown and falling on her neck in the long curls of a bygone fashion, was a warm auburn, and the curves of her bare neck and shoulders were exquisite.

"The other picture is that of the man to whom she was betrothed. Tell me, Amy, do you think him handsome?"

I looked at the other portrait critically. It was that of a young man of about twenty-five; he was undeniably handsome, but there was something I did not like in his face and I said so.

Aunt Winnifred made no reply—she was taking out the remaining contents of the box. There was a white silk fan with delicately carved ivory sticks, a packet of old letters and a folded paper containing some dried and crumpled flowers. Aunt laid the box aside and unpacked the chest in silence. First came a ball dress of pale-yellow satin brocade, made with the trained skirt, "baby" waist and full puffed sleeves of a former generation. Beneath it was a case containing a necklace of small but perfect pearls and a pair of tiny satin slippers. The rest of the compartment was filled with household linen, fine and costly but yellowed with age—damask table linen and webs of the uncut fabric.

In the second compartment lay a dress. Aunt Winnifred lifted it out reverently. It was a gown of rich silk that had once been white, but now, like the linen, it was yellow with age. It was simply made and trimmed with cobwebby old lace. Wrapped around it was a long white bridal veil, redolent with some strange, old-time perfume that had kept its sweetness all through the years.

"Well, Amy, this is all," said Aunt Winnifred with a quiver in her voice. "And now for the story. Where shall I begin?"

"At the very beginning, Aunty. You see I know nothing at all except her name. Tell me who she was and why she put her wedding dress away here."

"Poor Eliza!" said Aunt dreamily. "It is a sorrowful story, Amy, and it seems so long ago now. I must be an old woman. Forty years ago—and I was only twenty then. Eliza Laurance was my cousin, the only daughter of Uncle Henry Laurance. My father—your grandfather, Amy, you don't remember him—had two brothers, each of whom had an only daughter. Both these girls were called Eliza after your great-grandmother. I never saw Uncle George's Eliza but once. He was a rich man and his daughter was much sought after, but she was no beauty, I promise you that, and proud and vain to the last degree. Her home was in a distant city and she never came to Wyther Grange.

"The other Eliza Laurance was a poor man's daughter. She and I were of the same age and did not look unlike each other, although I was not so pretty by half. You can see by the portrait how beautiful she was, and it does her scant justice, for half her charm lay in her arch expression and her vivacious ways. She had her little faults, of course, and was rather over much given to romance and sentiment. This did not seem much of a defect to me then, Amy, for I was young and romantic too. Mother never cared much for Eliza, I think, but everyone else liked her. One winter Eliza came to Wyther Grange for a long visit. The Grange was a very lively place then, Amy. Eliza kept the old house ringing with merriment. We went out a great deal and she was always the belle of any festivity we attended. Yet she wore her honours easily; all the flattery and homage she received did not turn her head.

"That winter we first met Willis Starr. He was a newcomer, and nobody knew much about him, but one or two of the best families took him up, and his own fascinations did the rest. He became what you would call the rage. He was considered very handsome, his manners were polished and easy, and people said he was rich.

"I don't think, Amy, that I ever trusted Willis Starr. But like all the rest, I was blinded by his charm. Mother was almost the only one who did not worship at his shrine, and very often she dropped hints about penniless adventurers that made Eliza very indignant.

"From the first he had paid Eliza marked attention and seemed utterly bewitched by her. Well, his was an easy winning. Eliza loved him with her whole impulsive, girlish heart and made no attempt to hide it.

"I shall never forget the night they were first engaged. It was Eliza's birthday, and we were invited to a ball that evening. This yellow gown is the very one she wore. I suppose that is why she put it away here—the gown she wore on the happiest night of her life. I had never seen her look more beautiful—her neck and arms were bare, and she wore this string of pearls and carried a bouquet of her favourite white roses.

"When we reached home after the dance, Eliza had her happy secret to tell us. She was engaged to Willis Starr, and they were to be married in early spring.

"Willis Starr certainly seemed to be an ideal lover, and Eliza was so perfectly happy that she seemed to grow more beautiful and radiant every day.

"Well, Amy, the wedding day was set. Eliza was to be married from the Grange, as her own mother was dead, and I was to be bridesmaid. We made her wedding dress together, she and I. Girls were not above making their own gowns then, and not a stitch was set in Eliza's save those put there by loving fingers and blessed by loving wishes. It was I who draped the veil over her sunny curls—see how yellow and creased it is now, but it was as white as snow that day.

"A week before the wedding, Willis Starr was spending the evening at the Grange. We were all chattering gaily about the coming event, and in speaking of the invited guests Eliza said something about the other Eliza Laurance, the great heiress, looking archly at Willis over her shoulder as she spoke. It was some merry badinage about the cousin whose namesake she was but whom she so little resembled.

"We all laughed, but I shall never forget the look that came over Willis Starr's face. It passed quickly, but the chill fear that it gave me remained. A few minutes later I left the room on some trifling errand, and as I returned through the dim hall I was met by Willis Starr. He laid his hand on my arm and bent his evil face—for it *was* evil then, Amy—close to mine.

"'Tell me,' he said in a low but rude tone, 'is there another Eliza Laurance who is an heiress?'

"'Certainly there is,' I said sharply. 'She is our cousin and the daughter of our Uncle George. Our Eliza is not an heiress. You surely did not suppose she was!'

"Willis stepped aside with a mocking smile.

"'I did—what wonder? I had heard much about the great heiress, Eliza Laurance, and the great beauty, Eliza Laurance. I supposed they were one and the same. You have all been careful not to undeceive me.'

"'You forget yourself, Mr. Starr, when you speak so to me,' I retorted coldly. 'You have deceived yourself. We have never dreamed of allowing anyone to think that Eliza was an heiress. She is sweet and lovely enough to be loved for her own sake.'

"I went back to the parlour full of dismay. Willis Starr remained gloomy and taciturn all the rest of the evening, but nobody seemed to notice it but myself.

"The next day we were all so busy that I almost forgot the incident of the previous evening. We girls were up in the sewing room putting the last touches to the wedding gown. Eliza tried it and her veil on and was standing so, in all her silken splendour, when a letter was brought in. I guessed by her blush who was the writer. I laughed and ran downstairs, leaving her to read it.

"When I returned she was still standing just where I had left her in the middle of the room, holding the letter in her hand. Her face was as white as her veil, and her wide-open eyes had a dazed, agonized look as of someone who had been stricken a mortal blow. All the soft happiness and sweetness had gone out of them. They were the eyes of an old woman, Amy.

"'Eliza, what is the matter?' I said. 'Has anything happened to Willis?'

"She made no answer, but walked to the fireplace, dropped the letter in a bed of writhing blue flame and watched it burn to white ashes. Then she turned to me.

"'Help me take off this gown, Winnie,' she said dully. 'I shall never wear it again. There will be no wedding. Willis is gone.'

"'Gone!' I echoed stupidly.

"'Yes. I am not the heiress, Winnie. It was the fortune, not the girl, he loved. He says he is too poor for us to dream of marrying when I have nothing. Oh, such a cruel, heartless letter! Why did he not kill me? It would have been so much more merciful! I loved him so—I trusted him so! Oh, Winnie, Winnie, what am I to do!'

"There was something terrible in the contrast between her passionate words and her calm face and lifeless voice. I wanted to call Mother, but she would not let me. She went away to her own room, trailing along the dark hall in her dress and veil, and locked herself in.

"Well, I told it all to the others in some fashion. You can imagine their anger and dismay. Your father, Amy—he was a hot-blooded, impetuous, young fellow then—went at once to seek Willis Starr. But he was gone, no one knew where, and the whole country rang with the gossip and scandal of the affair. Eliza knew nothing of this, for she was ill and unconscious for many a day. In a novel or story she would have died, I suppose, and that would have been the end of it. But this was in real life, and Eliza did not die, although many times we thought she would.

"When she did recover, how frightfully changed she was! It almost broke my heart to see her. Her very nature seemed to have changed too—all her joyousness and light-heartedness were dead. From that time she was a faded, dispirited creature, no more like the Eliza we had known than the merest stranger. And then after a while came other news—Willis Starr was married to the other Eliza Lau-Laurance, the true heiress. He had made no second mistake. We tried to keep it from Eliza but she found it out at last. That was the day she came up here alone and packed this old chest. Nobody ever knew just what she put into it. But you and I see now, Amy—her ball dress, her wedding gown, her love letters and, more than all else, her youth and happiness—this old chest was the tomb of it all. Eliza Laurance was really buried here.

"She went home soon after. Before she went she exacted a promise from Mother that the old chest should be left at the Grange unopened until she came for it herself. But she never came back, and I do not think she ever intended to, and I never saw her again.

"That is the story of the old chest. It was all over so long ago—the heartbreak and the misery—but it all seems to come back to me now. Poor Eliza!"

My own eyes were full of tears as Aunt Winnifred went down the stairs, leaving me sitting dreamily there in the sunset light, with the old yellowed bridal veil across my lap and the portrait of Eliza Laurance in my hand. Around me were the relics of her pitiful story—the old, oft-repeated story of a faithless love and a woman's broken heart—the gown she had worn, the slippers in which she had danced light-heartedly at her betrothal ball, her fan, her pearls, her gloves—and it somehow seemed to me as if I were living in those old years myself, as if the love and happiness, the betrayal and pain were part of my own life. Presently Aunt Winnifred came back through the twilight shadows.

"Let us put all these things back in their grave, Amy," she said. "They are of no use to anyone now. The linen might be bleached and used, I dare say—but it would seem like a sacrilege. It was Mother's wedding present to Eliza. And the pearls—would you care to have them, Amy?"

"Oh, no, no," I said with a little shiver. "I would never wear them, Aunt Winnifred. I should feel like a ghost if I did. Put everything back just as we found it—only her portrait. I would like to keep that."

Reverently we put gowns and letters and trinkets back into the old blue chest. Aunt Winnifred closed the lid and turned the key softly. She bowed her head over it for a minute and then we went together in silence down the shadowy garret stairs of Wyther Grange.

The Osbornes' Christmas

Cousin Myra had come to spend Christmas at "The Firs," and all the junior Osbornes were ready to stand on their heads with delight. Darby—whose real name was Charles—did it, because he was only eight, and at eight you have no dignity to keep up. The others, being older, couldn't.

But the fact of Christmas itself awoke no great enthusiasm in the hearts of the junior Osbornes. Frank voiced their opinion of it the day after Cousin Myra had arrived. He was sitting on the table with his hands in his pockets and a cynical sneer on his face. At least, Frank flattered himself that it was cynical. He knew that Uncle Edgar was said to wear a cynical sneer, and Frank admired Uncle Edgar very much and imitated him in every possible way. But to you and me it would have looked just as it did to Cousin Myra—a very discontented and unbecoming scowl.

"I'm awfully glad to see you, Cousin Myra," explained Frank carefully, "and your being here may make some things worth while. But Christmas is just a bore—a regular bore."

That was what Uncle Edgar called things that didn't interest him, so that Frank felt pretty sure of his word. Nevertheless, he wondered uncomfortably what made Cousin Myra smile so queerly.

"Why, how dreadful!" she said brightly. "I thought all boys and girls looked upon Christmas as the very best time in the year."

"We don't," said Frank gloomily. "It's just the same old thing year in and year out. We know just exactly what is going to happen. We even know pretty well what presents we are going to get. And Christmas Day itself is always the same. We'll get up in the morning, and our stockings will be full of things, and half of them we don't want. Then there's dinner. It's always so poky. And all the uncles and aunts come to dinner—just the same old crowd, every year, and they say just the same things. Aunt Desda always says, 'Why, Frankie, how you have grown!' She knows I hate to be called Frankie. And after dinner they'll sit round and talk the rest of the day, and that's all. Yes, I call Christmas a nuisance."

"There isn't a single bit of fun in it," said Ida discontentedly.

"Not a bit!" said the twins, both together, as they always said things.

"There's lots of candy," said Darby stoutly. He rather liked Christmas, although he was ashamed to say so before Frank.

Cousin Myra smothered another of those queer smiles.

"You've had too much Christmas, you Osbornes," she said seriously. "It has palled on your taste, as all good things will if you overdo them. Did you ever try giving Christmas to somebody else?"

The Osbornes looked at Cousin Myra doubtfully. They didn't understand.

"We always send presents to all our cousins," said Frank hesitatingly. "That's a bore, too. They've all got so many things already it's no end of bother to think of something new."

"That isn't what I mean," said Cousin Myra. "How much Christmas do you suppose those little Rolands down there in the hollow have? Or Sammy Abbott with his lame back? Or French Joe's family over the hill? If you have too much Christmas, why don't you give some to them?"

The Osbornes looked at each other. This was a new idea.

"How could we do it?" asked Ida.

Whereupon they had a consultation. Cousin Myra explained her plan, and the Osbornes grew enthusiastic over it. Even Frank forgot that he was supposed to be wearing a cynical sneer.

"I move we do it, Osbornes," said he.

"If Father and Mother are willing," said Ida.

"Won't it be jolly!" exclaimed the twins.

"Well, rather," said Darby scornfully. He did not mean to be scornful. He had heard Frank saying the same words in the same tone, and thought it signified approval.

Cousin Myra had a talk with Father and Mother Osborne that night, and found them heartily in sympathy with her plans.

For the next week the Osbornes were agog with excitement and interest. At first Cousin Myra made the suggestions, but their enthusiasm soon outstripped her, and they thought out things for themselves. Never did a week pass so quickly. And the Osbornes had never had such fun, either.

Christmas morning there was not a single present given or received at "The Firs" except those which Cousin Myra and Mr. and Mrs. Osborne gave to each other. The junior Osbornes had asked that the money which their parents had planned to spend in presents for them be given to them the previous week; and given it was, without a word.

The uncles and aunts arrived in due time, but not with them was the junior Osbornes' concern. They were the guests of Mr. and Mrs. Osborne. The junior Osbornes were having a Christmas dinner party of their own. In the small dining room a table was spread and loaded with good things. Ida and the twins cooked that dinner all by themselves. To be sure, Cousin Myra had helped some, and Frank and Darby had stoned all the raisins and helped pull the home-made candy; and all together they had decorated the small dining room royally with Christmas greens.

Then their guests came. First, all the little Rolands from the Hollow arrived—seven in all, with very red, shining faces and not a word to say for themselves, so shy were they. Then came a troop from French Joe's—four black-eyed lads, who never knew what shyness meant. Frank drove down to the village in the cutter and brought lame Sammy back with him, and soon after the last guest arrived—little Tillie Mather, who was Miss Rankin's "orphan 'sylum girl" from over the road. Everybody knew that Miss Rankin never kept Christmas. She did not believe in it, she said, but she did not prevent Tillie from going to the Osbornes' dinner party.

Just at first the guests were a little stiff and unsocial; but they soon got acquainted, and so jolly was Cousin Myra—who had her dinner with the children in preference to the grown-ups—and so friendly the junior Osbornes, that all stiffness vanished. What a merry dinner it was! What peals of laughter went up, reaching to the big dining room across the hall, where the grown-ups sat in rather solemn state. And how those guests did eat and frankly enjoy the good things before them! How nicely they all behaved, even to the French Joes! Myra had secretly been a little dubious about those four mischievous-looking lads, but their manners were quite flawless. Mrs. French Joe had been drilling them for three days—ever since they had been invited to "de Chrismus dinner at de beeg house."

After the merry dinner was over, the junior Osbornes brought in a Christmas tree, loaded with presents. They had bought them with the money that Mr. and Mrs. Osborne had meant for their own presents, and a splendid assortment they were. All the French-Joe boys got a pair of skates apiece, and Sammy a set of beautiful books, and Tillie was made supremely happy with a big wax doll. Every little Roland got just what his or her small heart had been longing for. Besides, there were nuts and candies galore.

Then Frank hitched up his pony again, but this time into a great pung sleigh, and the junior Osbornes took their guests for a sleigh-drive, chaperoned by Cousin Myra. It was just dusk when they got back, having driven the Rolands and the French Joes and Sammy and Tillie to their respective homes.

"This has been the jolliest Christmas I ever spent," said Frank, emphatically.

"I thought we were just going to give the others a good time, but it was they who gave it to us," said Ida.

"Weren't the French Joes jolly?" giggled the twins. "Such cute speeches as they would make!"

"Me and Teddy Roland are going to be chums after this," announced Darby. "He's an inch taller than me, but I'm wider."

That night Frank and Ida and Cousin Myra had a little talk after the smaller Osbornes had been haled off to bed.

"We're not going to stop with Christmas, Cousin Myra," said Frank, at the end of it. "We're just going to keep on through the year. We've never had such a delightful old Christmas before."

"You've learned the secret of happiness," said Cousin Myra gently.

And the Osbornes understood what she meant.

The Romance of Aunt Beatrice

Margaret always maintains that it was a direct inspiration of Providence that took her across the street to see Aunt Beatrice that night. And Aunt Beatrice believes that it was too. But the truth of the matter is that Margaret was feeling very unhappy, and went over to talk to Aunt Beatrice as the only alternative to a fit of crying. Margaret's unhappiness has nothing further to do with this story, so it may be dismissed with the remark that it did not amount to much, in spite of Margaret's tragical attitude, and was dissipated at once and forever by the arrival of a certain missent letter the next day.

Aunt Beatrice was alone. Her brother and his wife had gone to the "at home" which Mrs. Cunningham was giving that night in honour of the Honourable John Reynolds, M.P. The children were upstairs in bed, and Aunt Beatrice was darning their stockings, a big basketful of which loomed up aggressively on the table beside her. Or, to speak more correctly, she had been darning them. Just when Margaret was sliding across the icy street Aunt Beatrice was bent forward in her chair, her hands over her face, while soft, shrinking little sobs shook her from head to foot.

When Margaret's imperative knock came at the front door, Aunt Beatrice started guiltily and wished earnestly that she had waited until she went to bed before crying, if cry she must. She knew Margaret's knock, and she did not want her gay young niece, of all people in the world, to suspect the fact or the cause of her tears.

"I hope she won't notice my eyes," she thought, as she hastily plumped a big ugly dark-green shade, with an almond-eyed oriental leering from it, over the lamp, before going out to let Margaret in.

Margaret did not notice at first. She was too deeply absorbed in her own troubles to think that anyone else in the world could be miserable too. She curled up in the deep easy-chair by the fire, and clasped her hands behind her curly head with a sigh of physical comfort and mental unhappiness, while Aunt Beatrice, warily sitting with her back to the light, took up her work again.

"You didn't go to Mrs. Cunningham's 'at home,' Auntie," said Margaret lazily, feeling that she must make some conversation to justify her appearance. "You were invited, weren't you?"

Aunt Beatrice nodded. The hole she was darning in the knee of Willie Hayden's stocking must be done very carefully. Mrs. George Hayden was particular about such matters. Perhaps this was why Aunt Beatrice did not speak.

"Why didn't you go?" asked Margaret absently, wondering why there had been no letter for her that morning—and this was the third day too! Could Gilbert be ill? Or was he flirting with some other girl and forgetting her? Margaret swallowed a big lump in her throat, and resolved that she would go home next week—no, she wouldn't, either—if he was as hateful and fickle as that—what was Aunt Beatrice saying?

"Well, I'm—I'm not used to going to parties now, my dear. And the truth is I have no dress fit to wear. At least Bella said so, because the party was to be a very fashionable affair. She said my old grey silk wouldn't do at all. Of course she knows. She had to have a new dress for it, and, we couldn't both have that. George couldn't afford it these hard times. And, as Bella said, it would be very foolish of me to get an expensive dress that would be no use to me afterward. But it doesn't matter. And, of course, somebody had to stay with the children."

"Of course," assented Margaret dreamily. Mrs. Cunningham's "at home" was of no particular interest. The guests were all middle-aged people whom the M.P. had known in his boyhood and Margaret, in her presumptuous youth, thought it would be a very prosy affair, although it had made quite a sensation in quiet little Murraybridge, where people still called an "at home" a party plain and simple.

"I saw Mr. Reynolds in church Sunday afternoon," she went on. "He is very fine-looking, I think. Did you ever meet him?"

"I used to know him very well long ago," answered Aunt Beatrice, bowing still lower over her work. "He used to live down in Wentworth, you know, and he visited his married sister here very often. He was only a boy at that time. Then—he went out to British Columbia and—and—we never heard much more about him."

"He's very rich and owns dozens of mines and railroads and things like that," said Margaret, "and he's a member of the Dominion Parliament, too. They say he's one of the foremost men in the House and came very near getting a portfolio in the new cabinet. I like men like that. They are so interesting. Wouldn't it be awfully nice and complimentary to have one of them in love with you? Is he married?"

"I—I don't know," said Aunt Beatrice faintly. "I have never heard that he was."

"There, you've run the needle into your finger," said Margaret sympathetically.

"It's of no consequence," said Aunt Beatrice hastily.

She wiped away the drop of blood and went on with her work. Margaret watched her dreamily. What lovely hair Aunt Beatrice had! It was so thick and glossy, with warm bronze tones where the lamp-light fell on it under that hideous weird old shade. But Aunt Beatrice wore it in such an unbecoming way. Margaret idly wondered if she would comb her hair straight back and prim when she was thirty-five. She thought it very probable if that letter did not come tomorrow.

From Aunt Beatrice's hair Margaret's eyes fell to Aunt Beatrice's face. She gave a little jump. Had Aunt Beatrice been crying? Margaret sat bolt upright.

"Aunt Beatrice, did you want to go to that party?" she demanded explosively. "Now tell me the truth."

"I did," said Aunt Beatrice weakly. Margaret's sudden attack fairly startled the truth out of her. "It is very silly of me, I know, but I did want to go. I didn't care about a new dress. I'd have been quite willing to wear my grey silk, and I could have fixed the sleeves. What difference would it have made? Nobody would ever have noticed me, but Bella thought it wouldn't do."

She paused long enough to give a little sob which she could not repress. Margaret made use of the opportunity to exclaim violently, "It's a shame!"

"I suppose you don't understand why I wanted to go to this particular party so much," went on Aunt Beatrice shyly. "I'll tell you why—if you won't laugh at me. I wanted to see John Reynolds—not to talk to him—oh, I dare say he wouldn't remember me—but just to see him. Long ago—fifteen years ago—we were engaged. And—and—I loved him so much then, Margaret."

"You poor dear!" said Margaret sympathetically. She reached over and patted her aunt's hand. She thought that this little bit of romance, long hidden and unsuspected, blossoming out under her eyes, was charming. In her interest she quite forgot her own pet grievance.

"Yes—and then we quarrelled. It was a dreadful quarrel and it was about such a trifle. We parted in anger and he went away. He never came back. It was all my fault. Well, it is all over long ago and everybody has forgotten. I—I don't mind it now. But I just wanted to see him once more and then come quietly away."

"Aunt Beatrice, you are going to that party yet," said Margaret decisively.

"Oh, it is impossible, my dear."

"No, it isn't. Nothing is impossible when I make up my mind. You must go. I'll drag you there by main force if it comes to that. Oh, I have such a jolly plan, Auntie. You know my black and yellow dinner dress—no, you don't either, for I've never worn it here. The folks at home all said it was too severe for me—and so it is. Nothing suits me but the fluffy, chuffy things with a tilt to them. Gil—er—I mean—well, yes, Gilbert always declared that dress made me look like a cross between an unwilling nun and a ballet girl, so I took a dislike to it. But it's as lovely as a dream. Oh, when you see it your eyes will stick out. You must wear it tonight. It's just your style, and I'm sure it will fit you, for our figures are so much alike."

"But it is too late."

"'Tisn't. It's not more than half an hour since Uncle George and Aunt Bella went. I'll have you ready in a twinkling."

"But the fire—and the children!"

"I'll stay here and look after both. I won't burn the house down, and if the twins wake up I'll give them—what is it you give them—soothing syrup? So go at once and get you ready, while I fly over for the dress. I'll fix your hair up when I get back."

Margaret was gone before Aunt Beatrice could speak again. Her niece's excitement seized hold of her too. She flung the stockings into the basket and the basket into the closet.

"I will go—and I won't do another bit of darning tonight. I hate it—I hate it—I hate it! Oh, how much good it does me to say it!"

When Margaret came flying up the stairs Aunt Beatrice was ready save for hair and dress. Margaret cast the gown on the bed, revealing all its beauty of jetted lace and soft yellow silk with a dextrous sweep of her arm. Aunt Beatrice gave a little cry of admiration.

"Isn't it lovely?" demanded Margaret. "And I've brought you my opera cape and my fascinator and my black satin slippers with the cunningest gold buckles, and some sweet pale yellow roses that Uncle Ned gave me yesterday. Oh, Aunt Beatrice! What magnificent arms and shoulders you have! They're like marble. Mine are so scrawny I'm just ashamed to have people know they belong to me."

Margaret's nimble fingers were keeping time with her tongue. Aunt Beatrice's hair went up as if by magic into soft puffs and waves and twists, and a golden rose was dropped among the bronze masses. Then the lovely dress was put on and pinned and looped and pulled until it fell into its simple, classical lines around the tall, curving figure. Margaret stepped back and clapped her hands admiringly.

"Oh, Auntie, you're beautiful! Now I'll pop down for the cloak and fascinator. I left them hanging by the fire."

When Margaret had gone Aunt Beatrice caught up the lamp and tiptoed shamefacedly across the hall to the icy-cold spare room. In the long mirror she saw herself reflected from top to toe—or was it herself! Could it be—that gracious woman with the sweet eyes and flushed cheeks, with rounded arms gleaming through their black laces and the cluster of roses nestling against the warm white flesh of the shoulder?

"I do look nice," she said aloud, with a little curtsey to the radiant reflection. "It is all the dress, I know. I feel like a queen in it—no, like a girl again—and that's better."

Margaret went to Mrs. Cunningham's door with her.

"How I wish I could go in and see the sensation you'll make, Aunt Beatrice," she whispered.

"You dear, silly child! It's just the purple and fine linen," laughed Aunt Beatrice. But she did not altogether think so, and she rang the doorbell unquailingly. In the hall Mrs. Cunningham herself came beamingly to greet her.

"My dear Beatrice! I'm so glad. Bella said you could not come because you had a headache."

"My headache got quite better after they left, and so I thought I would get ready and come, even if it were rather late," said Beatrice glibly, wondering if Sapphira had ever worn a black-and-yellow dress, and if so, might not her historic falsehood be traced to its influence?

When they came downstairs together, Beatrice, statuesque and erect in her trailing draperies, and Mrs. Cunningham secretly wondering where on earth Beatrice Hayden had got such a magnificent dress and what she had done to herself to make her look as she did—a man came through the hall. At the foot of the stairs they met. He put out his hand.

"Beatrice! It must be Beatrice! How little you have changed!"

Mrs. Cunningham was not particularly noted in Murraybridge for her tact, but she had a sudden visitation of the saving grace at that moment, and left the two alone.

Beatrice put her hand into the M.P.'s.

"I am glad to see you," she said simply, looking up at him.

She could not say that he had not changed, for there was little in this tall, broad-shouldered man of the world, with grey glints in his hair, to suggest the slim, boyish young lover whose image she had carried in her heart all the long years.

But the voice, though deeper and mellower, was the same, and the thin, clever mouth that went up at one corner and down at the other in a humorous twist; and one little curl of reddish hair fell over his forehead away from its orderly fellows, just as it used to when she had loved to poke her fingers through it; and, more than all, the deep-set grey eyes looking down into her blue ones were unchanged. Beatrice felt her heart beating to her fingertips.

"I thought you were not coming," he said. "I expected to meet you here and I was horribly disappointed. I thought the bitterness of that foolish old quarrel must be strong enough to sway you yet."

"Didn't Bella tell you I had a headache?" faltered Beatrice.

"Bella? Oh, your brother's wife! I wasn't talking to her. I've been sulking in corners ever since I concluded you were not coming. How beautiful you are, Beatrice! You'll let an old friend say that much, won't you?"

Beatrice laughed softly. She had forgotten for years that she was beautiful, but the sweet old knowledge had come back to her again. She could not help knowing that he spoke the simple truth, but she said mirthfully,

"You've learned to flatter since the old days, haven't you? Don't you remember you used to tell me I was too thin to be pretty? But I suppose a bit of blarney is a necessary ingredient in the composition of an M.P."

He was still holding her hand. With a glance of dissatisfaction at the open parlour door, he drew her away to the little room at the end of the hall, which Mrs. Cunningham, for reasons known only to herself, called her library.

"Come in here with me," he said masterfully. "I want to have a long talk with you before the other people get hold of you."

When Beatrice got home from the party ten minutes before her brother and his wife, Margaret was sitting Turk fashion in the big armchair, with her eyes very wide open and owlish.

"You dear girlie, were you asleep?" asked Aunt Beatrice indulgently.

Margaret nodded. "Yes, and I've let the fire go out. I hope you're not cold. I must run before Aunt Bella gets here, or she'll scold. Had a nice time?"

"Delightful. You were a dear to lend me this dress. It was so funny to see Bella staring at it."

When Margaret had put on her hat and jacket she went as far as the street door, and then tiptoed back to the sitting-room. Aunt Beatrice was leaning back in the armchair, with a drooping rose held softly against her lips, gazing dreamily into the dull red embers.

"Auntie," said Margaret contritely, "I can't go home without confessing, although I know it is a heinous offence to interrupt the kind of musing that goes with dying embers and faded roses in the small hours. But it would weigh on my conscience all night if I didn't. I was asleep, but I wakened up just before you came in and went to the window. I didn't mean to spy upon anyone—but that street was bright as day! And if you will let an M.P. kiss you on the doorstep in glaring moonlight, you must expect to be seen."

"I wouldn't have cared if there had been a dozen onlookers," said Aunt Beatrice frankly, "and I don't believe he would either."

Margaret threw up her hands. "Well, my conscience is clear, at least. And remember, Aunt Beatrice, I'm to be bridesmaid—I insist upon that. And, oh, won't you ask me to visit you when you go down to Ottawa next winter? I'm told it's such a jolly place when the House is in session. And you'll need somebody to help you entertain, you know. The wife of a cabinet minister has to do lots of that. But I forgot—he isn't a cabinet minister yet. But he will be, of course. Promise that you'll have me, Aunt Beatrice, promise quick. I hear Uncle George and Aunt Bella coming."

Aunt Beatrice promised. Margaret flew to the door.

"You'd better keep that dress," she called back softly, as she opened it.

The Running Away of Chester

Chester did the chores with unusual vim that night. His lips were set and there was an air of resolution as plainly visible on his small, freckled face as if it had been stamped there. Mrs. Elwell saw him flying around, and her grim features took on a still grimmer expression.

"Ches is mighty lively tonight," she muttered. "I s'pose he's in a gog to be off on some foolishness with Henry Wilson. Well, he won't, and he needn't think it."

Lige Barton, the hired man, also thought this was Chester's purpose, but he took a more lenient view of it than did Mrs. Elwell.

"The little chap is going through things with a rush this evening," he reflected. "Guess he's laying out for a bit of fun with the Wilson boy."

But Chester was not planning anything connected with Henry Wilson, who lived on the other side of the pond and was the only chum he possessed. After the chores were done, he lingered a little while around the barns, getting his courage keyed up to the necessary pitch.

Chester Stephens was an orphan without kith or kin in the world, unless his father's stepsister, Mrs. Harriet Elwell, could be called so. His parents had died in his babyhood, and Mrs. Elwell had taken him to bring up. She was a harsh woman, with a violent temper, and she had scolded and worried the boy all his short life. Upton people said it was a shame, but nobody felt called upon to interfere. Mrs. Elwell was not a person one would care to make an enemy of.

She eyed Chester sourly when he went in, expecting some request to be allowed to go with Henry, and prepared to refuse it sharply.

"Aunt Harriet," said Chester suddenly, "can I go to school this year? It begins tomorrow."

"No," said Mrs. Elwell, when she had recovered from her surprise at this unexpected question. "You've had schoolin' in plenty—more'n I ever had, and all you're goin' to get!"

"But, Aunt Harriet," persisted Chester, his face flushed with earnestness, "I'm nearly thirteen, and I can barely read and write a little. The other boys are ever so far ahead of me. I don't know anything."

"You know enough to be disrespectful!" exclaimed Mrs. Elwell. "I suppose you want to go to school to idle away your time, as you do at home—lazy good-for-nothing that you are!" Chester thought of the drudgery that had been his portion all his life. He resented being called lazy when he was willing enough to work, but he made one more appeal.

"If you'll let me go to school this year, I'll work twice as hard out of school to make up for it—indeed, I will. Do let me go, Aunt Harriet. I haven't been to school a day for over a year."

"Let's hear no more of this nonsense," said Mrs. Elwell, taking a bottle from the shelf above her with the air of one who closes a discussion. "Here, run down to the Bridge and get me this bottle full of vinegar at Jacob's store. Be smart, too, d'ye hear! I ain't going to have you idling around the Bridge neither. If you ain't back in twenty minutes, it won't be well for you."

Chester did his errand at the Bridge with a heart full of bitter disappointment and anger.

"I won't stand it any longer!" he muttered. "I'll run away—I don't care where, so long as it's away from her. I wish I could get out West on the harvest excursions."

On his return home, as he crossed the yard in the dusk, he stumbled over a stick of wood and fell. The bottle of vinegar slipped from his hand and was broken on the doorstep. Mrs. Elwell saw the accident from the window. She rushed out and jerked the unlucky lad to his feet.

"Take that, you sulky little cub!" she exclaimed, cuffing his ears soundly. "I'll teach you to break and spill things you're sent for! You did it on purpose. Get off to bed with you this instant."

Chester crept off to his garret chamber with a very sullen face. He was too used to being sent to bed without any supper to care much for that, although he was hungry. But his whole being was in a tumult of rebellion over the injustice that was meted out to him.

"I won't stand it!" he muttered over and over again. "I'll run away. I won't stay here."

To talk of running away was one thing. To do it without a cent in your pocket or a place to run to was another. But Chester had a great deal of determination in his make-up when it was fairly roused, and his hard upbringing had made him older and shrewder than his years. He lay awake late that night, thinking out ways and means, but could arrive at no satisfactory conclusion.

The next day Mrs. Elwell said, "Ches, Abner Stearns wants you to go up there for a fortnight while Tom Bixby is away, and drive the milk wagon of mornings and do the chores for Mrs. Stearns. You might as well put in the time 'fore harvest that way as any other. So hustle off—and mind you behave yourself."

Chester heard the news gladly. He had not yet devised any feasible plan for running away, and he always liked to work at the Stearns' place. To be sure, Mrs. Elwell received all the money he earned, but Mrs. Stearns was kind to him, and though he had to work hard and constantly, he was well fed and well treated by all.

The following fortnight was a comparatively happy one for the lad. But he did not forget his purpose of shaking the dust of Upton from his feet as soon as possible, and he cudgelled his brains trying to find a way.

On the evening when he left the Stearns' homestead, Mr. Stearns paid him for his fortnight's work, much to the boy's surprise, for Mrs. Elwell had always insisted that all such money should be paid directly to her. Chester found himself the possessor of four dollars—an amount of riches that almost took away his breath. He had never in his whole life owned more than ten cents at a time. As he tramped along the road home, he kept his hand in his pocket, holding fast to the money, as if he feared it would otherwise dissolve into thin air.

His mind was firmly made up. He would run away once and for all. This money was rightly his; he had earned every cent of it. It would surely last him until he found employment elsewhere. At any rate, he would go; and even if he starved, he would never come back to Aunt Harriet's!

When he reached home, he found Mrs. Elwell in an unusual state of worry. Lige had given warning—and this on the verge of harvest!

"Did Stearns say anything about coming down tomorrow to pay me for your work?" she asked.

"No, ma'am. He didn't say a word about it," said Chester boldly.

"Well, I hope he will. Take yourself off to bed, Ches. I'm sick of seeing you standing there, on one foot or t'other, like a gander."

Chester had been shifting about uneasily. He realized that, if his project did not miscarry, he would not see his aunt again, and his heart softened to her. Harsh as she was, she was the only protector he had ever known, and the boy had a vague wish to carry away with him some kindly word or look from her. Such, however, was not forthcoming, and Chester obeyed her command and took himself off to the garret. Here he sat down and reflected on his plans.

He must go that very night. When Mr. Stearns failed to appear on the morrow, Mrs. Elwell was quite likely to march up and demand the amount of Chester's wages. It would all come out then, and he would lose his money—besides, no doubt, getting severely punished into the bargain.

His preparations did not take long. He had nothing to carry with him. The only decent suit of clothes he possessed was his well-worn Sunday one. This he put on, carefully stowing away in his pocket the precious four dollars.

He had to wait until he thought his aunt was asleep, and it was about eleven when he crept downstairs, his heart quaking within him, and got out by the porch window. When he found himself alone in the clear moonlight of the August night, a sense of elation filled his cramped little heart. He was free, and he would never come back here—never!

"Wisht I could have seen Henry to say good-by to him, though," he muttered with a wistful glance at the big house across the pond where the unconscious Henry was sleeping soundly with never a thought of moonlight flittings for anyone in his curly head.

Chester meant to walk to Roxbury Station ten miles away. Nobody knew him there, and he could catch the morning train. Late as it was, he kept to fields and wood-roads lest he might be seen and recognized. It was three o'clock when he reached Roxbury, and he knew the train did not pass through until six. With the serenity of a philosopher who is starting out to win his way in the world and means to make the best of things, Chester curled himself up in the hollow space of a big lumber pile behind the station, and so tired was he that he fell soundly asleep in a few minutes.

Chester was awakened by the shriek of the express at the last crossing before the station. In a panic of haste he scrambled out of his lumber and dashed into the station house, where a sleepy, ill-natured agent stood behind the ticket window. He looked sharply enough at the freckled, square-jawed boy who asked for a second-class ticket to Belltown. Chester's heart quaked within him at the momentary thought that the ticket agent recognized him. He had an agonized vision of being collared without ceremony and haled straightway back to Aunt Harriet. When the ticket and his change were pushed out to him, he snatched them and fairly ran.

"Bolted as if the police were after him," reflected the agent, who did not sell many tickets and so had time to take a personal interest in the purchasers thereof. "I've seen that youngster before, though I can't recollect where. He's got a most fearful determined look."

Chester drew an audible sigh of relief when the train left the station. He was fairly off now and felt that he could defy even curious railway officials.

It was not his first train ride, for Mrs. Elwell had once taken him to Belltown to get an aching tooth extracted, but it was certainly his first under such exhilarating circumstances, and he meant to enjoy it. To be sure, he was very hungry, but that, he reflected, was only what he would probably be many times before he made his fortune, and it was just as well to get used to it. Meanwhile, it behooved him to keep his eyes open. On the road from Roxbury to Belltown there was not much to be seen that morning that Chester did not see.

The train reached Belltown about noon. He did not mean to stop long there—it was too near Upton. From the conductor on the train, he found that a boat left Belltown for Montrose at two in the afternoon. Montrose was a hundred miles from Upton, and Chester thought he would be safe there. To Montrose, accordingly, he decided to go, but the first thing was to get some dinner. He went into a grocery store and bought some crackers and a bit of cheese. He had somewhere picked up the idea that crackers and cheese were about as economical food as you could find for adventurous youths starting out on small capital.

He found his way to the only public square Belltown boasted, and munched his food hungrily on a bench under the trees. He would go to Montrose and there find something to do. Later on he would gradually work his way out West, where there was more room for an ambitious small boy to expand and grow. Chester dreamed some dazzling dreams as he sat there on the bench under the Belltown chestnuts. Passers-by, if they noticed him at all, saw merely a rather small, poorly clad boy, with a great many freckles, a square jaw and shrewd, level-gazing grey eyes. But this same lad was mapping out a very brilliant future for himself as people passed him heedlessly by. He would get out West, somehow or other, some time or other, and make a fortune. Then, perhaps, he would go back to Upton for a visit and shine in his splendour before all his old neighbours. It all seemed very easy and alluring, sitting there in the quiet little Belltown square. Chester, you see, possessed imagination. That, together with the crackers and cheese, so cheered him up that he felt ready for anything. He was aroused from a dream of passing Aunt Harriet by in lofty scorn and a glittering carriage, by the shrill whistle of the boat. Chester pocketed his remaining crackers and cheese and his visions also, and was once more his alert, wide-awake self. He had inquired the way to the wharf from the grocer, so he found no difficulty in reaching it. When the boat steamed down the muddy little river, Chester was on board of her.

He was glad to be out of Belltown, for he was anything but sure that he would not encounter some Upton people as long as he was in it. They often went to Belltown on business, but never to Montrose.

There were not many passengers on the boat, and Chester scrutinized them all so sharply in turn that he could have sworn to each and every one of them for years afterwards had it been necessary. The one he liked best was a middle-aged lady who sat just before him on the opposite side of the deck She was plump and motherly looking, with a fresh, rosy face and beaming blue eyes.

"If I was looking for anyone to adopt me I'd pick her," said Chester to himself. The more he looked at her, the better he liked her. He labelled her in his mind as "the nice, rosy lady."

The nice, rosy lady noticed Chester staring at her after awhile. She smiled promptly at him—a smile that seemed fairly to irradiate her round face—and then began fumbling in an old-fashioned reticule she carried, and from which she presently extracted a chubby little paper bag.

"If you like candy, little boy," she said to Chester, "here is some of my sugar taffy for you."

Chester did not exactly like being called a little boy. But her voice and smile were irresistible and won his heart straightway. He took the candy with a shy, "Thank you, ma'am," and sat holding it in his hand.

"Eat it," commanded the rosy lady authoritatively. "That is what taffy is for, you know."

So Chester ate it. It was the most delicious thing he had ever tasted in his life, and filled a void which even the crackers and cheese had left vacant. The rosy lady watched every mouthful he ate as if she enjoyed it more than he did. When he had finished the taffy she smiled one of her sociable smiles again and said, "Well, what do you think of it?"

"It's the nicest taffy I ever ate," answered Chester enthusiastically, as if he were a connoisseur in all kinds of taffies. The rosy lady nodded, well pleased.

"That is just what everyone says about my sugar taffy. Nobody up our way can match it, though goodness knows they try hard enough. My great-grandmother invented the recipe herself, and it has been in our family ever since. I'm real glad you liked it."

She smiled at him again, as if his appreciation of her taffy was a bond of good fellowship between them. She did not know it but, nevertheless, she was filling the heart of a desperate small boy, who had run away from home, with hope and encouragement and self-reliance. If there were such kind folks as this in the world, why, he would get along all right. The rosy lady's smiles and taffy—the smiles much more than the taffy—went far to thaw out of him a certain hardness and resentfulness against people in general that Aunt Harriet's harsh treatment had instilled into him. Chester instantly made a resolve that when he grew stout and rosy and prosperous he would dispense smiles and taffy and good cheer generally to all forlorn small boys on boats and trains.

It was almost dark when they reached Montrose. Chester lost sight of the rosy lady when they left the boat, and it gave him a lonesome feeling; but he could not indulge in that for long at a time. Here he was at his destination—at dark, in a strange city a hundred miles from home.

"The first thing is to find somewhere to sleep," he said to himself, resolutely declining to feel frightened, although the temptation was very strong.

Montrose was not really a very big place. It was only a bustling little town of some twenty thousand inhabitants, but to Chester's eyes it was a vast metropolis. He had never been in any place bigger than Belltown, and in Belltown you could see one end of it, at least, no matter where you were. Montrose seemed endless to Chester as he stood at the head of Water Street and gazed in bewilderment along one of its main business avenues—a big, glittering, whirling place where one small boy could so easily be swallowed up that he would never be heard of again.

Chester, after paying his fare to Montrose and buying his cheese and crackers, had just sixty cents left. This must last him until he found work, so that the luxury of lodgings was out of the question, even if he had known where to look for them. To be sure, there were benches in a public square right in front of him; but Chester was afraid that if he curled up on one of them for the night, a policeman might question him, and he did not believe he could give a very satisfactory account of himself. In his perplexity, he thought of his cosy lumber pile at Roxbury Station and remembered that when he had left the boat he had noticed a large vacant lot near the wharf which was filled with piles of lumber. Back to this he went and soon succeeded in finding a place to stow himself. His last waking thought was that he must be up and doing bright and early the next morning, and that it must surely be longer than twenty-four hours since he had crept downstairs and out of Aunt Harriet's porch window at Upton.

Montrose seemed less alarming by daylight, which was not so bewildering as the blinking electric lights. Chester was up betimes, ate the last of his cheese and crackers and started out at once to look for work. He determined to be thorough, and he went straight into every place of business he came to, from a blacksmith's forge to a department store, and boldly asked the first person he met if they wanted a boy there. There was, however, one class of places Chester shunned determinedly. He never went into a liquor saloon. The last winter he had been allowed to go to school in Upton, his teacher had been a pale, patient little woman who hated the liquor traffic with all her heart. She herself had suffered bitterly through it, and she instilled into her pupils a thorough aversion to it. Chester would have chosen death by starvation before he would have sought for employment in a liquor saloon. But there certainly did not seem room for him anywhere else. Nobody wanted a boy. The answer to his question was invariably "No." As the day wore on, Chester's hopes and courage went down to zero, but he still tramped doggedly about. He would be thorough, at least. Surely somewhere in this big place, where everyone seemed so busy, there must be something for him to do.

Once there seemed a chance of success. He had gone into a big provision store and asked the clerk behind the counter if they wanted a boy.

"Well, we do," said the clerk, looking him over critically, "but I hardly think you'll fill the bill. However, come in and see the boss."

He took Chester into a dark, grimy little inner office where a fat, stubby man was sitting before a desk with his feet upon it.

"Hey? What!" he said when the clerk explained. "Looking for the place? Why, sonny, you're not half big enough."

"Oh, I'm a great deal bigger than I look," cried Chester breathlessly. "That is, sir—I mean I'm ever so much stronger than I look. I'll work hard, sir, ever so hard—and I'll grow."

The fat, stubby man roared with laughter. What was grim earnest to poor Chester was a joke to him.

"No doubt you will, my boy," he said genially, "but I'm afraid you'll hardly grow fast enough to suit us. Boys aren't like pigweed, you know. No, no, our boy must be a big, strapping fellow of eighteen or nineteen. He'll have a deal of heavy lifting to do."

Chester went out of the store with a queer choking in his throat. For one horrible moment he thought he was going to cry—he, Chester Stephens, who had run away from home to do splendid things! A nice ending that would be to his fine dreams! He thrust his hands into his pockets and strode along the street, biting his lips fiercely. He would not cry—no, he would not! And he *would* find work!

Chester did not cry, but neither, alas, did he find work. He parted with ten cents of his precious hoard for more crackers, and he spend the night again in the lumber yard.

Perhaps I'll have better luck tomorrow, he thought hopefully.

But it really seemed as if there were to be no luck for Chester except bad luck. Day after day passed and, although he tramped resolutely from street to street and visited every place that seemed to offer any chance, he could get no employment. In spite of his pluck, his heart began to fail him.

At the end of a week Chester woke up among his lumber to a realization that he was at the end of his resources. He had just five cents left out of the four dollars that were to have been the key to his fortune. He sat gloomily on the wall of his sleeping apartment and munched the one solitary cracker he had left. It must carry him through the day unless he got work. The five cents must be kept for some dire emergency.

He started uptown rather aimlessly. In his week's wanderings he had come to know the city very well and no longer felt confused with its size and bustle. He envied every busy boy he saw. Back in Upton he had sometimes resented the fact that he was kept working continually and was seldom allowed an hour off. Now he was burdened with spare time. It certainly did not seem as if things were fairly divided, he thought. And then he thought no more just then, for one of the queer spells in his head came on. He had experienced them at intervals during the last three days. Something seemed to break loose in his head and spin wildly round and round, while houses and people and trees danced and wobbled all about him. Chester vaguely wondered if this could be what Aunt Harriet had been wont to call a "judgement." But then, he had done nothing very bad—nothing that would warrant a judgement, he thought. It was surely no harm to run away from a place where you were treated so bad and where they did not seem to want you. Chester felt bitter whenever he thought of Aunt Harriet.

Presently he found himself in the market square of Montrose. It was market day, and the place was thronged with people from the surrounding country settlements. Chester had hoped that he might pick up a few cents, holding a horse or cow for somebody or carrying a market basket, but no such chance offered itself. He climbed up on some bales of pressed hay in one corner and sat there moodily; there was dejection in the very dangle of his legs over the bales. Chester, you see, was discovering what many a boy before him has discovered—that it is a good deal easier to sit down and make a fortune in dreams than it is to go out into the world and make it.

Two men were talking to each other near him. At first Chester gave no heed to their conversation, but presently a sentence made him prick up his ears.

"Yes, there's a pretty fair crop out at Hopedale," one man was saying, "but whether it's going to be got in in good shape is another matter. It's terrible hard to get any help. Every spare man-jack far and wide has gone West on them everlasting harvest excursions. Salome Whitney at the Mount Hope Farm is in a predicament. She's got a hired man, but he can't harvest grain all by himself. She spent the whole of yesterday driving around, trying to get a couple of men or boys to help him, but I dunno if she got anyone or not."

The men moved out of earshot at this juncture, but Chester got down from the bales with a determined look. If workers were wanted in Hopedale, that was the place for him. He had done a man's work at harvest time in Upton the year before. Lige Barton had said so himself. Hope and courage returned with a rush.

He accosted the first man he met and asked if he could tell him the way to Hopedale.

"Reckon I can, sonny. I live in the next district. Want to go there? If you wait till evening, I can give you a lift part of the way. It's five miles out."

"Thank you, sir," said Chester firmly, "but I must go at once if you'll kindly direct me. It's important."

"Well, it's a straight road. That's Albemarle Street down there—follow it till it takes you out to the country, and then keep straight on till you come to a church painted yellow and white. Turn to your right, and over the hill is Hopedale. But you'd better wait for me. You don't look fit to walk five miles."

But Chester was off. Walk five miles! Pooh! He could walk twenty with hope to lure him on. Albemarle Street finally frayed off into a real country road. Chester was glad to find himself out in the country once more, with the great golden fields basking on either side and the wooded hills beyond, purple with haze. He had grown to hate the town with its cold, unheeding faces. It was good to breathe clear air again and feel the soft, springy soil of the ferny roadside under his tired little feet.

Long before the five miles were covered, Chester began to wonder if he would hold out to the end of them. He had to stop and rest frequently, when those queer dizzy spells came on. His feet seemed like lead. But he kept doggedly on. He would not give in now! The white and yellow church was the most welcome sight that had ever met his eyes.

Over the hill he met a man and inquired the way to Mount Hope Farm. Fortunately, it was nearby. At the gate Chester had to stop again to recover from his dizziness.

He liked the look of the place, with its great, comfortable barns and quaint, roomy old farmhouse, all set down in a trim quadrangle of beeches and orchards. There was an appearance of peace and prosperity about it.

If only Miss Salome Whitney will hire me! thought Chester wistfully, as he crept up the slope. I'm afraid she'll say I'm too small. Wisht I could stretch three inches all at once. Wisht I wasn't so dizzy. Wisht—

What Chester's third wish was will never be known, for just as he reached the kitchen door the worst dizzy spell of all came on. Trees, barns, well-sweep, all whirled around him with the speed of wind. He reeled and fell, a limp, helpless little body, on Miss Salome Whitney's broad, spotless sandstone doorstep.

In the Mount Hope kitchen Miss Salome was at that moment deep in discussion with her "help" over the weighty question of how the damsons were to be preserved. Miss Salome wanted them boiled; Clemantiny Bosworth, the help, insisted that they ought to be baked. Clemantiny was always very positive. She had "bossed" Miss Salome for years, and both knew that in the end the damsons would be baked, but the argument had to be carried out for dignity's sake.

"They're so sour when they're baked," protested Miss Salome.

"Well, you don't want damsons sweet, do you?" retorted Clemantiny scornfully. "That's the beauty of damsons—their tartness. And they keep ever so much better baked, Salome—you know they do. My grandmother *always* baked hers, and they would keep for three years."

Miss Salome knew that when Clemantiny dragged her grandmother into the question, it was time to surrender. Beyond that, dignity degenerated into stubbornness. It would be useless to say that she did not want to keep her damsons for three years, and that she was content to eat them up and trust to Providence for the next year's supply.

"Well, well, bake them then," she said placidly. "I don't suppose it makes much difference one way or another. Only, I insist—what was that noise, Clemantiny? It sounded like something falling against the porch door."

"It's that worthless dog of Martin's, I suppose," said Clemantiny, grasping a broom handle with a grimness that boded ill for the dog. "Mussing up my clean doorstep with his dirty paws again. I'll fix him!"

Clemantiny swept out through the porch and jerked open the door. There was a moment's silence. Then Miss Salome heard her say, "For the land's sake! Salome Whitney, come here."

What Miss Salome saw when she hurried out was a white-faced boy stretched on the doorstep at Clemantiny's feet.

"Is he dead?" she gasped.

"Dead? No," sniffed Clemantiny. "He's fainted, that's what he is. Where on earth did he come from? He ain't a Hopedale boy."

"He must be carried right in," exclaimed Miss Salome in distress. "Why, he may die there. He must be very ill."

"Looks more to me as if he had fainted from sheer starvation," returned Clemantiny brusquely as she picked him up in her lean, muscular arms. "Why, he's skin and bone. He ain't hardly heavier than a baby. Well, this is a mysterious piece of work. Where'll I put him?"

"Lay him on the sofa," said Miss Salome as soon as she had recovered from the horror into which Clemantiny's starvation dictum had thrown her. A child starving to death on her doorstep! "What do you do for people in a faint, Clemantiny?"

"Wet their face—and hist up their feet—and loosen their collar," said Clemantiny in a succession of jerks, doing each thing as she mentioned it. "And hold ammonia to their nose. Run for the ammonia, Salome. Look, will you? Skin and bone!"

But Miss Salome had gone for the ammonia. There was a look on the boy's thin, pallid face that tugged painfully at her heart-strings.

When Chester came back to consciousness with the pungency of the ammonia reeking through his head, he found himself lying on very soft pillows in a very big white sunny kitchen, where everything was scoured to a brightness that dazzled you. Bending over him was a tall, gaunt woman with a thin, determined face and snapping black eyes, and, standing beside her with a steaming bowl in her hand, was the nice rosy lady who had given him the taffy on the boat!

When he opened his eyes, Miss Salome knew him.

"Why, it's the little boy I saw on the boat!" she exclaimed.

"Well, you've come to!" said Clemantiny, eyeing Chester severely. "And now perhaps you'll explain what you mean by fainting away on doorsteps and scaring people out of their senses."

Chester thought that this must be the mistress of Mount Hope Farm, and hastened to propitiate her.

"I'm sorry," he faltered feebly. "I didn't mean to—I—"

"You're not to do any talking until you've had something to eat," snapped Clemantiny inconsistently. "Here, open your mouth and take this broth. Pretty doings, I say!"

Clemantiny spoke as sharply as Aunt Harriet had ever done, but somehow or other Chester did not feel afraid of her and her black eyes. She sat down by his side and fed him from the bowl of hot broth with a deft gentleness oddly in contrast with her grim expression.

Chester thought he had never in all his life tasted anything so good as that broth. The boy was really almost starved. He drank every drop of it. Clemantiny gave a grunt of satisfaction as she handed the empty bowl and spoon to the silent, smiling Miss Salome.

"Now, who are you and what do you want?" she said.

Chester had been expecting this question, and while coming along the Hopedale road he had thought out an answer to it. He began now, speaking the words slowly and gaspingly, as if reciting a hastily learned lesson.

"My name is Chester Benson. I belong to Upton up the country. My folks are dead and I came to Montrose to look for work, I've been there a week and couldn't get anything to do. I heard a man say that you wanted men to help in the harvest, so I came out to see if you'd hire me."

In spite of his weakness, Chester's face turned very red before he got to the end of his speech. He was new to deception. To be sure, there was not, strictly speaking, an untrue word in it. As for his name, it was Chester Benson Stephens. But for all that, Chester could not have felt or looked more guilty if he had been telling an out-and-out falsehood at every breath.

"Humph!" said Clemantiny in a dissatisfied tone. "What on earth do you suppose a midget like you can do in the harvest field? And we don't want any more help, anyway. We've got enough."

Chester grew sick with disappointment. But at this moment Miss Salome spoke up.

"No, we haven't, Clemantiny. We want another hand, and I'll hire you, Chester—that's your name, isn't it? I'll give you good wages, too."

"Now, Salome!" protested Clemantiny.

But Miss Salome only said, "I've made up my mind, Clemantiny."

Clemantiny knew that when Miss Salome did make up her mind and announced it in that very quiet, very unmistakable tone, she was mistress of the situation and intended to remain so.

"Oh, very well," she retorted. "You'll please yourself, Salome, of course. I think it would be wiser to wait until you found out a little more about him."

"And have him starving on people's doorsteps in the meantime?" questioned Miss Salome severely.

"Well," returned Clementiny with the air of one who washes her hands of a doubtful proposition, "don't blame me if you repent of it."

By this time Chester had grasped the wonderful fact that his troubles were ended—for a while, at least. He raised himself up on one arm and looked gratefully at Miss Salome.

"Thank you," he said. "I'll work hard. I'm used to doing a lot."

"There, there!" said Miss Salome, patting his shoulder gently. "Lie down and rest. Dinner will be ready soon, and I guess you'll be ready for it."

To Clementiny she added in a low, gentle tone, "There's a look on his face that reminded me of Johnny. It came out so strong when he sat up just now that it made me feel like crying. Don't you notice it, Clementiny?"

"Can't say that I do," replied that energetic person, who was flying about the kitchen with a speed that made Chester's head dizzy trying to follow her with his eyes. "All I can see is freckles and bones—but if you're satisfied, I am. For law's sake, don't fluster me, Salome. There's a hundred and one things to be done out of hand. This frolic has clean dundered the whole forenoon's work."

After dinner Chester decided that it was time to make himself useful.

"Can't I go right to work now?" he asked.

"We don't begin harvest till tomorrow," said Miss Salome. "You'd better rest this afternoon."

"Oh, I'm all right now," insisted Chester. "I feel fine. Please give me something to do."

"You can go out and cut me some wood for my afternoon's baking," said Clementiny. "And see you cut it short enough. Any other boy that's tried always gets it about two inches too long."

When he had gone out, she said scornfully to Miss Salome, "Well, what do you expect that size to accomplish in a harvest field, Salome Whitney?"

"Not very much, perhaps," said Miss Salome mildly. "But what could I do? You wouldn't have me turn the child adrift on the world again, would you, Clementiny?"

Clementiny did not choose to answer this appeal. She rattled her dishes noisily into the dishpan.

"Well, where are you going to put him to sleep?" she demanded. "The hands you've got will fill the kitchen chamber. There's only the spare room left. You'll hardly put him there, I suppose? Your philanthropy will hardly lead you as far as *that*."

When Clementiny employed big words and sarcasm at the same time, the effect was tremendous. But Miss Salome didn't wilt.

"What makes you so prejudiced against him?" she asked curiously.

"I'm *not* prejudiced against him. But that story about himself didn't ring true. I worked in Upton years ago, and there weren't any Bensons there then. There's more behind that he hasn't told. I'd find out what it was before I took him into my house, that's all. But I'm not prejudiced."

"Well, well," said Miss Salome soothingly, "we must do the best we can for him. It's a sort of duty. And as for a room for him—why, I'll put him in Johnny's."

Clemantiny opened her mouth and shut it again. She understood that it would be a waste of breath to say anything more. If Miss Salome had made up her mind to put this freckled, determined-looking waif, dropped on her doorstep from heaven knew where, into Johnny's room, that was an end of the matter.

"But I'll not be surprised at anything after this," she muttered as she carried her dishes into the pantry. "First a skinny little urchin goes and faints on her doorstep. Then she hires him and puts him in Johnny's room. Johnny's room! Salome Whitney, what *do* you mean?"

Perhaps Miss Salome hardly knew what she meant. But somehow her heart went out warmly to this boy. In spite of Clemantiny's sniffs, she held to the opinion that he looked like Johnny. Johnny was a little nephew of hers. She had taken him to bring up when his parents died, and she had loved him very dearly. He had died four years ago, and since that time the little front room over the front porch had never been occupied. It was just as Johnny had left it. Beyond keeping it scrupulously clean, Miss Salome never allowed it to be disturbed. And now a somewhat ragged lad from nowhere was to be put into it! No wonder Clemantiny shook her head when Miss Salome went up to air it.

Even Clemantiny had to admit that Chester was willing to work. He split wood until she called him to stop. Then he carried in the wood-box full, and piled it so neatly that even the grim handmaiden was pleased. After that, she sent him to the garden to pick the early beans. In the evening he milked three cows and did all the chores, falling into the ways of the place with a deft adaptability that went far to soften Clemantiny's heart.

"He's been taught to work somewheres," she admitted grudgingly, "and he's real polite and respectful. But he looks too cute by half. And his name isn't Benson any more than mine. When I called him 'Chester Benson' out there in the cow-yard, he stared at me fer half a minute 'sif I'd called him Nebuchadnezzar."

When bedtime came, Miss Salome took Chester up to a room whose whiteness and daintiness quite took away the breath of a lad who had been used to sleeping in garrets or hired men's kitchen chambers all his life. Later on Miss Salome came in to see if he was comfortable, and stood, with her candle in her hand, looking down very kindly at the thin, shrewd little face on the pillow.

"I hope you'll sleep real well here, Chester," she said. "I had a little boy once who used to sleep here. You—you look like him. Good night."

She bent over him and kissed his forehead. Chester had never been kissed by anyone before, so far as he could remember. Something came up in his throat that felt about as big as a pumpkin. At the same moment he wished he could have told Miss Salome the whole truth about himself. I might tell her in the morning, he thought, as he watched her figure passing out of the little porch chamber.

But on second thought he decided that this would never do. He felt sure she would disapprove of his running away, and would probably insist upon his going straight back to Upton or, at least, informing Aunt Harriet of his whereabouts. No, he could not tell her.

Clemantiny was an early riser, but when she came into the kitchen the next morning the fire was already made and Chester was out in the yard with three of the five cows milked.

"Humph!" said Clemantiny amiably. "New brooms sweep clean."

But she gave him cream with his porridge that morning. Generally, all Miss Salome's hired hands got from Clemantiny was skim milk.

Miss Salome's regular hired man lived in a little house down in the hollow. He soon turned up, and the other two men she had hired for harvest also arrived. Martin, the man, looked Chester over quizzically.

"What do you think you can do, sonny?"

"Anything," said Chester sturdily. "I'm used to work."

"He's right," whispered Clemantiny aside. "He's smart as a steel trap. But just you keep an eye on him all the same, Martin."

Chester soon proved his mettle in the harvest field. In the brisk three weeks that followed, even Clemantiny had to admit that he earned every cent of his wages. His active feet were untiring and his wiry arms could pitch and stock with the best. When the day's work was ended, he brought in wood and water for Clemantiny, helped milk the cows, gathered the eggs, and made on his own responsibility a round of barns and outhouses to make sure that everything was snug and tight for the night.

"Freckles-and-Bones has been well trained somewhere," said Clemantiny again.

It was hardly fair to put the bones in now, for Chester was growing plump and hearty. He had never been so happy in his life. Upton drudgery and that dreadful week in Montrose seemed like a bad dream. Here, in the golden meadows of Mount Hope Farm, he worked with a right good will. The men liked him, and he soon became a favourite with them. Even Clemantiny relented somewhat. To be sure, she continued very grim, and still threw her words at him as if they were so many missiles warranted to strike home. But Chester soon learned that Clemantiny's bark was worse than her bite. She was really very good to him and fed him lavishly. But she declared that this was only to put some flesh on him.

"It offends me to see bones sticking through anybody's skin like that. We aren't used to such objects at Mount Hope Farm, thank goodness. Yes, you may smile, Salome. I like him well enough, and I'll admit that he knows how to make himself useful, but I don't trust him any more than ever I did. He's mighty close about his past life. You can't get any more out of him than juice out of a post. I've tried, and I know."

But it was Miss Salome who had won Chester's whole heart. He had never loved anybody in his hard little life before. He loved her with an almost dog-like devotion. He forgot that he was working to earn money—and make his fortune. He worked to please Miss Salome. She was good and kind and gentle to him, and his starved heart thawed and expanded in the sunshine of her atmosphere. She went to the little porch room every night to kiss him good night. Chester would have been bitterly disappointed if she had failed to go.

She was greatly shocked to find out that he had never said his prayers before going to bed. She insisted on teaching him the simple little one she had used herself when a child. When Chester found that it would please her, he said it every night. There was nothing he would not have done for Miss Salome.

She talked a good deal to him about Johnny and she gave him the jack-knife that Johnny had owned.

"It belonged to a good, manly little boy once," she said, "and now I hope it belongs to another such."

"I ain't very good," said Chester repentantly, "but I'll try to be, Miss Salome—honest, I will."

One day he heard Miss Salome speaking of someone who had run away from home. "A wicked, ungrateful boy," she called him. Chester blushed until his freckles were drowned out in a sea of red, and Clemantiny saw it, of course. When did anything ever escape those merciless black eyes of Clemantiny's?

"Do you think it's always wrong for a fellow to run away, Miss Salome?" he faltered.

"It can't ever be right," said Miss Salome decidedly.

"But if he wasn't treated well—and was jawed at—and not let go to school?" pleaded Chester.

Clemantiny gave Miss Salome a look as of one who would say, You're bat-blind if you can't read between the lines of that; but Miss Salome was placidly unconscious. She was not really thinking of the subject at all, and did not guess that Chester meant anything more than generalities.

"Not even then," she said firmly. "Nothing can justify a boy for running away—especially as Jarvis Colemen did—never even left a word behind him to say where he'd gone. His aunt thought he'd fallen into the river."

"Don't suppose she would have grieved much if he had," said Clemantiny sarcastically, all the while watching Chester, until he felt as if she were boring into his very soul and reading all his past life.

When the harvest season drew to a close, dismay crept into the soul of our hero. Where would he go now? He hated to think of leaving Mount Hope Farm and Miss Salome. He would have been content to stay there and work as hard as he had ever worked at Upton, merely for the roof over his head and the food he ate. The making of a fortune seemed a small thing compared to the privilege of being near Miss Salome.

"But I suppose I must just up and go," he muttered dolefully.

One day Miss Salome had a conference with Clemantiny. At the end of it the latter said, "Do as you please," in the tone she might have used to a spoiled child. "But if you'd take my advice—which you won't and never do—you'd write to somebody in Upton and make inquiries about him first. What he says is all very well and he sticks to it marvellous, and there's no tripping him up. But there's something behind, Salome Whitney—mark my words, there's something behind."

"He looks so like Johnny," said Miss Salome wistfully.

"And I suppose you think that covers a multitude of sins," said Clemantiny contemptuously.

On the day when the last load of rustling golden sheaves was carried into the big barn and stowed away in the dusty loft, Miss Salome called Chester into the kitchen. Chester's heart sank as he obeyed the summons.

His time was up, and now he was to be paid his wages and sent away. To be sure, Martin had told him that morning that a man in East Hopedale wanted a boy for a spell, and that he, Martin, would see that he got the place if he wanted it. But that did not reconcile him to leaving Mount Hope Farm.

Miss Salome was sitting in her favourite sunny corner of the kitchen and Clemantiny was flying around with double briskness. The latter's thin lips were tightly set and disapproval was writ large in every flutter of her calico skirts.

"Chester," said Miss Salome kindly, "your time is up today."

Chester nodded. For a moment he felt as he had felt when he left the provision store in Montrose. But he would not let Clemantiny see him cry. Somehow, he would not have minded Miss Salome.

"What are you thinking of doing now?" Miss Salome went on.

"There's a man at East Hopedale wants a boy," said Chester, "and Martin says he thinks I'll suit."

"That is Jonas Smallman," said Miss Salome thoughtfully. "He has the name of being a hard master. It isn't right of me to say so, perhaps. I really don't know much about him. But wouldn't you rather stay here with me for the winter, Chester?"

"Ma'am? Miss Salome?" stammered Chester. He heard Clemantiny give a snort behind him and mutter, "Clean infatuated—clean infatuated," without in the least knowing what she meant.

"We really need a chore boy all the year round," said Miss Salome. "Martin has all he can do with the heavy work. And there are the apples to be picked. If you care to stay, you shall have your board and clothes for doing the odd jobs, and you can go to school all winter. In the spring we will see what need be done then."

If he would care to stay! Chester could have laughed aloud. His eyes were shining with joy as he replied, "Oh, Miss Salome, I'll be so glad to stay! I—I—didn't want to go away. I'll try to do everything you want me to do. I'll work ever so hard."

"Humph!"

This, of course, was from Clemantiny, as she set a pan of apples on the stove with an emphatic thud. "Nobody ever doubted your willingness to work. Pity everything else about you isn't as satisfactory."

"Clemantiny!" said Miss Salome rebukingly. She put her arms about Chester and drew him to her. "Then it is all settled, Chester. You are my boy now, and of course I shall expect you to be a good boy."

If ever a boy was determined to be good, that boy was Chester. That day was the beginning of a new life for him. He began to go to the Hopedale school the next week. Miss Salome gave him all Johnny's old school books and took an eager interest in his studies.

Chester ought to have been very happy, and at first he was; but as the bright, mellow days of autumn passed by, a shadow came over his happiness. He could not help thinking that he had really deceived Miss Salome, and was deceiving her still—Miss Salome, who had such confidence in him. He was not what he pretended to be. And as for his running away, he felt sure that Miss Salome would view that with horror. As the time passed by and he learned more and more what a high standard of honour and truth she had, he felt more and more ashamed of himself. When she looked at him with her clear, trustful, blue eyes, Chester felt as guilty as if he had systematically deceived her with intent to do harm. He began to wish that he had the courage to tell her the whole truth about himself.

Moreover, he began to think that perhaps he had not done right, after all, in running away from Aunt Harriet. In Miss Salome's code nothing could be right that was underhanded, and Chester was very swiftly coming to look at things through Miss Salome's eyes. He felt sure that Johnny would never have acted as he had, and if Chester now had one dear ambition on earth, it was to be as good and manly a fellow as Johnny must have been. But he could never be that as long as he kept the truth about himself from Miss Salome.

"That boy has got something on his mind," said the terrible Clemantiny, who, Chester felt convinced, could see through a stone wall.

"Nonsense! What could he have on his mind?" said Miss Salome. But she said it a little anxiously. She, too, had noticed Chester's absent ways and abstracted face.

"Goodness me, I don't know! I don't suppose he has robbed a bank or murdered anybody. But he is worrying over something, as plain as plain."

"He is getting on very well at school," said Miss Salome. "His teacher says so, and he is very eager to learn. I don't know what can be troubling him."

She was fated not to know for a fortnight longer. During that time Chester fought out his struggle with himself, and conquered. He must tell Miss Salome, he decided, with a long sigh. He knew that it would mean going back to Upton and Aunt Harriet and the old, hard life, but he would not sail under false colours any longer.

Chester went into the kitchen one afternoon when he came home from school, with his lips set and his jaws even squarer than usual. Miss Salome was making some of her famous taffy, and Clemantiny was spinning yarn on the big wheel.

"Miss Salome," said Chester desperately, "if you're not too busy, there is something I'd like to tell you."

"What is it?" asked Miss Salome good-humouredly, turning to him with her spoon poised in midair over her granite saucepan.

"It's about myself. I—I—oh, Miss Salome, I didn't tell you the truth about myself. I've got to tell it now. My name isn't Benson—exactly—and I ran away from home."

"Dear me!" said Miss Salome mildly. She dropped her spoon, handle and all, into the taffy and never noticed it. "Dear me, Chester!"

"I knew it," said Clemantiny triumphantly. "I knew it—and I always said it. Run away, did you?"

"Yes'm. My name is Chester Benson Stephens, and I lived at Upton with Aunt Harriet Elwell. But she ain't any relation to me, really. She's only father's stepsister. She—she—wasn't kind to me and she wouldn't let me go to school—so I ran away."

"But, dear me, Chester, didn't you know that was very wrong?" said Miss Salome in bewilderment.

"No'm—I didn't know it then. I've been thinking lately that maybe it was. I'm—I'm real sorry."

"What did you say your real name was?" demanded Clemantiny.

"Stephens, ma'am."

"And your mother's name before she was married?"

"Mary Morrow," said Chester, wondering what upon earth Clemantiny meant.

Clemantiny turned to Miss Salome with an air of surrendering a dearly cherished opinion.

"Well, ma'am, I guess you must be right about his looking like Johnny. I must say I never could see the resemblance, but it may well be there, for he—that very fellow there—and Johnny are first cousins. Their mothers were sisters!"

"Clemantiny!" exclaimed Miss Salome.

"You may well say 'Clemantiny.' Such a coincidence! It doesn't make you and him any relation, of course—the cousinship is on the mother's side. But it's there. Mary Morrow was born and brought up in Hopedale. She went to Upton when I did, and married Oliver Stephens there. Why, I knew his father as well as I know you."

"This is wonderful," said Miss Salome. Then she added sorrowfully, "But it doesn't make your running away right, Chester."

"Tell us all about it," demanded Clemantiny, sitting down on the wood-box. "Sit down, boy, sit down—don't stand there looking as if you were on trial for your life. Tell us all about it."

Thus adjured, Chester sat down and told them all about it—his moonlight flitting and his adventures in Montrose. Miss Salome exclaimed with horror over the fact of his sleeping in a pile of lumber for seven nights, but Clemantiny listened in silence, never taking her eyes from the boy's pale face. When Chester finished, she nodded.

"We've got it all now. There's nothing more behind, Salome. It would have been better for you to have told as straight a story at first, young man."

Chester knew that, but, having no reply to make, made none. Miss Salome looked at him wistfully.

"But, with it all, you didn't do right to run away, Chester," she said firmly. "I dare say your aunt was severe with you—but two wrongs never make a right, you know."

"No'm," said Chester.

"You must go back to your aunt," continued Miss Salome sadly.

Chester nodded. He knew this, but he could not trust himself to speak. Then did Clemantiny arise in her righteous indignation.

"Well, I never heard of such nonsense, Salome Whitney! What on earth do you want to send him back for? I knew Harriet Elwell years ago, and if she's still what she was then, it ain't much wonder Chester ran away from her. I'd say 'run,' too. Go back, indeed! You keep him right here, as you should, and let Harriet Elwell look somewhere else for somebody to scold!"

"Clemantiny!" expostulated Miss Salome.

"Oh, I must and will speak my mind, Salome. There's no one else to take Chester's part, it seems. You have as much claim on him as Harriet Elwell has. She ain't any real relation to him any more than you are."

Miss Salome looked troubled. Perhaps there was something in Clemantiny's argument. And she hated to think of seeing Chester go. He looked more like Johnny than ever, as he stood there with his flushed face and wistful eyes.

"Chester," she said gravely, "I leave it to you to decide. If you think you ought to go back to your aunt, well and good. If not, you shall stay here."

This was the hardest yet. Chester wished she had not left the decision to him. It was like cutting off his own hand. But he spoke up manfully.

"I—I think I ought to go back, Miss Salome, and I want to pay back the money, too."

"I think so, too, Chester, although I'm sorry as sorry can be. I'll go back to Upton with you. We'll start tomorrow. If, when we get there, your aunt is willing to let you stay with me, you can come back."

"There's a big chance of that!" said Clemantiny sourly. "A woman's likely to give up a boy like Chester—a good, steady worker and as respectful and obliging as there is between this and sunset—very likely, isn't she! Well, this taffy is all burnt to the saucepan and clean ruined—but what's the odds! All I hope, Salome Whitney, is that the next time you adopt a boy and let him twine himself 'round a person's heart, you'll make sure first that you are going to stick to it. I don't like having my affections torn up by the roots."

Clemantiny seized the saucepan and disappeared with it into the pantry amid a whirl of pungent smoke.

Mount Hope Farm was a strangely dismal place that night. Miss Salome sighed heavily and often as she made her preparations for the morrow's journey.

Clemantiny stalked about with her grim face grimmer than ever. As for Chester, when he went to bed that night in the little porch chamber, he cried heartily into his pillows. He didn't care for pride any longer; he just cried and didn't even pretend he wasn't crying when Miss Salome came in to sit by him a little while and talk to him. That talk comforted Chester. He realized that, come what might, he would always have a good friend in Miss Salome—aye, and in Clemantiny, too.

Chester never knew it, but after he had fallen asleep, with the tears still glistening on his brown cheeks, Clemantiny tiptoed silently in with a candle in her hand and bent over him with an expression of almost maternal tenderness on her face. It was late and an aroma of boiling sugar hung about her. She had sat up long after Miss Salome was abed, to boil another saucepan of taffy for Chester to eat on his journey.

"Poor, dear child!" she said, softly touching one of his crisp curls. "It's a shame in Salome to insist on his going back. She doesn't know what she's sending him to, or she wouldn't. He didn't say much against his aunt, and Salome thinks she was only just a little bit cranky. But *I* could guess."

Early in the morning Miss Salome and Chester started. They were to drive to Montrose, leave their team there and take the boat for Belltown. Chester bade farewell to the porch chamber and the long, white kitchen and the friendly barns with a full heart. When he climbed into the wagon, Clemantiny put a big bagful of taffy into his hands.

"Good-by, Chester," she said. "And remember, you've always got a friend in me, anyhow."

Then Clemantiny went back into the kitchen and cried—good, rough-spoken, tender-hearted Clemantiny sat down and cried.

It was an ideal day for travelling—crisp, clear and sunny—but neither Chester nor Miss Salome was in a mood for enjoyment.

Back over Chester's runaway route they went, and reached Belltown on the boat that evening.

They stayed in Belltown overnight and in the morning took the train to Roxbury Station. Here Miss Salome hired a team from the storekeeper and drove out to Upton.

Chester felt his heart sink as they drove into the Elwell yard. How well he knew it!

Miss Salome tied her hired nag to the gatepost and took Chester by the hand. They went to the door and knocked. It was opened with a jerk and Mrs. Elwell stood before them. She had probably seen them from the window, for she uttered no word of surprise at seeing Chester again. Indeed, she said nothing at all, but only stood rigidly before them.

Dear me, what a disagreeable-looking woman! thought Miss Salome. But she said courteously, "Are you Mrs. Elwell?"

"I am," said that lady forbiddingly.

"I've brought your nephew home," continued Miss Salome, laying her hand encouragingly on Chester's shrinking shoulder. "I have had him hired for some time on my farm at Hopedale, but I didn't know until yesterday that he had run away from you. When he told me about it, I thought he ought to come straight back and return your four dollars, and so did he. So I have brought him."

"You might have saved yourself the trouble then!" cried Mrs. Elwell shrilly. Her black eyes flashed with anger. "I'm done with him and don't want the money. Run away when there was work to do, and thinks he can come back now that it's all done and loaf all winter, does he? He shall never enter my house again."

"That he shall not!" cried Miss Salome, at last finding her tongue. Her gentle nature was grievously stirred by the heartlessness shown in the face and voice of Mrs. Elwell. "That he shall not!" she cried again. "But he shall not want for a home as long as I have one to give him. Come, Chester, we'll go home."

"I wish you well of him," Mrs. Elwell said sarcastically.

Miss Salome already repented her angry retort. She was afraid she had been undignified, but she wished for a moment that Clemantiny was there. Wicked as she feared it was, Miss Salome thought she could have enjoyed a tilt between her ancient handmaid and Mrs. Elwell.

"I beg your pardon, Mrs. Elwell, if I have used any intemperate expressions," she said with great dignity. "You provoked me more than was becoming by your remarks. I wish you good morning."

Mrs. Elwell slammed the door shut.

With her cheeks even more than usually rosy, Miss Salome led Chester down to the gate, untied her horse and drove out of the yard. Not until they reached the main road did she trust herself to speak to the dazed lad beside her.

"What a disagreeable women!" she ejaculated at last. "I don't wonder you ran away, Chester—I don't, indeed! Though, mind you, I don't think it was right, for all that. But I'm gladder than words can say that she wouldn't take you back. You are mine now, and you will stay mine. I want you to call me Aunt Salome after this. Get up, horse! If we can catch that train at Roxbury, we'll be home by night yet."

Chester was too happy to speak. He had never felt so glad and grateful in his life before.

They got home that night just as the sun was setting redly behind the great maples on the western hill. As they drove into the yard, Clemantiny's face appeared, gazing at them over the high board fence of the cow-yard. Chester waved his hand at her gleefully.

"Lawful heart!" said Clemantiny. She set down her pail and came out to the lane on a run. She caught Chester as he sprang from the wagon and gave him a hearty hug.

"I'm glad clean down to my boot soles to see you back again," she said.

"He's back for good," said Miss Salome. "Chester, you'd better go in and study up your lessons for tomorrow."

The Strike at Putney

The church at Putney was one that gladdened the hearts of all the ministers in the presbytery whenever they thought about it. It was such a satisfactory church. While other churches here and there were continually giving trouble in one way or another, the Putneyites were never guilty of brewing up internal or presbyterial strife.

The Exeter church people were always quarrelling among themselves and carrying their quarrels to the courts of the church. The very name of Exeter gave the members of presbytery the cold creeps. But the Putney church people never quarrelled.

Danbridge church was in a chronic state of ministerlessness. No minister ever stayed in Danbridge longer than he could help. The people were too critical, and they were also noted heresy hunters. Good ministers fought shy of Danbridge, and poor ones met with a chill welcome. The harassed presbytery, worn out with "supplying," were disposed to think that the millennium would come if ever the Danbridgians got a minister whom they liked. At Putney they had had the same minister for fifteen years and hoped and expected to have him for fifteen more. They looked with horror-stricken eyes on the Danbridge theological coquetries.

Bloom Valley church was over head and heels in debt and had no visible prospect of ever getting out. The moderator said under his breath that they did overmuch praying and too little hoeing. He did not believe in faith without works. Tarrytown Road kept its head above water but never had a cent to spare for missions or the schemes of the church.

In bright and shining contradistinction to these the Putney church had always paid its way and gave liberally to all departments of church work. If other springs of supply ran dry the Putneyites enthusiastically got up a "tea" or a "social," and so raised the money. Naturally the "heft" of this work fell on the women, but they did not mind—in very truth, they enjoyed it. The Putney women had the reputation of being "great church workers," and they plumed themselves on it, putting on airs at conventions among the less energetic women of the other churches.

They were especially strong on societies. There was the Church Aid Society, the Girls' Flower Band, and the Sewing Circle. There was a Mission Band and a Helping Hand among the children. And finally there was the Women's Foreign Mission Auxiliary, out of which the whole trouble grew which convulsed the church at Putney for a brief time and furnished a standing joke in presbyterial circles for years afterwards. To this day ministers and elders tell the story of the Putney church strike with sparkling eyes and subdued chuckles. It never grows old or stale. But the Putney elders are an exception. They never laugh at it. They never refer to it. It is not in the wicked, unregenerate heart of man to make a jest of his own bitter defeat.

It was in June that the secretary of the Putney W.F.M. Auxiliary wrote to a noted returned missionary who was touring the country, asking her to give an address on mission work before their society. Mrs. Cotterell wrote back saying that her brief time was so taken up already that she found it hard to make any further engagements, but she could not refuse the Putney people who were so well and favourably known in mission circles for their perennial interest and liberality. So, although she could not come on the date requested, she would, if acceptable, come the following Sunday.

This suited the Putney Auxiliary very well. On the Sunday referred to there was to be no evening service in the church owing to Mr. Sinclair's absence. They therefore appointed the missionary meeting for that night, and made arrangements to hold it in the church itself, as the classroom was too small for the expected audience.

Then the thunderbolt descended on the W.F.M.A. of Putney from a clear sky. The elders of the church rose up to a man and declared that no woman should occupy the pulpit of the Putney church. It was in direct contravention to the teachings of St. Paul.

To make matters worse, Mr. Sinclair declared himself on the elders' side. He said that he could not conscientiously give his consent to a woman occupying his pulpit, even when that woman was Mrs. Cotterell and her subject foreign missions.

The members of the Auxiliary were aghast. They called a meeting extraordinary in the classroom and, discarding all forms and ceremonies in their wrath, talked their indignation out.

Out of doors the world basked in June sunshine and preened itself in blossom. The birds sang and chirped in the lichened maples that cupped the little church in, and peace was over all the Putney valley. Inside the classroom disgusted women buzzed like angry bees.

"What on earth are we to do?" sighed the secretary plaintively. Mary Kilburn was always plaintive. She sat on the steps of the platform, being too wrought up in her mind to sit in her chair at the desk, and her thin, faded little face was twisted with anxiety. "All the arrangements are made and Mrs. Cotterell is coming on the tenth. How can we tell her that the men won't let her speak?"

"There was never anything like this in Putney church before," groaned Mrs. Elder Knox. "It was Andrew McKittrick put them up to it. I always said that man would make trouble here yet, ever since he moved to Putney from Danbridge. I've talked and argued with Thomas until I'm dumb, but he is as set as a rock."

"I don't see what business the men have to interfere with us anyhow," said her daughter Lucy, who was sitting on one of the window-sills. "We don't meddle with them, I'm sure. As if Mrs. Cotterell would contaminate the pulpit!"

"One would think we were still in the dark ages," said Frances Spenslow sharply. Frances was the Putney schoolteacher. Her father was one of the recalcitrant elders and Frances felt it bitterly—all the more that she had tried to argue with him and had been sat upon as a "child who couldn't understand."

"I'm more surprised at Mr. Sinclair than at the elders," said Mrs. Abner Keech, fanning herself vigorously. "Elders are subject to queer spells periodically. They think they assert their authority that way. But Mr. Sinclair has always seemed so liberal and broad-minded."

"You never can tell what crotchet an old bachelor will take into his head," said Alethea Craig bitingly.

The others nodded agreement. Mr. Sinclair's inveterate celibacy was a standing grievance with the Putney women.

"If he had a wife who could be our president this would never have happened, I warrant you," said Mrs. King sagely.

"But what are we going to do, ladies?" said Mrs. Robbins briskly. Mrs. Robbins was the president. She was a big, bustling woman with clear blue eyes and crisp, incisive ways. Hitherto she had held her peace. "They must talk themselves out before they can get down to business," she had reflected sagely. But she thought the time had now come to speak.

"You know," she went on, "we can talk and rage against the men all day if we like. They are not trying to prevent us. But that will do no good. Here's Mrs. Cotterell invited, and all the neighbouring auxiliaries notified—and the men won't let us have the church. The point is, how are we going to get out of the scrape?"

A helpless silence descended upon the classroom. The eyes of every woman present turned to Myra Wilson. Everyone could talk, but when it came to action they had a fashion of turning to Myra.

She had a reputation for cleverness and originality. She never talked much. So far today she had not said a word. She was sitting on the sill of the window across from Lucy Knox. She swung her hat on her knee, and loose, moist rings of dark hair curled around her dark, alert face. There was a sparkle in her grey eyes that boded ill to the men who were peaceably pursuing their avocations, rashly indifferent to what the women might be saying in the maple-shaded classroom.

"Have you any suggestion to make, Miss Wilson?" said Mrs. Robbins, with a return to her official voice and manner.

Myra put her long, slender index finger to her chin.

"I think," she said decidedly, "that we must strike."

When Elder Knox went in to tea that evening he glanced somewhat apprehensively at his wife. They had had an altercation before she went to the meeting, and he supposed she had talked herself into another rage while there. But Mrs. Knox was placid and smiling. She had made his favourite soda biscuits for him and inquired amiably after his progress in hoeing turnips in the southeast meadow.

She made, however, no reference to the Auxiliary meeting, and when the biscuits and the maple syrup and two cups of matchless tea had nerved the elder up, his curiosity got the better of his prudence—for even elders are human and curiosity knows no gender—and he asked what they had done at the meeting.

"We poor men have been shaking in our shoes," he said facetiously.

"Were you?" Mrs. Knox's voice was calm and faintly amused. "Well, you didn't need to. We talked the matter over very quietly and came to the conclusion that the session knew best and that women hadn't any right to interfere in church business at all."

Lucy Knox turned her head away to hide a smile. The elder beamed. He was a peace-loving man and disliked "ructions" of any sort and domestic ones in particular. Since the decision of the session Mrs. Knox had made his life a burden to him. He did not understand her sudden change of base, but he accepted it very thankfully.

"That's right—that's right," he said heartily. "I'm glad to hear you coming out so sensible, Maria. I was afraid you'd work yourselves up at that meeting and let Myra Wilson or Alethea Craig put you up to some foolishness or other. Well, I guess I'll jog down to the Corner this evening and order that barrel of pastry flour you want."

"Oh, you needn't," said Mrs. Knox indifferently. "We won't be needing it now."

"Not needing it! But I thought you said you had to have some to bake for the social week after next."

"There isn't going to be any social."

"Not any social?"

Elder Knox stared perplexedly at his wife. A month previously the Putney church had been recarpeted, and they still owed fifty dollars for it. This, the women declared, they would speedily pay off by a big cake and ice-cream social in the hall. Mrs. Knox had been one of the foremost promoters of the enterprise.

"Not any social?" repeated the elder again. "Then how is the money for the carpet to be got? And *why* isn't there going to be a social?"

"The men can get the money somehow, I suppose," said Mrs. Knox. "As for the social, why, of course, if women aren't good enough to speak in church they are not good enough to work for it either. Lucy, dear, will you pass me the cookies?"

"Lucy dear" passed the cookies and then rose abruptly and left the table. Her father's face was too much for her.

"What confounded nonsense is this?" demanded the elder explosively.

Mrs. Knox opened her mellow brown eyes widely, as if in amazement at her husband's tone.

"I don't understand you," she said. "Our position is perfectly logical."

She had borrowed that phrase from Myra Wilson, and it floored the elder. He got up, seized his hat, and strode from the room.

That night, at Jacob Wherrison's store at the Corner, the Putney men talked over the new development. The social was certainly off—for a time, anyway.

"Best let 'em alone, I say," said Wherrison. "They're mad at us now and doing this to pay us out. But they'll cool down later on and we'll have the social all right."

"But if they don't," said Andrew McKittrick gloomily, "who is going to pay for that carpet?"

This was an unpleasant question. The others shirked it.

"I was always opposed to this action of the session," said Alec Craig. "It wouldn't have hurt to have let the woman speak. 'Tisn't as if it was a regular sermon."

"The session knew best," said Andrew sharply. "And the minister—you're not going to set your opinion up against his, are you, Craig?"

"Didn't know they taught such reverence for ministers in Danbridge," retorted Craig with a laugh.

"Best let 'em alone, as Wherrison says," said Abner Keech.

"Don't see what else we can do," said John Wilson shortly.

On Sunday morning the men were conscious of a bare, deserted appearance in the church. Mr. Sinclair perceived it himself. After some inward wondering he concluded that it was because there were no flowers anywhere. The table before the pulpit was bare. On the organ a vase held a sorry, faded bouquet left over from the previous week. The floor was' unswept. Dust lay thickly on the pulpit Bible, the choir chairs, and the pew backs.

"This church looks disgraceful," said John Robbins in an angry undertone to his daughter Polly, who was president of the Flower Band. "What in the name of common sense is the good of your Flower Banders if you can't keep the place looking decent?"

"There is no Flower Band now, Father," whispered Polly in turn. "We've disbanded. Women haven't any business to meddle in church matters. You know the session said so."

It was well for Polly that she was too big to have her ears boxed. Even so, it might not have saved her if they had been anywhere else than in church.

Meanwhile the men who were sitting in the choir—three basses and two tenors—were beginning to dimly suspect that there was something amiss here too. Where were the sopranos and the altos? Myra Wilson and Alethea Craig and several other members of the choir were sitting down in their pews with perfectly unconscious faces. Myra was looking out of the window into the tangled sunlight and shadow of the great maples. Alethea Craig was reading her Bible.

Presently Frances Spenslow came in. Frances was organist, but today, instead of walking up to the platform, she slipped demurely into her father's pew at one side of the pulpit. Eben Craig, who was the Putney singing master and felt himself responsible for the choir, fidgeted uneasily. He tried to catch Frances's eye, but she was absorbed in reading the mission report she had found in the rack, and Eben was finally forced to tiptoe down to the Spenslow pew and whisper, "Miss

Spenslow, the minister is waiting for the doxology. Aren't you going to take the organ?"

Frances looked up calmly. Her clear, placid voice was audible not only to those in the nearby pews, but to the minister.

"No, Mr. Craig. You know if a woman isn't fit to speak in the church she can't be fit to sing in it either."

Eben Craig looked exceedingly foolish. He tiptoed gingerly back to his place. The minister, with an unusual flush on his thin, ascetic face, rose suddenly and gave out the opening hymn.

Nobody who heard the singing in Putney church that day ever forgot it. Untrained basses and tenors, unrelieved by a single female voice, are not inspiring.

There were no announcements of society meetings for the forthcoming week. On the way home from church that day irate husbands and fathers scolded, argued, or pleaded, according to their several dispositions. One and all met with the same calm statement that if a noble, self-sacrificing woman like Mrs. Cotterell were not good enough to speak in the Putney church, ordinary, everyday women could not be fit to take any part whatever in its work.

Sunday School that afternoon was a harrowing failure. Out of all the corps of teachers only one was a man, and he alone was at his post. In the Christian Endeavour meeting on Tuesday night the feminine element sat dumb and unresponsive. The Putney women never did things by halves.

The men held out for two weeks. At the end of that time they "happened" to meet at the manse and talked the matter over with the harassed minister. Elder Knox said gloomily, "It's this way. Nothing can move them women. I know, for I've tried. My authority has been set at naught in my own household. And I'm laughed at if I show my face in any of the other settlements."

The Sunday School superintendent said the Sunday School was going to wrack and ruin, also the Christian Endeavour. The condition of the church for dust was something scandalous, and strangers were making a mockery of the singing. And the carpet had to be paid for. He supposed they would have to let the women have their own way.

The next Sunday evening after service Mr. Sinclair arose hesitatingly. His face was flushed, and Alethea Craig always declared that he looked "just plain everyday cross." He announced briefly that the session after due deliberation had concluded that Mrs. Cotterell might occupy the pulpit on the evening appointed for her address.

The women all over the church smiled broadly. Frances Spenslow got up and went to the organ stool. The singing in the last hymn was good and hearty. Going down the steps after dismissal Mrs. Elder Knox caught the secretary of the Church Aid by the arm.

"I guess," she whispered anxiously, "you'd better call a special meeting of the Aids at my house tomorrow afternoon. If we're to get that social over before haying begins we've got to do some smart scurrying."

The strike in the Putney church was over.

The Unhappiness of Miss Farquhar

Frances Farquhar was a beauty and was sometimes called a society butterfly by people who didn't know very much about it. Her father was wealthy and her mother came of an extremely blue-blooded family. Frances had been out for three years, and was a social favourite. Consequently, it may be wondered why she was unhappy.

In plain English, Frances Farquhar had been jilted—just a commonplace, everyday jilting! She had been engaged to Paul Holcomb; he was a very handsome fellow, somewhat too evidently aware of the fact, and Frances was very deeply in love with him—or thought herself so, which at the time comes to pretty much the same thing. Everybody in her set knew of her engagement, and all her girl friends envied her, for Holcomb was a matrimonial catch.

Then the crash came. Nobody outside the family knew exactly what did happen, but everybody knew that the Holcomb-Farquhar match was off, and everybody had a different story to account for it.

The simple truth was that Holcomb was fickle and had fallen in love with another girl. There was nothing of the man about him, and it did not matter to his sublimely selfish caddishness whether he broke Frances Farquhar's heart or not. He got his freedom and he married Maud Carroll in six months' time.

The Farquhars, especially Ned, who was Frances's older brother and seldom concerned himself about her except when the family honour was involved, were furious at the whole affair. Mr. Farquhar stormed, and Ned swore, and Della lamented her vanished role of bridemaid. As for Mrs. Farquhar, she cried and said it would ruin Frances's future prospects.

The girl herself took no part in the family indignation meetings. But she believed that her heart was broken. Her love and her pride had suffered equally, and the effect seemed disastrous.

After a while the Farquhars calmed down and devoted themselves to the task of cheering Frances up. This they did not accomplish. She got through the rest of the season somehow and showed a proud front to the world, not even flinching when Holcomb himself crossed her path. To be sure, she was pale and thin, and had about as much animation as a mask, but the same might be said of a score of other girls who were not suspected of having broken hearts.

When the summer came Frances asserted herself. The Farquhars went to Green Harbour every summer. But this time Frances said she would not go, and stuck to it. The whole family took turns coaxing her and had nothing to show for their pains.

"I'm going up to Windy Meadows to stay with Aunt Eleanor while you are at the Harbour," she declared. "She has invited me often enough."

Ned whistled. "Jolly time you'll have of it, Sis. Windy Meadows is about as festive as a funeral. And Aunt Eleanor isn't lively, to put it in the mildest possible way."

"I don't care if she isn't. I want to get somewhere where people won't look at me and talk about—that," said Frances, looking ready to cry.

Ned went out and swore at Holcomb again, and then advised his mother to humour Frances. Accordingly, Frances went to Windy Meadows.

Windy Meadows was, as Ned had said, the reverse of lively. It was a pretty country place, with a sort of fag-end by way of a little fishing village, huddled on a wind-swept bit of beach, locally known as the "Cove." Aunt Eleanor was one of those delightful people, so few and far between in this world, who have perfectly mastered the art of minding their own business exclusively. She left Frances in peace.

She knew that her niece had had "some love trouble or other," and hadn't gotten over it rightly.

"It's always best to let those things take their course," said this philosophical lady to her "help" and confidant, Margaret Ann Peabody. "She'll get over it in time—though she doesn't think so now, bless you."

For the first fortnight Frances revelled in a luxury of unhindered sorrow. She could cry all night—and all day too, if she wished—without having to stop because people might notice that her eyes were red. She could mope in her room all she liked. And there were no men who demanded civility.

When the fortnight was over, Aunt Eleanor took crafty counsel with herself. The letting-alone policy was all very well, but it would not do to have the girl die on her hands. Frances was getting paler and thinner every day—and she was spoiling her eyelashes by crying.

"I wish," said Aunt Eleanor one morning at breakfast, while Frances pretended to eat, "that I could go and take Corona Sherwood out for a drive today. I promised her last week that I would, but I've never had time yet. And today is baking and churning day. It's a shame. Poor Corona!"

"Who is she?" asked Frances, trying to realize that there was actually someone in the world besides herself who was to be pitied.

"She is our minister's sister. She has been ill with rheumatic fever. She is better now, but doesn't seem to get strong very fast. She ought to go out more, but she isn't able to walk. I really must try and get around tomorrow. She keeps house for her brother at the manse. He isn't married, you know."

Frances didn't know, nor did she in the least degree care. But even the luxury of unlimited grief palls, and Frances was beginning to feel this vaguely. She offered to go and take Miss Sherwood out driving.

"I've never seen her," she said, "but I suppose that doesn't matter. I can drive Grey Tom in the phaeton, if you like."

It was just what Aunt Eleanor intended, and she saw Frances drive off that afternoon with a great deal of satisfaction.

"Give my love to Corona," she told her, "and say for me that she isn't to go messing about among those shore people until she's perfectly well. The manse is the fourth house after you turn the third corner."

Frances kept count of the corners and the houses and found the manse. Corona Sherwood herself came to the door. Frances had been expecting an elderly personage with spectacles and grey crimps; she was surprised to find that the minister's sister was a girl of about her own age and possessed of a distinct worldly prettiness. Corona was dark, with a different darkness from that of Frances, who had ivory outlines and blue-black hair, while Corona was dusky and piquant.

Her eyes brightened with delight when Frances told her errand.

"How good of you and Miss Eleanor! I am not strong enough to walk far yet—or do anything useful, in fact, and Elliott so seldom has time to take me out."

"Where shall we go?" asked Frances when they started. "I don't know much about this locality."

"Can we drive to the Cove first? I want to see poor little Jacky Hart. He has been so sick—"

"Aunt Eleanor positively forbade that," said Frances dubiously. "Will it be safe to disobey her?"

Corona laughed.

"Miss Eleanor blames my poor shore people for making me sick at first, but it was really not that at all. And I want to see Jacky Hart so much. He has been ill for some time with some disease of the spine and he is worse lately. I'm sure Miss Eleanor won't mind my calling just to see him."

Frances turned Grey Tom down the shore road that ran to the Cove and past it to silvery, wind-swept sands, rimming sea expanses crystal clear. Jacky Hart's home proved to be a tiny little place overflowing with children. Mrs. Hart was a pale, tired-looking woman with the patient, farseeing eyes so often found among the women who watch sea and shore every day and night of their lives for those who sometimes never return.

She spoke of Jacky with the apathy of hopelessness. The doctor said he would not last much longer. She told all her troubles unreservedly to Corona in her monotonous voice. Her "man" was drinking again and the mackerel catch was poor.

When Mrs. Hart asked Corona to go in and see Jacky, Frances went too. The sick boy, a child with a delicate, wasted face and large, bright eyes, lay in a tiny bedroom off the kitchen. The air was hot and heavy. Mrs. Hart stood at the foot of the bed with her tragic face.

"We have to set up nights with him now," she said. "It's awful hard on me and my man. The neighbours are kind enough and come sometimes, but most of them have enough to do. His medicine has to be given every half hour. I've been up for three nights running now. Jabez was off to the tavern for two. I'm just about played out."

She suddenly broke down and began to cry, or rather whimper, in a heart-broken way.

Corona looked troubled. "I wish I could come tonight, Mrs. Hart, but I'm afraid I'm really not strong enough yet."

"I don't know much about sickness," spoke up Frances firmly, "but if to sit by the child and give him his medicine regularly is all that is necessary, I am sure I can do that. I'll come and sit up with Jacky tonight if you care to have me."

Afterwards, when she and Corona were driving away, she wondered a good deal at herself. But Corona was so evidently pleased with her offer, and took it all so much as a matter of course, that Frances had not the courage to display her wonder. They had their drive through the great green bowl of the country valley, brimming over with sunshine, and afterwards Corona made Frances go home with her to tea.

Rev. Elliott Sherwood had got back from his pastoral visitations, and was training his sweet peas in the way they should go against the garden fence. He was in his shirt sleeves and wore a big straw hat, and seemed in nowise disconcerted thereby. Corona introduced him, and he took Grey Tom away and put him in the barn. Then he went back to his sweet peas. He had had his tea, he said, so that Frances did not see him again until she went home. She thought he was a very indifferent young man, and not half so nice as his sister.

But she went and sat up with Jacky Hart that night, getting to the Cove at dark, when the sea was a shimmer of fairy tints and the boats were coming in from the fishing grounds. Jacky greeted her with a wonderful smile, and later on she found herself watching alone by his bed. The tiny lamp on the table burned dim, and outside, on the rocks, there was loud laughing and talking until a late hour.

Afterwards a silence fell, through which the lap of the waves on the sands and the far-off moan of the Atlantic surges came sonorously. Jacky was restless and wakeful, but did not suffer, and liked to talk. Frances listened to him with a new-born power of sympathy, which she thought she must have caught from Corona. He told her all the tragedy of his short life, and how bad he felt, about Dad's taking to drink and Mammy's having to work so hard.

The pitiful little sentences made Frances's heart ache. The maternal instinct of the true woman awoke in her. She took a sudden liking to the child. He was a spiritual little creature, and his sufferings had made him old and wise. Once in the night he told Frances that he thought the angels must look like her.

"You are so sweet pretty," he said gravely. "I never saw anyone so pretty, not even Miss C'rona. You look like a picture I once saw on Mr. Sherwood's table when I was up at the manse one day 'fore I got so bad I couldn't walk. It was a woman with a li'l baby in her arms and a kind of rim round her head. I would like something most awful much."

"What is it, dear?" said Frances gently. "If I can get or do it for you, I will."

"You could," he said wistfully, "but maybe you won't want to. But I do wish you'd come here just once every day and sit here five minutes and let me look at you—just that. Will it be too much trouble?"

Frances stooped and kissed him. "I will come every day, Jacky," she said; and a look of ineffable content came over the thin little face. He put up his hand and touched her cheek.

"I knew you were good—as good as Miss C'rona, and she is an angel. I love you."

When morning came Frances went home. It was raining, and the sea was hidden in mist. As she walked along the wet road, Elliott Sherwood came splashing along in a little two-wheeled gig and picked her up. He wore a raincoat and a small cap, and did not look at all like a minister—or, at least, like Frances's conception of one.

Not that she knew much about ministers. Her own minister at home—that is to say, the minister of the fashionable uptown church which she attended—was a portly, dignified old man with silvery hair and gold-rimmed glasses, who preached scholarly, cultured sermons and was as far removed from Frances's personal life as a star in the Milky Way.

But a minister who wore rubber coats and little caps and drove about in a two-wheeled gig, very much mud-bespattered, and who talked about the shore people as if they were household intimates of his, was absolutely new to Frances.

She could not help seeing, however, that the crisp brown hair under the edges of the unclerical-looking cap curled around a remarkably well-shaped forehead, beneath which flashed out a pair of very fine dark-grey eyes; he had likewise a good mouth, which was resolute and looked as if it might be stubborn on occasion; and, although he was not exactly handsome, Frances decided that she liked his face.

He tucked the wet, slippery rubber apron of his conveyance about her and then proceeded to ask questions. Jacky Hart's case had to be reported on, and then Mr. Sherwood took out a notebook and looked over its entries intently.

"Do you want any more work of that sort to do?" he asked her abruptly.

Frances felt faintly amused. He talked to her as he might have done to Corona, and seemed utterly oblivious of the fact that her profile was classic and her eyes delicious. His indifference piqued Frances a little in spite of her murdered heart. Well, if there was anything she could do she might as well do it, she told him briefly, and he, with equal brevity, gave her directions for finding some old lady who lived on the Elm Creek road and to whom Corona had read tracts.

"Tracts are a mild dissipation of Aunt Clorinda's," he said. "She fairly revels in them. She is half blind and has missed Corona very much."

There were other matters also—a dozen or so of factory girls who needed to be looked after and a family of ragged children to be clothed. Frances, in some dismay, found herself pledged to help in all directions, and then ways and means had to be discussed. The long, wet road, sprinkled with houses, from whose windows people were peering to see "what girl the minister was driving," seemed very short. Frances did not know it, but Elliott Sherwood drove a full mile out of his way that morning to take her home, and risked being late for a very important appointment—from which it may be inferred that he was not quite so blind to the beautiful as he had seemed.

Frances went through the rain that afternoon and read tracts to Aunt Clorinda. She was so dreadfully tired that night that she forgot to cry, and slept well and soundly.

In the morning she went to church for the first time since coming to Windy Meadows. It did not seem civil not to go to hear a man preach when she had gone slumming with his sister and expected to assist him with his difficulties over factory girls. She was surprised at Elliott Sherwood's sermon, and mentally wondered why such a man had been allowed to remain for four years in a little country pulpit. Later on Aunt Eleanor told her it was for his health.

"He was not strong when he left college, so he came here. But he is as well as ever now, and I expect he will soon be gobbled up by some of your city churches. He preached in Castle Street church last winter, and I believe they were delighted with him."

This was all of a month later. During that time Frances thought that she must have been re-created, so far was her old self left behind. She seldom had an idle moment; when she had, she spent it with Corona. The two girls had become close friends, loving each other with the intensity of exceptional and somewhat exclusive natures.

Corona grew strong slowly, and could do little for her brother's people, but Frances was an excellent proxy, and Elliott Sherwood kept her employed. Incidentally, Frances had come to know the young minister, with his lofty ideals and earnest efforts, very well. He had got into a ridiculous habit of going to her—her, Frances Farquhar!—for advice in many perplexities.

Frances had nursed Jacky Hart and talked temperance to his father and read tracts to Aunt Clorinda and started a reading circle among the factory girls and fitted out all the little Jarboes with dresses and coaxed the shore children to go to school and patched up a feud between two 'longshore families and done a hundred other things of a similar nature.

Aunt Eleanor said nothing, as was her wise wont, but she talked it over with Margaret Ann Peabody, and agreed with that model domestic when she said: "Work'll keep folks out of trouble and help 'em out of it when they are in. Just as long as that girl brooded over her own worries and didn't think of anyone but herself she was miserable. But as soon as she found other folks were unhappy, too, and tried to help 'em out a bit, she helped herself most of all. She's getting fat and rosy, and it is plain to be seen that the minister thinks there isn't the like of her on this planet."

One night Frances told Corona all about Holcomb. Elliott Sherwood was away, and Frances had gone up to stay all night with Corona at the manse. They were sitting in the moonlit gloom of Corona's room, and Frances felt confidential. She had expected to feel badly and cry a little while she told it. But she did not, and before she was half through, it did not seem as if it were worth telling after all. Corona was deeply sympathetic. She did not say a great deal, but what she did say put Frances on better terms with herself.

"Oh, I shall get over it," the latter declared finally. "Once I thought I never would—but the truth is, I'm getting over it now. I'm very glad—but I'm horribly ashamed, too, to find myself so fickle."

"I don't think you are fickle, Frances," said Corona gravely, "because I don't think you ever really loved that man at all. You only imagined you did. And he was not worthy of you. You are so good, dear; those shore people just worship you. Elliott says you can do anything you like with them."

Frances laughed and said she was not at all good. Yet she was pleased. Later on, when she was brushing her hair before the mirror and smiling absently at her reflection, Corona said: "Frances, what is it like to be as pretty as you are?"

"Nonsense!" said Frances by way of answer.

"It is not nonsense at all. You must know you are very lovely, Frances. Elliott says you are the most beautiful girl he has ever seen."

For a girl who has told herself a dozen times that she would never care again for masculine admiration, Frances experienced a very odd thrill of delight on hearing that the minister of Windy Meadows thought her beautiful. She knew he admired her intellect and had immense respect for what he called her "genius for influencing people," but she had really believed all along that, if Elliott Sherwood had been asked, he could not have told whether she was a whit better looking than Kitty Martin of the Cove, who taught a class in Sunday school and had round rosy cheeks and a snub nose.

The summer went very quickly. One day Jacky Hart died—drifted out with the ebb tide, holding Frances's hand. She had loved the patient, sweet-souled little creature and missed him greatly.

When the time to go home came Frances felt dull. She hated to leave Windy Meadows and Corona and her dear shore people and Aunt Eleanor and—and—well, Margaret Ann Peabody.

Elliott Sherwood came up the night before she went away. When Margaret Ann showed him reverentially in, Frances was sitting in a halo of sunset light, and the pale, golden chrysanthemums in her hair shone like stars in the blue-black coils.

Elliott Sherwood had been absent from Windy Meadows for several days. There was a subdued jubilance in his manner.

"You think I have come to say good-bye, but I haven't," he told her. "I shall see you again very soon, I hope. I have just received a call to Castle Street church, and it is my intention to accept. So Corona and I will be in town this winter."

Frances tried to tell him how glad she was, but only stammered. Elliott Sherwood came close up to her as she stood by the window in the fading light, and said—

But on second thoughts I shall not record what he said—or what she said either. Some things should be left to the imagination.

Why Mr. Cropper Changed His Mind

"Well, Miss Maxwell, how did you get along today?" asked Mr. Baxter affably, when the new teacher came to the table.

She was a slight, dark girl, rather plain-looking, but with a smart, energetic way. Mr. Baxter approved of her; he "liked her style," as he would have said.

The summer term had just opened in the Maitland district. Esther Maxwell was a stranger, but she was a capable girl, and had no doubt of her own ability to get and keep the school in good working order. She smiled brightly at Mr. Baxter.

"Very well for a beginning. The children seem bright and teachable and not hard to control."

Mr. Baxter nodded. "There are no bad children in the school except the Cropper boys—and they can be good enough if they like. Reckon they weren't there today?"

"No."

"Well, Miss Maxwell, I think it only fair to tell you that you may have trouble with those boys when they do come. Forewarned is forearmed, you know. Mr. Cropper was opposed to our hiring you. Not, of course, that he had any personal objection to you, but he is set against female teachers, and when a Cropper is set there is nothing on earth can change him. He says female teachers can't keep order. He's started in with a spite at you on general principles, and the boys know it. They know he'll back them up in secret, no matter what they do, just to prove his opinions. Cropper is sly and slippery, and it is hard to corner him."

"Are the boys big?" queried Esther anxiously.

"Yes. Thirteen and fourteen and big for their age. You can't whip 'em—that is the trouble. A man might, but they'd twist you around their fingers. You'll have your hands full, I'm afraid. But maybe they'll behave all right after all."

Mr. Baxter privately had no hope that they would, but Esther hoped for the best. She could not believe that Mr. Cropper would carry his prejudices into a personal application. This conviction was strengthened when he overtook her walking from school the next day and drove her home. He was a big, handsome man with a very suave, polite manner. He asked interestedly about her school and her work, hoped she was getting on well, and said he had two young rascals of his own to send soon. Esther felt relieved. She thought that Mr. Baxter had exaggerated matters a little.

"That plum tree of Mrs. Charley's is loaded with fruit again this year," remarked Mr. Baxter at the tea table that evening. "I came past it today on my way 'cross lots home from the woods. There will be bushels of plums on it."

"I don't suppose poor Mrs. Charley will get one of them any more than she ever has," said Mrs. Baxter indignantly. "It's a burning shame, that's what it is! I just wish she could catch the Croppers once."

"You haven't any proof that it is really them, Mary," objected her husband, "and you shouldn't make reckless accusations before folks."

"I know very well it is them," retorted Mrs. Baxter, "and so do you, Adoniram. And Mrs. Charley knows it too, although she can't prove it—more's the pity! I don't say Isaac Cropper steals those plums with his own hands. But he knows who does—and the plums go into Mehitable Cropper's preserving kettle; there's nothing surer."

"You see, Miss Maxwell, it's this way," explained Mr. Baxter, turning to Esther. "Mrs. Charley Cropper's husband was Isaac's brother. They never got on well together, and when Charley died there was a tremendous fuss about the property. Isaac acted mean and scandalous clear through, and public opinion has been down on him ever since. But Mrs. Charley is a pretty smart woman, and he didn't get the better of her in everything. There was a strip of disputed land between the two farms, and she secured it. There's a big plum tree growing on it close to the line fence. It's the finest one in Maitland. But Mrs. Charley never gets a plum from it."

"But what becomes of them?" asked Esther.

"They disappear," said Mr. Baxter, with a significant nod. "When the plums are anything like ripe Mrs. Charley discovers some day that there isn't one left on the tree. She has never been able to get a scrap of proof as to who took them, or she'd make it hot for them. But nobody in Maitland has any doubt in his own mind that Isaac Cropper knows where those plums go."

"I don't think Mr. Cropper would steal," protested Esther.

"Well, he doesn't consider it stealing, you know. He claims the land and says the plums are his. I don't doubt that he is quite clear in his own mind that they are. And he does hate Mrs. Charley. I'd give considerable to see the old sinner fairly caught, but he is too deep."

"I think Mr. Baxter is too hard on Mr. Cropper," said Esther to herself later on. "He has probably some private prejudice against him."

But a month later she had changed her opinion. During that time the Cropper boys had come to school.

At first Esther had been inclined to like them. They were handsome lads, with the same smooth way that characterized their father, and seemed bright and intelligent. For a few days all went well, and Esther felt decidedly relieved.

But before long a subtle spirit of insubordination began to make itself felt in the school. Esther found herself powerless to cope with it. The Croppers never openly defied her, but they did precisely as they pleased. The other pupils thought themselves at liberty to follow this example, and in a month's time poor Esther had completely lost control of her little kingdom. Some complaints were heard among the ratepayers and even Mr. Baxter looked dubious. She knew that unless she could regain her authority she would be requested to hand in her resignation, but she was baffled by the elusive system of defiance which the Cropper boys had organized.

One day she resolved to go to Mr. Cropper himself and appeal to his sense of justice, if he had any. It had been an especially hard day in school. When she had been absent at the noon hour all the desks in the schoolroom had been piled in a pyramid on the floor, books and slates interchanged, and various other pranks played. When questioned every pupil denied having done or helped to do it. Alfred and Bob Cropper looked her squarely in the eyes and declared their innocence in their usual gentlemanly fashion, yet Esther felt sure that they were the guilty ones. She also knew what exaggerated accounts of the affair would be taken home to Maitland tea tables, and she felt like sitting down to cry. But she did not. Instead she set her mouth firmly, helped the children restore the room to order, and after school went up to Isaac Cropper's house.

That gentleman himself came in from the harvest field looking as courtly as usual, even in his rough working clothes. He shook hands heartily, told her he was glad to see her, and began talking about the weather. Esther was not to be turned from her object thus, although she felt her courage ebbing away from her as it always did in the presence of the Cropper imperviousness.

"I have come up to see you about Alfred and Robert, Mr. Cropper," she said. "They are not behaving well in school."

"Indeed!" Mr. Cropper's voice expressed bland surprise. "That is strange. As a rule I do not think Alfred and Robert have been troublesome to their teachers. What have they been doing now?"

"They refuse to obey my orders," said Esther faintly.

"Ah, well, Miss Maxwell, perhaps you will pardon my saying that a teacher should be able to enforce her orders. My boys are high-spirited fellows and need a strong, firm hand to restrain them. I have always said I considered it advisable to employ a male teacher in Maitland school. We should have better order. Not that I disapprove of you personally—far from it. I should be glad to see you succeed. But I have heard many complaints regarding the order in school at present."

"I had no trouble until your boys came," retorted Esther, losing her temper a little, "and I believe that if you were willing to co-operate with me that I could govern them."

"Well, you see," said Mr. Cropper easily, "when I send my boys to school I naturally expect that the teacher will be capable of doing the work she has been hired to do."

"Then you refuse to help me?" said Esther in a trembling voice.

"Why, my dear young lady, what can I do? Boys soon know when they can disobey a teacher with impunity. No doubt you will be able to secure a school easier to control and will do good work. But here, as I have already said, we need a firm hand at the helm. But you are not going yet, Miss Maxwell? You need some refreshment after your long walk. Mrs. Cropper will bring you in something."

"No, thank you," said poor Esther. She felt that she must get away at once or she would burst into heartsick tears under those steely, bland blue eyes. When she got home she shut herself up in her room and cried. There was nothing for her to do but resign, she thought dismally.

On the following Saturday Esther went for an afternoon walk, carrying her kodak with her. It was a brilliantly fine autumn day, and woods and fields were basking in a mellow haze. Esther went across lots to Mrs. Charley Cropper's house, intending to make a call. But the house was locked up and evidently deserted, so she rambled past it to the back fields. Passing through a grove of maples she came out among leafy young saplings on the other side. Just beyond her, with its laden boughs hanging over the line fence, was the famous plum tree. Esther looked at it for a moment. Then an odd smile gleamed over her face and she lifted her kodak.

Monday evening Esther called on Mr. Cropper again. After the preliminary remarks in which he indulged, she said, with seeming irrelevance, that Saturday had been a fine day.

"There was an excellent light for snapshots," she went on coolly. "I went out with my kodak and was lucky enough to get a good negative. I have brought you up a proof. I thought you would be interested in it."

She rose and placed the proof on the table before Mr. Cropper. The plum tree came out clearly. Bob and Alf Cropper were up among the boughs picking the plums. On the ground beneath them stood their father with a basket of fruit in his hand.

Mr. Cropper looked at the proof and from it to Esther. His eyes had lost their unconcerned glitter, but his voice was defiant.

"The plums are mine by right," he said.

"Perhaps," said Esther calmly, "but there are some who do not think so. Mrs. Charley, for instance—she would like to see this proof, I think."

"Don't show it to her," cried Mr. Cropper hastily. "I tell you, Miss Maxwell, the plums are mine. But I am tired of fighting over them and I had decided before this that I'd let her have them after this. It's only a trifle, anyhow. And about that little matter we were discussing the other night, Miss Maxwell. I have been thinking it over, and I admit I was somewhat unreasonable. I'll talk to Alfred and Robert and see what I can do."

"Very well," said Esther quietly. "The matter of the plums isn't my business and I don't wish to be involved in your family feuds, especially as you say that you mean to allow Mrs. Charley to enjoy her own in future. As for the school, we will hope that matters will improve."

"You'll leave the proof with me, won't you?" said Mr. Cropper eagerly.

"Oh, certainly," said Esther, smiling. "I have the negative still, you know."

From that time out the Cropper boys were models of good behaviour and the other turbulent spirits, having lost their leaders, were soon quelled. Complaint died away, and at the end of the term Esther was re-engaged.

"You seem to have won old Cropper over to your side entirely," Mr. Baxter told her that night. "He said at the meeting today that you were the best teacher we had ever had and moved to raise your salary. I never knew Isaac Cropper to change his opinions so handsomely."

Esther smiled. She knew it had taken a powerful lever to change Mr. Cropper's opinion, but she kept her own counsel.

LUCY MAUD MONTGOMERY SHORT STORIES, 1904

A Fortunate Mistake

"Oh, dear! oh, dear!" fretted Nan Wallace, twisting herself about uneasily on the sofa in her pretty room. "I never thought before that the days could be so long as they are now."

"Poor you!" said her sister Maude sympathetically. Maude was moving briskly about the room, putting it into the beautiful order that Mother insisted on. It was Nan's week to care for their room, but Nan had sprained her ankle three days ago and could do nothing but lie on the sofa ever since. And very tired of it, too, was wide-awake, active Nan.

"And the picnic this afternoon, too!" she sighed. "I've looked forward to it all summer. And it's a perfect day—and I've got to stay here and nurse this foot."

Nan looked vindictively at the bandaged member, while Maude leaned out of the window to pull a pink climbing rose. As she did so she nodded to someone in the village street below.

"Who is passing?" asked Nan.

"Florrie Hamilton."

"Is she going to the picnic?" asked Nan indifferently.

"No. She wasn't asked. Of course, I don't suppose she expected to be. She knows she isn't in our set. She must feel horribly out of place at school. A lot of the girls say it is ridiculous of her father to send her to Miss Braxton's private school—a factory overseer's daughter."

"She ought to have been asked to the picnic all the same," said Nan shortly. "She is in our class if she isn't in our set. Of course I don't suppose she would have enjoyed herself—or even gone at all, for that matter. She certainly doesn't push herself in among us. One would think she hadn't a tongue in her head."

"She is the best student in the class," admitted Maude, arranging her roses in a vase and putting them on the table at Nan's elbow. "But Patty Morrison and Wilhelmina Patterson had the most to say about the invitations, and they wouldn't have her. There, Nannie dear, aren't those lovely? I'll leave them here to be company for you."

"I'm going to have more company than that," said Nan, thumping her pillow energetically. "I'm not going to mope here alone all the afternoon, with you off having a jolly time at the picnic. Write a little note for me to Florrie Hastings, will you? I'll do as much for you when you sprain your foot."

"What shall I put in it?" said Maude, rummaging out her portfolio obligingly.

"Oh, just ask her if she will come down and cheer a poor invalid up this afternoon. She'll come, I know. And she is such good company. Get Dickie to run right out and mail it."

"I do wonder if Florrie Hamilton will feel hurt over not being asked to the picnic," speculated Maude absently as she slipped her note into an envelope and addressed it.

Florrie Hamilton herself could best have answered that question as she walked along the street in the fresh morning sunshine. She did feel hurt—much more keenly than she would acknowledge even to herself. It was not that she cared about the picnic itself: as Nan Wallace had said, she would not have been likely to enjoy herself if she had gone among a crowd of girls many of whom looked down on her and ignored her. But to be left out when every other girl in the school was invited! Florrie's lip quivered as she thought of it.

"I'll get Father to let me to go to the public school after vacation," she murmured. "I hate going to Miss Braxton's."

Florrie was a newcomer in Winboro. Her father had recently come to take a position in the largest factory of the small town. For this reason Florrie was slighted at school by some of the ruder girls and severely left alone by most of the others. Some, it is true, tried at the start to be friends, but Florrie, too keenly sensitive to the atmosphere around her to respond, was believed to be decidedly dull and mopy. She retreated further and further into herself and was almost as solitary at Miss Braxton's as if she had been on a desert island.

"They don't like me because I am plainly dressed and because my father is not a wealthy man," thought Florrie bitterly. And there was enough truth in this in regard to many of Miss Braxton's girls to make a very uncomfortable state of affairs.

"Here's a letter for you, Flo," said her brother Jack at noon. "Got it at the office on my way home. Who is your swell correspondent?"

Florrie opened the dainty, perfumed note and read it with a face that, puzzled at first, suddenly grew radiant.

"Listen, Jack," she said excitedly.

"Dear Florrie:

> "Nan is confined to house, room, and sofa with a sprained foot. As she will be all alone this afternoon, won't you come down and spend it with her? She very much wants you to come—she is so lonesome and thinks you will be just the one to cheer her up.
>
> "Yours cordially,
> "Maude Wallace."

"Are you going?" asked Jack.

"Yes—I don't know—I'll think about it," said Florrie absently. Then she hurried upstairs to her room.

"Shall I go?" she thought. "Yes, I will. I dare say Nan has asked me just out of pity because I was not invited to the picnic. But even so it was sweet of her. I've always thought I would like those Wallace girls if I could get really acquainted with them. They've always been nice to me, too—I don't know why I am always so tongue-tied and stupid with them. But I'll go anyway."

That afternoon Mrs. Wallace came into Nan's room.

"Nan, dear, Florrie Hamilton is downstairs asking for you."

"Florrie—Hamilton?"

"Yes. She said something about a note you sent her this morning. Shall I ask her to come up?"

"Yes, of course," said Nan lamely. When her mother had gone out she fell back on her pillows and thought rapidly.

"Florrie Hamilton! Maude must have addressed that note to her by mistake. But she mustn't know it was a mistake—mustn't suspect it. Oh, dear! What shall I ever find to talk to her about? She is so quiet and shy."

Further reflections were cut short by Florrie's entrance. Nan held out her hand with a chummy smile.

"It's good of you to give your afternoon up to visiting a cranky invalid," she said heartily. "You don't know how lonesome I've been since Maude went away. Take off your hat and pick out the nicest chair you can find, and let's be comfy."

Somehow, Nan's frank greeting did away with Florrie's embarrassment and made her feel at home. She sat down in Maude's rocker, then, glancing over to a vase filled with roses, her eyes kindled with pleasure. Seeing this, Nan said, "Aren't they lovely? We Wallaces are very fond of our climbing roses. Our great-grandmother brought the roots out from England with her sixty years ago, and they grow nowhere else in this country."

"I know," said Florrie, with a smile. "I recognized them as soon as I came into the room. They are the same kind of roses as those which grow about Grandmother Hamilton's house in England. I used to love them so."

"In England! Were you ever in England?"

"Oh, yes," laughed Florrie. "And I've been in pretty nearly every other country upon earth—every one that a ship could get to, at least."

"Why, Florrie Hamilton! Are you in earnest?"

"Indeed, yes. Perhaps you don't know that our 'now-mother,' as Jack says sometimes, is Father's second wife. My own mother died when I was a baby, and my aunt, who had no children of her own, took me to bring up. Her husband was a sea-captain, and she always went on his sea-voyages with him. So I went too. I almost grew up on shipboard. We had delightful times. I never went to school. Auntie had been a teacher before her marriage, and she taught me. Two years ago, when I was fourteen, Father married again, and then he wanted me to go home to him and Jack and our new mother. So I did, although at first I was very sorry to leave Auntie and the dear old ship and all our lovely wanderings."

"Oh, tell me all about them," demanded Nan. "Why, Florrie Hamilton, to think you've never said a word about your wonderful experiences! I love to hear about foreign countries from people who have really been there. Please just talk—and I'll listen and ask questions."

Florrie did talk. I'm not sure whether she or Nan was the more surprised to find that she could talk so well and describe her travels so brightly and humorously. The afternoon passed quickly, and when Florrie went away at dusk, after a dainty tea served up in Nan's room, it was with a cordial invitation to come again soon.

"I've enjoyed your visit so much," said Nan sincerely. "I'm going down to see you as soon as I can walk. But don't wait for that. Let us be good, chummy friends without any ceremony."

When Florrie, with a light heart and a happy smile, had gone, came Maude, sunburned and glowing from her picnic.

"Such a nice time as we had!" she exclaimed. "Wasn't I sorry to think of you cooped up here! Did Florrie come?"

"One Florrie did. Maude, you addressed that note to Florrie Hamilton today instead of Florrie Hastings."

"Nan, surely not! I'm sure—"

"Yes, you did. And she came here. Was I not taken aback at first, Maude!"

"I was thinking about her when I addressed it, and I must have put her name down by mistake. I'm so sorry—"

"You needn't be. I haven't been entertained so charmingly for a long while. Why, Maude, she has travelled almost everywhere—and is so bright and witty when she thaws out. She didn't seem like the same girl at all. She is just perfectly lovely!"

"Well, I'm glad you had such a nice time together. Do you know, some of the girls were very much vexed because she wasn't asked to the picnic. They said that it was sheer rudeness not to ask her, and that it reflected on us all, even if Patty and Wilhelmina were responsible for it. I'm afraid we girls at Miss Braxton's have been getting snobbish, and some of us are beginning to find it out and be ashamed of it."

"Just wait until school opens," said Nan—vaguely enough, it would seem. But Maude understood.

However, they did not have to wait until school opened. Long before that time Winboro girlhood discovered that the Wallace girls were taking Florrie Hamilton into their lives. If the Wallace girls liked her, there must be something in the girl more than was at first thought—thus more than one of Miss Braxton's girls reasoned. And gradually the other girls found, as Nan had found, that Florrie was full of fun and an all-round good companion when drawn out of her diffidence. When Miss Braxton's school reopened Florrie was the class favourite. Between her and Nan Wallace a beautiful and helpful friendship had been formed which was to grow and deepen through their whole lives.

"And all because Maude in a fit of abstraction wrote 'Hamilton' for 'Hastings,'" said Nan to herself one day. But that is something Florrie Hamilton will never know.

An Unpremeditated Ceremony

Selwyn Grant sauntered in upon the assembled family at the homestead as if he were returning from an hour's absence instead of a western sojourn of ten years. Guided by the sound of voices on the still, pungent autumnal air, he went around to the door of the dining room which opened directly on the poppy walk in the garden.

Nobody noticed him for a moment and he stood in the doorway looking at them with a smile, wondering what was the reason of the festal air that hung about them all as visibly as a garment. His mother sat by the table, industriously polishing the best silver spoons, which, as he remembered, were only brought forth upon some great occasion. Her eyes were as bright, her form as erect, her nose—the Carston nose—as pronounced and aristocratic as of yore.

Selwyn saw little change in her. But was it possible that the tall, handsome young lady with the sleek brown pompadour and a nose unmistakably and plebeianly Grant, who sat by the window doing something to a heap of lace and organdy in her lap, was the little curly-headed, sunburned sister of thirteen whom he remembered? The young man leaning against the sideboard must be Leo, of course; a fine-looking, broad-shouldered young fellow who made Selwyn think suddenly that he must be growing old. And there was the little, thin, grey father in the corner, peering at his newspaper with nearsighted eyes. Selwyn's heart gave a bound at the sight of him which not even his mother had caused. Dear old Dad! The years had been kind to him.

Mrs. Grant held up a glistening spoon and surveyed it complacently. "There, I think that is bright enough even to suit Margaret Graham. I shall take over the whole two dozen teas and one dozen desserts. I wish, Bertha, that you would tie a red cord around each of the handles for me. The Carmody spoons are the same pattern and I shall always be convinced that Mrs. Carmody carried off two of ours the time that Jenny Graham was married. I don't mean to take any more risks. And, Father——"

Something made the mother look around, and she saw her first-born!

When the commotion was over Selwyn asked why the family spoons were being rubbed up.

"For the wedding, of course," said Mrs. Grant, polishing her gold-bowed spectacles and deciding that there was no more time for tears and sentiment just then.

"And there, they're not half done—and we'll have to dress in another hour. Bertha is no earthly use—she is so taken up with her bridesmaid finery."

"Wedding? Whose wedding?" demanded Selwyn, in bewilderment.

"Why, Leo's, of course. Leo is to be married tonight. Didn't you get your invitation? Wasn't that what brought you home?"

"Hand me a chair, quick," implored Selwyn. "Leo, are *you* going to commit matrimony in this headlong fashion? Are you sure you're grown up?"

"Six feet is a pretty good imitation of it, isn't it?" grinned Leo. "Brace up, old fellow. It's not so bad as it might be. She's quite a respectable girl. We wrote you all about it three weeks ago and broke the news as gently as possible."

"I left for the East a month ago and have been wandering around preying on old college chums ever since. Haven't seen a letter. There, I'm better now. No, you needn't fan me, Sis. Well, no family can get through the world without its seasons of tribulations. Who is the party of the second part, little brother?"

"Alice Graham," replied Mrs. Grant, who had a habit of speaking for her children, none of whom had the Carston nose.

"Alice Graham! That child!" exclaimed Selwyn in astonishment.

Leo roared. "Come, come, Sel, perhaps we're not very progressive here in Croyden, but we don't actually stand still. Girls are apt to stretch out some between ten and twenty, you know. You old bachelors think nobody ever grows up. Why, Sel, you're grey around your temples."

"Too well I know it, but a man's own brother shouldn't be the first to cast such things up to him. I'll admit, since I come to think of it, that Alice has probably grown bigger. Is she any better-looking than she used to be?"

"Alice is a charming girl," said Mrs. Grant impressively. "She is a beauty and she is also sweet and sensible, which beauties are not always. We are all very much pleased with Leo's choice. But we have really no more time to spare just now. The wedding is at seven o'clock and it is four already."

"Is there anybody you can send to the station for my luggage?" asked Selwyn. "Luckily I have a new suit, otherwise I shouldn't have the face to go."

"Well, I must be off," said Mrs. Grant. "Father, take Selwyn away so that I shan't be tempted to waste time talking to him."

In the library father and son looked at each other affectionately.

"Dad, it's a blessing to see you just the same. I'm a little dizzy with all these changes. Bertha grown up and Leo within an inch of being married! To Alice Graham at that, whom I can't think of yet as anything else than the long-legged, black-eyed imp of mischief she was when a kiddy. To tell you the truth, Dad, I don't feel in a mood for going to a wedding at Wish-ton-wish tonight. I'm sure you don't either. You've always hated fusses. Can't we shirk it?"

They smiled at each other with chummy remembrance of many a family festival they had "shirked" together in the old days. But Mr. Grant shook his head. "Not this time, sonny. There are some things a decent man can't shirk and one of them is his own boy's wedding. It's a nuisance, but I must go through with it. You'll understand how it is when you're a family man yourself. By the way, why aren't you a family man by this time? Why haven't I been put to the bother and inconvenience of attending your wedding before now, son?"

Selwyn laughed, with a little vibrant note of bitterness in the laughter, which the father's quick ears detected. "I've been too busy with law books, Dad, to find me a wife."

Mr. Grant shook his bushy grey head. "That's not the real reason, son. The world has a wife for every man; if he hasn't found her by the time he's thirty-five, there's some real reason for it. Well, I don't want to pry into yours, but I hope it's a sound one and not a mean, sneaking, selfish sort of reason. Perhaps you'll choose a Madam Selwyn some day yet. In case you should I'm going to give you a small bit of good advice. Your mother—now, she's a splendid woman, Selwyn, a splendid woman. She can't be matched as a housekeeper and she has improved my finances until I don't know them when I meet them. She's been a good wife and a good mother. If I were a young man I'd court her and marry her over again, that I would. But, son, when *you* pick a wife pick one with a nice little commonplace nose, not a family nose. Never marry a woman with a family nose, son."

A woman with a family nose came into the library at this juncture and beamed maternally upon them both. "There's a bite for you in the dining room. After you've eaten it you must dress. Mind you brush your hair well down, Father. The green room is ready for you, Selwyn. Tomorrow I'll have a good talk with you, but tonight I'll be too busy to remember you're around. How are we all going to get over to Wish-ton-wish? Leo and Bertha are going in the pony carriage. It won't hold a third passenger. You'll have to squeeze in with Father and me in the buggy, Selwyn."

"By no means," replied Selwyn briskly. "I'll walk over to Wish-ton-wish. Ifs only half a mile across lots. I suppose the old way is still open?"

"It ought to be," answered Mr. Grant drily; "Leo has kept it well trodden. If you've forgotten how it runs he can tell you."

"I haven't forgotten," said Selwyn, a little brusquely. He had his own reasons for remembering the wood path. Leo had not been the first Grant to go courting to Wish-ton-wish.

When he started, the moon was rising round and red and hazy in an eastern hill-gap. The autumn air was mild and spicy. Long shadows stretched across the fields on his right and silvery mosaics patterned the floor of the old beechwood lane. Selwyn walked slowly. He was thinking of Esme Graham or, rather, of the girl who had been Esme Graham, and wondering if he would see her at the wedding. It was probable, and he did not want to see her. In spite of ten years' effort, he did not think he could yet look upon Tom St. Clair's wife with the proper calm indifference. At the best, it would taint his own memory of her; he would never again be able to think of her as Esme Graham but only as Esme St. Clair.

The Grahams had come to Wish-ton-wish eleven years before. There was a big family of girls of whom the tall, brown-haired Esme was the oldest. There was one summer during which Selwyn Grant had haunted Wish-ton-wish, the merry comrade of the younger girls, the boyishly, silently devoted lover of Esme. Tom

St. Clair had always been there too, in his right as second cousin, Selwyn had supposed. One day he found out that Tom and Esme had been engaged ever since she was sixteen; one of her sisters told him. That had been all. He had gone away soon after, and some time later a letter from home made casual mention of Tom St. Clair's marriage.

He narrowly missed being late for the wedding ceremony. The bridal party entered the parlour at Wish-ton-wish at the same moment as he slipped in by another door. Selwyn almost whistled with amazement at sight of the bride. *That* Alice Graham, that tall, stately, blushing young woman, with her masses of dead-black hair, frosted over by the film of wedding veil! Could that be the scrawny little tomboy of ten years ago? She looked not unlike Esme, with that subtle family resemblance that is quite independent of feature and colouring.

Where was Esme? Selwyn cast his eyes furtively over the assembled guests while the minister read the marriage ceremony. He recognized several of the Graham girls but he did not see Esme, although Tom St. Clair, stout and florid and prosperous-looking, was standing on a chair in a faraway corner, peering over the heads of the women.

After the turmoil of handshakings and congratulations, Selwyn fled to the cool, still outdoors, where the rosy glow of Chinese lanterns mingled with the waves of moonshine to make fairyland. And there he met her, as she came out of the house by a side door, a tall, slender woman in some glistening, clinging garment, with white flowers shining like stars in the coils of her brown hair. In the soft glow she looked even more beautiful than in the days of her girlhood, and Selwyn's heart throbbed dangerously at sight of her.

"Esme!" he said involuntarily.

She started, and he had an idea that she changed colour, although it was too dim to be sure. "Selwyn!" she exclaimed, putting out her hands. "Why, Selwyn Grant! Is it really you? Or are you such stuff as dreams are made of? I did not know you were here. I did not know you were home."

He caught her hands and held them tightly, drawing her a little closer to him, forgetting that she was Tom St. Clair's wife, remembering only that she was the woman to whom he had given all his love and life's devotion, to the entire beggaring of his heart.

"I reached home only four hours ago, and was haled straightway here to Leo's wedding. I'm dizzy, Esme. I can't adjust my old conceptions to this new state of affairs all at once. It seems ridiculous to think that Leo and Alice are married. I'm sure they can't be really grown up."

Esme laughed as she drew away her hands. "We are all ten years older," she said lightly.

"Not you. You are more beautiful than ever, Esme. That sunflower compliment is permissible in an old friend, isn't it?"

"This mellow glow is kinder to me than sunlight now. I am thirty, you know, Selwyn."

"And I have some grey hairs," he confessed. "I knew I had them but I had a sneaking hope that other folks didn't until Leo destroyed it today. These young brothers and sisters who won't stay children are nuisances. You'll be telling me next thing that 'Baby' is grown up."

"'Baby' is eighteen and has a beau," laughed Esme. "And I give you fair warning that she insists on being called Laura now. Do you want to come for a walk with me—down under the beeches to the old lane gate? I came out to see if the fresh air would do my bit of a headache good. I shall have to help with the supper later on."

They went slowly across the lawn and turned into a dim, moonlight lane beyond, their old favourite ramble. Selwyn felt like a man in a dream, a pleasant dream from which he dreads to awaken. The voices and laughter echoing out from the house died away behind them and the great silence of the night fell about them as they came to the old gate, beyond which was a range of shining, moonlight-misted fields.

For a little while neither of them spoke. The woman looked out across the white spaces and the man watched the glimmering curve of her neck and the soft darkness of her rich hair. How virginal, how sacred, she looked! The thought of Tom St. Clair was a sacrilege.

"It's nice to see you again, Selwyn," said Esme frankly at last. "There are so few of our old set left, and so many of the babies grown up. Sometimes I don't know my own world, it has changed so. It's an uncomfortable feeling. You give me a pleasant sensation of really belonging here. I'd be lonesome tonight if I dared. I'm going to miss Alice so much. There will be only Mother and Baby and I left now. Our family circle has dwindled woefully."

"Mother and Baby and you!" Selwyn felt his head whirling again. "Why, where is Tom?"

He felt that it was an idiotic question, but it slipped from his tongue before he could catch it. Esme turned her head and looked at him wonderingly. He knew that in the sunlight her eyes were as mistily blue as early meadow violets, but here they looked dark and unfathomably tender.

"Tom?" she said perplexedly. "Do you mean Tom St. Clair? He is here, of course, he and his wife. Didn't you see her? That pretty woman in pale pink, Lil Meredith. Why, you used to know Lil, didn't you? One of the Uxbridge Merediths?"

To the day of his death Selwyn Grant will firmly believe that if he had not clutched fast hold of the top bar of the gate he would have tumbled down on the moss under the beeches in speechless astonishment. All the surprises of that surprising evening were as nothing to this. He had a swift conviction that there were no words in the English language that could fully express his feelings and that it would be a waste of time to try to find any. Therefore he laid hold of the first baldly commonplace ones that came handy and said tamely, "I thought you were married to Tom."

"You—thought—I—was—married—to—Tom!" repeated Esme slowly. "And have you thought *that* all these years, Selwyn Grant?"

"Yes, I have. Is it any wonder? You were engaged to Tom when I went away, Jenny told me you were. And a year later Bertha wrote me a letter in which she made some reference to Tom's marriage. She didn't say to *whom*, but hadn't I the right to suppose it was to you?"

"Oh!" The word was partly a sigh and partly a little cry of long-concealed, long-denied pain. "It's been all a funny misunderstanding. Tom and I *were* engaged once—a boy-and-girl affair in the beginning. Then we both found out that we had made a mistake—that what we had thought was love was merely the affection of good comrades. We broke our engagement shortly before you went away. All the older girls knew it was broken but I suppose nobody mentioned the matter to Jen. She was such a child, we never thought about her. And you've thought I was Tom's wife all this time? It's—funny."

"Funny. You mean tragic! Look here, Esme, I'm not going to risk any more misunderstanding. There's nothing for it but plain talk when matters get to such a state as this. I love you—and I've loved you ever since I met you. I went away because I could not stay here and see you married to another man. I've stayed away for the same reason. Esme, is it too late? Did you ever care anything for me?"

"Yes, I did," she said slowly.

"Do you care still?" he asked.

She hid her face against his shoulder. "Yes," she whispered.

"Then we'll go back to the house and be married," he said joyfully.

Esme broke away and stared at him. "Married!"

"Yes, married. We've wasted ten years and we're not going to waste another minute. We're *not*, I say."

"Selwyn! It's impossible."

"I have expurgated that word from my dictionary. It's the very simplest thing when you look at it in an unprejudiced way. Here is a ready-made wedding and decorations and assembled guests, a minister on the spot and a state where no licence is required. You have a very pretty new dress on and you love me. I have a plain gold ring on my little finger that will fit you. Aren't all the conditions fulfilled? Where is the sense of waiting and having another family upheaval in a few weeks' time?"

"I understand why you have made such a success of the law," said Esme, "but—"

"There are no buts. Come with me, Esme. I'm going to hunt up your mother and mine and talk to them."

Half an hour later an astonishing whisper went circulating among the guests. Before they could grasp its significance Tom St. Clair and Jen's husband, broadly smiling, were hustling scattered folk into the parlour again and making clear a passage in the hall. The minister came in with his blue book, and then Selwyn Grant and Esme Graham walked in hand in hand.

When the second ceremony was over, Mr. Grant shook his son's hand vigorously. "There's no need to wish you happiness, son; you've got it. And you've made one fuss and bother do for both weddings, that's what I call genius. And"—this in a careful whisper, while Esme was temporarily obliterated in Mrs. Grant's capacious embrace—"she's got the right sort of a nose. But your mother is a grand woman, son, a grand woman."

At the Bay Shore Farm

The Newburys were agog with excitement over the Governor's picnic. As they talked it over on the verandah at sunset, they felt that life could not be worth living to those unfortunate people who had not been invited to it. Not that there were many of the latter in Claymont, for it was the Governor's native village, and the Claymonters were getting up the picnic for him during his political visit to the city fifteen miles away.

Each of the Newburys had a special reason for wishing to attend the Governor's picnic. Ralph and Elliott wanted to see the Governor himself. He was a pet hero of theirs. Had he not once been a Claymont lad just like themselves? Had he not risen to the highest office in the state by dint of sheer hard work and persistency? Had he not won a national reputation by his prompt and decisive measures during the big strike at Campden? And was he not a man, personally and politically, whom any boy might be proud to imitate? Yes, to all of these questions. Hence to the Newbury boys the interest of the picnic centred in the Governor.

"I shall feel two inches taller just to get a look at him," said Ralph enthusiastically.

"He isn't much to look at," said Frances, rather patronizingly. "I saw him once at Campden—he came to the school when his daughter was graduated. He is bald and fat. Oh, of course, he is famous and all that! But I want to go to the picnic to see Sara Beaumont. She's to be there with the Chandlers from Campden, and Mary Spearman, who knows her by sight, is going to point her out to me. I suppose it would be too much to expect to be introduced to her. I shall probably have to content myself with just looking at her."

Ralph resented hearing the Governor called bald and fat. Somehow it seemed as if his hero were being reduced to the level of common clay.

"That's like a girl," he said loftily; "thinking more about a woman who writes books than about a man like the Governor!"

"I'd rather see Sara Beaumont than forty governors," retorted Frances. "Why, she's famous—and her books are perfect! If I could ever hope to write anything like them! It's been the dream of my life just to see her ever since I read *The Story of Idlewild*. And now to think that it is to be fulfilled! It seems too good to be true that tomorrow—tomorrow, Newburys,—I shall see Sara Beaumont!"

"Well," said Cecilia gently—Cecilia was always gentle even in her enthusiasm—"I shall like to see the Governor and Sara Beaumont too. But I'm going to the picnic more for the sake of seeing Nan Harris than anything else. It's three years since she went away, you know, and I've never had another chum whom I love so dearly. I'm just looking forward to meeting her and talking over all our dear, good old times. I do wonder if she has changed much. But I am sure I shall know her."

"By her red hair and her freckles?" questioned Elliott teasingly. "They'll be the same as ever, I'll be bound."

Cecilia flushed and looked as angry as she could—which isn't saying much, after all. She didn't mind when Elliott teased her about her pug nose and her big mouth, but it always hurt her when he made fun of Nan.

Nan's family had once lived across the street from the Newburys. Nan and Cecilia had been playmates all through childhood, but when both girls were fourteen the Harrises had moved out west. Cecilia had never seen Nan since. But now the latter had come east for a visit, and was with her relatives in Campden. She was to be at the picnic, and Cecilia's cup of delight brimmed over.

Mrs. Newbury came briskly into the middle of their sunset plans. She had been down to the post office, and she carried an open letter in her hand.

"Mother," said Frances, straightening up anxiously, "you have a pitying expression on your face. Which of us is it for—speak out—don't keep us in suspense. Has Mary Spearman told you that Sara Beaumont isn't going to be at the picnic?"

"Or that the Governor isn't going to be there?"

"Or that Nan Harris isn't coming?"

"Or that something's happened to put off the affair altogether?" cried Ralph and Cecilia and Elliott all at once.

Mrs. Newbury laughed. "No, it's none of those things. And I don't know just whom I do pity, but it is one of you girls. This is a letter from Grandmother Newbury. Tomorrow is her birthday, and she wants either Frances or Cecilia to go out to Ashland on the early morning train and spend the day at the Bay Shore Farm."

There was silence on the verandah of the Newburys for the space of ten seconds. Then Frances burst out with: "Mother, you know neither of us can go tomorrow. If it were any other day! But the day of the picnic!"

"I'm sorry, but one of you must go," said Mrs. Newbury firmly. "Your father said so when I called at the store to show him the letter. Grandmother Newbury would be very much hurt and displeased if her invitation were disregarded—you know that. But we leave it to yourselves to decide which one shall go."

"Don't do that," implored Frances miserably. "Pick one of us yourself—pull straws—anything to shorten the agony."

"No; you must settle it for yourselves," said Mrs. Newbury. But in spite of herself she looked at Cecilia. Cecilia was apt to be looked at, someway, when things were to be given up. Mostly it was Cecilia who gave them up. The family had come to expect it of her; they all said that Cecilia was very unselfish.

Cecilia knew that her mother looked at her, but did not turn her face. She couldn't, just then; she looked away out over the hills and tried to swallow something that came up in her throat.

"Glad I'm not a girl," said Ralph, when Mrs. Newbury had gone into the house. "Whew! Nothing could induce me to give up that picnic—not if a dozen Grandmother Newburys were offended. Where's your sparkle gone now, Fran?"

"It's too bad of Grandmother Newbury," declared Frances angrily.

"Oh, Fran, she didn't know about the picnic," said Cecilia—but still without turning round.

"Well, she needn't always be so annoyed if we don't go when we are invited. Another day would do just as well," said Frances shortly. Something in her voice sounded choked too. She rose and walked to the other end of the verandah, where she stood and scowled down the road; Ralph and Elliott, feeling uncomfortable, went away.

The verandah was very still for a little while. The sun had quite set, and it was growing dark when Frances came back to the steps.

"Well, what are you going to do about it?" she said shortly. "Which of us is to go to the Bay Shore?"

"I suppose I had better go," said Cecilia slowly—very slowly indeed.

Frances kicked her slippered toe against the fern *jardinière*.

"You may see Nan Harris somewhere else before she goes back," she said consolingly.

"Yes, I may," said Cecilia. She knew quite well that she would not. Nan would return to Campden on the special train, and she was going back west in three days.

It was hard to give the picnic up, but Cecilia was used to giving things up. Nobody ever expected Frances to give things up; she was so brilliant and popular that the good things of life came her way naturally. It never seemed to matter so much about quiet Cecilia.

Cecilia cried herself to sleep that night. She felt that it was horribly selfish of her to do so, but she couldn't help it. She awoke in the morning with a confused idea that it was very late. Why hadn't Mary called her, as she had been told to do?

Through the open door between her room and Frances's she could see that the latter's bed was empty. Then she saw a little note, addressed to her, pinned on the pillow.

Dear Saint Cecilia [it ran], when you read this I shall be on the train to Ashland to spend the day with Grandmother Newbury. You've been giving up things so often and so long that I suppose you think you have a monopoly of it; but you see you haven't. I didn't tell you this last night because I hadn't quite made up my mind. But after you went upstairs, I fought it out to a finish and came to a decision. Sara Beaumont would keep, but Nan Harris wouldn't, so you must go to the picnic. I told Mary to call me instead of you this morning, and now I'm off. You needn't spoil your fun pitying me. Now that the wrench is over, I feel a most delightful glow of virtuous satisfaction!

Fran.

If by running after Frances Cecilia could have brought her back, Cecilia would have run. But a glance at her watch told her that Frances must already be halfway to Ashland. So she could only accept the situation.

"Well, anyway," she thought, "I'll get Mary to point Sara Beaumont out to me, and I'll store up a description of her in my mind to tell Fran tonight. I must remember to take notice of the colour of her eyes. Fran has always been exercised about that."

It was mid-forenoon when Frances arrived at Ashland station. Grandmother Newbury's man, Hiram, was waiting for her with the pony carriage, and Frances heartily enjoyed the three-mile drive to the Bay Shore Farm.

Grandmother Newbury came to the door to meet her granddaughter. She was a tall, handsome old lady with piercing black eyes and thick white hair. There was no savour of the traditional grandmother of caps and knitting about her. She was like a stately old princess and, much as her grandchildren admired her, they were decidedly in awe of her.

"So it is Frances," she said, bending her head graciously that Frances might kiss her still rosy cheek. "I expected it would be Cecilia. I heard after I had written you that there was to be a gubernatorial picnic in Claymont today, so I was quite sure it would be Cecilia. Why isn't it Cecilia?"

Frances flushed a little. There was a meaning tone in Grandmother Newbury's voice.

"Cecilia was very anxious to go to the picnic today to see an old friend of hers," she answered. "She was willing to come here, but you know, Grandmother, that Cecilia is always willing to do the things somebody else ought to do, so I decided I would stand on my rights as 'Miss Newbury' for once and come to the Bay Shore."

Grandmother Newbury smiled. She understood. Frances had always been her favourite granddaughter, but she had never been blind, clear-sighted old lady that she was, to the little leaven of easy-going selfishness in the girl's nature. She was pleased to see that Frances had conquered it this time.

"I'm glad it is you who have come—principally because you are cleverer than Cecilia," she said brusquely. "Or at least you are the better talker. And I want a clever girl and a good talker to help me entertain a guest today. She's clever herself, and she likes young girls. She is a particular friend of your Uncle Robert's family down south, and that is why I have asked her to spend a few days with me. You'll like her."

Here Grandmother Newbury led Frances into the sitting-room.

"Mrs. Kennedy, this is my granddaughter, Frances Newbury. I told you about her and her ambitions last night. You see, Frances, we have talked you over."

Mrs. Kennedy was a much younger woman than Grandmother Newbury. She was certainly no more than fifty and, in spite of her grey hair, looked almost girlish, so bright were her dark eyes, so clear-cut and fresh her delicate face, and so smart her general appearance. Frances, although not given to sudden likings, took one for Mrs. Kennedy. She thought she had never seen so charming a face.

She found herself enjoying the day immensely. In fact, she forgot the Governor's picnic and Sara Beaumont altogether. Mrs. Kennedy proved to be a delightful companion. She had travelled extensively and was an excellent *raconteur*. She had seen much of men and women and crystallized her experiences into sparkling little sentences and epigrams which made Frances feel as if she were listening to one of the witty people in clever books. But under all her sparkling wit there was a strongly felt undercurrent of true womanly sympathy and kind-heartedness which won affection as speedily as her brilliance won admiration. Frances listened and laughed and enjoyed. Once she found time to think that she would have missed a great deal if she had not come to Bay Shore Farm that day. Surely talking to a woman like Mrs. Kennedy was better than looking at Sara Beaumont from a distance.

"I've been 'rewarded' in the most approved storybook style," she thought with amusement.

In the afternoon, Grandmother Newbury packed Mrs. Kennedy and Frances off for a walk.

"The old woman wants to have her regular nap," she told them. "Frances, take Mrs. Kennedy to the fern walk and show her the famous 'Newbury Bubble' among the rocks. I want to be rid of you both until tea-time."

Frances and Mrs. Kennedy went to the fern walk and the beautiful "Bubble"—a clear, round spring of amber-hued water set down in a cup of rock overhung with ferns and beeches. It was a spot Frances had always loved. She found herself talking freely to Mrs. Kennedy of her hopes and plans. The older woman drew the girl out with tactful sympathy until she found that Frances's dearest ambition was some day to be a writer of books like Sara Beaumont.

"Not that I expect ever to write books like hers," she said hurriedly, "and I know it must be a long while before I can write anything worth while at all. But do you think—if I try hard and work hard—that I might do something in this line some day?"

"I think so," said Mrs. Kennedy, smiling, "if, as you say, you are willing to work hard and study hard. There will be a great deal of both and many disappointments. Sara Beaumont herself had a hard time at first—and for a very long first too. Her family was poor, you know, and Sara earned enough money to send away her first manuscripts by making a pot of jelly for a neighbour. The manuscripts came back, and Sara made more jelly and wrote more stories. Still they came back. Once she thought she had better give up writing stories and stick to the jelly alone. There did seem some little demand for the one and none at all for the other. But she determined to keep on until she either succeeded or proved to her own satisfaction that she could make better jelly than stories. And you see she did succeed. But it means perseverance and patience and much hard work. Prepare yourself for that, Frances, and one day you will win your place. Then you will look back to the 'Newbury Bubble,' and you will tell me what a good prophetess I was."

They talked longer—an earnest, helpful talk that went far to inspire Frances's hazy ambition with a definite purpose. She understood that she must not write merely to win fame for herself or even for the higher motive of pure pleasure in her work. She must aim, however humbly, to help her readers to higher planes of thought and endeavour. Then and only then would it be worth while.

"Mrs. Kennedy is going to drive you to the station," said Grandmother Newbury after tea. "I am much obliged to you, Frances, for giving up the picnic today and coming to the Bay Shore to gratify an old woman's inconvenient whim. But I shall not burden you with too much gratitude, for I think you have enjoyed yourself."

"Indeed, I have," said Frances heartily. Then she added with a laugh, "I think I would feel much more meritorious if it had not been so pleasant. It has robbed me of all the self-sacrificing complacency I felt this morning. You see, I wanted to go to that picnic to see Sara Beaumont, and I felt quite like a martyr at giving it up."

Grandmother Newbury's eyes twinkled. "You would have been beautifully disappointed had you gone. Sara Beaumont was not there. Mrs. Kennedy, I see you haven't told our secret. Frances, my dear, let me introduce you two over again. This lady is Mrs. Sara Beaumont Kennedy, the writer of *The Story of Idlewild* and all those other books you so much admire."

The Newburys were sitting on the verandah at dusk, too tired and too happy to talk. Ralph and Elliott had seen the Governor; more than that, they had been introduced to him, and he had shaken hands with them both and told them that their father and he had been chums when just their size. And Cecilia had spent a whole day with Nan Harris, who had not changed at all except to grow taller. But there was one little cloud on her content.

"I wanted to see Sara Beaumont to tell Frances about her, but I couldn't get a glimpse of her. I don't even know if she was there."

"There comes Fran up the station road now," said Ralph. "My eyes, hasn't she a step!"

Frances came smiling over the lawn and up the steps.

"So you are all home safe," she said gaily. "I hope you feasted your eyes on your beloved Governor, boys. I can tell that Cecilia forgathered with Nan by the beatific look on her face."

"Oh, Fran, it was lovely!" cried Cecilia. "But I felt so sorry—why didn't you let me go to Ashland? It was too bad you missed it—and Sara Beaumont."

"Sara Beaumont was at the Bay Shore Farm," said Frances. "I'll tell you all about it when I get my breath—I've been breathless ever since Grandmother Newbury told me of it. There's only one drawback to my supreme bliss—the remembrance of how complacently self-sacrificing I felt this morning. It humiliates me wholesomely to remember it!"

Elizabeth's Child

The Ingelows, of Ingelow Grange, were not a marrying family. Only one of them, Elizabeth, had married, and perhaps it was her "poor match" that discouraged the others. At any rate, Ellen and Charlotte and George Ingelow at the Grange were single, and so was Paul down at Greenwood Farm.

It was seventeen years since Elizabeth had married James Sheldon in the face of the most decided opposition on the part of her family. Sheldon was a handsome, shiftless ne'er-do-well, without any violent bad habits, but also "without any backbone," as the Ingelows declared. "There is sometimes hope of a man who is actively bad," Charlotte Ingelow had said sententiously, "but who ever heard of reforming a jellyfish?"

Elizabeth and her husband had gone west and settled on a prairie farm in Manitoba. She had never been home since. Perhaps her pride kept her away, for she had the Ingelow share of that, and she soon discovered that her family's estimate of James Sheldon had been the true one. There was no active resentment on either side, and once in a long while letters were exchanged. Still, ever since her marriage, Elizabeth had been practically an outsider and an alien. As the years came and went the Ingelows at home remembered only at long intervals that they had a sister on the western prairies.

One of these remembrances came to Charlotte Ingelow on a spring afternoon when the great orchards about the Grange were pink and white with apple and cherry blossoms, and over every hill and field was a delicate, flower-starred green. A soft breeze was blowing loose petals from the August Sweeting through the open door of the wide hall when Charlotte came through it. Ellen and George were standing on the steps outside.

"This kind of a day always makes me think of Elizabeth," said Charlotte dreamily. "It was in apple-blossom time she went away." The Ingelows always spoke of Elizabeth's going away, never of her marrying.

"Seventeen years ago," said Ellen. "Why, Elizabeth's oldest child must be quite a young woman now! I—I—" a sudden idea swept over and left her a little breathless. "I would really like to see her."

"Then why don't you write and ask her to come east and visit us?" asked George, who did not often speak, but who always spoke to some purpose when he did.

Ellen and Charlotte looked at each other. "I would like to see Elizabeth's child," repeated Ellen firmly.

"Do you think she would come?" asked Charlotte. "You know when James Sheldon died five years ago, we wrote to Elizabeth and asked her to come home and live with us, and she seemed almost resentful in the letter she wrote back. I've never said so before, but I've often thought it."

"Yes, she did," said Ellen, who had often thought so too, but never said so.

"Elizabeth was always very independent," remarked George. "Perhaps she thought your letter savoured of charity or pity. No Ingelow would endure that."

"At any rate, you know she refused to come, even for a visit. She said she could not leave the farm. She may refuse to let her child come."

"It won't do any harm to ask her," said George.

In the end, Charlotte wrote to Elizabeth and asked her to let her daughter visit the old homestead. The letter was written and mailed in much perplexity and distrust when once the glow of momentary enthusiasm in the new idea had passed.

"What if Elizabeth's child is like her father?" queried Charlotte in a half-whisper.

"Let us hope she won't be!" cried Ellen fervently. Indeed, she felt that a feminine edition of James Sheldon would be more than she could endure.

"She may not like us, or our ways," sighed Charlotte. "We don't know how she has been brought up. She will seem like a stranger after all. I really long to see Elizabeth's child, but I can't help fearing we have done a rash thing, Ellen."

"Perhaps she may not come," suggested Ellen, wondering whether she hoped it or feared it.

But Worth Sheldon did come. Elizabeth wrote back a prompt acceptance, with no trace of the proud bitterness that had permeated her answer to the former invitation. The Ingelows at the Grange were thrown into a flutter when the letter came. In another week Elizabeth's child would be with them.

"If only she isn't like her father," said Charlotte with foreboding, as she aired and swept the southeast spare room for their expected guest. They had three spare rooms at the Grange, but the aunts had selected the southeast one for their niece because it was done in white, "and white seems the most appropriate for a young girl," Ellen said, as she arranged a pitcher of wild roses on the table.

"I think everything is ready," announced Charlotte. "I put the very finest sheets on the bed, they smell deliciously of lavender, and we had very good luck doing up the muslin curtains. It is pleasant to be expecting a guest, isn't it, Ellen? I have often thought, although I have never said so before, that our lives were too self-centred. We seemed to have no interests outside of ourselves. Even Elizabeth has been really nothing to us, you know. She seemed to have become a stranger. I hope her child will be the means of bringing us nearer together again."

"If she has James Sheldon's round face and big blue eyes and curly yellow hair I shall never really like her, no matter how Ingelowish she may be inside," said Ellen decidedly.

When Worth Sheldon came, each of her aunts drew a long breath of relief. Worth was not in the least like her father in appearance. Neither did she resemble her mother, who had been a sprightly, black-haired and black-eyed girl. Worth was tall and straight, with a long braid of thick, wavy brown hair, large, level-gazing grey eyes, a square jaw, and an excellent chin with a dimple in it.

"She is the very image of Mother's sister, Aunt Alice, who died so long ago," said Charlotte. "You don't remember her, Ellen, but I do very well. She was the sweetest woman that ever drew breath. She was Paul's favourite aunt, too," Charlotte added with a sigh. Paul's antagonistic attitude was the only drawback to the joy of this meeting. How delightful it would have been if he had not refused to be there too, to welcome Elizabeth's child.

Worth came to hearts prepared to love her, but they must have loved her in any case. In a day Aunt Charlotte and Aunt Ellen and shy, quiet Uncle George had yielded wholly to her charm. She was girlishly bright and merry, frankly delighted with the old homestead and the quaint, old-fashioned, daintily kept rooms. Yet there was no suggestion of gush about her; she did not go into raptures, but her pleasure shone out in eyes and tones. There was so much to tell and ask and remember the first day that it was not until the second morning after her arrival that Worth asked the question her aunts had been dreading. She asked it out in the orchard, in the emerald gloom of a long arcade of stout old trees that Grandfather Ingelow had planted fifty years ago.

"Aunt Charlotte, when is Uncle Paul coming up to see me? I long to see him; Mother has talked so much to me about him. She was his favourite sister, wasn't she?"

Charlotte and Ellen looked at each other. Ellen nodded slyly. It would be better to tell Worth the whole truth at once. She would certainly find it out soon.

"I do not think, my dear," said Aunt Charlotte quietly, "that your Uncle Paul will be up to see you at all."

"Why not?" asked Worth, her serious grey eyes looking straight into Aunt Charlotte's troubled dark ones. Aunt Charlotte understood that Elizabeth had never told Worth anything about her family's resentment of her marriage. It was not a pleasant thing to have to explain it all to Elizabeth's child, but it must be done.

"I think, my dear," she said gently, "that I will have to tell you a little bit of our family history that may not be very pleasant to hear or tell. Perhaps you don't know that when your mother married we—we—did not exactly approve of her marriage. Perhaps we were mistaken; at any rate it was wrong and foolish to let it come between us and her as we have done. But that is how it was. None of us approved, as I have said, but none of us was so bitter as your Uncle Paul. Your mother was his favourite sister, and he was very deeply attached to her. She was only a year younger than he. When he bought the Greenwood farm she went and kept house for him for three years before her marriage. When she married, Paul was terribly angry. He was always a strange man, very determined and unyielding. He said he would never forgive her, and he never has. He has never married, and he has lived so long alone at Greenwood with only deaf old Mrs. Bree to keep house for him that he has grown odder than ever. One of us wanted to go and keep house for him, but he would not let us. And—I must tell you this although I hate to—he was very angry when he heard we had invited you to visit us, and he said he would not come near the Grange as long as you were here. Oh, you can't realize how bitter and obstinate he is. We pleaded with him, but I think that only made him worse. We have felt so bad over it, your Aunt Ellen and your Uncle George and I, but we can do nothing at all."

Worth had listened gravely. The story was all new to her, but she had long thought there must be a something at the root of her mother's indifferent relations with her old home and friends. When Aunt Charlotte, flushed and half-tearful, finished speaking, a little glimmer of fun came into Worth's grey eyes, and her dimple was very pronounced as she said,

"Then, if Uncle Paul will not come to see me, I must go to see him."

"My dear!" cried both her aunts together in dismay. Aunt Ellen got her breath first.

"Oh, my dear child, you must not think of such a thing," she cried nervously. "It would never do. He would—I don't know what he would do—order you off the premises, or say something dreadful. No! No! Wait. Perhaps he will come after all—we will see. You must have patience."

Worth shook her head and the smile in her eyes deepened.

"I don't think he will come," she said. "Mother has told me something about the Ingelow stubbornness. She says I have it in full measure, but I like to call it determination, it sounds so much better. No, the mountain will not come to Mohammed, so Mohammed will go to the mountain. I think I will walk down to Greenwood this afternoon. There, dear aunties, don't look so troubled. Uncle Paul won't run at me with a pitchfork, will he? He can't do worse than order me off his premises, as you say."

Aunt Charlotte shook her head. She understood that no argument would turn the girl from her purpose if she had the Ingelow will, so she said nothing more. In the afternoon Worth set out for Greenwood, a mile away.

"Oh, what will Paul say?" exclaimed the aunts, with dismal forebodings.

Worth met her Uncle Paul at the garden gate. He was standing there when she came up the slope of the long lane, a tall, massive figure of a man, with deep-set black eyes, a long, prematurely white beard, and a hooked nose. Handsome and stubborn enough Paul Ingelow looked. It was not without reason that his neighbours called him the oddest Ingelow of them all.

Behind him was a fine old farmhouse in beautiful grounds. Worth felt almost as much interested in Greenwood as in the Grange. It had been her mother's home for three years, and Elizabeth Ingelow had loved it and talked much to her daughter of it.

Paul Ingelow did not move or speak, although he probably guessed who his visitor was. Worth held out her hand. "How do you do, Uncle Paul?" she said.

Paul ignored the outstretched hand. "Who are you?" he asked gruffly.

"I am Worth Sheldon, your sister Elizabeth's daughter," she answered. "Won't you shake hands with me, Uncle Paul?"

"I have no sister Elizabeth," he answered unbendingly.

Worth folded her hands on the gatepost and met his frowning gaze unshrinkingly. "Oh, yes, you have," she said calmly. "You can't do away with natural ties by simply ignoring them, Uncle Paul. They go on existing. I never knew until this morning that you were at enmity with my mother. She never told me. But she has talked a great deal of you to me. She has told me often how much you and she loved each other and how good you always were to her. She sent her love to you."

"Years ago I had a sister Elizabeth," said Paul Ingelow harshly. "I loved her very tenderly, but she married against my will a shiftless scamp who—"

Worth lifted her hand slightly. "He was my father, Uncle Paul, and he was always kind to me; whatever his faults may have been I cannot listen to a word against him."

"You shouldn't have come here, then," he said, but he said it less harshly. There was even a certain reluctant approval of this composed, independent niece in his eyes. "Didn't they tell you at the Grange that I didn't want to see you?"

"Yes, they told me this morning, but *I* wanted to see you, so I came. Why cannot we be friends, Uncle Paul, not because we are uncle and niece, but simply because you are you and I am I? Let us leave my father and mother out of the question and start fair on our own account."

For a moment Uncle Paul looked at her. She met his gaze frankly and firmly, with a merry smile lurking in her eyes. Then he threw back his head and laughed a hearty laugh that was good to hear. "Very well," he said. "It is a bargain."

He put his hand over the gate and shook hers. Then he opened the gate and invited her into the house. Worth stayed to tea, and Uncle Paul showed her all over Greenwood.

"You are to come here as often as you like," he told her. "When a young lady and I make a compact of friendship I am going to live up to it. But you are not to talk to me about your mother. Remember, we are friends because I am I and you are you, and there is no question of anybody else."

The Grange Ingelows were amazed to see Paul bringing Worth home in his buggy that evening. When Worth had gone into the house Charlotte told him that she was glad to see that he had relented towards Elizabeth's child.

"I have not," he made stern answer. "I don't know whom you mean by Elizabeth's child. That young woman and I have taken a liking for each other which we mean to cultivate on our own account. Don't call her Elizabeth's child to me again."

As the days and weeks went by Worth grew dearer and dearer to the Grange folk. The aunts often wondered to themselves how they had existed before Worth came and, oftener yet, how they could do without her when the time came for her to go home. Meanwhile, the odd friendship between her and Uncle Paul deepened and grew. They read and drove and walked together. Worth spent half her time at Greenwood. Once Uncle Paul said to her, as if speaking half to himself,

"To think that James Sheldon could have a daughter like you!"

Up went Worth's head. Worth's grey eyes flashed. "I thought we were not to speak of my parents?" she said. "You ought not to have been the first to break the compact, Uncle Paul."

"I accept the rebuke and beg your pardon," he said. He liked her all the better for those little flashes of spirit across her girlish composure.

One day in September they were together in the garden at Greenwood. Worth, looking lovingly and regretfully down the sun-flecked avenue of box, said with a sigh, "Next month I must go home. How sorry I shall be to leave the Grange and Greenwood. I have had such a delightful summer, and I have learned to love all the old nooks and corners as well as if I had lived here all my life."

"Stay here!" said Uncle Paul abruptly. "Stay here with me. I want you, Worth. Let Greenwood be your home henceforth and adopt your crusty old bachelor uncle for a father."

"Oh, Uncle Paul," cried Worth, "I don't know—I don't think—oh, you surprise me!"

"I surprise myself, perhaps. But I mean it, Worth. I am a rich, lonely old man and I want to keep this new interest you have brought into my life. Stay with me. I will try to give you a very happy life, my child, and all I have shall be yours."

Seeing her troubled face, he added, "There, I don't ask you to decide right here. I suppose you have other claims to adjust. Take time to think it over."

"Thank you," said Worth. She went back to the Grange as one in a dream and shut herself up in the white southeast room to think. She knew that she wanted to accept this unexpected offer of Uncle Paul's. Worth's loyal tongue had never betrayed, even to the loving aunts, any discontent in the prairie farm life that had always been hers. But it had been a hard life for the girl, narrow and poverty-bounded. She longed to put forth her hand and take this other life which opened so temptingly before her. She knew, too, that her mother, ambitious for her child, would not be likely to interpose any objections. She had only to go to Uncle Paul and all that she longed for would be given her, together with the faithful, protecting fatherly love and care that in all its strength and sweetness had never been hers.

She must decide for herself. Not even of Aunt Charlotte or Aunt Ellen could she ask advice. She knew they would entreat her to accept, and she needed no such incentive to her own wishes. Far on into the night Worth sat at the white-curtained dormer window, looking at the stars over the apple trees, and fighting her battle between inclination and duty. It was a hard and stubbornly contested battle, but with that square chin and those unfaltering grey eyes it could end in only one way. Next day Worth went down to Greenwood.

"Well, what is it to be?" said Uncle Paul without preface, as he met her in the garden.

"I cannot come, Uncle Paul," said Worth steadily. "I cannot give up my mother."

"I don't ask you to give her up," he said gruffly. "You can write to her and visit her. I don't want to come between parent and child."

"That isn't the point exactly, Uncle Paul. I hope you will not be angry with me for not accepting your offer. I wanted to—you don't know how much I wanted to—but I cannot. Mother and I are so much to each other, Uncle Paul, more, I am sure, than even most mothers and daughters. You have never let me speak of her, but I must tell you this. Mother has often told me that when I came to her things were going very hard with her and that I was heaven's own gift to comfort and encourage her. Then, in the ten years that followed, the three other babies that came to her all died before they were two years old. And with each loss Mother said I grew dearer to her. Don't you see, Uncle Paul, I'm not merely just one child to her but I'm *all* those children? Six years ago the twins were born, and they are dear, bright little lads, but they are very small yet, so Mother has really nobody but me. I know she would consent to let me stay here, because she would think it best for me, but it wouldn't be really best for me; it couldn't be best for a girl to do what wasn't right. I love you, Uncle Paul, and I love Greenwood, and I want to stay so much, but I cannot. I have thought it all over and I must go back to Mother."

Uncle Paul did not say one word. He turned his back on Worth and walked the full length of the box alley twice. Worth watched him wistfully. Was he very angry? Would he forgive her?

"You are an Ingelow, Worth," he said when he came back. That was all, but Worth understood that her decision was not to cause any estrangement between them.

A month later Worth's last day at the Grange came. She was to leave for the West the next morning. They were all out in Grandfather Ingelow's arcade, Uncle George and Aunt Charlotte and Aunt Ellen and Worth, enjoying the ripe mellow sunshine of the October day, when Paul Ingelow came up the slope. Worth went to meet him with outstretched hands. He took them both in his and looked at her very gravely.

"I have not come to say goodbye, Worth. I will not say it. You are coming back to me."

Worth shook her brown head sadly. "Oh, I cannot, Uncle Paul. You know—I told you—"

"Yes, I know," he interrupted. "I have been thinking it all over every day since. You know yourself what the Ingelow determination is. It's a good thing in a good cause but a bad thing in a bad one. And it is no easy thing to conquer when you've let it rule you for years as I have done. But I have conquered it, or you have conquered it for me. Child, here is a letter. It is to your mother—my sister Elizabeth. In it I have asked her to forgive me, and to forget our long estrangement. I have asked her to come back to me with you and her boys. I want you all—all—at Greenwood and I will do the best I can for you all."

"Oh, Uncle Paul," cried Worth, her face aglow and quivering with smiles and tears and sunshine.

"Do you think she will forgive me and come?"

"I know she will," cried Worth. "I know how she has longed for you and home. Oh, I am so happy, Uncle Paul!"

He smiled at her and put his arm over her shoulder. Together they walked up the golden arcade to tell the others. That night Charlotte and Ellen cried with happiness as they talked it over in the twilight.

"How beautiful!" murmured Charlotte softly. "We shall not lose Worth after all. Ellen, I could not have borne it to see that girl go utterly out of our lives again."

"I always hoped and believed that Elizabeth's child would somehow bring us all together again," said Ellen happily.

Freda's Adopted Grave

North Point, where Freda lived, was the bleakest settlement in the world. Even its inhabitants, who loved it, had to admit that. The northeast winds swept whistling up the bay and blew rawly over the long hill that sloped down to it, blighting everything that was in their way. Only the sturdy firs and spruces could hold their own against it. So there were no orchards or groves or flower gardens in North Point.

Just over the hill, in a sheltered southwest valley, was the North Point church with the graveyard behind it, and this graveyard was the most beautiful spot in North Point or near it. The North Point folk loved flowers. They could not have them about their homes, so they had them in their graveyard. It was a matter of pride with each family to keep the separate plot neatly trimmed and weeded and adorned with beautiful blossoms.

It was one of the unwritten laws of the little community that on some selected day in May everybody would repair to the graveyard to plant, trim and clip. It was not an unpleasant duty, even to those whose sorrow was fresh. It seemed as if they were still doing something for the friends who had gone when they made their earthly resting places beautiful.

As for the children, they looked forward to "Graveyard Day" as a very delightful anniversary, and it divided its spring honours with the amount of the herring catch.

"Tomorrow is Graveyard Day," said Minnie Hutchinson at school recess, when all the little girls were sitting on the fence. "Ain't I glad! I've got the loveliest big white rosebush to plant by Grandma Hutchinson's grave. Uncle Robert sent it out from town."

"My mother has ten tuberoses to set out," said Nan Gray proudly.

"We're going to plant a row of lilies right around our plot," said Katie Morris.

Every little girl had some boast to make, that is, every little girl but Freda. Freda sat in a corner all by herself and felt miserably outside of everything. She had no part or lot in Graveyard Day.

"Are you going to plant anything, Freda?" asked Nan, with a wink at the others.

Freda shook her head mutely.

"Freda can't plant anything," said Winnie Bell cruelly, although she did not mean to be cruel. "She hasn't got a grave."

Just then Freda felt as if her gravelessness were a positive disgrace and crime, as if not to have an interest in a single grave in North Point cemetery branded you as an outcast forever and ever. It very nearly did in North Point. The other little girls pitied Freda, but at the same time they rather looked down upon her for it with the complacency of those who had been born into a good heritage of family graves and had an undisputed right to celebrate Graveyard Day.

Freda felt that her cup of wretchedness was full. She sat miserably on the fence while the other girls ran off to play, and she walked home alone at night. It seemed to her that she could *not* bear it any longer.

Freda was ten years old. Four years ago Mrs. Wilson had taken her from the orphan asylum in town. Mrs. Wilson lived just this side of the hill from the graveyard, and everybody in North Point called her a "crank." They pitied any child she took, they said. It would be worked to death and treated like a slave. At first they tried to pump Freda concerning Mrs. Wilson's treatment of her, but Freda was not to be pumped. She was a quiet little mite, with big, wistful dark eyes that had a disconcerting fashion of looking the gossips out of countenance. But if Freda had been disposed to complain, the North Point people would have found out that they had been only too correct in their predictions.

"Mrs. Wilson," Freda said timidly that night, "why haven't we got a grave?"

Mrs. Wilson averred that such a question gave her the "creeps."

"You ought to be very thankful that we haven't," she said severely. "That Graveyard Day is a heathenish custom, anyhow. They make a regular picnic of it, and it makes me sick to hear those school girls chattering about what they mean to plant, each one trying to outblow the other. If I *had* a grave there, I wouldn't make a flower garden of it!"

Freda did not go to the graveyard the next day, although it was a holiday. But in the evening, when everybody had gone home, she crept over the hill and through the beech grove to see what had been done. The plots were all very neat and prettily set out with plants and bulbs. Some perennials were already in bud. The grave of Katie Morris' great-uncle, who had been dead for forty years, was covered with blossoming purple pansies. Every grave, no matter how small or old, had its share of promise—every grave except one. Freda came across it with a feeling of surprise. It was away down in the lower corner where there were no plots. It was shut off from the others by a growth of young poplars and was sunken and overgrown with blueberry shrubs. There was no headstone, and it looked dismally neglected. Freda felt a sympathy for it. She had no grave, and this grave had nobody to tend it or care for it.

When she went home she asked Mrs. Wilson whose it was.

"Humph!" said Mrs. Wilson. "If you have so much spare time lying round loose, you'd better put it into your sewing instead of prowling about graveyards. Do you expect me to work my fingers to the bone making clothes for you? I wish I'd left you in the asylum. That grave is Jordan Slade's, I suppose. He died twenty years ago, and a worthless, drunken scamp he was. He served a term in the penitentiary for breaking into Andrew Messervey's store, and after it he had the face to come back to North Point. But respectable people would have nothing to do with him, and he went to the dogs altogether—had to be buried on charity when he died. He hasn't any relations here. There was a sister, a little girl of ten, who used to live with the Cogswells over at East Point. After Jord died, some rich folks saw her and was so struck with her good looks that they took her away with them. I don't know what become of her, and I don't care. Go and bring the cows up."

When Freda went to bed that night her mind was made up. She would adopt Jordan Slade's grave.

Thereafter, Freda spent her few precious spare-time moments in the graveyard. She clipped the blueberry shrubs and long, tangled grasses from the grave with a pair of rusty old shears that blistered her little brown hands badly. She brought ferns from the woods to plant about it. She begged a root of heliotrope from Nan Gray, a clump of day lilies from Katie Morris, a rosebush slip from Nellie Bell, some pansy seed from old Mrs. Bennett, and a geranium shoot from Minnie Hutchinson's big sister. She planted, weeded and watered faithfully, and her efforts were rewarded. "Her" grave soon looked as nice as any in the graveyard.

Nobody but Freda knew about it. The poplar growth concealed the corner from sight, and everybody had quite forgotten poor, disreputable Jordan Slade's grave. At least, it seemed as if everybody had. But one evening, when Freda slipped down to the graveyard with a little can of water and rounded the corner of the poplars, she saw a lady standing by the grave—a strange lady dressed in black, with the loveliest face Freda had ever seen, and tears in her eyes.

The lady gave a little start when she saw Freda with her can of water.

"Can you tell me who has been looking after this grave?" she said.

"It—it was I," faltered Freda, wondering if the lady would be angry with her. "Pleas'm, it was I, but I didn't mean any harm. All the other little girls had a grave, and I hadn't any, so I just adopted this one."

"Did you know whose it was?" asked the lady gently.

"Yes'm—Jordan Slade's. Mrs. Wilson told me."

"Jordan Slade was my brother," said the lady. "He went sadly astray, but he was not all bad. He was weak and too easily influenced. But whatever his faults, he was good and kind—oh! so good and kind—to me when I was a child. I loved him with all my heart. It has always been my wish to come back and visit his grave, but I have never been able to come, my home has been so far away. I expected to find it neglected. I cannot tell you how pleased and touched I am to find it kept so beautifully. Thank you over and over again, my dear child!"

"Then you're not cross, ma'am?" said Freda eagerly. "And I may go on looking after it, may I? Oh, it just seems as if I couldn't bear not to!"

"You may look after it as long as you want to, my dear. I will help you, too. I am to be at East Point all summer. This will be our grave—yours and mine."

That summer was a wonderful one for Freda. She had found a firm friend in Mrs. Halliday. The latter was a wealthy woman. Her husband had died a short time previously and she had no children. When she went away in the fall, Freda went with her "to be her own little girl for always." Mrs. Wilson consented grudgingly to give Freda up, although she grumbled a great deal about ingratitude.

Before they went they paid a farewell visit to their grave. Mrs. Halliday had arranged with some of the North Point people to keep it well attended to, but Freda cried at leaving it.

"Don't feel badly about it, dear," comforted Mrs. Halliday. "We are coming back every summer to see it. It will always be our grave."

Freda slipped her hand into Mrs. Halliday's and smiled up at her.

"I'd never have found you, Aunty, if it hadn't been for this grave," she said happily. "I'm so glad I adopted it."

How Don Was Saved

Will Barrie went whistling down the lane of the Locksley farm, took a short cut over a field of clover aftermath and through a sloping orchard where the trees were laden with apples, and emerged into the farmhouse yard where Curtis Locksley was sitting on a pile of logs, idly whittling at a stick.

"You look as if you had a corner in time, Curt," said Will. "I call that luck, for I want you to go chestnutting up to Grier's Hill with me. I met old Tom Grier on the road yesterday, and he told me I might go any day. Nice old man, Tom Grier."

"Good!" said Curtis heartily, as he sprang up. "If I haven't exactly a corner in time, I have a day off, at least. Uncle doesn't need me today. Wait till I whistle for Don. May as well take him with us."

Curtis whistled accordingly, but Don, his handsome Newfoundland dog, did not appear. After calling and whistling about the yard and barns for several minutes, Curtis turned away disappointedly.

"He can't be anywhere around. It is very strange. Don never used to go away from home without me, but lately he has been missing several times, and twice last week he wasn't here in the morning and didn't turn up until midday."

"I'd keep him shut up until I broke him of the habit of playing truant, if I were you," said Will, as they turned into the lane.

"Don hates to be shut up, howls all the time so mournfully that I can't stand it," responded Curtis.

"Well," said Will, hesitatingly, "maybe that would be better after all than letting him stray away with other dogs who may teach him bad habits. I saw Don myself one evening last week ambling down the Harbour road with that big brown dog of Sam Ventnor's. Ventnor's dog is beginning to have a bad reputation, you know. There have been several sheep worried lately, and—"

"Don wouldn't touch a sheep!" interrupted Curtis hotly.

"I daresay not, not yet. But Ventnor's dog is under suspicion, and if Don runs with him he'll learn the trick sure as preaching. The farmers are growling a good bit already, and if they hear of Don and Ventnor's dog going about in company, they'll put it on them both. Better keep Don shut up awhile, let him howl as he likes."

"I believe I will," said Curtis soberly. "I don't want Don to fall under suspicion of sheep-worrying, though I'm sure he would never do it. Anyhow, I don't want him to run with Ventnor's dog. I'll chain him up in the barn when I go home. I couldn't stand it if anything happened to Don. After you, he's the only chum I've got—and he's a good one."

Will agreed. He was almost as fond of Don as Curtis was. But he did not feel so sure that the dog would not worry a sheep. Will knew that Don was suspected already, but he did not like to tell Curtis so. And of course there was as yet no positive proof—merely mutterings and suggestions among the Bayside farmers who had lost sheep and were anxious to locate their slayer. There were many other dogs in Bayside and the surrounding districts who were just as likely to be the guilty animals, and Will hoped that if Don were shut up for a time, suspicion might be averted from him, especially if the worryings still went on.

He had felt a little doubtful about hinting the truth to Curtis, who was a high-spirited lad and always resented any slur cast upon Don much more bitterly than if it were meant for himself. But he knew that Curtis would take it better from him than from the other Bayside boys, one or the other of whom would be sure soon to cast something up to Curtis about his dog. Will felt decidedly relieved to find that Curtis took his advice in the spirit in which it was offered.

"Who have lost sheep lately?" queried Curtis, as they left the main road and struck into a wood path through the ranks of beeches on Tom Grier's land.

"Nearly everybody on the Hollow farms," answered Will. "Until last week nobody on the Hill farms had lost any. But Tuesday night old Paul Stockton had six fine sheep killed in his upland pasture behind the fir woods. He is furious about it, I believe, and vows he'll find out what dog did it and have him shot."

Curtis looked grave. Paul Stockton's farm was only about a quarter of a mile from the Locksley homestead, and he knew that Paul had an old family grudge against his Uncle Arnold, which included his nephew and all belonging to him. Moreover, Curtis remembered with a sinking heart that Wednesday morning had been one of the mornings upon which Don was missing.

"But I don't care!" he thought miserably. "I know Don didn't kill those sheep."

"Talking of old Paul," said Will, who thought it advisable to turn the conversation, "reminds me that they are getting anxious at the Harbour about George Finley's schooner, the *Amy Reade*. She was due three days ago and there's no sign of her yet. And there have been two bad gales since she left Morro. Oscar Stockton is on board of her, you know, and his father is worried about him. There are five other men on her, all from the Harbour, and their folks down there are pretty wild about the schooner."

Nothing more was said about the sheep, and soon, in the pleasures of chestnutting, Curtis forgot his anxiety. Old Tom Grier had called to the boys as they passed his house to come back and have dinner there when the time came. This they did, and it was late in the afternoon when Curtis, with his bag of chestnuts over his shoulder, walked into the Locksley yard.

His uncle was standing before the open barn doors, talking to an elderly, grizzled man with a thin, shrewd face.

Curtis's heart sank as he recognized old Paul Stockton. What could have brought him over?

"Curtis," called his uncle, "come here."

As Curtis crossed the yard, Don came bounding down the slope from the house to meet him. He put his hand on the dog's big head and the two of them walked slowly to the barn. Old Paul included them both in a vindictive scowl.

"Curtis," said his uncle gravely, "here's a bad business. Mr. Stockton tells me that your dog has been worrying his sheep."

"It's a—" began Curtis angrily. Then he checked himself and went on more calmly.

"That can't be so, Mr. Stockton. My dog would not harm anything."

"He killed or helped to kill six of the finest sheep in my flock!" retorted old Paul.

"What proof have you of it?" demanded Curtis, trying to keep his anger within bounds.

"Abner Peck saw your dog and Ventnor's running together through my sheep pasture at sundown on Tuesday evening," answered old Paul. "Wednesday morning I found this in the corner of the pasture where the sheep were worried. Your uncle admits that it was tied around your dog's neck on Tuesday."

And old Paul held out triumphantly a faded red ribbon. Curtis recognized it at a glance. It was the ribbon his little cousin, Lena, had tied around Don's neck Tuesday afternoon. He remembered how they had laughed at the effect of that frivolous red collar and bow on Don's massive body.

"I'm sure Don isn't guilty!" he cried passionately.

Mr. Locksley shook his head.

"I'm afraid he is, Curtis. The case looks very black against him, and sheep-stealing is a serious offence."

"The dog must be shot," said old Paul decidedly. "I leave the matter in your hands, Mr. Locksley. I've got enough proof to convict the dog and, if you don't have him killed, I'll make you pay for the sheep he worried."

As old Paul strode away, Curtis looked beseechingly at his uncle.

"Don mustn't be shot, Uncle!" he said desperately. "I'll chain him up all the time."

"And have him howling night and day as if we had a brood of banshees about the place?" said Mr. Locksley sarcastically. He was a stern man with little sentiment in his nature and no understanding whatever of Curtis's affection for Don. The Bayside people said that Arnold Locksley had always been very severe with his nephew. "No, no, Curtis, you must look at the matter sensibly. The dog is a nuisance and must be shot. You can't keep him shut up forever, and, if he has once learned the trick of sheep-worrying, he will never forget it. You can get another dog if you must have one. I'll get Charles Pippey to come and shoot Don tomorrow. No sulking now, Curtis. You are too big a boy for that. Tie the dog up for the night and then go and put the calves in. There is a storm coming. The wind is blowing hard from the northeast now."

His uncle walked away, leaving the boy white and miserable in the yard. He looked at Don, who sat on his haunches and returned his gaze frankly and open-heartedly. He did not look like a guilty dog. Could it be possible that he had really worried those sheep?

"I'll never believe it of you, old fellow!" Curtis said, as he led the dog into a corner of the carriage house and tied him up there. Then he flung himself down on a pile of sacks beside him and buried his face in Don's curly black fur. The boy felt sullen, rebellious and wretched.

He lay there until dark, thinking his own bitter thoughts and listening to the rapidly increasing gale. Finally he got up and flung off after the calves, with Don's melancholy howls at finding himself deserted ringing in his ears.

He'll be quiet enough tomorrow night, thought Curtis wretchedly, as he went upstairs to bed after housing the calves. For a long while he lay awake, but finally dropped into a heavy slumber which lasted until his aunt called him for milking.

The wind was blowing more furiously than ever. Up over the fields came the roar and crash of the surges on the outside shore. The Harbour to the east of Bay-side was rough and stormy.

They were just rising from breakfast when Will Barrie burst into the kitchen.

"The *Amy Reade* is ashore on Gleeson's rocks!" he shouted. "Struck there at daylight this morning! Come on, Curt!"

Curtis sprang for his cap, his uncle following suit more deliberately. As the two boys ran through the yard, Curtis heard Don howling.

"I'll take him with me!" he muttered. "Wait a minute, Will."

The Harbour road was thronged with people hurrying to the outside shore, for the news of the *Amy Readers* disaster had spread rapidly. As the boys, with the rejoicing Don at their heels, pelted along, Sam Morrow overtook them in a cart and told them to jump in. Sam had already been down to the shore and had gone back to tell his father. As they jolted along, he screamed information at them over the shriek of the gale.

"Bad business, this! She's pounding on a reef 'bout a quarter of a mile out. They're sure she's going to break up—old tub, you know—leaky—rotten. The sea's tremenjus high, and the surfs going dean over her. There can't be no boat launched for hours yet—they'll all be drowned. Old Paul's down there like a madman—offering everything he's got to the man who'll save Oscar, but it can't be done."

By this time they had reached the shore, which was black with excited people. Out on Gleeson's Reef the ill-fated little schooner was visible amid the flying spray. A grizzled old Harbour fisherman, to whom Sam shouted a question, shook his head.

"No, can't do nothin'! No boat c'd live in that surf f'r a moment. The schooner'll go to pieces mighty soon, I'm feared. It's turrible! turrible! to stan' by an' watch yer neighbours drown like this!"

Curtis and Will elbowed their way down to the water's edge. The relatives of the crew were all there in various stages of despair, but old Paul Stockton seemed like a man demented. He ran up and down the beach, crying and praying. His only son was on the *Amy Reade*, and he could do nothing to save him!

"What are they doing?" asked Will of Martin Clark.

"Trying to get a line ashore by throwing out a small rope with a stick tied to it," answered Martin. "It's young Stockton that's trying now. But it isn't any use. The cross-currents on that reef are too powerful."

"Why, Don will bring that line ashore!" exclaimed Curtis. "Here, Don! Don, I say!"

The dog bounded back along the shore with a quick bark. Curtis grasped him by the collar and pointed to the stick which young Stockton had just hurled again into the water. Don, with another bark of comprehension, dashed into the sea. The onlookers, grasping the situation, gave a cheer and then relapsed into silence. Only the shriek of the gale and the crash of the waves could be heard as they watched the magnificent dog swimming out through the breakers, his big black head now rising on the crest of a wave and now disappearing in the hollow behind it. When Don finally reached the tossing stick, grasped it in his mouth and turned shoreward, another great shout went up from the beach. A woman behind Curtis, whose husband was on the schooner, dropped on her knees on the pebbles, sobbing and thanking God. Curtis himself felt the stinging tears start to his eyes.

When Don reached the shore he dropped the stick at Curtis's feet and gave himself a tremendous shake. Curtis caught at the stick, while a dozen men and women threw themselves bodily on Don, hugging him and kissing his wet fur like distracted creatures. Old Paul Stockton was among them. Over his shoulder Don's big black head looked up, his eyes asking as plainly as speech what all this fuss was about.

Meanwhile some of the men had already pulled a big hawser ashore and made it fast. In half an hour the crew of the *Amy Reade* were safe on shore, chilled and dripping. Before they were hurried away to warmth and shelter, old Paul Stockton caught Curtis's hand. The tears were running freely down his hard, old face.

"Tell your uncle he is not to lay a finger on that dog!" he said. "He never killed a sheep of mine—he couldn't! And if he did I don't care! He's welcome to kill them all, if nothing but mutton'll serve his turn."

Curtis walked home with a glad heart. Mr. Locksley heard old Paul's message with a smile. He, too, had been touched by Don's splendid feat.

"Well, Curtis, I'm very glad that it has turned old Paul in his favour. But we must shut Don up for a week or so, no matter how hard he takes it. You can see that for yourself. After all, he might have worried the sheep. And, anyway, he must be broken of his intimacy with Ventnor's dog."

Curtis acknowledged the justice of this and poor Don was tied up again. His captivity was not long, however, for Ventnor's dog was soon shot. When Don was released, Curtis had an anxious time for a week or two. But no more sheep were worried, and Don's innocence was triumphantly established. As for old Paul Stockton, it seemed as if he could not do enough for Curtis and Don. His ancient grudge against the Locksleys was completely forgotten, and from that date he was a firm friend of Curtis. In regard to Don, old Paul would say:

"Why, there never was such a dog before, sir, never! He just talks with his eyes, that dog does. And if you'd just 'a' seen him swimming out to that schooner! Bones? Yes, sir! Every time that dog comes here he's to get the best bones we've got for him—and more'n bones, too. That dog's a hero, sir, that's what he is!"

Miss Madeline's Proposal

"Auntie, I have something to tell you," said Lina, with a blush that made her look more than ever like one of the climbing roses that nodded about the windows of the "old Churchill place," as it was always called in Lower Wentworth.

Miss Madeline, sitting in the low rocker by the parlour window, seemed like the presiding genius of the place. Everything about her matched her sweet old-fashionedness, from the crown of her soft brown hair, dressed in the style of her long ago girlhood, to the toes of her daintily slippered feet. Outside of the old Churchill place, in the busy streets of the up-to-date little town, Miss Madeline might have seemed out of harmony with her surroundings. But here, in this dim room, faintly scented with whiffs from the rose garden outside, she was like a note in some sweet, perfect melody of old time.

Lina, sitting on a little stool at Miss Madeline's feet with her curly head in her aunt's lap, was as pretty as Miss Madeline herself had once been. She was also very happy, and her happiness seemed to envelop her as in an atmosphere and lend her a new radiance and charm. Miss Madeline loved her pretty niece very dearly and patted the curly head tenderly with her slender white hands.

"What is it, my dear?"

"I'm—I'm engaged," whispered Lina, hiding her face in Miss Madeline's flowered muslin lap.

"Engaged!" Miss Madeline's tone was one of surprise and awe. She blushed as she said the word as deeply as Lina had done. Then she went on, with a little quiver of excitement in her voice, "To whom, my dear?"

"Oh, you don't know him, Auntie, but I hope you will soon. His name is Ralph Wylde. Isn't it pretty? I met him last winter, and we became very good friends. But we had a quarrel before I came down here and, oh, I have been so unhappy over it. Three weeks ago he wrote me and begged my pardon—so nice of him, because I was really all to blame, you know. And he said he loved me and—all that, you know."

"No, I don't know," said Miss Madeline gently. "But—but—I can imagine."

"Oh, I was so happy. I wrote back and I had this letter from him today. He is coming down tomorrow. You'll be glad to see him, won't you, Auntie?"

"Oh, yes, my dear, and I am glad for your sake—very glad. You are sure you love him?"

"Yes, indeed," said Lina, with a little laugh, as if wondering how anyone could doubt it.

Presently, Miss Madeline said in a shy voice, "Lina, did—did you ever receive a proposal of marriage from anybody besides Mr. Wylde?"

Lina laughed roguishly. "Why, yes, Auntie, ever so many. A dozen, at least."

"Oh, my dear!" cried Miss Madeline in a slightly shocked tone.

"But I did, really. Sometimes it was horrid and sometimes it was funny. It all depended on the man. Dear me, how red and uncomfortable most of them looked—all but the fifth. He was so cool and business like that he almost surprised me into accepting him."

"And—and what did you feel like, Lina?"

"Oh, frightened, mostly—but I always wanted to laugh too. You must know how it is yourself, Auntie. What did you feel like when somebody proposed to you?"

Miss Madeline flushed from chin to brow.

"Oh, Lina," she faltered as if she were confessing something very disgraceful, yet to which she was impelled by her strict truthfulness, "I—I—never had a proposal in my life—not one."

Lina opened her big brown eyes in amazement. "Why, Aunt Madeline! And you so pretty! What was the reason?"

"I've often wondered," said Miss Madeline faintly. "I *was* pretty, as you say—it's so long ago I can say that now. And I had many gentlemen friends. But nobody ever wanted to marry me. I sometimes wish that—that I could have had just one proposal. Not that I wanted to marry, you know, I do not mean that, but just so that it wouldn't have seemed that I was different from anybody else. It is very foolish of me to wish it, I know, and even wicked—for if I had not cared for the person it would have made him very unhappy. But then, he would have forgotten and I would have remembered. It would always have been something to be a little proud of."

"Yes," said Lina absently; her thoughts had gone back to Ralph.

That evening a letter was left at the front door of the old Churchill place. It was addressed in a scholarly hand to Miss Madeline Churchill, and Amelia Kent took it in. Amelia had been Miss Madeline's "help" for years and had grown grey in her service. In Amelia's loyal eyes Miss Madeline was still young and beautiful; she never doubted that the letter was for her mistress. Nobody else there was ever addressed as "Miss Madeline."

Miss Madeline was sitting by the window of her own room watching the sunset through the elms and reading her evening portion of Thomas à Kempis. She never liked to be disturbed when so employed but she read her letter after Amelia had gone out.

When she came to a certain paragraph, she turned very pale and Thomas à Kempis fell to the floor unheeded. When she had finished the letter she laid it on her lap, clasped her hands, and said, "Oh, oh, oh," in a faint, tremulous voice. Her cheeks were very pink and her eyes very bright. She did not even pick up Thomas à Kempis but went to the door and called Lina.

"What is it, Auntie?" asked Lina curiously, noticing the signs of unusual excitement about Miss Madeline.

Miss Madeline held out her letter with a trembling hand.

"Lina, dear, this is a letter from the Rev. Cecil Thorne. It—it is—a proposal of marriage. I feel terribly upset. How very strange that it should come so soon after our talk this morning! I want you to read it! Perhaps I ought not to show it to anyone—but I would like you to see it."

Lina took the letter and read it through. It was unmistakably a proposal of marriage and was, moreover, a very charming epistle of its kind, albeit a little stiff and old-fashioned.

"How funny!" said Lina when she came to the end.

"Funny!" exclaimed Miss Madeline, with a trace of indignation in her gentle voice.

"Oh, I didn't mean that the letter was funny," Lina hastened to explain, "only that, as you said, it is odd to think of it coming so soon after our talk."

But this was a little fib on Lina's part. She *had* thought that the letter or, rather, the fact that it had been written to Miss Madeline, funny. The Rev. Cecil Thorne was Miss Madeline's pastor. He was a handsome, scholarly man of middle age, and Lina had seen a good deal of him during her summer in Lower Wentworth. She had taught the infant class in Sunday School and sometimes she had thought that the minister was in love with her. But she must have been mistaken, she reflected; it must have been her aunt after all, and the Rev. Cecil Thorne's shyly displayed interest in her must have been purely professional.

"What a goose I was to be afraid he was in love with me!" she thought. Aloud she said, "He says he will call tomorrow evening to receive your answer."

"And, oh, what can I say to him?" murmured Miss Madeline in dismay. She wished she had a little of Lina's experience.

"You are going to—you will accept him, won't you?" asked Lina curiously.

"Oh, my dear, no!" cried Miss Madeline almost vehemently. "I couldn't think of such a thing. I am very sorry; do you think he will feel badly?"

"Judging from his letter I feel sure he will," said Lina decidedly.

Miss Madeline sighed. "Oh, dear me! It is very unpleasant. But of course I must refuse him. What a beautiful letter he writes too. I feel very much disturbed by this."

Miss Madeline picked up Thomas à Kempis, smoothed him out repentantly, and placed the letter between his leaves.

When the Rev. Cecil Thorne called at the old Churchill place next evening at sunset and asked for Miss Madeline Churchill, Amelia showed him into the parlour and went to call her mistress. Mr. Thorne sat down by the window that looked out on the lawn. His heart gave a bound as he caught a glimpse of an airy white muslin among the trees and a ripple of distant laughter. The next minute Lina appeared, strolling down the secluded path that curved about the birches. A young man was walking beside her with his arm around her. They crossed the green square before the house and disappeared in the rose garden.

Mr. Thorne leaned back in his chair and put his hand over his eyes. He felt that he had received his answer, and it was a very bitter moment for him. He had hardly dared hope that this bright, beautiful child could care for him, yet the realization came home to him none the less keenly. When Miss Madeline, paling and flushing by turns, came shyly in he had recovered his self-control sufficiently to be able to say "good evening" in a calm voice.

Miss Madeline sat down opposite to him. At that moment she was devoutly thankful that she had never had any other proposal to refuse. It was a dreadful ordeal. If he would only help her out! But he did not speak and every moment of silence made it worse.

"I—received your letter, Mr. Thorne," she faltered at last, looking distressfully down at the floor.

"My letter!" Mr. Thorne turned towards her. In her agitation Miss Madeline did not notice the surprise in his face and tone.

"Yes," she said, gaining a little courage since the ice was broken. "It—it—was a very great surprise to me. I never thought you—you cared for me as—as you said. And I am very sorry because—because I cannot return your affection. And so, of course, I cannot marry you."

Mr. Thorne put his hand over his eyes again. He understood now that there had been some mistake and that Miss Madeline had received the letter he had written to her niece. Well, it did not matter—the appearance of the young man in the garden had settled that. Would he tell Miss Madeline of her mistake? No, it would only humiliate her and it made no difference, since she had refused him.

"I suppose it is of no use to ask you to reconsider your decision?" he said.

"Oh, no," cried Miss Madeline almost aghast. She was afraid he might ask it after all. "Not in the least use. I am sorry—so very sorry—but I could not answer differently. We—I hope—this will make no difference in our friendly relations, Mr. Thorne?"

"Not at all," said Mr. Thorne gravely. "We will try to forget that it has happened."

He bowed sadly and went out. Miss Madeline watched him guiltily as he walked across the lawn. He looked heart-broken. How dreadful it had been! And Lina had refused twelve men! How could she have lived through it?

"Perhaps one gets accustomed to doing it," reflected Miss Madeline. "But I am sure I never could."

"Did Mr. Thorne feel very badly?" whispered Lina that night.

"I'm afraid he did," confessed Miss Madeline sorrowfully. "He looked so pale and sad, Lina, that my heart ached for him. I am very thankful that I have never had any other proposals to decline. It is a very unpleasant experience. But," she added, with a little tinge of satisfaction in her sweet voice, "I am glad I had one. It—it has made me feel more like other people, you know, dear."

Miss Sally's Company

"How beautiful!" said Mary Seymour delightedly, as they dismounted from their wheels on the crest of the hill. "Ida, who could have supposed that such a view would be our reward for climbing that long, tedious hill with its ruts and stones? Don't you feel repaid?"

"Yes, but I am dreadfully thirsty," said Ida, who was always practical and never as enthusiastic over anything as Mary was. Yet she, too, felt a keen pleasure in the beauty of the scene before them. Almost at their feet lay the sea, creaming and shimmering in the mellow sunshine. Beyond, on either hand, stretched rugged brown cliffs and rocks, here running out to sea in misty purple headlands, there curving into bays and coves that seemed filled up with sunlight and glamour and pearly hazes; a beautiful shore and, seemingly, a lonely one. The only house visible from where the girls stood was a tiny grey one, with odd, low eaves and big chimneys, that stood down in the little valley on their right, where the cliffs broke away to let a brook run out to sea and formed a small cove, on whose sandy shore the waves lapped and crooned within a stone's throw of the house. On either side of the cove a headland made out to sea, curving around to enclose the sparkling water as in a cup.

"What a picturesque spot!" said Mary.

"But what a lonely one!" protested Ida. "Why, there isn't another house in sight. I wonder who lives in it. Anyway, I'm going down to ask them for a drink of water."

"I'd like to ask for a square meal, too," said Mary, laughing. "I am discovering that I am hungry. Fine scenery is very satisfying to the soul, to be sure, but it doesn't still the cravings of the inner girl. And we've wheeled ten miles this afternoon. I'm getting hungrier every minute."

They reached the little grey house by way of a sloping, grassy lane. Everything about it was very neat and trim. In front a white-washed paling shut in the garden which, sheltered as it was by the house, was ablaze with poppies and hollyhocks and geraniums. A path, bordered by big white clam shells, led through it to the front door, whose steps were slabs of smooth red sandstone from the beach.

"No children here, certainly," whispered Ida. "Every one of those clam shells is placed just so. And this walk is swept every day. No, we shall never dare to ask for anything to eat here. They would be afraid of our scattering crumbs."

Ida lifted her hand to knock, but before she could do so, the door was thrown open and a breathless little lady appeared on the threshold.

She was very small, with an eager, delicately featured face and dark eyes twinkling behind gold-rimmed glasses. She was dressed immaculately in an old-fashioned gown of grey silk with a white muslin fichu crossed over her shoulders, and her silvery hair fell on each side of her face in long, smooth curls that just touched her shoulders and bobbed and fluttered with her every motion; behind, it was caught up in a knot on her head and surmounted by a tiny lace cap.

She looks as if she had just stepped out of a bandbox of last century, thought Mary.

"Are you Cousin Abner's girls?" demanded the little lady eagerly. There was such excitement and expectation in her face and voice that both the Seymour girls felt uncomfortably that they ought to be "Cousin Abner's girls."

"No," said Mary reluctantly, "we're not. We are only—Martin Seymour's girls."

All the light went out of the little lady's face, as if some illuminating lamp had suddenly been quenched behind it. She seemed fairly to droop under her disappointment. As for the rest, the name of Martin Seymour evidently conveyed no especial meaning to her ears. How could she know that he was a multi-millionaire who was popularly supposed to breakfast on railroads and lunch on small corporations, and that his daughters were girls whom all people delighted to honour?

"No, of course you are not Cousin Abner's girls," she said sorrowfully. "I'd have known you couldn't be if I had just stopped to think. Because you are dark and they would be fair, of course; Cousin Abner and his wife were both fair. But when I saw you coming down the lane—I was peeking through the hall window upstairs, you know, I and Juliana—I was sure you were Helen and Beatrice at last. And I can't help wishing you were!"

"I wish we were, too, since you expected them," said Mary, smiling. "But—"

"Oh, I wasn't really expecting them," broke in the little lady. "Only I am always hoping that they will come. They never have yet, but Trenton isn't so very far away, and it is so lonely here. I just long for company—I and Juliana—and I thought I was going to have it today. Cousin Abner came to see me once since I moved here and he said the girls would come, too, but that was six months ago and they haven't come yet. But perhaps they will soon. It is always something to look forward to, you know."

She talked in a sweet, chirpy voice like a bird's. There were pathetic notes in it, too, as the girls instinctively felt. How very quaint and sweet and unworldly she was! Mary found herself feeling indignant at Cousin Abner's girls, whoever they were, for their neglect.

"We are out for a spin on our wheels," said Ida, "and we are very thirsty. We thought perhaps you would be kind enough to give us a drink of water."

"Oh, my dear, anything—anything I have is at your service," said the little lady delightedly. "If you will come in, I will get you some lemonade."

"I am afraid it is too much trouble," began Mary.

"Oh, no, no," cried the little lady. "It is a pleasure. I love doing things for people, I wish more of them would come to give me the chance. I never have any company, and I do so long for it. It's very lonesome here at Golden Gate. Oh, if you would only stay to tea with me, it would make me so happy. I am all prepared. I prepare every Saturday morning, in particular, so that if Cousin Abner's girls did come, I would be all ready. And when nobody comes, Juliana and I have to eat everything up ourselves. And that is bad for us—it gives Juliana indigestion. If you would only stay!"

"We will," agreed Ida promptly. "And we're glad of the chance. We are both terribly hungry, and it is very good of you to ask us."

"Oh, indeed, it isn't! It's just selfishness in me, that's what it is, pure selfishness! I want company so much. Come in, my dears, and I suppose I must introduce myself because you don't know me, do you now? I'm Miss Sally Temple, and this is Golden Gate Cottage. Dear me, this *is* something like living. You are special providences, that you are, indeed!"

She whisked them through a quaint little parlour, where everything was as dainty and neat and old-fashioned as herself, and into a spare bedroom beyond it, to put off their hats.

"Now, just excuse me a minute while I run out and tell Juliana that we are going to have company to tea. She will be so glad, Juliana will. Make yourselves at home, my dears."

"Isn't she delicious?" said Mary, when Miss Sally had tripped out. "I'd like to shake Cousin Abner's girls. This is what Dot Halliday would call an adventure, Ida."

"Isn't it! Miss Sally and this quaint old spot both seem like a chapter out of the novels our grandmothers cried over. Look here, Mary, she is lonely and our visit seems like a treat to her. Let us try to make it one. Let's just chum with her and tell her all about ourselves and our amusements and our dresses. That sounds frivolous, but you know what I mean. She'll like it. Let's be company in real earnest for her."

When Miss Sally came back, she was attended by Juliana carrying a tray of lemonade glasses. Juliana proved to be a diminutive lass of about fourteen whose cheerful, freckled face wore an expansive grin of pleasure. Evidently Juliana was as fond of "company" as her mistress was. Afterwards, the girls overheard a subdued colloquy between Miss Sally and Juliana out in the hall.

"Go set the table, Juliana, and put on Grandmother Temple's wedding china—be sure you dust it carefully—and the best tablecloth—and be sure you get the crease straight—and put some sweet peas in the centre—and be sure they are fresh. I want everything extra nice, Juliana."

"Yes'm, Miss Sally, I'll see to it. Isn't it great to have company, Miss Sally?" whispered Juliana.

The Seymour girls long remembered that tea table and the delicacies with which it was heaped. Privately, they did not wonder that Juliana had indigestion when she had to eat many such unaided. Being hungry, they did full justice to Miss Sally's good things, much to that little lady's delight.

She told them all about herself. She had lived at Golden Gate Cottage only a year.

"Before that, I lived away down the country at Millbridge with a cousin. My Uncle Ephraim owned Golden Gate Cottage, and when he died he left it to me and I came here to live. It is a pretty place, isn't it? You see those two headlands out there? In the morning, when the sun rises, the water between them is just a sea of gold, and that is why Uncle Ephraim had a fancy to call his place Golden Gate. I love it here. It is so nice to have a home of my own. I would be quite content if I had more company. But I have you today, and perhaps Beatrice and Helen will come next week. So I've really a great deal to be thankful for."

"What is your Cousin Abner's other name?" asked Mary, with a vague recollection of hearing of Beatrice and Helen—somebody—in Trenton.

"Reed—Abner Abimelech Reed," answered Miss Sally promptly. "A.A. Reed, he signs himself now. He is very well-to-do, I am told, and he carries on business in town. He was a very fine young man, my Cousin Abner. I don't know his wife."

Mary and Ida exchanged glances. Beatrice and Helen Reed! They knew them slightly as the daughters of a new-rich family who were hangers-on of the fashionable society in Trenton. They were regarded as decidedly vulgar, and so far their efforts to gain an entry into the exclusive circle where the Seymours and their like revolved had not been very successful.

"I'm afraid Miss Sally will wait a long while before she sees Cousin Abner's girls," said Mary, when they had gone back to the parlour and Miss Sally had excused herself to superintend the washing of Grandmother Temple's wedding china. "They probably look on her as a poor relation to be ignored altogether; whereas, if they were only like her, Trenton society would have made a place for them long ago."

The Seymour girls enjoyed that visit as much as Miss Sally did. She was eager to hear all about their girlish lives and amusements. They told her of their travels, of famous men and women they had seen, of parties they had attended, the dresses they wore, the little fads and hobbies of their set—all jumbled up together and all listened to eagerly by Miss Sally and also by Juliana, who was permitted to sit on the stairs out in the hall and so gather in the crumbs of this intellectual feast.

"Oh, you've been such pleasant company," said Miss Sally when the girls went away.

Mary took the little lady's hands in hers and looked affectionately down into her face.

"Would you like it—you and Juliana—if we came out to see you often? And perhaps brought some of our friends with us?"

"Oh, if you only would!" breathed Miss Sally.

Mary laughed and, obeying a sudden impulse, bent and kissed Miss Sally's cheek.

"We'll come then," she promised. "Please look upon us as your 'steady company' henceforth."

The girls kept their word. Thereafter, nearly every Saturday of the summer found them taking tea with Miss Sally at Golden Gate. Sometimes they came alone; sometimes they brought other girls. It soon became a decided "fad" in their set to go to see Miss Sally. Everybody who met her loved her at sight. It was considered a special treat to be taken by the Seymours to Golden Gate.

As for Miss Sally, her cup of happiness was almost full. She had "company" to her heart's content and of the very kind she loved—bright, merry, fun-loving girls who devoured her dainties with a frank zest that delighted her, filled the quaint old rooms with laughter and life, and chattered to her of all their plans and frolics and hopes. There was just one little cloud on Miss Sally's fair sky.

"If only Cousin Abner's girls would come!" she once said wistfully to Mary. "Nobody can quite take the place of one's own, you know. My heart yearns after them."

Mary was very silent and thoughtful as she drove back to Trenton that night. Two days afterwards, she went to Mrs. Gardiner's lawn party. The Reed girls were there. They were tall, fair, handsome girls, somewhat too lavishly and pronouncedly dressed in expensive gowns and hats, and looking, as they felt, very much on the outside of things. They brightened and bridled, however, when Mrs. Gardiner brought Mary Seymour up and introduced her. If there was one thing on earth that the Reed girls longed for more than another it was to "get in" with the Seymour girls.

After Mary had chatted with them for a few minutes in a friendly way, she said, "I think we have a mutual friend in Miss Sally Temple of Golden Gate, haven't we? I'm sure I've heard her speak of you."

The Reed girls flushed. They did not care to have the rich Seymour girls know of their connection with that queer old cousin of their father's who lived in that out-of-the-world spot up-country.

"She is a distant cousin of ours," said Beatrice carelessly, "but we've never met her."

"Oh, how much you have missed!" said Mary frankly. "She is the sweetest and most charming little lady I have ever met, and I am proud to number her among my friends. Golden Gate is such an idyllic little spot, too. We go there so often that I fear Miss Sally will think we mean to outwear our welcome. We hope to have her visit us in town this winter. Well, good-by for now. I'll tell Miss Sally I've met you. She will be pleased to hear about you."

When Mary had gone, the Reed girls looked at each other.

"I suppose we ought to have gone to see Cousin Sally before," said Beatrice. "Father said we ought to."

"How on earth did the Seymours pick her up?" said Helen. "Of course we must go and see her."

Go they did. The very next day Miss Sally's cup of happiness brimmed right over, for Cousin Abner's girls came to Golden Gate at last. They were very nice to her, too. Indeed, in spite of a good deal of snobbishness and false views of life, they were good-hearted girls under it all; and some plain common sense they had inherited from their father came to the surface and taught them to see that Miss Sally was a relative of whom anyone might be proud. They succumbed to her charm, as the others had done, and thoroughly enjoyed their visit to Golden Gate. They went away promising to come often again; and I may say right here that they kept their promise, and a real friendship grew up between Miss Sally and "Cousin Abner's girls" that was destined to work wonders for the latter, not only socially and mentally but spiritually as well, for it taught them that sincerity and honest kindliness of heart and manner are the best passports everywhere, and that pretence of any kind is a vulgarity not to be tolerated. This took time, of course. The Reed girls could not discard their snobbishness all at once. But in the end it was pretty well taken out of them.

Miss Sally never dreamed of this or the need for it. She loved Cousin Abner's girls from the first and always admired them exceedingly.

"And then it is so good to have your own folks coming as company," she told the Seymour girls. "Oh, I'm just in the seventh heaven of happiness. But, dearies, I think you will always be my favourites—mine and Juliana's. I've plenty of company now and it's all thanks to you."

"Oh, no," said Mary quickly. "Miss Sally, your company comes to you for just your own sake. You've made Golden Gate a veritable Mecca for us all. You don't know and you never will know how much good you have done us. You are so good and true and sweet that we girls all feel as if we were bound to live up to you, don't you see? And we all love you, Miss Sally."

"I'm so glad," breathed Miss Sally with shining eyes, "and so is Juliana."

Mrs. March's Revenge

"I declare, it is a real fall day," said Mrs. Stapp, dropping into a chair with a sigh of relief as Mrs. March ushered her into the cosy little sitting-room. "The wind would chill the marrow in your bones; winter'll be here before you know it."

"That's so," assented Mrs. March, bustling about to stir up the fire. "But I don't know as I mind it at all. Winter is real pleasant when it does come, but I must say, I don't fancy these betwixt-and-between days much. Sit up to the fire, Theodosia. You look real blue."

"I feel so too. Lawful heart, but this is comfort. This chimney-corner of yours, Anna, is the cosiest spot in the world."

"When did you get home from Maitland?" asked Mrs. March. "Did you have a pleasant time? And how did you leave Emily and the children?"

Mrs. Stapp took this trio of interrogations in calm detail.

"I came home Saturday," she said, as she unrolled her knitting. "Nice wet day it was too! And as for my visit, yes, I enjoyed myself pretty, well, not but what I worried over Peter's rheumatism a good deal. Emily is well, and the children ought to be, for such rampageous young ones I never saw! Emily can't do no more with them than an old hen with a brood of ducks. But, lawful heart, Anna, don't mind about my little affairs! The news Peter had for me about you when I got home fairly took my breath. He came down to the garden gate to shout it before I was out of the wagon. I couldn't believe but what he was joking at first. You should have seen Peter. He had an old red shawl tied round his rheumatic shoulder, and he was waving his arms like a crazy man. I declare, I thought the chimney was afire! Theodosia, Theodosia!' he shouted. 'Anna March has had a fortune left her by her brother in Australy, and she's bought the old Carroll place, and is going to move up there!' That was his salute when I got home. I'd have been over before this to hear all about it, but things were at such sixes and sevens in the house that I couldn't go visiting until I'd straightened them out a bit. Peter's real neat, as men go, but, lawful heart, such a mess as he makes of housekeeping! I didn't know you had a brother living."

"No more did I, Theodosia. I thought, as everyone else did, that poor Charles was at the bottom of the sea forty years ago. It's that long since he ran away from home. He had a quarrel with Father, and he was always dreadful high-spirited. He went to sea, and we heard that he had sailed for England in the *Helen Ray*. She was never heard of after, and we all supposed that my poor brother had perished with her. And four weeks ago I got a letter from a firm of lawyers in Melbourne, Australia, saying that my brother, Charles Bennett, had died and left all his fortune to me. I couldn't believe it at first, but they sent me some things of his that he had when he left home, and there was an old picture of myself among them with my name written on it in my own hand, so then I knew there was no mistake. But whether Charles did sail in the *Helen Ray*, or if he did, how he escaped from her and got to Australia, I don't know, and it isn't likely I ever will."

"Well, of all wonderful things!" commented Mrs. Stapp.

"I was glad to hear that I was heir to so much money," said Mrs. March firmly. "At first I felt as if it were awful of me to be glad when it came to me by my brother's death. But I mourned for poor Charles forty years ago, and I can't sense that he has only just died. Not but what I'd rather have seen him come home alive than have all the money in the world, but it has come about otherwise, and as the money is lawfully mine, I may as well feel pleased about it."

"And you've bought the Carroll place," said Mrs. Stapp, with the freedom of a privileged friend. "Whatever made you do it? I'm sure you are as cosy here as need be, and nobody but yourself. Isn't this house big enough for you?"

"No, it isn't. All my life I've been hankering for a good, big, roomy house, and all my life I've had to put up with little boxes of places, not big enough to turn round in. I've been contented, and made the best of what I had, but now that I can afford it, I mean to have a house that will suit me. The Carroll house is just what I want, for all it is a little old-fashioned. I've always had a notion of that house, although I never expected to own it any more than the moon."

"It's a real handsome place," admitted Mrs. Stapp, "but I expect it will need a lot of fixing up. Nobody has lived in it for six years. When are you going to move in?"

"In about three weeks, if all goes well. I'm having it all painted and done over inside. The outside can wait until the spring."

"It's queer how things come about," said Mrs. Stapp meditatively. "I guess old Mrs. Carroll never imagined her home was going to pass into other folks' hands as it has. When you and I were girls, and Louise Carroll was giving herself such airs over us, you didn't much expect to ever stand in her shoes, did you? Do you remember Lou?"

"Yes, I do," said Mrs. March sharply. A change came over her sonsy, smiling face. It actually looked hard and revengeful, and a cruel light flickered in her dark brown eyes. "I'll not forget Lou Carroll as long as I live. She is the only person in this world I ever hated. I suppose it is sinful to say it, but I hate her still, and always will."

"I never liked her myself," admitted Mrs. Stapp. "She thought herself above us all. Well, for that matter I suppose she was—but she needn't have rubbed it in so."

"Well, she might have been above me," said Mrs. March bitterly, "but she wasn't above twitting and snubbing me every chance she got. She always had a spite at me from the time we were children together at school. When we grew up it was worse. I couldn't begin to tell you all the times that girl insulted me. But there was once in particular—I'll never forgive her for it. I was at a party, and she was there too, and so was that young Trenham Manning, who was visiting the Ashleys. Do you remember him, Dosia? He was a handsome young fellow, and Lou had a liking for him, so all the girls said. But he never looked at her that night, and he kept by me the whole time. It made Lou furious, and at last she came up to me with a sneer on her face, and her black eyes just snapping, and said, 'Miss Bennett, Mother told me to tell you to tell your ma that if that plain sewing isn't done by tomorrow night she'll send for it and give it to somebody else; if people engage to have work done by a certain time and don't keep their word, they needn't expect to get it.' Oh, how badly I felt! Mother and I were poor, and had to work hard, but we had feelings just like other people, and to be insulted like that before Trenham Manning! I just burst out crying then and there, and ran away and hid. It was very silly of me, but I couldn't help it. That stings me yet. If I was ever to get a chance to pay Lou Carroll out for that, I'd take it without any compunction."

"Oh, but that is unchristian!" protested Mrs. Stapp feebly.

"Perhaps so, but it's the way I feel. Old Parson Jones used to say that people were marbled good and bad pretty even, but that in everybody there were one or two streaks just pure wicked. I guess Lou Carroll is my wicked streak. I haven't seen or heard of her for years—ever since she married that worthless Dency Baxter and went away. She may be dead for all I know. I don't expect ever to have a chance to pay her out. But mark what I say, Theodosia, if I ever have, I will."

Mrs. March snipped off her thread, as if she challenged the world. Mrs. Stapp felt uncomfortable over the unusual display of feeling she had evoked, and hastened to change the subject.

In three weeks' time Mrs. March was established in her new home, and the "old Carroll house" blossomed out into renewed splendour. Theodosia Stapp, who had dropped in to see it, was in a rapture of admiration.

"You have a lovely home now, Anna. I used to think it fine enough in the Carrolls' time, but it wasn't as grand as this. And that reminds me, I have something to tell you, but I don't want you to get as excited as you did the last time I mentioned her name. You remember the last day I was to see you we were talking of Lou Carroll? Well, next day I was downtown in a store, and who should sail in but Mrs. Joel Kent, from Oriental. You know Mrs. Joel—Sarah Chapple that was? She and her man keep a little hotel up at Oriental. They're not very well off. She is a cousin of old Mrs. Carroll, but, lawful heart, the Carrolls didn't used to make much of the relationship! Well, Mrs. Joel and I had a chat. She told me all her troubles—she always has lots of them. Sarah was always of a grumbling turn, and she had a brand-new stock of them this time. What do you think, Anna March? Lou Carroll—or Mrs. Baxter, I suppose I should say—is up there at Joel Kent's at Oriental, dying of consumption; leastwise, Mrs. Joel says she is."

"Lou Carroll dying at Oriental!" cried Mrs. March.

"Yes. She came there from goodness knows where, about a month ago—might as well have dropped from the clouds, Mrs. Joel says, for all she expected of it. Her husband is dead, and I guess he led her a life of it when he was alive, and she's as poor as second skimmings. She was aiming to come here, Mrs. Joel says, but when she got to Oriental she wasn't fit to stir a step further, and the Kents had to keep her. I gather from what Mrs. Joel said that she's rather touched in her mind too, and has an awful hankering to get home here—to this very house. She appears to have the idea that it is hers, and all just the same as it used to be. I guess she is a sight of trouble, and Mrs. Joel ain't the woman to like that. But there! She has to work most awful hard, and I suppose a sick person doesn't come handy in a hotel. I guess you've got your revenge, Anna, without lifting a finger to get it. Think of Lou Carroll coming to that!"

The next day was cold and raw. The ragged, bare trees in the old Carroll grounds shook and writhed in the gusts of wind. Now and then a drifting scud of rain dashed across the windows. Mrs. March looked out with a shiver, and turned thankfully to her own cosy fireside again.

Presently she thought she heard a low knock at the front door, and went to see. As she opened it a savage swirl of damp wind rushed in, and the shrinking figure leaning against one of the fluted columns of the Grecian porch seemed to cower before its fury. It was a woman who stood there, a woman whose emaciated face wore a piteous expression, as she lifted it to Mrs. March.

"You don't know me, of course," she said, with a feeble attempt at dignity. "I am Mrs. Baxter. I—I used to live here long ago. I thought I'd walk over today and see my old home."

A fit of coughing interrupted her words, and she trembled like a leaf.

"Gracious me!" exclaimed Mrs. March blankly. "You don't mean to tell me that you have walked over from Oriental today—and you a sick woman! For pity's sake, come in, quick. And if you're not wet to the skin!"

She fairly pulled her visitor into the hall, and led her to the sitting-room.

"Sit down. Take this big easy-chair right up to the fire—so. Let me take your bonnet and shawl. I must run right out to tell Hannah to get you a hot drink."

"You are very kind," whispered the other. "I don't know you, but you look like a woman I used to know when I was a girl. She was a Mrs. Bennett, and she had a daughter, Anna. Do you know what became of her? I forget. I forget everything now."

"My name is March," said Mrs. March briefly, ignoring the question. "I don't suppose you ever heard it before."

She wrapped her own warm shawl about the other woman's thin shoulders. Then she hastened to the kitchen and soon returned, carrying a tray of food and a steaming hot drink. She wheeled a small table up to her visitor's side and said, very kindly,

"Now, take a bite, my dear, and this raspberry vinegar will warm you right up. It is a dreadful day for you to be out. Why on earth didn't Joel Kent drive you over?"

"They didn't know I was coming," whispered Mrs. Baxter anxiously. "I—I ran away. Sarah wouldn't have let me come if she had known. But I wanted to come so much. It is so nice to be home again."

Mrs. March watched her guest as she ate and drank. It was plain enough that her mind, or rather her memory, was affected. She did not realize that this was no longer her home. At moments she seemed to fancy herself back in the past again. Once or twice she called Mrs. March "Mother."

Presently a sharp knock was heard at the hall door. Mrs. March excused herself and went out. In the porch stood Theodosia Stapp and a woman whom Mrs. March did not at first glance recognize—a tall, aggressive-looking person, whose sharp black eyes darted in past Mrs. March and searched every corner of the hall before anyone had time to speak.

"Lawful heart!" puffed Mrs. Stapp, as she stepped in out of the biting wind. "I'm right out of breath. Mrs. March, allow me to introduce Mrs. Kent. We're looking for Mrs. Baxter. She has run away, and we thought perhaps she came here. Did she?"

"She is in my sitting-room now," said Mrs. March quietly.

"Didn't I say so?" demanded Mrs. Kent, turning to Mrs. Stapp. She spoke in a sharp, high-pitched tone that grated on Mrs. March's nerves. "Doesn't she beat all! She slipped away this morning when I was busy in the kitchen. And to think of her walking six miles over here in this wind! I dunno how she did it. I don't believe she's half as sick as she pretends. Well, I've got my wagon out here, Mrs. March, and I'll be much obliged if you'll tell her I'm here to take her home. I s'pose we'll have a fearful scene."

"I don't see that there is any call for a scene," said Mrs. March firmly. "The poor woman has just got here, and she thinks she has got home. She might as well think so if it is of any comfort to her. You'd better leave her here."

Theodosia gave a stifled gasp of amazement, but Mrs. March went serenely on.

"I'll take care of the poor soul as long as she needs it—and that will not be very long in my opinion, for if ever I saw death in a woman's face, it is looking out of hers. I've plenty of time to look after her and make her comfortable."

Mrs. Joel Kent was voluble in her thanks. It was evident that she was delighted to get the sick woman off her hands. Mrs. March cut her short with an invitation to stay to tea, but Mrs. Kent declined.

"I've got to hurry home straight off and get the men's suppers. Such a scamper to have over that woman! I'm sure I'm thankful you're willing to let her stay, for she'd never be contented anywhere else. I'll send over what few things she has tomorrow."

When Mrs. Kent had gone, Mrs. March and Mrs. Stapp looked at each other.

"And so this is your revenge, Anna March?" said the latter solemnly. "Do you remember what you said to me about her?"

"Yes, I do, Theodosia, and I thought I meant every word of it. But I guess my wicked streak ran out just when I needed it to depend on. Besides, you see, I've thought of Lou Carroll all these years as she was when I knew her—handsome and saucy and proud. But that poor creature in there isn't any more like the Lou Carroll I knew than you are—not a mite. The old Lou Carroll is dead already, and my spite is dead with her. Will you come in and see her?"

"Well, no, not just now. She wouldn't know me, and Mrs. Joel says strangers kind of excite her—a pretty bad place the hotel would be for her at that rate, I should think. I must go and tell Peter about it, and I'll send up some of my black currant jam for her."

When Mrs. Stapp had gone, Mrs. March went back to her guest. Lou Baxter had fallen asleep with her head pillowed on the soft plush back of her chair. Mrs. March looked at the hollow, hectic cheeks and the changed, wasted features, and her bright brown eyes softened with tears.

"Poor Lou," she said softly, as she brushed a loose lock of grey hair back from the sleeping woman's brow.

Nan

Nan was polishing the tumblers at the pantry window, outside of which John Osborne was leaning among the vines. His arms were folded on the sill and his straw hat was pushed back from his flushed, eager face as he watched Nan's deft movements.

Beyond them, old Abe Stewart was mowing the grass in the orchard with a scythe and casting uneasy glances at the pair. Old Abe did not approve of John Osborne as a suitor for Nan. John was poor; and old Abe, although he was the wealthiest farmer in Granville, was bent on Nan's making a good match. He looked upon John Osborne as a mere fortune-hunter, and it was a thorn in the flesh to see him talking to Nan while he, old Abe, was too far away to hear what they were saying. He had a good deal of confidence in Nan, she was a sensible, level-headed girl. Still, there was no knowing what freak even a sensible girl might take into her head, and Nan was so determined when she did make up her mind. She was his own daughter in that.

However, old Abe need not have worried himself. It could not be said that Nan was helping John Osborne on in his wooing at all. Instead, she was teasing and snubbing him by turns.

Nan was very pretty. Moreover, Nan was well aware of the fact. She knew that the way her dark hair curled around her ears and forehead was bewitching; that her complexion was the envy of every girl in Granville; that her long lashes had a trick of drooping over very soft, dark eyes in a fashion calculated to turn masculine heads hopelessly. John Osborne knew all this too, to his cost. He had called to ask Nan to go with him to the Lone Lake picnic the next day. At this request Nan dropped her eyes and murmured that she was sorry, but he was too late—she had promised to go with somebody else. There was no need of Nan's making such a mystery about it. The somebody else was her only cousin, Ned Bennett, who had had a quarrel with his own girl; the latter lived at Lone Lake, and Ned had coaxed Nan to go over with him and try her hand at patching matters up between him and his offended lady-love. And Nan, who was an amiable creature and tender-hearted where anybody's lover except her own was concerned, had agreed to go.

But John Osborne at once jumped to the conclusion—as Nan had very possibly meant him to do—that the mysterious somebody was Bryan Lee, and the thought was gall and wormwood to him.

"Whom are you going with?" he asked.

"That would be telling," Nan said, with maddening indifference.

"Is it Bryan Lee?" demanded John.

"It might be," said Nan reflectively, "and then again, you know, it mightn't."

John was silent; he was no match for Nan when it came to a war of words. He scowled moodily at the shining tumblers.

"Nan, I'm going out west," he said finally.

Nan stared at him with her last tumbler poised in mid-air, very much as if he had announced his intention of going to the North Pole or Equatorial Africa.

"John Osborne, are you crazy?"

"Not quite. And I'm in earnest, I can tell you that."

Nan set the glass down with a decided thud. John's curtness displeased her. He needn't suppose that it made any difference to her if he took it into his stupid head to go to Afghanistan.

"Oh!" she remarked carelessly. "Well, I suppose if you've got the Western fever your case is hopeless. Would it be impertinent to inquire why you are going?"

"There's nothing else for me to do, Nan," said John, "Bryan Lee is going to foreclose the mortgage next month and I'll have to clear out. He says he can't wait any longer. I've worked hard enough and done my best to keep the old place, but it's been uphill work and I'm beaten at last."

Nan sat blankly down on the stool by the window. Her face was a study which John Osborne, watching old Abe's movements, missed.

"Well, I never!" she gasped. "John Osborne, do you mean to tell me that Bryan Lee is going to do that? How did he come to get your mortgage?"

"Bought it from old Townsend," answered John briefly. "Oh, he's within his rights, I'll admit. I've even got behind with the interest this past year. I'll go out west and begin over again."

"It's a burning shame!" said Nan violently.

John looked around in time to see two very red spots on her cheeks.

"You don't care though, Nan."

"I don't like to see anyone unjustly treated," declared Nan, "and that is what you've been. You've never had half a chance. And after the way you've slaved, too!"

"If Lee would wait a little I might do something yet, now that Aunt Alice is gone," said John bitterly. "I'm not afraid of work. But he won't; he means to take his spite out at last."

Nan hesitated.

"Surely Bryan isn't so mean as that," she stammered. "Perhaps he'll change his mind if—if—"

Osborne wheeled about with face aflame.

"Don't you say a word to him about it, Nan!" he cried. "Don't you go interceding with him for me. I've got some pride left. He can take the farm from me, and he can take you maybe, but he can't take my self-respect. I won't beg him for mercy. Don't you dare to say a word to him about it."

Nan's eyes flashed. She was offended to find her sympathy flung back in her face.

"Don't be alarmed," she said tartly. "I shan't bother myself about your concerns. I've no doubt you're able to look out for them yourself."

Osborne turned away. As he did so he saw Bryan Lee driving up the lane. Perhaps Nan saw it too. At any rate, she leaned out of the window.

"John! John!" Osborne half turned. "You'll be up again soon, won't you?"

His face hardened. "I'll come to say goodbye before I go, of course," he answered shortly.

He came face to face with Lee at the gate, where the latter was tying his sleek chestnut to a poplar. He acknowledged his rival's condescending nod with a scowl. Lee looked after him with a satisfied smile.

"Poor beggar!" he muttered. "He feels pretty cheap I reckon. I've spoiled his chances in this quarter. Old Abe doesn't want any poverty-stricken hangers-on about his place and Nan won't dream of taking him when she knows he hasn't a roof over his head."

He stopped for a chat with old Abe. Old Abe approved of Bryan Lee. He was a son-in-law after old Abe's heart.

Meanwhile, Nan had seated herself at the pantry window and was ostentatiously hemming towels in apparent oblivion of suitor No. 2. Nevertheless, when Bryan came up she greeted him with an unusually sweet smile and at once plunged into an animated conversation. Bryan had not come to ask her to go to the picnic—business prevented him from going. But he meant to find out if she were going with John Osborne. As Nan was serenely impervious to all hints, he was finally forced to ask her bluntly if she was going to the picnic.

Well, yes, she expected to.

Oh! Might he ask with whom?

Nan didn't know that it was a question of public interest at all.

"It isn't with that Osborne fellow, is it?" demanded Bryan incautiously.

Nan tossed her head. "Well, why not?" she asked.

"Look here, Nan," said Lee angrily, "if you're going to the picnic with John Osborne I'm surprised at you. What do you mean by encouraging him so? He's as poor as Job's turkey. I suppose you've heard that I've been compelled to foreclose the mortgage on his farm."

Nan kept her temper sweetly—a dangerous sign, had Bryan but known it.

"Yes; he was telling me so this morning," she answered slowly.

"Oh, was he? I suppose he gave me my character?"

"No; he didn't say very much about it at all. He said of course you were within your rights. But do you really mean to do it, Bryan?"

"Of course I do," said Bryan promptly. "I can't wait any longer for my money, and I'd never get it if I did. Osborne can't even pay the interest."

"It isn't because he hasn't worked hard enough, then," said Nan. "He has just slaved on that place ever since he grew up."

"Well, yes, he has worked hard in a way. But he's kind of shiftless, for all that—no manager, as you might say. Some folks would have been clear by now, but Osborne is one of those men that are bound to get behind. He hasn't got any business faculty."

"He isn't shiftless," said Nan quickly, "and it isn't his fault if he has got behind. It's all because of his care for his aunt. He has had to spend more on her doctor's bills than would have raised the mortgage. And now that she is dead and he might have a chance to pull up, you go and foreclose."

"A man must look out for Number One," said Bryan easily, admiring Nan's downcast eyes and rosy cheeks. "I haven't any spite against Osborne, but business is business, you know."

Nan opened her lips to say something but, remembering Osborne's parting injunction, she shut them again. She shot a scornful glance at Lee as he stood with his arms folded on the sill beside her.

Bryan lingered, talking small talk, until Nan announced that she must see about getting tea.

"And you won't tell me who is going to take you to the picnic?" he coaxed.

"Oh, it's Ned Bennett," said Nan indifferently.

Bryan felt relieved. He unpinned the huge cluster of violets on his coat and laid them down on the sill beside her before he went. Nan flicked them off with her fingers as she watched him cross the lawn, his own self-satisfied smile upon his face.

A week later the Osborne homestead had passed into Bryan Lee's hands and John Osborne was staying with his cousin at Thornhope, pending his departure for the west. He had never been to see Nan since that last afternoon, but Bryan Lee haunted the Stewart place. One day he suddenly stopped coming and, although Nan was discreetly silent, in due time it came to old Abe's ears by various driblets of gossip that Nan had refused him.

Old Abe marched straightway home to Nan in a fury and demanded if this were true. Nan curtly admitted that it was. Old Abe was so much taken aback by her coolness that he asked almost meekly what was her reason for doing such a fool trick.

"Because he turned John Osborne out of house and home," returned Nan composedly. "If he hadn't done that there is no telling what might have happened. I might even have married him, because I liked him very well and it would have pleased you. At any rate, I wouldn't have married John when you were against him. Now I mean to."

Old Abe stormed furiously at this, but Nan kept so provokingly cool that he was conscious of wasting breath. He went off in a rage, but Nan did not feel particularly anxious now that the announcement was over. He would cool down, she knew. John Osborne worried her more. She didn't see clearly how she was to marry him unless he asked her, and he had studiously avoided her since the foreclosure.

But Nan did not mean to be baffled or to let her lover slip through her fingers for want of a little courage. She was not old Abe Stewart's daughter for nothing.

One day Ned Bennett dropped in and said that John Osborne would start for the west in three days. That evening Nan went up to her room and dressed herself in the prettiest dress she owned, combed her hair around her sparkling face in bewitching curls, pinned a cluster of apple blossoms at her belt, and, thus equipped, marched down in the golden sunset light to the Mill Creek Bridge. John Osborne, on his return from Thornhope half an hour later, found her there, leaning over the rail among the willows.

Nan started in well-assumed surprise and then asked him why he had not been to see her. John blushed—stammered—didn't know—had been busy. Nan cut short his halting excuses by demanding to know if he were really going away, and what he intended to do.

"I'll go out on the prairies and take up a claim," said Osborne sturdily. "Begin life over again free of debt. It'll be hard work, but I'm not afraid of that. I will succeed if it takes me years."

They walked on in silence. Nan came to the conclusion that Osborne meant to hold his peace.

"John," she said tremulously, "won't—won't you find it very lonely out there?"

"Of course—I expect that. I shall have to get used to it."

Nan grew nervous. Proposing to a man was really very dreadful.

"Wouldn't it be—nicer for you"—she faltered—"that is—it wouldn't be so lonely for you—would it—if—if you had me out there with you?"

John Osborne stopped squarely in the dusty road and looked at her. "Nan!" he exclaimed.

"Oh, if you can't take a hint!" said Nan in despair.

It was all of an hour later that a man drove past them as they loitered up the hill road in the twilight. It was Bryan Lee; he had taken from Osborne his house and land, but he had not been able to take Nan Stewart, after all.

Natty of Blue Point

Natty Miller strolled down to the wharf where Bliss Ford was tying up the *Cockawee*. Bliss was scowling darkly at the boat, a trim new one, painted white, whose furled sails seemed unaccountably wet and whose glistening interior likewise dripped with moisture. A group of fishermen on the wharf were shaking their heads sagely as Natty drew near.

"Might as well split her up for kindlings, Bliss," said Jake McLaren. "You'll never get men to sail in her. It passed the first time, seeing as only young Johnson was skipper, but when a boat turns turtle with Captain Frank in command, there's something serious wrong with her."

"What's up?" asked Natty.

"The *Cockawee* upset out in the bay again this morning," answered Will Scott. "That's the second time. The *Grey Gull* picked up the men and towed her in. It's no use trying to sail her. Lobstermen ain't going to risk their lives in a boat like that. How's things over at Blue Point, Natty?"

"Pretty well," responded Natty laconically. Natty never wasted words. He had not talked a great deal in his fourteen years of life, but he was much given to thinking. He was rather undersized and insignificant looking, but there were a few boys of his own age on the mainland who knew that Natty had muscles.

"Has Everett heard anything from Ottawa about the lighthouse business yet?" asked Will.

Natty shook his head.

"Think he's any chance of getting the app'intment?" queried Adam Lewis.

"Not the ghost of a chance," said Cooper Creasy decidedly. "He's on the wrong side of politics, that's what. Er rather his father was. A Tory's son ain't going to get an app'intment from a Lib'ral government, that's what."

"Mr. Barr says that Everett is too young to be trusted in such a responsible position," quoted Natty gravely.

Cooper shrugged his shoulders.

"Mebbe—mebbe. Eighteen is kind of green, but everybody knows that Ev's been the real lighthouse keeper for two years, since your father took sick. Irving Elliott wants that light—has wanted it for years—and he's a pretty strong pull at headquarters, that's what. Barr owes him something for years of hard work at elections. I ain't saying anything against Elliott, either. He's a good man, but your father's son ought to have that light as sure as he won't get it, that's what."

"Any of you going to take in the sports tomorrow down at Summerside?" asked Will Scott, in order to switch Cooper away from politics, which were apt to excite him.

"I'm going, for one," said Adam. "There's to be a yacht race atween the Summerside and Charlottetown boat clubs. Yes, I am going. Give you a chance down to the station, Natty, if you want one."

Natty shook his head.

"Not going," he said briefly.

"You should celebrate Victoria Day," said Adam, patriotically. "'Twenty-fourth o' May's the Queen's birthday, Ef we don't get a holiday we'll all run away,' as we used to say at school. The good old Queen is dead, but the day's been ap-p'inted a national holiday in honour of her memory and you should celebrate it becoming, Natty-boy."

"Ev and I can't both go, and he's going," explained Natty. "Prue and I'll stay home to light up. Must be getting back now. Looks squally."

"I misdoubt if we'll have Queen's weather tomorrow," said Cooper, squinting critically at the sky. "Looks like a northeast blow, that's what. There goes Bliss, striding off and looking pretty mad. The *Cockawee's* a dead loss to him, that's what. Nat's off—he knows how to handle a boat middling well, too. Pity he's such a puny youngster. Not much to him, I reckon."

Natty had cast loose in his boat, the *Merry Maid*, and hoisted his sail. In a few minutes he was skimming gaily down the bay. The wind was fair and piping and the *Merry Maid* went like a bird. Natty, at the rudder, steered for Blue Point Island, a reflective frown on his face. He was feeling in no mood for Victoria Day sports. In a very short time he and Ev and Prue must leave Blue Point lighthouse, where they had lived all their lives. To Natty it seemed as if the end of all things would come then. Where would life be worth living away from lonely, windy Blue Point Island?

David Miller had died the preceding winter after a long illness. He had been lighthouse keeper at Blue Point for thirty years. His three children had been born and brought up there, and there, four years ago, the mother had died. But womanly little Prue had taken her place well, and the boys were devoted to their sister. When their father died, Everett had applied for the position of lighthouse keeper. The matter was not yet publicly decided, but old Cooper Creasy had sized the situation up accurately. The Millers had no real hope that Everett would be appointed.

Victoria Day, while not absolutely stormy, proved to be rather unpleasant. A choppy northeast wind blew up the bay, and the water was rough enough. The sky was overcast with clouds, and the May air was raw and chilly. At Blue Point the Millers were early astir, for if Everett wanted to sail over to the mainland in time to catch the excursion train, no morning naps were permissible. He was going alone. Since only one of the boys could go, Natty had insisted that it should be

Everett, and Prue had elected to stay home with Natty. Prue had small heart for Victoria Day that year. She did not feel even a thrill of enthusiasm when Natty hoisted a flag and wreathed the Queen's picture with creeping spruce. Prue felt as badly about leaving Blue Point Island as the boys did.

The day passed slowly. In the afternoon the wind fell away to a dead calm, but there was still a heavy swell on, and shortly before sunset a fog came creeping up from the east and spread over the bay and islands, so thick and white that Prue and Natty could not even see Little Bear Island on the right.

"I'm glad Everett isn't coming back tonight," said Prue. "He could never find his way cross the harbour in that fog."

"Isn't it thick, though," said Natty. "The light won't show far tonight."

At sunset they lighted the great lamps and then settled down to an evening of reading. But it was not long before Natty looked up from his book to say, "Hello, Prue, what was that? Thought I heard a noise."

"So did I," said Prue. "I sounded like someone calling."

They hurried to the door, which looked out on the harbour. The night, owing to the fog, was dark with a darkness that seemed almost tangible. From somewhere out of that darkness came a muffled shouting, like that of a person in distress.

"Prue, there's somebody in trouble out there!" exclaimed Natty.

"Oh, it's surely never Ev!" cried Prue.

Natty shook his head.

"Don't think so. Ev had no intention of coming back tonight. Get that lantern, Prue. I must go and see what and who it is."

"Oh, Natty, you mustn't," cried Prue in distress. "There's a heavy swell on yet—and the fog—oh, if you get lost—"

"I'll not get lost, and I must go, Prue. Maybe somebody is drowning out there. It's not Ev, of course, but suppose it were! That's a good girl."

Prue, with set face, had brought the lantern, resolutely choking back the words of fear and protest that rushed to her lips. They hurried down to the shore and Natty sprang into the little skiff he used for rowing. He hastily lashed the lantern in the stern, cast loose the painter, and lifted the oars.

"I'll be back as soon as possible," he called to Prue. "Wait here for me."

In a minute the shore was out of sight, and Natty found himself alone in the black fog, with no guide but the cries for help, which already were becoming fainter. They seemed to come from the direction of Little Bear, and thither Natty rowed. It was a tough pull, and the water was rough enough for the little dory. But Natty had been at home with the oars from babyhood, and his long training and tough sinews stood him in good stead now. Steadily and intrepidly he rowed along. The water grew rougher as he passed out from the shelter of Blue Point into the channel between the latter and Little Bear. The cries were becoming very faint. What if he should be too late? He bent to the oars with all his energy. Presently, by the smoother water, he knew he must be in the lea of Little Bear. The cries sounded nearer. He must already have rowed nearly a mile. The next minute he shot around a small headland and right before him, dimly visible in the faint light cast by the lantern through the fog, was an upturned boat with two men clinging to it, one on each side, evidently almost exhausted. Natty rowed cautiously up to the one nearest him, knowing that he must be wary lest the grip of the drowning man overturn his own light skiff.

"Let go when I say," he shouted, "and don't—grab—anything, do you hear? Don't—grab. Now, let go."

The next minute the man lay in the dory, dragged over the stern by Netty's grip on his collar.

"Lie still," ordered Natty, clutching the oars. To row around the overturned boat, amid the swirl of water about her, was a task that taxed Netty's skill and strength to the utmost. The other man was dragged in over the bow, and with a gasp of relief Natty pulled away from the sinking boat. Once clear of her he could not row for a few minutes; he was shaking from head to foot with the reaction from tremendous effort and strain.

"This'll never do," he muttered. "I'm not going to be a baby now. But will I ever be able to row back?"

Presently, however, he was able to grip his oars again and pull for the lighthouse, whose beacon loomed dimly through the fog like a great blur of whiter mist. The men, obedient to his orders, lay quietly where he had placed them, and before long Natty was back again at the lighthouse landing, where Prue was waiting, wild with anxiety. The men were helped out and assisted up to the lighthouse, where Natty went to hunt up dry clothes for them, and Prue flew about to prepare hot drinks.

"To think that that child saved us!" exclaimed one of the men. "Why, I didn't think a grown man had the strength to do what he did. He is your brother, I suppose, Miss Miller. You have another brother, I think?"

"Oh, yes—Everett—but he is away," explained Prue. "We heard your shouts and Natty insisted on going at once to your rescue."

"Well, he came just in time. I couldn't have held on another minute—was so done up I couldn't have moved or spoken all the way here even if he hadn't commanded me to keep perfectly still."

Natty returned at this moment and exclaimed, "Why, it is Mr. Barr. I didn't recognize you before."

"Barr it is, young man. This gentleman is my friend, Mr. Blackmore. We have been celebrating Victoria Day by a shooting tramp over Little Bear. We hired a boat from Ford at the Harbour Head this morning—the *Cockawee*, he called her—and sailed over. I don't know much about running a boat, but Blackmore here thinks he does. We were at the other side of the island when the fog came up. We hurried across it, but it was almost dark when we reached our boat. We sailed around the point and then the boat just simply upset—don't know why—"

"But I know why," interrupted Natty indignantly. "That *Cockawee* does nothing but upset. She has turned turtle twice out in the harbour in fine weather. Ford was a rascal to let her to you. He might have known what would happen. Why—why—it was almost murder to let you go!"

"I thought there must be something queer about her," declared Mr. Blackmore. "I do know how to handle a boat despite my friend's gibe, and there was no reason why she should have upset like that. That Ford ought to be horsewhipped."

Thanks to Prue's stinging hot decoctions of black currant drink, the two gentlemen were no worse for their drenching and exposure, and the next morning Natty took them to the mainland in the *Merry Maid*. When he parted with them, Mr. Barr shook his hand heartily and said: "Thank you, my boy. You're a plucky youngster and a skilful one, too. Tell your brother that if I can get the Blue Point lighthouse berth for him I will, and as for yourself, you will always find a friend in me, and if I can ever do anything for you I will."

Two weeks later Everett received an official document formally appointing him keeper of Blue Point Island light. Natty carried the news to the mainland, where it was joyfully received among the fishermen.

"Only right and fair," said Cooper Creasy. "Blue Point without a Miller to light up wouldn't seem the thing at all, that's what. And it's nothing but Ev's doo."

"Guess Natty had more to do with it than Ev," said Adam, perpetrating a very poor pun and being immensely applauded therefor. It keyed Will Scott up to rival Adam.

"You said that Irving had a pull and the Millers hadn't," he said jocularly. "But it looks as if 'twas Natty's pull did the business after all—his pull over to Bear Island and back."

"It was about a miracle that a boy could do what he did on such a night," said Charles Macey.

"Where's Ford?" asked Natty uncomfortably. He hated to have his exploit talked about.

"Ford has cleared out," said Cooper, "gone down to Summerside to go into Tobe Meekins's factory there. Best thing he could do, that's what. Folks here hadn't no use for him after letting that death trap to them two men—even if they was Lib'rals. The *Cockawee* druv ashore on Little Bear, and there she's going to remain, I guess. D'ye want a berth in my mackerel boat this summer, Natty?"

"I do," said Natty, "but I thought you said you were full."

"I guess I can make room for you," said Cooper. "A boy with such grit and muscle ain't to be allowed to go to seed on Blue Point, that's what. Yesser, we'll make room for you."

And Natty's cup of happiness was full.

Penelope's Party Waist

"It's perfectly horrid to be so poor," grumbled Penelope. Penelope did not often grumble, but just now, as she sat tapping with one pink-tipped finger her invitation to Blanche Anderson's party, she felt that grumbling was the only relief she had.

Penelope was seventeen, and when one is seventeen and cannot go to a party because one hasn't a suitable dress to wear, the world is very apt to seem a howling wilderness.

"I wish I could think of some way to get you a new waist," said Doris, with what these sisters called "the poverty pucker" coming in the centre of her pretty forehead. "If your black skirt were sponged and pressed and re-hung, it would do very well."

Penelope saw the poverty pucker and immediately repented with all her impetuous heart having grumbled. That pucker came often enough without being brought there by extra worries.

"Well, there is no use sitting here sighing for the unattainable," she said, jumping up briskly. "I'd better be putting my grey matter into that algebra instead of wasting it plotting for a party dress that I certainly can't get. It's a sad thing for a body to lack brains when she wants to be a teacher, isn't it? If I could only absorb algebra and history as I can music, what a blessing it would be! Come now, Dorrie dear, smooth that pucker out. Next year I shall be earning a princely salary, which we can squander on party gowns at will—if people haven't given up inviting us by that time, in sheer despair of ever being able to conquer our exclusiveness."

Penelope went off to her detested algebra with a laugh, but the pucker did not go out of Doris' forehead. She wanted Penelope to go to that party.

Penelope has studied so hard all winter and she hasn't gone anywhere, thought the older sister wistfully. She is getting discouraged over those examinations and she needs just a good, jolly time to hearten her up. If it could only be managed!

But Doris did not see how it could. It took every cent of her small salary as typewriter in an uptown office to run their tiny establishment and keep Penelope in school dresses and books. Indeed, she could not have done even that much if they had not owned their little cottage. Next year it would be easier if Penelope got through her examinations successfully, but just now there was absolutely not a spare penny.

"It is hard to be poor. We are a pair of misfits," said Doris, with a patient little smile, thinking of Penelope's uncultivated talent for music and her own housewifely gifts, which had small chance of flowering out in her business life.

Doris dreamed of pretty dresses all that night and thought about them all the next day. So, it must be confessed, did Penelope, though she would not have admitted it for the world.

When Doris reached home the next evening, she found Penelope hovering over a bulky parcel on the sitting-room table.

"I'm so glad you've come," she said with an exaggerated gasp of relief. "I really don't think my curiosity could have borne the strain for another five minutes. The expressman brought this parcel an hour ago, and there's a letter for you from Aunt Adella on the clock shelf, and I think they belong to each other. Hurry up and find out. Dorrie, darling, what if it should be a—a—present of some sort or other!"

"I suppose it can't be anything else," smiled Doris. She knew that Penelope had started out to say "a new dress." She cut the strings and removed the wrappings. Both girls stared.

"Is it—it isn't—yes, it is! Doris Hunter, I believe it's an old quilt!"

Doris unfolded the odd present with a queer feeling of disappointment. She did not know just what she had expected the package to contain, but certainly not this. She laughed a little shakily.

"Well, we can't say after this that Aunt Adella never gave us anything," she said, when she had opened her letter. "Listen, Penelope."

My Dear Doris:

I have decided to give up housekeeping and go out West to live with Robert. So I am disposing of such of the family heirlooms as I do not wish to take with me. I am sending you by express your Grandmother Hunter's silk quilt. It is a handsome article still and I hope you will prize it as you should. It took your grandmother five years to make it. There is a bit of the wedding dress of every member of the family in it. Love to Penelope and yourself.

Your affectionate aunt,
Adella Hunter.

"I don't see its beauty," said Penelope with a grimace. "It may have been pretty once, but it is all faded now. It is a monument of patience, though. The pattern is what they call 'Little Thousands,' isn't it? Tell me, Dorrie, does it argue a lack of proper respect for my ancestors that I can't feel very enthusiastic over this heirloom—especially when Grandmother Hunter died years before I was born?"

"It was very kind of Aunt Adella to send it," said Doris dutifully.

"Oh, very," agreed Penelope drolly. "Only don't ever ask me to sleep under it. It would give me the nightmare. O-o-h!"

This last was a little squeal of admiration as Doris turned the quilt over and brought to view the shimmering lining.

"Why, the wrong side is ever so much prettier than the right!" exclaimed Penelope. "What lovely, old-timey stuff! And not a bit faded."

The lining was certainly very pretty. It was a soft, creamy yellow silk, with a design of brocaded pink rosebuds all over it.

"That was a dress Grandmother Hunter had when she was a girl," said Doris absently. "I remember hearing Aunt Adella speak of it. When it became old-fashioned, Grandmother used it to line her quilt. I declare, it is as good as new."

"Well, let us go and have tea," said Penelope. "I'm decidedly hungry. Besides, I see the poverty pucker coming. Put the quilt in the spare room. It is something to possess an heirloom, after all. It gives one a nice, important-family feeling."

After tea, when Penelope was patiently grinding away at her studies and thinking dolefully enough of the near-approaching examinations, which she dreaded, and of teaching, which she confidently expected to hate, Doris went up to the tiny spare room to look at the wrong side of the quilt again.

"It would make the loveliest party waist," she said under her breath. "Creamy yellow is Penelope's colour, and I could use that bit of old black lace and those knots of velvet ribbon that I have to trim it. I wonder if Grandmother Hunter's reproachful spirit will forever haunt me if I do it."

Doris knew very well that she would do it—had known it ever since she had looked at that lovely lining and a vision of Penelope's vivid face and red-brown hair rising above a waist of the quaint old silk had flashed before her mental sight. That night, after Penelope had gone to bed, Doris ripped the lining out of Grandmother Hunter's silk quilt.

"If Aunt Adella saw me now!" she laughed softly to herself as she worked.

In the three following evenings Doris made the waist. She thought it a wonderful bit of good luck that Penelope went out each of the evenings to study some especially difficult problems with a school chum.

"It will be such a nice surprise for her," the sister mused jubilantly.

Penelope was surprised as much as the tender, sisterly heart could wish when Doris flashed out upon her triumphantly on the evening of the party with the black skirt nicely pressed and re-hung, and the prettiest waist imaginable—a waist that was a positive "creation" of dainty rose-besprinkled silk, with a girdle and knots of black velvet.

"Doris Hunter, you are a veritable little witch! Do you mean to tell me that you conjured that perfectly lovely thing for me out of the lining of Grandmother Hunter's quilt?"

So Penelope went to Blanche's party and her dress was the admiration of every girl there. Mrs. Fairweather, who was visiting Mrs. Anderson, looked closely at it also. She was a very sweet old lady, with silver hair, which she wore in delightful, old-fashioned puffs, and she had very bright, dark eyes. Penelope thought her altogether charming.

"She looks as if she had just stepped out of the frame of some lovely old picture," she said to herself. "I wish she belonged to me. I'd just love to have a grandmother like her. And I do wonder who it is I've seen who looks so much like her."

A little later on the knowledge came to her suddenly, and she thought with inward surprise: Why, it is Doris, of course. If my sister Doris lives to be seventy years old and wears her hair in pretty white puffs, she will look exactly as Mrs. Fairweather does now.

Mrs. Fairweather asked to have Penelope introduced to her, and when they found themselves alone together she said gently, "My dear, I am going to ask a very impertinent question. Will you tell me where you got the silk of which your waist is made?"

Poor Penelope's pretty young face turned crimson. She was not troubled with false pride by any means, but she simply could not bring herself to tell Mrs. Fairweather that her waist was made out of the lining of an old heirloom quilt.

"My Aunt Adella gave me—gave us—the material," she stammered. "And my elder sister Doris made the waist for me. I think the silk once belonged to my Grandmother Hunter."

"What was your grandmother's maiden name?" asked Mrs. Fairweather eagerly.

"Penelope Saverne. I am named after her."

Mrs. Fairweather suddenly put her arm about Penelope and drew the young girl to her, her lovely old face aglow with delight and tenderness.

"Then you are my grandniece," she said. "Your grandmother was my half-sister. When I saw your dress, I felt sure you were related to her. I should recognize that rosebud silk if I came across it in Thibet. Penelope Saverne was the daughter of my mother by her first husband. Penelope was four years older than I was, but we were devoted to each other. Oddly enough, our birthdays fell on the same day, and when Penelope was twenty and I sixteen, my father gave us each a silk dress of this very material. I have mine yet.

"Soon after this our mother died and our household was broken up. Penelope went to live with her aunt and I went West with Father. This was long ago, you know, when travelling and correspondence were not the easy, matter-of-course things they are now. After a few years I lost touch with my half-sister. I married out West and have lived there all my life. I never knew what had become of Penelope. But tonight, when I saw you come in in that waist made of the rosebud silk, the whole past rose before me and I felt like a girl again. My dear, I am a very lonely old woman, with nobody belonging to me. You don't know how delighted I am to find that I have two grandnieces."

Penelope had listened silently, like a girl in a dream. Now she patted Mrs. Fairweather's soft old hand affectionately.

"It sounds like a storybook," she said gaily. "You must come and see Doris. She is such a darling sister. I wouldn't have had this waist if it hadn't been for her. I will tell you the whole truth—I don't mind it now. Doris made my party waist for me out of the lining of an old silk quilt of Grandmother Hunter's that Aunt Adella sent us."

Mrs. Fairweather did go to see Doris the very next day, and quite wonderful things came to pass from that interview. Doris and Penelope found their lives and plans changed in the twinkling of an eye. They were both to go and live with Aunt Esther—as Mrs. Fairweather had said they must call her. Penelope was to have, at last, her longed-for musical education and Doris was to be the home girl.

"You must take the place of my own dear little granddaughter," said Aunt Esther. "She died six years ago, and I have been so lonely since."

When Mrs. Fairweather had gone, Doris and Penelope looked at each other.

"Pinch me, please," said Penelope. "I'm half afraid I'll wake up and find I have been dreaming. Isn't it all wonderful, Doris Hunter?"

Doris nodded radiantly.

"Oh, Penelope, think of it! Music for you—somebody to pet and fuss over for me—and such a dear, sweet aunty for us both!"

"And no more contriving party waists out of old silk linings," laughed Penelope. "But it was very fortunate that you did it for once, sister mine. And no more poverty puckers," she concluded.

The Girl and The Wild Race

"If Judith would only get married," Mrs. Theodora Whitney was wont to sigh dolorously.

Now, there was no valid reason why Judith ought to get married unless she wanted to. But Judith was twenty-seven and Mrs. Theodora thought it was a terrible disgrace to be an old maid.

"There has never been an old maid in our family so far back as we know of," she lamented. "And to think that there should be one now! It just drags us down to the level of the McGregors. They have always been noted for their old maids."

Judith took all her aunt's lamentations good-naturedly. Sometimes she argued the subject placidly.

"Why are you in such a hurry to be rid of me, Aunt Theo? I'm sure we're very comfortable here together and you know you would miss me terribly if I went away."

"If you took the right one you wouldn't go so very far," said Mrs. Theodora, darkly significant. "And, anyhow, I'd put up with any amount of lonesomeness rather than have an old maid in the family. It's all very fine now, when you're still young enough and good looking, with lots of beaus at your beck and call. But that won't last much longer and if you go on with your dilly-dallying you'll wake up some fine day to find that your time for choosing has gone by. Your mother used to be dreadful proud of your good looks when you was a baby. I told her she needn't be. Nine times out of ten a beauty don't marry as well as an ordinary girl."

"I'm not much set on marrying at all," declared Judith sharply. Any reference to the "right one" always disturbed her placidity. The real root of the trouble was that Mrs. Theodora's "right one" and Judith's "right one" were two different people.

The Ramble Valley young men were very fond of dancing attendance on Judith, even if she were verging on old maidenhood. Her prettiness was undeniable; the Stewarts came to maturity late and at twenty-seven Judith's dower of milky-white flesh, dimpled red lips and shining bronze hair was at its fullest splendor. Besides, she was "jolly," and jollity went a long way in Ramble Valley popularity.

Of all Judith's admirers Eben King alone found favor in Mrs. Theodora's eyes. He owned the adjoining farm, was well off and homely—so homely that Judith declared it made her eyes ache to look at him.

Bruce Marshall, Judith's "right one" was handsome, but Mrs. Theodora looked upon him with sour disapproval. He owned a stony little farm at the remote end of Ramble Valley and was reputed to be fonder of many things than of work. To be sure, Judith had enough capability and energy for two; but Mrs. Theodora detested a lazy man. She ordered Judith not to encourage him and Judith obeyed. Judith generally obeyed her aunt; but, though she renounced Bruce Marshall, she would have nothing to do with Eben King or anybody else and all Mrs. Theodora's grumblings did not mend matters.

The afternoon that Mrs. Tony Mack came in Mrs. Theodora felt more aggrieved than ever. Ellie McGregor had been married the previous week—Ellie, who was the same age as Judith and not half so good looking. Mrs. Theodora had been nagging Judith ever since.

"But I might as well talk to the trees down there in that hollow," she complained to Mrs. Tony. "That girl is so set and contrary minded. She doesn't care a bit for my feelings."

This was not said behind Judith's back. The girl herself was standing at the open door, drinking in all the delicate, evasive beauty of the spring afternoon. The Whitney house crested a bare hill that looked down on misty intervals, feathered with young firs that were golden green in the pale sunlight. The fields were bare and smoking, although the lanes and shadowy places were full of moist snow. Judith's face was aglow with the delight of mere life and she bent out to front the brisk, dancing wind that blew up from the valley, resinous with the odors of firs and damp mosses.

At her aunt's words the glow went out of her face. She listened with her eyes brooding on the hollow and a glowing flame of temper smouldering in them. Judith's long patience was giving way. She had been flicked on the raw too often of late. And now her aunt was confiding her grievances to Mrs. Tony Mack—the most notorious gossip in Ramble Valley or out of it!

"I can't sleep at nights for worrying over what will become of her when I'm gone," went on Mrs. Theodora dismally. "She'll just have to live on alone here—a lonesome, withered-up old maid. And her that might have had her pick, Mrs. Tony, though I do say it as shouldn't. You must feel real thankful to have all your girls married off—especially when none of them was extry good-looking. Some people have all the luck. I'm tired of talking to Judith. Folks'll be saying soon that nobody ever really wanted her, for all her flirting. But she just won't marry."

"I will!"

Judith whirled about on the sun warm door step and came in. Her black eyes were flashing and her round cheeks were crimson.

"Such a temper you never saw!" reported Mrs. Tony afterwards. "Though 'tweren't to be wondered at. Theodora was most awful aggravating."

"I will," repeated Judith stormily. "I'm tired of being nagged day in and day out. I'll marry—and what is more I'll marry the very first man that asks me—that I will, if it is old Widower Delane himself! How does that suit you, Aunt Theodora?"

Mrs. Theodora's mental processes were never slow. She dropped her knitting ball and stooped for it. In that time she had decided what to do. She knew that Judith would stick to her word, Stewart-like, and she must trim her sails to catch this new wind.

"It suits me real well, Judith," she said calmly, "you can marry the first man that asks you and I'll say no word to hinder."

The color went out of Judith's face, leaving it pale as ashes. Her hasty assertion had no sooner been uttered than it was repented of, but she must stand by it now. She went out of the kitchen without another glance at her aunt or the delighted Mrs. Tony and dashed up the stairs to her own little room which looked out over the whole of Ramble Valley. It was warm with the March sunshine and the leafless boughs of the creeper that covered the end of the house were tapping a gay tattoo on the window panes to the music of the wind.

Judith sat down in her little rocker and dropped her pointed chin in her hands. Far down the valley, over the firs on the McGregor hill and the blue mirror of the Cranston pond, Bruce Marshall's little gray house peeped out from a semicircle of white-stemmed birches. She had not seen Bruce since before Christmas. He had been angry at her then because she had refused to let him drive her home from prayer meeting. Since then she had heard a rumor that he was going to see Kitty Leigh at the Upper Valley.

Judith looked sombrely down at the Marshall homestead. She had always loved the quaint, picturesque old place, so different from all the commonplace spick and span new houses of the prosperous valley. Judith had never been able to decide whether she really cared very much for Bruce Marshall or not, but she knew that she loved that rambling, cornery house of his, with the gable festooned with the real ivy that Bruce Marshall's great-grandmother had brought with her from England. Judith thought contrastingly of Eben King's staring, primrose-colored house in all its bare, intrusive grandeur. She gave a little shrug of distaste.

"I wish Bruce knew of this," she thought, flushing even in her solitude at the idea. "Although if it is true that he is going to see Kitty Leigh I don't suppose he'd care. And Aunt Theo will be sure to send word to Eben by hook or crook. Whatever possessed me to say such a mad thing? There goes Mrs. Tony now, all agog to spread such a delectable bit of gossip."

Mrs. Tony had indeed gone, refusing Mrs. Theodora's invitation to stay to tea, so eager was she to tell her story. And Mrs. Theodora, at that very minute, was out in her kitchen yard, giving her instructions to Potter Vane, the twelve year old urchin who cut her wood and did sundry other chores for her.

"Potter," she said, excitedly, "run over to the Kings' and tell Eben to come over here immediately—no matter what he's at. Tell him I want to see him about something of the greatest importance."

Mrs. Theodora thought that this was a master stroke.

"That match is as good as made," she thought triumphantly as she picked up chips to start the tea fire. "If Judith suspects that Eben is here she is quite likely to stay in her room and refuse to come down. But if she does I'll march him upstairs to her door and make him ask her through the keyhole. You can't stump Theodora Whitney."

Alas! Ten minutes later Potter returned with the unwelcome news that Eben was away from home.

"He went to Wexbridge about half an hour ago, his ma said. She said she'd tell him to come right over as soon as he kem home."

Mrs. Theodora had to content herself with this, but she felt troubled. She knew Mrs. Tony Mack's capabilities for spreading news. What if Bruce Marshall should hear it before Eben?

That evening Jacob Plowden's store at Wexbridge was full of men, sitting about on kegs and counters or huddling around the stove, for the March air had grown sharp as the sun lowered in the creamy sky over the Ramble Valley hills. Eben King had a keg in the corner. He was in no hurry to go home for he loved gossip dearly and the Wexbridge stores abounded with it. He had exhausted the news of Peter Stanley's store across the bridge and now he meant to hear what was saying at Plowden's. Bruce Marshall was there, too, buying groceries and being waited on by Nora Plowden, who was by no means averse to the service, although as a rule her father's customers received scanty tolerance at her hands.

"What are the Valley roads like, Marshall?" asked a Wexbridge man, between two squirts of tobacco juice.

"Bad," said Bruce briefly. "Another warm day will finish the sleighing."

"Are they crossing at Malley's Creek yet?" asked Plowden.

"No, Jack Carr got in there day before yesterday. Nearly lost his mare. I came round by the main road," responded Bruce.

The door opened at this point and Tony Mack came in. As soon as he closed the door he doubled up in a fit of chuckles, which lasted until he was purple in the face.

"Is the man crazy?" demanded Plowden, who had never seen lean little Tony visited like this before.

"Crazy nothin'," retorted Tony. "You'll laugh too, when you hear it. Such a joke! Hee-tee-tee-hee-e. Theodora Whitney has been badgering Judith Stewart so much about bein' an old maid that Judith's got mad and vowed she'll marry the first man that asks her. Hee-tee-tee-hee-e-e-e! My old woman was there and heard her. She'll keep her word, too. She ain't old Joshua Stewart's daughter for nothin'. If he said he'd do a thing he did it if it tuck the hair off. If I was a young feller now! Hee-tee-tee-hee-e-e-e!"

Bruce Marshall swung round on one foot. His face was crimson and if looks could kill, Tony Mack would have fallen dead in the middle of his sniggers.

"You needn't mind doing up that parcel for me," he said to Nora. "I'll not wait for it."

On his way to the door Eben King brushed past him. A shout of laughter from the assembled men followed them. The others streamed out in their wake, realizing that a race was afoot. Tony alone remained inside, helpless with chuckling.

Eben King's horse was tied at the door. He had nothing to do but step in and drive off. Bruce had put his mare in at Billy Bender's across the bridge, intending to spend the evening there. He knew that this would handicap him seriously, but he strode down the road with a determined expression on his handsome face. Fifteen minutes later he drove past the store, his gray mare going at a sharp gait. The crowd in front of Plowden's cheered him, their sympathies were with him for King was not popular. Tony had come out and shouted, "Here's luck to you, brother," after which he doubled up with renewed laughter. Such a lark! And he, Tony, had set it afoot! It would be a story to tell for years.

Marshall, with his lips set and his dreamy gray eyes for once glittering with a steely light, urged Lady Jane up the Wexbridge hill. From its top it was five miles to Ramble Valley by the main road. A full mile ahead of him he saw Eben King, getting along through mud and slush, and occasional big slumpy drifts of old snow, as fast as his clean-limbed trotter could carry him. As a rule Eben was exceedingly careful of his horses, but now he was sending Bay Billy along for all that was in him.

For a second Bruce hesitated. Then he turned his mare down the field cut to Malley's Creek. It was taking Lady Jane's life and possibly his own in his hand, but it was his only chance. He could never have overtaken Bay Billy on the main road.

"Do your best, Lady Jane," he muttered, and Lady Jane plunged down the steep hillside, through the glutinous mud of a ploughed field as if she meant to do it.

Beyond the field was a ravine full of firs, through which Malley's Creek ran. To cross it meant a four-mile cut to Ramble Valley. The ice looked black and rotten. To the left was the ragged hole where Jack Carr's mare had struggled for her life. Bruce headed Lady Jane higher up. If a crossing could be made at all it was only between Malley's spring-hole and the old ice road. Lady Jane swerved at the bank and whickered.

"On, old girl," said Bruce, in a tense voice. Unwillingly she advanced, picking her steps with cat-like sagacity. Once her foot went through, Bruce pulled her up with hands that did not tremble. The next moment she was scrambling up the opposite bank. Glancing back, Bruce saw the ice parting in her footprints and the black water gurgling up.

But the race was not yet decided. By crossing the creek he had won no more than an equal chance with Eben King. And the field road before him was much worse than the main road. There was little snow on it and some bad sloughs. But Lady Jane was good for it. For once she should not be spared.

Just as the red ball of the sun touched the wooded hills of the valley, Mrs. Theodora, looking from the cowstable door, saw two sleighs approaching, the horses of which were going at a gallop. One was trundling down the main road, headlong through old drifts and slumpy snow, where a false step might send the horse floundering to the bottom. The other was coming up from the direction of the creek, full tilt through Tony Mack's stump land, where not a vestige of snow coated the huge roots over which the runners bumped.

For a moment Mrs. Theodora stood at a gaze. Then she recognized both drivers. She dropped her milking pail and ran to the house, thinking as she ran. She knew that Judith was alone in the kitchen. If Eben King got there first, well and good, but if Bruce Marshall won the race he must encounter her, Mrs. Theodora.

"He won't propose to Judith as long as I'm round," she panted. "I know him—he's too shy. But Eben won't mind—I'll tip him the wink."

Potter Vane was chopping wood before the door. Mrs. Theodora recognizing in him a further obstacle to Marshall's wooing, caught him unceremoniously by the arm and hauled him, axe and all, over the doorstone and into the kitchen, just as Bruce Marshall and Eben King drove into the yard with not a second to spare between them. There was a woeful cut on Bay Billy's slender foreleg and the reeking Lady Jane was trembling like a leaf. The staunch little mare had brought her master over that stretch of sticky field road in time, but she was almost exhausted.

Both men sprang from their sleighs and ran to the door. Bruce Marshall won it by foot-room and burst into the kitchen with his rival hot on his heels. Mrs. Theodora stood defiantly in the middle of the room, still grasping the dazed and dismayed Potter. In a corner Judith turned from the window whence she had been watching the finish of the race. She was pale and tense from excitement. In those few gasping moments she had looked on her heart as on an open book; she knew at last that she loved Bruce Marshall and her eyes met his fiery gray ones as he sprang over the threshold.

"Judith, will you marry me?" gasped Bruce, before Eben, who had first looked at Mrs. Theodora and the squirming Potter, had located the girl.

"Yes," said Judith. She burst into hysterical tears as she said it and sat limply down in a chair.

Mrs. Theodora loosed her grip on Potter.

"You can go back to your work," she said dully. She followed him out and Eben King followed her. On the step she reached behind him and closed the door.

"Trust a King for being too late!" she said bitterly and unjustly.

Eben went home with Bay Billy. Potter gazed after him until Mrs. Theodora ordered him to put Marshall's mare in the stable and rub her down.

"Anyway, Judith won't be an old maid," she comforted herself.

The Promise of Lucy Ellen

Cecily Foster came down the sloping, fir-fringed road from the village at a leisurely pace. Usually she walked with a long, determined stride, but to-day the drowsy, mellowing influence of the Autumn afternoon was strong upon her and filled her with placid content. Without being actively conscious of it, she was satisfied with the existing circumstances of her life. It was half over now. The half of it yet to be lived stretched before her, tranquil, pleasant and uneventful, like the afternoon, filled with unhurried duties and calmly interesting days, Cecily liked the prospect.

When she came to her own lane she paused, folding her hands on the top of the whitewashed gate, while she basked for a moment in the warmth that seemed cupped in the little grassy hollow hedged about with young fir-trees.

Before her lay sere, brooding fields sloping down to a sandy shore, where long foamy ripples were lapping with a murmur that threaded the hushed air like a faint minor melody.

On the crest of the little hill to her right was her home—hers and Lucy Ellen's. The house was an old-fashioned, weather-gray one, low in the eaves, with gables and porches overgrown with vines that had turned to wine-reds and rich bronzes in the October frosts. On three sides it was closed in by tall old spruces, their outer sides bared and grim from long wrestling with the Atlantic winds, but their inner green and feathery. On the fourth side a trim white paling shut in the flower garden before the front door. Cecily could see the beds of purple and scarlet asters, making rich whorls of color under the parlor and sitting-room windows. Lucy Ellen's bed was gayer and larger than Cecily's. Lucy Ellen had always had better luck with flowers.

She could see old Boxer asleep on the front porch step and Lucy Ellen's white cat stretched out on the parlor window-sill. There was no other sign of life about the place. Cecily drew a long, leisurely breath of satisfaction.

"After tea I'll dig up those dahlia roots," she said aloud. "They'd ought to be up. My, how blue and soft that sea is! I never saw such a lovely day. I've been gone longer than I expected. I wonder if Lucy Ellen's been lonesome?"

When Cecily looked back from the misty ocean to the house, she was surprised to see a man coming with a jaunty step down the lane under the gnarled spruces. She looked at him perplexedly. He must be a stranger, for she was sure no man in Oriental walked like that.

"Some agent has been pestering Lucy Ellen, I suppose," she muttered vexedly.

The stranger came on with an airy briskness utterly foreign to Orientalites. Cecily opened the gate and went through. They met under the amber-tinted sugar maple in the heart of the hollow. As he passed, the man lifted his hat and bowed with an ingratiating smile.

He was about forty-five, well, although somewhat loudly dressed, and with an air of self-satisfied prosperity pervading his whole personality. He had a heavy gold watch chain and a large seal ring on the hand that lifted his hat. He was bald, with a high, Shaksperian forehead and a halo of sandy curls. His face was ruddy and weak, but good-natured: his eyes were large and blue, and he had a little straw-colored moustache, with a juvenile twist and curl in it.

Cecily did not recognize him, yet there was something vaguely familiar about him. She walked rapidly up to the house. In the sitting-room she found Lucy Ellen peering out between the muslin window curtains. When the latter turned there was an air of repressed excitement about her.

"Who was that man, Lucy Ellen?" Cecily asked.

To Cecily's amazement, Lucy Ellen blushed—a warm, Spring-like flood of color that rolled over her delicate little face like a miracle of rejuvenescence.

"Didn't you know him? That was Cromwell Biron," she simpered. Although Lucy Ellen was forty and, in most respects, sensible, she could not help simpering upon occasion.

"Cromwell Biron," repeated Cecily, in an emotionless voice. She took off her bonnet mechanically, brushed the dust from its ribbons and bows and went to put it carefully away in its white box in the spare bedroom. She felt as if she had had a severe shock, and she dared not ask anything more just then. Lucy Ellen's blush had frightened her. It seemed to open up dizzying possibilities of change.

"But she promised—she promised," said Cecily fiercely, under her breath.

While Cecily was changing her dress, Lucy Ellen was getting the tea ready in the little kitchen. Now and then she broke out into singing, but always checked herself guiltily. Cecily heard her and set her firm mouth a little firmer.

"If a man had jilted me twenty years ago, I wouldn't be so overwhelmingly glad to see him when he came back—especially if he had got fat and bald-headed," she added, her face involuntarily twitching into a smile. Cecily, in spite of her serious expression and intense way of looking at life, had an irrepressible sense of humor.

Tea that evening was not the pleasant meal it usually was. The two women were wont to talk animatedly to each other, and Cecily had many things to tell Lucy Ellen. She did not tell them. Neither did Lucy Ellen ask any questions, her ill-concealed excitement hanging around her like a festal garment.

Cecily's heart was on fire with alarm and jealousy. She smiled a little cruelly as she buttered and ate her toast.

"And so that was Cromwell Biron," she said with studied carelessness. "I thought there was something familiar about him. When did he come home?"

"He got to Oriental yesterday," fluttered back Lucy Ellen. "He's going to be home for two months. We—we had such an interesting talk this afternoon. He—he's as full of jokes as ever. I wished you'd been here."

This was a fib. Cecily knew it.

"I don't, then," she said contemptuously. "You know I never had much use for Cromwell Biron. I think he had a face of his own to come down here to see you uninvited, after the way he treated you."

Lucy Ellen blushed scorchingly and was miserably silent.

"He's changed terrible in his looks," went on Cecily relentlessly. "How bald he's got—and fat! To think of the spruce Cromwell Biron got to be bald and fat! To be sure, he still has the same sheepish expression. Will you pass me the currant jell, Lucy Ellen?"

"I don't think he's so very fat," she said resentfully, when Cecily had left the table. "And I don't care if he is."

Twenty years before this, Biron had jilted Lucy Ellen Foster. She was the prettiest girl in Oriental then, but the new school teacher over at the Crossways was prettier, with a dash of piquancy, which Lucy Ellen lacked, into the bargain. Cromwell and the school teacher had run away and been married, and Lucy Ellen was left to pick up the tattered shreds of her poor romance as best she could.

She never had another lover. She told herself that she would always be faithful to the one love of her life. This sounded romantic, and she found a certain comfort in it.

She had been brought up by her uncle and aunt. When they died she and her cousin, Cecily Foster, found themselves, except for each other, alone in the world.

Cecily loved Lucy Ellen as a sister. But she believed that Lucy Ellen would yet marry, and her heart sank at the prospect of being left without a soul to love and care for.

It was Lucy Ellen that had first proposed their mutual promise, but Cecily had grasped at it eagerly. The two women, verging on decisive old maidenhood, solemnly promised each other that they would never marry, and would always live together. From that time Cecily's mind had been at ease. In her eyes a promise was a sacred thing.

The next evening at prayer-meeting Cromwell Biron received quite an ovation from old friends and neighbors. Cromwell had been a favorite in his boyhood. He had now the additional glamour of novelty and reputed wealth.

He was beaming and expansive. He went into the choir to help sing. Lucy Ellen sat beside him, and they sang from the same book. Two red spots burned on her thin cheeks, and she had a cluster of lavender chrysanthemums pinned on her jacket. She looked almost girlish, and Cromwell Biron gazed at her with sidelong admiration, while Cecily watched them both fiercely from her pew. She knew that Cromwell Biron had come home, wooing his old love.

"But he sha'n't get her," Cecily whispered into her hymnbook. Somehow it was a comfort to articulate the words, "She promised."

On the church steps Cromwell offered his arm to Lucy Ellen with a flourish. She took it shyly, and they started down the road in the crisp Autumn moonlight. For the first time in ten years Cecily walked home from prayer-meeting alone. She went up-stairs and flung herself on her bed, reckless for once, of her second best hat and gown.

Lucy Ellen did not venture to ask Cromwell in. She was too much in awe of Cecily for that. But she loitered with him at the gate until the grandfather's clock in the hall struck eleven. Then Cromwell went away, whistling gaily, with Lucy Ellen's chrysanthemum in his buttonhole, and Lucy Ellen went in and cried half the night. But Cecily did not cry. She lay savagely awake until morning.

"Cromwell Biron is courting you again," she said bluntly to Lucy Ellen at the breakfast table.

Lucy Ellen blushed nervously.

"Oh, nonsense, Cecily," she protested with a simper.

"It isn't nonsense," said Cecily calmly. "He is. There is no fool like an old fool, and Cromwell Biron never had much sense. The presumption of him!"

Lucy Ellen's hands trembled as she put her teacup down.

"He's not so very old," she said faintly, "and everybody but you likes him—and he's well-to-do. I don't see that there's any presumption."

"Maybe not—if you look at it so. You're very forgiving, Lucy Ellen. You've forgotten how he treated you once."

"No—o—o, I haven't," faltered Lucy Ellen.

"Anyway," said Cecily coldly, "you shouldn't encourage his attentions, Lucy Ellen; you know you couldn't marry him even if he asked you. You promised."

All the fitful color went out of Lucy Ellen's face. Under Cecily's pitiless eyes she wilted and drooped.

"I know," she said deprecatingly, "I haven't forgotten. You are talking nonsense, Cecily. I like to see Cromwell, and he likes to see me because I'm almost the only one of his old set that is left. He feels lonesome in Oriental now."

Lucy Ellen lifted her fawn-colored little head more erectly at the last of her protest. She had saved her self-respect.

In the month that followed Cromwell Biron pressed his suit persistently, unintimidated by Cecily's antagonism. October drifted into November and the chill, drear days came. To Cecily the whole outer world seemed the dismal reflex of her pain-bitten heart. Yet she constantly laughed at herself, too, and her laughter was real if bitter.

One evening she came home late from a neighbor's. Cromwell Biron passed her in the hollow under the bare boughs of the maple that were outlined against the silvery moonlit sky.

When Cecily went into the house, Lucy Ellen opened the parlor door. She was very pale, but her eyes burned in her face and her hands were clasped before her.

"I wish you'd come in here for a few minutes, Cecily," she said feverishly.

Cecily followed silently into the room.

"Cecily," she said faintly, "Cromwell was here to-night. He asked me to marry him. I told him to come to-morrow night for his answer."

She paused and looked imploringly at Cecily. Cecily did not speak. She stood tall and unrelenting by the table. The rigidity of her face and figure smote Lucy Ellen like a blow. She threw out her bleached little hands and spoke with a sudden passion utterly foreign to her.

"Cecily, I want to marry him. I—I—love him. I always have. I never thought of this when I promised. Oh, Cecily, you'll let me off my promise, won't you?"

"No," said Cecily. It was all she said. Lucy Ellen's hands fell to her sides, and the light went out of her face.

"You won't?" she said hopelessly.

Cecily went out. At the door she turned.

"When John Edwards asked me to marry him six years ago, I said no for your sake. To my mind a promise is a promise. But you were always weak and romantic, Lucy Ellen."

Lucy Ellen made no response. She stood limply on the hearth-rug like a faded blossom bitten by frost.

After Cromwell Biron had gone away the next evening, with all his brisk jauntiness shorn from him for the time, Lucy Ellen went up to Cecily's room. She stood for a moment in the narrow doorway, with the lamplight striking upward with a gruesome effect on her wan face.

"I've sent him away," she said lifelessly. "I've kept my promise, Cecily."

There was silence for a moment. Cecily did not know what to say. Suddenly Lucy Ellen burst out bitterly.

"I wish I was dead!"

Then she turned swiftly and ran across the hall to her own room. Cecily gave a little moan of pain. This was her reward for all the love she had lavished on Lucy Ellen.

"Anyway, it is all over," she said, looking dourly into the moonlit boughs of the firs; "Lucy Ellen'll get over it. When Cromwell is gone she'll forget all about him. I'm not going to fret. She promised, and she wanted the promise first."

During the next fortnight tragedy held grim sway in the little weather-gray house among the firs—a tragedy tempered with grim comedy for Cecily, who, amid all her agony, could not help being amused at Lucy Ellen's romantic way of sorrowing.

Lucy Ellen did her mornings' work listlessly and drooped through the afternoons. Cecily would have felt it as a relief if Lucy Ellen had upbraided her, but after her outburst on the night she sent Cromwell away, Lucy Ellen never uttered a word of reproach or complaint.

One evening Cecily made a neighborly call in the village. Cromwell Biron happened to be there and gallantly insisted upon seeing her home.

She understood from Cromwell's unaltered manner that Lucy Ellen had not told him why she had refused him. She felt a sudden admiration for her cousin.

When they reached the house Cromwell halted suddenly in the banner of light that streamed from the sitting-room window. They saw Lucy Ellen sitting alone before the fire, her arms folded on the table, and her head bowed on them. Her white cat sat unnoticed at the table beside her. Cecily gave a gasp of surrender.

"You'd better come in," she said, harshly. "Lucy Ellen looks lonesome."

Cromwell muttered sheepishly, "I'm afraid I wouldn't be company for her. Lucy Ellen doesn't like me much—"

"Oh, doesn't she!" said Cecily, bitterly. "She likes you better than she likes me for all I've—but it's no matter. It's been all my fault—she'll explain. Tell her I said she could. Come in, I say."

She caught the still reluctant Cromwell by the arm and fairly dragged him over the geranium beds and through the front door. She opened the sitting-room door and pushed him in. Lucy Ellen rose in amazement. Over Cromwell's bald head loomed Cecily's dark face, tragic and determined.

"Here's your beau, Lucy Ellen," she said, "and I give you back your promise."

She shut the door upon the sudden illumination of Lucy Ellen's face and went up-stairs with the tears rolling down her cheeks.

"It's my turn to wish I was dead," she muttered. Then she laughed hysterically.

"That goose of a Cromwell! How queer he did look standing there, frightened to death of Lucy Ellen. Poor little Lucy Ellen! Well, I hope he'll be good to her."

The Pursuit of the Ideal

Freda's snuggery was aglow with the rose-red splendour of an open fire which was triumphantly warding off the stealthy approaches of the dull grey autumn twilight. Roger St. Clair stretched himself out luxuriously in an easy-chair with a sigh of pleasure.

"Freda, your armchairs are the most comfy in the world. How do you get them to fit into a fellow's kinks so splendidly?"

Freda smiled at him out of big, owlish eyes that were the same tint as the coppery grey sea upon which the north window of the snuggery looked.

"Any armchair will fit a lazy fellow's kinks," she said.

"I'm not lazy," protested Roger. "That you should say so, Freda, when I have wheeled all the way out of town this dismal afternoon over the worst bicycle road in three kingdoms to see you, bonnie maid!"

"I like lazy people," said Freda softly, tilting her spoon on a cup of chocolate with a slender brown hand.

Roger smiled at her chummily.

"You are such a comfortable girl," he said. "I like to talk to you and tell you things."

"You have something to tell me today. It has been fairly sticking out of your eyes ever since you came. Now, 'fess."

Freda put away her cup and saucer, got up, and stood by the fireplace, with one arm outstretched along the quaintly carved old mantel. She laid her head down on its curve and looked expectantly at Roger.

"I have seen my ideal, Freda," said Roger gravely.

Freda lifted her head and then laid it down again. She did not speak. Roger was glad of it. Even at the moment he found himself thinking that Freda had a genius for silence. Any other girl he knew would have broken in at once with surprised exclamations and questions and spoiled his story.

"You have not forgotten what my ideal woman is like?" he said.

Freda shook her head. She was not likely to forget. She remembered only too keenly the afternoon he had told her. They had been sitting in the snuggery, herself in the inglenook, and Roger coiled up in his big pet chair that nobody else ever sat in.

"'What must my lady be that I must love her?'" he had quoted. "Well, I will paint my dream-love for you, Freda. She must be tall and slender, with chestnut hair of wonderful gloss, with just the suggestion of a ripple in it. She must have an oval face, colourless ivory in hue, with the expression of a Madonna; and her eyes must be 'passionless, peaceful blue,' deep and tender as a twilight sky."

Freda, looking at herself along her arm in the mirror, recalled this description and smiled faintly. She was short and plump, with a piquant, irregular little face, vivid tinting, curly, unmanageable hair of ruddy brown, and big grey eyes. Certainly, she was not his ideal.

"When and where did you meet your lady of the Madonna face and twilight eyes?" she asked.

Roger frowned. Freda's face was solemn enough but her eyes looked as if she might be laughing at him.

"I haven't met her yet. I have only seen her. It was in the park yesterday. She was in a carriage with the Mandersons. So beautiful, Freda! Our eyes met as she drove past and I realized that I had found my long-sought ideal. I rushed back to town and hunted up Pete Manderson at the club. Pete is a donkey but he has his ways of being useful. He told me who she was. Her name is Stephanie Gardiner; she is his cousin from the south and is visiting his mother. And, Freda, I am to dine at the Mandersons' tonight. I shall meet her."

"Do goddesses and ideals and Madonnas eat?" said Freda in an awed whisper. Her eyes were certainly laughing now. Roger got up stiffly.

"I must confess I did not expect that you would ridicule my confidence, Freda," he said frigidly. "It is very unlike you. But if you are not interested I will not bore you with any further details. And it is time I was getting back to town anyhow."

When he had gone Freda ran to the west window and flung it open. She leaned out and waved both hands at him over the spruce hedge.

"Roger, Roger, I was a horrid little beast. Forget it immediately, please. And come out tomorrow and tell me all about her."

Roger came. He bored Freda terribly with his raptures but she never betrayed it. She was all sympathy—or, at least, as much sympathy as a woman can be who must listen while the man of men sings another woman's praises to her. She sent Roger away in perfect good humour with himself and all the world, then she curled herself up in the snuggery, pulled a rug over her head, and cried.

Roger came out to Lowlands oftener than ever after that. He had to talk to somebody about Stephanie Gardiner and Freda was the safest vent. The "pursuit of the Ideal," as she called it, went on with vim and fervour. Sometimes Roger would be on the heights of hope and elation; the next visit he would be in the depths of despair and humility. Freda had learned to tell which it was by the way he opened the snuggery door.

One day when Roger came he found six feet of young man reposing at ease in his particular chair. Freda was sipping chocolate in her corner and looking over the rim of her cup at the intruder just as she had been wont to look at Roger. She had on a new dark red gown and looked vivid and rose-hued.

She introduced the stranger as Mr. Grayson and called him Tim. They seemed to be excellent friends. Roger sat bolt upright on the edge of a fragile, gilded chair which Freda kept to hide a shabby spot in the carpet, and glared at Tim until the latter said goodbye and lounged out.

"You'll be over tomorrow?" said Freda.

"Can't I come this evening?" he pleaded.

Freda nodded. "Yes—and we'll make taffy. You used to make such delicious stuff, Tim."

"Who is that fellow, Freda?" Roger inquired crossly, as soon as the door closed.

Freda began to make a fresh pot of chocolate. She smiled dreamily as if thinking of something pleasant.

"Why, that was Tim Grayson—dear old Tim. He used to live next door to us when we were children. And we were such chums—always together, making mud pies, and getting into scrapes. He is just the same old Tim, and is home from the west for a long visit. I was so glad to see him again."

"So it would appear," said Roger grumpily. "Well, now that 'dear old Tim' is gone, I suppose I can have my own chair, can I? And do give me some chocolate. I didn't know you made taffy."

"Oh, I don't. It's Tim. He can do everything. He used to make it long ago, and I washed up after him and helped him eat it. How is the pursuit of the Ideal coming on, Roger-boy?"

Roger did not feel as if he wanted to talk about the Ideal. He noticed how vivid Freda's smile was and how lovable were the curves of her neck where the dusky curls were caught up from it. He had also an inner vision of Freda making taffy with Tim and he did not approve of it.

He refused to talk about the Ideal. On his way back to town he found himself thinking that Freda had the most charming, glad little laugh of any girl he knew. He suddenly remembered that he had never heard the Ideal laugh. She smiled placidly—he had raved to Freda about that smile—but she did not laugh. Roger began to wonder what an ideal without any sense of humour would be like when translated into the real.

He went to Lowlands the next afternoon and found Tim there—in his chair again. He detested the fellow but he could not deny that he was good-looking and had charming manners. Freda was very nice to Tim. On his way back to town Roger decided that Tim was in love with Freda. He was furious at the idea. The presumption of the man!

He also remembered that he had not said a word to Freda about the Ideal. And he never did say much more—perhaps because he could not get the chance. Tim was always there before him and generally outstayed him.

One day when he went out he did not find Freda at home. Her aunt told him that she was out riding with Mr. Grayson. On his way back he met them. As they cantered by, Freda waved her riding whip at him. Her face was full of warm, ripe, kissable tints, her loose lovelocks were blowing about it, and her eyes shone like grey pools mirroring stars. Roger turned and watched them out of sight behind the firs that cupped Lowlands.

That night at Mrs. Crandall's dinner table somebody began to talk about Freda. Roger strained his ears to listen. Mrs. Kitty Carr was speaking—Mrs. Kitty knew everything and everybody.

"She is simply the most charming girl in the world when you get really acquainted with her," said Mrs. Kitty, with the air of having discovered and patented Freda. "She is so vivid and unconventional and lovable—'spirit and fire and dew,' you know. Tim Grayson is a very lucky fellow."

"Are they engaged?" someone asked.

"Not yet, I fancy. But of course it is only a question of time. Tim simply adores her. He is a good soul and has lots of money, so he'll do. But really, you know, I think a prince wouldn't be good enough for Freda."

Roger suddenly became conscious that the Ideal was asking him a question of which he had not heard a word. He apologized and was forgiven. But he went home a very miserable man.

He did not go to Lowlands for two weeks. They were the longest, most wretched two weeks he had ever lived through. One afternoon he heard that Tim Grayson had gone back west. Mrs. Kitty told it mournfully.

"Of course, this means that Freda has refused him," she said. "She is such an odd girl."

Roger went straight out to Lowlands. He found Freda in the snuggery and held out his hands to her.

"Freda, will you marry me? It will take a lifetime to tell you how much I love you."

"But the Ideal?" questioned Freda.

"I have just discovered what my ideal is," said Roger. "She is a dear, loyal, companionable little girl, with the jolliest laugh and the warmest, truest heart in the world. She has starry grey eyes, two dimples, and a mouth I must and will kiss—there—there—there! Freda, tell me you love me a little bit, although I've been such a besotted idiot."

"I will not let you call my husband-that-is-to-be names," said Freda, snuggling down into the curve of his shoulder. "But indeed, Roger-boy, you will have to make me very, very happy to square matters up. You have made me so unutterably unhappy for two months."

"The pursuit of the Ideal is ended," declared Roger.

The Softening of Miss Cynthia

"I wonder if I'd better flavour this cake with lemon or vanilla. It's the most perplexing thing I ever heard of in my life."

Miss Cynthia put down the bottles with a vexed frown; her perplexity had nothing whatever to do with flavouring the golden mixture in her cake bowl. Mrs. John Joe knew that; the latter had dropped in in a flurry of curiosity concerning the little boy whom she had seen about Miss Cynthia's place for the last two days. Her daughter Kitty was with her; they both sat close together on the kitchen sofa.

"It *is* too bad," said Mrs. John Joe sympathetically. "I don't wonder you are mixed up. So unexpected, too! When did he come?"

"Tuesday night," said Miss Cynthia. She had decided on the vanilla and was whipping it briskly in. "I saw an express wagon drive into the yard with a boy and a trunk in it and I went out just as he got down. 'Are you my Aunt Cynthia?' he said. 'Who in the world are you?' I asked. And he says, 'I'm Wilbur Merrivale, and my father was John Merrivale. He died three weeks ago and he said I was to come to you, because you were his sister.' Well, you could just have knocked me down with a feather!"

"I'm sure," said Mrs. John Joe. "But I didn't know you had a brother. And his name—Merrivale?"

"Well, he wasn't any relation really. I was about six years old when my father married his mother, the Widow Merrivale. John was just my age, and we were brought up together just like brother and sister. He was a real nice fellow, I must say. But he went out to Californy years ago, and I haven't heard a word of him for fifteen years—didn't know if he was alive or dead. But it seems from what I can make out from the boy, that his mother died when he was a baby, and him and John roughed it along together—pretty poor, too, I guess—till John took a fever and died. And he told some of his friends to send the boy to me, for he'd no relations there and not a cent in the world. And the child came all the way from Californy, and here he is. I've been just distracted ever since. I've never been used to children, and to have the house kept in perpetual uproar is more than I can stand. He's about twelve and a born mischief. He'll tear through the rooms with his dirty feet, and he's smashed one of my blue vases and torn down a curtain and set Towser on the cat half a dozen times already—I never was so worried. I've got him out on the verandah shelling peas now, to keep him quiet for a little spell."

"I'm really sorry for you," said Mrs. John Joe. "But, poor child, I suppose he's never had anyone to look after him. And come all the way from Californy alone, too—he must be real smart."

"Too smart, I guess. He must take after his mother, whoever she was, for there ain't a bit of Merrivale in him. And he's been brought up pretty rough."

"Well, it'll be a great responsibility for you, Cynthia, of course. But he'll be company, too, and he'll be real handy to run errands and—"

"*I'm* not going to keep him," said Miss Cynthia determinedly. Her thin lips set themselves firmly and her voice had a hard ring.

"Not going to keep him?" said Mrs. John Joe blankly. "You can't send him back to Californy!"

"I don't intend to. But as for having him here to worry my life out and keep me in a perpetual stew, I just won't do it. D'ye think I'm going to trouble myself about children at my age? And all he'd cost for clothes and schooling, too! I can't afford it. I don't suppose his father expected it either. I suppose he expected me to look after him a bit—and of course I will. A boy of his age ought to be able to earn his keep, anyway. If I look out a place for him somewhere where he can do odd jobs and go to school in the winter, I think it's all anyone can expect of me, when he ain't really no blood relation."

Miss Cynthia flung the last sentence at Mrs. John Joe rather defiantly, not liking the expression on that lady's face.

"I suppose nobody could expect more, Cynthy," said Mrs. John Joe deprecatingly. "He would be an awful bother, I've no doubt, and you've lived alone so long with no one to worry you that you wouldn't know what to do with him. Boys are always getting into mischief—my four just keep me on the dead jump. Still, it's a pity for him, poor little fellow! No mother or father—it seems hard."

Miss Cynthia's face grew grimmer than ever as she went to the door with her callers and watched them down the garden path. As soon as Mrs. John Joe saw that the door was shut, she unburdened her mind to her daughter.

"Did you ever hear tell of the like? I thought I knew Cynthia Henderson well, if anybody in Wilmot did, but this beats me. Just think, Kitty—there she is, no one knows how rich, and not a soul in the world belonging to her, and she won't even take in her brother's child. She must be a hard woman. But it's just meanness, pure and simple; she grudges him what he'd eat and wear. The poor mite doesn't look as if he'd need much. Cynthia didn't used to be like that, but it's growing on her every day. She's got hard as rocks."

That afternoon Miss Cynthia harnessed her fat grey pony into the phaeton herself—she kept neither man nor maid, but lived in her big, immaculate house in solitary state—and drove away down the dusty, buttercup-bordered road, leaving Wilbur sitting on the verandah. She returned in an hour's time and drove into the yard, shutting the gate behind her with a vigorous snap. Wilbur was not in sight and, fearful lest he should be in mischief, she hurriedly tied the pony to the railing and went in search of him. She found him sitting by the well, his chin in his hands; he was pale and his eyes were red. Miss Cynthia hardened her heart and took him into the house.

"I've been down to see Mr. Robins this afternoon, Wilbur," she said, pretending to brush some invisible dust from the bottom of her nice black cashmere skirt for an excuse to avoid looking at him, "and he's agreed to take you on trial. It's a real good chance—better than you could expect. He says he'll board and clothe you and let you go to school in the winter."

The boy seemed to shrink.

"Daddy said that I would stay with you," he said wistfully. "He said you were so good and kind and would love me for his sake."

For a moment Miss Cynthia softened. She had been very fond of her step-brother; it seemed that his voice appealed to her across the grave in behalf of his child. But the crust of years was not to be so easily broken.

"Your father meant that I would look after you," she said, "and I mean to, but I can't afford to keep you here. You'll have a good place at Mr. Robins', if you behave yourself. I'm going to take you down now, before I unharness the pony, so go and wash your face while I put up your things. Don't look so woebegone, for pity's sake! I'm not taking you to prison."

Wilbur turned and went silently to the kitchen. Miss Cynthia thought she heard a sob. She went with a firm step into the little bedroom off the hall and took a purse out of a drawer.

"I s'pose I ought," she said doubtfully. "I don't s'pose he has a cent. I daresay he'll lose or waste it."

She counted out seventy-five cents carefully. When she came out, Wilbur was at the door. She put the money awkwardly into his hand.

"There, see that you don't spend it on any foolishness."

Miss Cynthia's Action made a good deal of talk in Wilmot. The women, headed by Mrs. John Joe—who said behind Cynthia's back what she did not dare say to her face—condemned her. The men laughed and said that Cynthia was a shrewd one; there was no getting round her. Miss Cynthia herself was far from easy. She could not forget Wilbur's wistful eyes, and she had heard that Robins was a hard master.

A week after the boy had gone she saw him one day at the store. He was lifting heavy bags from a cart. The work was beyond his strength, and he was flushed and panting. Miss Cynthia's conscience gave her a hard stab. She bought a roll of peppermints and took them over to him. He thanked her timidly and drove quickly away.

"Robins hasn't any business putting such work on a child," she said to herself indignantly. "I'll speak to him about it."

And she did—and got an answer that made her ears tingle. Mr. Robins bluntly told her he guessed he knew what was what about his hands. He weren't no nigger driver. If she wasn't satisfied, she might take the boy away as soon as she liked.

Miss Cynthia did not get much comfort out of life that summer. Almost everywhere she went she was sure to meet Wilbur, engaged in some hard task. She could not help seeing how miserably pale and thin he had become. The worry had its effect on her. The neighbours said that Cynthy was sharper than ever. Even her church-going was embittered. She had always enjoyed walking up the aisle with her rich silk skirt rustling over the carpet, her cashmere shawl folded correctly over her shoulders, and her lace bonnet set precisely on her thin shining crimps. But she could take no pleasure in that or in the sermon now, when Wilbur sat right across from her pew, between hard-featured Robins and his sulky-looking wife. The boy's eyes had grown too large for his thin face.

The softening of Miss Cynthia was a very gradual process, but it reached a climax one September morning, when Mrs. John Joe came into the former's kitchen with an important face. Miss Cynthia was preserving her plums.

"No, thank you, I'll not sit down—I only run in—I suppose you've heard it. That little Merrivale boy has took awful sick with fever, they say. He's been worked half to death this summer—everyone knows what Robins is with his help—and they say he has fretted a good deal for his father and been homesick, and he's run down, I s'pose. Anyway, Robins took him over to the hospital at Stanford last night—good gracious, Cynthy, are you sick?"

Miss Cynthia had staggered to a seat by the table; her face was pallid.

"No, it's only your news gave me a turn—it came so suddenly—I didn't know."

"I must hurry back and see to the men's dinners. I thought I'd come and tell you, though I didn't know as you'd care."

This parting shot was unheeded by Miss Cynthia. She laid her face in her hands. "It's a judgement on me," she moaned. "He's going to die, and I'm his murderess. This is the account I'll have to give John Merrivale of his boy. I've been a wicked, selfish woman, and I'm justly punished."

It was a humbled Miss Cynthia who met the doctor at the hospital that afternoon. He shook his head at her eager questions.

"It's a pretty bad case. The boy seems run down every way. No, it is impossible to think of moving him again. Bringing him here last night did him a great deal of harm. Yes, you may see him, but he will not know you, I fear—he is delirious and raves of his father and California."

Miss Cynthia followed the doctor down the long ward. When he paused by a cot, she pushed past him. Wilbur lay tossing restlessly on his pillow. He was thin to emaciation, but his cheeks were crimson and his eyes burning bright.

Miss Cynthia stooped and took the hot, dry hands in hers.

"Wilbur," she sobbed, "don't you know me—Aunt Cynthia?"

"You are not my Aunt Cynthia," said Wilbur. "Daddy said Aunt Cynthia was good and kind—you are a cross, bad woman. I want Daddy. Why doesn't he come? Why doesn't he come to little Wilbur?"

Miss Cynthia got up and faced the doctor.

"He's *got* to get better," she said stubbornly. "Spare no expense or trouble. If he dies, I will be a murderess. He must live and give me a chance to make it up for him."

And he did live; but for a long time it was a hard fight, and there were days when it seemed that death must win. Miss Cynthia got so thin and wan that even Mrs. John Joe pitied her.

The earth seemed to Miss Cynthia to laugh out in prodigal joyousness on the afternoon she drove home when Wilbur had been pronounced out of danger. How tranquil the hills looked, with warm October sunshine sleeping on their sides and faint blue hazes on their brows! How gallantly the maples flaunted their crimson flags! How kind and friendly was every face she met! Afterwards, Miss Cynthia said she began to live that day.

Wilbur's recovery was slow. Every day Miss Cynthia drove over with some dainty, and her loving gentleness sat none the less gracefully on her because of its newness. Wilbur grew to look for and welcome her coming. When it was thought safe to remove him, Miss Cynthia went to the hospital with a phaeton-load of shawls and pillows.

"I have come to take you away," she said.

Wilbur shrank back. "Not to Mr. Robins," he said piteously. "Oh, not there, Aunt Cynthia!"

Them Notorious Pigs

John Harrington was a woman-hater, or thought that he was, which amounts to the same thing. He was forty-five and, having been handsome in his youth, was a fine-looking man still. He had a remarkably good farm and was a remarkably good farmer. He also had a garden which was the pride and delight of his heart or, at least, it was before Mrs. Hayden's pigs got into it.

Sarah King, Harrington's aunt and housekeeper, was deaf and crabbed, and very few visitors ever came to the house. This suited Harrington. He was a good citizen and did his duty by the community, but his bump of sociability was undeveloped. He was also a contented man, looking after his farm, improving his stock, and experimenting with new bulbs in undisturbed serenity. This, however, was all too good to last. A man is bound to have some troubles in this life, and Harrington's were near their beginning when Perry Hayden bought the adjoining farm from the heirs of Shakespeare Ely, deceased, and moved in.

To be sure, Perry Hayden, poor fellow, did not bother Harrington much, for he died of pneumonia a month after he came there, but his widow carried on the farm with the assistance of a lank hired boy. Her own children, Charles and Theodore, commonly known as Bobbles and Ted, were as yet little more than babies.

The real trouble began when Mary Hayden's pigs, fourteen in number and of half-grown voracity, got into Harrington's garden. A railing, a fir grove, and an apple orchard separated the two establishments, but these failed to keep the pigs within bounds.

Harrington had just got his garden planted for the season, and to go out one morning and find a horde of enterprising porkers rooting about in it was, to put it mildly, trying. He was angry, but as it was a first offence he drove the pigs out with tolerable calmness, mended the fence, and spent the rest of the day repairing damages.

Three days later the pigs got in again. Harrington relieved his mind by some scathing reflections on women who tried to run farms. Then he sent Mordecai, his hired man, over to the Hayden place to ask Mrs. Hayden if she would be kind enough to keep her pigs out of his garden. Mrs. Hayden sent back word that she was very sorry and would not let it occur again. Nobody, not even John Harrington, could doubt that she meant what she said. But she had reckoned without the pigs. They had not forgotten the flavour of Egyptian fleshpots as represented by the succulent young shoots in the Harrington domains. A week later Mordecai came in and told Harrington that "them notorious pigs" were in his garden again.

There is a limit to everyone's patience. Harrington left Mordecai to drive them out, while he put on his hat and stalked over to the Haydens' place. Ted and Bobbles were playing at marbles in the lane and ran when they saw him coming. He got close up to the little low house among the apple trees before Mordecai appeared in the yard, driving the pigs around the barn. Mrs. Hayden was sitting on her doorstep, paring her dinner potatoes, and stood up hastily when she saw her visitor.

Harrington had never seen his neighbour at close quarters before. Now he could not help seeing that she was a very pretty little woman, with wistful, dark blue eyes and an appealing expression. Mary Hayden had been next to a beauty in her girlhood, and she had a good deal of her bloom left yet, although hard work and worry were doing their best to rob her of it. But John Harrington was an angry man and did not care whether the woman in question was pretty or not. Her pigs had rooted up his garden—that fact filled his mind.

"Mrs. Hayden, those pigs of yours have been in my garden again. I simply can't put up with this any longer. Why in the name of reason don't you look after your animals better? If I find them in again I'll set my dog on them, I give you fair warning."

A faint colour had crept into Mary Hayden's soft, milky-white cheeks during this tirade, and her voice trembled as she said, "I'm very sorry, Mr. Harrington. I suppose Bobbles forgot to shut the gate of their pen again this morning. He is so forgetful."

"I'd lengthen his memory, then, if I were you," returned Harrington grimly, supposing that Bobbles was the hired man. "I'm not going to have my garden ruined just because he happens to be forgetful. I am speaking my mind plainly, madam. If you can't keep your stock from being a nuisance to other people you ought not to try to run a farm at all."

Then did Mrs. Hayden sit down upon the doorstep and burst into tears. Harrington felt, as Sarah King would have expressed it, "every which way at once." Here was a nice mess! What a nuisance women were—worse than the pigs!

"Oh, don't cry, Mrs. Hayden," he said awkwardly. "I didn't mean—well, I suppose I spoke too strongly. Of course I know you didn't mean to let the pigs in. There, do stop crying! I beg your pardon if I've hurt your feelings."

"Oh, it isn't that," sobbed Mrs. Hayden, wiping away her tears. "It's only—I've tried so hard—and everything seems to go wrong. I make such mistakes. As for your garden, sir. I'll pay for the damage my pigs have done if you'll let me know what it comes to."

She sobbed again and caught her breath like a grieved child. Harrington felt like a brute. He had a queer notion that if he put his arm around her and told her not to worry over things women were not created to attend to he would be expressing his feelings better than in any other way. But of course he couldn't do that. Instead, he muttered that the damage didn't amount to much after all, and he hoped she wouldn't mind what he said, and then he got himself away and strode through the orchard like a man in a desperate hurry.

Mordecai had gone home and the pigs were not to be seen, but a chubby little face peeped at him from between two scrub, bloom-white cherry trees.

"G'way, you bad man!" said Bobbles vindictively. "G'way! You made my mommer cry—I saw you. I'm only Bobbles now, but when I grow up I'll be Charles Henry Hayden and you won't dare to make my mommer cry then."

Harrington smiled grimly. "So you're the lad who forgets to shut the pigpen gate, are you? Come out here and let me see you. Who is in there with you?"

"Ted is. He's littler than me. But I won't come out. I don't like you. G'way home."

Harrington obeyed. He went home and to work in his garden. But work as hard as he would, he could not forget Mary Hayden's grieved face.

"I was a brute!" he thought. "Why couldn't I have mentioned the matter gently? I daresay she has enough to trouble her. Confound those pigs!"

After that there was a time of calm. Evidently something had been done to Bobbles' memory or perhaps Mrs. Hayden attended to the gate herself. At all events the pigs were not seen and Harrington's garden blossomed like the rose. But Harrington himself was in a bad state.

For one thing, wherever he looked he saw the mental picture of his neighbour's tired, sweet face and the tears in her blue eyes. The original he never saw, which only made matters worse. He wondered what opinion she had of him and decided that she must think him a cross old bear. This worried him. He wished the pigs would break in again so that he might have a chance to show how forbearing he could be.

One day he gathered a nice mess of tender young greens and sent them over to Mrs. Hayden by Mordecai. At first he had thought of sending her some flowers, but that seemed silly, and besides, Mordecai and flowers were incongruous. Mrs. Hayden sent back a very pretty message of thanks, whereat Harrington looked radiant and Mordecai, who could see through a stone wall as well as most people, went out to the barn and chuckled.

"Ef the little widder hain't caught him! Who'd a-thought it?"

The next day one adventurous pig found its way alone into the Harrington garden. Harrington saw it get in and at the same moment he saw Mrs. Hayden running through her orchard. She was in his yard by the time he got out.

Her sunbonnet had fallen back and some loose tendrils of her auburn hair were curling around her forehead. Her cheeks were so pink and her eyes so bright from running that she looked almost girlish.

"Oh, Mr. Harrington," she said breathlessly, "that pet pig of Bobbles' is in your garden again. He only got in this minute. I saw him coming and I ran right after him."

"He's there, all right," said Harrington cheerfully, "but I'll get him out in a jiffy. Don't tire yourself. Won't you go into the house and rest while I drive him around?"

Mrs. Hayden, however, was determined to help and they both went around to the garden, set the gate open, and tried to drive the pig out. But Harrington was not thinking about pigs, and Mrs. Hayden did not know quite so much about driving them as Mordecai did; as a consequence they did not make much headway. In her excitement Mrs. Hayden ran over beds and whatever came in her way, and Harrington, in order to keep near her, ran after her. Between them they spoiled things about as much as a whole drove of pigs would have done.

But at last the pig grew tired of the fun, bolted out of the gate, and ran across the yard to his own place. Mrs. Hayden followed slowly and Harrington walked beside her.

"Those pigs are all to be shut up tomorrow," she said. "Hiram has been fixing up a place for them in his spare moments and it is ready at last."

"Oh, I wouldn't," said Harrington hastily. "It isn't good for pigs to be shut up so young. You'd better let them run a while yet."

"No," said Mrs. Hayden decidedly. "They have almost worried me to death already. In they go tomorrow."

They were at the lane gate now, and Harrington had to open it and let her pass through. He felt quite desperate as he watched her trip up through the rows of apple trees, her blue gingham skirt brushing the lush grasses where a lacy tangle of sunbeams and shadows lay. Bobbles and Ted came running to meet her and the three, hand in hand, disappeared from sight.

Harrington went back to the house, feeling that life was flat, stale, and unprofitable. That evening at the tea table he caught himself wondering what it would be like to see Mary Hayden sitting at his table in place of Sarah King, with Bobbles and Ted on either hand. Then he found out what was the matter with him. He was in love, fathoms deep, with the blue-eyed widow!

Presumably the pigs were shut up the next day, for Harrington's garden was invaded no more. He stood it for a week and then surrendered at discretion. He filled a basket with early strawberries and went across to the Hayden place, boldly enough to all appearance, but with his heart thumping like any schoolboy's.

The front door stood hospitably open, flanked by rows of defiant red and yellow hollyhocks. Harrington paused on the step, with his hand outstretched to knock. Somewhere inside he heard a low sobbing. Forgetting all about knocking, he stepped softly in and walked to the door of the little sitting-room. Bobbles was standing behind him in the middle of the kitchen but Harrington did not see him. He was looking at Mary Hayden, who was sitting by the table in the room with her arms flung out over it and her head bowed on them. She was crying softly in a hopeless fashion.

Harrington put down his strawberries. "Mary!" he exclaimed.

Mrs. Hayden straightened herself up with a start and looked at him, her lips quivering and her eyes full of tears.

"What is the matter?" said Harrington anxiously. "Is anything wrong?"

"Oh, nothing much," Said Mrs. Hayden, trying to recover herself. "Yes, there is too. But it is very foolish of me to be going on like this. I didn't know anyone was near. And I was feeling so discouraged. The colt broke his leg in the swamp pasture today and Hiram had to shoot him. It was Ted's colt. But there, there is no use in crying over it."

And by way of proving this, the poor, tired, overburdened little woman began to cry again. She was past caring whether Harrington saw her or not.

The woman-hater was so distressed that he forgot to be nervous. He sat down and put his arm around her and spoke out what was in his mind without further parley.

"Don't cry, Mary. Listen to me. You were never meant to run a farm and be killed with worry. You ought to be looked after and petted. I want you to marry me and then everything will be all right. I've loved you ever since that day I came over here and made you cry. Do you think you can like me a little, Mary?"

It may be that Mrs. Hayden was not very much surprised, because Harrington's face had been like an open book the day they chased the pig out of the garden together. As for what she said, perhaps Bobbles, who was surreptitiously gorging himself on Harrington's strawberries, may tell you, but I certainly shall not.

The little brown house among the apple trees is shut up now and the boundary fence belongs to ancient history. Sarah King has gone also and Mrs. John Harrington reigns royally in her place. Bobbles and Ted have a small, blue-eyed, much-spoiled sister, and there is a pig on the estate who may die of old age, but will never meet his doom otherwise. It is Bobbles' pig and one of the famous fourteen.

Mordecai still shambles around and worships Mrs. Harrington. The garden is the same as of yore, but the house is a different place and Harrington is a different man. And Mordecai will tell you with a chuckle, "It was them notorious pigs as did it all."

Why Not Ask Miss Price?

Frances Allen came in from the post office and laid an open letter on the table beside her mother, who was making mincemeat. Alma Allen looked up from the cake she was frosting to ask, "What is the matter? You look as if your letter contained unwelcome news, Fan."

"So it does. It is from Aunt Clara, to say she cannot come. She has received a telegram that her sister-in-law is very ill and she must go to her at once."

Mrs. Allen looked regretful, and Alma cast her spoon away with a tragic air.

"That is too bad. I feel as if our celebration were spoiled. But I suppose it can't be helped."

"No," agreed Frances, sitting down and beginning to peel apples. "So there is no use in lamenting, or I would certainly sit down and cry, I feel so disappointed."

"Is Uncle Frank coming?"

"Yes, Aunt Clara says he will come down from Stellarton if Mrs. King does not get worse. So that will leave just one vacant place. We must invite someone to fill it up. Who shall it be?"

Both girls looked rather puzzled. Mrs. Allen smiled a quiet little smile all to herself and went on chopping suet. She had handed the Thanksgiving dinner over to Frances and Alma this year. They were to attend to all the preparations and invite all the guests. But although they had made or planned several innovations in the dinner itself, they had made no change in the usual list of guests.

"It must just be the time-honoured family affair," Frances had declared. "If we begin inviting other folks, there is no knowing when to draw the line. We can't have more than fourteen, and some of our friends would be sure to feel slighted."

So the same old list it was. But now Aunt Clara—dear, jolly Aunt Clara, whom everybody in the connection loved and admired—could not come, and her place must be filled.

"We can't invite the new minister, because we would have to have his sister, too," said Frances. "And there is no reason for asking any one of our girl chums more than another."

"Mother, you will have to help us out," said Alma. "Can't you suggest a substitute guest?"

Mrs. Allen looked down at the two bright, girlish faces turned up to her and said slowly, "I think I can, but I am not sure my choice will please you. Why not ask Miss Price?"

Miss Price! They had never thought of her! She was the pale, timid-looking little teacher in the primary department of the Hazelwood school.

"Miss Price?" repeated Frances slowly. "Why, Mother, we hardly know her. She is dreadfully dull and quiet, I think."

"And so shy," said Alma. "Why, at the Wards' party the other night she looked startled to death if anyone spoke to her. I believe she would be frightened to come here for Thanksgiving."

"She is a very lonely little creature," said Mrs. Allen gently, "and doesn't seem to have anyone belonging to her. I think she would be very glad to get an invitation to spend Thanksgiving elsewhere than in that cheerless little boarding-house where she lives."

"Of course, if you would like to have her, Mother, we will ask her," said Frances.

"No, girls," said Mrs. Allen seriously. "You must not ask Miss Price on my account, if you do not feel prepared to make her welcome for her own sake. I had hoped that your own kind hearts might have prompted you to extend a little Thanksgiving cheer in a truly Thanksgiving spirit to a lonely, hard-working girl whose life I do not think is a happy one. But there, I shall not preach. This is your dinner, and you must please yourselves as to your guests."

Frances and Alma had both flushed, and they now remained silent for a few minutes. Then Frances sprang up and threw her arms around her mother.

"You're right, Mother dear, as you always are, and we are very selfish girls. We will ask Miss Price and try to give her a nice time. I'll go down this very evening and see her."

In the grey twilight of the chilly autumn evening Bertha Price walked home to her boarding-house, her pale little face paler, and her grey eyes sadder than ever, in the fading light. Only two days until Thanksgiving—but there would be no real Thanksgiving for her. Why, she asked herself rebelliously, when there seemed so much love in the world, was she denied her share?

Her landlady met her in the hall.

"Miss Allen is in the parlour, Miss Price. She wants to see you."

Bertha went into the parlour somewhat reluctantly. She had met Frances Allen only once or twice and she was secretly almost afraid of the handsome, vivacious girl who was so different from herself.

"I am sorry you have had to wait, Miss Allen," she said shyly. "I went to see a pupil of mine who is ill and I was kept later than I expected."

"My errand won't take very long," said Frances brightly. "Mother wants you to spend Thanksgiving Day with us, Miss Price, if you have no other engagement. We will have a few other guests, but nobody outside our own family except Mr. Seeley, who is the law partner and intimate friend of my brother Ernest in town. You'll come, won't you?"

"Oh, thank you, yes," said Bertha, in pleased surprise. "I shall be very glad to go. Why, it is so nice to think of it. I expected my Thanksgiving Day to be lonely and sad—not a bit Thanksgivingy."

"We shall expect you then," said Frances, with a cordial little hand-squeeze. "Come early in the morning, and we will have a real friendly, pleasant day."

That night Frances said to her mother and sister, "You never saw such a transfigured face as Miss Price's when I asked her up. She looked positively pretty—such a lovely pink came out on her cheeks and her eyes shone like stars. She reminded me so much of somebody I've seen, but I can't think who it is. I'm so glad we've asked her here for Thanksgiving!"

Thanksgiving came, as bright and beautiful as a day could be, and the Allens' guests came with it. Bertha Price was among them, paler and shyer than ever. Ernest Allen and his friend, Maxwell Seeley, came out from town on the morning train.

After all the necessary introductions had been made, Frances flew to the kitchen.

"I've found out who it is Miss Price reminds me of," she said, as she bustled about the range. "It's Max Seeley. You needn't laugh, Al. It's a fact. I noticed it the minute I introduced them. He's plump and prosperous and she's pinched and pale, but there's a resemblance nevertheless. Look for yourself and see if it isn't so."

Back in the big, cheery parlour the Thanksgiving guests were amusing themselves in various ways. Max Seeley had given an odd little start when he was introduced to Miss Price, and as soon as possible he followed her to the corner where she had taken refuge. Ernest Allen was out in the kitchen talking to his sisters, the "uncles and cousins and aunts" were all chattering to each other, and Mr. Seeley and Miss Price were quite unnoticed.

"You will excuse me, won't you, Miss Price, if I ask you something about yourself?" he said eagerly. "The truth is, you look so strikingly like someone I used to know that I feel sure you must be related to her. I do not think I have any relatives of your name. Have you any of mine?"

Bertha flushed, hesitated for an instant, then said frankly, "No, I do not think so. But I may as well tell you that Price is not my real name and I do not know what it is, although I think it begins with S. I believe that my parents died when I was about three years old, and I was then taken to an orphan asylum. The next year I was taken from there and adopted by Mrs. Price. She was very kind to me and treated me as her own daughter. I had a happy home with her, although we were poor. Mrs. Price wished me to bear her name, and I did so. She never told me my true surname, perhaps she did not know it. She died when I was sixteen, and since then I have been quite alone in the world. That is all I know about myself."

Max Seeley was plainly excited.

"Why do you think your real name begins with S?" he asked.

"I have a watch which belonged to my mother, with the monogram 'B.S.' on the case. It was left with the matron of the asylum and she gave it to Mrs. Price for me. Here it is."

Max Seeley almost snatched the old-fashioned little silver watch, from her hand and opened the case. An exclamation escaped him as he pointed to some scratches on the inner side. They looked like the initials M.A.S.

"Let me tell my story now," he said. "My name is Maxwell Seeley. My father died when I was seven years old, and my mother a year later. My little sister, Bertha, then three years old, and I were left quite alone and very poor. We had no relatives. I was adopted by a well-to-do old bachelor, who had known my father. My sister was taken to an orphan asylum in a city some distance away. I was very much attached to her and grieved bitterly over our parting. My adopted father was very kind to me and gave me a good education. I did not forget my sister, and as soon as I could I went to the asylum. I found that she had been taken away long before, and I could not even discover who had adopted her, for the original building, with all its records, had been destroyed by fire two years previous to my visit. I never could find any clue to her whereabouts, and long since gave up all hope of finding her. But I have found her at last. You are Bertha Seeley, my little sister!"

"Oh—can it be possible!"

"More than possible—it is certain. You are the image of my mother, as I remember her, and as an old daguerreotype I have pictures her. And this is her watch—see, I scratched my own initials on the case one day. There is no doubt in the world. Oh, Bertha, are you half as glad as I am?"

"Glad!"

Bertha's eyes were shining like stars. She tried to smile, but burst into tears instead and her head went down on her brother's shoulder. By this time everybody in the room was staring at the extraordinary tableau, and Ernest, coming through the hall, gave a whistle of astonishment that brought the two in the corner back to a sense of their surroundings.

"I haven't suddenly gone crazy, Ernest, old fellow," smiled Max. "Ladies and gentlemen all, this little school-ma'am was introduced to you as Miss Price, but that was a mistake. Let me introduce her again as Miss Bertha Seeley, my long-lost and newly-found sister."

Well they had an amazing time then, of course. They laughed and questioned and explained until the dinner was in imminent danger of getting stone-cold on the dining-room table. Luckily, Alma and Frances remembered it just in the nick of time, and they all got out, somehow, and into their places. It was a splendid dinner, but I believe that Maxwell and Bertha Seeley didn't know what they were eating, any more than if it had been sawdust. However, the rest of the guests made up for that, and did full justice to the girls' cookery.

In the afternoon they all went to church, and at least two hearts were truly and devoutly thankful that day.

When the dusk came, Ernest and Maxwell had to catch the last train for town, and the other guests went home, with the exception of Bertha, who was to stay all night. Just as soon as her resignation could be effected, she was to join her brother.

"Meanwhile, I'll see about getting a house to put you in," said Max. "No more boarding out for me, Ernest. You may consider me as a family man henceforth."

Frances and Alma talked it all over before they went to sleep that night.

"Just think," said Frances, "if we hadn't asked her here today she might never have found her brother! It's all Mother's doing, bless her! Things do happen like a storybook sometimes, don't they, Al? And didn't I tell you they looked alike?"

LUCY MAUD MONTGOMERY SHORT STORIES, 1905 TO 1906

A Correspondence and A Climax

At sunset Sidney hurried to her room to take off the soiled and faded cotton dress she had worn while milking. She had milked eight cows and pumped water for the milk-cans afterward in the fag-end of a hot summer day. She did that every night, but tonight she had hurried more than usual because she wanted to get her letter written before the early farm bedtime. She had been thinking it out while she milked the cows in the stuffy little pen behind the barn. This monthly letter was the only pleasure and stimulant in her life. Existence would have been, so Sidney thought, a dreary, unbearable blank without it. She cast aside her milking-dress with a thrill of distaste that tingled to her rosy fingertips. As she slipped into her blue-print afternoon dress her aunt called to her from below. Sidney ran out to the dark little entry and leaned over the stair railing. Below in the kitchen there was a hubbub of laughing, crying, quarrelling children, and a reek of bad tobacco smoke drifted up to the girl's disgusted nostrils.

Aunt Jane was standing at the foot of the stairs with a lamp in one hand and a year-old baby clinging to the other. She was a big shapeless woman with a round good-natured face—cheerful and vulgar as a sunflower was Aunt Jane at all times and occasions.

"I want to run over and see how Mrs. Brixby is this evening, Siddy, and you must take care of the baby till I get back."

Sidney sighed and went downstairs for the baby. It never would have occurred to her to protest or be petulant about it. She had all her aunt's sweetness of disposition, if she resembled her in nothing else. She had not grumbled because she had to rise at four that morning, get breakfast, milk the cows, bake bread, prepare seven children for school, get dinner, preserve twenty quarts of strawberries, get tea, and milk the cows again. All her days were alike as far as hard work and dullness went, but she accepted them cheerfully and uncomplainingly. But she did resent having to look after the baby when she wanted to write her letter.

She carried the baby to her room, spread a quilt on the floor for him to sit on, and gave him a box of empty spools to play with. Fortunately he was a phlegmatic infant, fond of staying in one place, and not given to roaming about in search of adventures; but Sidney knew she would have to keep an eye on him, and it would be distracting to literary effort.

She got out her box of paper and sat down by the little table at the window with a small kerosene lamp at her elbow. The room was small—a mere box above the kitchen which Sidney shared with two small cousins. Her bed and the cot where the little girls slept filled up almost all the available space. The furniture was poor, but everything was neat—it was the only neat room in the house, indeed, for tidiness was no besetting virtue of Aunt Jane's.

Opposite Sidney was a small muslined and befrilled toilet-table, above which hung an eight-by-six-inch mirror, in which Sidney saw herself reflected as she devoutly hoped other people did not see her. Just at that particular angle one eye appeared to be as large as an orange, while the other was the size of a pea, and the mouth zigzagged from ear to ear. Sidney hated that mirror as virulently as she could hate anything. It seemed to her to typify all that was unlovely in her life. The mirror of existence into which her fresh young soul had looked for twenty years gave back to her wistful gaze just such distortions of fair hopes and ideals.

Half of the little table by which she sat was piled high with books—old books, evidently well read and well-bred books, classics of fiction and verse every one of them, and all bearing on the flyleaf the name of Sidney Richmond, thereby meaning not the girl at the table, but her college-bred young father who had died the day before she was born. Her mother had died the day after, and Sidney thereupon had come into the hands of good Aunt Jane, with those books for her dowry, since nothing else was left after the expenses of the double funeral had been paid.

One of the books had Sidney Richmond's name printed on the title-page instead of written on the flyleaf. It was a thick little volume of poems, published in his college days—musical, unsubstantial, pretty little poems, every one of which the girl Sidney loved and knew by heart.

Sidney dropped her pointed chin in her hands and looked dreamily out into the moonlit night, while she thought her letter out a little more fully before beginning to write. Her big brown eyes were full of wistfulness and romance; for Sidney was romantic, albeit a faithful and understanding acquaintance with her father's books had given to her romance refinement and reason, and the delicacy of her own nature had imparted to it a self-respecting bias.

Presently she began to write, with a flush of real excitement on her face. In the middle of things the baby choked on a small twist spool and Sidney had to catch him up by the heels and hold him head downward until the trouble was ejected. Then she had to soothe him, and finally write the rest of her letter holding him on one arm and protecting the epistle from the grabs of his sticky little fingers. It was certainly letter-writing under difficulties, but Sidney seemed to deal with them mechanically. Her soul and understanding were elsewhere.

Four years before, when Sidney was sixteen, still calling herself a schoolgirl by reason of the fact that she could be spared to attend school four months in the winter when work was slack, she had been much interested in the "Maple Leaf" department of the Montreal weekly her uncle took. It was a page given over to youthful Canadians and filled with their contributions in the way of letters, verses, and prize essays. Noms de plume were signed to these, badges were sent to those who joined the Maple Leaf Club, and a general delightful sense of mystery pervaded the department.

Often a letter concluded with a request to the club members to correspond with the writer. One such request went from Sidney under the pen-name of "Ellen Douglas." The girl was lonely in Plainfield; she had no companions or associates such as she cared for; the Maple Leaf Club represented all that her life held of outward interest, and she longed for something more.

Only one answer came to "Ellen Douglas," and that was forwarded to her by the long-suffering editor of "The Maple Leaf." It was from John Lincoln of the Bar N Ranch, Alberta. He wrote that, although his age debarred him from membership in the club (he was twenty, and the limit was eighteen), he read the letters of the department with much interest, and often had thought of answering some of the requests for correspondents. He never had done so, but "Ellen Douglas's" letter was so interesting that he had decided to write to her. Would she be kind enough to correspond with him? Life on the Bar N, ten miles from the outposts of civilization, was lonely. He was two years out from the east, and had not yet forgotten to be homesick at times.

Sidney liked the letter and answered it. Since then they had written to each other regularly. There was nothing sentimental, hinted at or implied, in the correspondence. Whatever the faults of Sidney's romantic visions were, they did not tend to precocious flirtation. The Plainfield boys, attracted by her beauty and repelled by her indifference and aloofness, could have told that. She never expected to meet John Lincoln, nor did she wish to do so. In the correspondence itself she found her pleasure.

John Lincoln wrote breezy accounts of ranch life and adventures on the far western plains, so alien and remote from snug, humdrum Plainfield life that Sidney always had the sensation of crossing a gulf when she opened a letter from the Bar N. As for Sidney's own letter, this is the way it read as she wrote it:

"The Evergreens," Plainfield.

> Dear Mr. Lincoln:
>
> The very best letter I can write in the half-hour before the carriage will be at the door to take me to Mrs. Braddon's dance shall be yours tonight. I am sitting here in the library arrayed in my smartest, newest, whitest, silkiest gown, with a string of pearls which Uncle James gave me today about my throat—the dear, glistening, sheeny things! And I am looking forward to the "dances and delight" of the evening with keen anticipation.
>
> You asked me in your last letter if I did not sometimes grow weary of my endless round of dances and dinners and social functions. No, no, never! I enjoy every one of them, every minute of them. I love life and its bloom and brilliancy; I love meeting new people; I love the ripple of music, the hum of laughter and conversation. Every morning when I awaken the new day seems to me to be a good fairy who will bring me some beautiful gift of joy.

The gift she gave me today was my sunset gallop on my grey mare Lady. The thrill of it is in my veins yet. I distanced the others who rode with me and led the homeward canter alone, rocking along a dark, gleaming road, shadowy with tall firs and pines, whose balsam made all the air resinous around me. Before me was a long valley filled with purple dusk, and beyond it meadows of sunset and great lakes of saffron and rose where a soul might lose itself in colour. On my right was the harbour, silvered over with a rising moon. Oh, it was all glorious—the clear air with its salt-sea tang, the aroma of the pines, the laughter of my friends behind me, the spring and rhythm of Lady's grey satin body beneath me! I wanted to ride on so forever, straight into the heart of the sunset.

Then home and to dinner. We have a houseful of guests at present—one of them an old statesman with a massive silver head, and eyes that have looked into people's thoughts so long that you have an uncanny feeling that they can see right through your soul and read motives you dare not avow even to yourself. I was terribly in awe of him at first, but when I got acquainted with him I found him charming. He is not above talking delightful nonsense even to a girl. I sat by him at dinner, and he talked to me—not nonsense, either, this time. He told me of his political contests and diplomatic battles; he was wise and witty and whimsical. I felt as if I were drinking some rare, stimulating mental wine. What a privilege it is to meet such men and take a peep through their wise eyes at the fascinating game of empire-building!

I met another clever man a few evenings ago. A lot of us went for a sail on the harbour. Mrs. Braddon's house party came too. We had three big white boats that skimmed down the moonlit channel like great white sea birds. There was another boat far across the harbour, and the people in it were singing. The music drifted over the water to us, so sad and sweet and beguiling that I could have cried for very pleasure. One of Mrs. Braddon's guests said to me:

"That is the soul of music with all its sense and earthliness refined away."

I hadn't thought about him before—I hadn't even caught his name in the general introduction. He was a tall, slight man, with a worn, sensitive face and iron-grey hair—a quiet man who hadn't laughed or talked. But he began to talk to me then, and I forgot all about the others. I never had listened to anybody in the least like him. He talked of books and music, of art and travel. He had been all over the world, and had seen everything everybody else had seen and everything they hadn't too, I think. I seemed to be looking into an enchanted mirror where all my own dreams and ideals were reflected back to me, but made, oh, so much more beautiful!

On my way home after the Braddon people had left us somebody asked me how I liked Paul Moore! The man I had been talking with was Paul Moore, the great novelist! I was almost glad I hadn't known it while he was talking to me—I should have been too awed and reverential to have really enjoyed his conversation. As it was, I had contradicted him twice, and he had laughed and liked it. But his books will always have a new meaning to me henceforth, through the insight he himself has given me.

It is such meetings as these that give life its sparkle for me. But much of its abiding sweetness comes from my friendship with Margaret Raleigh. You will be weary of my rhapsodies over her. But she is such a rare and wonderful woman; much older then I am, but so young in heart and soul and freshness of feeling! She is to me mother and sister and wise, clear-sighted friend. To her I go with all my perplexities and hopes and triumphs. She has sympathy and understanding for my every mood. I love life so much for giving me such a friendship!

This morning I wakened at dawn and stole away to the shore before anyone else was up. I had a delightful run-away. The long, lowlying meadows between "The Evergreens" and the shore were dewy and fresh in that first light, that was as fine and purely tinted as the heart of one of my white roses. On the beach the water was purring in little blue ripples, and, oh, the sunrise out there beyond the harbour! All the eastern Heaven was abloom with it. And there was a wind that came dancing and whistling up the channel to replace the beautiful silence with a music more beautiful still.

The rest of the folks were just coming downstairs when I got back to breakfast. They were all yawny, and some were grumpy, but I had washed my being in the sunrise and felt as blithesome as the day. Oh, life is so good to live!

Tomorrow Uncle James's new vessel, the *White Lady*, is to be launched. We are going to make a festive occasion of it, and I am to christen her with a bottle of cobwebby old wine.

But I hear the carriage, and Aunt Jane is calling me. I had a great deal more to say—about your letter, your big "round-up" and your tribulations with your Chinese cook—but I've only time now to say goodbye. You wish me a lovely time at the dance and a full programme, don't you?

Yours sincerely,
Sidney Richmond.

Aunt Jane came home presently and carried away her sleeping baby. Sidney said her prayers, went to bed, and slept soundly and serenely.

She mailed her letter the next day, and a month later an answer came. Sidney read it as soon as she left the post office, and walked the rest of the way home as in a nightmare, staring straight ahead of her with wide-open, unseeing brown eyes.

John Lincoln's letter was short, but the pertinent paragraph of it burned itself into Sidney's brain. He wrote:

> I am going east for a visit. It is six years since I was home, and it seems like three times six. I shall go by the C.P.R., which passes through Plainfield, and I mean to stop off for a day. You will let me call and see you, won't you? I shall have to take your permission for granted, as I shall be gone before a letter from you can reach the Bar N. I leave for the east in five days, and shall look forward to our meeting with all possible interest and pleasure.

Sidney did not sleep that night, but tossed restlessly about or cried in her pillow. She was so pallid and hollow-eyed the next morning that Aunt Jane noticed it, and asked her what the matter was.

"Nothing," said Sidney sharply. Sidney had never spoken sharply to her aunt before. The good woman shook her head. She was afraid the child was "taking something."

"Don't do much today, Siddy," she said kindly. "Just lie around and take it easy till you get rested up. I'll fix you a dose of quinine."

Sidney refused to lie around and take it easy. She swallowed the quinine meekly enough, but she worked fiercely all day, hunting out superfluous tasks to do. That night she slept the sleep of exhaustion, but her dreams were unenviable and the awakening was terrible.

Any day, any hour, might bring John Lincoln to Plainfield. What should she do? Hide from him? Refuse to see him? But he would find out the truth just the same; she would lose his friendships and respect just as surely. Sidney trod the way of the transgressor, and found that its thorns pierced to bone and marrow. Everything had come to an end—nothing was left to her! In the untried recklessness of twenty untempered years she wished she could die before John Lincoln came to Plainfield. The eyes of youth could not see how she could possibly live afterward.

Some days later a young man stepped from the C.P.R. train at Plainfield station and found his way to the one small hotel the place boasted. After getting his supper he asked the proprietor if he could direct him to "The Evergreens."

Caleb Williams looked at his guest in bewilderment. "Never heerd o' such a place," he said.

"It is the name of Mr. Conway's estate—Mr. James Conway," explained John Lincoln.

"Oh, Jim Conway's place!" said Caleb. "Didn't know that was what he called it. Sartin I kin tell you whar' to find it. You see that road out thar'? Well, just follow it straight along for a mile and a half till you come to a blacksmith's forge. Jim Conway's house is just this side of it on the right—back from the road a smart piece and no other handy. You can't mistake it."

John Lincoln did not expect to mistake it, once he found it; he knew by heart what it appeared like from Sidney's description: an old stately mansion of mellowed brick, covered with ivy and set back from the highway amid fine ancestral trees, with a pine-grove behind it, a river to the left, and a harbour beyond.

He strode along the road in the warm, ruddy sunshine of early evening. It was not a bad-looking road at all; the farmsteads sprinkled along it were for the most part snug and wholesome enough; yet somehow it was different from what he had expected it to be. And there was no harbour or glimpse of distant sea visible. Had the hotel-keeper made a mistake? Perhaps he had meant some other James Conway.

Presently he found himself before the blacksmith's forge. Beside it was a rickety, unpainted gate opening into a snake-fenced lane feathered here and there with scrubby little spruces. It ran down a bare hill, crossed a little ravine full of young white-stemmed birches, and up another bare hill to an equally bare crest where a farmhouse was perched—a farmhouse painted a stark, staring yellow and the ugliest thing in farmhouses that John Lincoln had ever seen, even among the log shacks of the west. He knew now that he had been misdirected, but as there seemed to be nobody about the forge he concluded that he had better go to the yellow house and inquire within. He passed down the lane and over the little rustic bridge that spanned the brook. Just beyond was another home-made gate of poles.

Lincoln opened it, or rather he had his hand on the hasp of twisted withes which secured it, when he was suddenly arrested by the apparition of a girl, who flashed around the curve of young birch beyond and stood before him with panting breath and quivering lips.

"I beg your pardon," said John Lincoln courteously, dropping the gate and lifting his hat. "I am looking for the house of Mr. James Conway—'The Evergreens.' Can you direct me to it?"

"That is Mr. James Conway's house," said the girl, with the tragic air and tone of one driven to desperation and an impatient gesture of her hand toward the yellow nightmare above them.

"I don't think he can be the one I mean," said Lincoln perplexedly. "The man I am thinking of has a niece, Miss Richmond."

"There is no other James Conway in Plainfield," said the girl. "This is his place—nobody calls it 'The Evergreens' but myself. I am Sidney Richmond."

For a moment they looked at each other across the gate, sheer amazement and bewilderment holding John Lincoln mute. Sidney, burning with shame, saw that this stranger was exceedingly good to look upon—tall, clean-limbed, broad-shouldered, with clear-cut bronzed features and a chin and eyes that would have done honour to any man. John Lincoln, among all his confused sensations, was aware that this slim, agitated young creature before him was the loveliest thing he ever had seen, so lithe was her figure, so glossy and dark and silken her bare, wind-ruffled hair, so big and brown and appealing her eyes, so delicately oval her flushed cheeks. He felt that she was frightened and in trouble, and he wanted to comfort and reassure her. But how could she be Sidney Richmond?

"I don't understand," he said perplexedly.

"Oh!" Sidney threw out her hands in a burst of passionate protest. "No, and you never will understand—I can't make you understand."

"I don't understand," said John Lincoln again. "Can you be Sidney Richmond—the Sidney Richmond who has written to me for four years?"

"I am."

"Then, those letters—"

"Were all lies," said Sidney bluntly and desperately. "There was nothing true in them—nothing at all. This is my home. We are poor. Everything I told you about it and my life was just imagination."

"Then why did you write them?" he asked blankly. "Why did you deceive me?"

"Oh, I didn't mean to deceive you! I never thought of such a thing. When you asked me to write to you I wanted to, but I didn't know what to write about to a stranger. I just couldn't write you about my life here, not because it was hard, but it was so ugly and empty. So I wrote instead of the life I wanted to live—the life I did live in imagination. And when once I had begun, I had to keep it up. I found it so fascinating, too! Those letters made that other life seem real to me. I never expected to meet you. These last four days since your letter came have been dreadful to me. Oh, please go away and forgive me if you can! I know I can never make you understand how it came about."

Sidney turned away and hid her burning face against the cool white bark of the birch tree behind her. It was worse than she had even thought it would be. He was so handsome, so manly, so earnest-eyed! Oh, what a friend to lose!

John Lincoln opened the gate and went up to her. There was a great tenderness in his face, mingled with a little kindly, friendly amusement.

"Please don't distress yourself so, Sidney," he said, unconsciously using her Christian name. "I think I do understand. I'm not such a dull fellow as you take me for. After all, those letters were true—or, rather, there was truth in them. You revealed yourself more faithfully in them than if you had written truly about your narrow outward life."

Sidney turned her flushed face and wet eyes slowly toward him, a little smile struggling out amid the clouds of woe. This young man was certainly good at understanding. "You—you'll forgive me then?" she stammered.

"Yes, if there is anything to forgive. And for my own part, I am glad you are not what I have always thought you were. If I had come here and found you what I expected, living in such a home as I expected, I never could have told you or even thought of telling you what you have come to mean to me in these lonely years during which your letters have been the things most eagerly looked forward to. I should have come this evening and spent an hour or so with you, and then have gone away on the train tomorrow morning, and that would have been all.

"But I find instead just a dreamy romantic little girl, much like my sisters at home, except that she is a great deal cleverer. And as a result I mean to stay a week at Plainfield and come to see you every day, if you will let me. And on my way back to the Bar N I mean to stop off at Plainfield again for another week, and then I shall tell you something more—something it would be a little too bold to say now, perhaps, although I could say it just as well and truly. All this if I may. May I, Sidney?"

He bent forward and looked earnestly into her face. Sidney felt a new, curious, inexplicable thrill at her heart. "Oh, yes.—I suppose so," she said shyly.

"Now, take me up to the house and introduce me to your Aunt Jane," said John Lincoln in satisfied tone.

An Adventure on Island Rock

"Who was the man I saw talking to you in the hayfield?" asked Aunt Kate, as Uncle Richard came to dinner.

"Bob Marks," said Uncle Richard briefly. "I've sold Laddie to him."

Ernest Hughes, the twelve-year-old orphan boy whom Uncle "boarded and kept" for the chores he did, suddenly stopped eating.

"Oh, Mr. Lawson, you're not going to sell Laddie?" he cried chokily.

Uncle Richard stared at him. Never before, in the five years that Ernest had lived with him, had the quiet little fellow spoken without being spoken to, much less ventured to protest against anything Uncle Richard might do.

"Certainly I am," answered the latter curtly. "Bob offered me twenty dollars for the dog, and he's coming after him next week."

"Oh, Mr. Lawson," said Ernest, rising to his feet, his small, freckled face crimson. "Oh, don't sell Laddie! *Please*, Mr. Lawson, don't sell him!"

"What nonsense is this?" said Uncle Richard sharply. He was a man who brooked no opposition from anybody, and who never changed his mind when it was once made up.

"Don't sell Laddie!" pleaded Ernest miserably. "He is the only friend I've got. I can't live if Laddie goes away. Oh, don't sell him, Mr. Lawson!"

"Sit down and hold your tongue," said Uncle Richard sternly. "The dog is mine, and I shall do with him as I think fit. He is sold, and that is all there is about it. Go on with your dinner."

But Ernest for the first time did not obey. He snatched his cap from the back of his chair, dashed it down over his eyes, and ran from the kitchen with a sob choking his breath. Uncle Richard looked angry, but Aunt Kate hastened to soothe him.

"Don't be vexed with the boy, Richard," she said. "You know he is very fond of Laddie. He's had to do with him ever since he was a pup, and no doubt he feels badly at the thought of losing him. I'm rather sorry myself that you have sold the dog."

"Well, he *is* sold and there's an end of it. I don't say but that the dog is a good dog. But he is of no use to us, and twenty dollars will come in mighty handy just now. He's worth that to Bob, for he is a good watch dog, so we've both made a fair bargain."

Nothing more was said about Ernest or Laddie. I had taken no part in the discussion, for I felt no great interest in the matter. Laddie was a nice dog; Ernest was a quiet, inoffensive little fellow, five years younger than myself; that was all I thought about either of them.

I was spending my vacation at Uncle Richard's farm on the Nova Scotian Bay of Fundy shore. I was a great favourite with Uncle Richard, partly because he had been much attached to my mother, his only sister, partly because of my strong resemblance to his only son, who had died several years before. Uncle Richard was a stern, undemonstrative man, but I knew that he entertained a deep and real affection for me, and I always enjoyed my vacation sojourns at his place.

"What are you going to do this afternoon, Ned?" he asked, after the disturbance caused by Ernest's outbreak had quieted down.

"I think I'll row out to Island Rock," I replied. "I want to take some views of the shore from it."

Uncle Richard nodded. He was much interested in my new camera.

"If you're on it about four o'clock, you'll get a fine view of the 'Hole in the Wall' when the sun begins to shine on the water through it," he said. "I've often thought it would make a handsome picture."

"After I've finished taking the pictures, I think I'll go down shore to Uncle Adam's and stay all night," I said. "Jim's dark room is more convenient than mine, and he has some pictures he is going to develop tonight, too."

I started for the shore about two o'clock. Ernest was sitting on the woodpile as I passed through the yard, with his arms about Laddie's neck and his face buried in Laddie's curly hair. Laddie was a handsome and intelligent black-and-white Newfoundland, with a magnificent coat. He and Ernest were great chums. I felt sorry for the boy who was to lose his pet.

"Don't take it so hard, Ern," I said, trying to comfort him. "Uncle will likely get another pup."

"I don't want any other pup!" Ernest blurted out. "Oh, Ned, won't you try and coax your uncle not to sell him? Perhaps he'd listen to you."

I shook my head. I knew Uncle Richard too well to hope that.

"Not in this case, Ern," I said. "He would say it did not concern me, and you know nothing moves him when he determines on a thing. You'll have to reconcile yourself to losing Laddie, I'm afraid."

Ernest's tow-coloured head went down on Laddie's neck again, and I, deciding that there was no use in saying anything more, proceeded towards the shore, which was about a mile from Uncle Richard's house. The beach along his farm and for several farms along shore was a lonely, untenanted one, for the fisher-folk all lived two miles further down, at Rowley's Cove. About three hundred yards from the shore was the peculiar formation known as Island Rock. This was a large rock that stood abruptly up out of the water. Below, about the usual water-line, it was seamed and fissured, but its summit rose up in a narrow, flat-topped peak. At low tide twenty feet of it was above water, but at high tide it was six feet and often more under water.

I pushed Uncle Richard's small flat down the rough path and rowed out to Island Rock. Arriving there, I thrust the painter deep into a narrow cleft. This was the usual way of mooring it, and no doubt of its safety occurred to me.

I scrambled up the rock and around to the eastern end, where there was a broader space for standing and from which some capital views could be obtained. The sea about the rock was calm, but there was quite a swell on and an off-shore breeze was blowing. There were no boats visible. The tide was low, leaving bare the curious caves and headlands along shore, and I secured a number of excellent snapshots. It was now three o'clock. I must wait another hour yet before I could get the best view of the "Hole in the Wall"—a huge, arch-like opening through a jutting headland to the west of me. I went around to look at it, when I saw a sight that made me stop short in dismay. This was nothing less than the flat, drifting outward around the point. The swell and suction of the water around the rock must have pulled her loose—and I was a prisoner! At first my only feeling was one of annoyance. Then a thought flashed into my mind that made me dizzy with fear. The tide would be high that night. If I could not escape from Island Rock I would inevitably be drowned.

I sat down limply on a ledge and tried to look matters fairly in the face. I could not swim; calls for help could not reach anybody; my only hope lay in the chance of somebody passing down the shore or of some boat appearing.

I looked at my watch. It was a quarter past three. The tide would begin to turn about five, but it would be at least ten before the rock would be covered. I had, then, little more than six hours to live unless rescued.

The flat was by this time out of sight around the point. I hoped that the sight of an empty flat drifting down shore might attract someone's attention and lead to investigation. That seemed to be my only hope. No alarm would be felt at Uncle Richard's because of my non-appearance. They would suppose I had gone to Uncle Adam's.

I have heard of time seeming long to a person in my predicament, but to me it seemed fairly to fly, for every moment decreased my chance of rescue. I determined I would not give way to cowardly fear, so, with a murmured prayer for help, I set myself to the task of waiting for death as bravely as possible. At intervals I shouted as loudly as I could and, when the sun came to the proper angle for the best view of the "Hole in the Wall," I took the picture. It afterwards turned out to be a great success, but I have never been able to look at it without a shudder.

At five the tide began to come in. Very, very slowly the water rose around Island Rock. Up, up, up it came, while I watched it with fascinated eyes, feeling like a rat in a trap. The sun fell lower and lower; at eight o'clock the moon rose large and bright; at nine it was a lovely night, dear, calm, bright as day, and the water was swishing over the highest ledge of the rock. With some difficulty I climbed to the top and sat there to await the end. I had no longer any hope of rescue but, by a great effort, I preserved self-control. If I had to die, I would at least face death staunchly. But when I thought of my mother at home, it tasked all my energies to keep from breaking down utterly.

Suddenly I heard a whistle. Never was sound so sweet. I stood up and peered eagerly shoreward. Coming around the "Hole in the Wall" headland, on top of the cliffs, I saw a boy and a dog. I sent a wild halloo ringing shoreward.

The boy started, stopped and looked out towards Island Rock. The next moment he hailed me. It was Ernest's voice, and it was Laddie who was barking beside him.

"Ernest," I shouted wildly, "run for help—quick! quick! The tide will be over the rock in half an hour! Hurry, or you will be too late!"

Instead of starting off at full speed, as I expected him to do, Ernest stood still for a moment, and then began to pick his steps down a narrow path over the cliff, followed by Laddie.

"Ernest," I shouted frantically, "what are you doing? Why don't you go for help?"

Ernest had by this time reached a narrow ledge of rock just above the waterline. I noticed that he was carrying something over his arm.

"It would take too long," he shouted. "By the time I got to the Cove and a boat could row back here, you'd be drowned. Laddie and I will save you. Is there anything there you can tie a rope to? I've a coil of rope here that I think will be long enough to reach you. I've been down to the Cove and Alec Martin sent it up to your uncle."

I looked about me; a smooth, round hole had been worn clean through a thin part of the apex of the rock.

"I could fasten the rope if I had it!" I called. "But how can you get it to me?"

For answer Ernest tied a bit of driftwood to the rope and put it into Laddie's mouth. The next minute the dog was swimming out to me. As soon as he came close I caught the rope. It was just long enough to stretch from shore to rock, allowing for a couple of hitches which Ernest gave around a small boulder on the ledge. I tied my camera case on my head by means of some string I found in my pocket, then I slipped into the water and, holding to the rope, went hand over hand to the shore with Laddie swimming beside me. Ernest held on to the shoreward end of the rope like grim death, a task that was no light one for his small arms. When I finally scrambled up beside him, his face was dripping with perspiration and he trembled like a leaf.

"Ern, you are a brick!" I exclaimed. "You've saved my life!"

"No, it was Laddie," said Ernest, refusing to take any credit at all.

We hurried home and arrived at Uncle Richard's about ten, just as they were going to bed. When Uncle Richard heard what had happened, he turned very pale, and murmured, "Thank God!" Aunt Kate got me out of my wet clothes as quickly as possible, put me away to bed in hot blankets and dosed me with ginger tea. I slept like a top and felt none the worse for my experience the next morning.

At the breakfast table Uncle Richard scarcely spoke. But, just as we finished, he said abruptly to Ernest, "I'm not going to sell Laddie. You and the dog saved Ned's life between you, and no dog who helped do that is ever going to be sold by me. Henceforth he belongs to you. I give him to you for your very own."

"Oh, Mr. Lawson!" said Ernest, with shining eyes.

I never saw a boy look so happy. As for Laddie, who was sitting beside him with his shaggy head on Ernest's knee, I really believe the dog understood, too. The look in his eyes was almost human. Uncle Richard leaned over and patted him.

"Good dog!" he said. "Good dog!"

At Five O'Clock in the Morning

Fate, in the guise of Mrs. Emory dropping a milk-can on the platform under his open window, awakened Murray that morning. Had not Mrs. Emory dropped that can, he would have slumbered peacefully until his usual hour for rising—a late one, be it admitted, for of all the boarders at Sweetbriar Cottage Murray was the most irregular in his habits.

"When a young man," Mrs. Emory was wont to remark sagely and a trifle severely, "prowls about that pond half of the night, a-chasing of things what he calls 'moonlight effecks,' it ain't to be wondered at that he's sleepy in the morning. And it ain't the convenientest thing, nuther and noways, to keep the breakfast table set till the farm folks are thinking of dinner. But them artist men are not like other people, say what you will, and allowance has to be made for them. And I must say that I likes him real well and approves of him every other way."

If Murray had slept late that morning—well, he shudders yet over that "if." But aforesaid Fate saw to it that he woke when the hour of destiny and the milk-can struck, and having awakened he found he could not go to sleep again. It suddenly occurred to him that he had never seen a sunrise on the pond. Doubtless it would be very lovely down there in those dewy meadows at such a primitive hour; he decided to get up and see what the world looked like in the young daylight.

He scowled at a letter lying on his dressing table and thrust it into his pocket that it might be out of sight. He had written it the night before and the writing of it was going to cost him several things—a prospective million among others. So it is hardly to be wondered at if the sight of it did not reconcile him to the joys of early rising.

"Dear life and heart!" exclaimed Mrs. Emory, pausing in the act of scalding a milk-can when Murray emerged from a side door. "What on earth is the matter, Mr. Murray? You ain't sick now, surely? I told you them pond fogs was p'isen after night! If you've gone and got—"

"Nothing is the matter, dear lady," interrupted Murray, "and I haven't gone and got anything except an acute attack of early rising which is not in the least likely to become chronic. But at what hour of the night do you get up, you wonderful woman? Or rather do you ever go to bed at all? Here is the sun only beginning to rise and—positively yes, you have all your cows milked."

Mrs. Emory purred with delight.

"Folks as has fourteen cows to milk has to rise betimes," she answered with proud humility. "Laws, I don't complain—I've lots of help with the milking. How Mrs. Palmer manages, I really cannot comperhend—or rather, how she has managed. I suppose she'll be all right now since her niece came last night. I saw her posting to the pond pasture not ten minutes ago. She'll have to milk all them seven cows herself. But dear life and heart! Here I be palavering away and not a bite of breakfast ready for you!"

"I don't want any breakfast until the regular time for it," assured Murray. "I'm going down to the pond to see the sun rise."

"Now don't you go and get caught in the ma'sh," anxiously called Mrs. Emory, as she never failed to do when she saw him starting for the pond. Nobody ever had got caught in the marsh, but Mrs. Emory lived in a chronic state of fear lest someone should.

"And if you once got stuck in that black mud you'd be sucked right down and never seen or heard tell of again till the day of judgment, like Adam Palmer's cow," she was wont to warn her boarders.

Murray sought his favourite spot for pond dreaming—a bloomy corner of the pasture that ran down into the blue water, with a dump of leafy maples on the left. He was very glad he had risen early. A miracle was being worked before his very eyes. The world was in a flush and tremor of maiden loveliness, instinct with all the marvellous fleeting charm of girlhood and spring and young morning. Overhead the sky was a vast high-sprung arch of unstained crystal. Down over the sand dunes, where the pond ran out into the sea, was a great arc of primrose smitten through with auroral crimsonings. Beneath it the pond waters shimmered with a hundred fairy hues, but just before him they were clear as a flawless mirror. The fields around him glistened with dews, and a little wandering wind, blowing lightly from some bourne in the hills, strayed down over the slopes, bringing with it an unimaginable odour and freshness, and fluttered over the pond, leaving a little path of dancing silver ripples across the mirror-glory of the water. Birds were singing in the beech woods over on Orchard Knob Farm, answering to each other from shore to shore, until the very air was tremulous with the elfin music of this wonderful midsummer dawn.

"I will get up at sunrise every morning of my life hereafter," exclaimed Murray rapturously, not meaning a syllable of it, but devoutly believing he did.

Just as the fiery disc of the sun peered over the sand dunes Murray heard music that was not of the birds. It was a girl's voice singing beyond the maples to his left—a clear sweet voice, blithely trilling out the old-fashioned song, "Five O'Clock in the Morning."

"Mrs. Palmer's niece!"

Murray sprang to his feet and tiptoed cautiously through the maples. He had heard so much from Mrs. Palmer about her niece that he felt reasonably well acquainted with her. Moreover, Mrs. Palmer had assured him that Mollie was a very pretty girl. Now a pretty girl milking cows at sunrise in the meadows sounded well.

Mrs. Palmer had not over-rated her niece's beauty. Murray said so to himself with a little whistle of amazement as he leaned unseen on the pasture fence and looked at the girl who was milking a placid Jersey less than ten yards away from him. Murray's artistic instinct responded to the whole scene with a thrill of satisfaction.

He could see only her profile, but that was perfect, and the colouring of the oval cheek and the beautiful curve of the chin were something to adore. Her hair, ruffled into lovable little ringlets by the morning wind, was coiled in glistening chestnut masses high on her bare head, and her arms, bare to the elbow, were as white as marble. Presently she began to sing again, and this time Murray joined in. She half rose from her milking stool and cast a startled glance at the maples. Then she dropped back again and began to milk determinedly, but Murray could have sworn that he saw a demure smile hovering about her lips. That, and the revelation of her full face, decided him. He sprang over the fence and sauntered across the intervening space of lush clover blossoms.

"Good morning," he said coolly. He had forgotten her other name, and it did not matter; at five o'clock in the morning people who met in dewy clover fields might disregard the conventionalities. "Isn't it rather a large contract for you to be milking seven cows all alone? May I help you?"

Mollie looked up at him over her shoulder. She had glorious grey eyes. Her face was serene and undisturbed. "Can you milk?" she asked.

"Unlikely as it may seem, I can," said Murray. "I have never confessed it to Mrs. Emory, because I was afraid she would inveigle me into milking her fourteen cows. But I don't mind helping you. I learned to milk when I was a shaver on my vacations at a grandfatherly farm. May I have that extra pail?"

Murray captured a milking stool and rounded up another Jersey. Before sitting down he seemed struck with an idea.

"My name is Arnold Murray. I board at Sweetbriar Cottage, next farm to Orchard Knob. That makes us near neighbours."

"I suppose it does," said Mollie.

Murray mentally decided that her voice was the sweetest he had ever heard. He was glad he had arranged his cow at such an angle that he could study her profile. It was amazing that Mrs. Palmer's niece should have such a profile. It looked as if centuries of fine breeding were responsible for it.

"What a morning!" he said enthusiastically. "It harks back to the days when earth was young. They must have had just such mornings as this in Eden."

"Do you always get up so early?" asked Mollie practically.

"Always," said Murray without a blush. Then—"But no, that is a fib, and I cannot tell fibs to you. The truth is your tribute. I never get up early. It was fate that roused me and brought me here this morning. The morning is a miracle—and you, I might suppose you were born of the sunrise, if Mrs. Palmer hadn't told me all about you."

"What did she tell you about me?" asked Mollie, changing cows. Murray discovered that she was tall and that the big blue print apron shrouded a singularly graceful figure.

"She said you were the best-looking girl in Bruce county. I have seen very few of the girls in Bruce county, but I know she is right."

"That compliment is not nearly so pretty as the sunrise one," said Mollie reflectively. "Mrs. Palmer has told me things about you," she added.

"Curiosity knows no gender," hinted Murray.

"She said you were good-looking and lazy and different from other people."

"All compliments," said Murray in a gratified tone.

"Lazy?"

"Certainly. Laziness is a virtue in these strenuous days, I was not born with it, but I have painstakingly acquired it, and I am proud of my success. I have time to enjoy life."

"I think that I like you," said Mollie.

"You have the merit of being able to enter into a situation," he assured her.

When the last Jersey was milked they carried the pails down to the spring where the creamers were sunk and strained the milk into them. Murray washed the pails and Mollie wiped them and set them in a gleaming row on the shelf under a big maple.

"Thank you," she said.

"You are not going yet," said Murray resolutely. "The time I saved you in milking three cows belongs to me. We will spend it in a walk along the pond shore. I will show you a path I have discovered under the beeches. It is just wide enough for two. Come."

He took her hand and drew her through the copse into a green lane, where the ferns grew thickly on either side and the pond waters plashed dreamily below them. He kept her hand in his as they went down the path, and she did not try to withdraw it. About them was the great, pure silence of the morning, faintly threaded with caressing sounds—croon of birds, gurgle of waters, sough of wind. The spirit of youth and love hovered over them and they spoke no word.

When they finally came out on a little green nook swimming in early sunshine and arched over by maples, with the wide shimmer of the pond before it and the gold dust of blossoms over the grass, the girl drew a long breath of delight.

"It is a morning left over from Eden, isn't it?" said Murray.

"Yes," said Mollie softly.

Murray bent toward her. "You are Eve," he said. "You are the only woman in the world—for me. Adam must have told Eve just what he thought about her the first time he saw her. There were no conventionalities in Eden—and people could not have taken long to make up their minds. We are in Eden just now. One can say what he thinks in Eden without being ridiculous. You are divinely fair, Eve. Your eyes are stars of the morning—your cheek has the flush it stole from the sunrise-your lips are redder than the roses of paradise. And I love you, Eve."

Mollie lowered her eyes and the long fringe of her lashes lay in a burnished semi-circle on her cheek.

"I think," she said slowly, "that it must have been very delightful in Eden. But we are not really there, you know—we are only playing that we are. And it is time for me to go back. I must get the breakfast—that sounds too prosaic for paradise."

Murray bent still closer.

"Before we remember that we are only playing at paradise, will you kiss me, dear Eve?"

"You are very audacious," said Mollie coldly.

"We are in Eden yet," he urged. "That makes all the difference."

"Well," said Mollie. And Murray kissed her.

They had passed back over the fern path and were in the pasture before either spoke again. Then Murray said, "We have left Eden behind—but we can always return there when we will. And although we were only playing at paradise, I was not playing at love. I meant all I said, Mollie."

"Have you meant it often?" asked Mollie significantly.

"I never meant it—or even played at it—before," he answered. "I did—at one time—contemplate the possibility of playing at it. But that was long ago—as long ago as last night. I am glad to the core of my soul that I decided against it before I met you, dear Eve. I have the letter of decision in my coat pocket this moment. I mean to mail it this afternoon."

"'Curiosity knows no gender,'" quoted Mollie.

"Then, to satisfy your curiosity, I must bore you with some personal history. My parents died when I was a little chap, and my uncle brought me up. He has been immensely good to me, but he is a bit of a tyrant. Recently he picked out a wife for me—the daughter of an old sweetheart of his. I have never even seen her. But she has arrived in town on a visit to some relatives there. Uncle Dick wrote to me to return home at once and pay my court to the lady; I protested. He wrote again—a letter, short and the reverse of sweet. If I refused to do my best to win Miss Mannering he would disown me—never speak to me again—cut me off with a quarter. Uncle always means what he says—that is one of our family traits, you understand. I spent some miserable, undecided days. It was not the threat of disinheritance that worried me, although when you have been brought up to regard yourself as a prospective millionaire it is rather difficult to adjust your vision to a pauper focus. But it was the thought of alienating Uncle Dick. I love the dear, determined old chap like a father. But last night my guardian angel was with me and I decided to remain my own man. So I wrote to Uncle Dick, respectfully but firmly declining to become a candidate for Miss Mannering's hand."

"But you have never seen her," said Mollie. "She may be—almost—charming."

"'If she be not fair to me, what care I how fair she be?'" quoted Murray. "As you say, she may be—almost charming; but she is not Eve. She is merely one of a million other women, as far as I am concerned. Don't let's talk of her. Let us talk only of ourselves—there is nothing else that is half so interesting."

"And will your uncle really cast you off?" asked Mollie.

"Not a doubt of it."

"What will you do?"

"Work, dear Eve. My carefully acquired laziness must be thrown to the winds and I shall work. That is the rule outside of Eden. Don't worry. I've painted pictures that have actually been sold. I'll make a living for us somehow."

"Us?"

"Of course. You are engaged to me."

"I am not," said Mollie indignantly.

"Mollie! Mollie! After that kiss! Fie, fie!"

"You are very absurd," said Mollie, "But your absurdity has been amusing. I have—yes, positively—I have enjoyed your Eden comedy. But now you must not come any further with me. My aunt might not approve. Here is my path to Orchard Knob farmhouse. There, I presume, is yours to Sweetbriar Cottage. Good morning."

"I am coming over to see you this afternoon," said Murray coolly. "But you needn't be afraid. I will not tell tales out of Eden. I will be a hypocrite and pretend to Mrs. Palmer that we have never met before. But you and I will know and remember. Now, you may go. I reserve to myself the privilege of standing here and watching you out of sight."

That afternoon Murray strolled over to Orchard Knob, going into the kitchen without knocking as was the habit in that free and easy world. Mrs. Palmer was lying on the lounge with a pungent handkerchief bound about her head, but keeping a vigilant eye on a very pretty, very plump brown-eyed girl who was stirring a kettleful of cherry preserve on the range.

"Good afternoon, Mrs. Palmer," said Murray, wondering where Mollie was. "I'm sorry to see that you look something like an invalid."

"I've a raging, ramping headache," said Mrs. Palmer solemnly. "I had it all night and I'm good for nothing. Mollie, you'd better take them cherries off. Mr. Murray, this is my niece, Mollie Booth."

"What?" said Murray explosively.

"Miss Mollie Booth," repeated Mrs. Palmer in a louder tone.

Murray regained outward self-control and bowed to the blushing Mollie.

"And what about Eve?" he thought helplessly. "Who—what was she? Did I dream her? Was she a phantom of delight? No, no, phantoms don't milk cows. She was flesh and blood. No chilly nymph exhaling from the mists of the marsh could have given a kiss like that."

"Mollie has come to stay the rest of the summer with me," said Mrs. Palmer. "I hope to goodness my tribulations with hired girls is over at last. They have made a wreck of me."

Murray rapidly reflected. This development, he decided, released him from his promise to tell no tales. "I met a young lady down in the pond pasture this morning," he said deliberately. "I talked with her for a few minutes. I supposed her to be your niece. Who was she?"

"Oh, that was Miss Mannering," said Mrs. Palmer.

"What?" said Murray again.

"Mannering—Dora Mannering," said Mrs. Palmer loudly, wondering if Mr. Murray were losing his hearing. "She came here last night just to see me. I haven't seen her since she was a child of twelve. I used to be her nurse before I was married. I was that proud to think she thought it worth her while to look me up. And, mind you, this morning, when she found me crippled with headache and not able to do a hand's turn, that girl, Mr. Murray, went and milked seven cows"—"only four," murmured Murray, but Mrs. Palmer did not hear him—"for me. Couldn't prevent her. She said she had learned to milk for fun one summer when she was in the country, and she did it. And then she got breakfast for the men—Mollie didn't come till the ten o'clock train. Miss Mannering is as capable as if she had been riz on a farm."

"Where is she now?" demanded Murray.

"Oh, she's gone."

"What?"

"Gone," shouted Mrs. Palmer, "gone. She left on the train Mollie come on. Gracious me, has the man gone crazy? He hasn't seemed like himself at all this afternoon."

Murray had bolted madly out of the house and was striding down the lane.

Blind fool—unspeakable idiot that he had been! To take her for Mrs. Palmer's niece—that peerless creature with the calm acceptance of any situation, which marked the woman of the world, with the fine appreciation and quickness of repartee that spoke of generations of culture—to imagine that she could be Mollie Booth! He had been blind, besottedly blind. And now he had lost her! She would never forgive him; she had gone without a word or sign.

As he reached the last curve of the lane where it looped about the apple trees, a plump figure came flying down the orchard slope.

"Mr. Murray, Mr. Murray," Mollie Booth called breathlessly. "Will you please come here just a minute?"

Murray crossed over to the paling rather grumpily. He did not want to talk with Mollie Booth just then. Confound it, what did the girl want? Why was she looking so mysterious?

Mollie produced a little square grey envelope from some feminine hiding place and handed it over the paling.

"She give me this at the station—Miss Mannering did," she gasped, "and asked me to give it to you without letting Aunt Emily Jane see. I couldn't get a chanst when you was in, but as soon as you went I slipped out by the porch door and followed you. You went so fast I near died trying to head you off."

"You dear little soul," said Murray, suddenly radiant. "It is too bad you have had to put yourself so out of breath on my account. But I am immensely obliged to you. The next time your young man wants a trusty private messenger just refer him to me."

"Git away with you," giggled Mollie. "I must hurry back 'fore Aunt Emily Jane gits wind I'm gone. I hope there's good news in your girl's letter. My, but didn't you look flat when Aunt said she'd went!"

Murray beamed at her idiotically. When she had vanished among the trees he opened his letter.

> "Dear Mr. Murray," it ran, "your unblushing audacity of the morning deserves some punishment. I hereby punish you by prompt departure from Orchard Knob. Yet I do not dislike audacity, at some times, in some places, in some people. It is only from a sense of duty that I punish it in this case. And it was really pleasant in Eden. If you do not mail that letter, and if you still persist in your very absurd interpretation of the meaning of Eve's kiss, we may meet again in town. Until then I remain,
>
> "Very sincerely yours,
> "Dora Lynne Mannering."

Murray kissed the grey letter and put it tenderly away in his pocket. Then he took his letter to his uncle and tore it into tiny fragments. Finally he looked at his watch.

"If I hurry, I can catch the afternoon train to town," he said.

Aunt Susanna's Birthday Celebration

Good afternoon, Nora May. I'm real glad to see you. I've been watching you coming down the hill and I hoping you'd turn in at our gate. Going to visit with me this afternoon? That's good. I'm feeling so happy and delighted and I've been hankering for someone to tell it all to.

Tell you about it? Well, I guess I might as well. It ain't any breach of confidence.

You didn't know Anne Douglas? She taught school here three years ago, afore your folks moved over from Talcott. She belonged up Montrose way and she was only eighteen when she came here to teach. She boarded with us and her and me were the greatest chums. She was just a sweet girl.

She was the prettiest teacher we ever had, and that's saying a good deal, for Springdale has always been noted for getting good-looking schoolmarms, just as Miller's Road is noted for its humly ones.

Anne had *yards* of brown wavy hair and big, dark blue eyes. Her face was kind o' pale, but when she smiled you would have to smile too, if you'd been chief mourner at your own funeral. She was a well-spring of joy in the house, and we all loved her.

Gilbert Martin began to drive her the very first week she was here. Gilbert is my sister Julia's son, and a fine young fellow he is. It ain't good manners to brag of your own relations, but I'm always forgetting and doing it. Gil was a great pet of mine. He was so bright and nice-mannered everybody liked him. Him and Anne were a fine-looking couple, Nora May. Not but what they had their shortcomings. Anne's nose was a mite too long and Gil had a crooked mouth. Besides, they was both pretty proud and sperrited and high-strung.

But they thought an awful lot of each other. It made me feel young again to see 'em. Anne wasn't a mossel vain, but nights she expected Gil she'd prink for hours afore her glass, fixing her hair this way and that, and trying on all her good clothes to see which become her most. I used to love her for it. And I used to love to see the way Gil's face would light up when she came into a room or place where he was. Amanda Perkins, she says to me once, "Anne Douglas and Gil Martin are most terrible struck on each other." And she said it in a tone that indicated that it was a dreadful disgraceful and unbecoming state of affairs. Amanda had a disappointment once and it soured her. I immediately responded, "Yes, they are most terrible struck on each other," and I said it in a tone that indicated I thought it a most beautiful and lovely thing that they should be so.

And so it was. You're rather too young to be thinking of such things, Nora May, but you'll remember my words when the time comes.

Another nephew of mine, James Ebenezer Lawson—he calls himself James E. back there in town, and I don't blame him, for I never could stand Ebenezer for a name myself; but that's neither here nor there. Well, he said their love was idyllic, I ain't very sure what that means. I looked it up in the dictionary after James Ebenezer left—I wouldn't display my ignorance afore him—but I can't say that I was much the wiser for it. Anyway, it meant something real nice; I was sure of that by the way James Ebenezer spoke and the wistful look in his eyes. James Ebenezer isn't married; he was to have been, and she died a month afore the wedding day. He was never the same man again.

Well, to get back to Gilbert and Anne. When Anne's school year ended in June she resigned and went home to get ready to be married. The wedding was to be in September, and I promised Anne faithful I'd go over to Montrose in August for two weeks and help her to get her quilts ready. Anne thought that nobody could quilt like me. I was as tickled as a girl at the thought of visiting with Anne for two weeks, but I never went; things happened before August.

I don't know rightly how the trouble began. Other folks—jealous folks—made mischief. Anne was thirty miles away and Gilbert couldn't see her every day to keep matters clear and fair. Besides, as I've said, they were both proud and high-sperrited. The upshot of it was they had a terrible quarrel and the engagement was broken.

When two people don't care overly much for each other, Nora May, a quarrel never amounts to much between them, and it's soon made up. But when they love each other better than life it cuts so deep and hurts so much that nine times out of ten they won't ever forgive each other. The more you love anybody, Nora May, the more he can hurt you. To be sure, you're too young to be thinking of such things.

It all came like a thunderclap on Gil's friends here at Greendale, because we hadn't ever suspected things were going wrong. The first thing we knew was that Anne had gone up west to teach school again at St. Mary's, eighty miles away, and Gilbert, he went out to Manitoba on a harvest excursion and stayed there. It just about broke his parents' hearts. He was their only child and they just worshipped him.

Gil and Anne both wrote to me off and on, but never a word, not so much as a name, did they say of each other. I'd 'a' writ and asked 'em the rights of the fuss if I could, in hopes of patching it up, but I can't write now—my hand is too shaky—and mebbe it was just as well, for meddling is terribly risky work in a love trouble, Nora May. Ninety-nine times out of a hundred the last state of a meddler and them she meddles with is worse than the first.

So I just set tight and said nothing, while everybody else in the clan was talking Anne and Gil sixty words to the minute.

Well, last birthday morning I was feeling terrible disperrited. I had made up my mind that my birthday was always to be a good thing for other people, and there didn't seem one blessed thing I could do to make anybody glad. Emma Matilda and George and the children were all well and happy and wanted for nothing that I could give them. I begun to be afraid I'd lived long enough, Nora May. When a woman gets to the point where she can't give a gift of joy to anyone, there ain't much use in her living. I felt real old and worn out and useless.

I was sitting here under these very trees—they was just budding out in leaf then, as young and cheerful as if they wasn't a hundred years old. And I sighed right out loud and said, "Oh, Grandpa Holland, it's time I was put away up on the hill there with you." And with that the gate banged and there was Nancy Jane Whitmore's boy, Sam, with two letters for me.

One was from Anne up at St. Mary's and the other was from Gil out in Manitoba.

I read Anne's first. She just struck right into things in the first paragraph. She said her year at St. Mary's was nearly up, and when it was she meant to quit teaching and go away to New York and learn to be a trained nurse. She said she was just broken-hearted about Gilbert, and would always love him to the day of her death. But she knew he didn't care anything more about her after the way he had acted, and there was nothing left for her in life but to do something for other people, and so on and so on, for twelve mortal pages. Anne is a fine writer, and I just cried like a babe over that letter, it was so touching, although I was enjoying myself hugely all the time, I was so delighted to find out that Anne loved Gilbert still. I was getting skeered she didn't, her letters all winter had been so kind of jokey and frivolous, all about the good times she was having, and the parties she went to, and the new dresses she got. New dresses! When I read that letter of Anne's, I knew that all the purple and fine linen in the world was just like so much sackcloth and ashes to her as long as Gilbert was sulking out on a prairie farm.

Well, I wiped my eyes and polished up my specs, but I might have spared myself the trouble, for in five minutes, Nora May, there was I sobbing again; over Gilbert's letter. By the most curious coincidence he had opened his heart to me too. Being a man, he wasn't so discursive as Anne; he said his say in four pages, but I could read the heartache between the lines. He wrote that he was going to Klondike and would start in a month's time. He was sick of living now that he'd lost Anne. He said he loved her better than his life and always would, and could never forget her, but he knew she didn't care anything about him now after the way she'd acted, and he wanted to get as far away from her and the torturing thought of her as he could. So he was going to Klondike—going to Klondike, Nora May, when his mother was writing to him to come home every week and Anne was breaking her heart for him at St. Mary's.

Well, I folded up them letters and, says I, "Grandpa Holland, I guess my birthday celebration is here ready to hand." I thought real hard. I couldn't write myself to explain to those two people that they each thought the world of each other still—my hands are too stiff; and I couldn't get anyone else to write because I couldn't let out what they'd told me in confidence. So I did a mean, dishonourable thing, Nora May. I sent Anne's letter to Gilbert and Gilbert's to Anne. I asked Emma Matilda to address them, and Emma Matilda did it and asked no questions. I brought her up that way.

Then I settled down to wait. In less than a month Gilbert's mother had a letter from him saying that he was coming home to settle down and marry Anne. He arrived home yesterday and last night Anne came to Springdale on her way home from St. Mary's. They came to see me this morning and said things to me I ain't going to repeat because they would sound fearful vain. They were so happy that they made me feel as if it was a good thing to have lived eighty years in a world where folks could be so happy. They said their new joy was my birthday gift to them. The wedding is to be in September and I'm going to Montrose in August to help Anne with her quilts. I don't think anything will happen to prevent this time—no quarrelling, anyhow. Those two young creatures have learned their lesson. You'd better take it to heart too, Nora May. It's less trouble to learn it at second hand. Don't you ever quarrel with your real beau—it don't matter about the sham ones, of course. Don't take offence at trifles or listen to what other people tell you about him—outsiders, that is, that want to make mischief. What you think about him is of more importance than what they do. To be sure, you're too young yet to be thinking of such things at all. But just mind what old Aunt Susanna told you when your time comes.

Bertie's New Year

He stood on the sagging doorstep and looked out on the snowy world. His hands were clasped behind him, and his thin face wore a thoughtful, puzzled look. The door behind him opened jerkingly, and a scowling woman came out with a pan of dishwater in her hand.

"Ain't you gone yet, Bert?" she said sharply. "What in the world are you hanging round for?"

"It's early yet," said Bertie cheerfully. "I thought maybe George Fraser'd be along and I'd get a lift as far as the store."

"Well, I never saw such laziness! No wonder old Sampson won't keep you longer than the holidays if you're no smarter than that. Goodness, if I don't settle that boy!"—as the sound of fretful crying came from the kitchen behind her.

"What is wrong with William John?" asked Bertie.

"Why, he wants to go out coasting with those Robinson boys, but he can't. He hasn't got any mittens and he would catch his death of cold again."

Her voice seemed to imply that William John had died of cold several times already.

Bertie looked soberly down at his old, well-darned mittens. It was very cold, and he would have a great many errands to run. He shivered, and looked up at his aunt's hard face as she stood wiping her dish-pan with a grim frown which boded no good to the discontented William John. Then he suddenly pulled off his mittens and held them out.

"Here—he can have mine. I'll get on without them well enough."

"Nonsense!" said Mrs. Ross, but less unkindly. "The fingers would freeze off you. Don't be a goose."

"It's all right," persisted Bertie. "I don't need them—much. And William John doesn't hardly ever get out."

He thrust them into her hand and ran quickly down the street, as though he feared that the keen air might make him change his mind in spite of himself. He had to stop a great many times that day to breathe on his purple hands. Still, he did not regret having lent his mittens to William John—poor, pale, sickly little William John, who had so few pleasures.

It was sunset when Bertie laid an armful of parcels down on the steps of Doctor Forbes's handsome house. His back was turned towards the big bay window at one side, and he was busy trying to warm his hands, so he did not see the two small faces looking at him through the frosty panes.

"Just look at that poor little boy, Amy," said the taller of the two. "He is almost frozen, I believe. Why doesn't Caroline hurry and open the door?"

"There she goes now," said Amy. "Edie, couldn't we coax her to let him come in and get warm? He looks so cold." And she drew her sister out into the hall, where the housekeeper was taking Bertie's parcels.

"Caroline," whispered Edith timidly, "please tell that poor little fellow to come in and get warm—he looks very cold."

"He's used to the cold, I warrant you," said the housekeeper rather impatiently. "It won't hurt him."

"But it is Christmas week," said Edith gravely, "and you know, Caroline, when Mamma was here she used to say that we ought to be particularly thoughtful of others who were not so happy or well-off as we were at this time."

Perhaps Edith's reference to her mother softened Caroline, for she turned to Bertie and said cordially enough, "Come in, and warm yourself before you go. It's a cold day."

Bertie shyly followed her to the kitchen.

"Sit up to the fire," said Caroline, placing a chair for him, while Edith and Amy came round to the other side of the stove and watched him with friendly interest.

"What's your name?" asked Caroline.

"Robert Ross, ma'am."

"Oh, you're Mrs. Ross's nephew then," said Caroline, breaking eggs into her cake-bowl, and whisking them deftly round. "And you're Sampson's errand boy just now? My goodness," as the boy spread his blue hands over the fire, "where are your mittens, child? You're never out without mittens a day like this!"

"I lent them to William John—he hadn't any," faltered Bertie. He did not know but that the lady might consider it a grave crime to be mittenless.

"No mittens!" exclaimed Amy in dismay. "Why, I have three pairs. And who is William John?"

"He is my cousin," said Bertie. "And he's awful sickly. He wanted to go out to play, and he hadn't any mittens, so I lent him mine. I didn't miss them—much."

"What kind of a Christmas did you have?"

"We didn't have any."

"No Christmas!" said Amy, quite overcome. "Oh, well, I suppose you are going to have a good time on New Year's instead."

Bertie shook his head.

"No'm, I guess not. We never have it different from other times."

Amy was silent from sheer amazement. Edith understood better, and she changed the subject.

"Have you any brothers or sisters, Bertie?"

"No'm," returned Bertie cheerfully. "I guess there's enough of us without that. I must be going now. I'm very much obliged to you."

Edith slipped from the room as he spoke, and met him again at the door. She held out a pair of warm-looking mittens.

"These are for William John," she said simply, "so that you can have your own. They are a pair of mine which are too big for me. I know Papa will say it is all right. Goodbye, Bertie."

"Goodbye—and thank you," stammered Bertie, as the door closed. Then he hastened home to William John.

That evening Doctor Forbes noticed a peculiarly thoughtful look on Edith's face as she sat gazing into the glowing coal fire after dinner. He laid his hand on her dark curls inquiringly.

"What are you musing over?"

"There was a little boy here today," began Edith.

"Oh, such a dear little boy," broke in Amy eagerly from the corner, where she was playing with her kitten. "His name was Bertie Ross. He brought up the parcels, and we asked him in to get warm. He had no mittens, and his hands were almost frozen. And, oh, Papa, just think!—he said he never had any Christmas or New Year at all."

"Poor little fellow!" said the doctor. "I've heard of him; a pretty hard time he has of it, I think."

"He was so pretty, Papa. And Edie gave him her blue mittens for William John."

"The plot deepens. Who is William John?"

"Oh, a cousin or something, didn't he say Edie? Anyway, he is sick, and he wanted to go coasting, and Bertie gave him his mittens. And I suppose he never had any Christmas either."

"There are plenty who haven't," said the doctor, taking up his paper with a sigh. "Well, girlies, you seem interested in this little fellow so, if you like, you may invite him and his cousin to take dinner with you on New Year's night."

"Oh, Papa!" said Edith, her eyes shining like stars.

The doctor laughed. "Write him a nice little note of invitation—you are the lady of the house, you know—and I'll see that he gets it tomorrow."

And this was how it came to pass that Bertie received the next day his first invitation to dine out. He read the little note through three times in order fully to take in its contents, and then went around the rest of the day in deep abstraction as though he was trying to decide some very important question. It was with the same expression that he opened the door at home in the evening. His aunt was stirring some oatmeal mush on the stove.

"Is that you, Bert?" She spoke sharply. She always spoke sharply, even when not intending it; it had grown to be a habit.

"Yes'm," said Bertie meekly, as he hung up his cap.

"I s'pose you've only got one day more at the store," said Mrs. Ross. "Sampson didn't say anything about keeping you longer, did he?"

"No. He said he couldn't—I asked him."

"Well, I didn't expect he would. You'll have a holiday on New Year's anyhow; whether you'll have anything to eat or not is a different question."

"I've an invitation to dinner," said Bertie timidly, "me and William John. It's from Doctor Forbes's little girls—the ones that gave me the mittens."

He handed her the little note, and Mrs. Ross stooped down and read it by the fitful gleam of light which came from the cracked stove.

"Well, you can please yourself," she said as she handed it back, "but William John couldn't go if he had ten invitations. He caught cold coasting yesterday. I told him he would, but he was bound to go, and now he's laid up for a week. Listen to him barking in the bedroom there."

"Well, then, I won't go either," said Bertie with a sigh, it might be of relief, or it might be of disappointment. "I wouldn't go there all alone."

"You're a goose!" said his aunt. "They wouldn't eat you. But as I said, please yourself. Anyhow, hold your tongue about it to William John, or you'll have him crying and bawling to go too."

The caution came too late. William John had already heard it, and when his mother went in to rub his chest with liniment, she found him with the ragged quilt over his head crying.

"Come, William John, I want to rub you."

"I don't want to be rubbed—g'way," sobbed William John. "I heard you out there—you needn't think I didn't. Bertie's going to Doctor Forbes's to dinner and I can't go."

"Well, you've only yourself to thank for it," returned his mother. "If you hadn't persisted in going out coasting yesterday when I wanted you to stay in, you'd have been able to go to Doctor Forbes's. Little boys who won't do as they're told always get into trouble. Stop crying, now. I dare say if Bertie goes they'll send you some candy, or something."

But William John refused to be comforted. He cried himself to sleep that night, and when Bertie went in to see him next morning, he found him sitting up in bed with his eyes red and swollen and the faded quilt drawn up around his pinched face.

"Well, William John, how are you?"

"I ain't any better," replied William John mournfully. "I s'pose you'll have a great time tomorrow night, Bertie?"

"Oh, I'm not going since you can't," said Bertie cheerily. He thought this would comfort William John, but it had exactly the opposite effect. William John had cried until he could cry no more, but he turned around and sobbed.

"There now!" he said in tearless despair. "That's just what I expected. I did s'pose if I couldn't go you would, and tell me about it. You're mean as mean can be."

"Come now, William John, don't be so cross. I thought you'd rather have me home, but I'll go, if you want me to."

"Honest, now?"

"Yes, honest. I'll go anywhere to please you. I must be off to the store now. Goodbye."

Thus committed, Bertie took his courage in both hands and went. The next evening at dusk found him standing at Doctor Forbes's door with a very violently beating heart. He was carefully dressed in his well-worn best suit and a neat white collar. The frosty air had crimsoned his cheeks and his hair was curling round his face.

Caroline opened the door and showed him into the parlour, where Edith and Amy were eagerly awaiting him.

"Happy New Year, Bertie," cried Amy. "And—but, why, where is William John?"

"He couldn't come," answered Bertie anxiously—he was afraid he might not be welcome without William John. "He's real sick. He caught cold and has to stay in bed; but he wanted to come awful bad."

"Oh, dear me! Poor William John!" said Amy in a disappointed tone. But all further remarks were cut short by the entrance of Doctor Forbes.

"How do you do?" he said, giving Bertie's hand a hearty shake. "But where is the other little fellow my girls were expecting?"

Bertie patiently reaccounted for William John's non-appearance.

"It's a bad time for colds," said the doctor, sitting down and attacking the fire. "I dare say, though, you have to run so fast these days that a cold couldn't catch you. I suppose you'll soon be leaving Sampson's. He told me he didn't need you after the holiday season was over. What are you going at next? Have you anything in view?"

Bertie shook his head sorrowfully.

"No, sir; but," he added more cheerfully, "I guess I'll find something if I hunt around lively. I almost always do."

He forgot his shyness; his face flushed hopefully, and he looked straight at the doctor with his bright, earnest eyes. The doctor poked the fire energetically and looked very wise. But just then the girls came up and carried Bertie off to display their holiday gifts. And there was a fur cap and a pair of mittens for him! He wondered whether he was dreaming.

"And here's a picture-book for William John," said Amy, "and there is a sled out in the kitchen for him. Oh, there's the dinner-bell. I'm awfully hungry. Papa says that is my 'normal condition,' but I don't know what that means."

As for that dinner—Bertie might sometimes have seen such a repast in delightful dreams, but certainly never out of them. It was a feast to be dated from.

When the plum pudding came on, the doctor, who had been notably silent, leaned back in his chair, placed his finger-tips together, and looked critically at Bertie.

"So Mr. Sampson can't keep you?"

Bertie's face sobered at once. He had almost forgotten his responsibilities.

"No, sir. He says I'm too small for the heavy work."

"Well, you are rather small—but no doubt you will grow. Boys have a queer habit of doing that. I think you know how to make yourself useful. I need a boy here to run errands and look after my horse. If you like, I'll try you. You can live here, and go to school. I sometimes hear of places for boys in my rounds, and the first good one that will suit you, I'll bespeak for you. How will that do?"

"Oh, sir, you are too good," said Bertie with a choke in his voice.

"Well, that is settled," said the doctor genially. "Come on Monday then. And perhaps we can do something for that other little chap, William, or John, or whatever his name is. Will you have some more pudding, Bertie?"

"No, thank you," said Bertie. Pudding, indeed! He could not have eaten another mouthful after such wonderful and unexpected good fortune.

After dinner they played games, and cracked nuts, and roasted apples, until the clock struck nine; then Bertie got up to go.

"Off, are you?" said the doctor, looking up from his paper. "Well, I'll expect you on Monday, remember."

"Yes, sir," said Bertie happily. He was not likely to forget.

As he went out Amy came through the hall with a red sled.

"Here is William John's present. I've tied all the other things on so that they can't fall off."

Edith was at the door-with a parcel. "Here are some nuts and candies for William John," she said. "And tell him we all wish him a 'Happy New Year.'"

"Thank you," said Bertie. "I've had a splendid time. I'll tell William John. Goodnight."

He stepped out. It was frostier than ever. The snow crackled and snapped, the stars were keen and bright, but to Bertie, running down the street with William John's sled thumping merrily behind him, the world was aglow with rosy hope and promise. He was quite sure he could never forget this wonderful New Year.

Between the Hill and the Valley

It was one of the moist, pleasantly odorous nights of early spring. There was a chill in the evening air, but the grass was growing green in sheltered spots, and Jeffrey Miller had found purple-petalled violets and pink arbutus on the hill that day. Across a valley filled with beech and fir, there was a sunset afterglow, creamy yellow and pale red, with a new moon swung above it. It was a night for a man to walk alone and dream of his love, which was perhaps why Jeffrey Miller came so loiteringly across the springy hill pasture, with his hands full of the mayflowers.

He was a tall, broad-shouldered man of forty, and looking no younger, with dark grey eyes and a tanned, clean-cut face, clean-shaven save for a drooping moustache. Jeffrey Miller was considered a handsome man, and Bayside people had periodical fits of wondering why he had never married. They pitied him for the lonely life he must lead alone there at the Valley Farm, with only a deaf old housekeeper as a companion, for it did not occur to the Bayside people in general that a couple of shaggy dogs could be called companions, and they did not know that books make very excellent comrades for people who know how to treat them.

One of Jeffrey's dogs was with him now—the oldest one, with white breast and paws and a tawny coat. He was so old that he was half-blind and rather deaf, but, with one exception, he was the dearest of living creatures to Jeffrey Miller, for Sara Stuart had given him the sprawly, chubby little pup years ago.

They came down the hill together. A group of men were standing on the bridge in the hollow, discussing Colonel Stuart's funeral of the day before. Jeffrey caught Sara's name and paused on the outskirts of the group to listen. Sometimes he thought that if he were lying dead under six feet of turf and Sara Stuart's name were pronounced above him, his heart would give a bound of life.

"Yes, the old kunnel's gone at last," Christopher Jackson was saying. "He took his time dyin', that's sartain. Must be a kind of relief for Sara—she's had to wait on him, hand and foot, for years. But no doubt she'll feel pretty lonesome. Wonder what she'll do?"

"Is there any particular reason for her to do anything?" asked Alec Churchill.

"Well, she'll have to leave Pinehurst. The estate's entailed and goes to her cousin, Charles Stuart."

There were exclamations of surprise from the other men on hearing this. Jeffrey drew nearer, absently patting his dog's head. He had not known it either.

"Oh, yes," said Christopher, enjoying all the importance of exclusive information. "I thought everybody knew that. Pinehurst goes to the oldest male heir. The old kunnel felt it keen that he hadn't a son. Of course, there's plenty of money and Sara'll get that. But I guess she'll feel pretty bad at leaving her old home. Sara ain't as young as she used to be, neither. Let me see—she must be thirty-eight. Well, she's left pretty lonesome."

"Maybe she'll stay on at Pinehurst," said Job Crowe. "It'd only be right for her cousin to give her a home there."

Christopher shook his head.

"No, I understand they're not on very good terms. Sara don't like Charles Stuart or his wife—and I don't blame her. She won't stay there, not likely. Probably she'll go and live in town. Strange she never married. She was reckoned handsome, and had plenty of beaus at one time."

Jeffrey swung out of the group and started homeward with his dog. To stand by and hear Sara Stuart discussed after this fashion was more than he could endure. The men idly watched his tall, erect figure as he went along the valley.

"Queer chap, Jeff," said Alec Churchill reflectively.

"Jeff's all right," said Christopher in a patronizing way. "There ain't a better man or neighbour alive. I've lived next farm to him for thirty years, so I ought to know. But he's queer sartainly—not like other people—kind of unsociable. He don't care for a thing 'cept dogs and reading and mooning round woods and fields. That ain't natural, you know. But I must say he's a good farmer. He's got the best farm in Bayside, and that's a real nice house he put up on it. Ain't it an odd thing he never married? Never seemed to have no notion of it. I can't recollect of Jeff Miller's ever courting anybody. That's another unnatural thing about him."

"I've always thought that Jeff thought himself a cut or two above the rest of us," said Tom Scovel with a sneer. "Maybe he thinks the Bayside girls ain't good enough for him."

"There ain't no such dirty pride about Jeff," pronounced Christopher conclusively. "And the Millers *are* the best family hereabouts, leaving the kunnel's out. And Jeff's well off—nobody knows how well, I reckon, but I can guess, being his land neighbour. Jeff ain't no fool nor loafer, if he is a bit queer."

Meanwhile, the object of these remarks was striding homeward and thinking, not of the men behind him, but of Sara Stuart. He must go to her at once. He had not intruded on her since her father's death, thinking her sorrow too great for him to meddle with. But this was different. Perhaps she needed the advice or assistance only he could give. To whom else in Bayside could she turn for it but to him, her old friend? Was it possible that she must leave Pinehurst? The thought struck cold dismay to his soul. How could he bear his life if she went away?

He had loved Sara Stuart from childhood. He remembered vividly the day he had first seen her—a spring day, much like this one had been; he, a boy of eight, had gone with his father to the big, sunshiny hill field and he had searched for birds' nests in the little fir copses along the crest while his father plowed. He had so come upon her, sitting on the fence under the pines at the back of Pinehurst—a child of six in a dress of purple cloth. Her long, light brown curls fell over her shoulders and rippled sleekly back from her calm little brow; her eyes were large and greyish blue, straight-gazing and steadfast. To the end of his life the boy was to carry in his heart the picture she made there under the pines.

"Little boy," she had said, with a friendly smile, "will you show me where the mayflowers grow?"

Shyly enough he had assented, and they set out together for the barrens beyond the field, where the arbutus trailed its stars of sweetness under the dusty dead grasses and withered leaves of the old year. The boy was thrilled with delight. She was a fairy queen who thus graciously smiled on him and chattered blithely as they searched for mayflowers in the fresh spring sunshine. He thought it a wonderful thing that it had so chanced. It overjoyed him to give the choicest dusters he found into her slim, waxen little fingers, and watch her eyes grow round with pleasure in them. When the sun began to lower over the beeches she had gone home with her arms full of arbutus, but she had turned at the edge of the pineland and waved her hand at him.

That night, when he told his mother of the little girl he had met on the hill, she had hoped anxiously that he had been "very polite," for the little girl was a daughter of Colonel Stuart, newly come to Pinehurst. Jeffrey, reflecting, had not been certain that he had been polite; "But I am sure she liked me," he said gravely.

A few days later a message came from Mrs. Stuart on the hill to Mrs. Miller in the valley. Would she let her little boy go up now and then to play with Sara? Sara was very lonely because she had no playmates. So Jeff, overjoyed, had gone to his divinity's very home, where the two children played together many a day. All through their childhood they had been fast friends. Sara's parents placed no bar to their intimacy. They had soon concluded that little Jeff Miller was a very good playmate for Sara. He was gentle, well-behaved, and manly.

Sara never went to the district school which Jeff attended; she had her governess at home. With no other boy or girl in Bayside did she form any friendship, but her loyalty to Jeff never wavered. As for Jeff, he worshipped her and would have done anything she commanded. He belonged to her from the day they had hunted arbutus on the hill.

When Sara was fifteen she had gone away to school. Jeff had missed her sorely. For four years he saw her only in the summers, and each year she had seemed taller, statelier, further from him. When she graduated her father took her abroad for two years; then she came home, a lovely, high-bred girl, dimpling on the threshold of womanhood; and Jeffrey Miller was face to face with two bitter facts. One was that he loved her—not with the boy-and-girl love of long ago, but with the love of a man for the one woman in the world; and the other was that she was as far beyond his reach as one of those sunset stars of which she had always reminded him in her pure, clear-shining loveliness.

He looked these facts unflinchingly in the face until he had grown used to them, and then he laid down his course for himself. He loved Sara—and he did not wish to conquer his love, even if it had been possible. It were better to love her, whom he could never win, than to love and be loved by any other woman. His great office in life was to be her friend, humble and unexpectant; to be at hand if she should need him for ever so trifling a service; never to presume, always to be faithful.

Sara had not forgotten her old friend. But their former comradeship was now impossible; they could be friends, but never again companions. Sara's life was full and gay; she had interests in which he had no share; her social world was utterly apart from his; she was of the hill and its traditions, he was of the valley and its people. The democracy of childhood past, there was no common ground on which they might meet. Only one thing Jeffrey had found it impossible to contemplate calmly. Some day Sara would marry—a man who was her equal, who sat at her father's table as a guest. In spite of himself, Jeffrey's heart filled with hot rebellion at the thought; it was like a desecration and a robbery.

But, as the years went by, this thing he dreaded did not happen. Sara did not marry, although gossip assigned her many suitors not unworthy of her. She and Jeffrey were always friends, although they met but seldom. Sometimes she sent him a book; it was his custom to search for the earliest mayflowers and take them to her; once in a long while they met and talked of many things. Jeffrey's calendar from year to year was red-lettered by these small happenings, of which nobody knew, or, knowing, would have cared.

So he and Sara drifted out of youth, together yet apart. Her mother had died, and Sara was the gracious, stately mistress of Pinehurst, which grew quieter as the time went on; the lovers ceased to come, and holiday friends grew few; with the old colonel's failing health the gaieties and lavish entertaining ceased. Jeffrey thought that Sara must often be lonely, but she never said so; she remained sweet, serene, calm-eyed, like the child he had met on the hill. Only, now and then, Jeffrey fancied he saw a shadow on her face—a shadow so faint and fleeting that only the eye of an unselfish, abiding love, made clear-sighted by patient years, could have seen it. It hurt him, that shadow; he would have given anything in his power to have banished it.

And now this long friendship was to be broken. Sara was going away. At first he had thought only of her pain, but now his own filled his heart. How could he live without her? How could he dwell in the valley knowing that she had gone from the hill? Never to see her light shine down on him through the northern gap in the pines at night! Never to feel that perhaps her eyes rested on him now and then as he went about his work in the valley fields! Never to stoop with a glad thrill over the first spring flowers because it was his privilege to take them to her! Jeffrey groaned aloud. No, he could not go up to see her that night; he must wait—he must strengthen himself.

Then his heart rebuked him. This was selfishness; this was putting his own feelings before hers—a thing he had sworn never to do. Perhaps she needed him—perhaps she had wondered why he had not come to offer her such poor service as might be in his power. He turned and went down through the orchard lane, taking the old field-path across the valley and up the hill, which he had traversed so often and so joyfully in boyhood. It was dark now, and a few stars were shining in the silvery sky. The wind sighed among the pines as he walked under them. Sometimes he felt that he must turn back—that his pain was going to master him; then he forced himself to go on.

The old grey house where Sara lived seemed bleak and stricken in the dull light, with its leafless vines clinging to it. There were no lights in it. It looked like a home left soulless.

Jeffrey went around to the garden door and knocked. He had expected the maid to open it, put Sara herself came.

"Why, Jeff," she said, with pleasure in her tones. "I am so glad to see you. I have been wondering why you had not come before."

"I did not think you would want to see me yet," he said hurriedly. "I have thought about you every hour—but I feared to intrude."

"*You* couldn't intrude," she said gently. "Yes, I have wanted to see you, Jeff. Come into the library."

He followed her into the room where they had always sat in his rare calls. Sara lighted the lamp on the table. As the light shot up she stood clearly revealed in it—a tall, slender woman in a trailing gown of grey. Even a stranger, not knowing her age, would have guessed it to be what it was, yet it would have been hard to say what gave the impression of maturity. Her face was quite unlined—a little pale, perhaps, with more finely cut outlines than those of youth. Her eyes were clear and bright; her abundant brown hair waved back from her face in the same curves that Jeffrey had noted in the purple-gowned child of six, under the pines. Perhaps it was the fine patience and serenity in her face that told her tale of years. Youth can never acquire it.

Her eyes brightened when she saw the mayflowers he carried. She came and took them from him, and her hands touched his, sending a little thrill of joy through him.

"How lovely they are! And the first I have seen this spring. You always bring me the first, don't you, Jeff? Do you remember the first day we spent picking mayflowers together?"

Jeff smiled. Could he forget? But something held him back from speech.

Sara put the flowers in a vase on the table, but slipped one starry pink cluster into the lace on her breast. She came and sat down beside Jeffrey; he saw that her beautiful eyes had been weeping, and that there were lines of pain around her lips. Some impulse that would not be denied made him lean over and take her hand. She left it unresistingly in his clasp.

"I am very lonely now, Jeff," she said sadly. "Father has gone. I have no friends left."

"You have me," said Jeffrey quietly.

"Yes. I shouldn't have said that. You are my friend, I know, Jeff. But, but—I must leave Pinehurst, you know."

"I learned that tonight for the first time," he answered.

"Did you ever come to a place where *everything* seemed ended—where it seemed that there was nothing—simply nothing—left, Jeff?" she said wistfully. "But, no, it couldn't seem so to a man. Only a woman could fully understand what I mean. That is how I feel now. While I had Father to live for it wasn't so hard. But now there is nothing. And I must go away."

"Is there anything I can do?" muttered Jeffrey miserably. He knew now that he had made a mistake in coming tonight; he could not help her. His own pain had unmanned him. Presently he would say something foolish or selfish in spite of himself.

Sara turned her eyes on him.

"There is nothing anybody can do, Jeff," she said piteously. Her eyes, those clear child-eyes, filled with tears. "I shall be braver—stronger—after a while. But just now I have no strength left. I feel like a lost, helpless child. Oh, Jeff!"

She put her slender hands over her face and sobbed. Every sob cut Jeffrey to the heart.

"Don't—don't, Sara," he said huskily. "I can't bear to see you suffer so. I'd die for you if it would do you any good. I love you—I love you! I never meant to tell you so, but it is the truth. I oughtn't to tell you now. Don't think that I'm trying to take any advantage of your loneliness and sorrow. I know—I have always known—that you are far above me. But that couldn't prevent my loving you—just humbly loving you, asking nothing else. You may be angry with my presumption, but I can't help telling you that I love you. That's all. I just want you to know it."

Sara had turned away her head. Jeffrey was overcome with contrition. Ah, he had no business to speak so—he had spoiled the devotion of years. Who was he that he should have dared to love her? Silence alone had justified his love, and now he had lost that justification. She would despise him. He had forfeited her friendship for ever.

"Are you angry, Sara?" he questioned sadly, after a silence.

"I think I am," said Sara. She kept her stately head averted. "If—if you have loved me, Jeff, why did you never tell me so before?"

"How could I dare?" he said gravely. "I knew I could never win you—that I had no right to dream of you so. Oh, Sara, don't be angry! My love has been reverent and humble. I have asked nothing. I ask nothing now but your friendship. Don't take that from me, Sara. Don't be angry with me."

"I *am* angry," repeated Sara, "and I think I have a right to be."

"Perhaps so," he said simply, "but not because I have loved you. Such love as mine ought to anger no woman, Sara. But you have a right to be angry with me for presuming to put it into words. I should not have done so—but I could not help it. It rushed to my lips in spite of me. Forgive me."

"I don't know whether I can forgive you for not telling me before," said Sara steadily. "*That* is what I have to forgive—not your speaking at last, even if it was dragged from you against your will. Did you think I would make you such a very poor wife, Jeff, that you would not ask me to marry you?"

"Sara!" he said, aghast. "I—I—you were as far above me as a star in the sky—I never dreamed—I never hoped——"

"That I could care for you?" said Sara, looking round at last. "Then you were more modest than a man ought to be, Jeff. I did not know that you loved me, or I should have found some way to make you speak out long ago. I should not have let you waste all these years. I've loved you—ever since we picked mayflowers on the hill, I think—ever since I came home from school, I know. I never cared for anyone else—although I tried to, when I thought you didn't care for me. It mattered nothing to me that the world may have thought there was some social difference between us. There, Jeff, you cannot accuse me of not making my meaning plain."

"Sara," he whispered, wondering, bewildered, half-afraid to believe this unbelievable joy. "I'm not half worthy of you—but—but"—he bent forward and put his arm around her, looking straight into her clear, unshrinking eyes. "Sara, will you be my wife?"

"Yes." She said the word clearly and truly. "And I will think myself a proud and happy and honoured woman to be so, Jeff. Oh, I don't shrink from telling you the truth, you see. You mean too much to me for me to dissemble it. I've hidden it for eighteen years because I didn't think you wanted to hear it, but I'll give myself the delight of saying it frankly now."

She lifted her delicate, high-bred face, fearless love shining in every lineament, to his, and they exchanged their first kiss.

Clorinda's Gifts

"It is a dreadful thing to be poor a fortnight before Christmas," said Clorinda, with the mournful sigh of seventeen years.

Aunt Emmy smiled. Aunt Emmy was sixty, and spent the hours she didn't spend in a bed, on a sofa or in a wheel chair; but Aunt Emmy was never heard to sigh.

"I suppose it is worse then than at any other time," she admitted.

That was one of the nice things about Aunt Emmy. She always sympathized and understood.

"I'm worse than poor this Christmas ... I'm stony broke," said Clorinda dolefully. "My spell of fever in the summer and the consequent doctor's bills have cleaned out my coffers completely. Not a single Christmas present can I give. And I did so want to give some little thing to each of my dearest people. But I simply can't afford it ... that's the hateful, ugly truth."

Clorinda sighed again.

"The gifts which money can purchase are not the only ones we can give," said Aunt Emmy gently, "nor the best, either."

"Oh, I know it's nicer to give something of your own work," agreed Clorinda, "but materials for fancy work cost too. That kind of gift is just as much out of the question for me as any other."

"That was not what I meant," said Aunt Emmy.

"What did you mean, then?" asked Clorinda, looking puzzled.

Aunt Emmy smiled.

"Suppose you think out my meaning for yourself," she said. "That would be better than if I explained it. Besides, I don't think I *could* explain it. Take the beautiful line of a beautiful poem to help you in your thinking out: 'The gift without the giver is bare.'"

"I'd put it the other way and say, 'The giver without the gift is bare,'" said Clorinda, with a grimace. "That is my predicament exactly. Well, I hope by next Christmas I'll not be quite bankrupt. I'm going into Mr. Callender's store down at Murraybridge in February. He has offered me the place, you know."

"Won't your aunt miss you terribly?" said Aunt Emmy gravely.

Clorinda flushed. There was a note in Aunt Emmy's voice that disturbed her.

"Oh, yes, I suppose she will," she answered hurriedly. "But she'll get used to it very soon. And I will be home every Saturday night, you know. I'm dreadfully tired of being poor, Aunt Emmy, and now that I have a chance to earn something for myself I mean to take it. I can help Aunt Mary, too. I'm to get four dollars a week."

"I think she would rather have your companionship than a part of your salary, Clorinda," said Aunt Emmy. "But of course you must decide for yourself, dear. It is hard to be poor. I know it. I am poor."

"You poor!" said Clorinda, kissing her. "Why, you are the richest woman I know, Aunt Emmy—rich in love and goodness and contentment."

"And so are you, dearie ... rich in youth and health and happiness and ambition. Aren't they all worth while?"

"Of course they are," laughed Clorinda. "Only, unfortunately, Christmas gifts can't be coined out of them."

"Did you ever try?" asked Aunt Emmy. "Think out that question, too, in your thinking out, Clorinda."

"Well, I must say bye-bye and run home. I feel cheered up—you always cheer people up, Aunt Emmy. How grey it is outdoors. I do hope we'll have snow soon. Wouldn't it be jolly to have a white Christmas? We always have such faded brown Decembers."

Clorinda lived just across the road from Aunt Emmy in a tiny white house behind some huge willows. But Aunt Mary lived there too—the only relative Clorinda had, for Aunt Emmy wasn't really her aunt at all. Clorinda had always lived with Aunt Mary ever since she could remember.

Clorinda went home and upstairs to her little room under the eaves, where the great bare willow boughs were branching athwart her windows. She was thinking over what Aunt Emmy had said about Christmas gifts and giving.

"I'm sure I don't know what she could have meant," pondered Clorinda. "I do wish I could find out if it would help me any. I'd love to remember a few of my friends at least. There's Miss Mitchell ... she's been so good to me all this year and helped me so much with my studies. And there's Mrs. Martin out in Manitoba. If I could only send her something! She must be so lonely out there. And Aunt Emmy herself, of course; and poor old Aunt Kitty down the lane; and Aunt Mary and, yes—Florence too, although she did treat me so meanly. I shall never feel the same to her again. But she gave me a present last Christmas, and so out of mere politeness I ought to give her something."

Clorinda stopped short suddenly. She had just remembered that she would not have liked to say that last sentence to Aunt Emmy. Therefore, there was something wrong about it. Clorinda had long ago learned that there was sure to be something wrong in anything that could not be said to Aunt Emmy. So she stopped to think it over.

Clorinda puzzled over Aunt Emmy's meaning for four days and part of three nights. Then all at once it came to her. Or if it wasn't Aunt Emmy's meaning it was a very good meaning in itself, and it grew clearer and expanded in meaning during the days that followed, although at first Clorinda shrank a little from some of the conclusions to which it led her.

"I've solved the problem of my Christmas giving for this year," she told Aunt Emmy. "I have some things to give after all. Some of them quite costly, too; that is, they will cost me something, but I know I'll be better off and richer after I've paid the price. That is what Mr. Grierson would call a paradox, isn't it? I'll explain all about it to you on Christmas Day."

On Christmas Day, Clorinda went over to Aunt Emmy's. It was a faded brown Christmas after all, for the snow had not come. But Clorinda did not mind; there was such joy in her heart that she thought it the most delightful Christmas Day that ever dawned.

She put the queer cornery armful she carried down on the kitchen floor before she went into the sitting room. Aunt Emmy was lying on the sofa before the fire, and Clorinda sat down beside her.

"I've come to tell you all about it," she said.

Aunt Emmy patted the hand that was in her own.

"From your face, dear girl, it will be pleasant hearing and telling," she said.

Clorinda nodded.

"Aunt Emmy, I thought for days over your meaning ... thought until I was dizzy. And then one evening it just came to me, without any thinking at all, and I knew that I could give some gifts after all. I thought of something new every day for a week. At first I didn't think I *could* give some of them, and then I thought how selfish I was. I would have been willing to pay any amount of money for gifts if I had had it, but I wasn't willing to pay what I had. I got over that, though, Aunt Emmy. Now I'm going to tell you what I did give.

"First, there was my teacher, Miss Mitchell. I gave her one of father's books. I have so many of his, you know, so that I wouldn't miss one; but still it was one I loved very much, and so I felt that that love made it worth while. That is, I felt that on second thought. At first, Aunt Emmy, I thought I would be ashamed to offer Miss Mitchell a shabby old book, worn with much reading and all marked over with father's notes and pencillings. I was afraid she would think it queer of me to give her such a present. And yet somehow it seemed to me that it was better than something brand new and unmellowed—that old book which father had loved and which I loved. So I gave it to her, and she understood. I think it pleased her so much, the real meaning in it. She said it was like being given something out of another's heart and life.

"Then you know Mrs. Martin ... last year she was Miss Hope, my dear Sunday School teacher. She married a home missionary, and they are in a lonely part of the west. Well, I wrote her a letter. Not just an ordinary letter; dear me, no. I took a whole day to write it, and you should have seen the postmistress's eyes stick out when I mailed it. I just told her everything that had happened in Greenvale since she went away. I made it as newsy and cheerful and loving as I possibly could. Everything bright and funny I could think of went into it.

"The next was old Aunt Kitty. You know she was my nurse when I was a baby, and she's very fond of me. But, well, you know, Aunt Emmy, I'm ashamed to confess it, but really I've never found Aunt Kitty very entertaining, to put it mildly. She is always glad when I go to see her, but I've never gone except when I couldn't help it. She is very deaf, and rather dull and stupid, you know. Well, I gave her a whole day. I took my knitting yesterday, and sat with her the whole time and just talked and talked. I told her all the Greenvale news and gossip and everything else I thought she'd like to hear. She was so pleased and proud; she told me when I came away that she hadn't had such a nice time for years.

"Then there was ... Florence. You know, Aunt Emmy, we were always intimate friends until last year. Then Florence once told Rose Watson something I had told her in confidence. I found it out and I was so hurt. I couldn't forgive Florence, and I told her plainly I could never be a real friend to her again. Florence felt badly, because she really did love me, and she asked me to forgive her, but it seemed as if I couldn't. Well, Aunt Emmy, that was my Christmas gift to her ... my forgiveness. I went down last night and just put my arms around her and told her that I loved her as much as ever and wanted to be real close friends again.

"I gave Aunt Mary her gift this morning. I told her I wasn't going to Murraybridge, that I just meant to stay home with her. She was so glad—and I'm glad, too, now that I've decided so."

"Your gifts have been real gifts, Clorinda," said Aunt Emmy. "Something of you—the best of you—went into each of them."

Clorinda went out and brought her cornery armful in.

"I didn't forget you, Aunt Emmy," she said, as she unpinned the paper.

There was a rosebush—Clorinda's own pet rosebush—all snowed over with fragrant blossoms.

Aunt Emmy loved flowers. She put her finger under one of the roses and kissed it.

"It's as sweet as yourself, dear child," she said tenderly. "And it will be a joy to me all through the lonely winter days. You've found out the best meaning of Christmas giving, haven't you, dear?"

"Yes, thanks to you, Aunt Emmy," said Clorinda softly.

Cyrilla's Inspiration

It was a rainy Saturday afternoon and all the boarders at Mrs. Plunkett's were feeling dull and stupid, especially the Normal School girls on the third floor, Cyrilla Blair and Carol Hart and Mary Newton, who were known as The Trio, and shared the big front room together.

They were sitting in that front room, scowling out at the weather. At least, Carol and Mary were scowling. Cyrilla never scowled; she was sitting curled up on her bed with her Greek grammar, and she smiled at the rain and her grumbling chums as cheerfully as possible.

"For pity's sake, Cyrilla, put that grammar away," moaned Mary. "There is something positively uncanny about a girl who can study Greek on Saturday afternoons—at least, this early in the term."

"I'm not really studying," said Cyrilla, tossing the book away. "I'm only pretending to. I'm really just as bored and lonesome as you are. But what else is there to do? We can't stir outside the door; we've nothing to read; we can't make candy since Mrs. Plunkett has forbidden us to use the oil stove in our room; we'll probably quarrel all round if we sit here in idleness; so I've been trying to brush up my Greek verbs by way of keeping out of mischief. Have you any better employment to offer me?"

"If it were only a mild drizzle we might go around and see the Patterson girls," sighed Carol. "But there is no venturing out in such a downpour. Cyrilla, you are supposed to be the brainiest one of us. Prove your claim to such pre-eminence by thinking of some brand-new amusement, especially suited to rainy afternoons. That will be putting your grey matter to better use than squandering it on Greek verbs out of study limits."

"If only I'd got a letter from home today," said Mary, who seemed determined to persist in gloom. "I wouldn't mind the weather. Letters are such cheery things:—especially the letters my sister writes. They're so full of fun and nice little news. The reading of one cheers me up for the day. Cyrilla Blair, what is the matter? You nearly frightened me to death!" Cyrilla had bounded from her bed to the centre of the floor, waving her Greek grammar wildly in the air.

"Girls, I have an inspiration!" she exclaimed.

"Good! Let's hear it," said Carol.

"Let's write letters—rainy-day letters—to everyone in the house," said Cyrilla. "You may depend all the rest of the folks under Mrs. Plunkett's hospitable roof are feeling more or less blue and lonely too, as well as ourselves. Let's write them the jolliest, nicest letters we can compose and get Nora Jane to take them to their rooms. There's that pale little sewing girl, I don't believe she ever gets letters from anybody, and Miss Marshall, I'm sure *she* doesn't, and poor old Mrs. Johnson, whose only son died last month, and the new music teacher who came yesterday, a letter of welcome to her—and old Mr. Grant, yes, and Mrs. Plunkett too, thanking her for all her kindness to us. You knew she has been awfully nice to us in spite of the oil stove ukase. That's six—two apiece. Let's do it, girls."

Cyrilla's sudden enthusiasm for her plan infected the others.

"It's a nice idea," said Mary, brightening up. "But who's to write to whom? I'm willing to take anybody but Miss Marshall. I couldn't write a line to her to save my life. She'd be horrified at anything funny or jokey and our letters will have to be mainly nonsense—nonsense of the best brand, to be sure, but still nonsense."

"Better leave Miss Marshall out," suggested Carol. "You know she disapproves of us anyhow. She'd probably resent a letter of the sort, thinking we were trying to play some kind of joke on her."

"It would never do to leave her out," said Cyrilla decisively. "Of course, she's a bit queer and unamiable, but, girls, think of thirty years of boarding-house life, even with the best of Plunketts. Wouldn't that sour anybody? You know it would. You'd be cranky and grumbly and disagreeable too, I dare say. I'm really sorry for Miss Marshall. She's had a very hard life. Mrs. Plunkett told me all about her one day. I don't think we should mind her biting little speeches and sharp looks. And anyway, even if she is really as disagreeable as she sometimes seems to be, why, it must make it all the harder for her, don't you think? So she needs a letter most of all. I'll write to her, since it's my suggestion. We'll draw lots for the others."

Besides Miss Marshall, the new music teacher fell to Cyrilla's share. Mary drew Mrs. Plunkett and the dressmaker, and Carol drew Mrs. Johnson and old Mr. Grant. For the next two hours the girls wrote busily, forgetting all about the rainy day, and enjoying their epistolary labours to the full. It was dusk when all the letters were finished.

"Why, hasn't the afternoon gone quickly after all!" exclaimed Carol. "I just let my pen run on and jotted down any good working idea that came into my head. Cyrilla Blair, that big fat letter is never for Miss Marshall! What on earth did you find to write her?"

"It wasn't so hard when I got fairly started," said Cyrilla, smiling. "Now, let's hunt up Nora Jane and send the letters around so that everybody can read his or hers before tea-time. We should have a choice assortment of smiles at the table instead of all those frowns and sighs we had at dinner." Miss Emily Marshall was at that moment sitting in her little back room, all alone in the dusk, with the rain splashing drearily against the windowpanes outside. Miss Marshall was feeling as lonely and dreary as she looked—and as she had often felt in her life of sixty years. She told herself bitterly that she hadn't a friend in the world—not even one who cared enough for her to come and see her or write her a letter now and then. She thought her boarding-house acquaintances disliked her and she resented their dislike, without admitting to herself that her ungracious ways were responsible for it. She smiled sourly when little ripples of laughter came faintly down the hall from the front room where The Trio were writing their letters and laughing over the fun they were putting into them.

"If they were old and lonesome and friendless they wouldn't see much in life to laugh at, I guess," said Miss Marshall bitterly, drawing her shawl closer about her sharp shoulders. "They never think of anything but themselves and if a day passes that they don't have 'some fun' they think it's a fearful thing to put up with. I'm sick and tired of their giggling and whispering."

In the midst of these amiable reflections Miss Marshall heard a knock at her door. When she opened it there stood Nora Jane, her broad red face beaming with smiles.

"Please, Miss, here's a letter for you," she said.

"A letter for me!" Miss Marshall shut her door and stared at the fat envelope in amazement. Who could have written it? The postman came only in the morning. Was it some joke, perhaps? Those giggling girls? Miss Marshall's face grew harder as she lighted her lamp and opened the letter suspiciously.

"Dear Miss Marshall," it ran in Cyrilla's pretty girlish writing, "we girls are so lonesome and dull that we have decided to write rainy-day letters to everybody in the house just to cheer ourselves up. So I'm going to write to you just a letter of friendly nonsense."

Pages of "nonsense" followed, and very delightful nonsense it was, for Cyrilla possessed the happy gift of bright and easy letter-writing. She commented wittily on all the amusing episodes of the boarding-house life for the past month; she described a cat-fight she had witnessed from her window that morning and illustrated it by a pen-and-ink sketch of the belligerent felines; she described a lovely new dress her mother had sent her from home and told all about the class party to which she had worn it; she gave an account of her vacation camping trip to the mountains and pasted on one page a number of small snapshots taken during the outing; she copied a joke she had read in the paper that morning and discussed the serial story in the boarding-house magazine which all the boarders were reading; she wrote out the directions for a new crocheted tidy her sister had made—Miss Marshall had a mania for crocheting; and she finally wound up with "all the good will and good wishes that Nora Jane will consent to carry from your friend, Cyrilla Blair."

Before Miss Marshall had finished reading that letter she had cried three times and laughed times past counting. More tears came at the end—happy, tender tears such as Miss Marshall had not shed for years. Something warm and sweet and gentle seemed to thrill to life within her heart. So those girls were not such selfish, heedless young creatures as she had supposed! How kind it had been in Cyrilla Blair to think of her and write so to her. She no longer felt lonely and neglected.

Her whole sombre world had been brightened to sunshine by that merry friendly letter.

Mrs. Plunkett's table was surrounded by a ring of smiling faces that night. Everybody seemed in good spirits in spite of the weather. The pale little dressmaker, who had hardly uttered a word since her arrival a week before, talked and laughed quite merrily and girlishly, thanking Cyrilla unreservedly for her "jolly letter." Old Mr. Grant did not grumble once about the rain or the food or his rheumatism and he told Carol that she might be a good letter writer in time if she looked after her grammar more carefully—which, from Mr. Grant, was high praise. All the others declared that they were delighted with their letters—all except Miss Marshall. She said nothing but later on, when Cyrilla was going upstairs, she met Miss Marshall in the shadows of the second landing.

"My dear," said Miss Marshall gently, "I want to thank you for your letter, I don't think you can realize just what it has meant to me. I was so—so lonely and tired and discouraged. It heartened me right up. I—I know you have thought me a cross and disagreeable person. I'm afraid I have been, too. But—but—I shall try to be less so in future. If I can't succeed all at once don't mind me because, under it all, I shall always be your friend. And I mean to keep your letter and read it over every time I feel myself getting bitter and hard again." "Dear Miss Marshall, I'm so glad you liked it," said Cyrilla frankly. "We're all your friends and would be glad to be chummy with you. Only we thought perhaps we bothered you with our nonsense."

"Come and see me sometimes," said Miss Marshall with a smile. "I'll try to be 'chummy'—perhaps I'm not yet too old to learn the secret of friendliness. Your letter has made me think that I have missed much in shutting all young life out from mine as I have done. I want to reform in this respect if I can."

When Cyrilla reached the front room she found Mrs. Plunkett there.

"I've just dropped in, Miss Blair," said that worthy woman, "to say that I dunno as I mind your making candy once in a while if you want to. Only do be careful not to set the place on fire. Please be *particularly* careful not to set it on fire."

"We'll try," promised Cyrilla with dancing eyes. When the door closed behind Mrs. Plunkett the three girls looked at each other.

"Cyrilla, that idea of yours was a really truly inspiration," said Carol solemnly.

"I believe it was," said Cyrilla, thinking of Miss Marshall.

Dorinda's Desperate Deed

Dorinda had been home for a whole wonderful week and the little Pages were beginning to feel acquainted with her. When a girl goes away when she is ten and doesn't come back until she is fifteen, it is only to be expected that her family should regard her as somewhat of a stranger, especially when she is really a Page, and they are really all Carters except for the name. Dorinda had been only ten when her Aunt Mary—on the Carter side—had written to Mrs. Page, asking her to let Dorinda come to her for the winter.

Mrs. Page, albeit she was poor—nobody but herself knew how poor—and a widow with five children besides Dorinda, hesitated at first. She was afraid, with good reason, that the winter might stretch into other seasons; but Mary had lost her own only little girl in the summer, and Mrs. Page shuddered at the thought of what her loneliness must be. So, to comfort her, Mrs. Page had let Dorinda go, stipulating that she must come home in the spring. In the spring, when Dorinda's bed of violets was growing purple under the lilac bush, Aunt Mary wrote again. Dorinda was contented and happy, she said. Would not Emily let her stay for the summer? Mrs. Page cried bitterly over that letter and took sad counsel with herself. To let Dorinda stay with her aunt for the summer really meant, she knew, to let her stay altogether. Mrs. Page was finding it harder and harder to get along; there was so little and the children needed so much; Dorinda would have a good home with her Aunt Mary if she could only prevail on her rebellious mother heart to give her up. In the end she agreed to let Dorinda stay for the summer—and Dorinda had never been home since.

But now Dorinda had come back to the little white house on the hill at Willowdale, set back from the road in a smother of apple trees and vines. Aunt Mary had died very suddenly and her only son, Dorinda's cousin, had gone to Japan. There was nothing for Dorinda to do save to come home, to enter again into her old unfilled place in her mother's heart, and win a new place in the hearts of the brothers and sisters who barely remembered her at all. Leicester had been nine and Jean seven when Dorinda went away; now they were respectively fourteen and twelve.

At first they were a little shy with this big, practically brand-new sister, but this soon wore off. Nobody could be shy long with Dorinda; nobody could help liking her. She was so brisk and jolly and sympathetic—a real Page, so everybody said—while the brothers and sisters were Carter to their marrow; Carters with fair hair and blue eyes, and small, fine, wistful features; but Dorinda had merry black eyes, plump, dusky-red cheeks, and a long braid of glossy dark hair, which was perpetually being twitched from one shoulder to another as Dorinda whisked about the house on domestic duties intent.

In a week Dorinda felt herself one of the family again, with all the cares and responsibilities thereof resting on her strong young shoulders. Dorinda and her mother talked matters out fully one afternoon over their sewing, in the sunny south room where the winds got lost among the vines halfway through the open window. Mrs. Page sighed and said she really did not know what to do. Dorinda did not sigh; she did not know just what to do either, but there must be something that could be done—there is always something that can be done, if one can only find it. Dorinda sewed hard and pursed up her red lips determinedly.

"Don't you worry, Mother Page," she said briskly. "We'll be like that glorious old Roman who found a way or made it. I like overcoming difficulties. I've lots of old Admiral Page's fighting blood in me, you know. The first step is to tabulate just exactly what difficulties among our many difficulties must be ravelled out first—the capital difficulties, as it were. Most important of all comes—"

"Leicester," said Mrs. Page.

Dorinda winked her eyes as she always did when she was doubtful.

"Well, I knew he was one of them, but I wasn't going to put him the very first. However, we will. Leicester's case stands thus. He is a pretty smart boy—if he wasn't my brother, I'd say he was a very smart boy. He has gone as far in his studies as Willowdale School can take him, has qualified for entrance into the Blue Hill Academy, wants to go there this fall and begin the beginnings of a college course. Well, of course, Mother Page, we can't send Leicester to Blue Hill any more than we can send him to the moon."

"No," mourned Mrs. Page, "and the poor boy feels so badly over it. His heart is set on going to college and being a doctor like his father. He believes he could work his way through, if he could only get a start. But there isn't any chance. And I can't afford to keep him at school any longer. He is going into Mr. Churchill's store at Willow Centre in the fall. Mr. Churchill has very kindly offered him a place. Leicester hates the thought of it—I know he does, although he never says so."

"Next to Leicester's college course we want—"

"Music lessons for Jean."

Dorinda winked again.

"Are music lessons for Jean really a difficulty?" she said. "That is, one spelled with a capital?"

"Oh, yes, Dorinda dear. At least, I'm worried over it. Jean loves music so, and she has never had anything, poor child, not even as much school as she ought to have had. I've had to keep her home so much to help me with the work. She has been such a good, patient little girl too, and her heart is set on music lessons."

"Well, she must have them then—after we get Leicester's year at the academy for him. That's two. The third is a new—"

"The roof *must* be shingled this fall," said Mrs. Page anxiously. "It really must, Dorinda. It is no better than a sieve. We are nearly drowned every time it rains. But I don't know where the money to do it is going to come from."

"Shingles for the roof, three," said Dorinda, as if she were carefully jotting down something in a mental memorandum. "And fourth—now, Mother Page, I *will* have my say this time—fourthly, biggest capital of all, a Nice, New Dress and a Warm Fur Coat for Mother Page this winter. Yes, yes, you must have them, dearest. It's absolutely necessary. We can wait a year or so for college courses and music lessons to grow; we can set basins under the leaks and borrow some more if we haven't enough. But a new dress and coat for you we must, shall, and will have, however it is to be brought about."

"I wouldn't mind if I never got another new stitch, if I could only manage the other things," said Mrs. Page stoutly. "If your Uncle Eugene would only help us a little, until Leicester got through! He really ought to. But of course he never will."

"Have you ever asked him?" said Dorinda.

"Oh, my dear, no; of course not," said Mrs. Page in a horrified tone, as if Dorinda had asked if she had ever stolen a neighbour's spoons.

"I don't see why you shouldn't," said Dorinda seriously.

"Oh, Dorinda, Uncle Eugene hates us all. He is terribly bitter against us. He would never, never listen to any request for help, even if I could bring myself to make it."

"Mother, what was the trouble between us and Uncle Eugene? I have never known the rights of it. I was too small to understand when I was home before. All I remember is that Uncle Eugene never came to see us or spoke to us when he met us anywhere, and we were all afraid of him somehow. I used to think of him as an ogre who would come creeping up the back stairs after dark and carry me off bodily if I wasn't good. What made him our enemy? And how did he come to get all of Grandfather Page's property when Father got nothing?"

"Well, you know, Dorinda, that your Grandfather Page was married twice. Eugene was his first wife's son, and your father the second wife's. Eugene was a great deal older than your father—he was twenty-five when your father was born. He was always an odd man, even in his youth, and he had been much displeased at his father's second marriage. But he was very fond of your father—whose mother, as you know, died at his birth—and they were good friends and comrades until just before your father went to college. They then quarrelled; the cause of the quarrel was insignificant; with anyone else than Eugene a reconciliation would soon have been effected. But Eugene never was friendly with your father from that time. I think he was jealous of old Grandfather's affection; thought the old man loved your father best. And then, as I have said, he was very eccentric and stubborn. Well, your father went away to college and graduated, and then—we were married. Grandfather Page was very angry with him for marrying me. He wanted him to marry somebody else. He told him he would disinherit him if he married me. I did not know this until we were married. But Grandfather Page kept his word. He sent for a lawyer and had a new will made, leaving everything to Eugene. I think, nay, I am sure, that he would have relented in time, but he died the very next week; they found him dead in his bed one morning, so Eugene got everything; and that is all there is of the story, Dorinda."

"And Uncle Eugene has been our enemy ever since?"

"Yes, ever since. So you see, Dorinda dear, that I cannot ask any favours of Uncle Eugene."

"Yes, I see," said Dorinda understandingly. To herself she added, "But I don't see why *I* shouldn't."

Dorinda thought hard and long for the next few days about the capital difficulties. She could think of only one thing to do and, despite old Admiral Page's fighting blood, she shrank from doing it. But one night she found Leicester with his head down on his books and—no, it couldn't be tears in his eyes, because Leicester laughed scornfully at the insinuation.

"I wouldn't cry over it, Dorinda; I hope I'm more of a man than *that*. But I do really feel rather cut up because I've no chance of getting to college. And I hate the thought of going into a store. But I know I must for Mother's sake, and I mean to pitch in and like it in spite of myself when the time comes. Only—only—"

And then Leicester got up and whistled and went to the window and stood with his back to Dorinda.

"That settles it," said Dorinda out loud, as she brushed her hair before the glass that night. "I'll do it."

"Do what?" asked Jean from the bed.

"A desperate deed," said Dorinda solemnly, and that was all she would say.

Next day Mrs. Page and Leicester went to town on business. In the afternoon Dorinda put on her best dress and hat and started out. Admiral Page's fighting blood was glowing in her cheeks as she walked briskly up the hill road, but her heart beat in an odd fashion.

"I wonder if I am a little scared, 'way down deep," said Dorinda. "I believe I am. But I'm going to do it for all that, and the scareder I get the more I'll do it."

Oaklawn, where Uncle Eugene lived, was two miles away. It was a fine old place in beautiful grounds. But Dorinda did not quail before its splendours; nor did her heart fail her, even after she had rung the bell and had been shown by a maid into a very handsome parlour, but it still continued to beat in that queer fashion halfway up her throat.

Presently Uncle Eugene came in, a tall, black-eyed old man, with a fine head of silver hair that should have framed a ruddy, benevolent face, instead of Uncle Eugene's hard-lipped, bushy-browed countenance.

Dorinda stood up, dusky and crimson, with brave, glowing eyes. Uncle Eugene looked at her sharply.

"Who are you?" he said bluntly.

"I am your niece, Dorinda Page," said Dorinda steadily.

"And what does my niece, Dorinda Page, want with me?" demanded Uncle Eugene, motioning to her to sit down and sitting down himself. But Dorinda remained standing. It is easier to fight on your feet.

"I want you to do four things, Uncle Eugene," she said, as calmly as if she were making the most natural and ordinary request in the world. "I want you to lend us the money to send Leicester to Blue Hill Academy; he will pay it back to you when he gets through college. I want you to lend Jean the money for music lessons; she will pay you back when she gets far enough along to give lessons herself. And I want you to lend me the money to shingle our house and get Mother a new dress and fur coat for the winter. I'll pay you back sometime for that, because I am going to set up as a dressmaker pretty soon."

"Anything more?" said Uncle Eugene, when Dorinda stopped.

"Nothing more just now, I think," said Dorinda reflectively.

"Why don't you ask for something for yourself?" said Uncle Eugene.

"I don't want anything for myself," said Dorinda promptly. "Or—yes, I do, too. I want your friendship, Uncle Eugene."

"Be kind enough to sit down," said Uncle Eugene.

Dorinda sat.

"You are a Page," said Uncle Eugene. "I saw that as soon as I came in. I will send Leicester to college and I shall not ask or expect to be paid back. Jean shall have her music lessons, and a piano to practise them on as well. The house shall be shingled, and the money for the new dress and coat shall be forthcoming. You and I will be friends."

"Thank you," gasped Dorinda, wondering if, after all, it wasn't a dream.

"I would have gladly assisted your mother before," said Uncle Eugene, "if she had asked me. I had determined that she must ask me first. I knew that half the money should have been your father's by rights. I was prepared to hand it over to him or his family, if I were asked for it. But I wished to humble his pride, and the Carter pride, to the point of asking for it. Not a very amiable temper, you will say? I admit it. I am not amiable and I never have been amiable. You must be prepared to find me very unamiable. I see that you are waiting for a chance to say something polite and pleasant on that score, but you may save yourself the trouble. I shall hope and expect to have you visit me often. If your mother and your brothers and sisters see fit to come with you, I shall welcome them also. I think that this is all it is necessary to say just now. Will you stay to tea with me this evening?"

Dorinda stayed to tea, since she knew that Jean was at home to attend to matters there. She and Uncle Eugene got on famously. When she left, Uncle Eugene, grim and hard-lipped as ever, saw her to the door.

"Good evening, Niece Dorinda. You are a Page and I am proud of you. Tell your mother that many things in this life are lost through not asking for them. I don't think you are in need of the information for yourself."

Her Own People

The Taunton School had closed for the summer holidays. Constance Foster and Miss Channing went down the long, elm-shaded street together, as they generally did, because they happened to board on the same block downtown.

Constance was the youngest teacher on the staff, and had charge of the Primary Department. She had taught in Taunton school a year, and at its close she was as much of a stranger in the little corps of teachers as she had been at the beginning. The others thought her stiff and unapproachable; she was unpopular in a negative way with all except Miss Channing, who made it a profession to like everybody, the more so if other people disliked them. Miss Channing was the oldest teacher on the staff, and taught the fifth grade. She was short and stout and jolly; nothing, not even the iciest reserve, ever daunted Miss Channing.

"Isn't it good to think of two whole blessed months of freedom?" she said jubilantly. "Two months to dream, to be lazy, to go where one pleases, no exercises to correct, no reports to make, no pupils to keep in order. To be sure, I love them every one, but I'll love them all the more for a bit of a rest from them. Isn't it good?"

A little satirical smile crossed Constance Foster's dark, discontented face, looking just then all the more discontented in contrast to Miss Channing's rosy, beaming countenance.

"It's very good, if you have anywhere to go, or anybody who cares where you go," she said bitterly. "For my own part, I'm sorry school is closed. I'd rather go on teaching all summer."

"Heresy!" said Miss Channing. "Rank heresy! What are your vacation plans?"

"I haven't any," said Constance wearily. "I've put off thinking about vacation as long as I possibly could. You'll call that heresy, too, Miss Channing."

"It's worse than heresy," said Miss Channing briskly. "It's a crying necessity for blue pills, that's what it is. Your whole mental and moral and physical and spiritual system must be out of kilter, my child. No vacation plans! You *must* have vacation plans. You must be going *somewhere*."

"Oh, I suppose I'll hunt up a boarding place somewhere in the country, and go there and mope until September."

"Have you no friends, Constance?"

"No—no, I haven't anybody in the world. That is why I hate vacation, that is why I've hated to hear you and the others discussing your vacation plans. You all have somebody to go to. It has just filled me up with hatred of my life."

Miss Channing swallowed her honest horror at such a state of feeling.

"Constance, tell me about yourself. I've often wanted to ask you, but I was always a little afraid to. You seem so reserved and—and, as if you didn't want to be asked about yourself."

"I know it. I know I'm stiff and hateful, and that nobody likes me, and that it is all my own fault. No, never mind trying to smooth it over, Miss Channing. It's the truth, and it hurts me, but I can't help it. I'm getting more bitter and pessimistic and unwholesome every day of my life. Sometimes it seems as if I hated all the world because I'm so lonely in it. I'm nobody. My mother died when I was born—and Father—oh, I don't know. One can't say anything against one's father, Miss Channing. But I had a hard childhood—or rather, I didn't have any childhood at all. We were always moving about. We didn't seem to have any friends at all. My mother might have had relatives somewhere, but I never heard of any. I don't even know where her home was. Father never would talk of her. He died two years ago, and since then I've been absolutely alone."

"Oh, you poor girl," said Miss Channing softly.

"I want friends," went on Constance, seeming to take a pleasure in open confession now that her tongue was loosed. "I've always just longed for somebody belonging to me to love. I don't love anybody, Miss Channing, and when a girl is in that state, she is all wrong. She gets hard and bitter and resentful—I have, anyway. I struggled against it at first, but it has been too much for me. It poisons everything. There is nobody to care anything about me, whether I live or die."

"Oh, yes, there is One," said Miss Channing gently. "God cares, Constance."

Constance gave a disagreeable little laugh.

"That sounds like Miss Williams—she is so religious. God doesn't mean anything to me, Miss Channing. I've just the same resentful feeling toward him that I have for all the world, if he exists at all. There, I've shocked you in good earnest now. You should have left me alone, Miss Channing."

"God means nothing to you because you've never had him translated to you through human love, Constance," said Miss Channing seriously. "No, you haven't shocked me—at least, not in the way you mean. I'm only terribly sorry."

"Oh, never mind me," said Constance, freezing up into her reserve again as if she regretted her confidences. "I'll get along all right. This is one of my off days, when everything looks black."

Miss Channing walked on in silence. She must help Constance, but Constance was not easily helped. When school reopened, she might be able to do something worthwhile for the girl, but just now the only thing to do was to put her in the way of a pleasant vacation.

"You spoke of boarding," she said, when Constance paused at the door of her boarding-house. "Have you any particular place in view? No? Well, I know a place which I am sure you would like. I was there two summers ago. It is a country place about a hundred miles from here. Pine Valley is its name. It's restful and homey, and the people are so nice. If you like, I'll give you the address of the family I boarded with."

"Thank you," said Constance indifferently. "I might as well go there as anywhere else."

"Yes, but listen to me, dear. Don't take your morbidness with you. Open your heart to the summer, and let its sunshine in, and when you come back in the fall, come prepared to let us all be your friends. We'd like to be, and while friendship doesn't take the place of the love of one's own people, still it is a good and beautiful thing. Besides, there are other unhappy people in the world—try to help them when you meet them, and you'll forget about yourself. Good-by for now, and I hope you'll have a pleasant vacation in spite of yourself."

Constance went to Pine Valley, but she took her evil spirit with her. Not even the beauty of the valley, with its great balmy pines, and the cheerful friendliness of its people could exorcise it.

Nevertheless, she liked the place and found a wholesome pleasure in the long tramps she took along the piney roads.

"I saw such a pretty spot in my ramble this afternoon," she told her landlady one evening. "It is about three miles from here at the end of the valley. Such a picturesque, low-eaved little house, all covered over with honeysuckle. It was set between a big orchard and an old-fashioned flower garden with great pines at the back."

"Heartsease Farm," said Mrs. Hewitt promptly. "Bless you, there's only one place around here of that description. Mr. and Mrs. Bruce, Uncle Charles and Aunt Flora, as we all call them, live there. They are the dearest old couple alive. You ought to go and see them, they'd be delighted. Aunt Flora just loves company. They're real lonesome by times."

"Haven't they any children?" asked Constance indifferently. Her interest was in the place, not in the people.

"No. They had a niece once, though. They brought her up and they just worshipped her. She ran away with a worthless fellow—I forget his name, if I ever knew it. He was handsome and smooth-tongued, but he was a scamp. She died soon after and it just broke their hearts. They don't even know where she was buried, and they never heard anything more about her husband. I've heard that Aunt Flora's hair turned snow-white in a month. I'll take you up to see her some day when I find time."

Mrs. Hewitt did not find time, but thereafter Constance ordered her rambles that she might frequently pass Heartsease Farm. The quaint old spot had a strange attraction for her. She found herself learning to love it, and so unused was this unfortunate girl to loving anything that she laughed at herself for her foolishness.

One evening a fortnight later Constance, with her arms full of ferns and wood-lilies, came out of the pine woods above Heartsease Farm just as heavy raindrops began to fall. She had prolonged her ramble unseasonably, and it was now nearly night, and very certainly a rainy night at that. She was three miles from home and without even an extra wrap.

She hurried down the lane, but by the time she reached the main road, the few drops had become a downpour. She must seek shelter somewhere, and Heartsease Farm was the nearest. She pushed open the gate and ran up the slope of the yard between the hedges of sweetbriar. She was spared the trouble of knocking, for as she came to a breathless halt on the big red sandstone doorstep, the door was flung open, and the white-haired, happy-faced little woman standing on the threshold had seized her hand and drawn her in bodily before she could speak a word.

"I saw you coming from upstairs," said Aunt Flora gleefully, "and I just ran down as fast as I could. Dear, dear, you are a little wet. But we'll soon dry you. Come right in—I've a bit of a fire in the grate, for the evening is chilly. They laughed at me for loving a fire so, but there's nothing like its snap and sparkle. You're rained in for the night, and I'm as glad as I can be. I know who you are—you are Miss Foster. I'm Aunt Flora, and this is Uncle Charles."

Constance let herself be put into a cushiony chair and fussed over with an unaccustomed sense of pleasure. The rain was coming down in torrents, and she certainly was domiciled at Heartsease Farm for the night. Somehow, she felt glad of it. Mrs. Hewitt was right in calling Aunt Flora sweet, and Uncle Charles was a big, jolly, ruddy-faced old man with a hearty manner. He shook Constance's hand until it ached, threw more pine knots in the fire and told her he wished it would rain every night if it rained down a nice little girl like her.

She found herself strangely attracted to the old couple. The name of their farm was in perfect keeping with their atmosphere. Constance's frozen soul expanded in it. She chatted merrily and girlishly, feeling as if she had known them all her life.

When bedtime came, Aunt Flora took her upstairs to a little gable room.

"My spare room is all in disorder just now, dearie, we have been painting its floor. So I'm going to put you here in Jeannie's room. Someway you remind me of her, and you are just about the age she was when she left us. If it wasn't for that, I don't think I could put you in her room, not even if every other floor in the house were being painted. It is so sacred to me. I keep it just as she left it, not a thing is changed. Good night dearie, and I hope you'll have pleasant dreams."

When Constance found herself alone in the room, she looked about her with curiosity. It was a very dainty, old-fashioned little room. The floor was covered with braided mats; the two square, small-paned windows were draped with snowy muslin. In one corner was a little white bed with white curtains and daintily ruffled pillows, and in the other a dressing table with a gilt-framed mirror and the various knick-knacks of a girlish toilet. There was a little blue rocker and an ottoman with a work-basket on it. In the work-basket was a bit of unfinished, yellowed lace with a needle sticking in it. A small bookcase under the sloping ceiling was filled with books.

Constance picked up one and opened it at the yellowing title-page. She gave a little cry of surprise. The name written across the page in a fine, dainty script was "Jean Constance Irving," her mother's name!

For a moment Constance stood motionless. Then she turned impulsively and hurried downstairs again. Mr. and Mrs. Bruce were still in the sitting room talking to each other in the firelight.

"Oh," cried Constance excitedly. "I must know, I must ask you. This is my mother's name, Jean Constance Irving, can it be possible she was your little Jeannie?"

A fortnight later Miss Channing received a letter from Constance.

"I am so happy," she wrote. "Oh, Miss Channing, I have found 'mine own people,' and Heartsease Farm is to be my own, own dear home for always.

"It was such a strange coincidence, no, Aunt Flora says it was Providence, and I believe it was, too. I came here one rainy night, and Aunty put me in my mother's room, think of it! My own dear mother's room, and I found her name in a book. And now the mystery is all cleared up, and we are so happy.

"Everything is dear and beautiful, and almost the dearest and most beautiful thing is that I am getting acquainted with my mother, the mother I never knew before. She no longer seems dead to me. I feel that she lives and loves me, and I am learning to know her better every day. I have her room and her books and all her little girlish possessions. When I read her books, with their passages underlined by her hand, I feel as if she were speaking to me. She was very good and sweet, in spite of her one foolish, bitter mistake, and I want to be as much like her as I can.

"I said that this was *almost* the dearest and most beautiful thing. The very dearest and most beautiful is this—God means something to me now. He means so much! I remember that you said to me that he meant nothing to me because I had no human love in my heart to translate the divine. But I have now, and it has led me to Him.

"I am not going back to Taunton. I have sent in my resignation. I am going to stay home with Aunty and Uncle. It is so sweet to say *home* and know what it means.

"Aunty says you must come and spend all your next vacation with us. You see, I have lots of vacation plans now, even for a year ahead. After all, there is no need of the blue pills!

"I feel like a new creature, made over from the heart and soul out. I look back with shame and contrition on the old Constance. I want you to forget her and only remember your grateful friend, the *new* Constance."

Ida's New Year Cake

Mary Craig and Sara Reid and Josie Pye had all flocked into Ida Mitchell's room at their boarding-house to condole with each other because none of them was able to go home for New Year's. Mary and Josie had been home for Christmas, so they didn't really feel so badly off. But Ida and Sara hadn't even that consolation.

Ida was a third-year student at the Clifton Academy; she had holidays, and nowhere, so she mournfully affirmed, to spend them. At home three brothers and a sister were down with the measles, and, as Ida had never had them, she could not go there; and the news had come too late for her to make any other arrangements.

Mary and Josie were clerks in a Clifton bookstore, and Sara was stenographer in a Clifton lawyer's office. And they were all jolly and thoughtless and very fond of one another.

"This will be the first New Year's I have ever spent away from home," sighed Sara, nibbling chocolate fudge. "It does make me so blue to think of it. And not even a holiday—I'll have to go to work just the same. Now Ida here, she doesn't really need sympathy. She has holidays—a whole fortnight—and nothing to do but enjoy them."

"Holidays are dismal things when you've nowhere to holiday," said Ida mournfully. "The time drags horribly. But never mind, girls, I've a plummy bit of news for you. I'd a letter from Mother today and, bless the dear woman, she is sending me a cake—a New Year's cake—a great big, spicy, mellow, delicious fruit cake. It will be along tomorrow and, girls, we'll celebrate when it comes. I've asked everybody in the house up to my room for New Year's Eve, and we'll have a royal good time."

"How splendid!" said Mary. "There's nothing I like more than a slice of real countrified home-made fruit cake, where they don't scrimp on eggs or butter or raisins. You'll give me a good big piece, won't you, Ida?"

"As much as you can eat," promised Ida. "I can warrant Mother's fruit cake. Yes, we'll have a jamboree. Miss Monroe has promised to come in too. She says she has a weakness for fruit cake."

"Oh!" breathed all the girls. Miss Monroe was their idol, whom they had to be content to worship at a distance as a general thing. She was a clever journalist, who worked on a paper, and was reputed to be writing a book. The girls felt they were highly privileged to be boarding in the same house, and counted that day lost on which they did not receive a businesslike nod or an absent-minded smile from Miss Monroe. If she ever had time to speak to one of them about the weather, that fortunate one put on airs for a week. And now to think that she had actually promised to drop into Ida's room on New Year's Eve and eat fruit cake!

"There goes that funny little namesake of yours, Ida," said Josie, who was sitting by the window. "She seems to be staying in town over the holidays too. Wonder why. Perhaps she doesn't belong anywhere. She really is a most forlorn-appearing little mortal."

There were two Ida Mitchells attending the Clifton Academy. The other Ida was a plain, quiet, pale-faced little girl of fifteen who was in the second year. Beyond that, none of the third-year Ida Mitchell's set knew anything about her, or tried to find out.

"She must be very poor," said Ida carelessly. "She dresses so shabbily, and she always looks so pinched and subdued. She boards in a little house out on Marlboro Road, and I pity her if she has to spend her holidays there, for a more dismal place I never saw. I was there once on the trail of a book I had lost. Going, girls? Well, don't forget tomorrow night."

Ida spent the next day decorating her room and watching for the arrival of her cake. It hadn't come by tea-time, and she concluded to go down to the express office and investigate. It would be dreadful if that cake didn't turn up in time, with all the girls and Miss Monroe coming in. Ida felt that she would be mortified to death.

Inquiry at the express office discovered two things. A box had come in for Miss Ida Mitchell, Clifton; and said box had been delivered to Miss Ida Mitchell, Clifton.

"One of our clerks said he knew you personally—boarded next door to you—and he'd take it round himself," the manager informed her.

"There must be some mistake," said Ida in perplexity. "I don't know any of the clerks here. Oh—why—there's another Ida Mitchell in town! Can it be possible my cake has gone to her?"

The manager thought it very possible, and offered to send around and see. But Ida said it was on her way home and she would call herself.

At the dismal little house on Marlboro Road she was sent up three flights of stairs to the other Ida Mitchell's small hall bedroom. The other Ida Mitchell opened the door for her. Behind her, on the table, was the cake—such a fine, big, brown cake, with raisins sticking out all over it!

"Why, how do you do, Miss Mitchell!" exclaimed the other Ida with shy pleasure. "Come in. I didn't know you were in town. It's real good of you to come and see me. And just see what I've had sent to me! Isn't it a beauty? I was so surprised when it came—and, oh, so glad! I was feeling so blue and lonesome—as if I hadn't a friend in the world. I—I—yes, I was crying when that cake came. It has just made the world over for me. Do sit down and I'll cut you a piece. I'm sure you're as fond of fruit cake as I am."

Ida sat down in a chair, feeling bewildered and awkward. This was a nice predicament! How could she tell that other Ida that the cake didn't belong to her? The poor thing was so delighted. And, oh, what a bare, lonely little room! The big, luxurious cake seemed to emphasize the bareness and loneliness.

"Who—who sent it to you?" she asked lamely.

"It must have been Mrs. Henderson, because there is nobody else who would," answered the other Ida. "Two years ago I was going to school in Trenton and I boarded with her. When I left her to come to Clifton she told me she would send me a cake for Christmas. Well, I expected that cake last year—and it didn't come. I can't tell you how disappointed I was. You'll think me very childish. But I was so lonely, with no home to go to like the other girls. But she sent it this year, you see. It is so nice to think that somebody has remembered me at New Year's. It isn't the cake itself—it's the thought behind it. It has just made all the difference in the world. There—just sample it, Miss Mitchell."

The other Ida cut a generous slice from the cake and passed it to her guest. Her eyes were shining and her cheeks were flushed. She was really a very sweet-looking little thing—not a bit like her usual pale, timid self.

Ida ate the cake slowly. What was she to do? She couldn't tell the other Ida the truth about the cake. But the girls she had asked in to help eat it that very evening! And Miss Monroe! Oh, dear, it was too bad. But it couldn't be helped. She wouldn't blot out that light on the other Ida's face for anything! Of course, she would find out the truth in time—probably after she had written to thank Mrs. Henderson for the cake; but meanwhile she would have enjoyed the cake, and the supposed kindness back of it would tide her over her New Year loneliness.

"It's delicious," said Ida heartily, swallowing her own disappointment with the cake. "I'm—I'm glad I happened to drop in as I was passing." Ida hoped that speech didn't come under the head of a fib.

"So am I," said the other Ida brightly. "Oh, I've been so lonesome and downhearted this week. I'm so alone, you see—there isn't anybody to care. Father died three years ago, and I don't remember my mother at all. There is nobody but myself, and it is dreadfully lonely at times. When the Academy is open and I have my lessons to study, I don't mind so much. But the holidays take all the courage out of me."

"We should have fraternized more this week," smiled Ida, regretting that she hadn't thought of it before. "I couldn't go home because of the measles, and I've moped a lot. We might have spent the time together and had a real nice, jolly holiday."

The other Ida blushed with delight.

"I'd love to be friends with you," she said slowly. "I've often thought I'd like to know you. Isn't it odd that we have the same name? It was so nice of you to come and see me. I—I'd love to have you come often."

"I will," said Ida heartily.

"Perhaps you will stay the evening," suggested the other Ida. "I've asked some of the girls who board here in to have some cake, I'm so glad to be able to give them something—they've all been so good to me. They are all clerks in stores and some of them are so tired and lonely. It's so nice to have a pleasure to share with them. Won't you stay?"

"I'd like to," laughed Ida, "but I have some guests of my own invited in for to-night. I must hurry home, for they will most surely be waiting for me."

She laughed again as she thought what else the guests would be waiting for. But her face was sober enough as she walked home.

"But I'm glad I left the cake with her," she said resolutely. "Poor little thing! It means so much to her. It meant only 'a good feed,' as Josie says, to me. I'm simply going to make it my business next term to be good friends with the other Ida Mitchell. I'm afraid we third-year girls are very self-centred and selfish. And I know what I'll do! I'll write to Abby Morton in Trenton to send me Mrs. Henderson's address, and I'll write her a letter and ask her not to let Ida know she didn't send the cake."

Ida went into a confectionery store and invested in what Josie Pye was wont to call "ready-to-wear eatables"—fancy cakes, fruit, and candies. When she reached her room she found it full of expectant girls, with Miss Monroe enthroned in the midst of them—Miss Monroe in a wonderful evening dress of black lace and yellow silk, with roses in her hair and pearls on her neck—all donned in honour of Ida's little celebration. I won't say that, just for a moment, Ida didn't regret that she had given up her cake.

"Good evening, Miss Mitchell," cried Mary Craig gaily. "Walk right in and make yourself at home in your own room, do! We all met in the hall, and knocked and knocked. Finally Miss Monroe came, so we made bold to walk right in. Where is the only and original fruit cake, Ida? My mouth has been watering all day."

"The other Ida Mitchell is probably entertaining her friends at this moment with my fruit cake," said Ida, with a little laugh.

Then she told the whole story.

"I'm so sorry to disappoint you," she concluded, "but I simply couldn't tell that poor, lonely child that the cake wasn't intended for her. I've brought all the goodies home with me that I could buy, and we'll have to do the best we can without the fruit cake."

Their "best" proved to be a very good thing. They had a jolly New Year's Eve, and Miss Monroe sparkled and entertained most brilliantly. They kept their celebration up until twelve to welcome the new year in, and then they bade Ida good night. But Miss Monroe lingered for a moment behind the others to say softly:

"I want to tell you how good and sweet I think it was of you to give up your cake to the other Ida. That little bit of unselfishness was a good guerdon for your new year."

And Ida, radiant-faced at this praise from her idol, answered heartily:

"I'm afraid I'm anything but unselfish, Miss Monroe. But I mean to try to be more this coming year and think a little about the girls outside of my own little set who may be lonely or discouraged. The other Ida Mitchell isn't going to have to depend on that fruit cake alone for comfort and encouragement for the next twelve months."

In the Old Valley

The man halted on the crest of the hill and looked sombrely down into the long valley below. It was evening, and although the hills around him were still in the light the valley was already filled with kindly, placid shadows. A wind that blew across it from the misty blue sea beyond was making wild music in the rugged firs above his head as he stood in an angle of the weather-grey longer fence, knee-deep in bracken. It had been by these firs he had halted twenty years ago, turning for one last glance at the valley below, the home valley which he had never seen since. But then the firs had been little more than vigorous young saplings; they were tall, gnarled trees now, with lichened trunks, and their lower boughs were dead. But high up their tops were green and caught the saffron light of the west. He remembered that when a boy he had thought there was nothing more beautiful than the evening sunshine falling athwart the dark green fir boughs on the hills.

As he listened to the swish and murmur of the wind, the earth-old tune with the power to carry the soul back to the dawn of time, the years fell away from him and he forgot much, remembering more. He knew now that there had always been a longing in his heart to hear the wind-chant in the firs. He had called that longing by other names, but he knew it now for what it was when, hearing, he was satisfied.

He was a tall man with iron-grey hair and the face of a conqueror—strong, pitiless, unswerving. Eagle eyes, quick to discern and unfaltering to pursue; jaw square and intrepid; mouth formed to keep secrets and cajole men to his will—a face that hid much and revealed little. It told of power and intellect, but the soul of the man was a hidden thing. Not in the arena where he had fought and triumphed, giving fierce blow for blow, was it to be shown; but here, looking down on the homeland, with the strength of the hills about him, it rose dominantly and claimed its own. The old bond held. Yonder below him was home—the old house that had sheltered him, the graves of his kin, the wide fields where his boyhood dreams had been dreamed.

Should he go down to it? This was the question he asked himself. He had come back to it, heartsick of his idols of the marketplace. For years they had satisfied him, the buying and selling and getting gain, the pitting of strength and craft against strength and craft, the tireless struggle, the exultation of victory. Then, suddenly, they had failed their worshipper; they ceased to satisfy; the sacrifices he had heaped on their altars availed him nothing in this new need and hunger of his being. His gods mocked him and he wearied of their service. Were there not better things than these, things he had once known and loved and forgotten? Where were the ideals of his youth, the lofty aspirations that had upborne him then? Where was the eagerness and zest of new dawns, the earnestness of well-filled, purposeful hours of labour, the satisfaction of a good day worthily lived, at eventide the unbroken rest of long, starry nights? Where might he find them again? Were they yet to be had for the seeking in the old valley? With the thought came a great yearning for home. He had had many habitations, but he realized now that he had never thought of any of these places as home. That name had all unconsciously been kept sacred to the long, green, seaward-looking glen where he had been born.

So he had come back to it, drawn by a longing not to be resisted. But at the last he felt afraid. There had been many changes, of that he felt sure. Would it still be home? And if not, would not the loss be most irreparable and bitter? Would it not be better to go away, having looked at it from the hill and having heard the saga of the firs, keeping his memory of it unblurred, than risk the probable disillusion of a return to the places that had forgotten him and friends whom the varying years must certainly have changed as he had changed himself? No, he would not go down. It had been a foolish whim to come at all—foolish, because the object of his quest was not to be found there or elsewhere. He could not enter again into the heritage of boyhood and the heart of youth. He could not find there the old dreams and hopes that had made life sweet. He understood that he could not bring back to the old valley what he had taken from it. He had lost that intangible, all-real wealth of faith and idealism and zest; he had bartered it away for the hard, yellow gold of the marketplace, and he realized at last how much poorer he was than when he had left that home valley. His was a name that stood for millions, but he was beggared of hope and purpose.

No, he would not go down. There was no one left there, unchanged and unchanging, to welcome him. He would be a stranger there, even among his kin. He would stay awhile on the hill, until the night came down over it, and then he would go back to his own place.

Down below him, on the crest of a little upland, he saw his old home, a weather-grey house, almost hidden among white birch and apple trees, with a thick fir grove to the north of it. He had been born in that old house; his earliest memory was of standing on its threshold and looking afar up to the long green hills.

"What is over the hills?" he had asked of his mother. With a smile she had made answer,

"Many things, laddie. Wonderful things, beautiful things, heart-breaking things."

"Some day I shall go over the hills and find them all, Mother," he had said stoutly.

She had laughed and sighed and caught him to her heart. He had no recollection of his father, who had died soon after his son's birth, but how well he remembered his mother, his little, brown-eyed, girlish-faced mother!

He had lived on the homestead until he was twenty. He had tilled the broad fields and gone in and out among the people, and their life had been his life. But his heart was not in his work. He wanted to go beyond the hills and seek what he knew must be there. The valley was too narrow, too placid. He longed for conflict and accomplishment. He felt power and desire and the lust of endeavour stirring in him. Oh, to go over the hills to a world where men lived! Such had been the goal of all his dreams.

When his mother died he sold the farm to his cousin, Stephen Marshall. He supposed it still belonged to him. Stephen had been a good sort of a fellow, a bit slow and plodding, perhaps, bovinely content to dwell within the hills, never hearkening or responding to the lure of the beyond. Yet it might be he had chosen the better part, to dwell thus on the land of his fathers, with a wife won in youth, and children to grow up around him. The childless, wifeless man looking down from the hill wondered if it might have been so with him had he been content to stay in the valley. Perhaps so. There had been Joyce.

He wondered where Joyce was now and whom she had married, for of course she had married. Did she too live somewhere down there in the valley, the matronly, contented mother of lads and lassies? He could see her old home also, not so far from his own, just across a green meadow by way of a footpath and stile and through the firs beyond it. How often he had traversed that path in the old days, knowing that Joyce would be waiting at the end of it among the firs—Joyce, the playmate of childhood, the sweet confidante and companion of youth! They had never been avowed lovers, but he had loved her then, as a boy loves, although he had never said a word of love to her. Joyce alone knew of his longings and his ambitions and his dreams; he had told them all to her freely, sure of the understanding and sympathy no other soul in the valley could give him. How true and strong and womanly and gentle she had always been!

When he left home he had meant to go back to her some day. They had parted without pledge or kiss, yet he knew she loved him and that he loved her. At first they corresponded, then the letters began to grow fewer. It was his fault; he had gradually forgotten. The new, fierce, burning interests that came into his life crowded the old ones out. Boyhood's love was scorched up in that hot flame of ambition and contest. He had not heard from or of Joyce for many years. Now, again, he remembered as he looked down on the homeland fields.

The old places had changed little, whatever he might fear of the people who lived in them. There was the school he had attended, a small, low-eaved, whitewashed building set back from the main road among green spruces. Beyond it, amid tall elms, was the old church with its square tower hung with ivy. He felt glad to see it; he had expected to see a new church, offensively spick-and-span and modern, for this church had been old when he was a boy. He recalled the many times he had walked to it on the peaceful Sunday afternoons, sometimes with his mother, sometimes with Joyce.

The sun set far out to sea and sucked down with it all the light out of the winnowed dome of sky. The stars came out singly and crystal clear over the far purple curves of the hills. Suddenly, glancing over his shoulder, he saw through an arch of black fir boughs a young moon swung low in a lake of palely tinted saffron sky. He smiled a little, remembering that in boyhood it had been held a good omen to see the new moon over the right shoulder.

Down in the valley the lights began to twinkle out here and there like earth-stars. He would wait until he saw the kitchen light from the window of his old home. Then he would go. He waited until the whole valley was zoned with a glittering girdle, but no light glimmered out through his native trees. Why was it lacking, that light he had so often hailed at dark, coming home from boyish rambles on the hills? He felt anxious and dissatisfied, as if he could not go away until he had seen it.

When it was quite dark he descended the hill resolutely. He must know why the homelight had failed him. When he found himself in the old garden his heart grew sick and sore with disappointment and a bitter homesickness. It needed but a glance, even in the dimness of the summer night, to see that the old house was deserted and falling to decay. The kitchen door swung open on rusty hinges; the windows were broken and lifeless; weeds grew thickly over the yard and crowded wantonly up to the very threshold through the chinks of the rotten platform.

Cuthbert Marshall sat down on the old red sandstone step of the door and bowed his head in his hands. This was what he had come back to—this ghost and wreck of his past! Oh, bitterness!

From where he sat he saw the new house that Stephen had built beyond the fir grove, with a cheerful light shining from its window. After a long time he went over to it and knocked at the door. Stephen came to it, a stout grizzled farmer, with a chubby boy on his shoulder. He was not much changed; Cuthbert easily recognized him, but to Stephen Marshall no recognition came of this man with whom he had played and worked for years. Cuthbert was obliged to tell who he was. He was made instantly and warmly welcome. Stephen was unfeignedly glad to see him, and Stephen's comely wife, whom he remembered as a slim, fresh-cheeked valley girl, extended a kind and graceful hospitality. The boys and girls, too, soon made friends with him. Yet he felt himself the stranger and the alien, whom the long, swift-passing years had shut forever from his old place.

He and Stephen talked late that night, and in the morning he yielded to their entreaties to stay another day with them. He spent it wandering about the farm and the old haunts of wood and stream. Yet he could not find himself. This valley had his past in its keeping, but it could not give it back to him; he had lost the master word that might have compelled it.

He asked Stephen fully about all his old friends and neighbours with one exception. He could not ask him what had become of Joyce Cameron. The question was on his lips a dozen times, but he shrank from uttering it. He had a vague, secret dread that the answer, whatever it might be, would hurt him.

In the evening he yielded to a whim and went across to the Cameron homestead, by the old footpath which was still kept open. He walked slowly and dreamily, with his eyes on the far hills scarfed in the splendour of sunset. So he had walked in the old days, but he had no dreams now of what lay beyond the hills, and Joyce would not be waiting among the firs.

The stile he remembered was gone, replaced by a little rustic gate. As he passed through it he lifted his eyes and there before him he saw her, standing tall and gracious among the grey trees, with the light from the west falling over her face. So she had stood, so she had looked many an evening of the long-ago. She had not changed; he realized that in the first amazed, incredulous glance. Perhaps there were lines on her face, a thread or two of silver in the soft brown hair, but those splendid steady blue eyes were the same, and the soul of her looked out through them, true to itself, the staunch, brave, sweet soul of the maiden ripened to womanhood.

"Joyce!" he said, stupidly, unbelievingly.

She smiled and put out her hand. "I am glad to see you, Cuthbert," she said simply. "Stephen's Mary told me you had come. And I thought you would be over to see us this evening."

She had offered him only one hand but he took both and held her so, looking hungrily down at her as a man looks at something he knows must be his salvation if salvation exists for him.

"Is it possible you are here still, Joyce?" he said slowly. "And you have not changed at all."

She coloured slightly and pulled away her hands, laughing. "Oh, indeed I have. I have grown old. The twilight is so kind it hides that, but it is true. Come into the house, Cuthbert. Father and Mother will be glad to see you."

"After a little," he said imploringly. "Let us stay here awhile first, Joyce. I want to make sure that this is no dream. Last night I stood on those hills yonder and looked down, but I meant to go away because I thought there would be no one left to welcome me. If I had known you were here! You have lived here in the old valley all these years?"

"All these years," she said gently, "I suppose you think it must have been a very meagre life?"

"No. I am much wiser now than I was once, Joyce. I have learned wisdom beyond the hills. One learns there—in time—but sometimes the lesson is learned too late. Shall I tell you what I have learned, Joyce? The gist of the lesson is that I left happiness behind me in the old valley, when I went away from it, happiness and peace and the joy of living. I did not miss these things for a long while; I did not even know I had lost them. But I have discovered my loss."

"Yet you have been a very successful man," she said wonderingly.

"As the world calls success," he answered bitterly. "I have place and wealth and power. But that is not success, Joyce. I am tired of these things; they are the toys of grown-up children; they do not satisfy the man's soul. I have come back to the old valley seeking for what might satisfy, but I have little hope of finding it, unless—unless—"

He was silent, remembering that he had forfeited all right to her help in the quest. Yet he realized clearly that only she could help him, only she could guide him back to the path he had missed. It seemed to him that she held in her keeping all the good of his life, all the beauty of his past, all the possibilities of his future. Hers was the master word, but how should he dare ask her to utter it?

They walked among the firs until the stars came out, and they talked of many things. She had kept her freshness of soul and her ideals untarnished. In the peace of the old valley she had lived a life, narrow outwardly, wondrously deep and wide in thought and aspiration. Her native hills bounded the vision of her eyes, but the outlook of the soul was far and unhindered. In the quiet places and the green ways she had found what he had failed to find—the secret of happiness and content. He knew that if this woman had walked hand in hand with him through the years, life, even in the glare and tumult of that world beyond the hills, would never have lost its meaning for him. Oh, fool and blind that he had been! While he had sought and toiled afar, the best that God had meant for him had been here in the home of youth. When darkness came down through the firs he told her all this, haltingly, blunderingly, yearningly.

"Joyce, is it too late? Can you forgive my mistake, my long blindness? Can you care for me again—a little?"

She turned her face upward to the sky between the swaying fir tops and he saw the reflection of a star in her eyes. "I have never ceased to care," she said in a low tone. "I never really wanted to cease. It would have left life too empty. If my love means so much to you it is yours, Cuthbert—it always has been yours."

He drew her close into his arms, and as he felt her heart beating against his he understood that he had found the way back to simple happiness and true wisdom, the wisdom of loving and the happiness of being loved.

Jane Lavinia

Jane Lavinia put her precious portfolio down on the table in her room, carefully, as if its contents were fine gold, and proceeded to unpin and take off her second-best hat. When she had gone over to the Whittaker place that afternoon, she had wanted to wear her best hat, but Aunt Rebecca had vetoed that uncompromisingly.

"Next thing you'll be wanting to wear your best muslin to go for the cows," said Aunt Rebecca sarcastically. "You go right back upstairs and take off that chiffon hat. If I was fool enough to be coaxed into buying it for you, I ain't going to have you spoil it by traipsing hither and yon with it in the dust and sun. Your last summer's sailor is plenty good enough to go to the Whittakers' in, Jane Lavinia."

"But Mr. Stephens and his wife are from New York," pleaded Jane Lavinia, "and she's so stylish."

"Well, it's likely they're used to seeing chiffon hats," Aunt Rebecca responded, more sarcastically than ever. "It isn't probable that yours would make much of a sensation. Mr. Stephens didn't send for you to show him your chiffon hat, did he? If he did, I don't see what you're lugging that big portfolio along with you for. Go and put on your sailor hat, Jane Lavinia."

Jane Lavinia obeyed. She always obeyed Aunt Rebecca. But she took off the chiffon hat and pinned on the sailor with bitterness of heart. She had always hated that sailor. Anything ugly hurt Jane Lavinia with an intensity that Aunt Rebecca could never understand; and the sailor hat was ugly, with its stiff little black bows and impossible blue roses. It jarred on Jane Lavinia's artistic instincts. Besides, it was very unbecoming.

I look horrid in it, Jane Lavinia had thought sorrowfully; and then she had gone out and down the velvet-green springtime valley and over the sunny birch hill beyond with a lagging step and a rebellious heart.

But Jane Lavinia came home walking as if on the clear air of the crystal afternoon, her small, delicate face aglow and every fibre of her body and spirit thrilling with excitement and delight. She forgot to fling the sailor hat into its box with her usual energy of dislike. Just then Jane Lavinia had a soul above hats. She looked at herself in the glass and nodded with friendliness.

"You'll do something yet," she said. "Mr. Stephens said you would. Oh, I like you, Jane Lavinia, you dear thing! Sometimes I haven't liked you because you're nothing to look at, and I didn't suppose you could really do anything worthwhile. But I do like you now after what Mr. Stephens said about your drawings."

Jane Lavinia smiled radiantly into the little cracked glass. Just then she was pretty, with the glow on her cheeks and the sparkle in her eyes. Her uncertainly tinted hair and an all-too-certain little tilt of her nose no longer troubled her. Such things did not matter; nobody would mind them in a successful artist. And Mr. Stephens had said that she had talent enough to win success.

Jane Lavinia sat down by her window, which looked west into a grove of firs. They grew thickly, close up to the house, and she could touch their wide, fan-like branches with her hand. Jane Lavinia loved those fir trees, with their whispers and sighs and beckonings, and she also loved her little shadowy, low-ceilinged room, despite its plainness, because it was gorgeous for her with visions and peopled with rainbow fancies.

The stained walls were covered with Jane Lavinia's pictures—most of them pen-and-ink sketches, with a few flights into water colour. Aunt Rebecca sniffed at them and deplored the driving of tacks into the plaster. Aunt Rebecca thought Jane Lavinia's artistic labours a flat waste of time, which would have been much better put into rugs and crochet tidies and afghans. All the other girls in Chestercote made rugs and tidies and afghans. Why must Jane Lavinia keep messing with ink and crayons and water colours?

Jane Lavinia only knew that she *must*—she could not help it. There was something in her that demanded expression thus.

When Mr. Stephens, who was a well-known artist and magazine illustrator, came to Chestercote because his wife's father, Nathan Whittaker, was ill, Jane Lavinia's heart had bounded with a shy hope. She indulged in some harmless manoeuvring which, with the aid of good-natured Mrs. Whittaker, was crowned with success. One day, when Mr. Whittaker was getting better, Mr. Stephens had asked her to show him some of her work. Jane Lavinia, wearing the despised sailor hat, had gone over to the Whittaker place with some of her best sketches. She came home again feeling as if all the world and herself were transfigured.

She looked out from the window of her little room with great dreamy brown eyes, seeing through the fir boughs the golden western sky beyond, serving as a canvas whereon her fancy painted glittering visions of her future. She would go to New York—and study—and work, oh, so hard—and go abroad—and work harder—and win success—and be great and admired and famous—if only Aunt Rebecca—ah! if only Aunt Rebecca! Jane Lavinia sighed. There was spring in the world and spring in Jane Lavinia's heart; but a chill came with the thought of Aunt Rebecca, who considered tidies and afghans nicer than her pictures.

"But I'm going, anyway," said Jane Lavinia decidedly. "If Aunt Rebecca won't give me the money, I'll find some other way. I'm not afraid of any amount of work. After what Mr. Stephens said, I believe I could work twenty hours out of the twenty-four. I'd be content to live on a crust and sleep in a garret—yes, and wear sailor hats with stiff bows and blue roses the year round."

Jane Lavinia sighed in luxurious renunciation. Oh, it was good to be alive—to be a girl of seventeen, with wonderful ambitions and all the world before her! The years of the future sparkled and gleamed alluringly. Jane Lavinia, with her head on the window sill, looked out into the sunset splendour and dreamed.

Athwart her dreams, rending in twain their frail, rose-tinted fabric, came Aunt Rebecca's voice from the kitchen below, "Jane Lavinia! Jane Lavinia! Ain't you going for the cows tonight?"

Jane Lavinia started up guiltily; she had forgotten all about the cows. She slipped off her muslin dress and hurried into her print; but with all her haste it took time, and Aunt Rebecca was grimmer than ever when Jane Lavinia ran downstairs.

"It'll be dark before we get the cows milked. I s'pose you've been day-dreaming again up there. I do wish, Jane Lavinia, that you had more sense."

Jane Lavinia made no response. At any other time she would have gone out with a lump in her throat; but now, after what Mr. Stephens had said, Aunt Rebecca's words had no power to hurt her.

"After milking I'll ask her about it," she said to herself, as she went blithely down the sloping yard, across the little mossy bridge over the brook, and up the lane on the hill beyond, where the ferns grew thickly and the grass was beset with tiny blue-eyes like purple stars. The air was moist and sweet. At the top of the lane a wild plum tree hung out its branches of feathery bloom against the crimson sky. Jane Lavinia lingered, in spite of Aunt Rebecca's hurry, to look at it. It satisfied her artistic instinct and made her glad to be alive in the world where wild plums blossomed against springtime skies. The pleasure of it went with her through the pasture and back to the milking yard; and stayed with her while she helped Aunt Rebecca milk the cows.

When the milk was strained into the creamers down at the spring, and the pails washed and set in a shining row on their bench, Jane Lavinia tried to summon up her courage to speak to Aunt Rebecca. They were out on the back verandah; the spring twilight was purpling down over the woods and fields; down in the swamp the frogs were singing a silvery, haunting chorus; a little baby moon was floating in the clear sky above the white-blossoming orchard on the slope.

Jane Lavinia tried to speak and couldn't. For a wonder, Aunt Rebecca spared her the trouble.

"Well, what did Mr. Stephens think of your pictures?" she asked shortly.

"Oh!" Everything that Jane Lavinia wanted to say came rushing at once and together to her tongue's end. "Oh, Aunt Rebecca, he was delighted with them! And he said I had remarkable talent, and he wants me to go to New York and study in an art school there. He says Mrs. Stephens finds it hard to get good help, and if I'd be willing to work for her in the mornings, I could live with them and have my afternoons off. So it won't cost much. And he said he would help me—and, oh, Aunt Rebecca, can't I go?"

Jane Lavinia's breath gave out with a gasp of suspense.

Aunt Rebecca was silent for so long a space that Jane Lavinia had time to pass through the phases of hope and fear and despair and resignation before she said, more grimly than ever, "If your mind is set on going, go you will, I suppose. It doesn't seem to me that I have anything to say in the matter, Jane Lavinia."

"But, oh, Aunt Rebecca," said Jane Lavinia tremulously. "I can't go unless you'll help me. I'll have to pay for my lessons at the art school, you know."

"So that's it, is it? And do you expect me to give you the money to pay for them, Jane Lavinia?"

"Not give—exactly," stammered Jane Lavinia. "I'll pay it back some time, Aunt Rebecca. Oh, indeed, I will—when I'm able to earn money by my pictures!"

"The security is hardly satisfactory," said Aunt Rebecca immovably. "You know well enough I haven't much money, Jane Lavinia. I thought when I was coaxed into giving you two quarters' lessons with Miss Claxton that it was as much as you could expect me to do for you. I didn't suppose the next thing would be that you'd be for betaking yourself to New York and expecting me to pay your bills there."

Aunt Rebecca turned and went into the house. Jane Lavinia, feeling sore and bruised in spirit; fled to her own room and cried herself to sleep.

Her eyes were swollen the next morning, but she was not sulky. Jane Lavinia never sulked. She did her morning's work faithfully, although there was no spring in her step. That afternoon, when she was out in the orchard trying to patch up her tattered dreams, Aunt Rebecca came down the blossomy avenue, a tall, gaunt figure, with an uncompromising face.

"You'd better go down to the store and get ten yards of white cotton, Jane Lavinia," she said. "If you're going to New York, you'll have to get a supply of underclothing made."

Jane Lavinia opened her eyes.

"Oh, Aunt Rebecca, am I going?"

"You can go if you want to. I'll give you all the money I can spare. It ain't much, but perhaps it'll be enough for a start."

"Oh, Aunt Rebecca, thank you!" exclaimed Jane Lavinia, crimson with conflicting feelings. "But perhaps I oughtn't to take it—perhaps I oughtn't to leave you alone—"

If Aunt Rebecca had shown any regret at the thought of Jane Lavinia's departure, Jane Lavinia would have foregone New York on the spot. But Aunt Rebecca only said coldly, "I guess you needn't worry over that. I can get along well enough."

And with that it was settled. Jane Lavinia lived in a whirl of delight for the next week. She felt few regrets at leaving Chestercote. Aunt Rebecca would not miss her; Jane Lavinia thought that Aunt Rebecca regarded her as a nuisance—a foolish girl who wasted her time making pictures instead of doing something useful. Jane Lavinia had never thought that Aunt Rebecca had any affection for her. She had been a very little girl when her parents had died, and Aunt Rebecca had taken her to bring up. Accordingly she had been "brought up," and she was grateful to Aunt Rebecca, but there was no closer bond between them. Jane Lavinia would have given love for love unstintedly, but she never supposed that Aunt Rebecca loved her.

On the morning of departure Jane Lavinia was up and ready early. Her trunk had been taken over to Mr. Whittaker's the night before, and she was to walk over in the morning and go with Mr. and Mrs. Stephens to the station. She put on her chiffon hat to travel in, and Aunt Rebecca did not say a word of protest. Jane Lavinia cried when she said good-by, but Aunt Rebecca did not cry. She shook hands and said stiffly, "Write when you get to New York. You needn't let Mrs. Stephens work you to death either."

Jane Lavinia went slowly over the bridge and up the lane. If only Aunt Rebecca had been a little sorry! But the morning was perfect and the air clear as crystal, and she was going to New York, and fame and fortune were to be hers for the working. Jane Lavinia's spirits rose and bubbled over in a little trill of song. Then she stopped in dismay. She had forgotten her watch—her mother's little gold watch; she had left it on her dressing table.

Jane Lavinia hurried down the lane and back to the house. In the open kitchen doorway she paused, standing on a mosaic of gold and shadow where the sunshine fell through the morning-glory vines. Nobody was in the kitchen, but Aunt Rebecca was in the little bedroom that opened off it, crying bitterly and talking aloud between her sobs, "Oh, she's gone and left me all alone—my girl has gone! Oh, what shall I do? And she didn't care—she was glad to go—glad to get away. Well, it ain't any wonder. I've always been too cranky with her. But I loved her so much all the time, and I was so proud of her! I liked her picture-making real well, even if I did complain of her wasting her time. Oh, I don't know how I'm ever going to keep on living now she's gone!"

Jane Lavinia listened with a face from which all the sparkle and excitement had gone. Yet amid all the wreck and ruin of her tumbling castles in air, a glad little thrill made itself felt. Aunt Rebecca was sorry—Aunt Rebecca did love her after all!

Jane Lavinia turned and walked noiselessly away. As she went swiftly up the wild plum lane, some tears brimmed up in her eyes, but there was a smile on her lips and a song in her heart. After all, it was nicer to be loved than to be rich and admired and famous.

When she reached Mr. Whittaker's, everybody was out in the yard ready to start.

"Hurry up, Jane Lavinia," said Mr. Whittaker. "Blest if we hadn't begun to think you weren't coming at all. Lively now."

"I am not going," said Jane Lavinia calmly.

"Not going?" they all exclaimed.

"No. I'm very sorry, and very grateful to you, Mr. Stephens, but I can't leave Aunt Rebecca. She'd miss me too much."

"Well, you little goose!" said Mrs. Whittaker.

Mrs. Stephens said nothing, but frowned coldly. Perhaps her thoughts were less of the loss to the world of art than of the difficulty of hunting up another housemaid. Mr. Stephens looked honestly regretful.

"I'm sorry, very sorry, Miss Slade," he said. "You have exceptional talent, and I think you ought to cultivate it."

"I am going to cultivate Aunt Rebecca," said Jane Lavinia.

Nobody knew just what she meant, but they all understood the firmness of her tone. Her trunk was taken down out of the express wagon, and Mr. and Mrs. Stephens drove away. Then Jane Lavinia went home. She found Aunt Rebecca washing the breakfast dishes, with the big tears rolling down her face.

"Goodness me!" she cried, when Jane Lavinia walked in. "What's the matter? You ain't gone and been too late!"

"No, I've just changed my mind, Aunt Rebecca. They've gone without me. I am not going to New York—I don't want to go. I'd rather stay at home with you."

For a moment Aunt Rebecca stared at her. Then she stepped forward and flung her arms about the girl.

"Oh, Jane Lavinia," she said with a sob, "I'm so glad! I couldn't see how I was going to get along without you, but I thought you didn't care. You can wear that chiffon hat everywhere you want to, and I'll get you a pink organdy dress for Sundays."

SHE EYED CHESTER SOURLY.

Mackereling Out in the Gulf

The mackerel boats were all at anchor on the fishing grounds; the sea was glassy calm—a pallid blue, save for a chance streak of deeper azure where some stray sea breeze ruffled it.

It was about the middle of the afternoon, and intensely warm and breathless. The headlands and coves were blurred by a purple heat haze. The long sweep of the sandshore was so glaringly brilliant that the pained eye sought relief among the rough rocks, where shadows were cast by the big red sandstone boulders. The little cluster of fishing houses nearby were bleached to a silvery grey by long exposure to wind and rain. Far off were several "Yankee" fishing schooners, their sails dimly visible against the white horizon.

Two boats were hauled upon the "skids" that ran from the rocks out into the water. A couple of dories floated below them. Now and then a white gull, flashing silver where its plumage caught the sun, soared landward.

A young man was standing by the skids, watching the fishing boats through a spyglass. He was tall, with a straight, muscular figure clad in a rough fishing suit. His face was deeply browned by the gulf breezes and was attractive rather than handsome, while his eyes, as blue and clear as the gulf waters, were peculiarly honest and frank.

Two wiry, dark-faced French-Canadian boys were perched on one of the boats, watching the fishing fleet with lazy interest in their inky-black eyes, and wondering if the "Yanks" had seined many mackerel that day.

Presently three people came down the steep path from the fish-houses. One of them, a girl, ran lightly forward and touched Benjamin Selby's arm. He lowered his glass with a start and looked around. A flash of undisguised delight transfigured his face.

"Why, Mary Stella! I didn't expect you'd be down this hot day. You haven't been much at the shore lately," he added reproachfully.

"I really haven't had time, Benjamin," she answered carelessly, as she took the glass from his hand and tried to focus it on the fishing fleet. Benjamin steadied it for her; the flush of pleasure was still glowing on his bronzed cheek, "Are the mackerel biting now?"

"Not just now. Who is that stranger with your father, Mary Stella?"

"That is a cousin of ours—a Mr. Braithwaite. Are you very busy, Benjamin?"

"Not busy at all—idle as you see me. Why?"

"Will you take me out for a little row in the dory? I haven't been out for so long."

"Of course. Come—here's the dory—your namesake, you know. I had her fresh painted last week. She's as clean as an eggshell."

The girl stepped daintily off the rocks into the little cream-coloured skiff, and Benjamin untied the rope and pushed off.

"Where would you like to go, Mary Stella?"

"Oh, just upshore a little way—not far. And don't go out into very deep water, please, it makes me feel frightened and dizzy."

Benjamin smiled and promised. He was rowing along with the easy grace of one used to the oar. He had been born and brought up in sound of the gulf's waves; its never-ceasing murmur had been his first lullaby. He knew it and loved it in every mood, in every varying tint and smile, in every change of wind and tide. There was no better skipper alongshore than Benjamin Selby.

Mary Stella waved her hand gaily to the two men on the rocks. Benjamin looked back darkly.

"Who is that young fellow?" he asked again. "Where does he belong?"

"He is the son of Father's sister—his favourite sister, although he has never seen her since she married an American years ago and went to live in the States. She made Frank come down here this summer and hunt us up. He is splendid, I think. He is a New York lawyer and very clever."

Benjamin made no response. He pulled in his oars and let the dory float amid the ripples. The bottom of white sand, patterned over with coloured pebbles, was clear and distinct through the dark-green water. Mary Stella leaned over to watch the distorted reflection of her face by the dory's side.

"Have you had pretty good luck this week, Benjamin? Father couldn't go out much—he has been so busy with his hay, and Leon is such a poor fisherman."

"We've had some of the best hauls of the summer this week. Some of the Rustler boats caught six hundred to a line yesterday. We had four hundred to the line in our boat."

Mary Stella began absently to dabble her slender brown hand in the water. A silence fell between them, with which Benjamin was well content, since it gave him a chance to feast his eyes on the beautiful face before him.

He could not recall the time when he had not loved Mary Stella. It seemed to him that she had always been a part of his inmost life. He loved her with the whole strength and fidelity of a naturally intense nature. He hoped that she loved him, and he had no rival that he feared. In secret he exalted and deified her as something almost too holy for him to aspire to. She was his ideal of all that was beautiful and good; he was jealously careful over all his words and thoughts and actions that not one might make him more unworthy of her. In all the hardship and toil of his life his love was as his guardian angel, turning his feet from every dim and crooked byway; he trod in no path where he would not have the girl he loved to follow. The roughest labour was glorified if it lifted him a step nearer the altar of his worship.

But today he felt faintly disturbed. In some strange, indefinable way it seemed to him that Mary Stella was different from her usual self. The impression was vague and evanescent—gone before he could decide wherein the difference lay. He told himself that he was foolish, yet the vexing, transient feeling continued to come and go.

Presently Mary Stella said it was time to go back. Benjamin was in no hurry, but he never disputed her lightest inclination. He turned the dory about and rowed shoreward.

Back on the rocks, Mosey Louis and Xavier, the French Canadians, were looking through the spyglass by turns and making characteristic comments on the fleet. Mr. Murray and Braithwaite were standing by the skids, watching the dory.

"Who is that young fellow?" asked the latter. "What a splendid physique he has! It's a pleasure to watch him rowing."

"That," said the older man, with a certain proprietary pride in his tone, "is Benjamin Selby—the best mackerel fisherman on the island. He's been high line all along the gulf shore for years. I don't know a finer man every way you take him. Maybe you'll think I'm partial," he continued with a smile. "You see, he and Mary Stella think a good deal of each other. I expect to have Benjamin for a son-in-law some day if all goes well."

Braithwaite's expression changed slightly. He walked over to the dory and helped Mary Stella out of it while Benjamin made the painter fast. When the latter turned, Mary Stella was walking across the rocks with her cousin. Benjamin's blue eyes darkened, and he strode moodily over to the boats.

"You weren't out this morning, Mr. Murray?"

"No, that hay had to be took in. Reckon I missed it—pretty good catch, they tell me. Are they getting any now?"

"No. It's not likely the fish will begin to bite again for another hour."

"I see someone standing up in that off boat, don't I?" said Mr. Murray, reaching for the spyglass.

"No, that's only Rob Leslie's crew trying to fool us. They've tried it before this afternoon. They think it would be a joke to coax us out there to broil like themselves."

"Frank," shouted Mr. Murray, "come here, I want you."

Aside to Benjamin he said, "He's my nephew—a fine young chap. You'll like him, I know."

Braithwaite came over, and Mr. Murray put one hand on his shoulder and one on Benjamin's.

"Boys, I want you to know each other. Benjamin, this is Frank Braithwaite. Frank, this is Benjamin Selby, the high line of the gulf shore, as I told you."

While Mr. Murray was speaking, the two men looked steadily at each other. The few seconds seemed very long; when they had passed, Benjamin knew that the other man was his rival.

Braithwaite was the first to speak. He put out his hand with easy cordiality.

"I am glad to meet you, Mr. Selby," he said heartily, "although I am afraid I should feel very green in the presence of such a veteran fisherman as yourself."

His frank courtesy compelled some return. Benjamin took the proffered hand with restraint.

"I'm sorry there's no mackerel going this afternoon," continued the American. "I wanted to have a chance at them. I never saw mackerel caught before. I suppose I'll be very awkward at first."

"It's not a very hard thing to do," said Benjamin stiffly, speaking for the first time since their meeting. "Most anybody could catch mackerel for a while—it's the sticking to it that counts."

He turned abruptly and went back to his boat. He could not force himself to talk civilly to the stranger, with that newly born demon of distrust gnawing at his heart.

"I think I'll go out," he said. "It's freshening up. I shouldn't wonder if the mackerel schooled soon."

"I'll go, too, then," said Mr. Murray. "Hi, up there! Leon and Pete! Hi, I say!"

Two more French Canadians came running down from the Murray fish-house, where they had been enjoying a siesta. They fished in the Murray boat. A good deal of friendly rivalry as to catch went on between the two boats, while Leon and Mosey Louis were bitter enemies on their own personal account.

"Think you'll try it, Frank?" shouted Mr. Murray.

"Well, not this afternoon," was the answer. "It's rather hot. I'll see what it is like tomorrow."

The boats were quickly launched and glided out from the shadow of the cliffs. Benjamin stood at his mast. Mary Stella came down to the water's edge and waved her hand gaily.

"Good luck to you and the best catch of the season," she called out.

Benjamin waved his hat in response. His jealousy was forgotten for the moment and he felt that he had been churlish to Braithwaite.

"You'll wish you'd come," he shouted to him. "It's going to be a great evening for fish."

When the boats reached the fishing grounds, they came to and anchored, their masts coming out in slender silhouette against the sky. A row of dark figures was standing up in every boat; the gulfs shining expanse was darkened by odd black streaks—the mackerel had begun to school.

Frank Braithwaite went out fishing the next day and caught 30 mackerel. He was boyishly proud of it. He visited the shore daily after that and soon became very popular. He developed into quite an expert fisherman; nor, when the boats came in, did he shirk work, but manfully rolled up his trousers and helped carry water and "gib" mackerel as if he enjoyed it. He never put on any "airs," and he stoutly took Leon's part against the aggressive Mosey Louis. Even the French Canadians, those merciless critics, admitted that the "Yankee" was a good fellow. Benjamin Selby alone held stubbornly aloof.

One evening the loaded boats came in at sunset. Benjamin sprang from his as it bumped against the skids, and ran up the path. At the corner of his fish-house he stopped and stood quite still, looking at Braithwaite and Mary Stella, who were standing by the rough picket fence of the pasture land. Braithwaite's back was to Benjamin; he held the girl's hand in his and was talking earnestly. Mary Stella was looking up at him, her delicate face thrown back a little. There was a look in her eyes that Benjamin had never seen there before—but he knew what it meant.

His face grew pale and rigid; he clenched his hands and a whirlpool of agony and bitterness surged up in his heart. All the great blossoms of the hope that had shed beauty and fragrance over his rough life seemed suddenly to shrivel up into black unsightliness.

He turned and went swiftly and noiselessly down the road to his boat. The murmur of the sea sounded very far off. Mosey Louis was busy counting out the mackerel, Xavier was dipping up buckets of water and pouring it over the silvery fish. The sun was setting in a bank of purple cloud, and the long black headland to the west cut the golden seas like a wedge of ebony. It was all real and yet unreal. Benjamin went to work mechanically.

Presently Mary Stella came down to her father's boat. Braithwaite followed slowly, pausing a moment to exchange some banter with saucy Mosey Louis. Benjamin bent lower over his table; now and then he caught the dear tones of Mary Stella's voice or her laughter at some sally of Pete or Leon. He knew when she went up the road with Braithwaite; he caught the last glimpse of her light dress as she passed out of sight on the cliffs above, but he worked steadily on and gave no sign.

It was late when they finished. The tired French Canadians went quickly off to their beds in the fish-house loft. Benjamin stood by the skids until all was quiet, then he walked down the cove to a rocky point that jutted out into the water. He leaned against a huge boulder and laid his head on his arm, looking up into the dark sky. The stars shone calmly down on his misery; the throbbing sea stretched out before him; its low, murmuring moan seemed to be the inarticulate voice of his pain.

The air was close and oppressive; fitful flashes of heat lightning shimmered here and there over the heavy banks of cloud on the horizon; little wavelets sobbed at the base of the rocks.

When Benjamin lifted his head he saw Frank Braithwaite standing between him and the luminous water. He took a step forward, and they came face to face as Braithwaite turned with a start.

Benjamin clenched his hands and fought down a hideous temptation to thrust his rival off the rock.

"I saw you today," he said in a low, intense tone. "What do you think of yourself, coming down here to steal the girl I loved from me? Weren't there enough girls where you came from to choose among? I hate you. I'd kill you—"

"Selby, stop! You don't know what you are saying. If I have wronged you, I swear I did it unintentionally. I loved Stella from the first—who could help it?

But I thought she was virtually bound to you, and I did not try to win her away. You don't know what it cost me to remain passive. I know that you have always distrusted me, but hitherto you have had no reason to. But today I found that she was free—that she did not care for you! And I found—or thought I found—that there was a chance for me. I took it. I forgot everything else then."

"So she loves you?" said Benjamin dully.

"Yes," said Braithwaite softly.

Benjamin turned on him with sudden passion.

"I hate you—and I am the most miserable wretch alive, but if she is happy, it is no matter about me. You've won easily what I've slaved and toiled all my life for. You won't value it as I'd have done—but if you make her happy, nothing else matters. I've only one favour to ask of you. Don't let her come to the shore after this. I can't stand it."

August throbbed and burned itself out. Affairs along shore continued as usual. Benjamin shut his sorrow up in himself and gave no outward sign of suffering. As if to mock him, the season was one of phenomenal prosperity; it was a "mackerel year" to be dated from. He worked hard and unceasingly, sparing himself in no way.

Braithwaite seldom came to the shore now. Mary Stella never. Mr. Murray had tried to speak of the matter, but Benjamin would not let him.

"It's best that nothing be said," he told him with simple dignity. He was so calm that Mr. Murray thought he did not care greatly, and was glad of it. The older man regretted the turn of affairs. Braithwaite would take his daughter far away from him, as his sister had been taken, and he loved Benjamin as his own son.

One afternoon Benjamin stood by his boat and looked anxiously at sea and sky. The French Canadians were eager to go out, for the other boats were catching.

"I don't know about it," said Benjamin doubtfully. "I don't half like the look of things. I believe we're in for a squall before long. It was just such a day three years ago when that terrible squall came up that Joe Otway got drowned in."

The sky was dun and smoky, the glassy water was copper-hued, the air was heavy and breathless. The sea purred upon the shore, lapping it caressingly like some huge feline creature biding its time to seize and crunch its victim.

"I reckon I'll try it," said Benjamin after a final scrutiny. "If a squall does come up, we'll have to run for the shore mighty quick, that's all."

They launched the boat speedily; as there was no wind, they had to row. As they pulled out, Braithwaite and Leon came down the road and began to launch the Murray boat.

"If dem two gits caught in a squall dey'll hav a tam," grinned Mosey Louis. "Dat Leon, he don't know de fust ting 'bout a boat, no more dan a cat!"

Benjamin came to anchor close in, but Braithwaite and Leon kept on until they were further out than any other boat.

"Reckon dey's after cod," suggested Xavier.

The mackerel bit well, but Benjamin kept a close watch on the sky. Suddenly he saw a dark streak advancing over the water from the northwest. He wheeled around.

"Boys, the squall's coming! Up with the anchor—quick!"

"Dere's plenty tam," grumbled Mosey Louis, who hated to leave the fish. "None of de oder boats is goin' in yit."

The squall struck the boat as he spoke. She lurched and staggered. The water was tossing choppily. There was a sudden commotion all through the fleet and sails went rapidly up. Mosey Louis turned pale and scrambled about without delay. Benjamin was halfway to the shore before the sail went up in the Murray boat.

"Don' know what dey're tinkin' of," growled Mosey Louis. "Dey'll be drown fust ting!"

Benjamin looked back anxiously. Every boat was making for the shore. The gale was steadily increasing. He had his doubts about making a landing himself, and Braithwaite would be twenty minutes later.

"But it isn't my lookout," he muttered.

Benjamin had landed and was hauling up his boat when Mr. Murray came running down the road.

"Frank?" he gasped. "Him and Leon went out, the foolish boys! They neither of them know anything about a time like this."

"I guess they'll be all right," said Benjamin reassuringly. "They were late starting. They may find it rather hard to land."

The other boats had all got in with more or less difficulty. The Murray boat alone was out. Men came scurrying along the shore in frightened groups of two and three.

The boat came swiftly in before the wind. Mr. Murray was half beside himself.

"It'll be all right, sir," said one of the men. "If they can't land here, they can beach her on the sandshore."

"If they only knew enough to do that," wailed the old man. "But they don't—they'll come right on to the rocks."

"Why don't they lower their sail?" said another. "They will upset if they don't."

"They're lowering it now," said Benjamin.

The boat was now about 300 yards from the shore. The sail did not go all the way down—it seemed to be stuck.

"Good God, what's wrong?" exclaimed Mr. Murray.

As he spoke, the boat capsized. A yell of horror rose I from the beach. Mr. Murray sprang toward Benjamin's boat, but one of the men held him back.

"You can't do it, sir. I don't know that anybody can."

Braithwaite and Leon were clinging to the boat. Benjamin Selby, standing in the background, his lips set, his hands clenched, was fighting the hardest battle of his life. He knew that he alone, out of all the men there, possessed the necessary skill and nerve to reach the boat if she could be reached at all. There was a bare chance and a great risk. This man whom he hated was drowning before his eyes.

Let him drown, then! Why should he risk—ay, and perchance lose—his life for his enemy? No one could blame him for refusing—and if Braithwaite were out of the way, Mary Stella might yet be his!

The temptation and victory passed in a few brief seconds. He stepped forward, cool and self-possessed.

"I'm going out. I want one man with me. No one with child or wife. Who'll go?"

"I will," shouted Mosey Louis. "I haf some spat wid dat Leon, but I not lak to see him drown for all dat!"

Benjamin offered no objection. The French Canadian's arm was strong and he possessed skill and experience. Mr. Murray caught Benjamin's arm.

"No, no, Benjamin—not you—I can't see both my boys drowned."

Benjamin gently loosed the old man's hold.

"It's for Mary Stella's sake," he said hoarsely. "If I don't come back, tell her that."

They launched the large dory with difficulty and pulled out into the surf. Benjamin did not lose his nerve. His quick arm, his steady eye did not fail. A dozen times the wild-eyed watchers thought the boat was doomed, but as often she righted triumphantly.

At last the drowning men were reached and somehow or other hauled on board Benjamin's craft. It was easier to come back, for they beached the boat on the sand. With a wild cheer the men on the shore rushed into the surf and helped to carry the half-unconscious Braithwaite and Leon ashore and up to the Murray fish-house. Benjamin went home before anyone knew he had gone. Mosey Louis was left behind to reap the honours; he sat in a circle of admiring lads and gave all the details of the rescue.

"Dat Leon, he not tink he know so much now!" he said.

Braithwaite came to the shore next day somewhat pale and shaky. He went straight to Benjamin and held out his hand.

"Thank you," he said simply.

Benjamin bent lower over his work.

"You needn't thank me," he said gruffly. "I wanted to let you drown. But I went out for Mary Stella's sake. Tell me one thing—I couldn't bring myself to ask it of anyone else. When are you to be—married?"

"The 12th of September."

Benjamin did not wince. He turned away and looked out across the sea for a few moments. The last agony of his great renunciation was upon him. Then he turned and held out his hand.

"For her sake," he said earnestly.

Frank Braithwaite put his slender white hand into the fisherman's hard brown palm. There were tears in both men's eyes. They parted in silence.

On the morning of the 12th of September Benjamin Selby went out to the fishing grounds as usual. The catch was good, although the season was almost over. In the afternoon the French Canadians went to sleep. Benjamin intended to row down the shore for salt. He stood by his dory, ready to start, but he seemed to be waiting for something. At last it came: a faint train whistle blew, a puff of white smoke floated across a distant gap in the sandhills.

Mary Stella was gone at last—gone forever from his life. The honest blue eyes looking out over the sea did not falter; bravely he faced his desolate future.

The white gulls soared over the water, little swishing ripples lapped on the sand, and through all the gentle, dreamy noises of the shore came the soft, unceasing murmur of the gulf.

Millicent's Double

"'Nonsense,' said Millicent, pointing to their reflected faces"

When Millicent Moore and Worth Gordon met each other on the first day of the term in the entrance hall of the Kinglake High School, both girls stopped short, startled. Millicent Moore had never seen Worth Gordon before, but Worth Gordon's face she had seen every day of her life, looking at her out of her own mirror!

They were total strangers, but when two girls look enough alike to be twins, it is not necessary to stand on ceremony. After the first blank stare of amazement, both laughed outright. Millicent held out her hand.

"We ought to know each other right away," she said frankly. "My name is Millicent Moore, and yours is—?"

"Worth Gordon," responded Worth, taking the proffered hand with dancing eyes. "You actually frightened me when you came around that corner. For a moment I had an uncanny feeling that I was a disembodied spirit looking at my own outward shape. I know now what it feels like to have a twin."

"Isn't it odd that we should look so much alike?" said Millicent. "Do you suppose we can be any relation? I never heard of any relations named Gordon."

Worth shook her head. "I'm quite sure we're not," she said. "I haven't any relatives except my father's stepsister with whom I've lived ever since the death of my parents when I was a baby."

"Well, you'll really have to count me as a relative after this," laughed Millicent. "I'm sure a girl who looks as much like you as I do must be at least as much relation as a stepaunt."

From that moment they were firm friends, and their friendship was still further cemented by the fact that Worth found it necessary to change her boarding-house and became Millicent's roommate. Their odd likeness was the wonder of the school and occasioned no end of amusing mistakes, for all the students found it hard to distinguish between them. Seen apart it was impossible to tell which was which except by their clothes and style of hairdressing. Seen together there were, of course, many minor differences which served to distinguish them. Both girls were slight, with dark-brown hair, blue eyes and fair complexions. But Millicent had more colour than Worth. Even in repose, Millicent's face expressed mirth and fun; when Worth was not laughing or talking, her face was rather serious. Worth's eyes were darker, and her nose in profile slightly more aquiline. But still, the resemblance between them was very striking. In disposition they were also very similar. Both were merry, fun-loving girls, fond of larks and jokes. Millicent was the more heedless, but both were impulsive and too apt to do or say anything that came into their heads without counting the cost. One late October evening Millicent came in, her cheeks crimson after her walk in the keen autumn air, and tossed two letters on the study table. "It's a perfect evening, Worth. We had the jolliest tramp. You should have come with us instead of staying in moping over your books."

Worth smiled ruefully. "I simply had to prepare those problems for tomorrow," she said. "You see, Millie dear, there is a big difference between us in some things at least. I'm poor. I simply have to pass my exams and get a teacher's licence. So I can't afford to take any chances. You're just attending high school for the sake of education alone, so you don't really have to grind as I do."

"I'd like to do pretty well in the exams, though, for Dad's sake," answered Millicent, throwing aside her wraps. "But I don't mean to kill myself studying, just the same. Time enough for that when exams draw nigh. They're comfortably far off yet. But I'm in a bit of a predicament, Worth, and I don't know what to do. Here are two invitations for Saturday afternoon and I simply *must* accept them both. Now, how can I do it? You're a marvel at mathematics—so work out that problem for me.

"See, here's a note from Mrs. Kirby inviting me to tea at Beechwood. She called on me soon after the term opened and invited me to tea the next week. But I had another engagement for that afternoon, so couldn't go. Mr. Kirby is a business friend of Dad's, and they are very nice people. The other invitation is to the annual autumn picnic of the Alpha Gammas. Now, Worth Gordon, I simply *must* go to that. I wouldn't miss it for anything. But I don't want to offend Mrs. Kirby, and I'm afraid I shall if I plead another engagement a second time. Mother will be fearfully annoyed at me in that case. Dear me, I wish there were two of me, one to go to the Alpha Gammas and one to Beechwood—Worth Gordon!"

"What's the matter?"

"There *are* two of me! What's the use of a double if not for a quandary like this! Worth, you must go to tea at Beechwood Saturday afternoon in my place. They'll think you are my very self. They'll never know the difference. Go and keep my place warm for me, there's a dear."

"Impossible," cried Worth. "I'd never dare! They'd know there was something wrong."

"They wouldn't—they couldn't. None of the Kirbys have ever seen me except Mrs. Kirby, and she only for a few minutes one evening at dusk. They don't know I have a double and they can't possibly suspect. *Do* go, Worth. Why, it'll be a regular lark, the best little joke ever! And you'll oblige me immensely besides. Worthie, *please*."

Worth did not consent all at once; but the idea rather appealed to her for its daring and excitement. It would be a lark—just at that time Worth did not see it in any other light. Besides, she wanted to oblige Millicent, who coaxed vehemently. Finally, Worth yielded and promised Millicent that she would go to Beechwood in her place.

"You darling!" said Millicent emphatically, flying to her table to write acceptances of both invitations.

Saturday afternoon Worth got ready to keep Millicent's engagement. "Suppose I am found out and expelled from Beechwood in disgrace," she suggested laughingly, as she arranged her lace bertha before the glass.

"Nonsense," said Millicent, pointing to their reflected faces. "The Kirbys can never suspect. Why, if it weren't for the hair and the dresses, I'd hardly know myself which of those reflections belonged to which."

"What if they begin asking me about the welfare of the various members of your family?"

"They won't ask any but the most superficial questions. We're not intimate enough for anything else. I've coached you pretty thoroughly, and I think you'll get on all right."

Worth's courage carried her successfully through the ordeal of arriving at Beechwood and meeting Mrs. Kirby. She was unsuspectingly accepted as Millicent Moore, and found her impersonation of that young lady not at all difficult. No dangerous subject of conversation was introduced and nothing personal was said until Mr. Kirby came in. He looked so scrutinizingly at Worth as he shook hands with her that the latter felt her heart beating very fast. Did he suspect?

"Upon my word, Miss Moore," he said genially, "you gave me quite a start at first. You are very like what a half-sister of mine used to be when a girl long ago. Of course the resemblance must be quite accidental."

"Of course," said Worth, without any very clear sense of what she was saying. Her face was uncomfortably flushed and she was glad when tea was announced.

As nothing more of an embarrassing nature was said, Worth soon recovered her self-possession and was able to enter into the conversation. She liked the Kirbys; still, under her enjoyment, she was conscious of a strange, disagreeable feeling that deepened as the evening wore on. It was not fear—she was not at all afraid of betraying herself now. It had even been easier than she had expected. Then what was it? Suddenly Worth flushed again. She knew now—it was shame. She was a guest in that house as an impostor! What she had done seemed no longer a mere joke. What would her host and hostess say if they knew? That they would never know made no difference. *She* herself could not forget it, and her realization of the baseness of the deception grew stronger under Mrs. Kirby's cordial kindness.

Worth never forgot that evening. She compelled herself to chat as brightly as possible, but under it all was that miserable consciousness of falsehood, deepening every instant. She was thankful when the time came to leave. "You must come up often, Miss Moore," said Mrs. Kirby kindly. "Look upon Beechwood as a second home while you are in Kinglake. We have no daughter of our own, so we make a hobby of cultivating other people's."

When Millicent returned home from the Alpha Gamma outing, she found Worth in their room, looking soberly at the mirror. Something in her chum's expression alarmed her. "Worth, what is it? Did they suspect?"

"No," said Worth slowly. "They never suspected. They think I am what I pretended to be—Millicent Moore. But, but, I wish I'd never gone to Beechwood, Millie. It wasn't right. It was mean and wrong. It was acting a lie. I can't tell you how ashamed I felt when I realized that."

"Nonsense," said Millicent, looking rather sober, nevertheless. "No harm was done. It's only a good joke, Worth."

"Yes, harm *has* been done. I've done harm to myself, for one thing. I've lost my self-respect. I don't blame you, Millie. It's all my own fault. I've done a dishonourable thing, dishonourable."

Millicent sighed. "The Alpha Gamma picnic was horribly slow," she said. "I didn't enjoy myself a bit. I wish I had gone to Beechwood. I didn't think about it's being a practical falsehood before. I suppose it was. And I've always prided myself on my strict truthfulness! It wasn't your fault, Worth! It was mine. But it can't be undone now."

"No, it can't be undone," said Worth slowly, "but it might be confessed. We might tell Mrs. Kirby the truth and ask her to forgive us."

"I couldn't do such a thing," cried Millicent. "It isn't to be thought of!"

Nevertheless, Millicent did think of it several times that night and all through the following Sunday. She couldn't help thinking of it. A dishonourable trick! That thought stung Millicent. Monday evening Millicent flung down the book from which she was vainly trying to study.

"Worthie, it's no use. You were right. There's nothing to do but go and 'fess up to Mrs. Kirby. I can't respect Millicent Moore again until I do. I'm going right up now."

"I'll go with you," said Worth quietly. "I was equally to blame and I must take my share of the humiliation."

When the girls reached Beechwood, they were shown into the library where the family were sitting. Mrs. Kirby came smilingly forward to greet Millicent when her eyes fell upon Worth. "Why! *why*!" she said. "I didn't know you had a twin sister, Miss Moore."

"Neither I have," said Millicent, laughing nervously. "This is my chum, Worth Gordon, but she is no relation whatever."

At the mention of Worth's name, Mr. Kirby started slightly, but nobody noticed it. Millicent went on in a trembling voice. "We've come up to confess something, Mrs. Kirby. I'm sure you'll think it dreadful, but we didn't mean any harm. We just didn't realize, until afterwards."

Then Millicent, with burning cheeks, told the whole story and asked to be forgiven. "I, too, must apologize," said Worth, when Millicent had finished. "Can you pardon me, Mrs. Kirby?"

Mrs. Kirby had listened in amazed silence, but now she laughed. "Certainly," she said kindly. "I don't suppose it was altogether right for you girls to play such a trick on anybody. But I can make allowances for schoolgirl pranks. I was a school girl once myself, and far from a model one. You have atoned for your mistake by coming so frankly and confessing, and now we'll forget all about it. I think you have learned your lesson. Both of you must just sit down and spend the evening with us. Dear me, but you *are* bewilderingly alike!"

"I've something I want to say," interposed Mr. Kirby suddenly. "You say your name is Worth Gordon," he added, turning to Worth. "May I ask what your mother's name was?"

"Worth Mowbray," answered Worth wonderingly.

"I was sure of it," said Mr. Kirby triumphantly, "when I heard Miss Moore mention your name. Your mother was my half-sister, and you are my niece."

Everybody exclaimed and for a few moments they all talked and questioned together. Then Mr. Kirby explained fully. "I was born on a farm up-country. My mother was a widow when she married my father, and she had one daughter, Worth Mowbray, five years older than myself. When I was three years old, my mother died. Worth went to live with our mother's only living relative, an aunt. My father and I removed to another section of the country. He, too, died soon after, and I was brought up with an uncle's family. My sister came to see me once when she was a girl of seventeen and, as I remember her, very like you are now. I never saw her again and eventually lost trace of her. Many years later I endeavoured to find out her whereabouts. Our aunt was dead, and the people in the village where she had lived informed me that my sister was also dead. She had married a man named Gordon and had gone away, both she and her husband had died, and I was informed that they left no children, so I made no further inquiries. There is no doubt that you are her daughter. Well, well, this is a pleasant surprise, to find a little niece in this fashion!"

It was a pleasant surprise to Worth, too, who had thought herself all alone in the world and had felt her loneliness keenly. They had a wonderful evening, talking and questioning and explaining. Mr. Kirby declared that Worth must come and live with them. "We have no daughter," he said. "You must come to us in the place of one, Worth."

Mrs. Kirby seconded this with a cordiality that won Worth's affection at once. The girl felt almost bewildered by her happiness.

"I feel as if I were in a dream," she said to Millicent as they walked to their boarding-house. "It's really all too wonderful to grasp at once. You don't know, Millie, how lonely I've felt often under all my nonsense and fun. Aunt Delia was kind to me, but she was really no relation, she had a large family of her own, and I have always felt that she looked upon me as a rather inconvenient duty. But now I'm so happy!"

"I'm so glad for you, Worth," said Millicent warmly, "although your gain will certainly be my loss, for I shall miss my roommate terribly when she goes to live at Beechwood. Hasn't it all turned out strangely? If you had never gone to Beechwood in my place, this would never have happened."

"Say rather that if we hadn't gone to confess our fault, it would never have happened," said Worth gently. "I'm very, very glad that I have found Uncle George and such a loving welcome to his home. But I'm gladder still that I've got my self-respect back. I feel that I can look Worth Gordon in the face again."

"I've learned a wholesome lesson, too," admitted Millicent.

The Blue North Room

"This," said Sara, laying Aunt Josephina's letter down on the kitchen table with such energy that in anybody but Sara it must have been said she threw it down, "this is positively the last straw! I have endured all the rest. I have given up my chance of a musical education, when Aunt Nan offered it, that I might stay home and help Willard pay the mortgage off—if it doesn't pay us off first—and I have, which was much harder, accepted the fact that we can't possibly afford to send Ray to the Valley Academy, even if I wore the same hat and coat for four winters. I did not grumble when Uncle Joel came here to live because he wanted to be 'near his dear nephew's children.' I felt it my Christian duty to look pleasant when we had to give Cousin Caroline a home to save her from the poorhouse. But my endurance and philosophy, and worst of all, my furniture, has reached a limit. I cannot have Aunt Josephina come here to spend the winter, because I have no room to put her in."

"Hello, Sally, what's the matter?" asked Ray, coming in with a book. It would have been hard to catch Ray without a book; he generally took one even to bed with him. Ray had a headful of brains, and Sara thought it was a burning shame that there seemed to be no chance for his going to college. "You look all rumpled up in your conscience, beloved sis," the boy went on, chaffingly.

"My conscience is all right," said Sara severely. "It's worse than that. If you please, here's a letter from Aunt Josephina! She writes that she is very lonesome. Her son has gone to South America, and won't be back until spring, and she wants to come and spend the winter with us."

"Well, why not?" asked Ray serenely. Nothing ever bothered Ray. "The more the merrier."

"Ray Sheldon! Where are we to put her? We have no spare room, as you well know."

"Can't she room with Cousin Caroline?"

"Cousin Caroline's room is too small for two. It's full to overflowing with her belongings now, and Aunt Josephina will bring two trunks at least. Try again, bright boy."

"What's the matter with the blue north room?"

"There is nothing the matter with it—oh, nothing at all! We could put Aunt Josephina there, but where will she sleep? Where will she wash her face? Will it not seem slightly inhospitable to invite her to sit on a bare floor? Have you forgotten that there isn't a stick of furniture in the blue north room and, worse still, that we haven't a spare cent to buy any, not even the cheapest kind?"

"I'll give it up," said Ray. "I might have a try at squaring the circle if you asked me, but the solution of the Aunt Josephina problem is beyond me."

"The solution is simply that we must write to Aunt Josephina, politely but firmly, that we can't have her come, owing to lack of accommodation. You must write the letter, Ray. Make it as polite as you can, but above all make it firm."

"Oh, but Sally, dear," protested Ray, who didn't relish having to write such a letter, "isn't this rather hasty, rather inhospitable? Poor Aunt Josephina must really be rather lonely, and it's only natural she should want to visit her relations."

"We're *not* her relations," cried Sara. "We're not a speck of relation really. She's only the half-sister of Mother's half-brother. That sounds nice and relationy, doesn't it? And she's fussy and interfering, and she will fight with Cousin Caroline, everybody fights with Cousin Caroline—"

"Except Sara," interrupted Ray, but Sara went on with a rush, "And we won't have a minute's peace all winter. Anyhow, where could we put her even if we wanted her to come? No, we can't have her!"

"Mother was always very fond of Aunt Josephina," said Ray reflectively. Sara had her lips open, all ready to answer whatever Ray might say, but she shut them suddenly and the boy went on. "Aunt Josephina thought a lot of Mother, too. She used to say she knew there was always a welcome for her at Maple Hollow. It does seem a pity, Sally dear, for your mother's daughter to send word to Aunt Josephina, per my mother's son, that there isn't room for her any longer at Maple Hollow."

"I shall leave it to Willard," said Sara abruptly. "If he says to let her come, come she shall, even if Dorothy and I have to camp in the barn."

"I'm going to have a prowl around the garret," said Ray, apropos of nothing.

"And I shall get the tea ready," answered Sara briskly. "Dorothy will be home from school very soon, and I hear Uncle Joel stirring. Willard won't be back till dark, so there is no use waiting for him."

At twilight Sara decided to walk up the lane and meet Willard. She always liked to meet him thus when he had been away for a whole day. Sara thought there was nobody in the world as good and dear as Willard.

It was a dull grey November twilight; the maples in the hollow were all leafless, and the hawthorn hedge along the lane was sere and frosted; a little snow had fallen in the afternoon, and lay in broad patches on the brown fields. The world looked very dull and dispirited, and Sara sighed. She could not help thinking of the dark side of things just then. "Everything is wrong," said poor Sara dolefully. "Willard has to work like a slave, and yet with all his efforts he can barely pay the interest on the mortgage. And Ray ought to go to college. But I don't see how we can ever manage. To be sure, he won't be ready until next fall, but we won't have the money then any more than now. It would take every bit of a hundred and fifty dollars to fit him out with books and clothes, and pay for board and tuition at the academy. If he could just have a year there he could teach and earn his own way through college. But we might as well hope for the moon as one hundred and fifty dollars."

Sara sighed again. She was only eighteen, but she felt very old. Willard was nineteen, and Willard had never had a chance to be young. His father had died when he was twelve, and he had run the farm since then, he and Sara together indeed, for Sara was a capital planner and manager and worker. The little mother had died two years ago, and the household cares had all fallen on Sara's shoulders since. Sometimes, as now, they pressed very heavily, but a talk with Willard always heartened her up. Willard had his blue spells too, but Sara thought it a special Providence that their blue turns never came together. When one got downhearted the other was always ready to do the cheering up.

Sara was glad to hear Willard whistling when he drove into the lane; it was a sign he was in good spirits. He pulled up, and Sara climbed into the wagon.

"Things go all right today, Sally?" he asked cheerfully.

"There was a letter from Aunt Josephina," answered Sara, anxious to get the worst over, "and she wants to come to Maple Hollow for the winter. I thought at first we just couldn't have her, but I decided to leave it to you."

"Well, we've got a pretty good houseful already," said Willard thoughtfully. "But I suppose if Aunt Josephina wants to come we'd better have her. I always liked Aunt Josephina, and so did Mother, you know."

"I don't know where we can put her. We haven't any spare room, Will."

"Ray and I can sleep in the kitchen loft. You and Dolly take our room, and let Aunt Josephina take yours."

"The kitchen loft isn't really fit to sleep in," said Sara pessimistically. "It's awfully cold, and there're mice and rats—ugh! You and Ray will get nibbled in spots. But it's the only thing to do if we must have Aunt Josephina. I'll get Ray to write to her tomorrow. I couldn't put enough cordiality into the letter if I wrote it myself."

Ray came in while Willard was at supper. There were cobwebs all over him from his head to his heels. "I've solved the Aunt J. problem," he announced cheerfully. "We will furnish the blue north room."

"With what?" asked Sara disbelievingly.

"I've been poking about in the garret and in the carriage house loft," said Ray, "and I've found furniture galore. It's very old and cobwebby—witness my appearance—and very much in want of scrubbing and a few nails. But it will do."

"I'd forgotten about those old things," said Sara slowly. "They've never been used since I can remember, and long before. They were discarded before Mother came here. But I thought they were all broken and quite useless."

"Not at all. I believe we can furbish them up sufficiently to make the room habitable. It will be rather old-fashioned, but then it's Hobson's choice. There are the pieces of an old bed out in the loft, and they can be put together. There's an old corner cupboard out there too, with leaded glass doors, two old solid wooden armchairs, and a funny old chest of drawers with a writing desk in place of the top drawer, all full of yellow old letters and trash. I found it under a pile of old carpet. Then there's a washstand, and also a towel rack up in the garret, and the funniest old table with three claw legs, and a tippy top. One leg is broken off, but I hunted around and found it, and I guess we can fix it on. And there are two more old chairs and a queer little oval table with a cracked swing mirror on it."

"I have it," exclaimed Sara, with a burst of inspiration, "let us fix up a real old-fashioned room for Aunt Josephina. It won't do to put anything modern with those old things. One would kill the other. I'll put Mother's rag carpet down in it, and the four braided mats Grandma Sheldon gave me, and the old brass candlestick and the Irish chain coverlet. Oh, I believe it will be lots of fun."

It was. For a week the Sheldons hammered and glued and washed and consulted. The north room was already papered with a blue paper of an old-fashioned stripe-and-diamond pattern. The rag carpet was put down, and the braided rugs laid on it. The old bedstead was set up in one corner and, having been well cleaned and polished with beeswax and turpentine, was really a handsome piece of furniture. On the washstand Sara placed a quaint old basin and ewer which had been Grandma Sheldon's. Ray had fixed up the table as good as new; Sara had polished the brass claws, and on the table she put the brass tray, two candlesticks, and snuffers which had been long stowed away in the kitchen loft. The dressing table and swing mirror, with its scroll frame of tarnished gilt, was in the window corner, and opposite it was the old chest of drawers. The cupboard was set up in a corner, and beside it stood the spinning-wheel from the kitchen loft. The big grandfather clock, which had always stood in the hall below was carried up, and two platters of blue willow-ware were set up over the mantel. Above them was hung the faded sampler that Grandma Sheldon had worked ninety years ago when she was a little girl.

"Do you know," said Sara, when they stood in the middle of the room and surveyed the result, "I expected to have a good laugh over this, but it doesn't look funny after all. The things all seem to suit each other, some way, and they look good, don't they? I mean they look *real*, clear through. I believe that table and those drawers are solid mahogany. And look at the carving on those bedposts. Cleaning them has made such a difference. I do hope Aunt Josephina won't mind their being so old."

Aunt Josephina didn't. She was very philosophical about it when Sara explained that Cousin Caroline had the spare room, and the blue north room was all they had left. "Oh, it will be all right," she said, plainly determined to make the best of things. "Those old things are thought a lot of now, anyhow. I can't say I fancy them much myself—I like something a little brighter. But the rich folks have gone cracked over them. I know a woman in Boston that's got her whole house furnished with old truck, and as soon as she hears of any old furniture anywhere she's not contented till she's got it. She says it's her hobby, and she spends a heap on it. She'd be in raptures if she saw this old room of yours, Sary."

"Do you mean," said Sara slowly, "that there are people who would buy old things like these?"

"Yes, and pay more for them than would buy a real nice set with a marble-topped burey. You may well say there's lots of fools in the world, Sary." Sara was not saying or thinking any such thing. It was a new idea to her that any value was attached to old furniture, for Sara lived very much out of the world of fads and collectors. But she did not forget what Aunt Josephina had said.

The winter passed away. Aunt Josephina plainly enjoyed her visit, whatever the Sheldons felt about it. In March her son returned, and Aunt Josephina went home to him. Before she left, Sara asked her for the address of the woman whose hobby was old furniture, and the very afternoon after Aunt Josephina had gone Sara wrote and mailed a letter. For a week she looked so mysterious that Willard and Ray could not guess what she was plotting. At the end of that time Mrs. Stanton came.

Mrs. Stanton always declared afterwards that the mere sight of that blue north room gave her raptures. Such a find! Such a discovery! A bedstead with carved posts, a claw-footed table, real old willow-ware plates with the birds' bills meeting! Here was luck, if you like!

When Willard and Ray came home to tea Sara was sitting on the stairs counting her wealth.

"Sally, where did you discover all that long-lost treasure?" demanded Ray.

"Mrs. Stanton of Boston was here today," said Sara, enjoying the moment of revelation hugely. "She makes a hobby of collecting old furniture. I sold her every blessed thing in the blue north room except Mother's carpet and Grandma's mats and sampler. She wanted those too, but I couldn't part with them. She bought everything else and," Sara lifted her hands, full of bills, dramatically, "here are two hundred and fifty dollars to take you to the Valley Academy next fall, Ray."

"It wouldn't be fair to take it for that," said Ray, flushing. "You and Will—"

"Will and I say you must take it," said Sara. "Don't we, Will? There is nothing we want so much as to give you a college start. It is an enormous burden off my mind to think it is so nicely provided for. Besides, most of those old things were yours by the right of rediscovery, and you voted first of all to have Aunt Josephina come."

"You must take it, of course, Ray," said Willard. "Nothing else would give Sara and me so much pleasure. A blessing on Aunt Josephina."

"Amen," said Sara and Ray.

The Christmas Surprise at Enderly Road

"Phil, I'm getting fearfully hungry. When are we going to strike civilization?"

The speaker was my chum, Frank Ward. We were home from our academy for the Christmas holidays and had been amusing ourselves on this sunshiny December afternoon by a tramp through the "back lands," as the barrens that swept away south behind the village were called. They were grown over with scrub maple and spruce, and were quite pathless save for meandering sheep tracks that crossed and recrossed, but led apparently nowhere.

Frank and I did not know exactly where we were, but the back lands were not so extensive but that we would come out somewhere if we kept on. It was getting late and we wished to go home.

"I have an idea that we ought to strike civilization somewhere up the Enderly Road pretty soon," I answered.

"Do you call *that* civilization?" said Frank, with a laugh.

No Blackburn Hill boy was ever known to miss an opportunity of flinging a slur at Enderly Road, even if no Enderly Roader were by to feel the sting.

Enderly Road was a miserable little settlement straggling back from Blackburn Hill. It was a forsaken looking place, and the people, as a rule, were poor and shiftless. Between Blackburn Hill and Enderly Road very little social intercourse existed and, as the Road people resented what they called the pride of Blackburn Hill, there was a good deal of bad feeling between the two districts.

Presently Frank and I came out on the Enderly Road. We sat on the fence a few minutes to rest and discuss our route home. "If we go by the road it's three miles," said Frank. "Isn't there a short cut?"

"There ought to be one by the wood-lane that comes out by Jacob Hart's," I answered, "but I don't know where to strike it."

"Here is someone coming now; we'll inquire," said Frank, looking up the curve of the hard-frozen road. The "someone" was a little girl of about ten years old, who was trotting along with a basketful of school books on her arm. She was a pale, pinched little thing, and her jacket and red hood seemed very old and thin.

"Hello, missy," I said, as she came up, and then I stopped, for I saw she had been crying.

"What is the matter?" asked Frank, who was much more at ease with children than I was, and had always a warm spot in his heart for their small troubles. "Has your teacher kept you in for being naughty?"

The mite dashed her little red knuckles across her eyes and answered indignantly, "No, indeed. I stayed after school with Minnie Lawler to sweep the floor."

"And did you and Minnie quarrel, and is that why you are crying?" asked Frank solemnly.

"Minnie and I *never* quarrel. I am crying because we can't have the school decorated on Monday for the examination, after all. The Dickeys have gone back on us ... after promising, too," and the tears began to swell up in the blue eyes again.

"Very bad behaviour on the part of the Dickeys," commented Frank. "But can't you decorate the school without them?"

"Why, of course not. They are the only big boys in the school. They said they would cut the boughs, and bring a ladder tomorrow and help us nail the wreaths up, and now they won't ... and everything is spoiled ... and Miss Davis will be so disappointed."

By dint of questioning Frank soon found out the whole story. The semi-annual public examination was to be held on Monday afternoon, the day before Christmas. Miss Davis had been drilling her little flock for the occasion; and a program of recitations, speeches, and dialogues had been prepared. Our small informant, whose name was Maggie Bates, together with Minnie Lawler and several other little girls, had conceived the idea that it would be a fine thing to decorate the schoolroom with greens. For this it was necessary to ask the help of the boys. Boys were scarce at Enderly school, but the Dickeys, three in number, had promised to see that the thing was done.

"And now they won't," sobbed Maggie. "Matt Dickey is mad at Miss Davis 'cause she stood him on the floor today for not learning his lesson, and he says he won't do a thing nor let any of the other boys help us. Matt just makes all the boys do as he says. I feel dreadful bad, and so does Minnie."

"Well, I wouldn't cry any more about it," said Frank consolingly. "Crying won't do any good, you know. Can you tell us where to find the wood-lane that cuts across to Blackburn Hill?" Maggie could, and gave us minute directions. So, having thanked her, we left her to pursue her disconsolate way and betook ourselves homeward.

"I would like to spoil Matt Dickey's little game," said Frank. "He is evidently trying to run things at Enderly Road school and revenge himself on the teacher. Let us put a spoke in his wheel and do Maggie a good turn as well."

"Agreed. But how?"

Frank had a plan ready to hand and, when we reached home, we took his sisters, Carrie and Mabel, into our confidence; and the four of us worked to such good purpose all the next day, which was Saturday, that by night everything was in readiness.

At dusk Frank and I set out for the Enderly Road, carrying a basket, a small step-ladder, an unlit lantern, a hammer, and a box of tacks. It was dark when we reached the Enderly Road schoolhouse. Fortunately, it was quite out of sight of any inhabited spot, being surrounded by woods. Hence, mysterious lights in it at strange hours would not be likely to attract attention.

The door was locked, but we easily got in by a window, lighted our lantern, and went to work. The schoolroom was small, and the old-fashioned furniture bore marks of hard usage; but everything was very snug, and the carefully swept floor and dusted desks bore testimony to the neatness of our small friend Maggie and her chum Minnie.

Our basket was full of mottoes made from letters cut out of cardboard and covered with lissome sprays of fir. They were, moreover, adorned with gorgeous pink and red tissue roses, which Carrie and Mabel had contributed. We had considerable trouble in getting them tacked up properly, but when we had succeeded, and had furthermore surmounted doors, windows, and blackboard with wreaths of green, the little Enderly Road schoolroom was quite transformed.

"It looks nice," said Frank in a tone of satisfaction. "Hope Maggie will like it."

We swept up the litter we had made, and then scrambled out of the window.

"I'd like to see Matt Dickey's face when he comes Monday morning," I laughed, as we struck into the back lands.

"I'd like to see that midget of a Maggie's," said Frank. "See here, Phil, let's attend the examination Monday afternoon. I'd like to see our decorations in daylight."

We decided to do so, and also thought of something else. Snow fell all day Sunday, so that, on Monday morning, sleighs had to be brought out. Frank and I drove down to the store and invested a considerable share of our spare cash in a varied assortment of knick-knacks. After dinner we drove through to the Enderly Road schoolhouse, tied our horse in a quiet spot, and went in. Our arrival created quite a sensation for, as a rule, Blackburn Hillites did not patronize Enderly Road functions. Miss Davis, the pale, tired-looking little teacher, was evidently pleased, and we were given seats of honour next to the minister on the platform.

Our decorations really looked very well, and were further enhanced by two large red geraniums in full bloom which, it appeared, Maggie had brought from home to adorn the teacher's desk. The side benches were lined with Enderly Road parents, and all the pupils were in their best attire. Our friend Maggie was there, of course, and she smiled and nodded towards the wreaths when she caught our eyes.

The examination was a decided success, and the program which followed was very creditable indeed. Maggie and Minnie, in particular, covered themselves with glory, both in class and on the platform. At its close, while the minister was making his speech, Frank slipped out; when the minister sat down the door opened and Santa Claus himself, with big fur coat, ruddy mask, and long white beard, strode into the room with a huge basket on his arm, amid a chorus of surprised "Ohs" from old and young.

Wonderful things came out of that basket. There was some little present for every child there—tops, knives, and whistles for the boys, dolls and ribbons for the girls, and a "prize" box of candy for everybody, all of which Santa Claus presented with appropriate remarks. It was an exciting time, and it would have been hard to decide which were the most pleased, parents, pupils, or teacher.

In the confusion Santa Claus discreetly disappeared, and school was dismissed. Frank, having tucked his toggery away in the sleigh, was waiting for us outside, and we were promptly pounced upon by Maggie and Minnie, whose long braids were already adorned with the pink silk ribbons which had been their gifts.

"*You* decorated the school," cried Maggie excitedly. "I know you did. I told Minnie it was you the minute I saw it."

"You're dreaming, child," said Frank.

"Oh, no, I'm not," retorted Maggie shrewdly, "and wasn't Matt Dickey mad this morning! Oh, it was such fun. I think you are two real nice boys and so does Minnie—don't you Minnie?"

Minnie nodded gravely. Evidently Maggie did the talking in their partnership.

"This has been a splendid examination," said Maggie, drawing a long breath. "Real Christmassy, you know. We never had such a good time before."

"Well, it has paid, don't you think?" asked Frank, as we drove home.

"Rather," I answered.

It did "pay" in other ways than the mere pleasure of it. There was always a better feeling between the Roaders and the Hillites thereafter. The big brothers of the little girls, to whom our Christmas surprise had been such a treat, thought it worthwhile to bury the hatchet, and quarrels between the two villages became things of the past.

The Dissipation of Miss Ponsonby

We hadn't been very long in Glenboro before we managed to get acquainted with Miss Ponsonby. It did not come about in the ordinary course of receiving and returning calls, for Miss Ponsonby never called on anybody; neither did we meet her at any of the Glenboro social functions, for Miss Ponsonby never went anywhere except to church, and very seldom there. Her father wouldn't let her. No, it simply happened because her window was right across the alleyway from ours. The Ponsonby house was next to us, on the right, and between us were only a fence, a hedge of box, and a sprawly acacia tree that shaded Miss Ponsonby's window, where she always sat sewing—patchwork, as I'm alive—when she wasn't working around the house. Patchwork seemed to be Miss Ponsonby's sole and only dissipation of any kind.

We guessed her age to be forty-five at least, but we found out afterward that we were mistaken. She was only thirty-five. She was tall and thin and pale, one of those drab-tinted persons who look as if they had never felt a rosy emotion in their lives. She had any amount of silky, fawn-coloured hair, always combed straight back from her face, and pinned in a big, tight bun just above her neck—the last style in the world for any woman with Miss Ponsonby's nose to adopt. But then I doubt if Miss Ponsonby had any idea what her nose was really like. I don't believe she ever looked at herself critically in a mirror in her life. Her features were rather nice, and her expression tamely sweet; her eyes were big, timid, china-blue orbs that looked as if she had been badly scared when she was little and had never got over it; she never wore anything but black, and, to crown all, her first name was Alicia.

Miss Ponsonby sat and sewed at her window for hours at a time, but she never looked our way, partly, I suppose, from habit induced by modesty, since the former occupants of our room had been two gay young bachelors, whose names Jerry and I found out all over our window-panes with a diamond.

Jerry and I sat a great deal at ours, laughing and talking, but Miss Ponsonby never lifted her head or eyes. Jerry couldn't stand it long; she declared it got on her nerves; besides, she felt sorry to see a fellow creature wasting so many precious moments of a fleeting lifetime at patchwork. So one afternoon she hailed Miss Ponsonby with a cheerful "hello," and Miss Ponsonby actually looked over and said "good afternoon," as prim as an eighteen-hundred-and-forty fashion plate.

Then Jerry, whose name is Geraldine only in the family Bible, talked to her about the weather. Jerry can talk interestingly about anything. In five minutes she had performed a miracle—she had made Miss Ponsonby laugh. In five minutes more she was leaning half out of the window showing Miss Ponsonby a new, white, fluffy, frivolous, chiffony waist of hers, and Miss Ponsonby was leaning halfway out of hers looking at it eagerly. At the end of a quarter of an hour they were exchanging confidences about their favourite books. Jerry was a confirmed Kiplingomaniac, but Miss Ponsonby adored Laura Jean Libbey. She said sorrowfully she supposed she ought not to read novels at all since her father disapproved. We found out later on that Mr. Ponsonby's way of expressing disapproval was to burn any he got hold of, and storm at his daughter about them like the confirmed old crank he was. Poor Miss Ponsonby had to keep her Laura Jeans locked up in her trunk, and it wasn't often she got a new one.

From that day dated our friendship with Miss Ponsonby, a curious friendship, only carried on from window to window. We never saw Miss Ponsonby anywhere else; we asked her to come over but she said her father didn't allow her to visit anybody. Miss Ponsonby was one of those meek women who are ruled by whomsoever happens to be nearest them, and woe be unto them if that nearest happen to be a tyrant. Her meekness fairly infuriated Jerry.

But we liked Miss Ponsonby and we pitied her. She confided to us that she was very lonely and that she wrote poetry. We never asked to see the poetry, although I think she would have liked to show it. But, as Jerry says, there are limits.

We told Miss Ponsonby all about our dances and picnics and beaus and pretty dresses; she was never tired of hearing of them; we smuggled new library novels—Jerry got our cook to buy them—and boxes of chocolates, from our window to hers; we sat there on moonlit nights and communed with her while other girls down the street were entertaining callers on their verandahs; we did everything we could for her except to call her Alicia, although she begged us to do so. But it never came easily to our tongues; we thought she must have been born and christened Miss Ponsonby; "Alicia" was something her mother could only have dreamed about her.

We thought we knew all about Miss Ponsonby's past; but even pale, drab, china-blue women can have their secrets and keep them. It was a full half year before we discovered Miss Ponsonby's.

In October, Stephen Shaw came home from the west to visit his father and mother after an absence of fifteen years. Jerry and I met him at a party at his brother-in-law's. We knew he was a bachelor of forty-five or so and had made heaps of money in the lumber business, so we expected to find him short and round and bald, with bulgy blue eyes and a double chin. On the contrary, he was a tall, handsome man with clear-cut features, laughing black eyes like a boy's, and iron-grey hair. That iron-grey hair nearly finished Jerry; she thinks there is nothing so distinguished and she had the escape of her life from falling in love with Stephen Shaw.

He was as gay as the youngest, danced splendidly, went everywhere, and took all the Glenboro girls about impartially. It was rumoured that he had come east to look for a wife but he didn't seem to be in any particular hurry to find her.

One evening he called on Jerry; that is to say, he did ask for both of us, but within ten minutes Jerry had him mewed up in the cosy corner to the exclusion of all the rest of the world. I felt that I was a huge crowd, so I obligingly decamped upstairs and sat down by my window to "muse," as Miss Ponsonby would have said.

It was a glorious moonlight night, with just a hint of October frost in the air—enough to give sparkle and tang. After a few moments I became aware that Miss Ponsonby was also "musing" at her window in the shadow of the acacia tree. In that dim light she looked quite pretty. It was suddenly borne in upon me for the first time that, when Miss Ponsonby was young, she must have been very pretty, with that delicate elusive fashion of beauty which fades so early if the life is not kept in it by love and tenderness. It seemed odd, somehow, to think of Miss Ponsonby as young and pretty. She seemed so essentially middle-aged and faded.

"Lovely night, Miss Ponsonby," I said brilliantly.

"A very beautiful night, dear Elizabeth," answered Miss Ponsonby in that tired little voice of hers that always seemed as drab-coloured as the rest of her.

"I'm mopy," I said frankly. "Jerry has concentrated herself on Stephen Shaw for the evening and I'm left on the fringe of things."

Miss Ponsonby didn't say anything for a few moments. When she spoke some strange and curious note had come into her voice, as if a chord, long unswept and silent, had been suddenly thrilled by a passing hand.

"Did I understand you to say that Geraldine was—entertaining Stephen Shaw?"

"Yes. He's home from the west and he's delightful," I replied. "All the Glenboro girls are quite crazy over him. Jerry and I are as bad as the rest. He isn't at all young but he's very fascinating."

"Stephen Shaw!" repeated Miss Ponsonby faintly. "So Stephen Shaw is home again!"

"Why, I suppose you would know him long ago," I said, remembering that Stephen Shaw's youth must have been contemporaneous with Miss Ponsonby's.

"Yes, I used to know him," said Miss Ponsonby very slowly.

She did not say anything more, which I thought a little odd, for she was generally full of mild curiosity about all strangers and sojourners in Glenboro. Presently she got up and went away from her window. Deserted even by Miss Ponsonby, I went grumpily to bed.

Then Mrs. George Hubbard gave a big dance. Jerry and I were pleasantly excited. The Hubbards were the smartest of the Glenboro smart set and their entertainments were always quite brilliant affairs for a small country village like ours. This party was professedly given in honour of Stephen Shaw, who was to leave for the west again in a week's time.

On the evening of the party Jerry and I went to our room to dress. And there, across at her window in the twilight, sat Miss Ponsonby, crying. I had never seen Miss Ponsonby cry before.

"What is the matter?" I called out softly and anxiously.

"Oh, nothing," sobbed Miss Ponsonby, "only—only—I'm invited to the party tonight—Susan Hubbard is my cousin, you know—and I would like so much to go."

"Then why don't you?" said Jerry briskly.

"My father won't let me," said Miss Ponsonby, swallowing a sob as if she were a little girl of ten years old. Jerry had to dodge behind the curtain to hide a smile.

"It's too bad," I said sympathetically, but wondering a little why Miss Ponsonby seemed so worked up about it. I knew she had sometimes been invited out before and had not been allowed to go, but she had never cared apparently.

"Well, what is to be done?" I whispered to Jerry.

"Take Miss Ponsonby to the party with us, of course," said Jerry, popping out from behind the curtain.

I didn't ask her if she expected to fly through the air with Miss Ponsonby, although short of that I couldn't see how the latter was to be got out of the house without her father knowing. The old gentleman had a den off the hall where he always sat in the evening and smoked fiercely, after having locked all the doors to keep the servants in. He was a delightful sort of person, that old Mr. Ponsonby.

Jerry poked her head as far as she could out of the window. "Miss Ponsonby, you are going to the dance," she said in a cautious undertone, "so don't cry any more or your eyes will be dreadfully red."

"It is impossible," said Miss Ponsonby resignedly.

"Nothing is impossible when I make up my mind," said Jerry firmly. "You must get dressed, climb down that acacia tree, and join us in our yard. It will be pitch dark in a few minutes and your father will never know."

I had a frantic vision of Miss Ponsonby scrambling down that acacia tree like an eloping damsel. But Jerry was in dead earnest, and really it was quite possible if Miss Ponsonby only thought so. I did not believe she would think so, but I was mistaken. Her thorough course in Libbey heroines and their marvellous escapades had quite prepared her to contemplate such an adventure calmly—in the abstract at least. But another obstacle presented itself.

"It's impossible," she said again, after her first flash hope. "I haven't a fit dress to wear—I've nothing at all but my black cashmere and it is three years old."

But the more hindrances in Jerry's way when she sets out to accomplish something the more determined and enthusiastic she becomes. I listened to her with amazement.

"I have a dress I'll lend you," she said resolutely. "And I'll go over and fix you up as soon as it's a little darker. Go now and bathe your eyes and just trust to me."

Miss Ponsonby's long habit of obedience to whatever she was told stood her in good stead now. She obeyed Jerry without another word. Jerry seized me by the waist and waltzed me around the room in an ecstasy.

"Jerry Elliott, how are you going to carry this thing through?" I demanded sternly.

"Easily enough," responded Jerry. "You know that black lace dress of mine—the one with the apricot slip. I've never worn it since I came to Glenboro, so nobody will know it's mine, and I never mean to wear it again for it's got too tight. It's a trifle old-fashioned, but that won't matter for Glenboro, and it will fit Miss Ponsonby all right. She's about my height and figure. I'm determined that poor soul shall have a dissipation for once in her life since she hankers for it. Come on now, Elizabeth. It will be a lark."

I caught Jerry's enthusiasm, and while she hunted out the box containing the black lace dress, I hastily gathered together some other odds and ends I thought might be useful—a black aigrette, a pair of black şilk gloves, a spangled gauze fan, and a pair of slippers. They wouldn't have stood daylight, but they looked all right after night. As we left the room I caught up some pale pink roses on my table.

We pushed through a little gap in the privet hedge and found ourselves under the acacia tree with Miss Ponsonby peering anxiously at us from above. I wanted to shriek with laughter, the whole thing seemed so funny and unreal. Jerry, although she hasn't climbed trees since she was twelve, went up that acacia as nimbly as a pussy-cat, took the box and things from me, passed them to Miss Ponsonby, and got in at the window while I went back to my own room to dress, hoping old Mr. Ponsonby wouldn't be running out to ring the fire alarm.

In a very short time I heard Miss Ponsonby and Jerry at the opposite window, and I rushed to mine to see the sight. But Miss Ponsonby, with a red fascinator over her head and a big cape wrapped round her, slipped out of the window and down that blessed acacia tree as neatly and nimbly as if she had been accustomed to doing it for exercise every day of her life. There were possibilities in Miss Ponsonby. In two more minutes they were both safe in our room.

Then Jerry threw off Miss Ponsonby's wraps and stepped back. I know I stared until my eyes stuck out of my head. Was that Miss Ponsonby—that!

The black lace dress, with the pinkish sheen of its slip beneath, suited her slim shape to perfection and clung around her in lovely, filmy curves that made her look willowy and girlish. It was high-necked, just cut away slightly at the throat, and had great, loose, hanging frilly sleeves of lace. Jerry had shaken out her hair and piled it high on her head in satiny twists and loops, with a pompadour such as Miss Ponsonby could never have thought about. It suited her tremendously and seemed to alter the whole character of her face, giving verve and piquancy to her delicate little features. The excitement had flushed her cheeks into positive pinkness and her eyes were starry. The roses were pinned on her shoulder. Miss Ponsonby, as she stood there, was a pretty woman, with fifteen apparent birthdays the less.

"Oh, Alicia, you look just lovely!" I gasped. The name slipped out quite naturally. I never thought about it at all.

"My dear Elizabeth," she said, "it's like a dream of lost youth."

We got Jerry ready and then we started for the Hubbards', out by our back door and through our neighbour-on-the-left's lane to avoid all observation. Miss Ponsonby was breathless with terror. She was sure every footstep she heard behind her was her father's in pursuit. She almost fainted on the spot when a belated man came tearing along the street. Jerry and I breathed a sigh of devout thanksgiving when we found ourselves safely in the Hubbard parlour.

We were early, but Stephen Shaw was there before us. He came up to us at once, and just then Miss Ponsonby turned around.

"Alicia!" he said.

"How do you do, Stephen?" she said tremulously.

And there he was looking down at her with an expression on his face that none of the Glenboro girls he had been calling on had ever seen. Jerry and I just simply melted away. We can see through grindstones when there are holes in them!

We went out and sat down on the stairs.

"There's a mystery here," said Jerry, "but Miss Ponsonby shall explain it to us before we let her climb up that acacia tree tonight. Now that I come to think of it, the first night he called he asked me about her. Wanted to know if her father were the same old blustering tyrant he always was, and if we knew her at all. I'm afraid I made a little mild fun of her, and he didn't say anything more. Well, I'm awfully glad now that I didn't fall in love with him. I could have, but I wouldn't."

Miss Ponsonby's appearance at the Hubbards' party was the biggest sensation Glenboro had had for years. And in her way, she was a positive belle. She didn't dance, but all the middle-aged men, widowers, wedded, and bachelors, who had known her in her girlhood crowded around her, and she laughed and chatted as I hadn't even imagined Miss Ponsonby could laugh and chat. Jerry and I revelled in her triumph, for did we not feel that it was due to us? At last Miss Ponsonby disappeared; shortly after Jerry and I blundered into the library to fix some obstreperous hairpins, and there we found her and Stephen Shaw in the cosy corner.

There were no explanations on the road home, for Miss Ponsonby walked behind us with Stephen Shaw in the pale, late-risen October moonshine. But when we had sneaked through the neighbour-to-the-left's lane and reached our side verandah we waited for her, and as soon as Stephen Shaw had gone we laid violent hands on Miss Ponsonby and made her 'fess up there on the dark, chilly verandah, at one o'clock in the morning.

"Miss Ponsonby," said Jerry, "before we assist you in returning to those ancestral halls of yours you've simply got to tell us what all this means."

Miss Ponsonby gave a little, shy, nervous laugh.

"Stephen Shaw and I were engaged to be married long ago," she said simply. "But Father disapproved. Stephen was poor then. And so—and so—I sent him away. What else could I do?"—for Jerry had snorted—"Father had to be obeyed.

But it broke my heart. Stephen went away—he was very angry—and I have never seen him since. When Susan Hubbard invited me to the party I felt as if I must go—I must see Stephen once more. I never thought for a minute that he remembered me—or cared still...."

"But he does?" said Jerry breathlessly. Jerry never scruples to ask anything right out that she wants to know.

"Yes," said Miss Ponsonby softly. "Isn't it wonderful? I could hardly believe it—I am so changed. But he said tonight he had never thought of any other woman. He—he came home to see me. But when I never went anywhere, even when I must know he was home, he thought I didn't want to see him. If I hadn't gone tonight—oh, I owe it all to you two dear girls!"

"When are you to be married?" demanded that terrible Jerry.

"As soon as possible," said Miss Ponsonby. "Stephen was going away next week, but he says he will wait until I can get ready."

"Do you think your father will object this time?" I queried.

"No, I don't think so. Stephen is a rich man now, you know. That wouldn't make any difference with me—but Father is very—practical. Stephen is going to see him tomorrow."

"But what if he does object?" I persisted anxiously.

"The acacia tree will still be there," said Miss Ponsonby firmly.

The Falsoms' Christmas Dinner

"Well, so it's all settled," said Stephen Falsom.

"Yes," assented Alexina. "Yes, it is," she repeated, as if somebody had questioned it.

Then Alexina sighed. Whatever "it" was, the fact of its being settled did not seem to bring Alexina any great peace of mind—nor Stephen either, judging from his face, which wore a sort of "suffer and be strong" expression just then. "When do you go?" said Alexina, after a pause, during which she had frowned out of the window and across the Tracy yard. Josephine Tracy and her brother Duncan were strolling about the yard in the pleasant December sunshine, arm in arm, laughing and talking. They appeared to be a nice, harmless pair of people, but the sight of them did not seem to please Alexina.

"Just as soon as we can sell the furniture and move away," said Stephen moodily. "Heigh-ho! So this is what all our fine ambitions have come to, Lexy, your music and my M.D. A place in a department store for you, and one in a lumber mill for me."

"I don't dare to complain," said Alexina slowly. "We ought to be so thankful to get the positions. I *am* thankful. And I don't mind so very much about my music. But I do wish you could have gone to college, Stephen."

"Never mind me," said Stephen, brightening up determinedly. "I'm going to go into the lumber business enthusiastically. You don't know what unsuspected talents I may develop along that line. The worst of it is that we can't be together. But I'll keep my eyes open, and perhaps I'll find a place for you in Lessing."

Alexina said nothing. Her separation from Stephen was the one point in their fortunes she could not bear to discuss. There were times when Alexina did not see how she was going to exist without Stephen. But she never said so to him. She thought he had enough to worry him without her making matters worse. "Well," said Stephen, getting up, "I'll run down to the office. And see here, Lexy. Day after tomorrow is Christmas. Are we going to celebrate it at all? If so I'd better order the turkey."

Alexina looked thoughtful. "I don't know, Stephen. We're short of money, you know, and the fund is dwindling every day. Don't you think it's a little extravagant to have a turkey for two people? And somehow I don't feel a bit Christmassy. I think I'd rather spend it just like any other day and try to forget that it *is* Christmas. Everything would be so different."

"That's true, Lexy. And we must look after the bawbees closely, I'll admit." When Stephen had gone out Alexina cried a little, not very much, because she didn't want her eyes to be red against Stephen's return. But she had to cry a little. As she had said, everything was so different from what it had been a year ago. Their father had been alive then and they had been very cosy and happy in the little house at the end of the street. There had been no mother there since Alexina's birth sixteen years ago. Alexina had kept house for her father and Stephen since she was ten. Stephen was a clever boy and intended to study medicine. Alexina had a good voice, and something was to be done about training it. The Tracys lived next door to them. Duncan Tracy was Stephen's particular chum, and Josephine Tracy was Alexina's dearest friend. Alexina was never lonely when Josie was near by to laugh and chat and plan with.

Then, all at once, troubles came. In June the firm of which Mr. Falsom was a member failed. There was some stigma attached to the failure, too, although the blame did not rest upon Mr. Falsom, but with his partner. Worry and anxiety aggravated the heart trouble from which he had suffered for some time, and a month later he died. Alexina and Stephen were left alone to face the knowledge that they were penniless, and must look about for some way of supporting themselves. At first they hoped to be able to get something to do in Thorndale, so that they might keep their home. This proved impossible. After much discouragement and disappointment Stephen had secured a position in the lumber mill at Lessing, and Alexina was promised a place in a departmental store in the city.

To make matters worse, Duncan Tracy and Stephen had quarrelled in October. It was only a boyish disagreement over some trifle, but bitter words had passed. Duncan, who was a quick-tempered lad, had twitted Stephen with his father's failure, and Stephen had resented it hotly. Duncan was sorry for and ashamed of his words as soon as they were uttered, but he would not humble himself to say so. Alexina had taken Stephen's part and her manner to Josie assumed a tinge of coldness. Josie quickly noticed and resented it, and the breach between the two girls widened almost insensibly, until they barely spoke when they met. Each blamed the other and cherished bitterness in her heart.

When Stephen came home from the post office he looked excited.

"Were there any letters?" asked Alexina.

"Well, rather! One from Uncle James!"

"Uncle James," exclaimed Alexina, incredulously.

"Yes, beloved sis. Oh, you needn't try to look as surprised as I did. And I ordered the turkey after all. Uncle James has invited himself here to dinner on Christmas Day. You'll have a chance to show your culinary skill, for you know we've always been told that Uncle James was a gourmand."

Alexina read the letter in a maze. It was a brief epistle, stating that the writer wished to make the acquaintance of his niece and nephew, and would visit them on Christmas Day. That was all. But Alexina instantly saw a future of rosy possibilities. For Uncle James, who lived in the city and was really a great-uncle, had never taken the slightest notice of their family since his quarrel with their father twenty years ago; but this looked as if Uncle James were disposed to hold out the olive branch.

"Oh, Stephen, if he likes you, and if he offers to educate you!" breathed Alexina. "Perhaps he will if he is favourably impressed. But we'll have to be so careful, he is so whimsical and odd, at least everybody has always said so. A little thing may turn the scale either way. Anyway, we must have a good dinner for him. I'll have plum pudding and mince pie."

For the next thirty-six hours Alexina lived in a whirl. There was so much to do. The little house was put in apple pie order from top to bottom, and Stephen was set to stoning raisins and chopping meat and beating eggs. Alexina was perfectly reckless; no matter how big a hole it made in their finances Uncle James must have a proper Christmas dinner. A favourable impression must be made. Stephen's whole future—Alexina did not think about her own at all just then—might depend on it.

Christmas morning came, fine and bright and warm. It was more like a morning in early spring than in December, for there was no snow or frost, and the air was moist and balmy. Alexina was up at daybreak, cleaning and decorating at a furious rate. By eleven o'clock everything was finished or going forward briskly. The plum pudding was bubbling in the pot, the turkey—Burton's plumpest—was sizzling in the oven. The shelf in the pantry bore two mince pies upon which Alexina was willing to stake her culinary reputation. And Stephen had gone to the train to meet Uncle James.

From her kitchen window Alexina could see brisk preparations going on in the Tracy kitchen. She knew Josie and Duncan were all alone; their parents had gone to spend Christmas with friends in Lessing. In spite of her hurry and excitement Alexina found time to sigh. Last Christmas Josie and Duncan had come over and eaten their dinner with them. But now last Christmas seemed very far away. And Josie had behaved horridly. Alexina was quite clear on that point.

Then Stephen came with Uncle James. Uncle James was a rather pompous, fussy old man with red cheeks and bushy eyebrows. "H'm! Smells nice in here," was his salutation to Alexina. "I hope it will taste as good as it smells. I'm hungry."

Alexina soon left Uncle James and Stephen talking in the parlour and betook herself anxiously to the kitchen. She set the table in the little dining room, now and then pausing to listen with a delighted nod to the murmur of voices and laughter in the parlour. She felt sure that Stephen was making a favourable impression. She lifted the plum pudding and put it on a plate on the kitchen table; then she took out the turkey, beautifully done, and put it on a platter; finally, she popped the two mince pies into the oven. Just at this moment Stephen stuck his head in at the hall door.

"Lexy, do you know where that letter of Governor Howland's to Father is? Uncle James wants to see it."

Alexina, not waiting to shut the oven door—for delay might impress Uncle James unfavourably—rushed upstairs to get the letter. She was ten minutes finding it. Then, remembering her pies, she flew back to the kitchen. In the middle of the floor she stopped as if transfixed, staring at the table. The turkey was gone. And the plum pudding was gone! And the mince pies were gone! Nothing was left but the platters! For a moment Alexina refused to believe her eyes. Then she saw a trail of greasy drops on the floor to the open door, out over the doorstep, and along the boards of the walk to the back fence.

Alexina did not make a fuss. Even at that horrible moment she remembered the importance of making a favourable impression. But she could not quite keep the alarm and excitement out of her voice as she called Stephen, and Stephen knew that something had gone wrong as he came quickly through the hall. "Is the turkey burned, Lexy?" he cried.

"Burned! No, it's ten times worse," gasped Alexina. "It's gone—gone, Stephen. And the pudding and the mince pies, too. Oh, what shall we do? Who can have taken them?"

It may be stated right here and now that the Falsoms never really *knew* anything more about the disappearance of their Christmas dinner than they did at that moment. But the only reasonable explanation of the mystery was that a tramp had entered the kitchen and made off with the good things. The Falsom house was right at the end of the street. The narrow backyard opened on a lonely road. Across the road was a stretch of pine woods. There was no house very near except the Tracy one.

Stephen reached this conclusion with a bound. He ran out to the yard gate followed by the distracted Alexina. The only person visible was a man some distance down the road. Stephen leaped over the gate and tore down the road in pursuit of him. Alexina went back to the doorstep, sat down upon it, and began to cry. She couldn't help it. Her hopes were all in ruins around her. There was no dinner for Uncle James.

Josephine Tracy saw her crying. Now, Josie honestly thought that she had a grievance against Alexina. But an Alexina walking unconcernedly by with a cool little nod and her head held high was a very different person from an Alexina sitting on a back doorstep, on Christmas morning, crying. For a moment Josie hesitated. Then she slowly went out and across the yard to the fence. "What is the trouble?" she asked.

Alexina forgot that there was such a thing as dignity to be kept up; or, if she remembered it, she was past caring for such a trifle. "Our dinner is gone," she sobbed. "And there is nothing to give Uncle James to eat except vegetables—and I do so want to make a favourable impression!"

This was not particularly lucid, but Josie, with a flying mental leap, arrived at the conclusion that it was very important that Uncle James, whoever he was, should have a dinner, and she knew where one was to be had. But before she could speak Stephen returned, looking rueful. "No use, Lexy. That man was only old Mr. Byers, and he had seen no signs of a tramp. There is a trail of grease right across the road. The tramp must have taken directly to the woods. We'll simply have to do without our Christmas dinner."

"By no means," said Josie quickly, with a little red spot on either cheek. "Our dinner is all ready—turkey, pudding and all. Let us lend it to you. Don't say a word to your uncle about the accident."

Alexina flushed and hesitated. "It's very kind of you," she stammered, "but I'm afraid—it would be too much—"

"Not a bit of it," Josie interrupted warmly. "Didn't Duncan and I have Christmas dinner at your house last year? Just come and help us carry it over."

"If you lend us your dinner you and Duncan must come and help us eat it," said Alexina, resolutely.

"I'll come of course," said Josie, "and I think that Duncan will too if—if—" She looked at Stephen, the scarlet spots deepening. Stephen coloured too.

"Duncan must come," he said quietly. "I'll go and ask him."

Two minutes later a peculiar procession marched out of the Tracy kitchen door, across the two yards, and into the Falsom house. Josie headed it, carrying a turkey on a platter. Alexina came next with a plum pudding. Stephen and Duncan followed with a hot mince pie apiece. And in a few more minutes Alexina gravely announced to Uncle James that dinner was ready.

The dinner was a pronounced success, marked by much suppressed hilarity among the younger members of the party. Uncle James ate very heartily and seemed to enjoy everything, especially the mince pie.

"This is the best mince pie I have ever sampled," he told Alexina. "I am glad to know that I have a niece who can make such a mince pie." Alexina cast an agonized look at Josie, and was on the point of explaining that she wasn't the maker of the pie. But Josie frowned her into silence.

"I felt so guilty to sit there and take the credit—*your* credit," she told Josie afterwards, as they washed up the dishes.

"Nonsense," said Josie. "It wasn't as if you couldn't make mince pies. Your mince pies are better than mine, if it comes to that. It might have spoiled everything if you'd said a word. I must go home now. Won't you and Stephen come over after your uncle goes, and spend the evening with us? We'll have a candy pull."

When Josie and Duncan had gone, Uncle James called his nephew and niece into the parlour, and sat down before them with approving eyes. "I want to have a little talk with you two. I'm sorry I've let so many years go by without making your acquaintance, because you seem worth getting acquainted with. Now, what are your plans for the future?"

"I'm going into a lumber mill at Lessing and Alexina is going into the T. Morson store," said Stephen quietly.

"Tut, tut, no, you're not. And she's not. You're coming to live with me, both of you. If you have a fancy for cutting and carving people up, young man, you must be trained to cut and carve them scientifically, anyhow. As for you, Alexina, Stephen tells me you can sing. Well, there's a good Conservatory of Music in town. Wouldn't you rather go there instead of behind a counter?"

"Oh, Uncle James!" exclaimed Alexina with shining eyes. She jumped up, put her arms about Uncle James' neck and kissed him.

Uncle James said, "Tut, tut," again, but he liked it.

When Stephen had seen his uncle off on the six o'clock train he returned home and looked at the radiant Alexina.

"Well, you made your favourable impression, all right, didn't you?" he said gaily. "But we owe it to Josie Tracy. Isn't she a brick? I suppose you're going over this evening?"

"Yes, I am. I'm so tired that I feel as if I couldn't crawl across the yard, but if I can't you'll have to carry me. Go I will. I can't begin to tell you how glad I am about everything, but really the fact that you and Duncan and Josie and I are good friends again seems the best of all. I'm glad that tramp stole the dinner and I hope he enjoyed it. I don't grudge him one single bite!"

The Fraser Scholarship

Elliot Campbell came down the main staircase of Marwood College and found himself caught up with a whoop into a crowd of Sophs who were struggling around the bulletin board. He was thumped on the back and shaken hands with amid a hurricane of shouts and congratulations.

"Good for you, Campbell! You've won the Fraser. See your little name tacked up there at the top of the list, bracketed off all by itself for the winner? 'Elliott H. Campbell, ninety-two per cent.' A class yell for Campbell, boys!"

While the yell was being given with a heartiness that might have endangered the roof, Elliott, with flushed face and sparkling eyes, pushed nearer to the important typewritten announcement on the bulletin board. Yes, he had won the Fraser Scholarship. His name headed the list of seven competitors.

Roger Brooks, who was at his side, read over the list aloud:

"'Elliott H. Campbell, ninety-two.' I said you'd do it, my boy. 'Edward Stone, ninety-one'—old Ned ran you close, didn't he? But of course with that name he'd no show. 'Kay Milton, eighty-eight.' Who'd have thought slow-going old Kay would have pulled up so well? 'Seddon Brown, eighty-seven; Oliver Field, eighty-four; Arthur McIntyre, eighty-two'—a very respectable little trio. And 'Carl McLean, seventy.' Whew! what a drop! Just saved his distance. It was only his name took him in, of course. He knew you weren't supposed to be strong in mathematics."

Before Elliott could say anything, a professor emerged from the president's private room, bearing the report of a Freshman examination, which he proceeded to post on the Freshman bulletin board, and the rush of the students in that direction left Elliott and Roger free of the crowd. They seized the opportunity to escape.

Elliott drew a long breath as they crossed the campus in the fresh April sunshine, where the buds were swelling on the fine old chestnuts and elms that surrounded Marwood's red brick walls.

"That has lifted a great weight off my mind," he said frankly. "A good deal depended on my winning the Fraser. I couldn't have come back next year if I hadn't got it. That four hundred will put me through the rest of my course."

"That's good," said Roger Brooks heartily.

He liked Elliott Campbell, and so did all the Sophomores. Yet none of them was at all intimate with him. He had no chums, as the other boys had. He boarded alone, "dug" persistently, and took no part in the social life of the college. Roger Brooks came nearest to being his friend of any, yet even Roger knew very little about him. Elliott had never before said so much about his personal affairs as in the speech just recorded.

"I'm poor—woefully poor," went on Elliott gaily. His success seemed to have thawed his reserve for the time being. "I had just enough money to bring me through the Fresh and Soph years by dint of careful management. Now I'm stone broke, and the hope of the Fraser was all that stood between me and the dismal certainty of having to teach next year, dropping out of my class and coming back in two or three years' time, a complete, rusty stranger again. Whew! I made faces over the prospect."

"No wonder," commented Roger. "The class would have been sorry if you had had to drop out, Campbell. We want to keep all our stars with us to make a shining coruscation at the finish. Besides, you know we all like you for yourself. It would have been an everlasting shame if that little cad of a McLean had won out. Nobody likes him."

"Oh, I had no fear of him," answered Elliott. "I don't see what induced him to go in, anyhow. He must have known he'd no chance. But I was afraid of Stone—he's a born dabster at mathematics, you know, and I only hold my own in them by hard digging."

"Why, Stone couldn't have taken the Fraser over you in any case, if you made over seventy," said Roger with a puzzled look. "You must have known that. McLean was the only competitor you had to fear."

"I don't understand you," said Elliott blankly.

"You must know the conditions of the Fraser!" exclaimed Roger.

"Certainly," responded Elliott. "'The Fraser scholarship, amounting to four hundred dollars, will be offered annually in the Sophomore class. The competitors will be expected to take a special examination in mathematics, and the winner will be awarded two hundred dollars for two years, payable in four annual instalments, the payment of any instalment to be conditional on the winner's attending the required classes for undergraduates and making satisfactory progress therein.' Isn't that correct?"

"So far as it goes, old man. You forget the most important part of all. 'Preference is to be given to competitors of the name Fraser, Campbell or McLean, provided that such competitor makes at least seventy per cent in his examination.' You don't mean to tell me that you didn't know that!"

"Are you joking?" demanded Elliott with a pale face.

"Not a joke. Why, man, it's in the calendar."

"I didn't know it," said Elliott slowly. "I read the calendar announcement only once, and I certainly didn't notice that condition."

"Well, that's curious. But how on earth did you escape hearing it talked about? It's always discussed extensively among the boys, especially when there are two competitors of the favoured names, which doesn't often happen."

"I'm not a very sociable fellow," said Elliott with a faint smile. "You know they call me 'the hermit.' As it happened, I never talked the matter over with anyone or heard it referred to. I—I wish I had known this before."

"Why, what difference does it make? It's all right, anyway. But it is odd to think that if your name hadn't been Campbell, the Fraser would have gone to McLean over the heads of Stone and all the rest. Their only hope was that you would both fall below seventy. It's an absurd condition, but there it is in old Professor Fraser's will. He was rich and had no family. So he left a number of bequests to the college on ordinary conditions. I suppose he thought he might humour his whim in one. His widow is a dear old soul, and always makes a special pet of the boy who wins the Fraser. Well, here's my street. So long, Campbell."

Elliott responded almost curtly and walked onward to his boarding-house with a face from which all the light had gone. When he reached his room he took down the Marwood calendar and whirled over the leaves until he came to the announcement of bursaries and scholarships. The Fraser announcement, as far as he had read it, ended at the foot of the page. He turned the leaf and, sure enough, at the top of the next page, in a paragraph by itself, was the condition: "Preference shall be given to candidates of the name Fraser, Campbell or McLean, provided that said competitor makes at least seventy per cent in his examination."

Elliott flung himself into a chair by his table and bowed his head on his hands. He had no right to the Fraser Scholarship. His name was not Campbell, although perhaps nobody in the world knew it save himself, and he remembered it only by an effort of memory.

He had been born in a rough mining camp in British Columbia, and when he was a month old his father, John Hanselpakker, had been killed in a mine explosion, leaving his wife and child quite penniless and almost friendless. One of the miners, an honest, kindly Scotchman named Alexander Campbell, had befriended Mrs. Hanselpakker and her little son in many ways, and two years later she had married him. They returned to their native province of Nova Scotia and settled in a small country village. Here Elliott had grown up, bearing the name of the man who was a kind and loving father to him, and whom he loved as a father. His mother had died when he was ten years old and his stepfather when he was fifteen. On his deathbed he asked Elliott to retain his name.

"I've cared for you and loved you since the time you were born, lad," he said. "You seem like my own son, and I've a fancy to leave you my name. It's all I can leave you, for I'm a poor man, but it's an honest name, lad, and I've kept it free from stain. See that you do likewise, and you'll have your mother's blessing and mine."

Elliott fought a hard battle that spring evening.

"Hold your tongue and keep the Fraser," whispered the tempter. "Campbell *is* your name. You've borne it all your life. And the condition itself is a ridiculous one—no fairness about it. You made the highest marks and you ought to be the winner. It isn't as if you were wronging Stone or any of the others who worked hard and made good marks. If you throw away what you've won by your own hard labour, the Fraser goes to McLean, who made only seventy. Besides, you need the money and he doesn't. His father is a rich man."

"But I'll be a cheat and a cad if I keep it," Elliott muttered miserably. "Campbell isn't my legal name, and I'd never again feel as if I had even the right of love to it if I stained it by a dishonest act. For it *would* be stained, even though nobody but myself knew it. Father said it was a clean name when he left it, and I cannot soil it."

The tempter was not silenced so easily as that. Elliott passed a sleepless night of indecision. But next day he went to Marwood and asked for a private interview with the president. As a result, an official announcement was posted that afternoon on the bulletin board to the effect that, owing to a misunderstanding, the Fraser Scholarship had been wrongly awarded. Carl McLean was posted as winner.

The story soon got around the campus, and Elliott found himself rather overwhelmed with sympathy, but he did not feel as if he were very much in need of it after all. It was good to have done the right thing and be able to look your conscience in the face. He was young and strong and could work his own way through Marwood in time.

"No condolences, please," he said to Roger Brooks with a smile. "I'm sorry I lost the Fraser, of course, but I've my hands and brains left. I'm going straight to my boarding-house to dig with double vim, for I've got to take an examination next week for a provincial school certificate. Next winter I'll be a flourishing pedagogue in some up-country district."

He was not, however. The next afternoon he received a summons to the president's office. The president was there, and with him was a plump, motherly-looking woman of about sixty.

"Mrs. Fraser, this is Elliott Hanselpakker, or Campbell, as I understand he prefers to be called. Elliott, I told your story to Mrs. Fraser last evening, and she was greatly interested when she heard your rather peculiar name. She will tell you why herself."

"I had a young half-sister once," said Mrs. Fraser eagerly. "She married a man named John Hanselpakker and went West, and somehow I lost all trace of her. There was, I regret to say, a coolness between us over her marriage. I disapproved of it because she married a very poor man. When I heard your name, it struck me that you might be her son, or at least know something about her. Her name was Mary Helen Rodney, and I loved her very dearly in spite of our foolish quarrel."

There was a tremour in Mrs. Fraser's voice and an answering one in Elliott's as he replied: "Mary Helen Rodney was my dear mother's name, and my father was John Hanselpakker."

"Then you are my nephew," exclaimed Mrs. Fraser. "I am your Aunt Alice. My boy, you don't know how much it means to a lonely old woman to have found you. I'm the happiest person in the world!"

She slipped her arm through Elliott's and turned to the sympathetic president with shining eyes.

"He is my boy forever, if he will be. Blessings on the Fraser Scholarship!"

"Blessings rather on the manly boy who wouldn't keep it under false colours," said the president with a smile. "I think you are fortunate in your nephew, Mrs. Fraser."

So Elliott Hanselpakker Campbell came back to Marwood the next year after all.

The Girl at the Gate

Something very strange happened the night old Mr. Lawrence died. I have never been able to explain it and I have never spoken of it except to one person and she said that I dreamed it. I did not dream it ... I saw and heard, waking.

We had not expected Mr. Lawrence to die then. He did not seem very ill ... not nearly so ill as he had been during his previous attack. When we heard of his illness I went over to Woodlands to see him, for I had always been a great favourite with him. The big house was quiet, the servants going about their work as usual, without any appearance of excitement. I was told that I could not see Mr. Lawrence for a little while, as the doctor was with him. Mrs. Yeats, the housekeeper, said the attack was not serious and asked me to wait in the blue parlour, but I preferred to sit down on the steps of the big, arched front door. It was an evening in June. Woodlands was very lovely; to my right was the garden, and before me was a little valley abrim with the sunset. In places under the big trees it was quite dark even then.

There was something unusually still in the evening ... a stillness as of waiting. It set me thinking of the last time Mr. Lawrence had been ill ... nearly a year ago in August. One night during his convalescence I had watched by him to relieve the nurse. He had been sleepless and talkative, telling me many things about his life. Finally he told me of Margaret.

I knew a little about her ... that she had been his sweetheart and had died very young. Mr. Lawrence had remained true to her memory ever since, but I had never heard him speak of her before.

"She was very beautiful," he said dreamily, "and she was only eighteen when she died, Jeanette. She had wonderful pale-golden hair and dark-brown eyes. I have a little ivory miniature of her. When I die it is to be given to you, Jeanette. I have waited a long while for her. You know she promised she would come."

I did not understand his meaning and kept silence, thinking that he might be wandering a little in his mind.

"She promised she would come and she will keep her word," he went on. "I was with her when she died. I held her in my arms. She said to me, 'Herbert, I promise that I will be true to you forever, through as many years of lonely heaven as I must know before you come. And when your time is at hand I will come to make your deathbed easy as you have made mine. I will come, Herbert.' She solemnly promised, Jeanette. We made a death-tryst of it. And I know she will come."

He had fallen asleep then and after his recovery he had not alluded to the matter again. I had forgotten it, but I recalled it now as I sat on the steps among the geraniums that June evening. I liked to think of Margaret ... the lovely girl who had died so long ago, taking her lover's heart with her to the grave. She had been a sister of my grandfather, and people told me that I resembled her slightly. Perhaps that was why old Mr. Lawrence had always made such a pet of me.

Presently the doctor came out and nodded to me cheerily. I asked him how Mr. Lawrence was.

"Better ... better," he said briskly. "He will be all right tomorrow. The attack was very slight. Yes, of course you may go in. Don't stay longer than half an hour."

Mrs. Stewart, Mr. Lawrence's sister, was in the sickroom when I went in. She took advantage of my presence to lie down on the sofa a little while, for she had been up all the preceding night. Mr. Lawrence turned his fine old silver head on the pillow and smiled a greeting. He was a very handsome old man; neither age nor illness had marred his finely modelled face or impaired the flash of his keen, steel-blue eyes. He seemed quite well and talked naturally and easily of many commonplace things.

At the end of the doctor's half-hour I rose to go. Mrs. Stewart had fallen asleep and he would not let me wake her, saying he needed nothing and felt like sleeping himself. I promised to come up again on the morrow and went out.

It was dark in the hall, where no lamp had been lighted, but outside on the lawn the moonlight was bright as day. It was the clearest, whitest night I ever saw. I turned aside into the garden, meaning to cross it, and take the short way over the west meadow home. There was a long walk of rose bushes leading across the garden to a little gate on the further side ... the way Mr. Lawrence had been wont to take long ago when he went over the fields to woo Margaret. I went along it, enjoying the night. The bushes were white with roses, and the ground under my feet was all snowed over with their petals. The air was still and breezeless; again I felt that sensation of waiting ... of expectancy. As I came up to the little gate I saw a young girl standing on the other side of it. She stood in the full moonlight and I saw her distinctly.

She was tall and slight and her head was bare. I saw that her hair was a pale gold, shining somewhat strangely about her head as if catching the moonbeams. Her face was very lovely and her eyes large and dark. She was dressed in something white and softly shimmering, and in her hand she held a white rose ... a very large and perfect one. Even at the time I found myself wondering where she could have picked it. It was not a Woodlands rose. All the Woodlands roses were smaller and less double.

She was a stranger to me, yet I felt that I had seen her or someone very like her before. Possibly she was one of Mr. Lawrence's many nieces who might have come up to Woodlands upon hearing of his illness.

As I opened the gate I felt an odd chill of positive fear. Then she smiled as if I had spoken my thought.

"Do not be frightened," she said. "There is no reason you should be frightened. I have only come to keep a tryst."

The words reminded me of something, but I could not recall what it was. The strange fear that was on me deepened. I could not speak.

She came through the gateway and stood for a moment at my side.

"It is strange that you should have seen me," she said, "but now behold how strong and beautiful a thing is faithful love—strong enough to conquer death. We who have loved truly love always—and this makes our heaven."

She walked on after she had spoken, down the long rose path. I watched her until she reached the house and went up the steps. In truth I thought the girl was someone not quite in her right mind. When I reached home I did not speak of the matter to anyone, not even to inquire who the girl might possibly be. There seemed to be something in that strange meeting that demanded my silence.

The next morning word came that old Mr. Lawrence was dead. When I hurried down to Woodlands I found all in confusion, but Mrs. Yeats took me into the blue parlour and told me what little there was to tell.

"He must have died soon after you left him, Miss Jeanette," she sobbed, "for Mrs. Stewart wakened at ten o'clock and he was gone. He lay there, smiling, with such a strange look on his face as if he had just seen something that made him wonderfully happy. I never saw such a look on a dead face before."

"Who is here besides Mrs. Stewart?" I asked.

"Nobody," said Mrs. Yeats. "We have sent word to all his friends but they have not had time to arrive here yet."

"I met a young girl in the garden last night," I said slowly. "She came into the house. I did not know her but I thought she must be a relative of Mr. Lawrence's."

Mrs. Yeats shook her head.

"No. It must have been somebody from the village, although I didn't know of anyone calling after you went away."

I said nothing more to her about it.

After the funeral Mrs. Stewart gave me Margaret's miniature. I had never seen it or any picture of Margaret before. The face was very lovely—also strangely like my own, although I am not beautiful. It was the face of the young girl I had met at the gate!

The Light on the Big Dipper

"Don't let Nellie run out of doors, Mary Margaret, and be careful of the fire, Mary Margaret. I expect we'll be back pretty soon after dark, so don't be lonesome, Mary Margaret."

Mary Margaret laughed and switched her long, thick braid of black hair from one shoulder to the other.

"No fear of my being lonesome, Mother Campbell. I'll be just as careful as can be and there are so many things to be done that I'll be as busy and happy as a bee all day long. Nellie and I will have just the nicest kind of a time. I won't get lonesome, but if I should feel just tempted to, I'll think, Father is on his way home. He will soon be here.' And that would drive the lonesomeness away before it dared to show its face. Don't you worry, Mother Campbell."

Mother Campbell smiled. She knew she could trust Mary Margaret—careful, steady, prudent little Mary Margaret. Little! Ah, that was just the trouble. Careful and steady and prudent as Mary Margaret might be, she was only twelve years old, after all, and there would not be another soul besides her and Nellie on the Little Dipper that whole day. Mrs. Campbell felt that she hardly dared to go away under such circumstances. And yet she *must* dare it. Oscar Bryan had sailed over from the mainland the evening before with word that her sister Nan—her only sister, who lived in Cartonville—was ill and about to undergo a serious operation. She must go to see her, and Uncle Martin was waiting with his boat to take her over to the mainland to catch the morning train for Cartonville.

If five-year-old Nellie had been quite well Mrs. Campbell would have taken both her and Mary Margaret and locked up the house. But Nellie had a very bad cold and was quite unfit to go sailing across the harbour on a raw, chilly November day. So there was nothing to do but leave Mary Margaret in charge, and Mary Margaret was quite pleased at the prospect.

"You know, Mother Campbell, I'm not afraid of anything except tramps. And no tramps ever come to the Dippers. You see what an advantage it is to live on an island! There, Uncle Martin is waving. Run along, little mother."

Mary Margaret watched the boat out of sight from the window and then betook herself to the doing of her tasks, singing blithely all the while. It was rather nice to be left in sole charge like this—it made you feel so important and grown-up.

She would do everything very nicely and Mother would see when she came back what a good housekeeper her daughter was.

Mary Margaret and Nellie and Mrs. Campbell had been living on the Little Dipper ever since the preceding April. Before that they had always lived in their own cosy home at the Harbour Head. But in April Captain Campbell had sailed in the *Two Sisters* for a long voyage and, before he went, Mrs. Campbell's brother, Martin Clowe, had come to them with a proposition. He ran a lobster cannery on the Little Dipper, and he wanted his sister to go and keep house for him while her husband was away. After some discussion it was so arranged, and Mrs. Campbell and her two girls moved to the Little Dipper. It was not a lonesome place then, for the lobstermen and their families lived on it, and boats were constantly sailing to and fro between it and the mainland. Mary Margaret enjoyed her summer greatly; she bathed and sailed and roamed over the rocks, and on fine days her Uncle George, who kept the lighthouse on the Big Dipper, and lived there all alone, often came over and took her across to the Big Dipper. Mary Margaret thought the lighthouse was a wonderful place. Uncle George taught her how to light the lamps and manage the light.

When the lobster season dosed, the men took up codfishing and carried this on till October, when they all moved back to the mainland. But Uncle Martin was building a house for himself at Harbour Head and did not wish to move until the ice formed over the bay because it would then be so much easier to transport his goods and chattels; so the Campbells stayed with him until the Captain should return.

Mary Margaret found plenty to do that day and wasn't a bit lonesome. But when evening came she didn't feel quite so cheerful. Nellie had fallen asleep, and there wasn't another living creature except the cat on the Little Dipper. Besides, it looked like a storm. The harbour was glassy calm, but the sky was very black and dour in the northeast—like snow, thought weather-wise Mary Margaret. She hoped her mother would get home before it began, and she wished the lighthouse star would gleam out on the Big Dipper. It would seem like the bright eye of a steady old friend. Mary Margaret always watched for it every night; just as soon as the sun went down the big lighthouse star would flash goldenly out in the northeastern sky.

"I'll sit down by the window and watch for it," said Mary Margaret to herself. "Then, when it is lighted, I'll get up a nice warm supper for Mother and Uncle Martin."

Mary Margaret sat down by the kitchen window to watch. Minute after minute passed, but no light flashed out on the Big Dipper. What was the matter? Mary Margaret began to feel uneasy. It was too cloudy to tell just when the sun had set, but she was sure it must be down, for it was quite dark in the house. She lighted a lamp, got the almanac, and hunted out the exact time of sunsetting. The sun had been down fifteen minutes!

And there was no light on the Big Dipper!

Mary Margaret felt alarmed and anxious. What was wrong at the Big Dipper? Was Uncle George away? Or had something happened to him? Mary Margaret was sure he had never forgotten!

Fifteen minutes longer did Mary Margaret watch restlessly at the window. Then she concluded that something was desperately wrong somewhere. It was half an hour after sunset and the Big Dipper light, the most important one along the whole coast, was not lighted. What would she do? What *could* she do?

The answer came swift and dear into Mary Margaret's steady, sensible little mind. She must go to the Big Dipper and light the lamps!

But could she? Difficulties came crowding thick and fast into her thoughts. It was going to snow; the soft broad flakes were falling already. Could she row the two miles to the Big Dipper in the darkness and the snow? If she could, dare she leave Nellie all alone in the house? Oh, she couldn't! Somebody at the Harbour Head would surely notice that the Big Dipper light was unlighted and would go over to investigate the cause. But suppose they shouldn't? If the snow came thicker they might never notice the absence of the light. And suppose there was a ship away out there, as there nearly always was, with the dangerous rocks and shoals of the outer harbour to pass, with precious lives on board and no guiding beacon on the Big Dipper.

Mary Margaret hesitated no longer. She must go.

Bravely, briskly and thoughtfully she made her preparations. First, the fire was banked and the draughts dosed; then she wrote a little note for her mother and laid it on the table. Finally she wakened Nellie.

"Nellie," said Mary Margaret, speaking very kindly and determinedly, "there is no light on the Big Dipper and I've got to row over and see about it. I'll be back as quickly as I can, and Mother and Uncle Martin will soon be here. You won't be afraid to stay alone, will you, dearie? You mustn't be afraid, because I have to go. And, Nellie, I'm going to tie you in your chair; it's necessary, because I can't lock the door, so you mustn't cry; nothing will hurt you, and I want you to be a brave little girl and help sister all you can."

Nellie, too sleepy and dazed to understand very clearly what Mary Margaret was about, submitted to be wrapped up in quilts and bound securely in her chair. Then Mary Margaret tied the chair fast to the wall so that Nellie couldn't upset it. That's safe, she thought. Nellie can't run out now or fall on the stove or set herself afire.

Mary Margaret put on her jacket, hood and mittens, and took Uncle Martin's lantern. As she went out and closed the door, a little wail from Nellie sounded on her ear. For a moment she hesitated, then the blackness of the Big Dipper confirmed her resolution. She must go. Nellie was really quite safe and comfortable. It would not hurt her to cry a little, and it might hurt somebody a great deal if the Big Dipper light failed. Setting her lips firmly, Mary Margaret ran down to the shore.

Like all the Harbour girls, Mary Margaret could row a boat from the time she was nine years old. Nevertheless, her heart almost failed her as she got into the little dory and rowed out. The snow was getting thick. Could she pull across those black two miles between the Dippers before it got so much thicker that she would lose her way? Well, she must risk it. She had set the light in the kitchen window; she must keep it fair behind her and then she would land on the lighthouse beach. With a murmured prayer for help and guidance she pulled staunchly away.

It was a long, hard row for the little twelve-year-old arms. Fortunately there was no wind. But thicker and thicker came the snow; finally the kitchen light was hidden in it. For a moment Mary Margaret's heart sank in despair; the next it gave a joyful bound, for, turning, she saw the dark tower of the lighthouse directly behind her. By the aid of her lantern she rowed to the landing, sprang out and made her boat fast. A minute later she was in the lighthouse kitchen.

The door leading to the tower stairs was open and at the foot of the stairs lay Uncle George, limp and white.

"Oh, Uncle George," gasped Mary Margaret, "what is the matter? What has happened?"

"Mary Margaret! Thank God! I was just praying to Him to send somebody to 'tend the light. Who's with you?"

"Nobody.... I got frightened because there was no light and I rowed over. Mother and Uncle Martin are away."

"You don't mean to say you rowed yourself over here alone in the dark and snow! Well, you are the pluckiest little girl about this harbour! It's a mercy I've showed you how to manage the light. Run up and start it at once. Don't mind about me. I tumbled down those pesky stairs like the awkward old fool I am and I've broke my leg and hurt my back so bad I can't crawl an inch. I've been lying here for three mortal hours and they've seemed like three years. Hurry with the light, Mary Margaret."

Mary Margaret hurried. Soon the Big Dipper light was once more gleaming cheerfully athwart the stormy harbour. Then she ran back to her uncle. There was not much she could do for him beyond covering him warmly with quilts, placing a pillow under his head, and brewing him a hot drink of tea.

"I left a note for Mother telling her where I'd gone, Uncle George, so I'm sure Uncle Martin will come right over as soon as they get home."

"He'll have to hurry. It's blowing up now ... hear it ... and snowing thick. If your mother and Martin haven't left the Harbour Head before this, they won't leave it tonight. But, anyhow, the light is lit. I don't mind my getting smashed up compared to that. I thought I'd go crazy lying here picturing to myself a vessel out on the reefs."

That night was a very long and anxious one. The storm grew rapidly worse, and snow and wind howled around the lighthouse. Uncle George soon grew feverish and delirious, and Mary Margaret, between her anxiety for him and her dismal thoughts of poor Nellie tied in her chair over at the Little Dipper, and the dark possibility of her mother and Uncle Martin being out in the storm, felt almost distracted. But the morning came at last, as mornings blessedly will, be the nights never so long and anxious, and it dawned fine and clear over a white world. Mary

Margaret ran to the shore and gazed eagerly across at the Little Dipper. No smoke was visible from Uncle Martin's house!

She could not leave Uncle George, who was raving wildly, and yet it was necessary to obtain assistance somehow. Suddenly she remembered the distress signal. She must hoist it. How fortunate that Uncle George had once shown her how!

Ten minutes later there was a commotion over at Harbour Head where the signal was promptly observed, and very soon—although it seemed long enough to Mary Margaret—a boat came sailing over to the Big Dipper. When the men landed they were met by a very white-faced little girl who gasped out a rather disjointed story of a light that hadn't been lighted and an uncle with a broken leg and a sister tied in her chair, and would they please see to Uncle George at once, for she must go straight over to the other Dipper?

One of the men rowed her over, but before they were halfway there another boat went sailing across the harbour, and Mary Margaret saw a woman and two men land from it and hurry up to the house.

That is Mother and Uncle Martin, but who can the other man be? wondered Mary Margaret.

When she reached the cottage her mother and Uncle Martin were reading her note, and Nellie, just untied from the chair where she had been found fast asleep, was in the arms of a great, big, brown, bewhiskered man. Mary Margaret just gave one look at the man. Then she flew across the room with a cry of delight.

"Father!"

For ten minutes not one intelligible word was said, what with laughing and crying and kissing. Mary Margaret was the first to recover herself and say briskly, "Now, *do* explain, somebody. Tell me how it all happened."

"Martin and I got back to Harbour Head too late last night to cross over," said her mother. "It would have been madness to try to cross in the storm, although I was nearly wild thinking of you two children. It's well I didn't know the whole truth or I'd have been simply frantic. We stayed at the Head all night, and first thing this morning came your father."

"We came in last night," said Captain Campbell, "and it was pitch dark, not a light to be seen and beginning to snow. We didn't know where we were and I was terribly worried, when all at once the Big Dipper light I'd been looking for so vainly flashed out, and everything was all right in a moment. But, Mary Margaret, if that light hadn't appeared, we'd never have got in past the reefs. You've saved your father's ship and all the lives in her, my brave little girl."

"Oh!" Mary Margaret drew a long breath and her eyes were starry with tears of happiness. "Oh, I'm so thankful I went over. And I *had* to tie Nellie in her chair, Mother, there was no other way. Uncle George broke his leg and is very sick this morning, and there's no breakfast ready for anyone and the fire black out ... but that doesn't matter when Father is safe ... and oh, I'm so tired!"

And then Mary Margaret sat down just for a moment, intending to get right up and help her mother light the fire, laid her head on her father's shoulder, and fell sound asleep before she ever suspected it.

The Prodigal Brother

Miss Hannah was cutting asters in her garden. It was a very small garden, for nothing would grow beyond the shelter of the little, grey, low-eaved house which alone kept the northeast winds from blighting everything with salt spray; but small as it was, it was a miracle of blossoms and a marvel of neatness. The trim brown paths were swept clean of every leaf or fallen petal, each of the little square beds had its border of big white quahog clamshells, and not even a sweet-pea vine would have dared to straggle from its appointed course under Miss Hannah's eye.

Miss Hannah had always lived in the little grey house down by the shore, so far away from all the other houses in Prospect and so shut away from them by a circle of hills that it had a seeming isolation. Not another house could Miss Hannah see from her own doorstone; she often declared she could not have borne it if it had not been for the lighthouse beacon at night flaming over the northwest hill behind the house like a great unwinking, friendly star that never failed even on the darkest night. Behind the house a little tongue of the St. Lawrence gulf ran up between the headlands until the wavelets of its tip almost lapped against Miss Hannah's kitchen doorstep. Beyond, to the north, was the great crescent of the gulf, whose murmur had been Miss Hannah's lullaby all her life. When people wondered to her how she could endure living in such a lonely place, she retorted that the loneliness was what she loved it for, and that the lighthouse star and the far-away call of the gulf had always been company enough for her and always would be ... until Ralph came back. When Ralph came home, of course, he might like a livelier place and they might move to town or up-country as he wished.

"Of course," said Miss Hannah with a proud smile, "a rich man mightn't fancy living away down here in a little grey house by the shore. He'll be for building me a mansion, I expect, and I'd like it fine. But until he comes I must be contented with things as they are."

People always smiled to each other when Miss Hannah talked like this. But they took care not to let her see the smile.

Miss Hannah snipped her white and purple asters off ungrudgingly and sang, as she snipped, an old-fashioned song she had learned long ago in her youth. The day was one of October's rarest, and Miss Hannah loved fine days. The air was clear as golden-hued crystal, and all the slopes around her were mellow and hazy in the autumn sunshine. She knew that beyond those sunny slopes were woods glorying in crimson and gold, and she would have the delight of a walk through them later on when she went to carry the asters to sick Millie Starr at the Bridge. Flowers were all Miss Hannah had to give, for she was very poor, but she gave them with a great wealth of friendliness and goodwill.

Presently a wagon drove down her lane and pulled up outside of her white garden paling. Jacob Delancey was in it, with a pretty young niece of his who was a visitor from the city, and Miss Hannah, her sheaf of asters in her arms, went over to the paling with a sparkle of interest in her faded blue eyes. She had heard a great deal of the beauty of this strange girl. Prospect people had been talking of nothing else for a week, and Miss Hannah was filled with a harmless curiosity concerning her. She always liked to look at pretty people, she said; they did her as much good as her flowers.

"Good afternoon, Miss Hannah," said Jacob Delancey. "Busy with your flowers, as usual, I see."

"Oh, yes," said Miss Hannah, managing to stare with unobtrusive delight at the girl while she talked. "The frost will soon be coming now, you know; so I want to live among them as much as I can while they're here."

"That's right," assented Jacob, who made a profession of cordial agreement with everybody and would have said the same words in the same tone had Miss Hannah announced a predilection for living in the cellar. "Well, Miss Hannah, it's flowers I'm after myself just now. We're having a bit of a party at our house tonight, for the young folks, and my wife told me to call and ask you if you could let us have a few for decoration."

"Of course," said Miss Hannah, "you can have these. I meant them for Millie, but I can cut the west bed for her."

She opened the gate and carried the asters over to the buggy. Miss Delancey took them with a smile that made Miss Hannah remember the date forever.

"Lovely day," commented Jacob genially.

"Yes," said Miss Hannah dreamily. "It reminds me of the day Ralph went away twenty years ago. It doesn't seem so long. Don't you think he'll be coming back soon, Jacob?"

"Oh, sure," said Jacob, who thought the very opposite.

"I have a feeling that he's coming very soon," said Miss Hannah brightly. "It will be a great day for me, won't it, Jacob? I've been poor all my life, but when Ralph comes back everything will be so different. He will be a rich man and he will give me everything I've always wanted. He said he would. A fine house and a carriage and a silk dress. Oh, and we will travel and see the world. You don't know how I look forward to it all. I've got it all planned out, all I'm going to do and have. And I believe he will be here very soon. A man ought to be able to make a fortune in twenty years, don't you think, Jacob?"

"Oh, sure," said Jacob. But he said it a little uncomfortably. He did not like the job of throwing cold water, but it seemed to him that he ought not to encourage Miss Hannah's hopes. "Of course, you shouldn't think too much about it, Miss Hannah. He mightn't ever come back, or he might be poor."

"How can you say such things, Jacob?" interrupted Miss Hannah indignantly, with a little crimson spot flaming out in each of her pale cheeks. "You know quite well he will come back. I'm as sure of it as that I'm standing here. And he will be rich, too. People are always trying to hint just as you've done to me, but I don't mind them. I know."

She turned and went back into her garden with her head held high. But her sudden anger floated away in a whiff of sweet-pea perfume that struck her in the face; she waved her hand in farewell to her callers and watched the buggy down the lane with a smile.

"Of course, Jacob doesn't know, and I shouldn't have snapped him up so quick. It'll be my turn to crow when Ralph does come. My, but isn't that girl pretty. I feel as if I'd been looking at some lovely picture. It just makes a good day of this. Something pleasant happens to me most every day and that girl is today's pleasant thing. I just feel real happy and thankful that there are such beautiful creatures in the world and that we can look at them."

"Well, of all the queer delusions!" Jacob Delancey was ejaculating as he and his niece drove down the lane.

"What is it all about?" asked Miss Delancey curiously.

"Well, it's this way, Dorothy. Long ago Miss Hannah had a brother who ran away from home. It was before their father and mother died. Ralph Walworth was as wild a young scamp as ever was in Prospect and a spendthrift in the bargain. Nobody but Hannah had any use for him, and she just worshipped him. I must admit he was real fond of her too, but he and his father couldn't get on at all. So finally he ups and runs away; it was generally supposed he went to the mining country. He left a note for Hannah bidding her goodbye and telling her that he was going to make his fortune and would come back to her a rich man. There's never been a word heard tell of him since, and in my opinion it's doubtful if he's still alive. But Miss Hannah, as you saw, is sure and certain he'll come back yet with gold dropping out of his pockets. She's as sane as anyone everyway else, but there is no doubt she's a little cracked on that p'int. If he never turns up she'll go on hoping quite happy to her death. But if he should turn up and be poor, as is ten times likelier than anything else, I believe it'd most kill Miss Hannah. She's terrible proud for all she's so sweet, and you saw yourself how mad she got when I kind of hinted he mightn't be rich. If he came back poor, after all her boasting about him, I don't fancy he'd get much of a welcome from her. And she'd never hold up her head again, that's certain. So it's to be hoped, say I, that Ralph Walworth never will turn up, unless he comes in a carriage and four, which is about as likely, in my opinion, as that he'll come in a pumpkin drawn by mice."

When October had passed and the grey November days came, the glory of Miss Hannah's garden was over. She was very lonely without her flowers. She missed them more this year than ever. On fine days she paced up and down the walks and looked sadly at the drooping, unsightly stalks and vines. She was there one afternoon when the northeast wind was up and doing, whipping the gulf waters into whitecaps and whistling up the inlet and around the grey eaves. Miss

Hannah was mournfully patting a frosted chrysanthemum under its golden chin when she saw a man limping slowly down the lane.

"Now, who can that be?" she murmured. "It isn't any Prospect man, for there's nobody lame around here."

She went to the garden gate to meet him. He came haltingly up the slope and paused before her, gazing at her wistfully. He looked old and bent and broken, and his clothes were poor and worn. Who was he? Miss Hannah felt that she ought to know him, and her memory went groping back amongst all her recollections. Yet she could think of nobody but her father, who had died fifteen years before.

"Don't ye know me, Hannah?" said the man wistfully. "Have I changed so much as all that?"

"Ralph!"

It was between a cry and a laugh. Miss Hannah flew through the gate and caught him in her arms. "Ralph, my own dear brother! Oh, I always knew you'd come back. If you knew how I've looked forward to this day!" She was both laughing and crying now. Her face shone with a soft gladness. Ralph Walworth shook his head sadly.

"It's a poor wreck of a man I am come back to you, Hannah," he said. "I've never accomplished anything and my health's broken and I'm a cripple as ye see. For a time I thought I'd never show my face back here, such a failure as I be, but the longing to see you got too strong. It's naught but a wreck I am, Hannah."

"You're my own dear brother," cried Miss Hannah. "Do you think I care how poor you are? And if your health is poor I'm the one to nurse you up, who else than your only sister, I'd like to know! Come right in. You're shivering in this wind. I'll mix you a good hot currant drink. I knew them black currants didn't bear so plentiful for nothing last summer. Oh, this is a good day and no mistake!"

In twenty-four hours' time everybody in Prospect knew that Ralph Walworth had come home, crippled and poor. Jacob Delancey shook his head as he drove away from the station with Ralph's shabby little trunk standing on end in his buggy. The station master had asked him to take it down to Miss Hannah's, and Jacob did not fancy the errand. He was afraid Miss Hannah would be in a bad way and he did not know what to say to her.

She was in her garden, covering her pansies with seaweed, when he drove up, and she came to the garden gate to meet him, all smiles.

"So you've brought Ralph's trunk, Mr. Delancey. Now, that was real good of you. He was going over to the station to see about it himself, but he had such a cold I persuaded him to wait till tomorrow. He's lying down asleep now. He's just real tired. He brought this seaweed up from the shore for me this morning and it played him out. He ain't strong. But didn't I tell you he was coming back soon? You only laughed at me, but I knew."

"He isn't very rich, though," said Jacob jokingly. He was relieved to find that Miss Hannah did not seem to be worrying over this.

"That doesn't matter," cried Miss Hannah. "Why, he's my brother! Isn't that enough? I'm rich if he isn't, rich in love and happiness. And I'm better pleased in a way than if he had come back rich. He might have wanted to take me away or build a fine house, and I'm too old to be making changes. And then he wouldn't have needed me. I'd have been of no use to him. As it is, it's just me he needs to look after him and coddle him. Oh, it's fine to have somebody to do things for, somebody that belongs to you. I was just dreading the loneliness of the winter, and now it's going to be such a happy winter. I declare last night Ralph and I sat up till morning talking over everything. He's had a hard life of it. Bad luck and illness right along. And last winter in the lumber woods he got his leg broke. But now he's come home and we're never going to be parted again as long as we live. I could sing for joy, Jacob."

"Oh, sure," assented Jacob cordially. He felt a little dazed. Miss Hannah's nimble change of base was hard for him to follow, and he had an injured sense of having wasted a great deal of commiseration on her when she didn't need it at all. "Only I kind of thought, we all thought, you had such plans."

"Well, they served their turn," interrupted Miss Hannah briskly. "They amused me and kept me interested till something real would come in their place. If I'd had to carry them out I dare say they'd have bothered me a lot. Things are more comfortable as they are. I'm happy as a bird, Jacob."

"Oh, sure," said Jacob. He pondered the business deeply all the way back home, but could make nothing of it.

"But I ain't obliged to," he concluded sensibly. "Miss Hannah's satisfied and happy and it's nobody else's concern. However, I call it a curious thing."

The Redemption of John Churchill

John Churchill walked slowly, not as a man walks who is tired, or content to saunter for the pleasure of it, but as one in no haste to reach his destination through dread of it. The day was well on to late afternoon in mid-spring, and the world was abloom. Before him and behind him wound a road that ran like a red ribbon through fields of lush clovery green. The orchards scattered along it were white and fragrant, giving of their incense to a merry south-west wind; fence-corner nooks were purple with patches of violets or golden-green with the curly heads of young ferns. The roadside was sprinkled over with the gold dust of dandelions and the pale stars of wild strawberry blossoms. It seemed a day through which a man should walk lightly and blithely, looking the world and his fellows frankly in the face, and opening his heart to let the springtime in.

But John Churchill walked laggingly, with bent head. When he met other wayfarers or was passed by them, he did not lift his face, but only glanced up under his eyebrows with a furtive look that was replaced by a sort of shamed relief when they had passed on without recognizing him. Some of them he knew for friends of the old time. Ten years had not changed them as he had been changed. They had spent those ten years in freedom and good repute, under God's blue sky, in His glad air and sunshine. He, John Churchill, had spent them behind the walls of a prison.

His close-clipped hair was grey; his figure, encased in an ill-fitting suit of coarse cloth, was stooped and shrunken; his face was deeply lined; yet he was not an old man in years. He was only forty; he was thirty when he had been convicted of embezzling the bank funds for purposes of speculation and had been sent to prison, leaving behind a wife and father who were broken-hearted and a sister whose pride had suffered more than her heart.

He had never seen them since, but he knew what had happened in his absence. His wife had died two months later, leaving behind her a baby boy; his father had died within the year. He had killed them; he, John Churchill, who loved them, had killed them as surely as though his hand had struck them down in cold blood. His sister had taken the baby, his little son whom he had never seen, but for whom he had prepared such a birthright of dishonour. She had never forgiven her brother and she never wrote to him. He knew that she would have brought the boy up either in ignorance of his father's crime or in utter detestation of it. When he came back to the world after his imprisonment, there was not a single friendly hand to clasp his and help him struggle up again. The best his friends had been able to do for him was to forget him.

He was filled with bitterness and despair and a gnawing hatred of the world of brightness around him. He had no place in it; he was an ugly blot on it. He was a friendless, wifeless, homeless man who could not so much as look his fellow men in the face, who must henceforth consort with outcasts. In his extremity he hated God and man, burning with futile resentment against both.

Only one feeling of tenderness yet remained in his heart; it centred around the thought of his little son.

When he left the prison he had made up his mind what to do. He had a little money which his father had left him, enough to take him west. He would go there, under a new name. There would be novelty and adventure to blot out the memories of the old years. He did not care what became of him, since there was no one else to care. He knew in his heart that his future career would probably lead him still further and further downward, but that did not matter. If there had been anybody to care, he might have thought it worthwhile to struggle back to respectability and trample his shame under feet that should henceforth walk only in the ways of honour and honesty. But there was nobody to care. So he would go to his own place.

But first he must see little Joey, who must be quite a big boy now, nearly ten years old. He would go home and see him just once, even although he dreaded meeting aversion in the child's eyes. Then, when he had bade him good-bye, and, with him, good-bye to all that remained to make for good in his desolated existence, he would go out of his life forever.

"I'll go straight to the devil then," he said sullenly. "That's where I belong, a jail-bird at whom everybody except other jail-birds looks askance. To think what I was once, and what I am now! It's enough to drive a man mad! As for repenting, bah! Who'd believe that I really repented, who'd give me a second chance on the faith of it? Not a soul. Repentance won't blot out the past. It won't give me back my wife whom I loved above everything on earth and whose heart I broke. It won't restore me my unstained name and my right to a place among honourable men. There's no chance for a man who has fallen as low as I have. If Emily were living, I could struggle for her sake. But who'd be fool enough to attempt such a fight with no motive and not one chance of success in a hundred. Not I. I'm down and I'll stay down. There's no climbing up again."

He celebrated his first day of freedom by getting drunk, although he had never before been an intemperate man. Then, when the effects of the debauch wore off, he took the train for Alliston; he would go home and see little Joey once.

Nobody at the station where he alighted recognized him or paid any attention to him. He was as a dead man who had come back to life to find himself effaced from recollection and his place knowing him no more. It was three miles from the station to where his sister lived, and he resolved to walk the distance. Now that the critical moment drew near, he shrank from it and wished to put it off as long as he could.

When he reached his sister's home he halted on the road and surveyed the place over its snug respectability of iron fence. His courage failed him at the thought of walking over that trim lawn and knocking at that closed front door. He would slip around by the back way; perhaps, who knew, he might come upon Joey without running the gauntlet of his sister's cold, offended eyes. If he might only find the boy and talk to him for a little while without betraying his identity, meet his son's clear gaze without the danger of finding scorn or fear in it—his heart beat high at the thought.

He walked furtively up the back way between high, screening hedges of spruce. When he came to the gate of the yard, he paused. He heard voices just beyond the thick hedge, children's voices, and he crept as near as he could to the sound and peered through the hedge, with a choking sensation in his throat and a smart in his eyes. Was that Joey, could that be his little son? Yes, it was; he would have known him anywhere by his likeness to Emily. Their boy had her curly brown hair, her sensitive mouth, above all, her clear-gazing, truthful grey eyes, eyes in which there was never a shadow of falsehood or faltering.

Joey Churchill was sitting on a stone bench in his aunt's kitchen yard, holding one of his black-stockinged knees between his small, brown hands. Jimmy Morris was standing opposite to him, his back braced against the trunk of a big, pink-blossomed apple tree, his hands in his pockets, and a scowl on his freckled face. Jimmy lived next door to Joey and as a rule they were very good friends, but this afternoon they had quarrelled over the right and proper way to construct an Indian ambush in the fir grove behind the pig-house. The argument was long and warm and finally culminated in personalities. Just as John Churchill dropped on one knee behind the hedge, the better to see Joey's face, Jimmy Morris said scornfully:

"I don't care what you say. Nobody believes you. Your father is in the penitentiary."

The taunt struck home as it always did. It was not the first time that Joey had been twitted with his father by his boyish companions. But never before by Jimmy! It always hurt him, and he had never before made any response to it. His face would flush crimson, his lips would quiver, and his big grey eyes darken miserably with the shadow that was on his life; he would turn away in silence. But that Jimmy, his best beloved chum, should say such a thing to him; oh, it hurt terribly.

There is nothing so merciless as a small boy. Jimmy saw his advantage and vindictively pursued it.

"Your father stole money, that's what he did! You know he did. I'm pretty glad *my* father isn't a thief. *Your* father is. And when he gets out of prison, he'll go on stealing again. My father says he will. Nobody'll have anything to do with him, my father says. His own sister won't have anything to do with him. So there, Joey Churchill!"

"There *will* somebody have something to do with him!" cried Joey hotly. He slid off the bench and faced Jimmy proudly and confidently. The unseen watcher on the other side of the hedge saw his face grow white and intense and set-lipped, as if it had been the face of a man. The grey eyes were alight with a steady, fearless glow.

"*I'll* have something to do with him. He is my father and I love him. I don't care what he did, I love him just as well as if he was the best man in the world. I love him better than if he was as good as your father, because he needs it more. I've always loved him ever since I found out about him. I'd write to him and tell him so, if Aunt Beatrice would tell me where to send the letter. Aunt Beatrice won't ever talk about him or let me talk about him, but I *think* about him all the time. And he's going to be a good man yet, yes, he is, just as good as your father, Jimmy Morris. I'm going to *make* him good. I made up my mind years ago what I would do and I'm going to do it, so there, Jimmy."

"I don't see what you can do," muttered Jimmy, already ashamed of what he had said and wishing he had let Joey's father alone.

"I'll tell you what I can do!" Joey was confronting all the world now, with his head thrown back and his face flushed with his earnestness. "I can love him and stand by him, and I will. When he gets out of—of prison, he'll come to see me, I know he will. And I'm just going to hug him and kiss him and say, 'Never mind, Father. I know you're sorry for what you've done, and you're never going to do it any more. You're going to be a good man and I'm going to stand by you.' Yes, sir, that's just what I'm going to say to him. I'm all the children he has and there's nobody else to love him, because I know Aunt Beatrice doesn't. And I'm going with him wherever he goes."

"You can't," said Jimmy in a scared tone. "Your Aunt Beatrice won't let you."

"Yes, she will. She'll have to. I belong to my father. And I think he'll be coming pretty soon some way. I'm pretty sure the time must be 'most up. I wish he would come. I want to see him as much as can be, 'cause I know he'll need me. And I'll be proud of him yet, Jimmy Morris, yes, I'll be just as proud as you are of your father. When I get bigger, nobody will call my father names, I can tell you. I'll fight them if they do, yes, sir, I will. My father and I are going to stand by each other like bricks. Aunt Beatrice has lots of children of her own and I don't believe she'll be a bit sorry when I go away. She's ashamed of my father 'cause he did a bad thing. But I'm not, no, sir. I'm going to love him so much that I'll make up to him for everything else. And you can just go home, Jimmy Morris, so there!"

Jimmy Morris went home, and when he had gone, Joey flung himself face downward in the grass and fallen apple blossoms and lay very still.

On the other side of the spruce hedge knelt John Churchill with bowed head. The tears were running freely down his face, but there was a new, tender light in his eyes. The bitterness and despair had fallen out of his heart, leaving a great peace and a dawning hope in their place. Bless that loyal little soul! There was something to live for after all—there was a motive to make the struggle worthwhile. He must justify his son's faith in him; he must strive to make himself worthy of this sweet, pure, unselfish love that was offered to him, as a divine draught is offered to the parched lips of a man perishing from thirst. Aye, and,

God helping him, he would. He would redeem the past. He would go west, but under his own name. His little son should go with him; he would work hard; he would pay back the money he had embezzled, as much of it as he could, if it took the rest of his life to do so. For his boy's sake he must cleanse his name from the dishonour he had brought on it. Oh, thank God, there was somebody to care, somebody to love him, somebody to believe him when he said humbly, "I repent." Under his breath he said, looking heavenward:

"God be merciful to me, a sinner."

Then he stood up erectly, went through the gate and over the grass to the motionless little figure with its face buried in its arms.

"Joey boy," he said huskily. "Joey boy."

Joey sprang to his feet with tears still glistening in his eyes. He saw before him a bent, grey-headed man looking at him lovingly and wistfully. Joey knew who it was—the father he had never seen. With a glad cry of welcome he sprang into the outstretched arms of the man whom his love had already won back to God.

The Schoolmaster's Letters

At sunset the schoolmaster went up to his room to write a letter to her. He always wrote to her at the same time—when the red wave of the sunset, flaming over the sea, surged in at the little curtainless window and flowed over the pages he wrote on. The light was rose-red and imperial and spiritual, like his love for her, and seemed almost to dye the words of the letters in its own splendid hues—the letters to her which she never was to see, whose words her eyes never were to read, and whose love and golden fancy and rainbow dreams never were to be so much as known by her. And it was because she never was to see them that he dared to write them, straight out of his full heart, taking the exquisite pleasure of telling her what he never could permit himself to tell her face to face. Every evening he wrote thus to her, and the hour so spent glorified the entire day. The rest of the hours—all the other hours of the commonplace day—he was merely a poor schoolmaster with a long struggle before him, one who might not lift his eyes to gaze on a star. But at this hour he was her equal, meeting her soul to soul, telling out as a man might all his great love for her, and wearing the jewel of it on his brow. What wonder indeed that the precious hour which made him a king, crowned with a mighty and unselfish passion, was above all things sacred to him? And doubly sacred when, as tonight, it followed upon an hour spent with her? Its mingled delight and pain were almost more than he could bear.

He went through the kitchen and the hall and up the narrow staircase with a glory in his eyes that thus were held from seeing his sordid surroundings. Link Houseman, sprawled out on the platform before the kitchen door, saw him pass with that rapt face, and chuckled. Link was ill enough to look at any time, with his sharp, freckled features and foxy eyes. When he chuckled his face was that of an unholy imp.

But the schoolmaster took no heed of him. Neither did he heed the girl whom he met in the hall. Her handsome, sullen face flushed crimson under the sting of his utter disregard, and her black eyes followed him up the stairs with a look that was not good to see.

"Sis," whispered Link piercingly, "come out here! I've got a joke to tell you, something about the master and his girl. You ain't to let on to him you know, though. I found it out last night when he was off to the shore. That old key of Uncle Jim's was just the thing. He's a softy, and no mistake."

Upstairs in his little room, the schoolmaster was writing his letter. The room was as bare and graceless as all the other rooms of the farmhouse where he had boarded during his term of teaching; but it looked out on the sea, and was hung with such priceless tapestry of his iris dreams and visions that it was to him an apartment in a royal palace. From it he gazed afar on bays that were like great cups of sapphire brimming over with ruby wine for gods to drain, on headlands that were like amethyst, on wide sweeps of sea that were blue and far and mysterious; and ever the moan and call of the ocean's heart came up to his heart as of one great, hopeless love and longing crying out to another love and longing, as great and hopeless. And here, in the rose-radiance of the sunset, with the sea-music in the dim air, he wrote his letter to her.

My Lady: How beautiful it is to think that there is nothing to prevent my loving you! There is much—everything—to prevent me from telling you that I love you. But nothing has any right to come between my heart and its own; it is permitted to love you forever and ever and serve and reverence you in secret and silence. For so much, dear, I thank life, even though the price of the permission must always be the secret and the silence.

I have just come from you, my lady. Your voice is still in my ears; your eyes are still looking into mine, gravely yet half smilingly, sweetly yet half provokingly. Oh, how dear and human and girlish and queenly you are—half saint and half very womanly woman! And how I love you with all there is of me to love—heart and soul and brain, every fibre of body and spirit thrilling to the wonder and marvel and miracle of it! You do not know it, my sweet, and you must never know it. You would not even wish to know it, for I am nothing to you but one of many friends, coming into your life briefly and passing out of it, of no more account to you than a sunshiny hour, a bird's song, a bursting bud in your garden. But the hour and the bird and the flower gave you a little delight in their turn, and when you remembered them once before forgetting, that was their reward and blessing. That is all I ask, dear lady, and I ask that only in my own heart. I am content to love you and be forgotten. It is sweeter to love you and be forgotten than it would be to love any other woman and live in her lifelong remembrance: so humble has love made me, sweet, so great is my sense of my own unworthiness.

Yet love must find expression in some fashion, dear, else it is only pain, and hence these letters to you which you will never read. I put all my heart into them; they are the best and highest of me, the buds of a love that can never bloom openly in the sunshine of your life. I weave a chaplet of them, dear, and crown you with it. They will never fade, for such love is eternal.

It is a whole summer since I first met you. I had been waiting for you all my life before and did not know it. But I knew it when you came and brought with you a sense of completion and fulfilment. This has been the precious year of my life, the turning-point to which all things past tended and all things future must look back. Oh, my dear, I thank you for this year! It has been your royal gift to me, and I shall be rich and great forever because of it. Nothing can ever take it from me, nothing can mar it. It were well to have lived a lifetime of loneliness for such a boon—the price would not be too high. I would not give my one perfect summer for a generation of other men's happiness.

There are those in the world who would laugh at me, who would pity me, Una. They would say that the love I have poured out in secret at your feet has been wasted, that I am a poor weak fool to squander all my treasure of affection on a woman who does not care for me and who is as far above me as that great white star that is shining over the sea. Oh, my dear, they do not know, they cannot understand. The love I have given you has not left me poorer. It has enriched my life unspeakably; it has opened my eyes and given me the gift of clear vision for those things that matter; it has been a lamp held before my stumbling feet whereby I have avoided snares and pitfalls of baser passions and unworthy dreams. For all this I thank you, dear, and for all this surely the utmost that I can give of love and reverence and service is not too much.

I could not have helped loving you. But if I could have helped it, knowing with just what measure of pain and joy it would brim my cup, I would have chosen to love you, Una. There are those who strive to forget a hopeless love. To me, the greatest misfortune that life could bring would be that I should forget you. I want to remember you always and love you and long for you. That would be unspeakably better than any happiness that could come to me through forgetting.

Dear lady, good night. The sun has set; there is now but one fiery dimple on the horizon, as if a golden finger had dented it—now it is gone; the mists are coming up over the sea.

A kiss on each of your white hands, dear. Tonight I am too humble to lift my thoughts to your lips.

The schoolmaster folded up his letter and held it against his cheek for a little space while he gazed out on the silver-shining sea with his dark eyes full of dreams. Then he took from his shabby trunk a little inlaid box and unlocked it with a twisted silver key. It was full of letters—his letters to Una. The first had been written months ago, in the early promise of a northern spring. They linked together the golden weeks of the summer. Now, in the purple autumn, the box was full, and the schoolmaster's term was nearly ended.

He took out the letters reverently and looked over them, now and then murmuring below his breath some passages scattered through the written pages. He had laid bare his heart in those letters, writing out what he never could have told her, even if his love had been known and returned, for dead and gone generations of stern and repressed forefathers laid their unyielding fingers of reserve on his lips, and the shyness of dreamy, book-bred youth stemmed the language of eye and tone.

> I will love you forever and ever. And even though you know it not, surely such love will hover around you all your life. Like an invisible benediction, not understood but dimly felt, guarding you from ill and keeping far from you all things and thoughts of harm and evil!
>
> Sometimes I let myself dream. And in those dreams you love me, and we go out to meet life together. I have dreamed that you kissed me—dreamed it so reverently that the dream did your womanhood no wrong. I have dreamed that you put your hands in mine and said, "I love you." Oh, the rapture of it!
>
> We may give all we will if we do not ask for a return. There should be no barter in love. If, by reason of the greatness of my love for you, I were to ask your love in return, I should be a base creature. It is only because I am content to love and serve for the sake of loving and serving that I have the right to love you.
>
> I have a memory of a blush of yours—a rose of the years that will bloom forever in my garden of remembrance. Tonight you blushed when I came upon you suddenly among the flowers. You were startled—perhaps I had broken too rudely on some girlish musing; and straightway your round, pale curve of cheek and your white arch of brow were made rosy as with the dawn of beautiful sunrise. I shall see you forever as you looked at that time. In my mad moments I shall dream, knowing all the while that it is only a dream, that you blushed with delight at my coming. I shall be able to picture forevermore how you would look at one you loved.
>
> Tonight the moon was low in the west. It hung over the sea like a shallop of ruddy gold moored to a star in the harbour of the night. I lingered long and watched it, for I knew that you, too, were watching it from your window that looks on the sea. You told me once that you always watched the moon set. It has been a bond between us ever since.
>
> This morning I rose at dawn and walked on the shore to think of you, because it seemed the most fitting time. It was before sunrise, and the world was virgin. All the east was a shimmer of silver and the morning star floated in it like a dissolving pearl. The sea was a great miracle. I walked up and down by it and said your name over and over again. The hour was sacred to you. It was as pure and unspoiled as your own soul. Una, who will bring into your life the sunrise splendour and colour of love?

Do you know how beautiful you are, Una? Let me tell you, dear. You are tall, yet you have to lift your eyes a little to meet mine. Such dear eyes, Una! They are dark blue, and when you smile they are like wet violets in sunshine. But when you are pensive they are more lovely still—the spirit and enchantment of the sea at twilight passes into them then. Your hair has the gloss and brownness of ripe nuts, and your face is always pale. Your lips have a trick of falling apart in a half-smile when you listen. They told me before I knew you that you were pretty. Pretty! The word is cheap and tawdry. You are beautiful, with the beauty of a pearl or a star or a white flower.

Do you remember our first meeting? It was one evening last spring. You were in your garden. The snow had not all gone, but your hands were full of pale, early flowers. You wore a white shawl over your shoulders and head. Your face was turned upward a little, listening to a robin's call in the leafless trees above you. I thought God had never made anything so lovely and love-deserving. I loved you from that moment, Una.

This is your birthday. The world has been glad of you for twenty years. It is fitting that there have been bird songs and sunshine and blossom today, a great light and fragrance over land and sea. This morning I went far afield to a long, lonely valley lying to the west, girt round about with dim old pines, where feet of men seldom tread, and there I searched until I found some rare flowers meet to offer you. I sent them to you with a little book, an old book. A new book, savouring of the shop and marketplace, however beautiful it might be, would not do for you. So I sent the book that was my mother's. She read it and loved it—the faded rose-leaves she placed in it are there still. At first, dear, I almost feared to send it. Would you miss its meaning? Would you laugh a little at the shabby volume with its pencil marks and its rose-leaves? But I knew you would not; I knew you would understand.

Today I saw you with the child of your sister in your arms. I felt as the old painters must have felt when they painted their Madonnas. You bent over his shining golden head, and on your face was the mother passion and tenderness that is God's finishing touch to the beauty of womanhood. The next moment you were laughing with him—two children playing together. But I had looked upon you in that brief space. Oh, the pain and joy of it!

It is so sweet, dear, to serve you a little, though it be only in opening a door for you to pass through, or handing you a book or a sheet of music! Love wishes to do so much for the beloved! I can do so little for you, but that little is sweet.

This evening I read to you the poem which you had asked me to read. You sat before me with your brown head leaning on your hands and your eyes cast down. I stole dear glances at you between the lines. When I finished I put a red, red rose from your garden between the pages and crushed the book close on it. That poem will always be dear to me, stained with the life-blood of a rose-like hour.

I do not know which is the sweeter, your laughter or your sadness. When you laugh you make me glad, but when you are sad I want to share in your sadness and soothe it. I think I am nearer to you in your sorrowful moods.

Today I met you by accident at the turn of the lane. Nothing told me that you were coming—not even the wind, that should have known. I was sad, and then all at once I saw you, and wondered how I could have been sad. You walked past me with a smile, as if you had tossed me a rose. I stood and watched you out of sight. That meeting was the purple gift the day gave me.

Today I tried to write a poem to you, Una, but I could not find words fine enough, as a lover could find no raiment dainty enough for his bride. The old words other men have used in singing to their loves seemed too worn and common for you. I wanted only new words, crystal clear or coloured only by the iris of the light, not words that have been steeped and stained with all the hues of other men's thoughts. So I burned the verses that were so unworthy of you.

Una, some day you will love. You will watch for him; you will blush at his coming, be sad at his going. Oh, I cannot think of it!

Today I saw you when you did not see me. I was walking on the shore, and as I came around a rock you were sitting on the other side. I drew back a little and looked at you. Your hands were clasped over your knees; your hat had fallen back, and the sea wind was ruffling your hair. Your face was lifted to the sky, your lips were parted, your eyes were full of light. You seemed to be listening to something that made you happy. I crept gently away, that I might not mar your dream. Of what were you thinking, Una?

I must leave you soon. Sometimes I think I cannot bear it. Oh, Una, how selfish it is of me to wish that you might love me! Yet I do wish it, although I have nothing to offer you but a great love and all my willing work of hand and brain. If you loved me, I fear I should be weak enough to do you the wrong of wooing you. I want you so much, dear!

The schoolmaster added the last letter to the others and locked the box. When he unlocked it again, two days later, the letters were gone.

He gazed at the empty box with dilated eyes. At first he could not realize what had happened. The letters could not be gone! He must have made a mistake, have put them in some other place! With trembling fingers he ransacked his trunk. There was no trace of the letters. With a groan he dropped his face in his hands and tried to think.

His letters were gone—those precious letters, held almost too sacred for his own eyes to read after they were written—had been stolen from him! The inmost secrets of his soul had been betrayed. Who had done this hideous thing?

He rose and went downstairs. In the farmyard he found Link tormenting his dog. Link was happy only when he was tormenting something. He never had been afraid of anything in his life before, but now absolute terror took possession of him at sight of the schoolmaster's face. Physical strength and force had no power to frighten the sullen lad, but all the irresistible might of a fine soul roused to frenzy looked out in the young man's blazing eyes, dilated nostrils, and tense white mouth. It cowed the boy, because it was something he could not understand. He only realized that he was in the presence of a force that was not to be trifled with.

"Link, where are my letters?" said the schoolmaster.

"I didn't take 'em, Master!" cried Link, crumpling up visibly in his sheer terror. "I didn't. I never teched 'em! It was Sis. I told her not to—I told her you'd be awful mad, but she wouldn't tend to me. It was Sis took 'em. Ask her, if you don't believe me."

The schoolmaster believed him. Nothing was too horrible to believe just then. "What has she done with them?" he said hoarsely.

"She—she sent 'em to Una Clifford," whimpered Link. "I told her not to. She's mad at you, cause you went to see Una and wouldn't go with her. She thought Una would be mad at you for writing 'em, cause the Cliffords are so proud and think themselves above everybody else. So she sent 'em. I—I told her not to."

The schoolmaster said not another word. He turned his back on the whining boy and went to his room. He felt sick with shame. The indecency of the whole thing revolted him. It was as if his naked heart had been torn from his breast and held up to the jeers of a vulgar world by the merciless hand of a scorned and jealous woman. He felt stunned as if by a physical blow.

After a time his fierce anger and shame died into a calm desperation. The deed was done beyond recall. It only remained for him to go to Una, tell her the truth, and implore her pardon. Then he must go from her sight and presence forever.

It was dusk when he went to her home. They told him that she was in the garden, and he found her there, standing at the curve of the box walk, among the last late-blooming flowers of the summer.

Have you thought from his letters that she was a wonderful woman of marvellous beauty? Not so. She was a sweet and slender slip of girlhood, with girlhood's own charm and freshness. There were thousands like her in the world—thank God for it!—but only one like her in one man's eyes.

He stood before her mute with shame, his boyish face white and haggard. She had blushed crimson all over her dainty paleness at sight of him, and laid her hand quickly on the breast of her white gown. Her eyes were downcast and her breath came shortly.

He thought her silence the silence of anger and scorn. He wished that he might fling himself in the dust at her feet.

"Una—Miss Clifford—forgive me!" he stammered miserably. "I—I did not send them. I never meant that you should see them. A shameful trick has been played upon me. Forgive me!"

"For what am I to forgive you?" she asked gravely. She did not look up, but her lips parted in the little half-smile he loved. The blush was still on her face.

"For my presumption," he whispered. "I—I could not help loving you, Una. If you have read the letters you know all the rest."

"I have read the letters, every word," she answered, pressing her hand a little more closely to her breast. "Perhaps I should not have done so, for I soon discovered that they were not meant for me to read. I thought at first you had sent them, although the writing of the address on the packet did not look like yours; but even when I knew you did not I could not help reading them all. I do not know who sent them, but I am very grateful to the sender."

"Grateful?" he said wonderingly.

"Yes. I have something to forgive you, but not—not your presumption. It is your blindness, I think—and—and your cruel resolution to go away and never tell me of your—your love for me. If it had not been for the sending of these letters I might never have known. How can I forgive you for that?"

"Una!" he said. He had been very blind, but he was beginning to see. He took a step nearer and took her hands. She threw up her head and gazed, blushingly, steadfastly, into his eyes. From the folds of her gown she drew forth the little packet of letters and kissed it.

"Your dear letters!" she said bravely. "They have given me the right to speak out. I will speak out! I love you, dear! I will be content to wait through long years until you can claim me. I—I have been so happy since your letters came!"

He put his arms around her and drew her head close to his. Their lips met.

The Story of Uncle Dick

I had two schools offered me that summer, one at Rocky Valley and one at Bayside. At first I inclined to Rocky Valley; it possessed a railway station and was nearer the centres of business and educational activity. But eventually I chose Bayside, thinking that its country quietude would be a good thing for a student who was making school-teaching the stepping-stone to a college course.

I had reason to be glad of my choice, for in Bayside I met Uncle Dick. Ever since it has seemed to me that not to have known Uncle Dick would have been to miss a great sweetness and inspiration from my life. He was one of those rare souls whose friendship is at once a pleasure and a benediction, showering light from their own crystal clearness into all the dark corners in the souls of others until, for the time being at least, they reflected his own simplicity and purity. Uncle Dick could no more help bringing delight into the lives of his associates than could the sunshine or the west wind or any other of the best boons of nature.

I had been in Bayside three weeks before I met him, although his farm adjoined the one where I boarded and I passed at a little distance from his house every day in my short cut across the fields to school. I even passed his garden unsuspectingly for a week, never dreaming that behind that rank of leafy, rustling poplars lay a veritable "God's acre" of loveliness and fragrance. But one day as I went by, a whiff of something sweeter than the odours of Araby brushed my face and, following the wind that had blown it through the poplars, I went up to the white paling and found there a trellis of honeysuckle, and beyond it Uncle Dick's garden. Thereafter I daily passed close by the fence that I might have the privilege of looking over it.

It would be hard to define the charm of that garden. It did not consist in order or system, for there was no trace of either, except, perhaps, in that prim row of poplars growing about the whole domain and shutting it away from all idle and curious eyes. For the rest, I think the real charm must have been in its unexpectedness. At every turn and in every nook you stumbled on some miracle of which you had never dreamed. Or perhaps the charm was simply that the whole garden was an expression of Uncle Dick's personality.

In one corner a little green dory, filled with earth, overflowed in a wave of gay annuals. In the centre of the garden an old birch-bark canoe seemed sailing through a sea of blossoms, with a many-coloured freight of geraniums. Paths twisted and turned among flowering shrubs, and clumps of old-fashioned perennials were mingled with the latest fads of the floral catalogues. The mid-garden was a pool of sunshine, with finely sifted winds purring over it, but under the poplars there were shadows and growing things that loved the shadows, crowding about the old stone benches at each side. Somehow, my daily glimpse of Uncle Dick's garden soon came to symbolize for me a meaning easier to translate into life and soul than into words. It was a power for good within me, making its influence felt in many ways.

Finally I caught Uncle Dick in his garden. On my way home one evening I found him on his knees among the rosebushes, and as soon as he saw me he sprang up and came forward with outstretched hand. He was a tall man of about fifty, with grizzled hair, but not a thread of silver yet showed itself in the ripples of his long brown beard. Later I discovered that his splendid beard was Uncle Dick's only vanity. So fine and silky was it that it did not hide the candid, sensitive curves of his mouth, around which a mellow smile, tinged with kindly, quizzical humour, always lingered. His face was tanned even more deeply than is usual among farmers, for he had an inveterate habit of going about hatless in the most merciless sunshine; but the line of forehead under his hair was white as milk, and his eyes were darkly blue and as tender as a woman's.

"How do you do, Master?" he said heartily. (The Bayside pedagogue was invariably addressed as "Master" by young and old.) "I'm glad to see you. Here I am, trying to save my rosebushes. There are green bugs on 'em, Master—green bugs, and they're worrying the life out of me."

I smiled, for Uncle Dick looked very unlike a worrying man, even over such a serious accident as green bugs.

"Your roses don't seem to mind, Mr. Oliver," I said. "They are the finest I have ever seen."

The compliment to his roses, well-deserved as it was, did not at first engage his attention. He pretended to frown at me.

"Don't get into any bad habit of mistering me, Master," he said. "You'd better begin by calling me Uncle Dick from the start and then you won't have the trouble of changing. Because it would come to that—it always does. But come in, come in! There's a gate round here. I want to get acquainted with you. I have a taste for schoolmasters. I didn't possess it when I was a boy" (a glint of fun appeared in his blue eyes). "It's an acquired taste."

I accepted his invitation and went, not only into his garden but, as was proved later, into his confidence and affection. He linked his arm with mine and piloted me about to show me his pets.

"I potter about this garden considerable," he said. "It pleases the women folks to have lots of posies."

I laughed, for Uncle Dick was a bachelor and considered to be a hopeless one.

"Don't laugh, Master," he said, pressing my arm. "I've no woman folk of my own about me now, 'tis true. But all the girls in the district come to Uncle Dick when they want flowers for their little diversions. Besides—perhaps—sometimes—"

Uncle Dick broke off and stood in a brown study, looking at an old stump aflame with nasturtiums for fully three minutes. Later on I was to learn the significance of that pause and reverie.

I spent the whole evening with Uncle Dick. After we had explored the garden he took me into his house and into his "den." The house was a small white one and wonderfully neat inside, considering the fact that Uncle Dick was his own housekeeper. His "den" was a comfortable place, its one window so shadowed by a huge poplar that the room had a grotto-like effect of emerald gloom. I came to know it well, for, at Uncle Dick's invitation, I did my studying there and browsed at will among his classics. We soon became close friends. Uncle Dick had always "chummed with the masters," as he said, but our friendship went deeper. For my own part, I preferred his company to that of any young man I knew. There was a perennial spring of youth in Uncle Dick's soul that yet had all the fascinating flavour of ripe experience. He was clever, kindly, humorous and, withal, so crystal clear of mind and heart that an atmosphere partaking of childhood hung around him.

I knew Uncle Dick's outward history as the Bayside people knew it. It was not a very eventful one. He had lost his father in boyhood; before that there had been some idea of Dick's going to college. After his father's death he seemed quietly to have put all such hopes away and settled down to look after the farm and take care of his invalid stepmother. This woman, as I learned from others, but never from Uncle Dick, had been a peevish, fretful, exacting creature, and for nearly thirty years Uncle Dick had been a very slave to her whims and caprices.

"Nobody knows what he had to put up with, for he never complained," Mrs. Lindsay, my landlady, told me. "She was out of her mind once and she was liable to go out of it again if she was crossed in anything. He was that good and patient with her. She was dreadful fond of him too, for all she did almost worry his life out. No doubt she was the reason he never married. He couldn't leave her and he knew no woman would go in there. Uncle Dick never courted anyone, unless it was Rose Lawrence. She was a cousin of my man's. I've heard he had a kindness for her; it was years ago, before I came to Bayside. But anyway, nothing came of it. Her father's health failed and he had to go out to California. Rose had to go with him, her mother being dead, and that was the end of Uncle Dick's love affair."

But that was not the end of it, as I discovered when Uncle Dick gave me his confidence. One evening I went over and, piloted by the sound of shrieks and laughter, found Uncle Dick careering about the garden, pursued by half a dozen schoolgirls who were pelting him with overblown roses. At sight of the master my pupils instantly became prim and demure and, gathering up their flowery spoil, they beat a hasty retreat down the lane.

"Those little girls are very sweet," said Uncle Dick abruptly. "Little blossoms of life! Have you ever wondered, Master, why I haven't some of my own blooming about the old place instead of just looking over the fence of other men's gardens, coveting their human roses?"

"Yes, I have," I answered frankly. "It has been a puzzle to me why you, Uncle Dick, who seem to me fitted above all men I have ever known for love and husbandhood and fatherhood, should have elected to live your life alone."

"It has not been a matter of choice," said Uncle Dick gently. "We can't always order our lives as we would, Master. I loved a woman once and she loved me. And we love each other still. Do you think I could bear life else? I've an interest in it that the Bayside folk know nothing of. It has kept youth in my heart and joy in my soul through long, lonely years. And it's not ended yet, Master—it's not ended yet! Some day I hope to bring a wife here to my old house—my wife, my rose of joy!"

He was silent for a space, gazing at the stars. I too kept silence, fearing to intrude into the holy places of his thought, although I was tingling with interest in this unsuspected outflowering of romance in Uncle Dick's life.

After a time he said gently,

"Shall I tell you about it, Master? I mean, do you care to know?"

"Yes," I answered, "I do care to know. And I shall respect your confidence, Uncle Dick."

"I know that. I couldn't tell you, otherwise," he said. "I don't want the Bayside folk to know—it would be a kind of desecration. They would laugh and joke me about it, as they tease other people, and I couldn't bear that. Nobody in Bayside knows or suspects, unless it's old Joe Hammond at the post office. And he has kept my secret, or what he knows of it, well. But somehow I feel that I'd like to tell you, Master.

"Twenty-five years ago I loved Rose Lawrence. The Lawrences lived where you are boarding now. There was just the father, a sickly man, and Rose, my "Rose of joy," as I called her, for I knew my Emerson pretty well even then. She was sweet and fair, like a white rose with just a hint of pink in its cup. We loved each other, but we couldn't marry then. My mother was an invalid, and one time, before I had learned to care for Rose, she, the mother, had asked me to promise her that I'd never marry as long as she lived. She didn't think then that she would live long, but she lived for twenty years, Master, and she held me to my promise all the time. Yes, it was hard"—for I had given an indignant exclamation—"but you see, Master, I had promised and I had to keep my word. Rose said I was right in doing it. She said she was willing to wait for me, but she didn't know, poor girl, how long the waiting was to be. Then her father's health failed completely, and the doctor ordered him to another climate. They went to California. That was a hard parting, Master. But we promised each other that we would be true, and we have been. I've never seen my Rose of joy since then, but I've had a letter from her every week. When the mother died, five years ago, I wanted to move to California and marry Rose. But she wrote that her father was so poorly she couldn't marry me yet. She has to wait on him every minute, and he's restless, and they move here and there—a hard life for my poor girl. So I had to take a new lease of patience, Master. One learns how to wait in twenty years. But I shall have her some day, God willing. Our love will be crowned yet. So I wait, Master, and try to keep my life and soul clean and wholesome and young for her.

"That's my story, Master, and we'll not say anything more about it just now, for I dare say you don't exactly know what to say. But at times I'll talk of her to you and that will be a rare pleasure to me; I think that was why I wanted you to know about her."

He did talk often to me of her, and I soon came to realize what this far-away woman meant in his life. She was for him the centre of everything. His love was strong, pure, and idyllic—the ideal love of which the loftiest poets sing. It glorified his whole inner life with a strange, unfailing radiance. I found that everything he did was done with an eye single to what she would think of it when she came. Especially did he put his love into his garden.

"Every flower in it stands for a thought of her, Master," he said. "It is a great joy to think that she will walk in this garden with me some day. It will be complete then—my Rose of joy will be here to crown it."

That summer and winter passed away, and when spring came again, lettering her footsteps with violets in the meadows and waking all the sleeping loveliness of old homestead gardens, Uncle Dick's long deferred happiness came with her. One evening when I was in our "den," mid-deep in study of old things that seemed musty and unattractive enough in contrast with the vivid, newborn, out-of-doors, Uncle Dick came home from the post office with an open letter in his hand. His big voice trembled as he said,

"Master, she's coming home. Her father is dead and she has nobody in the world now but me. In a month she will be here. Don't talk to me of it yet—I want to taste the joy of it in silence for a while."

He hastened away to his garden and walked there until darkness fell, with his face uplifted to the sky, and the love rapture of countless generations shining in his eyes. Later on, we sat on one of the old stone benches and Uncle Dick tried to talk practically.

Bayside people soon found out that Rose Lawrence was coming home to marry Uncle Dick. Uncle Dick was much teased, and suffered under it; it seemed, as he had said, desecration. But the real goodwill and kindly feeling in the banter redeemed it.

He went to the station to meet Rose Lawrence the day she came. When I went home from school Mrs. Lindsay told me she was in the parlour and took me in to be introduced. I was bitterly disappointed. Somehow, I had expected to meet, not indeed a young girl palpitating with youthful bloom, but a woman of ripe maturity, dowered with the beauty of harmonious middle-age—the feminine counterpart of Uncle Dick. Instead, I found in Rose Lawrence a small, faded woman of forty-five, gowned in shabby black. She had evidently been very pretty once, but bloom and grace were gone. Her face had a sweet and gentle expression, but was tired and worn, and her fair hair was plentifully streaked with grey. Alas, I thought compassionately, for Uncle Dick's dreams! What a shock the change to her must have given him! Could this be the woman on whom he had lavished such a life-wealth of love and reverence? I tried to talk to her, but I found her shy and timid. She seemed to me uninteresting and commonplace. And this was Uncle Dick's Rose of joy!

I was so sorry for Uncle Dick that I shrank from meeting him. Nevertheless, I went over after tea, fearing that he might misunderstand, nay, rather, understand, my absence. He was in the garden, and he came down the path where the buds were just showing. There was a smile on his face and the glory in his eyes was quite undimmed.

"Master, she's come. And she's not a bit changed. I feared she would be, but she is just the same—my sweet little Rose of joy!"

I looked at Uncle Dick in some amazement. He was thoroughly sincere, there was no doubt of that, and I felt a great throb of relief. He had found no disillusioning change. I saw Rose Lawrence merely with the cold eyes of the stranger. He saw her through the transfiguring medium of a love that made her truly his Rose of joy. And all was well.

They were married the next morning and walked together over the clover meadow to their home. In the evening I went over, as I had promised Uncle Dick to do. They were in the garden, with a great saffron sky over them and a glory of sunset behind the poplars. I paused unseen at the gate. Uncle Dick was big and splendid in his fine new wedding suit, and his faded little bride was hanging on his arm. Her face was upturned to him; it was a glorified face, so transformed by the tender radiance of love shining through it that I saw her then as Uncle Dick must always see her, and no longer found it hard to understand how she could be his Rose of joy. Happiness clothed them as a garment; they were crowned king and queen in the bridal realm of the springtime.

The Understanding of Sister Sara

June First.

I began this journal last New Year's—wrote two entries in it and then forgot all about it. I came across it today in a rummage—Sara insists on my cleaning things out thoroughly every once in so long—and I'm going to keep it up. I feel the need of a confidant of some kind, even if it is only an inanimate journal. I have no other. And I cannot talk my thoughts over with Sara—she is so unsympathetic.

Sara is a dear good soul and I love her as much as she will let me. I am also very grateful to her. She brought me up when our mother died. No doubt she had a hard time of it, poor dear, for I never was easily brought up, perversely preferring to come up in my own way. But Sara did her duty unflinchingly and—well, it's not for me to say that the result does her credit. But it really does, considering the material she had to work with. I'm a bundle of faults as it is, but I tremble to think what I would have been if there had been no Sara.

Yes, I love Sara, and I'm grateful to her. But she doesn't understand me in the least. Perhaps it is because she is so much older than I am, but it doesn't seem to me that Sara could really ever have been young. She laughs at things I consider the most sacred and calls me a romantic girl, in a tone of humorous toleration. I am chilled and thrown back on myself, and the dreams and confidences I am bubbling over with have no outlet. Sara couldn't understand—she is so practical. When I go to her with some beautiful thought I have found in a book or poem she is quite likely to say, "Yes, yes, but I noticed this morning that the braid was loose on your skirt, Beatrice. Better go and sew it on before you forget again. 'A stitch in time saves nine.'"

When I come home from a concert or lecture, yearning to talk over the divine music or the wonderful new ideas with her, she will say, "Yes, yes, but are you sure you didn't get your feet damp? Better go and change your stockings, my dear. 'An ounce of prevention is worth a pound of cure.'"

So I have given up trying to talk things over with Sara. This old journal will be better.

Last night Sara and I went to Mrs. Trent's musicale. I had to sing and I had the loveliest new gown for the occasion. At first Sara thought my old blue dress would do. She said we must economize this summer and told me I was entirely too extravagant in the matter of clothes. I cried about it after I went to bed. Sara looked at me very sharply the next morning without saying anything. In the afternoon she went uptown and bought some lovely pale yellow silk organdie. She made it up herself—Sara is a genius at dressmaking—and it was the prettiest gown at the musicale. Sara wore her old grey silk made over. Sara doesn't care anything about dress, but then she is forty.

Walter Shirley was at the Trents'. The Shirleys are a new family here; they moved to Atwater two months ago. Walter is the oldest son and has been at college in Marlboro all winter so that nobody here knew him until he came home a fortnight ago. He is very handsome and distinguished-looking and everybody says he is so clever. He plays the violin just beautifully and has such a melting, sympathetic voice and the loveliest deep, dark, inscrutable eyes. I asked Sara when we came home if she didn't think he was splendid.

"He'd be a nice boy if he wasn't rather conceited," said Sara.

After that it was impossible to say anything more about Mr. Shirley.

I am glad he is going to be in Atwater all summer. We have so few really nice young men here; they go away just as soon as they grow up and those who stay are just the muffs. I wonder if I shall see Mr. Shirley soon again.

June Thirtieth.

It does not seem possible that it is only a month since my last entry. It seems more like a year—a delightful year. I can't believe that I am the same Beatrice Mason who wrote then. And I am not, either. She was just a simple little girl, knowing nothing but romantic dreams. I feel that I am very much changed. Life seems so grand and high and beautiful. I want to be a true noble woman. Only such a woman could be worthy of—of—a fine, noble man. But when I tried to say something like this to Sara she replied calmly:

"My dear child, the average woman is quite good enough for the average man. If she can cook his meals decently and keep his buttons sewed on and doesn't nag him he will think that life is a pretty comfortable affair. And that reminds me, I saw holes in your black lace stockings yesterday. Better go and darn them at once. 'Procrastination is the thief of time.'"

Sara cannot understand.

Blanche Lawrence was married yesterday to Ted Martin. I thought it the most solemn and sacred thing I had ever listened to—the marriage ceremony, I mean. I had never thought much about it before. I don't see how Blanche could care anything for Ted—he is so stout and dumpy; with shallow blue eyes and a little pale moustache. I must say I do not like fair men. But there is no doubt that he and Blanche love each other devotedly and that fact sufficed to make the service very beautiful to me—those two people pledging each other to go through life together, meeting its storm and sunshine hand in hand, thinking joy the sweeter because they shared it, finding sorrow sacred because it came to them both.

When Sara and I walked home from the church Sara said, "Well, considering the chances she has had, Blanche Lawrence hasn't done so well after all."

"Oh, Sara," I cried, "she has married the man she loves and who loves her. What better is there to do? I thought it beautiful."

"They should have waited another year at least," said Sara severely. "Ted Martin has only been practising law for a year, and he had nothing to begin with. He can't have made enough in one year in Atwater to justify him in setting up housekeeping. I think a man ought to be ashamed of himself to take a girl from a good home to an uncertainty like that."

"Not if she loved him and was willing to share the uncertainty," I said softly.

"Love won't pay the butcher's bill," said Sara with a sniff, "and landlords have an unfeeling preference for money over affection. Besides, Blanche is a mere child, far too young to be burdened with the responsibilities of life."

Blanche is twenty—two years older than I am. But Sara talks as if I were a mere infant.

July Thirtieth.

Oh, I am so happy! I wonder if there is another girl in the world as happy as I am tonight. No, of course there cannot be, because there is only one Walter!

Walter and I are engaged. It happened last night when we were sitting out in the moonlight under the silver maple on the lawn. I cannot write down what he said—the words are too sacred and beautiful to be kept anywhere but in my own heart forever and ever as long as I live. And I don't remember just what I said. But we understood each other perfectly at last.

Of course Sara had to do her best to spoil things. Just as Walter had taken my hand in his and bent forward with his splendid earnest eyes just burning into mine, and my heart was beating so furiously, Sara came to the front door and called out, "Beatrice! Beatrice! Have you your rubbers on? And don't you think it is too damp out there for you in that heavy dew? Better come into the house, both of you. Walter has a cold now."

"Oh, we'll be in soon, Sara," I said impatiently. But we didn't go in for an hour, and when we did Sara was cross, and after Walter had gone she told me I was a very silly girl to be so reckless of my health and risk getting pneumonia loitering out in the dew with a sentimental boy.

I had had some vague thoughts of telling Sara all about my new happiness, for it was so great I wanted to talk it over with somebody, but I couldn't after that. Oh, I wish I had a mother! She could understand. But Sara cannot.

Walter and I have decided to keep our engagement a secret for a month—just our own beautiful secret unshared by anyone. Then before he goes back to college he is going to tell Sara and ask her consent. I don't think Sara will refuse it exactly. She really likes Walter very well. But I know she will be horrid and I just dread it. She will say I am too young and that a boy like Walter has no business to get engaged until he is through college and that we haven't known each other long enough to know anything about each other and that we are only a pair of romantic children. And after she has said all this and given a disapproving consent she will begin to train me up in the way a good housekeeper should go, and talk to me about table linen and the best way to manage a range and how to tell if a chicken is really a chicken or only an old hen. Oh, I know Sara! She will set the teeth of my spirit on edge a dozen times a day and rub all the bloom off my dear, only, little romance with her horrible practicalities. I know one must learn about those things of course and I do want to make Walter's home the best and dearest and most comfortable spot on earth for him and be the very best little wife and housekeeper I can be when the time comes. But I want to dream my dreams first and Sara will wake me up so early to realities.

This is why we determined to keep one month sacred to ourselves. Walter will graduate next spring—he is to be a doctor—and then he intends to settle down in Atwater and work up a practice. I am sure he will succeed for everyone likes him so much. But we are to be married as soon as he is through college because he has a little money of his own—enough to set up housekeeping in a modest way with care and economy. I know Sara will talk about risk and waiting and all that just as she did in Ted Martin's case. But then Sara does not understand.

Oh, I am so happy! It almost frightens me—I don't see how anything so wonderful can last. But it will last, for nothing can ever separate Walter and me, and as long as we are together and love each other this great happiness will be mine. Oh, I want to be so good and noble for his sake. I want to make life "one grand sweet song." I have gone about the house today feeling like a woman consecrated and set apart from other women by Walter's love. Nothing could spoil it, not even when Sara scolded me for letting the preserves burn in the kettle because I forgot to stir them while I was planning out our life together. Sara said she really did not know what would happen to me some day if I was so careless and forgetful. But then, Sara does not understand.

August Twentieth.

It is all over. Life is ended for me and I do not know how I can face the desolate future. Walter and I have quarrelled and our engagement is broken. He is gone and my heart is breaking.

I hardly know how it began. I'm sure I never meant to flirt with Jack Ray. I never did flirt with him either, in spite of Walter's unmanly accusations. But Walter has been jealous of Jack all summer, although he knew perfectly well he needn't be, and two nights ago at the Morley dance poor Jack seemed so dull and unhappy that I tried to cheer him up a little and be kind to him. I danced with him three times and sat out another dance just to talk with him in a real sisterly fashion. But Walter was furious and last night when he came up he said horrid things—things no girl of any spirit could endure, and things he could never have said to me if he had really cared one bit for me. We had a frightful quarrel and when I saw plainly that Walter no longer loved me I told him that he was free and that I never wanted to see him again and that I hated him. He glared at me and said that I should have my wish—I never should see him again and he hoped he would never again meet such a faithless, fickle girl. Then he went away and slammed the front door.

I cried all night, but today I went about the house singing. I would not for the world let other people know how Walter has treated me. I will hide my broken heart under a smiling face bravely. But, oh, I am so miserable! Just as soon as I am old enough I mean to go away and be a trained nurse. There is nothing else left in life for me. Sara does not suspect that anything is wrong and I am so thankful she does not. She would not understand.

September Sixth.

Today I read this journal over and thought I would burn it, it is so silly. But on second thought I concluded to keep it as a reminder of how blind and selfish I was and how good Sara is. For I am happy again and everything is all right, thanks to Sara. The very day after our quarrel Walter left Atwater. He did not have to return to college for three weeks, but he went to visit some friends down in Charlotteville and I heard—Mollie Roach told me—Mollie Roach was always wild about Walter herself—that he was not coming back again, but would go right on to Marlboro from Charlotteville. I smiled squarely at Mollie as if I didn't care a particle, but I can't describe how I felt. I knew then that I had really been hoping that something would happen in three weeks to make our quarrel up. In a small place like Atwater people in the same set can't help meeting. But Walter had gone and I should never see him again, and what was worse I knew he didn't care or he wouldn't have gone.

I bore it in silence for three weeks, but I will shudder to the end of my life when I remember those three weeks. Night before last Sara came up to my room where I was lying on my bed with my face in the pillow. I wasn't crying—I couldn't cry. There was just a dreadful dull ache in everything. Sara sat down on the rocker in front of the window and the sunset light came in behind her and made a sort of nimbus round her head, like a motherly saint's in a cathedral.

"Beatrice," she said gently, "I want to know what the trouble is. You can't hide it from me that something is wrong. I've noticed it for some time. You don't eat anything and you cry all night—oh, yes, I know you do. What is it, dear?"

"Oh, Sara!"

I just gave a little cry, slipped from the bed to the floor, laid my head in her lap, and told her everything. It was such a relief, and such a relief to feel those good motherly arms around me and to realize that here was a love that would never fail me no matter what I did or how foolish I was. Sara heard me out and then she said, without a word of reproach or contempt, "It will all come out right yet, dear. Write to Walter and tell him you are sorry."

"Sara, I never could! He doesn't love me any longer—he said he hoped he'd never see me again."

"Didn't you say the same to him, child? He meant it as little as you did. Don't let your foolish pride keep you miserable."

"If Walter won't come back to me without my asking him he'll never come, Sara," I said stubbornly.

Sara didn't scold or coax any more. She patted my head and kissed me and made me bathe my face and go to bed. Then she tucked me in just as she used to do when I was a little girl.

"Now, don't cry, dear," she said, "it will come right yet."

Somehow, I began to hope it would when Sara thought so, and anyhow it was such a comfort to have talked it all over with her. I slept better than I had for a long time, and it was seven o'clock yesterday morning when I woke to find that it was a dull grey day outside and that Sara was standing by my bed with her hat and jacket on.

"I'm going down to Junction Falls on the 7:30 train to see Mr. Conway about coming to fix the back kitchen floor," she said, "and I have some other business that may keep me for some time, so don't be anxious if I'm not back till late. Give the bread a good kneading in an hour's time and be careful not to bake it too much."

That was a dismal day. It began to rain soon after Sara left and it just poured. I never saw a soul all day except the milkman, and I was really frantic by night. I never was so glad of anything as when I heard Sara's step on the verandah. I flew to the front door to let her in—and there was Walter all dripping wet—and his arms were about me and I was crying on the shoulder of his mackintosh.

I only guessed then what I knew later on. Sara had heard from Mrs. Shirley that Walter was going to Marlboro that day without coming back to Atwater. Sara knew that he must change trains at Junction Falls and she went there to meet him. She didn't know what train he would come on so she went to meet the earliest and had to wait till the last, hanging around the dirty little station at the Falls all day while it poured rain, and she hadn't a thing to eat except some fancy biscuits she had bought on the train. But Walter came at last on the 7:50 train and there was Sara to pounce on him. He told me afterwards that no angel could have been so beautiful a vision to him as Sara was, standing there on the wet platform with her tweed skirt held up and a streaming umbrella over her head, telling him he must come back to Atwater because Beatrice wanted him to.

But just at the moment of his coming I didn't care how he had come or who had brought him. I just realized that he was there and that was enough. Sara came in behind him. Walter's wet arms were about me and I was standing there with my thin-slippered feet in a little pool of water that dripped from his umbrella. But Sara never said a word about colds and dampness. She just smiled, went on into the sitting-room, and shut the door. Sara understood.

The Unforgotten One

It was Christmas Eve, but there was no frost, or snow, or sparkle. It was a green Christmas, and the night was mild and dim, with hazy starlight. A little wind was laughing freakishly among the firs around Ingleside and rustling among the sere grasses along the garden walks. It was more like a night in early spring or late fall than in December; but it was Christmas Eve, and there was a light in every window of Ingleside, the glow breaking out through the whispering darkness like a flame-red blossom swung against the background of the evergreens; for the children were coming home for the Christmas reunion, as they always came—Fritz and Margaret and Laddie and Nora, and Robert's two boys in the place of Robert, who had died fourteen years ago—and the old house must put forth its best of light and good cheer to welcome them.

Doctor Fritz and his brood were the last to arrive, driving up to the hall door amid a chorus of welcoming barks from the old dogs and a hail of merry calls from the group in the open doorway.

"We're all here now," said the little mother, as she put her arms about the neck of her stalwart firstborn and kissed his bearded face. There were handshakings and greetings and laughter. Only Nanny, far back in the shadows of the firelit hall, swallowed a resentful sob, and wiped two bitter tears from her eyes with her little red hand.

"We're not all here," she murmured under her breath. "Miss Avis isn't here. Oh, how can they be so glad? How can they have forgotten?"

But nobody heard or heeded Nanny—she was only the little orphan "help" girl at Ingleside. They were all very good to her, and they were all very fond of her, but at the times of family reunion Nanny was unconsciously counted out. There was no bond of blood to unite her to them, and she was left on the fringe of things. Nanny never resented this—it was all a matter of course to her; but on this Christmas Eve her heart was broken because she thought that nobody remembered Miss Avis.

After supper they all gathered around the open fireplace of the hall, hung with its berries and evergreens in honour of the morrow. It was their unwritten law to form a fireside circle on Christmas Eve and tell each other what the year had brought them of good and ill, sorrow and joy. The circle was smaller by one than it had been the year before, but none spoke of that. There was a smile on every face and happiness in every voice.

The father and mother sat in the centre, grey-haired and placid, their fine old faces written over with the history of gracious lives. Beside the mother, Doctor Fritz sat like a boy, on the floor, with his massive head, grey as his father's, on her lap, and one of his smooth, muscular hands, that were as tender as a woman's at the operating table, clasped in hers. Next to him sat sweet Nora, the twenty-year-old "baby," who taught in a city school; the rosy firelight gleamed lovingly over her girlish beauty of burnished brown hair, dreamy blue eyes, and soft, virginal curves of cheek and throat. Doctor Fritz's spare arm was about her, but Nora's own hands were clasped over her knee, and on one of them sparkled a diamond that had not been there at the last Christmas reunion. Laddie, who figured as Archibald only in the family Bible, sat close to the inglenook—a handsome young fellow with a daring brow and rollicking eyes. On the other side sat Margaret, hand in hand with her father, a woman whose gracious sweetness of nature enveloped her as a garment; and Robert's two laughing boys filled up the circle, looking so much alike that it was hard to say which was Cecil and which was Sid.

Margaret's husband and Fritz's wife were playing games with the children in the parlour, whence shrieks of merriment drifted out into the hall. Nanny might have been with them had she chosen, but she preferred to sit alone in the darkest corner of the hall and gaze with jealous, unhappy eyes at the mirthful group about the fire, listening to their story and jest and laughter with unavailing protest in her heart. Oh, how could they have forgotten so soon? It was not yet a full year since Miss Avis had gone. Last Christmas Eve she had sat there, a sweet and saintly presence, in the inglenook, more, so it had almost seemed, the centre of the home circle than the father and mother; and now the December stars were shining over her grave, and not one of that heedless group remembered her; not once was her name spoken; even her old dog had forgotten her—he sat with his nose in Margaret's lap, blinking with drowsy, aged contentment at the fire.

"Oh, I can't bear it!" whispered Nanny, under cover of the hearty laughter which greeted a story Doctor Fritz had been telling. She slipped out into the kitchen, put on her hood and cloak, and took from a box under the table a little wreath of holly. She had made it out of the bits left over from the decorations. Miss Avis had loved holly; Miss Avis had loved every green, growing thing.

As Nanny opened the kitchen door something cold touched her hand, and there stood the old dog, wagging his tail and looking up at her with wistful eyes, mutely pleading to be taken, too.

"So you do remember her, Gyppy," said Nanny, patting his head. "Come along then. We'll go together."

They slipped out into the night. It was quite dark, but it was not far to the graveyard—just out through the evergreens and along a field by-path and across the road. The old church was there, with its square tower, and the white stones gleaming all around it. Nanny went straight to a shadowy corner and knelt on the sere grasses while she placed her holly wreath on Miss Avis's grave. The tears in her eyes brimmed over.

"Oh, Miss Avis! Miss Avis!" she sobbed. "I miss you so—I miss you so! It can't ever seem like Christmas to me without you. You were always so sweet and kind to me. There ain't a day passes but I think of you and all the things you used to say to me, and I try to be good like you'd want me to be. But I hate them for forgetting you—yes, I do! I'll never forget you, darling Miss Avis! I'd rather be here alone with you in the dark than back there with them."

Nanny sat down by the grave. The old dog lay down by her side with his fore-paws on the turf and his eyes fixed on the tall white marble shaft. It was too dark for Nanny to read the inscription but she knew every word of it: "In loving remembrance of Avis Maywood, died January 20, 1902, aged 45." And underneath the lines of her own choosing:

"Say not good night, but in some brighter clime
Bid me good morning."

But they had forgotten her—oh, they had forgotten her already!

When half an hour had passed, Nanny was startled by approaching footsteps. Not wishing to be seen, she crept softly behind the headstones into the shadow of the willow on the farther side, and the old dog followed. Doctor Fritz, coming to the grave, thought himself alone with the dead. He knelt down by the headstone and pressed his face against it.

"Avis," he said gently, "dear Avis, I have come to visit your grave tonight because you seem nearer to me here than elsewhere. And I want to talk to you, Avis, as I have always talked to you every Christmastide since we were children together. I have missed you so tonight, dear friend and sympathizer—no words can tell how I have missed you—your welcoming handclasp and your sweet face in the firelight shadows. I could not bear to speak your name, the aching sense of loss was so bitter. Amid all the Christmas mirth and good fellowship I felt the sorrow of your vacant chair. Avis, I wanted to tell you what the year had brought to me. My theory has been proved; it has made me a famous man. Last Christmas, Avis, I told you of it, and you listened and understood and believed in it. Dear Avis, once again I thank you for all you have been to me—all you are yet. I have brought you your roses; they are as white and pure and fragrant as your life."

Other footsteps came so quickly on Doctor Fritz' retreating ones that Nanny could not rise. It was Laddie this time—gay, careless, thoughtless Laddie.

"Roses? So Fritz has been here! I have brought you lilies, Avis. Oh, Avis, I miss you so! You were so jolly and good—you understood a fellow so well. I had to come here tonight to tell you how much I miss you. It doesn't seem half home without you. Avis, I'm trying to be a better chap—more the sort of man you'd have me be. I've given the old set the go-by—I'm trying to live up to your standard. It would be easier if you were here to help me. When I was a kid it was always easier to be good for awhile after I'd talked things over with you. I've got the best mother a fellow ever had, but you and I were such chums, weren't we, Avis? I thought I'd just break down in there tonight and put a damper on everything by crying like a baby. If anybody had spoken about you, I should have. Hello!"

Laddie wheeled around with a start, but it was only Robert's two boys, who came shyly up to the grave, half hanging back to find anyone else there.

"Hello, boys," said Laddie huskily. "So you've come to see her grave too?"

"Yes," said Cecil solemnly. "We—we just had to. We couldn't go to bed without coming. Oh, isn't it lonesome without Cousin Avis?"

"She was always so good to us," said Sid.

"She used to talk to us so nice," said Cecil chokily. "But she liked fun, too."

"Boys," said Laddie gravely, "never forget what Cousin Avis used to say to you. Never forget that you have *got* to grow up into men she'd be proud of."

They went away then, the boys and their boyish uncle; and when they had gone Nora came, stealing timidly through the shadows, starting at the rustle of the wind in the trees.

"Oh, Avis," she whispered. "I want to see you so much! I want to tell you all about it—about *him*. You would understand so well. He is the best and dearest lover ever a girl had. You would think so too. Oh, Avis, I miss you so much! There's a little shadow even on my happiness because I can't talk it over with you in the old way. Oh, Avis, it was dreadful to sit around the fire tonight and not see you. Perhaps you were there in spirit. I love to think you were, but I wanted to see you. You were always there to come home to before, Avis, dear."

Sobbing, she went away; and then came Margaret, the grave, strong Margaret.

"Dear cousin, dear to me as a sister, it seemed to me that I must come to you here tonight. I cannot tell you how much I miss your wise, clear-sighted advice and judgment, your wholesome companionship. A little son was born to me this past year, Avis. How glad you would have been, for you knew, as none other did, the bitterness of my childless heart. How we would have delighted to talk over my baby together, and teach him wisely between us! Avis, Avis, your going made a blank that can never be filled for me!"

Margaret was still standing there when the old people came.

"Father! Mother! Isn't it too late and chilly for you to be here?"

"No, Margaret, no," said the mother. "I couldn't go to my bed without coming to see Avis's grave. I brought her up from a baby—her dying mother gave her to me. She was as much my own child as any of you. And oh! I miss her so. You only miss her when you come home, but I miss her all the time—every day!"

"We all miss her, Mother," said the old father, tremulously. "She was a good girl—Avis was a good girl. Good night, Avis!"

"'Say not good night, but in some brighter clime bid her good morning,'" quoted Margaret softly. "That was her own wish, you know. Let us go back now. It is getting late."

When they had gone Nanny crept out from the shadows. It had not occurred to her that perhaps she should not have listened—she had been too shy to make her presence known to those who came to Avis's grave. But her heart was full of joy.

"Oh, Miss Avis, I'm so glad, I'm so glad! They haven't forgotten you after all, Miss Avis, dear, not one of them. I'm sorry I was so cross at them; and I'm so glad they haven't forgotten you. I love them for it."

Then the old dog and Nanny went home together.

The Wooing of Bessy

When Lawrence Eastman began going to see Bessy Houghton the Lynnfield people shrugged their shoulders and said he might have picked out somebody a little younger and prettier—but then, of course, Bessy was well off. A two-hundred-acre farm and a substantial bank account were worth going in for. Trust an Eastman for knowing upon which side his bread was buttered.

Lawrence was only twenty, and looked even younger, owing to his smooth, boyish face, curly hair, and half-girlish bloom. Bessy Houghton was in reality no more than twenty-five, but Lynnfield people had the impression that she was past thirty. She had always been older than her years—a quiet, reserved girl who dressed plainly and never went about with other young people. Her mother had died when Bessy was very young, and she had always kept house for her father. The responsibility made her grave and mature. When she was twenty her father died and Bessy was his sole heir. She kept the farm and took the reins of government in her own capable hands. She made a success of it too, which was more than many a man in Lynnfield had done.

Bessy had never had a lover. She had never seemed like other girls, and passed for an old maid when her contemporaries were in the flush of social success and bloom.

Mrs. Eastman, Lawrence's mother, was a widow with two sons. George, the older, was the mother's favourite, and the property had been willed to him by his father. To Lawrence had been left the few hundreds in the bank. He stayed at home and hired himself to George, thereby adding slowly to his small hoard. He had his eye on a farm in Lynnfield, but he was as yet a mere boy, and his plans for the future were very vague until he fell in love with Bessy Houghton.

In reality nobody was more surprised over this than Lawrence himself. It had certainly been the last thing in his thoughts on the dark, damp night when he had overtaken Bessy walking home alone from prayer meeting and had offered to drive her the rest of the way.

Bessy assented and got into his buggy. At first she was very silent, and Lawrence, who was a bashful lad at the best of times, felt tongue-tied and uncomfortable. But presently Bessy, pitying his evident embarrassment, began to talk to him. She could talk well, and Lawrence found himself entering easily into the spirit of her piquant speeches. He had an odd feeling that he had never known

Bessy Houghton before; he had certainly never guessed that she could be such good company. She was very different from the other girls he knew, but he decided that he liked the difference.

"Are you going to the party at Baileys' tomorrow night?" he asked, as he helped her to alight at her door.

"I don't know," she answered. "I'm invited—but I'm all alone—and parties have never been very much in my line."

There was a wistful note in her voice, and Lawrence detecting it, said hurriedly, not giving himself time to get frightened: "Oh, you'd better go to this one. And if you like, I'll call around and take you."

He wondered if she would think him very presumptuous. He thought her voice sounded colder as she said: "I am afraid that it would be too much trouble for you."

"It wouldn't be any trouble at all," he stammered. "I'll be very pleased to take you."

In the end Bessy had consented to go, and the next evening Lawrence called for her in the rose-red autumn dusk.

Bessy was ready and waiting. She was dressed in what was for her unusual elegance, and Lawrence wondered why people called Bessy Houghton so plain. Her figure was strikingly symmetrical and softly curved. Her abundant, dark-brown hair, instead of being parted plainly and drawn back into a prim coil as usual, was dressed high on her head, and a creamy rose nestled amid the becoming puffs and waves. She wore black, as she usually did, but it was a lustrous black silk, simply and fashionably made, with frost-like frills of lace at her firm round throat and dainty wrists. Her cheeks were delicately flushed, and her wood-brown eyes were sparkling under her long lashes.

She offered him a half-opened bud for his coat and pinned it on for him. As he looked down at her he noticed what a sweet mouth she had—full and red, with a half child-like curve.

The fact that Lawrence Eastman took Bessy Houghton to the Baileys' party made quite a sensation at that festal scene. People nodded and winked and wondered. "An old maid and her money," said Milly Fiske spitefully. Milly, as was well known, had a liking for Lawrence herself.

Lawrence began to "go with" Bessy Houghton regularly after that. In his single-mindedness he never feared that Bessy would misjudge his motives or imagine him to be prompted by mercenary designs. He never thought of her riches himself, and it never occurred to him that she would suppose he did.

He soon realized that he loved her, and he ventured to hope timidly that she loved him in return. She was always rather reserved, but the few favours that meant nothing from other girls meant a great deal from Bessy. The evenings he spent with her in her pretty sitting-room, their moonlight drives over long, satin-smooth stretches of snowy roads, and their walks home from church and prayer meeting under the winter stars, were all so many moments of supreme happiness to Lawrence.

Matters had gone thus far before Mrs. Eastman got her eyes opened. At Mrs. Tom Bailey's quilting party an officious gossip took care to inform her that Lawrence was supposed to be crazy over Bessy Houghton, who was, of course, en-encouraging him simply for the sake of having someone to beau her round, and who would certainly throw him over in the end since she knew perfectly well that it was her money he was after.

Mrs. Eastman was a proud woman and a determined one. She had always disliked Bessy Houghton, and she went home from the quilting resolved to put an instant stop to "all such nonsense" on her son's part.

"Where is Lawrie?" she asked abruptly; as she entered the small kitchen where George Eastman was lounging by the fire.

"Out in the stable grooming up Lady Grey," responded her older son sulkily. "I suppose he's gadding off to see Bessy Houghton again, the young fool that he is! Why don't you put a stop to it?"

"I am going to put a stop to it," said Mrs. Eastman grimly. "I'd have done it before if I'd known. You should have told me of it if you knew. I'm going out to see Lawrence right now."

George Eastman muttered something inaudible as the door closed behind her. He was a short, thickset man, not in the least like Lawrence, who was ten years his junior. Two years previously he had made a furtive attempt to pay court to Bessy Houghton for the sake of her wealth, and her decided repulse of his advances was a remembrance that made him grit his teeth yet. He had hated her bitterly ever since.

Lawrence was brushing his pet mare's coat until it shone like satin, and whistling "Annie Laurie" until the rafters rang. Bessy had sung it for him the night before. He could see her plainly still as she had looked then, in her gown of vivid red—a colour peculiarly becoming to her—with her favourite laces at wrist and throat and a white rose in her hair, which was dressed in the high, becoming knot she had always worn since the night he had shyly told her he liked it so.

She had played and sung many of the sweet old Scotch ballads for him, and when she had gone to the door with him he had taken both her hands in his and, emboldened by the look in her brown eyes, he had stooped and kissed her. Then he had stepped back, filled with dismay at his own audacity. But Bessy had said no word of rebuke, and only blushed hotly crimson. She must care for him, he thought happily, or else she would have been angry.

When his mother came in at the stable door her face was hard and uncompromising.

"Lawrie," she said sharply, "where are you going again tonight? You were out last night."

"Well, Mother, I promise you I wasn't in any bad company. Come now, don't quiz a fellow too close."

"You are going to dangle after Bessy Houghton again. It's time you were told what a fool you were making of yourself. She's old enough to be your mother. The whole settlement is laughing at you."

Lawrence looked as if his mother had struck him a blow in the face. A dull, purplish flush crept over his brow.

"This is some of George's work," he broke out fiercely. "He's been setting you on me, has he? Yes, he's jealous—he wanted Bessy himself, but she would not look at him. He thinks nobody knows it, but I do. Bessy marry him? It's very likely!"

"Lawrie Eastman, you are daft. George hasn't said anything to me. You surely don't imagine Bessy Houghton would marry you. And if she would, she is too old for you. Now, don't you hang around her any longer."

"I will," said Lawrence flatly. "I don't care what anybody says. You needn't worry over me. I can take care of myself."

Mrs. Eastman looked blankly at her son. He had never defied or disobeyed her in his life before. She had supposed her word would be law. Rebellion was something she had not dreamed of. Her lips tightened ominously and her eyes narrowed.

"You're a bigger fool than I took you for," she said in a voice that trembled with anger. "Bessy Houghton laughs at you everywhere. She knows you're just after her money, and she makes fun—"

"Prove it," interrupted Lawrence undauntedly, "I'm not going to put any faith in Lynnfield gossip. Prove it if you can."

"I can prove it. Maggie Hatfield told me what Bessy Houghton said to her about you. She said you were a lovesick fool, and she only went with you for a little amusement, and that if you thought you had nothing to do but marry her and hang up your hat there you'd find yourself vastly mistaken."

Possibly in her calmer moments Mrs. Eastman might have shrunk from such a deliberate falsehood, although it was said of her in Lynnfield that she was not one to stick at a lie when the truth would not serve her purpose. Moreover, she felt quite sure that Lawrence would never ask Maggie Hatfield anything about it.

Lawrence turned white to the lips, "Is that true, Mother?" he asked huskily.

"I've warned you," replied his mother, not choosing to repeat her statement. "If you go after Bessy any more you can take the consequences."

She drew her shawl about her pale, malicious face and left him with a parting glance of contempt.

"I guess that'll settle him," she thought grimly. "Bessy Houghton turned up her nose at George, but she shan't make a fool of Lawrence too."

Alone in the stable Lawrence stood staring out at the dull red ball of the winter sun with unseeing eyes. He had implicit faith in his mother, and the stab had gone straight to his heart. Bessy Houghton listened in vain that night for his well-known footfall on the verandah.

The next night Lawrence went home with Milly Fiske from prayer meeting, taking her out from a crowd of other girls under Bessy Houghton's very eyes as she came down the steps of the little church.

Bessy walked home alone. The light burned low in her sitting-room, and in the mirror over the mantel she saw her own pale face, with its tragic, pain-stricken eyes. Annie Hillis, her "help," was out. She was alone in the big house with her misery and despair.

She went dizzily upstairs to her own room and flung herself on the bed in the chill moonlight.

"It is all over," she said dully. All night she lay there, fighting with her pain. In the wan, grey morning she looked at her mirrored self with pitying scorn—at the pallid face, the lifeless features, the dispirited eyes with their bluish circles.

"What a fool I have been to imagine he could care for me!" she said bitterly. "He has only been amusing himself with my folly. And to think that I let him kiss me the other night!"

She thought of that kiss with a pitiful shame. She hated herself for the weakness that could not check her tears. Her lonely life had been brightened by the companionship of her young lover. The youth and girlhood of which fate had cheated her had come to her with love; the future had looked rosy with promise; now it had darkened with dourness and greyness.

Maggie Hatfield came that day to sew. Bessy had intended to have a dark-blue silk made up and an evening waist of pale pink cashmere. She had expected to wear the latter at a party which was to come off a fortnight later, and she had got it to please Lawrence, because he had told her that pink was his favourite colour. She would have neither it nor the silk made up now. She put them both away and instead brought out an ugly pattern of snuff-brown stuff, bought years before and never used.

"But where is your lovely pink, Bessy?" asked the dressmaker. "Aren't you going to have it for the party?"

"No, I'm not going to have it made up at all," said Bessy listlessly. "It's too gay for me. I was foolish to think it would ever suit me. This brown will do for a spring suit. It doesn't make much difference what I wear."

Maggie Hatfield, who had not been at prayer meeting the night beforehand knew nothing of what had occurred, looked at her curiously, wondering what Lawrence Eastman could see in her to be as crazy about her as some people said he was. Bessy was looking her oldest and plainest just then, with her hair combed severely back from her pale, dispirited face.

"It must be her money he is after," thought the dressmaker. "She looks over thirty, and she can't pretend to be pretty. I believe she thinks a lot of him, though."

For the most part, Lynnfield people believed that Bessy had thrown Lawrence over. This opinion was borne out by his woebegone appearance. He was thin and pale; his face had lost its youthful curves and looked hard and mature. He was moody and taciturn and his speech and manner were marked by a new cynicism.

In April a well-to-do storekeeper from an adjacent village began to court Bessy Houghton. He was over fifty, and had never been a handsome man in his best days, but Lynnfield oracles opined that Bessy would take him. She couldn't expect to do any better, they said, and she was looking terribly old and dowdy all at once.

In June Maggie Hatfield went to the Eastmans' to sew. The first bit of news she imparted to Mrs. Eastman was that Bessy Houghton had refused Jabez Lea—at least, he didn't come to see her any more.

Mrs. Eastman twitched her thread viciously. "Bessy Houghton was born an old maid," she said sharply. "She thinks nobody is good enough for her, that is what's the matter. Lawrence got some silly boy-notion into his head last winter, but I soon put a stop to that."

"I always had an idea that Bessy thought a good deal of Lawrence," said Maggie. "She has never been the same since he left off going with her. I was up there the morning after that prayer-meeting night people talked so much of, and she looked positively dreadful, as if she hadn't slept a wink the whole night."

"Nonsense!" said Mrs. Eastman decisively. "She would never think of taking a boy like him when she'd turned up her nose at better men. And I didn't want her for a daughter-in-law anyhow. I can't bear her. So I put my foot down in time. Lawrence sulked for a spell, of course—boy-fashion—and he's been as fractious as a spoiled baby ever since."

"Well, I dare say you're right," assented the dressmaker. "But I must say I had always imagined that Bessy had a great notion of Lawrence. Of course, she's so quiet it is hard to tell. She never says a word about herself."

There was an unsuspected listener to this conversation. Lawrence had come in from the field for a drink, and was standing in the open kitchen doorway, within easy earshot of the women's shrill tones.

He had never doubted his mother's word at any time in his life, but now he knew beyond doubt that there had been crooked work somewhere. He shrank from believing his mother untrue, yet where else could the crookedness come in?

When Mrs. Eastman had gone to the kitchen to prepare dinner, Maggie Hatfield was startled by the appearance of Lawrence at the low open window of the sitting-room.

"Mercy me, how you scared me!" she exclaimed nervously.

"Maggie," said Lawrence seriously, "I want to ask you a question. Did Bessy Houghton ever say anything to you about me or did you ever say that she did? Give me a straight answer."

The dressmaker peered at him curiously.

"No. Bessy never so much as mentioned your name to me," she said, "and I never heard that she did to anyone else. Why?"

"Thank you. That was all I wanted to know," said Lawrence, ignoring her question, and disappearing as suddenly as he had come.

That evening at moonrise he passed through the kitchen dressed in his Sunday best. His mother met him at the door.

"Where are you going?" she asked querulously.

Lawrence looked her squarely in the face with accusing eyes, before which her own quailed.

"I'm going to see Bessy Houghton, Mother," he said sternly, "and to ask her pardon for believing the lie that has kept us apart so long."

Mrs. Eastman flushed crimson and opened her lips to speak. But something in Lawrence's grave, white face silenced her. She turned away without a word, knowing in her secret soul that her youngest-born was lost to her forever.

Lawrence found Bessy in the orchard under apple trees that were pyramids of pearly bloom. She looked at him through the twilight with reproach and aloofness in her eyes. But he put out his hands and caught her reluctant ones in a masterful grasp.

"Listen to me, Bessy. Don't condemn me before you've heard me. I've been to blame for believing falsehoods about you, but I believe them no longer, and I've come to ask you to forgive me."

He told his story simply and straightforwardly. In strict justice he could not keep his mother's name out of it, but he merely said she had been mistaken. Perhaps Bessy understood none the less. She knew what Mrs. Eastman's reputation in Lynnfield was.

"You might have had a little more faith in me," she cried reproachfully.

"I know—I know. But I was beside myself with pain and wretchedness. Oh, Bessy, won't you forgive me? I love you so! If you send me away I'll go to the dogs. Forgive me, Bessy."

And she, being a woman, did forgive him.

"I've loved you from the first, Lawrence," she said, yielding to his kiss.

Their Girl Josie

When Paul Morgan, a rising young lawyer with justifiable political aspirations, married Elinor Ashton, leading woman at the Green Square Theatre, his old schoolmates and neighbours back in Spring Valley held up their hands in horror, and his father and mother up in the weather-grey Morgan homestead were crushed in the depths of humiliation. They had been too proud of Paul ... their only son and such a clever fellow ... and this was their punishment! He had married an actress! To Cyrus and Deborah Morgan, brought up and nourished all their lives on the strictest and straightest of old-fashioned beliefs both as regards this world and that which is to come, this was a tragedy.

They could not be brought to see it in any other light. As their neighbours said, "Cy Morgan never hilt up his head again after Paul married the play-acting woman." But perhaps it was less his humiliation than his sorrow which bowed down his erect form and sprinkled grey in his thick black hair that fifty years had hitherto spared. For Paul, forgetting the sacrifices his mother and father had made for him, had bitterly resented the letter of protest his father had written concerning his marriage. He wrote one angry, unfilial letter back and then came silence. Between grief and shame Cyrus and Deborah Morgan grew old rapidly in the year that followed.

At the end of that time Elinor Morgan, the mother of an hour, died; three months later Paul Morgan was killed in a railroad collision. After the funeral Cyrus Morgan brought home to his wife their son's little daughter, Joscelyn Morgan.

Her aunt, Annice Ashton, had wanted the baby. Cyrus Morgan had been almost rude in his refusal. His son's daughter should never be brought up by an actress; it was bad enough that her mother had been one and had doubtless transmitted the taint to her child. But in Spring Valley, if anywhere, it might be eradicated.

At first neither Cyrus nor Deborah cared much for Joscelyn. They resented her parentage, her strange, un-Morgan-like name, and the pronounced resemblance she bore to the dark-haired, dark-eyed mother they had never seen. All the Morgans had been fair. If Joscelyn had had Paul's blue eyes and golden curls her grandfather and grandmother would have loved her sooner.

But the love came ... it had to. No living mortal could have resisted Joscelyn. She was the most winsome and lovable little mite of babyhood that ever toddled.

Her big dark eyes overflowed with laughter before she could speak, her puckered red mouth broke constantly into dimples and cooing sounds. She had ways that no orthodox Spring Valley baby ever thought of having. Every smile was a caress, every gurgle of attempted speech a song. Her grandparents came to worship her and were stricter than ever with her by reason of their love. Because she was so dear to them she must be saved from her mother's blood.

Joscelyn shot up through a roly-poly childhood into slim, bewitching girlhood in a chill repressive atmosphere. Cyrus and Deborah were nothing if not thorough. The name of Joscelyn's mother was never mentioned to her; she was never called anything but Josie, which sounded more "Christian-like" than Joscelyn; and all the flowering out of her alien beauty was repressed as far as might be in the plainest and dullest of dresses and the primmest arrangement possible to riotous ripe-brown curls.

The girl was never allowed to visit her Aunt Annice, although frequently invited. Miss Ashton, however, wrote to her occasionally, and every Christmas sent a box of presents which even Cyrus and Deborah Morgan could not forbid her to accept, although they looked with disapproving eyes and ominously set lips at the dainty, frivolous trifles the actress woman sent. They would have liked to cast those painted fans and lace frills and beflounced lingerie into the fire as if they had been infected rags from a pest-house.

The path thus set for Joscelyn's dancing feet to walk in was indeed sedate and narrow. She was seldom allowed to mingle with the young people of even quiet, harmless Spring Valley; she was never allowed to attend local concerts, much less take part in them; she was forbidden to read novels, and Cyrus Morgan burned an old copy of Shakespeare which Paul had given him years ago and which he had himself read and treasured, lest its perusal should awaken unlawful instincts in Joscelyn's heart. The girl's passion for reading was so marked that her grandparents felt that it was their duty to repress it as far as lay in their power.

But Joscelyn's vitality was such that all her bonds and bands served but little to check or retard the growth of her rich nature. Do what they might they could not make a Morgan of her. Her every step was a dance, her every word and gesture full of a grace and virility that filled the old folks with uneasy wonder. She seemed to them charged with dangerous tendencies all the more potent from repression. She was sweet-tempered and sunny, truthful and modest, but she was as little like the trim, simple Spring Valley girls as a crimson rose is like a field daisy, and her unlikeness bore heavily on her grandparents.

Yet they loved her and were proud of her. "Our girl Josie," as they called her, was more to them than they would have admitted even to themselves, and in the main they were satisfied with her, although the grandmother grumbled because Josie did not take kindly to patchwork and rug-making and the grandfather would fain have toned down that exuberance of beauty and vivacity into the meeker pattern of maidenhood he had been accustomed to.

When Joscelyn was seventeen Deborah Morgan noticed a change in her. The girl became quieter and more brooding, falling at times into strange, idle reveries, with her hands clasped over her knee and her big eyes fixed unseeingly on space; or she would creep away for solitary rambles in the beech wood, going away droopingly and returning with dusky glowing cheeks and a nameless radiance, as of some newly discovered power, shining through every muscle and motion. Mrs. Morgan thought the child needed a tonic and gave her sulphur and molasses.

One day the revelation came. Cyrus and Deborah had driven across the valley to visit their married daughter. Not finding her at home they returned. Mrs. Morgan went into the house while her husband went to the stable. Joscelyn was not in the kitchen, but the grandmother heard the sound of voices and laughter in the sitting room across the hall.

"What company has Josie got?" she wondered, as she opened the hall door and paused for a moment on the threshold to listen. As she listened her old face grew grey and pinched; she turned noiselessly and left the house, and flew to her husband as one distracted.

"Cyrus, Josie is play-acting in the room ... laughing and reciting and going on. I heard her. Oh, I've always feared it would break out in her and it has! Come you and listen to her."

The old couple crept through the kitchen and across the hall to the open parlour door as if they were stalking a thief. Joscelyn's laugh rang out as they did so ... a mocking, triumphant peal. Cyrus and Deborah shivered as if they had heard sacrilege.

Joscelyn had put on a trailing, clinging black skirt which her aunt had sent her a year ago and which she had never been permitted to wear. It transformed her into a woman. She had cast aside her waist of dark plum-coloured homespun and wrapped a silken shawl about herself until only her beautiful arms and shoulders were left bare. Her hair, glossy and brown, with burnished red lights where the rays of the dull autumn sun struck on it through the window, was heaped high on her head and held in place by a fillet of pearl beads. Her cheeks were crimson, her whole body from head to foot instinct and alive with a beauty that to Cyrus and Deborah, as they stood mute with horror in the open doorway, seemed akin to some devilish enchantment.

Joscelyn, rapt away from her surroundings, did not perceive her grandparents. Her face was turned from them and she was addressing an unseen auditor in passionate denunciation. She spoke, moved, posed, gesticulated, with an inborn genius shining through every motion and tone like an illuminating lamp.

"Josie, what are you doing?"

It was Cyrus who spoke, advancing into the room like a stern, hard impersonation of judgment. Joscelyn's outstretched arm fell to her side and she turned sharply around; fear came into her face and the light went out of it. A moment before she had been a woman, splendid, unafraid; now she was again the schoolgirl, too confused and shamed to speak.

"What are you doing, Josie?" asked her grandfather again, "dressed up in that indecent manner and talking and twisting to yourself?"

Joscelyn's face, that had grown pale, flamed scarlet again. She lifted her head proudly.

"I was trying Aunt Annice's part in her new play," she answered. "I have not been doing anything wrong, Grandfather."

"Wrong! It's your mother's blood coming out in you, girl, in spite of all our care! Where did you get that play?"

"Aunt Annice sent it to me," answered Joscelyn, casting a quick glance at the book on the table. Then, when her grandfather picked it up gingerly, as if he feared contamination, she added quickly, "Oh, give it to me, please, Grandfather. Don't take it away."

"I am going to burn it," said Cyrus Morgan sternly.

"Oh, don't, Grandfather," cried Joscelyn, with a sob in her voice. "Don't burn it, please. I ... I ... won't practise out of it any more. I'm sorry I've displeased you. Please give me my book."

"No," was the stern reply. "Go to your room, girl, and take off that rig. There is to be no more play-acting in my house, remember that."

He flung the book into the fire that was burning in the grate. For the first time in her life Joscelyn flamed out into passionate defiance.

"You are cruel and unjust, Grandfather. I have done no wrong ... it is not doing wrong to develop the one gift I have. It's the only thing I can do ... and I am going to do it. My mother was an actress and a good woman. So is Aunt Annice. So I mean to be."

"Oh, Josie, Josie," said her grandmother in a scared voice. Her grandfather only repeated sternly, "Go, take that rig off, girl, and let us hear no more of this."

Joscelyn went but she left consternation behind her. Cyrus and Deborah could not have been more shocked if they had discovered the girl robbing her grandfather's desk. They talked the matter over bitterly at the kitchen hearth that night.

"We haven't been strict enough with the girl, Mother," said Cyrus angrily. "We'll have to be stricter if we don't want to have her disgracing us. Did you hear how she defied me? 'So I mean to be,' she says. Mother, we'll have trouble with that girl yet."

"Don't be too harsh with her, Pa ... it'll maybe only drive her to worse," sobbed Deborah.

"I ain't going to be harsh. What I do is for her own good, you know that, Mother. Josie is as dear to me as she is to you, but we've got to be stricter with her."

They were. From that day Josie was watched and distrusted. She was never permitted to be alone. There were no more solitary walks. She felt herself under the surveillance of cold, unsympathetic eyes every moment and her very soul writhed. Joscelyn Morgan, the high-spirited daughter of high-spirited parents, could not long submit to such treatment. It might have passed with a child; to a woman, thrilling with life and conscious power to her very fingertips, it was galling beyond measure. Joscelyn rebelled, but she did nothing secretly ... that was not her nature. She wrote to her Aunt Annice, and when she received her reply she went straight and fearlessly to her grandparents with it.

"Grandfather, this letter is from my aunt. She wishes me to go and live with her and prepare for the stage. I told her I wished to do so. I am going."

Cyrus and Deborah looked at her in mute dismay.

"I know you despise the profession of an actress," the girl went on with heightened colour. "I am sorry you think so about it because it is the only one open to me. I must go ... I must."

"Yes, you must," said Cyrus cruelly. "It's in your blood ... your bad blood, girl."

"My blood isn't bad," cried Joscelyn proudly. "My mother was a sweet, true, good woman. You are unjust, Grandfather. But I don't want you to be angry with me. I love you both and I am very grateful indeed for all your kindness to me. I wish that you could understand what...."

"We understand enough," interrupted Cyrus harshly. "This is all I have to say. Go to your play-acting aunt if you want to. Your grandmother and me won't hinder you. But you'll come back here no more. We'll have nothing further to do with you. You can choose your own way and walk in it."

With this dictum Joscelyn went from Spring Valley. She clung to Deborah and wept at parting, but Cyrus did not even say goodbye to her. On the morning of her departure he went away on business and did not return until evening.

Joscelyn went on the stage. Her aunt's influence and her mother's fame helped her much. She missed the hard experiences that come to the unassisted beginner. But her own genius must have won in any case. She had all her mother's gifts, deepened by her inheritance of Morgan intensity and sincerity ... much, too, of the Morgan firmness of will. When Joscelyn Morgan was twenty-two she was famous over two continents.

When Cyrus Morgan returned home on the evening after his granddaughter's departure he told his wife that she was never to mention the girl's name in his hearing again. Deborah obeyed. She thought her husband was right, albeit she might in her own heart deplore the necessity of such a decree. Joscelyn had disgraced them; could that be forgiven?

Nevertheless both the old people missed her terribly. The house seemed to have lost its soul with that vivid, ripely tinted young life. They got their married daughter's oldest girl, Pauline, to come and stay with them. Pauline was a quiet, docile maiden, industrious and commonplace—just such a girl as they had vainly striven to make of Joscelyn, to whom Pauline had always been held up as a model. Yet neither Cyrus nor Deborah took to her, and they let her go unregretfully when they found that she wished to return home.

"She hasn't any of Josie's gimp," was old Cyrus's unspoken fault. Deborah spoke, but all she said was, "Polly's a good girl, Father, only she hasn't any snap."

Joscelyn wrote to Deborah occasionally, telling her freely of her plans and doings. If it hurt the girl that no notice was ever taken of her letters she still wrote them. Deborah read the letters grimly and then left them in Cyrus's way. Cyrus would not read them at first; later on he read them stealthily when Deborah was out of the house.

When Joscelyn began to succeed she sent to the old farmhouse papers and magazines containing her photographs and criticisms of her plays and acting. Deborah cut them out and kept them in her upper bureau drawer with Joscelyn's letters. Once she overlooked one and Cyrus found it when he was kindling the fire. He got the scissors and cut it out carefully. A month later Deborah discovered it between the leaves of the family Bible.

But Joscelyn's name was never mentioned between them, and when other people asked them concerning her their replies were cold and ungracious. In a way they had relented towards her, but their shame of her remained. They could never forget that she was an actress.

Once, six years after Joscelyn had left Spring Valley, Cyrus, who was reading a paper by the table, got up with an angry exclamation and stuffed it into the stove, thumping the lid on over it with grim malignity.

"That fool dunno what he's talking about," was all he would say. Deborah had her share of curiosity. The paper was the *National Gazette* and she knew that their next-door neighbour, James Pennan, took it. She went over that evening and borrowed it, saying that their own had been burned before she had had time to read the serial in it. With one exception she read all its columns carefully without finding anything to explain her husband's anger. Then she doubtfully plunged into the exception ... a column of "Stage Notes." Halfway down she came upon an adverse criticism of Joscelyn Morgan and her new play. It was malicious and vituperative. Deborah Morgan's old eyes sparkled dangerously as she read it.

"I guess somebody is pretty jealous of Josie," she muttered. "I don't wonder Pa was riled up. But I guess she can hold her own. She's a Morgan."

No long time after this Cyrus took a notion he'd like a trip to the city. He'd like to see the Horse Fair and look up Cousin Hiram Morgan's folks.

"Hiram and me used to be great chums, Mother. And we're getting kind of mossy, I guess, never stirring out of Spring Valley. Let's go and dissipate for a week—what say?"

Deborah agreed readily, albeit of late years she had been much averse to going far from home and had never at any time been very fond of Cousin Hiram's wife. Cyrus was as pleased as a child over their trip. On the second day of their sojourn in the city he slipped away when Deborah had gone shopping with Mrs. Hiram and hurried through the streets to the Green Square Theatre with a hang-dog look. He bought a ticket apologetically and sneaked in to his seat. It was a matinee performance, and Joscelyn Morgan was starring in her famous new play.

Cyrus waited for the curtain to rise, feeling as if every one of his Spring Valley neighbours must know where he was and revile him for it. If Deborah were ever to find out ... but Deborah must never find out! For the first time in their married life the old man deliberately plotted to deceive his old wife. He must see his girl Josie just once; it was a terrible thing that she was an actress, but she was a successful one, nobody could deny that, except fools who yapped in the *National Gazette*.

The curtain went up and Cyrus rubbed his eyes. He had certainly braced his nerves to behold some mystery of iniquity; instead he saw an old kitchen so like his own at home that it bewildered him; and there, sitting by the cheery wood stove, in homespun gown, with primly braided hair, was Joscelyn—his girl Josie, as he had seen her a thousand times by his own ingle-side. The building rang with applause; one old man pulled out a red bandanna and wiped tears of joy and pride from his eyes. She hadn't changed—Josie hadn't changed. Play-acting hadn't spoiled her—couldn't spoil her. Wasn't she Paul's daughter! And all this applause was for her—for Josie.

Joscelyn's new play was a homely, pleasant production with rollicking comedy and heart-moving pathos skilfully commingled. Joscelyn pervaded it all with a convincing simplicity that was really the triumph of art. Cyrus Morgan listened and exulted in her; at every burst of applause his eyes gleamed with pride. He wanted to go on the stage and box the ears of the villain who plotted against her; he wanted to shake hands with the good woman who stood by her; he wanted to pay off the mortgage and make Josie happy. He wiped tears from his eyes in the third act when Josie was turned out of doors and, when the fourth left her a happy, blushing bride, hand in hand with her farmer lover, he could have wept again for joy.

Cyrus Morgan went out into the daylight feeling as if he had awakened from a dream. At the outer door he came upon Mrs. Hiram and Deborah. Deborah's face was stained with tears, and she caught at his hand.

"Oh, Pa, wasn't it splendid—wasn't our girl Josie splendid! I'm so proud of her. Oh, I was bound to hear her. I was afraid you'd be mad, so I didn't let on and when I saw you in the seat down there I couldn't believe my eyes. Oh, I've just been crying the whole time. Wasn't it splendid! Wasn't our girl Josie splendid?"

The crowd around looked at the old pair with amused, indulgent curiosity, but they were quite oblivious to their surroundings, even to Mrs. Hiram's anxiety to decoy them away. Cyrus Morgan cleared his throat and said, "It was great, Mother, great. She took the shine off the other play-actors all right. I knew that *National Gazette* man didn't know what he was talking about. Mother, let us go and see Josie right off. She's stopping with her aunt at the Maberly Hotel—I saw it in the paper this morning. I'm going to tell her she was right and we were wrong. Josie's beat them all, and I'm going to tell her so!"

When Jack and Jill Took a Hand

Jack's Side of It

Jill says I have to begin this story because it was me—I mean it was I—who made all the trouble in the first place. That is so like Jill. She is such a good hand at forgetting. Why, it was she who suggested the plot to me. I should never have thought of it myself—not that Jill is any smarter than I am, either, but girls are such creatures for planning up mischief and leading other folks into it and then laying the blame on them when things go wrong. How could I tell Dick would act so like a mule? I thought grown-up folks had more sense. Aunt Tommy was down on me for weeks, while she thought Jill a regular heroine. But there! Girls don't know anything about being fair, and I am determined I will never have anything more to do with them and their love affairs as long as I live. Jill says I will change my mind when I grow up, but I won't.

Still, Jill is a pretty good sort of girl. I have to scold her sometimes, but if any other chap tried to I would punch his head for him.

I suppose it *is* time I explained who Dick and Aunt Tommy are. Dick is our minister. He hasn't been it very long. He only came a year ago. I shall never forget how surprised Jill and I were that first Sunday we went to church and saw him. We had always thought that ministers had to be old. All the ministers we knew were. Mr. Grinnell, the one before Dick came, must have been as old as Methuselah. But Dick was young—and good-looking. Jill said she thought it a positive sin for a minister to be so good-looking, it didn't seem Christian; but that was just because all the ministers we knew happened to be homely so that it didn't appear natural.

Dick was tall and pale and looked as if he had heaps of brains. He had thick curly brown hair and big dark blue eyes—Jill said his eyes were like an archangel's, but how could she tell? She never saw an archangel. I liked his nose. It was so straight and finished-looking. Mr. Grinnell had the worst-looking nose you ever saw. Jill and I used to make poetry about it in church to keep from falling asleep when he preached such awful long sermons.

Dick preached great sermons. They were so nice and short. It was such fun to hear him thump the pulpit when he got excited; and when he got more excited still he would lean over the pulpit, his face all white, and talk so low and solemn that it would just send the most gorgeous thrills through you.

Dick came to Owlwood—that's our place; I hate these explanations—quite a lot, even before Aunt Tommy came. He and Father were chums; they had been in college together and Father said Dick was the best football player he ever knew. Jill and I soon got acquainted with him and this was another uncanny thing. We had never thought it possible to get acquainted with a minister. Jill said she didn't think it proper for a real live minister to be so chummy. But then Jill was a little jealous because Dick and I, being both men; were better friends than he and she could be. He taught me to skate that winter and fence with canes and do long division. I could never understand long division before Dick came, although I was away on in fractions.

Jill has just been in and says I ought to explain that Dick's name wasn't Dick. I do wish Jill would mind her own business. Of course it wasn't. His real name was the Reverend Stephen Richmond, but Jill and I always called him Dick behind his back; it seemed so jolly and venturesome, somehow, to speak of a minister like that. Only we had to be careful not to let Father and Mother hear us. Mother wouldn't even let Father call Dick "Stephen"; she said it would set a bad example of familiarity to the children. Mother is an old darling. She won't believe we're half as bad as we are.

Well, early in May comes Aunt Tommy. I must explain who Aunt Tommy is or Jill will be at me again. She is Father's youngest sister and her real name is Bertha Gordon, but Father has always called her Tommy and she likes it.

Jill and I had never seen Aunt Tommy before, but we took to her from the start because she was so pretty and because she talked to us just as if we were grown up. She called Jill Elizabeth, and Jill would adore a Hottentot who called her Elizabeth.

Aunt Tommy is the prettiest girl I ever saw. If Jill is half as good-looking when she gets to be twenty—she's only ten now, same age as I am, we're twins—I shall be proud of her for a sister.

Aunt Tommy is all white and dimpled. She has curly red hair and big jolly brown eyes and scrumptious freckles. I do like freckles in a girl, although Jill goes wild if she thinks she has one on her nose. When we talked of writing this story Jill said I wasn't to say that Aunt Tommy had freckles because it wouldn't sound romantic. But I don't care. She has freckles and I think they are all right.

We went to church with Aunt Tommy the first Sunday after she came, one on each side of her. Aunt Tommy is the only girl in the world I'd walk hand in hand with before people. She looked fine that day. She had on a gorgeous dress, all frills and ruffles, and a big white floppy hat. I was proud of her for an aunt, I can tell you, and I was anxious for Dick to see her. When he came up to speak to me and Jill after church came out I said, "Aunt Tommy, this is Mr. Richmond," just like the grown-up people say. Aunt Tommy and Dick shook hands and Dick got as red as anything. It was funny to see him.

The very next evening he came down to Owlwood. We hadn't expected him until Tuesday, for he never came Monday night before. That is Father's night for going to a lodge meeting. Mother was away this time too. I met Dick on the porch and took him into the parlour, thinking what a bully talk we could have all alone together, without Jill bothering around. But in a minute Aunt Tommy came in and she and Dick began to talk, and I just couldn't get a word in edgewise. I got so disgusted I started out, but I don't believe they ever noticed I was gone. I liked Aunt Tommy very well, but I didn't think she had any business to monopolize Dick like that when he and I were such old chums.

Outside I came across Jill. She was sitting all alone in the dark, curled up on the edge of the verandah just where she could see into the parlour through the big glass door. I sat down beside her, for I wanted sympathy.

"Dick's in there talking to Aunt Tommy," I said. "I don't see what makes him want to talk to her."

"What a goose you are!" said Jill in that aggravatingly patronizing way of hers. "Why, Dick has fallen in love with Aunt Tommy!"

Honest, I jumped. I never was so surprised.

"How do you know?" I asked.

"Because I do," said Jill. "I knew it yesterday at church and I think it is so romantic."

"I don't see how you can tell," I said—and I didn't.

"You'll understand better when you get older," said Jill. Sometimes Jill talks as if she were a hundred years older than I am, instead of being a twin. And really, sometimes I think she *is* older.

"I didn't think ministers ever fell in love," I protested.

"Some do," said Jill sagely. "Mr. Grinnell wouldn't ever, I suppose. But Dick is different. I'd like him for a husband myself. But he'd be too old for me by the time I grew up, so I suppose I'll have to let Aunt Tommy have him. It will be all in the family anyhow—that is one comfort. I think Aunt Tommy ought to have me for a flower girl and I'll wear pink silk clouded over with white chiffon and carry a big bouquet of roses."

"Jill, you take my breath away," I said, and she did. My imagination couldn't travel as fast as that. But after I had thought the idea over a bit I liked it. It was a good deal like a book; and, besides, a minister is a respectable thing to have in a family.

"We must help them all we can," said Jill.

"What can we do?" I asked.

"We must praise Dick to Aunt Tommy and Aunt Tommy to Dick and we must keep out of the way—we mustn't ever hang around when they want to be alone," said Jill.

"I don't want to give up being chums with Dick," I grumbled.

"We must be self-sacrificing," said Jill. And that sounded so fine it reconciled me to the attempt.

We sat there and watched Dick and Aunt Tommy for an hour. I thought they were awfully prim and stiff. If I'd been Dick I'd have gone over and hugged her. I said so to Jill and Jill was shocked. She said it wouldn't be proper when they weren't even engaged.

When Dick went away Aunt Tommy came out to the verandah and discovered us. She sat down between us and put her arms about us. Aunt Tommy has such cute ways.

"I like your minister very much," she said.

"He's bully," I said.

"He's as handsome as a prince," Jill said.

"He preaches splendid sermons—he makes people sit up in church, I can tell you," I said.

"He has a heavenly tenor voice," Jill said.

"He's got a magnificent muscle," I said.

"He has the most poetical eyes," Jill said.

"He swims like a duck," I said.

"He looks just like a Greek god," Jill said.

I'm sure Jill couldn't have known what a Greek god looked like, but I suppose she got the comparison out of some novel. Jill is always reading novels. She borrows them from the cook.

Aunt Tommy laughed and said, "You darlings."

For the next three months Jill and I were wild. It was just like reading a serial story to watch Dick and Aunt Tommy. One day when Dick came Aunt Tommy wasn't quite ready to come down, so Jill and I went in to the parlour to help things along. We knew we hadn't much time, so we began right off.

"Aunt Tommy is the jolliest girl I know," I said.

"She is as beautiful as a dream," Jill said.

"She can play games as good as a boy," I said.

"She does the most elegant fancy work," Jill said.

"She never gets mad," I said.

"She plays and sings divinely," Jill said.

"She can cook awfully good things," I said, for I was beginning to run short of compliments. Jill was horrified; she said afterwards that it wasn't a bit romantic. But I don't care—I believe Dick liked it, for he smiled with his eyes I just as he always does when he's pleased. Girls don't understand everything.

But at the end of three months we began to get anxious. Things were going so slow. Dick and Aunt Tommy didn't seem a bit further ahead than at first. Jill said it was because Aunt Tommy didn't encourage Dick enough.

"I do wish we could hurry them up a little," she said. "At this rate they will never be married this year and by next I'll be too big to be a flower girl. I'm stretching out horribly as it is. Mother has had to let down my frocks again."

"I wish they would get engaged and have done with it," I said. "My mind would be at rest then. It's all Dick's fault. Why doesn't he ask Aunt Tommy to marry him? What's making him so slow about it? If I wanted a girl to marry me—but I wouldn't ever—I'd tell her so right spang off."

"I suppose ministers have to be more dignified," said Jill, "but three months ought to be enough time for anyone. And Aunt Tommy is only going to be here another month. If Dick could be made a little jealous it would hurry him up. And he could be made jealous if you had any spunk about you."

"I guess I've got more spunk than you have," I said.

"The trouble with Dick is this," said Jill. "There is nobody else coming to see Aunt Tommy and he thinks he is sure of her. If you could tell him something different it would stir him up."

"Are you sure it would?" I asked.

"It always does in novels," said Jill. And that settled it, of course.

Jill and I fixed up what I was to say and Jill made me say it over and over again to be sure I had it right. I told her—sarcastically—that she'd better say it herself and then it would be done properly. Jill said she would if it were Aunt Tommy, but when it was Dick it was better for a man to do it. So of course I agreed.

I didn't know when I would have a chance to stir Dick up, but Providence—so Jill said—favoured us. Aunt Tommy didn't expect Dick down the next night, so she and Father and Mother all went away somewhere. Dick came after all, and Jill sent me into the parlour to tell him. He was standing before the mantel looking at Aunt Tommy's picture. There was such an adoring look in his eyes. I could see it quite plain in the mirror before him. I practised that look a lot before my own glass after that—because I thought it might come in handy some time, you know—but I guess I couldn't have got it just right because when I tried it on Jill she asked me if I had a pain.

"Well, Jack, old man," said Dick, sitting down on the sofa. I sat down before him.

"Aunt Tommy is out," I said, to get the worst over. "I guess you like Aunt Tommy pretty well, don't you, Mr. Richmond?"

"Yes," said Dick softly.

"So do other men," I said—mysterious, as Jill had ordered me.

Dick thumped one of the sofa pillows.

"Yes, I suppose so," he said.

"There's a man in New York who just worships Aunt Tommy," I said. "He writes her most every day and sends her books and music and elegant presents. I guess she's pretty fond of him too. She keeps his photograph on her bedroom table and I've seen her kissing it."

I stopped there, not because I had said all I had to say, but because Dick's face scared me—honest, it did. It had all gone white, like it does in the pulpit sometimes when he is tremendously in earnest, only ten times worse. But all he said was,

"Is your Aunt Bertha engaged to this—this man?"

"Not exactly engaged," I said, "but I guess anybody else who wants to marry her will have to reckon with him."

Dick got up.

"I think I won't wait this evening," he said.

"I wish you'd stay and have a talk with me," I said. "I haven't had a talk with you for ages and I have a million things to tell you."

Dick smiled as if it hurt him to smile.

"I can't tonight, Jacky. Some other time we'll have a good powwow, old chap."

He took his hat and went out. Then Jill came flying in to hear all about it. I told her as well as I could, but she wasn't satisfied. If Dick took it so quietly, she declared, I couldn't have made it strong enough.

"If you had seen Dick's face," I said, "you would have thought I made it plenty strong. And I'd like to know what Aunt Tommy will say to all this when she finds out."

"Well, you didn't tell a thing but what was true," said Jill.

The next evening was Dick's regular night for coming, but he didn't come, although Jill and I went down the lane a dozen times to watch for him. The night after that was prayer-meeting night. Dick had always walked home with Aunt Tommy and us, but that night he didn't. He only just bowed and smiled as he passed us in the porch. Aunt Tommy hardly spoke all the way home, only just held tight to Jill's and my hands. But after we got home she seemed in great spirits and laughed and chatted with Father and Mother.

"What does this mean?" asked Jill, grabbing me in the hall on our way to bed.

"You'd better get another novel from the cook and find out," I said grouchily. I was disgusted with things in general and Dick in particular.

The three weeks that followed were awful. Dick never came near Owlwood. Jill and I fought every day, we were so cross and disappointed. Nothing had come out right, and Jill blamed it all on me. She said I must have made it too strong. There was no fun in anything, not even in going to church. Dick hardly thumped the pulpit at all and when he did it was only a measly little thump. But Aunt Tommy didn't seem to worry any. She sang and laughed and joked from morning to night.

"She doesn't mind Dick's making an ass of himself, anyway, that's one consolation," I said to Jill.

"She is breaking her heart about it," said Jill, "and that's your consolation!"

"I don't believe it," I said. "What makes you think so?"

"She cries every night," said Jill. "I can tell by the look of her eyes in the morning."

"She doesn't look half as woebegone over it as you do," I said.

"If I had her reason for looking woebegone I wouldn't look it either," said Jill.

I asked her to explain her meaning, but she only said that little boys couldn't understand those things.

Things went on like this for another week. Then they reached—so Jill says—a climax. If Jill knows what that means I don't. But Pinky Carewe was the climax. Pinky's name is James, but Jill and I always called him Pinky because we couldn't bear him. He took to calling at Owlwood and one evening he took Aunt Tommy out driving. Then Jill came to me.

"Something has got to be done," she said resolutely. "I am not going to have Pinky Carewe for an Uncle Tommy and that is all there is about it. You must go straight to Dick and tell him the truth about the New York man."

I looked at Jill to see if she were in earnest. When I saw that she was I said, "I wouldn't take all the gems of Golconda and go and tell Dick that I'd been hoaxing him. You can do it yourself, Jill Gordon."

"You didn't tell him anything that wasn't true," said Jill.

"I don't know how a minister might look upon it," I said. "Anyway, I won't go."

"Then I suppose I've got to," said Jill very dolefully.

"Yes, you'll have to," I said.

And this finishes my part of the story, and Jill is going to tell the rest. But you needn't believe everything she says about me in it.

Jill's Side of It

Jacky has made a fearful muddle of his part, but I suppose I shall just have to let it go. You couldn't expect much better of a boy. But I am determined to re-describe Aunt Tommy, for the way Jacky has done it is just disgraceful. I know exactly how to do it, the way it is always done in stories.

Aunt Tommy is divinely beautiful. Her magnificent wealth of burnished auburn hair flows back in amethystine waves from her sun-kissed brow. Her eyes are gloriously dark and deep, like midnight lakes mirroring the stars of heaven; her features are like sculptured marble and her mouth is like a trembling, curving Cupid's bow (this is a classical allusion) luscious and glowing as a dewy rose. Her creamy skin is as fair and flawless as the inner petals of a white lily. (She may have a weeny teeny freckle or two in summer, but you'd never notice.) Her slender form is matchless in its symmetry and her voice is like the ripple of a woodland brook.

There, I'm sure that's ever so much better than Jacky's description, and now I can proceed with a clear conscience.

Well, I didn't like the idea of going and explaining to Dick very much, but it had to be done unless I wanted to run the risk of having Pinky Carewe in the family. So I went the next morning.

I put on my very prettiest pink organdie dress and did my hair the new way, which is very becoming to me. When you are going to have an important interview with a man it is always well to look your very best. I put on my big hat with the wreath of pink roses that Aunt Tommy had brought me from New York and took my spandy ruffled parasol.

"With your shield or upon it, Jill," said Jacky when I started. (This is another classical allusion.)

I went straight up the hill and down the road to the manse where Dick lived with his old housekeeper, Mrs. Dodge. She came to the door when I knocked and I said, very politely, "Can I see the Reverend Stephen Richmond, if you please?"

Mrs. Dodge went upstairs and came right back saying would I please go up to the study. Up I went, my heart in my mouth, I can tell you, and there was Dick among his books, looking so pale and sorrowful and interesting, for all the world like Lord Algernon Francis in the splendid serial in the paper cook took. There was a Madonna on his desk that looked just like Aunt Tommy.

"Good evening, Miss Elizabeth," said Dick, just as if I were grown up, you know. "Won't you sit down? Try that green velvet chair. I am sure it was created for a pink dress and unfortunately neither Mrs. Dodge nor I possess one. How are all your people?"

"We are all pretty well; thank you," I said, "except Aunt Tommy. She—" I was going to say, "She cries every night after she goes to bed," but I remembered just in time that if I were in Aunt Tommy's place I wouldn't want a man to know I cried about him even if I did. So I said instead "—she has got a cold."

"Ah, indeed, I am sorry to hear it," said Dick, politely but coldly, as if it were part of his duty as a minister to be sorry for anybody who had a cold, but as if, apart from that, it was not a concern of his if Aunt Tommy had galloping consumption.

"And Jack and I are terribly harrowed up in our minds," I went on. "That is what I've come up to see you about."

"Well, tell me all about it," said Dick.

"I'm afraid to," I said. "I know you'll be cross even if you are a minister. It's about what Jack told you about that man in New York and Aunt Tommy."

Dick turned as red as fire.

"I'd rather not discuss your Aunt Bertha's affairs," he said stiffly.

"You must hear this," I cried, feeling thankful that Jacky hadn't come after all, for he'd never have got any further ahead after that snub. "It's all a mistake. There is a man in New York and he just worships Aunt Tommy and she just adores him. But he's seventy years old and he's her Uncle Matthew who brought her up ever since her father died and you've heard her talking about him a hundred times. That's all, cross my heart solemn and true."

You never saw anything like Dick's face when I stopped. It looked just like a sunrise. But he said slowly, "Why did Jacky tell me such a—tell me it in such a way?"

"We wanted to make you jealous," I said. "I put Jacky up to it."

"I didn't think it was in either of you to do such a thing," said Dick reproachfully.

"Oh, Dick," I cried—fancy my calling him Dick right to his face! Jacky will never believe I really did it. He says I would never have dared. But it wasn't daring at all, it was just forgetting. "Oh, Dick, we didn't mean any harm. We thought you weren't getting on fast enough and we wanted to stir you up like they do in books. We thought if we made you jealous it would work all right. We didn't mean any harm. Oh, please forgive us!"

I was just ready to cry. But that dear Dick leaned over the table and patted my hand.

"There, there, it's all right. I understand and of course I forgive you. Don't cry, sweetheart."

The way Dick said "sweetheart" was perfectly lovely. I envied Aunt Tommy, and I wanted to keep on crying so that he would go on comforting me.

"And you'll come back to see Aunt Tommy again?" I said.

Dick's face clouded over; he got up and walked around the room several times before he said a word. Then he came and sat down beside me and explained it all to me, just as if I were grown up.

"Sweetheart, we'll talk this all out. You see, it is this way. Your Aunt Bertha is the sweetest woman in the world. But I'm only a poor minister and I have no right to ask her to share my life of hard work and self-denial. And even if I dared I know she wouldn't do it. She doesn't care anything for me except as a friend. I never meant to tell her I cared for her but I couldn't help going to Owlwood, even though I knew it was a weakness on my part. So now that I'm out of the habit of going I think it would be wisest to stay out. It hurts dreadfully, but it would hurt worse after a while. Don't you agree with me, Miss Elizabeth?"

I thought hard and fast. If I were in Aunt Tommy's place I mightn't want a man to know I cried about him, but I was quite sure I'd rather have him know than have him stay away because he didn't know. So I spoke right up.

"No, I don't, Mr. Richmond; Aunt Tommy does care—you just ask her. She cries every blessed night because you never come to Owlwood."

"Oh, Elizabeth!" said Dick.

He got up and stalked about the room again.

"You'll come back?" I said.

"Yes," he answered.

I drew a long breath. It was such a responsibility off my mind.

"Then you'd better come down with me right off," I said, "for Pinky Carewe had her out driving last night and I want a stop put to that as soon as possible. Even if he is rich he's a perfect pig."

Dick got his hat and came. We walked up the road in lovely creamy yellow twilight and I was, oh, so happy.

"Isn't it just like a novel?" I said.

"I am afraid, Elizabeth," said Dick preachily, "that you read too many novels, and not the right kind, either. Some of these days I am going to ask you to promise me that you will read no more books except those your mother and I pick out for you."

You don't know how squelched I felt. And I knew I would have to promise, too, for Dick can make me do anything he likes.

When we got to Owlwood I left Dick in the parlour and flew up to Aunt Tommy's room. I found her all scrunched up on her bed in the dark with her face in the pillows.

"Aunt Tommy, Dick is down in the parlour and he wants to see you," I said.

Didn't Aunt Tommy fly up, though!

"Oh, Jill—but I'm not fit to be seen—tell him I'll be down in a few minutes."

I knew Aunt Tommy wanted to fix her hair and dab rose-water on her eyes, so I trotted meekly down and told Dick. Then I flew out to Jacky and dragged him around to the glass door. It was all hung over with vines and a wee bit ajar so that we could see and hear everything that went on.

Jacky said it was only sneaks that listened—but he didn't say it until next day. At the time he listened just as hard as I did. I didn't care if it was mean. I just had to listen. I was perfectly wild to hear how a man would propose and how a girl would accept and it was too good a chance to lose.

Presently in sweeps Aunt Tommy, in an elegant dress, not a hair out of place. She looked perfectly sweet, only her nose was a little red. Dick looked at her for just a moment, then he stepped forward and took her right into his arms.

Aunt Tommy drew back her head for just a second as if she were going to crush him in the dust, and then she just all kind of crumpled up and her face went down on his shoulder.

"Oh—Bertha—I—love—you—I—love you," he said, just like that, all quick and jerky.

"You—you have taken a queer way of showing it," said Aunt Tommy, all muffled.

"I—I—was led to believe that there was another man—whom you cared for—and I thought you were only trifling with me. So I sulked like a jealous fool. Bertha, darling, you do love me a little, don't you?"

Aunt Tommy lifted her head and stuck up her mouth and he kissed her. And there it was, all over, and they were engaged as quick as that, mind you. He didn't even go down on his knees. There was nothing romantic about it and I was never so disgusted in my life. When I grow up and anybody proposes to me he will have to be a good deal more flowery and eloquent than that, I can tell you, if he wants me to listen to him.

I left Jacky peeking still and I went to bed. After a long time Aunt Tommy came up to my room and sat down on my bed in the moonlight.

"You dear blessed Elizabeth!" she said.

"It's all right then, is it?" I asked.

"Yes, it is all right, thanks to you, dearie. We are to be married in October and somebody must be my little flower girl."

"I think Dick will make a splendid husband," I said. "But Aunt Tommy, you mustn't be too hard on Jacky. He only wanted to help things along, and it was I who put him up it in the first place."

"You have atoned by going and confessing," said Aunt Tommy with a hug, "Jacky had no business to put that off on you. I'll forgive him, of course, but I'll punish him by not letting him know that I will for a little while. Then I'll ask him to be a page at my wedding."

Well, the wedding came off last week. It was a perfectly gorgeous affair. Aunt Tommy's dress was a dream—and so was mine, all pink silk and chiffon and carnations. Jacky made a magnificent page too, in a suit of white velvet. The wedding cake was four stories high, and Dick looked perfectly handsome. He kissed me too, right after he kissed Aunt Tommy.

So everything turned out all right, and I believe Dick would never have dared to speak up if we hadn't helped things along. But Jacky and I have decided that we will never meddle in an affair of the kind again. It is too hard on the nerves.

LUCY MAUD MONTGOMERY SHORT STORIES, 1907 TO 1908

A Millionaire's Proposal

Thrush Hill, Oct. 5, 18—.

It is all settled at last, and in another week I shall have left Thrush Hill. I am a little bit sorry and a great bit glad. I am going to Montreal to spend the winter with Alicia.

Alicia—it used to be plain Alice when she lived at Thrush Hill and made her own dresses and trimmed her own hats—is my half-sister. She is eight years older than I am. We are both orphans, and Aunt Elizabeth brought us up here at Thrush Hill, the most delightful old country place in the world, half smothered in big willows and poplars, every one of which I have climbed in the early tomboy days of gingham pinafores and sun-bonnets.

When Alicia was eighteen she married Roger Gresham, a man of forty. The world said that she married him for his money. I dare say she did. Alicia was tired of poverty.

I don't blame her. Very likely I shall do the same thing one of these days, if I get the chance—for I too am tired of poverty.

When Alicia went to Montreal she wanted to take me with her, but I wanted to be outdoors, romping in the hay or running wild in the woods with Jack.

Jack Willoughby—Dr. John H. Willoughby, it reads on his office door—was the son of our nearest neighbour. We were chums always, and when he went away to college I was heartbroken.

The vacations were the only joy of my life then.

I don't know just when I began to notice a change in Jack, but when he came home two years ago, a full-fledged M.D.—a great, tall, broad-shouldered fellow, with the sweetest moustache, and lovely thick black hair, just made for poking one's fingers through—I realized it to the full. Jack was grown up. The dear old days of bird-nesting and nutting and coasting and fishing and general delightful goings-on were over forever.

I was sorry at first. I wanted "Jack." "Dr. Willoughby" seemed too distinguished and far away.

I suppose he found a change in me, too. I had put on long skirts and wore my hair up. I had also found out that I had a complexion, and that sunburn was not becoming. I honestly thought I looked pretty, but Jack surveyed me with decided disapprobation.

"What have you done to yourself? You don't look like the same girl. I'd never know you in that rig-out, with all those flippery-trippery curls all over your head. Why don't you comb your hair straight back, and let it hang in a braided tail, like you used to?"

This didn't suit me at all. When I expect a compliment and get something quite different I always get snippy. So I said, with what I intended to be crushing dignity, "that I supposed I wasn't the same girl; I had grown up, and if he didn't like my curls he needn't look at them. For my part, I thought them infinitely preferable to that horrid, conceited-looking moustache he had grown."

"I'll shave it off if it doesn't suit you," said Jack amiably.

Jack is always so provokingly good-humoured. When you've taken pains and put yourself out—even to the extent of fibbing about a moustache—to exasperate a person, there is nothing more annoying than to have him keep perfectly angelic.

But after a while Jack and I adjusted ourselves to the change in each other and became very good friends again. It was quite a different friendship from the old, but it was very pleasant. Yes, it was; I *will* admit that much.

I was provoked at Jack's determination to settle down for life in Valleyfield, a horrible, humdrum, little country village.

"You'll never make your fortune there, Jack," I said spitefully. "You'll just be a poor, struggling country doctor all your life, and you'll be grey at forty."

"I don't expect to make a fortune, Kitty," said Jack quietly. "Do you think that is the one desirable thing? I shall never be a rich man. But riches are not the only thing that makes life pleasant."

"Well, I think they have a good deal to do with it, anyhow," I retorted. "It's all very well to pretend to despise wealth, but it's generally a case of sour grapes. *I* will own up honestly that I'd *love* to be rich."

It always seems to make Jack blue and grumpy when I talk like that. I suppose that is one reason why he never asked me to settle down in life as a country doctor's wife. Another was, no doubt, that I always nipped his sentimental sproutings religiously in the bud.

Three weeks ago Alicia wrote to me, asking me to spend the winter with her. Her letters always make me just gasp with longing for the life they describe.

Jack's face, when I told him about it, was so woebegone that I felt a stab of remorse, even in the heyday of my delight.

"Do you really mean it, Kitty? Are you going away to leave me?"

"You won't miss me much," I said flippantly—I had a creepy, crawly presentiment that a scene of some kind was threatening—"and I'm awfully tired of Thrush Hill and country life, Jack. I suppose it is horribly ungrateful of me to say so, but it is the truth."

"I shall miss you," he said soberly.

Somehow he had my hands in his. *How* did he ever get them? I was sure I had them safely tucked out of harm's way behind me. "You know, Kitty, that I love you. I am a poor man—perhaps I may never be anything else—and this may seem to you very presumptuous. But I cannot let you go like this. Will you be my wife, dear?"

Wasn't it horribly straightforward and direct? So like Jack! I tried to pull my hands away, but he held them fast. There was nothing to do but answer him. That "no" I had determined to say must be said, but, oh! how woefully it did stick in my throat!

And I honestly believe that by the time I got it out it would have been transformed into a "yes," in spite of me, had it not been for a certain paragraph in Alicia's letter which came providentially to my mind:

> Not to flatter you, Katherine, you are a beauty, my dear—if your photo is to be trusted. If you have not discovered that fact before—how should you, indeed, in a place like Thrush Hill?—you soon will in Montreal. With your face and figure you will make a sensation.
>
> There is to be a nephew of the Sinclairs here this winter. He is an American, immensely wealthy, and will be the catch of the season. A word to the wise, etc. Don't get into any foolish entanglement down there. I have heard some gossip of you and our old playfellow, Jack Willoughby. I hope it is nothing but gossip. You can do better than that, Katherine.

That settled Jack's fate, if there ever had been any doubt.

"Don't talk like that, Jack," I said hurriedly. "It is all nonsense. I think a great deal of you as a friend and—and—all that, you know. But I can never marry you."

"Are you sure, Kitty?" said Jack earnestly. "Don't you care for me at all?"

It was horrid of Jack to ask that question!

"No," I said miserably, "not—not in that way, Jack. Oh, don't ever say anything like this to me again."

He let go of my hands then, white to the lips.

"Oh, don't look like that, Jack," I entreated.

"I can't help it," he said in a low voice. "But I won't bother you again, dear. It was foolish of me to expect—to hope for anything of the sort. You are a thousand times too good for me, I know."

"Oh, indeed I'm not, Jack," I protested. "If you knew how horrid I am, really, you'd be glad and thankful for your escape. Oh, Jack, I wish people never grew up."

Jack smiled sadly.

"Don't feel badly over this, Kitty. It isn't your fault. Good night, dear."

He turned my face up and kissed me squarely on the mouth. He had never kissed me since the summer before he went away to college. Somehow it didn't seem a bit the same as it used to; it was—nicer now.

After he went away I came upstairs and had a good, comfortable howl. Then I buried the whole affair decently. I am not going to think of it any more.

I shall always have the highest esteem for Jack, and I hope he will soon find some nice girl who will make him happy. Mary Carter would jump at him, I know. To be sure, she is as homely as she can be and live. But, then, Jack is always telling me how little he cares for beauty, so I have no doubt she will suit him admirably.

As for myself—well, I am ambitious. I don't suppose my ambition is a very lofty one, but such as it is I mean to hunt it down. Come. Let me put it down in black and white, once for all, and see how it looks:

I mean to marry the rich nephew of the Sinclairs.

There! It is out, and I feel better. How mercenary and awful it looks written out in cold blood like that. I wouldn't have Jack or Aunt Elizabeth—dear, unworldly old soul—see it for the world. But I wouldn't mind Alicia.

Poor dear Jack!

Montreal, Dec. 16, 18—.

This is a nice way to keep a journal. But the days when I could write regularly are gone by. That was when I was at Thrush Hill.

I am having a simply divine time. How in the world did I ever contrive to live at Thrush Hill?

To be sure, I felt badly enough that day in October when I left it. When the train left Valleyfield I just cried like a baby.

Alicia and Roger welcomed me very heartily, and after the first week of homesickness—I shiver yet when I think of it—was over, I settled down to my new life as if I had been born to it.

Alicia has a magnificent home and everything heart could wish for—jewels, carriages, servants, opera boxes, and social position. Roger is a model husband apparently. I must also admit that he is a model brother-in-law.

I could feel Alicia looking me over critically the moment we met. I trembled with suspense, but I was soon relieved.

"Do you know, Katherine, I am glad to see that your photograph didn't flatter you. Photographs so often do, I am positively surprised at the way you have developed, my dear; you used to be such a scrawny little brown thing. By the way, I hope there is nothing between you and Jack Willoughby?"

"No, of course not," I answered hurriedly. I had intended to tell Alicia all about Jack, but when it came to the point I couldn't.

"I am glad of that," said Alicia, with a relieved air. "Of course, I've no doubt Jack is a good fellow enough. He was a nice boy. But he would not be a suitable husband for you, Katherine."

I knew that very well. That was just why I had refused him. But it made me wince to hear Alicia say it. I instantly froze up—Alicia says dignity is becoming to me—and Jack's name has never been mentioned between us since.

I made my bow to society at an "At Home" which Alicia gave for that purpose. She drilled me well beforehand, and I think I acquitted myself decently. Charlie Vankleek, whose verdict makes or mars every debutante in his set, has approved of me. He called me a beauty, and everybody now believes that I am one, and greets me accordingly.

I met Gus Sinclair at Mrs. Brompton's dinner. Alicia declares it was a case of love at first sight. If so, I must confess that it was all on one side.

Mr. Sinclair is undeniably ugly—even Alicia has to admit that—and can't hold a candle to Jack in point of looks, for Jack, poor boy, was handsome, if he were nothing else. But, as Alicia does not fail to remind me, Mr. Sinclair's homeliness is well gilded.

Apart from his appearance, I really liked him very much. He is a gentlemanly little fellow—his head reaches about to my shoulder—cultured and travelled, and can talk splendidly, which Jack never could.

He took me into dinner at Mrs. Brompton's, and was very attentive. You may imagine how many angelic glances I received from the other candidates for his favour.

Since then I have been having the gayest time imaginable. Dances, dinners, luncheons, afternoon teas, "functions" to no end, and all delightful.

Aunt Elizabeth writes to me, but I have never heard a word from Jack. He seems to have forgotten my existence completely. No doubt he has consoled himself with Mary Carter.

Well, that is all for the best, but I must say I did not think Jack could have forgotten me so soon or so absolutely. Of course it does not make the least difference to me.

The Sinclairs and the Bromptons and the Curries are to dine here tonight. I can see myself reflected in the long mirror before me, and I really think my appearance will satisfy even Gus Sinclair's critical eye. I am pale, as usual, I never have any colour. That used to be one of Jack's grievances. He likes pink and white milkmaidish girls. My "magnificent pallor" didn't suit him at all.

But, what is more to the purpose, it suits Gus Sinclair. He admires the statuesque style.

Montreal, Jan. 20, 18—.

Here it is a whole month since my last entry. I am sitting here decked out in "gloss of satin and glimmer of pearls" for Mrs. Currie's dance. These few minutes, after I emerge from the hands of my maid and before the carriage is announced, are almost the only ones I ever have to myself.

I am having a good time still. Somehow, though, it isn't as exciting as it used to be. I'm afraid I'm very changeable. I believe I must be homesick.

I'd love to get a glimpse of dear old Thrush Hill and Aunt Elizabeth, and J—but, no! I will not write that.

Mr. Sinclair has not spoken yet, but there is no doubt that he soon will. Of course, I shall accept him when he does, and I coolly told Alicia so when she just as coolly asked me what I meant to do.

"Certainly, I shall marry him," I said crossly, for the subject always irritates me. "Haven't I been laying myself out all winter to catch him? That is the bold, naked truth, and ugly enough it is. My dearly beloved sister, I mean to accept Mr. Sinclair, without any hesitation, whenever I get the chance."

"I give you credit for more sense than to dream of doing anything else," said Alicia in relieved tones. "Katherine, you are a very lucky girl."

"Because I am going to marry a rich man for his money?" I said coldly.

Sometimes I get snippy with Alicia these days.

"No," said my half-sister in an exasperated way. "Why will you persist in speaking in that way? You are very provoking. It is not likely I would wish to see you throw yourself away on a poor man, and I'm sure you must like Gus."

"Oh, yes, I like him well enough," I said listlessly. "To be sure, I did think once, in my salad days, that liking wasn't quite all in an affair of this kind. I was absurd enough to imagine that love had something to do with it."

"Don't talk so nonsensically," said Alicia sharply. "Love! Well, of course, you ought to love your husband, and you will. He loves you enough, at all events."

"Alicia," I said earnestly, looking her straight in the face and speaking bluntly enough to have satisfied even Jack's love of straightforwardness, "you married for money and position, so people say. Are you happy?"

For the first time that I remembered, Alicia blushed. She was very angry.

"Yes, I did marry for money," she said sharply, "and I don't regret it. Thank heaven, I never was a fool."

"Don't be vexed, Alicia," I entreated. "I only asked because—well, it is no matter."

Montreal, Jan. 25, 18—.

It is bedtime, but I am too excited and happy and miserable to sleep. Jack has been here—dear old Jack! How glad I was to see him.

His coming was so unexpected. I was sitting alone in my room this afternoon—I believe I was moping—when Bessie brought up his card. I gave it one rapturous look and tore downstairs, passing Alicia in the hall like a whirlwind, and burst into the drawing-room in a most undignified way.

"Jack!" I cried, holding out both hands to him in welcome.

There he was, just the same old Jack, with his splendid big shoulders and his lovely brown eyes. And his necktie was crooked, too; as soon as I could get my hands free I put them up and straightened it out for him. How nice and old-timey that was!

"So you are glad to see me, Kitty?" he said as he squeezed my hands in his big strong paws.

"'Deed and 'deed I am, Jack. I thought you had forgotten me altogether. And I've been so homesick and so—so everything," I said incoherently. "And, oh, Jack, I've so many questions to ask I don't know where to begin. Tell me all the Thrush Hill and Valleyfield news, tell me everything that has happened since I left. How many people have you killed off? And, oh, why didn't you come to see me before?"

"I didn't think I should be wanted, Kitty," Jack answered quietly. "You seemed to be so absorbed in your new life that old friends and interests were crowded out."

"So I was at first," I answered penitently. "I was dazzled, you know. The glare was too much for my Thrush Hill brown. But it's different now. How did you happen to come, Jack?"

"I had to come to Montreal on business, and I thought it would be too bad if I went back without coming to see what they had been doing in Vanity Fair to my little playmate."

"Well, what do you think they have been doing?" I asked saucily.

I had on a particularly fetching gown and knew I was looking my best. Jack, however, looked me over with his head on one side.

"Well, I don't know, Kitty," he said slowly. "That is a stunning sort of dress you have on—not so pretty, though, as that old blue muslin you used to wear last summer—and your hair is pretty good. But you look rather disdainful and, after all, I believe I prefer Thrush Hill Kitty."

How like Jack that was. He never thought me really pretty, and he is too honest to pretend he does.

But I didn't care. I just laughed, and we sat down together and had a long, delightful, chummy talk.

Jack told me all the Valleyfield gossip, not forgetting to mention that Mary Carter was going to be married to a minister in June. Jack didn't seem to mind it a bit, so I guess he couldn't have been particularly interested in Mary.

In due time Alicia sailed in. I suppose she had found out from Bessie who my caller was, and felt rather worried over the length of our tête-à-tête.

She greeted Jack very graciously, but with a certain polite condescension of which she is past mistress. I am sure Jack felt it, for, as soon as he decently could, he got up to go. Alicia asked him to remain to dinner.

"We are having a few friends to dine with us, but it is quite an informal affair," she said sweetly.

I felt that Jack glanced at me for the fraction of a second. But I remembered that Gus Sinclair was coming too, and I did not look at him.

Then he declined quietly. He had a business engagement, he said.

I suppose Alicia had noticed that look at me, for she showed her claws.

"Don't forget to call any time you are in Montreal," she said more sweetly than ever. "I am sure Katherine will always be glad to see any of her old friends, although some of her new ones *are* proving very absorbing—one, in especial. Don't blush, Katherine, I am sure Mr. Willoughby won't tell any tales out of school to your old Valleyfield friends."

I was not blushing, and I was furious. It was really too bad of Alicia, although I don't see why I need have cared.

Alicia kept her eye on us both until Jack was fairly gone. Then she remarked in the patronizing tone which I detest:

"Really, Katherine, Jack Willoughby has developed into quite a passable-looking fellow, although he is rather shabby. But I suppose he is poor."

"Yes," I answered curtly, "he is poor, in everything except youth and manhood and goodness and truth! But I suppose those don't count for anything."

Whereupon Alicia lifted her eyebrows and looked me over.

Just at dusk a box arrived with Jack's compliments. It was full of lovely white carnations, and must have cost the extravagant fellow more than he has any business to waste on flowers. I was beast enough to put them on when I went down to listen to another man's love-making.

This evening I sparkled and scintillated with unusual brilliancy, for Jack's visit and my consequent crossing of swords with Alicia had produced a certain elation of spirits. When Gus Sinclair was leaving he asked if he might see me alone tomorrow afternoon.

I knew what that meant, and a cold shiver went up and down my backbone. But I looked down at him—spick-and-span and glossy—*his* neckties are never crooked—and said, yes, he might come at three o'clock.

Alicia had noticed our aside—when did anything ever escape her?—and when he was gone she asked, significantly, what secret he had been telling me.

"He wants to see me alone tomorrow afternoon. I suppose you know what that means, Alicia?"

"Ah," purred Alicia, "I congratulate you, my dear."

"Aren't your congratulations a little premature?" I asked coldly. "I haven't accepted him yet."

"But you will?"

"Oh, certainly. Isn't it what we've schemed and angled for? I'm very well satisfied."

And so I am. But I wish it hadn't come so soon after Jack's visit, because I feel rather upset yet. Of course I like Gus Sinclair very much, and I am sure I shall be very fond of him.

Well, I must go to bed now and get my beauty sleep. I don't want to be haggard and hollow-eyed at that important interview tomorrow—an interview that will decide my destiny.

Thrush Hill, May 6, 18—.

Well, it did decide it, but not exactly in the way I anticipated. I can look back on the whole affair quite calmly now, but I wouldn't live it over again for all the wealth of Ind.

That day when Gus Sinclair came I was all ready for him. I had put on my very prettiest new gown to do honour to the occasion, and Alicia smilingly assured me I was looking very well.

"And *so* cool and composed. Will you be able to keep that up? Don't you really feel a little nervous, Katherine?"

"Not in the least," I said. "I suppose I ought to be, according to traditions, but I never felt less flustered in my life."

When Bessie brought up Gus Sinclair's card Alicia dropped a pecky little kiss on my cheek, and pushed me toward the door. I went down calmly, although I'll admit that my heart *was* beating wildly. Gus Sinclair was plainly nervous, but I was composed enough for both. You would really have thought that I was in the habit of being proposed to by a millionaire every day.

"I suppose you know what I have come to say," he said, standing before me, as I leaned gracefully back in a big chair, having taken care that the folds of my dress fell just as they should.

And then he proceeded to say it in a rather jumbled-up fashion, but very sincerely.

I remember thinking at the time that he must have composed the speech in his head the night before, and rehearsed it several times, but was forgetting it in spots.

When he ended with the self-same question that Jack had asked me three months before at Thrush Hill he stopped and took my hands.

I looked up at him. His good, homely face was close to mine, and in his eyes was an unmistakable look of love and tenderness.

I opened my mouth to say yes.

And then there came over me in one rush the most awful realization of the sacrilege I was going to commit.

I forgot everything except that I loved Jack Willoughby, and that I could never, never marry anybody in the world except him.

Then I pulled my hands away and burst into hysterical, undignified tears.

"I beg your pardon," said Mr. Sinclair. "I did not mean to startle you. Have I been too abrupt? Surely you must have known—you must have expected—"

"Yes—yes—I knew," I cried miserably, "and I intended right up to this very minute to marry you. I'm so sorry—but I can't—I can't."

"I don't understand," he said in a bewildered tone. "If you expected it, then why—why—don't you care for me?"

"No, that's just it," I sobbed. "I don't love you at all—and I do love somebody else. But he is poor, and I hate poverty. So I refused him, and I meant to marry you just because you are rich."

Such a pained look came over his face. "I did not think this of you," he said in a low tone.

"Oh, I know I have acted shamefully," I said. "You can't think any worse of me than I do of myself. How you must despise me!"

"No," he said, with a grim smile, "if I did it would be easier for me. I might not love you then. Don't distress yourself, Katherine. I do not deny that I feel greatly hurt and disappointed, but I am glad you have been true to yourself at last. Don't cry, dear."

"You're very good," I answered disconsolately, "but all the same the fact remains that I have behaved disgracefully to you, and I know you think so. Oh, Mr. Sinclair, please, please, go away. I feel so miserably ashamed of myself that I cannot look you in the face."

"I am going, dear," he said gently. "I know all this must be very painful to you, but it is not easy for me, either."

"Can you forgive me?" I said wistfully.

"Yes, my dear, completely. Do not let yourself be unhappy over this. Remember that I will always be your friend. Goodbye."

He held out his hand and gave mine an earnest clasp. Then he went away.

I remained in the drawing-room, partly because I wanted to finish out my cry, and partly because, miserable coward that I was, I didn't dare face Alicia. Finally she came in, her face wreathed with anticipatory smiles. But when her eyes fell on my forlorn, crumpled self she fairly jumped.

"Katherine, what is the matter?" she asked sharply. "Didn't Mr. Sinclair—"

"Yes, he did," I said desperately. "And I've refused him. There now, Alicia!"

Then I waited for the storm to burst. It didn't all at once. The shock was too great, and at first quite paralyzed my half-sister.

"Katherine," she gasped, "are you crazy? Have you lost your senses?"

"No, I've just come to them. It's true enough, Alicia. You can scold all you like. I know I deserve it, and I won't flinch. I did really intend to take him, but when it came to the point I couldn't. I didn't love him."

Then, indeed, the storm burst. I never saw Alicia so angry before, and I never got so roundly abused. But even Alicia has her limits, and at last she grew calmer.

"You have behaved disgracefully," she concluded. "I am disgusted with you. You have encouraged Gus Sinclair markedly right along, and now you throw him over like this. I never dreamed that you were capable of such unwomanly behaviour."

"That's a hard word, Alicia," I protested feebly.

She dealt me a withering glance. "It does not begin to be as hard as your shameful conduct merits. To think of losing a fortune like that for the sake of sentimental folly! I didn't think you were such a consummate fool."

"I suppose you absorbed all the sense of our family," I said drearily. "There now, Alicia, do leave me alone. I'm down in the very depths already."

"What do you mean to do now?" said Alicia scornfully. "Go back to Valleyfield and marry that starving country doctor of yours, I suppose?"

I flared up then; Alicia might abuse me all she liked, but I wasn't going to hear a word against Jack.

"Yes, I will, if he'll have me," I said, and I marched out of the room and upstairs, with my head very high.

Of course I decided to leave Montreal as soon as I could. But I couldn't get away within a week, and it was a very unpleasant one. Alicia treated me with icy indifference, and I knew I should never be reinstated in her good graces.

To my surprise, Roger took my part. "Let the girl alone," he told Alicia. "If she doesn't love Sinclair, she was right in refusing him. I, for one, am glad that she has got enough truth and womanliness in her to keep her from selling herself."

Then he came to the library where I was moping, and laid his hand on my head.

"Little girl," he said earnestly, "no matter what anyone says to you, never marry a man for his money or for any other reason on earth except because you love him."

This comforted me greatly, and I did not cry myself to sleep that night as usual.

At last I got away. I had telegraphed to Jack: "Am coming home Wednesday; meet me at train," and I knew he would be there. How I longed to see him again—dear, old, badly treated Jack.

I got to Valleyfield just at dusk. It was a rainy evening, and everything was slush and fog and gloom. But away up I saw the home light at Thrush Hill, and Jack was waiting for me on the platform.

"Oh, Jack!" I said, clinging to him, regardless of appearances. "Oh, I'm so glad to be back."

"That's right, Kitty. I knew you wouldn't forget us. How well you are looking!"

"I suppose I ought to be looking wretched," I said penitently. "I've been behaving very badly, Jack. Wait till we get away from the crowd and I'll tell you all about it."

And I did.

I didn't gloss over anything, but just confessed the whole truth. Jack heard me through in silence, and then he kissed me.

"Can you forgive me, Jack, and take me back?" I whispered, cuddling up to him.

And he said—but, on second thought, I will not write down what he said.

We are to be married in June.

A Substitute Journalist

Clifford Baxter came into the sitting-room where Patty was darning stockings and reading a book at the same time. Patty could do things like that. The stockings were well darned too, and Patty understood and remembered what she read.

Clifford flung himself into a chair with a sigh of weariness. "Tired?" queried Patty sympathetically.

"Yes, rather. I've been tramping about the wharves all day gathering longshore items. But, Patty, I've got a chance at last. Tonight as I was leaving the office Mr. Harmer gave me a real assignment for tomorrow—two of them in fact, but only one of importance. I'm to go and interview Mr. Keefe on this new railroad bill that's up before the legislature. He's in town, visiting his old college friend, Mr. Reid, and he's quite big game. I wouldn't have had the assignment, of course, if there'd been anyone else to send, but most of the staff will be away all day tomorrow to see about that mine explosion at Midbury or the teamsters' strike at Bainsville, and I'm the only one available. Harmer gave me a pretty broad hint that it was my chance to win my spurs, and that if I worked up a good article out of it I'd stand a fair show of being taken on permanently next month when Alsop leaves. There'll be a shuffle all round then, you know. Everybody on the staff will be pushed up a peg, and that will leave a vacant space at the foot."

Patty threw down her darning needle and clapped her hands with delight. Clifford gazed at her admiringly, thinking that he had the prettiest sister in the world—she was so bright, so eager, so rosy.

"Oh, Clifford, how splendid!" she exclaimed. "Just as we'd begun to give up hope too. Oh, you must get the position! You must hand in a good write-up. Think what it means to us."

"Yes, I know." Clifford dropped his head on his hand and stared rather moodily at the lamp. "But my joy is chastened, Patty. Of course I want to get the permanency, since it seems to be the only possible thing, but you know my heart isn't really in newspaper work. The plain truth is I don't like it, although I do my best. You know Father always said I was a born mechanic. If I only could get a position somewhere among machinery—that would be my choice. There's one vacant in the Steel and Iron Works at Bancroft—but of course I've no chance of getting it."

"I know. It's too bad," said Patty, returning to her stockings with a sigh. "I wish I were a boy with a foothold on the *Chronicle*. I firmly believe that I'd make a good newspaper woman, if such a thing had ever been heard of in Aylmer."

"That you would. You've twice as much knack in that line as I have. You seem to know by instinct just what to leave out and put in. I never do, and Harmer has to blue-pencil my copy mercilessly. Well, I'll do my best with this, as it's very necessary I should get the permanency, for I fear our family purse is growing very slim. Mother's face has a new wrinkle of worry every day. It hurts me to see it."

"And me," sighed Patty. "I do wish I could find something to do too. If only we both could get positions, everything would be all right. Mother wouldn't have to worry so. Don't say anything about this chance to her until you see what comes of it. She'd only be doubly disappointed if nothing did. What is your other assignment?"

"Oh, I've got to go out to Bancroft on the morning train and write up old Mr. Moreland's birthday celebration. He is a hundred years old, and there's going to be a presentation and speeches and that sort of thing. Nothing very exciting about it. I'll have to come back on the three o'clock train and hurry out to catch my politician before he leaves at five. Take a stroll down to meet my train, Patty. We can go out as far as Mr. Reid's house together, and the walk will do you good."

The Baxters lived in Aylmer, a lively little town with two newspapers, the *Chronicle* and the *Ledger*. Between these two was a sharp journalistic rivalry in the matter of "beats" and "scoops." In the preceding spring Clifford had been taken on the *Chronicle* on trial, as a sort of general handyman. There was no pay attached to the position, but he was getting training and there was the possibility of a permanency in September if he proved his mettle. Mr. Baxter had died two years before, and the failure of the company in which Mrs. Baxter's money was invested had left the little family dependent on their own resources. Clifford, who had cherished dreams of a course in mechanical engineering, knew that he must give them up and go to the first work that offered itself, which he did staunchly and uncomplainingly. Patty, who hitherto had had no designs on a "career," but had been sunnily content to be a home girl and Mother's right hand, also realized that it would be well to look about her for something to do. She was not really needed so far as the work of the little house went, and the whole burden must not be allowed to fall on Clifford's eighteen-year-old shoulders. Patty was his senior by a year, and ready to do her part unflinchingly.

The next afternoon Patty went down to meet Clifford's train. When it came, no Clifford appeared. Patty stared about her at the hurrying throngs in bewilderment. Where was Clifford? Hadn't he come on the train? Surely he must have, for there was no other until seven o'clock. She must have missed him somehow. Patty waited until everybody had left the station, then she walked slowly homeward. As the *Chronicle* office was on her way, she dropped in to see if Clifford had reported there.

She found nobody in the editorial offices except the office boy, Larry Brown, who promptly informed her that not only had Clifford not arrived, but that there was a telegram from him saying that he had missed his train. Patty gasped in dismay. It was dreadful!

"Where is Mr. Harmer?" she asked.

"He went home as soon as the afternoon edition came out. He left before the telegram came. He'll be furious when he finds out that nobody has gone to interview that foxy old politician," said Larry, who knew all about Clifford's assignment and its importance.

"Isn't there anyone else here to go?" queried Patty desperately.

Larry shook his head. "No, there isn't a soul in. We're mighty short-handed just now on account of the explosion and the strike."

Patty went downstairs and stood for a moment in the hall, rapt in reflection. If she had been at home, she verily believed she would have sat down and cried. Oh, it was too bad, too disappointing! Clifford would certainly lose all chance of the permanency, even if the irate news editor did not discharge him at once. What could she do? Could she do anything? She *must* do something.

"If I only could go in his place," moaned Patty softly to herself.

Then she started. Why not? Why not go and interview the big man herself? To be sure, she did not know a great deal about interviewing, still less about railroad bills, and nothing at all about politics. But if she did her best it might be better than nothing, and might at least save Clifford his present hold.

With Patty, to decide was to act. She flew back to the reporters' room, pounced on a pencil and tablet, and hurried off, her breath coming quickly, and her eyes shining with excitement. It was quite a long walk out to Mr. Reid's place and Patty was tired when she got there, but her courage was not a whit abated. She mounted the steps and rang the bell undauntedly.

"Can I see Mr.—Mr.—Mr.—" Patty paused for a moment in dismay. She had forgotten the name. The maid who had come to the door looked her over so superciliously that Patty flushed with indignation. "The gentleman who is visiting Mr. Reid," she said crisply. "I can't remember his name, but I've come to interview him on behalf of the *Chronicle*. Is he in?"

"If you mean Mr. Reefer, he is," said the maid quite respectfully. Evidently the *Chronicle*'s name carried weight in the Reid establishment. "Please come into the library. I'll go and tell him."

Patty had just time to seat herself at the table, spread out her paper imposingly, and assume a businesslike air when Mr. Reefer came in. He was a tall, handsome old man with white hair, jet-black eyes, and a mouth that made Patty hope she wouldn't stumble on any questions he wouldn't want to answer. Patty knew she would waste her breath if she did. A man with a mouth like that would never tell anything he didn't want to tell.

"Good afternoon. What can I do for you, madam?" inquired Mr. Reefer with the air and tone of a man who means to be courteous, but has no time or information to waste.

Patty was almost overcome by the "Madam." For a moment, she quailed. She couldn't ask that masculine sphinx questions! Then the thought of her mother's pale, careworn face flashed across her mind, and all her courage came back with an inspiriting rush. She bent forward to look eagerly into Mr. Reefer's carved, granite face, and said with a frank smile:

"I have come to interview you on behalf of the *Chronicle* about the railroad bill. It was my brother who had the assignment, but he has missed his train and I have come in his place because, you see, it is so important to us. So much depends on this assignment. Perhaps Mr. Harmer will give Clifford a permanent place on the staff if he turns in a good article about you. He is only handyman now. I just couldn't let him miss the chance—he might never have another. And it means so much to us and Mother."

"Are you a member of the *Chronicle* staff yourself?" inquired Mr. Reefer with a shade more geniality in his tone.

"Oh, no! I've nothing to do with it, so you won't mind my being inexperienced, will you? I don't know just what I should ask you, so won't you please just tell me everything about the bill, and Mr. Harmer can cut out what doesn't matter?"

Mr. Reefer looked at Patty for a few moments with a face about as expressive as a graven image. Perhaps he was thinking about the bill, and perhaps he was thinking what a bright, vivid, plucky little girl this was with her waiting pencil and her air that strove to be businesslike, and only succeeded in being eager and hopeful and anxious.

"I'm not used to being interviewed myself," he said slowly, "so I don't know very much about it. We're both green hands together, I imagine. But I'd like to help you out, so I don't mind telling you what I think about this bill, and its bearing on certain important interests."

Mr. Reefer proceeded to tell her, and Patty's pencil flew as she scribbled down his terse, pithy sentences. She found herself asking questions too, and enjoying it. For the first time, Patty thought she might rather like politics if she understood them—and they did not seem so hard to understand when a man like Mr. Reefer explained them. For half an hour he talked to her, and at the end of that time Patty was in full possession of his opinion on the famous railroad bill in all its aspects.

"There now, I'm talked out," said Mr. Reefer. "You can tell your news editor that you know as much about the railroad bill as Andrew Reefer knows. I hope you'll succeed in pleasing him, and that your brother will get the position he wants. But he shouldn't have missed that train. You tell him that. Boys with important things to do mustn't miss trains. Perhaps it's just as well he did in this case though, but tell him not to let it happen again."

Patty went straight home, wrote up her interview in ship-shape form, and took it down to the *Chronicle* office. There she found Mr. Harmer, scowling blackly. The little news editor looked to be in a rather bad temper, but he nodded not unkindly to Patty. Mr. Harmer knew the Baxters well and liked them, although he would have sacrificed them all without a qualm for a "scoop."

"Good evening, Patty. Take a chair. That brother of yours hasn't turned up yet. The next time I give him an assignment, he'll manage to be on hand in time to do it."

"Oh," cried Patty breathlessly, "please, Mr. Harmer, I have the interview here. I thought perhaps I could do it in Clifford's place, and I went out to Mr. Reid's and saw Mr. Reefer. He was very kind and—"

"Mr. who?" fairly shouted Mr. Harmer.

"Mr. Reefer—Mr. Andrew Reefer. He told me to tell you that this article contained all he knew or thought about the railroad bill and—"

But Mr. Harmer was no longer listening. He had snatched the neatly written sheets of Patty's report and was skimming over them with a practised eye. Then Patty thought he must have gone crazy. He danced around the office, waving the sheets in the air, and then he dashed frantically up the stairs to the composing room.

Ten minutes later, he returned and shook the mystified Patty by the hand.

"Patty, it's the biggest beat we've ever had! We've scooped not only the *Ledger*, but every other newspaper in the country. How did you do it? How did you ever beguile or bewitch Andrew Reefer into giving you an interview?"

"Why," said Patty in utter bewilderment, "I just went out to Mr. Reid's and asked for the gentleman who was visiting there—I'd forgotten his name—and Mr. Reefer came down and I told him my brother had been detailed to interview him on behalf of the *Chronicle* about the bill, and that Clifford had missed his train, and wouldn't he let me interview him in his place and excuse my inexperience—and he did."

"It wasn't Andrew Reefer I told Clifford to interview," laughed Mr. Harmer. "It was John C. Keefe. I didn't know Reefer was in town, but even if I had I wouldn't have thought it a particle of use to send a man to him. He has never consented to be interviewed before on any known subject, and he's been especially close-mouthed about this bill, although men from all the big papers in the country have been after him. He is notorious on that score. Why, Patty, it's the biggest journalistic fish that has ever been landed in this office. Andrew Reefer's opinion on the bill will have a tremendous influence. We'll run the interview as a leader in a special edition that is under way already. Of course, he must have been ready to give the information to the public or nothing would have induced him to open his mouth. But to think that we should be the first to get it! Patty, you're a brick!"

Clifford came home on the seven o'clock train, and Patty was there to meet him, brimful of her story. But Clifford also had a story to tell and got his word in first.

"Now, Patty, don't scold until you hear why I missed the train. I met Mr. Peabody of the Steel and Iron Company at Mr. Moreland's and got into conversation with him. When he found out who I was, he was greatly interested and said Father had been one of his best friends when they were at college together. I told him about wanting to get the position in the company, and he had me go right out to the works and see about it. And, Patty, I have the place. Goodbye to the grind of newspaper items and fillers. I tried to get back to the station at Bancroft in time to catch the train but I couldn't, and it was just as well, for Mr. Keefe was suddenly summoned home this afternoon, and when the three-thirty train from town stopped at Bancroft he was on it. I found that out and I got on, going to the next station with him and getting my interview after all. It's here in my notebook, and I must hurry up to the office and hand it in. I suppose Mr. Harmer will be very much vexed until he finds that I have it."

"Oh, no. Mr. Harmer is in a very good humour," said Patty with dancing eyes. Then she told her story.

The interview with Mr. Reefer came out with glaring headlines, and the *Chronicle* had its hour of fame and glory. The next day Mr. Harmer sent word to Patty that he wanted to see her.

"So Clifford is leaving," he said abruptly when she entered the office. "Well, do you want his place?"

"Mr. Harmer, are you joking?" demanded Patty in amazement.

"Not I. That stuff you handed in was splendidly written—I didn't have to use the pencil more than once or twice. You have the proper journalist instinct all right. We need a lady on the staff anyhow, and if you'll take the place it's yours for saying so, and the permanency next month."

"I'll take it," said Patty promptly and joyfully.

"Good. Go down to the Symphony Club rehearsal this afternoon and report it. You've just ten minutes to get there," and Patty joyfully and promptly departed.

Anna's Love Letters

"Are you going to answer Gilbert's letter tonight, Anna?" asked Alma Williams, standing in the pantry doorway, tall, fair, and grey-eyed, with the sunset light coming down over the dark firs, through the window behind her, and making a primrose nimbus around her shapely head.

Anna, dark, vivid, and slender, was perched on the edge of the table, idly swinging her slippered foot at the cat's head. She smiled wickedly at Alma before replying.

"I am not going to answer it tonight or any other night," she said, twisting her full, red lips in a way that Alma had learned to dread. Mischief was ripening in Anna's brain when that twist was out.

"What do you mean?" asked Alma anxiously.

"Just what I say, dear," responded Anna, with deceptive meekness. "Poor Gilbert is gone, and I don't intend to bother my head about him any longer. He was amusing while he lasted, but of what use is a beau two thousand miles away, Alma?"

Alma was patient—outwardly. It was never of any avail to show impatience with Anna.

"Anna, you are talking foolishly. Of course you are going to answer his letter. You are as good as engaged to him. Wasn't that practically understood when he left?"

"No, no, dear," and Anna shook her sleek black head with the air of explaining matters to an obtuse child. "*I* was the only one who understood. Gil *mis*understood. He thought that I would really wait for him until he should have made enough money to come home and pay off the mortgage. I let him think so, because I hated to hurt his little feelings. But now it's off with the old love and on with a new one for me."

"Anna, you cannot be in earnest!" exclaimed Alma.

But she was afraid that Anna was in earnest. Anna had a wretched habit of being in earnest when she said flippant things.

"You don't mean that you are not going to write to Gilbert at all—after all you promised?"

Anna placed her elbows daintily on the top of the rocking chair, dropped her pointed chin in her hands, and looked at Alma with black demure eyes.

"I—do—mean—just—that," she said slowly. "I never mean to marry Gilbert Murray. This is final, Alma, and you need not scold or coax, because it would be a waste of breath. Gilbert is safely out of the way, and now I am going to have a good time with a few other delightful men creatures in Exeter."

Anna nodded decisively, flashed a smile at Alma, picked up her cat, and went out. At the door she turned and looked back, with the big black cat snuggled under her chin.

"If you think Gilbert will feel very badly over his letter not being answered, you might answer it yourself, Alma," she said teasingly. "There it is"—she took the letter from the pocket of her ruffled apron and threw it on a chair. "You may read it if you want to; it isn't really a love letter. I told Gilbert he wasn't to write silly letters. Come, pussy, I'm going to get ready for prayer meeting. We've got a nice, new, young, good-looking minister in Exeter, pussy, and that makes prayer meeting *very* interesting."

Anna shut the door, her departing laugh rippling mockingly through the dusk. Alma picked up Gilbert Murray's letter and went to her room. She wanted to cry, since she could not shake Anna. Even if she could have shook her, it would only have made her more perverse. Anna was in earnest; Alma knew that, even while she hoped and believed that it was but the earnestness of a freak that would pass in time. Anna had had one like it a year ago, when she had cast Gilbert off for three months, driving him distracted by flirting with Charlie Moore. Then she had suddenly repented and taken him back. Alma thought that this whim would run its course likewise and leave a repentant Anna. But meanwhile everything might be spoiled. Gilbert might not prove forgiving a second time.

Alma would have given much if she could only have induced Anna to answer Gilbert's letter, but coaxing Anna to do anything was a very sure and effective way of preventing her from doing it.

Alma and Anna had lived alone at the old Williams homestead ever since their mother's death four years before. Exeter matrons thought this hardly proper, since Alma, in spite of her grave ways, was only twenty-four. The farm was rented, so that Alma's only responsibilities were the post office which she kept, and that harum-scarum beauty of an Anna.

The Murray homestead adjoined theirs. Gilbert Murray had grown up with Alma; they had been friends ever since she could remember. Alma loved Gilbert with a love which she herself believed to be purely sisterly, and which nobody else doubted could be, since she had been at pains to make a match—Exeter matrons' phrasing—between Gil and Anna, and was manifestly delighted when Gilbert obligingly fell in love with the latter.

There was a small mortgage on the Murray place which Mr. Murray senior had not been able to pay off. Gilbert determined to get rid of it, and his thoughts turned to the west. His father was an active, hale old man, quite capable of managing the farm in Gilbert's absence. Alexander MacNair had gone to the west two years previously and got work on a new railroad. He wrote to Gilbert to come too, promising him plenty of work and good pay. Gilbert went, but before going he had asked Anna to marry him.

It was the first proposal Anna had ever had, and she managed it quite cleverly, from her standpoint. She told Gilbert that he must wait until he came home again before settling that, meanwhile, they would be *very* good friends—emphasized with a blush—and that he might write to her. She kissed him goodbye, and Gilbert, honest fellow, was quite satisfied. When an Exeter girl had allowed so much to be inferred, it was understood to be equivalent to an engagement. Gilbert had never discerned that Anna was not like the other Exeter girls, but was a law unto herself.

Alma sat down by her window and looked out over the lane where the slim wild cherry trees were bronzing under the autumn frosts. Her lips were very firmly set. Something must be done. But what?

Alma's heart was set on this marriage for two reasons. Firstly, if Anna married Gilbert she would be near her all her life. She could not bear the thought that some day Anna might leave her and go far away to live. In the second and largest place, she desired the marriage because Gilbert did. She had always been desirous, even in the old, childish play-days, that Gilbert should get just exactly what he wanted. She had always taken a keen, strange delight in furthering his wishes.

Anna's falseness would surely break his heart, and Alma winced at the thought of his pain.

There was one thing she could do. Anna's tormenting suggestion had fallen on fertile soil. Alma balanced pros and cons, admitting the risk. But she would have taken a tenfold larger risk in the hope of holding secure Anna's place in Gilbert's affections until Anna herself should come to her senses.

When it grew quite dark and Anna had gone lilting down the lane on her way to prayer meeting, Alma lighted her lamp, read Gilbert's letter—and answered it. Her handwriting was much like Anna's. She signed the letter "A. Williams," and there was nothing in it that might not have been written by her to Gilbert; but she knew that Gilbert would believe Anna had written it, and she intended him so to believe. Alma never did a thing halfway when she did it at all. At first she wrote rather constrainedly but, reflecting that in any case Anna would have written a merely friendly letter, she allowed her thoughts to run freely, and the resulting epistle was an excellent one of its kind. Alma had the gift of expression and more brains than Exeter people had ever imagined she possessed. When Gilbert read that letter a fortnight later he was surprised to find that Anna was so clever. He had always, with a secret regret, thought her much inferior to Alma in this respect, but that delightful letter, witty, wise, fanciful, was the letter of a clever woman.

When a year had passed Alma was still writing to Gilbert the letters signed "A. Williams." She had ceased to fear being found out, and she took a strange pleasure in the correspondence for its own sake. At first she had been quakingly afraid of discovery. When she smuggled the letters addressed in Gilbert's handwriting to Miss Anna Williams out of the letter packet and hid them from Anna's eyes, she felt as guilty as if she were breaking all the laws of the land at once. To be sure, she knew that she would have to confess to Anna some day, when the latter repented and began to wish she had written to Gilbert, but that was a very different thing from premature disclosure.

But Anna had as yet given no sign of such repentance, although Alma looked for it anxiously. Anna was having the time of her life. She was the acknowledged beauty of five settlements, and she went forward on her career of conquest quite undisturbed by the jealousies and heart-burnings she provoked on every side.

One moonlight night she went for a sleigh-drive with Charlie Moore of East Exeter—and returned to tell Alma that they were married!

"I knew you would make a fuss, Alma, because you don't like Charlie, so we just took matters into our own hands. It was so much more romantic, too. I'd always said I'd never be married in any of your dull, commonplace ways. You might as well forgive me and be nice right off, Alma, because you'd have to do it anyway, in time. Well, you do look surprised!"

Alma accepted the situation with an apathy that amazed Anna. The truth was that Alma was stunned by a thought that had come to her even while Anna was speaking.

"Gilbert will find out about the letters now, and despise me."

Nothing else, not even the fact that Anna had married shiftless Charlie Moore, seemed worth while considering beside this. The fear and shame of it haunted her like a nightmare; she shrank every morning from the thought of all the mail that was coming that day, fearing that there would be an angry, puzzled letter from Gilbert. He must certainly soon hear of Anna's marriage; he would see it in the home paper, other correspondents in Exeter would write him of it. Alma grew sick at heart thinking of the complications in front of her.

When Gilbert's letter came she left it for a whole day before she could summon courage to open it. But it was a harmless epistle after all; he had not yet heard of Anna's marriage. Alma had at first no thought of answering it, yet her fingers ached to do so. Now that Anna was gone, her loneliness was unbearable. She realized how much Gilbert's letters had meant to her, even when written to another woman. She could bear her life well enough, she thought, if she only had his letters to look forward to.

No more letters came from Gilbert for six weeks. Then came one, alarmed at Anna's silence, anxiously asking the reason for it; Gilbert had heard no word of the marriage. He was working in a remote district where newspapers seldom penetrated. He had no other correspondent in Exeter now; except his mother, and she, not knowing that he supposed himself engaged to Anna had forgotten to mention it.

Alma answered that letter. She told herself recklessly that she would keep on writing to him until he found out. She would lose his friendship anyhow, when that occurred, but meanwhile she would have the letters a little longer. She could not learn to live without them until she had to.

The correspondence slipped back into its old groove. The harassed look which Alma's face had worn, and which Exeter people had attributed to worry over Anna, disappeared. She did not even feel lonely, and reproached herself for lack of proper feeling in missing Anna so little. Besides, to her horror and dismay, she detected in herself a strange undercurrent of relief at the thought that Gilbert could never marry Anna now! She could not understand it. Had not that marriage been her dearest wish for years? Why then should she feel this strange gladness at the impossibility of its fulfilment? Altogether, Alma feared that her condition of mind and morals must be sadly askew. Perhaps, she thought mournfully, this perversion of proper feeling was her punishment for the deception she had practised. She had deliberately done evil that good might come, and now the very imaginations of her heart were stained by that evil. Alma cried herself to sleep many a night in her repentance, but she kept on writing to Gilbert, for all that.

The winter passed, and the spring and summer waned, and Alma's outward life flowed as smoothly as the currents of the seasons, broken only by vivid eruptions from Anna, who came over often from East Exeter, glorying in her young matronhood, "to cheer Alma up." Alma, so said Exeter people, was becoming unsociable and old maidish. She lost her liking for company, and seldom went anywhere among her neighbours. Her once frequent visits across the yard to chat with old Mrs. Murray became few and far between. She could not bear to hear the old lady talking about Gilbert, and she was afraid that some day she would be told that he was coming home. Gilbert's home-coming was the nightmare dread that darkened poor Alma's whole horizon.

One October day, two years after Gilbert's departure, Alma, standing at her window in the reflected glow of a red maple outside, looked down the lane and saw him striding up it! She had had no warning of his coming. His last letter, dated three weeks back, had not hinted at it. Yet there he was—and with him Alma's Nemesis.

She was very calm. Now that the worst had come, she felt quite strong to meet it. She would tell Gilbert the truth, and he would go away in anger and never forgive her, but she deserved it. As she went downstairs, the only thing that really worried her was the thought of the pain Gilbert would suffer when she told him of Anna's faithlessness. She had seen his face as he passed under her window, and it was the face of a blithe man who had not heard any evil tidings. It was left to her to tell him; surely, she thought apathetically, that was punishment enough for what she had done.

With her hand on the doorknob, she paused to wonder what she should say when he asked her why she had not told him of Anna's marriage when it occurred—why she had still continued the deception when it had no longer an end to serve. Well, she would tell him the truth—that it was because she could not bear the thought of giving up writing to him. It was a humiliating thing to confess, but that did not matter—nothing mattered now. She opened the door.

Gilbert was standing on the big round door-stone under the red maple—a tall, handsome young fellow with a bronzed face and laughing eyes. His exile had improved him. Alma found time and ability to reflect that she had never known Gilbert was so fine-looking.

He put his arm around her and kissed her cheek in his frank delight at seeing her again. Alma coldly asked him in. Her face was still as pale as when she came downstairs, but a curious little spot of fiery red blossomed out where Gilbert's lips had touched it.

Gilbert followed her into the sitting-room and looked about eagerly.

"When did you come home?" she said slowly. "I did not know you were expected."

"Got homesick, and just came! I wanted to surprise you all," he answered, laughing. "I arrived only a few minutes ago. Just took time to hug my mother, and here I am. Where's Anna?"

The pent-up retribution of two years descended on Alma's head in the last question of Gilbert's. But she did not flinch. She stood straight before him, tall and fair and pale, with the red maple light streaming in through the open door behind her, staining her light house-dress and mellowing the golden sheen of her hair. Gilbert reflected that Alma Williams was really a very handsome girl. These two years had improved her. What splendid big grey eyes she had! He had always wished that Anna's eyes had not been quite so black.

"Anna is not here," said Alma. "She is married."

"Married!"

Gilbert sat down suddenly on a chair and looked at Alma in bewilderment.

"She has been married for a year," said Alma steadily. "She married Charlie Moore of East Exeter, and has been living there ever since."

"Then," said Gilbert, laying hold of the one solid fact that loomed out of the mist of his confused understanding, "why did she keep on writing letters to me after she was married?"

"She never wrote to you at all. It was I that wrote the letters."

Gilbert looked at Alma doubtfully. Was she crazy? There was something odd about her, now that he noticed, as she stood rigidly there, with that queer red spot on her face, a strange fire in her eyes, and that weird reflection from the maple enveloping her like an immaterial flame.

"I don't understand," he said helplessly.

Still standing there, Alma told the whole story, giving full explanations, but no excuses. She told it clearly and simply, for she had often pictured this scene to herself and thought out what she must say. Her memory worked automatically, and her tongue obeyed it promptly. To herself she seemed like a machine, talking mechanically, while her soul stood on one side and listened.

When she had finished there was a silence lasting perhaps ten seconds. To Alma it seemed like hours. Would Gilbert overwhelm her with angry reproaches, or would he simply rise up and leave her in unutterable contempt? It was the most tragic moment of her life, and her whole personality was strung up to meet it and withstand it.

"Well, they were good letters, anyhow," said Gilbert finally; "interesting letters," he added, as if by way of a meditative afterthought.

It was so anti-climactic that Alma broke into an hysterical giggle, cut short by a sob. She dropped into a chair by the table and flung her hands over her face, laughing and sobbing softly to herself. Gilbert rose and walked to the door, where he stood with his back to her until she regained her self-control. Then he turned and looked down at her quizzically.

Alma's hands lay limply in her lap, and her eyes were cast down, with tears glistening on the long fair lashes. She felt his gaze on her.

"Can you ever forgive me, Gilbert?" she said humbly.

"I don't know that there is much to forgive," he answered. "I have some explanations to make too and, since we're at it, we might as well get them all over and have done with them. Two years ago I did honestly think I was in love with Anna—at least when I was round where she was. She had a taking way with her. But, somehow, even then, when I wasn't with her she seemed to kind of grow dim and not count for so awful much after all. I used to wish she was more like you—quieter, you know, and not so sparkling. When I parted from her that last night before I went west, I did feel very bad, and she seemed very dear to me, but it was six weeks from that before her—your—letter came, and in that time she seemed to have faded out of my thoughts. Honestly, I wasn't thinking much about her at all. Then came the letter—and it was a splendid one, too. I had never thought that Anna could write a letter like that, and I was as pleased as Punch about it. The letters kept coming, and I kept on looking for them more and more all the time. I fell in love all over again—with the writer of those letters. I thought it was Anna, but since you wrote the letters, it must have been with you, Alma. I thought it was because she was growing more womanly that she could write such letters. That was why I came home. I wanted to get acquainted all over again, before she grew beyond me altogether—I wanted to find the real Anna the letters showed me. I—I—didn't expect this. But I don't care if Anna is married, so long as the girl who wrote those letters isn't. It's you I love, Alma."

He bent down and put his arm about her, laying his cheek against hers. The little red spot where his kiss had fallen was now quite drowned out in the colour that rushed over her face.

"If you'll marry me, Alma, I'll forgive you," he said.

A little smile escaped from the duress of Alma's lips and twitched her dimples.

"I'm willing to do anything that will win your forgiveness, Gilbert," she said meekly.

Aunt Caroline's Silk Dress

Patty came in from her walk to the post office with cheeks finely reddened by the crisp air. Carry surveyed her with pleasure. Of late Patty's cheeks had been entirely too pale to please Carry, and Patty had not had a very good appetite. Once or twice she had even complained of a headache. So Carry had sent her to the office for a walk that night, although the post office trip was usually Carry's own special constitutional, always very welcome to her after a weary day of sewing on other people's pretty dresses.

Carry never sewed on pretty dresses for herself, for the simple reason that she never had any pretty dresses. Carry was twenty-two—and feeling forty, her last pretty dress had been when she was a girl of twelve, before her father had died. To be sure, there was the silk organdie Aunt Kathleen had sent her, but that was fit only for parties, and Carry never went to any parties.

"Did you get any mail, Patty?" she asked unexpectantly. There was never much mail for the Lea girls.

"Yes'm," said Patty briskly. "Here's the *Weekly Advocate*, and a patent medicine almanac with all your dreams expounded, *and* a letter for Miss Carry M. Lea. It's postmarked Enfield, and has a suspiciously matrimonial look. I'm sure it's an invitation to Chris Fairley's wedding. Hurry up and see, Caddy."

Carry, with a little flush of excitement on her face, opened her letter. Sure enough, it contained an invitation "to be present at the marriage of Christine Fairley."

"How jolly!" exclaimed Patty. "Of course you'll go, Caddy. You'll have a chance to wear that lovely organdie of yours at last."

"It was sweet of Chris to invite me," said Carry. "I really didn't expect it."

"Well, I did. Wasn't she your most intimate friend when she lived in Enderby?"

"Oh, yes, but it is four years since she left, and some people might forget in four years. But I might have known Chris wouldn't. Of course I'll go."

"And you'll make up your organdie?"

"I shall have to," laughed Carry, forgetting all her troubles for a moment, and feeling young and joyous over the prospect of a festivity. "I haven't another thing that would do to wear to a wedding. If I hadn't that blessed organdie I couldn't go, that's all."

"But you have it, and it will look lovely made up with a tucked skirt. Tucks are so fashionable now. And there's that lace of mine you can have for a bertha. I want you to look just right, you see. Enfield is a big place, and there will be lots of grandees at the wedding. Let's get the last fashion sheet and pick out a design right away. Here's one on the very first page that would be nice. You could wear it to perfection, Caddy you're so tall and slender. It wouldn't suit a plump and podgy person like myself at all."

Carry liked the pattern, and they had an animated discussion over it. But, in the end, Carry sighed, and pushed the sheet away from her, with all the brightness gone out of face.

"It's no use, Patty. I'd forgotten for a few minutes, but it's all come back now. I can't think of weddings and new dresses, when the thought of that interest crowds everything else out. It's due next month—fifty dollars—and I've only ten saved up. I can't make forty dollars in a month, even if I had any amount of sewing, and you know hardly anyone wants sewing done just now. I don't know what we shall do. Oh, I suppose we can rent a couple of rooms in the village and *exist* in them. But it breaks my heart to think of leaving our old home."

"Perhaps Mr. Kerr will let us have more time," suggested Patty, not very hopefully. The sparkle had gone out of her face too. Patty loved their little home as much as Carry did.

"You know he won't. He has been only too anxious for an excuse to foreclose, this long time. He wants the land the house is on. Oh, if I only hadn't been sick so long in the summer—just when everybody had sewing to do. I've tried so hard to catch up, but I couldn't." Carry's voice broke in a sob.

Patty leaned over the table and patted her sister's glossy dark hair gently.

"You've worked too hard, dearie. You've just gone to skin and bone. Oh, I know how hard it is! I can't bear to think of leaving this dear old spot either. If we could only induce Mr. Kerr to give us a year's grace! I'd be teaching then, and we could easily pay the interest and some of the principal too. Perhaps he will if we both go to him and coax very hard. Anyway, don't worry over it till after the wedding. I want you to go and have a good time. You never have good times, Carry."

"Neither do you," said Carry rebelliously. "You never have anything that other girls have, Patty—not even pretty clothes."

"Deed, and I've lots of things to be thankful for," said Patty cheerily. "Don't you fret about me. I'm vain enough to think I've got some brains anyway, and I'm a-meaning to do something with them too. Now I think I'll go upstairs and study this evening. It will be warm enough there tonight, and the noise of the machine rather bothers me."

Patty whisked out, and Carry knew she should go to her sewing. But she sat a long while at the table in dismal thought. She was so tired, and so hopeless. It had been such a hard struggle, and it seemed now as if it would all come to naught. For five years, ever since her mother's death, Carry had supported herself and Patty by dressmaking. They had been a hard five years of pinching and economizing and going without, for Enderby was only a small place, and there were two other dressmakers. Then there was always the mortgage to devour everything. Carry had kept it at bay till now, but at last she was conquered. She had had typhoid fever in the spring and had not been able to work for a long time. Indeed, she had gone to work before she should. The doctor's bill was yet unpaid, but Dr. Hamilton had told her to take her time. Carry knew she would not be pressed for that, and next year Patty would be able to help her. But next year would be too late. The dear little home would be lost then.

When Carry roused herself from her sad reflections, she saw a crumpled note lying on the floor. She picked it up and absently smoothed it out. Seeing Patty's name at the top she was about to lay it aside without reading it, but the lines were few, and the sense of them flashed into Carry's brain. The note was an invitation to Clare Forbes's party! The Lea girls had known that the Forbes girls were going to give a party, but they had not expected that Patty would be invited. Of course, Clare Forbes was in Patty's class at school and was always very nice and friendly with her. But then the Forbes set was not the Lea set.

Carry ran upstairs to Patty's room. "Patty, you dropped this on the floor. I couldn't help seeing what it was. Why didn't you tell me Clare had invited you?"

"Because I knew I couldn't go, and I thought you would feel badly over that. Caddy, I wish you hadn't seen it."

"Oh, Patty, I *do* wish you could go to the party. It was so sweet of Clare to invite you, and perhaps she will be offended if you don't go—she won't understand. Clare Forbes isn't a girl whose friendship is to be lightly thrown away when it is offered."

"I know that. But, Caddy dear, it is impossible. I don't think that I have any foolish pride about clothes, but you know it is out of the question to think of going to Clare Forbes's party in my last winter's plaid dress, which is a good two inches too short and skimpy in proportion. Putting my own feelings aside, it would be an insult to Clare. There, don't think any more about it."

But Carry did think about it. She lay awake half the night wondering if there might not be some way for Patty to go to that party. She knew it was impossible, unless Patty had a new dress, and how could a new dress be had? Yet she did so want Patty to go. Patty never had any good times, and she was studying so hard. Then, all at once, Carry thought of a way by which Patty might have a new dress. She had been tossing restlessly, but now she lay very still, staring with wide-open eyes at the moonlit window, with the big willow boughs branching darkly across it. Yes, it was a way, but could she? *Could* she? Yes, she could, and she would. Carry buried her face in her pillow with a sob and a gulp. But she had decided what must be done, and how it must be done.

"Are you going to begin on your organdie today?" asked Patty in the morning, before she started for school.

"I must finish Mrs. Pidgeon's suit first," Carry answered. "Next week will be time enough to think about my wedding garments."

She tried to laugh and failed. Patty thought with a pang that Carry looked horribly pale and tired—probably she had worried most of the night over the interest.

"I'm so glad she's going to Chris's wedding," thought Patty, as she hurried down the street. "It will take her out of herself and give her something nice to think of for ever so long."

Nothing more was said that week about the organdie, or the wedding, or the Forbes's party. Carry sewed fiercely, and sat at her machine for hours after Patty had gone to bed. The night before the party she said to Patty, "Braid your hair to-night, Patty. You'll want it nice and wavy to go to the Forbes's tomorrow night."

Patty thought that Carry was actually trying to perpetrate a weak joke, and endeavoured to laugh. But it was a rather dreary laugh. Patty, after a hard evening's study, felt tired and discouraged, and she was really dreadfully disappointed about the party, although she wouldn't have let Carry suspect it for the world.

"You're going, you know," said Carry, as serious as a judge, although there was a little twinkle in her eyes.

"In a faded plaid two inches too short?" Patty smiled as brightly as possible.

"Oh, no. I have a dress all ready for you." Carry opened the wardrobe door and took out—the loveliest girlish dress of creamy organdie, with pale pink roses scattered over it, made with the daintiest of ruffles and tucks, with a bertha of soft creamy lace, and a girdle of white silk. "This is for you," said Carry.

Patty gazed at the dress with horror-stricken eyes. "Caroline Lea, *that is your organdie!* And you've gone and made it up for *me*! Carry Lea, what are you going to wear to the wedding?"

"Nothing. I'm not going."

"You are—you must—you shall. I won't take the organdie."

"You'll have to now, because it's made to fit you. Come, Patty dear, I've set my heart on your going to that party. You mustn't disappoint me—you *can't*, for what good would it do? I can never wear the dress now."

Patty realized that. She knew she might as well go to the party, but she did not feel much pleasure in the prospect. Nevertheless, when she was ready for it the next evening, she couldn't help a little thrill of delight. The dress was so pretty, and dainty, and becoming.

"You look sweet," exclaimed Carry admiringly. "There, I hear the Browns' carriage. Patty, I want you to promise me this—that you'll not let any thought of me, or my not going to the wedding, spoil your enjoyment this evening. I gave you the dress that you might have a good time, so don't make my gift of no effect."

"I'll try," promised Patty, flying downstairs, where her next-door neighbours were waiting for her.

At two o'clock that night Carry was awakened to see Patty bending over her, flushed and radiant. Carry sat sleepily up. "I hope you had a good time," she said.

"I had—oh, I had—but I didn't waken you out of your hard-earned slumbers at this wee sma' hour to tell you that. Carry, I've thought of a way for you to go to the wedding. It just came to me at supper. Mrs. Forbes was sitting opposite to me, and her dress suggested it. You must make over Aunt Caroline's silk dress."

"Nonsense," said Carry, a little crossly; even sweet-tempered people are sometimes cross when they are wakened up for—as it seemed—nothing.

"It's good plain sense. Of course, you must make it over and—"

"Patty Lea, you're crazy. I wouldn't dream of wearing that hideous thing. Bright green silk, with huge yellow brocade flowers as big as cabbages all over it! I think I see myself in it."

"Caddy, listen to me. You know there's enough of that black lace of mother's for the waist, and the big black lace shawl of Grandmother Lea's will do for the skirt. Make it over—"

"A plain slip of the silk," gasped Carry, her quick brain seizing on all the possibilities of the plan. "Why didn't I think of it before? It will be just the thing, the greens and yellow will be toned down to a nice shimmer under the black lace. And I'll make cuffs of black velvet with double puffs above—and just cut out a wee bit at the throat with a frill of lace and a band of black velvet ribbon around my neck. Patty Lea, it's an inspiration."

Carry was out of bed by daylight the next morning and, while Patty still slumbered, she mounted to the garret, and took Aunt Caroline's silk dress from the chest where it had lain forgotten for three years. Carry held it up at arm's length, and looked at it with amusement.

"It is certainly ugly, but with the lace over it it will look very different. There's enough of it, anyway, and that skirt is stiff enough to stand alone. Poor Aunt Caroline, I'm afraid I wasn't particularly grateful for her gift at the time, but I really am now."

Aunt Caroline, who had given the dress to Carry three years before, was, an old lady of eighty, the aunt of Carry's father. She had once possessed a snug farm but in an evil hour she had been persuaded to deed it to her nephew, Edward Curry, whom she had brought up. Poor Aunt Caroline had lived to regret this step, for everyone in Enderby knew that Edward Curry and his wife had repaid her with ingratitude and greed.

Carry, who was named for her, was her favourite grandniece and often went to see her, though such visits were coldly received by the Currys, who always took especial care never to leave Aunt Caroline alone with any of her relatives. On one occasion, when Carry was there, Aunt Caroline had brought out this silk dress.

"I'm going to give this to you, Carry," she said timidly. "It's a good silk, and not so very old. Mr. Greenley gave it to me for a birthday present fifteen years ago. Maybe you can make it over for yourself."

Mrs. Edward, who was on duty at the time, sniffed disagreeably, but she said nothing. The dress was of no value in her eyes, for the pattern was so ugly and old-fashioned that none of her smart daughters would have worn it. Had it been otherwise, Aunt Caroline would probably not have been allowed to give it away.

Carry had thanked Aunt Caroline sincerely. If she did not care much for the silk, she at least prized the kindly motive behind the gift. Perhaps she and Patty laughed a little over it as they packed it away in the garret. It was so very ugly, but Carry thought it was sweet of Aunt Caroline to have given her something.

Poor old Aunt Caroline had died soon after, and Carry had not thought about the silk dress again. She had too many other things to think of, this poor worried Carry.

After breakfast Carry began to rip the skirt breadths apart. Snip, snip, went her scissors, while her thoughts roamed far afield—now looking forward with renewed pleasure to Christine's wedding, now dwelling dolefully on the mortgage. Patty, who was washing the dishes, knew just what her thoughts were by the light and shadow on her expressive face.

"Why!—what?" exclaimed Carry suddenly. Patty wheeled about to see Carry staring at the silk dress like one bewitched. Between the silk and the lining which she had just ripped apart was a twenty-dollar bill, and beside it a sheet of letter paper covered with writing in a cramped angular hand, both secured very carefully to the silk.

"Carry Lea!" gasped Patty.

With trembling fingers Carry snipped away the stitches that held the letter, and read it aloud.

> "My dear Caroline," it ran, "I do not know when you will find this letter and this money, but when you do it belongs to you. I have a hundred dollars which I always meant to give you because you were named for me. But Edward and his wife do not know I have it, and I don't want them to find out. They would not let me give it to you if they knew, so I have thought of this way of getting it to you. I have sewed five twenty-dollar bills under the lining of this skirt, and they are all yours, with your Aunt Caroline's best love. You were always a good girl, Carry, and you've worked hard, and I've given Edward enough. Just take this money and use it as you like.
>
> "Aunt Caroline Greenley."

"Carry Lea, are we both dreaming?" gasped Patty.

With crimson cheeks Carry ripped the other breadths apart, and there were the other four bills. Then she slipped down in a little heap on the sofa cushions and began to cry—happy tears of relief and gladness.

"We can pay the interest," said Patty, dancing around the room, "and get yourself a nice new dress for the wedding."

"Indeed I won't," said Carry, sitting up and laughing through her tears. "I'll make over this dress and wear it out of gratitude to the memory of dear Aunt Caroline."

Aunt Susanna's Thanksgiving Dinner.

"Here's Aunt Susanna, girls," said Laura who was sitting by the north window—nothing but north light does for Laura who is the artist of our talented family.

Each of us has a little pet new-fledged talent which we are faithfully cultivating in the hope that it will amount to something and soar highly some day. But it is difficult to cultivate four talents on our tiny income. If Laura wasn't such a good manager we never could do it.

Laura's words were a signal for Kate to hang up her violin and for me to push my pen and portfolio out of sight. Laura had hidden her brushes and water colors as she spoke. Only Margaret continued to bend serenely over her Latin grammar. Aunt Susanna frowns on musical and literary and artistic ambitions but she accords a faint approval to Margaret's desire for an education. A college course, with a tangible diploma at the end, and a sensible pedagogic aspiration is something Aunt Susanna can understand when she tries hard. But she cannot understand messing with paints, fiddling, or scribbling, and she has only unmeasured contempt for messers, fiddlers, and scribblers. Time was when we had paid no attention to Aunt Susanna's views on these points; but ever since she had, on one incautious day when she was in high good humor, dropped a pale, anemic little hint that she might send Margaret to college if she were a good girl we had been bending all our energies towards securing Aunt Susanna's approval. It was not enough that Aunt Susanna should approve of Margaret; she must approve of the whole four of us or she would not help Margaret. That is Aunt Susanna's way. Of late we had been growing a little discouraged. Aunt Susanna had recently read a magazine article which stated that the higher education of women was ruining our country and that a woman who was a B.A. couldn't, in the very nature of things, ever be a housewifely, cookly creature. Consequently, Margaret's chances looked a little foggy; but we hadn't quite given up hope. A very little thing might sway Aunt Susanna one way or the other, so that we walked very softly and tried to mingle serpents' wisdom and doves' harmlessness in practical portions.

When Aunt Susanna came in Laura was crocheting, Kate was sewing, and I was poring over a recipe book. That was not deception at all, since we did all these things frequently—much more frequently, in fact, than we painted or fiddled or wrote. But Aunt Susanna would never believe it. Nor did she believe it now.

She threw back her lovely new sealskin cape, looked around the sitting-room and then smiled—a truly Aunt Susannian smile.

"What a pity you forgot to wipe that smudge of paint off your nose, Laura," she said sarcastically. "You don't seem to get on very fast with your lace. How long is it since you began it? Over three months, isn't it?"

"This is the third piece of the same pattern I've done in three months, Aunt Susanna," said Laura presently. Laura is an old duck. She never gets cross and snaps back. I do; and it's so hard not to with Aunt Susanna sometimes. But I generally manage it for I'd do anything for Margaret. Laura did not tell Aunt Susanna that she sold her lace at the Women's Exchange in town and made enough to buy her new hats. She makes enough out of her water colors to dress herself.

Aunt Susanna took a second breath and started in again.

"I notice your violin hasn't quite as much dust on it as the rest of the things in this room, Kate. It's a pity you stopped playing just as I came in. I don't enjoy fiddling much but I'd prefer it to seeing anyone using a needle who isn't accustomed to it."

Kate is really a most dainty needlewoman and does all the fine sewing in our family. She colored and said nothing—that being the highest pitch of virtue to which our Katie, like myself, can attain.

"And there's Margaret ruining her eyes over books," went on Aunt Susanna severely. "Will you kindly tell me, Margaret Thorne, what good you ever expect Latin to do you?"

"Well, you see, Aunt Susanna," said Margaret gently—Magsie and Laura are birds of a feather—"I want to be a teacher if I can manage to get through, and I shall need Latin for that."

All the girls except me had now got their accustomed rap, but I knew better than to hope I should escape.

"So you're reading a recipe book, Agnes? Well, that's better than poring over a novel. I'm afraid you haven't been at it very long though. People generally don't read recipes upside down—and besides, you didn't quite cover up your portfolio. I see a corner of it sticking out. Was genius burning before I came in? It's too bad if I quenched the flame."

"A cookery book isn't such a novelty to me as you seem to think, Aunt Susanna," I said, as meekly as it was possible for me. "Why I'm a real good cook—'if I do say it as hadn't orter.'"

I am, too.

"Well, I'm glad to hear it," said Aunt Susanna skeptically, "because that has to do with my errand her to-day. I'm in a peck of troubles. Firstly, Miranda Mary's mother has had to go and get sick and Miranda Mary must go home to wait on her. Secondly, I've just had a telegram from my sister-in-law who has been ordered west for her health, and I'll have to leave on to-night's train to see her before she goes. I can't get back until the noon train Thursday, and that is Thanksgiving, and I've invited Mr. and Mrs. Gilbert to dinner that day. They'll come on the same train. I'm dreadfully worried. There doesn't seem to be anything I can do except get on of you girls to go up to the Pinery Thursday morning and cook the dinner for us. Do you think you can manage it?"

We all felt rather dismayed, and nobody volunteered with a rush. But as I had just boasted that I could cook it was plainly my duty to step into the breach, and I did it with fear and trembling.

"I'll go, Aunt Susanna," I said.

"And I'll help you," said Kate.

"Well, I suppose I'll have to try you," said Aunt Susanna with the air of a woman determined to make the best of a bad business. "Here is the key of the kitchen door. You'll find everything in the pantry, turkey and all. The mince pies are all ready made so you'll only have to warm them up. I want dinner sharp at twelve for the train is due at 11:50. Mr. and Mrs. Gilbert are very particular and I do hope you will have things right. Oh, if I could only be home myself! Why will people get sick at such inconvenient times?"

"Don't worry, Aunt Susanna," I said comfortingly. "Kate and I will have your Thanksgiving dinner ready for you in tiptop style."

"Well I'm sure I hope so. Don't get to mooning over a story, Agnes. I'll lock the library up and fortunately there are no fiddles at the Pinery. Above all, don't let any of the McGinnises in. They'll be sure to be prowling around when I'm not home. Don't give that dog of theirs any scraps either. That is Miranda Mary's one fault. She will feed that dog in spite of all I can do and I can't walk out of my own back door without falling over him."

We promise to eschew the McGinnises and all their works, including the dog, and when Aunt Susanna had gone we looked at each other with mingled hope and fear.

"Girls, this is the chance of your lives," said Laura. "If you can only please Aunt Susanna with this dinner it will convince her that you are good cooks in spite of your nefarious bent for music and literature. I consider the illness of Miranda Mary's mother a Providential interposition—that is, if she isn't too sick."

"It's all very well for you to be pleased, Lolla," I said dolefully. "But I don't feel jubilant over the prospect at all. Something will probably go wrong. And then there's our own nice little Thanksgiving celebration we've planned, and pinched and economized for weeks to provide. That is half spoiled now."

"Oh, what is that compared to Margaret's chance of going to college?" exclaimed Kate. "Cheer up, Aggie. You know we can cook. I feel that it is now or never with Aunt Susanna."

I cheered up accordingly. We are not given to pessimism which is fortunate. Ever since father died four years ago we have struggled on here, content to give up a good deal just to keep our home and be together. This little gray house—oh, how we do love it and its apple trees—is ours and we have, as aforesaid, a tiny income and our ambitions; not very big ambitions but big enough to give zest to our lives and hope to the future. We've been very happy as a rule. Aunt Susanna has a big house and lots of money but she isn't as happy as we are. She nags us a good deal—just as she used to nag father—but we don't mind it very much after all. Indeed, I sometimes suspect that we really like Aunt Susanna tremendously if she'd only leave us alone long enough to find it out.

Thursday morning was an ideal Thanksgiving morning—bright, crisp and sparkling. There had been a white frost in the night, and the orchard and the white birch wood behind it looked like fairyland. We were all up early. None of us had slept well, and both Kate and I had had the most fearful dreams of spoiling Aunt Susanna's Thanksgiving dinner.

"Never mind, dreams always go by contraries, you know," said Laura cheerfully. "You'd better go up to the Pinery early and get the fires on, for the house will be cold. Remember the McGinnises and the dog. Weigh the turkey so that you'll know exactly how long to cook it. Put the pies in the oven in time to get piping hot—lukewarm mince pies are an abomination. Be sure—"

"Laura, don't confuse us with any more cautions," I groaned, "or we shall get hopelessly fuddled. Come on, Kate, before she has time to."

It wasn't very far up to the Pinery—just ten minutes' walk, and such a delightful walk on that delightful morning. We went through the orchard and then through the white birch wood where the loveliness of the frosted boughs awed us. Beyond that there was a lane between ranks of young, balsamy, white-misted firs and then an open pasture field, sere and crispy. Just across it was the Pinery, a lovely old house with dormer windows in the roof, surrounded by pines that were dark and glorious against the silvery morning sky.

The McGinnis dog was sitting on the back-door steps when we arrived. He wagged his tail ingratiatingly, but we ruthlessly pushed him off, went in and shut the door in his face. All the little McGinnises were sitting in a row on their fence, and they whooped derisively. The McGinnis manners are not those which appertain to the caste of Vere de Vere; but we rather like the urchins—there are eight of them—and we would probably have gone over to talk to them if we had not had the fear of Aunt Susanna before our eyes.

We kindled the fires, weighed the turkey, put it in the oven and prepared the vegetables. Then we set the dining-room table and decorated it with Aunt Susanna's potted ferns and dishes of lovely red apples. Everything went so smoothly that we soon forgot to be nervous. When the turkey was done, we took it out, set it on the back of the range to keep warm and put the mince pies in. The potatoes, cabbage and turnips were bubbling away cheerfully, and everything was going as merrily as a marriage bell. Then, all at once, things happened.

In an evil hour we went to the yard window and looked out. We saw a quiet scene. The McGinnis dog was still sitting on his haunches by the steps, just as he had been sitting all the morning. Down in the McGinnis yard everything wore an unusually peaceful aspect. Only one McGinnis was in sight—Tony, aged eight, who was perched up on the edge of the well box, swinging his legs and singing at the top of his melodious Irish voice. All at once, just as we were looking at him, Tony went over backward and apparently tumbled head foremost down his father's well.

Kate and I screamed simultaneously. We tore across the kitchen, flung open the door, plunged down over Aunt Susanna's yard, scrambled over the fence and flew to the well. Just as we reached it, Tony's red head appeared as he climbed serenely out over the box. I don't know whether I felt more relieved or furious. He had merely fallen on the blank guard inside the box: and there are times when I am tempted to think he fell on purpose because he saw Kate and me looking out at the window. At least he didn't seem at all frightened, and grinned most impishly at us.

Kate and I turned on our heels and marched back in as dignified a manner as was possible under the circumstances. Half way up Aunt Susanna's yard we forgot dignity and broke into a run. We had left the door open and the McGinnis dog had disappeared.

Never shall I forget the sight we saw or the smell we smelled when we burst into that kitchen. There on the floor was the McGinnis dog and what was left of Aunt Susanna's Thanksgiving turkey. As for the smell, imagine a commingled odor of scorching turnips and burning mince pies, and you have it.

The dog fled out with a guilty yelp. I groaned and snatched the turnips off. Kate threw open the oven door and dragged out the pies. Pies and turnips were ruined as irretrievably as the turkey.

"Oh, what shall we do?" I cried miserably. I knew Margaret's chance of college was gone forever.

"Do!" Kate was superb. She didn't lose her wits for a second. "We'll go home and borrow the girls' dinner. Quick—there's just ten minutes before train time. Throw those pies and turnips into this basket—the turkey too—we'll carry them with us to hide them."

I might not be able to evolve an idea like that on the spur of the moment, but I can at least act up to it when it is presented. Without a moment's delay we shut the door and ran. As we went I saw the McGinnis dog licking his chops over in their yard. I have been ashamed ever since of my feelings toward that dog. They were murderous. Fortunately I had no time to indulge them.

It is ten minutes walk from the Pinery to our house, but you can run it in five. Kate and I burst into the kitchen just as Laura and Margaret were sitting down to dinner. We had neither time nor breath for explanations. Without a word I grasped the turkey platter and the turnip tureen. Kate caught one hot mince pie from the oven and whisked a cold one out of the pantry.

"We've—got—to have—them," was all she said.

I've always said that Laura and Magsie would rise to any occasion. They saw us carry their Thanksgiving dinner off under their very eyes and they never interfered by word or motion. They didn't even worry us with questions. They realized that something desperate had happened and that the emergency called for deed not words.

"Aggie," gasped Kate behind me as we tore through the birch wood, "the border—of these pies—is crimped—differently—from Aunt Susanna's."

"She—won't know—the difference," I panted. "Miranda—Mary—crimps them."

We got back to the Pinery just as the train whistle blew. We had ten minutes to transfer turkey and turnips to Aunt Susanna's dishes, hide our own, air the kitchen, and get back our breath. We accomplished it. When Aunt Susanna and her guests came we were prepared for them: we were calm—outwardly—and the second mince pie was getting hot in the oven. It was ready by the time it was needed. Fortunately our turkey was the same size as Aunt Susanna's, and Laura had cooked a double supply of turnips, intending to warm them up the next day. Still, all things considered, Kate and I didn't enjoy that dinner much. We kept thinking of poor Laura and Magsie at home, dining off potatoes on Thanksgiving!

But at least Aunt Susanna was satisfied. When Kate and I were washing the dishes she came out quite beamingly.

"Well, my dears, I must admit that you made a very good job of the dinner, indeed. The turkey was done to perfection. As for the mince pies—well, of course Miranda Mary made them, but she must have had extra good luck with them, for they were excellent and heated to just the right degree. You didn't give anything to the McGinnis dog, I hope?"

"No, we didn't give him anything," said Kate.

Aunt Susanna did not notice the emphasis.

When we had finished the dishes we smuggled our platter and tureen out of the house and went home. Laura and Margaret were busy painting and studying and were just as sweet-tempered as if we hadn't robbed them of their dinner. But we had to tell them the whole story before we even took off our hats.

"There is a special Providence for children and idiots," said Laura gently. We didn't ask her whether she meant us or Tony McGinnis or both. There are some things better left in obscurity. I'd have probably said something much sharper than that if anybody had made off with my Thanksgiving turkey so unceremoniously.

Aunt Susanna came down the next day and told Margaret that she would send her to college. Also she commissioned Laura to paint her a water-color for her dining-room and said she'd pay her five dollars for it.

Kate and I were rather left out in the cold in this distribution of favors, but when you come to reflect that Laura and Magsie had really cooked that dinner, it was only just.

Anyway, Aunt Susanna has never since insinuated that we can't cook, and that is as much as we deserve.

By Grace of Julius Caesar

Melissa sent word on Monday evening that she thought we had better go round with the subscription list for cushioning the church pews on Tuesday. I sent back word that I thought we had better go on Thursday. I had no particular objection to Tuesday, but Melissa is rather fond of settling things without consulting anyone else, and I don't believe in always letting her have her own way. Melissa is my cousin and we have always been good friends, and I am really very fond of her; but there's no sense in lying down and letting yourself be walked over. We finally compromised on Wednesday.

I always have a feeling of dread when I hear of any new church-project for which money will be needed, because I know perfectly well that Melissa and I will be sent round to collect for it. People say we seem to be able to get more than anybody else; and they appear to think that because Melissa is an unencumbered old maid, and I am an unencumbered widow, we can spare the time without any inconvenience to ourselves. Well, we have been canvassing for building funds, and socials, and suppers for years, but it is needed now; at least, I have had enough of it, and I should think Melissa has, too.

We started out bright and early on Wednesday morning, for Jersey Cove is a big place and we knew we should need the whole day. We had to walk because neither of us owned a horse, and anyway it's more nuisance getting out to open and shut gates than it is worth while. It was a lovely day then, though promising to be hot, and our hearts were as light as could be expected, considering the disagreeable expedition we were on.

I was waiting at my gate for Melissa when she came, and she looked me over with wonder and disapproval. I could see she thought I was a fool to dress up in my second best flowered muslin and my very best hat with the pale pink roses in it to walk about in the heat and dust; but I wasn't. All my experience in canvassing goes to show that the better dressed and better looking you are the more money you'll get—that is, when it's the men you have to tackle, as in this case. If it had been the women, however, I would have put on the oldest and ugliest things, consistent with decency, I had. This was what Melissa had done, as it was, and she did look fearfully prim and dowdy, except for her front hair, which was as soft and fluffy and elaborate as usual. I never could understand how Melissa always got it arranged so beautifully.

Nothing particular happened the first part of the day. Some few growled and wouldn't subscribe anything, but on the whole we did pretty well. If it had been a missionary subscription we should have fared worse; but when it was something touching their own comfort, like cushioning the pews, they came down handsomely. We reached Daniel Wilson's by noon, and had to have dinner there. We didn't eat much, although we were hungry enough—Mary Wilson's cooking is a by-word in Jersey Cove. No wonder Daniel is dyspeptic; but dyspeptic or not, he gave us a big subscription for our cushions and told us we looked younger than ever. Daniel is always very complimentary, and they say Mary is jealous.

When we left the Wilson's Melissa said, with an air of a woman nerving herself to a disagreeable duty:

"I suppose we might as well go to Isaac Appleby's now and get it over."

I agreed with her. I had been dreading that call all day. It isn't a very pleasant thing to go to a man you have recently refused to marry and ask him for money; and Melissa and I were both in that predicament.

Isaac was a well-to-do old bachelor who had never had any notion of getting married until his sister died in the winter. And then, as soon as the spring planting was over, he began to look round for a wife. He came to me first and I said "No" good and hard. I liked Isaac well enough; but I was snug and comfortable, and didn't feel like pulling up my roots and moving into another lot; besides, Isaac's courting seemed to me a shade too business-like. I can't get along without a little romance; it's my nature.

Isaac was disappointed and said so, but intimated that it wasn't crushing and that the next best would do very well. The next best was Melissa, and he proposed to her after the decent interval of a fortnight. Melissa also refused him. I admit I was surprised at this, for I knew Melissa was rather anxious to marry; but she has always been down on Isaac Appleby, from principle, because of a family feud on her mother's side; besides, an old beau of hers, a widower at Kingsbridge, was just beginning to take notice again, and I suspected Melissa had hopes concerning him. Finally, I imagine Melissa did not fancy being second choice.

Whatever her reasons were, she refused poor Isaac, and that finished his matrimonial prospects as far as Jersey Cove was concerned, for there wasn't another eligible woman in it—that is, for a man of Isaac's age. I was the only widow, and the other old maids besides Melissa were all hopelessly old-maiden.

This was all three months ago, and Isaac had been keeping house for himself ever since. Nobody knew much about how he got along, for the Appleby house is half a mile from anywhere, down near the shore at the end of a long lane—the lonesomest place, as I did not fail to remember when I was considering Isaac's offer.

"I heard Jarvis Aldrich say Isaac had got a dog lately," said Melissa, when we finally came in sight of the house—a handsome new one, by the way, put up only ten years ago. "Jarvis said it was an imported breed. I do hope it isn't cross."

I have a mortal horror of dogs, and I followed Melissa into the big farmyard with fear and trembling. We were halfway across the yard when Melissa shrieked:

"Anne, there's the dog!"

There was the dog; and the trouble was that he didn't stay there, but came right down the slope at a steady, business-like trot. He was a bull-dog and big enough to bite a body clean in two, and he was the ugliest thing in dogs I had ever seen.

Melissa and I both lost our heads. We screamed, dropped our parasols, and ran instinctively to the only refuge that was in sight—a ladder leaning against the old Appleby house. I am forty-five and something more than plump, so that climbing ladders is not my favorite form of exercise. But I went up that one with the agility and grace of sixteen. Melissa followed me, and we found ourselves on the roof—fortunately it was a flat one—panting and gasping, but safe, unless that diabolical dog could climb a ladder.

I crept cautiously to the edge and peered over. The beast was sitting on his haunches at the foot of the ladder, and it was quite evident he was not short on time. The gleam in his eye seemed to say:

"I've got you two unprincipled subscription hunters beautifully treed and it's treed you're going to stay. That is what I call satisfying."

I reported the state of the case to Melissa.

"What shall we do?" I asked.

"Do?" said Melissa, snappishly. "Why, stay here till Isaac Appleby comes out and takes that brute away? What else can we do?"

"What if he isn't at home?" I suggested.

"We'll stay here till he comes home. Oh, this is a nice predicament. This is what comes of cushioning churches!"

"It might be worse," I said comfortingly. "Suppose the roof hadn't been flat?"

"Call Isaac," said Melissa shortly.

I didn't fancy calling Isaac, but call him I did, and when that failed to bring him Melissa condescended to call, too; but scream as we might, no Isaac appeared, and that dog sat there and smiled internally.

"It's no use," said Melissa sulkily at last. "Isaac Appleby is dead or away."

Half an hour passed; it seemed as long as a day. The sun just boiled down on that roof and we were nearly melted. We were dreadfully thirsty, and the heat made our heads ache, and I could see my muslin dress fading before my very eyes. As for the roses on my best hat—but that was too harrowing to think about.

Then we saw a welcome sight—Isaac Appleby coming through the yard with a hoe over his shoulder. He had probably been working in his field at the back of the house. I never thought I should have been so glad to see him.

"Isaac, oh, Isaac!" I called joyfully, leaning over as far as I dared.

Isaac looked up in amazement at me and Melissa craning our necks over the edge of the roof. Then he saw the dog and took in the situation. The creature actually grinned.

"Won't you call off your dog and let us get down, Isaac?" I said pleadingly.

Isaac stood and reflected for a moment or two. Then he came slowly forward and, before we realized what he was going to do, he took that ladder down and laid it on the ground.

"Isaac Appleby, what do you mean?" demanded Melissa wrathfully.

Isaac folded his arms and looked up. It would be hard to say which face was the more determined, his or the dog's. But Isaac had the advantage in point of looks, I will say that for him.

"I mean that you two women will stay up on that roof until one of you agrees to marry me," said Isaac solemnly.

I gasped.

"Isaac Appleby, you can't be in earnest?" I cried incredulously. "You couldn't be so mean?"

"I am in earnest. I want a wife, and I am going to have one. You two will stay up there, and Julius Caesar here will watch you until one of you makes up her mind to take me. You can settle it between yourselves, and let me know when you have come to a decision."

And with that Isaac walked jauntily into his new house.

"The man can't mean it!" said Melissa. "He is trying to play a joke on us."

"He does mean it," I said gloomily. "An Appleby never says anything he doesn't mean. He will keep us here until one of us consents to marry him."

"It won't be me, then," said Melissa in a calm sort of rage. "I won't marry him if I have to sit on this roof for the rest of my life. You can take him. It's really you he wants, anyway; he asked you first."

I always knew that rankled with Melissa.

I thought the situation over before I said anything more. We certainly couldn't get off that roof, and if we could, there was Julius Caesar. The place was out of sight of every other house in Jersey Cove, and nobody might come near it for a week. To be sure, when Melissa and I didn't turn up the Covites might get out and search for us; but that wouldn't be for two or three days anyhow.

Melissa had turned her back on me and was sitting with her elbows propped up on her knees, looking gloomily out to sea. I was afraid I couldn't coax her into marrying Isaac. As for me, I hadn't any real objection to marrying him, after all, for if he was short of romance he was good-natured and has a fat bank account; but I hated to be driven into it that way.

"You'd better take him, Melissa," I said entreatingly. "I've had one husband and that is enough."

"More than enough for me, thank you," said Melissa sarcastically.

"Isaac is a fine man and has a lovely house; and you aren't sure the Kingsbridge man really means anything," I went on.

"I would rather," said Melissa, with the same awful calmness, "jump down from this roof and break my neck, or be devoured piecemeal by that fiend down there than marry Isaac Appleby."

It didn't seem worth while to say anything more after that. We sat there in stony silence and the time dragged by. I was hot, hungry, thirsty, cross; and besides, I felt that I was in a ridiculous position, which was worse than all the rest. We could see Isaac sitting in the shade of one of his apple trees in the front orchard comfortably reading a newspaper. I think if he hadn't aggravated me by doing that I'd have given in sooner. But as it was, I was determined to be as stubborn as everybody else. We were four obstinate creatures—Isaac and Melissa and Julius Caesar and I.

At four o'clock Isaac got up and went into the house; in a few minutes he came out again with a basket in one hand and a ball of cord in the other.

"I don't intend to starve you, of course, ladies," he said politely, "I will throw this ball up to you and you can then draw up the basket."

I caught the ball, for Melissa never turned her head. I would have preferred to be scornful, too, and reject the food altogether; but I was so dreadfully thirsty that I put my pride in my pocket and hauled the basket up. Besides, I thought it might enable us to hold out until some loophole of escape presented itself.

Isaac went back into the house and I unpacked the basket. There was a bottle of milk, some bread and butter, and a pie. Melissa wouldn't take a morsel of the food, but she was so thirsty she had to take a drink of milk.

She tried to lift her veil—and something caught; Melissa gave it a savage twitch, and off came veil and hat—and all her front hair!

You never saw such a sight. I'd always suspected Melissa wore a false front, but I'd never had any proof before.

Melissa pinned on her hair again and put on her hat and drank the milk, all without a word; but she was purple. I felt sorry for her.

And I felt sorry for Isaac when I tried to eat that bread. It was sour and dreadful. As for the pie, it was hopeless. I tasted it, and then threw it down to Julius Caesar. Julius Caesar, not being over particular, ate it up. I thought perhaps it would kill him, for anything might come of eating such a concoction. That pie was a strong argument for Isaac. I thought a man who had to live on such cookery did indeed need a wife and might be pardoned for taking desperate measures to get one. I was dreadfully tired of broiling on the roof anyhow.

But it was the thunderstorm that decided me. When I saw it coming up, black and quick, from the northwest, I gave in at once. I had endured a good deal and was prepared to endure more; but I had paid ten dollars for my hat and I was not going to have it ruined by a thunderstorm. I called to Isaac and out he came.

"If you will let us down and promise to dispose of that dog before I come here I will marry you, Isaac," I said, "but I'll make you sorry for it afterwards, though."

"I'll take the risk of that, Anne," he said; "and, of course, I'll sell the dog. I won't need him when I have you."

Isaac meant to be complimentary, though you mightn't have thought so if you had seen the face of that dog.

Isaac ordered Julius Caesar away and put up the ladder, and turned his back, real considerately, while we climbed down. We had to go in his house and stay till the shower was over. I didn't forget the object of our call and I produced our subscription list at once.

"How much have you got?" asked Isaac.

"Seventy dollars and we want a hundred and fifty," I said.

"You may put me down for the remaining eighty, then," said Isaac calmly.

The Applebys are never mean where money is concerned, I must say.

Isaac offered to drive us home when it cleared up, but I said "No." I wanted to settle Melissa before she got a chance to talk.

On the way home I said to her:

"I hope you won't mention this to anyone, Melissa. I don't mind marrying Isaac, but I don't want people to know how it came about."

"Oh, I won't say anything about it," said Melissa, laughing a little disagreeably.

"Because," I said, to clinch the matter, looking significantly at her front hair as I said it, "I have something to tell, too."

Melissa will hold her tongue.

By the Rule of Contrary

"Look here, Burton," said old John Ellis in an ominous tone of voice, "I want to know if what that old busybody of a Mary Keane came here today gossiping about is true. If it is—well, I've something to say about the matter! Have you been courting that niece of Susan Oliver's all summer on the sly?"

Burton Ellis's handsome, boyish face flushed darkly crimson to the roots of his curly black hair. Something in the father's tone roused anger and rebellion in the son. He straightened himself up from the turnip row he was hoeing, looked his father squarely in the face, and said quietly,

"Not on the sly, sir, I never do things that way. But I have been going to see Madge Oliver for some time, and we are engaged. We are thinking of being married this fall, and we hope you will not object."

Burton's frankness nearly took away his father's breath. Old John fairly choked with rage.

"You young fool," he spluttered, bringing down his hoe with such energy that he sliced off half a dozen of his finest young turnip plants, "have you gone clean crazy? No, sir, I'll never consent to your marrying an Oliver, and you needn't have any idea that I will."

"Then I'll marry her without your consent," retorted Burton angrily, losing the temper he had been trying to keep.

"Oh, will you indeed! Well, if you do, out you go, and not a cent of my money or a rod of my land do you ever get."

"What have you got against Madge?" asked Burton, forcing himself to speak calmly, for he knew his father too well to doubt for a minute that he meant and would do just what he said.

"She's an Oliver," said old John crustily, "and that's enough." And considering that he had settled the matter, John Ellis threw down his hoe and left the field in a towering rage.

Burton hoed away savagely until his anger had spent itself on the weeds. Give up Madge—dear, sweet little Madge? Not he! Yet if his father remained of the same mind, their marriage was out of the question at present. And Burton knew quite well that his father would remain of the same mind. Old John Ellis had the reputation of being the most contrary man in Greenwood.

When Burton had finished his row he left the turnip field and went straight across lots to see Madge and tell her his dismal story. An hour later Miss Susan Oliver went up the stairs of her little brown house to Madge's room and found her niece lying on the bed, her pretty curls tumbled, her soft cheeks flushed crimson, crying as if her heart would break.

Miss Susan was a tall, grim, angular spinster who looked like the last person in the world to whom a love affair might be confided. But never were appearances more deceptive than in this case. Behind her unprepossessing exterior Miss Susan had a warm, sympathetic heart filled to the brim with kindly affection for her pretty niece. She had seen Burton Ellis going moodily across the fields homeward and guessed that something had gone wrong.

"Now, dearie, what is the matter?" she said, tenderly patting the brown head.

Madge sobbed out the whole story disconsolately. Burton's father would not let him marry her because she was an Oliver. And, oh, what would she do?

"Don't worry, Madge," said Miss Susan comfortingly. "I'll soon settle old John Ellis."

"Why, what can you do?" asked Madge forlornly.

Miss Susan squared her shoulders and looked amused.

"You'll see. I know old John Ellis better than he knows himself. He is the most contrary man the Lord ever made. I went to school with him. I learned how to manage him then, and I haven't forgotten how. I'm going straight up to interview him."

"Are you sure that will do any good?" said Madge doubtfully. "If you go to him and take Burton's and my part, won't it only make him worse?"

"Madge, dear," said Miss Susan, busily twisting her scanty, iron-grey hair up into a hard little knob at the back of her head before Madge's glass, "you just wait. I'm not young, and I'm not pretty, and I'm not in love, but I've more gumption than you and Burton have or ever will have. You keep your eyes open and see if you can learn something. You'll need it if you go up to live with old John Ellis."

Burton had returned to the turnip field, but old John Ellis was taking his ease with a rampant political newspaper on the cool verandah of his house. Looking up from a bitter editorial to chuckle over a cutting sarcasm contained therein, he saw a tall, angular figure coming up the lane with aggressiveness written large in every fold and flutter of shawl and skirt.

"Old Susan Oliver, as sure as a gun," said old John with another chuckle. "She looks mad clean through. I suppose she's coming here to blow me up for refusing to let Burton take that girl of hers. She's been angling and scheming for it for years, but she will find who she has to deal with. Come on, Miss Susan."

John Ellis laid down his paper and stood up with a sarcastic smile.

Miss Susan reached the steps and skimmed undauntedly up them. She did indeed look angry and disturbed. Without any preliminary greeting she burst out into a tirade that simply took away her complacent foe's breath.

"Look here, John Ellis, I want to know what this means. I've discovered that that young upstart of a son of yours, who ought to be in short trousers yet, has been courting my niece, Madge Oliver, all summer. He has had the impudence to tell me that he wants to marry her. I won't have it, I tell you, and you can tell your son so. Marry my niece indeed! A pretty pass the world is coming to! I'll never consent to it."

Perhaps if you had searched Greenwood and all the adjacent districts thoroughly you might have found a man who was more astonished and taken aback than old John Ellis was at that moment, but I doubt it. The wind was completely taken out of his sails and every bit of the Ellis contrariness was roused.

"What have you got to say against my son?" he fairly shouted in his rage. "Isn't he good enough for your girl, Susan Oliver, I'd like to know?"

"No, he isn't," retorted Miss Susan deliberately and unflinchingly. "He's well enough in his place, but you'll please to remember, John Ellis, that my niece is an Oliver, and the Olivers don't marry beneath them."

Old John was furious. "Beneath them indeed! Why, woman, it is condescension in my son to so much as look at your niece—condescension, that is what it is. You are as poor as church mice."

"We come of good family, though," retorted Miss Susan. "You Ellises are nobodies. Your grandfather was a hired man! And yet you have the presumption to think you're fit to marry into an old, respectable family like the Olivers. But talking doesn't signify. I simply won't allow this nonsense to go on. I came here today to tell you so plump and plain. It's your duty to stop it; if you don't I will, that's all."

"Oh, will you?" John Ellis was at a white heat of rage and stubbornness now. "We'll see, Miss Susan, we'll see. My son shall marry whatever girl he pleases, and I'll back him up in it—do you hear that? Come here and tell me my son isn't good enough for your niece indeed! I'll show you he can get her anyway."

"You've heard what I've said," was the answer, "and you'd better go by it, that's all. I shan't stay to bandy words with you, John Ellis. I'm going home to talk to my niece and tell her her duty plain, and what I want her to do, and she'll do it, I haven't a fear."

Miss Susan was halfway down the steps, but John Ellis ran to the railing of the verandah to get the last word.

"I'll send Burton down this evening to talk to her and tell her what *he* wants her to do, and we'll see whether she'll sooner listen to you than to him," he shouted.

Miss Susan deigned no reply. Old John strode out to the turnip field. Burton saw him coming and looked for another outburst of wrath, but his father's first words almost took away his breath.

"See here, Burt, I take back all I said this afternoon. I want you to marry Madge Oliver now, and the sooner, the better. That old cat of a Susan had the face to come up and tell me you weren't good enough for her niece. I told her a few plain truths. Don't you mind the old crosspatch. I'll back you up."

By this time Burton had begun hoeing vigorously, to hide the amused twinkle of comprehension in his eyes. He admired Miss Susan's tactics, but he did not say so.

"All right, Father," he answered dutifully.

When Miss Susan reached home she told Madge to bathe her eyes and put on her new pink muslin, because she guessed Burton would be down that evening.

"Oh, Auntie, how did you manage it?" cried Madge.

"Madge," said Miss Susan solemnly, but with dancing eyes, "do you know how to drive a pig? Just try to make it go in the opposite direction and it will bolt the way you want it. Remember that, my dear."

Fair Exchange and No Robbery

Katherine Rangely was packing up. Her chum and roommate, Edith Wilmer, was sitting on the bed watching her in that calm disinterested fashion peculiarly maddening to a bewildered packer.

"It does seem too provoking," said Katherine, as she tugged at an obstinate shawl strap, "that Ned should be transferred here now, just when I'm going away. The powers that be might have waited until vacation was over. Ned won't know a soul here and he'll be horribly lonesome."

"I'll do my best to befriend him, with your permission," said Edith consolingly.

"Oh, I know. You're a special Providence, Ede. Ned will be up tonight first thing, of course, and I'll introduce him. Try to keep the poor fellow amused until I get back. Two months! Just fancy! And Aunt Elizabeth won't abate one jot or tittle of the time I promised to stay with her. Harbour Hill is so frightfully dull, too."

Then the talk drifted around to Edith's affairs. She was engaged to a certain Sidney Keith, who was a professor in some college.

"I don't expect to see much of Sidney this summer," said Edith. "He's writing another book. He is so terribly addicted to literature."

"How lovely," sighed Katherine, who had aspirations in that line herself. "If only Ned were like him I should be perfectly happy. But Ned is so prosaic. He doesn't care a rap for poetry, and he laughs when I enthuse. It makes him quite furious when I talk of taking up writing seriously. He says women writers are an abomination on the face of the earth. Did you ever hear anything so ridiculous?"

"He is very handsome, though," said Edith, with a glance at his photograph on Katherine's dressing table. "And that is what Sid is not. He is rather distinguished looking, but as plain as he can possibly be."

Edith sighed. She had a weakness for handsome men and thought it rather hard that fate should have allotted her so plain a lover.

"He has lovely eyes," said Katherine comfortingly, "and handsome men are always vain. Even Ned is. I have to snub him regularly. But I think you'll like him."

Edith thought so too when Ned Ellison appeared that night. He was a handsome off-handed young fellow, who seemed to admire Katherine immensely, and be a little afraid of her into the bargain.

"Edith will try to make Riverton pleasant for you while I am away," she told him in their good-bye chat. "She is a dear girl—you'll like her, I know. It's really too bad I have to go away now, but it can't be helped."

"I shall be awfully lonesome," grumbled Ned. "Don't you forget to write regularly, Kitty."

"Of course I'll write, but for pity's sake, Ned, don't call me Kitty. It sounds so childish. Well, bye-bye, dear boy. I'll be back in two months and then we'll have a lovely time."

When Katherine had been at Harbour Hill for a week she wondered how upon earth she was going to put in the remaining seven. Harbour Hill was noted for its beauty, but not every woman can live by scenery alone.

"Aunt Elizabeth," said Katherine one day, "does anybody ever die in Harbour Hill? Because it doesn't seem to me it would be any change for them if they did."

Aunt Elizabeth's only reply to this was a shocked look.

To pass the time Katherine took to collecting seaweeds, and this involved long tramps along the shore. On one of these occasions she met with an adventure. The place was a remote spot far up the shore. Katherine had taken off her shoes and stockings, tucked up her skirt, rolled her sleeves high above her dimpled elbows, and was deep in the absorbing process of fishing up seaweeds off a craggy headland. She looked anything but dignified while so employed, but under the circumstances dignity did not matter.

Presently she heard a shout from the shore and, turning around in dismay, she beheld a man on the rocks behind her. He was evidently shouting at her. What on earth could the creature want?

"Come in," he called, gesticulating wildly. "You'll be in the bottomless pit in another moment if you don't look out."

"He certainly must be a lunatic," said Katherine to herself, "or else he's drunk. What am I to do?"

"Come in, I tell you," insisted the stranger. "What in the world do you mean by wading out to such a place? Why, it's madness."

Katherine's indignation got the better of her fear.

"I do not think I am trespassing," she called back as icily as possible.

The stranger did not seem to be snubbed at all. He came down to the very edge of the rocks where Katherine could see him plainly. He was dressed in a somewhat well-worn grey suit and wore spectacles. He did not look like a lunatic, and he did not seem to be drunk.

"I implore you to come in," he said earnestly. "You must be standing on the very brink of the bottomless pit."

He is certainly off his balance, thought Katherine. He must be some revivalist who has gone insane on one point. I suppose I'd better go in. He looks quite capable of wading out here after me if I don't.

She picked her steps carefully back with her precious specimens. The stranger eyed her severely as she stepped on the rocks.

"I should think you would have more sense than to risk your life in that fashion for a handful of seaweeds," he said.

"I haven't the faintest idea what you mean," said Miss Rangely. "You don't look crazy, but you talk as if you were."

"Do you mean to say you don't know that what the people hereabouts call the Bottomless Pit is situated right off that point—the most dangerous spot along the whole coast?"

"No, I didn't," said Katherine, horrified. She remembered now that Aunt Elizabeth had warned her to be careful of some bad hole along shore, but she had not been paying much attention and had supposed it to be in quite another direction. "I am a stranger here."

"Well, I hardly thought you'd be foolish enough to be out there if you knew," said the other in mollified accents. "The place ought not to be left without warning, anyhow. It is the most careless thing I ever heard of. There is a big hole right off that point and nobody has ever been able to find the bottom of it. A person who got into it would never be heard of again. The rocks there form an eddy that sucks everything right down."

"I am very grateful to you for calling me in," said Katherine humbly. "I had no idea I was in such danger."

"You have a very fine bunch of seaweeds, I see," said the unknown.

But Katherine was in no mood to converse on seaweeds. She suddenly realized what she must look like—bare feet, draggled skirts, dripping arms. And this creature whom she had taken for a lunatic was undoubtedly a gentleman. Oh, if he would only go and give her a chance to put on her shoes and stockings!

Nothing seemed further from his intentions. When Katherine had picked up the aforesaid articles and turned homeward, he walked beside her, still discoursing on seaweeds as eloquently as if he were commonly accustomed to walking with barefooted young women. In spite of herself, Katherine couldn't help listening to him, for he managed to invest seaweeds with an absorbing interest. She finally decided that as he didn't seem to mind her bare feet, she wouldn't either.

He knew so much about seaweeds that Katherine felt decidedly amateurish beside him. He looked over her specimens and pointed out the valuable ones. He explained the best method of preserving and mounting them, and told her of other and less dangerous places along the shore where she might get some new varieties.

When they came in sight of Harbour Hill, Katherine began to wonder what on earth she would do with him. It wasn't exactly permissible to snub a man who had practically saved your life, but, on the other hand, the prospect of walking through the principal street of Harbour Hill barefooted and escorted by a scholarly looking gentleman discoursing on seaweeds was not to be calmly contemplated.

The unknown cut the Gordian knot himself. He said that he must really go back or he would be late for dinner, lifted his hat politely, and departed. Katherine waited until he was out of sight, then sat down on the sand and put on her shoes and stockings.

"Who on earth can he be?" she said to herself. "And where have I seen him before? There was certainly something familiar about his appearance. He is very nice, but he must have thought me crazy. I wonder if he belongs to Harbour Hill."

The mystery was solved when she got home and found a letter from Edith awaiting her.

"I see Ned quite often," wrote the latter, "and I think he is perfectly splendid. You are a lucky girl, Kate. But oh, do you know that Sidney is actually at Harbour Hill, too, or at least quite near it? I had a letter from him yesterday. He has gone down there to spend his vacation, because it is so quiet, and to finish up some horrid scientific book he is working at. He's boarding at some little farmhouse up the shore. I've written to him today to hunt you up and consider himself introduced to you. I think you'll like him, for he's just your style."

Katherine smiled when Sidney Keith's card was brought up to her that evening and went down to meet him. Her companion of the morning rose to meet her.

"You!" he said.

"Yes, me," said Miss Rangely cheerfully and ungrammatically. "You didn't expect it, did you? I was sure I had seen you before—only it wasn't you but your photograph."

When Professor Keith went away it was with a cordial invitation to call again. He did not fail to avail himself of it—in fact, he became a constant visitor at Sycamore Villa. Katherine wrote all about it to Edith and cultivated Professor Keith with a dear conscience.

They got on capitally together. They went on long expeditions up shore after seaweeds, and when seaweeds were exhausted they began to make a collection of the Harbour Hill flora. This involved more long, companionable expeditions. Katherine sometimes wondered when Professor Keith found time to work on his book, but as he made no reference to the subject, neither did she.

Once in a while, when she had time to think of them, she wondered how Ned and Edith were getting on. At first Edith's letters had been full of Ned, but in her last two or three she had said little about him. Katherine wrote and jokingly asked Edith if she and Ned had quarreled. Edith wrote back and said, "What nonsense." She and Ned were as good friends as ever, but he was getting acquainted in Riverton now and wasn't so dependent on her society, etc.

Katherine sighed and went on a fern hunt with Professor Keith. It was getting near the end of her vacation and she had only two weeks more. They were sitting down to rest on the side of the road when she mentioned this fact inconsequently. The professor prodded the harmless dust with his cane. Well, he supposed she would find a return to work pleasant and would doubtless be glad to see her Riverton friends again.

"I'm dying to see Edith," said Katherine.

"And Ned?" suggested Professor Keith.

"Oh yes. Ned, of course," assented Katherine without enthusiasm. There didn't seem to be anything more to say. One cannot talk everlastingly about ferns, so they got up and went home.

Katherine wrote a particularly affectionate letter to Ned that night. Then she went to bed and cried.

When Professor Keith came up to bid Miss Rangely good-bye on the eve of her departure from Harbour Hill, he looked like a man who was being led to execution without benefit of clergy. But he kept himself well in hand and talked calmly on impersonal subjects. After all, it was Katherine who made the first break when she got up to say good-bye. She was in the middle of some conventional sentence when she suddenly stopped short, and her voice trailed off in a babyish quiver.

The professor put out his arm and drew her close to him. His hat dropped under their feet and was trampled on, but I doubt if Professor Keith knows the difference to this day, for he was fully absorbed in kissing Katherine's hair. When she became cognizant of this fact, she drew herself away.

"Oh, Sidney, don't!—think of Edith! I feel like a traitor."

"Do you think she would care very much if I—if you—if we—" hesitated the professor.

"Oh, it would break her heart," cried Katherine with convincing earnestness. "I know it would—and Ned's too. They must never know."

The professor stooped and began hunting for his maltreated hat. He was a long time finding it, and when he did he went softly to the door. With his hand on the knob, he paused and looked back.

"Good-bye, Miss Rangely," he said softly.

But Katherine, whose face was buried in the cushions of the lounge, did not hear him and when she looked up he was gone.

Katharine felt that life was stale, flat and unprofitable when she alighted at Riverton station in the dusk of the next evening. She was not expected until a later train and there was no one to meet her. She walked drearily through the streets to her boarding house and entered her room unannounced. Edith, who was lying on the bed, sprang up with a surprised greeting. It was too dark to be sure, but Katherine had an uncomfortable suspicion that her friend had been crying, and her heart quaked guiltily. Could Edith have suspected anything?

"Why, we didn't think you'd be up till the 8:30 train, and Ned and I were going to meet you."

"I found I could catch an earlier train, so I took it," said Katherine, as she dropped listlessly into a chair. "I am tired to death and I have such a headache. I can't see anyone tonight, not even Ned."

"You poor dear," said Edith sympathetically, beginning a search for the cologne. "Lie down on the bed and I'll bathe your poor head. Did you have a good time at Harbour Hill? And how did you leave Sid? Did he say anything about coming up?"

"Oh, he was quite well," said Katherine wearily. "I didn't hear him say if he intended to come up or not. There, thanks—that will do nicely."

After Edith had gone down, Katherine tossed about restlessly. She knew Ned had come and she did not want to see him. But, after all, it was only putting off the evil day, and it was treating him rather shabbily. She would go down for a minute.

There were two doors to the parlour, and Katherine went by way of the library one, over which a portiere was hanging. Her hand was lifted to draw it back when she heard something that arrested the movement.

A woman was crying in the room beyond. It was Edith—and what was she saying?

"Oh, Ned, it is all perfectly dreadful! I couldn't look Catherine in the face when she came home. I'm so ashamed of myself and I never meant to be so false. We must never let her suspect for a minute."

"It's pretty rough on a fellow," said another voice—Ned's voice—in a choked sort of a way. "Upon my word, Edith, I don't see how I'm going to keep it up."

"You must," sobbed Edith. "It would break her heart—and Sidney's too. We must just make up our minds to forget each other, Ned, and you must marry Katherine."

Just at this point Katherine became aware that she was eavesdropping and she went away noiselessly. She did not look in the least like a person who has received a mortal blow, and she had forgotten her headache altogether.

When Edith came up half an hour later, she found the worn-out invalid sitting up and reading a novel.

"How is your headache, dear?" she asked, carefully keeping her face turned away from Katherine.

"Oh, it's all gone," said Miss Rangely cheerfully.

"Why didn't you come down then? Ned was here."

"Well, Ede, I did go down, but I thought I wasn't particularly wanted, so I came back."

Edith faced her friend in dismay, forgetful of swollen lids and tear-stained cheeks.

"Katherine!"

"Don't look so conscience stricken, my dear child. There is no harm done."

"You heard—"

"Some surprising speeches. So you and Ned have gone and fallen in love with one another?"

"Oh, Katherine," sobbed Edith, "we—we—couldn't help it—but it's all over. Oh, don't be angry with me!"

"Angry? My dear, I'm delighted."

"Delighted?"

"Yes, you dear goose. Can't you guess, or must I tell you? Sidney and I did the very same, and had just such a melancholy parting last night as I suspect you and Ned had tonight."

"Katherine!"

"Yes, it's quite true. And of course we made up our minds to sacrifice ourselves on the altar of duty and all that. But now, thank goodness, there is no need of such wholesale immolation. So just let's forgive each other."

"Oh," sighed Edith happily, "it is almost too good to be true."

"It is really providentially ordered, isn't it?" said Katherine. "Ned and I would never have got on together in the world, and you and Sidney would have bored each other to death. As it is, there will be four perfectly happy people instead of four miserable ones. I'll tell Ned so tomorrow."

Four Winds

Alan Douglas threw down his pen with an impatient exclamation. It was high time his next Sunday's sermon was written, but he could not concentrate his thoughts on his chosen text. For one thing he did not like it and had selected it only because Elder Trewin, in his call of the evening before, had hinted that it was time for a good stiff doctrinal discourse, such as his predecessor in Rexton, the Rev. Jabez Strong, had delighted in. Alan hated doctrines—"the soul's staylaces," he called them—but Elder Trewin was a man to be reckoned with and Alan preached an occasional sermon to please him.

"It's no use," he said wearily. "I could have written a sermon in keeping with that text in November or midwinter, but now, when the whole world is reawakening in a miracle of beauty and love, I can't do it. If a northeast rainstorm doesn't set in before next Sunday, Mr. Trewin will not have his sermon. I shall take as my text instead, 'The flowers appear on the earth, the time of the singing of birds has come.'"

He rose and went to his study window, outside of which a young vine was glowing in soft tender green tints, its small dainty leaves casting quivering shadows on the opposite wall where the portrait of Alan's mother hung. She had a fine, strong, sweet face; the same face, cast in a masculine mould, was repeated in her son, and the resemblance was striking as he stood in the searching evening sunshine. The black hair grew around his forehead in the same way; his eyes were steel blue, like hers, with a similar expression, half brooding, half tender, in their depths. He had the mobile, smiling mouth of the picture, but his chin was deeper and squarer, dented with a dimple which, combined with a certain occasional whimsicality of opinion and glance, had caused Elder Trewin some qualms of doubt regarding the fitness of this young man for his high and holy vocation. The Rev. Jabez Strong had never indulged in dimples or jokes; but then, as Elder Trewin, being a just man, had to admit, the Rev. Jabez Strong had preached many a time and oft to more empty pews than full ones, while now the church was crowded to its utmost capacity on Sundays and people came to hear Mr. Douglas who had not darkened a church door for years. All things considered, Elder Trewin decided to overlook the dimple. There was sure to be some drawback in every minister.

Alan from his study looked down on all the length of the Rexton valley, at the head of which the manse was situated, and thought that Eden might have looked so in its innocence, for all the orchards were abloom and the distant hills were tremulous and aerial in springtime gauzes of pale purple and pearl. But in any garden, despite its beauty, is an element of tameness and domesticity, and Alan's eyes, after a moment's delighted gazing, strayed wistfully off to the north where the hills broke away into a long sloping lowland of pine and fir. Beyond it stretched the wide expanse of the lake, flashing in the molten gold and crimson of evening. Its lure was irresistible. Alan had been born and bred beside a faraway sea and the love of it was strong in his heart—so strong that he knew he must go back to it sometime. Meanwhile, the great lake, mimicking the sea in its vast expanse and the storms that often swept over it, was his comfort and solace. As often as he could he stole away to its wild and lonely shore, leaving the snug bounds of cultivated home lands behind him with something like a sense of relief. Down there by the lake was a primitive wilderness where man was as naught and man-made doctrines had no place. There one might walk hand in hand with nature and so come very close to God. Many of Alan's best sermons were written after he had come home, rapt-eyed, from some long shore tramp where the wilderness had opened its heart to him and the pines had called to him in their soft, sibilant speech.

With a half guilty glance at the futile sermon, he took his hat and went out. The sun of the cool spring evening was swinging low over the lake as he turned into the unfrequented, deep-rutted road leading to the shore. It was two miles to the lake, but half way there Alan came to where another road branched off and struck down through the pines in a northeasterly direction. He had sometimes wondered where it led but he had never explored it. Now he had a sudden whim to do so and turned into it. It was even rougher and lonelier than the other; between the ruts the grasses grew long and thickly; sometimes the pine boughs met overhead; again, the trees broke away to reveal wonderful glimpses of gleaming water, purple islets, dark feathery coasts. Still, the road seemed to lead nowhere and Alan was half repenting the impulse which had led him to choose it when he suddenly came out from the shadow of the pines and found himself gazing on a sight which amazed him.

Before him was a small peninsula running out into the lake and terminating in a long sandy point. Beyond it was a glorious sweep of sunset water. The peninsula itself seemed barren and sandy, covered for the most part with scrub firs and spruces, through which the narrow road wound on to what was the astonishing; feature in the landscape—a grey and weather-beaten house built almost at the extremity of the point and shadowed from the western light by a thick plantation of tall pines behind it.

It was the house which puzzled Alan. He had never known there was any house near the lake shore—had never heard mention made of any; yet here was one, and one which was evidently occupied, for a slender spiral of smoke was curling upward from it on the chilly spring air. It could not be a fisherman's dwelling, for it was large and built after a quaint tasteful design. The longer Alan looked at it the more his wonder grew. The people living here were in the bounds of his congregation. How then was it that he had never seen or heard of them?

He sauntered slowly down the road until he saw that it led directly to the house and ended in the yard. Then he turned off in a narrow path to the shore. He was not far from the house now and he scanned it observantly as he went past. The barrens swept almost up to its door in front but at the side, sheltered from the lake winds by the pines, was a garden where there was a fine show of gay tulips and golden daffodils. No living creature was visible and, in spite of the blossoming geraniums and muslin curtains at the windows and the homely spiral of smoke, the place had a lonely, almost untenanted, look.

When Alan reached the shore he found that it was of a much more open and less rocky nature than the part which he had been used to frequent. The beach was of sand and the scrub barrens dwindled down to it almost insensibly. To right and left fir-fringed points ran out into the lake, shaping a little cove with the house in its curve.

Alan walked slowly towards the left headland, intending to follow the shore around to the other road. As he passed the point he stopped short in astonishment. The second surprise and mystery of the evening confronted him.

A little distance away a girl was standing—a girl who turned a startled face at his unexpected appearance. Alan Douglas had thought he knew all the girls in Rexton, but this lithe, glorious creature was a stranger to him. She stood with her hand on the head of a huge, tawny collie dog; another dog was sitting on his haunches beside her.

She was tall, with a great braid of shining chestnut hair, showing ruddy burnished tints where the sunlight struck it, hanging over her shoulder. The plain dark dress she wore emphasized the grace and strength of her supple form. Her face was oval and pale, with straight black brows and a finely cut crimson mouth—a face whose beauty bore the indefinable stamp of race and breeding mingled with a wild sweetness, as of a flower growing in some lonely and inaccessible place. None of the Rexton girls looked like that. Who, in the name of all that was amazing, could she be?

As the thought crossed Alan's mind the girl turned, with an air of indifference that might have seemed slightly overdone to a calmer observer than was the young minister at that moment and, with a gesture of command to her dogs, walked quickly away into the scrub spruces. She was so tall that her uncovered head was visible over them as she followed some winding footpath, and Alan stood like a man rooted to the ground until he saw her enter the grey house. Then he went homeward in a maze, all thought of sermons, doctrinal or otherwise, for the moment knocked out of his head.

She is the most beautiful woman I ever saw, he thought. How is it possible that I have lived in Rexton for six months and never heard of her or of that house? Well, I daresay there's some simple explanation of it all. The place may have been unoccupied until lately—probably it is the summer residence of people who have only recently come to it. I'll ask Mrs. Danby. She'll know if anybody will. That good woman knows everything about everybody in Rexton for three generations back.

Alan found Isabel King with his housekeeper when he got home. His greeting was tinged with a slight constraint. He was not a vain man, but he could not help knowing that Isabel looked upon him with a favour that had in it much more than professional interest. Isabel herself showed it with sufficient distinctness. Moreover, he felt a certain personal dislike of her and of her hard, insistent beauty, which seemed harder and more insistent than ever contrasted with his recollection of the girl of the lake shore.

Isabel had a trick of coming to the manse on plausible errands to Mrs. Danby and lingering until it was so dark that Alan was in courtesy bound to see her home. The ruse was a little too patent and amused Alan, although he carefully hid his amusement and treated Isabel with the fine unvarying deference which his mother had engrained into him for womanhood—a deference that flattered Isabel even while it annoyed her with the sense of a barrier which she could not break down or pass. She was the daughter of the richest man in Rexton and inclined to give herself airs on that account, but Alan's gentle indifference always brought home to her an unwelcome feeling of inferiority.

"You've been tiring yourself out again tramping that lake shore, I suppose," said Mrs. Danby, who had kept house for three bachelor ministers and consequently felt entitled to hector them in a somewhat maternal fashion.

"Not tiring myself—resting and refreshing myself rather," smiled Alan. "I was tired when I went out but now I feel like a strong man rejoicing to run a race. By the way, Mrs. Danby, who lives in that quaint old house away down at the very shore? I never knew of its existence before."

Alan's "by the way" was not quite so indifferent as he tried to make it. Isabel King, leaning back posingly among the cushions of the lounge, sat quickly up as he asked his question.

"Dear me, you don't mean to say you've never heard of Captain Anthony—Captain Anthony Oliver?" said Mrs. Danby. "He lives down there at Four Winds, as they call it—he and his daughter and an old cousin."

Isabel King bent forward, her brown eyes on Alan's face.

"Did you see Lynde Oliver?" she asked with suppressed eagerness.

Alan ignored the question—perhaps he did not hear it.

"Have they lived there long?" he asked.

"For eighteen years," said Mrs. Danby placidly. "It's funny you haven't heard them mentioned. But people don't talk much about the Captain now—he's an old story—and of course they never go anywhere, not even to church. The Captain is a rank infidel and they say his daughter is just as bad. To be sure, nobody knows much about her, but it stands to reason that a girl who's had her bringing up must be odd, to say no worse of her. It's not really her fault, I suppose—her wicked old scalawag of a father is to blame for it. She's never darkened a church or school door in her life and they say she's always been a regular tomboy—running wild outdoors with dogs, and fishing and shooting like a man. Nobody ever goes there—the Captain doesn't want visitors. He must have done something dreadful in his time, if it was only known, when he's so set on living like a hermit away down on that jumping-off place. Did you see any of them?"

"I saw Miss Oliver, I suppose," said Alan briefly. "At least I met a young lady on the shore. But where did these people come from? Surely more is known of them than this."

"Precious little. The truth is, Mr. Douglas, folks don't think the Olivers respectable and don't want to have anything to do with them. Eighteen years ago Captain Anthony came from goodness knows where, bought the Four Winds point, and built that house. He said he'd been a sailor all his life and couldn't live away from the water. He brought his wife and child and an old cousin of his with him. This Lynde wasn't more than two years old then. People went to call but they never saw any of the women and the Captain let them see they weren't wanted. Some of the men who'd been working round the place saw his wife and said she was sickly but real handsome and like a lady, but she never seemed to want to see anyone or be seen herself. There was a story that the Captain had been a smuggler and that if he was caught he'd be sent to prison. Oh, there were all sorts of yarns, mostly coming from the men who worked there, for nobody else ever got inside the house. Well, four years ago his wife disappeared—it wasn't known how or when. She just wasn't ever seen again, that's all. Whether she died or was murdered or went away nobody ever knew. There was some talk of an investigation but nothing came of it. As for the girl, she's always lived there with her father. She must be a perfect heathen. He never goes anywhere, but there used to be talk of strangers visiting him—queer sort of characters who came up the lake in vessels from the American side. I haven't heard any reports of such these past few years, though—not since his wife disappeared. He keeps a yacht and goes sailing in it—sometimes he cruises about for weeks—that's about all he ever does. And now you know as much about the Olivers as I do, Mr. Douglas."

Alan had listened to this gossipy narrative with an interest that did not escape Isabel King's observant eyes. Much of it he mentally dismissed as improbable surmise, but the basic facts were probably as Mrs. Danby had reported them. He had known that the girl of the shore could be no commonplace, primly nurtured young woman.

"Has no effort ever been made to bring these people into touch with the church?" he asked absently.

"Bless you, yes. Every minister that's ever been in Rexton has had a try at it. The old cousin met every one of them at the door and told him nobody was at home. Mr. Strong was the most persistent—he didn't like being beaten. He went again and again and finally the Captain sent him word that when he wanted parsons or pill-dosers he'd send for them, and till he did he'd thank them to mind their own business. They say Mr. Strong met Lynde once along shore and wanted to know if she wouldn't come to church, and she laughed in his face and told him she knew more about God now than he did or ever would. Perhaps the story isn't true. Or if it was maybe he provoked her into saying it. Mr. Strong wasn't overly tactful. I believe in judging the poor girl as charitably as possible and making allowances for her, seeing how she's been brought up. You couldn't expect her to know how to behave."

Somehow, Alan resented Mrs. Danby's charity. Then, his sense of humour being strongly developed, he smiled to think of this commonplace old lady "making allowances" for the splendid bit of femininity he had seen on the shore. A plump barnyard fowl might as well have talked of making allowances for a seagull!

Alan walked home with Isabel King but he was very silent as they went together down the long, dark, sweet-smelling country road bordered by its white orchards. Isabel put her own construction on his absent replies to her remarks and presently she asked him, "Did you think Lynde Oliver handsome?"

The question gave Alan an annoyance out of all proportion to its significance. He felt an instinctive reluctance to discuss Lynde Oliver with Isabel King.

"I saw her only for a moment," he said coldly, "but she impressed me as being a beautiful woman."

"They tell queer stories about her—but maybe they're not all true," said Isabel, unable to keep the sneer of malice out of her voice. At that moment Alan's secret contempt for her crystallized into pronounced aversion. He made no reply and they went the rest of the way in silence. At her gate Isabel said, "You haven't been over to see us very lately, Mr. Douglas."

"My congregation is a large one and I cannot visit all my people as often as I might wish," Alan answered, all the more coldly for the personal note in her tone. "A minister's time is not his own, you know."

"Shall you be going to see the Olivers?" asked Isabel bluntly.

"I have not considered that question. Good-night, Miss King."

On his way back to the manse Alan did consider the question. Should he make any attempt to establish friendly relations with the residents of Four Winds? It surprised him to find how much he wanted to, but he finally concluded that he would not. They were not adherents of his church and he did not believe that even a minister had any right to force himself upon people who plainly wished to be let alone.

When he got home, although it was late, he went to his study and began work on a new text—for Elder Trewin's seemed utterly out of the question. Even with the new one he did not get on very well. At last in exasperation he leaned back in his chair.

Why can't I stop thinking of those Four Winds people? Here, let me put these haunting thoughts into words and see if that will lay them. That girl had a beautiful face but a cold one. Would I like to see it lighted up with the warmth of her soul set free? Yes, frankly, I would. She looked upon me with indifference. Would I like to see her welcome me as a friend? I have a conviction that I would, although no doubt everybody in my congregation would look upon her as a most unsuitable friend for me. Do I believe that she is wild, unwomanly, heathenish, as Mrs. Danby says? No, I do not, most emphatically. I believe she is a lady in the truest sense of that much abused word, though she is doubtless unconventional. Having said all this, I do not see what more there is to be said. And—I—am—going—to—write—this—sermon.

Alan wrote it, putting all thought of Lynde Oliver sternly out of his mind for the time being. He had no notion of falling in love with her. He knew nothing of love and imagined that it counted for nothing in his life. He admitted that his curiosity was aflame about the girl, but it never occurred to him that she meant or could mean anything to him but an attractive enigma which once solved would lose its attraction. The young women he knew in Rexton, whose simple, pleasant friendship he valued, had the placid, domestic charm of their own sweet-breathed, windless orchards. Lynde Oliver had the fascination of the lake shore—wild, remote, untamed—the lure of the wilderness and the primitive. There was nothing more personal in his thought of her, and yet when he recalled Isabel King's sneer he felt an almost personal resentment.

During the following fortnight Alan made many trips to the shore—and he always went by the branch road to the Four Winds point. He did not attempt to conceal from himself that he hoped to meet Lynde Oliver again. In this he was unsuccessful. Sometimes he saw her at a distance along the shore but she always disappeared as soon as seen. Occasionally as he crossed the point he saw her working in her garden but he never went very near the house, feeling that he had no right to spy on it or her in any way. He soon became convinced that she avoided him purposely and the conviction piqued him. He felt an odd masterful desire to meet her face to face and make her look at him. Sometimes he called himself a fool and vowed he would go no more to the Four Winds shore. Yet he inevitably went. He did not find in the shore the comfort and inspiration he had formerly found. Something had come between his soul and the soul of the wilderness—something he did not recognize or formulate—a nameless, haunting longing that shaped itself about the memory of a cold sweet face and starry, indifferent eyes, grey as the lake at dawn.

Of Captain Anthony he never got even a glimpse, but he saw the old cousin several times, going and coming about the yard and its environs. Finally one day he met her, coming up a path which led to a spring down in a firry hollow. She was carrying two heavy pails of water and Alan asked permission to help her.

He half expected a repulse, for the tall, grim old woman had a rather stern and forbidding look, but after gazing at him a moment in a somewhat scrutinizing manner she said briefly, "You may, if you like."

Alan took the pails and followed her, the path not being wide enough for two. She strode on before him at a rapid, vigorous pace until they came out into the yard by the house. Alan felt his heart beating foolishly. Would he see Lynde Oliver? Would—

"You may carry the water there," the old woman said, pointing to a little outhouse near the pines. "I'm washing—the spring water is softer than the well water. Thank you"—as Alan set the pails down on a bench—"I'm not so young as I was and bringing the water so far tires me. Lynde always brings it for me when she's home."

She stood before him in the narrow doorway, blocking his exit, and looked at him with keen, deep-set dark eyes. In spite of her withered aspect and wrinkled face, she was not an uncomely old woman and there was about her a dignity of carriage and manner that pleased Alan. It did not occur to him to wonder why it should please him. If he had hunted that feeling down he might have been surprised to discover that it had its origin in a curious gratification over the thought that the woman who lived with Lynde had a certain refinement about her. He preferred her unsmiling dourness to vulgar garrulity.

"Are you the young minister up at Rexton?" she asked bluntly.

"Yes."

"I thought so. Lynde said she had seen you on the shore once. Well"—she cast an uncertain glance over her shoulder at the house—"I'm much obliged to you."

Alan had an idea that that was not what she had thought of saying, but as she had turned aside and was busying herself with the pails, there seemed nothing for him to do but to go.

"Wait a moment." She faced him again, and if Alan had been a vain man he might have thought that admiration looked from her piercing eyes. "What do you think of us? I suppose they've told you tales of us up there?"—with a scornful gesture of her hand in the direction of Rexton. "Do you believe them?"

"I believe no ill of anyone until I have absolute proof of it," said Alan, smiling—he was quite unconscious what a winning smile he had, which was the best of it—"and I never put faith in gossip. Of course you are gossipped about—you know that."

"Yes, I know it"—grimly—"and I don't care what they say about the Captain and me. We are a queer pair—just as queer as they make us out. You can believe what you like about us, but don't you believe a word they say against Lynde. She's sweet and good and beautiful. It's not her fault that she never went to church—it's her father's. Don't you hold that against her."

The fierce yet repressed energy of her tone prevented Alan from feeling any amusement over her simple defence of Lynde. Moreover, it sounded unreasonably sweet in his ears.

"I won't," he promised, "but I don't suppose it would matter much to Miss Oliver if I did. She did not strike me as a young lady who would worry very much about other people's opinions."

If his object were to prolong the conversation about Lynde, he was disappointed, for the old woman had turned abruptly to her work again and, though Alan lingered for a few moments longer, she took no further notice of him. But when he had gone she peered stealthily after him from the door until he was lost to sight among the pines.

"A well-looking man," she muttered. "I wish Lynde had been home. I didn't dare ask him to the house for I knew Anthony was in one of his moods. But it's time something was done. She's woman grown and this is no life for her. And there's nobody to do anything but me and I'm not able, even if I knew what to do. I wonder why she hates men so. Perhaps it's because she never knew any that were real gentlemen. This man is—but then he's a minister and that makes a wide gulf between them in another way. I've seen the love of man and woman bridge some wider gulfs though. But it can't with Lynde, I'm fearing. She's so bitter at the mere speaking of love and marriage. I can't think why. I'm sure her mother and Anthony were happy together, and that was all she's ever seen of marriage. But I thought when she told me of meeting this young man on the shore there was something in her look I'd never noticed before—as if she'd found something in herself she'd never known was there. But she'll never make friends with him and I can't. If the Captain wasn't so queer—"

She stopped abruptly, for a tall lithe figure was coming up from the shore. Lynde waved her hand as she drew near.

"Oh, Emily, I've had such a splendid sail. It was glorious. Bad Emily, you've been carrying water. Didn't I tell you never to do that when I was away?"

"I didn't have to do it. That young minister up at Rexton met me and brought it up. He's nice, Lynde."

Lynde's brow darkened. She turned and walked away to the house without a word.

On his way home that night Alan met Isabel King on the main shore road. She carried an armful of pine boughs and said she wanted the needles for a cushion. Yet the thought came into Alan's mind that she was spying on him and, although he tried to dismiss it as unworthy, it continued to lurk there.

For a week he avoided the shore, but there came a day when its inexplicable lure drew him to it again irresistibly. It was a warm, windy evening and the air was sweet and resinous, the lake misty and blue. There was no sign of life about Four Winds and the shore seemed as lonely and virgin as if human foot had never trodden it. The Captain's yacht was gone from the little harbour where it was generally anchored and, though every flutter of wind in the scrub firs made Alan's heart beat expectantly, he saw nothing of Lynde Oliver. He was on the point of turning homeward, with an unreasoning sense of disappointment, when one of Lynde's dogs broke down through the hedge of spruces, barking loudly.

Alan looked for Lynde to follow, but she did not, and he speedily saw that there was something unusual about the dog's behaviour. The animal circled around him, still barking excitedly, then ran off for a short distance, stopped, barked again, and returned, repeating the manoeuvre. It was plain that he wanted Alan to follow him, and it occurred to the young minister that the dog's mistress must be in danger of some kind. Instantly he set off after him; and the dog, with a final sharp bark of satisfaction, sprang up the low bank into the spruces.

Alan followed him across the peninsula and then along the further shore, which rapidly grew steep and high. Half a mile down the cliffs were rocky and precipitous, while the beach beneath them was heaped with huge boulders. Alan followed the dog along one of the narrow paths with which the barrens abounded until nearly a mile from Four Winds. Then the animal halted, ran to the edge of the cliff and barked.

It was an ugly-looking place where a portion of the soil had evidently broken away recently, and Alan stepped cautiously out to the brink and looked down. He could not repress an exclamation of dismay and alarm.

A few feet below him Lynde Oliver was lying on a mass of mossy soil which was apparently on the verge of slipping over a sloping shelf of rock, below which was a sheer drop of thirty feet to the cruel boulders below. The extreme danger of her position was manifest at a glance; the soil on which she lay was stationary, yet it seemed as if the slightest motion on her part would send it over the brink.

Lynde lay movelessly; her face was white, and both fear and appeal were visible in her large dilated eyes. Yet she was quite calm and a faint smile crossed her pale lips as she saw the man and the dog.

"Good faithful Pat, so you did bring help," she said.

"But how can I help you, Miss Oliver?" said Alan hoarsely. "I cannot reach you—and it looks as if the slightest touch or jar would send that broken earth over the brink."

"I fear it would. You must go back to Four Winds and get a rope."

"And leave you here alone—in such danger?"

"Pat will stay with me. Besides, there is nothing else to do. You will find a rope in that little house where you put the water for Emily. Father and Emily are away. I think I am quite safe here if I don't move at all."

Alan's own common sense told him that, as she said, there was nothing else to do and, much as he hated to leave her alone thus, he realized that he must lose no time in doing it.

"I'll be back as quickly as possible," he said hurriedly.

Alan had been a noted runner at college and his muscles had not forgotten their old training. Yet it seemed to him an age ere he reached Four Winds, secured the rope, and returned. At every flying step he was haunted by the thought of the girl lying on the brink of the precipice and the fear that she might slip over it before he could rescue her. When he reached the scene of the accident he dreaded to look over the broken edge, but she was lying there safely and she smiled when she saw him—a brave smile that softened her tense white face into the likeness of a frightened child's.

"If I drop the rope down to you, are you strong enough to hold to it while the earth goes and then draw yourself up the slope hand over hand?" asked Alan anxiously.

"Yes," she answered fearlessly.

Alan passed down one end of the rope and then braced himself firmly to hold it, for there was no tree near enough to be of any assistance. The next moment the full weight of her body swung from it, for at her first movement the soil beneath her slipped away. Alan's heart sickened; what if she went with it? Could she cling to the rope while he drew her up?

Then he saw she was still safe on the sloping shelf. Carefully and painfully she drew herself to her knees and, dinging to the rope, crept up the rock hand over hand. When she came within his reach he grasped her arms and lifted her up into safety beside him.

"Thank God," he said, with whiter lips than her own.

For a few moments Lynde sat silent on the sod, exhausted with fright and exertion, while her dog fawned on her in an ecstasy of joy. Finally she looked up into Alan's anxious face and their eyes met. It was something more than the physical reaction that suddenly flushed the girl's cheeks. She sprang lithely to her feet.

"Can you walk back home?" Alan asked.

"Oh, yes, I am all right now. It was very foolish of me to get into such a predicament. Father and Emily went down the lake in the yacht this afternoon and I started out for a ramble. When I came here I saw some junebells growing right out on the ledge and I crept out to gather them. I should have known better. It broke away under me and the more I tried to scramble back the faster it slid down, carrying me with it. I thought it would go right over the brink"—she gave a little involuntary shudder—"but just at the very edge it stopped. I knew I must lie very still or it would go right over. It seemed like days. Pat was with me and I told him to go for help, but I knew there was no one at home—and I was horribly afraid," she concluded with another shiver. "I never was afraid in my life before—at least not with that kind of fear."

"You have had a terrible experience and a narrow escape," said Alan lamely. He could think of nothing more to say; his usual readiness of utterance seemed to have failed him.

"You saved my life," she said, "you and Pat—for doggie must have his share of credit."

"A much larger share than mine," said Alan, smiling. "If Pat had not come for me, I would not have known of your danger. What a magnificent fellow he is!"

"Isn't he?" she agreed proudly. "And so is Laddie, my other dog. He went with Father today. I love my dogs more than people." She looked at him with a little defiance in her eyes. "I suppose you think that terrible."

"I think many dogs are much more lovable—and worthy of love—than many people," said Alan, laughing.

How childlike she was in some ways! That trace of defiance—it was so like a child who expected to be scolded for some wrong attitude of mind. And yet there were moments when she looked the tall proud queen. Sometimes, when the path grew narrow, she walked before him, her hand on the dog's head. Alan liked this, since it left him free to watch admiringly the swinging grace of her step and the white curves of her neck beneath the thick braid of hair, which today was wound about her head. When she dropped back beside him in the wider spaces, he could only have stolen glances at her profile, delicately, strongly cut, virginal in its soft curves, childlike in its purity. Once she looked around and caught his glance; again she flushed, and something strange and exultant stirred in Alan's heart. It was as if that maiden blush were the involuntary, unconscious admission of some power he had over her—a power which her hitherto unfettered spirit had never before felt. The cold indifference he had seen in her face at their first meeting was gone, and something told him it was gone forever.

When they came in sight of Four Winds they saw two people walking up the road from the harbour and a few further steps brought them face to face with Captain Anthony Oliver and his old housekeeper.

The Captain's appearance was a fresh surprise to Alan. He had expected to meet a rough, burly sailor, loud of voice and forbidding of manner. Instead, Captain Anthony was a tall, well-built man of perhaps fifty. His face, beneath its shock of iron-grey hair, was handsome but wore a somewhat forbidding expression, and there was something in it, apart from line or feature, which did not please Alan. He had no time to analyze this impression, for Lynde said hurriedly, "Father, this is Mr. Douglas. He has just done me a great service."

She briefly explained her accident; when she had finished, the Captain turned to Alan and held out his hand, a frank smile replacing the rather suspicious and contemptuous scowl which had previously overshadowed it.

"I am much obliged to you, Mr. Douglas," he said cordially. "You must come up to the house and let me thank you at leisure. As a rule I'm not very partial to the cloth, as you may have heard. In this case it is the man, not the minister, I invite."

The front door of Four Winds opened directly into a wide, low-ceilinged living room, furnished with simplicity and good taste. Leaving the two men there, Lynde and the old cousin vanished, and Alan found himself talking freely with the Captain who could, as it appeared, talk well on many subjects far removed from Four Winds. He was evidently a clever, self-educated man, somewhat opinionated and given to sarcasm; he never made any references to his own past life or experiences, but Alan discovered him to be surprisingly well read in politics and science. Sometimes in the pauses of the conversation Alan found the older man looking at him in a furtive way he did not like, but the Captain was such an improvement on what he had been led to expect that he was not inclined to be over critical. At least, this was what he honestly thought. He did not suspect that it was because this man was Lynde's father that he wished to think as well as possible of him.

Presently Lynde came in. She had changed her outdoor dress, stained with moss and soil in her fall, for a soft clinging garment of some pale yellow material, and her long, thick braid of hair hung over her shoulder. She sat mutely down in a dim corner and took no part in the conversation except to answer briefly the remarks which Alan addressed to her. Emily came in and lighted the lamp on the table. She was as grim and unsmiling as ever, yet she cast a look of satisfaction on Alan as she passed out. One dog lay down at Lynde's feet, the other sat on his haunches by her side and laid his head on her lap. Rexton and its quiet round of parish duties seemed thousands of miles away from Alan, and he wondered a little if this were not all a dream.

When he went away the Captain invited him back.

"If you like to come, that is," he said brusquely, "and always as the man, not the priest, remember. I don't want you by and by to be slyly slipping in the thin end of any professional wedges. You'll waste your time if you do. Come as man to man and you'll be welcome, for I like you—and it's few men I like. But don't try to talk religion to me."

"I never talk religion," said Alan emphatically. "I try to live it. I'll not come to your house as a self-appointed missionary, sir, but I shall certainly act and speak at all times as my conscience and my reverence for my vocation demands. If I respect your beliefs, whatever they may be, I shall expect you to respect mine, Captain Oliver."

"Oh, I won't insult your God," said the Captain with a faint sneer.

Alan went home in a tumult of contending feelings. He did not altogether like Captain Anthony—that was very clear to him, and yet there was something about the man that attracted him. Intellectually he was a worthy foeman, and Alan had often longed for such since coming to Rexton. He missed the keen, stimulating debates of his college days and, now there seemed a chance of renewing them, he was eager to grasp it. And Lynde—how beautiful she was! What though she shared—as was not unlikely—in her father's lack of belief? She could not be essentially irreligious—that were impossible in a true woman. Might not this be his opportunity to help her—to lead her into dearer light? Alan Douglas was a sincere man, with himself as well as with others, yet there are some motives that lie, in their first inception, too deep even for the probe of self-analysis. He had not as yet the faintest suspicion as to the real source of his interest in Lynde Oliver—in his sudden forceful desire to be of use and service to her—to rescue her from spiritual peril as he had that day rescued her from bodily danger.

She must have a lonely, unsatisfying life, he thought. It is my duty to help her if I can.

It did not then occur to him that duty in this instance wore a much more pleasing aspect than it had sometimes worn in his experience.

Alan did not mean to be oversoon in going back to Four Winds, but three days later a book came to him which Captain Anthony had expressed a wish to see. It furnished an excuse for an earlier call. After that he went often. He always found the Captain courteous and affable, old Emily grimly cordial, Lynde sometimes remote and demure, sometimes frankly friendly. Occasionally, when the Captain was away in his yacht, he went for a walk with her and her dogs along the shore or through the sweet-smelling pinelands up the lake. He found that she loved books and was avid for more of them than she could obtain; he was glad to take her several and discuss them with her. She liked history and travels best. With novels she had no patience, she said disdainfully. She seldom spoke of herself or her past life and Alan fancied she avoided any personal reference. But once she said abruptly, "Why do you never ask me to go to church? I've always been afraid you would."

"Because I do not think it would do you any good to go if you didn't want to," said Alan gravely. "Souls should not be rudely handled any more than bodies."

She looked at him reflectively, her finger denting her chin in a meditative fashion she had.

"You are not at all like Mr. Strong. He always scolded me, when he got a chance, for not going to church. I would have hated him if it had been worthwhile. I told him one day that I was nearer to God under these pines than I could be in any building fashioned by human hands. He was very much shocked. But I don't want you to misunderstand me. Father does not go to church because he does not believe there is a God. But I know there is. Mother taught me so. I have never gone to church because Father would not allow me, and I could not go now in Rexton where the people talk about me so. Oh, I know they do—you know it, too—but I do not care for them. I know I'm not like other girls. I would like to be but I can't be—I never can be—now."

There was some strange passion in her voice that Alan did not quite understand—a bitterness and a revolt which he took to be against the circumstances that hedged her in.

"Is not some other life possible for you if your present life does not content you?" he said gently.

"But it does content me," said Lynde imperiously. "I want no other—I wish this life to go on forever—forever, do you understand? If I were sure that it would—if I were sure that no change would ever come to me, I would be perfectly content. It is the fear that a change will come that makes me wretched. Oh!" She shuddered and put her hands over her eyes.

Alan thought she must mean that when her father died she would be alone in the world. He wanted to comfort her—reassure her—but he did not know how.

One evening when he went to Four Winds he found the door open and, seeing the Captain in the living room, he stepped in unannounced. Captain Anthony was sitting by the table, his head in his hands; at Alan's entrance he turned upon him a haggard face, blackened by a furious scowl beneath which blazed eyes full of malevolence.

"What do you want here?" he said, following up the demand with a string of vile oaths.

Before Alan could summon his scattered wits, Lynde glided in with a white, appealing face. Wordlessly she grasped Alan's arm, drew him out, and shut the door.

"Oh, I've been watching for you," she said breathlessly. "I was afraid you might come tonight—but I missed you."

"But your father?" said Alan in amazement. "How have I angered him?"

"Hush. Come into the garden. I will explain there."

He followed her into the little enclosure where the red and white roses were now in full blow.

"Father isn't angry with you," said Lynde in a low shamed voice. "It's just—he takes strange moods sometimes. Then he seems to hate us all—even me—and he is like that for days. He seems to suspect and dread everybody as if they were plotting against him. You—perhaps you think he has been drinking? No, that is not the trouble. These terrible moods come on without any cause that we know of. Even Mother could not do anything with him when he was like that. You must go away now—and do not come back until his dark mood has passed. He will be just as glad to see you as ever then, and this will not make any difference with him. Don't come back for a week at least."

"I do not like to leave you in such trouble, Miss Oliver."

"Oh, it doesn't matter about me—I have Emily. And there is nothing you could do. Please go at once. Father knows I am talking to you and that will vex him still more."

Alan, realizing that he could not help her and that his presence only made matters worse, went away perplexedly. The following week was a miserable one for him. His duties were distasteful to him and meeting his people a positive torture. Sometimes Mrs. Danby looked dubiously at him and seemed on the point of saying something—but never said it. Isabel King watched him when they met, with bold probing eyes. In his abstraction he did not notice this any more than he noticed a certain subtle change which had come over the members of his congregation—as if a breath of suspicion had blown across them and troubled their confidence and trust. Once Alan would have been keenly and instantly conscious of this slight chill; now he was not even aware of it.

When he ventured to go back to Four Winds he found the Captain on the point of starting off for a cruise in his yacht. He was urbane and friendly, utterly ignoring the incident of Alan's last visit and regretting that business compelled him to go down the lake. Alan saw him off with small regret and turned joyfully to Lynde, who was walking under the pines with her dogs. She looked pale and tired and her eyes were still troubled, but she smiled proudly and made no reference to what had happened.

"I'm going to put these flowers on Mother's grave," she said, lifting her slender hands filled with late white roses. "Mother loved flowers and I always keep them near her when I can. You may come with me if you like."

Alan had known Lynde's mother was buried under the pines but he had never visited the spot before. The grave was at the westernmost end of the pine wood, where it gave out on the lake, a beautiful spot, given over to silence and shadow.

"Mother wished to be buried here," Lynde said, kneeling to arrange her flowers. "Father would have taken her anywhere but she said she wanted to be near us and near the lake she had loved so well. Father buried her himself. He wouldn't have anyone else do anything for her. I am so glad she is here. It would have been terrible to have seen her taken far away—my sweet little mother."

"A mother is the best thing in the world—I realized that when I lost mine," said Alan gently. "How long is it since your mother died?"

"Three years. Oh, I thought I should die too when she did. She was very ill—she was never strong, you know—but I never thought she could die. There was a year then—part of the time I didn't believe in God at all and the rest I hated Him. I was very wicked but I was so unhappy. Father had so many dreadful moods and—there was something else. I used to wish to die."

She bowed her head on her hands and gazed moodily on the ground. Alan, leaning against a pine tree, looked down at her. The sunlight fell through the swaying boughs on her glory of burnished hair and lighted up the curve of cheek and chin against the dark background of wood brown. All the defiance and wildness had gone from her for the time and she seemed like a helpless, weary child. He wanted to take her in his arms and comfort her.

"You must resemble your mother," he said absently, as if thinking aloud. "You don't look at all like your father."

Lynde shook her head.

"No, I don't look like Mother either. She was tiny and dark—she had a sweet little face and velvet-brown eyes and soft curly dark hair. Oh, I remember her look so well. I wish I did resemble her. I loved her so—I would have done anything to save her suffering and trouble. At least, she died in peace."

There was a curious note of fierce self-gratulation in the girl's voice as she spoke the last sentence. Again Alan felt the unpleasant impression that there was much in her that he did not understand—might never understand—although such understanding was necessary to perfect friendship. She had never spoken so freely of her past life to him before, yet he felt somehow that something was being kept back in jealous repression. It must be something connected with her father, Alan thought. Doubtless, Captain Anthony's past would not bear inspection, and his daughter knew it and dwelt in the shadow of her knowledge. His heart filled with aching pity for her; he raged secretly because he was so powerless to help her. Her girlhood had been blighted, robbed of its meed of happiness and joy. Was she likewise to miss her womanhood? Alan's hands clenched involuntarily at the unuttered question.

On his way home that evening he again met Isabel King. She turned and walked back with him but she made no reference to Four Winds or its inhabitants. If Alan had troubled himself to look, he would have seen a malicious glow in her baleful brown eyes. But the only eyes which had any meaning for him just then were the grey ones of Lynde Oliver.

During Alan's next three visits to Four Winds he saw nothing of Lynde, either in the house or out of it. This surprised and worried him. There was no apparent difference in Captain Anthony, who continued to be suave and friendly. Alan always enjoyed his conversations with the Captain, who was witty, incisive, and pungent; yet he disliked the man himself more at every visit. If he had been compelled to define his impression, he would have said the Captain was a charming scoundrel.

But it occurred to him that Emily was disturbed about something. Sometimes he caught her glance, full of perplexity and—it almost seemed—distrust. She looked as if she felt hostile towards him. But Alan dismissed the idea as absurd. She had been friendly from the first and he had done nothing to excite her disapproval. Lynde's mysterious absence was a far more perplexing problem. She had not gone away, for when Alan asked the Captain concerning her, he responded indifferently that she was out walking. Alan caught a glint of amusement in the older man's eyes as he spoke. He could have sworn it was malicious amusement.

One evening he went to Four Winds around the shore. As he turned the headland of the cove, he saw Lynde and her dogs not a hundred feet away. The moment she saw him she darted up the bank and disappeared among the firs.

Alan was thunderstruck. There was no room for doubt that she meant to avoid him. He walked up to the house in a tumult of mingled feelings which he did not even then understand. He only realized that he felt bitterly hurt and grieved—puzzled as well. What did it all mean?

He met Emily in the yard of Four Winds on her way to the spring and stopped her resolutely.

"Miss Oliver," he said bluntly, "is Miss Lynde angry with me? And why?"

Emily looked at him piercingly.

"Have you no idea why?" she asked shortly.

"None in the world."

She looked at him through and through a moment longer. Then, seeming satisfied with her scrutiny, she picked up her pail.

"Come down to the spring with me," she said.

As soon as they were out of sight of the house, Emily began abruptly.

"If you don't know why Lynde is acting so, I can't tell you, for I don't know either. I don't even know if she is angry. I only thought perhaps she was—that you had done or said something to vex her—plaguing her to go to church maybe. But if you didn't, it may not be anger at all. I don't understand that girl. She's been different ever since her mother died. She used to tell me everything before that. You must go and ask her right out yourself what is wrong. But maybe I can tell you something. Did you write her a letter a fortnight ago?"

"A letter? No."

"Well, she got one then. I thought it came from you—I didn't know who else would be writing to her. A boy brought it and gave it to her at the door. She's been acting strange ever since. She cries at night—something Lynde never did before except when her mother died. And in daytime she roams the shore and woods like one possessed. You must find out what was in that letter, Mr. Douglas."

"Have you any idea who the boy was?" Alan asked, feeling somewhat relieved. The mystery was clearing up, he thought. No doubt it was the old story of some cowardly anonymous letter. His thoughts flew involuntarily to Isabel King.

Emily shook her head.

"No. He was just a half-grown fellow with reddish hair and he limped a little."

"Oh, that is the postmaster's son," said Alan disappointedly. "That puts us further off the scent than ever. The letter was probably dropped in the box at the office and there will consequently be no way of tracing the writer."

"Well, I can't tell you anything more," said Emily. "You'll have to ask Lynde for the truth."

This Alan was determined to do whenever he should meet her. He did not go to the house with Emily but wandered about the shore, watching for Lynde and not seeing her. At length he went home, a prey to stormy emotions. He realized at last that he loved Lynde Oliver. He wondered how he could have been so long blind to it. He knew that he must have loved her ever since he had first seen her. The discovery amazed but did not shock him. There was no reason why he should not love her—should not woo and win her for his wife if she cared for him. She was good and sweet and true. Anything of doubt in her antecedents could not touch her. Probably the world would look upon Captain Anthony as a somewhat undesirable father-in-law for a minister, but that aspect of the question did not disturb Alan. As for the trouble of the letter, he felt sure he would easily be able to clear it away. Probably some malicious busybody had become aware of his frequent calls at Four Winds and chose to interfere in his private affairs thus. For the first time it occurred to him that there had been a certain lack of cordiality among his people of late. If it were really so, doubtless this was the reason. At any other time this would have been of moment to him. But now his thoughts were too wholly taken up with Lynde and the estrangement on her part to attach much importance to anything else. What she thought mattered incalculably more to Alan than what all the people in Rexton put together thought. He had the right, like any other man, to woo the woman of his choice and he would certainly brook no outside interference in the matter.

After a sleepless night he went back to Four Winds in the morning. Lynde would not expect him at that time and he would have more chance of finding her. The result justified his idea, for he met her by the spring.

Alan felt shocked at the change in her appearance. She looked as if years of suffering had passed over her. Her lips were pallid, and hollow circles under her eyes made them appear unnaturally large. He had last left the girl in the bloom of her youth; he found her again a woman on whom life had laid its heavy hand.

A burning flood of colour swept over her face as they met, then receded as quickly, leaving her whiter than before. Without any waste of words, Alan plunged abruptly into the subject.

"Miss Oliver, why have you avoided me so of late? Have I done anything to offend you?"

"No." She spoke as if the word hurt her, her eyes persistently cast down.

"Then what is the trouble?"

There was no answer. She gave an unvoluntary glance around as if seeking some way of escape. There was none, for the spring was set about with thick young firs and Alan blocked the only path.

He leaned forward and took her hands in his.

"Miss Oliver, you must tell me what the trouble is," he said firmly.

She pulled her hands away and flung them up to her face, her form shaken by stormy sobs. In distress he put his arm about her and drew her closer.

"Tell me, Lynde," he whispered tenderly.

She broke away from him, saying passionately, "You must not come to Four Winds any more. You must not have anything more to do with us—any of us. We have done you enough harm already. But I never thought it could hurt you—oh, I am sorry, sorry!"

"Miss Oliver, I want to see that letter you received the other evening. Oh"—as she started with surprise—"I know about it—Emily told me. Who wrote it?"

"There was no name signed to it," she faltered.

"Just as I thought. Well, you must let me see it."

"I cannot—I burned it."

"Then tell me what was in it. You must. This matter must be cleared up—I am not going to have our beautiful friendship spoiled by the malice of some coward. What did that letter say?"

"It said that everybody in your congregation was talking about your frequent visits here—that it had made a great scandal—that it was doing you a great deal of injury and would probably end in your having to leave Rexton."

"That would be a catastrophe indeed," said Alan drily. "Well, what else?"

"Nothing more—at least, nothing about you. The rest was about myself—I did not mind it—much. But I was so sorry to think that I had done you harm. It is not too late to undo it. You must not come here any more. Then they will forget."

"Perhaps—but I should not forget. It's a little too late for me. Lynde, you must not let this venomous letter come between us. I love you, dear—I've loved you ever since I met you and I want you for my wife."

Alan had not intended to say that just then, but the words came to his lips in spite of himself. She looked so sad and appealing and weary that he wanted to have the right to comfort and protect her.

She turned her eyes full upon him with no hint of maidenly shyness or shrinking in them. Instead, they were full of a blank, incredulous horror that swallowed up every other feeling. There was no mistaking their expression and it struck an icy chill to Alan's heart. He had certainly not expected a too ready response on her part—he knew that even if she cared for him he might find it a matter of time to win her avowal of it—but he certainly had not expected to see such evident abject dismay as her blanched face betrayed. She put up her hand as if warding a blow.

"Don't—don't," she gasped. "You must not say that—you must never say it. Oh, I never dreamed of this. If I had thought it possible you could—love me, I would never have been friends with you. Oh, I've made a terrible mistake."

She wrung her hands piteously together, looking like a soul in torment. Alan could not bear to see her pain.

"Don't feel such distress," he implored. "I suppose I've spoken too abruptly—but I'll be so patient, dear, if you'll only try to care for me a little. Can't you, dear?"

"I can't marry you," said Lynde desperately. She leaned against a slim white bole of a young birch behind her and looked at him wretchedly. "Won't you please go away and forget me?"

"I can't forget you," Alan said, smiling a little in spite of his suffering. "You are the only woman I can ever love—and I can't give you up unless I have to.

Won't you be frank with me, dear? Do you honestly think you can never learn to love me?"

"It is not that," said Lynde in a hard, unnatural voice. "I am married already."

Alan stared at her, not in the least comprehending the meaning of her words. Everything—pain, hope, fear, passion—had slipped away from him for a moment, as if he had been stunned by a physical blow. He could not have heard aright.

"Married?" he said dully. "Lynde, you cannot mean it?"

"Yes, I do. I was married three years ago."

"Why was I not told this?" Alan's voice was stern, although he did not mean it to be so, and she shrank and shivered. Then she began in a low monotonous tone from which all feeling of any sort seemed to have utterly faded.

"Three years ago Mother was very ill—so ill that any shock would kill her, so the doctor Father brought from the lake told us. A man—a young sea captain—came here to see Father. His name was Frank Harmon and he had known Father well in the past. They had sailed together. Father seemed to be afraid of him—I had never seen him afraid of anybody before. I could not think much about anybody except Mother then, but I knew I did not quite like Captain Harmon, although he was very polite to me and I suppose might have been called handsome. One day Father came to me and told me I must marry Captain Harmon. I laughed at the idea at first but when I looked at Father's face I did not laugh. It was all white and drawn. He implored me to marry Captain Harmon. He said if I did not it would mean shame and disgrace for us all—that Captain Harmon had some hold on him and would tell what he knew if I did not marry him. I don't know what it was but it must have been something dreadful. And he said it would kill Mother. I knew it would, and that was what drove me to consent at last. Oh, I can't tell you what I suffered. I was only seventeen and there was nobody to advise me. One day Father and Captain Harmon and I went down the lake to Crosse Harbour and we were married there. As soon as the ceremony was over, Captain Harmon had to sail in his vessel. He was going to China. Father and I came back home. Nobody knew—not even Emily. He said we must not tell Mother until she was better. But she was never better. She only lived three months more—she lived them happily and at rest. When I think of that, I am not sorry for what I did. Captain Harmon said he would be back in the fall to claim me. I waited, sick at heart. But he did not come—he has never come. We have never heard a word of or about him since. Sometimes I feel sure he cannot be still living. But never a day dawns that I don't say to myself, 'Perhaps he will come today'—and, oh—"

She broke down again, sobbing bitterly. Amid all the daze of his own pain Alan realized that, at any cost, he must not make it harder for her by showing his suffering. He tried to speak calmly, wisely, as a disinterested friend.

"Could it not be discovered whether your—this man—is or is not living? Surely your father could find out."

Lynde shook her head.

"No, he says he has no way of doing so. We do not know if Captain Harmon had any relatives or even where his home was, and it was his own ship in which he sailed. Father would be glad to think that Frank Harmon was dead, but he does not think he is. He says he was always a fickle-minded fellow, one fancy driving another out of his mind. Oh, I can bear my own misery—but to think what I have brought on you! I never dreamed that you could care for me. I was so lonely and your friendship was so pleasant—can you ever forgive me?"

"There is nothing to forgive, as far as you are concerned, Lynde," said Alan steadily. "You have done me no wrong. I have loved you sincerely and such love can be nothing but a blessing to me. I only wish that I could help you. It wrings my heart to think of your position. But I can do nothing—nothing. I must not even come here any more. You understand that?"

"Yes."

There was an unconscious revelation in the girl's mournful eyes as she turned them on Alan. It thrilled him to the core of his being. She loved him. If it were not for that empty marriage form, he could win her, but the knowledge was only an added mocking torment. Alan had not known a man could endure such misery and live. A score of wild questions rushed to his lips but he crushed them back for Lynde's sake and held out his hand.

"Good-bye, dear," he said almost steadily, daring to say no more lest he should say too much.

"Good-bye," Lynde answered faintly.

When he had gone she flung herself down on the moss by the spring and lay there in an utter abandonment of misery and desolation.

Pain and indignation struggled for mastery in Alan's stormy soul as he walked homeward. So this was Captain Anthony's doings! He had sacrificed his daughter to some crime of his dubious past. Alan never dreamed of blaming Lynde for having kept her marriage a secret; he put the blame where it belonged—on the Captain's shoulders. Captain Anthony had never warned him by so much as a hint that Lynde was not free to be won. It had all probably seemed a good joke to him. Alan thought the furtive amusement he had so often detected in the Captain's eyes was explained now.

He found Elder Trewin in his study when he got home. The good Elder's face was stern and anxious; he had called on a distasteful errand—to tell the young minister of the scandal his intimacy with the Four Winds people was making in the congregation and remonstrate with him concerning it. Alan listened absently, with none of the resentment he would have felt at the interference a day previously. A man does not mind a pin-prick when a limb is being wrenched away.

"I can promise you that my objectionable calls at Four Winds will cease," he said sarcastically, when the Elder had finished. Elder Trewin got himself away, feeling snubbed but relieved.

"Took it purty quiet," he reflected. "Don't believe there was much in the yarns after all. Isabel King started them and probably she exaggerated a lot. I suppose he's had some notion like as not of bringing the Captain over to the church. But that's foolish, for he'd never manage it, and meanwhile was giving occasion for gossip. It's just as well to stop it. He's a good pastor and he works hard—too hard, mebbe. He looked real careworn and worried today."

The Rexton gossip soon ceased with the cessation of the young minister's visits to Four Winds. A month later it suffered a brief revival when a tall grim-faced old woman, whom a few recognized as Captain Anthony's housekeeper, was seen to walk down the Rexton road and enter the manse. She did not stay there long—watchers from a dozen different windows were agreed upon that—and nobody, not even Mrs. Danby, who did her best to find out, ever knew why she had called.

Emily looked at Alan with grim reproach when she was shown into his study, and as soon as they were alone she began with her usual abruptness, "Mr. Douglas, why have you given up coming to Four Winds?"

Alan flinched.

"You must ask Lynde that, Miss Oliver," he said quietly.

"I have asked her—and she says nothing."

"Then I cannot tell you."

Anger glowed in Emily's eyes.

"I thought you were a gentleman," she said bitterly. "You are not. You are breaking Lynde's heart. She's gone to a shadow of herself and she's fretting night and day. You went there and made her like you—oh, I've eyes—and then you left her."

Alan bent over his desk and looked the old woman in the face unflinchingly.

"You are mistaken, Miss Oliver," he said earnestly. "I love Lynde and would be only too happy if it were possible that I could marry her. I am not to blame for what has come about—she will tell you that herself if you ask her."

His look and tone convinced Emily.

"Who is to blame then? Lynde herself?"

"No, no."

"The Captain then?"

"Not in the sense you mean. I can tell you nothing more."

A baffled expression crossed the old woman's face. "There's a mystery here—there always has been—and I'm shut out of it. Lynde won't confide in me—in me who'd give my life's blood to help her. Perhaps I can help her—I could tell you something. Have you stopped coming to Four Winds—has she made you stop coming—because she's got such a wicked old scamp for a father? Is that the reason?"

Alan shook his head.

"No, that has nothing to do with it."

"And you won't come back?"

"It is not a question of will. I cannot—must not go."

"Lynde will break her heart then," said Emily in a tone of despair.

"I think not. She is too strong and fine for that. Help her all you can with sympathy but don't torment her with any questions. You may tell her if you like that I advise her to confide the whole story to you, but if she cannot don't tease her to. Be very gentle with her."

"You don't need to tell me that. I'd rather die than hurt her. I came here full of anger against you—but I see now you are not to blame. You are suffering too—your face tells that. All the same, I wish you'd never set foot in Four Winds. She wasn't happy before but she wasn't so miserable as she is now. Oh, I know Anthony is at the bottom of it all in some way but I won't ask you any more questions since you don't feel free to answer them. But are you sure that nothing can be done to clear up the trouble?"

"Too sure," said Alan's white lips.

The autumn dragged away. Alan found out how much a man may suffer and yet go on living and working. As for that, his work was all that made life possible for him now and he flung himself into it with feverish energy, growing so thin and hollow-eyed over it that even Elder Trewin remonstrated and suggested a vacation—a suggestion at which Alan merely smiled. A vacation which would take him away from Lynde's neighbourhood—the thought was not to be entertained.

He never saw Lynde, for he never went to any part of the shore now; yet he hungered constantly for the sight of her, the sound of her voice, the glance of her luminous eyes. When he pictured her eating her heart out in the solitude of Four Winds, he clenched his hands in despair. As for the possibility of Harmon's return, Alan could never face it for a moment. When it thrust its ugly presence into his thoughts, he put it away desperately. The man was dead—or his fickle fancy had veered elsewhere. Nothing else could explain his absence. But they could never know, and the uncertainty would forever stand between him and Lynde like a spectre. But he thought more of Lynde's pain than his own. He would have elected to bear any suffering if by so doing he could have freed her from the nightmare dread of Harmon's returning to claim her. That dread had always hung over her and now it must be intensified to agony by her love for another man. And he could do nothing—nothing. He groaned aloud in his helplessness.

One evening in late November Alan flung aside his pen and yielded to the impulse that urged him to the lake shore. He did not mean to seek Lynde—he would go to a part of the shore where there would be no likelihood of meeting her. But get away by himself he must. A November storm was raging and there would be a certain satisfaction in breasting its buffets and fighting his way through it. Besides, he knew that Isabel King was in the house and he dreaded meeting her. Since his conviction that she had written that letter to Lynde, he could not tolerate the girl and it tasked his self-control to keep from showing his contempt openly. Perhaps Isabel felt it beneath all his outward courtesy. At least she did not seek his society as she had formerly done.

It was the second day of the storm; a wild northeast gale was blowing and cold rain and freezing sleet fell in frequent showers. Alan shivered as he came out into its full fury on the lake shore. At first he could not see the water through the driving mist. Then it cleared away for a moment and he stopped short, aghast at the sight which met his eyes.

Opposite him was a long low island known as Philip's Point, dwindling down at its northeastern side to two long narrow bars of quicksand. Alan's horrified eyes saw a small schooner sunk between the bars; her hull was entirely under water and in the rigging clung one solitary figure. So much he saw before the Point was blotted out in a renewed downpour of sleet.

Without a moment's hesitation Alan turned and ran for Four Winds, which was only about a quarter of a mile away around a headland. With the Captain's assistance, something might be done. Other help could not be obtained before darkness would fall and then it would be impossible to do anything. He dashed up the steps of Four Winds and met Emily, who had flung the door open. Behind her was Lynde's pale face with its alarmed questioning eyes.

"Where is the Captain?" gasped Alan. "There's a vessel on Philip's Point and one man at least on her."

"The Captain's away on a cruise," said Emily blankly. "He went three days ago."

"Then nothing can be done," said Alan despairingly. "It will be dark long before I can get to the village."

Lynde stepped out, tying a shawl around her head.

"Let us go around to the Point," she said. "Have you matches? No? Emily, get some. We must light a bonfire at least. And bring Father's glass."

"It is not a fit night for you to be out," said Alan anxiously. "You are sheltered here—you don't feel it—but it's a fearful storm down there."

"I am not afraid of the storm. It will not hurt me. Let us hurry. It is growing dark already."

In silence they breasted their way to the shore and around the headland. Arriving opposite Philip's Point, a lull in the sleet permitted them to see the sunken schooner and the clinging figure. Lynde waved her hand to him and they saw him wave back.

"It won't be necessary to light a fire now that he has seen us," said Lynde. "Nothing can be done with village help till morning and that man can never cling there so long. He will freeze to death, for it is growing colder every minute. His only chance is to swim ashore if he can swim. The danger will be when he comes near shore; the undertow of the backwater on the quicksand will sweep him away and in his probably exhausted condition he may not be able to make head against it."

"He knows that, doubtless, and that is why he hasn't attempted to swim ashore before this," said Alan. "But I'll meet him in the backwater and drag him in."

"You—you'll risk your own life," cried Lynde.

"There is a little risk certainly, but I don't think there is a great one. Anyhow, the attempt must be made," said Alan quietly.

Suddenly Lynde's composure forsook her. She wrung her hands.

"I can't let you do it," she cried wildly. "You might be drowned—there's every risk. You don't know the force of that backwater. Alan, Alan, don't think of it."

She caught his arm in her white wet hands and looked into his face with passionate pleading.

Emily, who had said nothing, now spoke harshly.

"Lynde is right, Mr. Douglas. You have no right to risk your life for a stranger. My advice is to go to the village for help, and Lynde and I will make a fire and watch here. That is all that can be expected of you or us."

Alan paid no heed to Emily. Very tenderly he loosened Lynde's hold on his arm and looked into her quivering face.

"You know it is my duty, Lynde," he said gently. "If anything can be done for that poor man, I am the only one who can do it. I will come back safe, please God. Be brave, dear."

Lynde, with a little moan of resignation, turned away. Old Emily looked on with a face of grim disapproval as Alan waded out into the surf that boiled and swirled around him in a mad whirl of foam. The shower of sleet had again slackened, and the wreck half a mile away, with its solitary figure, was dearly visible. Alan beckoned to the man to jump overboard and swim ashore, enforcing his appeal by gestures that commanded haste before the next shower should come. For a few moments it seemed as if the seaman did not understand or lacked the courage or power to obey. The next minute he had dropped from the rigging on the crest of a mighty wave and was being borne onward to the shore.

Speedily the backwater was reached and the man, sucked down by the swirl of the wave, threw up his arms and disappeared. Alan dashed in, groping, swimming; it seemed an eternity before his hand clutched the drowning man and wrenched him from the undertow. And, with the seaman in his arms, he staggered back through the foam and dropped his burden on the sand at Lynde's feet. Alan was reeling from exhaustion and chilled to the marrow, but he thought only of the man he had rescued. The latter was unconscious and, as Alan bent over him, he heard Lynde give a choking little cry.

"He is living still," said Alan. "We must get him up to the house as soon as possible. How shall we manage it?"

"Lynde and I can go and bring the Captain's mattress down," said Emily. Now that Alan was safe she was eager to do all she could. "Then you and I can carry him up to the house."

"That will be best," said Alan. "Go quickly."

He did not look at Lynde or he would have been shocked by the agony on her face. She cast one glance at the prostrate man and followed Emily. In a short time they returned with the mattress, and Alan and Emily carried the sailor on it to Four Winds. Lynde walked behind them, seemingly unconscious of both. She watched the stranger's face as one fascinated.

At Four Winds they carried the man to a room where Emily and Alan worked over him, while Lynde heated water and hunted out stimulants in a mechanical fashion. When Alan came down she asked no questions but looked at him with the same strained horror on her face which it had borne ever since Alan had dropped his burden at her feet.

"Is he—conscious?" asked Lynde, as if she forced herself to ask the question.

"Yes, he has come back to life. But he is delirious and doesn't realize his surroundings at all. He thinks he is still on board the vessel. He'll probably come round all right. Emily is going to watch him and I'll go up to Rexton and send Dr. Ames down."

"Do you know who that man you have saved is?" asked Lynde.

"No. I asked him his name but could not get any sensible answer."

"I can tell you who he is—he is Frank Harmon."

Alan stared at her. "Frank Harmon. Your—your—the man you married? Impossible!"

"It is he. Do you think I could be mistaken?"

Dr. Ames came to Four Winds that night and again the next day. He found Harmon delirious in a high fever.

"It will be several days before he comes to his senses," he said. "Shall I send you help to nurse him?"

"It isn't necessary," said Emily stiffly. "I can look after him—and the Captain ought to be back tomorrow."

"You've no idea who he is, I suppose?" asked the doctor.

"No." Emily was quite sincere. Lynde had not told her, and Emily did not recognize him.

"Well, Mr. Douglas did a brave thing in rescuing him," said Dr. Ames. "I'll be back tomorrow."

Harmon remained delirious for a week. Alan went every day to Four Winds, his interest in a man he had rescued explaining his visits to the Rexton people. The Captain had returned and, though not absolutely uncivil, was taciturn and moody. Alan reflected grimly that Captain Anthony probably owed him a grudge for saving Harmon's life. He never saw Lynde alone, but her strained, tortured face made his heart ache. Old Emily only seemed her natural self. She waited on Harmon and Dr. Ames considered her a paragon of a nurse. Alan thought it was well that Emily knew nothing more of Harmon than that he was an old friend of Captain Anthony's. He felt sure that she would have walked out of the sick room and never reentered it had she guessed that the patient was the man whom, above all others, Lynde dreaded and feared.

One afternoon when Alan went to Four Winds Emily met him at the door.

"He's better," she announced. "He had a good sleep this afternoon and when he woke he was quite himself. You'd better go up and see him. I told him all I could but he wants to see you. Anthony and Lynde are away to Crosse Harbour. Go up and talk to him."

Harmon turned his head as the minister approached and held out his hand with a smile.

"You're the preacher, I reckon. They tell me you were the man who pulled me out of that hurly-burly. I wasn't hardly worth saving but I'm as grateful to you as if I was."

"I only—did—what any man would have done," said Alan, taking the offered hand.

"I don't know about that. Anyhow, it's not every man could have done it. I'd been hanging in that rigging all day and most of the night before. There were five more of us but they dropped off. I knew it was no use to try to swim ashore alone—the backwater would be too much for me. I must have been a lot of trouble. That old woman says I've been raving for a week. And, by the way I feel, I fancy I'll be stretched out here another week before I'll be able to use my pins. Who are these Olivers anyhow? The old woman wouldn't talk about the family."

"Don't you know them?" asked Alan in astonishment. "Isn't your name Harmon?"

"That's right—Harmon—Alfred Harmon, first mate of the schooner, *Annie M.*"

"Alfred! I thought your name was Frank!"

"Frank was my twin brother. We were so much alike our own mammy couldn't tell us apart. Did you know Frank?"

"No. This family did. Miss Oliver thought you were Frank when she saw you."

"I don't feel much like myself but I'm not Frank anyway. He's dead, poor chap—got shot in a spat with Chinese pirates three years ago."

"Dead! Man, are you speaking the truth? Are you certain?"

"Pop sure. His mate told me the whole story. Say, preacher, what's the matter? You look as if you were going to keel over."

Alan hastily drank a glass of water.

"I—I am all right now. I haven't been feeling well of late."

"Guess you didn't do yourself any good going out into that freezing water and dragging me in."

"I shall thank God every day of my life that I did do it," said Alan gravely, new light in his eyes, as Emily entered the room. "Miss Oliver, when will the Captain and Lynde be back?"

"They said they would be home by four."

She looked at Alan curiously.

"I will go and meet her," he said quickly.

He came upon Lynde, sitting on a grey boulder under the shadow of an overhanging fir coppice, with her dogs beside her.

She turned her head indifferently as Alan's footsteps sounded on the pebbles, and then stood slowly up.

"Are you looking for me?" she asked.

"I have some news for you, Lynde," Alan said.

"Has he—has he come to himself?" she whispered.

"Yes, he has come to himself. Lynde, he is not Frank Harmon—he is his twin brother. He says Frank Harmon was killed three years ago in the China seas."

For a moment Lynde's great grey eyes stared into Alan's, questioning. Then, as the truth seized on her comprehension, she sat down on the boulder and put her hands over her face without a word. Alan walked down to the water's edge to give her time to recover herself. When he came back he took her hands and said quietly, "Lynde, do you realize what this means for us—for us? You are free—free to love me—to be my wife."

Lynde shook her head.

"Oh, that can't be. I am not fit to be your wife."

"Don't talk nonsense, dear," he smiled.

"It isn't nonsense. You are a minister and it would ruin you to marry a girl like me. Think what the Rexton people would say of it."

"Rexton isn't the world, dearest. Last week I had a letter from home asking me to go to a church there. I did not think of accepting then—now I will go—we will both go—and a new life will begin for you, clear of the shadows of the old."

"That isn't possible. No, Alan, listen—I love you too well to do you the wrong of marrying you. It would injure you. There is Father. I love him and he has always been very kind to me. But—but—there's something wrong—you know it—some crime in his past—"

"The only man who knew that is dead."

"We do not know that he was the only man. I am the daughter of a criminal and I am no fit wife for Alan Douglas. No, Alan, don't plead, please. I won't think differently—I never can."

There was a ring of finality in her tone that struck dismay to Alan's heart. He prepared to entreat and argue, but before he could utter a word, the boughs behind them parted and Captain Anthony stepped down from the bank.

"I've been listening," he announced coolly, "and I think it high time I took a share in the conversation. You seem to have run up against a snag, Mr. Douglas. You say Frank Harmon is dead. That's good riddance if it's true. Is it true?"

"His brother declares it is."

"Well, then, I'll help you all I can. I like you, Mr. Douglas, and I happen to be fond of Lynde, too—though you mayn't believe it. I'm fond of her for her mother's sake and I'd like to see her happy. I didn't want to give her to Harmon that time three years ago but I couldn't help myself. He had the upper hand, curse him. It wasn't for my own sake, though—it was for my wife's. However, that's all over and done with and I'll do the best I can to atone for it. So you won't marry your minister because your father was not a good man, Lynde? Well, I don't suppose he was a very good man—a man who makes his wife's life a hell, even in a refined way, isn't exactly a saint, to my way of thinking. But that's the worst that could be said of him and it doesn't entail any indelible disgrace on his family, I suppose. I am not your father, Lynde."

"Not my father?" Lynde echoed the words blankly.

"No. Your father was your mother's first husband. She never told you of him. When I said he made her life a hell, I said the truth, no more, no less. I had loved your mother ever since I was a boy, Lynde. But she was far above me in station and I never dreamed it was possible to win her love. She married James Ashley. He was a gentleman, so called—and he didn't kick or beat her. Oh no, he just tormented her refined womanhood to the verge of frenzy, that was all. He died when you were a baby. And a year later I found out your mother could love me, rough sailor and all as I was. I married her and brought her here. We had fifteen years of happiness together. I'm not a good man—but I made your mother happy in spite of her wrecked health and her dark memories. It was her wish that you should be known as my daughter, but under the present circumstances I know she would wish that you should be told the truth. Marry your man, Lynde, and go away with him. Emily will go with you if you like. I'm going back to the sea. I've been hankering for it ever since your mother died. I'll go out of your life. There, don't cry—I hate to see a woman cry. Mr. Douglas, I'll leave you to dry her tears and I'll go up to the house and have a talk with Harmon."

When Captain Anthony had disappeared behind the Point, Alan turned to Lynde. She was sobbing softly and her face was wet with tears. Alan drew her head down on his shoulder.

"Sweetheart, the dark past is all put by. Our future begins with promise. All is well with us, dear Lynde."

Like a child, she put her arms about his neck and their lips met.

Marcella's Reward

Dr. Clark shook his head gravely. "She is not improving as fast as I should like to see," he said. "In fact—er—she seems to have gone backward the past week. You must send her to the country, Miss Langley. The heat here is too trying for her."

Dr. Clark might as well have said, "You must send her to the moon"—or so Marcella thought bitterly. Despair filled her heart as she looked at Patty's white face and transparent hands and listened to the doctor's coolly professional advice. Patty's illness had already swept away the scant savings of three years. Marcella had nothing left with which to do anything more for her.

She did not make any answer to the doctor—she could not. Besides, what could she say, with Patty's big blue eyes, bigger and bluer than ever in her thin face, looking at her so wistfully? She dared not say it was impossible. But Aunt Emma had no such scruples. With a great clatter and racket, that lady fell upon the dishes that held Patty's almost untasted dinner and whisked them away while her tongue kept time to her jerky movements.

"Goodness me, doctor, do you think you're talking to millionaires? Where do you suppose the money is to come from to send Patty to the country? *I* can't afford it, that is certain. I think I do pretty well to give Marcella and Patty their board free, and I have to work my fingers to the bone to do *that*. It's all nonsense about Patty, anyhow. What she ought to do is to make an effort to get better. She doesn't—she just mopes and pines. She won't eat a thing I cook for her. How can anyone expect to get better if she doesn't eat?"

Aunt Emma glared at the doctor as if she were triumphantly sure that she had propounded an unanswerable question. A dull red flush rose to Marcella's face.

"Oh, Aunt Emma, I *can't* eat!" said Patty wearily. "It isn't because I won't—indeed, I can't."

"Humph! I suppose my cooking isn't fancy enough for you—that's the trouble. Well, I haven't the time to put any frills on it. I think I do pretty well to wait on you at all with all that work piling up before me. But some people imagine that they were born to be waited on."

Aunt Emma whirled the last dish from the table and left the room, slamming the door behind her.

The doctor shrugged his shoulders. He had become used to Miss Gibson's tirades during Patty's illness. But Marcella had never got used to them—never, in all the three years she had lived with her aunt. They flicked on the raw as keenly as ever. This morning it seemed unbearable. It took every atom of Marcella's self-control to keep her from voicing her resentful thoughts. It was only for Patty's sake that she was able to restrain herself. It was only for Patty's sake, too, that she did not, as soon as the doctor had gone, give way to tears. Instead, she smiled bravely into the little sister's eyes.

"Let me brush your hair now, dear, and bathe your face."

"Have you time?" said Patty anxiously.

"Yes, I think so."

Patty gave a sigh of content.

"I'm so glad! Aunt Emma always hurts me when she brushes my hair—she is in such a hurry. You're so gentle, Marcella, you don't make my head ache at all. But oh! I'm so tired of being sick. I wish I could get well faster. Marcy, do you think I can be sent to the country?"

"I—I don't know, dear. I'll see if I can think of any way to manage it," said Marcella, striving to speak hopefully.

Patty drew a long breath.

"Oh, Marcy, it would be lovely to see the green fields again, and the woods and brooks, as we did that summer we spent in the country before Father died. I wish we could live in the country always. I'm sure I would soon get better if I could go—if it was only for a little while. It's so hot here—and the factory makes such a noise—my head seems to go round and round all the time. And Aunt Emma scolds so."

"You mustn't mind Aunt Emma, dear," said Marcella. "You know she doesn't really mean it—it is just a habit she has got into. She was really very good to you when you were so sick. She sat up night after night with you, and made me go to bed. There now, dearie, you're fresh and sweet, and I must hurry to the store, or I'll be late. Try and have a little nap, and I'll bring you home some oranges tonight."

Marcella dropped a kiss on Patty's cheek, put on her hat and went out. As soon as she left the house, she quickened her steps almost to a run. She feared she would be late, and that meant a ten-cent fine. Ten cents loomed as large as ten dollars now to Marcella's eyes when every dime meant so much. But fast as she went, her distracted thoughts went faster. She could not send Patty to the country. There was no way, think, plan, worry as she might. And if she could not! Marcella remembered Patty's face and the doctor's look, and her heart sank like lead. Patty was growing weaker every day instead of stronger, and the weather was getting hotter. Oh, if Patty were to—to—but Marcella could not complete the sentence even in thought.

If they were not so desperately poor! Marcella's bitterness overflowed her soul at the thought. Everywhere around her were evidences of wealth—wealth often lavishly and foolishly spent—and she could not get money enough anywhere to save her sister's life! She almost felt that she hated all those smiling, well-dressed people who thronged the streets. By the time she reached the store, poor Marcella's heart was seething with misery and resentment.

Three years before, when Marcella had been sixteen and Patty nine, their parents had died, leaving them absolutely alone in the world except for their father's half-sister, Miss Gibson, who lived in Canning and earned her livelihood washing and mending for the hands employed in the big factory nearby. She had grudgingly offered the girls a home, which Marcella had accepted because she must. She obtained a position in one of the Canning stores at three dollars a week, out of which she contrived to dress herself and Patty and send the latter to school. Her life for three years was one of absolute drudgery, yet until now she had never lost courage, but had struggled bravely on, hoping for better times in the future when she should get promotion and Patty would be old enough to teach school.

But now Marcella's courage and hopefulness had gone out like a spent candle. She was late at the store, and that meant a fine; her head ached, and her feet felt like lead as she climbed the stairs to her department—a hot, dark, stuffy corner behind the shirtwaist counter. It was warm and close at any time, but today it was stifling, and there was already a crowd of customers, for it was the day of a bargain sale. The heat and noise and chatter got on Marcella's tortured nerves. She felt that she wanted to scream, but instead she turned calmly to a waiting customer—a big, handsome, richly dressed woman. Marcella noted with an ever-increasing bitterness that the woman wore a lace collar the price of which would have kept Patty in the country for a year.

She was Mrs. Liddell—Marcella knew her by sight—and she was in a very bad temper because she had been kept waiting. For the next half hour she badgered and worried Marcella to the point of distraction. Nothing suited her. Pile after pile, box after box, of shirtwaists did Marcella take down for her, only to have them flung aside with sarcastic remarks. Mrs. Liddell seemed to hold Marcella responsible for the lack of waists that suited her; her tongue grew sharper and sharper and her comments more trying. Then she mislaid her purse, and was disagreeable about that until it turned up.

Marcella shut her lips so tightly that they turned white to keep back the impatient retort that rose momentarily to her lips. The insolence of some customers was always trying to the sensitive, high-spirited girl, but today it seemed unbearable. Her head throbbed fiercely with the pain of the ever-increasing ache, and—what was the lady on her right saying to a friend?

"Yes, she had typhoid, you know—a very bad form. She rallied from it, but she was so exhausted that she couldn't really recover, and the doctor said—"

"Really," interrupted Mrs. Liddell's sharp voice, "may I ask you to attend to me, if you please? No doubt gossip may be very interesting to you, but I am accustomed to having a clerk pay *some* small attention to my requirements. If you cannot attend to your business, I shall go to the floor walker and ask him to direct me to somebody who can. The laziness and disobligingness of the girls in this store is really getting beyond endurance."

A passionate answer was on the point of Marcella's tongue. All her bitterness and suffering and resentment flashed into her face and eyes. For one moment she was determined to speak out, to repay Mrs. Liddell's insolence in kind. A retort was ready to her hand. Everyone knew that Mrs. Liddell, before her marriage to a wealthy man, had been a working girl. What could be easier than to say contemptuously: "You should be a judge of a clerk's courtesy and ability, madam. You were a shop girl yourself once?"

But if she said it, what would follow? Prompt and instant dismissal. And Patty? The thought of the little sister quelled the storm in Marcella's soul. For Patty's sake she must control her temper—and she did. With an effort that left her white and tremulous she crushed back the hot words and said quietly: "I beg your pardon, Mrs. Liddell. I did not mean to be inattentive. Let me show you some of our new lingerie waists, I think you will like them."

But Mrs. Liddell did not like the new lingerie waists which Marcella brought to her in her trembling hands. For another half hour she examined and found fault and sneered. Then she swept away with the scornful remark that she didn't see a thing there that was fit to wear, and she would go to Markwell Bros. and see if they had anything worth looking at.

When she had gone, Marcella leaned against the counter, pale and exhausted. She must have a breathing spell. Oh, how her head ached! How hot and stifling and horrible everything was! She longed for the country herself. Oh, if she and Patty could only go away to some place where there were green clover meadows and cool breezes and great hills where the air was sweet and pure!

During all this time a middle-aged woman had been sitting on a stool beside the bargain counter. When a clerk asked her if she wished to be waited on, she said, "No, I'm just waiting here for a friend who promised to meet me."

She was tall and gaunt and grey haired. She had square jaws and cold grey eyes and an aggressive nose, but there was something attractive in her plain face, a mingling of common sense and kindliness. She watched Marcella and Mrs. Liddell closely and lost nothing of all that was said and done on both sides. Now and then she smiled grimly and nodded.

When Mrs. Liddell had gone, she rose and leaned over the counter. Marcella opened her burning eyes and pulled herself wearily together.

"What can I do for you?" she said.

"Nothing. I ain't looking for to have anything done for me. You need to have something done for you, I guess, by the looks of you. You seem dead beat out. Aren't you awful tired? I've been listening to that woman jawing you till I felt like rising up and giving her a large and wholesome piece of my mind. I don't know how you kept your patience with her, but I can tell you I admired you for it, and I made up my mind I'd tell you so."

The kindness and sympathy in her tone broke Marcella down. Tears rushed to her eyes. She bowed her head on her hands and said sobbingly, "Oh, I *am* tired! But it's not that. I'm—I'm in such trouble."

"I knew you were," said the other, with a nod of her head. "I could tell that right off by your face. Do you know what I said to myself? I said, 'That girl has got somebody at home awful sick.' *That's* what I said. Was I right?"

"Yes, indeed you were," said Marcella.

"I knew it"—another triumphant nod. "Now, you just tell me all about it. It'll do you good to talk it over with somebody. Here, I'll pretend I'm looking at shirt-waists, so that floor walker won't be coming down on you, and I'll be as hard to please as that other woman was, so's you can take your time. Who's sick—and what's the matter?"

Marcella told the whole story, choking back her sobs and forcing herself to speak calmly, having the fear of the floor walker before her eyes.

"And I can't afford to send Patty to the country—I *can't*—and I know she won't get better if she doesn't go," she concluded.

"Dear, dear, but that's too bad! Something must be done. Let me see—let me put on my thinking cap. What is your name?"

"Marcella Langley."

The older woman dropped the lingerie waist she was pretending to examine and stared at Marcella.

"You don't say! Look here, what was your mother's name before she was married?"

"Mary Carvell."

"Well, I *have* heard of coincidences, but this beats all! Mary Carvell! Well, did you ever hear your mother speak of a girl friend of hers called Josephine Draper?"

"I should think I did! You don't mean—"

"I *do* mean it. I'm Josephine Draper. Your mother and I went to school together, and we were as much as sisters to each other until she got married. Then she went away, and after a few years I lost trace of her. I didn't even know she was dead. Poor Mary! Well, *my* duty is plain—that's one comfort—my duty and my pleasure, too. Your sister is coming out to Dalesboro to stay with me. Yes, and you are too, for the whole summer. You needn't say you're not, because you *are*. I've said so. There's room at Fir Cottage for you both. Yes, Fir Cottage—I guess you've heard your mother speak of *that*. There's her old room out there that we always slept in when she came to stay all night with me. It's all ready for you. What's that? You can't afford to lose your place here? Bless your heart, child, you won't lose it! The owner of this store is my nephew, and he'll do considerable to oblige me, as well he might, seeing as I brought him up. To think that Mary Carvell's daughter has been in his store for three years, and me never suspecting it! And I might never have found you out at all if you hadn't been so patient with that woman. If you'd sassed her back, I'd have thought she deserved it and wouldn't have blamed you a mite, but I wouldn't have bothered coming to talk to you either. Well, well well! Poor child, don't cry. You just pick up and go home. I'll make it all right with Tom. You're pretty near played out yourself, I can see that. But a summer in Fir Cottage, with plenty of cream and eggs and *my* cookery, will soon make another girl of you. Don't you dare to *thank* me. It's a privilege to be able to do something for Mary Carvell's girls. I just loved Mary."

The upshot of the whole matter was that Marcella and Patty went, two days later, to Dalesboro, where Miss Draper gave them a hearty welcome to Fir Cottage—a quaint, delightful little house circled by big Scotch firs and overgrown with vines. Never were such delightful weeks as those that followed. Patty came rapidly back to health and strength. As for Marcella, Miss Draper's prophecy was also fulfilled; she soon looked and felt like another girl. The dismal years of drudgery behind her were forgotten like a dream, and she lived wholly in the beautiful present, in the walks and drives, the flowers and grass slopes, and in the pleasant household duties which she shared with Miss Draper.

"I love housework," she exclaimed one September day. "I don't like the thought of going back to the store a bit."

"Well, you're not going back," calmly said Miss Draper, who had a habit of arranging other people's business for them that might have been disconcerting had it not been for her keen insight and hearty good sense. "You're going to stay here with me—you and Patty. I don't propose to die of lonesomeness losing you, and I need somebody to help me about the house. I've thought it all out. You are to call me Aunt Josephine, and Patty is to go to school. I had this scheme in mind from the first, but I thought I'd wait to see how we got along living in the same house, and how you liked it here, before I spoke out. No, you needn't thank me this time either. I'm doing this every bit as much for my sake as yours. Well, that's all settled. Patty won't object, bless her rosy cheeks!"

"Oh!" said Marcella, with eyes shining through her tears. "I'm so happy, dear Miss Draper—I mean Aunt Josephine. I'll love to stay here—and I *will* thank you."

"Fudge!" remarked Miss Draper, who felt uncomfortably near crying herself. "You might go out and pick a basket of Golden Gems. I want to make some jelly for Patty."

Margaret's Patient

"DID DR. FORBES THINK SHE OUGHT TO GIVE UP HER TRIP?"

Margaret paused a moment at the gate and looked back at the quaint old house under its snowy firs with a thrill of proprietary affection. It was her home; for the first time in her life she had a real home, and the long, weary years of poorly paid drudgery were all behind her. Before her was a prospect of independence and many of the delights she had always craved; in the immediate future was a trip to Vancouver with Mrs. Boyd.

For I shall go, of course, thought Margaret, as she walked briskly down the snowy road. I've always wanted to see the Rockies, and to go there with Mrs. Boyd will double the pleasure. She is such a delightful companion.

Margaret Campbell had been an orphan ever since she could remember. She had been brought up by a distant relative of her father's—that is, she had been given board, lodging, some schooling and indifferent clothes for the privilege of working like a little drudge in the house of the grim cousin who sheltered her. The death of this cousin flung Margaret on her own resources. A friend had procured her employment as the "companion" of a rich, eccentric old lady, infirm of health and temper. Margaret lived with her for five years, and to the young girl they seemed treble the time. Her employer was fault-finding, peevish, unreasonable, and many a time Margaret's patience almost failed her—almost, but not quite. In the end it brought her a more tangible reward than sometimes falls to the lot of the toiler. Mrs. Constance died, and in her will she left to Margaret her little up-country cottage and enough money to provide her an income for the rest of her life.

Margaret took immediate possession of her little house and, with the aid of a capable old servant, soon found herself very comfortable. She realized that her days of drudgery were over, and that henceforth life would be a very different thing from what it had been. Margaret meant to have "a good time." She had never had any pleasure and now she was resolved to garner in all she could of the joys of existence.

"I'm not going to do a single useful thing for a year," she had told Mrs. Boyd gaily. "Just think of it—a whole delightful year of vacation, to go and come at will, to read, travel, dream, rest. After that, I mean to see if I can find something to do for other folks, but I'm going to have this one golden year. And the first thing in it is our trip to Vancouver. I'm so glad I have the chance to go with you. It's a wee bit short notice, but I'll be ready when you want to start."

Altogether, Margaret felt pretty well satisfied with life as she tripped blithely down the country road between the ranks of snow-laden spruces, with the blue sky above and the crisp, exhilarating air all about. There was only one drawback, but it was a pretty serious one.

It's so lonely by spells, Margaret sometimes thought wistfully. All the joys my good fortune has brought me can't quite fill my heart. There's always one little empty, aching spot. Oh, if I had somebody of my very own to love and care for, a mother, a sister, even a cousin. But there's nobody. I haven't a relative in the world, and there are times when I'd give almost anything to have one. Well, I must try to be satisfied with friendship, instead.

Margaret's meditations were interrupted by a brisk footstep behind her, and presently Dr. Forbes came up.

"Good afternoon, Miss Campbell. Taking a constitutional?"

"Yes. Isn't it a lovely day? I suppose you are on your professional rounds. How are all your patients?"

"Most of them are doing well. But I'm sorry to say I have a new one and am very much worried about her. Do you know Freda Martin?"

"The little teacher in the Primary Department who boards with the Wayes? Yes, I've met her once or twice. Is she ill?"

"Yes, seriously. It's typhoid, and she has been going about longer than she should. I don't know what is to be done with her. It seems she is like yourself in one respect, Miss Campbell; she is utterly alone in the world. Mrs. Waye is crippled with rheumatism and can't nurse her, and I fear it will be impossible to get a nurse in Blythefield. She ought to be taken from the Wayes'. The house is overrun with children, is right next door to that noisy factory, and in other respects is a poor place for a sick girl."

"It is too bad, I am very sorry," said Margaret sympathetically.

Dr. Forbes shot a keen look at her from his deep-set eyes. "Are you willing to show your sympathy in a practical form, Miss Campbell?" he said bluntly. "You told me the other day you meant to begin work for others next year. Why not begin now? Here's a splendid chance to befriend a friendless girl. Will you take Freda Martin into your home during her illness?"

"Oh, I couldn't," cried Margaret blankly. "Why, I'm going away next week. I'm going with Mrs. Boyd to Vancouver, and my house will be shut up."

"Oh, I did not know. That settles it, I suppose," said the doctor with a sigh of regret. "Well, I must see what else I can do for poor Freda. If I had a home of my own, the problem would be easily solved, but as I'm only a boarder myself, I'm helpless in that respect. I'm very much afraid she will have a hard time to pull through, but I'll do the best I can for her. Well, I must run in here and have a look at Tommy Griggs' eyes. Good morning, Miss Campbell."

Margaret responded rather absently and walked on with her eyes fixed on the road. Somehow all the joy had gone out of the day for her, and out of her prospective trip. She stopped on the little bridge and gazed unseeingly at the ice-bound creek. Did Dr. Forbes really think she ought to give up her trip in order to take Freda Martin into her home and probably nurse her as well, since skilled nursing of any kind was almost unobtainable in Blythefield? No, of course, Dr. Forbes did not mean anything of the sort. He had not known she intended to go away. Margaret tried to put the thought out of her mind, but it came insistently back.

She knew—none better—what it was to be alone and friendless. Once she had been ill, too, and left to the ministration of careless servants. Margaret shuddered whenever she thought of that time. She was very, very sorry for Freda Martin, but she certainly couldn't give up her plans for her.

"Why, I'd never have the chance to go with Mrs. Boyd again," she argued with her troublesome inward promptings.

Altogether, Margaret's walk was spoiled. But when she went to bed that night, she was firmly resolved to dismiss all thought of Freda Martin. In the middle of the night she woke up. It was calm and moonlight and frosty. The world was very still, and Margaret's heart and conscience spoke to her out of that silence, where all worldly motives were hushed and shamed. She listened, and knew that in the morning she must send for Dr. Forbes and tell him to bring his patient to Fir Cottage.

The evening of the next day found Freda in Margaret's spare room and Margaret herself installed as nurse, for as Dr. Forbes had feared, he had found it impossible to obtain anyone else. Margaret had a natural gift for nursing, and she had had a good deal of experience in sick rooms. She was skilful, gentle and composed, and Dr. Forbes nodded his head with satisfaction as he watched her.

A week later Mrs. Boyd left for Vancouver, and Margaret, bending over her delirious patient, could not even go to the station to see her off. But she thought little about it. All her hopes were centred on pulling Freda Martin through; and when, after a long, doubtful fortnight, Dr. Forbes pronounced her on the way to recovery, Margaret felt as if she had given the gift of life to a fellow creature. "Oh, I am so glad I stayed," she whispered to herself.

During Freda's convalescence Margaret learned to love her dearly. She was such a sweet, brave little creature, full of a fine courage to face the loneliness and trials of her lot.

"I can never repay you for your kindness, Miss Campbell," she said wistfully.

"I am more than repaid already," said Margaret sincerely. "Haven't I found a dear little friend?"

One day Freda asked Margaret to write a note for her to a certain school chum.

"She will like to know I am getting better. You will find her address in my writing desk."

Freda's modest trunk had been brought to Fir Cottage, and Margaret went to it for the desk. As she turned over the loose papers in search of the address, her eye was caught by a name signed to a faded and yellowed letter—Worth Spencer. Her mother's name!

Margaret gave a little exclamation of astonishment. Could her mother have written that letter? It was not likely another woman would have that uncommon name. Margaret caught up the letter and ran to Freda's room.

"Freda, I couldn't help seeing the name signed to this letter, it is my mother's. To whom was it written?"

"That is one of my mother's old letters," said Freda. "She had a sister, my Aunt Worth. She was a great deal older than Mother. Their parents died when Mother was a baby. Aunt Worth went to her father's people, while Mother's grandmother took her. There was not very good feeling between the two families, I think. Mother said she lost trace of her sister after her sister married, and then, long after, she saw Aunt Worth's death in the papers."

"Can you tell me where your mother and her sister lived before they were separated?" asked Margaret excitedly.

"Ridgetown."

"Then my mother must have been your mother's sister, and, oh, Freda, Freda, you are my cousin."

Eventually this was proved to be the fact. Margaret investigated the matter and discovered beyond a doubt that she and Freda were cousins. It would be hard to say which of the two girls was the more delighted.

"Anyhow, we'll never be parted again," said Margaret happily. "Fir Cottage is your home henceforth, Freda. Oh, how rich I am. I have got somebody who really belongs to me. And I owe it all to Dr. Forbes. If he hadn't suggested you coming here, I should never have found out that we were cousins."

"And I don't think I should ever have got better at all," whispered Freda, slipping her hand into Margaret's.

"I think we are going to be the two happiest girls in the world," said Margaret. "And Freda, do you know what we are going to do when your summer vacation comes? We are going to have a trip through the Rockies, yes, indeedy. It would have been nice going with Mrs. Boyd, but it will be ten times nicer to go with you."

Matthew Insists on Puffed Sleeves

Matthew was having a bad ten minutes of it. He had come into the kitchen, in the twilight of a cold, grey December evening, and had sat down in the wood-box corner to take off his heavy boots, unconscious of the fact that Anne and a bevy of her schoolmates were having a practice of "The Fairy Queen" in the sitting-room. Presently they came trooping through the hall and out into the kitchen, laughing and chattering gaily. They did not see Matthew, who shrank bashfully back into the shadows beyond the wood-box with a boot in one hand and a bootjack in the other, and he watched them shyly for the aforesaid ten minutes as they put on caps and jackets and talked about the dialogue and the concert. Anne stood among them, bright eyed and animated as they; but Matthew suddenly became conscious that there was something about her different from her mates. And what worried Matthew was that the difference impressed him as being something that should not exist. Anne had a brighter face, and bigger, starrier eyes, and more delicate features than the others; even shy, unobservant Matthew had learned to take note of these things; but the difference that disturbed him did not consist in any of these respects. Then in what did it consist?

Matthew was haunted by this question long after the girls had gone, arm in arm, down the long, hard-frozen lane and Anne had betaken herself to her books. He could not refer it to Marilla, who, he felt, would be quite sure to sniff scornfully and remark that the only difference she saw between Anne and the other girls was that they sometimes kept their tongues quiet while Anne never did. This, Matthew felt, would be no great help.

He had recourse to his pipe that evening to help him study it out, much to Marilla's disgust. After two hours of smoking and hard reflection Matthew arrived at a solution of his problem. Anne was not dressed like the other girls!

The more Matthew thought about the matter the more he was convinced that Anne never had been dressed like the other girls—never since she had come to Green Gables. Marilla kept her clothed in plain, dark dresses, all made after the same unvarying pattern. If Matthew knew there was such a thing as fashion in dress it is as much as he did; but he was quite sure that Anne's sleeves did not look at all like the sleeves the other girls wore. He recalled the cluster of little girls he had seen around her that evening—all gay in waists of red and blue and pink and white—and he wondered why Marilla always kept her so plainly and soberly gowned.

Of course, it must be all right. Marilla knew best and Marilla was bringing her up. Probably some wise, inscrutable motive was to be served thereby. But surely it would do no harm to let the child have one pretty dress—something like Diana Barry always wore. Matthew decided that he would give her one; that surely could not be objected to as an unwarranted putting in of his oar. Christmas was only a fortnight off. A nice new dress would be the very thing for a present. Matthew, with a sigh of satisfaction, put away his pipe and went to bed, while Marilla opened all the doors and aired the house.

The very next evening Matthew betook himself to Carmody to buy the dress, determined to get the worst over and have done with it. It would be, he felt assured, no trifling ordeal. There were some things Matthew could buy and prove himself no mean bargainer; but he knew he would be at the mercy of shopkeepers when it came to buying a girl's dress.

After much cogitation Matthew resolved to go to Samuel Lawson's store instead of William Blair's. To be sure, the Cuthberts always had gone to William Blair's; it was almost as much a matter of conscience with them as to attend the Presbyterian church and vote Conservative. But William Blair's two daughters frequently waited on customers there and Matthew held them in absolute dread. He could contrive to deal with them when he knew exactly what he wanted and could point it out; but in such a matter as this, requiring explanation and consultation, Matthew felt that he must be sure of a man behind the counter. So he would go to Lawson's, where Samuel or his son would wait on him.

Alas! Matthew did not know that Samuel, in the recent expansion of his business, had set up a lady clerk also; she was a niece of his wife's and a very dashing young person indeed, with a huge, drooping pompadour, big, rolling brown eyes, and a most extensive and bewildering smile. She was dressed with exceeding smartness and wore several bangle bracelets that glittered and rattled and tinkled with every movement of her hands. Matthew was covered with confusion at finding her there at all; and those bangles completely wrecked his wits at one fell swoop.

"What can I do for you this evening. Mr. Cuthbert?" Miss Lucilla Harris inquired, briskly and ingratiatingly, tapping the counter with both hands.

"Have you any—any—any—well now, say any garden rakes?" stammered Matthew.

Miss Harris looked somewhat surprised, as well she might, to hear a man inquiring for garden rakes in the middle of December.

"I believe we have one or two left over," she said, "but they're upstairs in the lumber-room. I'll go and see."

During her absence Matthew collected his scattered senses for another effort.

When Miss Harris returned with the rake and cheerfully inquired: "Anything else tonight, Mr. Cuthbert?" Matthew took his courage in both hands and replied:

"Well now, since you suggest it, I might as well—take—that is—look at—buy some—some hayseed."

Miss Harris had heard Matthew Cuthbert called odd. She now concluded that he was entirely crazy.

"We only keep hayseed in the spring," she explained loftily. "We've none on hand just now."

"Oh, certainly—certainly—just as you say," stammered unhappy Matthew, seizing the rake and making for the door. At the threshold he recollected that he had not paid for it and he turned miserably back. While Miss Harris was counting out his change he rallied his powers for a final desperate attempt.

"Well now—if it isn't too much trouble—I might as well—that is—I'd like to look at—at—some sugar."

"White or brown?" queried Miss Harris patiently.

"Oh—well now—brown," said Matthew feebly.

"There's a barrel of it over there," said Miss Harris, shaking her bangles at it. "It's the only kind we have."

"I'll—I'll take twenty pounds of it," said Matthew, with beads of perspiration standing on his forehead.

Matthew had driven halfway home before he was his own man again. It had been a gruesome experience, but it served him right, he thought, for committing the heresy of going to a strange store. When he reached home he hid the rake in the tool-house, but the sugar he carried in to Marilla.

"Brown sugar!" exclaimed Marilla. "Whatever possessed you to get so much? You know I never use it except for the hired man's porridge or black fruit-cake. Jerry's gone and I've made my cake long ago. It's not good sugar, either—it's coarse and dark—William Blair doesn't usually keep sugar like that."

"I—I thought it might come in handy sometime," said Matthew, making good his escape.

When Matthew came to think the matter over he decided that a woman was required to cope with the situation. Marilla was out of the question. Matthew felt sure she would throw cold water on his project at once. Remained only Mrs. Lynde; for of no other woman in Avonlea would Matthew have dared to ask advice. To Mrs. Lynde he went accordingly, and that good lady promptly took the matter out of the harassed man's hands.

"Pick out a dress for you to give Anne? To be sure I will. I'm going to Carmody tomorrow and I'll attend to it. Have you something particular in mind? No? Well, I'll just go by my own judgment then. I believe a nice rich brown would just suit Anne, and William Blair has some new gloria in that's real pretty. Perhaps you'd like me to make it up for her, too, seeing that if Marilla was to make it Anne would probably get wind of it before the time and spoil the surprise? Well, I'll do it. No, it isn't a mite of trouble. I like sewing. I'll make it to fit my niece, Jenny Gillis, for she and Anne are as like as two peas as far as figure goes."

"Well now, I'm much obliged," said Matthew, "and—and—I dunno—but I'd like—I think they make the sleeves different nowadays to what they used to be. If it wouldn't be asking too much I—I'd like them made in the new way."

"Puffs? Of course. You needn't worry a speck more about it, Matthew. I'll make it up in the very latest fashion," said Mrs. Lynde. To herself she added when Matthew had gone:

"It'll be a real satisfaction to see that poor child wearing something decent for once. The way Marilla dresses her is positively ridiculous, that's what, and I've ached to tell her so plainly a dozen times. I've held my tongue though, for I can see Marilla doesn't want advice and she thinks she knows more about bringing children up than I do for all she's an old maid. But that's always the way. Folks that has brought up children know that there's no hard and fast method in the world that'll suit every child. But them as never have think it's all as plain and easy as Rule of Three—just set your three terms down so fashion, and the sum'll work out correct. But flesh and blood don't come under the head of arithmetic and that's where Marilla Cuthbert makes her mistake. I suppose she's trying to cultivate a spirit of humility in Anne by dressing her as she does: but it's more likely to cultivate envy and discontent. I'm sure the child must feel the difference between her clothes and the other girls'. But to think of Matthew taking notice of it! That man is waking up after being asleep for over sixty years."

Marilla knew all the following fortnight that Matthew had something on his mind, but what it was she could not guess, until Christmas Eve, when Mrs. Lynde brought up the new dress. Marilla behaved pretty well on the whole, although it is very likely she distrusted Mrs. Lynde's diplomatic explanation that she had made the dress because Matthew was afraid Anne would find out about it too soon if Marilla made it.

"So this is what Matthew has been looking so mysterious over and grinning about to himself for two weeks, is it?" she said a little stiffly but tolerantly. "I knew he was up to some foolishness. Well, I must say I don't think Anne needed any more dresses. I made her three good, warm, serviceable ones this fall, and anything more is sheer extravagance. There's enough material in those sleeves alone to make a waist, I declare there is. You'll just pamper Anne's vanity, Matthew, and she's as vain as a peacock now. Well, I hope she'll be satisfied at last, for I know she's been hankering after those silly sleeves ever since they came in, although she never said a word after the first. The puffs have been getting bigger and more ridiculous right along; they're as big as balloons now. Next year anybody who wears them will have to go through a door sideways."

Christmas morning broke on a beautiful white world. It had been a very mild December and people had looked forward to a green Christmas; but just enough snow fell softly in the night to transfigure Avonlea. Anne peeped out from her frosted gable window with delighted eyes. The firs in the Haunted Wood were all feathery and wonderful; the birches and wild cherry trees were outlined in pearl; the ploughed fields were stretches of snowy dimples; and there was a crisp tang in the air that was glorious. Anne ran downstairs singing until her voice re-echoed through Green Gables.

"Merry Christmas, Marilla! Merry Christmas, Matthew! Isn't it a lovely Christmas? I'm so glad it's white. Any other kind of Christmas doesn't seem real, does it? I don't like green Christmases. They're *not* green—they're just nasty faded browns and greys. What makes people call them green? Why—why—Matthew, is that for me? Oh, Matthew!"

Matthew had sheepishly unfolded the dress from its paper swathings and held it out with a deprecatory glance at Marilla, who feigned to be contemptuously filling the teapot, but nevertheless watched the scene out of the corner of her eye with a rather interested air.

Anne took the dress and looked at it in reverent silence. Oh, how pretty it was—a lovely soft brown gloria with all the gloss of silk; a skirt with dainty frills and shirrings; a waist elaborately pin-tucked in the most fashionable way, with a little ruffle of filmy lace at the neck. But the sleeves—they were the crowning glory! Long elbow cuffs, and above them two beautiful puffs divided by rows of shirring and bows of brown silk ribbon.

"That's a Christmas present for you, Anne," said Matthew shyly. "Why—why—Anne, don't you like it? Well now—well now."

For Anne's eyes had suddenly filled with tears.

"*Like* it! Oh, Matthew!" Anne laid the dress over a chair and clasped her hands. "Matthew, it's perfectly exquisite. Oh, I can never thank you enough. Look at those sleeves! Oh, it seems to me this must be a happy dream."

"Well, well, let us have breakfast," interrupted Marilla. "I must say, Anne, I don't think you needed the dress; but since Matthew has got it for you, see that you take good care of it. There's a hair ribbon Mrs. Lynde left for you. It's brown, to match the dress. Come now, sit in."

"I don't see how I'm going to eat breakfast," said Anne rapturously. "Breakfast seems so commonplace at such an exciting moment. I'd rather feast my eyes on that dress. I'm so glad that puffed sleeves are still fashionable. It did seem to me that I'd never get over it if they went out before I had a dress with them. I'd never have felt quite satisfied, you see. It was lovely of Mrs. Lynde to give me the ribbon, too. I feel that I ought to be a very good girl indeed. It's at times like this I'm sorry I'm not a model little girl; and I always resolve that I will be in future. But somehow it's hard to carry out your resolutions when irresistible temptations come. Still, I really will make an extra effort after this."

When the commonplace breakfast was over Diana appeared, crossing the white log bridge in the hollow, a gay little figure in her crimson ulster. Anne flew down the slope to meet her.

"Merry Christmas, Diana! And oh, it's a wonderful Christmas. I've something splendid to show you. Matthew has given me the loveliest dress, with *such* sleeves. I couldn't even imagine any nicer."

"I've got something more for you," said Diana breathlessly. "Here—this box. Aunt Josephine sent us out a big box with ever so many things in it—and this is for you. I'd have brought it over last night, but it didn't come until after dark, and I never feel very comfortable coming through the Haunted Wood in the dark now."

Anne opened the box and peeped in. First a card with "For the Anne-girl and Merry Christmas," written on it; and then, a pair of the daintiest little kid slippers, with beaded toes and satin bows and glistening buckles.

"Oh," said Anne, "Diana, this is too much, I must be dreaming."

"*I* call it providential," said Diana. "You won't have to borrow Ruby's slippers now, and that's a blessing, for they're two sizes too big for you, and it would be awful to hear a fairy shuffling. Josie Pye would be delighted. Mind you, Rob Wright went home with Gertie Pye from the practice night before last. Did you ever hear anything equal to that?"

All the Avonlea scholars were in a fever of excitement that day, for the hall had to be decorated and a last grand rehearsal held.

The concert came off in the evening and was a pronounced success. The little hall was crowded; all the performers did excellently well, but Anne was the bright particular star of the occasion, as even envy, in the shape of Josie Pye, dared not deny.

"Oh, hasn't it been a brilliant evening?" sighed Anne, when it was all over and she and Diana were walking home together under a dark, starry sky.

"Everything went off very well," said Diana practically. "I guess we must have made as much as ten dollars. Mind you, Mr. Allan is going to send an account of it to the Charlottetown papers."

"Oh, Diana, will we really see our names in print? It makes me thrill to think of it. Your solo was perfectly elegant, Diana. I felt prouder than you did when it was encored. I just said to myself, 'It is my dear bosom friend who is so honoured.'"

"Well, your recitations just brought down the house, Anne. That sad one was simply splendid."

"Oh, I was so nervous, Diana. When Mr. Allan called out my name I really cannot tell how I ever got up on that platform. I felt as if a million eyes were looking at me and through me, and for one dreadful moment I was sure I couldn't begin at all. Then I thought of my lovely puffed sleeves and took courage. I knew that I must live up to those sleeves, Diana. So I started in, and my voice seemed to be coming from ever so far away. I just felt like a parrot. It's providential that I practised those recitations so often up in the garret, or I'd never have been able to get through. Did I groan all right?"

"Yes, indeed, you groaned lovely," assured Diana.

"I saw old Mrs. Sloane wiping away tears when I sat down. It was splendid to think I had touched somebody's heart. It's so romantic to take part in a concert isn't it? Oh, it's been a very memorable occasion indeed."

"Wasn't the boys' dialogue fine?" said Diana. "Gilbert Blythe was just splendid. Anne, I do think it's awful mean the way you treat Gil. Wait till I tell you. When you ran off the platform after the fairy dialogue one of your roses fell out of your hair. I saw Gil pick it up and put it in his breast pocket. There now. You're so romantic that I'm sure you ought to be pleased at that."

"It's nothing to me what that person does," said Anne loftily. "I simply never waste a thought on him, Diana."

That night Marilla and Matthew, who had been out to a concert for the first time in twenty years, sat for awhile by the kitchen fire after Anne had gone to bed.

"Well now, I guess our Anne did as well as any of them," said Matthew proudly.

"Yes, she did," admitted Marilla. "She's a bright child, Matthew. And she looked real nice, too. I've been kind of opposed to this concert scheme, but I suppose there's no real harm in it after all. Anyhow, I was proud of Anne tonight, although I'm not going to tell her so."

"Well now, I was proud of her and I did tell her so 'fore she went upstairs," said Matthew. "We must see what we can do for her some of these days, Marilla. I guess she'll need something more than Avonlea school by and by."

"There's time enough to think of that," said Marilla. "She's only thirteen in March. Though tonight it struck me she was growing quite a big girl. Mrs. Lynde made that dress a mite too long, and it makes Anne look so tall. She's quick to learn and I guess the best thing we can do for her will be to send her to Queen's after a spell. But nothing need be said about that for a year or two yet."

"Well now, it'll do no harm to be thinking it over off and on," said Matthew. "Things like that are all the better for lots of thinking over."

Missy's Room

Mrs. Falconer and Miss Bailey walked home together through the fine blue summer afternoon from the Ladies' Aid meeting at Mrs. Robinson's. They were talking earnestly; that is to say, Miss Bailey was talking earnestly and volubly, and Mrs. Falconer was listening. Mrs. Falconer had reduced the practice of listening to a fine art. She was a thin, wistful-faced mite of a woman, with sad brown eyes, and with snow-white hair that was a libel on her fifty-five years and girlish step. Nobody in Lindsay ever felt very well acquainted with Mrs. Falconer, in spite of the fact that she had lived among them forty years. She kept between her and her world a fine, baffling reserve which no one had ever been able to penetrate. It was known that she had had a bitter sorrow in her life, but she never made any reference to it, and most people in Lindsay had forgotten it. Some foolish ones even supposed that Mrs. Falconer had forgotten it.

"Well, I do not know what on earth is to be done with Camilla Clark," said Miss Bailey, with a prodigious sigh. "I suppose that we will simply have to trust the whole matter to Providence."

Miss Bailey's tone and sigh really seemed to intimate to the world at large that Providence was a last resort and a very dubious one. Not that Miss Bailey meant anything of the sort; her faith was as substantial as her works, which were many and praiseworthy and seasonable.

The case of Camilla Clark was agitating the Ladies' Aid of one of the Lindsay churches. They had talked about it through the whole of that afternoon session while they sewed for their missionary box—talked about it, and come to no conclusion.

In the preceding spring James Clark, one of the hands in the lumber mill at Lindsay, had been killed in an accident. The shock had proved nearly fatal to his young wife. The next day Camilla Clark's baby was born dead, and the poor mother hovered for weeks between life and death. Slowly, very slowly, life won the battle, and Camilla came back from the valley of the shadow. But she was still an invalid, and would be so for a long time.

The Clarks had come to Lindsay only a short time before the accident. They were boarding at Mrs. Barry's when it happened, and Mrs. Barry had shown every kindness and consideration to the unhappy young widow. But now the Barrys were very soon to leave Lindsay for the West, and the question was, what was to be done with Camilla Clark? She could not go west; she could not even do work of any sort yet in Lindsay; she had no relatives or friends in the world; and she was absolutely penniless. As she and her husband had joined the church to which the aforesaid Ladies' Aid belonged, the members thereof felt themselves bound to take up her case and see what could be done for her.

The obvious solution was for some of them to offer her a home until such time as she would be able to go to work. But there did not seem to be anyone who could offer to do this—unless it was Mrs. Falconer. The church was small, and the Ladies' Aid smaller. There were only twelve members in it; four of these were unmarried ladies who boarded, and so were helpless in the matter; of the remaining eight seven had large families, or sick husbands, or something else that prevented them from offering Camilla Clark an asylum. Their excuses were all valid; they were good, sincere women who would have taken her in if they could, but they could not see their way clear to do so. However, it was probable they would eventually manage it in some way if Mrs. Falconer did not rise to the occasion.

Nobody liked to ask Mrs. Falconer outright to take Camilla Clark in, yet everyone thought she might offer. She was comfortably off, and though her house was small, there was nobody to live in it except herself and her husband. But Mrs. Falconer sat silent through all the discussion of the Ladies' Aid, and never opened her lips on the subject of Camilla Clark despite the numerous hints which she received.

Miss Bailey made one more effort as aforesaid. When her despairing reference to Providence brought forth no results, she wished she dared ask Mrs. Falconer openly to take Camilla Clark, but somehow she did not dare. There were not many things that could daunt Miss Bailey, but Mrs. Falconer's reserve and gentle aloofness always could.

When Miss Bailey had gone on down the village street, Mrs. Falconer paused for a few moments at her gate, apparently lost in deep thought. She was perfectly well aware of all the hints that had been thrown out for her benefit that afternoon. She knew that the Aids, one and all, thought that she ought to take Camilla Clark. But she had no room to give her—for it was out of the question to think of putting her in Missy's room.

"I couldn't do such a thing," she said to herself piteously. "They don't understand—they can't understand—but I *couldn't* give her Missy's room. I'm sorry for poor Camilla, and I wish I could help her. But I can't give her Missy's room, and I have no other."

The little Falconer cottage, set back from the road in the green seclusion of an apple orchard and thick, leafy maples, was a very tiny one. There were just two rooms downstairs and two upstairs. When Mrs. Falconer entered the kitchen an old-looking man with long white hair and mild blue eyes looked up with a smile from the bright-coloured blocks before him.

"Have you been lonely, Father?" said Mrs. Falconer tenderly.

He shook his head, still smiling.

"No, not lonely. These"—pointing to the blocks—"are so pretty. See my house, Mother."

This man was Mrs. Falconer's husband. Once he had been one of the smartest, most intelligent men in Lindsay, and one of the most trusted employees of the railroad company. Then there had been a train collision. Malcolm Falconer was taken out of the wreck fearfully injured. He eventually recovered physical health, but he was from that time forth merely a child in intellect—a harmless, kindly creature, docile and easily amused.

Mrs. Falconer tried to dismiss the thought of Camilla Clark from her mind, but it would not be dismissed. Her conscience reproached her continually. She tried to compromise with it by saying that she would go down and see Camilla that evening and take her some nice fresh Irish moss jelly. It was so good for delicate people.

She found Camilla alone in the Barry sitting-room, and noticed with a feeling that was almost like self-reproach how thin and frail and white the poor young creature looked. Why, she seemed little more than a child! Her great dark eyes were far too big for her wasted face, and her hands were almost transparent.

"I'm not much better yet," said Camilla tremulously, in response to Mrs. Falconer's inquiries. "Oh, I'm so slow getting well! And I know—I feel that I'm a burden to everybody."

"But you mustn't think that, dear," said Mrs. Falconer, feeling more uncomfortable than ever. "We are all glad to do all we can for you."

Mrs. Falconer paused suddenly. She was a very truthful woman and she instantly realized that that last sentence was not true. She was not doing all she could for Camilla—she would not be glad, she feared, to do all she could.

"If I were only well enough to go to work," sighed Camilla. "Mr. Marks says I can have a place in the shoe factory whenever I'm able to. But it will be so long yet. Oh, I'm so tired and discouraged!"

She put her hands over her face and sobbed. Mrs. Falconer caught her breath. What if Missy were somewhere alone in the world—ill, friendless, with never a soul to offer her a refuge or a shelter? It was so very, very probable. Before she could check herself Mrs. Falconer spoke. "My dear, don't cry! I want you to come and stay with me until you get perfectly well. You won't be a speck of trouble, and I'll be glad to have you for company."

Mrs. Falconer's Rubicon was crossed. She could not draw back now if she wanted to. But she was not at all sure that she did want to. By the time she reached home she was sure she didn't want to. And yet—to give Missy's room to Camilla! It seemed a great sacrifice to Mrs. Falconer.

She went up to it the next morning with firmly set lips to air and dust it. It was just the same as when Missy had left it long ago. Nothing had ever been moved or changed, but everything had always been kept beautifully neat and clean. Snow-white muslin curtains hung before the small square window. In one corner was a little white bed. Missy's pictures hung on the walls; Missy's books and work-basket were lying on the square stand; there was a bit of half-finished fancy work, yellow from age, lying in the basket. On a small bureau before the gilt-framed mirror were several little girlish knick-knacks and boxes whose contents had never been disturbed since Missy went away. One of Missy's gay pink ribbons—Missy had been so fond of pink ribbons—hung over the top of the mirror. On a chair lay Missy's hat, bright with ribbons and roses, just as Missy had laid it there on the night before she left her home.

Mrs. Falconer's lips quivered as she looked about the room, and tears came to her eyes. Oh, how could she put these things away and bring a stranger here—here, where no one save herself had entered for fifteen years, here in this room, sacred to Missy's memory, waiting for her return when she should be weary of wandering? It almost seemed to the mother's vague fancy, distorted by long, silent brooding, that her daughter's innocent girlhood had been kept here for her and would be lost forever if the room were given to another.

"I suppose it's dreadful foolishness," said Mrs. Falconer, wiping her eyes. "I know it is, but I can't help it. It just goes to my heart to think of putting these things away. But I must do it. Camilla is coming here today, and this room must be got ready for her. Oh, Missy, my poor lost child, it's for your sake I'm doing this—because you may be suffering somewhere as Camilla is now, and I'd wish the same kindness to be shown to you."

She opened the window and put fresh linen on the bed. One by one Missy's little belongings were removed and packed carefully away. On the gay, foolish little hat with its faded wreath of roses the mother's tears fell as she put it in a box. She remembered so plainly the first time Missy had worn it. She could see the pretty, delicately tinted face, the big shining brown eyes, and the riotous golden curls under the drooping, lace-edged brim. Oh, where was Missy now? What roof sheltered her? Did she ever think of her mother and the little white cottage under the maples, and the low-ceilinged, dim room where she had knelt to say her childhood's prayer?

Camilla Clark came that afternoon.

"Oh, it is lovely here," she said gratefully, looking out into the rustling shade of the maples. "I'm sure I shall soon get well here. Mrs. Barry was so kind to me—I shall never forget her kindness—but the house is so close to the factory, and there was such a whirring of wheels all the time, it seemed to get into my head and make me wild with nervousness. I'm so weak that sounds like that worry me. But it is so still and green and peaceful here. It just rests me."

When bedtime came, Mrs. Falconer took Camilla up to Missy's room. It was not as hard as she had expected it to be after all. The wrench was over with the putting away of Missy's things, and it did not hurt the mother to see the frail, girlish Camilla in her daughter's place.

"What a dear little room!" said Camilla, glancing around. "It is so white and sweet. Oh, I know I am going to sleep well here, and dream sweet dreams."

"It was my daughter's room," said Mrs. Falconer, sitting down on the chintz-covered seat by the open window.

Camilla looked surprised.

"I did not know you had a daughter," she said.

"Yes—I had just the one child," said Mrs. Falconer dreamily.

For fifteen years she had never spoken of Missy to a living soul except her husband. But now she felt a sudden impulse to tell Camilla about her, and about the room.

"Her name was Isabella, after her father's mother, but we never called her anything but Missy. That was the little name she gave herself when she began to talk. Oh, I've missed her so!"

"When did she die?" asked Camilla softly, sympathy shining, starlike, in her dark eyes.

"She—she didn't die," said Mrs. Falconer. "She went away. She was a pretty girl and gay and fond of fun—but such a good girl. Oh, Missy was always a good girl! Her father and I were so proud of her—too proud, I suppose. She had her little faults—she was too fond of dress and gaiety, but then she was so young, and we indulged her. Then Bert Williams came to Lindsay to work in the factory. He was a handsome fellow, with taking ways about him, but he was drunken and profane, and nobody knew anything about his past life. He fascinated Missy. He kept coming to see her until her father forbade him the house. Then our poor, foolish child used to meet him elsewhere. We found this out afterwards. And at last she ran away with him, and they were married over at Peterboro and went there to live, for Bert had got work there. We—we were too hard on Missy. But her father was so dreadful hurt about it. He'd been so fond and proud of her, and he felt that she had disgraced him. He disowned her, and sent her word never to show her face here again, for he'd never forgive her. And I was angry too. I didn't send her any word at all. Oh, how I've wept over that! If I had just sent her one little word of forgiveness, everything might have been different. But Father forbade me to.

"Then in a little while there was a dreadful trouble. A woman came to Peterboro and claimed to be Bert Williams's wife—and she was—she proved it. Bert cleared out and was never seen again in these parts. As soon as we heard about it Father relented, and I went right down to Peterboro to see Missy and bring her home. But she wasn't there—she had gone, nobody knew where. I got a letter from her the next week. She said her heart was broken, and she knew we would never forgive her, and she couldn't face the disgrace, so she was going away where nobody would ever find her. We did everything we could to trace her, but we never could. We've never heard from her since, and it is fifteen years ago. Sometimes I am afraid she is dead, but then again I feel sure she isn't. Oh, Camilla, if I could only find my poor child and bring her home!

"This was her room. And when she went away I made up my mind I would keep it for her just as she left it, and I have up to now. Nobody has ever been inside the door but myself. I've always hoped that Missy would come home, and I would lead her up here and say, 'Missy, here is your room just as you left it, and here is your place in your mother's heart just as you left it,' But she never came. I'm afraid she never will."

Mrs. Falconer dropped her face in her hands and sobbed softly. Camilla came over to her and put her arms about her.

"I think she will," she said. "I think—I am sure your love and prayers will bring Missy home yet. And I understand how good you have been in giving me her room—oh, I know what it must have cost you! I will pray tonight that God will bring Missy back to you."

When Mrs. Falconer returned to the kitchen to close the house for the night, her husband being already sound asleep; she heard a low, timid knock at the door. Wondering who it could be so late, she opened it. The light fell on a shrinking, shabby figure on the step, and on a pale, pinched face in which only a mother could have recognized the features of her child. Mrs. Falconer gave a cry.

"Missy! Missy! Missy!"

She caught the poor wanderer to her heart and drew her in.

"Oh, Missy, Missy, have you come back at last? Thank God! Oh, thank God!"

"I *had* to come back. I was starving for a glimpse of your face and of the old home, Mother," sobbed Missy. "But I didn't mean you should know—I never meant to show myself to you. I've been sick, and just as soon as I got better I came here. I meant to creep home after dark and look at the dear old house, and perhaps get a glimpse of you and Father through the window if you were still here. I didn't know if you were. And then I meant to go right away on the night train. I was under the window and I heard you telling my story to someone. Oh, Mother, when I knew that you had forgiven me, that you loved me still and had always kept my room for me, I made up my mind that I'd show myself to you."

The mother had got her child into a rocking-chair and removed the shabby hat and cloak. How ill and worn and faded Missy looked! Yet her face was pure and fine, and there was in it something sweeter than had ever been there in her beautiful girlhood.

"I'm terribly changed, am I not, Mother?" said Missy, with a faint smile. "I've had a hard life—but an honest one, Mother. When I went away I was almost mad with the disgrace my wilfulness had brought on you and Father and myself. I went as far as I could get away from you, and I got work in a factory. I've worked there ever since, just making enough to keep body and soul together. Oh, I've starved for a word from you—the sight of your face! But I thought Father would spurn me from his door if I should ever dare to come back."

"Oh, Missy!" sobbed the mother. "Your poor father is just like a child. He got a terrible hurt ten years ago, and never got over it. I don't suppose he'll even know you—he's clean forgot everything. But he forgave you before it happened. You poor child, you're done right out. You're too weak to be travelling. But never mind, you're home now, and I'll soon nurse you up. I'll put on the kettle and get you a good cup of tea first thing. And you're not to do any more talking till the morning. But, oh, Missy, I can't take you to your own room after all. Camilla Clark has it, and she'll be asleep by now; we mustn't disturb her, for she's been real sick. I'll fix up a bed for you on the sofa, though. Missy, Missy, let us kneel down here and thank God for His mercy!"

Late that night, when Missy had fallen asleep in her improvised bed, the wakeful mother crept in to gloat over her.

"Just to think," she whispered, "if I hadn't taken Camilla Clark in, Missy wouldn't have heard me telling about the room, and she'd have gone away again and never have known. Oh, I don't deserve such a blessing when I was so unwilling to take Camilla! But I know one thing: this is going to be Camilla's home. There'll be no leaving it even when she does get well. She shall be my daughter, and I'll love her next to Missy."

Ted's Afternoon Off

Ted was up at five that morning, as usual. He always had to rise early to kindle the fire and go for the cows, but on this particular morning there was no "had to" about it. He had awakened at four o'clock and had sprung eagerly to the little garret window facing the east, to see what sort of a day was being born. Thrilling with excitement, he saw that it was going to be a glorious day. The sky was all rosy and golden and clear beyond the sharp-pointed, dark firs on Lee's Hill. Out to the north the sea was shimmering and sparkling gaily, with little foam crests here and there ruffled up by the cool morning breeze. Oh, it would be a splendid day!

And he, Ted Melvin, was to have a half holiday for the first time since he had come to live in Brookdale four years ago—a whole afternoon off to go to the Sunday School picnic at the beach beyond the big hotel. It almost seemed too good to be true!

The Jacksons, with whom he had lived ever since his mother had died, did not think holidays were necessities for boys. Hard work and cast-off clothes, and three grudgingly allowed months of school in the winter, made up Ted's life year in and year out—his outer life at least. He had an inner life of dreams, but nobody knew or suspected anything about that. To everybody in Brookdale he was simply Ted Melvin, a shy, odd-looking little fellow with big dreamy black eyes and a head of thick tangled curls which could never be made to look tidy and always annoyed Mrs. Jackson exceedingly.

It was as yet too early to light the fire or go for the cows. Ted crept softly to a corner in the garret and took from the wall an old brown fiddle. It had been his father's. He loved to play on it, and his few rare spare moments were always spent in the garret corner or the hayloft, with his precious fiddle. It was his one link with the old life he had lived in a little cottage far away, with a mother who had loved him and a merry young father who had made wonderful music on the old brown violin.

Ted pushed open his garret window and, seating himself on the sill, began to play, with his eyes fixed on the glowing eastern sky. He played very softly, since Mrs. Jackson had a pronounced dislike to being wakened by "fiddling at all unearthly hours."

The music he made was beautiful and would have astonished anybody who knew enough to know how wonderful it really was. But there was nobody to hear this little neglected urchin of all work, and he fiddled away happily, the music floating out of the garret window, over the treetops and the dew-wet clover fields, until it mingled with the winds and was lost in the silver skies of the morning.

Ted worked doubly hard all that forenoon, since there was a double share of work to do if, as Mrs. Jackson said, he was to be gadding to picnics in the afternoon. But he did it all cheerily and whistled for joy as he worked.

After dinner Mrs. Ross came in. Mrs. Ross lived down on the shore road and made a living for herself and her two children by washing and doing days' work out. She was not a very cheerful person and generally spoke as if on the point of bursting into tears. She looked more doleful than ever today, and lost no time in explaining why.

"I've just got word that my sister over at White Sands is sick with pendikis"—this was the nearest Mrs. Ross could get to appendicitis—"and has to go to the hospital. I've got to go right over and see her, Mrs. Jackson, and I've run in to ask if Ted can go and stay with Jimmy till I get back. There's no one else I can get, and Amelia is away. I'll be back this evening. I don't like leaving Jimmy alone."

"Ted's been promised that he could go to the picnic this afternoon," said Mrs. Jackson shortly. "Mr. Jackson said he could go, so he'll have to please himself. If he's willing to stay with Jimmy instead, he can. *I* don't care."

"Oh, I've *got* to go to the picnic," cried Ted impulsively. "I'm awful sorry for Jimmy—but I *must* go to the picnic."

"I s'pose you feel so," said Mrs. Ross, sighing heavily. "I dunno's I blame you. Picnics is more cheerful than staying with a poor little lame boy, I don't doubt. Well, I s'pose I can put Jimmy's supper on the table clost to him, and shut the cat in with him, and mebbe he'll worry through. He was counting on having you to fiddle for him, though. Jimmy's crazy about music, and he don't never hear much of it. Speaking of fiddling, there's a great fiddler stopping at the hotel now. His name is Blair Milford, and he makes his living fiddling at concerts. I knew him well when he was a child—I was nurse in his father's family. He was a taking little chap, and I was real fond of him. Well, I must be getting. Jimmy'll feel bad at staying alone, but I'll tell him he'll just have to put up with it."

Mrs. Ross sighed herself away, and Ted flew up to his garret corner with a choking in his throat. He couldn't go to stay with Jimmy—he couldn't give up the picnic! Why, he had never been at a picnic; and they were going to drive to the hotel beach in wagons, and have swings, and games, and ice cream, and a boat sail to Curtain Island! He had been looking forward to it, waking and dreaming, for a fortnight. He *must* go. But poor little Jimmy! It was too bad for him to be left all alone.

"I wouldn't like it myself," said Ted miserably, trying to swallow a lump that persisted in coming up in his throat. "It must be dreadful to have to lie on the sofa all the time and never be able to run, climb trees or play, or do a single thing. And Jimmy doesn't like reading much. He'll be dreadful lonesome. I'll be thinking of him all the time at the picnic—I know I will. I suppose I *could* go and stay with him, if I just made up my mind to it."

Making up his mind to it was a slow and difficult process. But when Ted was finally dressed in his shabby, "skimpy" Sunday best, he tucked his precious fiddle under his arm and slipped downstairs. "Please, I think I'll go and stay with Jimmy," he said to Mrs. Jackson timidly, as he always spoke to her.

"Well, if you're to waste the afternoon, I s'pose it's better to waste it that way than in going to a picnic and eating yourself sick," was Mrs. Jackson's ungracious response.

Ted reached Mrs. Ross's little house just as that good lady was locking the door on Jimmy and the cat. "Well, I'm real glad," she said, when Ted told her he had come to stay. "I'd have worried most awful if I'd had to leave Jimmy all alone. He's crying in there this minute. Come now, Jimmy, dry up. Here's Ted come to stop with you after all, and he's brought his fiddle, too."

Jimmy's tears were soon dried, and he welcomed Ted joyfully. "I've been thinking awful long to hear you fiddling," said Jimmy, with a sigh of content. "Seems like the ache ain't never half so bad when I'm listening to music—and when it's your music, I forget there's any ache at all."

Ted took his violin and began to play. After all, it was almost as good as a picnic to have a whole afternoon for his music. The stuffy little room, with its dingy plaster and shabby furniture, was filled with wonderful harmonies. Once he began, Ted could play for hours at a stretch and never be conscious of fatigue. Jimmy lay and listened in rapturous content while Ted's violin sang and laughed and dreamed and rippled.

There was another listener besides Jimmy. Outside, on the red sandstone doorstep, a man was sitting—a tall, well-dressed man with a pale, beautiful face and long, supple white hands. Motionless, he sat there and listened to the music until at last it stopped. Then he rose and knocked at the door. Ted, violin in hand, opened it.

An expression of amazement flashed into the stranger's face, but he only said, "Is Mrs. Ross at home?"

"No, sir," said Ted shyly. "She went over to White Sands and she won't be back till night. But Jimmy is here—Jimmy is her little boy. Will you come in?"

"I'm sorry Mrs. Ross is away," said the stranger, entering. "She was an old nurse of mine. I must confess I've been sitting on the step out there for some time, listening to your music. Who taught you to play, my boy?"

"Nobody," said Ted simply. "I've always been able to play."

"He makes it up himself out of his own head, sir," said Jimmy eagerly.

"No, I don't make it—it makes itself—it just *comes*," said Ted, a dreamy gaze coming into his big black eyes.

The caller looked at him closely. "I know a little about music myself," he said. "My name is Blair Milford and I am a professional violinist. Your playing is wonderful. What is your name?"

"Ted Melvin."

"Well, Ted, I think that you have a great talent, and it ought to be cultivated. You should have competent instruction. Come, you must tell me all about yourself."

Ted told what little he thought there was to tell. Blair Milford listened and nodded, guessing much that Ted didn't tell and, indeed, didn't know himself. Then he made Ted play for him again. "Amazing!" he said softly, under his breath.

Finally he took the violin and played himself. Ted and Jimmy listened breathlessly. "Oh, if I could only play like that!" said Ted wistfully.

Blair Milford smiled. "You will play much better some day if you get the proper training," he said. "You have a wonderful talent, my boy, and you should have it cultivated. It will never in the world do to waste such genius. Yes, that is the right word," he went on musingly, as if talking to himself, "'genius.' Nature is always taking us by surprise. This child has what I have never had and would make any sacrifice for. And yet in him it may come to naught for lack of opportunity. But it must not, Ted. You must have a musical training."

"I can't take lessons, if that is what you mean, sir," said Ted wonderingly. "Mr. Jackson wouldn't pay for them."

"I think we needn't worry about the question of payment if you can find time to practise," said Blair Milford. "I am to be at the beach for two months yet. For once I'll take a music pupil. But will you have time to practise?"

"Yes, sir, I'll make time," said Ted, as soon as he could speak at all for the wonder of it. "I'll get up at four in the morning and have an hour's practising before the time for the cows. But I'm afraid it'll be too much trouble for you, sir, I'm afraid—"

Blair Milford laughed and put his slim white hand on Ted's curly head. "It isn't much trouble to train an artist. It is a privilege. Ah, Ted, you have what I once hoped I had, what I know now I never can have. You don't understand me. You will some day."

"Ain't he an awful nice man?" said Jimmy, when Blair Milford had gone. "But what did he mean by all that talk?"

"I don't know exactly," said Ted dreamily. "That is, I seem to *feel* what he meant but I can't quite put it into words. But, oh, Jimmy, I'm so happy. I'm to have lessons—I have always longed to have them."

"I guess you're glad you didn't go to the picnic?" said Jimmy.

"Yes, but I was glad before, Jimmy, honest I was."

Blair Milford kept his promise. He interviewed Mr. and Mrs. Jackson and, by means best known to himself, induced them to consent that Ted should take music lessons every Saturday afternoon. He was a pupil to delight a teacher's heart and, after every lesson, Blair Milford looked at him with kindly eyes and murmured, "Amazing," under his breath. Finally he went again to the Jacksons, and the next day he said to Ted, "Ted, would you like to come away with me—live with me—be my boy and have your gift for music thoroughly cultivated?"

"What do you mean, sir?" said Ted tremblingly.

"I mean that I want you—that I must have you, Ted. I've talked to Mr. Jackson, and he has consented to let you come. You shall be educated, you shall have the best masters in your art that the world affords, you shall have the career I once dreamed of. Will you come, Ted?"

Ted drew a long breath. "Yes, sir," he said. "But it isn't so much because of the music—it's because I love you, Mr. Milford, and I'm so glad I'm to be always with you."

The Doctor's Sweetheart

Just because I am an old woman outwardly it doesn't follow that I am one inwardly. Hearts don't grow old—or shouldn't. Mine hasn't, I am thankful to say. It bounded like a girl's with delight when I saw Doctor John and Marcella Barry drive past this afternoon. If the doctor had been my own son I couldn't have felt more real pleasure in his happiness. I'm only an old lady who can do little but sit by her window and knit, but eyes were made for seeing, and I use mine for that purpose. When I see the good and beautiful things—and a body need never look for the other kind, you know—the things God planned from the beginning and brought about in spite of the counter plans and schemes of men, I feel such a deep joy that I'm glad, even at seventy-five, to be alive in a world where such things come to pass. And if ever God meant and made two people for each other, those people were Doctor John and Marcella Barry; and that is what I always tell folk who come here commenting on the difference in their ages. "Old enough to be her father," sniffed Mrs. Riddell to me the other day. I didn't say anything to Mrs. Riddell. I just looked at her. I presume my face expressed what I felt pretty clearly. How any woman can live for sixty years in the world, as Mrs. Riddell has, a wife and mother at that, and not get some realization of the beauty and general satisfactoriness of a real and abiding love, is something I cannot understand and never shall be able to.

Nobody in Bridgeport believed that Marcella would ever come back, except Doctor John and me—not even her Aunt Sara. I've heard people laugh at me when I said I knew she would; but nobody minds being laughed at when she is sure of a thing and I was sure that Marcella Barry would come back as that the sun rose and set. I hadn't lived beside her for eight years to know so little about her as to doubt her. Neither had Doctor John.

Marcella was only eight years old when she came to live in Bridgeport. Her father, Chester Barry, had just died. Her mother, who was a sister of Miss Sara Bryant, my next door neighbor, had been dead for four years. Marcella's father left her to the guardianship of his brother, Richard Barry; but Miss Sara pleaded so hard to have the little girl that the Barrys consented to let Marcella live with her aunt until she was sixteen. Then, they said, she would have to go back to them, to be properly educated and take the place of her father's daughter in *his* world. For, of course, it is a fact that Miss Sara Bryant's world was and is a very different one from Chester Barry's world. As to which side the difference favors, that isn't for me to say. It all depends on your standard of what is really worth while, you know.

So Marcella came to live with us in Bridgeport. I say "us" advisedly. She slept and ate in her aunt's house, but every house in the village was a home to her; for, with all our little disagreements and diverse opinions, we are really all one big family, and everybody feels an interest in and a good working affection for everybody else. Besides, Marcella was one of those children whom everybody loves at sight, and keeps on loving. One long, steady gaze from those big grayish-blue black-lashed eyes of hers went right into your heart and stayed there.

She was a pretty child and as good as she was pretty. It was the right sort of goodness, too, with just enough spice of original sin in it to keep it from spoiling by reason of over-sweetness. She was a frank, loyal, brave little thing, even at eight, and wouldn't have said or done a mean or false thing to save her life.

She and I were right good friends from the beginning. She loved me and she loved her Aunt Sara; but from the very first her best and deepest affection went out to Doctor John Haven, who lived in the big brick house on the other side of Miss Sara's.

Doctor John was a Bridgeport boy, and when he got through college he came right home and settled down here, with his widowed mother. The Bridgeport girls were fluttered, for eligible young men were scarce in our village; there was considerable setting of caps, I must say that, although I despise ill-natured gossip; but neither the caps nor the wearers thereof seemed to make any impression on Doctor John. Mrs. Riddell said that he was a born old bachelor; I suppose she based her opinion on the fact that Doctor John was always a quiet, bookish fellow, who didn't care a button for society, and had never been guilty of a flirtation in his life. I knew Doctor John's heart far better than Martha Riddell could know anybody's; and I knew there was nothing of the old bachelor in his nature. He just had to wait for the right woman, that was all, not being able to content himself with less as some men can and do. If she never came Doctor John would never marry; but he wouldn't be an old bachelor for all that.

He was thirty when Marcella came to Bridgeport—a tall, broad-shouldered man with a mane of thick brown curls and level, dark hazel eyes. He walked with a little stoop, his hands clasped behind him; and he had the sweetest, deepest voice. Spoken music, if ever a voice was. He was kind and brave and gentle, but a little distant and reserved with most people. Everybody in Bridgeport liked him, but only a very few ever passed the inner gates of his confidence or were admitted to any share in his real life. I am proud to say I was one; I think it is something for an old woman to boast of.

Doctor John was always fond of children, and they of him. It was natural that he and little Marcella should take to each other. He had the most to do with bringing her up, for Miss Sara consulted him in everything. Marcella was not hard to manage for the most part; but she had a will of her own, and when she did set it up in opposition to the powers that were, nobody but the doctor could influence her at all; she never resisted him or disobeyed his wishes.

Marcella was one of those girls who develop early. I suppose her constant association with us elderly folks had something to do with it, too. But, at fifteen, she was a woman, loving, beautiful, and spirited.

And Doctor John loved her—loved the woman, not the child. I knew it before he did—but not, as I think, before Marcella did, for those young, straight-gazing eyes of hers were wonderfully quick to read into other people's hearts. I watched them together and saw the love growing between them, like a strong, fair, perfect flower, whose fragrance was to endure for eternity. Miss Sara saw it, too, and was half-pleased and half-worried; even Miss Sara thought the Doctor too old for Marcella; and besides, there were the Barrys to be reckoned with. Those Barrys were the nightmare dread of poor Miss Sara's life.

The time came when Doctor John's eyes were opened. He looked into his own heart and read there what life had written for him. As he told me long afterwards, it came to him with a shock that left him white-lipped. But he was a brave, sensible fellow and he looked the matter squarely in the face. First of all, he put away to one side all that the world might say; the thing concerned solely him and Marcella, and the world had nothing to do with it. That disposed of, he asked himself soberly if he had a right to try to win Marcella's love. He decided that he had not; it would be taking an unfair advantage of her youth and inexperience. He knew that she must soon go to her father's people—she must not go bound by any ties of his making. Doctor John, for Marcella's sake, gave the decision against his own heart.

So much did Doctor John tell me, his old friend and confidant. I said nothing and gave no advice, not having lived seventy-five years for nothing. I knew that Doctor John's decision was manly and right and fair; but I also knew it was all nullified by the fact that Marcella already loved him.

So much I knew; the rest I was left to suppose. The Doctor and Marcella told me much, but there were some things too sacred to be told, even to me. So that to this day I don't know how the doctor found out that Marcella loved him. All I know is that one day, just a month before her sixteenth birthday, the two came hand in hand to Miss Sara and me, as we sat on Miss Sara's veranda in the twilight, and told us simply that they had plighted their troth to each other.

I looked at them standing there with that wonderful sunrise of life and love on their faces—the doctor, tall and serious, with a sprinkle of silver in his brown hair and the smile of a happy man on his lips—Marcella, such a slip of a girl, with her black hair in a long braid and her lovely face all dewed over with tears and sunned over with smiles—I, an old woman, looked at them and thanked the good God for them and their delight.

Miss Sara laughed and cried and kissed—and forboded what the Barrys would do. Her forebodings proved only too true. When the doctor wrote to Richard Barry, Marcella's guardian, asking his consent to their engagement, Richard Barry promptly made trouble—the very worst kind of trouble. He descended on Bridgeport and completely overwhelmed poor Miss Sara in his wrath. He laughed at the idea of countenancing an engagement between a child like Marcella and an obscure country doctor. And he carried Marcella off with him!

She had to go, of course. He was her legal guardian and he would listen to no pleadings. He didn't know anything about Marcella's character, and he thought that a new life out in the great world would soon blot out her fancy.

After the first outburst of tears and prayers Marcella took it very calmly, as far as outward eye could see. She was as cool and dignified and stately as a young queen. On the night before she went away she came over to say good-bye to me. She did not even shed any tears, but the look in her eyes told of bitter hurt. "It is goodbye for five years, Miss Tranquil," she said steadily. "When I am twenty-one I will come back. That is the only promise I can make. They will not let me write to John or Aunt Sara and I will do nothing underhanded. But I will not forget and I will come back."

Richard Barry would not even let her see Doctor John alone again. She had to bid him good-bye beneath the cold, contemptuous eyes of the man of the world. So there was just a hand-clasp and one long deep look between them that was tenderer than any kiss and more eloquent than any words.

"I will come back when I am twenty-one," said Marcella. And I saw Richard Barry smile.

So Marcella went away and in all Bridgeport there were only two people who believed she would ever return. There is no keeping a secret in Bridgeport, and everybody knew all about the love affair between Marcella and the doctor and about the promise she had made. Everybody sympathized with the doctor because everybody believed he had lost his sweetheart.

"For of course she'll never come back," said Mrs. Riddell to me. "She's only a child and she'll soon forget him. She's to be sent to school and taken abroad and between times she'll live with the Richard Barrys; and they move, as everyone knows, in the very highest and gayest circles. I'm sorry for the doctor, though. A man of his age doesn't get over a thing like that in a hurry and he was perfectly silly over Marcella. But it really serves him right for falling in love with a child."

There are times when Martha Riddell gets on my nerves. She's a good-hearted woman, and she means well; but she rasps—rasps terribly.

Even Miss Sara exasperated me. But then she had her excuse. The child she loved as her own had been torn from her and it almost broke her heart. But even so, I thought she ought to have had a little more faith in Marcella.

"Oh, no, she'll never come back," sobbed Miss Sara. "Yes, I know she promised. But they'll wean her away from me. She'll have such a gay, splendid life she'll not want to come back. Five years is a lifetime at her age. No, don't try to comfort me, Miss Tranquil, because I *won't* be comforted!"

When a person has made up her mind to be miserable you just have to *let* her be miserable.

I almost dreaded to see Doctor John for fear he would be in despair, too, without any confidence in Marcella. But when he came I saw I needn't have worried.

The light had all gone out of his eyes, but there was a calm, steady patience in them.

"She will come back to me, Miss Tranquil," he said. "I know what people are saying, but that does not trouble me. They do not know Marcella as I do. She promised and she will keep her word—keep it joyously and gladly, too. If I did not know that I would not wish its fulfilment. When she is free she will turn her back on that brilliant world and all it offers her and come back to me. My part is to wait and believe."

So Doctor John waited and believed. After a little while the excitement died away and people forgot Marcella. We never heard from or about her, except a paragraph now and then in the society columns of the city paper the doctor took. We knew she was sent to school for three years; then the Barrys took her abroad. She was presented at court. When the doctor read this—he was with me at the time—he put his hand over his eyes and sat very silent for a long time. I wondered if at last some momentary doubt had crept into his mind—if he did not fear that Marcella must have forgotten him. The paper told of her triumph and her beauty and hinted at a titled match. Was it probable or even possible that she would be faithful to him after all this?

The doctor must have guessed my thoughts, for at last he looked up with a smile.

"She will come back," was all he said. But I saw that the doubt, if doubt it were, had gone. I watched him as he went away, that tall, gentle, kindly-eyed man, and I prayed that his trust might not be misplaced; for if it should be it would break his heart.

Five years seems a long time in looking forward. But they pass quickly. One day I remembered that it was Marcella's twenty-first birthday. Only one other person thought of it. Even Miss Sara did not. Miss Sara remembered Marcella only as a child that had been loved and lost. Nobody else in Bridgeport thought about her at all. The doctor came in that evening. He had a rose in his buttonhole and he walked with a step as light as a boy's.

"She is free to-day," he said. "We shall soon have her again, Miss Tranquil."

"Do you think she will be the same?" I said.

I don't know what made me say it. I hate to be one of those people who throw cold water on other peoples' hopes. But it slipped out before I thought. I suppose the doubt had been vaguely troubling me always, under all my faith in Marcella, and now made itself felt in spite of me.

But the doctor only laughed.

"How could she be changed?" he said. "Some women might be—most women would be—but not Marcella. Dear Miss Tranquil, don't spoil your beautiful record of confidence by doubting her now. We shall have her again soon—how soon I don't know, for I don't even know where she is, whether in the old world or the new—but just as soon as she can come to us."

We said nothing more—neither of us. But every day the light in the doctor's eyes grew brighter and deeper and tenderer. He never spoke of Marcella, but I knew she was in his thoughts every moment. He was much calmer than I was. I trembled when the postman knocked, jumped when the gate latch clicked, and fairly had a cold chill if I saw a telegraph boy running down the street.

One evening, a fortnight later, I went over to see Miss Sara. She was out somewhere, so I sat down in her little sitting room to wait for her. Presently the doctor came in and we sat in the soft twilight, talking a little now and then, but silent when we wanted to be, as becomes real friendship. It was such a beautiful evening. Outside in Miss Sara's garden the roses were white and red, and sweet with dew; the honeysuckle at the window sent in delicious breaths now and again; a few sleepy birds were twittering; between the trees the sky was all pink and silvery blue and there was an evening star over the elm in my front yard. We heard somebody come through the door and down the hall. I turned, expecting to see Miss Sara—and I saw Marcella! She was standing in the doorway, tall and beautiful, with a ray of sunset light falling athwart her black hair under her travelling hat. She was looking past me at Doctor John and in her splendid eyes was the look of the exile who had come home to her own.

"Marcella!" said the doctor.

I went out by the dining-room door and shut it behind me, leaving them alone together.

The wedding is to be next month. Miss Sara is beside herself with delight. The excitement has been really terrible, and the way people have talked and wondered and exclaimed has almost worn my patience clean out. I've snubbed more persons in the last ten days than I ever did in all my life before.

Nothing of this worries Doctor John or Marcella. They are too happy to care for gossip or outside curiosity. The Barrys are not coming to the wedding, I understand. They refuse to forgive Marcella or countenance her folly, as they call it, in any way. Folly! When I see those two together and realize what they mean to each other I have some humble, reverent idea of what true wisdom is.

The End of the Young Family Feud

A week before Christmas, Aunt Jean wrote to Elizabeth, inviting her and Alberta and me to eat our Christmas dinner at Monkshead. We accepted with delight. Aunt Jean and Uncle Norman were delightful people, and we knew we should have a jolly time at their house. Besides, we wanted to see Monkshead, where Father had lived in his boyhood, and the old Young homestead where he had been born and brought up and where Uncle William still lived. Father never said much about it, but we knew he loved it very dearly, and we had always greatly desired to get at least a glimpse of what Alberta liked to call "our ancestral halls."

Since Monkshead was only sixty miles away, and Uncle William lived there as aforesaid, it may be pertinently asked what there was to prevent us from visiting it and the homestead as often as we wished. We answer promptly: the family feud.

Father and Uncle William were on bad terms, or rather on no terms at all, and had been ever since we could remember. After Grandfather Young's death there had been a wretched quarrel over the property. Father always said that he had been as much to blame as Uncle William, but Great-aunt Emily told us that Uncle William had been by far the most to blame, and that he had behaved scandalously to Father. Moreover, she said that Father had gone to him when cooling-down time came, apologized for what he had said, and asked Uncle William to be friends again; and that William, simply turned his back on Father and walked into the house without saying a word, but, as Great-aunt Emily said, with the Young temper sticking out of every kink and curve of his figure. Great-aunt Emily is our aunt on Mother's side, and she does not like any of the Youngs except Father and Uncle Norman.

This was why we had never visited Monkshead. We had never seen Uncle William, and we always thought of him as a sort of ogre when we thought of him at all. When we were children, our old nurse, Margaret Hannah, used to frighten us into good behaviour by saying ominously, "If you 'uns aint good your Uncle William'll cotch you."

What he would do to us when he "cotched" us she never specified, probably reasoning that the unknown was always more terrible than the known. My private opinion in those days was that he would boil us in oil and pick our bones.

Uncle Norman and Aunt Jean had been living out west for years. Three months before this Christmas they had come east, bought a house in Monkshead, and settled there. They had been down to see us, and Father and Mother and the boys had been up to see them, but we three girls had not; so we were pleasantly excited at the thought of spending Christmas there.

Christmas morning was fine, white as a pearl and clear as a diamond. We had to go by the seven o'clock train, since there was no other before eleven, and we reached Monkshead at eight-thirty.

When we stepped from the train the stationmaster asked us if we were the three Miss Youngs. Alberta pleaded guilty, and he said, "Well, here's a letter for you then."

We took the letter and went into the waiting room with sundry misgivings. What had happened? Were Uncle Norman and Aunt Jean quarantined for scarlet fever, or had burglars raided the pantry and carried off the Christmas supplies? Elizabeth opened and read the letter aloud. It was from Aunt Jean to the following effect:

> DEAR GIRLS: I am so sorry to disappoint you, but I cannot help it. Word has come from Streatham that my sister has met with a serious accident and is in a very critical condition. Your uncle and I must go to Streatham immediately and are leaving on the eight o'clock express. I know you have started before this, so there is no use in telegraphing. We want you to go right to the house and make yourself at home. You will find the key under the kitchen doorstep, and the dinner in the pantry all ready to cook. There are two mince pies on the third shelf, and the plum pudding only needs to be warmed up. You will find a little Christmas remembrance for each of you on the dining-room table. I hope you will make as merry as you possibly can and we will have you down again as soon as we come back.
>
> Your hurried and affectionate,
> AUNT JEAN

We looked at each other somewhat dolefully. But, as Alberta pointed out, we might as well make the best of it, since there was no way of getting home before the five o'clock train. So we trailed out to the stationmaster, and asked him limply if he could direct us to Mr. Norman Young's house.

He was a rather grumpy individual, very busy with pencil and notebook over some freight; but he favoured us with his attention long enough to point with his pencil and say jerkily, "Young's? See that red house on the hill? That's it."

The red house was about a quarter of a mile from the station, and we saw it plainly. Accordingly, to the red house we betook ourselves. On nearer view it proved to be a trim, handsome place, with nice grounds and very fine old trees.

We found the key under the kitchen doorstep and went in. The fire was black out, and somehow things wore a more cheerless look than I had expected to find. I may as well admit that we marched into the dining room first of all, to find our presents.

There were three parcels, two very small and one pretty big, lying on the table, but when we came to look for names there were none.

"Evidently Aunt Jean, in her hurry and excitement, forgot to label them," said Elizabeth. "Let us open them. We may be able to guess from the contents which belongs to whom."

I must say we were surprised when we opened those parcels. "We had known that Aunt Jean's gifts would be nice, but we had not expected anything like this. There was a magnificent stone marten collar, a dear little gold watch and pearl chatelaine, and a gold chain bracelet set with turquoises.

"The collar must be for you, Elizabeth, because Mary and I have one already, and Aunt Jean knows it," said Alberta; "the watch must be for you, Mary, because I have one; and by the process of exhaustion the bracelet must be for me. Well, they are all perfectly sweet."

Elizabeth put on her collar and paraded in front of the sideboard mirror. It was so dusty she had to take her handkerchief and wipe it before she could see herself properly. Everything in the room was equally dusty. As for the lace curtains, they looked as if they hadn't been washed for years, and one of them had a long ragged hole in it. I couldn't help feeling secretly surprised, for Aunt Jean had the reputation of being a perfect housekeeper. However, I didn't say anything, and neither did the other girls. Mother had always impressed upon us that it was the height of bad manners to criticize anything we might not like in a house where we were guests.

"Well, let's see about dinner," said Alberta, practically, snapping her bracelet on her wrist and admiring the effect.

We went to the kitchen, where Elizabeth proceeded to light the fire, that being one of her specialties, while Alberta and I explored the pantry. We found the dinner supplies laid out as Aunt Jean had explained. There was a nice fat turkey all stuffed, and vegetables galore. The mince pies were in their place, but they were almost the only things about which that could be truthfully said, for the disorder of that pantry was enough to give a tidy person nightmares for a month. "I never in all my life saw—" began Alberta, and then stopped short, evidently remembering Mother's teaching.

"Where is the plum pudding?" said I, to turn the conversation into safer channels.

It was nowhere to be seen, so we concluded it must be in the cellar. But we found the cellar door padlocked good and fast.

"Never mind," said Elizabeth. "You know none of us really likes plum pudding. We only eat it because it is the proper traditional dessert. The mince pies will suit us better."

We hurried the turkey into the oven, and soon everything was going merrily. We had lots of fun getting up that dinner, and we made ourselves perfectly at home, as Aunt Jean had commanded. We kindled a fire in the dining room and dusted everything in sight. We couldn't find anything remotely resembling a duster, so we used our handkerchiefs. When we got through, the room looked like something, for the furnishings were really very handsome, but our handkerchiefs—well!

Then we set the table with all the nice dishes we could find. There was only one long tablecloth in the sideboard drawer, and there were three holes in it, but we covered them with dishes and put a little potted palm in the middle for a centrepiece. At one o'clock dinner was ready for us and we for it. Very nice that table looked, too, as we sat down to it.

Just as Alberta was about to spear the turkey with a fork and begin carving, that being one of *her* specialties, the kitchen door opened and somebody walked in. Before we could move, a big, handsome, bewhiskered man in a fur coat appeared in the dining-room doorway.

I wasn't frightened. He seemed quite respectable, I thought, and I supposed he was some intimate friend of Uncle Norman's. I rose politely and said, "Good day."

You never saw such an expression of amazement as was on that poor man's face. He looked from me to Alberta and from Alberta to Elizabeth and from Elizabeth to me again as if he doubted the evidence of his eyes.

"Mr. and Mrs. Norman Young are not at home," I explained, pitying him. "They went to Streatham this morning because Mrs. Young's sister is very ill."

"What does all this mean?" said the big man gruffly. "This isn't Norman Young's house ... it is mine. I'm William Young. Who are you? And what are you doing here?"

I fell back into my chair, speechless. My very first impulse was to put up my hand and cover the gold watch. Alberta had dropped the carving knife and was trying desperately to get the gold bracelet off under the table. In a flash we had realized our mistake and its awfulness. As for me, I felt positively frightened; Margaret Hannah's warnings of old had left an ineffaceable impression.

Elizabeth rose to the occasion. Rising to the occasion is another of Elizabeth's specialties. Besides, she was not hampered by the tingling consciousness that she was wearing a gift that had not been intended for her.

"We have made a mistake, I fear," she said, with a dignity which I appreciated even in my panic, "and we are very sorry for it. We were invited to spend Christmas with Mr. and Mrs. Norman Young. When we got off the train we were given a letter from them stating that they were summoned away but telling us to go to their house and make ourselves at home. The stationmaster told us that this was the house, so we came here. We have never been in Monkshead, so we did not know the difference. Please pardon us."

I had got off the watch by this time and laid it on the table, unobserved, as I thought. Alberta, not having the key of the bracelet, had not been able to get it off, and she sat there crimson with shame. As for Uncle William, there was positively a twinkle in his eye. He did not look in the least ogreish.

"Well, it has been quite a fortunate mistake for me," he said. "I came home expecting to find a cold house and a raw dinner, and I find this instead. I'm very much obliged to you."

Alberta rose, went to the mantel piece, took the key of the bracelet therefrom, and unlocked it. Then she faced Uncle William. "Mrs. Young told us in her letter that we would find our Christmas gifts on the table, so we took it for granted that these things belonged to us," she said desperately. "And now, if you will kindly tell us where Mr. Norman Young does live, we won't intrude on you any longer. Come, girls."

Elizabeth and I rose with a sigh. There was nothing else to be done, of course, but we were fearfully hungry, and we did not feel enthusiastic over the prospect of going to another empty house and cooking another dinner.

"Wait a bit," said Uncle William. "I think since you have gone to all the trouble of cooking the dinner it's only fair you should stay and help to eat it. Accidents seem to be rather fashionable just now. My housekeeper's son broke his leg down at Weston, and I had to take her there early this morning. Come, introduce yourselves. To whom am I indebted for this pleasant surprise?"

"We are Elizabeth, Alberta, and Mary Young of Green Village," I said; and then I looked to see the ogre creep out if it were ever going to.

But Uncle William merely looked amazed for the first moment, foolish for the second, and the third he was himself again.

"Robert's daughters?" he said, as if it were the most natural thing in the world that Robert's daughters should be there in his house. "So you are my nieces? Well, I'm very glad to make your acquaintance. Sit down and we'll have dinner as soon as I can get my coat off. I want to see if you are as good cooks as your mother used to be long ago."

We sat down, and so did Uncle William. Alberta had her chance to show what she could do at carving, for Uncle William said it was something he never did; he kept a housekeeper just for that. At first we felt a bit stiff and awkward; but that soon wore off, for Uncle William was genial, witty, and entertaining. Soon, to our surprise, we found that we were enjoying ourselves. Uncle William seemed to be, too. When we had finished he leaned back and looked at us.

"I suppose you've been brought up to abhor me and all my works?" he said abruptly.

"Not by Father and Mother," I said frankly. "They never said anything against you. Margaret Hannah did, though. She brought us up in the way we should go through fear of you."

Uncle William laughed.

"Margaret Hannah was a faithful old enemy of mine," he said. "Well, I acted like a fool—and worse. I've been sorry for it ever since. I was in the wrong. I couldn't have said this to your father, but I don't mind saying it to you, and you can tell him if you like."

"He'll be delighted to hear that you are no longer angry with him," said Alberta. "He has always longed to be friends with you again, Uncle William. But he thought you were still bitter against him."

"No—no—nothing but stubborn pride," said Uncle William. "Now, girls, since you are my guests I must try to give you a good time. We'll take the double sleigh and have a jolly drive this afternoon. And about those trinkets there—they are yours. I did get them for some young friends of mine here, but I'll give them something else. I want you to have these. That watch looked very nice on your blouse, Mary, and the bracelet became Alberta's pretty wrist very well. Come and give your cranky old uncle a hug for them."

Uncle William got his hugs heartily; then we washed up the dishes and went for our drive. We got back just in time to catch the evening train home. Uncle William saw us off at the station, under promise to come back and stay a week with him when his housekeeper came home.

"One of you will have to come and stay with me altogether, pretty soon," he said. "Tell your father he must be prepared to hand over one of his girls to me as a token of his forgiveness. I'll be down to talk it over with him shortly."

When we got home and told our story, Father said, "Thank God!" very softly. There were tears in his eyes. He did not wait for Uncle William to come down, but went to Monkshead himself the next day.

In the spring Alberta is to go and live with Uncle William. She is making a supply of dusters now. And next Christmas we are going to have a grand family reunion at the old homestead. Mistakes are not always bad.

The Genesis of the Doughnut Club

When John Henry died there seemed to be nothing for me to do but pack up and go back east. I didn't want to do it, but forty-five years of sojourning in this world have taught me that a body has to do a good many things she doesn't want to do, and that most of them turn out to be for the best in the long run. But I knew perfectly well that it wasn't best for me or anybody else that I should go back to live with William and Susanna, and I couldn't think what Providence was about when things seemed to point that way.

I wanted to stay in Carleton. I loved the big, straggling, bustling little town that always reminded me of a lanky, overgrown schoolboy, all arms and legs, but full to the brim with enthusiasm and splendid ideas. I knew Carleton was bound to grow into a magnificent city, and I wanted to be there and see it grow and watch it develop; and I loved the whole big, breezy golden west, with the rush and tingle of its young life. And, more than all, I loved my boys, and what I was going to do without them or they without me was more than I knew, though I tried to think Providence might know.

But there was no place in Carleton for me; the only thing to do was to go back east, and I knew that all the time, even when I was desperately praying that I might find a way to remain. There's not much comfort, or help either, praying one way and believing another.

I'd lived down east in Northfield all my life—until five years ago—lived with my brother William and his wife. Northfield was a little pinched-up village where everybody knew more about you than you did about yourself, and you couldn't turn around without being commented upon. William and Susanna were kind to me, but I was just the old maid sister, of no importance to anybody, and I never felt as if I were really living. I was simply vegetating on, and wouldn't be missed by a single soul if I died. It is a horrible feeling, but I didn't expect it would ever be any different, and I had made up my mind that when I died I would have the word "Wasted" carved on my tombstone. It wouldn't be conventional at all, but I'd been conventional all my life, and I was determined I'd have something done out of the common even if I had to wait until I was dead to have it.

Then all at once the letter came from John Henry, my brother out west. He wrote that his wife had died and he wanted me to go out and keep house for him. I sat right down and wrote him I'd go and in a week's time I started.

It made quite a commotion; I had that much satisfaction out of it to begin with. Susanna wasn't any too well pleased. I was only the old maid sister, but I was a good cook, and help was scarce in Northfield. All the neighbours shook their heads, and warned me I wouldn't like it. I was too old to change my ways, and I'd be dreadfully homesick, and I'd find the west too rough and boisterous. I just smiled and said nothing.

Well, I came out here to Carleton, and from the time I got here I was perfectly happy. John Henry had a little rented house, and he was as poor as a church mouse, being the ne'er-do-well of our family, and the best loved, as ne'er-do-wells are so apt to be. He'd nearly died of lonesomeness since his wife's death, and he was so glad to see me. That was delightful in itself, and I was just in my element getting that little house fixed up cosy and homelike, and cooking the most elegant meals. There wasn't much work to do, just for me and him, and I got a squaw in to wash and scrub. I never thought about Northfield except to thank goodness I'd escaped from it, and John Henry and I were as happy as a king and queen.

Then after awhile my activities began to sprout and branch out, and the direction they took was *boys*. Carleton was full of boys, like all the western towns, overflowing with them as you might say, young fellows just let loose from home and mother, some of them dying of homesickness and some of them beginning to run wild and get into risky ways, some of them smart and some of them lazy, some ugly and some handsome; but all of them boys, lovable, rollicking boys, with the makings of good men in them if there was anybody to take hold of them and cut the pattern right, but liable to be spoiled just because there wasn't anybody.

Well, I did what I could. It began with John Henry bringing home some of them that worked in his office to spend the evening now and again, and they told other fellows and asked leave to bring them in too. And before long it got to be that there never was an evening there wasn't some of them there, "Aunt-Pattying" me. I told them from the start I would *not* be called Miss. When a woman has been Miss for forty-five years she gets tired of it.

So Aunt Patty it was, and Aunt Patty it remained, and I loved all those dear boys as if they'd been my own. They told me all their troubles, and I mothered them and cheered them up and scolded them, and finally topped off with a jolly good supper; for, talk as you like, you can't preach much good into a boy if he's got an aching void in his stomach. Fill *that* up with tasty victuals, and then you can do something with his spiritual nature. If a boy is well stuffed with good things and then won't listen to advice, you might as well stop wasting your breath on him, because there is something radically wrong with him. Probably his grandfather had dyspepsia. And a dyspeptic ancestor is worse for a boy than predestination, in my opinion.

Anyway, most of my boys took to going to church and Bible class of their own accord, after I'd been their aunt for awhile. The young minister thought it was all his doings, and I let him think so to keep him cheered up. He was a nice boy himself, and often dropped in of an evening too; but I never would let him talk theology until after supper. His views always seemed so much mellower then, and didn't puzzle the other boys more than was wholesome for them.

This went on for five glorious years, the only years of my life I'd ever *lived*, and then came, as I thought, the end of everything. John Henry took typhoid and died. At first that was all I could think of; and when I got so that I could think of other things, there was, as I have said, nothing for me to do but go back east.

The boys, who had been as good as gold to me all through my trouble, felt dreadfully bad over this, and coaxed me hard to stay. They said if I'd start a boarding house I'd have all the boarders I could accommodate; but I knew it was no use to think of that, because I wasn't strong enough, and help was so hard to get. No, there was nothing for it but Northfield and stagnation again, with not a stray boy anywhere to mother. I looked the dismal prospect square in the face and made up my mind to it.

But I was determined to give my boys one good celebration before I went, anyway. It was near Thanksgiving, and I resolved they should have a dinner that would keep my memory green for awhile, a real old-fashioned Thanksgiving dinner such as they used to have at home. I knew it would cost more than I could really afford, but I shut my eyes to that aspect of the question. I was going back to strict eastern economy for the rest of my days, and I meant to indulge in one wild, blissful riot of extravagance before I was cooped up again.

I counted up the boys I must have, and there were fifteen, including the minister. I invited them a fortnight ahead to make sure of getting them, though I needn't have worried, for they all said they would have broken an engagement to dine with the king for one of my dinners. The minister said he had been feeling so homesick he was afraid he wouldn't be able to preach a real thankful sermon, but now he was comfortably sure that his sermon would be overflowing with gratitude.

I just threw myself heart and soul into the preparations for that dinner. I had three turkeys and two sucking pigs, and mince pies and pumpkin pies and apple pies, and doughnuts and fruit cake and cranberry sauce and brown bread, and ever so many other things to fill up the chinks. The night before Thanksgiving everything was ready, and I was so tired I could hardly talk to Jimmy Nelson when he dropped in.

Jimmy had something on his mind, I saw that. So I said, "'Fess up, Jimmy, and then you'll be able to enjoy your call."

"I want to ask a favour of you, Aunt Patty," said Jimmy.

I knew I should have to grant it; nobody could refuse Jimmy anything, he looked so much like a nice, clean, pink-and-white little schoolboy whose mother had just scrubbed his face and told him to be good. At the same time he was one of the wildest young scamps in Carleton, or had been until a year ago. I'd got him well set on the road to reformation, and I felt worse about leaving him than any of the rest of them. I knew he was just at the critical point. With somebody to tide him over the next half year he'd probably go straight for the rest of his life, but if he were left to himself he'd likely just slip back to his old set and ways.

"I want you to let me bring my Uncle Joe to dinner tomorrow," said Jimmy. "The poor old fellow is stranded here for Thanksgiving, and he hates hotels. May I?"

"Of course," I said heartily, wondering why Jimmy seemed to think I mightn't want his Uncle Joe. "Bring him right along."

"Thanks," said Jimmy. "He'll be more than pleased. Your sublime cookery will delight him. He adores the west, but he can't endure its cooking. He's always harping on his mother's pantry and the good old down-east dinners. He's dyspeptic and pessimistic most of the time, and he's got half a dozen cronies just like himself. All they think of is railroads and bills of fare."

"Railroads!" I cried. And then an awful thought assailed me. "Jimmy Nelson, your uncle isn't—isn't—he can't be Joseph P. Nelson, the *rich* Joseph P. Nelson!"

"Oh, he's rich enough," said Jimmy; getting up and reaching for his hat. "In dollars, that is. Some ways he's poor enough. Well, I must be going. Thanks ever so much for letting me bring Uncle Joe."

And that rascal was gone, leaving me crushed. Joseph Nelson was coming to my house to dinner—Joseph P. Nelson, the millionaire railroad king, who kept his own chef and was accustomed to dining with the great ones of the earth!

I was afraid I should never be able to forgive Jimmy. I couldn't sleep a wink that night, and I cooked that dinner next day in a terrible state of mind. Every ring that came at the door made my heart jump,—but in the end Jimmy didn't ring at all, but just walked in with his uncle in tow. The minute I saw Joseph P. I knew I needn't be scared of *him*; he just looked real common. He was little and thin and kind of bored-looking, with grey hair and whiskers, and his clothes were next door to downright shabbiness. If it hadn't been for the thought of that chef, I wouldn't have felt a bit ashamed of my old-fashioned Thanksgiving spread.

When Joseph P. sat down to that table he stopped looking bored. All the time the minister was saying grace that man simply stared at a big plate of doughnuts near my end of the table, as if he'd never seen anything like them before.

All the boys talked and laughed while they were eating, but Joseph P. just *ate*, tucking away turkey and vegetables and keeping an anxious eye on those doughnuts, as if he was afraid somebody else would get hold of them before his turn came. I wished I was sure it was etiquette to tell him not to worry because there were plenty more in the pantry. By the time he'd been helped three times to mince pie I gave up feeling bad about the chef. He finished off with the doughnuts, and I shan't tell how many of them he devoured, because I would not be believed.

Most of the boys had to go away soon after dinner. Joseph P. shook hands with me absently and merely said, "Good afternoon, Miss Porter." I didn't think he seemed at all grateful for his dinner, but that didn't worry me because it was for my boys I'd got it up, and not for dyspeptic millionaires whose digestion had been spoiled by private chefs. And my boys had appreciated it, there wasn't any doubt about that. Peter Crockett and Tommy Gray stayed to help me wash the dishes, and we had the jolliest time ever. Afterward we picked the turkey bones.

But that night I realized that I was once more a useless, lonely old woman. I cried myself to sleep, and next morning I hadn't spunk enough to cook myself a dinner. I dined off some crackers and the remnants of the apple pies, and I was sitting staring at the crumbs when the bell rang. I wiped away my tears and went to the door. Joseph P. Nelson was standing there, and he said, without wasting any words—it was easy to see how that man managed to get railroads built where nobody else could manage it—that he had called to see me on a little matter of business.

He took just ten minutes to make it clear to me, and when I saw the whole project I was the happiest woman in Carleton or out of it. He said he had never eaten such a Thanksgiving dinner as mine, and that I was the woman he'd been looking for for years. He said that he had a few business friends who had been brought up on a down-east farm like himself, and never got over their hankering for old-fashioned cookery.

"That is something we can't get here, with all our money," he said. "Now, Miss Porter, my nephew tells me that you wish to remain in Carleton, if you can find some way of supporting yourself. I have a proposition to make to you. These aforesaid friends of mine and I expect to spend most of our time in Carleton for the next few years. In fact we shall probably make it our home eventually. It's going to be *the* city of the west after awhile, and the centre of a dozen railroads. Well, we mean to equip a small private restaurant for ourselves and we want you to take charge of it. You won't have to do much except oversee the business and arrange the bills of fare. We want plain, substantial old-time meals and cookery. When we have a hankering for doughnuts and apple pies and cranberry tarts, we want to know just where to get them and have them the right kind. We're all horribly tired of hotel fare and fancy fol-de-rols with French names. A place where we could get a dinner such as you served yesterday would be a boon to us. We'd have started the restaurant long ago if we could have got a suitable person to take charge of it."

He named the salary the club would pay and the very sound of it made me feel rich. You may be sure I didn't take long to decide. That was a year ago, and today the Doughnut Club, as they call themselves, is a huge success, and the fame of it has gone abroad in the land, although they are pretty exclusive and keep all their good things close enough to themselves. Joseph P. took a Scotch peer there to dinner one day last week. Jimmy Nelson told me afterward that the man said it was the only satisfying meal he'd had since he left the old country.

As for me, I have my little house, my very own and no rented one, and all my dear boys, and I'm a happy old busybody. You see, Providence did answer my prayers in spite of my lack of faith; but of course He used means, and that Thanksgiving dinner of mine was the earthly instrument of it all.

The Girl Who Drove the Cows

"I wonder who that pleasant-looking girl who drives cows down the beech lane every morning and evening is," said Pauline Palmer, at the tea table of the country farmhouse where she and her aunt were spending the summer. Mrs. Wallace had wanted to go to some fashionable watering place, but her husband had bluntly told her he couldn't afford it. Stay in the city when all her set were out she would not, and the aforesaid farmhouse had been the compromise.

"I shouldn't suppose it could make any difference to you who she is," said Mrs. Wallace impatiently. "I do wish, Pauline, that you were more careful in your choice of associates. You hobnob with everyone, even that old man who comes around buying eggs. It is very bad form."

Pauline hid a rather undutiful smile behind her napkin. Aunt Olivia's snobbish opinions always amused her.

"You've no idea what an interesting old man he is," she said. "He can talk more entertainingly than any other man I know. What is the use of being so exclusive, Aunt Olivia? You miss so much fun. You wouldn't be so horribly bored as you are if you fraternized a little with the 'natives,' as you call them."

"No, thank you," said Mrs. Wallace disdainfully.

"Well, I am going to try to get acquainted with that girl," said Pauline resolutely. "She looks nice and jolly."

"I don't know where you get your low tastes from," groaned Mrs. Wallace. "I'm sure it wasn't from your poor mother. What do you suppose the Morgan Knowles would think if they saw you taking up with some tomboy girl on a farm?"

"I don't see why it should make a great deal of difference what they would think, since they don't seem to be aware of my existence, or even of yours, Aunty," said Pauline, with twinkling eyes. She knew it was her aunt's dearest desire to get in with the Morgan Knowles' "set"—a desire that seemed as far from being realized as ever. Mrs. Wallace could never understand why the Morgan Knowles shut her from their charmed circle. They certainly associated with people much poorer and of more doubtful worldly station than hers—the Markhams, for instance, who lived on an unfashionable street and wore quite shabby clothes. Just before she had left Colchester, Mrs. Wallace had seen Mrs. Knowles and Mrs. Markham together in the former's automobile. James Wallace and Morgan

Knowles were associated in business dealings; but in spite of Mrs. Wallace's schemings and aspirations and heart burnings, the association remained a purely business one and never advanced an inch in the direction of friendship.

As for Pauline, she was hopelessly devoid of social ambitions and she did not in the least mind the Morgan Knowles' remote attitude.

"Besides," continued Pauline, "she isn't a tomboy at all. She looks like a very womanly, well-bred sort of girl. Why should you think her a tomboy because she drives cows? Cows are placid, useful animals—witness this delicious cream which I am pouring over my blueberries. And they have to be driven. It's an honest occupation."

"I daresay she is someone's servant," said Mrs. Wallace contemptuously. "But I suppose even that wouldn't matter to you, Pauline?"

"Not a mite," said Pauline cheerfully. "One of the very nicest girls I ever knew was a maid Mother had the last year of her dear life. I loved that girl, Aunt Olivia, and I correspond with her. She writes letters that are ten times more clever and entertaining than those stupid epistles Clarisse Gray sends me—and Clarisse Gray is a rich man's daughter and is being educated in Paris."

"You are incorrigible, Pauline," said Mrs. Wallace hopelessly.

"Mrs. Boyd," said Pauline to their landlady, who now made her appearance, "who is that girl who drives the cows along the beech lane mornings and evenings?"

"Ada Cameron, I guess," was Mrs. Boyd's response. "She lives with the Embrees down on the old Embree place just below here. They're pasturing their cows on the upper farm this summer. Mrs. Embree is her father's half-sister."

"Is she as nice as she looks?"

"Yes, Ada's a real nice sensible girl," said Mrs. Boyd. "There is no nonsense about her."

"That doesn't sound very encouraging," murmured Pauline, as Mrs. Boyd went out. "I like people with a little nonsense about them. But I hope better things of Ada, Mrs. Boyd to the contrary notwithstanding. She has a pair of grey eyes that can't possibly always look sensible. I think they must mellow occasionally into fun and jollity and wholesome nonsense. Well, I'm off to the shore. I want to get that photograph of the Cove this evening, if possible. I've set my heart on taking first prize at the Amateur Photographers' Exhibition this fall, and if I can only get that Cove with all its beautiful lights and shadows, it will be the gem of my collection."

Pauline, on her return from the shore, reached the beech lane just as the Embree cows were swinging down it. Behind them came a tall, brown-haired, brown-faced girl in a neat print dress. Her hat was hung over her arm, and the low evening sunlight shone redly over her smooth glossy head. She carried herself with a pretty dignity, but when her eyes met Pauline's, she looked as if she would smile on the slightest provocation.

Pauline promptly gave her the provocation.

"Good evening, Miss Cameron," she called blithely. "Won't you please stop a few moments and look me over? I want to see if you think me a likely person for a summer chum."

Ada Cameron did more than smile. She laughed outright and went over to the fence where Pauline was sitting on a stump. She looked down into the merry black eyes of the town girl she had been half envying for a week and said humorously: "Yes, I think you very likely, indeed. But it takes two to make a friendship—like a bargain. If I'm one, you'll have to be the other."

"I'm the other. Shake," said Pauline, holding out her hand.

That was the beginning of a friendship that made poor Mrs. Wallace groan outwardly as well as inwardly. Pauline and Ada found that they liked each other even more than they had expected to. They walked, rowed, berried and picnicked together. Ada did not go to Mrs. Boyd's a great deal, for some instinct told her that Mrs. Wallace did not look favourably on her, but Pauline spent half her time at the little, brown, orchard-embowered house at the end of the beech lane where the Embrees lived. She had never met any girl she thought so nice as Ada.

"She is nice every way," she told the unconvinced Aunt Olivia. "She's clever and well read. She is sensible and frank. She has a sense of humour and a great deal of insight into character—witness her liking for your niece! She can talk interestingly and she can also be silent when silence is becoming. And she has the finest profile I ever saw. Aunt Olivia, may I ask her to visit me next winter?"

"No, indeed," said Mrs. Wallace, with crushing emphasis. "You surely don't expect to continue this absurd intimacy past the summer, Pauline?"

"I expect to be Ada's friend all my life," said Pauline laughingly, but with a little ring of purpose in her voice. "Oh, Aunty, dear, can't you see that Ada is just the same girl in cotton print that she would be in silk attire? She is really far more distinguished looking than any girl in the Knowles' set."

"Pauline!" said Aunt Olivia, looking as shocked as if Pauline had committed blasphemy.

Pauline laughed again, but she sighed as she went to her room. Aunt Olivia has the kindest heart in the world, she thought. What a pity she isn't able to see things as they really are! My friendship with Ada can't be perfect if I can't invite her to my home. And she is such a dear girl—the first real friend after my own heart that I've ever had.

The summer waned, and August burned itself out.

"I suppose you will be going back to town next week? I shall miss you dreadfully," said Ada.

The two girls were in the Embree garden, where Pauline was preparing to take a photograph of Ada standing among the asters, with a great sheaf of them in her arms. Pauline wished she could have said: But you must come and visit me in the winter. Since she could not, she had to content herself with saying: "You won't miss me any more than I shall miss you. But we'll correspond, and I hope Aunt Olivia will come to Marwood again next summer."

"I don't think I shall be here then," said Ada with a sigh. "You see, it is time I was doing something for myself, Pauline. Aunt Jane and Uncle Robert have always been very kind to me, but they have a large family and are not very well off. So I think I'll try for a situation in one of the Remington stores this fall."

"It's such a pity you couldn't have gone to the Academy and studied for a teacher's licence," said Pauline, who knew what Ada's ambitions were.

"I should have liked that better, of course," said Ada quietly. "But it is not possible, so I must do my best at the next best thing. Don't let's talk of it. It might make me feel blueish and I want to look especially pleasant if I'm going to have my photo taken."

"You couldn't look anything else," laughed Pauline. "Don't smile too broadly—I want you to be looking over the asters with a bit of a dream on your face and in your eyes. If the picture turns out as beautiful as I fondly expect, I mean to put it in my exhibition collection under the title 'A September Dream.' There, that's the very expression. When you look like that, you remind me of somebody I have seen, but I can't remember who it is. All ready now—don't move—there, dearie, it is all over."

When Pauline went back to Colchester, she was busy for a month preparing her photographs for the exhibition, while Aunt Olivia renewed her spinning of all the little social webs in which she fondly hoped to entangle the Morgan Knowles and other desirable flies.

When the exhibition was opened, Pauline Palmer's collection won first prize, and the prettiest picture in it was one called "A September Dream"—a tall girl with a wistful face, standing in an old-fashioned garden with her arms full of asters.

The very day after the exhibition was opened the Morgan Knowles' automobile stopped at the Wallace door. Mrs. Wallace was out, but it was Pauline whom stately Mrs. Morgan Knowles asked for. Pauline was at that moment buried in her darkroom developing photographs, and she ran down just as she was—a fact which would have mortified Mrs. Wallace exceedingly if she had ever known it. But Mrs. Morgan Knowles did not seem to mind at all. She liked Pauline's simplicity of manner. It was more than she had expected from the aunt's rather vulgar affectations.

"I have called to ask you who the original of the photograph 'A September Dream' in your exhibit was, Miss Palmer," she said graciously. "The resemblance to a very dear childhood friend of mine is so startling that I am sure it cannot be accidental."

"That is a photograph of Ada Cameron, a friend whom I met this summer up in Marwood," said Pauline.

"Ada Cameron! She must be Ada Frame's daughter, then," exclaimed Mrs. Knowles in excitement. Then, seeing Pauline's puzzled face, she explained: "Years ago, when I was a child, I always spent my summers on the farm of my uncle, John Frame. My cousin, Ada Frame, was the dearest friend I ever had, but after we grew up we saw nothing of each other, for I went with my parents to Europe for several years, and Ada married a neighbour's son, Alec Cameron, and went out west. Her father, who was my only living relative other than my parents, died, and I never heard anything more of Ada until about eight years ago, when somebody told me she was dead and had left no family. That part of the report cannot have been true if this girl is her daughter."

"I believe she is," said Pauline quickly. "Ada was born out west and lived there until she was eight years old, when her parents died and she was sent east to her father's half-sister. And Ada looks like you—she always reminded me of somebody I had seen, but I never could decide who it was before. Oh, I hope it is true, for Ada is such a sweet girl, Mrs. Knowles."

"She couldn't be anything else if she is Ada Frame's daughter," said Mrs. Knowles. "My husband will investigate the matter at once, and if this girl is Ada's child we shall hope to find a daughter in her, as we have none of our own."

"What will Aunt Olivia say!" said Pauline with wickedly dancing eyes when Mrs. Knowles had gone.

Aunt Olivia was too much overcome to say anything. That good lady felt rather foolish when it was proved that the girl she had so despised was Mrs. Morgan Knowles' cousin and was going to be adopted by her. But to hear Aunt Olivia talk now, you would suppose that she and not Pauline had discovered Ada.

The latter sought Pauline out as soon as she came to Colchester, and the summer friendship proved a life-long one and was, for the Wallaces, the open sesame to the enchanted ground of the Knowles' "set."

"So everybody concerned is happy," said Pauline. "Ada is going to college and so am I, and Aunt Olivia is on the same committee as Mrs. Knowles for the big church bazaar. What about my 'low tastes' now, Aunt Olivia?"

"Well, who would ever have supposed that a girl who drove cows to pasture was connected with the Morgan Knowles?" said poor Aunt Olivia piteously.

The Growing Up of Cornelia

January First.

Aunt Jemima gave me this diary for a Christmas present. It's just the sort of gift a person named Jemima would be likely to make.

I can't imagine why Aunt Jemima thought I should like a diary. Probably she didn't think about it at all. I suppose it happened to be the first thing she saw when she started out to do her Christmas duty by me, and so she bought it. I'm sure I'm the last girl in the world to keep a diary. I'm not a bit sentimental and I never have time for soul outpourings. It's jollier to be out skating or snowshoeing or just tramping around. And besides, nothing ever happens to me worth writing in a diary.

Still, since Aunt Jemima gave it to me, I'm going to get the good out of it. I don't believe in wasting even a diary. Father ... it would be easier to write "Dad," but Dad sounds disrespectful in a diary ... says I have a streak of old Grandmother Marshall's economical nature in me. So I'm going to write in this book whenever I have anything that might, by any stretch of imagination, be supposed worth while.

Jen and Alice and Sue would have plenty to write about, I dare say. They certainly seem to have jolly times ... and as for the men ... but there! People say men are interesting. They may be. But I shall never get well enough acquainted with any of them to find out.

Mother says it is high time I gave up my tomboy ways and came "out" too, because I am eighteen. I coaxed off this winter. It wasn't very hard, because no mother with three older unmarried girls on her hands would be very anxious to bring out a fourth. The girls took my part and advised Mother to let me be a child as long as possible. Mother yielded for this time, but said I must be brought out next winter or people would talk. Oh, I hate the thought of it! People might talk about my not being brought out, but they will talk far more about the blunders I shall make.

The doleful fact is, I'm too wretchedly shy and awkward to live. It fills my soul with terror to think of donning long dresses and putting my hair up and going into society. I can't talk and men frighten me to death. I fall over things as it is, and what will it be with long dresses? As far back as I can remember it has been my one aim and object in life to escape company. Oh, if only one need never grow up! If I could only go back four years and stay there!

Mother laments over it muchly. She says she doesn't know what she has done to have such a shy, unpresentable daughter. *I* know. She married Grandmother Marshall's son, and Grandmother Marshall was as shy as she was economical. Mother triumphed over heredity with Jen and Sue and Alice, but it came off best with me. The other girls are noted for their grace and tact. But I'm the black sheep and always will be. It wouldn't worry me so much if they'd leave me alone and stop nagging me. "Oh, for a lodge in some vast wilderness," where there were no men, no parties, no dinners ... just quantities of dogs and horses and skating ponds and woods! I need never put on long dresses then, but just be a jolly little girl forever.

However, I've got one beautiful year before me yet, and I mean to make the most of it.

January Tenth.

It is rather good to have a diary to pour out your woes in when you feel awfully bad and have no one to sympathize with you. I've been used to shutting them all up in my soul and then they sometimes fermented and made trouble.

We had a lot of people here to dinner tonight, and that made me miserable to begin with. I had to dress up in a stiff white dress *with a sash*, and Jen tied two big white fly-away bows on my hair that kept rasping my neck and tickling my ears in a most exasperating way. Then an old lady whom I detest tried to make me talk before everybody, and all I could do was to turn as red as a beet and stammer: "Yes, ma'am," "no, ma'am." It made Mother furious, because it is so old-fashioned to say "ma'am." Our old nurse taught me to say it when I was small, and though it has been pretty well governessed out of me since then, it's sure to pop up when I get confused and nervous.

Sue ... may it be accounted unto her for righteousness ... contrived that I should go out to dinner with old Mr. Grant, because she knew he goes to dinners for the sake of eating and never talks or wants anybody else to. But when we were crossing the hall I stepped on Mrs. Burnett's train and something tore. Mrs. Burnett gave me a furious look and glowered all through dinner. The meal was completely spoiled for me and I could find no comfort, even in the Nesselrode pudding, which is my favourite dessert.

It was just when the pudding came on that I got the most unkindest cut of all. Mrs. Allardyce remarked that Sidney Elliot was coming home to Stillwater.

Everybody exclaimed and questioned and seemed delighted. I saw Mother give one quick, involuntary look at Jen, and then gaze steadfastly at Mr. Grant to atone for it. Jen is twenty-six, and Stillwater is next door to our place!

As for me, I was so vexed that I might as well have been eating chips for all the good that Nesselrode pudding was to me. If Sidney Elliot were coming home everything would be spoiled. There would be no more ramblings in the Stillwater woods, no more delightful skating on the Stillwater lake. Stillwater has been the only place in the world where I could find the full joy of solitude, and now this, too, was to be taken from me. We had no woods, no lake. I hated Sidney Elliot.

It is ten years since Sidney Elliot closed Stillwater and went abroad. He has stayed abroad ever since and nobody has missed him, I'm sure. I remember him dimly as a tall dark man who used to lounge about alone in his garden and was always reading books. Sometimes he came into our garden and teased us children. He is said to be a cynic and to detest society. If this latter item be a fact I almost feel a grim pity for him. He may detest it, but he will be dragged into it. Rich bachelors are few and far between in Riverton, and the mammas will hunt him down.

I feel like crying. If Sidney Elliot comes home I shall be debarred from Stillwater. I have roamed its demesnes for ten beautiful years, and I'm sure I love them a hundredfold better than he does, or can. It is flagrantly unfair. Oh, I hate him!

January Twentieth.

No, I don't. I believe I like him. Yet it's almost unbelievable. I've always thought men so detestable.

I'm tingling all over with the surprise and pleasure of a little unexpected adventure. For the first time I have something really worth writing in a diary ... and I'm glad I have a diary to write it in. Blessings on Aunt Jemima! May her shadow never grow less.

This evening I started out for a last long lingering ramble in my beloved Stillwater woods. The last, I thought, because I knew Sidney Elliot was expected home next week, and after that I'd have to be cooped up on our lawn. I dressed myself comfortably for climbing fences and skimming over snowy wastes. That is, I put on the shortest old tweed skirt I have and a red jacket with sleeves three years behind the fashion, but jolly pockets to put your hands in, and a still redder tam. Thus accoutred, I sallied forth.

It was such a lovely evening that I couldn't help enjoying myself in spite of my sorrows. The sun was low and creamy, and the snow was so white and the shadows so slender and blue. All through the lovely Stillwater woods was a fine frosty stillness. It was splendid to skim down those long wonderful avenues of crusted snow, with the mossy grey boles on either hand, and overhead the lacing, leafless boughs, I just drank in the air and the beauty until my very soul was thrilling, and I went on and on and on until I was most delightfully lost. That is, I didn't know just where I was, but the woods weren't so big but that I'd be sure to come out safely somewhere; and, oh, it was so glorious to be there all alone and never a creature to worry me.

At last I turned into a long aisle that seemed to lead right out into the very heart of a deep-red overflowing winter sunset. At its end I found a fence, and I climbed up on that fence and sat there, so comfortably, with my back against a big beech and my feet dangling.

Then I saw him!

I knew it was Sidney Elliot in a moment. He was just as tall and just as black-eyed; he was still given to lounging evidently, for he was leaning against the fence a panel away from me and looking at me with an amused smile. After my first mad impulse to rush away and bury myself in the wilderness that smile put me at ease. If he had looked grave or polite I would have been as miserably shy as I've always been in a man's presence. But it was the smile of a grandfather for a child, and I just grinned cheerfully back at him.

He ploughed along through the thick drift that was soft and spongy by the fence and came close up to me.

"You must be little Cornelia," he said with another aged smile. "Or rather, you *were* little Cornelia. I suppose you are big Cornelia now and want to be treated like a young lady?"

"Indeed, I don't," I protested. "I'm not grown up and I don't want to be. You are Mr. Elliot, I suppose. Nobody expected you till next week. What made you come so soon?"

"A whim of mine," he said. "I'm full of whims and crotchets. Old bachelors always are. But why did you ask that question in a tone which seemed to imply that you resented my coming so soon, Miss Cornelia?"

"Oh, don't tack the Miss on," I implored. "Call me Cornelia ... or better still, Nic, as Dad does. I *do* resent your coming so soon. I resent your coming at all. And, oh, it is such a satisfaction to tell you so."

He smiled with his eyes ... a deep, black, velvety smile. But he shook his head sorrowfully.

"I must be getting very old," he said. "It's a sign of age when a person finds himself unwelcome and superfluous."

"Your age has nothing to do with it," I retorted. "It is because Stillwater is the only place I have to run wild in ... and running wild is all I'm fit for. It's so lovely and roomy I can lose myself in it. I shall die or go mad if I'm cooped up on our little pocket handkerchief of a lawn."

"But why should you be?" he inquired gravely.

I reflected ... and was surprised.

"After all, I don't know ... now ... why I should be," I admitted. "I thought you wouldn't want me prowling about your domains. Besides, I was afraid I'd meet you ... and I don't like meeting men. I hate to have them around ... I'm so shy and awkward."

"Do you find me very dreadful?" he asked.

I reflected again ... and was again surprised.

"No, I don't. I don't mind you a bit ... any more than if you were Dad."

"Then you mustn't consider yourself an exile from Stillwater. The woods are yours to roam in at will, and if you want to roam them alone you may, and if you'd like a companion once in a while command me. Let's be good friends, little lass. Shake hands on it."

I slipped down from the fence and shook hands with him. I did like him very much ... he was so nice and unaffected and brotherly ... just as if I'd known him all my life. We walked down the long white avenue, where everything was growing dusky, and I had told him all my troubles before we got to the end of it. He was so sympathetic and agreed with me that it was a pity people had to grow up. He promised to come over tomorrow and look at Don's leg. Don is one of my dogs, and he has got a bad leg. I've been doctoring it myself, but it doesn't get any better. Sidney thinks he can cure it. He says I must call him Sidney if I want him to call me Nic.

When we got to the lake, there it lay all gleaming and smooth as glass ... the most tempting thing.

"What a glorious possible slide," he said. "Let us have it, little lass."

He took my hand and we ran down the slope and went skimming over the ice. It *was* glorious. The house came in sight as we reached the other side. It was big and dark and silent.

"So the old place is still standing," said Sidney, looking up at it. In the dusk I thought his face had a tender, reverent look instead of the rather mocking expression it had worn all along.

"Haven't you been there yet?" I asked quickly.

"No. I'm stopping at the hotel over in Croyden. The house will need some fixing up before it's fit to live in. I just came down tonight to look at it and took a short cut through the woods. I'm glad I did. It was worth while to see you come tramping down that long white avenue when you thought yourself alone with the silence. I thought I had never seen a child so full of the pure joy of existence. Hold fast to that, little lass, as long as you can. You'll never find anything to take its place after it goes. You jolly little child!"

"I'm eighteen," I said suddenly. I don't know what made me say it.

He laughed and pulled his coat collar up around his ears.

"Never," he mocked. "You're about twelve ... stay twelve, and always wear red caps and jackets, you vivid thing: Good night."

He was off across the lake, and I came home. Yes, I do like him, even if he is a man.

February Twentieth.

I've found out what diaries are for ... to work off blue moods in, moods that come on without any reason whatever and therefore can't be confided to any fellow creature. You scribble away for a while ... and then it's all gone ... and your soul feels clear as crystal once more.

I always go to Sidney now in a blue mood that has a real cause. He can cheer me up in five minutes. But in such a one as this, which is quite unaccountable, there's nothing for it but a diary.

Sidney has been living at Stillwater for a month. It seems as if he must have lived there always.

He came to our place the next day after I met him in the woods. Everybody made a fuss over him, but he shook them off with an ease I envied and whisked me out to see Don's leg. He has fixed it up so that it is as good as new now, and the dogs like him almost better than they like me.

We have had splendid times since then. We are just the jolliest chums and we tramp about everywhere together and go skating and snowshoeing and riding. We read a lot of books together too, and Sidney always explains everything I don't understand. I'm not a bit shy and I can always find plenty to say to him. He isn't at all like any other man I know.

Everybody likes him, but the women seem to be a little afraid of him. They say he is so terribly cynical and satirical. He goes into society a good bit, although he says it bores him. He says he only goes because it would bore him worse to stay home alone.

There's only one thing about Sidney that I hardly like. I think he rather overdoes it in the matter of treating me as if I were a little girl. Of course, I don't want him to look upon me as grown up. But there is a medium in all things, and he really needn't talk as if he thought I was a child of ten and had no earthly interest in anything but sports and dogs. These *are* the best things ... I suppose ... but I understand lots of other things too, only I can't convince Sidney that I do. I know he is laughing at me when I try to show him I'm not so childish as he thinks me. He's indulgent and whimsical, just as he would be with a little girl who was making believe to be grown up. Perhaps next winter, when I put on long dresses and come out, he'll stop regarding me as a child. But next winter is so horribly far off.

The day we were fussing with Don's leg I told Sidney that Mother said I'd have to be grown up next winter and how I hated it, and I made him promise that when the time came he would use all his influence to beg me off for another year. He said he would, because it was a shame to worry children about society. But somehow I've concluded not to bother making a fuss. I have to come out some time, and I might as well take the plunge and get it over.

Mrs. Burnett was here this evening fixing up some arrangements for a charity bazaar she and Jen are interested in, and she talked most of the time about Sidney ... for Jen's benefit, I suppose, although Jen and Sid don't get on at all. They fight every time they meet, so I don't see why Mrs. Burnett should think things.

"I wonder what he'll do when Mrs. Rennie comes to the Glasgows' next month," said Mrs. Burnett.

"Why should he do anything?" asked Jen.

"Oh, well, you know there was something between them ... an understanding if not an engagement ... before she married Rennie. They met abroad ... my sister told me all about it ... and Mr. Elliot was quite infatuated with her. She was a very handsome and fascinating girl. Then she threw him over and married old Jacob Rennie ... for his millions, of course, for he certainly had nothing else to recommend him. Amy says Mr. Elliot was never the same man again. But Jacob died obligingly two years ago and Mrs. Rennie is free now; so I dare say they'll make it up. No doubt that is why she is coming to Riverton. Well, it would be a very suitable match."

I'm so glad I never liked Mrs. Burnett.

I wonder if it is true that Sidney did care for that horrid woman ... of course she is horrid! Didn't she marry an old man for his money?... and cares for her still.

It is no business of mine, of course, and it doesn't matter to me at all. But I rather hope he doesn't ... because it would spoil everything if he got married. He wouldn't have time to be chums with me then.

I don't know why I feel so dull tonight. Writing in this diary doesn't seem to have helped me as much as I thought it would, either. I dare say it's the weather. It must be the weather. It is a wet, windy night and the rain is thudding against the window. I hate rainy nights.

I wonder if Mrs. Rennie is really as handsome as Mrs. Burnett says. I wonder how old she is. I wonder if she ever cared for Sidney ... no, she didn't. No woman who cared for Sidney could ever have thrown him over for an old moneybag. I wonder if I shall like her. No, I won't. I'm sure I shan't like her.

My head is aching and I'm going to bed.

March Tenth.

Mrs. Rennie was here to dinner tonight. My head was aching again, and Mother said I needn't go down to dinner if I'd rather not; but a dozen headaches could not have kept me back, or a dozen men either, even supposing I'd have to talk to them all. I wanted to see Mrs. Rennie. Nothing has been talked of in Riverton for the last fortnight but Mrs. Rennie. I've heard of her beauty and charm and costumes until I'm sick of the subject. Today I spoke to Sidney about her. Before I thought I said right out, "Mrs. Rennie is to dine with us tonight."

"Yes?" he said in a quiet voice.

"I'm dying to see her," I went on recklessly. "I've heard so much about her. They say she's so beautiful and fascinating. *Is* she? *You* ought to know."

Sidney swung the sled around and put it in position for another coast.

"Yes, I know her," he admitted tranquilly. "She is a very handsome woman, and I suppose most people would consider her fascinating. Come, Nic, get on the sled. We have just time for one more coast, and then you must go in."

"You were once a good friend ... a very good friend ... of Mrs. Rennie's, weren't you, Sid?" I said.

A little mocking gleam crept into his eyes, and I instantly realized that he was looking upon me as a rather impertinent child.

"You've been listening to gossip, Nic," he said. "It's a bad habit, child. Don't let it grow on you. Come."

I went, feeling crushed and furious and ashamed.

I knew her at once when I went down to the drawing-room. There were three other strange women there, but I knew she was the only one who could be Mrs. Rennie. I felt such a horrible queer sinking feeling at my heart when I saw her. Oh, she was beautiful ... I had never seen anyone so beautiful. And Sidney was standing beside her, talking to her, with a smile on his face, but none in his eyes ... I noticed *that* at a glance.

She was so tall and slender and willowy. Her dress was wonderful, and her bare throat and shoulders were like pearls. Her hair was pale, pale gold, and her eyes long-lashed and sweet, and her mouth like a scarlet blossom against her creamy face. I thought of how I must look beside her ... an awkward little girl in a short skirt with my hair in a braid and too many hands and feet, and I would have given anything then to be tall and grown-up and graceful.

I watched her all the evening and the queer feeling in me somewhere grew worse and worse. I couldn't eat anything. Sidney took Mrs. Rennie in; they sat opposite to me and talked all the time.

I was so glad when the dinner was over and everybody gone. The first thing I did when I escaped to my room was to go to the glass and look myself over just as critically and carefully as if I were somebody else. I saw a great rope of dark brown hair ... a brown skin with red cheeks ... a big red mouth ... a pair of grey eyes. That was all. And when I thought of that shimmering witch woman with her white skin and shining hair I wanted to put out the light and cry in the dark. Only I've never cried since I was a child and broke my last doll, and I've got so out of the habit that I don't know how to go about it.

April Fifth.

Aunt Jemima would not think I was getting the good out of my diary. A whole month and not a word! But there was nothing to write, and I've felt too miserable to write if there had been. I don't know what is the matter with me. I'm just cross and horrid to everyone, even to poor Sidney.

Mrs. Rennie has been queening it in Riverton society for the past month. People rave over her and I admire her horribly, although I don't like her. Mrs. Burnett says that a match between her and Sidney Elliot is a foregone conclusion.

It's plain to be seen that Mrs. Rennie loves Sidney. Even I can see that, and I don't know much about such things. But it puzzles me to know how Sidney regards her. I have never thought he showed any sign of really caring for her. But then, he isn't the kind that would.

"Nic, I wonder if you will ever grow up," he said to me today, laughing, when he caught me racing over the lawn with the dogs.

"I'm grown up now," I said crossly. "Why, I'm eighteen and a half and I'm two inches taller than any of the other girls."

Sidney laughed, as if he were heartily amused at something.

"You're a blessed baby," he said, "and the dearest, truest, jolliest little chum ever a fellow had. I don't know what I'd do without you, Nic. You keep me sane and wholesome. I'm a tenfold better man for knowing you, little girl."

I was rather pleased. It was nice to think I was some good to Sidney.

"Are you going to the Trents' dinner tonight?" I asked.

"Yes," he said briefly.

"Mrs. Rennie will be there," I said.

Sidney nodded.

"Do you think her so very handsome, Sidney?" I said. I had never mentioned Mrs. Rennie to him since the day we were coasting, and I didn't mean to now. The question just asked itself.

"Yes, very; but not as handsome as you will be ten years from now, Nic," said Sidney lightly.

"Do you think I'm handsome, Sidney?" I cried.

"You will be when you're grown up," he answered, looking at me critically.

"Will you be going to Mrs. Greaves' reception after the dinner?" I asked.

"Yes, I suppose so," said Sidney absently. I could see he wasn't thinking of me at all. I wondered if he were thinking of Mrs. Rennie.

April Sixth.

Oh, something so wonderful has happened. I can hardly believe it. There are moments when I quake with the fear that it is all a dream. I wonder if I can really be the same Cornelia Marshall I was yesterday. No, I'm *not* the same ... and the difference is so blessed.

Oh, I'm so happy! My heart bubbles over with happiness and song. It's so wonderful and lovely to be a woman and know it and know that other people know it.

You dear diary, you were made for this moment ... I shall write all about it in you and so fulfil your destiny. And then I shall put you away and never write anything more in you, because I shall not need you ... I shall have Sidney.

Last night I was all alone in the house ... and I was so lonely and miserable. I put my chin on my hands and I thought ... and thought ... and thought. I imagined Sidney at the Greaves', talking to Mrs. Rennie with that velvety smile in his eyes. I could see her, graceful and white, in her trailing, clinging gown, with diamonds about her smooth neck and in her hair. I suddenly wondered what I would look like in evening dress with my hair up. I wondered if Sidney would like me in it.

All at once I got up and rushed to Sue's room. I lighted the gas, rummaged, and went to work. I piled my hair on top of my head, pinned it there, and thrust a long silver dagger through it to hold a couple of pale white roses she had left on her table. Then I put on her last winter's party dress. It was such a pretty pale yellow thing, with touches of black lace, and it didn't matter about its being a little old-fashioned, since it fitted me like a glove. Finally I stepped back and looked at myself.

I saw a woman in that glass ... a tall, straight creature with crimson cheeks and glowing eyes ... and the thought in my mind was so insistent that it said itself aloud: "Oh, I wish Sidney could see me now!"

At that very moment the maid knocked at the door to tell me that Mr. Elliot was downstairs asking for me. I did not hesitate a second. With my heart beating wildly I trailed downstairs to Sidney.

He was standing by the fireplace when I went in, and looked very tired. When he heard me he turned his head and our eyes met.

All at once a terrible thing happened ... at least, I thought it a terrible thing then. *I knew why I had wanted Sidney to realize that I was no longer a child.* It was because I loved him! I knew it the moment I saw that strange, new expression leap into his eyes.

"Cornelia," he said in a stunned sort of voice. "Why ... Nic ... why, little girl ... you're a woman! How blind I've been! And now I've lost my little chum."

"Oh, no, no," I said wildly. I was so miserable and confused I didn't know what I said. "Never, Sidney. I'd rather be a little girl and have you for a friend ... I'll always be a little girl! It's all this hateful dress. I'll go and take it off ... I'll...."

And then I just put my hands up to my burning face and the tears that would never come before came in a flood.

All at once I felt Sidney's arms about me and felt my head drawn to his shoulder.

"Don't cry, dearest," I heard him say softly. "You can never be a little girl to me again ... my eyes are opened ... but I didn't want you to be. I want you to be my big girl ... mine, all mine, forever."

What happened after that isn't to be written in a diary. I won't even write down the things he said about how I looked, because it would seem so terribly vain, but I can't help thinking of them, for I am so happy.

The Old Fellow's Letter

Ruggles and I were down on the Old Fellow. It doesn't matter why and, since in a story of this kind we must tell the truth no matter what happens—or else where is the use of writing a story at all?—I'll have to confess that we had deserved all we got and that the Old Fellow did no more than his duty by us. Both Ruggles and I see that now, since we have had time to cool off, but at the moment we were in a fearful wax at the Old Fellow and were bound to hatch up something to get even with him.

Of course, the Old Fellow had another name, just as Ruggles has another name. He is principal of the Frampton Academy—the Old Fellow, not Ruggles—and his name is George Osborne. We have to call him Mr. Osborne to his face, but he is the Old Fellow everywhere else. He is quite old—thirty-six if he's a day, and whatever possessed Sylvia Grant—but there, I'm getting ahead of my story.

Most of the Cads like the Old Fellow. Even Ruggles and I like him on the average. The girls are always a little provoked at him because he is so shy and absent-minded, but when it comes to the point, they like him too. I heard Emma White say once that he was "so handsome"; I nearly whooped. Ruggles was mad because he's gone on Em. For the idea of calling a thin, pale, dark, dreamy-looking chap like the Old Fellow "handsome" was more than I could stand without guffawing. Em probably said it to provoke Ruggles; she couldn't really have thought it. "Micky," the English professor, now—if she had called him handsome there would have been some sense in it. He is splendid: big six-footer with magnificent muscles, red cheeks, and curly yellow hair. I can't see how he can be contented to sit down and teach mushy English literature and poetry and that sort of thing. It would have been more in keeping with the Old Fellow. There was a rumour running at large in the Academy that the Old Fellow wrote poetry, but he ran the mathematics and didn't make such a foozle of it as you might suppose, either.

Ruggles and I meant to get square with the Old Fellow, if it took all the term; at least, we said so. But if Providence hadn't sent Sylvia Grant walking down the street past our boarding house that afternoon, we should probably have cooled off before we thought of any working plan of revenge.

Sylvia Grant did go down the street, however. Ruggles, hanging halfway out of the window as usual, saw her, and called me to go and look. Of course I went.

Sylvia Grant was always worth looking at. There was no girl in Frampton who could hold a candle to her when it came to beauty. As for brains, that is another thing altogether. My private opinion is that Sylvia hadn't any, or she would never have preferred—but there, I'm getting on too fast again. Ruggles should have written this story; he can concentrate better.

Sylvia was the Latin professor's daughter; she wasn't a Cad girl, of course. She was over twenty and had graduated from it two years ago, but she was in all the social things that went on in the Academy; and all the unmarried professors, except the Old Fellow, were in love with her. Micky had it the worst, and we had all made up our minds that Sylvia would marry Micky. He was so handsome, we didn't see how she could help it. I tell you, they made a dandy-looking couple when they were together.

Well, as I said before, I toddled to the window to have a look at the fair Sylvia. She was all togged out in some new fall duds, and I guess she'd come out to show them off. They were brownish, kind of, and she'd a spanking hat on with feathers and things in it. Her hair was shining under it, all purply-black, and she looked sweet enough to eat. Then she saw Ruggles and me and she waved her hand and laughed, and her big blackish-blue eyes sparkled; but she hadn't been laughing before, or sparkling either.

I'd thought she looked kind of glum, and I wondered if she and Micky had had a falling out. I rather suspected it, for at the Senior Prom, three nights before, she had hardly looked at Micky, but had sat in a corner and talked to the Old Fellow. He didn't do much talking; he was too shy, and he looked mighty uncomfortable. I thought it kind of mean of Sylvia to torment him so, when she knew he hated to have to talk to girls, but when I saw Micky scowling at the corner, I knew she was doing it to make him jealous. Girls won't stick at anything when they want to provoke a chap; I know it to my cost, for Jennie Price—but that has nothing to do with this story.

Just across the square Sylvia met the Old Fellow and bowed. He lifted his hat and passed on, but after a few steps he turned and looked back; he caught Sylvia doing the same thing, so he wheeled and came on, looking mighty foolish. As he passed beneath our window Ruggles chuckled fiendishly.

"I've thought of something, Polly," he said—my name is Paul. "Bet you it will make the Old Fellow squirm. Let's write a letter to Sylvia Grant—a love letter—and sign the Old Fellow's name to it. She'll give him a fearful snubbing, and we'll be revenged."

"But who'll write it?" I said doubtfully. "I can't. You'll have to, Ruggles. You've had more practice."

Ruggles turned red. I know he writes to Em White in vacations.

"I'll do my best," he said, quite meekly. "That is, I'll compose it. But you'll have to copy it. You can imitate the Old Fellow's handwriting so well."

"But look here," I said, an uncomfortable idea striking me, "what about Sylvia? Won't she feel kind of flattish when she finds out he didn't write it? For of course he'll tell her. We haven't anything against her, you know."

"Oh, Sylvia won't care," said Ruggles serenely. "She's the sort of girl who can take a joke. I've seen her eyes shine over tricks we've played on the professors before now. She'll just laugh. Besides, she doesn't like the Old Fellow a bit. I know from the way she acts with him. She's always so cool and stiff when he's about, not a bit like she is with the other professors."

Well, Ruggles wrote the letter. At first he tried to pass it off on me as his own composition. But I know a few little things, and one of them is that Ruggles couldn't have made up that letter any more than he could have written a sonnet. I told him so, and made him own up. He had a copy of an old letter that had been written to his sister by her young man. I suppose Ruggles had stolen it, but there is no use inquiring too closely into these things. Anyhow, that letter just filled the bill. It was beautifully expressed. Ruggles's sister's young man must have possessed lots of ability. He was an English professor, something like Micky, so I suppose he was extra good at it. He started in by telling her how much he loved her, and what an angel of beauty and goodness he had always thought her; how unworthy he felt himself of her and how little hope he had that she could ever care for him; and he wound up by imploring her to tell him if she could possibly love him a little bit and all that sort of thing.

I copied the letter out on heliotrope paper in my best imitation of the Old Fellow's handwriting and signed it, "Yours devotedly and imploringly, George Osborne." Then we mailed it that very evening.

The next evening the Cad girls gave a big reception in the Assembly Hall to an Academy alumna who was visiting the Greek professor's wife. It was the smartest event of the term and everybody was there—students and faculty and, of course, Sylvia Grant. Sylvia looked stunning. She was all in white, with a string of pearls about her pretty round throat and a couple of little pink roses in her black hair. I never saw her so smiling and bright; but she seemed quieter than usual, and avoided poor Micky so skilfully that it was really a pleasure to watch her. The Old Fellow came in late, with his tie all crooked, as it always was; I saw Sylvia blush and nudged Ruggles to look.

"She's thinking of the letter," he said.

Ruggles and I never meant to listen, upon my word we didn't. It was pure accident. We were in behind the flags and palms in the Modern Languages Room, fixing up a plan how to get Em and Jennie off for a moonlit stroll in the grounds—these things require diplomacy I can tell you, for there are always so many other fellows hanging about—when in came Sylvia Grant and the Old Fellow arm in arm. The room was quite empty, or they thought it was, and they sat down just on the other side of the flags. They couldn't see us, but we could see them quite plainly. Sylvia still looked smiling and happy, not a bit mad as we had expected, but just kind of shy and radiant. As for the Old Fellow, he looked, as Em White would say, as Sphinx-like as ever. I'd defy any man alive to tell from the Old Fellow's expression what he was thinking about or what he felt like at any time.

Then all at once Sylvia said softly, with her eyes cast down, "I received your letter, Mr. Osborne."

Any other man in the world would have jumped, or said, "My letter!!!" or shown surprise in some way. But the Old Fellow has a nerve. He looked sideways at Sylvia for a moment and then he said kind of drily, "Ah, did you?"

"Yes," said Sylvia, not much above a whisper. "It—it surprised me very much. I never supposed that you—you cared for me in that way."

"Can you tell me how I could help caring?" said the Old Fellow in the strangest way. His voice actually trembled.

"I—I don't think I would tell you if I knew," said Sylvia, turning her head away. "You see—I don't want you to help caring."

"Sylvia!"

You never saw such a transformation as came over the Old Fellow. His eyes just blazed, but his face went white. He bent forward and took her hand.

"Sylvia, do you mean that you—you actually care a little for me, dearest? Oh, Sylvia, do you mean that?"

"Of course I do," said Sylvia right out. "I've always cared—ever since I was a little girl coming here to school and breaking my heart over mathematics, although I hated them, just to be in your class. Why—why—I've treasured up old geometry exercises you wrote out for me just because you wrote them. But I thought I could never make you care for me. I was the happiest girl in the world when your letter came today."

"Sylvia," said the Old Fellow, "I've loved you for years. But I never dreamed that you could care for me. I thought it quite useless to tell you of my love—before. Will you—can you be my wife, darling?"

At this point Ruggles and I differ as to what came next. He asserts that Sylvia turned square around and kissed the Old Fellow. But I'm sure she just turned her face and gave him a look and then he kissed her.

Anyhow, there they both were, going on at the silliest rate about how much they loved each other and how the Old Fellow thought she loved Micky and all that sort of thing. It was awful. I never thought the Old Fellow or Sylvia either could be so spooney. Ruggles and I would have given anything on earth to be out of that. We knew we'd no business to be there and we felt as foolish as flatfish. It was a tremendous relief when the Old Fellow and Sylvia got up at last and trailed away, both of them looking idiotically happy.

"Well, did you ever?" said Ruggles.

It was a girl's exclamation, but nothing else would have expressed his feelings.

"No, I never," I said. "To think that Sylvia Grant should be sweet on the Old Fellow when she could have Micky! It passes comprehension. Did she—did she really promise to marry him, Ruggles?"

"She did," said Ruggles gloomily. "But, I say, isn't that Old Fellow game? Tumbled to the trick in a jiff; never let on but what he wrote the letter, never will let on, I bet. Where does the joke come in, Polly, my boy?"

"It's on us," I said, "but nobody will know of it if we hold our tongues. We'll have to hold them anyhow, for Sylvia's sake, since she's been goose enough to go and fall in love with the Old Fellow. She'd go wild if she ever found out the letter was a hoax. We have made that match, Ruggles. He'd never have got up enough spunk to tell her he wanted her, and she'd probably have married Micky out of spite."

"Well, you know the Old Fellow isn't a bad sort after all," said Ruggles, "and he's really awfully gone on her. So it's all right. Let's go and find the girls."

The Parting of The Ways

Mrs. Longworth crossed the hotel piazza, descended the steps, and walked out of sight down the shore road with all the grace of motion that lent distinction to her slightest movement. Her eyes were very bright, and an unusual flush stained the pallor of her cheek. Two men who were lounging in one corner of the hotel piazza looked admiringly after her.

"She is a beautiful woman," said one.

"Wasn't there some talk about Mrs. Longworth and Cunningham last winter?" asked the other.

"Yes. They were much together. Still, there may have been nothing wrong. She was old Judge Carmody's daughter, you know. Longworth got Carmody under his thumb in money matters and put the screws on. They say he made Carmody's daughter the price of the old man's redemption. The girl herself was a mere child, I shall never forget her face on her wedding day. But she's been plucky since then, I must say. If she has suffered, she hasn't shown it. I don't suppose Longworth ever ill-treats her. He isn't that sort. He's simply a grovelling cad—that's all. Nobody would sympathise much with the poor devil if his wife did run off with Cunningham."

Meanwhile, Beatrice Longworth walked quickly down the shore road, her white skirt brushing over the crisp golden grasses by the way. In a sunny hollow among the sandhills she came upon Stephen Gordon, sprawled out luxuriously in the warm, sea-smelling grasses. The youth sprang to his feet at sight of her, and his big brown eyes kindled to a glow.

Mrs. Longworth smiled to him. They had been great friends all summer. He was a lanky, overgrown lad of fifteen or sixteen, odd and shy and dreamy, scarcely possessing a speaking acquaintance with others at the hotel. But he and Mrs. Longworth had been congenial from their first meeting. In many ways, he was far older than his years, but there was a certain inerradicable boyishness about him to which her heart warmed.

"You are the very person I was just going in search of. I've news to tell. Sit down."

He spoke eagerly, patting the big gray boulder beside him with his slim, brown hand. For a moment Beatrice hesitated. She wanted to be alone just then. But his clever, homely face was so appealing that she yielded and sat down.

Stephen flung himself down again contentedly in the grasses at her feet, pillowing his chin in his palms and looking up at her, adoringly.

"You are so beautiful, dear lady. I love to look at you. Will you tilt that hat a little more over the left eye-brow? Yes—so—some day I shall paint you."

His tone and manner were all simplicity.

"When you are a great artist," said Beatrice, indulgently.

He nodded.

"Yes, I mean to be that. I've told you all my dreams, you know. Now for my news. I'm going away to-morrow. I had a telegram from father to-day."

He drew the message from his pocket and flourished it up at her.

"I'm to join him in Europe at once. He is in Rome. Think of it—in Rome! I'm to go on with my art studies there. And I leave to-morrow."

"I'm glad—and I'm sorry—and you know which is which," said Beatrice, patting the shaggy brown head. "I shall miss you dreadfully, Stephen."

"We *have* been splendid chums, haven't we?" he said, eagerly.

Suddenly his face changed. He crept nearer to her, and bowed his head until his lips almost touched the hem of her dress.

"I'm glad you came down to-day," he went on in a low, diffident voice. "I want to tell you something, and I can tell it better here. I couldn't go away without thanking you. I'll make a mess of it—I can never explain things. But you've been so much to me—you mean so much to me. You've made me believe in things I never believed in before. You—you—I know now that there is such a thing as a good woman, a woman who could make a man better, just because he breathed the same air with her."

He paused for a moment; then went on in a still lower tone:

"It's hard when a fellow can't speak of his mother because he can't say anything good of her, isn't it? My mother wasn't a good woman. When I was eight years old she went away with a scoundrel. It broke father's heart. Nobody thought I understood, I was such a little fellow. But I did. I heard them talking. I knew she had brought shame and disgrace on herself and us. And I had loved her so! Then, somehow, as I grew up, it was my misfortune that all the women I had to do with were mean and base. They were hirelings, and I hated and feared them. There was an aunt of mine—she tried to be good to me in her way. But she told me a lie, and I never cared for her after I found it out. And then, father—we loved each other and were good chums. But he didn't believe in much either. He was bitter, you know. He said all women were alike. I grew up with that notion. I didn't care much for anything—nothing seemed worth while. Then I came here and met you."

He paused again. Beatrice had listened with a gray look on her face. It would have startled him had he glanced up, but he did not, and after a moment's silence the halting boyish voice went on:

"You have changed everything for me. I was nothing but a clod before. You are not the mother of my body, but you are of my soul. It was born of you. I shall always love and reverence you for it. You will always be my ideal. If I ever do anything worth while it will be because of you. In everything I shall ever attempt I shall try to do it as if you were to pass judgment upon it. You will be a lifelong inspiration to me. Oh, I am bungling this! I can't tell you what I feel—you are so pure, so good, so noble! I shall reverence all women for your sake henceforth."

"And if," said Beatrice, in a very low voice, "if I were false to your ideal of me—if I were to do anything that would destroy your faith in me—something weak or wicked—"

"But you couldn't," he interrupted, flinging up his head and looking at her with his great dog-like eyes, "you couldn't!"

"But if I could?" she persisted, gently, "and if I did—what then?"

"I should hate you," he said, passionately. "You would be worse than a murderess. You would kill every good impulse and belief in me. I would never trust anything or anybody again—but there," he added, his voice once more growing tender, "you will never fail me, I feel sure of that."

"Thank you," said Beatrice, almost in a whisper. "Thank you," she repeated, after a moment. She stood up and held out her hand. "I think I must go now. Good-bye, dear laddie. Write to me from Rome. I shall always be glad to hear from you wherever you are. And—and—I shall always try to live up to your ideal of me, Stephen."

He sprang to his feet and took her hand, lifting it to his lips with boyish reverence. "I know that," he said, slowly. "Good-bye, my sweet lady."

When Mrs. Longworth found herself in her room again, she unlocked her desk and took out a letter. It was addressed to Mr. Maurice Cunningham. She slowly tore it twice across, laid the fragments on a tray, and touched them with a lighted match. As they blazed up one line came out in writhing redness across the page: "I will go away with you as you ask." Then it crumbled into gray ashes.

She drew a long breath and hid her face in her hands.

The Promissory Note

Ernest Duncan swung himself off the platform of David White's store and walked whistling up the street. Life seemed good to Ernest just then. Mr. White had given him a rise in salary that day, and had told him that he was satisfied with him. Mr. White was not easy to please in the matter of clerks, and it had been with fear and trembling that Ernest had gone into his store six months before. He had thought himself fortunate to secure such a chance. His father had died the preceding year, leaving nothing in the way of worldly goods except the house he had lived in. For several years before his death he had been unable to do much work, and the finances of the little family had dwindled steadily. After his father's death Ernest, who had been going to school and expecting to go to college, found that he must go to work at once instead to support himself and his mother.

If George Duncan had not left much of worldly wealth behind him, he at least bequeathed to his son the interest of a fine, upright character and a reputation for honesty and integrity. None knew this better than David White, and it was on this account that he took Ernest as his clerk, over the heads of several other applicants who seemed to have a stronger "pull."

"I don't know anything about *you*, Ernest," he said bluntly. "You're only sixteen, and you may not have an ounce of real grit or worth in you. But it will be a queer thing if your father's son hasn't. I knew him all his life. A better man never lived nor, before his accident, a smarter one. I'll give his son a chance, anyhow. If you take after your dad you'll get on all right."

Ernest had not been in the store very long before Mr. White concluded, with a gratified chuckle, that he did take after his father. He was hard-working, conscientious, and obliging. Customers of all sorts, from the rough fishermen who came up from the harbour to the old Irishwomen from the back country roads, liked him. Mr. White was satisfied. He was beginning to grow old. This lad had the makings of a good partner in him by and by. No hurry; he must serves long apprenticeship first and prove his mettle; no use spoiling him by hinting at future partnerships before need was. That would all come in due time. David White was a shrewd man.

Ernest was unconscious of his employer's plans regarding him; but he knew that he stood well with him and, much to his surprise, he found that he liked the work, and was beginning to take a personal interest and pleasure in the store.

Hence, he went home to tea on this particular afternoon with buoyant step and smiling eyes. It was a good world, and he was glad to be alive in it, glad to have work to do and a dear little mother to work for. Most of the folks who met him smiled in friendly fashion at the bright-eyed, frank-faced lad. Only old Jacob Patterson scowled grimly as he passed him, emitting merely a surly grunt in response to Ernest's greeting. But then, old Jacob Patterson was noted as much for his surliness as for his miserliness. Nobody had ever heard him speak pleasantly to anyone; therefore his unfriendliness did not at all dash Ernest's high spirits.

"I'm sorry for him," the lad thought. "He has no interest in life save accumulating money. He has no other pleasure or affection or ambition. When he dies I don't suppose a single regret will follow him. Father died a poor man, but what love and respect went with him to his grave—aye, and beyond it. Jacob Patterson, I'm sorry for you. You have chosen the poorer part, and you are a poor man in spite of your thousands."

Ernest and his mother lived up on the hill, at the end of the straggling village street. The house was a small, old-fashioned one, painted white, set in the middle of a small but beautiful lawn. George Duncan, during the last rather helpless years of his life, had devoted himself to the cultivation of flowers, shrubs, and trees and, as a result, his lawn was the prettiest in Conway. Ernest worked hard in his spare moments to keep it looking as well as in his father's lifetime, for he loved his little home dearly, and was proud of its beauty.

He ran gaily into the sitting-room.

"Tea ready, lady mother? I'm hungry as a wolf. Good news gives one an appetite. Mr. White has raised my salary a couple of dollars per week. We must celebrate the event somehow this evening. What do you say to a sail on the river and an ice cream at Taylor's afterwards? When a little woman can't outlive her schoolgirl hankering for ice cream—why, Mother, what's the matter? Mother, dear!"

Mrs. Duncan had been standing before the window with her back to the room when Ernest entered. When she turned he saw that she had been crying.

"Oh, Ernest," she said brokenly, "Jacob Patterson has just been here—and he says—he says—"

"What has that old miser been saying to trouble you?" demanded Ernest angrily, taking her hands in his.

"He says he holds your father's promissory note for nine hundred dollars, overdue for several years," answered Mrs. Duncan. "Yes—and he showed me the note, Ernest."

"Father's promissory note for nine hundred!" exclaimed Ernest in bewilderment. "But Father paid that note to James Patterson five years ago, Mother—just before his accident. Didn't you tell me he did?"

"Yes, he did," said Mrs. Duncan, "but—"

"Then where is it?" interrupted Ernest. "Father would keep the receipted note, of course. We must look among his papers."

"You won't find it there, Ernest. We—we don't know where the note is. It—it was lost."

"Lost! That is unfortunate. But you say that Jacob Patterson showed you a promissory note of Father's still in existence? How can that be? It can't possibly be the note he paid. And there couldn't have been another note we knew nothing of?"

"I understand how this note came to be in Jacob Patterson's possession," said Mrs. Duncan more firmly, "but he laughed in my face when I told him. I must tell you the whole story, Ernest. But sit down and get your tea first."

"I haven't any appetite for tea now, Mother," said Ernest soberly. "Let me hear the whole truth about the matter."

"Seven years ago your father gave his note to old James Patterson, Jacob's brother," said Mrs. Duncan. "It was for nine hundred dollars. Two years afterwards the note fell due and he paid James Patterson the full amount with interest. I remember the day well. I have only too good reason to. He went up to the Patterson place in the afternoon with the money. It was a very hot day. James Patterson receipted the note and gave it to your father. Your father always remembered that much; he was also sure that he had the note with him when he left the house. He then went over to see Paul Sinclair. A thunderstorm came up while he was on the road. Then, as you know, Ernest, just as he turned in at Paul Sinclair's gate the lightning flash struck and stunned him. It was weeks before he came to himself at all. He never did come completely to himself again. When, weeks afterwards, I thought of the note and asked him about it, we could not find it; and, search as we did, we never found it. Your father could never remember what he did with it when he left James Patterson's. Neither Mr. Sinclair nor his wife could recollect seeing anything of it at the time of the accident. James Patterson had left for California the very morning after, and he never came back. We did not worry much about the loss of the note then; it did not seem of much moment, and your father was not in a condition to be troubled about the matter."

"But, Mother, this note that Jacob Patterson holds—I don't understand about this."

"I'm coming to that. I remember distinctly that on the evening when your father came home after signing the note he said that James Patterson drew up a note and he signed it, but just as he did so the old man's pet cat, which was sitting on the table, upset an ink bottle and the ink ran all over the table and stained one end of the note. Old James Patterson was the fussiest man who ever lived, and a stickler for neatness. 'Tut, tut,' he said, 'this won't do. Here, I'll draw up another note and tear this blotted one up.' He did so and your father signed it. He always supposed James Patterson destroyed the first one, and certainly he must have intended to, for there never was an honester man. But he must have neglected to do so for, Ernest, it was that blotted note Jacob Patterson showed me today. He said he found it among his brother's papers. I suppose it has been in the desk up at the Patterson place ever since James went to California. He died last winter and

Jacob is his sole heir. Ernest, that note with the compound interest on it for seven years amounts to over eleven hundred dollars. How can we pay it?"

"I'm afraid that this is a very serious business, Mother," said Ernest, rising and pacing the floor with agitated strides. "We shall have to pay the note if we cannot find the other—and even if we could, perhaps. Your story of the drawing up of the second note would not be worth anything as evidence in a court of law—and we have nothing to hope from Jacob Patterson's clemency. No doubt he believes that he really holds Father's unpaid note. He is not a dishonest man; in fact, he rather prides himself on having made all his money honestly. He will exact every penny of the debt. The first thing to do is to have another thorough search for the lost note—although I am afraid that it is a forlorn hope."

A forlorn hope it proved to be. The note did not turn up. Old Jacob Patterson proved obdurate. He laughed to scorn the tale of the blotted note and, indeed, Ernest sadly admitted to himself that it was not a story anybody would be in a hurry to believe.

"There's nothing for it but to sell our house and pay the debt, Mother," he said at last. Ernest had grown old in the days that had followed Jacob Patterson's demand. His boyish face was pale and haggard. "Jacob Patterson will take the case into the law courts if we don't settle at once. Mr. White offered to lend me the money on a mortgage on the place, but I could never pay the interest out of my salary when we have nothing else to live on. I would only get further and further behind. I'm not afraid of hard work, but I dare not borrow money with so little prospect of ever being able to repay it. We must sell the place and rent that little four-roomed cottage of Mr. Percy's down by the river to live in. Oh, Mother, it half kills me to think of your being turned out of your home like this!"

It was a bitter thing for Mrs. Duncan also, but for Ernest's sake she concealed her feelings and affected cheerfulness. The house and lot were sold, Mr. White being the purchaser thereof; and Ernest and his mother removed to the little riverside cottage with such of their household belongings as had not also to be sold to make up the required sum. Even then, Ernest had to borrow two hundred dollars from Mr. White, and he foresaw that the repayal of this sum would cost him much self-denial and privation. It would be necessary to cut their modest expenses down severely. For himself Ernest did not mind, but it hurt him keenly that his mother should lack the little luxuries and comforts to which she had been accustomed. He saw too, in spite of her efforts to hide it, that leaving her old home was a terrible blow to her. Altogether, Ernest felt bitter and disheartened; his step lacked spring and his face its smile. He did his work with dogged faithfulness, but he no longer found pleasure in it. He knew that his mother secretly pined after her lost home where she had gone as a bride, and the knowledge rendered him very unhappy.

Paul Sinclair, his father's friend and cousin, died that winter, leaving two small children. His wife had died the previous year. When his business affairs came to be settled they were found to be sadly involved. There were debts on all sides, and it was soon only too evident that nothing was left for the little boys. They were homeless and penniless.

"What will become of them, poor little fellows?" said Mrs. Duncan pityingly. "We are their only relatives, Ernest. We must give them a home at least."

"Mother, how can we!" exclaimed Ernest. "We are so poor. It's as much as we can do to get along now, and there is that two hundred to pay Mr. White. I'm sorry for Danny and Frank, but I don't see how we can possibly do anything for them."

Mrs. Duncan sighed.

"I know it isn't right to ask you to add to your burden," she said wistfully.

"It is of *you* I am thinking, Mother," said Ernest tenderly. "I can't have your burden added to. You deny yourself too much and work too hard now. What would it be if you took the care of those children upon yourself?"

"Don't think of me, Ernest," said Mrs. Duncan eagerly. "I wouldn't mind. I'd be glad to do anything I could for them, poor little souls. Their father was your father's best friend, and I feel as if it were our duty to do all we can for them. They're such little fellows. Who knows how they would be treated if they were taken by strangers? And they'd most likely be separated, and that would be a shame. But I leave it for you to decide, Ernest. It is your right, for the heaviest part will fall on you."

Ernest did not decide at once. For a week he thought the matter over, weighing pros and cons carefully. To take the two Sinclair boys meant a double portion of toil and self-denial. Had he not enough to bear now? But, on the other side, was it not his duty, nay, his privilege, to help the children if he could? In the end he said to his mother:

"We'll take the little fellows, Mother. I'll do the best I can for them. We'll manage a corner and a crust for them."

So Danny and Frank Sinclair came to the little cottage. Frank was eight and Danny six, and they were small and lively and mischievous. They worshipped Mrs. Duncan, and thought Ernest the finest fellow in the world. When his birthday came around in March, the two little chaps put their heads together in a grave consultation as to what they could give him.

"You know he gave us presents on our birthdays," said Frank. "So we must give him something."

"I'll div him my pottet-knife," said Danny, taking the somewhat battered and loose-jointed affair from his pocket, and gazing at it affectionately.

"I'll give him one of Papa's books," said Frank. "That pretty one with the red covers and the gold letters."

A few of Mr. Sinclair's books had been saved for the boys, and were stored in a little box in their room. The book Frank referred to was an old *History of the Turks*, and its gay cover was probably the best of it, since its contents were of no particular merit.

On Ernest's birthday both boys gave him their offerings after breakfast.

"Here's a pottet-knife for you," said Danny graciously. "It's a bully pottet-knife. It'll cut real well if you hold it dust the wight way. I'll show you."

"And here's a book for you," said Frank. "It's a real pretty book, and I guess it's pretty interesting reading too. It's all about the Turks."

Ernest accepted both gifts gravely, and after the children had gone out he and his mother had a hearty laugh.

"The dear, kind-hearted little lads!" said Mrs. Duncan. "It must have been a real sacrifice on Danny's part to give you his beloved 'pottet-knife.' I was afraid you were going to refuse it at first, and that would have hurt his little feelings terribly. I don't think the *History of the Turks* will keep you up burning the midnight oil. I remember that book of old—I could never forget that gorgeous cover. Mr. Sinclair lent it to your father once, and he said it was absolute trash. Why, Ernest, what's the matter?"

Ernest had been turning the book's leaves over carelessly. Suddenly he sprang to his feet with an exclamation, his face turning white as marble.

"Mother!" he gasped, holding out a yellowed slip of paper. "Look! It's the lost promissory note."

Mother and son looked at each other for a moment. Then Mrs. Duncan began to laugh and cry together.

"Your father took that book with him when he went to pay the note," she said. "He intended to return it to Mr. Sinclair. I remember seeing the gleam of the red binding in his hand as he went out of the gate. He must have slipped the note into it and I suppose the book has never been opened since. Oh, Ernest—do you think—will Jacob Patterson—"

"I don't know, Mother. I must see Mr. White about this. Don't be too sanguine. This doesn't prove that the note Jacob Patterson found wasn't a genuine note also, you know—that is, I don't think it would serve as proof in law. We'll have to leave it to his sense of justice. If he refuses to refund the money I'm afraid we can't compel him to do so."

But Jacob Patterson did not any longer refuse belief to Mrs. Patterson's story of the blotted note. He was a harsh, miserly man, but he prided himself on his strict honesty; he had been fairly well acquainted with his brother's business transactions, and knew that George Duncan had given only one promissory note.

"I'll admit, ma'am, since the receipted note has turned up, that your story about the blotted one must be true," he said surlily. "I'll pay your money back. Nobody can ever say Jacob Patterson cheated. I took what I believed to be my due. Since I'm convinced it wasn't I'll hand every penny over. Though, mind you, you couldn't make me do it by law. It's my honesty, ma'am, it's my honesty."

Since Jacob Patterson was so well satisfied with the fibre of his honesty, neither Mrs. Duncan nor Ernest was disposed to quarrel with it. Mr. White readily agreed to sell the old Duncan place back to them, and by spring they were settled again in their beloved little home. Danny and Frank were with them, of course.

"We can't be too good to them, Mother," said Ernest. "We really owe all our happiness to them."

"Yes, but, Ernest, if you had not consented to take the homeless little lads in their time of need this wouldn't have come about."

"I've been well rewarded, Mother," said Ernest quietly, "but, even if nothing of the sort had happened, I would be glad that I did the best I could for Frank and Danny. I'm ashamed to think that I was unwilling to do it at first. If it hadn't been for what you said, I wouldn't have. So it is your unselfishness we have to thank for it all, Mother dear."

The Revolt of Mary Isabel

"For a woman of forty, Mary Isabel, you have the least sense of any person I have ever known," said Louisa Irving.

Louisa had said something similar in spirit to Mary Isabel almost every day of her life. Mary Isabel had never resented it, even when it hurt her bitterly. Everybody in Latimer knew that Louisa Irving ruled her meek little sister with a rod of iron and wondered why Mary Isabel never rebelled. It simply never occurred to Mary Isabel to do so; all her life she had given in to Louisa and the thought of refusing obedience to her sister's Mede-and-Persian decrees never crossed her mind. Mary Isabel had only one secret from Louisa and she lived in daily dread that Louisa would discover it. It was a very harmless little secret, but Mary Isabel felt rightly sure that Louisa would not tolerate it for a moment.

They were sitting together in the dim living room of their quaint old cottage down by the shore. The window was open and the sea-breeze blew in, stirring the prim white curtains fitfully, and ruffling the little rings of dark hair on Mary Isabel's forehead—rings which always annoyed Louisa. She thought Mary Isabel ought to brush them straight back, and Mary Isabel did so faithfully a dozen times a day; and in ten minutes they crept down again, kinking defiance to Louisa, who might make Mary Isabel submit to her in all things but had no power over naturally curly hair. Louisa had never had any trouble with her own hair; it was straight and sleek and mouse-coloured—what there was of it.

Mary Isabel's face was flushed and her wood-brown eyes looked grieved and pleading. Mary Isabel was still pretty, and vanity is the last thing to desert a properly constructed woman.

"I can't wear a bonnet yet, Louisa," she protested. "Bonnets have gone out for everybody except really old ladies. I want a hat: one of those pretty, floppy ones with pale blue forget-me-nots."

Then it was that Louisa made the remark quoted above.

"I wore a bonnet before I was forty," she went on ruthlessly, "and so should every decent woman. It is absurd to be thinking so much of dress at your age, Mary Isabel. I don't know what sort of a way you'd bedizen yourself out if I'd let you, I'm sure. It's fortunate you have somebody to keep you from making a fool of yourself. I'm going to town tomorrow and I'll pick you out a suitable black bonnet. You'd look nice starring round in leghorn and forget-me-nots, now, wouldn't you?"

Mary Isabel privately thought she would, but she gave in, of course, although she did hate bitterly that unbought, unescapable bonnet.

"Well, do as you think best, Louisa," she said with a sigh. "I suppose it doesn't matter much. Nobody cares how I look anyhow. But can't I go to town with you? I want to pick out my new silk."

"I'm as good a judge of black silk as you," said Louisa shortly. "It isn't safe to leave the house alone."

"But I don't want a black silk," cried Mary Isabel. "I've worn black so long; both my silk dresses have been black. I want a pretty silver-grey, something like Mrs. Chester Ford's."

"Did anyone ever hear such nonsense?" Louisa wanted to know, in genuine amazement. "Silver-grey silk is the most unserviceable thing in the world. There's nothing like black for wear and real elegance. No, no, Mary Isabel, don't be foolish. You must let me choose for you; you know you never had any judgment. Mother told you so often enough. Now, get your sunbonnet and take a walk to the shore. You look tired. I'll get the tea."

Louisa's tone was kind though firm. She Was really good to Mary Isabel as long as Mary Isabel gave her her own way peaceably. But if she had known Mary Isabel's secret she would never have permitted those walks to the shore.

Mary Isabel sighed again, yielded, and went out. Across a green field from the Irving cottage Dr. Donald Hamilton's big house was hooding itself in the shadows of the thick fir grove that enabled the doctor to have a garden. There was no shelter at the cottage, so the Irving "girls" never tried to have a garden. Soon after Dr. Hamilton had come there to live he had sent a bouquet of early daffodils over by his housekeeper. Louisa had taken them gingerly in her extreme fingertips, carried them across the field to the lawn fence, and cast them over it, under the amused grey eyes of portly Dr. Hamilton, who was looking out of his office window. Then Louisa had come back to the porch door and ostentatiously washed her hands.

"I guess that will settle Donald Hamilton," she told the secretly sorry Mary Isabel triumphantly, and it did settle him—at least as far as any farther social advances were concerned.

Dr. Hamilton was an excellent physician and an equally excellent man. Louisa Irving could not have picked a flaw in his history or character. Indeed, against Dr. Hamilton himself she had no grudge, but he was the brother of a man she hated and whose relatives were consequently taboo in Louisa's eyes. Not that the brother was a bad man either; he had simply taken the opposite side to the Irvings in a notable church feud of a dozen years ago, and Louisa had never since held any intercourse with him or his fellow sinners.

Mary Isabel did not look at the Hamilton house. She kept her head resolutely turned away as she went down the shore lane with its wild sweet loneliness of salt-withered grasses and piping sea-winds. Only when she turned the corner of the fir-wood, which shut her out from view of the houses, did she look timidly over the line-fence. Dr. Hamilton was standing there, where the fence ran out to the sandy shingle, smoking his little black pipe, which he took out and put away when Mary Isabel came around the firs. Men did things like that instinctively in Mary Isabel's company. There was something so delicately virginal about her, in spite of her forty years, that they gave her the reverence they would have paid to a very young, pure girl.

Dr. Hamilton smiled at the little troubled face under the big sunbonnet. Mary Isabel had to wear a sunbonnet. She would never have done it from choice.

"What is the matter?" asked the doctor, in his big, breezy, old-bachelor voice. He had another voice for sick-beds and rooms of bereavement, but this one suited best with the purring of the waves and winds.

"How do you know that anything is the matter?" Mary Isabel parried demurely.

"By your face. Come now, tell me what it is."

"It is really nothing. I have just been foolish, that is all. I wanted a hat with forget-me-nots and a grey silk, and Louisa says I must have black and a bonnet."

The doctor looked indignant but held his peace. He and Mary Isabel had tacitly agreed never to discuss Louisa, because such discussion would not make for harmony. Mary Isabel's conscience would not let the doctor say anything uncomplimentary of Louisa, and the doctor's conscience would not let him say anything complimentary. So they left her out of the question and talked about the sea and the boats and poetry and flowers and similar non-combustible subjects.

These clandestine meetings had been going on for two months, ever since the day they had just happened to meet below the firs. It never occurred to Mary Isabel that the doctor meant anything but friendship; and if it had occurred to the doctor, he did not think there would be much use in saying so. Mary Isabel was too hopelessly under Louisa's thumb. She might keep tryst below the firs occasionally—so long as Louisa didn't know—but to no farther lengths would she dare go. Besides, the doctor wasn't quite sure that he really wanted anything more. Mary Isabel was a sweet little woman, but Dr. Hamilton had been a bachelor so long that it would be very difficult for him to get out of the habit; so difficult that it was hardly worth while trying when such an obstacle as Louisa Irving's tyranny loomed in the way. So he never tried to make love to Mary Isabel, though he probably would have if he had thought it of any use. This does not sound very romantic, of course, but when a man is fifty, romance, while it may be present in the fruit, is assuredly absent in blossom.

"I suppose you won't be going to the induction of my nephew Thursday week?" said the doctor in the course of the conversation.

"No. Louisa will not permit it. I had hoped," said Mary Isabel with a sigh, as she braided some silvery shore-grasses nervously together, "that when old Mr. Moody went away she would go back to the church here. And I think she would if—if—"

"If Jim hadn't come in Mr. Moody's place," finished the doctor with his jolly laugh.

Mary Isabel coloured prettily. "It is not because he is your nephew, doctor. It is because—because—"

"Because he is the nephew of my brother who was on the other side in that ancient church fracas? Bless you, I understand. What a good hater your sister is! Such a tenacity in holding bitterness from one generation to another commands admiration of a certain sort. As for Jim, he's a nice little chap, and he is coming to live with me until the manse is repaired."

"I am sure you will find that pleasant," said Mary Isabel primly.

She wondered if the young minister's advent would make any difference in regard to these shore-meetings; then decided quickly that it would not; then more quickly still that it wouldn't matter if it did.

"He will be company," admitted the doctor, who liked company and found the shore road rather lonesome. "I had a letter from him today saying that he'd come home with me from the induction. By the way, they're tearing down the old post office today. And that reminds me—by Jove, I'd all but forgotten. I promised to go up and see Mollie Marr this evening; Mollie's nerves are on the rampage again. I must rush."

With a wave of his hand the doctor hurried off. Mary Isabel lingered for some time longer, leaning against the fence, looking dreamily out to sea. The doctor was a very pleasant companion. If only Louisa would allow neighbourliness! Mary Isabel felt a faint, impotent resentment. She had never had anything other girls had: friends, dresses, beaus, and it was all Louisa's fault—Louisa who was going to make her wear a bonnet for the rest of her life. The more Mary Isabel thought of that bonnet the more she hated it.

That evening Warren Marr rode down to the shore cottage on horseback and handed Mary Isabel a letter; a strange, scrumpled, soiled, yellow letter. When Mary Isabel saw the handwriting on the envelope she trembled and turned as deadly pale as if she had seen a ghost:

"Here's a letter for you," said Warren, grinning. "It's been a long time on the way—nigh fifteen years. Guess the news'll be rather stale. We found it behind the old partition when we tore it down today."

"It is my brother Tom's writing," said Mary Isabel faintly. She went into the room trembling, holding the letter tightly in her clasped hands. Louisa had gone up to the village on an errand; Mary Isabel almost wished she were home; she hardly felt equal to the task of opening Tom's letter alone. Tom had been dead for ten years and this letter gave her an uncanny sensation; as of a message from the spirit-land.

Fifteen years, ago Thomas Irving had gone to California and five years later he had died there. Mary Isabel, who had idolized her brother, almost grieved herself to death at the time.

Finally she opened the letter with ice-cold fingers. It had been written soon after Tom reached California. The first two pages were filled with descriptions of the country and his "job."

On the third Tom began abruptly:

Look here, Mary Isabel, you are not to let Louisa boss you about as she was doing when I was at home. I was going to speak to you about it before I came away, but I forgot. Lou is a fine girl, but she is too domineering, and the more you give in to her the worse it makes her. You're far too easy-going for your own welfare, Mary Isabel, and for your own sake I Wish you had more spunk. Don't let Louisa live your life for you; just you live it yourself. Never mind if there is some friction at first; Lou will give in when she finds she has to, and you'll both be the better for it, I want you to be real happy, Mary Isabel, but you won't be if you don't assert your independence. Giving in the way you do is bad for both you and Louisa. It will make her a tyrant and you a poor-spirited creature of no account in the world. Just brace up and stand firm.

When she had read the letter through Mary Isabel took it to her own room and locked it in her bureau drawer. Then she sat by her window, looking out into a sea-sunset, and thought it over. Coming in the strange way it had, the letter seemed a message from the dead, and Mary Isabel had a superstitious conviction that she must obey it. She had always had a great respect for Tom's opinion. He was right—oh, she felt that he was right. What a pity she had not received the letter long ago, before the shackles of habit had become so firmly riveted. But it was not too late yet. She would rebel at last and—how had Tom phrased it—oh, yes, assert her independence. She owed it to Tom; It had been his wish—and he was dead—and she would do her best to fulfil it.

"I shan't get a bonnet," thought Mary Isabel determinedly. "Tom wouldn't have liked me in a bonnet. From this out I'm just going to do exactly as Tom would have liked me to do, no matter how afraid I am of Louisa. And, oh, I am horribly afraid of her."

Mary Isabel was every whit as much afraid the next morning after breakfast but she did not look it, by reason of the flush on her cheeks and the glint in her brown eyes. She had put Tom's letter in the bosom of her dress and she pressed her fingertips on it that the crackle might give her courage.

"Louisa," she said firmly, "I am going to town with you."

"Nonsense," said Louisa shortly.

"You may call it nonsense if you like, but I am going," said Mary Isabel unquailingly. "I have made up my mind on that point, Louisa, and nothing you can say will alter it."

Louisa looked amazed. Never before had Mary Isabel set her decrees at naught.

"Are you crazy, Mary Isabel?" she demanded.

"No, I am not crazy. But I am going to town and I am going to get a silver-grey silk for myself and a new hat. I will not wear a bonnet and you need never mention it to me again, Louisa."

"If you are going to town I shall stay home," said Louisa in a cold, ominous tone that almost made Mary Isabel quake. If it had not been for that reassuring crackle of Tom's letter I fear Mary Isabel would have given in. "This house can't be left alone. If you go, I'll stay."

Louisa honestly thought that would bring the rebel to terms. Mary Isabel had never gone to town alone in her life. Louisa did not believe she would dare to go. But Mary Isabel did not quail. Defiance was not so hard after all, once you had begun.

Mary Isabel went to town and she went alone. She spent the whole delightful day in the shops, unhampered by Louisa's scorn and criticism in her examination of all the pretty things displayed. She selected a hat she felt sure Tom would like—a pretty crumpled grey straw with forget-me-nots and ribbons. Then she bought a grey silk of a lovely silvery shade.

When she got back home she unwrapped her packages and showed her purchases to Louisa. But Louisa neither looked at them nor spoke to Mary Isabel. Mary Isabel tossed her head and went to her own room. Her draught of freedom had stimulated her, and she did not mind Louisa's attitude half as much as she would have expected. She read Tom's letter over again to fortify herself and then she dressed her hair in a fashion she had seen that day in town and pulled out all the little curls on her forehead.

The next day she took the silver-grey silk to the Latimer dressmaker and picked out a fashionable design for it. When the silk dress came home, Louisa, who had thawed out somewhat in the meantime, unbent sufficiently to remark that it fitted very well.

"I am going to wear it to the induction tomorrow," Mary Isabel said, boldly to all appearances, quakingly in reality. She knew that she was throwing down the gauntlet for good and all. If she could assert and maintain her independence in this matter Louisa's power would be broken forever.

Twelve years before this, the previously mentioned schism had broken out in the Latimer church. The minister had sided with the faction which Louisa Irving opposed. She had promptly ceased going to his church and withdrew all financial support. She paid to the Marwood church, fifteen miles away, and occasionally she hired a team and drove over there to service. But she never entered the Latimer church again nor allowed Mary Isabel to do so. For that matter, Mary Isabel did not wish to go. She had resented the minister's attitude almost as bitterly as Louisa. But when Mr. Moody accepted a call elsewhere Mary Isabel hoped that she and Louisa might return to their old church home. Possibly they might have done so had not the congregation called the young, newly fledged James Anderson. Mary Isabel would not have cared for this, but Louisa sternly said that neither she nor any of hers should ever darken the doors of a church where the nephew of Martin Hamilton preached. Mary Isabel had regretfully acquiesced at the time, but now she had made up her mind to go to church and she meant to begin with the induction service.

Louisa stared at her sister incredulously.

"Have you taken complete leave of your senses, Mary Isabel?"

"No. I've just come to them," retorted Mary Isabel recklessly, gripping a chair-back desperately so that Louisa should not see how she was trembling. "It is all foolishness to keep away from church just because of an old grudge. I'm tired of staying home Sundays or driving fifteen miles to Marwood to hear poor old Mr. Grattan. Everybody says Mr. Anderson is a splendid young man and an excellent preacher, and I'm going to attend his services regularly."

Louisa had taken Mary Isabel's first defiance in icy disdain. Now she lost her temper and raged. The storm of angry words beat on Mary Isabel like hail, but she fronted it staunchly. She seemed to hear Tom's voice saying, "Live your own life, Mary Isabel; don't let Louisa live it for you," and she meant to obey him.

"If you go to that man's induction I'll never forgive you," Louisa concluded.

Mary Isabel said nothing. She just primmed up her lips very determinedly, picked up the silk dress, and carried it to her room.

The next day was fine and warm. Louisa said no word all the morning. She worked fiercely and slammed things around noisily. After dinner Mary Isabel went to her room and came down presently, fine and dainty in her grey silk, with the forget-me-not hat resting on the soft loose waves of her hair. Louisa was blacking the kitchen stove.

She shot one angry glance at Mary Isabel, then gave a short, contemptuous laugh, the laugh of an angry woman who finds herself robbed of all weapons except ridicule.

Mary Isabel flushed and walked with an unfaltering step out of the house and up the lane. She resented Louisa's laughter. She was sure there was nothing so very ridiculous about her appearance. Women far older than she, even in Latimer, wore light dresses and fashionable hats. Really, Louisa was very disagreeable.

"I have put up with her ways too long," thought Mary Isabel, with a quick, unwonted rush of anger. "But I never shall again—no, never, let her be as vexed and scornful as she pleases."

The induction services were interesting, and Mary Isabel enjoyed them. Doctor Hamilton was sitting across from her and once or twice she caught him looking at her admiringly. The doctor noticed the hat and the grey silk and wondered how Mary Isabel had managed to get her own way concerning them. What a pretty woman she was! Really, he had never realized before how very pretty she was. But then, he had never seen her except in a sunbonnet or with her hair combed primly back.

But when the service was over Mary Isabel was dismayed to see that the sky had clouded over and looked very much like rain. Everybody hurried home, and Mary Isabel tripped along the shore road filled with anxious thoughts about her dress. That kind of silk always spotted, and her hat would be ruined if it got wet. How foolish she had been not to bring an umbrella!

She reached her own doorstep panting just as the first drop of rain fell.

"Thank goodness," she breathed.

Then she tried to open the door. It would not open.

She could see Louisa sitting by the kitchen window, calmly reading.

"Louisa, open the door quick," she called impatiently.

Louisa never moved a muscle, although Mary Isabel knew she must have heard.

"Louisa, do you hear what I say?" she cried, reaching over and tapping on the pane imperiously. "Open the door at once. It is going to rain—it is raining now. Be quick."

Louisa might as well have been a graven image for all the response she gave. Then did Mary Isabel realize her position. Louisa had locked her out purposely, knowing the rain was coming. Louisa had no intention of letting her in; she meant to keep her out until the dress and hat of her rebellion were spoiled. This was Louisa's revenge.

Mary Isabel turned with a gasp. What should she do? The padlocked doors of hen-house and well-house and wood-house: revealed the thoroughness of Louisa's vindictive design. Where should she go? She would go somewhere. She would not have her lovely new dress and hat spoiled!

She caught her ruffled skirts up in her hand and ran across the yard. She climbed the fence into the field and ran across that. Another drop of rain struck her cheek. She never glanced back or she would have seen a horrified face peering from the cottage kitchen window. Louisa had never dreamed that Mary Isabel would seek refuge over at Dr. Hamilton's.

Dr. Hamilton, who had driven home from church with the young minister, saw her coming and ran to open the door for her. Mary Isabel dashed up the verandah steps, breathless, crimson-cheeked, trembling with pent-up indignation and sense of outrage.

"Louisa locked me out, Dr. Hamilton," she cried almost hysterically. "She locked me out on purpose to spoil my dress. I'll never forgive her, I'll never go back to her, never, never, unless she asks me to. I had to come here. I was not going to have my dress ruined to please Louisa."

"Of course not—of course not," said Dr. Hamilton soothingly, drawing her into his big cosy living room. "You did perfectly right to come here, and you are just in time. There is the rain now in good earnest."

Mary Isabel sank into a chair and looked at Dr. Hamilton with tears in her eyes.

"Wasn't it an unkind, unsisterly thing to do?" she asked piteously. "Oh, I shall never feel the same towards Louisa again. Tom was right—I didn't tell you about Tom's letter but I will by and by. I shall not go back to Louisa after her locking me out. When it stops raining I'll go straight up to my cousin Ella's and stay with her until I arrange my plans. But one thing is certain, I shall not go back to Louisa."

"I wouldn't," said the doctor recklessly. "Now, don't cry and don't worry. Take off your hat—you can go to the spare room across the hall, if you like. Jim has gone upstairs to lie down; he has a bad headache and says he doesn't want any tea.

So I was going to get up a bachelor's snack for myself. My housekeeper is away. She heard, at church that her mother was ill and went over to Marwood."

When Mary Isabel came back from the spare room, a little calmer but with traces of tears on her pink cheeks, the doctor had as good a tea-table spread as any woman could have had. Mary Isabel thought it was fortunate that the little errand boy, Tommy Brewster, was there, or she certainly would have been dreadfully embarrassed, now that the flame of her anger had blown out. But later on, when tea was over and she and the doctor were left alone, she did not feel embarrassed after all. Instead, she felt delightfully happy and at home. Dr. Hamilton put one so at ease.

She told him all about Tom's letter and her subsequent revolt. Dr. Hamilton never once made the mistake of smiling. He listened and approved and sympathized.

"So I'm determined I won't go back," concluded Mary Isabel, "unless she asks me to—and Louisa will never do that. Ella will be glad enough to have me for a while; she has five children and can't get any help."

The doctor shrugged his shoulders. He thought of Mary Isabel as unofficial drudge to Ella Kemble and her family. Then he looked at the little silvery figure by the window.

"I think I can suggest a better plan," he said gently and tenderly. "Suppose you stay here—as my wife. I've always wanted to ask you that but I feared it was no use because I knew Louisa would oppose it and I did not think you would consent if she did not. I think," the doctor leaned forward and took Mary Isabel's fluttering hand in his, "I think we can be very happy here, dear."

Mary Isabel flushed crimson and her heart beat wildly. She knew now that she loved Dr. Hamilton—and Tom would have liked it—yes, Tom would. She remembered how Tom hated the thought of his sisters being old maids.

"I—think—so—too," she faltered shyly.

"Then," said the doctor briskly, "what is the matter with our being married right here and now?"

"Married!"

"Yes, of course. Here we are in a state where no licence is required, a minister in the house, and you all dressed in the most beautiful wedding silk imaginable. You must see, if you just look at it calmly, how much better it will be than going up to Mrs. Kemble's and thereby publishing your difference with Louisa to all the village. I'll give you fifteen minutes to get used to the idea and then I'll call Jim down."

Mary Isabel put her hands to her face.

"You—you're like a whirlwind," she gasped. "You take away my breath."

"Think it over," said the doctor in a businesslike voice.

Mary Isabel thought—thought very hard for a few moments.

What would Tom have said?

Was it probable that Tom would have approved of such marrying in haste?

Mary Isabel came to the decision that he would have preferred it to having family jars bruited abroad. Moreover, Mary Isabel had never liked Ella Kemble very much. Going to her was only one degree better than going back to Louisa.

At last Mary Isabel took her hands down from her face. "Well?" said the doctor persuasively as she did so.

"I will consent on one condition," said Mary Isabel firmly. "And that is, that you will let me send word over to Louisa that I am going to be married and that she may come and see the ceremony if she will. Louisa has behaved very unkindly in this matter, but after all she is my sister—and she has been good to me in some ways—and I am not going to give her a chance to say that I got married in this—this headlong-fashion and never let her know."

"Tommy can take the word over," said the doctor.

Mary Isabel went to the doctor's desk and wrote a very brief note.

Dear Louisa:

> I am going to be married to Dr. Hamilton right away. I've seen him often at the shore this summer. I would like you to be present at the ceremony if you choose.

Mary Isabel.

Tommy ran across the field with the note.

It had now ceased raining and the clouds were breaking. Mary Isabel thought that a good omen. She and the doctor watched Tommy from the window. They saw Louisa come to the door, take the note, and shut the door in Tommy's face. Ten minutes later she reappeared, habited in her mackintosh, with her second-best bonnet on.

"She's—coming," said Mary Isabel, trembling.

The doctor put his arm protectingly about the little lady.

Mary Isabel tossed her head. "Oh, I'm not—I'm only excited. I shall never be afraid of Louisa again."

Louisa came grimly over the field, up the verandah steps, and into the room without knocking.

"Mary Isabel," she said, glaring at her sister and ignoring the doctor entirely, "did you mean what you said in that letter?"

"Yes, I did," said Mary Isabel firmly.

"You are going to be married to that man in this shameless, indecent haste?"

"Yes."

"And nothing I can say will have the least effect on you?"

"Not the slightest."

"Then," said Louisa, more grimly than ever, "all I ask of you is to come home and be married from under your father's roof. Do have that much respect for your parents' memory, at least."

"Of course I will," cried Mary Isabel impulsively, softening at once. "Of course we will—won't we?" she asked, turning prettily to the doctor.

"Just as you say," he answered gallantly.

Louisa snorted. "I'll go home and air the parlour," she said. "It's lucky I baked that fruitcake Monday. You can come when you're ready."

She stalked home across the field. In a few minutes the doctor and Mary Isabel followed, and behind them came the young minister, carrying his blue book under his arm, and trying hard and not altogether successfully to look grave.

The Twins and a Wedding

Sometimes Johnny and I wonder what would really have happened if we had never started for Cousin Pamelia's wedding. I think that Ted would have come back some time; but Johnny says he doesn't believe he ever would, and Johnny ought to know, because Johnny's a boy. Anyhow, he couldn't have come back for four years. However, we *did* start for the wedding and so things came out all right, and Ted said we were a pair of twin special Providences.

Johnny and I fully expected to go to Cousin Pamelia's wedding because we had always been such chums with her. And she did write to Mother to be sure and bring us, but Father and Mother didn't want to be bothered with us. That is the plain truth of the matter. They are good parents, as parents go in this world; I don't think we could have picked out much better, all things considered; but Johnny and I have always known that they never want to take us with them anywhere if they can get out of it. Uncle Fred says that it is no wonder, since we are a pair of holy terrors for getting into mischief and keeping everybody in hot water. But I think we are pretty good, considering all the temptations we have to be otherwise. And, of course, twins have just twice as many as ordinary children.

Anyway, Father and Mother said we would have to stay home with Hannah Jane. This decision came upon us, as Johnny says, like a bolt from the blue. At first we couldn't believe they were not joking. Why, we felt that we simply *had* to go to Pamelia's wedding. We had never been to a wedding in our lives and we were just aching to see what it would be like. Besides, we had written a marriage ode to Pamelia and we wanted to present it to her. Johnny was to recite it, and he had been practising it out behind the carriage house for a week. I wrote the most of it. I can write poetry as slick as anything. Johnny helped me hunt out the rhymes. That is the hardest thing about writing poetry, it is so difficult to find rhymes. Johnny would find me a rhyme and then I would write a line to suit it, and we got on swimmingly.

When we realized that Father and Mother meant what they said we were just too miserable to live. When I went to bed that night I simply pulled the clothes over my face and howled quietly. I couldn't help it when I thought of Pamelia's white silk dress and tulle veil and flower girls and all the rest. Johnny said it was the wedding dinner *he* thought about. Boys are like that, you know.

Father and Mother went away on the early morning train, telling us to be good twins and not bother Hannah Jane. It would have been more to the point if they had told Hannah Jane not to bother us. She worries more about our bringing up than Mother does.

I was sitting on the front doorstep after they had gone when Johnny came around the corner, looking so mysterious and determined that I knew he had thought of something splendid.

"Sue," said Johnny impressively, "if you have any real sporting blood in you now is the time to show it. If you've enough grit we'll get to Pamelia's wedding after all."

"How?" I said as soon as I was able to say anything.

"We'll just go. We'll take the ten o'clock train. It will get to Marsden by eleven-thirty and that'll be in plenty of time. The wedding isn't until twelve."

"But we've never been on the train alone, and we've never been to Marsden at all!" I gasped.

"Oh, of course, if you're going to hatch up all sorts of difficulties!" said Johnny scornfully. "I thought you had more spunk!"

"Oh, I have, Johnny," I said eagerly. "I'm *all* spunk. And I'll do anything you'll do. But won't Father and Mother be perfectly savage?"

"Of course. But we'll be there and they can't send us home again, so we'll see the wedding. We'll be punished afterwards all right, but we'll have had the fun, don't you see?"

I saw. I went right upstairs to dress, trusting everything blindly to Johnny. I put on my best pale blue shirred silk hat and my blue organdie dress and my high-heeled slippers. Johnny whistled when he saw me, but he never said a word; there are times when Johnny is a duck.

We slipped away when Hannah Jane was feeding the hens.

"I'll buy the tickets," explained Johnny. "I've got enough money left out of my last month's allowance because I didn't waste it all on candy as you did. You'll have to pay me back when you get your next month's jink, remember. I'll ask the conductor to tell us when we get to Marsden. Uncle Fred's house isn't far from the station, and we'll be sure to know it by all the cherry trees round it."

It sounded easy, and it *was* easy. We had a jolly ride, and finally the conductor came along and said, "Here's your jumping-off place, kiddies."

Johnny didn't like being called a kiddy, but I saw the conductor's eye resting admiringly on my blue silk hat and I forgave him.

Marsden was a pretty little village, and away up the road we saw Uncle Fred's place, for it was fairly smothered in cherry trees all white with lovely bloom. We started for it as fast as we could go, for we knew we had no time to lose. It is perfectly dreadful trying to hurry when you have on high-heeled shoes, but I said nothing and just tore along, for I knew Johnny would have no sympathy for me. We finally reached the house and turned in at the open gate of the lawn. I thought everything looked very peaceful and quiet for a wedding to be under way and I had a sickening idea that it was too late and it was all over.

"Nonsense!" said Johnny, cross as a bear, because he was really afraid of it too. "I suppose everybody is inside the house. No, there are two people over there by that bench. Let us go and ask them if this is the right place, because if it isn't we have no time to lose."

We ran across the lawn to the two people. One of them was a young lady, the very prettiest young lady I had ever seen. She was tall and stately, just like the heroine in a book, and she had lovely curly brown hair and big blue eyes and the most dazzling complexion. But she looked very cross and disdainful and I knew the minute I saw her that she had been quarrelling with the young man. He was standing in front of her and he was as handsome as a prince. But he looked angry too. Altogether, you never saw a crosser-looking couple. Just as we came up we heard the young lady say, "What you ask is ridiculous and impossible, Ted. I *can't* get married at two days' notice and I don't mean to be."

And he said, "Very well, Una, I am sorry you think so. You would not think so if you really cared anything for me. It is just as well I have found out you don't. I am going away in two days' time and I shall not return in a hurry, Una."

"I do not care if you never return," she said.

That was a fib and well I knew it. But the young man didn't—men are so stupid at times. He swung around on one foot without replying and he would have gone in another second if he had not nearly fallen over Johnny and me.

"Please, sir," said Johnny respectfully, but hurriedly. "We're looking for Mr. Frederick Murray's place. Is this it?"

"No," said the young man a little gruffly. "This is Mrs. Franklin's place. Frederick Murray lives at Marsden, ten miles away."

My heart gave a jump and then stopped beating. I know it did, although Johnny says it is impossible.

"Isn't this Marsden?" cried Johnny chokily.

"No, this is Harrowsdeane," said the young man, a little more mildly.

I couldn't help it. I was tired and warm and so disappointed. I sat right down on the rustic seat behind me and burst into tears, as the story-books say.

"Oh, don't cry, dearie," said the young lady in a very different voice from the one she had used before. She sat down beside me and put her arms around me. "We'll take you over to Marsden if you've got off at the wrong station."

"But it will be too late," I sobbed wildly. "The wedding is to be at twelve—and it's nearly that now—and oh, Johnny, I do think you might try to comfort me!"

For Johnny had stuck his hands in his pockets and turned his back squarely on me. I thought it so unkind of him. I didn't know then that it was because he was afraid he was going to cry right there before everybody, and I felt deserted by all the world.

"Tell me all about it," said the young lady.

So I told her as well as I could all about the wedding and how wild we were to see it and why we were running away to it.

"And now it's all no use," I wailed. "And we'll be punished when they find out just the same. I wouldn't mind being punished if we hadn't missed the wedding.

We've never seen a wedding—and Pamelia was to wear a white silk dress—and have flower girls—and oh, my heart is just broken. I shall never get over this—never—if I live to be as old as Methuselah."

"What can we do for them?" said the young lady, looking up at the young man and smiling a little. She seemed to have forgotten that they had just quarrelled. "I can't bear to see children disappointed. I remember my own childhood too well."

"I really don't know what we can do," said the young man, smiling back, "unless we get married right here and now for their sakes. If it is a wedding they want to see and nothing else will do them, that is the only idea I can suggest."

"Nonsense!" said the young lady. But she said it as if she would rather like to be persuaded it wasn't nonsense.

I looked up at her. "Oh, if you have any notion of being married I wish you would right off," I said eagerly. "Any wedding would do just as well as Pamelia's. Please do."

The young lady laughed.

"One might just as well be married at two hours' notice as two days'," she said.

"Una," said the young man, bending towards her, "will you marry me here and now? Don't send me away alone to the other side of the world, Una."

"What on earth would Auntie say?" said Una helplessly.

"Mrs. Franklin wouldn't object if you told her you were going to be married in a balloon."

"I don't see how we could arrange—oh, Ted, it's absurd."

"'Tisn't. It's highly sensible. I'll go straight to town on my wheel for the licence and ring and I'll be back in an hour. You can be ready by that time."

For a moment Una hesitated. Then she said suddenly to me, "What is your name, dearie?"

"Sue Murray," I said, "and this is my brother, Johnny. We're twins. We've been twins for ten years."

"Well, Sue, I'm going to let you decide for me. This gentleman here, whose name is Theodore Prentice, has to start for Japan in two days and will have to remain there for four years. He received his orders only yesterday. He wants me to marry him and go with him. Now, I shall leave it to you to consent or refuse for me. Shall I marry him or shall I not?"

"Marry him, of course," said I promptly. Johnny says she knew I would say that when she left it to me.

"Very well," said Una calmly. "Ted, you may go for the necessaries. Sue, you must be my bridesmaid and Johnny shall be best man. Come, we'll go into the house and break the news to Auntie."

I never felt so interested and excited in my life. It seemed too good to be true. Una and I went into the house and there we found the sweetest, pinkest, plumpest old lady asleep in an easy-chair. Una wakened her and said, "Auntie, I'm going to be married to Mr. Prentice in an hour's time."

That was a most wonderful old lady! All she said was, "Dear me!" You'd have thought Una had simply told her she was going out for a walk.

"Ted has gone for licence and ring and minister," Una went on. "We shall be married out under the cherry trees and I'll wear my new white organdie. We shall leave for Japan in two days. These children are Sue and Johnny Murray who have come out to see a wedding—*any* wedding. Ted and I are getting married just to please them."

"Dear me!" said the old lady again. "This is rather sudden. Still—if you must. Well, I'll go and see what there is in the house to eat."

She toddled away, smiling, and Una turned to me. She was laughing, but there were tears in her eyes.

"You blessed accidents!" she said, with a little tremble in her voice. "If you hadn't happened just then Ted would have gone away in a rage and I might never have seen him again. Come now, Sue, and help me dress."

Johnny stayed in the hall and I went upstairs with Una. We had such an exciting time getting her dressed. She had the sweetest white organdie you ever saw, all frills and laces. I'm sure Pamelia's silk couldn't have been half so pretty. But she had no veil, and I felt rather disappointed about that. Then there was a knock at the door and Mrs. Franklin came in, with her arms full of something all fine and misty like a lacy cobweb.

"I've brought you my wedding veil, dearie," she said. "I wore it forty years ago. And God bless you, dearie. I can't stop a minute. The boy is killing the chickens and Bridget is getting ready to broil them. Mrs. Jenner's son across the road has just gone down to the bakery for a wedding cake."

With that she toddled off again. She was certainly a wonderful old lady. I just thought of Mother in her place. Well, Mother would simply have gone wild entirely.

When Una was dressed she looked as beautiful as a dream. The boy had finished killing the chickens, and Mrs. Franklin had sent him up with a basket of roses for us, and we had each the loveliest bouquet. Before long Ted came back with the minister, and the next thing we knew we were all standing out on the lawn under the cherry trees and Una and Ted were being married.

I was too happy to speak. I had never thought of being a bridesmaid in my wildest dreams and here I was one. How thankful I was that I had put on my blue organdie and my shirred hat! I wasn't a bit nervous and I don't believe Una was either. Mrs. Franklin stood at one side with a smudge of flour on her nose, and she had forgotten to take off her apron. Bridget and the boy watched us from the kitchen garden. It was all like a beautiful, bewildering dream. But the ceremony was horribly solemn. I am sure I shall never have the courage to go through with anything of the sort, but Johnny says I will change my mind when I grow up.

When it was all over I nudged Johnny and said "Ode" in a fierce whisper. Johnny immediately stepped out before Una and recited it. Pamelia's name was mentioned three times and of course he should have put Una in place of it, but he forgot. You can't remember everything.

"You dear funny darlings!" said Una, kissing us both. Johnny didn't like *that*, but he said he didn't mind it in a bride.

Then we had dinner, and I thought Mrs. Franklin more wonderful than ever. I couldn't have believed any woman could have got up such a spread at two hours' notice. Of course, some credit must be given to Bridget and the boy. Johnny and I were hungry enough by this time and we enjoyed that repast to the full.

We went home on the evening train. Ted and Una came to the station with us, and Una said she would write me when she got to Japan, and Ted said he would be obliged to us forever and ever.

When we got home we found Hannah Jane and Father and Mother—who had arrived there an hour before us—simply distracted. They were so glad to see us safe and sound that they didn't even scold us, and when Father heard our story he laughed until the tears came into his eyes.

"Some are born to luck, some achieve luck, and some have luck thrust upon them," he said.

LUCY MAUD MONTGOMERY SHORT STORIES, 1909 TO 1922

A Golden Wedding

The land dropped abruptly down from the gate, and a thick, shrubby growth of young apple orchard almost hid the little weather-grey house from the road. This was why the young man who opened the sagging gate could not see that it was boarded up, and did not cease his cheerful whistling until he had pressed through the crowding trees and found himself almost on the sunken stone doorstep over which in olden days honeysuckle had been wont to arch. Now only a few straggling, uncared-for vines clung forlornly to the shingles, and the windows were, as has been said, all boarded up.

The whistle died on the young man's lips and an expression of blank astonishment and dismay settled down on his face—a good, kindly, honest face it was, although perhaps it did not betoken any pronounced mental gifts on the part of its owner.

"What can have happened?" he said to himself. "Uncle Tom and Aunt Sally can't be dead—I'd have seen their deaths in the paper if they was. And I'd a-thought if they'd moved away it'd been printed too. They can't have been gone long—that flower-bed must have been made up last spring. Well, this is a kind of setback for a fellow. Here I've been tramping all the way from the station, a-thinking how good it would be to see Aunt Sally's sweet old face again, and hear Uncle Tom's laugh, and all I find is a boarded-up house going to seed. S'pose I might as well toddle over to Stetsons' and inquire if they haven't disappeared, too."

He went through the old firs back of the lot and across the field to a rather shabby house beyond. A cheery-faced woman answered his knock and looked at him in a puzzled fashion. "Have you forgot me, Mrs. Stetson? Don't you remember Lovell Stevens and how you used to give him plum tarts when he'd bring your turkeys home?"

Mrs. Stetson caught both his hands in a hearty clasp.

"I guess I haven't forgotten!" she declared. "Well, well, and you're Lovell! I think I ought to know your face, though you've changed a lot. Fifteen years have made a big difference in you. Come right in. Pa, this is Lovell—you mind Lovell, the boy Aunt Sally and Uncle Tom had for years?"

"Reckon I do," drawled Jonah Stetson with a friendly grin. "Ain't likely to forget some of the capers you used to be cutting up. You've filled out considerable.

Where have you been for the last ten years? Aunt Sally fretted a lot over you, thinking you was dead or gone to the bad."

Lovell's face clouded.

"I know I ought to have written," he said repentantly, "but you know I'm a terrible poor scholar, and I'd do most anything than try to write a letter. But where's Uncle Tom and Aunt Sally gone? Surely they ain't dead?"

"No," said Jonah Stetson slowly, "no—but I guess they'd rather be. They're in the poorhouse."

"The poorhouse! Aunt Sally in the poorhouse!" exclaimed Lovell.

"Yes, and it's a burning shame," declared Mrs. Stetson. "Aunt Sally's just breaking her heart from the disgrace of it. But it didn't seem as if it could be helped. Uncle Tom got so crippled with rheumatism he couldn't work and Aunt Sally was too frail to do anything. They hadn't any relations and there was a mortgage on the house."

"There wasn't any when I went away."

"No; they had to borrow money six years ago when Uncle Tom had his first spell of rheumatic fever. This spring it was clear that there was nothing for them but the poorhouse. They went three months ago and terrible hard they took it, especially Aunt Sally, I felt awful about it myself. Jonah and I would have took them if we could, but we just couldn't—we've nothing but Jonah's wages and we have eight children and not a bit of spare room. I go over to see Aunt Sally as often as I can and take her some little thing, but I dunno's she wouldn't rather not see anybody than see them in the poorhouse."

Lovell weighed his hat in his hands and frowned over it reflectively.

"Who owns the house now?"

"Peter Townley. He held the mortgage. And all the old furniture was sold too, and that most killed Aunt Sally. But do you know what she's fretting over most of all? She and Uncle Tom will have been married fifty years in a fortnight's time and Aunt Sally thinks it's awful to have to spend their golden wedding anniversary in the poorhouse. She talks about it all the time. You're not going, Lovell"—for Lovell had risen—"you must stop with us, since your old home is closed up. We'll scare you up a shakedown to sleep on and you're welcome as welcome. I haven't forgot the time you caught Mary Ellen just as she was tumbling into the well."

"Thank you, I'll stay to tea," said Lovell, sitting down again, "but I guess I'll make my headquarters up at the station hotel as long as I stay round here. It's kind of more central."

"Got on pretty well out west, hey?" queried Jonah.

"Pretty well for a fellow who had nothing but his two hands to depend on when he went out," said Lovell cautiously. "I've only been a labouring man, of course, but I've saved up enough to start a little store when I go back. That's why I came east for a trip now—before I'd be tied down to business. I was hankering to see Aunt Sally and Uncle Tom once more. I'll never forget how kind and good they was to me. There I was, when Dad died, a little sinner of eleven, just heading for destruction. They give me a home and all the schooling I ever had and all the love I ever got. It was Aunt Sally's teachings made as much a man of me as I am. I never forgot 'em and I've tried to live up to 'em."

After tea Lovell said he thought he'd stroll up the road and pay Peter Townley a call. Jonah Stetson and his wife looked at each other when he had gone.

"Got something in his eye," nodded Jonah. "Him and Peter weren't never much of friends."

"Maybe Aunt Sally's bread is coming back to her after all," said his wife. "People used to be hard on Lovell. But I always liked him and I'm real glad he's turned out so well."

Lovell came back to the Stetsons' the next evening. In the interval he had seen Aunt Sally and Uncle Tom. The meeting had been both glad and sad. Lovell had also seen other people.

"I've bought Uncle Tom's old house from Peter Townley," he said quietly, "and I want you folks to help me out with my plans. Uncle Tom and Aunt Sally ain't going to spend their golden wedding in the poorhouse—no, sir. They'll spend it in their own home with their old friends about them. But they're not to know anything about it till the very night. Do you s'pose any of the old furniture could be got back?"

"I believe every stick of it could," said Mrs. Stetson excitedly. "Most of it was bought by folks living handy and I don't believe one of them would refuse to sell it back. Uncle Tom's old chair is here to begin with—Aunt Sally give me that herself. She said she couldn't bear to have it sold. Mrs. Isaac Appleby at the station bought the set of pink-sprigged china and James Parker bought the grandfather's clock and the whatnot is at the Stanton Grays'."

For the next fortnight Lovell and Mrs. Stetson did so much travelling round together that Jonah said genially he might as well be a bachelor as far as meals and buttons went. They visited every house where a bit of Aunt Sally's belongings could be found. Very successful they were too, and at the end of their jaunting the interior of the little house behind the apple trees looked very much as it had looked when Aunt Sally and Uncle Tom lived there.

Meanwhile, Mrs. Stetson had been revolving a design in her mind, and one afternoon she did some canvassing on her own account. The next time she saw Lovell she said:

"We ain't going to let you do it all. The women folks around here are going to furnish the refreshments for the golden wedding and the girls are going to decorate the house with golden rod."

The evening of the wedding anniversary came. Everybody in Blair was in the plot, including the matron of the poorhouse. That night Aunt Sally watched the sunset over the hills through bitter tears.

"I never thought I'd be celebrating my golden wedding in the poorhouse," she sobbed. Uncle Tom put his twisted hand on her shaking old shoulder, but before he could utter any words of comfort Lovell Stevens stood before them.

"Just get your bonnet on, Aunt Sally," he cried jovially, "and both of you come along with me. I've got a buggy here for you ... and you might as well say good-bye to this place, for you're not coming back to it any more."

"Lovell, oh, what do you mean?" said Aunt Sally tremulously.

"I'll explain what I mean as we drive along. Hurry up—the folks are waiting."

When they reached the little old house, it was all aglow with light. Aunt Sally gave a cry as she entered it. All her old household goods were back in their places. There were some new ones too, for Lovell had supplied all that was lacking. The house was full of their old friends and neighbours. Mrs. Stetson welcomed them home again.

"Oh, Tom," whispered Aunt Sally, tears of happiness streaming down her old face, "oh, Tom, isn't God good?"

They had a right royal celebration, and a supper such as the Blair housewives could produce. There were speeches and songs and tales. Lovell kept himself in the background and helped Mrs. Stetson cut cake in the pantry all the evening. But when the guests had gone, he went to Aunt Sally and Uncle Tom, who were sitting by the fire.

"Here's a little golden wedding present for you," he said awkwardly, putting a purse into Aunt Sally's hand. "I reckon there's enough there to keep you from ever having to go to the poorhouse again and if not, there'll be more where that comes from when it's done."

There were twenty-five bright twenty-dollar gold pieces in the purse.

"We can't take it, Lovell," protested Aunt Sally. "You can't afford it."

"Don't you worry about that," laughed Lovell. "Out west men don't think much of a little wad like that. I owe you far more than can be paid in cash, Aunt Sally. You must take it—I want to know there's a little home here for me and two kind hearts in it, no matter where I roam."

"God bless you, Lovell," said Uncle Tom huskily. "You don't know what you've done for Sally and me."

That night, when Lovell went to the little bedroom off the parlour—for Aunt Sally, rejoicing in the fact that she was again mistress of a spare room, would not hear of his going to the station hotel—he gazed at his reflection in the gilt-framed mirror soberly.

"You've just got enough left to pay your passage back west, old fellow," he said, "and then it's begin all over again just where you begun before. But Aunt Sally's face was worth it all—yes, sir. And you've got your two hands still and an old couple's prayers and blessings. Not such a bad capital, Lovell, not such a bad capital."

A Redeeming Sacrifice

The dance at Byron Lyall's was in full swing. Toff Leclerc, the best fiddler in three counties, was enthroned on the kitchen table and from the glossy brown violin, which his grandfather brought from Grand Pré, was conjuring music which made even stiff old Aunt Phemy want to show her steps. Around the kitchen sat a row of young men and women, and the open sitting-room doorway was crowded with the faces of non-dancing guests who wanted to watch the sets.

An eight-hand reel had just been danced and the girls, giddy from the much swinging of the final figure, had been led back to their seats. Mattie Lyall came out with a dipper of water and sprinkled the floor, from which a fine dust was rising. Toff's violin purred under his hands as he waited for the next set to form. The dancers were slow about it. There was not the rush for the floor that there had been earlier in the evening, for the supper table was now spread in the dining-room and most of the guests were hungry.

"Fill up dere, boys," shouted the fiddler impatiently. "Bring out your gals for de nex' set."

After a moment Paul King led out Joan Shelley from the shadowy corner where they had been sitting. They had already danced several sets together; Joan had not danced with anybody else that evening. As they stood together under the light from the lamp on the shelf above them, many curious and disapproving eyes watched them. Connor Mitchell, who had been standing in the open outer doorway with the moonlight behind him, turned abruptly on his heel and went out.

Paul King leaned his head against the wall and watched the watchers with a smiling, defiant face as they waited for the set to form. He was a handsome fellow, with the easy, winning ways that women love. His hair curled in bronze masses about his head; his dark eyes were long and drowsy and laughing; there was a swarthy bloom on his round cheeks; and his lips were as red and beguiling as a girl's. A bad egg was Paul King, with a bad past and a bad future. He was shiftless and drunken; ugly tales were told of him. Not a man in Lyall's house that night but grudged him the privilege of standing up with Joan Shelley.

Joan was a slight, blossom-like girl in white, looking much like the pale, sweet-scented house rose she wore in her dark hair. Her face was colourless and young, very pure and softly curved. She had wonderfully sweet, dark blue eyes, generally dropped down, with notably long black lashes. There were many showier girls in the groups around her, but none half so lovely. She made all the rosy-cheeked beauties seem coarse and over-blown.

She left in Paul's clasp the hand by which he had led her out on the floor. Now and then he shifted his gaze from the faces before him to hers. When he did, she always looked up and they exchanged glances as if they had been utterly alone. Three other couples gradually took the floor and the reel began. Joan drifted through the figures with the grace of a wind-blown leaf. Paul danced with rollicking abandon, seldom taking his eyes from Joan's face. When the last mad whirl was over, Joan's brother came up and told her in an angry tone to go into the next room and dance no more, since she would dance with only one man. Joan looked at Paul. That look meant that she would do as he, and none other, told her. Paul nodded easily—he did not want any fuss just then—and the girl went obediently into the room. As she turned from him, Paul coolly reached out his hand and took the rose from her hair; then, with a triumphant glance around the room, he went out.

The autumn night was very clear and chill, with a faint, moaning wind blowing up from the northwest over the sea that lay shimmering before the door. Out beyond the cove the boats were nodding and curtsying on the swell, and over the shore fields the great red star of the lighthouse flared out against the silvery sky. Paul, with a whistle, sauntered down the sandy lane, thinking of Joan. How mightily he loved her—he, Paul King, who had made a mock of so many women and had never loved before! Ah, and she loved him. She had never said so in words, but eyes and tones had said it—she, Joan Shelley, the pick and pride of the Harbour girls, whom so many men had wooed, winning their trouble for their pains. He had won her; she was his and his only, for the asking. His heart was seething with pride and triumph and passion as he strode down to the shore and flung himself on the cold sand in the black shadow of Michael Brown's beached boat.

Byron Lyall, a grizzled, elderly man, half farmer, half fisherman, and Maxwell Holmes, the Prospect schoolteacher, came up to the boat presently. Paul lay softly and listened to what they were saying. He was not troubled by any sense of dishonour. Honour was something Paul King could not lose since it was something he had never possessed. They were talking of him and Joan.

"What a shame that a girl like Joan Shelley should throw herself away on a man like that," Holmes said.

Byron Lyall removed the pipe he was smoking and spat reflectively at his shadow.

"Darned shame," he agreed. "That girl's life will be ruined if she marries him, plum' ruined, and marry him she will. He's bewitched her—darned if I can understand it. A dozen better men have wanted her—Connor Mitchell for one. And he's a honest, steady fellow with a good home to offer her. If King had left her alone, she'd have taken Connor. She used to like him well enough. But that's all over. She's infatuated with King, the worthless scamp. She'll marry him and be sorry for it to her last day. He's bad clear through and always will be. Why, look you,

Teacher, most men pull up a bit when they're courting a girl, no matter how wild they've been and will be again. Paul hasn't. It hasn't made any difference. He was dead drunk night afore last at the Harbour head, and he hasn't done a stroke of work for a month. And yet Joan Shelley'll take him."

"What are her people thinking of to let her go with him?" asked Holmes.

"She hasn't any but her brother. He's against Paul, of course, but it won't matter. The girl's fancy's caught and she'll go her own gait to ruin. Ruin, I tell ye. If she marries that handsome ne'er-do-well, she'll be a wretched woman all her days and none to pity her."

The two moved away then, and Paul lay motionless, face downward on the sand, his lips pressed against Joan's sweet, crushed rose. He felt no anger over Byron Lyall's unsparing condemnation. He knew it was true, every word of it. He *was* a worthless scamp and always would be. He knew that perfectly well. It was in his blood. None of his race had ever been respectable and he was worse than them all. He had no intention of trying to reform because he could not and because he did not even want to. He was not fit to touch Joan's hand. Yet he had meant to marry her!

But to spoil her life! Would it do that? Yes, it surely would. And if he were out of the way, taking his baleful charm out of her life, Connor Mitchell might and doubtless would win her yet and give her all he could not.

The man suddenly felt his eyes wet with tears. He had never shed a tear in his daredevil life before, but they came hot and stinging now. Something he had never known or thought of before entered into his passion and purified it. He loved Joan. Did he love her well enough to stand aside and let another take the sweetness and grace that was now his own? Did he love her well enough to save her from the poverty-stricken, shamed life she must lead with him? Did he love her better than himself?

"I ain't fit to think of her," he groaned. "I never did a decent thing in my life, as they say. But how can I give her up—God, how can I?"

He lay still a long time after that, until the moonlight crept around the boat and drove away the shadow. Then he got up and went slowly down to the water's edge with Joan's rose, all wet with his unaccustomed tears, in his hands. Slowly and reverently he plucked off the petals and scattered them on the ripples, where they drifted lightly off like fairy shallops on moonshine. When the last one had fluttered from his fingers, he went back to the house and hunted up Captain Alec Matheson, who was smoking his pipe in a corner of the verandah and watching the young folks dancing through the open door. The two men talked together for some time.

When the dance broke up and the guests straggled homeward, Paul sought Joan. Rob Shelley had his own girl to see home and relinquished the guardianship of his sister with a scowl. Paul strode out of the kitchen and down the steps at the side of Joan, smiling with his usual daredeviltry. He whistled noisily all the way up the lane.

"Great little dance," he said. "My last in Prospect for a spell, I guess."

"Why?" asked Joan wonderingly.

"Oh, I'm going to take a run down to South America in Matheson's schooner. Lord knows when I'll come back. This old place has got too deadly dull to suit me. I'm going to look for something livelier."

Joan's lips turned ashen under the fringes of her white fascinator. She trembled violently and put one of her small brown hands up to her throat. "You—you are not coming back?" she said faintly.

"Not likely. I'm pretty well tired of Prospect and I haven't got anything to hold me here. Things'll be livelier down south."

Joan said nothing more. They walked along the spruce-fringed roads where the moonbeams laughed down through the thick, softly swaying boughs. Paul whistled one rollicking tune after another. The girl bit her lips and clenched her hands. He cared nothing for her—he had been making a mock of her as of others. Hurt pride and wounded love fought each other in her soul. Pride conquered. She would not let him, or anyone, see that she cared. She would *not* care!

At her gate Paul held out his hand.

"Well, good-bye, Joan. I'm sailing tomorrow so I won't see you again—not for years likely. You will be some sober old married woman when I come back to Prospect, if I ever do."

"Good-bye," said Joan steadily. She gave him her cold hand and looked calmly into his face without quailing. She had loved him with all her heart, but now a fatal scorn of him was already mingling with her love. He was what they said he was, a scamp without principle or honour.

Paul whistled himself out of the Shelley lane and over the hill. Then he flung himself down under the spruces, crushed his face into the spicy frosted ferns, and had his black hour alone.

But when Captain Alec's schooner sailed out of the harbour the next day, Paul King was on board of her, the wildest and most hilarious of a wild and hilarious crew. Prospect people nodded their satisfaction.

"Good riddance," they said. "Paul King is black to the core. He never did a decent thing in his life."

A Soul That Was Not at Home

There was a very fine sunset on the night Paul and Miss Trevor first met, and she had lingered on the headland beyond Noel's Cove to delight in it. The west was splendid in daffodil and rose; away to the north there was a mackerel sky of little fiery golden clouds; and across the water straight from Miss Trevor's feet ran a sparkling path of light to the sun, whose rim had just touched the throbbing edge of the purple sea. Off to the left were softly swelling violet hills and beyond the sandshore, where little waves were crisping and silvering, there was a harbour where scores of slender masts were nodding against the gracious horizon.

Miss Trevor sighed with sheer happiness in all the wonderful, fleeting, elusive loveliness of sky and sea. Then she turned to look back at Noel's Cove, dim and shadowy in the gloom of the tall headlands, and she saw Paul.

It did not occur to her that he could be a shore boy—she knew the shore type too well. She thought his coming mysterious, for she was sure he had not come along the sand, and the tide was too high for him to have come past the other headland. Yet there he was, sitting on a red sandstone boulder, with his bare, bronzed, shapely little legs crossed in front of him and his hands clasped around his knee. He was not looking at Miss Trevor but at the sunset—or, rather, it seemed as if he were looking through the sunset to still grander and more radiant splendours beyond, of which the things seen were only the pale reflections, not worthy of attention from those who had the gift of further sight.

Miss Trevor looked him over carefully with eyes that had seen a good many people in many parts of the world for more years than she found it altogether pleasant to acknowledge, and she concluded that he was quite the handsomest lad she had ever seen. He had a lithe, supple body, with sloping shoulders and a brown, satin throat. His hair was thick and wavy, of a fine reddish chestnut; his brows were very straight and much darker than his hair; and his eyes were large and grey and meditative. The modelling of chin and jaw was perfect and his mouth was delicious, being full without pouting, the crimson lips just softly touching, and curving into finely finished little corners that narrowly escaped being dimpled.

His attire was a blue cotton shirt and a pair of scanty corduroy knickerbockers, but he wore it with such an unconscious air of purple and fine linen that Miss Trevor was tricked into believing him much better dressed than he really was.

Presently he smiled dreamily, and the smile completed her subjugation. It was not merely an affair of lip and eye, as are most smiles; it seemed an illumination of his whole body, as if some lamp had suddenly burst into flame inside of him, irradiating him from his chestnut crown to the tips of his unspoiled toes. Best of all, it was involuntary, born of no external effort or motive, but simply the outflashing of some wild, delicious thought that was as untrammelled and freakish as the wind of the sea.

Miss Trevor made up her mind that she must find out all about him, and she stepped out from the shadows of the rocks into the vivid, eerie light that was glowing all along the shore. The boy turned his head and looked at her, first with surprise, then with inquiry, then with admiration. Miss Trevor, in a white dress with a lace scarf on her dark, stately head, was well worth admiring. She smiled at him and Paul smiled back. It was not quite up to his first smile, having more of the effect of being put on from the outside, but at least it conveyed the subtly flattering impression that it had been put on solely for her, and they were as good friends from that moment as if they had known each other for a hundred years. Miss Trevor had enough discrimination to realize this and know that she need not waste time in becoming acquainted.

"I want to know your name and where you live and what you were looking at beyond the sunset," she said.

"My name is Paul Hubert. I live over there. And I can't tell just what I saw in the sunset, but when I go home I'm going to write it all in my foolscap book."

In her surprise over the second clause of his answer, Miss Trevor forgot, at first, to appreciate the last. "Over there," according to his gesture, was up at the head of Noel's Cove, where there was a little grey house perched on the rocks and looking like a large seashell cast up by the tide. The house had a stovepipe coming out of its roof in lieu of a chimney, and two of its window panes were replaced by shingles. Could this boy, who looked as young princes should—and seldom do—live there? Then he was a shore boy after all.

"Who lives there with you?" she asked. "You see"—plaintively—"I must ask questions about you. I know we like each other, and that is all that really matters. But there are some tiresome items which it would be convenient to know. For example, have you a father—a mother? Are there any more of you? How long have you been yourself?"

Paul did not reply immediately. He clasped his hands behind him and looked at her affectionately.

"I like the way you talk," he said. "I never knew anybody did talk like that except folks in books and my rock people."

"Your rock people?"

"I'm eleven years old. I haven't any father or mother, they're dead. I live over there with Stephen Kane. Stephen is splendid. He plays the violin and takes me fishing in his boat. When I get bigger he's going shares with me. I love him, and I love my rock people too."

"What do you mean by your rock people?" asked Miss Trevor, enjoying herself hugely. This was the only child she had ever met who talked as she wanted children to talk and who understood her remarks without having to have them translated.

"Nora is one of them," said Paul, "the best one of them. I love her better than all the others because she came first. She lives around that point and she has black eyes and black hair and she knows all about the mermaids and water kelpies. You ought to hear the stories she can tell. Then there are the Twin Sailors. They don't live anywhere—they sail all the time, but they often come ashore to talk to me. They are a pair of jolly tars and they have seen everything in the world—and more than what's in the world, if you only knew it. Do you know what happened to the Youngest Twin Sailor once? He was sailing and he sailed right into a moonglade. A moonglade is the track the full moon makes on the water when it is rising from the sea, you know. Well, the Youngest Twin Sailor sailed along the moonglade till he came right up to the moon, and there was a little golden door in the moon and he opened it and sailed right through. He had some wonderful adventures inside the moon—I've got them all written down in my foolscap book. Then there is the Golden Lady of the Cave. One day I found a big cave down the shore and I went in and in and in—and after a while I found the Golden Lady. She has golden hair right down to her feet, and her dress is all glittering and glistening like gold that is alive. And she has a golden harp and she plays all day long on it—you might hear the music if you'd listen carefully, but prob'bly you'd think it was only the wind among the rocks. I've never told Nora about the Golden Lady, because I think it would hurt her feelings. It even hurts her feelings when I talk too long with the Twin Sailors. And I hate to hurt Nora's feelings, because I do love her best of all my rock people."

"Paul! How much of this is true?" gasped Miss Trevor.

"Why, none of it!" said Paul, opening his eyes widely and reproachfully. "I thought you would know that. If I'd s'posed you wouldn't I'd have warned you there wasn't any of it true. I thought you were one of the kind that would know."

"I am. Oh, I am!" said Miss Trevor eagerly. "I really would have known if I had stopped to think. Well, it's getting late now. I must go back, although I don't want to. But I'm coming to see you again. Will you be here tomorrow afternoon?"

Paul nodded.

"Yes. I promised to meet the Youngest Twin Sailor down at the striped rocks tomorrow afternoon, but the day after will do just as well. That is the beauty of the rock people, you know. You can always depend on them to be there just when you want them. The Youngest Twin Sailor won't mind—he's very good-tempered. If it was the Oldest Twin I dare say he'd be cross. I have my suspicions about that Oldest Twin sometimes. I b'lieve he'd be a pirate if he dared. You don't know how fierce he can look at times. There's really something very mysterious about him."

On her way back to the hotel Miss Trevor remembered the foolscap book.

"I must get him to show it to me," she mused, smiling. "Why, the boy is a born genius—and to think he should be a shore boy! I can't understand it. And here I am loving him already. Well, a woman has to love something—and you don't have to know people for years before you can love them."

Paul was waiting on the Noel's Cove rocks for Miss Trevor the next afternoon. He was not alone; a tall man, with a lined, strong-featured face and a grey beard, was with him. The man was clad in a rough suit and looked what he was, a 'longshore fisherman. But he had deep-set, kindly eyes, and Miss Trevor liked his face. He moved off to one side when she came and stood there for a little, apparently gazing out to sea, while Paul and Miss Trevor talked. Then he walked away up the cove and disappeared in his little grey house.

"Stephen came down to see if you were a suitable person for me to talk to," said Paul gravely.

"I hope he thinks I am," said Miss Trevor, amused.

"Oh, he does! He wouldn't have gone away and left us alone if he didn't. Stephen is very particular who he lets me 'sociate with. Why, even the rock people now—I had to promise I'd never let the Twin Sailors swear before he'd allow me to be friends with them. Sometimes I know by the look of the Oldest Twin that he's just dying to swear, but I never let him, because I promised Stephen. I'd do anything for Stephen. He's awful good to me. Stephen's bringing me up, you know, and he's bound to do it well. We're just perfectly happy here, only I wish I'd more books to read. We go fishing, and when we come home at night I help Stephen clean the fish and then we sit outside the door and he plays the violin for me. We sit there for hours sometimes. We never talk much—Stephen isn't much of a hand for talking—but we just sit and think. There's not many men like Stephen, I can tell you."

Miss Trevor did not get a glimpse of the foolscap book that day, nor for many days after. Paul blushed all over his beautiful face whenever she mentioned it.

"Oh, I couldn't show you that," he said uncomfortably. "Why, I've never even showed it to Stephen—or Nora. Let me tell you something else instead, something that happened to me once long ago. You'll find it more interesting than the foolscap book, only you must remember it isn't true! You won't forget that, will you?"

"I'll try to remember," Miss Trevor agreed.

"Well, I was sitting here one evening just like I was last night, and the sun was setting. And an enchanted boat came sailing over the sea and I got into her. The boat was all pearly like the inside of the mussel shells, and her sail was like moonshine. Well, I sailed right across to the sunset. Think of that—I've been in the sunset! And what do you suppose it is? The sunset is a land all flowers, like a great garden, and the clouds are beds of flowers. We sailed into a great big harbour, a thousand times bigger than the harbour over there at your hotel, and I stepped out of the boat on a 'normous meadow all roses. I stayed there for ever so long. It seemed almost a year, but the Youngest Twin Sailor says I was only away a few hours or so. You see, in Sunset Land the time is ever so much longer than it is here. But I was glad to come back too. I'm always glad to come back to the cove and Stephen. Now, you know this never really happened."

Miss Trevor would not give up the foolscap book so easily, but for a long time Paul refused to show it to her. She came to the cove every day, and every day Paul seemed more delightful to her. He was so quaint, so clever, so spontaneous. Yet there was nothing premature or unnatural about him. He was wholly boy, fond of fun and frolic, not too good for little spurts of quick temper now and again, though, as he was careful to explain to Miss Trevor, he never showed them to a lady.

"I get real mad with the Twin Sailors sometimes, and even with Stephen, for all he's so good to me. But I couldn't be mad with you or Nora or the Golden Lady. It would never do."

Every day he had some new story to tell of a wonderful adventure on rock or sea, always taking the precaution of assuring her beforehand that it wasn't true. The boy's fancy was like a prism, separating every ray that fell upon it into rainbows. He was passionately fond of the shore and water. The only world for him beyond Noel's Cove was the world of his imagination. He had no companions except Stephen and the "rock people."

"And now you," he told Miss Trevor. "I love you too, but I know you'll be going away before long, so I don't let myself love you as much—quite—as Stephen and the rock people."

"But you could, couldn't you?" pleaded Miss Trevor. "If you and I were to go on being together every day, you could love me just as well as you love them, couldn't you?"

Paul considered in a charming way he had.

"Of course I could love you better than the Twin Sailors and the Golden Lady," he announced finally. "And I think perhaps I could love you as much as I love Stephen. But not as much as Nora—oh, no, I wouldn't love you quite as much as Nora. She was first, you see; she's always been there. I feel sure I couldn't ever love anybody as much as Nora."

One day when Stephen was out to the mackerel grounds, Paul took Miss Trevor into the little grey house and showed her his treasures. They climbed the ladder in one corner to the loft where Paul slept. The window of it, small and square-paned, looked seaward, and the moan of the sea and the pipe of the wind sounded there night and day. Paul had many rare shells and seaweeds, curious flotsam and jetsam of shore storms, and he had a small shelf full of books.

"They're splendid," he said enthusiastically. "Stephen brought me them all. Every time Stephen goes to town to ship his mackerel he brings me home a new book."

"Were you ever in town yourself?" asked Miss Trevor.

"Oh, yes, twice. Stephen took me. It was a wonderful place. I tell you, when I next met the Twin Sailors it was me did the talking then. I had to tell them about all I saw and all that had happened. And Nora was ever so interested too. The Golden Lady wasn't, though—she didn't hardly listen. Golden people are like that."

"Would you like," said Miss Trevor, watching him closely, "to live always in a town and have all the books you wanted and play with real girls and boys—and visit those strange lands your twin sailors tell you of?"

Paul looked startled.

"I—don't—know," he said doubtfully. "I don't think I'd like it very well if Stephen and Nora weren't there too."

But the new thought remained in his mind. It came back to him at intervals, seeming less new and startling every time.

"And why not?" Miss Trevor asked herself. "The boy should have a chance. I shall never have a son of my own—he shall be to me in the place of one."

The day came when Paul at last showed her the foolscap book. He brought it to her as she sat on the rocks of the headland.

"I'm going to run around and talk to Nora while you read it," he said. "I'm afraid I've been neglecting her lately—and I think she feels it."

Miss Trevor took the foolscap book. It was made of several sheets of paper sewed together and encased in an oilcloth cover. It was nearly filled with writing in a round childish hand and it was very neat, although the orthography was rather wild and the punctuation capricious. Miss Trevor read it through in no very long time. It was a curious medley of quaint thoughts and fancies. Conversations with the Twin Sailors filled many of the pages; accounts of Paul's "adventures" occupied others. Sometimes it seemed impossible that a child of eleven should have written them, then would come an expression so boyish and naive that Miss Trevor laughed delightedly over it. When she finished the book and closed it she found Stephen Kane at her elbow. He removed his pipe and nodded at the foolscap book.

"What do you think of it?" he said.

"I think it is wonderful. Paul is a very clever child."

"I've often thought so," said Stephen laconically. He thrust his hands into his pockets and gazed moodily out to sea. Miss Trevor had never before had an opportunity to talk to him in Paul's absence and she determined to make the most of it.

"I want to know something about Paul," she said, "all about him. Is he any relation to you?"

"No. I expected to marry his mother once, though," said Stephen unemotionally. His hand in his pocket was clutching his pipe fiercely, but Miss Trevor could not know that. "She was a shore girl and very pretty. Well, she fell in love with a young fellow that came teaching up t' the harbour school and he with her. They got married and she went away with him. He was a good enough sort of chap. I know that now, though once I wasn't disposed to think much good of him. But 'twas a mistake all the same; Rachel couldn't live away from the shore. She fretted and pined and broke her heart for it away there in his world. Finally her husband died and she came back—but it was too late for her. She only lived a month—and there was Paul, a baby of two. I took him. There was nobody else. Rachel had no relatives nor her husband either. I've done what I could for him—not that it's been much, perhaps."

"I am sure you have done a great deal for him," said Miss Trevor rather patronizingly. "But I think he should have more than you can give him now. He should be sent to school."

Stephen nodded.

"Maybe. He never went to school. The harbour school was too far away. I taught him to read and write and bought him all the books I could afford. But I can't do any more for him."

"But I can," said Miss Trevor, "and I want to. Will you give Paul to me, Mr. Kane? I love him dearly and he shall have every advantage. I'm rich—I can do a great deal for him."

Stephen continued to gaze out to sea with an expressionless face. Finally he said: "I've been expecting to hear you say something of the sort. I don't know. If you took Paul away, he'd grow to be a cleverer man and a richer man maybe, but would he be any better—or happier? He's his mother's son—he loves the sea and its ways. There's nothing of his father in him except his hankering after books. But I won't choose for him—he can go if he likes—he can go if he likes."

In the end Paul "liked," since Stephen refused to influence him by so much as a word. Paul thought Stephen didn't seem to care much whether he went or stayed, and he was dazzled by Miss Trevor's charm and the lure of books and knowledge she held out to him.

"I'll go, I guess," he said, with a long sigh.

Miss Trevor clasped him close to her and kissed him maternally. Paul kissed her cheek shyly in return. He thought it very wonderful that he was to live with her always. He felt happy and excited—so happy and excited that the parting when it came slipped over him lightly. Miss Trevor even thought he took it too easily and had a vague wish that he had shown more sorrow. Stephen said farewell to the boy he loved better than life with no visible emotion.

"Good-bye, Paul. Be a good boy and learn all you can." He hesitated a moment and then said slowly, "If you don't like it, come back."

"Did you bid good-bye to your rock people?" Miss Trevor asked him with a smile as they drove away.

"No. I—couldn't—I—I—didn't even tell them I was going away. Nora would break her heart. I'd rather not talk of them anymore, if you please. Maybe I won't want them when I've plenty of books and lots of other boys and girls—real ones—to play with."

They drove the ten miles to the town where they were to take the train the next day. Paul enjoyed the drive and the sights of the busy streets at its end. He was all excitement and animation. After they had had tea at the house of the friend where Miss Trevor meant to spend the night, they went for a walk in the park. Paul was tired and very quiet when they came back. He was put away to sleep in a bedroom whose splendours frightened him, and left alone.

At first Paul lay very still on his luxurious perfumed pillows. It was the first night he had ever spent away from the little seaward-looking loft where he could touch the rafters with his hands. He thought of it now and a lump came into his throat and a strange, new, bitter longing came into his heart. He missed the sea plashing on the rocks below him—he could not sleep without that old lullaby. He turned his face into the pillow, and the longing and loneliness grew worse and hurt him until he moaned. Oh, he wanted to be back home! Surely he had not left it—he could never have meant to leave it. Out there the stars would be shining over the harbour. Stephen would be sitting at the door, all alone, with his violin. But he would not be playing it—all at once Paul knew he would not be playing it. He would be sitting there with his head bowed and the loneliness in his heart calling to the loneliness in Paul's heart over all the miles between them. Oh, he could never have really meant to leave Stephen.

And Nora? Nora would be down on the rocks waiting for him—for him, Paul, who would never come to her more. He could see her elfin little face peering around the point, watching for him wistfully.

Paul sat up in bed, choking with tears. Oh, what were books and strange countries?—what was even Miss Trevor, the friend of a month?—to the call of the sea and Stephen's kind, deep eyes and his dear rock people? He could not stay away from them—never—never.

He slipped out of bed very softly and dressed in the dark. Then he lighted the lamp timidly and opened the little brown chest Stephen had given him. It held his books and his treasures, but he took out only a pencil, a bit of paper and the foolscap book. With a hand shaking in his eagerness, he wrote:

dear miss Trever

> *Im going back home, dont be fritened about me because I know the way. Ive got to go. something is calling me. dont be cross. I love you, but I cant stay. Im leaving my foolscap book for you, you can keep it always but I must go back to Stephen and nora*

Paul

He put the note on the foolscap book and laid them on the table. Then he blew out the light, took his cap and went softly out. The house was very still. Holding his breath, he tiptoed downstairs and opened the front door. Before it ran the street which went, he knew, straight out to the country road that led home. Paul closed the door and stole down the steps, his heart beating painfully, but when he reached the sidewalk he broke into a frantic run under the limes. It was late and no one was out on that quiet street. He ran until his breath gave out, then walked miserably until he recovered it, and then ran again. He dared not stop running until he was out of that horrible town, which seemed like a prison closing around him, where the houses shut out the stars and the wind could only creep in a narrow space like a fettered, cringing thing, instead of sweeping grandly over great salt wastes of sea.

At last the houses grew few and scattered, and finally he left them behind. He drew a long breath; this was better—rather smothering yet, of course, with nothing but hills and fields and dark woods all about him, but at least his own sky was above him, looking just the same as it looked out home at Noel's Cove. He recognized the stars as friends; how often Stephen had pointed them out to him as they sat at night by the door of the little house.

He was not at all frightened now. He knew the way home and the kind night was before him. Every step was bringing him nearer to Stephen and Nora and the Twin Sailors. He whistled as he walked sturdily along.

The dawn was just breaking when he reached Noel's Cove. The eastern sky was all pale rose and silver, and the sea was mottled over with dear grey ripples. In the west over the harbour the sky was a very fine ethereal blue and the wind blew from there, salt and bracing. Paul was tired, but he ran lightly down the shelving rocks to the cove. Stephen was getting ready to launch his boat. When he saw Paul he started and a strange, vivid, exultant expression flashed across his face.

Paul felt a sudden chill—the upspringing fountain of his gladness was checked in mid-leap. He had known no doubt on the way home—all that long, weary walk he had known no doubt—but now?

"Stephen," he cried. "I've come back! I had to! Stephen, are you glad—are you glad?"

Stephen's face was as emotionless as ever. The burst of feeling which had frightened Paul by its unaccustomedness had passed like a fleeting outbreak of sunshine between dull clouds.

"I reckon I am," he said. "Yes, I reckon I am. I kind of—hoped—you would come back. You'd better go in and get some breakfast."

Paul's eyes were as radiant as the deepening dawn. He knew Stephen was glad and he knew there was nothing more to be said about it. They were back just where they were before Miss Trevor came—back in their perfect, unmarred, sufficient comradeship.

"I must just run around and see Nora first," said Paul.

Abel and His Great Adventure

"Come out of doors, master—come out of doors. I can't talk or think right with walls around me—never could. Let's go out to the garden." These were almost the first words I ever heard Abel Armstrong say. He was a member of the board of school trustees in Stillwater, and I had not met him before this late May evening, when I had gone down to confer with him upon some small matter of business. For I was "the new schoolmaster" in Stillwater, having taken the school for the summer term.

It was a rather lonely country district—a fact of which I was glad, for life had been going somewhat awry with me and my heart was sore and rebellious over many things that have nothing to do with this narration. Stillwater offered time and opportunity for healing and counsel. Yet, looking back, I doubt if I should have found either had it not been for Abel and his beloved garden.

Abel Armstrong (he was always called "Old Abel", though he was barely sixty) lived in a quaint, gray house close by the harbour shore. I heard a good deal about him before I saw him. He was called "queer", but Stillwater folks seemed to be very fond of him. He and his sister, Tamzine, lived together; she, so my garrulous landlady informed me, had not been sound of mind at times for many years; but she was all right now, only odd and quiet. Abel had gone to college for a year when he was young, but had given it up when Tamzine "went crazy". There was no one else to look after her. Abel had settled down to it with apparent content: at least he had never complained.

"Always took things easy, Abel did," said Mrs. Campbell. "Never seemed to worry over disappointments and trials as most folks do. Seems to me that as long as Abel Armstrong can stride up and down in that garden of his, reciting poetry and speeches, or talking to that yaller cat of his as if it was a human, he doesn't care much how the world wags on. He never had much git-up-and-git. His father was a hustler, but the family didn't take after him. They all favoured the mother's people—sorter shiftless and dreamy. 'Taint the way to git on in this world."

No, good and worthy Mrs. Campbell. It was not the way to get on in your world; but there are other worlds where getting on is estimated by different standards, and Abel Armstrong lived in one of these—a world far beyond the ken of the thrifty Stillwater farmers and fishers. Something of this I had sensed, even before I saw him; and that night in his garden, under a sky of smoky red, blossoming into stars above the harbour, I found a friend whose personality and philosophy were to calm and harmonize and enrich my whole existence. This sketch is my grateful tribute to one of the rarest and finest souls God ever clothed with clay.

He was a tall man, somewhat ungainly of figure and homely of face. But his large, deep eyes of velvety nut-brown were very beautiful and marvellously bright and clear for a man of his age. He wore a little pointed, well-cared-for beard, innocent of gray; but his hair was grizzled, and altogether he had the appearance of a man who had passed through many sorrows which had marked his body as well as his soul. Looking at him, I doubted Mrs. Campbell's conclusion that he had not "minded" giving up college. This man had given up much and felt it deeply; but he had outlived the pain and the blessing of sacrifice had come to him. His voice was very melodious and beautiful, and the brown hand he held out to me was peculiarly long and shapely and flexible.

We went out to the garden in the scented moist air of a maritime spring evening. Behind the garden was a cloudy pine wood; the house closed it in on the left, while in front and on the right a row of tall Lombardy poplars stood out in stately purple silhouette against the sunset sky.

"Always liked Lombardies," said Abel, waving a long arm at them. "They are the trees of princesses. When I was a boy they were fashionable. Anyone who had any pretensions to gentility had a row of Lombardies at the foot of his lawn or up his lane, or at any rate one on either side of his front door. They're out of fashion now. Folks complain they die at the top and get ragged-looking. So they do—so they do, if you don't risk your neck every spring climbing up a light ladder to trim them out as I do. My neck isn't worth much to anyone, which, I suppose, is why I've never broken it; and *my* Lombardies never look out-at-elbows. My mother was especially fond of them. She liked their dignity and their stand-offishness. *They* don't hobnob with every Tom, Dick and Harry. If it's pines for company, master, it's Lombardies for society."

We stepped from the front doorstone into the garden. There was another entrance—a sagging gate flanked by two branching white lilacs. From it a little dappled path led to a huge apple-tree in the centre, a great swelling cone of rosy blossom with a mossy circular seat around its trunk. But Abel's favourite seat, so he told me, was lower down the slope, under a little trellis overhung with the delicate emerald of young hop-vines. He led me to it and pointed proudly to the fine view of the harbour visible from it. The early sunset glow of rose and flame had faded out of the sky; the water was silvery and mirror-like; dim sails drifted along by the darkening shore. A bell was ringing in a small Catholic chapel across the harbour. Mellowly and dreamily sweet the chime floated through the dusk, blent with the moan of the sea. The great revolving light at the channel trembled and flashed against the opal sky, and far out, beyond the golden sand-dunes of the bar, was the crinkled gray ribbon of a passing steamer's smoke.

"There, isn't that view worth looking at?" said old Abel, with a loving, proprietary pride. "You don't have to pay anything for it, either. All that sea and sky free—'without money and without price'. Let's sit down here in the hop-vine arbour, master. There'll be a moonrise presently. I'm never tired of finding out what a moonrise sheen can be like over that sea. There's a surprise in it every time. Now, master, you're getting your mouth in the proper shape to talk business—but don't you do it. Nobody should talk business when he's expecting a moonrise. Not that I like talking business at any time."

"Unfortunately it has to be talked of sometimes, Mr. Armstrong," I said.

"Yes, it seems to be a necessary evil, master," he acknowledged. "But I know what business you've come upon, and we can settle it in five minutes after the moon's well up. I'll just agree to everything you and the other two trustees want. Lord knows why they ever put me on the school board. Maybe it's because I'm so ornamental. They wanted one good-looking man, I reckon."

His low chuckle, so full of mirth and so free from malice, was infectious. I laughed also, as I sat down in the hop-vine arbour.

"Now, you needn't talk if you don't want to," he said. "And I won't. We'll just sit here, sociable like, and if we think of anything worth while to say we'll say it. Otherwise, not. If you can sit in silence with a person for half an hour and feel comfortable, you and that person can be friends. If you can't, friends you'll never be, and you needn't waste time in trying."

Abel and I passed successfully the test of silence that evening in the hop-vine arbour. I was strangely content to sit and think—something I had not cared to do lately. A peace, long unknown to my stormy soul, seemed hovering near it. The garden was steeped in it; old Abel's personality radiated it. I looked about me and wondered whence came the charm of that tangled, unworldly spot.

"Nice and far from the market-place isn't it?" asked Abel suddenly, as if he had heard my unasked question. "No buying and selling and getting gain here. Nothing was ever sold out of *this* garden. Tamzine has her vegetable plot over yonder, but what we don't eat we give away. Geordie Marr down the harbour has a big garden like this and he sells heaps of flowers and fruit and vegetables to the hotel folks. He thinks I'm an awful fool because I won't do the same. Well, he gets money out of his garden and I get happiness out of mine. That's the difference. S'posing I could make more money—what then? I'd only be taking it from people that needed it more. There's enough for Tamzine and me. As for Geordie Marr, there isn't a more unhappy creature on God's earth—he's always stewing in a broth of trouble, poor man. O' course, he brews up most of it for himself, but I reckon that doesn't make it any easier to bear. Ever sit in a hop-vine arbour before, master?"

I was to grow used to Abel's abrupt change of subject. I answered that I never had.

"Great place for dreaming," said Abel complacently. "Being young, no doubt, you dream a-plenty."

I answered hotly and bitterly that I had done with dreams.

"No, you haven't," said Abel meditatively. "You may *think* you have. What then? First thing you know you'll be dreaming again—thank the Lord for it. I ain't going to ask you what's soured you on dreaming just now. After awhile you'll begin again, especially if you come to this garden as much as I hope you will. It's chockful of dreams—*any* kind of dreams. You take your choice. Now, *I* favour dreams of adventures, if you'll believe it. I'm sixty-one and I never do anything rasher than go out cod-fishing on a fine day, but I still lust after adventures. Then I dream I'm an awful fellow—blood-thirsty."

I burst out laughing. Perhaps laughter was somewhat rare in that old garden. Tamzine, who was weeding at the far end, lifted her head in a startled fashion and walked past us into the house. She did not look at us or speak to us. She was reputed to be abnormally shy. She was very stout and wore a dress of bright red-and-white striped material. Her face was round and blank, but her reddish hair was abundant and beautiful. A huge, orange-coloured cat was at her heels; as she passed us he bounded over to the arbour and sprang up on Abel's knee. He was a gorgeous brute, with vivid green eyes, and immense white double paws.

"Captain Kidd, Mr. Woodley." He introduced us as seriously as if the cat had been a human being. Neither Captain Kidd nor I responded very enthusiastically.

"You don't like cats, I reckon, master," said Abel, stroking the Captain's velvet back. "I don't blame you. I was never fond of them myself until I found the Captain. I saved his life and when you've saved a creature's life you're bound to love it. It's next thing to giving it life. There are some terrible thoughtless people in the world, master. Some of those city folks who have summer homes down the harbour are so thoughtless that they're cruel. It's the worst kind of cruelty, I think—the thoughtless kind. You can't cope with it. They keep cats there in the summer and feed them and pet them and doll them up with ribbons and collars; and then in the fall they go off and leave them to starve or freeze. It makes my blood boil, master."

"One day last winter I found a poor old mother cat dead on the shore, lying against the skin and bone bodies of her three little kittens. She had died trying to shelter them. She had her poor stiff claws around them. Master, I cried. Then I swore. Then I carried those poor little kittens home and fed 'hem up and found good homes for them. I know the woman who left the cat. When she comes back this summer I'm going to go down and tell her my opinion of her. It'll be rank meddling, but, lord, how I love meddling in a good cause."

"Was Captain Kidd one of the forsaken?" I asked.

"Yes. I found him one bitter cold day in winter caught in the branches of a tree by his darn-fool ribbon collar. He was almost starving. Lord, if you could have seen his eyes! He was nothing but a kitten, and he'd got his living somehow since he'd been left till he got hung up. When I loosed him he gave my hand a pitiful swipe with his little red tongue. He wasn't the prosperous free-booter you behold now. He was meek as Moses. That was nine years ago. His life has been long in the land for a cat. He's a good old pal, the Captain is."

"I should have expected you to have a dog," I said.

Abel shook his head.

"I had a dog once. I cared so much for him that when he died I couldn't bear the thought of ever getting another in his place. He was a *friend*—you understand? The Captain's only a pal. I'm fond of the Captain—all the fonder because of the spice of deviltry there is in all cats. But I *loved* my dog. There isn't any devil in a good dog. That's why they're more lovable than cats—but I'm darned if they're as interesting."

I laughed as I rose regretfully.

"Must you go, master? And we haven't talked any business after all. I reckon it's that stove matter you've come about. It's like those two fool trustees to start up a stove sputter in spring. It's a wonder they didn't leave it till dog-days and begin then."

"They merely wished me to ask you if you approved of putting in a new stove."

"Tell them to put in a new stove—any kind of a new stove—and be hanged to them," rejoined Abel. "As for you, master, you're welcome to this garden any time. If you're tired or lonely, or too ambitious or angry, come here and sit awhile, master. Do you think any man could keep mad if he sat and looked into the heart of a pansy for ten minutes? When you feel like talking, I'll talk, and when you feel like thinking, I'll let you. I'm a great hand to leave folks alone."

"I think I'll come often," I said, "perhaps too often."

"Not likely, master—not likely—not after we've watched a moonrise contentedly together. It's as good a test of compatibility as any I know. You're young and I'm old, but our souls are about the same age, I reckon, and we'll find lots to say to each other. Are you going straight home from here?"

"Yes."

"Then I'm going to bother you to stop for a moment at Mary Bascom's and give her a bouquet of my white lilacs. She loves 'em and I'm not going to wait till she's dead to send her flowers."

"She's very ill just now, isn't she?"

"She's got the Bascom consumption. That means she may die in a month, like her brother, or linger on for twenty years, like her father. But long or short, white lilac in spring is sweet, and I'm sending her a fresh bunch every day while it lasts. It's a rare night, master. I envy you your walk home in the moonlight along that shore."

"Better come part of the way with me," I suggested.

"No." Abel glanced at the house. "Tamzine never likes to be alone o' nights. So I take my moonlight walks in the garden. The moon's a great friend of mine, master. I've loved her ever since I can remember. When I was a little lad of eight I fell asleep in the garden one evening and wasn't missed. I woke up alone in the night and I was most scared to death, master. Lord, what shadows and queer noises there were! I darsn't move. I just sat there quaking, poor small mite. Then all at once I saw the moon looking down at me through the pine boughs, just like an old friend. I was comforted right off. Got up and walked to the house as brave as a lion, looking at her. Goodnight, master. Tell Mary the lilacs'll last another week yet."

From that night Abel and I were cronies. We walked and talked and kept silence and fished cod together. Stillwater people thought it very strange that I should prefer his society to that of the young fellows of my own age. Mrs. Campbell was quite worried over it, and opined that there had always been something queer about me. "Birds of a feather."

I loved that old garden by the harbour shore. Even Abel himself, I think, could hardly have felt a deeper affection for it. When its gate closed behind me it shut out the world and my corroding memories and discontents. In its peace my soul emptied itself of the bitterness which had been filling and spoiling it, and grew normal and healthy again, aided thereto by Abel's wise words. He never preached, but he radiated courage and endurance and a frank acceptance of the hard things of life, as well as a cordial welcome of its pleasant things. He was the sanest soul I ever met. He neither minimized ill nor exaggerated good, but he held that we should never be controlled by either. Pain should not depress us unduly, nor pleasure lure us into forgetfulness and sloth. All unknowingly he made me realize that I had been a bit of a coward and a shirker. I began to understand that my personal woes were not the most important things in the universe, even to myself. In short, Abel taught me to laugh again; and when a man can laugh wholesomely things are not going too badly with him.

That old garden was always such a cheery place. Even when the east wind sang in minor and the waves on the gray shore were sad, hints of sunshine seemed to be lurking all about it. Perhaps this was because there were so many yellow flowers in it. Tamzine liked yellow flowers. Captain Kidd, too, always paraded it in panoply of gold. He was so large and effulgent that one hardly missed the sun. Considering his presence I wondered that the garden was always so full of singing birds. But the Captain never meddled with them. Probably he understood that his master would not have tolerated it for a moment. So there was always a song or a chirp somewhere. Overhead flew the gulls and the cranes. The wind in the pines always made a glad salutation. Abel and I paced the walks, in high converse on matters beyond the ken of cat or king.

"I liked to ponder on all problems, though I can never solve them," Abel used to say. "My father held that we should never talk of things we couldn't understand. But, lord, master, if we didn't the subjects for conversation would be mighty few. I reckon the gods laugh many a time to hear us, but what matter? So long as we remember that we're only men, and don't take to fancying ourselves gods, really knowing good and evil, I reckon our discussions won't do us or anyone much harm. So we'll have another whack at the origin of evil this evening, master."

Tamzine forgot to be shy with me at last, and gave me a broad smile of welcome every time I came. But she rarely spoke to me. She spent all her spare time weeding the garden, which she loved as well as Abel did. She was addicted to bright colours and always wore wrappers of very gorgeous print. She worshipped Abel and his word was a law unto her.

"I am very thankful Tamzine is so well," said Abel one evening as we watched the sunset. The day had begun sombrely in gray cloud and mist, but it ended in a pomp of scarlet and gold. "There was a time when she wasn't, master—you've heard? But for years now she has been quite able to look after herself. And so, if I fare forth on the last great adventure some of these days Tamzine will not be left helpless."

"She is ten years older than you. It is likely she will go before you," I said.

Abel shook his head and stroked his smart beard. I always suspected that beard of being Abel's last surviving vanity. It was always so carefully groomed, while I had no evidence that he ever combed his grizzled mop of hair.

"No, Tamzine will outlive me. She's got the Armstrong heart. I have the Marwood heart—my mother was a Marwood. We don't live to be old, and we go quick and easy. I'm glad of it. I don't think I'm a coward, master, but the thought of a lingering death gives me a queer sick feeling of horror. There, I'm not going to say any more about it. I just mentioned it so that some day when you hear that old Abel Armstrong has been found dead, you won't feel sorry. You'll remember I wanted it that way. Not that I'm tired of life either. It's very pleasant, what with my garden and Captain Kidd and the harbour out there. But it's a trifle monotonous at times and death will be something of a change, master. I'm real curious about it."

"I hate the thought of death," I said gloomily.

"Oh, you're young. The young always do. Death grows friendlier as we grow older. Not that one of us really wants to die, though, master. Tennyson spoke truth when he said that. There's old Mrs. Warner at the Channel Head. She's had heaps of trouble all her life, poor soul, and she's lost almost everyone she cared about. She's always saying that she'll be glad when her time comes, and she doesn't want to live any longer in this vale of tears. But when she takes a sick spell, lord, what a fuss she makes, master! Doctors from town and a trained nurse and enough medicine to kill a dog! Life may be a vale of tears, all right, master, but there are some folks who enjoy weeping, I reckon."

Summer passed through the garden with her procession of roses and lilies and hollyhocks and golden glow. The golden glow was particularly fine that year. There was a great bank of it at the lower end of the garden, like a huge billow of sunshine. Tamzine revelled in it, but Abel liked more subtly-tinted flowers. There was a certain dark wine-hued hollyhock which was a favourite with him. He would sit for hours looking steadfastly into one of its shallow satin cups. I found him so one afternoon in the hop-vine arbour.

"This colour always has a soothing effect on me," he explained. "Yellow excites me too much—makes me restless—makes me want to sail 'beyond the bourne of sunset'. I looked at that surge of golden glow down there today till I got all worked up and thought my life had been an awful failure. I found a dead butterfly and had a little funeral—buried it in the fern corner. And I thought I hadn't been any more use in the world than that poor little butterfly. Oh, I was woeful, master. Then I got me this hollyhock and sat down here to look at it alone. When a man's alone, master, he's most with God—or with the devil. The devil rampaged around me all the time I was looking at that golden glow; but God spoke to me through the hollyhock. And it seemed to me that a man who's as happy as I am and has got such a garden has made a real success of living."

"I hope I'll be able to make as much of a success," I said sincerely.

"I want you to make a different kind of success, though, master," said Abel, shaking his head. "I want you to *do* things—the things I'd have tried to do if I'd had the chance. It's in you to do them—if you set your teeth and go ahead."

"I believe I *can* set my teeth and go ahead now, thanks to you, Mr. Armstrong," I said. "I was heading straight for failure when I came here last spring; but you've changed my course."

"Given you a sort of compass to steer by, haven't I?" queried Abel with a smile. "I ain't too modest to take some credit for it. I saw I could do *you* some good. But my garden has done more than I did, if you'll believe it. It's wonderful what a garden can do for a man when he lets it have its way. Come, sit down here and bask, master. The sunshine may be gone to-morrow. Let's just sit and think."

We sat and thought for a long while. Presently Abel said abruptly:

"You don't see the folks I see in this garden, master. You don't see anybody but me and old Tamzine and Captain Kidd. I see all who used to be here long ago. It was a lively place then. There were plenty of us and we were as gay a set of youngsters as you'd find anywhere. We tossed laughter backwards and forwards here like a ball. And now old Tamzine and older Abel are all that are left."

He was silent a moment, looking at the phantoms of memory that paced invisibly to me the dappled walks and peeped merrily through the swinging boughs. Then he went on:

"Of all the folks I see here there are two that are more vivid and real than all the rest, master. One is my sister Alice. She died thirty years ago. She was very beautiful. You'd hardly believe that to look at Tamzine and me, would you? But it is true. We always called her Queen Alice—she was so stately and handsome. She had brown eyes and red gold hair, just the colour of that nasturtium there. She was father's favourite. The night she was born they didn't think my mother would live. Father walked this garden all night. And just under that old apple-tree he knelt at sunrise and thanked God when they came to tell him that all was well.

"Alice was always a creature of joy. This old garden rang with her laughter in those years. She seldom walked—she ran or danced. She only lived twenty years, but nineteen of them were so happy I've never pitied her over much. She had everything that makes life worth living—laughter and love, and at the last sorrow. James Milburn was her lover. It's thirty-one years since his ship sailed out of that harbour and Alice waved him good-bye from this garden. He never came back. His ship was never heard of again.

"When Alice gave up hope that it would be, she died of a broken heart. They say there's no such thing; but nothing else ailed Alice. She stood at yonder gate day after day and watched the harbour; and when at last she gave up hope life went with it. I remember the day: she had watched until sunset. Then she turned away from the gate. All the unrest and despair had gone out of her eyes. There was a terrible peace in them—the peace of the dead. 'He will never come back now, Abel,' she said to me.

"In less than a week she was dead. The others mourned her, but I didn't, master. She had sounded the deeps of living and there was nothing else to linger through the years for. *My* grief had spent itself earlier, when I walked this garden in agony because I could not help her. But often, on these long warm summer afternoons, I seem to hear Alice's laughter all over this garden; though she's been dead so long."

He lapsed into a reverie which I did not disturb, and it was not until another day that I learned of the other memory that he cherished. He reverted to it suddenly as we sat again in the hop-vine arbour, looking at the glimmering radiance of the September sea.

"Master, how many of us are sitting here?"

"Two in the flesh. How many in the spirit I know not," I answered, humouring his mood.

"There is one—the other of the two I spoke of the day I told you about Alice. It's harder for me to speak of this one."

"Don't speak of it if it hurts you," I said.

"But I want to. It's a whim of mine. Do you know why I told you of Alice and why I'm going to tell you of Mercedes? It's because I want someone to remember them and think of them sometimes after I'm gone. I can't bear that their names should be utterly forgotten by all living souls.

"My older brother, Alec, was a sailor, and on his last voyage to the West Indies he married and brought home a Spanish girl. My father and mother didn't like the match. Mercedes was a foreigner and a Catholic, and differed from us in every way. But I never blamed Alec after I saw her. It wasn't that she was so very pretty. She was slight and dark and ivory-coloured. But she was very graceful, and there was a charm about her, master—a mighty and potent charm. The women couldn't understand it. They wondered at Alec's infatuation for her. I never did. I—I loved her, too, master, before I had known her a day. Nobody ever knew it. Mercedes never dreamed of it. But it's lasted me all my life. I never wanted to think of any other woman. She spoiled a man for any other kind of woman—that little pale, dark-eyed Spanish girl. To love her was like drinking some rare sparkling wine. You'd never again have any taste for a commoner draught.

"I think she was very happy the year she spent here. Our thrifty women-folk in Stillwater jeered at her because she wasn't what they called capable. They said she couldn't do anything. But she could do one thing well—she could love. She worshipped Alec. I used to hate him for it. Oh, my heart has been very full of black thoughts in its time, master. But neither Alec nor Mercedes ever knew. And I'm thankful now that they were so happy. Alec made this arbour for Mercedes—at least he made the trellis, and she planted the vines.

"She used to sit here most of the time in summer. I suppose that's why I like to sit here. Her eyes would be dreamy and far-away until Alec would flash his welcome. How that used to torture me! But now I like to remember it. And her pretty soft foreign voice and little white hands. She died after she had lived here a year. They buried her and her baby in the graveyard of that little chapel over the harbour where the bell rings every evening. She used to like sitting here and listening to it. Alec lived a long while after, but he never married again. He's gone now, and nobody remembers Mercedes but me."

Abel lapsed into a reverie—a tryst with the past which I would not disturb. I thought he did not notice my departure, but as I opened the gate he stood up and waved his hand.

Three days later I went again to the old garden by the harbour shore. There was a red light on a distant sail. In the far west a sunset city was built around a great deep harbour of twilight. Palaces were there and bannered towers of crimson and gold. The air was full of music; there was one music of the wind and another of the waves, and still another of the distant bell from the chapel near which Mercedes slept. The garden was full of ripe odours and warm colours. The Lombardies around it were tall and sombre like the priestly forms of some mystic band. Abel was sitting in the hop-vine arbour; beside him Captain Kidd slept. I thought Abel was asleep, too; his head leaned against the trellis and his eyes were shut.

But when I reached the arbour I saw that he was not asleep. There was a strange, wise little smile on his lips as if he had attained to the ultimate wisdom and were laughing in no unkindly fashion at our old blind suppositions and perplexities.

Abel had gone on his Great Adventure.

Akin To Love

David Hartley had dropped in to pay a neighbourly call on Josephine Elliott. It was well along in the afternoon, and outside, in the clear crispness of a Canadian winter, the long blue shadows from the tall firs behind the house were falling over the snow.

It was a frosty day, and all the windows of every room where there was no fire were covered with silver palms. But the big, bright kitchen was warm and cosy, and somehow seemed to David more tempting than ever before, and that is saying a good deal. He had an uneasy feeling that he had stayed long enough and ought to go. Josephine was knitting at a long gray sock with doubly aggressive energy, and that was a sign that she was talked out. As long as Josephine had plenty to say, her plump white fingers, where her mother's wedding ring was lost in dimples, moved slowly among her needles. When conversation flagged she fell to her work as furiously as if a husband and half a dozen sons were waiting for its completion. David often wondered in his secret soul what Josephine did with all the interminable gray socks she knitted. Sometimes he concluded that she put them in the home missionary barrels; again, that she sold them to her hired man. At any rate, they were very warm and comfortable looking, and David sighed as he thought of the deplorable state his own socks were generally in.

When David sighed Josephine took alarm. She was afraid David was going to have one of his attacks of foolishness. She must head him off someway, so she rolled up the gray sock, stabbed the big pudgy ball with her needles, and said she guessed she'd get the tea.

David got up.

"Now, you're not going before tea?" said Josephine hospitably. "I'll have it all ready in no time."

"I ought to go home, I s'pose," said David, with the air and tone of a man dallying with a great temptation. "Zillah'll be waiting tea for me; and there's the stock to tend to."

"I guess Zillah won't wait long," said Josephine. She did not intend it at all, but there was a certain scornful ring in her voice. "You must stay. I've a fancy for company to tea."

David sat down again. He looked so pleased that Josephine went down on her knees behind the stove, ostensibly to get a stick of firewood, but really to hide her smile.

"I suppose he's tickled to death to think of getting a good square meal, after the starvation rations Zillah puts him on," she thought.

But Josephine misjudged David just as much as he misjudged her. She had really asked him to stay to tea out of pity, but David thought it was because she was lonesome, and he hailed that as an encouraging sign. And he was not thinking about getting a good meal either, although his dinner had been such a one as only Zillah Hartley could get up. As he leaned back in his cushioned chair and watched Josephine bustling about the kitchen, he was glorying in the fact that he could spend another hour with her, and sit opposite to her at the table while she poured his tea for him and passed him the biscuits, just as if—just as if—

Here Josephine looked straight at him with such intent and stern brown eyes that David felt she must have read his thoughts, and he colored guiltily. But Josephine did not even notice that he was blushing. She had only paused to wonder whether she would bring out cherry or strawberry preserve; and, having decided on the cherry, took her piercing gaze from David without having seen him at all. But he allowed his thoughts no more vagaries.

Josephine set the table with her mother's wedding china. She used it because it was the anniversary of her mother's wedding day, but David thought it was out of compliment to him. And, as he knew quite well that Josephine prized that china beyond all her other earthly possessions, he stroked his smooth-shaven, dimpled chin with the air of a man to whom is offered a very subtly sweet homage.

Josephine whisked in and out of the pantry, and up and down cellar, and with every whisk a new dainty was added to the table. Josephine, as everybody in Meadowby admitted, was past mistress in the noble art of cookery. Once upon a time rash matrons and ambitious young wives had aspired to rival her, but they had long ago realised the vanity of such efforts and dropped comfortably back to second place.

Josephine felt an artist's pride in her table when she set the teapot on its stand and invited David to sit in. There were pink slices of cold tongue, and crisp green pickles and spiced gooseberry, the recipe for which Josephine had invented herself, and which had taken first prize at the Provincial Exhibition for six successive years; there was a lemon pie which was a symphony in gold and silver, biscuits as light and white as snow, and moist, plummy cubes of fruit cake. There was the ruby-tinted cherry preserve, a mound of amber jelly, and, to crown all, steaming cups of tea, in flavour and fragrance unequalled.

And Josephine, too, sitting at the head of the table, with her smooth, glossy crimps of black hair and cheeks as rosy clear as they had been twenty years ago, when she had been a slender slip of girlhood and bashful young David Hartley had looked at her over his hymn-book in prayer-meeting and tramped all the way home a few feet behind her, because he was too shy to go boldly up and ask if he might see her home.

All taken together, what wonder if David lost his head over that tea-table and determined to ask Josephine the same old question once more? It was eighteen years since he had asked it for the first time, and two years since the last. He would try his luck again; Josephine was certainly more gracious than he remembered her to ever have been before.

When the meal was over Josephine cleared the table and washed the dishes. When she had taken a dry towel and sat down by the window to polish her china David understood that his opportunity had come. He moved over and sat down beside her on the sofa by the window.

Outside the sun was setting in a magnificent arch of light and colour over the snow-clad hills and deep blue St. Lawrence gulf. David grasped at the sunset as an introductory factor.

"Isn't that fine, Josephine?" he said admiringly. "It makes me think of that piece of poetry that used to be in the old Fifth Reader when we went to school. D'ye mind how the teacher used to drill us up in it on Friday afternoons? It begun

'Slow sinks more lovely ere his race is run
Along Morea's hills the setting sun.'"

Then David declaimed the whole passage in a sing-song tone, accompanied by a few crude gestures recalled from long-ago school-boy elocution. Josephine knew what was coming. Every time David proposed to her he had begun by reciting poetry. She twirled her towel around the last plate resignedly. If it had to come, the sooner it was over the better. Josephine knew by experience that there was no heading David off, despite his shyness, when he had once got along as far as the poetry.

"But it's going to be for the last time," she said determinedly. "I'm going to settle this question so decidedly to-night that there'll never be a repetition."

When David had finished his quotation he laid his hand on Josephine's plump arm.

"Josephine," he said huskily, "I s'pose you couldn't—could you now?—make up your mind to have me. I wish you would, Josephine—I wish you would. Don't you think you could, Josephine?"

Josephine folded up her towel, crossed her hands on it, and looked her wooer squarely in the eyes.

"David Hartley," she said deliberately, "what makes you go on asking me to marry you every once in a while when I've told you times out of mind that I can't and won't?"

"Because I can't help hoping that you'll change your mind through time," David replied meekly.

"Well, you just listen to me. I will not marry you. That is in the first place. And in the second, this is to be final. It has to be. You are never to ask me this again under any circumstances. If you do I will not answer you—I will not let on I hear you at all; but (and Josephine spoke very slowly and impressively) I will never speak to you again—never. We are good friends now, and I like you real well, and like to have you drop in for a neighbourly chat as often as you wish to, but there'll be an end, short and sudden, to that, if you don't mind what I say."

"Oh, Josephine, ain't that rather hard?" protested David feebly. It seemed terrible to be cut off from all hope with such finality as this.

"I mean every word of it," returned Josephine calmly. "You'd better go home now, David. I always feel as if I'd like to be alone for a spell after a disagreeable experience."

David obeyed sadly and put on his cap and overcoat. Josephine kindly warned him not to slip and break his legs on the porch, because the floor was as icy as anything; and she even lighted a candle and held it up at the kitchen door to guide him safely out. David, as he trudged sorrowfully homeward across the fields, carried with him the mental picture of a plump, sonsy woman, in a trim dress of plum-coloured homespun and ruffled blue-check apron, haloed by candlelight. It was not a very romantic vision, perhaps, but to David it was more beautiful than anything else in the world.

When David was gone Josephine shut the door with a little shiver. She blew out the candle, for it was not yet dark enough to justify artificial light to her thrifty mind. She thought the big, empty house, in which she was the only living thing, was very lonely. It was so still, except for the slow tick of the "grandfather's clock" and the soft purr and crackle of the wood in the stove. Josephine sat down by the window.

"I wish some of the Sentners would run down," she said aloud. "If David hadn't been so ridiculous I'd have got him to stay the evening. He can be good company when he likes—he's real well-read and intelligent. And he must have dismal times at home there with nobody but Zillah."

She looked across the yard to the little house at the other side of it, where her French-Canadian hired man lived, and watched the purple spiral of smoke from its chimney curling up against the crocus sky. Would she run over and see Mrs. Leon Poirier and her little black-eyed, brown-skinned baby? No, they never knew what to say to each other.

"If 'twasn't so cold I'd go up and see Ida," she said. "As it is, I guess I'd better fall back on my knitting, for I saw Jimmy Sentner's toes sticking through his socks the other day. How setback poor David did look, to be sure! But I think I've settled that marrying notion of his once for all and I'm glad of it."

She said the same thing next day to Mrs. Tom Sentner, who had come down to help her pick her geese. They were at work in the kitchen with a big tubful of feathers between them, and on the table a row of dead birds, which Leon had killed and brought in. Josephine was enveloped in a shapeless print wrapper, and had an apron tied tightly around her head to keep the down out of her beautiful hair, of which she was rather proud.

"What do you think, Ida?" she said, with a hearty laugh at the recollection. "David Hartley was here to tea last night, and asked me to marry him again. There's a persistent man for you. I can't brag of ever having had many beaux, but I've certainly had my fair share of proposals."

Mrs. Tom did not laugh. Her thin little face, with its faded prettiness, looked as if she never laughed.

"Why won't you marry him?" she said fretfully.

"Why should I?" retorted Josephine. "Tell me that, Ida Sentner."

"Because it is high time you were married," said Mrs. Tom decisively. "I don't believe in women living single. And I don't see what better you can do than take David Hartley."

Josephine looked at her sister with the interested expression of a person who is trying to understand some mental attitude in another which is a standing puzzle to her. Ida's evident wish to see her married always amused Josephine. Ida had married very young and for fifteen years her life had been one of drudgery and ill-health. Tom Sentner was a lazy, shiftless fellow. He neglected his family and was drunk half his time. Meadowby people said that he beat his wife when "on the spree," but Josephine did not believe that, because she did not think that Ida could keep from telling her if it were so. Ida Sentner was not given to bearing her trials in silence.

Had it not been for Josephine's assistance, Tom Sentner's family would have stood an excellent chance of starvation. Josephine practically kept them, and her generosity never failed or stinted. She fed and clothed her nephews and nieces, and all the gray socks whose destination puzzled David so much went to the Sentners.

As for Josephine herself, she had a good farm, a comfortable house, a plump bank account, and was an independent, unworried woman. And yet, in the face of all this, Mrs. Tom Sentner could bewail the fact that Josephine had no husband to look out for her. Josephine shrugged her shoulders and gave up the conundrum, merely saying ironically, in reply to her sister's remark:

"And go to live with Zillah Hartley?"

"You know very well you wouldn't have to do that. Ever since John Hartley's wife at the Creek died he's been wanting Zillah to go and keep house for him, and if David got married Zillah'd go quick. Catch her staying there if you were mistress! And David has such a beautiful house! It's ten times finer than yours, though I don't deny yours is comfortable. And his farm is the best in Meadowby and joins yours. Think what a beautiful property they'd make together. You're all right now, Josephine, but what will you do when you get old and have nobody to take care of you? I declare the thought worries me at night till I can't sleep."

"I should have thought you had enough worries of your own to keep you awake at nights without taking over any of mine," said Josephine drily. "As for old age, it's a good ways off for me yet. When your Jack gets old enough to have some sense he can come here and live with me. But I'm not going to marry David Hartley, you can depend on that, Ida, my dear. I wish you could have heard him rhyming off that poetry last night. It doesn't seem to matter much what piece he recites—first thing that comes into his head, I reckon. I remember one time he went clean through that hymn beginning, 'Hark from the tombs a doleful sound,' and two years ago it was 'To Mary in Heaven,' as lackadaisical as you please. I never had such a time to keep from laughing, but I managed it, for I wouldn't hurt his feelings for the world. No, I haven't any intention of marrying anybody, but if I had it wouldn't be dear old sentimental, easy-going David."

Mrs. Tom thumped a plucked goose down on the bench with an expression which said that she, for one, wasn't going to waste any more words on an idiot. Easy-going, indeed! Did Josephine consider that a drawback? Mrs. Tom sighed. If Josephine, she thought, had put up with Tom Sentner's tempers for fifteen years she would know how to appreciate a good-natured man at his real value.

The cold snap which had set in on the day of David's call lasted and deepened for a week. On Saturday evening, when Mrs. Tom came down for a jug of cream, the mercury of the little thermometer thumping against Josephine's porch was below zero. The gulf was no longer blue, but white with ice. Everything outdoors was crackling and snapping. Inside Josephine had kept roaring fires all through the house but the only place really warm was the kitchen.

"Wrap your head up well, Ida," she said anxiously, when Mrs. Tom rose to go. "You've got a bad cold."

"There's a cold going," said Mrs. Tom. "Everyone has it. David Hartley was up at our place to-day barking terrible—a real churchyard cough, as I told him. He never takes any care of himself. He said Zillah had a bad cold, too. Won't she be cranky while it lasts?"

Josephine sat up late that night to keep fires on. She finally went to bed in the little room opposite the big hall stove, and she slept at once, and dreamed that the thumps of the thermometer flapping in the wind against the wall outside grew louder and more insistent until they woke her up. Some one was pounding on the porch door.

Josephine sprang out of bed and hurried on her wrapper and felt shoes. She had no doubt that some of the Sentners were sick. They had a habit of getting sick about that time of night. She hurried out and opened the door, expecting to see hulking Tom Sentner, or perhaps Ida herself, big-eyed and hysterical.

But David Hartley stood there, panting for breath. The clear moonlight showed that he had no overcoat on, and he was coughing hard. Josephine, before she spoke a word, clutched him by the arm and pulled him in out of the wind.

"For pity's sake, David Hartley, what is the matter?"

"Zillah's awful sick," he gasped. "I came here because 'twas nearest. Oh, won't you come over, Josephine? I've got to go for the doctor and I can't leave her alone. She's suffering dreadful. I know you and her ain't on good terms, but you'll come, won't you?"

"Of course I will," said Josephine sharply. "I'm not a barbarian, I hope, to refuse to go to the help of a sick person, if 'twas my worst enemy. I'll go in and get ready and you go straight to the hall stove and warm yourself. There's a good fire in it yet. What on earth do you mean, starting out on a bitter night like this without an overcoat or even mittens, and you with a cold like that?"

"I never thought of them, I was so frightened," said David apologetically. "I just lit up a fire in the kitchen stove as quick's I could and run. It rattled me to hear Zillah moaning so's you could hear her all over the house."

"You need someone to look after you as bad as Zillah does," said Josephine severely.

In a very few minutes she was ready, with a basket packed full of homely remedies, "for like as not there'll be no putting one's hand on anything there," she muttered. She insisted on wrapping her big plaid shawl around David's head and neck, and made him put on a pair of mittens she had knitted for Jack Sentner. Then she locked the door and they started across the gleaming, crusted field. It was so slippery that Josephine had to cling to David's arm to keep her feet. In the rapture of supporting her David almost forgot everything else.

In a few minutes they had passed under the bare, glistening boughs of the poplars on David's lawn, and for the first time Josephine crossed the threshold of David Hartley's house.

Years ago, in her girlhood, when the Hartley's lived in the old house and there were half a dozen girls at home, Josephine had frequently visited there. All the Hartley girls liked her except Zillah. She and Zillah never "got on" together. When the other girls had married and gone, Josephine gave up visiting there. She had never been inside the new house, and she and Zillah had not spoken to each other for years.

Zillah was a sick woman—too sick to be anything but civil to Josephine. David started at once for the doctor at the Creek, and Josephine saw that he was well wrapped up before she let him go. Then she mixed up a mustard plaster for Zillah and sat down by the bedside to wait.

When Mrs. Tom Sentner came down the next day she found Josephine busy making flaxseed poultices, with her lips set in a line that betokened she had made up her mind to some disagreeable course of duty.

"Zillah has got pneumonia bad," she said, in reply to Mrs. Tom's inquiries. "The Doctor is here and Mary Bell from the Creek. She'll wait on Zillah, but there'll have to be another woman here to see to the work. I reckon I'll stay. I suppose it's my duty and I don't see who else could be got. You can send Mamie and Jack down to stay at my house until I can go back. I'll run over every day and keep an eye on things."

At the end of a week Zillah was out of danger. Saturday afternoon Josephine went over home to see how Mamie and Jack were getting on. She found Mrs. Tom there, and the latter promptly despatched Jack and Mamie to the post-office that she might have an opportunity to hear Josephine's news.

"I've had an awful week of it, Ida," said Josephine solemnly, as she sat down by the stove and put her feet up on the glowing hearth.

"I suppose Zillah is pretty cranky to wait on," said Mrs. Tom sympathetically.

"Oh, it isn't Zillah. Mary Bell looks after her. No, it's the house. I never lived in such a place of dust and disorder in my born days. I'm sorrier for David Hartley than I ever was for anyone before."

"I suppose he's used to it," said Mrs. Tom with a shrug.

"I don't see how anyone could ever get used to it," groaned Josephine. "And David used to be so particular when he was a boy. The minute I went there the other night I took in that kitchen with a look. I don't believe the paint has even been washed since the house was built. I honestly don't. And I wouldn't like to be called upon to swear when the floor was scrubbed either. The corners were just full of rolls of dust—you could have shovelled it out. I swept it out next day and I thought I'd be choked. As for the pantry—well, the less said about *that* the better. And it's the same all through the house. You could write your name on everything. I couldn't so much as clean up. Zillah was so sick there couldn't be a bit of noise made. I did manage to sweep and dust, and I cleaned out the pantry. And, of course, I saw that the meals were nice and well cooked. You should have seen David's face. He looked as if he couldn't get used to having things clean and tasty. I darned his socks—he hadn't a whole pair to his name—and I've done everything I could to give him a little comfort. Not that I could do much. If Zillah heard me moving round she'd send Mary Bell out to ask what the matter was. When I wanted to go upstairs I'd have to take off my shoes and tiptoe up on my stocking feet, so's she wouldn't know it. And I'll have to stay there another fortnight yet. Zillah won't be able to sit up till then. I don't really know if I can stand it without falling to and scrubbing the house from garret to cellar in spite of her."

Mrs. Tom Sentner did not say much to Josephine. To herself she said complacently:

"She's sorry for David. Well, I've always heard that pity was akin to love. We'll see what comes of this."

Josephine did manage to live through that fortnight. One morning she remarked to David at the breakfast table:

"Well, I think that Mary Bell will be able to attend to the work after today, David. I guess I'll go home tonight."

David's face clouded over.

"Well, I s'pose we oughtn't to keep you any longer, Josephine. I'm sure it's been awful good of you to stay this long. I don't know what we'd have done without you."

"You're welcome," said Josephine shortly.

"Don't go for to walk home," said David; "the snow is too deep. I'll drive you over when you want to go."

"I'll not go before the evening," said Josephine slowly.

David went out to his work gloomily. For three weeks he had been living in comfort. His wants were carefully attended to; his meals were well cooked and served, and everything was bright and clean. And more than all, Josephine had been there, with her cheerful smile and companionable ways. Well, it was all ended now.

Josephine sat at the breakfast table long after David had gone out. She scowled at the sugar-bowl and shook her head savagely at the tea-pot.

"I'll have to do it," she said at last.

"I'm so sorry for him that I can't do anything else."

She got up and went to the window, looking across the snowy field to her own home, nestled between the grove of firs and the orchard.

"It's awful snug and comfortable," she said regretfully, "and I've always felt set on being free and independent. But it's no use. I'd never have a minute's peace of mind again, thinking of David living here in dirt and disorder, and him so particular and tidy by nature. No, it's my duty, plain and clear, to come here and make things pleasant for him—the pointing of Providence, as you might say. The worst of it is, I'll have to tell him so myself. He'll never dare to mention the subject again, after what I said to him that night he proposed last. I wish I hadn't been so dreadful emphatic. Now I've got to say it myself if it is ever said. But I'll not begin by quoting poetry, that's one thing sure!"

Josephine threw back her head, crowned with its shining braids of jet-black hair, and laughed heartily. She bustled back to the stove and poked up the fire.

"I'll have a bit of corned beef and cabbage for dinner," she said, "and I'll make David that pudding he's so fond of. After all, it's kind of nice to have someone to plan and think for. It always did seem like a waste of energy to fuss over cooking things when there was nobody but myself to eat them."

Josephine sang over her work all day, and David went about his with the face of a man who is going to the gallows without benefit of clergy. When he came in to supper at sunset his expression was so woe-begone that Josephine had to dodge into the pantry to keep from laughing outright. She relieved her feelings by pounding the dresser with the potato masher, and then went primly out and took her place at the table.

The meal was not a success from a social point of view. Josephine was nervous and David glum. Mary Bell gobbled down her food with her usual haste, and then went away to carry Zillah hers. Then David said reluctantly:

"If you want to go home now, Josephine, I'll hitch up Red Rob and drive you over."

Josephine began to plait the tablecloth. She wished again that she had not been so emphatic on the occasion of his last proposal. Without replying to David's suggestion she said crossly (Josephine always spoke crossly when she was especially in earnest):

"I want to tell you what I think about Zillah. She's getting better, but she's had a terrible shaking up, and it's my opinion that she won't be good for much all winter. She won't be able to do any hard work, that's certain. If you want my advice, I tell you fair and square that I think she'd better go off for a visit as soon as she's fit. She thinks so herself. Clementine wants her to go and stay a spell with her in town. 'Twould be just the thing for her."

"She can go if she wants to, of course," said David dully. "I can get along by myself for a spell."

"There's no need of your getting along by yourself," said Josephine, more crossly than ever. "I'll—I'll come here and keep house for you if you like."

David looked at her uncomprehendingly.

"Wouldn't people kind of gossip?" he asked hesitatingly. "Not but what—"

"I don't see what they'd have to gossip about," broke in Josephine, "if we were—married."

David sprang to his feet with such haste that he almost upset the table.

"Josephine, do you mean that?" he exclaimed.

"Of course I mean it," she said, in a perfectly savage tone. "Now, for pity's sake, don't say another word about it just now. I can't discuss it for a spell. Go out to your work. I want to be alone for awhile."

For the first and last time David disobeyed her. Instead of going out, he strode around the table, caught Josephine masterfully in his arms, and kissed her. And Josephine, after a second's hesitation, kissed him in return.

Aunt Philippa and the Men

I knew quite well why Father sent me to Prince Edward Island to visit Aunt Philippa that summer. He told me he was sending me there "to learn some sense"; and my stepmother, of whom I was very fond, told me she was sure the sea air would do me a world of good. I did not want to learn sense or be done a world of good; I wanted to stay in Montreal and go on being foolish—and make up my quarrel with Mark Fenwick. Father and Mother did not know anything about this quarrel; they thought I was still on good terms with him—and that is why they sent me to Prince Edward Island.

I was very miserable. I did not want to go to Aunt Philippa's. It was not because I feared it would be dull—for without Mark, Montreal was just as much of a howling wilderness as any other place. But it was so horribly far away. When the time came for Mark to want to make up—as come I knew it would—how could he do it if I were seven hundred miles away?

Nevertheless, I went to Prince Edward Island. In all my eighteen years I had never once disobeyed Father. He is a very hard man to disobey. I knew I should have to make a beginning some time if I wanted to marry Mark, so I saved all my little courage up for that and didn't waste any of it opposing the visit to Aunt Philippa.

I couldn't understand Father's point of view. Of course, he hated old John Fenwick, who had once sued him for libel and won the case. Father had written an indiscreet editorial in the excitement of a red-hot political contest—and was made to understand that there are some things you can't say of another man even at election time. But then, he need not have hated Mark because of that; Mark was not even born when it happened.

Old John Fenwick was not much better pleased about Mark and me than Father was, though he didn't go to the length of forbidding it; he just acted grumpily and disagreeably. Things were unpleasant enough all round without a quarrel between Mark and me; yet quarrel we did—and over next to nothing, too, you understand. And now I had to set out for Prince Edward Island without even seeing him, for he was away in Toronto on business.

When my train reached Copely the next afternoon, Aunt Philippa was waiting for me. There was nobody else in sight, but I would have known her had there been a thousand. Nobody but Aunt Philippa could have that determined mouth, those piercing grey eyes, and that pronounced, unmistakable Goodwin nose. And certainly nobody but Aunt Philippa would have come to meet me arrayed in a wrapper of chocolate print with huge yellow roses scattered over it, and a striped blue-and-white apron!

She welcomed me kindly but absent-mindedly, her thoughts evidently being concentrated on the problem of getting my trunk home. I had only the one, and in Montreal it had seemed to be of moderate size; but on the platform of Copely station, sized up by Aunt Philippa's merciless eye, it certainly looked huge.

"I thought we could a-took it along tied on the back of the buggy," she said disapprovingly, "but I guess we'll have to leave it, and I'll send the hired boy over for it tonight. You can get along without it till then, I s'pose?"

There was a fine irony in her tone. I hastened to assure her meekly that I could, and that it did not matter if my trunk could not be taken up till next day.

"Oh, Jerry can come for it tonight as well as not," said Aunt Philippa, as we climbed into her buggy. "I'd a good notion to send him to meet you, for he isn't doing much today, and I wanted to go to Mrs. Roderick MacAllister's funeral. But my head was aching me so bad I thought I wouldn't enjoy the funeral if I did go. My head is better now, so I kind of wish I had gone. She was a hundred and four years old and I'd always promised myself that I'd go to her funeral."

Aunt Philippa's tone was melancholy. She did not recover her good spirits until we were out on the pretty, grassy, elm-shaded country road, garlanded with its ribbon of buttercups. Then she suddenly turned around and looked me over scrutinizingly.

"You're not as good-looking as I expected from your picture, but them photographs always flatter. That's the reason I never had any took. You're rather thin and brown. But you've good eyes and you look clever. Your father writ me you hadn't much sense, though. He wants me to teach you some, but it's a thankless business. People would rather be fools."

Aunt Philippa struck her steed smartly with the whip and controlled his resultant friskiness with admirable skill.

"Well, you know it's pleasanter," I said, wickedly. "Just think what a doleful world it would be if everybody were sensible."

Aunt Philippa looked at me out of the corner of her eye and disdained any skirmish of flippant epigram.

"So you want to get married?" she said. "You'd better wait till you're grown up."

"How old must a person be before she is grown up?" I asked gravely.

"Humph! That depends. Some are grown up when they're born, and others ain't grown up when they're eighty. That same Mrs. Roderick I was speaking of never grew up. She was as foolish when she was a hundred as when she was ten."

"Perhaps that's why she lived so long," I suggested. All thought of seeking sympathy in Aunt Philippa had vanished. I resolved I would not even mention Mark's name.

"Mebbe 'twas," admitted Aunt Philippa with a grim smile. "*I'd* rather live fifty sensible years than a hundred foolish ones."

Much to my relief, she made no further reference to my affairs. As we rounded a curve in the road where two great over-arching elms met, a buggy wheeled by us, occupied by a young man in clerical costume. He had a pleasant boyish face, and he touched his hat courteously. Aunt Philippa nodded very frostily and gave her horse a quite undeserved cut.

"There's a man you don't want to have much to do with," she said portentously. "He's a Methodist minister."

"Why, Auntie, the Methodists are a very nice denomination," I protested. "My stepmother is a Methodist, you know."

"No, I didn't know, but I'd believe anything of a stepmother. I've no use for Methodists or their ministers. This fellow just came last spring, and it's *my* opinion he smokes. And he thinks every girl who looks at him falls in love with him—as if a Methodist minister was any prize! Don't you take much notice of him, Ursula."

"I'll not be likely to have the chance," I said, with an amused smile.

"Oh, you'll see enough of him. He boards at Mrs. John Callman's, just across the road from us, and he's always out sunning himself on her verandah. Never studies, of course. Last Sunday they say he preached on the iron that floated. If he'd confine himself to the Bible and leave sensational subjects alone it would be better for him and his poor congregation, and so I told Mrs. John Callman to her face. I should think *she* would have had enough of his sex by this time. She married John Callman against her father's will, and he had delirious trembles for years. That's the men for you."

"They're not *all* like that, Aunt Philippa," I protested.

"Most of 'em are. See that house over there? Mrs. Jane Harrison lives there. Her husband took tantrums every few days or so and wouldn't get out of bed. She had to do all the barn work till he'd got over his spell. That's men for you. When he died, people writ her letters of condolence but *I* just sot down and writ her one of congratulation. There's the Presbyterian manse in the hollow. Mr. Bentwell's our minister. He's a good man and he'd be a rather nice one if he didn't think it was his duty to be a little miserable all the time. He won't let his wife wear a fashionable hat, and his daughter can't fix her hair the way she wants to. Even being a minister can't prevent a man from being a crank. Here's Ebenezer Milgrave coming. You take a good look at him. He used to be insane for years. He believed he was dead and used to rage at his wife because she wouldn't bury him. *I'd* a-done it."

Aunt Philippa looked so determinedly grim that I could almost see her with a spade in her hand. I laughed aloud at the picture summoned up.

"Yes, it's funny, but I guess his poor wife didn't find it very humorsome. He's been pretty sane for some years now, but you never can tell when he'll break out again. He's got a brother, Albert Milgrave, who's been married twice. They say he was courting his second wife while his first was dying. Let that be as it may, he used his first wife's wedding ring to marry the second. That's the men for you."

"Don't you know *any* good husbands, Aunt Philippa?" I asked desperately.

"Oh, yes, lots of 'em—over there," said Aunt Philippa sardonically, waving her whip in the direction of a little country graveyard on a distant hill.

"Yes, but *living*—walking about in the flesh?"

"Precious few. Now and again you'll come across a man whose wife won't put up with any nonsense and he *has* to be respectable. But the most of 'em are poor bargains—poor bargains."

"And are all the wives saints?" I persisted.

"Laws, no, but they're too good for the men," retorted Aunt Philippa, as she turned in at her own gate. Her house was close to the road and was painted such a vivid green that the landscape looked faded by contrast. Across the gable end of it was the legend, "Philippa's Farm," emblazoned in huge black letters two feet long. All its surroundings were very neat. On the kitchen doorstep a patchwork cat was making a grave toilet. The groundwork of the cat was white, and its spots were black, yellow, grey, and brown.

"There's Joseph," said Aunt Philippa. "I call him that because his coat is of many colours. But I ain't no lover of cats. They're too much like the men to suit me."

"Cats have always been supposed to be peculiarly feminine," I said, descending.

"'Twas a man that supposed it, then," retorted Aunt Philippa, beckoning to her hired boy. "Here, Jerry, put Prince away. Jerry's a good sort of boy," she confided to me as we went into the house. "I had Jim Spencer last summer and the only good thing about *him* was his appetite. I put up with him till harvest was in, and then one day my patience give out. He upsot a churnful of cream in the back yard—and was just as cool as a cowcumber over it—laughed and said it was good for the land. I told him I wasn't in the habit of fertilizing my back yard with cream. But that's the men for you. Come in. I'll have tea ready in no time. I sot the table before I left. There's lemon pie. Mrs. John Cantwell sent it over. I never make lemon pie myself. Ten years ago I took the prize for lemon pies at the county fair, and I've never made any since for fear I'd lose my reputation for them."

The first month of my stay passed not unpleasantly. The summer weather was delightful, and the sea air was certainly splendid. Aunt Philippa's little farm ran right down to the shore, and I spent much of my time there. There were also several families of cousins to be visited in the farmhouses that dotted the pretty, seaward-sloping valley, and they came back to see me at "Philippa's Farm." I picked spruce gum and berries and ferns, and Aunt Philippa taught me to make butter. It was all very idyllic—or would have been if Mark had written. But Mark did not write. I supposed he must be very angry because I had run off to Prince Edward Island without so much as a note of goodbye. But I had been so sure he would understand!

Aunt Philippa never made any further reference to the reason Father had sent me to her, but she allowed no day to pass without holding up to me some horrible example of matrimonial infelicity. The number of unhappy wives who walked or drove past "Philippa's Farm" every afternoon, as we sat on the verandah, was truly pitiable.

We always sat on the verandah in the afternoon, when we were not visiting or being visited. I made a pretence of fancy work, and Aunt Philippa spun diligently on a little old-fashioned spinning-wheel that had been her grandmother's. She always sat before the wood stand which held her flowers, and the gorgeous blots of geranium blossom and big green leaves furnished a pretty background. She always wore her shapeless but clean print wrappers, and her iron-grey hair was always combed neatly down over her ears. Joseph sat between us, sleeping or purring. She spun so expertly that she could keep a close watch on the road as well, and I got the biography of every individual who went by. As for the poor young Methodist minister, who liked to read or walk on the verandah of our neighbour's house, Aunt Philippa never had a good word for him. I had met him once or twice socially and had liked him. I wanted to ask him to call but dared not—Aunt Philippa had vowed he should never enter her house.

"If I was dead and he came to my funeral I'd rise up and order him out," she said.

"I thought he made a very nice prayer at Mrs. Seaman's funeral the other day," I said.

"Oh, I've no doubt he can pray. I never heard anyone make more beautiful prayers than old Simon Kennedy down at the harbour, who was always drunk or hoping to be—and the drunker he was the better he prayed. It ain't no matter how well a man prays if his preaching isn't right. That Methodist man preaches a lot of things that ain't true, and what's worse they ain't sound doctrine. At least, that's what I've heard. I never was in a Methodist church, thank goodness."

"Don't you think Methodists go to heaven as well as Presbyterians, Aunt Philippa?" I asked gravely.

"That ain't for us to decide," said Aunt Philippa solemnly. "It's in higher hands than ours. But I ain't going to associate with them on *earth*, whatever I may have to do in heaven. The folks round here mostly don't make much difference and go to the Methodist church quite often. But *I* say if you are a Presbyterian, *be* a Presbyterian. Of course, if you ain't, it don't matter much what you do. As for that minister man, he has a grand-uncle who was sent to the penitentiary for embezzlement. I found out *that* much."

And evidently Aunt Philippa had taken an unholy joy in finding it out.

"I dare say some of our own ancestors deserved to go to the penitentiary, even if they never did," I remarked. "Who is that woman driving past, Aunt Philippa? She must have been very pretty once."

"She was—and that was all the good it did her. 'Favour is deceitful and beauty is vain,' Ursula. She was Sarah Pyatt and she married Fred Proctor. He was one of your wicked, fascinating men. After she married him he give up being fascinating but he kept on being wicked. *That's* the men for you. Her sister Flora weren't much luckier. *Her* man was that domineering she couldn't call her soul her own. Finally he couldn't get his own way over something and he just suicided by jumping into the well. A good riddance—but of course the well was spoiled. Flora could never abide the thought of using it again, poor thing. *That's* men for you.

"And there's that old Enoch Allan on his way to the station. He's ninety if he's a day. You can't kill some folks with a meat axe. His wife died twenty years ago. He'd been married when he was twenty so they'd lived together for fifty years. She was a faithful, hard-working creature and kept him out of the poorhouse, for he was a shiftless soul, not lazy, exactly, but just too fond of sitting. But he weren't grateful. She had a kind of bitter tongue and they did use to fight scandalous. O' course it was all his fault. Well, she died, and old Enoch and my father drove together to the graveyard. Old Enoch was awful quiet all the way there and back, but just afore they got home, he says solemnly to Father: 'You mayn't believe it, Henry, but this is the happiest day of my life.' *That's* men for you. His brother, Scotty Allan, was the meanest man ever lived in these parts. When his wife died she was buried with a little gold brooch in her collar unbeknownst to him. When he found it out he went one night to the graveyard and opened up the grave and the casket to get that brooch."

"Oh, Aunt Philippa, that is a horrible story," I cried, recoiling with a shiver over the gruesomeness of it.

"'Course it is, but what would you expect of a man?" retorted Aunt Philippa.

Somehow, her stories began to affect me in spite of myself. There were times when I felt very dreary. Perhaps Aunt Philippa was right. Perhaps men possessed neither truth nor constancy. Certainly Mark had forgotten me. I was ashamed of myself because this hurt me so much, but I could not help it. I grew pale and listless. Aunt Philippa sometimes peered at me sharply, but she held her peace. I was grateful for this.

But one day a letter did come from Mark. I dared not read it until I was safely in my own room. Then I opened it with trembling fingers.

The letter was a little stiff. Evidently Mark was feeling sore enough over things. He made no reference to our quarrel or to my sojourn in Prince Edward Island. He wrote that his firm was sending him to South Africa to take charge of their interests there. He would leave in three weeks' time and could not return for five years. If I still cared anything for him, would I meet him in Halifax, marry him, and go to South Africa with him? If I would not, he would understand that I had ceased to love him and that all was over between us.

That, boiled down, was the gist of Mark's letter. When I had read it I cast myself on the bed and wept out all the tears I had refused to let myself shed during my weeks of exile.

For I could not do what Mark asked—I *could not*. I couldn't run away to be married in that desolate, unbefriended fashion. It would be a disgrace. I would feel ashamed of it all my life and be unhappy over it. I thought that Mark was rather unreasonable. He knew what my feelings about run-away marriages were.

And was it absolutely necessary for him to go to South Africa? Of course his father was behind it somewhere, but surely he could have got out of it if he had really tried.

Well, if he went to South Africa he must go alone. But my heart would break.

I cried the whole afternoon, cowering among my pillows. I never wanted to go out of that room again. I never wanted to see anybody again. I hated the thought of facing Aunt Philippa with her cold eyes and her miserable stories that seemed to strip life of all beauty and love of all reality. I could hear her scornful, "That's the men for you," if she heard what was in Mark's letter.

"What is the matter, Ursula?"

Aunt Philippa was standing by my bed. I was too abject to resent her coming in without knocking.

"Nothing," I said spiritlessly.

"If you've been crying for three mortal hours over nothing you want a good spanking and you'll get it," observed Aunt Philippa placidly, sitting down on my trunk. "Get right up off that bed this minute and tell me what the trouble is. I'm bound to know, for I'm in your father's place at present."

"There, then!" I flung her Mark's letter. There wasn't anything in it that it was sacrilege to let another person see. That was one reason why I had been crying.

Aunt Philippa read it over twice. Then she folded it up deliberately and put it back in the envelope.

"What are you going to do?" she asked in a matter-of-fact tone.

"I'm not going to run away to be married," I answered sullenly.

"Well, no, I wouldn't advise you to," said Aunt Philippa reflectively. "It's a kind of low-down thing to do, though there's been a terrible lot of romantic nonsense talked and writ about eloping. It may be a painful necessity sometimes, but it ain't in this case. You write to your young man and tell him to come here and be married respectable under my roof, same as a Goodwin ought to."

I sat up and stared at Aunt Philippa. I was so amazed that it is useless to try to express my amazement.

"Aunt—Philippa," I gasped. "I thought—I thought—"

"You thought I was a hard old customer, and so I am," said Aunt Philippa. "But I don't take my opinions from your father nor anybody else. It didn't prejudice me any against your young man that your father didn't like him. I knew your father of old. I have some other friends in Montreal and I writ to them and asked them what he was like. From what they said I judged he was decent enough as men go. You're too young to be married, but if you let him go off to South Africa he'll slip through your fingers for sure, and I s'pose you're like some of the rest of us—nobody'll do you but the one. So tell him to come here and be married."

"I don't see how I can," I gasped. "I can't get ready to be married in three weeks. I can't—"

"I should think you have enough clothes in that trunk to do you for a spell," said Aunt Philippa sarcastically. "You've more than my mother ever had in all her life. We'll get you a wedding dress of some kind. You can get it made in Charlottetown, if country dressmakers aren't good enough for you, and I'll bake you a wedding cake that'll taste as good as anything you could get in Montreal, even if it won't look so stylish."

"What will Father say?" I questioned.

"Lots o' things," conceded Aunt Philippa grimly. "But I don't see as it matters when neither you nor me'll be there to have our feelings hurt. I'll write a few things to your father. He hasn't got much sense. He ought to be thankful to get a decent young man for his son-in-law in a world where most every man is a wolf in sheep's clothing. But that's the men for you."

And that was Aunt Philippa for you. For the next three weeks she was a blissfully excited, busy woman. I was allowed to choose the material and fashion of my wedding suit and hat myself, but almost everything else was settled by Aunt Philippa. I didn't mind; it was a relief to be rid of all responsibility; I did protest when she declared her intention of having a big wedding and asking all the cousins and semi-cousins on the island, but Aunt Philippa swept my objections lightly aside.

"I'm bound to have one good wedding in this house," she said. "Not likely I'll ever have another chance."

She found time amid all the baking and concocting to warn me frequently not to take it too much to heart if Mark failed to come after all.

"I know a man who jilted a girl on her wedding day. That's the men for you. It's best to be prepared."

But Mark did come, getting there the evening before our wedding day. And then a severe blow fell on Aunt Philippa. Word came from the manse that Mr. Bentwell had been suddenly summoned to Nova Scotia to his mother's deathbed; he had started that night.

"That's the men for you," said Aunt Philippa bitterly. "Never can depend on one of them, not even on a minister. What's to be done now?"

"Get another minister," said Mark easily.

"Where'll you get him?" demanded Aunt Philippa. "The minister at Cliftonville is away on his vacation, and Mercer is vacant, and that leaves none nearer than town. It won't do to depend on a town minister being able to come. No, there's no help for it. You'll have to have that Methodist man."

Aunt Philippa's tone was tragic. Plainly she thought the ceremony would scarcely be legal if that Methodist man married us. But neither Mark nor I cared. We were too happy to be disturbed by any such trifles.

The young Methodist minister married us the next day in the presence of many beaming guests. Aunt Philippa, splendid in black silk and point-lace collar, neither of which lost a whit of dignity or lustre by being made ten years before, was composure itself while the ceremony was going on. But no sooner had the minister pronounced us man and wife than she spoke up.

"Now that's over I want someone to go right out and put out the fire on the kitchen roof. It's been on fire for the last ten minutes."

Minister and bridegroom headed the emergency brigade, and Aunt Philippa pumped the water for them. In a short time the fire was out, all was safe, and we were receiving our deferred congratulations.

"Now, young man," said Aunt Philippa solemnly as she shook hands with Mark, "don't you ever try to get out of this, even if a Methodist minister did marry you."

She insisted on driving us to the train and said goodbye to us as we stood on the car steps. She had caught more of the shower of rice than I had, and as the day was hot and sunny she had tied over her head, atop of that festal silk dress, a huge, home-made, untrimmed straw hat. But she did not look ridiculous. There was a certain dignity about Aunt Philippa in any costume and under any circumstance.

"Aunt Philippa," I said, "tell me this: why have you helped me to be married?"

The train began to move.

"I refused once to run away myself, and I've repented it ever since." Then, as the train gathered speed and the distance between us widened, she shouted after us, "But I s'pose if I had run away I'd have repented of that too."

Bessie's Doll

Tommy Puffer, sauntering up the street, stopped to look at Miss Octavia's geraniums. Tommy never could help stopping to look at Miss Octavia's flowers, much as he hated Miss Octavia. Today they were certainly worth looking at. Miss Octavia had set them all out on her verandah—rows upon rows of them, overflowing down the steps in waves of blossom and colour. Miss Octavia's geraniums were famous in Arundel, and she was very proud of them. But it was her garden which was really the delight of her heart. Miss Octavia always had the prettiest garden in Arundel, especially as far as annuals were concerned. Just now it was like faith—the substance of things hoped for. The poppies and nasturtiums and balsams and morning glories and sweet peas had been sown in the brown beds on the lawn, but they had not yet begun to come up.

Tommy was still feasting his eyes on the geraniums when Miss Octavia herself came around the corner of the house. Her face darkened the minute she saw Tommy. Most people's did. Tommy had the reputation of being a very bad, mischievous boy; he was certainly very poor and ragged, and Miss Octavia disapproved of poverty and rags on principle. Nobody, she argued, not even a boy of twelve, need be poor and ragged if he is willing to work.

"Here, you, get away out of this," she said sharply. "I'm not going to have you hanging over my palings."

"I ain't hurting your old palings," retorted Tommy sullenly. "I was jist a-looking at the flowers."

"Yes, and picking out the next one to throw a stone at," said Miss Octavia sarcastically. "It was you who threw that stone and broke my big scarlet geranium clear off the other day."

"It wasn't—I never chucked a stone at your flowers," said Tommy.

"Don't tell me any falsehoods, Tommy Puffer. It was you. Didn't I catch you firing stones at my cat a dozen times?"

"I might have fired 'em at an old cat, but I wouldn't tech a flower," avowed Tommy boldly—brazenly, Miss Octavia thought.

"You clear out of this or I'll make you," she said warningly.

Tommy had had his ears boxed by Miss Octavia more than once. He had no desire to have the performance repeated, so he stuck his tongue out at Miss Octavia and then marched up the street with his hands in his pockets, whistling jauntily.

"He's the most impudent brat I ever saw in my life," muttered Miss Octavia wrathfully. There was a standing feud between her and all the Arundel small boys, but Tommy was her special object of dislike.

Tommy's heart was full of wrath and bitterness as he marched away. He hated Miss Octavia; he wished something would happen to every one of her flowers; he knew it was Ned Williams who had thrown that stone, and he hoped Ned would throw some more and smash all the flowers. So Tommy raged along the street until he came to Mr. Blacklock's store, and in the window of it he saw something that put Miss Octavia and her disagreeable remarks quite out of his tow-coloured head.

This was nothing more or less than a doll. Now, Tommy was not a judge of dolls and did not take much interest in them, but he felt quite sure that this was a very fine one. It was so big; it was beautifully dressed in blue silk, with a ruffled blue silk hat; it had lovely long golden hair and big brown eyes and pink cheeks; and it stood right up in the showcase and held out its hands winningly.

"Gee, ain't it a beauty!" said Tommy admiringly. "It looks 'sif it was alive, and it's as big as a baby. I must go an' bring Bessie to see it."

Tommy at once hurried away to the shabby little street where what he called "home" was. Tommy's home was a very homeless-looking sort of place. It was the smallest, dingiest, most slatternly house on a street noted for its dingy and slatternly houses. It was occupied by a slatternly mother and a drunken father, as well as by Tommy; and neither the father nor the mother took much notice of Tommy except to scold or nag him. So it is hardly to be wondered at if Tommy was the sort of boy who was frowned upon by respectable citizens.

But one little white blossom of pure affection bloomed in the arid desert of Tommy's existence for all that. In the preceding fall a new family had come to Arundel and moved into the tiny house next to the Puffers'. It was a small, dingy house, just like the others, but before long a great change took place in it. The new family were thrifty, industrious folks, although they were very poor. The little house was white-washed, the paling neatly mended, the bit of a yard cleaned of all its rubbish. Muslin curtains appeared in the windows, and rows of cans, with blossoming plants, adorned the sills.

There were just three people in the Knox family—a thin little mother, who went out scrubbing and took in washing, a boy of ten, who sold newspapers and ran errands—and Bessie.

Bessie was eight years old and walked with a crutch, but she was a smart little lassie and kept the house wonderfully neat and tidy while her mother was away. The very first time she had seen Tommy she had smiled at him sweetly and said, "Good morning." From that moment Tommy was her devoted slave. Nobody had ever spoken like that to him before; nobody had ever smiled so at him. Tommy would have given his useless little life for Bessie, and thenceforth the time he was not devising mischief he spent in bringing little pleasures into her life. It was

Tommy's delight to bring that smile to her pale little face and a look of pleasure into her big, patient blue eyes. The other boys on the street tried to tease Bessie at first and shouted "Cripple!" after her when she limped out. But they soon stopped it. Tommy thrashed them all one after another for it, and Bessie was left in peace. She would have had a very lonely life if it had not been for Tommy, for she could not play with the other children. But Tommy was as good as a dozen playmates, and Bessie thought him the best boy in the world. Tommy, whatever he might be with others, was very careful to be good when he was with Bessie. He never said a rude word in her hearing, and he treated her as if she were a little princess. Miss Octavia would have been amazed beyond measure if she had seen how tender and thoughtful and kind and chivalrous that neglected urchin of a Tommy could be when he tried.

Tommy found Bessie sitting by the kitchen window, looking dreamily out of it. For just a moment Tommy thought uneasily that Bessie was looking very pale and thin this spring.

"Bessie, come for a walk up to Mr. Blacklock's store," he said eagerly. "There is something there I want to show you."

"What is it?" Bessie wanted to know. But Tommy only winked mysteriously.

"Ah, I ain't going to tell you. But it's something awful pretty. Just you wait."

Bessie reached for her crutch and the two went up to the store, Tommy carefully suiting his steps to Bessie's slow ones. Just before they reached the store he made her shut her eyes and led her to the window.

"Now—look!" he commanded dramatically.

Bessie looked and Tommy was rewarded. She flushed pinkly with delight and clasped her hands in ecstasy.

"Oh, Tommy, isn't she perfectly beautiful?" she breathed. "Oh, she's the very loveliest dolly I ever saw. Oh, Tommy!"

"I thought you'd like her," said Tommy exultantly. "Don't you wish you had a doll like that of your very own, Bessie?"

Bessie looked almost rebuking, as if Tommy had asked her if she wouldn't like a golden crown or a queen's palace.

"Of course I could never have a dolly like that," she said. "She must cost an awful lot. But it's enough just to look at her. Tommy, will you bring me up here every day just to look at her?"

"'Course," said Tommy.

Bessie talked about the blue-silk doll all the way home and dreamed of her every night. "I'm going to call her Roselle Geraldine," she said. After that she went up to see Roselle Geraldine every day, gazing at her for long moments in silent rapture. Tommy almost grew jealous of her; he thought Bessie liked the doll better than she did him.

"But it don't matter a bit if she does," he thought loyally, crushing down the jealousy. "If she likes to like it better than me, it's all right."

Sometimes, though, Tommy felt uneasy. It was plain to be seen that Bessie had set her heart on that doll. And what would she do when the doll was sold, as would probably happen soon? Tommy thought Bessie would feel awful sad, and he would be responsible for it.

What Tommy feared came to pass. One afternoon, when they went up to Mr. Blacklock's store, the doll was not in the window.

"Oh," cried Bessie, bursting into tears, "she's gone—Roselle Geraldine is gone."

"Perhaps she isn't sold," said Tommy comfortingly. "Maybe they only took her out of the window 'cause the blue silk would fade. I'll go in and ask."

A minute later Tommy came out looking sober.

"Yes, she's sold, Bessie," he said. "Mr. Blacklock sold her to a lady yesterday. Don't cry, Bessie—maybe they'll put another in the window 'fore long."

"It won't be mine," sobbed Bessie. "It won't be Roselle Geraldine. It won't have a blue silk hat and such cunning brown eyes."

Bessie cried quietly all the way home, and Tommy could not comfort her. He wished he had never shown her the doll in the window.

From that day Bessie drooped, and Tommy watched her in agony. She grew paler and thinner. She was too tired to go out walking, and too tired to do the little household tasks she had delighted in. She never spoke about Roselle Geraldine, but Tommy knew she was fretting about her. Mrs. Knox could not think what ailed the child.

"She don't take a bit of interest in nothing," she complained to Mrs. Puffer. "She don't eat enough for a bird. The doctor, he says there ain't nothing the matter with her as he can find out, but she's just pining away."

Tommy heard this, and a queer, big lump came up in his throat. He had a horrible fear that he, Tommy Puffer, was going to cry. To prevent it he began to whistle loudly. But the whistle was a failure, very unlike the real Tommy-whistle. Bessie was sick—and it was all his fault, Tommy believed. If he had never taken her to see that hateful, blue-silk doll, she would never have got so fond of it as to be breaking her heart because it was sold.

"If I was only rich," said Tommy miserably, "I'd buy her a cartload of dolls, all dressed in blue silk and all with brown eyes. But I can't do nothing."

By this time Tommy had reached the paling in front of Miss Octavia's lawn, and from force of habit he stopped to look over it. But there was not much to see this time, only the little green rows and circles in the brown, well-weeded beds, and the long curves of dahlia plants, which Miss Octavia had set out a few days before. All the geraniums were carried in, and the blinds were down. Tommy knew Miss Octavia was away. He had seen her depart on the train that morning, and heard her tell a friend that she was going down to Chelton to visit her brother's folks and wouldn't be back until the next day.

Tommy was still leaning moodily against the paling when Mrs. Jenkins and Mrs. Reid came by, and they too paused to look at the garden.

"Dear me, how cold it is!" shivered Mrs. Reid. "There's going to be a hard frost tonight. Octavia's flowers will be nipped as sure as anything. It's a wonder she'd stay away from them overnight when her heart's so set on them."

"Her brother's wife is sick," said Mrs. Jenkins. "We haven't had any frost this spring, and I suppose Octavia never thought of such a thing. She'll feel awful bad if her flowers get frosted, especially them dahlias. Octavia sets such store by her dahlias."

Mrs. Jenkins and Mrs. Reid moved away, leaving Tommy by the paling. It was cold—there was going to be a hard frost—and Miss Octavia's plants and flowers would certainly be spoiled. Tommy thought he ought to be glad, but he wasn't. He was sorry—not for Miss Octavia, but for her flowers. Tommy had a queer, passionate love for flowers in his twisted little soul. It was a shame that they should be nipped—that all the glory of crimson and purple and gold hidden away in those little green rows and circles should never have a chance to blossom out royally. Tommy could never have put this thought into words, but it was there in his heart. He wished he could save the flowers. And couldn't he? Newspapers spread over the beds and tied around the dahlias would save them, Tommy knew. He had seen Miss Octavia doing it other springs. And he knew there was a big box of newspapers in a little shed in her backyard. Ned Williams had told him there was, and that the shed was never locked.

Tommy hurried home as quickly as he could and got a ball of twine out of his few treasures. Then he went back to Miss Octavia's garden.

The next forenoon Miss Octavia got off the train at the Arundel station with a very grim face. There had been an unusually severe frost for the time of year. All along the road Miss Octavia had seen gardens frosted and spoiled. She knew what she should see when she got to her own—the dahlia stalks drooping and black and limp, the nasturtiums and balsams and poppies and pansies all withered and ruined.

But she didn't. Instead she saw every dahlia carefully tied up in a newspaper, and over all the beds newspapers spread out and held neatly in place with pebbles. Miss Octavia flew into her garden with a radiant face. Everything was safe—nothing was spoiled.

But who could have done it? Miss Octavia was puzzled. On one side of her lived Mrs. Kennedy, who had just moved in and, being a total stranger, would not be likely to think of Miss Octavia's flowers. On the other lived Miss Matheson, who was a "shut-in" and spent all her time on the sofa. But to Miss Matheson Miss Octavia went.

"Rachel, do you know who covered my plants up last night?"

Miss Matheson nodded. "Yes, it was Tommy Puffer. I saw him working away there with papers and twine. I thought you'd told him to do it."

"For the land's sake!" ejaculated Miss Octavia. "Tommy Puffer! Well, wonders will never cease."

Miss Octavia went back to her house feeling rather ashamed of herself when she remembered how she had always treated Tommy Puffer.

"But there must be some good in the child, or he wouldn't have done this," she said to herself. "I've been real mean, but I'll make it up to him."

Miss Octavia did not see Tommy that day, but when he passed the next morning she ran to the door and called him.

"Tommy, Tommy Puffer, come in here!"

Tommy came reluctantly. He didn't like Miss Octavia any better than he had, and he didn't know what she wanted of him. But Miss Octavia soon informed him without loss of words.

"Tommy, Miss Matheson tells me that it was you who saved my flowers from the frost the other night. I'm very much obliged to you indeed. Whatever made you think of doing it?"

"I hated to see the flowers spoiled," muttered Tommy, who was feeling more uncomfortable than he had ever felt in his life.

"Well, it was real thoughtful of you. I'm sorry I've been so hard on you, Tommy, and I believe now you didn't break my scarlet geranium. Is there anything I can do for you—anything you'd like to have? If it's in reason I'll get it for you, just to pay my debt."

Tommy stared at Miss Octavia with a sudden hopeful inspiration. "Oh, Miss Octavia," he cried eagerly, "will you buy a doll and give it to me?"

"Well, for the land's sake!" ejaculated Miss Octavia, unable to believe her ears. "A doll! What on earth do you want of a doll?"

"It's for Bessie," said Tommy eagerly. "You see, it's this way."

Then Tommy told Miss Octavia the whole story. Miss Octavia listened silently, sometimes nodding her head. When he had finished she went out of the room and soon returned, bringing with her the very identical doll that had been in Mr. Blacklock's window.

"I guess this is the doll," she said. "I bought it to give to a small niece of mine, but I can get another for her. You may take this to Bessie."

It would be of no use to try to describe Bessie's joy when Tommy rushed in and put Roselle Geraldine in her arms with a breathless account of the wonderful story. But from that moment Bessie began to pick up again, and soon she was better than she had ever been and the happiest little lassie in Arundel.

When a week had passed, Miss Octavia again called Tommy in; Tommy went more willingly this time. He had begun to like Miss Octavia.

That lady looked him over sharply and somewhat dubiously. He was certainly very ragged and unkempt. But Miss Octavia saw what she had never noticed before—that Tommy's eyes were bright and frank, that Tommy's chin was a good chin, and that Tommy's smile had something very pleasant about it.

"You're fond of flowers, aren't you, Tommy?" she asked.

"You bet," was Tommy's inelegant but heartfelt answer.

"Well," said Miss Octavia slowly, "I have a brother down at Chelton who is a florist. He wants a boy of your age to do handy jobs and run errands about his establishment, and he wants one who is fond of flowers and would like to learn the business. He asked me to recommend him one, and I promised to look out for a suitable boy. Would you like the place, Tommy? And will you promise to be a very good boy and learn to be respectable if I ask my brother to give you a trial and a chance to make something of yourself?"

"Oh, Miss Octavia!" gasped Tommy. He wondered if he were simply having a beautiful dream.

But it was no dream. And it was all arranged later on. No one rejoiced more heartily in Tommy's success than Bessie.

"But I'll miss you dreadfully, Tommy," she said wistfully.

"Oh, I'll be home every Saturday night, and we'll have Sunday together, except when I've got to go to Sunday school. 'Cause Miss Octavia says I must," said Tommy comfortingly. "And the rest of the time you'll have Roselle Geraldine."

"Yes, I know," said Bessie, giving the blue-silk doll a fond kiss, "and she's just lovely. But she ain't as nice as you, Tommy, for all."

Then was Tommy's cup of happiness full.

Charlotte's Ladies

Just as soon as dinner was over at the asylum, Charlotte sped away to the gap in the fence—the northwest corner gap. There was a gap in the southeast corner, too—the asylum fence was in a rather poor condition—but the southeast gap was interesting only after tea, and it was never at any time quite as interesting as the northwest gap.

Charlotte ran as fast as her legs could carry her, for she did not want any of the other orphans to see her. As a rule, Charlotte liked the company of the other orphans and was a favourite with them. But, somehow, she did not want them to know about the gaps. She was sure they would not understand.

Charlotte had discovered the gaps only a week before. They had not been there in the autumn, but the snowdrifts had lain heavily against the fence all winter, and one spring day when Charlotte was creeping through the shrubbery in the northwest corner in search of the little yellow daffodils that always grew there in spring, she found a delightful space where a board had fallen off, whence she could look out on a bit of woodsy road with a little footpath winding along by the fence under the widespreading boughs of the asylum trees. Charlotte felt a wild impulse to slip out and run fast and far down that lovely, sunny, tempting, fenceless road. But that would have been wrong, for it was against the asylum rules, and Charlotte, though she hated most of the asylum rules with all her heart, never disobeyed or broke them. So she subdued the vagrant longing with a sigh and sat down among the daffodils to peer wistfully out of the gap and feast her eyes on this glimpse of a world where there were no brick walls and prim walks and never-varying rules.

Then, as Charlotte watched, the Pretty Lady with the Blue Eyes came along the footpath. Charlotte had never seen her before and hadn't the slightest idea in the world who she was, but that was what she called her as soon as she saw her. The lady was so pretty, with lovely blue eyes that were very sad, although somehow as you looked at them you felt that they ought to be laughing, merry eyes instead. At least Charlotte thought so and wished at once that she knew how to make them laugh. Besides, the Lady had lovely golden hair and the most beautiful pink cheeks, and Charlotte, who had mouse-coloured hair and any number of freckles, had an unbounded admiration for golden locks and roseleaf complexions. The Lady was dressed in black, which Charlotte didn't like, principally because the matron of the asylum wore black and Charlotte didn't—exactly—like the matron.

When the Pretty Lady with the Blue Eyes had gone by, Charlotte drew a long breath.

"If I could pick out a mother I'd pick out one that looked just like her," she said.

Nice things sometimes happen close together, even in an orphan asylum, and that very evening Charlotte discovered the southeast gap and found herself peering into the most beautiful garden you could imagine, a garden where daffodils and tulips grew in great ribbon-like beds, and there were hedges of white and purple lilacs, and winding paths under blossoming trees. It was such a garden as Charlotte had pictured in happy dreams and never expected to see in real life. And yet here it had been all the time, divided from her only by a high board fence.

"I wouldn't have s'posed there could be such a lovely place so near an orphan asylum," mused Charlotte. "It's the very loveliest place I ever saw. Oh, I do wish I could go and walk in it. Well, I do declare! If there isn't a lady in it, too!"

Sure enough, there was a lady, helping an unruly young vine to run in the way it should go over a little arbour. Charlotte instantly named her the Tall Lady with the Black Eyes. She was not nearly so young or so pretty as the Lady with the Blue Eyes, but she looked very kind and jolly.

I'd like her for an aunt, reflected Charlotte. Not for a mother—oh, no, not for a mother, but for an aunt. I know she'd make a splendid aunt. And, oh, just look at her cat!

Charlotte looked at the cat with all her might and main. She loved cats, but cats were not allowed in an orphan asylum, although Charlotte sometimes wondered if there were no orphan kittens in the world which would be appropriate for such an institution.

The Tall Lady's cat was so big and furry, with a splendid tail and elegant stripes. A Very Handsome Cat, Charlotte called him mentally, seeing the capitals as plainly as if they had been printed out. Charlotte's fingers tingled to stroke his glossy coat, but she folded them sternly together.

"You know you can't," she said to herself reproachfully, "so what is the use of wanting to, Charlotte Turner? You ought to be thankful just to see the garden and the Very Handsome Cat."

Charlotte watched the Tall Lady and the Cat until they went away into a fine, big house further up the garden, then she sighed and went back through the cherry trees to the asylum playground, where the other orphans were playing games. But, somehow, games had lost their flavour compared with those fascinating gaps.

It did not take Charlotte long to discover that the Pretty Lady always walked past the northwest gap about one o'clock every day and never at any other time—at least at no other time when Charlotte was free to watch her; and that the Tall Lady was almost always in her garden at five in the afternoon, accompanied by the Very Handsome Cat, pruning and trimming some of her flowers. Charlotte never missed being at the gaps at the proper times, if she could possibly manage it, and her heart was full of dreams about her two Ladies. But the other orphans thought all the fun had gone out of her, and the matron noticed her absent-mindedness and dosed her with sulphur and molasses for it. Charlotte took the dose meekly, as she took everything else. It was all part and parcel with being an orphan in an asylum.

"But if the Pretty Lady with the Blue Eyes was my mother, she wouldn't make me swallow such dreadful stuff," sighed Charlotte. "I don't believe even the Tall Lady with the Black Eyes would—though perhaps she might, aunts not being quite as good as mothers."

"Do you know," said Maggie Brunt, coming up to Charlotte at this moment, "that Lizzie Parker is going to be adopted? A lady is going to adopt her."

"Oh!" cried Charlotte breathlessly. An adoption was always a wonderful event in the asylum, as well as a somewhat rare one. "Oh, how splendid!"

"Yes, isn't it?" said Maggie enviously. "She picked out Lizzie because she was pretty and had curls. I don't think it is fair."

Charlotte sighed. "Nobody will ever want to adopt me, because I've mousy hair and freckles," she said. "But somebody may want you some day, Maggie. You have such lovely black hair."

"But it isn't curly," said Maggie forlornly. "And the matron won't let me put it up in curl papers at night. I just wish I was Lizzie."

Charlotte shook her head. "I don't. I'd love to be adopted, but I wouldn't really like to be anybody but myself, even if I am homely. It's better to be yourself with mousy hair and freckles than somebody else who is ever so beautiful. But I do envy Lizzie, though the matron says it is wicked to envy anyone."

Envy of the fortunate Lizzie did not long possess Charlotte's mind, however, for that very day a wonderful thing happened at noon hour by the northwest gap. Charlotte had always been very careful not to let the Pretty Lady see her, but to-day, after the Pretty Lady had gone past, Charlotte leaned out of the gap to watch her as far as she could. And just at that very moment the Pretty Lady looked back; and there, peering at her from the asylum fence, was a little scrap of a girl, with mouse-coloured hair and big freckles, and the sweetest, brightest, most winsome little face the Pretty Lady had ever seen. The Pretty Lady smiled right down at Charlotte and for just a moment her eyes looked as Charlotte had always known they ought to look. Charlotte was feeling rather frightened down in her heart but she smiled bravely back.

"Are you thinking of running away?" said the Pretty Lady, and, oh, what a sweet voice she had—sweet and tender, just like a mother's voice ought to be!

"No," said Charlotte, shaking her head gravely. "I should like to run away but it would be of no use, because there is no place to run to."

"Why would you like to run away?" asked the Pretty Lady, still smiling. "Don't you like living here?"

Charlotte opened her big eyes very widely. "Why, it's an orphan asylum!" she exclaimed. "Nobody could like living in an orphan asylum. But, of course, orphans should be very thankful to have any place to live in and I *am* thankful. I'd be thankfuller still if the matron wouldn't make me take sulphur and molasses. If you had a little girl, would you make her take sulphur and molasses?"

"I didn't when I had a little girl," said the Pretty Lady wistfully, and her eyes were sad again.

"Oh, did you really have a little girl once?" asked Charlotte softly.

"Yes, and she died," said the Pretty Lady in a trembling voice.

"Oh, I am sorry," said Charlotte, more softly still. "Did she—did she have lovely golden hair and pink cheeks like yours?"

"No," the Pretty Lady smiled again, though it was a very sad smile. "No, she had mouse-coloured hair and freckles."

"Oh! And weren't you sorry?"

"No, I was glad of it, because it made her look like her father. I've always loved little girls with mouse-coloured hair and freckles ever since. Well, I must hurry along. I'm late now, and schools have a dreadful habit of going in sharp on time. If you should happen to be here tomorrow, I'm going to stop and ask your name."

Of course Charlotte was at the gap the next day and they had a lovely talk. In a week they were the best of friends. Charlotte soon found out that she could make the Pretty Lady's eyes look as they ought to for a little while at least, and she spent all her spare time and lay awake at nights devising speeches to make the Pretty Lady laugh.

Then another wonderful thing happened. One evening when Charlotte went to the southeast gap, the Tall Lady with the Black Eyes was not in the garden—at least, Charlotte thought she wasn't. But the Very Handsome Cat was, sitting gravely under a syringa bush and looking quite proud of himself for being a cat.

"You Very Handsome Cat," said Charlotte, "won't you come here and let me stroke you?"

The Very Handsome Cat did come, just as if he understood English, and he purred with delight when Charlotte took him in her arms and buried her face in his fur. Then—Charlotte thought she would really sink into the ground, for the Tall Lady herself came around a lilac bush and stood before the gap.

"Please, ma'am," stammered Charlotte in an agony of embarrassment, "I wasn't meaning to do any harm to your Very Handsome Cat. I just wanted to pat him. I—I am very fond of cats and they are not allowed in orphan asylums."

"I've always thought asylums weren't run on proper principles," said the Tall Lady briskly. "Bless your heart, child, don't look so scared. You're welcome to pat the cat all you like. Come in and I'll give you some flowers."

"Thank you, but I am not allowed to go off the grounds," said Charlotte firmly, "and I think I'd rather not have any flowers because the matron might want to know where I got them, and then she would have this gap closed up. I live in mortal dread for fear it will be closed anyhow. It's very uncomfortable—living in mortal dread."

The Tall Lady laughed a very jolly laugh. "Yes, I should think it would be," she agreed. "I haven't had that experience."

Then they had a jolly talk, and every evening after that Charlotte went to the gap and stroked the Very Handsome Cat and chatted to the Tall Lady.

"Do you live all alone in that big house?" she asked wonderingly one day.

"All alone," said the Tall Lady.

"Did you always live alone?"

"No. I had a sister living with me once. But I don't want to talk about her. You'll oblige me, Charlotte, by *not* talking about her."

"I won't then," agreed Charlotte. "I can understand why people don't like to have their sisters talked about sometimes. Lily Mitchell has a big sister who was sent to jail for stealing. Of course Lily doesn't like to talk about her."

The Tall Lady laughed a little bitterly. "My sister didn't steal. She married a man I detested, that's all."

"Did he drink?" asked Charlotte gravely. "The matron's husband drank and that was why she left him and took to running an orphan asylum. I think I'd rather put up with a drunken husband than live in an orphan asylum."

"My sister's husband didn't drink," said the Tall Lady grimly. "He was beneath her, that was all. I told her I'd never forgive her and I never shall. He's dead now—he died a year after she married him—and she's working for her living. I dare say she doesn't find it very pleasant. She wasn't brought up to that. Here, Charlotte, is a turnover for you. I made it on purpose for you. Eat it and tell me if you don't think I'm a good cook. I'm dying for a compliment. I never get any now that I've got old. It's a dismal thing to get old and have nobody to love you except a cat, Charlotte."

"I think it is just as bad to be young and have nobody to love you, not *even* a cat," sighed Charlotte, enjoying the turnover, nevertheless.

"I dare say it is," agreed the Tall Lady, looking as if she had been struck by a new and rather startling idea.

I like the tall lady with the Black Eyes ever so much, thought Charlotte that night as she lay in bed, but I love the Pretty Lady. I have more fun with the Tall Lady and the Very Handsome Cat, but I always feel nicer with the Pretty Lady. Oh, I'm so glad her little girl had mouse-coloured hair.

Then the most wonderful thing of all happened. One day a week later the Pretty Lady said, "Would you like to come and live with me, Charlotte?"

Charlotte looked at her. "Are you in earnest?" she asked in a whisper.

"Indeed I am. I want you for my little girl, and if you'd like to come, you shall. I'm poor, Charlotte, really, I'm dreadfully poor, but I can make my salary stretch far enough for two, and we'll love each other enough to cover the thin spots. Will you come?"

"Well, I should just think I will!" said Charlotte emphatically. "Oh, I wish I was sure I'm not dreaming. I do love you so much, and it will be so delightful to be your little girl."

"Very well, sweetheart. I'll come tomorrow afternoon—it is Saturday, so I'll have the whole blessed day off—and see the matron about it. Oh, we'll have lovely times together, dearest. I only wish I'd discovered you long ago."

Charlotte may have eaten and studied and played and kept rules the rest of that day and part of the next, but, if so, she has no recollection of it. She went about like a girl in a dream, and the matron concluded that something more than sulphur and molasses was needed and decided to speak to the doctor about her. But she never did, because a lady came that afternoon and told her she wanted to adopt Charlotte.

Charlotte obeyed the summons to the matron's room in a tingle of excitement. But when she went in, she saw only the matron and the Tall Lady with the Black Eyes. Before Charlotte could look around for the Pretty Lady the matron said, "Charlotte, this lady, Miss Herbert, wishes to adopt you. It is a splendid thing for you, and you ought to be a very thankful little girl."

Charlotte's head fairly whirled. She clasped her hands and the tears brimmed up in her eyes.

"Oh, I like the Tall Lady," she gasped, "but I *love* the Pretty Lady and I promised her I'd be her little girl. I can't break my promise."

"What on earth is the child talking about?" said the mystified matron.

And just then the maid showed in the Pretty Lady. Charlotte flew to her and flung her arms about her.

"Oh, tell them I am your little girl!" she begged. "Tell them I promised you first. I don't want to hurt the Tall Lady's feelings because I truly do like her so very much. But I want to be your little girl."

The Pretty Lady had given one glance at the Tall Lady and flushed red. The Tall Lady, on the contrary, had grown very pale. The matron felt uncomfortable. Everybody knew that Miss Herbert and Mrs. Bond hadn't spoken to each other for years, even if they were sisters and alone in the world except for each other.

Mrs. Bond turned to the matron. "I have come to ask permission to adopt this little girl," she said.

"Oh, I'm very sorry," stammered the matron, "but Miss Herbert has just asked for her, and I have consented."

Charlotte gave a great gulp of disappointment, but the Pretty Lady suddenly wheeled around to face the Tall Lady, with quivering lips and tearful eyes.

"Don't take her from me, Alma," she pleaded humbly. "She—she is so like my own baby and I'm so lonely. Any other child will suit you as well."

"Not at all," said the Tall Lady brusquely. "Not at all, Anna. No other child will suit me at all. And may I ask what you intend to keep her on? I know your salary is barely enough for yourself."

"That is my concern," said the Pretty Lady a little proudly.

"Humph!" The Tall Lady shrugged her shoulders. "Just as independent as ever, Anna, I see. Well, child, what do *you* say? Which of us will you come with? Remember, I have the cat on my side, and Anna can't make half as good turnovers as I can. Remember all this, Charlotte."

"Oh, I—I like you so much," stammered Charlotte, "and I wish I could live with you both. But since I can't, I must go with the Pretty Lady, because I promised, and because I loved her first."

"And best?" queried the Tall Lady.

"And best," admitted Charlotte, bound to be truthful, even at the risk of hurting the Tall Lady's feelings. "But I *do* like you, too—next best. And you really don't need me as much as she does, for you have your Very Handsome Cat and she hasn't anything."

"A cat no longer satisfies the aching void in my soul," said the Tall Lady stubbornly. "Nothing will satisfy it but a little girl with mouse-coloured hair and freckles. No, Anna, I've got to have Charlotte. But I think that with her usual astuteness, she has already solved the problem for us by saying she'd like to live with us both. Why can't she? You just come back home and we'll let bygones be bygones. We both have something to forgive, but I was an obstinate old fool and I've known it for years, though I never confessed it to anybody but the cat."

The Pretty Lady softened, trembled, smiled. She went right up to the Tall Lady and put her arms about her neck.

"Oh, I've wanted so much to be friends with you again," she sobbed. "But I thought you would never relent—and—and—I've been so lonely—"

"There, there," whispered the Tall Lady, "don't cry under the matron's eye. Wait till we get home. I may have some crying to do myself then. Charlotte, go and get your hat and come right over with us. We can sign the necessary papers later on, but we must have you right off. The cat is waiting for you on the back porch, and there is a turnover cooling on the pantry window that is just your size."

"I am so happy," remarked Charlotte, "that I feel like crying myself."

Christmas at Red Butte

"Of course Santa Claus will come," said Jimmy Martin confidently. Jimmy was ten, and at ten it is easy to be confident. "Why, he's *got* to come because it is Christmas Eve, and he always *has* come. You know that, twins."

Yes, the twins knew it and, cheered by Jimmy's superior wisdom, their doubts passed away. There had been one terrible moment when Theodora had sighed and told them they mustn't be too much disappointed if Santa Claus did not come this year because the crops had been poor, and he mightn't have had enough presents to go around.

"That doesn't make any difference to Santa Claus," scoffed Jimmy. "You know as well as I do, Theodora Prentice, that Santa Claus is rich whether the crops fail or not. They failed three years ago, before Father died, but Santa Claus came all the same. Prob'bly you don't remember it, twins, 'cause you were too little, but I do. Of course he'll come, so don't you worry a mite. And he'll bring my skates and your dolls. He knows we're expecting them, Theodora, 'cause we wrote him a letter last week, and threw it up the chimney. And there'll be candy and nuts, of course, and Mother's gone to town to buy a turkey. I tell you we're going to have a ripping Christmas."

"Well, don't use such slangy words about it, Jimmy-boy," sighed Theodora. She couldn't bear to dampen their hopes any further, and perhaps Aunt Elizabeth might manage it if the colt sold well. But Theodora had her painful doubts, and she sighed again as she looked out of the window far down the trail that wound across the prairie, red-lighted by the declining sun of the short wintry afternoon.

"Do people always sigh like that when they get to be sixteen?" asked Jimmy curiously. "You didn't sigh like that when you were only fifteen, Theodora. I wish you wouldn't. It makes me feel funny—and it's not a nice kind of funniness either."

"It's a bad habit I've got into lately," said Theodora, trying to laugh. "Old folks are dull sometimes, you know, Jimmy-boy."

"Sixteen *is* awful old, isn't it?" said Jimmy reflectively. "I'll tell you what *I'm* going to do when I'm sixteen, Theodora. I'm going to pay off the mortgage, and buy mother a silk dress, and a piano for the twins. Won't that be elegant? I'll be able to do that 'cause I'm a man. Of course if I was only a girl I couldn't."

"I hope you'll be a good kind brave man and a real help to your mother," said Theodora softly, sitting down before the cosy fire and lifting the fat little twins into her lap.

"Oh, I'll be good to her, never you fear," assured Jimmy, squatting comfortably down on the little fur rug before the stove—the skin of the coyote his father had killed four years ago. "I believe in being good to your mother when you've only got the one. Now tell us a story, Theodora—a real jolly story, you know, with lots of fighting in it. Only please don't kill anybody. I like to hear about fighting, but I like to have all the people come out alive."

Theodora laughed, and began a story about the Riel Rebellion of '85—a story which had the double merit of being true and exciting at the same time. It was quite dark when she finished, and the twins were nodding, but Jimmy's eyes were wide open and sparkling.

"That was great," he said, drawing a long breath. "Tell us another."

"No, it's bedtime for you all," said Theodora firmly. "One story at a time is my rule, you know."

"But I want to sit up till Mother comes home," objected Jimmy.

"You can't. She may be very late, for she would have to wait to see Mr. Porter. Besides, you don't know what time Santa Claus might come—if he comes at all. If he were to drive along and see you children up instead of being sound asleep in bed, he might go right on and never call at all."

This argument was too much for Jimmy.

"All right, we'll go. But we have to hang up our stockings first. Twins, get yours."

The twins toddled off in great excitement, and brought back their Sunday stockings, which Jimmy proceeded to hang along the edge of the mantel shelf. This done, they all trooped obediently off to bed. Theodora gave another sigh, and seated herself at the window, where she could watch the moonlit prairie for Mrs. Martin's homecoming and knit at the same time.

I am afraid that you will think from all the sighing Theodora was doing that she was a very melancholy and despondent young lady. You couldn't think anything more unlike the real Theodora. She was the jolliest, bravest girl of sixteen in all Saskatchewan, as her shining brown eyes and rosy, dimpled cheeks would have told you; and her sighs were not on her own account, but simply for fear the children were going to be disappointed. She knew that they would be almost heartbroken if Santa Claus did not come, and that this would hurt the patient hardworking little mother more than all else.

Five years before this, Theodora had come to live with Uncle George and Aunt Elizabeth in the little log house at Red Butte. Her own mother had just died, and Theodora had only her big brother Donald left, and Donald had Klondike fever. The Martins were poor, but they had gladly made room for their little niece, and Theodora had lived there ever since, her aunt's right-hand girl and the beloved playmate of the children. They had been very happy until Uncle George's death two years before this Christmas Eve; but since then there had been hard times in the little log house, and though Mrs. Martin and Theodora did their best, it was a woefully hard task to make both ends meet, especially this year when their crops had been poor. Theodora and her aunt had made every sacrifice possible for the children's sake, and at least Jimmy and the twins had not felt the pinch very severely yet.

At seven Mrs. Martins bells jingled at the door and Theodora flew out. "Go right in and get warm, Auntie," she said briskly. "I'll take Ned away and unharness him."

"It's a bitterly cold night," said Mrs. Martin wearily. There was a note of discouragement in her voice that struck dismay to Theodora's heart.

"I'm afraid it means no Christmas for the children tomorrow," she thought sadly, as she led Ned away to the stable. When she returned to the kitchen Mrs. Martin was sitting by the fire, her face in her chilled hand, sobbing convulsively.

"Auntie—oh, Auntie, don't!" exclaimed Theodora impulsively. It was such a rare thing to see her plucky, resolute little aunt in tears. "You're cold and tired—I'll have a nice cup of tea for you in a trice."

"No, it isn't that," said Mrs. Martin brokenly "It was seeing those stockings hanging there. Theodora, I couldn't get a thing for the children—not a single thing. Mr. Porter would only give forty dollars for the colt, and when all the bills were paid there was barely enough left for such necessaries as we must have. I suppose I ought to feel thankful I could get those. But the thought of the children's disappointment tomorrow is more than I can bear. It would have been better to have told them long ago, but I kept building on getting more for the colt. Well, it's weak and foolish to give way like this. We'd better both take a cup of tea and go to bed. It will save fuel."

When Theodora went up to her little room her face was very thoughtful. She took a small box from her table and carried it to the window. In it was a very pretty little gold locket hung on a narrow blue ribbon. Theodora held it tenderly in her fingers, and looked out over the moonlit prairie with a very sober face. Could she give up her dear locket—the locket Donald had given her just before he started for the Klondike? She had never thought she could do such a thing. It was almost the only thing she had to remind her of Donald—handsome, merry, impulsive, warmhearted Donald, who had gone away four years ago with a smile on his bonny face and splendid hope in his heart.

"Here's a locket for you, Gift o' God," he had said gaily—he had such a dear loving habit of calling her by the beautiful meaning of her name. A lump came into Theodora's throat as she remembered it. "I couldn't afford a chain too, but when I come back I'll bring you a rope of Klondike nuggets for it."

Then he had gone away. For two years letters had come from him regularly. Then he wrote that he had joined a prospecting party to a remote wilderness. After that was silence, deepening into anguish of suspense that finally ended in hopelessness. A rumour came that Donald Prentice was dead. None had returned from the expedition he had joined. Theodora had long ago given up all hope of ever seeing Donald again. Hence her locket was doubly dear to her.

But Aunt Elizabeth had always been so good and loving and kind to her. Could she not make the sacrifice for her sake? Yes, she could and would. Theodora flung up her head with a gesture that meant decision. She took out of the locket the bits of hair—her mother's and Donald's—which it contained (perhaps a tear or two fell as she did so) and then hastily donned her warmest cap and wraps. It was only three miles to Spencer; she could easily walk it in an hour and, as it was Christmas Eve, the shops would be open late. She muse walk, for Ned could not be taken out again, and the mare's foot was sore. Besides, Aunt Elizabeth must not know until it was done.

As stealthily as if she were bound on some nefarious errand, Theodora slipped downstairs and out of the house. The next minute she was hurrying along the trail in the moonlight. The great dazzling prairie was around her, the mystery and splendour of the northern night all about her. It was very calm and cold, but Theodora walked so briskly that she kept warm. The trail from Red Butte to Spencer was a lonely one. Mr. Lurgan's house, halfway to town, was the only dwelling on it.

When Theodora reached Spencer she made her way at once to the only jewellery store the little town contained. Mr. Benson, its owner, had been a friend of her uncle's, and Theodora felt sure that he would buy her locket. Nevertheless her heart beat quickly, and her breath came and went uncomfortably fast as she went in. Suppose he wouldn't buy it. Then there would be no Christmas for the children at Red Butte.

"Good evening, Miss Theodora," said Mr. Benson briskly. "What can I do for you?"

"I'm afraid I'm not a very welcome sort of customer, Mr. Benson," said Theodora, with an uncertain smile. "I want to sell, not buy. Could you—will you buy this locket?"

Mr. Benson pursed up his lips, took up the locket, and examined it. "Well, I don't often buy second-hand stuff," he said, after some reflection, "but I don't mind obliging you, Miss Theodora. I'll give you four dollars for this trinket."

Theodora knew the locket had cost a great deal more than that, but four dollars would get what she wanted, and she dared not ask for more. In a few minutes the locket was in Mr. Benson's possession, and Theodora, with four crisp new bills in her purse, was hurrying to the toy store. Half an hour later she was on her way back to Red Butte, with as many parcels as she could carry—Jimmy's skates, two lovely dolls for the twins, packages of nuts and candy, and a nice plump turkey. Theodora beguiled her lonely tramp by picturing the children's joy in the morning.

About a quarter of a mile past Mr. Lurgan's house the trail curved suddenly about a bluff of poplars. As Theodora rounded the turn she halted in amazement. Almost at her feet the body of a man was lying across the road. He was clad in a big fur coat, and had a fur cap pulled well down over his forehead and ears. Almost all of him that could be seen was a full bushy beard. Theodora had no idea who he was, or where he had come from. But she realized that he was unconscious, and that he would speedily freeze to death if help were not brought. The footprints of a horse galloping across the prairie suggested a fall and a runaway, but Theodora did not waste time in speculation. She ran back at full speed to Mr. Lurgan's, and roused the household. In a few minutes Mr. Lurgan and his son had hitched a horse to a wood-sleigh, and hurried down the trail to the unfortunate man.

Theodora, knowing that her assistance was not needed, and that she ought to get home as quickly as possible, went on her way as soon as she had seen the stranger in safe keeping. When she reached the little log house she crept in, cautiously put the children's gifts in their stockings, placed the turkey on the table where Aunt Elizabeth would see it the first thing in the morning, and then slipped off to bed, a very weary but very happy girl.

The joy that reigned in the little log house the next day more than repaid Theodora for her sacrifice.

"Whoopee, didn't I tell you that Santa Claus would come all right!" shouted the delighted Jimmy. "Oh, what splendid skates!"

The twins hugged their dolls in silent rapture, but Aunt Elizabeth's face was the best of all.

Then the dinner had to be prepared, and everybody had a hand in that. Just as Theodora, after a grave peep into the oven, had announced that the turkey was done, a sleigh dashed around the house. Theodora flew to answer the knock at the door, and there stood Mr. Lurgan and a big, bewhiskered, fur-coated fellow whom Theodora recognized as the stranger she had found on the trail. But—*was* he a stranger? There was something oddly familiar in those merry brown eyes. Theodora felt herself growing dizzy.

"Donald!" she gasped. "Oh, Donald!"

And then she was in the big fellow's arms, laughing and crying at the same time.

Donald it was indeed. And then followed half an hour during which everybody talked at once, and the turkey would have been burned to a crisp had it not been for the presence of mind of Mr. Lurgan who, being the least excited of them all, took it out of the oven, and set it on the back of the stove.

"To think that it was you last night, and that I never dreamed it," exclaimed Theodora. "Oh, Donald, if I hadn't gone to town!"

"I'd have frozen to death, I'm afraid," said Donald soberly. "I got into Spencer on the last train last night. I felt that I must come right out—I couldn't wait till morning. But there wasn't a team to be got for love or money—it was Christmas Eve and all the livery rigs were out. So I came on horseback. Just by that bluff something frightened my horse, and he shied violently. I was half asleep and thinking of my little sister, and I went off like a shot. I suppose I struck my head against a tree. Anyway, I knew nothing more until I came to in Mr. Lurgan's kitchen. I wasn't much hurt—feel none the worse of it except for a sore head and shoulder. But, oh, Gift o' God, how you have grown! I can't realize that you are the little sister I left four years ago. I suppose you have been thinking I was dead?"

"Yes, and, oh, Donald, where *have* you been?"

"Well, I went way up north with a prospecting party. We had a tough time the first year, I can tell you, and some of us never came back. We weren't in a country where post offices were lying round loose either, you see. Then at last, just as we were about giving up in despair, we struck it rich. I've brought a snug little pile home with me, and things are going to look up in this log house, Gift o' God. There'll be no more worrying for you dear people over mortgages."

"I'm so glad—for Auntie's sake," said Theodora, with shining eyes. "But, oh, Donald, it's best of all just to have you back. I'm so perfectly happy that I don't know what to do or say."

"Well, I think you might have dinner," said Jimmy in an injured tone. "The turkey's getting stone cold, and I'm most starving. I just can't stand it another minute."

So, with a laugh, they all sat down to the table and ate the merriest Christmas dinner the little log house had ever known.

How We Went to the Wedding

"If it were to clear up I wouldn't know how to behave, it would seem so unnatural," said Kate. "Do you, by any chance, remember what the sun looks like, Phil?"

"Does the sun ever shine in Saskatchewan anyhow?" I asked with assumed sarcasm, just to make Kate's big, bonny black eyes flash.

They did flash; but Kate laughed immediately after, as she sat down on a chair in front of me and cradled her long, thin, spirited dark face in her palms.

"We have more sunny weather in Saskatchewan than in all the rest of Canada put together, in an average year," she said, clicking her strong, white teeth and snapping her eyes at me. "But I can't blame you for feeling sceptical about it, Phil. If I went to a new country and it rained every day—all day—all night—after I got there for three whole weeks I'd think things not lawful to be uttered about the climate too. So, little cousin, I forgive you. Remember that 'into each life some rain must fall, some days must be dark and dreary.' Oh, if you'd only come to visit me last fall. We had such a bee-yew-tiful September last year. We were drowned in sunshine. This fall we're drowned in water. Old settlers tell of a similar visitation in '72, though they claim even that wasn't quite as bad as this."

I was sitting rather disconsolately by an upper window of Uncle Kenneth Morrison's log house at Arrow Creek. Below was what in dry weather—so, at least, I was told—was merely a pretty, grassy little valley, but which was now a considerable creek of muddy yellow water, rising daily. Beyond was a cheerless prospect of sodden prairie and dripping "bluff."

"It would be a golden, mellow land, with purple hazes over the bluffs, in a normal fall," assured Kate. "Even now if the sun were just to shine out for a day and a good 'chinook' blow you'd see a surprising change. I feel like chanting continually that old rhyme I learned in the first primer,

'Rain, rain, go away,
Come again some other day:
—some other day next summer—
Phil and Katie want to play.'

Philippa, dear girl, don't look so dismal. It's bound to clear up sometime."

"I wish the 'sometime' would come soon, then," I said, rather grumpily.

"You know it hasn't really rained for three days," protested Kate. "It's been damp and horrid and threatening, but it hasn't rained. I defy you to say that it has actually rained."

"When it's so wet underfoot that you can't stir out without rubber boots it might as well be wet overhead too," I said, still grumpily.

"I believe you're homesick, girl," said Kate anxiously.

"No, I'm not," I answered, laughing, and feeling ashamed of my ungraciousness. "Nobody could be homesick with such a jolly good fellow as you around, Kate. It's only that this weather is getting on my nerves a bit. I'm fit for treasons, stratagems, and spoils. If your chinook doesn't come soon, Kitty, I'll do something quite desperate."

"I feel that way myself," admitted Kate. "Real reckless, Phil. Anyhow, let's put on our despised rubber boots and sally out for a wade."

"Here's Jim Nash coming on horseback down the trail," I said. "Let's wait and see if he's got the mail."

We hurried down, Kate humming, "Somewhere the sun is shining," solely, I believe, because she knew it aggravated me. At any other time I should probably have thrown a pillow at her, but just now I was too eager to see if Jim Nash had brought any mail.

I had come from Ontario, the first of September, to visit Uncle Kenneth Morrison's family. I had been looking forward to the trip for several years. My cousin Kate and I had always corresponded since they had "gone west" ten years before; and Kate, who revelled in the western life, had sung the praises of her adopted land rapturously and constantly. It was quite a joke on her that, when I did finally come to visit her, I should have struck the wettest autumn ever recorded in the history of the west. A wet September in Saskatchewan is no joke, however. The country was almost "flooded out." The trails soon became nearly impassable. All our plans for drives and picnics and inter-neighbour visiting—at that time a neighbour meant a man who lived at least six miles away—had to be given up. Yet I was not lonesome, and I enjoyed my visit in spite of everything. Kate was a host in herself. She was twenty-eight years old—eight years my senior—but the difference in our ages had never been any barrier to our friendship. She was a jolly, companionable, philosophical soul, with a jest for every situation, and a merry solution for every perplexity. The only fault I had to find with her was her tendency to make parodies. Kate's parodies were perfectly awful and always got on my nerves.

She was dreadfully ashamed of the way the Saskatchewan weather was behaving after all her boasting. She was thin at the best of times, but now she grew positively scraggy with the worry of it. I am afraid I took an unholy delight in teasing her, and abused the western weather even more than was necessary.

Jim Nash—the lank youth who was hired to look after the place during Uncle Kenneth's absence on a prolonged threshing expedition—had brought some mail. Kate's share was a letter, postmarked Bothwell, a rising little town about one hundred and twenty miles from Arrow Creek. Kate had several friends there, and one of our plans had been to visit Bothwell and spend a week with them. We had meant to drive, of course, since there was no other way of getting there, and equally of course the plan had been abandoned because of the wet weather.

"Mother," exclaimed Kate, "Mary Taylor is going to be married in a fortnight's time! She wants Phil and me to go up to Bothwell for the wedding."

"What a pity you can't go," remarked Aunt Jennie placidly. Aunt Jennie was always a placid little soul, with a most enviable knack of taking everything easy. Nothing ever worried her greatly, and when she had decided that a thing was inevitable it did not worry her at all.

"But I am going," cried Kate. "I will go—I must go. I positively cannot let Mary Taylor—my own beloved Molly—go and perpetrate matrimony without my being on hand to see it. Yes, I'm going—and if Phil has a spark of the old Blair pioneer spirit in her, she'll go too."

"Of course I'll go if you go," I said.

Aunt Jennie did not think we were in earnest, so she merely laughed at first, and said, "How do you propose to go? Fly—or swim?"

"We'll drive, as usual," said Kate calmly. "I'd feel more at home in that way of locomotion. We'll borrow Jim Nash's father's democrat, and take the ponies. We'll put on old clothes, raincoats, rubber caps and boots, and we'll start tomorrow. In an ordinary time we could easily do it in six days or less, but this fall we'll probably need ten or twelve."

"You don't really mean to go, Kate!" said Aunt Jennie, beginning to perceive that Kate did mean it.

"I do," said Kate, in a convincing tone.

Aunt Jennie felt a little worried—as much as she could feel worried over anything—and she tried her best to dissuade Kate, although she plainly did not have much hope of doing so, having had enough experience with her determined daughter to realize that when Kate said she was going to do a thing she did it. It was rather funny to listen to the ensuing dialogue.

"Kate, you can't do it. It's a crazy idea! The road is one hundred and twenty miles long."

"I've driven it twice, Mother."

"Yes, but not in such a wet year. The trail is impassable in places."

"Oh, there are always plenty of dry spots to be found if you only look hard for them."

"But you don't know where to look for them, and goodness knows what you'll get into while you are looking."

"We'll call at the M.P. barracks and get an Indian to guide us. Indians always know the dry spots."

"The stage driver has decided not to make another trip till the October frosts set in."

"But he always has such a heavy load. It will be quite different with us, you must remember. We'll travel light—just our provisions and a valise containing our wedding garments."

"What will you do if you get mired twenty miles from a human being?"

"But we won't. I'm a good driver and I haven't nerves—but I have nerve. Besides, you forget that we'll have an Indian guide with us."

"There was a company of Hudson Bay freighters ambushed and killed along that very trail by Blackfoot Indians in 1839," said Aunt Jennie dolefully.

"Fifty years ago! Their ghosts must have ceased to haunt it by this time," said Kate flippantly.

"Well, you'll get wet through and catch your deaths of cold," protested Aunt Jennie.

"No fear of it. We'll be cased in rubber. And we'll borrow a good tight tent from the M.P.s. Besides, I'm sure it's not going to rain much more. I know the signs."

"At least wait for a day or two until you're sure that it has cleared up," implored Aunt Jennie.

"Which being interpreted means, 'Wait for a day or two, because then your father may be home and he'll squelch your mad expedition,'" said Kate, with a sly glance at me. "No, no, my mother, your wiles are in vain. We'll hit the trail tomorrow at sunrise. So just be good, darling, and help us pack up some provisions. I'll send Jim for his father's democrat."

Aunt Jennie resigned herself to the inevitable and betook herself to the pantry with the air of a woman who washes her hands of the consequences. I flew upstairs to pack some finery. I was wild with delight over the proposed outing. I did not realize what it actually meant, and I had perfect confidence in Kate, who was an expert driver, an experienced camper out, and an excellent manager. If I could have seen what was ahead of us I would certainly not have been quite so jubilant and reckless, but I would have gone all the same. I would not miss the laughter-provoking memories of that trip out of my life for anything. I have always been glad I went.

We left at sunrise the next morning; there was a sunrise that morning, for a wonder. The sun came up in a pinky-saffron sky and promised us a fine day. Aunt Jennie bade us goodbye and, estimable woman that she was, did not trouble us with advice or forebodings.

Mr. Nash had sent over his "democrat," a light wagon with springs; and Kate's "shaganappies," Tom and Jerry—native ponies, the toughest horse flesh to be found in the world—were hitched to it. Kate and I were properly accoutred for our trip and looked—but I try to forget how we looked! The memory is not flattering.

We drove off in the gayest of spirits. Our difficulties began at the start, for we had to drive a mile before we could find a place to ford the creek. Beyond that, however, we had a passable trail for three miles to the little outpost of the Mounted Police, where five or six men were stationed on detachment duty.

"Sergeant Baker is a friend of mine," said Kate. "He'll be only too glad to lend me all we require."

The sergeant was a friend of Kate's, but he looked at her as if he thought she was crazy when she told him where we were going.

"You'd better take a canoe instead of a team," he said sarcastically. "I've a good notion to arrest you both as horse thieves and prevent you from going on such a mad expedition."

"You know nothing short of arrest would stop me," said Kate, nodding at him with laughing eyes, "and you really won't go to such an extreme, I know. So please be nice, even if it comes hard, and lend us some things. I've come a-borrying."

"I won't lend you a thing," declared the sergeant. "I won't aid and abet you in any such freak as this. Go home now, like a good girl."

"I'm not going home," said Kate. "I'm not a 'good girl'—I'm a wicked old maid, and I'm going to Bothwell. If you won't lend us a tent we'll go without—and sleep in the open—and our deaths will lie forever at your door. I'll come back and haunt you, if you don't lend me a tent. I'll camp on your very threshold and you won't be able to go out of your door without falling over my spook."

"I've more fear of being accountable for your death if I do let you go," said Sergeant Baker dubiously. "However, I see that nothing but physical force will prevent you. What do you want?"

"I want," said Kate, "a cavalry tent, a sheet-iron camp stove, and a good Indian guide—old Peter Crow for choice. He's such a respectable-looking old fellow, and his wife often works for us."

The sergeant gave us the tent and stove, and sent a man down to the Reserve for Peter Crow. Moreover, he vindicated his title of friend by making us take a dozen prairie chickens and a large ham—besides any quantity of advice. We didn't want the advice but we hugely welcomed the ham. Presently our guide appeared—quite a spruce old Indian, as Indians go. I had never been able to shake off my childhood conviction that an Indian was a fearsome creature, hopelessly addicted to scalping knives and tomahawks, and I secretly felt quite horrified at the idea of two defenceless females starting out on a lonely prairie trail with an Indian for guide. Even old Peter Crow's meek appearance did not quite reassure me; but I kept my qualms to myself, for I knew Kate would only laugh at me.

It was ten when we finally got away from the M.P. outpost. Sergeant Baker bade us goodbye in a tone which seemed to intimate that he never expected to see either of us again. What with his dismal predictions and my secret horror of Indians, I was beginning to feel anything but jubilant over our expedition. Kate, however, was as blithe and buoyant as usual. She knew no fear, being one of those enviable folk who can because they think they can. One hundred and twenty miles of half-flooded prairie trail—camping out at night in the solitude of the Great Lone Land—rain—muskegs—Indian guides—nothing had any terror for my dauntless cousin.

For the next three hours, however, we got on beautifully. The trail was fair, though somewhat greasy; the sun shone, though with a somewhat watery gleam, through the mists; and Peter Crow, coiled up on the folded tent behind the seat, slept soundly and snored mellifluously. That snore reassured me greatly. I had never thought of Indians as snoring. Surely one who did couldn't be dreaded greatly.

We stopped at one o'clock and had a cold lunch, sitting in our wagon, while Peter Crow wakened up and watered the ponies. We did not get on so well in the afternoon. The trail descended into low-lying ground where travelling was very difficult. I had to admit old Peter Crow was quite invaluable. He knew, as Kate had foretold, "all the dry spots"—that is to say, spots less wet than others. But, even so, we had to make so many detours that by sunset we were little more than six miles distant from our noon halting place.

"We'd better set camp now, before it gets any darker," said Kate. "There's a capital spot over there, by that bluff of dead poplar. The ground seems pretty dry too. Peter, cut us a set of tent poles and kindle a fire."

"Want my dollar first," said old Peter stolidly.

We had agreed to pay him a dollar a day for the trip, but none of the money was to be paid until we got to Bothwell. Kate told him this. But all the reply she got was a stolid, "Want dollar. No make fire without dollar."

We were getting cold and it was getting dark, so finally Kate, under the law of necessity, paid him his dollar. Then he carried out our orders at his own sweet leisure. In course of time he got a fire lighted, and while we cooked supper he set up the tent and prepared our beds, by cutting piles of brush and covering them with rugs.

Kate and I had a hilarious time cooking that supper. It was my first experience of camping out and, as I had become pretty well convinced that Peter Crow was not the typical Indian of old romance, I enjoyed it all hugely. But we were both very tired, and as soon as we had finished eating we betook ourselves to our tent and found our brush beds much more comfortable than I had expected. Old Peter coiled up on his blanket outside by the fire, and the great silence of a windless prairie enwrapped us. In a few minutes we were sound asleep and never wakened until seven o'clock.

When we arose and lifted the flap of the tent we saw a peculiar sight. The little elevation on which we had pitched our camp seemed to be an island in a vast sea of white mist, dotted here and there with other islands. On every hand to the far horizon stretched that strange, phantasmal ocean, and a hazy sun looked over the shifting billows. I had never seen a western mist before and I thought it extremely beautiful; but Kate, to whom it was no novelty, was more cumbered with breakfast cares.

"I'm ravenous," she said, as she bustled about among our stores. "Camping out always does give one such an appetite. Aren't you hungry, Phil?"

"Comfortably so," I admitted. "But where are our ponies? And where is Peter Crow?"

"Probably the ponies have strayed away looking for pea vines. They love and adore pea vines," said Kate, stirring up the fire from under its blanket of grey ashes. "And Peter Crow has gone to look for them, good old fellow. When you do get a conscientious Indian there is no better guide in the world, but they are rare. Now, Philippa-girl, just pry out the sergeant's ham and shave a few slices off it for our breakfast. Some savoury fried ham always goes well on the prairie."

I went for the ham but could not find it. A thorough search among our effects revealed it not.

"Kate, I can't find the ham," I called out. "It must have fallen out somewhere on the trail."

Kate ceased wrestling with the fire and came to help in the search for the missing delicacy.

"It couldn't have fallen out," she said incredulously. "That is impossible. The tent was fastened securely over everything. Nothing could have jolted out."

"Well, then, where is the ham?" I said.

That question was unanswerable, as Kate discovered after another thorough search. The ham was gone—that much was certain.

"I believe Peter Crow has levanted with the ham," I said decidedly.

"I don't believe Peter Crow could be so dishonest," said Kate rather shortly. "His wife has worked for us for years, and she's as honest as the sunlight."

"Honesty isn't catching," I remarked, but I said nothing more just then, for Kate's black eyes were snapping.

"Anyway, we can't have ham for breakfast," she said, twitching out the frying pan rather viciously. "We'll have to put up with canned chicken—if the cans haven't disappeared too."

They hadn't, and we soon produced a very tolerable breakfast. But neither of us had much appetite.

"Do you suppose Peter Crow has taken the horses as well as the ham?" I asked.

"No," gloomily responded Kate, who had evidently been compelled by the logic of hard facts to believe in Peter's guilt, "he would hardly dare to do that, because he couldn't dispose of them without being found out. They've probably strayed away on their own account when Peter decamped. As soon as this mist lifts I'll have a look for them. They can't have gone far."

We were spared this trouble, however, for when we were washing up the dishes the ponies returned of their own accord. Kate caught them and harnessed them.

"Are we going on?" I asked mildly.

"Of course we're going on," said Kate, her good humour entirely restored. "Do you suppose I'm going to be turned from my purpose by the defection of a miserable old Indian? Oh, wait till he comes round in the winter, begging."

"Will he come?" I asked.

"Will he? Yes, my dear, he will—with a smooth, plausible story to account for his desertion and a bland denial of ever having seen our ham. I shall know how to deal with him then, the old scamp."

"When you do get a conscientious Indian there's no better guide in the world, but they are rare," I remarked with a far-away look.

Kate laughed.

"Don't rub it in, Phil. Come, help me to break camp. We'll have to work harder and hustle for ourselves, that's all."

"But is it safe to go on without a guide?" I inquired dubiously. I hadn't felt very safe with Peter Crow, but I felt still more unsafe without him.

"Safe! Of course, it's safe—perfectly safe. I know the trail, and we'll just have to drive around the wet places. It would have been easier with Peter, and we'd have had less work to do, but we'll get along well enough without him. I don't think I'd have bothered with him at all, only I wanted to set Mother's mind at rest. She'll never know he isn't with us till the trip is over, so that is all right. We're going to have a glorious day. But, oh, for our lost ham! 'The Ham That Was Never Eaten.' There's a subject for a poem, Phil. You write one when we get back to civilization. Methinks I can sniff the savoury odour of that lost ham on all the prairie breezes."

"Of all sad words of tongue or pen,
The saddest are these—it might have been,"

I quoted, beginning to wash the dishes.

"Saw ye my wee ham, saw ye my ain ham,
Saw ye my pork ham down on yon lea?
Crossed it the prairie last night in the darkness
Borne by an old and unprincipled Cree?"

sang Kate, loosening the tent ropes. Altogether, we got a great deal more fun out of that ham than if we had eaten it.

As Kate had predicted, the day was glorious. The mists rolled away and the sun shone brightly. We drove all day without stopping, save for dinner—when the lost ham figured largely in our conversation—of course. We said so many witty things about it—at least, we thought them witty—that we laughed continuously through the whole meal, which we ate with prodigious appetite.

But with all our driving we were not getting on very fast. The country was exceedingly swampy and we had to make innumerable detours.

"'The longest way round is the shortest way to Bothwell,'" said Kate, when we drove five miles out of our way to avoid a muskeg. By evening we had driven fully twenty-five miles, but we were only ten miles nearer Bothwell than when we had broken camp in the morning.

"We'll have to camp soon," sighed Kate. "I believe around this bluff will be a good place. Oh, Phil, I'm tired—dead tired! My very thoughts are tired. I can't even think anything funny about the ham. And yet we've got to set up the tent ourselves, and attend to the horses; and we'll have to scrape some of the mud off this beautiful vehicle."

"We can leave that till the morning," I suggested.

"No, it will be too hard and dry then. Here we are—and here are two tepees of Indians also!"

There they were, right around the bluff. The inmates were standing in a group before them, looking at us as composedly as if we were not at all an unusual sight.

"I'm going to stay here anyhow," said Kate doggedly.

"Oh, don't," I said in alarm. "They're such a villainous-looking lot—so dirty—and they've got so little clothing on. I wouldn't sleep a wink near them. Look at that awful old squaw with only one eye. They'd steal everything we've got left, Kate. Remember the ham—oh, pray remember the fate of our beautiful ham."

"I shall never forget that ham," said Kate wearily, "but, Phil, we can't drive far enough to be out of their reach if they really want to steal our provisions. But I don't believe they will. I believe they have plenty of food—Indians in tepees mostly have. The men hunt, you know. Their looks are probably the worst of them. Anyhow, you can't judge Indians by appearances. Peter Crow looked respectable—and he was a whited sepulchre. Now, these Indians look as bad as Indians can look—so they may turn out to be angels in disguise."

"Very much disguised, certainly," I acquiesced satirically. "They seem to me to belong to the class of a neighbour of ours down east. Her family is always in rags, because she says, 'a hole is an accident, a patch is a disgrace,' Set camp here if you like, Kate. But I'll not sleep a wink with such neighbours."

I cheerfully ate my words later on. Never were appearances more deceptive than in the case of those Stoneys. There is an old saying that many a kind heart beats behind a ragged coat. The Indians had no coats for their hearts to beat behind—nothing but shirts—some of them hadn't even shirts! But the shirts were certainly ragged enough, and their hearts were kind.

Those Indians were gentlemen. They came forward and unhitched our horses, fed, and watered them; they pitched our tent, and built us a fire, and cut brush for our beds. Kate and I had simply nothing to do except sit on our rugs and tell them what we wanted done. They would have cooked our supper for us if we had allowed it. But, tired as we were, we drew the line at that. Their hearts were pure gold, but their hands! No, Kate and I dragged ourselves up and cooked our own suppers. And while we ate it, those Indians fell to and cleaned all the mud off our democrat for us. To crown all—it is almost unbelievable but it is true, I solemnly avow—they wouldn't take a cent of payment for it all, urge them as we might and did.

"Well," said Kate, as we curled up on our brush beds that night, "there certainly is a special Providence for unprotected females. I'd forgive Peter Crow for deserting us for the sake of those Indians, if he hadn't stolen our lovely ham into the bargain. That was altogether unpardonable."

In the morning the Indians broke camp for us and harnessed our shaganappies. We drove off, waving our hands to them, the delightful creatures. We never saw any of them again. I fear their kind is scarce, but as long as I live I shall remember those Stoneys with gratitude.

We got on fairly well that third day, and made about fifteen miles before dinner time. We ate three of the sergeant's prairie chickens for dinner, and enjoyed them.

"But only think how delicious the ham would have been," said Kate.

Our real troubles began that afternoon. We had not been driving long when the trail swooped down suddenly into a broad depression—a swamp, so full of mud-holes that there didn't seem to be anything but mud-holes. We pulled through six of them—but in the seventh we stuck, hard and fast. Pull as our ponies could and did, they could not pull us out.

"What are we to do?" I said, becoming horribly frightened all at once. It seemed to me that our predicament was a dreadful one.

"Keep cool," said Kate. She calmly took off her shoes and stockings, tucked up her skirt, and waded to the horses' heads.

"Can't I do anything?" I implored.

"Yes, take the whip and spare it not," said Kate. "I'll encourage them here with sundry tugs and inspiriting words. You urge them behind with a good lambasting."

Accordingly we encouraged and urged, tugged and lambasted, with a right good will, but all to no effect. Our ponies did their best, but they could not pull the democrat out of that slough.

"Oh, what—" I began, and then I stopped. I resolved that I would not ask that question again in that tone in that scrape. I would be cheerful and courageous like Kate—splendid Kate!

"I shall have to unhitch them, tie one of them to that stump, and ride off on the other for help," said Kate.

"Where to?" I asked.

"Till I find it," grinned Kate, who seemed to think the whole disaster a capital joke. "I may have to go clean back to the tepees—and further. For that matter, I don't believe there were any tepees. Those Indians were too good to be true—they were phantoms of delight—such stuff as dreams are made of. But even if they were real they won't be there now—they'll have folded their tents like the Arabs and as silently stolen away. But I'll find help somewhere."

"I can't stay here alone. You may be gone for hours," I cried, forgetting all my resolutions of courage and cheerfulness in an access of panic.

"Then ride the other pony and come with me," suggested Kate.

"I can't ride bareback," I moaned.

"Then you'll have to stay here," said Kate decidedly. "There's nothing to hurt you, Phil. Sit in the wagon and keep dry. Eat something if you get hungry. I may not be very long."

I realized that there was nothing else to do; and, rather ashamed of my panic, I resigned myself to the inevitable and saw Kate off with a smile of encouragement. Then I waited. I was tired and frightened—horribly frightened. I sat there and imagined scores of gruesome possibilities. It was no use telling myself to be brave. I couldn't be brave. I never was in such a blue funk before or since. Suppose Kate got lost—suppose she couldn't find me again—suppose something happened to her—suppose she couldn't get help—suppose it came on night and I there all alone—suppose Indians—not gentlemanly Stoneys or even Peter Crows, but genuine, old-fashioned Indians—should come along—suppose it began to pour rain!

It did begin to rain, the only one of my suppositions which came true. I hoisted an umbrella and sat there grimly, in that horseless wagon in the mud-hole.

Many a time since have I laughed over the memory of the appearance I must have presented sitting in that mud-hole, but there was nothing in the least funny about it at the time. The worst feature of it all was the uncertainty. I could have waited patiently enough and conquered my fears if I had known that Kate would find help and return within a reasonable time—at least before dark. But everything was doubtful. I was not composed of the stuff out of which heroines are fashioned and I devoutly wished we had never left Arrow Creek.

Shouts—calls—laughter—Kate's dear voice in an encouraging cry from the hill behind me!

"Halloo, honey! Hold the fort a few minutes longer. Here we are. Bless her, hasn't she been a brick to stay here all alone like this—and a tenderfoot at that?"

I could have cried with joy. But I saw that there were men with Kate—two men—white men—and I laughed instead. I had not been brave—I had been an arrant little coward, but I vowed that nobody, not even Kate, should suspect it. Later on Kate told me how she had fared in her search for assistance.

"When I left you, Phil, I felt much more anxious than I wanted to let you see. I had no idea where to go. I knew there were no houses along our trail and I might have to go clean back to the tepees—fifteen miles bareback. I didn't dare try any other trail, for I knew nothing of them and wasn't sure that there were even tepees on them. But when I had gone about six miles I saw a welcome sight—nothing less than a spiral of blue, homely-looking smoke curling up from the prairie far off to my right. I decided to turn off and investigate. I rode two miles and finally I came to a little log shack. There was a bee-yew-tiful big horse in a corral close by. My heart jumped with joy. But suppose the inmates of the shack were half-breeds! You can't realize how relieved I felt when the door opened and two white men came out. In a few minutes everything was explained. They knew who I was and what I wanted, and I knew that they were Mr. Lonsdale and Mr. Hopkins, owners of a big ranch over by Deer Run. They were 'shacking out' to put up some hay and Mrs. Hopkins was keeping house for them. She wanted me to stop and have a cup of tea right off, but I thought of you, Phil, and declined. As soon as they heard of our predicament those lovely men got their two biggest horses and came right with me."

It was not long before our democrat was on solid ground once more, and then our rescuers insisted that we go back to the shack with them for the night. Accordingly we drove back to the shack, attended by our two gallant deliverers on white horses. Mrs. Hopkins was waiting for us, a trim, dark-haired little lady in a very pretty gown, which she had donned in our honour. Kate and I felt like perfect tramps beside her in our muddy old raiment, with our hair dressed by dead reckoning—for we had not included a mirror in our baggage. There was a mirror in the shack, however—small but good—and we quickly made ourselves tidy at least, and Kate even went to the length of curling her bangs—bangs were in style then and Kate had long, thick ones—using the stem of a broken pipe of Mr. Hopkins's for a curler. I was so tired that my vanity was completely crushed out—for the time being—and I simply pinned my bangs back. Later on, when I discovered that Mr. Lonsdale was really the younger son of an English earl, I wished I had curled them, but it was too late then.

He didn't look in the least like a scion of aristocracy. He wore a cowboy rig and had a scrubby beard of a week's growth. But he was very jolly and played the violin beautifully. After tea—and a lovely tea it was, although, as Kate remarked to me later, there was no ham—we had an impromptu concert. Mr. Lonsdale played the violin; Mrs. Hopkins, who sang, was a graduate of a musical conservatory; Mr. Hopkins gave a comic recitation and did a Cree war-dance; Kate gave a spirited account of our adventures since leaving home and mother; and I described—with trimmings—how I felt sitting alone in the democrat in a mud-hole, in a pouring rain on a vast prairie.

Mrs. Hopkins, Kate, and I slept in the one bed the shack boasted, screened off from public view by a calico curtain. Mr. Lonsdale reposed in his accustomed bunk by the stove, but poor Mr. Hopkins had to sleep on the floor. He must have been glad Kate and I stayed only one night.

The fourth morning found us blithely hitting the trail in renewed confidence and spirits. We parted from our kind friends in the shack with mutual regret. Mr. Hopkins gave us a haunch of jumping deer and Mrs. Hopkins gave us a box of home-made cookies. Mr. Lonsdale at first thought he couldn't give us anything, for he said all he had with him was his pipe and his fiddle; but later on he said he felt so badly to see us go without any token of his good will that he felt constrained to ask us to accept a piece of rope that he had tied his outfit together with.

The fourth day we got on so nicely that it was quite monotonous. The sun shone, the chinook blew, our ponies trotted over the trail gallantly. Kate and I sang, told stories, and laughed immoderately over everything. Even a poor joke seems to have a subtle flavour on the prairie. For the first time I began to think Saskatchewan beautiful, with those far-reaching parklike meadows dotted with the white-stemmed poplars, the distant bluffs bannered with the airiest of purple hazes, and the little blue lakes that sparkled and shimmered in the sunlight on every hand.

The only thing approaching an adventure that day happened in the afternoon when we reached a creek which had to be crossed.

"We must investigate," said Kate decidedly. "It would never do to risk getting mired here, for this country is unsettled and we must be twenty miles from another human being."

Kate again removed her shoes and stockings and puddled about that creek until she found a safe fording place. I am afraid I must admit that I laughed most heartlessly at the spectacle she presented while so employed.

"Oh, for a camera, Kate!" I said, between spasms.

Kate grinned. "I don't care what I look like," she said, "but I feel wretchedly unpleasant. This water is simply swarming with wigglers."

"Goodness, what are they?" I exclaimed.

"Oh, they're tiny little things like leeches," responded Kate. "I believe they develop into mosquitoes later on, bad 'cess to them. What Mr. Nash would call my pedal extremities are simply being devoured by the brutes. Ugh! I believe the bottom of this creek is all soft mud. We may have to drive—no, as I'm a living, wiggler-haunted human being, here's firm bottom. Hurrah, Phil, we're all right!"

In a few minutes we were past the creek and bowling merrily on our way. We had a beautiful camping ground that night—a fairylike little slope of white poplars with a blue lake at its foot. When the sun went down a milk-white mist hung over the prairie, with a young moon kissing it. We boiled some slices of our jumping deer and ate them in the open around a cheery camp-fire. Then we sought our humble couches, where we slept the sleep of just people who had been driving over the prairie all day. Once in the night I wakened. It was very dark. The unearthly stillness of a great prairie was all around me. In that vast silence Kate's soft breathing at my side seemed an intrusion of sound where no sound should be.

"Philippa Blair, can you believe it's yourself?" I said mentally. "Here you are, lying on a brush bed on a western prairie in the middle of the night, at least twenty miles from any human being except another frail creature of your own sex. Yet you're not even frightened. You are very comfy and composed, and you're going right to sleep again."

And right to sleep again I went.

Our fifth day began ominously. We had made an early start and had driven about six miles when the calamity occurred. Kate turned a corner too sharply, to avoid a big boulder; there was a heart-breaking sound.

"The tongue of the wagon is broken," cried Kate in dismay. All too surely it was. We looked at each other blankly.

"What can we do?" I said.

"I'm sure I don't know," said Kate helplessly. When Kate felt helpless I thought things must be desperate indeed. We got out and investigated the damage.

"It's not a clean break," said Kate. "It's a long, slanting break. If we had a piece of rope I believe I could fix it."

"Mr. Lonsdale's piece of rope!" I cried.

"The very thing," said Kate, brightening up.

The rope was found and we set to work. With the aid of some willow withes and that providential rope we contrived to splice the tongue together in some shape.

Although the trail was good we made only twelve miles the rest of the day, so slowly did we have to drive. Besides, we were continually expecting that tongue to give way again, and the strain was bad for our nerves. When we came at sunset to the junction of the Black River trail with ours, Kate resolutely turned the shaganappies down it.

"We'll go and spend the night with the Brewsters," she said. "They live only ten miles down this trail. I went to school in Regina with Hannah Brewster, and though I haven't seen her for ten years I know she'll be glad to see us. She's a lovely person, and her husband is a very nice man. I visited them once after they were married."

We soon arrived at the Brewster place. It was a trim, white-washed little log house in a grove of poplars. But all the blinds were down and we discovered the door was locked. Evidently the Brewsters were not at home.

"Never mind," said Kate cheerfully, "we'll light a fire outside and cook our supper and then we'll spend the night in the barn. A bed of prairie hay will be just the thing."

But the barn was locked too. It was now dark and our plight was rather desperate.

"I'm going to get into the house if I have to break a window," said Kate resolutely. "Hannah would want us to do that. She'd never get over it, if she heard we came to her house and couldn't get in."

Fortunately we did not have to go to the length of breaking into Hannah's house. The kitchen window went up quite easily. We turned the shaganappies loose to forage for themselves, grass and water being abundant. Then we climbed in at the window, lighted our lantern, and found ourselves in a very snug little kitchen. Opening off it on one side was a trim, nicely furnished parlour and on the other a well-stocked pantry.

"We'll light the fire in the stove in a jiffy and have a real good supper," said Kate exultantly. "Here's cold roast beef—and preserves and cookies and cheese and butter."

Before long we had supper ready and we did full justice to the absent Hannah's excellent cheer. After all, it was quite nice to sit down once more to a well-appointed table and eat in civilized fashion.

Then we washed up all the dishes and made everything snug and tidy. I shall never be sufficiently thankful that we did so.

Kate piloted me upstairs to the spare room.

"This is fixed up much nicer than it was when I was here before," she said, looking around. "Of course, Hannah and Ted were just starting out then and they had to be economical. They must have prospered, to be able to afford such furniture as this. Well, turn in, Phil. Won't it be rather jolly to sleep between sheets once more?"

We slept long and soundly until half-past eight the next morning; and dear knows if we would have wakened then of our own accord. But I heard somebody saying in a very harsh, gruff voice, "Here, you two, wake up! I want to know what this means."

We two did wake up, promptly and effectually. I never wakened up so thoroughly in my life before. Standing in our room were three people, one of them a man. He was a big, grey-haired man with a bushy black beard and an angry scowl. Beside him was a woman—a tall, thin, angular personage with red hair and an indescribable bonnet. She looked even crosser and more amazed than the man, if that were possible. In the background was another woman—a tiny old lady who must have been at least eighty. She was, in spite of her tininess, a very striking-looking personage; she was dressed all in black, and had snow-white hair, a dead-white face, and snapping, vivid, coal-black eyes. She looked as amazed as the other two, but she didn't look cross.

I knew something must be wrong—fearfully wrong—but I didn't know what. Even in my confusion, I found time to think that if that disagreeable-looking red-haired woman was Hannah Brewster, Kate must have had a queer taste in school friends. Then the man said, more gruffly than ever, "Come now. Who are you and what business have you here?"

Kate raised herself on one elbow. She looked very wild. I heard the old black-and-white lady in the background chuckle to herself.

"Isn't this Theodore Brewster's place?" gasped Kate.

"No," said the big woman, speaking for the first time. "This place belongs to us. We bought it from the Brewsters in the spring. They moved over to Black River Forks. Our name is Chapman."

Poor Kate fell back on the pillow, quite overcome. "I—I beg your pardon," she said. "I—I thought the Brewsters lived here. Mrs. Brewster is a friend of mine. My cousin and I are on our way to Bothwell and we called here to spend the night with Hannah. When we found everyone away we just came in and made ourselves at home."

"A likely story," said the red woman.

"We weren't born yesterday," said the man.

Madam Black-and-White didn't say anything, but when the other two had made their pretty speeches she doubled up in a silent convulsion of mirth, shaking her head from side to side and beating the air with her hands.

If they had been nice to us, Kate would probably have gone on feeling confused and ashamed. But when they were so disagreeable she quickly regained her self-possession. She sat up again and said in her haughtiest voice, "I do not know when you were born, or where, but it must have been somewhere where very peculiar manners were taught. If you will have the decency to leave our room—this room—until we can get up and dress we will not transgress upon your hospitality" (Kate put a most satirical emphasis on that word) "any longer. And we shall pay you amply for the food we have eaten and the night's lodging we have taken."

The black-and-white apparition went through the motion of clapping her hands, but not a sound did she make. Whether he was cowed by Kate's tone, or appeased by the prospect of payment, I know not, but Mr. Chapman spoke more civilly. "Well, that's fair. If you pay up it's all right."

"They shall do no such thing as pay you," said Madam Black-and-White in a surprisingly clear, resolute, authoritative voice. "If you haven't any shame for yourself, Robert Chapman, you've got a mother-in-law who can be ashamed for you. No strangers shall be charged for food or lodging in any house where Mrs. Matilda Pitman lives. Remember that I've come down in the world, but I haven't forgot all decency for all that. I knew you was a skinflint when Amelia married you and you've made her as bad as yourself. But I'm boss here yet. Here, you,

Robert Chapman, take yourself out of here and let those girls get dressed. And you, Amelia, go downstairs and cook a breakfast for them."

I never, in all my life, saw anything like the abject meekness with which those two big people obeyed that mite. They went, and stood not upon the order of their going. As the door closed behind them, Mrs. Matilda Pitman laughed silently, and rocked from side to side in her merriment.

"Ain't it funny?" she said. "I mostly lets them run the length of their tether but sometimes I has to pull them up, and then I does it with a jerk. Now, you can take your time about dressing, my dears, and I'll go down and keep them in order, the mean scalawags."

When we descended the stairs we found a smoking-hot breakfast on the table. Mr. Chapman was nowhere to be seen, and Mrs. Chapman was cutting bread with a sulky air. Mrs. Matilda Pitman was sitting in an armchair, knitting. She still wore her bonnet and her triumphant expression. "Set right in, dears, and make a good breakfast," she said.

"We are not hungry," said Kate, almost pleadingly. "I don't think we can eat anything. And it's time we were on the trail. Please excuse us and let us go on."

Mrs. Matilda Pitman shook a knitting needle playfully at Kate. "Sit down and take your breakfast," she commanded. "Mrs. Matilda Pitman commands you. Everybody obeys Mrs. Matilda Pitman—even Robert and Amelia. You must obey her too."

We did obey her. We sat down and, such was the influence of her mesmeric eyes, we ate a tolerable breakfast. The obedient Amelia never spoke; Mrs. Matilda Pitman did not speak either, but she knitted furiously and chuckled. When we had finished Mrs. Matilda Pitman rolled up her knitting. "Now, you can go if you want to," she said, "but you don't have to go. You can stay here as long as you like, and I'll make them cook your meals for you."

I never saw Kate so thoroughly cowed.

"Thank you," she said faintly. "You are very kind, but we must go."

"Well, then," said Mrs. Matilda Pitman, throwing open the door, "your team is ready for you. I made Robert catch your ponies and harness them. And I made him fix that broken tongue properly. I enjoy making Robert do things. It's almost the only sport I have left. I'm eighty and most things have lost their flavour, except bossing Robert."

Our democrat and ponies were outside the door, but Robert was nowhere to be seen; in fact, we never saw him again.

"I do wish," said Kate, plucking up what little spirit she had left, "that you would let us—ah—uh"—Kate quailed before Mrs. Matilda Pitman's eye—"recompense you for our entertainment."

"Mrs. Matilda Pitman said before—and meant it—that she doesn't take pay for entertaining strangers, nor let other people where she lives do it, much as their meanness would like to do it."

We got away. The sulky Amelia had vanished, and there was nobody to see us off except Mrs. Matilda Pitman.

"Don't forget to call the next time you come this way," she said cheerfully, waving her knitting at us. "I hope you'll get safe to Bothwell. If I was ten years younger I vow I'd pack a grip and go along with you. I like your spunk. Most of the girls nowadays is such timid, skeery critters. When I was a girl I wasn't afraid of nothing or nobody."

We said and did nothing until we had driven out of sight and earshot. Then Kate laid down the reins and laughed until the tears came.

"Oh, Phil, Phil, will you ever forget this adventure?" she gasped.

"I shall never forget Mrs. Matilda Pitman," I said emphatically.

We had no further adventures that day. Robert Chapman had fixed the tongue so well—probably under Mrs. Matilda Pitman's watchful eyes—that we could drive as fast as we liked; and we made good progress. But when we pitched camp that night Kate scanned the sky with an anxious expression. "I don't like the look of it," she said. "I'm afraid we're going to have a bad day tomorrow."

We had. When we awakened in the morning rain was pouring down. This in itself might not have prevented us from travelling, but the state of the trail did. It had been raining the greater part of the night and the trail was little more than a ditch of slimy, greasy, sticky mud.

If we could have stayed in the tent the whole time it would not have been quite so bad. But we had to go out twice to take the ponies to the nearest pond and water them; moreover, we had to collect pea vines for them, which was not an agreeable occupation in a pouring rain. The day was very cold too, but fortunately there was plenty of dead poplar right by our camp. We kept a good fire on in the camp stove and were quite dry and comfortable as long as we stayed inside. Even when we had to go out we did not get very wet, as we were well protected. But it was a long dreary day. Finally when the dark came down and supper was over Kate grew quite desperate. "Let's have a game of checkers," she suggested.

"Where is your checkerboard?" I asked.

"Oh, I'll soon furnish that," said Kate.

She cut out a square of brown paper, in which a biscuit box had been wrapped, and marked squares off on it with a pencil. Then she produced some red and white high-bush cranberries for men. A cranberry split in two was a king.

We played nine games of checkers by the light of our smoky lantern. Our enjoyment of the game was heightened by the fact that it had ceased raining. Nevertheless, when morning came the trail was so drenched that it was impossible to travel on it.

"We must wait till noon," said Kate.

"That trail won't be dry enough to travel on for a week," I said disconsolately.

"My dear; the chinook is blowing up," said Kate. "You don't know how quickly a trail dries in a chinook. It's like magic."

I did not believe a chinook or anything else could dry up that trail by noon sufficiently for us to travel on. But it did. As Kate said, it seemed like magic. By one o'clock we were on our way again, the chinook blowing merrily against our faces.

It was a wind that blew straight from the heart of the wilderness and had in it all the potent lure of the wild. The yellow prairie laughed and glistened in the sun.

We made twenty-five miles that afternoon and, as we were again fortunate enough to find a bluff of dead poplar near which to camp, we built a royal campfire which sent its flaming light far and wide over the dark prairie.

We were in jubilant spirits. If the next day were fine and nothing dreadful happened to us, we would reach Bothwell before night.

But our ill luck was not yet at an end. The next morning was beautiful. The sun shone warm and bright; the chinook blew balmily and alluringly; the trail stretched before us dry and level. But we sat moodily before our tent, not even having sufficient heart to play checkers. Tom had gone lame—so lame that there was no use in thinking of trying to travel with him. Kate could not tell what was the matter.

"There is no injury that I can see," she said. "He must have sprained his foot somehow."

Wait we did, with all the patience we could command. But the day was long and wearisome, and at night Tom's foot did not seem a bit better.

We went to bed gloomily, but joy came with the morning. Tom's foot was so much improved that Kate decided we could go on, though we would have to drive slowly.

"There's no chance of making Bothwell today," she said, "but at least we shall be getting a little nearer to it."

"I don't believe there is such a place as Bothwell, or any other town," I said pessimistically. "There's nothing in the world but prairie, and we'll go on driving over it forever, like a couple of female Wandering Jews. It seems years since we left Arrow Creek."

"Well, we've had lots of fun out of it all, you know," said Kate. "Mrs. Matilda Pitman alone was worth it. She will be an amusing memory all our lives. Are you sorry you came?"

"No, I'm not," I concluded, after honest, soul-searching reflection. "No, I'm glad, Kate. But I think we were crazy to attempt it, as Sergeant Baker said. Think of all the might-have-beens."

"Nothing else will happen," said Kate. "I feel in my bones that our troubles are over."

Kate's bones proved true prophets. Nevertheless, that day was a weary one. There was no scenery. We had got into a barren, lakeless, treeless district where the world was one monotonous expanse of grey-brown prairie. We just crawled along. Kate had her hands full driving those ponies. Jerry was in capital fettle and couldn't understand why he mightn't tear ahead at full speed. He was so much disgusted over being compelled to walk that he was very fractious. Poor Tom limped patiently along. But by night his lameness had quite disappeared, and although we were still a good twenty-five miles from Bothwell we could see it quite distinctly far ahead on the level prairie.

"'Tis a sight for sore eyes, isn't it?" said Kate, as we pitched camp.

There is little more to be told. Next day at noon we rattled through the main and only street of Bothwell. Curious sights are frequent in prairie towns, so we did not attract much attention. When we drew up before Mr. Taylor's house Mary Taylor flew out and embraced Kate publicly.

"You darling! I knew you'd get here if anyone could. They telegraphed us you were on the way. You're a brick—two bricks."

"No, I'm not a brick at all, Miss Taylor," I confessed frankly. "I've been an arrant coward and a doubting Thomas and a wet blanket all through the expedition. But Kate is a brick and a genius and an all-round, jolly good fellow."

"Mary," said Kate in a tragic whisper, "have—you—any—ham—in—the—house?"

Jessamine

When the vegetable-man knocked, Jessamine went to the door wearily. She felt quite well acquainted with him. He had been coming all the spring, and his cheery greeting always left a pleasant afterglow behind him. But it was not the vegetable-man after all—at least, not the right one. This one was considerably younger. He was tall and sunburned, with a ruddy, smiling face, and keen, pleasant blue eyes; and he had a spray of honeysuckle pinned on his coat.

"Want any garden stuff this morning?"

Jessamine shook her head. "We always get ours from Mr. Bell. This is his day to come."

"Well, I guess you won't see Mr. Bell for a spell. He fell off a loft out at his place yesterday and broke his leg. I'm his nephew, and I'm going to fill his place till he gets 'round again."

"Oh, I'm so sorry—for Mr. Bell, I mean. Have you any green peas?"

"Yes, heaps of them. I'll bring them in. Anything else?"

"Not today," said Jessamine, with a wistful glance at the honeysuckle.

Mr. Bell, junior, saw it. In an instant the honeysuckle was unpinned and handed to her. "If you like posies, you're welcome to this. I guess you're fond of flowers," he added, as he noted the flash of delight that passed over her pale face.

"Yes, indeed; they put me so in mind of home—of the country. Oh, how sweet this is!"

"You're country-bred, then? Been in the city long?"

"Since last fall. I was born and brought up in the country. I wish I was back. I can't get over being homesick. This honeysuckle seems to bring it right back. We had honeysuckles around our porch at home."

"You don't like the city, then?"

"Oh, no. I sometimes feel as if I should smother here. I shall never feel at home, I am afraid."

"Where did you live before you came here?"

"Up at Middleton. It was an old-fashioned place, but pretty—our house was covered with vines, and there were trees all about it, and great green fields beyond. But I don't know what makes me tell you this. I forgot I was talking to a stranger."

"Pretty little woman," soliloquized Andrew Bell, as he drove away. "She doesn't look happy, though. I suppose she's married some city chap and has to live in town. I guess it don't agree with her. Her eyes had a real hungry look in them over that honeysuckle. She seemed near about crying when she talked of the country."

Jessamine felt more like crying than ever when she went back to her work. Her head ached and she was very tired. The tiny kitchen was hot and stifling. How she longed for the great, roomy kitchen in her old home, with its spotless floors and floods of sunshine streaming in through the maples outside. There was room to live and breathe there, and from the door one looked out over green wind-rippled meadows, under a glorious arch of pure blue sky, away to the purple hills in the distance.

Jessamine Stacy had always lived in the country. When her sister died and the old home had to go, Jessamine could only accept the shelter offered by her brother, John Stacy, who did business in the city.

Of her stylish sister-in-law Jessamine was absolutely in awe. At first Mrs. John was by no means pleased at the necessity of taking a country sister into her family circle. But one day, when the servant girl took a tantrum and left, Mrs. John found it very convenient to have in the house a person who could step into Eliza's place as promptly and efficiently as Jessamine could.

Indeed, she found it so convenient that Eliza never had a successor. Jessamine found herself in the position of maid-of-all-work and kitchen drudge for board and clothes.

She never complained, but she grew thinner and paler as the winter went by. She had worked as hard on the farm, but it was the close confinement and weary routine that told on her. Mrs. John was exacting and querulous. John was absorbed in his business worries and had no time to waste on his sister. Now, when the summer had come, her homesickness was almost unbearable.

The next day Mr. Bell came he handed her a big bunch of sweet-brier roses.

"Here you are," he said heartily. "I took the liberty to bring you these today, seeing you're so fond of posies. The country roads are pink with them now. Why don't you get your husband to bring you out for a drive some day? You'd be as welcome as a lark at my farm."

"I will when he comes along, but I haven't seen him yet."

Mr. Bell gave a prolonged whistle. "Excuse me. I thought you were Mrs. Something-or-other for sure. Aren't you mistress here?"

"Oh, no. My brother's wife is the mistress here. I'm only Jessamine."

She laughed again. She was holding the roses against her face, and her eyes sparkled over them roguishly. The vegetable-man looked at her admiringly.

"You're a country rose yourself, miss, and you ought to be blooming out in the fields, instead of wilting in here."

"I wish I was. Thank you so much for the roses, Mr. —— Mr. ——"

"Bell—Andrew Bell, that's my name. I live out at Pine Pastures. We're all Bells out there—can't throw a stone without hitting one. Glad you like the roses."

After that the vegetable-man brought Jessamine a bouquet every trip. Now it was a big bunch of field-daisies or golden buttercups, now a green glory of spicy ferns, now a cluster of old-fashioned garden flowers.

"They keep life in me," Jessamine told him.

They were great friends by this time. True, she knew little about him but she felt instinctively that he was manly and kind-hearted.

One day when he came Jessamine met him almost gleefully. "No, nothing to-day. There is no dinner to cook."

"You don't say. Where are the folks?"

"Gone on an excursion. They won't be back until tonight."

"They won't? Well, I'll tell you what to do. You get ready, and when I'm through my rounds we'll go for a drive up the country."

"Oh, Mr. Bell! But won't it be too much bother for you?"

"Well, I reckon not! You want an excursion as well as other folks, and you shall have it."

"Oh, thank you so much. Yes, I'll be ready. You don't know how much it means to me."

"Poor little creature," said Mr. Bell, as he drove away. "It's downright cruelty, that's what it is, to keep her penned up like that. You might as well coop up a lark in a hen-house and expect it to thrive and sing. I'd like to give that brother of hers a piece of my mind."

When he lifted her up to the high seat of his express wagon that afternoon he said, "Now, I want you to do something. Just shut your eyes and don't open them again until I tell you to."

Jessamine laughed and obeyed. Finally she heard him say, "Look."

Jessamine opened her eyes with a little cry. They were on a remote country road, cool and dim and quiet, in the very heart of the beech woods. Long banners of light fell athwart the grey boles. Along the roadsides grew sheets of feathery ferns. Above the sky was gloriously blue. The air was sweet with the wild woodsy smell of the forest.

Jessamine lifted and clasped her hands in rapture. "Oh, how lovely!"

"Do you know where we're going?" said Mr. Bell delightedly. "Out to my farm at Pine Pastures. My aunt keeps house for me, and she'll be real glad to see you. You're just going to have a real good time this afternoon."

They had a delightful drive to begin with, and presently Mr. Bell turned into a wide lane.

"This is Cloverside Farm. I'm proud of it, I'll admit. There isn't a finer place in the county. What do you think of it?"

"Oh, it is lovely—it is like home. Look at those great fields. I'd like to go and lie down in that clover."

Mr. Bell lifted her from the wagon and marched her up a flowery garden path. "You shall do it, and everything else you want to. Here, Aunt, this is the young lady I spoke of. Make her at home while I tend to the horses."

Miss Bell was a pleasant-faced woman with silver hair and kind blue eyes. She took Jessamine's hand in a friendly fashion.

"Come in, dear. You're welcome as a June rose."

When Mr. Bell returned, he found Jessamine standing on the porch with her hands full of honeysuckle and her cheeks pink with excitement.

"I declare, you've got roses already," he exclaimed. "If they'd only stay now, and not bleach out again. What's first now?"

"Oh, I don't know. There are so many things I want to do. Those flowers in the garden are calling me—and I want to go down to that hollow and pick buttercups—and I want to stay right here and look at things."

Mr. Bell laughed. "Come with me to the pasture and see my Jersey calves. They're something worth seeing. Come, Aunt. This way, Miss Stacy."

He led the way down the lane, the two women following together. Jessamine thought she must be in a pleasant dream. The whole afternoon was a feast of delight to her starved heart. When sunset came she sat down, tired out, but radiant, on the porch steps. Her hat had slipped back and her hair was curling around her face. Her dark eyes were aglow; the roses still bloomed in her cheeks.

Mr. Bell looked at her admiringly. "If a man could see that pretty sight every night!" he thought. "And, Great Scott, why can't he? What's to prevent, I'd like to know?"

When the moon rose, Mr. Bell brought his team around and they drove back through the clear night, past the wonderful stillness of the great beech woods and the wide fields. The farmer looked sideways at his companion.

"The little thing wants to be petted and looked after," he thought. "She's just pining away for home and love. And why can't she have it? She's dying by inches in that hole back in town."

Jessamine, quite unsuspecting the farmer's meditations, was living over again in fancy the joys of the afternoon: the ramble in the pasture, the drink of water from the spring under the hillside pines, the bountiful, old-fashioned country supper in the vine-shaded dining-room, the cup of new milk in the dairy at sunset, and all the glory of skies and meadows and trees. How could she go back to her cage again?

The next week Mr. Bell, senior, resumed his visits, and the young farmer came no more to the side door of No. 49. Jessamine missed him greatly. Mr. Bell, senior, never brought her clover or honeysuckle.

But one day his nephew suddenly reappeared. Jessamine opened the door for him, and her face lighted up, but Mr. Bell saw that she had been crying.

"Did you think I had forgotten you?" he asked. "Not a bit of it. Harvest was on and I couldn't get clear before. I've come to ask you when you intend to take another drive to Cloverside Farm. What have you been up to? You look as if you'd been working too hard."

"I—I—haven't felt very well. I'm glad you came today, Mr. Bell. Perhaps I shall not see you again, and I wanted to say goodbye and thank you for all your kindness."

"Goodbye? Why, where are you going?"

"My brother went west a week ago," faltered Jessamine. She could not bring herself to tell the clear-eyed farmer that John Stacy had failed and had been obliged to start for the west without saying goodbye to his creditors. "His wife and I—are going too—next week."

"Oh, Jessamine," exclaimed Mr. Bell in despair, "don't go—you mustn't. I want you at Cloverside Farm. I came today on purpose to ask you. I love you and I'll make you happy if you'll marry me. What do you say, Jessamine?"

Jessamine, by way of answer, sat down on the nearest chair and began to cry.

"Oh, don't," said the wooer in distress. "I didn't want to make you feel bad. If you don't like the idea, I won't mention it again."

"Oh, it isn't that—but I—I thought nobody cared what became of me. You are so kind—I'm afraid I'd only be a bother to you...."

"I'll risk that. You shall have a happy home, little girl. Will you come to it?"

"Ye-e-e-s." It was very indistinct and faltering, but Mr. Bell heard it and considered it a most eloquent answer.

Mrs. John fumed and sulked and chose to consider herself hoodwinked and injured. But Mr. Bell was a resolute man, and a few days later he came for the last time to No. 49 and took his bride away with him.

As they drove through the beech woods he put his arm tenderly around the shy, smiling little woman beside him and said, "You'll never be sorry for this, my dear."

And she never was.

Miss Sally's Letter

Miss Sally peered sharply at Willard Stanley, first through her gold-rimmed glasses and then over them. Willard continued to look very innocent. Joyce got up abruptly and went out of the room.

"So you have bought that queer little house with the absurd name?" said Miss Sally.

"You surely don't call Eden an absurd name," protested Willard.

"I do—for a house. Particularly such a house as that. Eden! There are no Edens on earth. And what are you going to do with it?"

"Live in it."

"Alone?"

Miss Sally looked at him suspiciously.

"No. The truth is, Miss Sally, I am hoping to be married in the fall and I want to fix up Eden for my bride."

"Oh!" Miss Sally drew a long breath, partly it seemed of relief and partly of triumph, and looked at Joyce, who had returned, with an expression that said, "I told you so"; but Joyce, whose eyes were cast down, did not see it.

"And," went on Willard calmly, "I want you to help me fix it up, Miss Sally. I don't know much about such things and you know everything. You will be able to tell me just what to do to make Eden habitable."

Miss Sally looked as pleased as she ever allowed herself to look over anything a man suggested. It was the delight of her heart to plan and decorate and contrive. Her own house was a model of comfort and good taste, and Miss Sally was quite ready for new worlds to conquer. Instantly Eden assumed importance in her eyes. She might be sorry for the misguided bride who was rashly going to trust her life's keeping to a man, but she would see, at least, that the poor thing should have a decent place to begin her martyrdom in.

"I'll be pleased to help you all I can," she said graciously.

Miss Sally could speak very graciously when she chose, even to men. You would not have thought she hated them, but she did. In all sincerity, too. Also, she had brought her niece up to hate and distrust them. Or, she had tried to do so. But at times Miss Sally was troubled with an uncomfortable suspicion that Joyce did not hate and distrust men quite as thoroughly as she ought. The suspicion had recurred several times this summer since Willard Stanley had come to take charge of the biological station at the harbour. Miss Sally did not distrust Willard on his own account. She merely distrusted him on principle and on Joyce's account. Nevertheless, she was rather nice to him. Miss Sally, dear, trim, dainty Miss Sally, with her snow-white curls and her big girlish black eyes, couldn't help being nice, even to a man.

Willard had come a great deal to Miss Sally's. If it were Joyce he were after Miss Sally blocked his schemes with much enjoyment. He never saw Joyce alone—that Miss Sally knew of, at least—and he did not make much apparent headway. But now all danger was removed, Miss Sally thought. He was going to be married to somebody else, and Joyce was safe.

"Thank you," said Willard. "I'll come up tomorrow afternoon, and you and I will take a prowl about Eden and see what must be done. I'm ever so much obliged, Miss Sally."

"I wonder who he is going to marry," said Miss Sally, careless of grammar, after he had gone. "Poor, poor girl!"

"I don't see why you should pity her," said Joyce, not looking up from her embroidery. There was just the merest tremor in her voice. Miss Sally looked at her sharply.

"I pity any woman who is foolish enough to marry," she said solemnly. "No man is to be trusted, Joyce—no man. They are all ready to break a trusting woman's heart for the sport of it. Never you allow any man the chance to break yours, Joyce. I shall never consent to your marrying anybody, so mind you don't take any such notion into your head. There oughtn't to be any danger, for I have instilled correct ideas on this subject into you from childhood. But girls are such fools. I know, because I was one myself once."

"Of course, I would never marry without your consent, Aunt Sally," said Joyce, smiling faintly but affectionately at her aunt. Joyce loved Miss Sally with her whole heart. Everybody did who knew her. There never was a more lovable creature than this pretty little old maid who hated the men so bitterly.

"That's a good girl," said Miss Sally approvingly. "I own that I have been a little afraid that this Willard Stanley was coming here to see you. But my mind is set at rest on that point now, and I shall help him fix up his doll house with a clear conscience. Eden, indeed!"

Miss Sally sniffed and tripped out of the room to hunt up a furniture catalogue. Joyce sighed and let her embroidery slip to the floor.

"Oh, I'm afraid Willard's plan won't succeed," she murmured. "I'm afraid Aunt Sally will never consent to our marriage. And I can't and won't marry him unless she does, for she would never forgive me and I couldn't bear that. I wonder what makes her so bitter against men. She is so sweet and loving, it seems simply unnatural that she should have such a feeling so deeply rooted in her. Oh, what will she say when she finds out—dear little Aunt Sally? I couldn't bear to have her angry with me."

The next day Willard came up from the harbour and took Miss Sally down to see Eden. Eden was a tiny, cornery, gabled grey house just across the road and down a long, twisted windy lane, skirting the edge of a beech wood. Nobody had lived in it for four years, and it had a neglected, out-at-elbow appearance.

"It's rather a box of a place, isn't it?" said Willard slowly. "I'm afraid she will think so. But it is all I can afford just now. I dream of giving her a palace some day, of course. But we'll have to begin humbly. Do you think anything can be made of it?"

Miss Sally was busily engaged in sizing up the possibilities of the place.

"It is pretty small," she said meditatively. "And the yard is small too—and there are far too many trees and shrubs all messed up together. They must be thinned out—and that paling taken down. I think a good deal can be done with it. As for the house—well, let us see the inside."

Willard unlocked the door and showed Miss Sally over the place. Miss Sally poked and pried and sniffed and wrinkled her forehead, and finally stood on the stairs and delivered her ultimatum.

"This house can be done up very nicely. Paint and paper will work wonders. But I wouldn't paint it outside. Leave it that pretty silver weather-grey and plant vines to run over it. Oh, we'll see what we can do. Of course it is small—a kitchen, a dining room, a living room, and two bedrooms. You won't want anything stuffy. You can do the painting yourself, and I'll help you hang the paper. How much money can you spend on it?"

Willard named the sum. It was not a large one.

"But I think it will do," mused Miss Sally. "We'll *make* it do. There's such satisfaction getting as much as you possibly can out of a dollar, and twice as much as anybody else would get. I enjoy that sort of thing. This will be a game, and we'll play it with a right good will. But I do wish you would give the place a sensible name."

"I think Eden is the most appropriate name in the world," laughed Willard. "It will be Eden for me when she comes."

"I suppose you tell her all that and she believes it," said Miss Sally sarcastically. "You'll both find out that there is a good deal more prose than poetry in life."

"But we'll find it out *together*," said Willard tenderly. "Won't that be worth something, Miss Sally? Prose, rightly written and read, is sometimes as beautiful as poetry."

Miss Sally deigned no reply. She carefully gathered up her grey silken skirts from the dusty floor and walked out. "Get Christina Bowes to come up tomorrow and scrub this place out," she said practically. "We can go to town and select paint and paper. I should like the dining room done in pale green and the living room in creamy tones, ranging from white to almost golden brown. But perhaps my taste won't be hers."

"Oh, yes, it will," said Willard with assurance. "I am quite certain she will like everything you like. I can never thank you enough for helping me. If you hadn't consented I should have had to put it into the hands of some outsider whom I couldn't have helped at all. And I *wanted* to help. I wanted to have a finger in everything, because it is for her, you see, Miss Sally. It will be such a delight to fix up this little house, knowing that she is coming to live in it."

"I wonder if you really mean it," said Miss Sally bitterly. "Oh, I dare say you think you do. But *do* you? Perhaps you do. Perhaps you are the exception that proves the rule."

This was a great admission for Miss Sally to make.

For the next two months Miss Sally was happy. Even Willard himself was not more keenly interested in Eden and its development. Miss Sally did wonders with his money. She was an expert at bargain hunting, and her taste was excellent. A score of times she mercilessly nipped Willard's suggestions in the bud. "Lace curtains for the living room—never! They would be horribly out of place in such a house. You don't want curtains at all—just a frill is all that quaint window needs, with a shelf above it for a few bits of pottery. I picked up a love of a brass platter in town yesterday—got it for next to nothing from that old Jew who would really rather *give* you a thing than suffer you to escape without taking something. Oh, I know how to manage them."

"You certainly do," laughed Willard. "It amazes me to see how far you can stretch a dollar."

Willard did the painting under Miss Sally's watchful eye, and they hung the paper together. Together they made trips to town or junketed over the country in search of furniture and dishes of which Miss Sally had heard. Day by day the little house blossomed into a home, and day by day Miss Sally's interest in it grew. She began to have a personal affection for its quaint rooms and their adornments. Moreover, in spite of herself, she felt a growing interest in Willard's bride. He never told her the name of the girl he hoped to bring to Eden, and Miss Sally never asked it. But he talked of her a great deal, in a shy, reverent, tender way.

"He certainly seems to be very much in love with her," Miss Sally told Joyce one evening when she returned from Eden. "I would believe in him if it were possible for me to believe in a man. Anyway, she will have a dear little home. I've almost come to love that Eden house. Why don't you come down and see it, Joyce?"

"Oh, I'll come some day—I hope," said Joyce lightly. "I think I'd rather not see it until it is finished."

"Willard is a nice boy," said Miss Sally suddenly. "I don't think I ever did him justice before. The finer qualities of his character come out in these simple, homely little doings and tasks. He is certainly very thoughtful and kind. Oh, I suppose he'll make a good husband, as husbands go. But he doesn't know the first thing about managing. If his wife isn't a good manager, I don't know what they'll do. And perhaps she won't like the way we've done up Eden. Willard says she will, of course, because he thinks her perfection. But she may have dreadful taste and want the lace curtains and that nightmare of a pink rug Willard admired, and I dare say she'd rather have a new flaunting set of china with rosebuds on it than that dear old dull blue I picked up for a mere song down at the Aldenbury auction. I stood in the rain for two mortal hours to make sure of it, and it was really worth all that Willard has spent on the dining room put together. It will break my heart if she sets to work altering Eden. It's simply perfect as it is—though I suppose I shouldn't say it."

In another week Eden was finished. Miss Sally stood in the tiny hall and looked about her.

"Well, it is done," she said with a sigh. "I'm sorry. I have enjoyed fixing it up tremendously, and now I feel that my occupation is gone. I hope you are satisfied, Willard."

"Satisfied is too mild a word, Miss Sally. I am delighted. I knew you could accomplish wonders, but I never hoped for *this*. Eden is a dream—the dearest, quaintest, sweetest little home that ever waited for a bride. When I bring her here—oh, Miss Sally, do you know what that thought means to me?"

Miss Sally looked curiously at the young man. His face was flushed and his voice trembled a little. There was a far-away shining look in his eyes as if he saw a vision.

"I hope you and she will be happy," said Miss Sally slowly. "When will she be coming, Willard?"

The flush went out of Willard's face, leaving it pale and determined.

"That is for her—and you—to say," he answered steadily.

"Me!" exclaimed Miss Sally. "What have I to do with it?"

"A great deal—for unless you consent she will never come here at all."

"Willard Stanley," said Miss Sally, with ominous calm, "who is the girl you mean to marry?"

"The girl I *hope* to marry is Joyce, Miss Sally. Wait—don't say anything till you hear me out." He came close to her and caught her hands in a boyish grip. "Joyce and I have loved each other ever since we met. But we despaired of winning your consent, and Joyce will not marry me without it. I thought if I could get you to help me fix up my little home that you might get so interested in it—and so well acquainted with me—that you would trust me with Joyce. Please do, Miss Sally. I love her so truly and I know I can make her happy. If you don't, Eden shall never have a mistress. I'll shut it up, just as it is, and leave it sacred to the dead hope of a bride that will never come to it."

"Oh, you wouldn't," protested Miss Sally. "It would be a shame—such a dear little house—and after all the trouble I've taken. But you have tricked me—oh, you men couldn't be straightforward in anything—"

"Wasn't it a fair device for a desperate lover, Miss Sally?" interrupted Willard. "Oh, you mustn't hold spite because of it, dear; And you will give me Joyce, won't you? Because if you don't, I really will shut up Eden forever."

Miss Sally looked wistfully around her. Through the open door on her left she saw the little living room with its quaint, comfortable furniture, its dainty pictures and adornments. Through the front door she saw the trim, velvet-swarded little lawn. Upstairs were two white rooms that only wanted a woman's living presence to make them jewels. And the kitchen on which she had expended so much thought and ingenuity—the kitchen furnished to the last detail, even to the kindling in the range and the match Willard had laid ready to light it! It gave Miss Sally a pang to think of that altar fire never being lighted. It was really the thought of the kitchen that finished Miss Sally.

"You've tricked me," she said again reproachfully. "You've tricked me into loving this house so much that I cannot bear the thought of it never living. You'll have to have Joyce, I suppose. And I believe I'm glad that it isn't a stranger who is to be the mistress of Eden. Joyce won't hanker after pink rugs and lace curtains. And her taste in china is the same as mine. In one way it's a great relief to my mind. But it's a fearful risk—a fearful risk. To think that you may make my dear child miserable!"

"You know you don't think that I will, Miss Sally. I'm not really such a bad fellow, now, am I?"

"You are a man—and I have no confidence whatever in men," declared Miss Sally, wiping some very real tears from her eyes with a very unreal sort of handkerchief—one of the cobwebby affairs of lace her daintiness demanded.

"Miss Sally, why have you such a rooted distrust of men?" demanded Willard curiously. "Somehow, it seems so foreign to your character."

"I suppose you think I am a perfect crank," said Miss Sally, sighing. "Well, I'll tell you why I don't trust men. I have a very good reason for it. A man broke my heart and embittered my life. I've never spoken about it to a living soul, but if you want to hear about it, you shall."

Miss Sally sat down on the second step of the stairs and tucked her wet handkerchief away. She clasped her slender white hands over her knee. In spite of her silvery hair and the little lines on her face she looked girlish and youthful. There was a pink flush on her cheeks, and her big black eyes sparkled with the anger her memories aroused in her.

"I was a young girl of twenty when I met him," she said, "and I was just as foolish as all young girls are—foolish and romantic and sentimental. He was very handsome and I thought him—but there, I won't go into that. It vexes me to recall my folly. But I loved him—yes, I did, with all my heart—with all there was of me to love. He made me love him. He deliberately set himself to win my love. For a whole summer he flirted with me. I didn't know he was flirting—I thought him in earnest. Oh, I was such a little fool—and so happy. Then—he went away. Went away suddenly without even a word of goodbye. But he had been summoned home by his father's serious illness, and I thought he would write—I waited—I hoped. I never heard from him—never saw him again. He had tired of his plaything and flung it aside. That is all," concluded Miss Sally passionately. "I never trusted any man again. When my sister died and gave me her baby, I determined to bring the dear child up safely, training her to avoid the danger I had fallen into. Well, I've failed. But perhaps it will be all right—perhaps there are some men who are true, though Stephen Merritt was false."

"Stephen—who?" demanded Willard abruptly. Miss Sally coloured.

"I didn't mean to tell you his name," she said, getting up. "It was a slip of the tongue. Never mind—forget it and him. He was not worthy of remembrance—and yet I do remember him. I can't forget him—and I hate him all the more for it—for having entered so deeply into my life that I could not cast him out when I knew him unworthy. It is humiliating. There—let us lock up Eden and go home. I suppose you are dying to see Joyce and tell her your precious plot has succeeded."

Willard did not appear to be at all impatient. He had relapsed into a brown study, during which he let Miss Sally lock up the house. Then he walked silently home with her. Miss Sally was silent too. Perhaps she was repenting her confidence—or perhaps she was thinking of her false lover. There was a pathetic droop to her lips, and her black eyes were sad and dreamy.

"Miss Sally," said Willard at last, as they neared her house, "had Stephen Merritt any sisters?"

Miss Sally threw him a puzzled glance.

"He had one—Jean Merritt—whom I disliked and who disliked me," she said crisply. "I don't want to talk of her—she was the only woman I ever hated. I never met any of the other members of his family—his home was in a distant part of the state."

Willard stayed with Joyce so brief a time that Miss Sally viewed his departure with suspicion. This was not very lover-like conduct.

"I dare say he's like all the rest—when his aim is attained the prize loses its value," reflected Miss Sally pessimistically. "Poor Joyce—poor child! But there—there isn't a single inharmonious thing in his house—that is one comfort. I'm so thankful I didn't let Willard buy those brocade chairs he wanted. They would have given Joyce the nightmare."

Meanwhile, Willard rushed down to the biological station and from there drove furiously to the station to catch the evening express. He did not return until three days later, when he appeared at Miss Sally's, dusty and triumphant.

"Joyce is out," said Miss Sally.

"I'm glad of it," said Willard recklessly. "It's you I want to see, Miss Sally. I have something to show you. I've been all the way home to get it."

From his pocketbook Willard drew something folded and creased and yellow that looked like a letter. He opened it carefully and, holding it in his fingers, looked over it at Miss Sally.

"My grandmother's maiden name was Jean Merritt," he said deliberately, "and Stephen Merritt was my great-uncle. I never saw him—he died when I was a child—but I've heard my father speak of him often."

Miss Sally turned very pale. She passed her cobwebby handkerchief across her lips and her hand trembled. Willard went on.

"My uncle never married. He and his sister Jean lived together until her late marriage. I was not very fond of my grandmother. She was a selfish, domineering woman—very unlike the grandmother of tradition. When she died everything she possessed came to me, as my father, her only child, was then dead. In looking over a box of old papers I found a letter—an old love letter. I read it with some interest, wondering whose it could be and how it came among Grandmother's private letters. It was signed 'Stephen,' so that I guessed my great-uncle had been the writer, but I had no idea who the Sally was to whom it was written, until the other day. Then I knew it was you—and I went home to bring you your letter—the letter you should have received long ago. Why you did not receive it I cannot ex-explain. I fear that my grandmother must have been to blame for that—she must have intercepted and kept the letter in order to part her brother and you. In so far as I can I wish to repair the wrong she has done you. I know it can never be repaired—but at least I think this letter will take the bitterness out of the memory of your lover."

He dropped the letter in Miss Sally's lap and went away.

Pale, Miss Sally picked it up and read it. It was from Stephen Merritt to "dearest Sally," and contained a frank, manly avowal of love. Would she be his wife? If she would, let her write and tell him so. But if she did not and could not love him, let her silence reveal the bitter fact; he would wish to spare her the pain of putting her refusal into words, and if she did not write he would understand that she was not for him.

When Willard and Joyce came back into the twilight room they found Miss Sally still sitting by the table, her head leaning pensively on her hand. She had been crying—the cobwebby handkerchief lay beside her, wrecked and ruined forever—but she looked very happy.

"I wonder if you know what you have done for me," she said to Willard. "But no—you can't know—you can't realize it fully. It means everything to me. You have taken away my humiliation and restored to me my pride of womanhood. He really loved me—he was not false—he was what I believed him to be. Nothing else matters to me at all now. Oh, I am very happy—but it would never have been if I had not consented to give you Joyce."

She rose and took their hands in hers, joining them.

"God bless you, dears," she said softly. "I believe you will be happy and that your love for each other will always be true and faithful and tender. Willard, I give you my dear child in perfect trust and confidence."

With her yellowed love letter clasped to her heart, and a raptured shining in her eyes, Miss Sally went out of the room.

My Lady Jane

The boat got into Broughton half an hour after the train had gone. We had been delayed by some small accident to the machinery; hence that lost half-hour, which meant a night's sojourn for me in Broughton. I am ashamed of the things I thought and said. When I think that fate might have taken me at my word and raised up a special train, or some such miracle, by which I might have got away from Broughton that night, I experience a cold chill. Out of gratitude I have never sworn over missing connections since.

At the time, however, I felt thoroughly exasperated. I was in a hurry to get on. Important business engagements would be unhinged by the delay. I was a stranger in Broughton. It looked like a stupid, stuffy little town. I went to a hotel in an atrocious humor. After I had fumed until I wanted a change, it occurred to me that I might as well hunt up Clark Oliver by way of passing the time. I had never been overly fond of Clark Oliver, although he was my cousin. He was a bit of a cad, and stupider than anyone belonging to our family had a right to be. Moreover, he was in politics, and I detest politics. But I rather wanted to see if he looked as much like me as he used to. I hadn't seen him for three years and I hoped that the time might have differentiated us to a saving degree. It was over a year since I had last been blown up by some unknown, excited individual on the ground that I was that scoundrel Oliver—politically speaking. I thought that was a good omen.

I went to Clark's office, found he had left, and followed him to his rooms. The minute I saw him I experienced the same nasty feeling of lost or bewildered individuality which always overcame me in his presence. He was so absurdly like me. I felt as if I were looking into a mirror where my reflection persisted in doing things I didn't do, thereby producing a most uncanny sensation.

Clark pretended he was glad to see me. He really couldn't have been, because his Great Idea hadn't struck him then, and we had always disliked each other.

"Hello, Elliott," he said, shaking me by the hand with a twist he had learned in election campaigns, whereby something like heartiness was simulated. "Glad to see you, old fellow. Gad, you're as like me as ever. Where did you drop from?"

I explained my predicament and we talked amiably and harmlessly for awhile about family gossip. I abhor family gossip, but it is a shade better than politics, and those two subjects are the only ones on which Clark can converse at all. I described Mary Alice's wedding, and Florence's new young man, and Tom-and-

Kate's twins. Clark tried to be interested but I saw he had something on what serves him for a mind. After awhile it came out. He looked at his watch with a frown.

"I'm in a bit of a puzzle," he said. "The Mark Kennedys are giving a dinner to-night. You don't know them, of course. They're the big people of Broughton. Kennedy runs the politics of the place, and Mrs. K. makes or mars people socially. It's my first invitation there and it's necessary I should accept it—necessary every way. Mrs. K. would never forgive me if I disappointed her at the last moment. Not that I, personally, am of much account—yet—to her. But it would leave a vacant place. Mrs. K. would never notice me again and, as she bosses Kennedy, I can't afford to offend her. Besides, there's a girl who'll be there. I've met her once. I want to meet her again. She's a beauty and no mistake. Toplofty as they make 'em, though. However, I think I've made an impression on her. It was at the Harvey's dance last week. She was the handsomest woman there, and she never took her eyes off me. I've given Mrs. Kennedy a pretty broad hint that I want to take her in to dinner. If I don't go I'll miss all round."

"Well, what is there to prevent you from going?" I asked, squiffily. I never could endure the way Clark talked about girls and hinted at his conquests.

"Just this. Herbert Bronson came to town this afternoon and is leaving on the 10.30 train to-night. He's sent me word to meet him at his hotel this evening and talk over a mining deal I've been trying to pull off. I simply must go. It's my one chance to corral Bronson. If I lose him it'll be all up, and I'll be thousands out of pocket."

"Well, you *are* in rather a predicament," I agreed, with the philosophical acceptance of the situation that marks the outsider. *I* wasn't hampered by the multiplicity of my business and social engagements that evening, so I could afford to pity Clark. It is always rather nice to be able to pity a person you dislike.

"I should say so. I can't make up my mind what to do. Hang it. I'll *have* to see Bronson. There's no question about that. A man ought to keep an understood substitute on hand to send to dinners when he can't go. By Jove! Elliott!"

Clark's Great Idea had arrived. He bounced up eagerly.

"Elliott, will *you* go to the Kennedys' in my place? They'll never know the difference. Do, now—there's a good fellow!"

"Nonsense!" I said.

"It isn't nonsense. The resemblance between us was foreordained for this hour. I'll lend you my dress suit—it'll fit you—your figure is as much like mine as your face. You've nothing to do with yourself this evening. I offer you a good dinner and an agreeable partner. Come now, to oblige me. You know you owe me a good turn for that Mulhenen business."

The Mulhenen business clinched the matter. Until he mentioned it I had no notion whatever of masquerading as Clark Oliver at the Kennedys' dinner. But, as Clark so delicately put it, he had done me a good turn in that affair and the obligation had rankled ever since. It is beastly to be indebted for a favor to a man you detest. Now was my chance to pay it off and I took it without more ado.

"But," I said doubtfully, "I don't know the Kennedys—nor any of the social stunts that are doing in Broughton; I won't dare to talk about anything, and I'll seem so stupid, even if I don't actually make some irremediable blunder, that the Kennedys will be disgusted with you. It will probably do your prospects more harm than your absence would."

"Not at all. Keep your mouth shut when you can and talk generalities when you can't, and you'll pass. If you take that girl in she's a stranger in Broughton and won't suspect your ignorance of what's going on. Nobody will suspect you. Nobody here knows I have a cousin so like me. Our own mothers haven't always been able to tell us apart. Our very voices are alike. Come now, get into my dinner togs. You haven't much time and Mrs. K. doesn't like late comers."

There seemed to be a number of things that Mrs. Kennedy did not like. I thought my chance of pleasing that critical lady extremely small, especially when I had to live up to Clark Oliver's personality. However, I dressed as expeditiously as possible. The novelty of the adventure rather pleased me. I always liked doing unusual things. Anything was better than lounging away the evening at my hotel. It couldn't do any harm. I owed Clark Oliver a good turn and I would save Mrs. Kennedy the annoyance of a vacant chair.

There was no disputing the fact that I looked most disgustingly like Clark when I got into his clothes. I actually felt a grudge against them for their excellent fit.

"You'll do," said Clark. "Remember you're a Conservative to-night and don't let your rank Liberal views crop out, or you'll queer me for all time with the great and only Mark. He doesn't talk politics at his dinners, though, so you're not likely to have trouble on that score. Mrs. Kennedy has a weakness for beer mugs. Her collection is considered very fine. Scandal whispers that Miss Harvey has a budding interest in settlement work—"

"Miss who?" I said sharply.

"Harvey. Christian name unknown. That's the girl I mentioned. You'll probably take her in. Be nice to her even if you have to make an effort. She's the one I've picked out as your future cousin, you know, so I don't want you to spoil her good opinion of me in any way."

The name had given me a jump. Once, in another world, I had known a Jane Harvey. But Clark's Miss Harvey couldn't be Jane. A month before I had read a newspaper item to the effect that Jane was on the Pacific coast. Moreover, Jane, when I knew her, had certainly no manifest vocation for settlement work. I didn't think two years could have worked such a transformation. Two years! Was it only two years? It seemed more like two centuries.

I went to the Kennedys' in a pleasantly excited frame of mind and a cab. I just missed being late by a hairbreadth. The house was a big one, and everybody pertaining to it was big, except the host. Mark Kennedy was a little, thin man with a bald head. He didn't look like a political power, but that was all the more reason for his being one in a world where things are not what they seem.

Mrs. Kennedy greeted me cordially and told me significantly that she had granted my request. This meant, as my card had already informed me, that I was to take Miss Harvey out. Of course there would be no introduction since Clark Oliver was already acquainted with the lady. I was wondering how I was to locate her when I got a shock that made me dizzy. Jane was over in a corner looking at me.

There was no time to collect my wits. The guests were moving out to the dining-room. I took my nerve in my hand, crossed the room, bowed, and the next moment was walking through the hall with Jane's hand on my arm. The hall was a good long one; I blessed the architect who had planned it. It gave me time to sort out my ideas.

Jane here! Jane going out to dinner with me, believing me to be Clark Oliver! Jane—but it was incredible! The whole thing was a dream—or I had gone crazy!

I looked at her sideways when we had got into our places at the table. She was more beautiful than ever, that tall, brown-haired, disdainful Jane. The settlement work story I was inclined to dismiss as a myth. Settlement work in a beautiful woman generally means crowsfeet or a broken heart. Jane, according to my sight and belief, possessed neither.

Once upon a time I had been engaged to Jane. I had been idiotically in love with her in those days and still more idiotically believed that she loved me. The trouble was that, although I had been cured of the latter phase of my idiocy, the former had become chronic. I had never been able to get over loving Jane. All through those two years I had hugged the fond hope that sometime I might stumble across her in a mild mood and make matters up. There was no such thing as seeking her out or writing to her, since she had icily forbidden me to do so, and Jane had a most detestable habit—in a woman—of meaning what she said. But the deity I had invoked was the god of chance—and this was how he had answered my prayers. I was eating my dinner beside Jane, who supposed me to be Clark Oliver!

What should I do? Confess the truth and plead my cause while she had to sit beside me? That would never do. Someone might overhear us. And, in any case, it would be no passport to Jane's favor that I was a guest in the house under false pretences. She would be certain to disapprove strongly. It was a maddening situation.

Jane, who was calmly eating soup—she was the only woman I had ever seen who could eat soup and look like a goddess at the same time—glanced around and caught me studying her profile. I thought she blushed slightly and I raged inwardly to think that blush was meant for Clark Oliver—Clark Oliver who had told me he thought Jane was smitten on him! Jane! On him!

"Do you know, Mr. Oliver," said Jane slowly, "that you are startlingly like a—a person I used to know? When I first saw you the other night I took you for him."

A *person* you used to know! Oh, Jane, that was the most unkindest cut of all.

"My cousin, Elliott Cameron, I suppose?" I answered as indifferently as I could. "We resemble each other very closely. You were acquainted with Cameron, Miss Harvey?"

"Slightly," said Jane.

"A fine fellow," I said unblushingly.

"A-h," said Jane.

"My favorite relative," I went on brazenly. "He's a thoroughly good sort—rather dull now to what he used to be, though. He had an unfortunate love affair two years ago and has never got over it."

"Indeed?" said Jane coldly, crumbling a bit of bread between her fingers. Her face was expressionless and her voice ditto; but I had heard her criticize nervous people who did things like that at table.

"I fear poor Elliott's life has been completely spoiled," I said, with a sigh. "It's a shame."

"Did he confide the affair to you?" asked Jane, a little scornfully.

"Well, after a fashion. He said enough for me to guess the rest. He never told me the lady's name. She was very beautiful, I understand, and very heartless. Oh, she used him very badly."

"Did he tell you that, too?" asked Jane.

"Not he. He won't listen to a word against her. But a chap can draw his own conclusions, you know."

"What went wrong between them?" asked Jane. She smiled at a lady across the table, as if she were merely asking questions to make conversation, but she went on crumbling bread.

"Simply a very stiff quarrel, I believe. Elliott never went into details. The lady was flirting with somebody else, I fancy."

"People have such different ideas about flirting," said Jane, languidly. "What one would call mere simple friendliness another construes into flirting. Possibly your friend—or is it your cousin?—is one of those men who become insanely jealous over every trifle and attempt to exert authority before they have any to exert. A woman of spirit would hardly fail to resent that."

"Of course Elliott was jealous," I admitted. "But then, you know, Miss Harvey, that jealousy is said to be the measure of a man's love. If he went beyond his rights I am sure he is bitterly sorry for it."

"Does he really care about her still?" asked Jane, eating most industriously, although somehow the contents of her plate did hot grow noticeably less. As for me, I didn't pretend to eat. I simply pecked.

"He loves her with all his heart," I answered fervently. "There never has been and never will be any other woman for Elliott Cameron."

"Why doesn't he go and tell her so?" inquired Jane, as if she felt rather bored over the whole subject.

"He doesn't dare to. She forbade him ever to cross her path again. Told him she hated him and always would hate him as long as she lived."

"She must have been an unpleasantly emphatic young woman," commented Jane.

"I'd like to hear anyone say so to Elliott," I responded. "He considers her perfection. I'm sorry for Elliott. His life is wrecked."

"Do you know," said Jane slowly, as if poking about in the recesses of her memory for something half forgotten. "I believe I know the—the girl in question."

"Really?" I said.

"Yes, she is a friend of mine. She—she never told me his name, but putting two and two together, I believe it must have been your cousin. But she—she thinks she was the one to blame."

"Does she?" It was my turn to ask questions now, but my heart thumped so that I could hardly speak.

"Yes, she says she was too hasty and unreasonable. She didn't mean to flirt at all—and she never cared for anyone but—him. But his jealousy irritated her. I suppose she said things to him she didn't really mean. She—she never supposed he was going to take her at her word."

"Do you think she cares for him still?" Considering what was at stake, I think I asked the question very well.

"I think she must," said Jane languidly. "She has never looked at any other man. She devotes most of her time to charitable work, but I feel sure she isn't really happy."

So the settlement story was true. Oh, Jane!

"What would you advise my cousin to do?" I asked. "Do you think he should go boldly to her? Would she listen to him—forgive him?"

"She might," said Jane.

"Have I your permission to tell Elliott Cameron this?" I demanded.

Jane selected and ate an olive with maddening deliberation.

"I suppose you may—if you are really convinced that he wants to hear it," she said at last, as if barely recollecting that I had asked the question two minutes previously.

"I'll tell him as soon as I go home," I said.

I had the satisfaction of startling Jane at last. She turned her head and looked at me. I got a good, square, satisfying gaze into her big, blackish-blue eyes.

"Yes," I said, compelling myself to look away. "He came in on the boat this afternoon too late for his train. Has to stay over till to-morrow night. I left him in my rooms when I came away. Doubtless to-morrow will see him speeding recklessly to his dear divinity. I wonder if he knows where she is at present."

"If he doesn't," said Jane, with the air of dismissing the subject once and forever from her mind, "I can give him the information. You may tell him I'm staying with the Duncan Moores, and shall be leaving day after to-morrow. By the way, have you seen Mrs. Kennedy's collection of steins? It is a remarkably fine one."

Clark Oliver couldn't come to our wedding—or wouldn't. Jane has never met him since, but she cannot understand why I have such an aversion to him, especially when he has such a good opinion of me. She says she thought him charming, and one of the most interesting conversationalists she ever went out to dinner with.

Robert Turner's Revenge

When Robert Turner came to the green, ferny triangle where the station road forked to the right and left under the birches, he hesitated as to which direction he would take. The left led out to the old Turner homestead, where he had spent his boyhood and where his cousin still lived; the right led down to the Cove shore where the Jameson property was situated. Since he had stopped off at Chiswick for the purpose of looking this property over before foreclosing the mortgage on it he concluded that he might as well take the Cove road; he could go around by the shore afterward—he had not forgotten the way even in forty years—and so on up through the old spruce wood in Alec Martin's field—if the spruces were there still and the field still Alec Martin's—to his cousin's place. He would just about have time to make the round before the early country supper hour. Then a brief visit with Tom—Tom had always been a good sort of a fellow although woefully dull and slow-going—and the evening express for Montreal. He swung with a businesslike stride into the Cove road.

As he went on, however, the stride insensibly slackened into an unaccustomed saunter. How well he remembered that old road, although it was forty years since he had last traversed it, a set-lipped boy of fifteen, cast on the world by the indifference of an uncle. The years had made surprisingly little difference in it or in the surrounding scenery. True, the hills and fields and lanes seemed lower and smaller and narrower than he remembered them; there were some new houses along the road, and the belt of woods along the back of the farms had become thinner in most places. But that was all. He had no difficulty in picking out the old familiar spots. There was the big cherry orchard on the Milligan place which had been so famous in his boyhood. It was snow-white with blossoms, as if the trees were possessed of eternal youth; they had been in blossom the last time he had seen them. Well, time had not stood still with him as it had with Luke Milligan's cherry orchard, he reflected grimly. His springtime had long gone by.

The few people he met on the road looked at him curiously, for strangers were not commonplace in Chiswick. He recognized some of the older among them but none of them knew him. He had been an awkward, long-limbed lad with fresh boyish colour and crisp black curls when he had left Chiswick. He returned to it a somewhat portly figure of a man, with close-cropped, grizzled hair, and a face that looked as if it might be carved out of granite, so immobile and unyielding it was—the face of a man who never faltered or wavered, who stuck at nothing that might advance his plans and purposes, a face known and dreaded in the business world where he reigned master. It was a cold, hard, selfish face, but the face of the boy of forty years ago had been neither cold nor hard nor selfish.

Presently the homesteads and orchard lands grew fewer and then ceased altogether. The fields were long and low-lying, sloping down to the misty blue rim of sea. A turn of the road brought him in sudden sight of the Cove, and there below him was the old Jameson homestead, built almost within wave-lap of the pebbly shore and shut away into a lonely grey world of its own by the sea and sands and those long slopes of tenantless fields.

He paused at the sagging gate that opened into the long, deep-rutted lane and, folding his arms on it, looked earnestly and scrutinizingly over the buildings. They were grey and faded, lacking the prosperous appearance that had characterized them once. There was an air of failure about the whole place as if the very land had become disheartened and discouraged.

Long ago, Neil Jameson, senior, had been a well-to-do man. The big Cove farm had been one of the best in Chiswick then. As for Neil Jameson, Junior, Robert Turner's face always grew something grimmer when he recalled him—the one person, boy and man, whom he had really hated in the world. They had been enemies from childhood, and once in a bout of wrestling at the Chiswick school Neil had thrown him by an unfair trick and taunted him continually thereafter on his defeat. Robert had made a compact with himself that some day he would pay Neil Jameson back. He had not forgotten it—he never forgot such things—but he had never seen or heard of Neil Jameson after leaving Chiswick. He might have been dead for anything Robert Turner knew. Then, when John Kesley failed and his effects turned over to his creditors, of whom Robert Turner was the chief, a mortgage on the Cove farm at Chiswick, owned by Neil Jameson, had been found among his assets. Inquiry revealed the fact that Neil Jameson was dead and that the farm was run by his widow. Turner felt a pang of disappointment. What satisfaction was there in wreaking revenge on a dead man? But at least his wife and children should suffer. That debt of his to Jameson for an ill-won victory and many a sneer must be paid in full, if not to him, why, then to his heirs.

His lawyers reported that Mrs. Jameson was two years behind with her interest. Turner instructed them to foreclose the mortgage promptly. Then he took it into his head to revisit Chiswick and have a good look at the Cove farm and other places he knew so well. He had a notion that it might be a decent place to spend a summer month or two in. His wife went to seaside and mountain resorts, but he liked something quieter. There was good fishing at the Cove and in Chiswick pond, as he remembered. If he liked the farm as well as his memory promised him he would do, he would bid it in himself. It would make Neil Jameson turn in his grave if the penniless lad he had jeered at came into the possession of his old ancestral property that had been owned by a Jameson for over one hundred years. There was a flavour in such a revenge that pleased Robert Turner. He smiled one of his occasional grim smiles over it. When Robert Turner smiled, weather prophets of the business sky foretold squalls.

Presently he opened the gate and went through. Halfway down the lane forked, one branch going over to the house, the other slanting across the field to the cove. Turner took the latter and soon found himself on the grey shore where the waves were tumbling in creamy foam just as he remembered them long ago. Nothing about the old cove had changed; he walked around a knobby headland, weatherworn with the wind and spray of years, which cut him off from sight of the Jameson house, and sat down on a rock. He thought himself alone and was annoyed to find a boy sitting on the opposite ledge with a book on his knee.

The lad lifted his eyes and looked Turner over with a clear, direct gaze. He was about twelve years old, tall for his age, slight, with a delicate, clear-cut face—a face that was oddly familiar to Turner, although he was sure he had never seen it before. The boy had oval cheeks, finely tinted with colour, big, shy blue eyes quilled about with long black lashes, and silvery-golden hair lying over his head in soft ringlets like a girl's. What girl's? Something far back in Robert Turner's dreamlike boyhood seemed to call to him like a note of a forgotten melody, sweet yet stirring like a pain. The more he looked at the boy the stronger the impression of a resemblance grew in every feature but the mouth. That was alien to his recollection of the face, yet there was something about it, when taken by itself, that seemed oddly familiar also—yes, and unpleasantly familiar, although the mouth was a good one—finely cut and possessing more firmness than was found in all the other features put together.

"It's a good place for reading, sonny, isn't it?" he inquired, more genially than he had spoken to a child for years. In fact, having no children of his own, he so seldom spoke to a child that his voice and manner when he did so were generally awkward and rusty.

The boy nodded a quick little nod. Somehow, Turner had expected that nod and the glimmer of a smile that accompanied it.

"What book are you reading?" he asked.

The boy held it out; it was an old *Robinson Crusoe*, that classic of boyhood.

"It's splendid," he said. "Billy Martin lent it to me and I have to finish it today because Ned Josephs is to have it next and he's in a hurry for it."

"It's a good while since I read *Robinson Crusoe*," said Turner reflectively. "But when I did it was on this very shore a little further along below the Miller place. There was a Martin and a Josephs in the partnership then too—the fathers, I dare say, of Billy and Ned. What is your name, my boy?"

"Paul Jameson, sir."

The name was a shock to Turner. This boy a Jameson—Neil Jameson's son? Why, yes, he had Neil's mouth. Strange he had nothing else in common with the black-browed, black-haired Jamesons. What business had a Jameson with those blue eyes and silvery-golden curls? It was flagrant forgery on Nature's part to fashion such things and label them Jameson by a mouth.

Hated Neil Jameson's son! Robert Turner's face grew so grey and hard that the boy involuntarily glanced upward to see if a cloud had crossed the sun.

"Your father was Neil Jameson, I suppose?" Turner said abruptly.

Paul nodded. "Yes, but he is dead. He has been dead for eight years. I don't remember him."

"Have you any brothers or sisters?"

"I have a little sister a year younger than I am. The other four are dead. They died long ago. I'm the only boy Mother had. Oh, I do so wish I was bigger and older! If I was I could do something to save the place—I'm sure I could. It is breaking Mother's heart to have to leave it."

"So she has to leave it, has she?" said Turner grimly, with the old hatred stirring in his heart.

"Yes. There is a mortgage on it and we're to be sold out very soon—so the lawyers told us. Mother has tried so hard to make the farm pay but she couldn't. I could if I was bigger—I know I could. If they would only wait a few years! But there is no use hoping for that. Mother cries all the time about it. She has lived at the Cove farm for over thirty years and she says she can't live away from it now. Elsie—that's my sister—and I do all we can to cheer her up, but we can't do much. Oh, if I was only a man!"

The lad shut his lips together—how much his mouth was like his father's—and looked out seaward with troubled blue eyes. Turner smiled another grim smile. Oh, Neil Jameson, your old score was being paid now!

Yet something embittered the sweetness of revenge. That boy's face—he could not hate it as he had accustomed himself to hate the memory of Neil Jameson and all connected with him.

"What was your mother's name before she married your father?" he demanded abruptly.

"Lisbeth Miller," answered the boy, still frowning seaward over his secret thoughts.

Turner started again. Lisbeth Miller! He might have known it. What woman in all the world save Lisbeth Miller could have given her son those eyes and curls? So Lisbeth had married Neil Jameson—little Lisbeth Miller, his schoolboy sweetheart. He had forgotten her—or thought he had; certainly he had not thought of her for years. But the memory of her came back now with a rush.

Little Lisbeth—pretty little Lisbeth—merry little Lisbeth! How clearly he remembered her! The old Miller place had adjoined his uncle's farm. Lisbeth and he had played together from babyhood. How he had worshipped her! When they were six years old they had solemnly promised to marry each other when they grew up, and Lisbeth had let him kiss her as earnest of their compact, made under a bloom-white apple tree in the Miller orchard. Yet she would always blush furiously and deny it ever afterwards; it made her angry to be reminded of it.

He saw himself going to school, carrying her books for her, the envied of all the boys. He remembered how he had fought Tony Josephs because Tony had the presumption to bring her spice apples: he had thrashed him too, so soundly that from that time forth none of the schoolboys presumed to rival him in Lisbeth's affections—roguish little Lisbeth! who grew prettier and saucier every year.

He recalled the keen competition of the old days when to be "head of the class" seemed the highest honour within mortal reach, and was striven after with might and main. He had seldom attained to it because he would never "go up past" Lisbeth. If she missed a word, he, Robert, missed it too, no matter how well he knew it. It was sweet to be thought a dunce for her dear sake. It was all the reward he asked to see her holding her place at the head of the class, her cheeks flushed pink and her eyes starry with her pride of position. And how sweetly she would lecture him on the way home from school about learning his spellings better, and wind up her sermon with the frank avowal, uttered with deliciously downcast lids, that she liked him better than any of the other boys after all, even if he couldn't spell as well as they could. Nothing of success that he had won since had ever thrilled him as that admission of little Lisbeth's!

She had been such a sympathetic little sweetheart too, never weary of listening to his dreams and ambitions, his plans for the future. She had always assured him that she knew he would succeed. Well, he had succeeded—and now one of the uses he was going to make of his success was to turn Lisbeth and her children out of their home by way of squaring matters with a dead man!

Lisbeth had been away from home on a long visit to an aunt when he had left Chiswick. She was growing up and the childish intimacy was fading. Perhaps, under other circumstances, it might have ripened into fruit, but he had gone away and forgotten her; the world had claimed him; he had lost all active remembrance of Lisbeth and, before this late return to Chiswick, he had not even known if she were living. And she was Neil Jameson's widow!

He was silent for a long time, while the waves purred about the base of the big red sandstone rock and the boy returned to his *Crusoe*. Finally Robert Turner roused himself from his reverie.

"I used to know your mother long ago when she was a little girl," he said. "I wonder if she remembers me. Ask her when you go home if she remembers Bobby Turner."

"Won't you come up to the house and see her, sir?" asked Paul politely. "Mother is always glad to see her old friends."

"No, I haven't time today." Robert Turner was not going to tell Neil Jameson's son that he did not care to look for the little Lisbeth of long ago in Neil Jameson's widow. The name spoiled her for him, just as the Jameson mouth spoiled her son for him. "But you may tell her something else. The mortgage will not be foreclosed. I was the power behind the lawyers, but I did not know that the present owner of the Cove farm was my little playmate, Lisbeth Miller. You and she shall have all the time you want. Tell her Bobby Turner does this in return for what she gave him under the big sweeting apple tree on her sixth birthday. I think she will remember and understand. As for you, Paul, be a good boy and good to your mother. I hope you'll succeed in your ambition of making the farm pay when you are old enough to take it in hand. At any rate, you'll not be disturbed in your possession of it."

"Oh, sir! oh, sir!" stammered Paul in an agony of embarrassed gratitude and delight. "Oh, it seems too good to be true. Do you really mean that we're not to be sold out? Oh, won't you come and tell Mother yourself? She'll be so happy—so grateful. Do come and let her thank you."

"Not today. I haven't time. Give her my message, that's all. There, run; the sooner she gets the news the better."

Turner watched the boy as he bounded away, until the headland hid him from sight.

"There goes my revenge—and a fine bit of property eminently suited for a summer residence—all for a bit of old, rusty sentiment," he said with a shrug. "I didn't suppose I was capable of such a mood. But then—little Lisbeth. There never was a sweeter girl. I'm glad I didn't go with the boy to see her. She's an old woman now—and Neil Jameson's widow. I prefer to keep my old memories of her undisturbed—little Lisbeth of the silvery-golden curls and the roguish blue eyes. Little Lisbeth of the old time! I'm glad to be able to have done you the small service of securing your home to you. It is my thanks to you for the friendship and affection you gave my lonely boyhood—my tribute to the memory of my first sweetheart."

He walked away with a smile, whose amusement presently softened to an expression that would have amazed his business cronies. Later on he hummed the air of an old love song as he climbed the steep spruce road to Tom's.

The Fillmore Elderberries

"I expected as much," said Timothy Robinson. His tone brought the blood into Ellis Duncan's face. The lad opened his lips quickly, as if for an angry retort, but as quickly closed them again with a set firmness oddly like Timothy Robinson's own.

"When I heard that lazy, worthless father of yours was dead, I expected you and your mother would be looking to me for help," Timothy Robinson went on harshly. "But you're mistaken if you think I'll give it. You've no claim on me, even if your father was my half-brother—no claim at all. And I'm not noted for charity."

Timothy Robinson smiled grimly. It was very true that he was far from being noted for charity. His neighbours called him "close" and "near." Some even went so far as to call him "a miserly skinflint." But this was not true. It was, however, undeniable that Timothy Robinson kept a tight clutch on his purse-strings, and although he sometimes gave liberally enough to any cause which really appealed to him, such causes were few and far between.

"I am not asking for charity, Uncle Timothy," said Ellis quietly. He passed over the slur at his father in silence, deeply as he felt it, for, alas, he knew that it was only too true. "I expect to support my mother by hard and honest work. And I am not asking you for work on the ground of our relationship. I heard you wanted a hired man, and I have come to you, as I should have gone to any other man about whom I had heard it, to ask you to hire me."

"Yes, I do want a man," said Uncle Timothy drily. "A *man*—not a half-grown boy of fourteen, not worth his salt. I want somebody able and willing to work."

Again Ellis flushed deeply and again he controlled himself. "I am willing to work, Uncle Timothy, and I think you would find me able also if you would try me. I'd work for less than a man's wages at first, of course."

"You won't work for any sort of wages from me," interrupted Timothy Robinson decidedly. "I tell you plainly that I won't hire you. You're the wrong man's son for that. Your father was lazy and incompetent and, worst of all, untrustworthy. I did try to help him once, and all I got was loss and ingratitude. I want none of his kind around my place. I don't believe in you, so you may as well take yourself off, Ellis. I've no more time to waste."

Ellis took himself off, his ears tingling. As he walked homeward his thoughts were very bitter. All Uncle Timothy had said about his father was true, and Ellis realized what a count it was against him in his efforts to obtain employment. Nobody wanted to be bothered with "Old Sam Duncan's son," though nobody had been so brutally outspoken as his Uncle Timothy.

Sam Duncan and Timothy Robinson had been half-brothers. Sam, the older, had been the son of Mrs. Robinson's former marriage. Never were two lads more dissimilar. Sam was a lazy, shiftless fellow, deserving all the hard things that came to be said of him. He would not work and nobody could depend on him, but he was a handsome lad with rather taking ways in his youth, and at first people had liked him better than the close, blunt, industrious Timothy. Their mother had died in their childhood, but Mr. Robinson had been fond of Sam and the boy had a good home. When he was twenty-two and Timothy eighteen, Mr. Robinson had died very suddenly, leaving no will. Everything he possessed went to Timothy. Sam immediately left. He said he would not stay there to be "bossed" by Timothy.

He rented a little house in the village, married a girl "far too good for him," and started in to support himself and his wife by days' work. He had lounged, borrowed, and shirked through life. Once Timothy Robinson, perhaps moved by pity for Sam's wife and baby, had hired him for a year at better wages than most hired men received in Dalrymple. Sam idled through a month of it, then got offended and left in the middle of haying. Timothy Robinson washed his hands of him after that.

When Ellis was fourteen Sam Duncan died, after a lingering illness of a year. During this time the family were kept by the charity of pitying neighbours, for Ellis could not be spared from attendance on his father to make any attempt at earning money. Mrs. Duncan was a fragile little woman, worn out with her hard life, and not strong enough to wait on her husband alone.

When Sam Duncan was dead and buried, Ellis straightened his shoulders and took counsel with himself. He must earn a livelihood for his mother and himself, and he must begin at once. He was tall and strong for his age, and had a fairly good education, his mother having determinedly kept him at school when he had pleaded to be allowed to go to work. He had always been a quiet fellow, and nobody in Dalrymple knew much about him. But they knew all about his father, and nobody would hire Ellis unless he were willing to work for a pittance that would barely clothe him.

Ellis had not gone to his Uncle Timothy until he had lost all hope of getting a place elsewhere. Now this hope too had gone. It was nearly the end of June and everybody who wanted help had secured it. Look where he would, Ellis could see no prospect of employment.

"If I could only get a chance!" he thought miserably. "I know I am not idle or lazy—I know I can work—if I could get a chance to prove it."

He was sitting on the fence of the Fillmore elderberry pasture as he said it, having taken a short cut across the fields. This pasture was rather noted in Dalrymple. Originally a mellow and fertile field, it had been almost ruined by a persistent, luxuriant growth of elderberry bushes. Old Thomas Fillmore had at first tried to conquer them by mowing them down "in the dark of the moon." But the elderberries did not seem to mind either moon or mowing, and flourished alike in all the quarters. For the past two years Old Thomas had given up the contest, and the elderberries had it all their own sweet way.

Thomas Fillmore, a bent old man with a shrewd, nutcracker face, came through the bushes while Ellis was sitting on the fence.

"Howdy, Ellis. Seen anything of my spotted calves? I've been looking for 'em for over an hour."

"No, I haven't seen any calves—but a good many might be in this pasture without being visible to the naked eye," said Ellis, with a smile.

Old Thomas shook his head ruefully. "Them elders have been too many for me," he said. "Did you ever see a worse-looking place? You'd hardly believe that twenty years ago there wasn't a better piece of land in Dalrymple than this lot, would ye? Such grass as grew here!"

"The soil must be as good as ever if anything had a chance to grow on it," said Ellis. "Couldn't those elders be rooted out?"

"It'd be a back-breaking job, but I reckon it could be done if anyone had the muscle and patience and time to tackle it. I haven't the first at my age, and my hired man hasn't the last. And nobody would do it for what I could afford to pay."

"What will you give me if I undertake to clean the elders out of this field for you, Mr. Fillmore?" asked Ellis quietly.

Old Thomas looked at him with a surprised face, which gradually reverted to its original shrewdness when he saw that Ellis was in earnest. "You must be hard up for a job," he said.

"I am," was Ellis's laconic answer.

"Well, lemme see." Old Thomas calculated carefully. He never paid a cent more for anything than he could help, and was noted for hard bargaining. "I'll give ye sixteen dollars if you clean out the whole field," he said at length.

Ellis looked at the pasture. He knew something about cleaning out elderberry brush, and he also knew that sixteen dollars would be very poor pay for it. Most of the elders were higher than a man's head, with big roots, thicker than his wrist, running deep into the ground.

"It's worth more, Mr. Fillmore," he said.

"Not to me," responded Old Thomas drily. "I've plenty more land and I'm an old fellow without any sons. I ain't going to pay out money for the benefit of some stranger who'll come after me. You can take it or leave it at sixteen dollars."

Ellis shrugged his shoulders. He had no prospect of anything else, and sixteen dollars were better than nothing. "Very well, I'll take it," he said.

"Well, now, look here," said Old Thomas shrewdly, "I'll expect you to do the work thoroughly, young man. Them roots ain't to be cut off, remember; they'll have to be dug out. And I'll expect you to finish the job if you undertake it too, and not drop it halfway through if you get a chance for a better one."

"I'll finish with your elderberries before I leave them," promised Ellis.

Ellis went to work the next day. His first move was to chop down all the brush and cart it into heaps for burning. This took two days and was comparatively easy work. The third day Ellis tackled the roots. By the end of the forenoon he had discovered just what cleaning out an elderberry pasture meant, but he set his teeth and resolutely persevered. During the afternoon Timothy Robinson, whose farm adjoined the Fillmore place, wandered by and halted with a look of astonishment at the sight of Ellis, busily engaged in digging and tearing out huge, tough, stubborn elder roots. The boy did not see his uncle, but worked away with a vim and vigour that were not lost on the latter.

"He never got that muscle from Sam," reflected Timothy. "Sam would have fainted at the mere thought of stumping elders. Perhaps I've been mistaken in the boy. Well, well, we'll see if he holds out."

Ellis did hold out. The elderberries tried to hold out too, but they were no match for the lad's perseverance. It was a hard piece of work, however, and Ellis never forgot it. Week after week he toiled in the hot summer sun, digging, cutting, and dragging out roots. The job seemed endless, and his progress each day was discouragingly slow. He had expected to get through in a month, but he soon found it would take two. Frequently Timothy Robinson wandered by and looked at the increasing pile of roots and the slowly extending stretch of cleared land. But he never spoke to Ellis and made no comment on the matter to anybody.

One evening, when the field was about half done, Ellis went home more than usually tired. It had been a very hot day. Every bone and muscle in him ached. He wondered dismally if he would ever get to the end of that wretched elderberry field. When he reached home Jacob Green from Westdale was there. Jacob lost no time in announcing his errand.

"My hired boy's broke his leg, and I must fill his place right off. Somebody referred me to you. Guess I'll try you. Twelve dollars a month, board, and lodging. What say?"

For a moment Ellis's face flushed with delight. Twelve dollars a month and permanent employment! Then he remembered his promise to Mr. Fillmore. For a moment he struggled with the temptation. Then he mastered it. Perhaps the discipline of his many encounters with those elderberry roots helped him to do so.

"I'm sorry, Mr. Green," he said reluctantly. "I'd like to go, but I can't. I promised Mr. Fillmore that I'd finish cleaning up his elderberry pasture when I'd once begun it, and I shan't be through for a month yet."

"Well, I'd see myself turning down a good offer for Old Tom Fillmore," said Jacob Green.

"It isn't for Mr. Fillmore—it's for myself," said Ellis steadily. "I promised and I must keep my word."

Jacob drove away grumblingly. On the road he met Timothy Robinson and stopped to relate his grievances.

It must be admitted that there were times during the next month when Ellis was tempted to repent having refused Jacob Green's offer. But at the end of the month the work was done and the Fillmore elderberry pasture was an elderberry pasture no longer. All that remained of the elders, root and branch, was piled into a huge heap ready for burning.

"And I'll come up and set fire to it when it's dry enough," Ellis told Mr. Fillmore. "I claim the satisfaction of that."

"You've done the job thoroughly," said Old Thomas. "There's your sixteen dollars, and every cent of it was earned, if ever money was, I'll say that much for you. There ain't a lazy bone in your body. If you ever want a recommendation just you come to me."

As Ellis passed Timothy Robinson's place on the way home that worthy himself appeared, strolling down his lane. "Ah, Ellis," he said, speaking to his nephew for the first time since their interview two months before, "so you've finished with your job?"

"Yes, sir."

"Got your sixteen dollars, I suppose? It was worth four times that. Old Tom cheated you. You were foolish not to have gone to Green when you had the chance."

"I'd promised Mr. Fillmore to finish with his pasture, sir!"

"Humph! Well, what are you going to do now?"

"I don't know. Harvest will be on next week. I may get in somewhere as an extra hand for a spell."

"Ellis," said his uncle abruptly, after a moment's silence, "I'm going to discharge my man. He's no earthly good. Will you take his place? I'll give you fifteen dollars a month and found."

Ellis stared at Timothy Robinson. "I thought you told me that you had no place for my father's son," he said slowly.

"I've changed my mind. I've seen how you went at that elderberry job. Great snakes, there couldn't be a better test for anybody than rooting out them things. I know you can work. When Jacob Green told me why you'd refused his offer I knew you could be depended on. You come to me and I'll do well by you. I've no kith or kin of my own except you. And look here, Ellis. I'm tired of hired housekeepers. Will your mother come up and live with us and look after things a bit? I've a good girl, and she won't have to work hard, but there must be somebody at the head of a household. She must have a good headpiece—for you have inherited good qualities from someone, and goodness knows it wasn't from your father."

"Uncle Timothy," said Ellis respectfully but firmly, "I'll accept your offer gratefully, and I am sure Mother will too. But there is one thing I must say. Perhaps my father deserves all you say of him—but he is dead—and if I come to you it must be with the understanding that nothing more is ever to be said against him."

Timothy Robinson smiled—a queer, twisted smile that yet had a hint of affection and comprehension in it. "Very well," he said. "I'll never cast his shortcomings up to you again. Come to me—and if I find you always as industrious and reliable as you've proved yourself to be negotiating them elders, I'll most likely forget that you ain't my own son some of these days."

The Finished Story

She always sat in a corner of the west veranda at the hotel, knitting something white and fluffy, or pink and fluffy, or pale blue and fluffy—always fluffy, at least, and always dainty. Shawls and scarfs and hoods the things were, I believe. When she finished one she gave it to some girl and began another. Every girl at Harbour Light that summer wore some distracting thing that had been fashioned by Miss Sylvia's slim, tireless, white fingers.

She was old, with that beautiful, serene old age which is as beautiful in its way as youth. Her girlhood and womanhood must have been very lovely to have ripened into such a beauty of sixty years. It was a surprise to everyone who heard her called *Miss* Sylvia. She looked so like a woman who ought to have stalwart, grown sons and dimpled little grandchildren.

For the first two days after the arrival at the hotel she sat in her corner alone. There was always a circle of young people around her; old folks and middle-aged people would have liked to join it, but Miss Sylvia, while she was gracious to all, let it be distinctly understood that her sympathies were with youth. She sat among the boys and girls, young men and maidens, like a fine white queen. Her dress was always the same and somewhat old-fashioned, but nothing else would have suited her half so well; she wore a lace cap on her snowy hair and a heliotrope shawl over her black silk shoulders. She knitted continually and talked a good deal, but listened more. We sat around her at all hours of the day and told her everything.

When you were first introduced to her you called her Miss Stanleymain. Her endurance of that was limited to twenty-four hours. Then she begged you to call her Miss Sylvia, and as Miss Sylvia you spoke and thought of her forevermore.

Miss Sylvia liked us all, but I was her favourite. She told us so frankly and let it be understood that when I was talking to her and her heliotrope shawl was allowed to slip under one arm it was a sign that we were not to be interrupted. I was as vain of her favour as any lovelorn suitor whose lady had honoured him, not knowing, as I came to know later, the reason for it.

Although Miss Sylvia had an unlimited capacity for receiving confidences, she never gave any. We were all sure that there must be some romance in her life, but our efforts to discover it were unsuccessful. Miss Sylvia parried tentative questions so skilfully that we knew she had something to defend. But one evening, when I had known her a month, as time is reckoned, and long years as affection and understanding are computed, she told me her story—at least, what there was to tell of it. The last chapter was missing.

We were sitting together on the veranda at sunset. Most of the hotel people had gone for a harbour sail; a few forlorn mortals prowled about the grounds and eyed our corner wistfully, but by the sign of the heliotrope shawl knew it was not for them.

I was reading one of my stories to Miss Sylvia. In my own excuse I must allege that she tempted me to do it. I did not go around with manuscripts under my arm, inflicting them on defenceless females. But Miss Sylvia had discovered that I was a magazine scribbler, and moreover, that I had shut myself up in my room that very morning and perpetrated a short story. Nothing would do but that I read it to her.

It was a rather sad little story. The hero loved the heroine, and she loved him. There was no reason why he should not love her, but there was a reason why he could not marry her. When he found that he loved her he knew that he must go away. But might he not, at least, tell her his love? Might he not, at least, find out for his consolation if she cared for him? There was a struggle; he won, and went away without a word, believing it to be the more manly course. When I began to read Miss Sylvia was knitting, a pale green something this time, of the tender hue of young leaves in May. But after a little her knitting slipped unheeded to her lap and her hands folded idly above it. It was the most subtle compliment I had ever received.

When I turned the last page of the manuscript and looked up, Miss Sylvia's soft brown eyes were full of tears. She lifted her hands, clasped them together and said in an agitated voice:

"Oh, no, no; don't let him go away without telling her—just telling her. Don't let him do it!"

"But, you see, Miss Sylvia," I explained, flattered beyond measure that my characters had seemed so real to her, "that would spoil the story. It would have no reason for existence then. Its *motif* is simply his mastery over self. He believes it to be the nobler course."

"No, no, it wasn't—if he loved her he should have told her. Think of her shame and humiliation—she loved him, and he went without a word and she could never know he cared for her. Oh, you must change it—you must, indeed! I cannot bear to think of her suffering what I have suffered."

Miss Sylvia broke down and sobbed. To appease her, I promised that I would remodel the story, although I knew that the doing so would leave it absolutely pointless.

"Oh, I'm so glad," said Miss Sylvia, her eyes shining through her tears. "You see, I know it would make her happier—I know it. I'm going to tell you my poor little story to convince you. But you—you must not tell it to any of the others."

"I am sorry you think the admonition necessary," I said reproachfully.

"Oh, I do not, indeed I do not," she hastened to assure me. "I know I can trust you. But it's such a poor little story. You mustn't laugh at it—it is all the romance I had. Years ago—forty years ago—when I was a young girl of twenty, I—learned to care very much for somebody. I met him at a summer resort like this. I was there with my aunt and he was there with his mother, who was delicate. We saw a great deal of each other for a little while. He was—oh, he was like no other man I had ever seen. You remind me of him somehow. That is partly why I like you so much. I noticed the resemblance the first time I saw you. I don't know in just what it consists—in your expression and the way you carry your head, I think. He was not strong—he coughed a good deal. Then one day he went away—suddenly. I had thought he cared for me, but he never said so—just went away. Oh, the shame of it! After a time I heard that he had been ordered to California for his health. And he died out there the next spring. My heart broke then, I never cared for anybody again—I couldn't. I have always loved him. But it would have been so much easier to bear if I had only known that he loved me—oh, it would have made all the difference in the world. And the sting of it has been there all these years. I can't even permit myself the joy of dwelling on his memory because of the thought that perhaps he did not care."

"He must have cared," I said warmly. "He couldn't have helped it, Miss Sylvia."

Miss Sylvia shook her head with a sad smile.

"I cannot be sure. Sometimes I think he did. But then the doubt creeps back again. I would give almost anything to know that he did—to know that I have not lavished all the love of my life on a man who did not want it. And I never can know, never—I can hope and almost believe, but I can never know. Oh, you don't understand—a man couldn't fully understand what my pain has been over it. You see now why I want you to change the story. I am sorry for that poor girl, but if you only let her know that he really loves her she will not mind all the rest so very much; she will be able to bear the pain of even life-long separation if she only knows."

Miss Sylvia picked up her knitting and went away. As for me, I thought savagely of the dead man she loved and called him a cad, or at best, a fool.

Next day Miss Sylvia was her serene, smiling self once more, and she did not again make any reference to what she had told me. A fortnight later she returned home and I went my way back to the world. During the following winter I wrote several letters to Miss Sylvia and received replies from her. Her letters were very like herself. When I sent her the third-rate magazine containing my story—nothing but a third-rate magazine would take it in its rewritten form—she wrote to say that she was so glad that I had let the poor girl know.

Early in April I received a letter from an aunt of mine in the country, saying that she intended to sell her place and come to the city to live. She asked me to go out to Sweetwater for a few weeks and assist her in the business of settling up the estate and disposing of such things as she did not wish to take with her.

When I arrived at Sweetwater I found it moist and chill with the sunny moisture and teasing chill of our Canadian springs. They are long and fickle and reluctant, these springs of ours, but, oh, the unnamable charm of them! There was something even in the red buds of the maples at Sweetwater and in the long, smoking stretches of hillside fields that sent a thrill through my veins, finer and subtler than any given by old wine.

A week after my arrival, when we had got the larger affairs pretty well straightened out, Aunt Mary suggested that I had better overhaul Uncle Alan's room.

"The things there have never been meddled with since he died," she said. "In particular, there's an old trunk full of his letters and his papers. It was brought home from California after his death. I've never examined them. I don't suppose there is anything of any importance among them. But I'm not going to carry all that old rubbish to town. So I wish you would look over them and see if there is anything that should be kept. The rest may be burned."

I felt no particular interest in the task. My Uncle Alan Blair was a mere name to me. He was my mother's eldest brother and had died years before I was born. I had heard that he had been very clever and that great things had been expected of him. But I anticipated no pleasure from exploring musty old letters and papers of forty neglected years.

I went up to Uncle Alan's room at dusk that night. We had been having a day of warm spring rain, but it had cleared away and the bare maple boughs outside the window were strung with glistening drops. The room looked to the north and was always dim by reason of the close-growing Sweetwater pines. A gap had been cut through them to the northwest, and in it I had a glimpse of the sea Uncle Alan had loved, and above it a wondrous sunset sky fleeced over with little clouds, pale and pink and golden and green, that suddenly reminded me of Miss Sylvia and her fluffy knitting. It was with the thought of her in my mind that I lighted a lamp and began the task of grubbing into Uncle Alan's trunkful of papers. Most of these were bundles of yellowed letters, of no present interest, from his family and college friends. There were several college theses and essays, and a lot of loose miscellania pertaining to boyish school days. I went through the collection rapidly, until at the bottom of the trunk, I came to a small book bound in dark-green leather. It proved to be a sort of journal, and I began to glance over it with a languid interest.

It had been begun in the spring after he had graduated from college. Although suspected only by himself, the disease which was to end his life had already fastened upon him. The entries were those of a doomed man, who, feeling the curse fall on him like a frost, blighting all the fair hopes and promises of life, seeks some help and consolation in the outward self-communing of a journal. There was nothing morbid, nothing unmanly in the record. As I read, I found myself liking Uncle Alan, wishing that he might have lived and been my friend.

His mother had not been well that summer and the doctor ordered her to the seashore. Alan accompanied her. Here occurred a hiatus in the journal. No leaves had been torn out, but a quire or so of them had apparently become loosened from the threads that held them in place. I found them later on in the trunk, but at the time I passed to the next page. It began abruptly:

> This girl is the sweetest thing that God ever made. I had not known a woman could be so fair and sweet. Her beauty awes me, the purity of her soul shines so clearly through it like an illuminating lamp. I love her with all my power of loving and I am thankful that it is so. It would have been hard to die without having known love. I am glad that it has come to me, even if its price is unspeakable bitterness. A man has not lived for nothing who has known and loved Sylvia Stanleymain.
>
> I must not seek her love—that is denied me. If I were well and strong I should win it; yes, I believe I could win it, and nothing in the world would prevent me from trying, but, as things are, it would be the part of a coward to try. Yet I cannot resist the delight of being with her, of talking to her, of watching her wonderful face. She is in my thoughts day and night, she dwells in my dreams. O, Sylvia, I love you, my sweet!

A week later there was another entry:

> July Seventeenth.
>
> I am afraid. To-day I met Sylvia's eyes. In them was a look which at first stirred my heart to its deeps with tumultuous delight, and then I remembered. I must spare her that suffering, at whatever cost to myself. I must not let myself dwell on the dangerous sweetness of the thought that her heart is turning to me. What would be the crowning joy to another man could be only added sorrow to me.

Then:

> July Eighteenth.
>
> This morning I took the train to the city. I was determined to know the worst once for all. The time had come when I must. My doctor at home had put me off with vague hopes and perhapses. So I went to a noted physician in the city. I told him I wanted the whole truth—I made him tell it. Stripped of all softening verbiage it is this: I have perhaps eight months or a year to live—no more!
>
> I had expected it, although not quite so soon. Yet the certainty was none the less bitter. But this is no time for self-pity. It is of Sylvia I must think now. I shall go away at once, before the sweet fancy which is possibly budding in her virgin heart shall have bloomed into a flower that might poison some of her fair years.
>
> July Nineteenth.

> It is over. I said good-bye to her to-day before others, for I dared not trust myself to see her alone. She looked hurt and startled, as if someone had struck her. But she will soon forget, even if I have not been mistaken in the reading of her eyes. As for me, the bitterness of death is already over in that parting. All that now remains is to play the man to the end.

From further entries in the journal I learned that Alan Blair had returned to Sweetwater and later on had been ordered to California. The entries during his sojourn there were few and far between. In all of them he spoke of Sylvia. Finally, after a long silence, he had written:

> I think the end is not far off now. I am not sorry for my suffering has been great of late. Last night I was easier. I slept and dreamed that I saw Sylvia. Once or twice I thought that I would arrange to have this book sent to her after my death. But I have decided that it would be unwise. It would only pain her, so I shall destroy it when I feel the time has come.
>
> It is sunset in this wonderful summer land. At home in Sweetwater it is only early spring as yet, with snow lingering along the edges of the woods. The sunsets there will be creamy-yellow and pale red now. If I could but see them once more! And Sylvia—

There was a little blot where the pen had fallen. Evidently the end had been nearer than Alan Blair had thought. At least, there were no more entries, and the little green book had not been destroyed. I was glad that it had not been; and I felt glad that it was thus put in my power to write the last chapter of Miss Sylvia's story for her.

As soon as I could leave Sweetwater I went to the city, three hundred miles away, where Miss Sylvia lived. I found her in her library, in her black silk dress and heliotrope shawl, knitting up cream wool, for all the world as if she had just been transplanted from the veranda corner of Harbour Light.

"My dear boy!" she said.

"Do you know why I have come?" I asked.

"I am vain enough to think it was because you wanted to see me," she smiled.

"I did want to see you; but I would have waited until summer if it had not been that I wished to bring you the missing chapter of your story, dear lady."

"I—I—don't understand," said Miss Sylvia, starting slightly.

"I had an uncle, Alan Blair, who died forty years ago in California," I said quietly. "Recently I have had occasion to examine some of his papers. I found a journal among them and I have brought it to you because I think that you have the best right to it."

I dropped the parcel in her lap. She was silent with surprise and bewilderment.

"And now," I added, "I am going away. You won't want to see me or anyone for a while after you have read this book. But I will come up to see you tomorrow."

When I went the next day Miss Sylvia herself met me at the door. She caught my hand and drew me into the hall. Her eyes were softly radiant.

"Oh, you have made me so happy!" she said tremulously. "Oh, you can never know how happy! Nothing hurts now—nothing ever can hurt, because I know he did care."

She laid her face down on my shoulder, as a girl might have nestled to her lover, and I bent and kissed her for Uncle Alan.

The Garden of Spices

Jims tried the door of the blue room. Yes, it was locked. He had hoped Aunt Augusta *might* have forgotten to lock it; but when did Aunt Augusta forget anything? Except, perhaps, that little boys were not born grown-ups—and *that* was something she never remembered. To be sure, she was only a half-aunt. Whole aunts probably had more convenient memories.

Jims turned and stood with his back against the door. It was better that way; he could not imagine things behind him then. And the blue room was so big and dim that a dreadful number of things could be imagined in it. All the windows were shuttered but one, and that one was so darkened by a big pine tree branching right across it that it did not let in much light.

Jims looked very small and lost and lonely as he shrank back against the door—so small and lonely that one might have thought that even the sternest of half-aunts should have thought twice before shutting him up in that room and telling him he must stay there the whole afternoon instead of going out for a promised ride. Jims hated being shut up alone—especially in the blue room. Its bigness and dimness and silence filled his sensitive little soul with vague horror. Sometimes he became almost sick with fear in it. To do Aunt Augusta justice, she never suspected this. If she had she would not have decreed this particular punishment, because she knew Jims was delicate and must not be subjected to any great physical or mental strain. That was why she shut him up instead of whipping him. But how was she to know it? Aunt Augusta was one of those people who never know anything unless it is told them in plain language and then hammered into their heads. There was no one to tell her but Jims, and Jims would have died the death before he would have told Aunt Augusta, with her cold, spectacled eyes and thin, smileless mouth, that he was desperately frightened when he was shut in the blue room. So he was always shut in it for punishment; and the punishments came very often, for Jims was always doing things that Aunt Augusta considered naughty. At first, this time, Jims did not feel quite so frightened as usual because he was very angry. As he put it, he was very mad at Aunt Augusta. He hadn't *meant* to spill his pudding over the floor and the tablecloth and his clothes; and how such a little bit of pudding—Aunt Augusta was mean with desserts—could ever have spread itself over so much territory Jims could not understand. But he had made a terrible mess and Aunt Augusta had been very angry and had said he must be cured of such carelessness. She said he must spend the afternoon in the blue room instead of going for a ride with Mrs. Loring in her new car.

Jims was bitterly disappointed. If Uncle Walter had been home Jims would have appealed to him—for when Uncle Walter could be really wakened up to a realization of his small nephew's presence in his home, he was very kind and indulgent. But it was so hard to waken him up that Jims seldom attempted it. He liked Uncle Walter, but as far as being acquainted with him went he might as well have been the inhabitant of a star in the Milky Way. Jims was just a lonely, solitary little creature, and sometimes he felt so friendless that his eyes smarted, and several sobs had to be swallowed.

There were no sobs just now, though—Jims was still too angry. It wasn't fair. It was so seldom he got a car ride. Uncle Walter was always too busy, attending to sick children all over the town, to take him. It was only once in a blue moon Mrs. Loring asked him to go out with her. But she always ended up with ice cream or a movie, and to-day Jims had had strong hopes that both were on the programme.

"I hate Aunt Augusta," he said aloud; and then the sound of his voice in that huge, still room scared him so that he only thought the rest. "I won't have any fun—and she won't feed my gobbler, either."

Jims had shrieked "Feed my gobbler," to the old servant as he had been hauled upstairs. But he didn't think Nancy Jane had heard him, and nobody, not even Jims, could imagine Aunt Augusta feeding the gobbler. It was always a wonder to him that she ate, herself. It seemed really too human a thing for her to do.

"I wish I had spilled that pudding *on purpose*," Jims said vindictively, and with the saying his anger evaporated—Jims never could stay angry long—and left him merely a scared little fellow, with velvety, nut-brown eyes full of fear that should have no place in a child's eyes. He looked so small and helpless as he crouched against the door that one might have wondered if even Aunt Augusta would not have relented had she seen him.

How that window at the far end of the room rattled! It sounded terribly as if somebody—or *something*—were trying to get in. Jims looked desperately at the unshuttered window. He must get to it; once there, he could curl up in the window seat, his back to the wall, and forget the shadows by looking out into the sunshine and loveliness of the garden over the wall. Jims would have likely have been found dead of fright in that blue room some time had it not been for the garden over the wall.

But to get to the window Jims must cross the room and pass by the bed. Jims held that bed in special dread. It was the oldest fashioned thing in the old-fashioned, old-furnitured house. It was high and rigid, and hung with gloomy blue curtains. *Anything* might jump out of such a bed.

Jims gave a gasp and ran madly across the room. He reached the window and flung himself upon the seat. With a sigh of relief he curled down in the corner. Outside, over the high brick wall, was a world where his imagination could roam, though his slender little body was pent a prisoner in the blue room.

Jims had loved that garden from his first sight of it. He called it the Garden of Spices and wove all sorts of yarns in fancy—yarns gay and tragic—about it. He had only known it for a few weeks. Before that, they had lived in a much smaller house away at the other side of the town. Then Uncle Walter's uncle—who had brought him up just as he was bringing up Jims—had died, and they had all come to live in Uncle Walter's old home. Somehow, Jims had an idea that Uncle Walter wasn't very glad to come back there. But he had to, according to great-uncle's will. Jims himself didn't mind much. He liked the smaller rooms in their former home better, but the Garden of Spices made up for all.

It was such a beautiful spot. Just inside the wall was a row of aspen poplars that always talked in silvery whispers and shook their dainty, heart-shaped leaves at him. Beyond them, under scattered pines, was a rockery where ferns and wild things grew. It was almost as good as a bit of woods—and Jims loved the woods, though he scarcely ever saw them. Then, past the pines, were roses just breaking into June bloom—roses in such profusion as Jims hadn't known existed, with dear little paths twisting about among the bushes. It seemed to be a garden where no frost could blight or rough wind blow. When rain fell it must fall very gently. Past the roses one saw a green lawn, sprinkled over now with the white ghosts of dandelions, and dotted with ornamental trees. The trees grew so thickly that they almost hid the house to which the garden pertained. It was a large one of grey-black stone, with stacks of huge chimneys. Jims had no idea who lived there. He had asked Aunt Augusta and Aunt Augusta had frowned and told him it did not matter who lived there and that he must never, on any account, mention the next house or its occupant to Uncle Walter. Jims would never have thought of mentioning them to Uncle Walter. But the prohibition filled him with an unholy and unsubduable curiosity. He was devoured by the desire to find out who the folks in that tabooed house were.

And he longed to have the freedom of that garden. Jims loved gardens. There had been a garden at the little house but there was none here—nothing but an old lawn that had been fine once but was now badly run to seed. Jims had heard Uncle Walter say that he was going to have it attended to but nothing had been done yet. And meanwhile here was a beautiful garden over the wall which looked as if it should be full of children. But no children were ever in it—or anybody else apparently. And so, in spite of its beauty, it had a lonely look that hurt Jims. He *wanted* his Garden of Spices to be full of laughter. He pictured himself running in it with imaginary playmates—and there was a mother in it—or a big sister—or, at the least, a whole aunt who would let you hug her and would never dream of shutting you up in chilly, shadowy, horrible blue rooms.

"It seems to me," said Jims, flattening his nose against the pane, "that I must get into that garden or bust."

Aunt Augusta would have said icily, "We do not use such expressions, James," but Aunt Augusta was not there to hear.

"I'm afraid the Very Handsome Cat isn't coming to-day," sighed Jims. Then he brightened up; the Very Handsome Cat was coming across the lawn. He was the only living thing, barring birds and butterflies, that Jims ever saw in the garden. Jims worshipped that cat. He was jet black, with white paws and dickey, and he had as much dignity as ten cats. Jims' fingers tingled to stroke him. Jims had never been allowed to have even a kitten because Aunt Augusta had a horror of cats. And you cannot stroke gobblers!

The Very Handsome Cat came through the rose garden paths on his beautiful paws, ambled daintily around the rockery, and sat down in a shady spot under a pine tree, right where Jims could see him, through a gap in the little poplars. He looked straight up at Jims and winked. At least, Jims always believed and declared he did. And that wink said, or seemed to say, plainly:

"Be a sport. Come down here and play with me. A fig for your Aunt Augusta!"

A wild, daring, absurd idea flashed into Jims' brain. Could he? He could! He would! He knew it would be easy. He had thought it all out many times, although until now he had never dreamed of really doing it. To unhook the window and swing it open, to step out on the pine bough and from it to another that hung over the wall and dropped nearly to the ground, to spring from it to the velvet sward under the poplars—why, it was all the work of a minute. With a careful, repressed whoop Jims ran towards the Very Handsome Cat.

The cat rose and retreated in deliberate haste; Jims ran after him. The cat dodged through the rose paths and eluded Jims' eager hands, just keeping tantalizingly out of reach. Jims had forgotten everything except that he must catch the cat. He was full of a fearful joy, with an elfin delight running through it. He had escaped from the blue room and its ghosts; he was in his Garden of Spices; he had got the better of mean old Aunt Augusta. But he *must* catch the cat.

The cat ran over the lawn and Jims pursued it through the green gloom of the thickly clustering trees. Beyond them came a pool of sunshine in which the old stone house basked like a huge grey cat itself. More garden was before it and beyond it, wonderful with blossom. Under a huge spreading beech tree in the centre of it was a little tea table; sitting by the table reading was a lady in a black dress.

The cat, having lured Jims to where he wanted him, sat down and began to lick his paws. He was quite willing to be caught now; but Jims had no longer any idea of catching him. He stood very still, looking at the lady. She did not see him then and Jims could only see her profile, which he thought very beautiful. She had wonderful ropes of blue-black hair wound around her head. She looked so sweet that Jims' heart beat. Then she lifted her head and turned her face and saw him. Jims felt something of a shock. She was not pretty after all. One side of her face was marked by a dreadful red scar. It quite spoilt her good looks, which Jims thought a great pity; but nothing could spoil the sweetness of her face or the loveliness of her peculiar soft, grey-blue eyes. Jims couldn't remember his mother and had no idea what she looked like, but the thought came into his head that he would have liked her to have eyes like that. After the first moment Jims did not mind the scar at all.

But perhaps that first moment had revealed itself in his face, for a look of pain came into the lady's eyes and, almost involuntarily it seemed, she put her hand up to hide the scar. Then she pulled it away again and sat looking at Jims half defiantly, half piteously. Jims thought she must be angry because he had chased her cat.

"I beg your pardon," he said gravely, "I didn't mean to hurt your cat. I just wanted to play with him. He is *such* a very handsome cat."

"But where did you come from?" said the lady. "It is so long since I saw a child in this garden," she added, as if to herself. Her voice was as sweet as her face. Jims thought he was mistaken in thinking her angry and plucked up heart of grace. Shyness was no fault of Jims.

"I came from the house over the wall," he said. "My name is James Brander Churchill. Aunt Augusta shut me up in the blue room because I spilled my pudding at dinner. I hate to be shut up. And I was to have had a ride this afternoon—and ice cream—and *maybe* a movie. So I was mad. And when your Very Handsome Cat came and looked at me I just got out and climbed down."

He looked straight at her and smiled. Jims had a very dear little smile. It seemed a pity there was no mother alive to revel in it. The lady smiled back.

"I think you did right," she said.

"*You* wouldn't shut a little boy up if you had one, would you?" said Jims.

"No—no, dear heart, I wouldn't," said the lady. She said it as if something hurt her horribly. She smiled again gallantly.

"Will you come here and sit down?" she added, pulling a chair out from the table.

"Thank you. I'd rather sit here," said Jims, plumping down on the grass at her feet. "Then maybe your cat will come to me."

The cat came over promptly and rubbed his head against Jims' knee. Jims stroked him delightedly; how lovely his soft fur felt and his round velvety head.

"I like cats," explained Jims, "and I have nothing but a gobbler. This is such a Very Handsome Cat. What is his name, please?"

"Black Prince. He loves me," said the lady. "He always comes to my bed in the morning and wakes me by patting my face with his paw. *He* doesn't mind my being ugly."

She spoke with a bitterness Jims couldn't understand.

"But you are not ugly," he said.

"Oh, I *am* ugly—I *am* ugly," she cried. "Just look at me—right at me. Doesn't it hurt you to look at me?"

Jims looked at her gravely and dispassionately.

"No, it doesn't," he said. "Not a bit," he added, after some further exploration of his consciousness.

Suddenly the lady laughed beautifully. A faint rosy flush came into her unscarred cheek.

"James, I believe you mean it."

"Of course I mean it. And, if you don't mind, please call me Jims. Nobody calls me James but Aunt Augusta. She isn't my whole aunt. She is just Uncle Walter's half-sister. *He* is my whole uncle."

"What does he call you?" asked the lady. She looked away as she asked it.

"Oh, Jims, when he thinks about me. He doesn't often think about me. He has too many sick children to think about. Sick children are all Uncle Walter cares about. He's the greatest children's doctor in the Dominion, Mr. Burroughs says. But he is a woman-hater."

"How do you know that?"

"Oh, I heard Mr. Burroughs say it. Mr. Burroughs is my tutor, you know. I study with him from nine till one. I'm not allowed to go to the public school. I'd like to, but Uncle Walter thinks I'm not strong enough yet. I'm going next year, though, when I'm ten. I have holidays now. Mr. Burroughs always goes away the first of June."

"How came he to tell you your uncle was a woman-hater?" persisted the lady.

"Oh, he didn't tell me. He was talking to a friend of his. He thought I was reading my book. So I was—but I heard it all. It was more interesting than my book. Uncle Walter was engaged to a lady, long, long ago, when he was a young man. She was devilishly pretty."

"Oh, Jims!"

"Mr. Burroughs said so. I'm only quoting," said Jims easily. "And Uncle Walter just worshipped her. And all at once she just jilted him without a word of explanation, Mr. Burroughs said. So that is why he hates women. It isn't any wonder, is it?"

"I suppose not," said the lady with a sigh. "Jims, are you hungry?"

"Yes, I am. You see, the pudding was spilled. But how did you know?"

"Oh, boys always used to be hungry when I knew them long ago. I thought they hadn't changed. I shall tell Martha to bring out something to eat and we'll have it here under this tree. You sit here—I'll sit there. Jims, it's so long since I talked to a little boy that I'm not sure that I know how."

"You know how, all right," Jims assured her. "But what am I to call you, please?"

"My name is Miss Garland," said the lady a little hesitatingly. But she saw the name meant nothing to Jims. "I would like you to call me Miss Avery. Avery is my first name and I never hear it nowadays. Now for a jamboree! I can't offer you a movie—and I'm afraid there isn't any ice cream either. I could have had some if I'd known you were coming. But I think Martha will be able to find something good."

A very old woman, who looked at Jims with great amazement, came out to set the table. Jims thought she must be as old as Methusaleh. But he did not mind her. He ran races with Black Prince while tea was being prepared, and rolled the delighted cat over and over in the grass. And he discovered a fragrant herb-garden in a far corner and was delighted. Now it was truly a garden of spices.

"Oh, it is so beautiful here," he told Miss Avery, who sat and looked at his revels with a hungry expression in her lovely eyes. "I wish I could come often."

"Why can't you?" said Miss Avery.

The two looked at each other with sly intelligence.

"I could come whenever Aunt Augusta shuts me up in the blue room," said Jims.

"Yes," said Miss Avery. Then she laughed and held out her arms. Jims flew into them. He put his arms about her neck and kissed her scarred face.

"Oh, I wish *you* were my aunt," he said.

Miss Avery suddenly pushed him away. Jims was horribly afraid he had offended her. But she took his hand.

"We'll just be chums, Jims," she said. "That's really better than being relations, after all. Come and have tea."

Over that glorious tea-table they became life-long friends. They had always known each other and always would. The Black Prince sat between them and was fed tit-bits. There was such a lot of good things on the table and nobody to say "You have had enough, James." James ate until *he* thought he had enough. Aunt Augusta would have thought he was doomed, could she have seen him.

"I suppose I must go back," said Jims with a sigh. "It will be our supper time in half an hour and Aunt Augusta will come to take me out."

"But you'll come again?"

"Yes, the first time she shuts me up. And if she doesn't shut me up pretty soon I'll be so bad she'll have to shut me up."

"I'll always set a place for you at the tea-table after this, Jims. And when you're not here I'll pretend you are. And when you can't come here write me a letter and bring it when you do come."

"Good-bye," said Jims. He took her hand and kissed it. He had read of a young knight doing that and had always thought he would like to try it if he ever got a chance. But who could dream of kissing Aunt Augusta's hands?

"You dear, funny thing," said Miss Avery. "Have you thought of how you are to get back? Can you reach that pine bough from the ground?"

"Maybe I can jump," said Jims dubiously.

"I'm afraid not. I'll give you a stool and you can stand on it. Just leave it there for future use. Good-bye, Jims. Jims, two hours ago I didn't know there was such a person in the world as you—and now I love you—I love you."

Jims' heart filled with a great warm gush of gladness. He had always wanted to be loved. And no living creature, he felt sure, loved him, except his gobbler—and a gobbler's love is not very satisfying, though it is better than nothing. He was blissfully happy as he carried his stool across the lawn. He climbed his pine and went in at the window and curled up on the seat in a maze of delight. The blue room was more shadowy than ever but that did not matter. Over in the Garden of Spices was friendship and laughter and romance galore. The whole world was transformed for Jims.

From that time Jims lived a shamelessly double life. Whenever he was shut in the blue room he escaped to the Garden of Spices—and he was shut in very often, for, Mr. Burroughs being away, he got into a good deal of what Aunt Augusta called mischief. Besides, it is a sad truth that Jims didn't try very hard to be good now. He thought it paid better to be bad and be shut up. To be sure there was always a fly in the ointment. He was haunted by a vague fear that Aunt Augusta might relent and come to the blue room before supper time to let him out.

"And *then* the fat would be in the fire," said Jims.

But he had a glorious summer and throve so well on his new diet of love and companionship that one day Uncle Walter, with fewer sick children to think about than usual, looked at him curiously and said:

"Augusta, that boy seems to be growing much stronger. He has a good color and his eyes are getting to look more like a boy's eyes should. We'll make a man of you yet, Jims."

"He may be getting stronger but he's getting naughtier, too," said Aunt Augusta, grimly. "I am sorry to say, Walter, that he behaves very badly."

"We were all young once," said Uncle Walter indulgently.

"Were *you*?" asked Jims in blank amazement.

Uncle Walter laughed.

"Do you think me an antediluvian, Jims?"

"I don't know what *that* is. But your hair is gray and your eyes are tired," said Jims uncompromisingly.

Uncle Walter laughed again, tossed Jims a quarter, and went out.

"Your uncle is only forty-five and in his prime," said Aunt Augusta dourly.

Jims deliberately ran across the room to the window and, under pretence of looking out, knocked down a flower pot. So he was exiled to the blue room and got into his beloved Garden of Spices where Miss Avery's beautiful eyes looked love into his and the Black Prince was a jolly playmate and old Martha petted and spoiled him to her heart's content.

Jims never asked questions but he was a wide-awake chap, and, taking one thing with another, he found out a good deal about the occupants of the old stone house. Miss Avery never went anywhere and no one ever went there. She lived all alone with two old servants, man and maid. Except these two and Jims nobody had ever seen her for twenty years. Jims didn't know why, but he thought it must be because of the scar on her face.

He never referred to it, but one day Miss Avery told him what caused it.

"I dropped a lamp and my dress caught fire and burned my face, Jims. It made me hideous. I was beautiful before that—very beautiful. Everybody said so. Come in and I will show you my picture."

She took him into her big parlor and showed him the picture hanging on the wall between the two high windows. It was of a young girl in white. She certainly was very lovely, with her rose-leaf skin and laughing eyes. Jims looked at the pictured face gravely, with his hands in his pockets and his head on one side. Then he looked at Miss Avery.

"You were prettier then—yes," he said, judicially, "but I like your face ever so much better now."

"Oh, Jims, you can't," she protested.

"Yes, I do," persisted Jims. "You look kinder and—nicer now."

It was the nearest Jims could get to expressing what he felt as he looked at the picture. The young girl was beautiful, but her face was a little hard. There was pride and vanity and something of the insolence of great beauty in it. There was nothing of that in Miss Avery's face now—nothing but sweetness and tenderness, and a motherly yearning to which every fibre of Jims' small being responded. How they loved each other, those two! And how they understood each other! To *love* is easy, and therefore common; but to *understand*—how rare that is! And oh! such good times as they had! They made taffy. Jims had always longed to make taffy, but Aunt Augusta's immaculate kitchen and saucepans might not be so desecrated. They read fairy tales together. Mr. Burroughs had disapproved of fairy tales. They blew soap-bubbles out on the lawn and let them float away over the garden and the orchard like fairy balloons. They had glorious afternoon teas under the beech tree. They made ice cream themselves. Jims even slid down the bannisters when he wanted to. And he could try out a slang word or two occasionally without anybody dying of horror. Miss Avery did not seem to mind it a bit.

At first Miss Avery always wore dark sombre dresses. But one day Jims found her in a pretty gown of pale primrose silk. It was very old and old-fashioned, but Jims did not know that. He capered round her in delight.

"You like me better in this?" she asked, wistfully.

"I like you just as well, no matter what you wear," said Jims, "but that dress is awfully pretty."

"Would you like me to wear bright colors, Jims?"

"You bet I would," said Jims emphatically.

After that she always wore them—pink and primrose and blue and white; and she let Jims wreathe flowers in her splendid hair. He had quite a knack of it. She never wore any jewelry except, always, a little gold ring with a design of two clasped hands.

"A friend gave that to me long ago when we were boy and girl together at school," she told Jims once. "I never take it off, night or day. When I die it is to be buried with me."

"You mustn't die till I do," said Jims in dismay.

"Oh, Jims, if we could only *live* together nothing else would matter," she said hungrily. "Jims—Jims—I see so little of you really—and some day soon you'll be going to school—and I'll lose you."

"I've got to think of some way to prevent it," cried Jims. "I won't have it. I won't—I won't."

But his heart sank notwithstanding.

One day Jims slipped from the blue room, down the pine and across the lawn with a tear-stained face.

"Aunt Augusta is going to kill my gobbler," he sobbed in Miss Avery's arms. "She says she isn't going to bother with him any longer—and he's getting old—and he's to be killed. And that gobbler is the only friend I have in the world except you. Oh, I can't *stand* it, Miss Avery."

Next day Aunt Augusta told him the gobbler had been sold and taken away. And Jims flew into a passion of tears and protest about it and was promptly incarcerated in the blue room. A few minutes later a sobbing boy plunged through the trees—and stopped abruptly. Miss Avery was reading under the beech and the Black Prince was snoozing on her knee—and a big, magnificent, bronze turkey was parading about on the lawn, twisting his huge fan of a tail this way and that.

"*My* gobbler!" cried Jims.

"Yes. Martha went to your uncle's house and bought him. Oh, she didn't betray you. She told Nancy Jane she wanted a gobbler and, having seen one over there, thought perhaps she could get him. See, here's your pet, Jims, and here he shall live till he dies of old age. And I have something else for you—Edward and Martha went across the river yesterday to the Murray Kennels and got it for you."

"Not a dog?" exclaimed Jims.

"Yes—a dear little bull pup. He shall be your very own, Jims, and I only stipulate that you reconcile the Black Prince to him."

It was something of a task but Jims succeeded. Then followed a month of perfect happiness. At least three afternoons a week they contrived to be together. It was all too good to be true, Jims felt. Something would happen soon to spoil it. Just *suppose* Aunt Augusta grew tender-hearted and ceased to punish! Or suppose she suddenly discovered that he was growing too big to be shut up! Jims began to stint himself in eating lest he grew too fast. And then Aunt Augusta worried about his loss of appetite and suggested to Uncle Walter that he should be sent to the country till the hot weather was over. Jims didn't want to go to the country now because his heart was elsewhere. He must eat again, if he grew like a weed. It was all very harassing.

Uncle Walter looked at him keenly.

"It seems to me you're looking pretty fit, Jims. Do you want to go to the country?"

"No, please."

"Are you happy, Jims?"

"Sometimes."

"A boy should be happy all the time, Jims."

"If I had a mother and someone to play with I would be."

"I have tried to be a mother to you, Jims," said Aunt Augusta, in an offended tone. Then she addressed Uncle Walter. "A younger woman would probably understand him better. And I feel that the care of this big place is too much for me. I would prefer to go to my own old home. If you had married long ago, as you should, Walter, James would have had a mother and some cousins to play with. I have always been of this opinion."

Uncle Walter frowned and got up.

"Just because one woman played you false is no good reason for spoiling your life," went on Aunt Augusta severely. "I have kept silence all these years but now I am going to speak—and speak plainly. You should marry, Walter. You are young enough yet and you owe it to your name."

"Listen, Augusta," said Uncle Walter sternly. "I loved a woman once. I believed she loved me. She sent me back my ring one day and with it a message saying she had ceased to care for me and bidding me never to try to look upon her face again. Well, I have obeyed her, that is all."

"There was something strange about all that, Walter. The life she has since led proves that. So you should not let it embitter you against all women."

"I haven't. It's nonsense to say I'm a woman-hater, Augusta. But that experience has robbed me of the power to care for another woman."

"Well, this isn't a proper conversation for a child to hear," said Aunt Augusta, recollecting herself. "Jims, go out."

Jims would have given one of his ears to stay and listen with the other. But he went obediently.

And then, the very next day, the dreaded something happened.

It was the first of August and very, very hot. Jims was late coming to dinner and Aunt Augusta reproved him and Jims, deliberately, and with malice aforethought, told her he thought she was a nasty old woman. He had never been saucy to Aunt Augusta before. But it was three days since he had seen Miss Avery and the Black Prince and Nip and he was desperate. Aunt Augusta crimsoned with anger and doomed Jims to an afternoon in the blue room for impertinence.

"And I shall tell your uncle when he comes home," she added.

That rankled, for Jims didn't want Uncle Walter to think him impertinent. But he forgot all his worries as he scampered through the Garden of Spices to the beech tree. And there Jims stopped as if he had been shot. Prone on the grass under the beech tree, white and cold and still, lay his Miss Avery—dead, stone dead!

At least Jims drought she was dead. He flew into the house like a mad thing, shrieking for Martha. Nobody answered. Jims recollected, with a rush of sickening dread, that Miss Avery had told him Martha and Edward were going away that day to visit a sister. He rushed blindly across the lawn again, through the little side gate he had never passed before and down the street home. Uncle Walter was just opening the door of his car.

"Uncle Walter—come—come," sobbed Jims, clutching frantically at his hand. "Miss Avery's dead—dead—oh, come quick."

"*Who* is dead?"

"Miss Avery—Miss Avery Garland. She's lying on the grass over there in her garden. And I love her so—and I'll die, too—oh, Uncle Walter, *come*."

Uncle Walter looked as if he wanted to ask some questions, but he said nothing. With a strange face he hurried after Jims. Miss Avery was still lying there. As Uncle Walter bent over her he saw the broad red scar and started back with an exclamation.

"She is dead?" gasped Jims.

"No," said Uncle Walter, bending down again—"no, she has only fainted, Jims—overcome by the heat, I suppose. I want help. Go and call somebody."

"There's no one home here to-day," said Jims, in a spasm of joy so great that it shook him like a leaf.

"Then go home and telephone over to Mr. Loring's. Tell them I want the nurse who is there to come here for a few minutes."

Jims did his errand. Uncle Walter and the nurse carried Miss Avery into the house and then Jims went back to the blue room. He was so unhappy he didn't care where he went. He wished something *would* jump at him out of the bed and put an end to him. Everything was discovered now and he would never see Miss Avery again. Jims lay very still on the window seat. He did not even cry. He had come to one of the griefs that lie too deep for tears.

"I think I must have been put under a curse at birth," thought poor Jims.

Over at the stone house Miss Avery was lying on the couch in her room. The nurse had gone away and Dr. Walter was sitting looking at her. He leaned forward and pulled away the hand with which she was hiding the scar on her face. He looked first at the little gold ring on the hand and then at the scar.

"Don't," she said piteously.

"Avery—why did you do it?—*why* did you do it?"

"Oh, you know—you must know now, Walter."

"Avery, did you break my heart and spoil my life—and your own—simply because your face was scarred?"

"I couldn't bear to have you see me hideous," she moaned. "You had been so proud of my beauty. I—I—thought you couldn't love me any more—I couldn't bear the thought of looking in your eyes and seeing aversion there."

Walter Grant leaned forward.

"Look in my eyes, Avery. Do you see any aversion?"

Avery forced herself to look. What she saw covered her face with a hot blush.

"Did you think my love such a poor and superficial thing, Avery," he said sternly, "that it must vanish because a blemish came on your fairness? Do you think *that* would change me? Was your own love for me so slight?"

"No—no," she sobbed. "I have loved you every moment of my life, Walter. Oh, don't look at me so sternly."

"If you had even told me," he said. "You said I was never to try to look on your face again—and they told me you had gone away. You sent me back my ring."

"I kept the old one," she interrupted, holding out her hand, "the first one you ever gave me—do you remember, Walter? When we were boy and girl."

"You robbed me of all that made life worth while, Avery. Do you wonder that I've been a bitter man?"

"I was wrong—I was wrong," she sobbed. "I should have believed in you. But don't you think I've paid, too? Forgive me, Walter—it's too late to atone—but forgive me."

"*Is* it too late?" he asked gravely.

She pointed to the scar.

"Could you endure seeing this opposite to you every day at your table?" she asked bitterly.

"Yes—if I could see your sweet eyes and your beloved smile with it, Avery," he answered passionately. "Oh, Avery, it was *you* I loved—not your outward favor. Oh, how foolish you were—foolish and morbid! You always put too high a value on beauty, Avery. If I had dreamed of the true state of the case—if I had known you were here all these years—why I heard a rumor long ago that you had married, Avery—but if I had known I would have come to you and *made* you be—sensible."

She gave a little laugh at his lame conclusion. That was so like the old Walter. Then her eyes filled with tears as he took her in his arms.

The door of the blue room opened. Jims did not look up. It was Aunt Augusta, of course—and she had heard the whole story.

"Jims, boy."

Jims lifted his miserable eyes. It was Uncle Walter—but a different Uncle Walter—an Uncle Walter with laughing eyes and a strange radiance of youth about him.

"Poor, lonely little fellow," said Uncle Walter unexpectedly. "Jims, would you like Miss Avery to come *here*—and live with us always—and be your real aunt?"

"Great snakes!" said Jims, transformed in a second. "Is there any chance of *that*?"

"There is a certainty, thanks to you," said Uncle Walter. "You can go over to see her for a little while. Don't talk her to death—she's weak yet—and attend to that menagerie of yours over there—she's worrying because the bull dog and gobbler weren't fed—and Jims—"

But Jims had swung down through the pine and was tearing across the Garden of Spices.

The Girl and the Photograph

When I heard that Peter Austin was in Vancouver I hunted him up. I had met Peter ten years before when I had gone east to visit my father's people and had spent a few weeks with an uncle in Croyden. The Austins lived across the street from Uncle Tom, and Peter and I had struck up a friendship, although he was a hobbledehoy of awkward sixteen and I, at twenty-two, was older and wiser and more dignified than I've ever been since or ever expect to be again. Peter was a jolly little round freckled chap. He was all right when no girls were around; when they were he retired within himself like a misanthropic oyster, and was about as interesting. This was the one point upon which we always disagreed. Peter couldn't endure girls; I was devoted to them by the wholesale. The Croyden girls were pretty and vivacious. I had a score of flirtations during my brief sojourn among them.

But when I went away the face I carried in my memory was not that of any girl with whom I had walked and driven and played the game of hearts.

It was ten years ago, but I had never been quite able to forget that girl's face. Yet I had seen it but once and then only for a moment. I had gone for a solitary ramble in the woods over the river and, in a lonely little valley dim with pines, where I thought myself alone, I had come suddenly upon her, standing ankle-deep in fern on the bank of a brook, the late evening sunshine falling yellowly on her uncovered dark hair. She was very young—no more than sixteen; yet the face and eyes were already those of a woman. Such a face! Beautiful? Yes, but I thought of that afterward, when I was alone. With that face before my eyes I thought only of its purity and sweetness, of the lovely soul and rich mind looking out of the great, greyish-blue eyes which, in the dimness of the pine shadows, looked almost black. There was something in the face of that child-woman I had never seen before and was destined never to see again in any other face. Careless boy though I was, it stirred me to the deeps. I felt that she must have been waiting forever in that pine valley for me and that, in finding her, I had found all of good that life could offer me.

I would have spoken to her, but before I could shape my greeting into words that should not seem rude or presumptuous, she had turned and gone, stepping lightly across the brook and vanishing in the maple copse beyond. For no more than ten seconds had I gazed into her face, and the soul of her, the real woman behind the fair outwardness, had looked back into my eyes; but I had never been able to forget it.

When I returned home I questioned my cousins diplomatically as to who she might be. I felt strangely reluctant to do so—it seemed in some way sacrilege; yet only by so doing could I hope to discover her. They could tell me nothing; nor did I meet her again during the remainder of my stay in Croyden, although I never went anywhere without looking for her, and haunted the pine valley daily, in the hope of seeing her again. My disappointment was so bitter that I laughed at myself.

I thought I was a fool to feel thus about a girl I had met for a moment in a chance ramble—a mere child at that, with her hair still hanging in its long glossy schoolgirl braid. But when I remembered her eyes, my wisdom forgave me.

Well, that was ten years ago; in those ten years the memory had, I must confess, grown dimmer. In our busy western life a man had not much time for sentimental recollections. Yet I had never been able to care for another woman. I wanted to; I wanted to marry and settle down. I had come to the time of life when a man wearies of drifting and begins to hanker for a calm anchorage in some snug haven of his own. But, somehow, I shirked the matter. It seemed rather easier to let things slide.

At this stage Peter came west. He was something in a bank, and was as round and jolly as ever; but he had evidently changed his attitude towards girls, for his rooms were full of their photos. They were stuck around everywhere and they were all pretty. Either Peter had excellent taste, or the Croyden photographers knew how to flatter. But there was one on the mantel which attracted my attention especially. If the photo were to be trusted the girl was quite the prettiest I had ever seen.

"Peter, what pretty girl's picture is this on your mantel?" I called out to Peter, who was in his bedroom, donning evening dress for some function.

"That's my cousin, Marian Lindsay," he answered. "She *is* rather nice-looking, isn't she. Lives in Croyden now—used to live up the river at Chiselhurst. Didn't you ever chance across her when you were in Croyden?"

"No," I said. "If I had I wouldn't have forgotten her face."

"Well, she'd be only a kid then, of course. She's twenty-six now. Marian is a mighty nice girl, but she's bound to be an old maid. She's got notions—ideals, she calls 'em. All the Croyden fellows have been in love with her at one time or another but they might as well have made up to a statue. Marian really hasn't a spark of feeling or sentiment in her. Her looks are the best part of her, although she's confoundedly clever."

Peter spoke rather squiffily. I suspected that he had been one of the smitten swains himself. I looked at the photo for a few minutes longer, admiring it more every minute and, when I heard Peter coming out, I did an unjustifiable thing—I took that photo and put it in my pocket.

I expected Peter would make a fuss when he missed it, but that very night the house in which he lived was burned to the ground. Peter escaped with the most important of his goods and chattels, but all the counterfeit presentments of his dear divinities went up in smoke. If he ever thought particularly of Marian Lindsay's photograph he must have supposed that it shared the fate of the others.

As for me, I propped my ill-gotten treasure up on my mantel and worshipped it for a fortnight. At the end of that time I went boldly to Peter and told him I wanted him to introduce me by letter to his dear cousin and ask her to agree to a friendly correspondence with me.

Oddly enough, I did not do this without some reluctance, in spite of the fact that I was as much in love with Marian Lindsay as it was possible to be through the medium of a picture. I thought of the girl I had seen in the pine wood and felt an inward shrinking from a step that might divide me from her forever. But I rated myself for this nonsense. It was in the highest degree unlikely that I should ever meet the girl of the pines again. If she were still living she was probably some other man's wife. I would think no more about it.

Peter whistled when he heard what I had to say.

"Of course I'll do it, old man," he said obligingly. "But I warn you I don't think it will be much use. Marian isn't the sort of girl to open up a correspondence in such a fashion. However, I'll do the best I can for you."

"Do. Tell her I'm a respectable fellow with no violent bad habits and all that. I'm in earnest, Peter. I want to make that girl's acquaintance, and this seems the only way at present. I can't get off just now for a trip east. Explain all this, and use your cousinly influence in my behalf if you possess any."

Peter grinned.

"It's not the most graceful job in the world you are putting on me, Curtis," he said. "I don't mind owning up now that I was pretty far gone on Marian myself two years ago. It's all over now, but it was bad while it lasted. Perhaps Marian will consider your request more favourably if I put it in the light of a favour to myself. She must feel that she owes me something for wrecking my life."

Peter grinned again and looked at the one photo he had contrived to rescue from the fire. It was a pretty, snub-nosed little girl. She would never have consoled me for the loss of Marian Lindsay, but every man to his taste.

In due time Peter sought me out to give me his cousin's answer.

"Congratulations, Curtis. You've out-Caesared Caesar. You've conquered without even going and seeing. Marian agrees to a friendly correspondence with you. I am amazed, I admit—even though I did paint you up as a sort of Sir Galahad and Lancelot combined. I'm not used to seeing proud Marian do stunts like that, and it rather takes my breath."

I wrote to Marian Lindsay after one farewell dream of the girl under the pines. When Marian's letters began to come regularly I forgot the other one altogether.

Such letters—such witty, sparkling, clever, womanly, delightful letters! They completed the conquest her picture had begun. Before we had corresponded six months I was besottedly in love with this woman whom I had never seen. Finally, I wrote and told her so, and I asked her to be my wife.

A fortnight later her answer came. She said frankly that she believed she had learned to care for me during our correspondence, but that she thought we should meet in person, before coming to any definite understanding. Could I not arrange to visit Croyden in the summer? Until then we would better continue on our present footing.

I agreed to this, but I considered myself practically engaged, with the personal meeting merely to be regarded as a sop to the Cerberus of conventionality. I permitted myself to use a decidedly lover-like tone in my letters henceforth, and I hailed it as a favourable omen that I was not rebuked for this, although Marian's own letters still retained their pleasant, simple friendliness.

Peter had at first tormented me mercilessly about the affair, but when he saw I did not like his chaff he stopped it. Peter was always a good fellow. He realized that I regarded the matter seriously, and he saw me off when I left for the east with a grin tempered by honest sympathy and understanding.

"Good luck to you," he said. "If you win Marian Lindsay you'll win a pearl among women. I haven't been able to grasp her taking to you in this fashion, though. It's so unlike Marian. But, since she undoubtedly has, you are a lucky man."

I arrived in Croyden at dusk and went to Uncle Tom's. There I found them busy with preparations for a party to be given that night in honour of a girl friend who was visiting my cousin Edna. I was secretly annoyed, for I wanted to hasten at once to Marian. But I couldn't decently get away, and on second thoughts I was consoled by the reflection that she would probably come to the party. I knew she belonged to the same social set as Uncle Tom's girls. I should, however, have preferred our meeting to have been under different circumstances.

From my stand behind the palms in a corner I eagerly scanned the guests as they arrived. Suddenly my heart gave a bound. Marian Lindsay had just come in.

I recognized her at once from her photograph. It had not flattered her in the least; indeed, it had not done her justice, for her exquisite colouring of hair and complexion were quite lost in it. She was, moreover, gowned with a taste and smartness eminently admirable in the future Mrs. Eric Curtis. I felt a thrill of proprietary pride as I stepped out from behind the palms. She was talking to Aunt Grace; but her eyes fell on me. I expected a little start of recognition, for I had sent her an excellent photograph of myself; but her gaze was one of blankest unconsciousness.

I felt something like disappointment at her non-recognition, but I consoled myself by the reflection that people often fail to recognize other people whom they have seen only in photographs, no matter how good the likeness may be. I waylaid Edna, who was passing at that time, and said, "Edna I want you to introduce me to the girl who is talking to your mother."

Edna laughed.

"So you have succumbed at first sight to our Croyden beauty? Of course I'll introduce you, but I warn you beforehand that she is the most incorrigible flirt in Croyden or out of it. So take care."

It jarred on me to hear Marian called a flirt. It seemed so out of keeping with her letters and the womanly delicacy and fineness revealed in them. But I reflected that women sometimes find it hard to forgive another woman who absorbs more than her share of lovers, and generally take their revenge by dubbing her a flirt, whether she deserves the name or not.

We had crossed the room during this reflection. Marian turned and stood before us, smiling at Edna, but evincing no recognition whatever of myself. It is a piquant experience to find yourself awaiting an introduction to a girl to whom you are virtually engaged.

"Dorothy dear," said Edna, "this is my cousin, Mr. Curtis, from Vancouver. Eric, this is Miss Armstrong."

I suppose I bowed. Habit carries us mechanically through many impossible situations. I don't know what I looked like or what I said, if I said anything. I don't suppose I betrayed my dire confusion, for Edna went off unconcernedly without another glance at me.

Dorothy Armstrong! Gracious powers—who—where—why? If this girl was Dorothy Armstrong who was Marian Lindsay? To whom was I engaged? There was some awful mistake somewhere, for it could not be possible that there were two girls in Croyden who looked exactly like the photograph reposing in my valise at that very moment. I stammered like a schoolboy.

"I—oh—I—your face seems familiar to me, Miss Armstrong. I—I—think I must have seen your photograph somewhere."

"Probably in Peter Austin's collection," smiled Miss Armstrong. "He had one of mine before he was burned out. How is he?"

"Peter? Oh, he's well," I replied vaguely. I was thinking a hundred words to the second, but my thoughts arrived nowhere. I was staring at Miss Armstrong like a man bewitched. She must have thought me a veritable booby. "Oh, by the way—can you tell me—do you know a Miss Lindsay in Croyden?"

Miss Armstrong looked surprised and a little bored. Evidently she was not used to having newly introduced young men inquiring about another girl.

"Marian Lindsay? Oh, yes."

"Is she here tonight?" I said.

"No, Marian is not going to parties just now, owing to the recent death of her aunt, who lived with them."

"Does she—oh—does she look like you at all?" I inquired idiotically.

Amusement glimmered but over Miss Armstrong's boredom. She probably concluded that I was some harmless lunatic.

"Like me? Not at all. There couldn't be two people more dissimilar. Marian is quite dark. I am fair. And our features are altogether unlike. Why, good evening, Jack. Yes, I believe I did promise you this dance."

She bowed to me and skimmed away with Jack. I saw Aunt Grace bearing down upon me and fled incontinently. In my own room I flung myself on a chair and tried to think the matter out. Where did the mistake come in? How had it happened? I shut my eyes and conjured up the vision of Peter's room that day. I remembered vaguely that, when I had picked up Dorothy Armstrong's picture, I had noticed another photograph that had fallen face downward beside it. That must have been Marian Lindsay's, and Peter had thought I meant it.

And now what a position I was in! I was conscious of bitter disappointment. I had fallen in love with Dorothy Armstrong's photograph. As far as external semblance goes it was she whom I loved. I was practically engaged to another woman—a woman who, in spite of our correspondence, seemed to me now, in the shock of this discovery, a stranger. It was useless to tell myself that it was the mind and soul revealed in those letters that I loved, and that that mind and soul were Marian Lindsay's. It was useless to remember that Peter had said she was pretty. Exteriorly, she was a stranger to me; hers was not the face which had risen before me for nearly a year as the face of the woman I loved. Was ever unlucky wretch in such a predicament before?

Well, there was only one thing to do. I must stand by my word. Marian Lindsay was the woman I had asked to marry me, whose answer I must shortly go to receive. If that answer were "yes" I must accept the situation and banish all thought of Dorothy Armstrong's pretty face.

Next evening at sunset I went to "Glenwood," the Lindsay place. Doubtless, an eager lover might have gone earlier, but an eager lover I certainly was not. Probably Marian was expecting me and had given orders concerning me, for the maid who came to the door conveyed me to a little room behind the stairs—a room which, as I felt as soon as I entered it, was a woman's pet domain. In its books and pictures and flowers it spoke eloquently of dainty femininity. Somehow, it suited the letters. I did not feel quite so much the stranger as I had felt. Nevertheless, when I heard a light footfall on the stairs my heart beat painfully. I stood up and turned to the door, but I could not look up. The footsteps came nearer; I knew that a white hand swept aside the *portière* at the entrance; I knew that she had entered the room and was standing before me.

With an effort I raised my eyes and looked at her. She stood, tall and gracious, in a ruby splendour of sunset falling through the window beside her. The light quivered like living radiance over a dark proud head, a white throat, and a face before whose perfect loveliness the memory of Dorothy Armstrong's laughing prettiness faded like a star in the sunrise, nevermore in the fullness of the day to be remembered. Yet it was not of her beauty I thought as I stood spellbound before her. I seemed to see a dim little valley full of whispering pines, and a girl standing under their shadows, looking at me with the same great, greyish-blue eyes which gazed upon me now from Marian Lindsay's face—the same face, matured into gracious womanhood, that I had seen ten years ago; and loved—aye, loved—ever since. I took an unsteady step forward.

"Marian?" I said.

When I got home that night I burned Dorothy Armstrong's photograph. The next day I went to my cousin Tom, who owns the fashionable studio of Croyden and, binding him over to secrecy, sought one of Marian's latest photographs from him. It is the only secret I have ever kept from my wife.

Before we were married Marian told me something.

"I always remembered you as you looked that day under the pines," she said. "I was only a child, but I think I loved you then and ever afterwards. When I dreamed my girl's dream of love your face rose up before me. I had the advantage of you that I knew your name—I had heard of you. When Peter wrote about you I knew who you were. That was why I agreed to correspond with you. I was afraid it was a forward—an unwomanly thing to do. But it seemed my chance for happiness and I took it. I am glad I did."

I did not answer in words, but lovers will know how I did answer.

The Gossip of Valley View

It was the first of April, and Julius Barrett, aged fourteen, perched on his father's gatepost, watched ruefully the low descending sun, and counted that day lost. He had not succeeded in "fooling" a single person, although he had tried repeatedly. One and all, old and young, of his intended victims had been too wary for Julius. Hence, Julius was disgusted and ready for anything in the way of a stratagem or a spoil.

The Barrett gatepost topped the highest hill in Valley View. Julius could see the entire settlement, from "Young" Thomas Everett's farm, a mile to the west, to Adelia Williams's weather-grey little house on a moonrise slope to the east. He was gazing moodily down the muddy road when Dan Chester, homeward bound from the post office, came riding sloppily along on his grey mare and pulled up by the Barrett gate to hand a paper to Julius.

Dan was a young man who took life and himself very seriously. He seldom smiled, never joked, and had a Washingtonian reputation for veracity. Dan had never told a conscious falsehood in his life; he never even exaggerated.

Julius, beholding Dan's solemn face, was seized with a perfectly irresistible desire to "fool" him. At the same moment his eye caught the dazzling reflection of the setting sun on the windows of Adelia Williams's house, and he had an inspiration little short of diabolical. "Have you heard the news, Dan?" he asked.

"No, what is it?" asked Dan.

"I dunno's I ought to tell it," said Julius reflectively. "It's kind of a family affair, but then Adelia didn't say not to, and anyway it'll be all over the place soon. So I'll tell you, Dan, if you'll promise never to tell who told you. Adelia Williams and Young Thomas Everett are going to be married."

Julius delivered himself of this tremendous lie with a transparently earnest countenance. Yet Dan, credulous as he was, could not believe it all at once.

"Git out," he said.

"It's true, 'pon my word," protested Julius. "Adelia was up last night and told Ma all about it. Ma's her cousin, you know. The wedding is to be in June, and Adelia asked Ma to help her get her quilts and things ready."

Julius reeled all this off so glibly that Dan finally believed the story, despite the fact that the people thus coupled together in prospective matrimony were the very last people in Valley View who could have been expected to marry each other. Young Thomas was a confirmed bachelor of fifty, and Adelia Williams was forty; they were not supposed to be even well acquainted, as the Everetts and the Williamses had never been very friendly, although no open feud existed between them.

Nevertheless, in view of Julius's circumstantial statements, the amazing news must be true, and Dan was instantly agog to carry it further. Julius watched Dan and the grey mare out of sight, fairly writhing with ecstasy. Oh, but Dan had been easy! The story would be all over Valley View in twenty-four hours. Julius laughed until he came near to falling off the gatepost.

At this point Julius and Danny drop out of our story, and Young Thomas enters.

It was two days later when Young Thomas heard that he was to be married to Adelia Williams in June. Eben Clark, the blacksmith, told him when he went to the forge to get his horse shod. Young Thomas laughed his big jolly laugh. Valley View gossip had been marrying him off for the last thirty years, although never before to Adelia Williams.

"It's news to me," he said tolerantly.

Eben grinned broadly. "Ah, you can't bluff it off like that, Tom," he said. "The news came too straight this time. Well, I was glad to hear it, although I was mighty surprised. I never thought of you and Adelia. But she's a fine little woman and will make you a capital wife."

Young Thomas grunted and drove away. He had a good deal of business to do that day, involving calls at various places—the store for molasses, the mill for flour, Jim Bentley's for seed grain, the doctor's for toothache drops for his housekeeper, the post office for mail—and at each and every place he was joked about his approaching marriage. In the end it rather annoyed Young Thomas, He drove home at last in what was for him something of a temper. How on earth had that fool story started? With such detailed circumstantiality of rugs and quilts, too? Adelia Williams must be going to marry somebody, and the Valley View gossips, unable to locate the man, had guessed Young Thomas.

When he reached home, tired, mud-bespattered, and hungry, his housekeeper, who was also his hired man's wife, asked him if it was true that he was going to be married. Young Thomas, taking in at a glance the ill-prepared, half-cold supper on the table, felt more annoyed than ever, and said it wasn't, with a strong expression—not quite an oath—for Young Thomas never swore, unless swearing be as much a matter of intonation as of words.

Mrs. Dunn sighed, patted her swelled face, and said she was sorry; she had hoped it was true, for her man had decided to go west. They were to go in a month's time. Young Thomas sat down to his supper with the prospect of having to look up another housekeeper and hired man before planting to destroy his appetite.

Next day, three people who came to see Young Thomas on business congratulated him on his approaching marriage. Young Thomas, who had recovered his usual good humour, merely laughed. There was no use in being too earnest in denial, he thought. He knew that his unusual fit of petulance with his housekeeper had only convinced her that the story was true. It would die away in time, as other similar stories had died, he thought. Valley View gossip was imaginative.

Young Thomas looked rather serious, however, when the minister and his wife called that evening and referred to the report. Young Thomas gravely said that it was unfounded. The minister looked graver still and said he was sorry—he had hoped it was true. His wife glanced significantly about Young Thomas's big, untidy sitting-room, where there were cobwebs on the ceiling and fluff in the corners and dust on the mop-board, and said nothing, but looked volumes.

"Dang it all," said Young Thomas, as they drove away, "they'll marry me yet in spite of myself."

The gossip made him think about Adelia Williams. He had never thought about her before; he was barely acquainted with her. Now he remembered that she was a plump, jolly-looking little woman, noted for being a good housekeeper. Then Young Thomas groaned, remembering that he must start out looking for a housekeeper soon; and housekeepers were not easily found, as Young Thomas had discovered several times since his mother's death ten years before.

Next Sunday in church Young Thomas looked at Adelia Williams. He caught Adelia looking at him. Adelia blushed and looked guiltily away.

"Dang it all," reflected Young Thomas, forgetting that he was in church. "I suppose she has heard that fool story too. I'd like to know the person who started it; man or woman, I'd punch their head."

Nevertheless, Young Thomas went on looking at Adelia by fits and starts, although he did not again catch Adelia looking at him. He noticed that she had round rosy cheeks and twinkling brown eyes. She did not look like an old maid, and Young Thomas wondered that she had been allowed to become one. Sarah Barnett, now, to whom report had married him a year ago, looked like a dried sour apple.

For the next four weeks the story haunted Young Thomas like a spectre. Down it would not. Everywhere he went he was joked about it. It gathered fresh detail every week. Adelia was getting her clothes ready; she was to be married in seal-brown cashmere; Vinnie Lawrence at Valley Centre was making it for her; she had got a new hat with a long ostrich plume; some said white, some said grey.

Young Thomas kept wondering who the man could be, for he was convinced that Adelia was going to marry somebody. More than that, once he caught himself wondering enviously. Adelia was a nice-looking woman, and he had not so far heard of any probable housekeeper.

"Dang it all," said Young Thomas to himself in desperation. "I wouldn't care if it was true."

His married sister from Carlisle heard the story and came over to investigate. Young Thomas denied it shortly, and his sister scolded. She had devoutly hoped it was true, she said, and it would have been a great weight off her mind.

"This house is in a disgraceful condition, Thomas," she said severely. "It would break Mother's heart if she could rise out of her grave to see it. And Adelia Williams is a perfect housekeeper."

"You didn't use to think so much of the Williams crowd," said Young Thomas drily.

"Oh, some of them don't amount to much," admitted Maria, "but Adelia is all right."

Catching sight of an odd look on Young Thomas's face, she added hastily, "Thomas Everett, I believe it's true after all. Now, is it? For mercy's sake don't be so sly. You might tell me, your own and only sister, if it is."

"Oh, shut up," was Young Thomas's unfeeling reply to his own and only sister.

Young Thomas told himself that night that Valley View gossip would drive him into an asylum yet if it didn't let up. He also wondered if Adelia was as much persecuted as himself. No doubt she was. He never could catch her eye in church now, but he would have been surprised had he realized how many times he tried to.

The climax came the third week in May, when Young Thomas, who had been keeping house for himself for three weeks, received a letter and an express box from his cousin, Charles Everett, out in Manitoba. Charles and he had been chums in their boyhood. They corresponded occasionally still, although it was twenty years since Charles had gone west.

The letter was to congratulate Young Thomas on his approaching marriage. Charles had heard of it through some Valley View correspondents of his wife. He was much pleased; he had always liked Adelia, he said—had been an old beau of hers, in fact. Thomas might give her a kiss for him if he liked. He forwarded a wedding present by express and hoped they would be very happy, etc.

The present was an elaborate hatrack of polished buffalo horns, mounted on red plush, with an inset mirror. Young Thomas set it up on the kitchen table and scowled moodily at his reflection in the mirror. If wedding presents were beginning to come, it was high time something was done. The matter was past being a joke. This affair of the present would certainly get out—things always got out in Valley View, dang it all—and he would never hear the last of it.

"I'll marry," said Young Thomas decisively. "If Adelia Williams won't have me, I'll marry the first woman who will, if it's Sarah Barnett herself."

Young Thomas shaved and put on his Sunday suit. As soon as it was safely dark, he hied him away to Adelia Williams. He felt very doubtful about his reception, but the remembrance of the twinkle in Adelia's brown eyes comforted him. She looked like a woman who had a sense of humour; she might not take him, but she would not feel offended or insulted because he asked her.

"Dang it all, though, I hope she will take me," said Young Thomas. "I'm in for getting married now and no mistake. And I can't get Adelia out of my head. I've been thinking of her steady ever since that confounded gossip began."

When he knocked at Adelia's door he discovered that his face was wet with perspiration. Adelia opened the door and started when she saw him; then she turned very red and stiffly asked him in. Young Thomas went in and sat down, wondering if all men felt so horribly uncomfortable when they went courting.

Adelia stooped low over the woodbox to put a stick of wood in the stove, for the May evening was chilly. Her shoulders were shaking; the shaking grew worse; suddenly Adelia laughed hysterically and, sitting down on the woodbox, continued to laugh. Young Thomas eyed her with a friendly grin.

"Oh, do excuse me," gasped poor Adelia, wiping tears from her eyes. "This is—dreadful—I didn't mean to laugh—I don't know why I'm laughing—but—I—can't help it."

She laughed helplessly again. Young Thomas laughed too. His embarrassment vanished in the mellowness of that laughter. Presently Adelia composed herself and removed from the woodbox to a chair, but there was still a suspicious twitching about the corners of her mouth.

"I suppose," said Young Thomas, determined to have it over with before the ice could form again, "I suppose, Adelia, you've heard the story that's been going about you and me of late?"

Adelia nodded. "I've been persecuted to the verge of insanity with it," she said. "Every soul I've seen has tormented me about it, and people have written me about it. I've denied it till I was black in the face, but nobody believed me. I can't find out how it started. I hope you believe, Mr. Everett, that it couldn't possibly have arisen from anything I said. I've felt dreadfully worried for fear you might think it did. I heard that my cousin, Lucilla Barrett, said I told her, but Lucilla vowed to me that she never said such a thing or even dreamed of it. I've felt dreadful bad over the whole affair. I even gave up the idea of making a quilt after a lovely new pattern I've got because they made such a talk about my brown dress."

"I've been kind of supposing that you must be going to marry somebody, and folks just guessed it was me," said Young Thomas—he said it anxiously.

"No, I'm not going to be married to anybody," said Adelia with a laugh, taking up her knitting.

"I'm glad of that," said Young Thomas gravely. "I mean," he hastened to add, seeing the look of astonishment on Adelia's face, "that I'm glad there isn't any other man because—because I want you myself, Adelia."

Adelia laid down her knitting and blushed crimson. But she looked at Young Thomas squarely and reproachfully.

"You needn't think you are bound to say that because of the gossip, Mr. Everett," she said quietly.

"Oh, I don't," said Young Thomas earnestly. "But the truth is, the story set me to thinking about you, and from that I got to wishing it was true—honest, I did—I couldn't get you out of my head, and at last I didn't want to. It just seemed to me that you were the very woman for me if you'd only take me. Will you, Adelia? I've got a good farm and house, and I'll try to make you happy."

It was not a very romantic wooing, perhaps. But Adelia was forty and had never been a romantic little body even in the heyday of youth. She was a practical woman, and Young Thomas was a fine looking man of his age with abundance of worldly goods. Besides, she liked him, and the gossip had made her think a good deal about him of late. Indeed, in a moment of candour she had owned to herself the very last Sunday in church that she wouldn't mind if the story were true.

"I'll—I'll think of it," she said.

This was practically an acceptance, and Young Thomas so understood it. Without loss of time he crossed the kitchen, sat down beside Adelia, and put his arms about her plump waist.

"Here's a kiss Charlie sent me to give you," he said, giving it.

The Letters

Just before the letter was brought to me that evening I was watching the red November sunset from the library window. It was a stormy, unrestful sunset, gleaming angrily through the dark fir boughs that were now and again tossed suddenly and distressfully in a fitful gust of wind. Below, in the garden, it was quite dark, and I could only see dimly the dead leaves that were whirling and dancing uncannily over the roseless paths. The poor dead leaves—yet not quite dead! There was still enough unquiet life left in them to make them restless and forlorn. They hearkened yet to every call of the wind, who cared for them no longer but only played freakishly with them and broke their rest. I felt sorry for the leaves as I watched them in that dull, weird twilight, and angry—in a petulant fashion that almost made me laugh—with the wind that would not leave them in peace. Why should they—and I—be vexed with these transient breaths of desire for a life that had passed us by?

I was in the grip of a bitter loneliness that evening—so bitter and so insistent that I felt I could not face the future at all, even with such poor fragments of courage as I had gathered about me after Father's death, hoping that they would, at least, suffice for my endurance, if not for my content. But now they fell away from me at sight of the emptiness of life.

The emptiness! Ah, it was from that I shrank. I could have faced pain and anxiety and heartbreak undauntedly, but I could not face that terrible, yawning, barren emptiness. I put my hands over my eyes to shut it out, but it pressed in upon my consciousness insistently, and would not be ignored longer.

The moment when a woman realizes that she has nothing to live for—neither love nor purpose nor duty—holds for her the bitterness of death. She is a brave woman indeed who can look upon such a prospect unquailingly, and I was not brave. I was weak and timid. Had not Father often laughed mockingly at me because of it?

It was three weeks since Father had died—my proud, handsome, unrelenting old father, whom I had loved so intensely and who had never loved me. I had always accepted this fact unresentfully and unquestioningly, but it had steeped my whole life in its tincture of bitterness. Father had never forgiven me for two things. I had cost my mother's life and I was not a son to perpetuate the old name and carry on the family feud with the Frasers.

I was a very lonely child, with no playmates or companions of any sort, and my girlhood was lonelier still. The only passion in my life was my love for my father. I would have done and suffered anything to win his affection in return. But all I ever did win was an amused tolerance—and I was grateful for that—almost content. It was much to have something to love and be permitted to love it.

If I had been a beautiful and spirited girl I think Father might have loved me, but I was neither. At first I did not think or care about my lack of beauty; then one day I was alone in the beech wood; I was trying to disentangle my skirt which had caught on some thorny underbrush. A young man came around the curve of the path and, seeing my predicament, bent with murmured apology to help me. He had to kneel to do it, and I saw a ray of sunshine falling through the beeches above us strike like a lance of light athwart the thick brown hair that pushed out from under his cap. Before I thought I put out my hand and touched it softly, then I blushed crimson with shame over what I had done. But he did not know—he never knew.

When he had released my dress he rose and our eyes met for a moment as I timidly thanked him. I saw that he was good to look upon—tall and straight, with broad, stalwart shoulders and a dark, clean-cut face. He had a firm, sensitive mouth and kindly, pleasant, dark blue eyes. I never quite forgot the look in those eyes. It made my heart beat strangely, but it was only for a moment, and the next he had lifted his cap and passed on.

As I went homeward I wondered who he might be. He must be a stranger, I thought—probably a visitor in some of our few neighbouring families. I wondered too if I should meet him again, and found the thought very pleasant.

I knew few men and they were all old, like Father, or at least elderly. They were the only people who ever came to our house, and they either teased me or overlooked me. None of them was at all like this young man I had met in the beech wood, nor ever could have been, I thought.

When I reached home I stopped before the big mirror that hung in the hall and did what I had never done before in my life—looked at myself very scrutinizingly and wondered if I had any beauty. I could only sorrowfully conclude that I had not—I was so slight and pale, and the thick black hair and dark eyes that might have been pretty in another woman seemed only to accentuate the lack of spirit and regularity in my features. I was still standing there, gazing wistfully at my mirrored face with a strange sinking of spirit, when Father came through the hall, his riding whip in his hand. Seeing me, he laughed.

"Don't waste your time gazing into mirrors, Isobel," he said carelessly. "That might have been excusable in former ladies of Shirley whose beauty might pardon and even adorn vanity, but with you it is only absurd. The needle and the cook-book are all that you need concern yourself with."

I was accustomed to such speeches from him, but they had never hurt me so cruelly before. At that moment I would have given all the world only to be beautiful.

The next Sunday I looked across the church, and in the Fraser pew I saw the young man I had met in the wood. He was looking at me with his arms folded over his breast and on his brow a little frown that seemed somehow indicative of pain and surprise. I felt a miserable sense of disappointment. If he were the Frasers' guest I could not expect to meet him again. Father hated the Frasers, all the Shirleys hated them; it was an old feud, bitter and lasting, that had been as much our inheritance for generations as land and money. The only thing Father had ever taken pains to teach me was detestation of the Frasers and all their works. I accepted this as I accepted all the other traditions of my race. I thought it did not matter much. The Frasers were not likely to come my way, and hatred was a good satisfying passion in the lack of all else. I think I rather took a pride in hating them as became my blood.

I did not look at the Fraser pew again, but outside, under the elms, we met him, standing in the dappling light and shadow. He looked very handsome and a little sad. I could not help glancing back over my shoulder as Father and I walked to the gate, and I saw him looking after us with that little frown which again made me think something had hurt him. I liked better the smile he had worn in the beech wood, but I had an odd liking for the frown too, and I think I had a foolish longing to go back to him, put up my fingers and smooth it away.

"So Alan Fraser has come home," said my father.

"Alan Fraser?" I repeated, with a strange, horrible feeling of coldness and chill coming over me like a shadow on a bright day. Alan Fraser, the son of old Malcolm Fraser of Glenellyn! The son of our enemy! He had been living since childhood with his dead mother's people, so much I knew. And this was he! Something stung and smarted in my eyes. I think the sting and smart might have turned to tears if Father had not been looking down at me.

"Yes. Didn't you see him in his father's pew? But I forgot. You are too demure to be looking at the young men in preaching—or out of it, Isobel. You are a model young woman. Odd that the men never like the model young women! Curse old Malcolm Fraser! What right has he to have a son like that when I have nothing but a puling girl? Remember, Isobel, that if you ever meet that young man you are not to speak to or look at him, or even intimate that you are aware of his existence. He is your enemy and the enemy of your race. You will show him that you realize this."

Of course that ended it all—though just what there had been to end would have been hard to say. Not long afterwards I met Alan Fraser again, when I was out for a canter on my mare. He was strolling through the beech wood with a couple of big collies, and he stopped short as I drew near. I had to do it—Father had decreed—my Shirley pride demanded—that I should do it. I looked him unseeingly in the face, struck my mare a blow with my whip, and dashed past him. I even felt angry, I think, that a Fraser should have the power to make me feel so badly in doing my duty.

After that I had forgotten. There was nothing to make me remember, for I never met Alan Fraser again. The years slipped by, one by one, so like each other in their colourlessness that I forgot to take account of them. I only knew that I grew older and that it did not matter since there was nobody to care. One day they brought Father in, white-lipped and groaning. His mare had thrown him, and he was never to walk again, although he lived for five years. Those five years had been the happiest of my life. For the first time I was necessary to someone—there was something for me to do which nobody else could do so well. I was Father's nurse and companion; and I found my pleasure in tending him and amusing him, soothing his hours of pain and brightening his hours of ease. People said I "did my duty" toward him. I had never liked that word "duty," since the day I had ridden past Alan Fraser in the beech wood. I could not connect it with what I did for Father. It was my delight because I loved him. I did not mind the moods and the irritable outbursts that drove others from him.

But now he was dead, and I sat in the sullen dusk, wishing that I need not go on with life either. The loneliness of the big echoing house weighed on my spirit. I was solitary, without companionship. I looked out on the outside world where the only sign of human habitation visible to my eyes was the light twinkling out from the library window of Glenellyn on the dark fir hill two miles away. By that light I knew Alan Fraser must have returned from his long sojourn abroad, for it only shone when he was at Glenellyn. He still lived there, something of a hermit, people said; he had never married, and he cared nothing for society. His companions were books and dogs and horses; he was given to scientific researches and wrote much for the reviews; he travelled a great deal. So much I knew in a vague way. I even saw him occasionally in church, and never thought the years had changed him much, save that his face was sadder and sterner than of old and his hair had become iron-grey. People said that he had inherited and cherished the old hatred of the Shirleys—that he was very bitter against us. I believed it. He had the face of a good hater—or lover—a man who could play with no emotion but must take it in all earnestness and intensity.

When it was quite dark the housekeeper brought in the lights and handed me a letter which, she said, a man had just brought up from the village post office. I looked at it curiously before I opened it, wondering from whom it was. It was postmarked from a city several miles away, and the firm, decided, rather peculiar handwriting was strange to me. I had no correspondents. After Father's death I had received a few perfunctory notes of condolence from distant relatives and family friends. They had hurt me cruelly, for they seemed to exhale a subtle spirit of congratulation on my being released from a long and unpleasant martyrdom of attendance on an invalid, that quite overrode the decorous phrases of conventional sympathy in which they were expressed. I hated those letters for their implied injustice. I was not thankful for my "release." I missed Father miserably and longed passionately for the very tasks and vigils that had evoked their pity.

This letter did not seem like one of those. I opened it and took out some stiff, blackly written sheets. They were undated and, turning to the last, I saw that they were unsigned. With a not unpleasant tingling of interest I sat down by my desk to read. The letter began abruptly:

> You will not know by whom this is written. Do not seek to know—now or ever. It is only from behind the veil of your ignorance of my identity that I can ever write to you fully and freely as I wish to write—can say what I wish to say in words denied to a formal and conventional expression of sympathy. Dear lady, let me say to you thus what is in my heart.
>
> I know what your sorrow is, and I think I know what your loneliness must be—the sorrow of a broken tie, the loneliness of a life thrown emptily back on itself. I know how you loved your father—how you must have loved him if those eyes and brow and mouth speak truth, for they tell of a nature divinely rich and deep, giving of its wealth and tenderness ungrudgingly to those who are so happy as to be the objects of its affection. To such a nature bereavement must bring a depth and an agony of grief unknown to shallower souls.
>
> I know what your father's helplessness and need of you meant to you. I know that now life must seem to you a broken and embittered thing and, knowing this, I venture to send this greeting across the gulf of strangerhood between us, telling you that my understanding sympathy is fully and freely yours, and bidding you take heart for the future, which now, it may be, looks so heartless and hopeless to you.
>
> Believe me, dear lady, it will be neither. Courage will come to you with the kind days. You will find noble tasks to do, beautiful and gracious duties waiting along your path. The pain and suffering of the world never dies, and while it lives there will be work for such as you to do, and in the doing of it you will find comfort and strength and the highest joy of living. I believe in you. I believe you will make of your life a beautiful and worthy thing. I give you Godspeed for the years to come. Out of my own loneliness I, an unknown friend, who has never clasped your hand, send this message to you. I understand—I have always understood—and I say to you: "Be of good cheer."

To say that this strange letter was a mystery to me seems an inadequate way of stating the matter. I was completely bewildered, nor could I even guess who the writer might be, think and ponder as I might.

The letter itself implied that the writer was a stranger. The handwriting was evidently that of a man, and I knew no man who could or would have sent such a letter to me.

The very mystery stung me to interest. As for the letter itself, it brought me an uplift of hope and inspiration such as I would not have believed possible an hour earlier. It rang so truly and sincerely, and the mere thought that somewhere I had a friend who cared enough to write it, even in such odd fashion, was so sweet that I was half ashamed of the difference it made in my outlook. Sitting there, I took courage and made a compact with myself that I would justify the writer's faith in me—that I would take up my life as something to be worthily lived for all good, to the disregard of my own selfish sorrow and shrinking. I would seek for something to do—for interests which would bind me to my fellow-creatures—for tasks which would lessen the pains and perils of humankind. An hour before, this would not have seemed to me possible; now it seemed the right and natural thing to do.

A week later another letter came. I welcomed it with an eagerness which I feared was almost childish. It was a much longer letter than the first and was written in quite a different strain. There was no apology for or explanation of the motive for writing. It was as if the letter were merely one of a permitted and established correspondence between old friends. It began with a witty, sparkling review of a new book the writer had just read, and passed from this to crisp comments on the great events, political, scientific, artistic, of the day. The whole letter was pungent, interesting, delightful—an impersonal essay on a dozen vital topics of life and thought. Only at the end was a personal note struck.

"Are you interested in these things?" ran the last paragraph. "In what is being done and suffered and attained in the great busy world? I think you must be—for I have seen you and read what is written in your face. I believe you care for these things as I do—that your being thrills to the 'still, sad music of humanity'—that the songs of the poets I love find an echo in your spirit and the aspirations of all struggling souls a sympathy in your heart. Believing this, I have written freely to you, taking a keen pleasure in thus revealing my thoughts and visions to one who will understand. For I too am friendless, in the sense of one standing alone, shut out from the sweet, intimate communion of feeling and opinion that may be held with the heart's friends. Shall you have read this as a friend, I wonder—a candid, uncritical, understanding friend? Let me hope it, dear lady."

I was expecting the third letter when it came—but not until it did come did I realize what my disappointment would have been if it had not. After that every week brought me a letter; soon those letters were the greatest interest in my life. I had given up all attempts to solve the mystery of their coming and was content to enjoy them for themselves alone. From week to week I looked forward to them with an eagerness that I would hardly confess, even to myself.

And such letters as they were, growing longer and fuller and freer as time went on—such wise, witty, brilliant, pungent letters, stimulating all my torpid life into tingling zest! I had begun to look abroad in my small world for worthy work and found plenty to do. My unknown friend evidently kept track of my expanding efforts, for he commented and criticized, encouraged and advised freely. There was a humour in his letters that I liked; it leavened them with its sanity and reacted on me most wholesomely, counteracting many of the morbid tendencies and influences of my life. I found myself striving to live up to the writer's ideal of philosophy and ambition, as pictured, often unconsciously, in his letters.

They were an intellectual stimulant as well. To understand them fully I found it necessary to acquaint myself thoroughly with the literature and art, the science and the politics they touched upon. After every letter there was something new for me to hunt out and learn and assimilate, until my old narrow mental attitude had so broadened and deepened, sweeping out into circles of thought I had never known or imagined, that I hardly knew myself.

They had been coming for a year before I began to reply to them. I had often wished to do so—there were so many things I wanted to say and discuss, but it seemed foolish to write letters that could not be sent. One day a letter came that kindled my imagination and stirred my heart and soul so deeply that they insistently demanded answering expression. I sat down at my desk and wrote a full reply to it. Safe in the belief that the mysterious friend to whom it was written would never see it, I wrote with a perfect freedom and a total lack of self-consciousness that I could never have attained otherwise. The writing of that letter gave me a pleasure second only to that which the reading of his brought. For the first time I discovered the delight of revealing my thought unhindered by the conventions. Also, I understood better why the writer of those letters had written them. Doubtless he had enjoyed doing so and was not impelled thereto simply by a purely philanthropic wish to help me.

When my letter was finished I sealed it up and locked it away in my desk with a smile at my middle-aged folly. What, I wondered, would all my sedate, serious friends, my associates of mission and hospital committees think if they knew. Well, everybody has, or should have, a pet nonsense in her life. I did not think mine was any sillier than some others I knew, and to myself I admitted that it was very sweet. I knew if those letters ceased to come all savour would go out of my life.

After that I wrote a reply to every letter I received and kept them all locked up together. It was delightful. I wrote out all my doings and perplexities and hopes and plans and wishes—yes, and my dreams. The secret romance of it all made me look on existence with joyous, contented eyes.

Gradually a change crept over the letters I received. Without ever affording the slightest clue to the identity of their writer they grew more intimate and personal. A subtle, caressing note of tenderness breathed from them and thrilled my heart curiously. I felt as if I were being drawn into the writer's life, admitted into the most sacred recesses of his thoughts and feelings. Yet it was all done so subtly, so delicately, that I was unconscious of the change until I discovered it in reading over the older letters and comparing them with the later ones.

Finally a letter came—my first love letter, and surely never was a love letter received under stranger circumstances. It began abruptly as all the letters had begun, plunging into the middle of the writer's strain of thought without any preface. The first words drove the blood to my heart and then sent it flying hotly all over my face.

> I love you. I must say it at last. Have you not guessed it before? It has trembled on my pen in every line I have written to you—yet I have never dared to shape it into words before. I know not how I dare now. I only know that I must. What a delight to write it out and know that you will read it. Tonight the mood is on me to tell it to you recklessly and lavishly, never pausing to stint or weigh words.

> Sweetheart, I love you—love you—love you—dear true, faithful woman soul, I love you with all the heart of a man.
>
> Ever since I first saw you I have loved you. I can never come to tell you so in spoken words; I can only love you from afar and tell my love under the guise of impersonal friendship. It matters not to you, but it matters more than all else in life to me. I am glad that I love you, dear—glad, glad, glad.

There was much more, for it was a long letter. When I had read it I buried my burning face in my hands, trembling with happiness. This strange confession of love meant so much to me; my heart leaped forth to meet it with answering love. What mattered it that we could never meet—that I could not even guess who my lover was? Somewhere in the world was a love that was mine alone and mine wholly and mine forever. What mattered his name or his station, or the mysterious barrier between us? Spirit leaped to spirit unhindered over the fettering bounds of matter and time. I loved and was beloved. Nothing else mattered.

I wrote my answer to his letter. I wrote it fearlessly and unstintedly. Perhaps I could not have written so freely if the letter were to have been read by him; as it was, I poured out the riches of my love as fully as he had done. I kept nothing back, and across the gulf between us I vowed a faithful and enduring love in response to his.

The next day I went to town on business with my lawyers. Neither of the members of the firm was in when I called, but I was an old client, and one of the clerks showed me into the private office to wait. As I sat down my eyes fell on a folded letter lying on the table beside me. With a shock of surprise I recognized the writing. I could not be mistaken—I should have recognized it anywhere.

The letter was lying by its envelope, so folded that only the middle third of the page was visible. An irresistible impulse swept over me. Before I could reflect that I had no business to touch the letter, that perhaps it was unfair to my unknown friend to seek to discover his identity when he wished to hide it, I had turned the letter over and seen the signature.

I laid it down again and stood up, dizzy, breathless, unseeing. Like a woman in a dream I walked through the outer office and into the street. I must have walked on for blocks before I became conscious of my surroundings. The name I had seen signed to that letter was Alan Fraser!

No doubt the reader has long ago guessed it—has wondered why I had not. The fact remains that I had not. Out of the whole world Alan Fraser was the last man whom I should have suspected to be the writer of those letters—Alan Fraser, my hereditary enemy, who, I had been told, cherished the old feud so faithfully and bitterly, and hated our very name.

And yet I now wondered at my long blindness. No one else could have written those letters—no one but him. I read them over one by one when I reached home and, now that I possessed the key, he revealed himself in every line, expression, thought. And he loved me!

I thought of the old feud and hatred; I thought of my pride and traditions. They seemed like the dust and ashes of outworn things—things to be smiled at and cast aside. I took out all the letters I had written—all except the last one—sealed them up in a parcel and directed it to Alan Fraser. Then, summoning my groom, I bade him ride to Glenellyn with it. His look of amazement almost made me laugh, but after he was gone I felt dizzy and frightened at my own daring.

When the autumn darkness came down I went to my room and dressed as the woman dresses who awaits the one man of all the world. I hardly knew what I hoped or expected, but I was all athrill with a nameless, inexplicable happiness. I admit I looked very eagerly into the mirror when I was done, and I thought that the result was not unpleasing. Beauty had never been mine, but a faint reflection of it came over me in the tremulous flush and excitement of the moment. Then the maid came up to tell me that Alan Fraser was in the library.

I went down with my cold hands tightly clasped behind me. He was standing by the library table, a tall, broad-shouldered man, with the light striking upward on his dark, sensitive face and iron-grey hair. When he saw me he came quickly forward.

"So you know—and you are not angry—your letters told me so much. I have loved you since that day in the beech wood, Isobel—Isobel."

His eyes were kindling into mine. He held my hands in a close, impetuous clasp. His voice was infinitely caressing as he pronounced my name. I had never heard it since Father died—I had never heard it at all so musically and tenderly uttered. My ancestors might have turned in their graves just then—but it mattered not. Living love had driven out dead hatred.

"Isobel," he went on, "there was *one* letter unanswered—the last."

I went to my desk, took out the last letter I had written and gave it to him in silence. While he read it I stood in a shadowy corner and watched him, wondering if life could always be as sweet as this. When he had finished he turned to me and held out his arms. I went to them as a bird to her nest, and with his lips against mine the old feud was blotted out forever.

The Life-Book of Uncle Jesse

Uncle Jesse! The name calls up the vision of him as I saw him so often in those two enchanted summers at Golden Gate; as I saw him the first time, when he stood in the open doorway of the little low-eaved cottage on the harbour shore, welcoming us to our new domicile with the gentle, unconscious courtesy that became him so well. A tall, ungainly figure, somewhat stooped, yet suggestive of great strength and endurance; a clean-shaven old face deeply lined and bronzed; a thick mane of iron-grey hair falling quite to his shoulders; and a pair of remarkably blue, deep-set eyes, which sometimes twinkled and sometimes dreamed, but oftener looked out seaward with a wistful question in them, as of one seeking something precious and lost. I was to learn one day what it was for which Uncle Jesse looked.

It cannot be denied that Uncle Jesse was a homely man. His spare jaws, rugged mouth, and square brow were not fashioned on the lines of beauty, but though at first sight you thought him plain you never thought anything more about it—the spirit shining through that rugged tenement beautified it so wholly.

Uncle Jesse was quite keenly aware of his lack of outward comeliness and lamented it, for he was a passionate worshipper of beauty in everything. He told Mother once that he'd rather like to be made over again and made handsome.

"Folks say I'm good," he remarked whimsically, "but I sometimes wish the Lord had made me only half as good and put the rest of it into looks. But I reckon He knew what He was about, as a good Captain should. Some of us have to be homely or the purty ones—like Miss Mary there—wouldn't show up so well."

I was not in the least pretty but Uncle Jesse was always telling me I was—and I loved him for it. He told the fib so prettily and sincerely that he almost made me believe it for the time being, and I really think he believed it himself. All women were lovely and of good report in his eyes, because of one he had loved. The only time I ever saw Uncle Jesse really angered was when someone in his hearing cast an aspersion on the character of a shore girl. The wretched man who did it fairly cringed when Uncle Jesse turned on him with lightning of eye and thundercloud of brow. At that moment I no longer found it hard to reconcile Uncle Jesse's simple, kindly personality with the wild, adventurous life he had lived.

We went to Golden Gate in the spring. Mother's health had not been good and her doctor recommended sea air and quiet. Uncle James, when he heard it, proposed that we take possession of a small cottage at Golden Gate, to which he had recently fallen heir by the death of an old aunt who had lived in it.

"I haven't been up to see it," he said, "but it is just as Aunt Elizabeth left it and she was the pink of neatness. The key is in the possession of an old sailor living nearby—Jesse Boyd is the name, I think. I imagine you can be very comfortable in it. It is built right on the harbour shore, inside the bar, and it is within five minutes' walk of the outside shore."

Uncle James's offer fitted in very opportunely with our limp family purse, and we straightway betook ourselves to Golden Gate. We telegraphed to Jesse Boyd to have the house opened for us and, one crisp spring day, when a rollicking wind was scudding over the harbour and the dunes, whipping the water into white caps and washing the sandshore with long lines of silvery breakers, we alighted at the little station and walked the half mile to our new home, leaving our goods and chattels to be carted over in the evening by an obliging station agent's boy.

Our first glimpse of Aunt Elizabeth's cottage was a delight to soul and sense; it looked so like a big grey seashell stranded on the shore. Between it and the harbour was only a narrow strip of shingle, and behind it was a gnarled and battered fir wood where the winds were in the habit of harping all sorts of weird and haunting music. Inside, it was to prove even yet more quaint and delightful, with its low, dark-beamed ceilings and square, deep-set windows by which, whether open or shut, sea breezes entered at their own sweet will. The view from our door was magnificent, taking in the big harbour and sweeps of purple hills beyond. The entrance of the harbour gave it its name—a deep, narrow channel between the bar of sand dunes on the one side and a steep, high, frowning red sandstone cliff on the other. We appreciated its significance the first time we saw a splendid golden sunrise flooding it, coming out of the wonderful sea and sky beyond and billowing through that narrow passage in waves of light. Truly, it was a golden gate through which one might sail to "faerie lands forlorn."

As we went along the path to our little house we were agreeably surprised to see a blue spiral of smoke curling up from its big, square chimney, and the next moment Uncle Jesse (we were calling him Uncle Jesse half an hour after we met him, so it seems scarcely worthwhile to begin with anything else) came to the door.

"Welcome, ladies," he said, holding out a big, hard, but scrupulously clean hand. "I thought you'd be feeling a bit tired and hungry, maybe, so when I came over to open up I put on a fire and brewed you up a cup of tea. I just delight in being neighbourly and 'tain't often I have the chance."

We found that Uncle Jesse's "cup of tea" meant a veritable spread. He had aired the little dining room, set out the table daintily with Aunt Elizabeth's china and linen—"knowed jest where to put my hands on 'em—often and often helped old Miss Kennedy wash 'em. We were cronies, her and me. I miss her terrible"—and adorned it with mayflowers which, as we afterwards discovered, he had tramped several miles to gather. There was good bread and butter, "store" biscuits, a dish of tea fit for the gods on high Olympus, and a platter of the most delicious sea trout, done to a turn.

"Thought they'd be tasty after travelling," said Uncle Jesse. "They're fresh as trout can be, ma'am. Two hours ago they was swimming in Johnson's pond yander. I caught 'em—yes, ma'am. It's about all I'm good for now, catching trout and cod occasional. But 'tweren't always so—not by no manner of means. I used to do other things, as you'd admit if you saw my life-book."

I was so hungry and tired that I did not then "rise to the bait" of Uncle Jesse's "life-book." I simply wanted to begin on those trout. Mother insisted that Uncle Jesse sit down and help us eat the repast he had prepared, and he assented without undue coaxing.

"Thank ye kindly. 'Twill be a real treat. I mostly has to eat my meals alone, with the reflection of my ugly old phiz in a looking glass opposite for company. 'Tisn't often I have the chance to sit down with two such sweet purty ladies."

Uncle Jesse's compliments look bald enough on paper, but he paid them with such gracious, gentle deference of tone and look that the woman who received them felt that she was being offered a queen's gift in kingly fashion.

He broke bread with us and from that moment we were all friends together and forever. After we had eaten all we could, we sat at our table for an hour and listened to Uncle Jesse telling us stories of his life.

"If I talk too much you must jest check me," he said seriously, but with a twinkle in his eyes. "When I do get a chance to talk to anyone I'm apt to run on terrible."

He had been a sailor from the time he was ten years old, and some of his adventures had such a marvellous edge that I secretly wondered if Uncle Jesse were not drawing a rather long bow at our credulous expense. But in this, as I found later, I did him injustice. His tales were all literally true, and Uncle Jesse had the gift of the born story-teller, whereby "unhappy, far-off things" can be brought vividly before the hearer and made to live again in all their pristine poignancy.

Mother and I laughed and shivered over Uncle Jesse's tales, and once we found ourselves crying. Uncle Jesse surveyed our tears with pleasure shining out through his face like an illuminating lamp.

"I like to make folks cry that way," he remarked. "It's a compliment. But I can't do justice to the things I've seen and helped do. I've got 'em all jotted down in my life-book but I haven't got the knack of writing them out properly. If I had, I could make a great book, if I had the knack of hitting on just the right words and stringing everything together proper on paper. But I can't. It's in this poor human critter," Uncle Jesse patted his breast sorrowfully, "but he can't get it out."

When Uncle Jesse went home that evening Mother asked him to come often to see us.

"I wonder if you'd give that invitation if you knew how likely I'd be to accept it," he remarked whimsically.

"Which is another way of saying you wonder if I meant it," smiled Mother. "I do, most heartily and sincerely."

"Then I'll come. You'll likely be pestered with me at any hour. And I'd be proud to have you drop over to visit me now and then too. I live on that point yander. Neither me nor my house is worth coming to see. It's only got one room and a loft and a stovepipe sticking out of the roof for a chimney. But I've got a few little things lying around that I picked up in the queer corners I used to be poking my nose into. Mebbe they'd interest you."

Uncle Jesse's "few little things" turned out to be the most interesting collection of curios I had ever seen. His one neat little living room was full of them—beautiful, hideous or quaint as the case might be, and almost all having some weird or exciting story attached.

Mother and I had a beautiful summer at Golden Gate. We lived the life of two children with Uncle Jesse as a playmate. Our housekeeping was of the simplest description and we spent our hours rambling along the shores, reading on the rocks or sailing over the harbour in Uncle Jesse's trim little boat. Every day we loved the simple-souled, true, manly old sailor more and more. He was as refreshing as a sea breeze, as interesting as some ancient chronicle. We never tired of listening to his stories, and his quaint remarks and comments were a continual delight to us. Uncle Jesse was one of those interesting and rare people who, in the picturesque phraseology of the shore folks, "never speak but they say something." The milk of human kindness and the wisdom of the serpent were mingled in Uncle Jesse's composition in delightful proportions.

One day he was absent all day and returned at nightfall.

"Took a tramp back yander." "Back yander" with Uncle Jesse might mean the station hamlet or the city a hundred miles away or any place between—"to carry Mr. Kimball a mess of trout. He likes one occasional and it's all I can do for a kindness he did me once. I stayed all day to talk to him. He likes to talk to me, though he's an eddicated man, because he's one of the folks that's *got* to talk or they're miserable, and he finds listeners scarce 'round here. The folks fight shy of him because they think he's an infidel. He ain't *that* far gone exactly—few men is, I reckon—but he's what you might call a heretic. Heretics are wicked but they're mighty interesting. It's just that they've got sorter lost looking for God, being under the impression that He's hard to find—which He ain't, never. Most of 'em blunder to Him after a while I guess. I don't think listening to Mr. Kimball's arguments is likely to do *me* much harm. Mind you, I believe what I was brought up to believe. It saves a vast of trouble—and back of it all, God is good. The trouble with Mr. Kimball is, he's a leetle *too* clever. He thinks he's bound to live up to his cleverness and that it's smarter to thrash out some new way of getting to heaven than to go by the old track the common, ignorant folks is travelling. But he'll get there sometime all right and then he'll laugh at himself."

Nothing ever seemed to put Uncle Jesse out or depress him in any way.

"I've kind of contracted a habit of enjoying things," he remarked once, when Mother had commented on his invariable cheerfulness. "It's got so chronic that I believe I even enjoy the disagreeable things. It's great fun thinking they can't last. 'Old rheumatiz,' I says, when it grips me hard, 'you've *got* to stop aching sometime. The worse you are the sooner you'll stop, perhaps. I'm bound to get the better of you in the long run, whether in the body or out of the body.'"

Uncle Jesse seldom came to our house without bringing us something, even if it were only a bunch of sweet grass.

"I favour the smell of sweet grass," he said. "It always makes me think of my mother."

"She was fond of it?"

"Not that I knows on. Dunno's she ever saw any sweet grass. No, it's because it has a kind of motherly perfume—not too young, you understand—something kind of seasoned and wholesome and dependable—just like a mother."

Uncle Jesse was a very early riser. He seldom missed a sunrise.

"I've seen all kinds of sunrises come in through that there Gate," he said dreamily one morning when I myself had made a heroic effort at early rising and joined him on the rocks halfway between his house and ours. "I've been all over the world and, take it all in all, I've never seen a finer sight than a summer sunrise out there beyant the Gate. A man can't pick his time for dying, Mary—jest got to go when the Captain gives his sailing orders. But if I could I'd go out when the morning comes in there at the Gate. I've watched it a many times and thought what a thing it would be to pass out through that great white glory to whatever was waiting beyant, on a sea that ain't mapped out on any airthly chart. I think, Mary, I'd find lost Margaret there."

He had already told me the story of "lost Margaret," as he always called her. He rarely spoke of her, but when he did his love for her trembled in every tone—a love that had never grown faint or forgetful. Uncle Jesse was seventy; it was fifty years since lost Margaret had fallen asleep one day in her father's dory and drifted—as was supposed, for nothing was ever known certainly of her fate—across the harbour and out of the Gate, to perish in the black thunder squall that had come up suddenly that long-ago afternoon. But to Uncle Jesse those fifty years were but as yesterday when it is past.

"I walked the shore for months after that," he said sadly, "looking to find her dear, sweet little body, but the sea never gave her back to me. But I'll find her sometime. I wisht I could tell you just how she looked but I can't. I've seen a fine silvery mist hanging over the Gate at sunrise that seemed like her—and then again I've seen a white birch in the woods back yander that made me think of her. She had pale brown hair and a little white face, and long slender fingers like yours, Mary, only browner, for she was a shore girl. Sometimes I wake up in the night and hear the sea calling to me in the old way and it seems as if lost Margaret called in it. And when there's a storm and the waves are sobbing and moaning I hear her lamenting among them. And when they laugh on a gay day it's *her* laugh—lost Margaret's sweet little laugh. The sea took her from me but some day I'll find her, Mary. It can't keep us apart forever."

I had not been long at Golden Gate before I saw Uncle Jesse's "life-book," as he quaintly called it. He needed no coaxing to show it and he proudly gave it to me to read. It was an old leather-bound book filled with the record of his voyages and adventures. I thought what a veritable treasure trove it would be to a writer. Every sentence was a nugget. In itself the book had no literary merit; Uncle Jesse's charm of story-telling failed him when he came to pen and ink; he could only jot down roughly the outlines of his famous tales, and both spelling and grammar were sadly askew. But I felt that if anyone possessing the gift could take that simple record of a brave, adventurous life, reading between the bald lines the tale of dangers staunchly faced and duties manfully done, a wonderful story might be made from it. Pure comedy and thrilling tragedy were both lying hidden in Uncle Jesse's "life-book," waiting for the touch of the magician's hand to waken the laughter and grief and horror of thousands. I thought of my cousin, Robert Kennedy, who juggled with words in a masterly fashion, but complained that he found it hard to create incidents or characters. Here were both ready to his hand, but Robert was in Japan in the interests of his paper.

In the fall, when the harbour lay black and sullen under November skies, Mother and I went back to town, parting with Uncle Jesse regretfully. We wanted him to visit us in town during the winter but he shook his head.

"It's too far away, Mary. If lost Margaret called me I mightn't hear her there. I must be here when my time comes. It can't be very far off now."

I wrote often to Uncle Jesse through the winter and sent him books and magazines. He enjoyed them but he thought—and truly enough—that none of them came up to his life-book for real interest.

"If my life-book could be took and writ by someone that knowed how, it would beat them holler," he wrote in one of his few letters to me.

In the spring we returned joyfully to Golden Gate. It was as golden as ever and the harbour as blue; the winds still rollicked as gaily and sweetly and the breakers boomed outside the bar as of yore. All was unchanged save Uncle Jesse. He had aged greatly and seemed frail and bent. After he had gone home from his first call on us, Mother cried.

"Uncle Jesse will soon be going to seek lost Margaret," she said.

In June Robert came. I took him promptly over to see Uncle Jesse, who was very much excited when he found that Robert was a "real writing man."

"Robert wants to hear some of your stories, Uncle Jesse," I said. "Tell him the one about the captain who went crazy and imagined he was the Flying Dutchman."

This was Uncle Jesse's best story. It was a compound of humour and horror, and though I had heard it several times, I laughed as heartily and shivered as fearsomely over it as Robert did. Other tales followed; Uncle Jesse told how his vessel had been run down by a steamer, how he had been boarded by Malay pirates, how his ship had caught fire, how he had helped a political prisoner escape from a South American republic. He never said a boastful word, but it was impossible to help seeing what a hero the man had been—brave, true, resourceful, unselfish, skilful. He sat there in his poor little room and made those things live again for us. By a lift of the eyebrow, a twist of the lip, a gesture, a word, he painted some whole scene or character so that we saw it as it was.

Finally, he lent Robert his life-book. Robert sat up all night reading it and came to the breakfast table in great excitement.

"Mary, this is a wonderful book. If I could take it and garb it properly—work it up into a systematic whole and string it on the thread of Uncle Jesse's romance of lost Margaret, it would be the novel of the year. Do you suppose he would let me do it?"

"Let you! I think he would be delighted," I answered.

And he was. He was as excited as a schoolboy over it. At last his cherished dream was to be realized and his life-book given to the world.

"We'll collaborate," said Robert. "You will give the soul and I the body. Oh, we'll write a famous book between us, Uncle Jesse. And we'll get right to work."

Uncle Jesse was a happy man that summer. He looked upon the little back room we gave up to Robert for a study as a sacred shrine. Robert talked everything over with Uncle Jesse but would not let him see the manuscript. "You must wait till it is published," he said. "Then you'll get it all at once in its best shape."

Robert delved into the treasures of the life-book and used them freely. He dreamed and brooded over lost Margaret until she became a vivid reality to him and lived in his pages. As the book progressed it took possession of him and he worked at it with feverish eagerness. He let me read the manuscript and criticize it; and the concluding chapter of the book, which the critics later on were pleased to call idyllic, was modelled after my suggestions, so that I felt as if I had a share in it too.

It was autumn when the book was finished. Robert went back to town, but Mother and I decided to stay at Golden Gate all winter. We loved the spot and, besides, I wished to remain for Uncle Jesse's sake. He was failing all the time, and after Robert went and the excitement of the book-making was past, he failed still more rapidly. His tramping expeditions were over and he seldom went out in his boat. Neither did he talk a great deal. He liked to come over and sit silently for hours at our seaward window, looking out wistfully toward the Gate with his swiftly whitening head leaning on his hand. The only keen interest he still had was in Robert's book. He waited and watched impatiently for its publication.

"I want to live till I see it," he said, "just that long—then I'll be ready to go. He said it would be out in the spring—I must hang on till it comes, Mary."

There were times when I doubted sadly if he would "hang on." As the winter wore away he grew frailer and frailer. But ever he looked forward to the coming of spring and "the book," *his* book, transformed and glorified.

One day in young April the book came at last. Uncle Jesse had gone to the post office faithfully every day for a month, expecting it, but this day he was too feeble to go and I went for him. The book was there. It was called simply, *The Life-Book of Jesse Boyd*, and on the title page the names of Robert Kennedy and Jesse Boyd were printed as collaborators.

I shall never forget Uncle Jesse's face as I handed it to him. I came away and left him reading it, oblivious to all else. All night the light burned in his window, and I looked out across the sands to it and pictured the delight of the old man poring over the printed pages whereon his own life was portrayed. I wondered how he would like the ending—the ending I had suggested. I was never to know.

After breakfast I went over to Uncle Jesse's house, taking some little delicacy Mother had cooked for him. It was an exquisite morning, full of delicate spring tints and sounds. The harbour was sparkling and dimpling like a girl, the winds were playing hide and seek roguishly among the stunted firs, and the silver-flashing gulls were soaring over the bar. Beyond the Gate was a shining, wonderful sea.

When I reached the little house on the point I saw the lamp still burning wanly in the window. A quick alarm struck at my heart. Without waiting to knock, I lifted the latch, and entered.

Uncle Jesse was lying on the old sofa by the window, with the book clasped to his heart. His eyes were closed and on his face was a look of the most perfect peace and happiness—the look of one who has long sought and found at last.

We could not know at what hour he had died, but somehow I think he had his wish and went out when the morning came in through the Golden Gate. Out on that shining tide his spirit drifted, over the sunrise sea of pearl and silver, to the haven where lost Margaret waited beyond the storms and calms.

The Little Black Doll

Everybody in the Marshall household was excited on the evening of the concert at the Harbour Light Hotel—everybody, even to Little Joyce, who couldn't go to the concert because there wasn't anybody else to stay with Denise. Perhaps Denise was the most excited of them all—Denise, who was slowly dying of consumption in the Marshall kitchen chamber because there was no other place in the world for her to die in, or anybody to trouble about her. Mrs. Roderick Marshall thought it very good of herself to do so much for Denise. To be sure, Denise was not much bother, and Little Joyce did most of the waiting on her.

At the tea table nothing was talked of but the concert; for was not Madame Laurin, the great French Canadian prima donna, at the hotel, and was she not going to sing? It was the opportunity of a lifetime—the Marshalls would not have missed it for anything. Stately, handsome old Grandmother Marshall was going, and Uncle Roderick and Aunt Isabella, and of course Chrissie, who was always taken everywhere because she was pretty and graceful, and everything that Little Joyce was not.

Little Joyce would have liked to go to the concert, for she was very fond of music; and, besides, she wanted to be able to tell Denise all about it. But when you are shy and homely and thin and awkward, your grandmother never takes you anywhere. At least, such was Little Joyce's belief.

Little Joyce knew quite well that Grandmother Marshall did not like her. She thought it was because she was so plain and awkward—and in part it was. Grandmother Marshall cared very little for granddaughters who did not do her credit. But Little Joyce's mother had married a poor man in the face of her family's disapproval, and then both she and her husband had been inconsiderate enough to die and leave a small orphan without a penny to support her. Grandmother Marshall fed and clothed the child, but who could make anything of such a shy creature with no gifts or graces whatever? Grandmother Marshall had no intention of trying. Chrissie, the golden-haired and pink-cheeked, was Grandmother Marshall's pet.

Little Joyce knew this. She did not envy Chrissie but, oh, how she wished Grandmother Marshall would love her a little, too! Nobody loved her but Denise and the little black doll. And Little Joyce was beginning to understand that Denise would not be in the kitchen chamber very much longer, and the little black doll couldn't *tell* you she loved you—although she did, of course. Little Joyce had no doubt at all on this point.

Little Joyce sighed so deeply over this thought that Uncle Roderick smiled at her. Uncle Roderick *did* smile at her sometimes.

"What is the matter, Little Joyce?" he asked.

"I was thinking about my black doll," said Little Joyce timidly.

"Ah, your black doll. If Madame Laurin were to see it, she'd likely want it. She makes a hobby of collecting dolls all over the world, but I doubt if she has in her collection a doll that served to amuse a little girl four thousand years ago in the court of the Pharaohs."

"I think Joyce's black doll is very ugly," said Chrissie. "My wax doll with the yellow hair is ever so much prettier."

"My black doll isn't ugly," cried Little Joyce indignantly. She could endure to be called ugly herself, but she could not bear to have her darling black doll called ugly. In her excitement she upset her cup of tea over the tablecloth. Aunt Isabella looked angry, and Grandmother Marshall said sharply: "Joyce, leave the table. You grow more awkward and careless every day."

Little Joyce, on the verge of tears, crept away and went up the kitchen stairs to Denise to be comforted. But Denise herself had been crying. She lay on her little bed by the low window, where the glow of the sunset was coming in; her hollow cheeks were scarlet with fever.

"Oh! I want so much to hear Madame Laurin sing," she sobbed. "I feel lak I could die easier if I hear her sing just one leetle song. She is Frenchwoman, too, and she sing all de ole French songs—de ole songs my mudder sing long 'go. Oh! I so want to hear Madame Laurin sing."

"But you can't, dear Denise," said Little Joyce very softly, stroking Denise's hot forehead with her cool, slender hand. Little Joyce had very pretty hands, only nobody had ever noticed them. "You are not strong enough to go to the concert. I'll sing for you, if you like. Of course, I can't sing very well, but I'll do my best."

"You sing lak a sweet bird, but you are not Madame Laurin," said Denise restlessly. "It is de great Madame I want to hear. I haf not long to live. Oh, I know, Leetle Joyce—I know what de doctor look lak—and I want to hear Madame Laurin sing 'fore I die. I know it is impossible—but I long for it so—just one leetle song."

Denise put her thin hands over her face and sobbed again. Little Joyce went and sat down by the window, looking out into the white birches. Her heart ached bitterly. Dear Denise was going to die soon—oh, very soon! Little Joyce, wise and knowing beyond her years, saw that. And Denise wanted to hear Madame Laurin sing. It seemed a foolish thing to think of, but Little Joyce thought hard about it; and when she had finished thinking, she got her little black doll and took it to bed with her, and there she cried herself to sleep.

At the breakfast table next morning the Marshalls talked about the concert and the wonderful Madame Laurin. Little Joyce listened in her usual silence; her crying the night before had not improved her looks any. Never, thought handsome

Grandmother Marshall, had she appeared so sallow and homely. Really, Grandmother Marshall could not have the patience to look at her. She decided that she would not take Joyce driving with her and Chrissie that afternoon, as she had thought of, after all.

In the forenoon it was discovered that Denise was much worse, and the doctor was sent for. He came, and shook his head, that being really all he could do under the circumstances. When he went away, he was waylaid at the back door by a small gypsy with big, black, serious eyes and long black hair.

"Is Denise going to die?" Little Joyce asked in the blunt, straightforward fashion Grandmother Marshall found so trying.

The doctor looked at her from under his shaggy brows and decided that here was one of the people to whom you might as well tell the truth first as last, because they are bound to have it.

"Yes," he said.

"Soon?"

"Very soon, I'm afraid. In a few days at most."

"Thank you," said Little Joyce gravely.

She went to her room and did something with the black doll. She did not cry, but if you could have seen her face you would have wished she would cry.

After dinner Grandmother Marshall and Chrissie drove away, and Uncle Roderick and Aunt Isabella went away, too. Little Joyce crept up to the kitchen chamber. Denise was lying in an uneasy sleep, with tear stains on her face. Then Little Joyce tiptoed down and sped away to the hotel.

She did not know just what she would say or do when she got there, but she thought hard all the way to the end of the shore road. When she came out to the shore, a lady was sitting alone on a big rock—a lady with a dark, beautiful face and wonderful eyes. Little Joyce stopped before her and looked at her meditatively. Perhaps it would be well to ask advice of this lady.

"If you please," said Little Joyce, who was never shy with strangers, for whose opinion she didn't care at all, "I want to see Madame Laurin at the hotel and ask her to do me a very great favour. Will you tell me the best way to go about seeing her? I shall be much obliged to you."

"What is the favour you want to ask of Madame Laurin?" inquired the lady, smiling.

"I want to ask her if she will come and sing for Denise before she dies—before Denise dies, I mean. Denise is our French girl, and the doctor says she cannot live very long, and she wishes with all her heart to hear Madame Laurin sing. It is very bitter, you know, to be dying and want something very much and not be able to get it."

"Do you think Madame Laurin will go?" asked the lady.

"I don't know. I am going to offer her my little black doll. If she will not come for that, there is nothing else I can do."

A flash of interest lighted up the lady's brown eyes. She bent forward.

"Is it your doll you have in that box? Will you let me see it?"

Little Joyce nodded. Mutely she opened the box and took out the black doll. The lady gave an exclamation of amazed delight and almost snatched it from Little Joyce. It was a very peculiar little doll indeed, carved out of some black polpolished wood.

"Child, where in the world did you get this?" she cried.

"Father got it out of a grave in Egypt," said Little Joyce. "It was buried with the mummy of a little girl who lived four thousand years ago, Uncle Roderick says. She must have loved her doll very much to have had it buried with her, mustn't she? But she could not have loved it any more than I do."

"And yet you are going to give it away?" said the lady, looking at her keenly.

"For Denise's sake," explained Little Joyce. "I would do anything for Denise because I love her and she loves me. When the only person in the world who loves you is going to die, there is nothing you would not do for her if you could. Denise was so good to me before she took sick. She used to kiss me and play with me and make little cakes for me and tell me beautiful stories."

The lady put the little black doll back in the box. Then she stood up and held out her hand.

"Come," she said. "I am Madame Laurin, and I shall go and sing for Denise."

Little Joyce piloted Madame Laurin home and into the kitchen and up the back stairs to the kitchen chamber—a proceeding which would have filled Aunt Isabella with horror if she had known. But Madame Laurin did not seem to mind, and Little Joyce never thought about it at all. It was Little Joyce's awkward, unMarshall-like fashion to go to a place by the shortest way there, even if it was up the kitchen stairs.

Madame Laurin stood in the bare little room and looked pityingly at the wasted, wistful face on the pillow.

"This is Madame Laurin, and she is going to sing for you, Denise," whispered Little Joyce.

Denise's face lighted up, and she clasped her hands.

"If you please," she said faintly. "A French song, Madame—de ole French song dey sing long 'go."

Then did Madame Laurin sing. Never had that kitchen chamber been so filled with glorious melody. Song after song she sang—the old folklore songs of the *habitant*, the songs perhaps that Evangeline listened to in her childhood.

Little Joyce knelt by the bed, her eyes on the singer like one entranced. Denise lay with her face full of joy and rapture—such joy and rapture! Little Joyce did not regret the sacrifice of her black doll—never could regret it, as long as she remembered Denise's look.

"T'ank you, Madame," said Denise brokenly, when Madame ceased. "Dat was so beautiful—de angel, dey cannot sing more sweet. I love music so much, Madame. Leetle Joyce, she sing to me often and often—she sing sweet, but not lak you—oh, not lak you."

"Little Joyce must sing for me," said Madame, smiling, as she sat down by the window. "I always like to hear fresh, childish voices. Will you, Little Joyce?"

"Oh, yes." Little Joyce was quite unembarrassed and perfectly willing to do anything she could for this wonderful woman who had brought that look to Denise's face. "I will sing as well as I can for you. Of course, I can't sing very well and I don't know anything but hymns. I always sing hymns for Denise, although she is a Catholic and the hymns are Protestant. But her priest told her it was all right, because all music was of God. Denise's priest is a very nice man, and I like him. He thought my little black doll—*your* little black doll—was splendid. I'll sing 'Lead, Kindly Light.' That is Denise's favourite hymn."

Then Little Joyce, slipping her hand into Denise's, began to sing. At the first note Madame Laurin, who had been gazing out of the window with a rather listless smile, turned quickly and looked at Little Joyce with amazed eyes. Delight followed amazement, and when Little Joyce had finished, the great Madame rose impulsively, her face and eyes glowing, stepped swiftly to Little Joyce and took the thin dark face between her gemmed hands.

"Child, do you know what a wonderful voice you have—what a marvellous voice? It is—it is—I never heard such a voice in a child of your age. Mine was nothing to it—nothing at all. You will be a great singer some day—far greater than I—yes. But you must have the training. Where are your parents? I must see them."

"I have no parents," said the bewildered Little Joyce. "I belong to Grandmother Marshall, and she is out driving."

"Then I shall wait until your Grandmother Marshall comes home from her drive," said Madame Laurin decidedly.

Half an hour later a very much surprised old lady was listening to Madame Laurin's enthusiastic statements.

"How is it I have never heard you sing, if you can sing so well?" asked Grandmother Marshall, looking at Little Joyce with something in her eyes that had never been in them before—as Little Joyce instantly felt to the core of her sensitive soul. But Little Joyce hung her head. It had never occurred to her to sing in Grandmother Marshall's presence.

"This child must be trained by-and-by," said Madame Laurin. "If you cannot afford it, Mrs. Marshall, I will see to it. Such a voice must not be wasted."

"Thank you, Madame Laurin," said Grandmother Marshall with a gracious dignity, "but I am quite able to give my granddaughter all the necessary advantages for the development of her gift. And I thank you very much for telling me of it."

Madame Laurin bent and kissed Little Joyce's brown cheek.

"Little gypsy, good-by. But come every day to this hotel to see me. And next summer I shall be back. I like you—because some day you will be a great singer and because today you are a loving, unselfish baby."

"You have forgotten the little black doll, Madame," said Little Joyce gravely.

Madame threw up her hands, laughing. "No, no, I shall not take your little black doll of the four thousand years. Keep it for a mascot. A great singer always needs a mascot. But do not, I command you, take it out of the box till I am gone, for if I were to see it again, I might not be able to resist the temptation. Some day I shall show you *my* dolls, but there is not such a gem among them."

When Madame Laurin had gone, Grandmother Marshall looked at Little Joyce.

"Come to my room, Joyce. I want to see if we cannot find a more becoming way of arranging your hair. It has grown so thick and long. I had no idea how thick and long. Yes, we must certainly find a better way than that stiff braid. Come!"

Little Joyce, taking Grandmother Marshall's extended hand, felt very happy. She realized that this strange, stately old lady, who never liked little girls unless they were pretty or graceful or clever, was beginning to love her at last.

The Man on the Train

When the telegram came from William George, Grandma Sheldon was all alone with Cyrus and Louise. And Cyrus and Louise, aged respectively twelve and eleven, were not very much good, Grandma thought, when it came to advising what was to be done. Grandma was "all in a flutter, dear, oh dear," as she said.

The telegram said that Delia, William George's wife, was seriously ill down at Green Village, and William George wanted Samuel to bring Grandma down immediately. Delia had always thought there was nobody like Grandma when it came to nursing sick folks.

But Samuel and his wife were both away—had been away for two days and intended to be away for five more. They had driven to Sinclair, twenty miles away, to visit with Mrs. Samuel's folks for a week.

"Dear, oh dear, what shall I do?" said Grandma.

"Go right to Green Village on the evening train," said Cyrus briskly.

"Dear, oh dear, and leave you two alone!" cried Grandma.

"Louise and I will do very well until tomorrow," said Cyrus sturdily. "We will send word to Sinclair by today's mail, and Father and Mother will be home by tomorrow night."

"But I never was on the cars in my life," protested Grandma nervously. "I'm—I'm so frightened to start alone. And you never know what kind of people you may meet on the train."

"You'll be all right, Grandma. I'll drive you to the station, get you your ticket, and put you on the train. Then you'll have nothing to do until the train gets to Green Village. I'll send a telegram to Uncle William George to meet you."

"I shall fall and break my neck getting off the train," said Grandma pessimistically. But she was wondering at the same time whether she had better take the black valise or the yellow, and whether William George would be likely to have plenty of flaxseed in the house.

It was six miles to the station, and Cyrus drove Grandma over in time to catch a train that reached Green Village at nine o'clock.

"Dear, oh dear," said Grandma, "what if William George's folks ain't there to meet me? It's all very well, Cyrus, to say that they will be there, but you don't know. And it's all very well to say not to be nervous because everything will be all right. If you were seventy-five years old and had never set foot on the cars in your life you'd be nervous too, and you can't be sure that everything will be all right. You never know what sort of people you'll meet on the train. I may get on the wrong train or lose my ticket or get carried past Green Village or get my pocket picked. Well, no, I won't do that, for not one cent will I carry with me. You shall take back home all the money you don't need to get my ticket. Then I shall be easier in my mind. Dear, oh dear, if it wasn't that Delia is so seriously ill I wouldn't go one step."

"Oh, you'll be all right, Grandma," assured Cyrus.

He got Grandma's ticket for her and Grandma tied it up in the corner of her handkerchief. Then the train came in and Grandma, clinging closely to Cyrus, was put on it. Cyrus found a comfortable seat for her and shook hands cheerily.

"Good-bye, Grandma. Don't be frightened. Here's the *Weekly Argus*. I got it at the store. You may like to look over it."

Then Cyrus was gone, and in a minute the station house and platform began to glide away.

Dear, oh dear, what has happened to it? thought Grandma in dismay. The next moment she exclaimed aloud, "Why, it's us that's moving, not it!"

Some of the passengers smiled pleasantly at Grandma. She was the variety of old lady at which people do smile pleasantly; a grandma with round, pink cheeks, soft, brown eyes, and lovely snow-white curls is a nice person to look at wherever she is found.

After a while Grandma, to her amazement, discovered that she liked riding on the cars. It was not at all the disagreeable experience she had expected it to be. Why, she was just as comfortable as if she were in her own rocking chair at home! And there was such a lot of people to look at, and many of the ladies had such beautiful dresses and hats. After all, the people you met on a train, thought Grandma, are surprisingly like the people you meet off it. If it had not been for wondering how she would get off at Green Village, Grandma would have enjoyed herself thoroughly.

Four or five stations farther on the train halted at a lonely-looking place consisting of the station house and a barn, surrounded by scrub woods and blueberry barrens. One passenger got on and, finding only one vacant seat in the crowded car, sat right down beside Grandma Sheldon.

Grandma Sheldon held her breath while she looked him over. Was he a pickpocket? He didn't appear like one, but you can never be sure of the people you meet on the train. Grandma remembered with a sigh of thankfulness that she had no money.

Besides, he seemed really very respectable and harmless. He was quietly dressed in a suit of dark-blue serge with a black overcoat. He wore his hat well down on his forehead and was clean shaven. His hair was very black, but his eyes were blue—nice eyes, Grandma thought. She always felt great confidence in a man who had bright, open, blue eyes. Grandpa Sheldon, who had died so long ago, four years after their marriage, had had bright blue eyes.

To be sure, he had fair hair, reflected Grandma. It's real odd to see such black hair with such light blue eyes. Well, he's real nice looking, and I don't believe there's a mite of harm in him.

The early autumn night had now fallen and Grandma could not amuse herself by watching the scenery. She bethought herself of the paper Cyrus had given her and took it out of her basket. It was an old weekly a fortnight back. On the first page was a long account of a murder case with scare heads, and into this Grandma plunged eagerly. Sweet old Grandma Sheldon, who would not have harmed a fly and hated to see even a mousetrap set, simply revelled in the newspaper accounts of murders. And the more shocking and cold-blooded they were, the more eagerly did Grandma read of them.

This murder story was particularly good from Grandma's point of view; it was full of "thrills." A man had been shot down, apparently in cold blood, and his supposed murderer was still at large and had eluded all the efforts of justice to capture him. His name was Mark Hartwell, and he was described as a tall, fair man, with full auburn beard and curly, light hair.

"What a shocking thing!" said Grandma aloud.

Her companion looked at her with a kindly, amused smile.

"What is it?" he asked.

"Why, this murder at Charlotteville," answered Grandma, forgetting, in her excitement, that it was not safe to talk to people you meet on the train. "It just makes my blood run cold to read about it. And to think that the man who did it is still around the country somewhere—plotting other murders, I haven't a doubt. What is the good of the police?"

"They're dull fellows," agreed the dark man.

"But I don't envy that man his conscience," said Grandma solemnly—and somewhat inconsistently, in view of her statement about the other murders that were being plotted. "What must a man feel like who has the blood of a fellow creature on his hands? Depend upon it, his punishment has begun already, caught or not."

"That is true," said the dark man quietly.

"Such a good-looking man too," said Grandma, looking wistfully at the murderer's picture. "It doesn't seem possible that he can have killed anybody. But the paper says there isn't a doubt."

"He is probably guilty," said the dark man, "but nothing is known of his provocation. The affair may not have been so cold-blooded as the accounts state. Those newspaper fellows never err on the side of undercolouring."

"I really think," said Grandma slowly, "that I would like to see a murderer—just one. Whenever I say anything like that, Adelaide—Adelaide is Samuel's wife—looks at me as if she thought there was something wrong about me. And perhaps there is, but I do, all the same. When I was a little girl, there was a man in our settlement who was suspected of poisoning his wife. She died very suddenly. I used to look at him with such interest. But it wasn't satisfactory, because you could never be sure whether he was really guilty or not. I never could believe that he was, because he was such a nice man in some ways and so good and kind to children. I don't believe a man who was bad enough to poison his wife could have any good in him."

"Perhaps not," agreed the dark man. He had absent-mindedly folded up Grandma's old copy of the *Argus* and put it in his pocket. Grandma did not like to ask him for it, although she would have liked to see if there were any more murder stories in it. Besides, just at that moment the conductor came around for tickets.

Grandma looked in the basket for her handkerchief. It was not there. She looked on the floor and on the seat and under the seat. It was not there. She stood up and shook herself—still no handkerchief.

"Dear, oh dear," exclaimed Grandma wildly, "I've lost my ticket—I always knew I would—I told Cyrus I would! Oh, where can it be?"

The conductor scowled unsympathetically. The dark man got up and helped Grandma search, but no ticket was to be found.

"You'll have to pay the money then, and something extra," said the conductor gruffly.

"I can't—I haven't a cent of money," wailed Grandma. "I gave it all to Cyrus because I was afraid my pocket would be picked. Oh, what shall I do?"

"Don't worry. I'll make it all right," said the dark man. He took out his pocketbook and handed the conductor a bill. That functionary grumblingly made the change and marched onward, while Grandma, pale with excitement and relief, sank back into her seat.

"I can't tell you how much I am obliged to you, sir," she said tremulously. "I don't know what I should have done. Would he have put me off right here in the snow?"

"I hardly think he would have gone to such lengths," said the dark man with a smile. "But he's a cranky, disobliging fellow enough—I know him of old. And you must not feel overly grateful to me. I am glad of the opportunity to help you. I had an old grandmother myself once," he added with a sigh.

"You must give me your name and address, of course," said Grandma, "and my son—Samuel Sheldon of Midverne—will see that the money is returned to you. Well, this is a lesson to me! I'll never trust myself on a train again, and all I wish is that I was safely off this one. This fuss has worked my nerves all up again."

"Don't worry, Grandma. I'll see you safely off the train when we get to Green Village."

"Will you, though? Will you, now?" said Grandma eagerly. "I'll be real easy in my mind, then," she added with a returning smile. "I feel as if I could trust you for anything—and I'm a real suspicious person too."

They had a long talk after that—or, rather, Grandma talked and the dark man listened and smiled. She told him all about William George and Delia and their baby and about Samuel and Adelaide and Cyrus and Louise and the three cats and the parrot. He seemed to enjoy her accounts of them too.

When they reached Green Village station he gathered up Grandma's parcels and helped her tenderly off the train.

"Anybody here to meet Mrs. Sheldon?" he asked of the station master.

The latter shook his head. "Don't think so. Haven't seen anybody here to meet anybody tonight."

"Dear, oh dear," said poor Grandma. "This is just what I expected. They've never got Cyrus's telegram. Well, I might have known it. What shall I do?"

"How far is it to your son's?" asked the dark man.

"Only half a mile—just over the hill there. But I'll never get there alone this dark night."

"Of course not. But I'll go with you. The road is good—we'll do finely."

"But that train won't wait for you," gasped Grandma, half in protest.

"It doesn't matter. The Starmont freight passes here in half an hour and I'll go on her. Come along, Grandma."

"Oh, but you're good," said Grandma. "Some woman is proud to have you for a son."

The man did not answer. He had not answered any of the personal remarks Grandma had made to him in her conversation.

They were not long in reaching William George Sheldon's house, for the village road was good and Grandma was smart on her feet. She was welcomed with eagerness and surprise.

"To think that there was no one to meet you!" exclaimed William George. "But I never dreamed of your coming by train, knowing how you were set against it. Telegram? No, I got no telegram. S'pose Cyrus forgot to send it. I'm most heartily obliged to you, sir, for looking after my mother so kindly."

"It was a pleasure," said the dark man courteously. He had taken off his hat, and they saw a curious scar, shaped like a large, red butterfly, high up on his forehead under his hair. "I am delighted to have been of any assistance to her."

He would not wait for supper—the next train would be in and he must not miss it.

"There are people looking for me," he said with his curious smile. "They will be much disappointed if they do not find me."

He had gone, and the whistle of the Starmont freight had blown before Grandma remembered that he had not given her his name and address.

"Dear, oh dear, how are we ever going to send that money to him?" she exclaimed. "And he so nice and goodhearted!"

Grandma worried over this for a week in the intervals of looking after Delia. One day William George came in with a large city daily in his hands. He looked curiously at Grandma and then showed her the front-page picture of a man, clean-shaven, with an oddly shaped scar high up on his forehead.

"Did you ever see that man, Mother?" he asked.

"Of course I did," said Grandma excitedly. "Why, it's the man I met on the train. Who is he? What is his name? Now, we'll know where to send—"

"That is Mark Hartwell, who shot Amos Gray at Charlotteville three weeks ago," said William George quietly.

Grandma looked at him blankly for a moment.

"It couldn't be," she gasped at last. "That man a murderer! I'll never believe it!"

"It's true enough, Mother. The whole story is here. He had shaved his beard and dyed his hair and came near getting clear out of the country. They were on his trail the day he came down in the train with you and lost it because of his getting off to bring you here. His disguise was so perfect that there was little fear of his being recognized so long as he hid that scar. But it was seen in Montreal and he was run to earth there. He has made a full confession."

"I don't care," cried Grandma valiantly. "I'll never believe he was all bad—a man who would do what he did for a poor old woman like me, when he was flying for his life too. No, no, there was good in him even if he did kill that man. And I'm sure he must feel terrible over it."

In this view Grandma persisted. She never would say or listen to a word against Mark Hartwell, and she had only pity for him whom everyone else condemned. With her own trembling hands she wrote him a letter to accompany the money Samuel sent before Hartwell was taken to the penitentiary for life. She thanked him again for his kindness to her and assured him that she knew he was sorry for what he had done and that she would pray for him every night of her life. Mark Hartwell had been hard and defiant enough, but the prison officials told that he cried like a child over Grandma Sheldon's little letter.

"There's nobody all bad," says Grandma when she relates the story. "I used to believe a murderer must be, but I know better now. I think of that poor man often and often. He was so kind and gentle to me—he must have been a good boy once. I write him a letter every Christmas and I send him tracts and papers. He's my own little charity. But I've never been on the cars since and I never will be again. You never can tell what will happen to you or what sort of people you'll meet if you trust yourself on a train."

The Romance of Jedediah

Jedediah was not a name that savoured of romance. His last name was Crane, which is little better. And it would be no use to call this story "Mattie Adams's Romance" because Mattie Adams is not a romantic name either. But names have really nothing to do with romance. The most exciting and tragic affair I ever knew was between a man named Silas Putdammer and a woman named Kezia Cullen—which has nothing to do with the present story.

Jedediah, to all outward seeming, did not appear to be any more romantic than his name. He looked distinctly commonplace as he rode comfortably along the winding country road that was dreaming in the haze and sunshine of a midsummer afternoon. He was perched on the seat of a bright red pedlar's wagon, above and behind a dusty, ambling, red pony of that peculiar gait and appearance pertaining to the ponies of country pedlars—a certain placid, unhasting leanness, as of a nag that has encountered troubles of his own and has lived them down by sheer patience and staying power. From the bright red wagon proceeded a certain metallic rumbling and clinking as it bowled along, and two or three nests of tin pans on its flat rope-encircled top flashed back the light so dazzlingly that Jedediah seemed the beaming sun of a little planetary system all his own. A new broom sticking up aggressively at each of the four corners gave the wagon a resemblance to a triumphal chariot.

Jedediah himself had not been in the tin-peddling business long enough to acquire the apologetic, out-at-elbows appearance which distinguishes a tin pedlar from other kinds of pedlars. In fact, this was his maiden venture in this line; hence he still looked plump and self-respecting. He had a round red face under his plug hat, twinkling blue eyes, and a little pursed-up mouth, the shape of which was partly due to nature and partly to much whistling. Jedediah's pudgy body was clothed in a suit of large, light checks, and he wore a bright pink necktie and an amethyst pin. Will I still be believed when I assert that, in spite of all this, Jedediah was full of, and bubbling over with, romance?

Romance cares not for appearances and apparently delights in contradictions. The homely shambling man you pass unnoticed on the street may have, tucked away in his past, a story more exciting and thrilling than anything you have ever read in fiction. So it was, in a measure, with Jedediah; poor, unknown to fame, afflicted with a double chin and bald spot, reduced to driving a tin-wagon for a living, he yet had his romance and he was still romantic.

As Jedediah rode through Amberley he looked about him with interest. He knew it well, although it was fifteen years since he had seen it. He had been born and brought up in Amberley; he had left it at the age of twenty-five to make his fortune. But Amberley was Amberley still. Jedediah found it hard to believe that it or himself was fifteen years older.

"There's the Stanton place," he said. "Charlie has painted the house yellow—it used to be white; and Bob Hollman has cut the trees down behind the blacksmith forge. Bob never had any poetry in his soul—no romance, as you might say. He was what you might call a plodder—you might call him that. Get up, my nag, get up. There's the old Harkness place—seems to be spruced up considerable. Folks used to say if ye wanted to see how the world looked the morning after the flood just go into George Harkness's barn-yard on a rainy day. The pond and the old hills ain't changed any. Get up, my nag, get up. There's the Adams homestead. Do I really behold it again?"

Jedediah thought the moment deliciously romantic. He revelled in it and, to match his exhilarated mood, he touched the pony with his whip and went clinking and glittering down the hill under the poplars at a dashing rate. He had not intended to offer his wares in Amberley that day. He meant to break the ice in Occidental, the village beyond. But he could not pass the Adams place. When he came to the open gate he turned in under the willows and drove down the wide, shady lane, girt on both sides with a trim white paling smothered in lavish sweet-briar bushes that were gay with bloom. Jedediah's heart was beating furiously under his checks.

"What a fool you are, Jed Crane," he told himself. "You used to be a young fool, and now you're an old one. Sad, that! Get up, my nag, get up. It's a poor lookout for a man of your years, Jed. Don't get excited. It ain't the least likely that Mattie Adams is here yet. She's married and gone years ago, no doubt. It's probable there's no Adamses here at all now. But it's romantic, yes, it's romantic. It's splendid. Get up, my nag, get up."

The Adams place itself was not unromantic. The house was a large, old-fashioned white one, with green shutters and a front porch with Grecian columns. These were thought very elegant in Amberley. Mrs. Carmody said they gave a house such a classical air. In this instance the classical effect was somewhat smothered in honeysuckle, which rioted over the whole porch and hung in pale yellow, fragrant festoons over the rows of potted scarlet geraniums that flanked the green steps. Beyond the house a low-boughed orchard covered the slope between it and the main road, and behind it there was a revel of colour betokening a flower garden.

Jedediah climbed down from his lofty seat and walked dubiously to a side door that looked more friendly, despite its prim screen, than the classical front porch. As he drew near he saw a woman sitting behind the screen—a woman who rose as he approached and opened the door. Jedediah's heart had been beating a wild tattoo as he crossed the yard. It now stopped altogether—at least he declared in later years it did.

The woman was Mattie Adams—Mattie Adams fifteen years older than when he had seen her last, plumper, rosier, somewhat broader-faced, but still unmistakably Mattie Adams. Jedediah felt that the situation was delicious.

"Mattie," he said, holding out his hand.

"Why, Jed, how are you?" said Mattie, as if they had parted the week before. It had always taken a great deal to disturb Mattie. Whatever happened she was calm. Even an old lover, and the only one she had ever possessed at that, dropping, so to speak, from the skies, after fifteen years' disappearance, did not ruffle her placidity.

"I didn't suppose you'd know me, Mattie," said Jedediah, still holding her hand foolishly.

"I knew you the minute I set eyes on you," returned Mattie. "You're some fatter and older—like myself—but you're Jed still. Where have you been all these years?"

"Pretty near everywhere, Mattie—pretty near everywhere. And ye see what it's come to—here I be driving a tin-wagon for Boone Brothers. Business is business—don't you want to buy some new tinware?"

To himself, Jed thought it was romantic, asking a woman whom he had loved all his life to buy tins on the occasion of their first meeting after fifteen years' separation.

"I don't know but I do want a quart measure," said Mattie, in her sweet, unchanged voice, "but all in good time. You must stay and have tea with me, Jed. I'm all alone now—Mother and Father have gone. Unhitch your horse and put him in the third stall in the stable."

Jed hesitated.

"I ought to be getting on, I s'pose," he said wistfully. "I hain't done much today—"

"You must stay to tea," interrupted Mattie. "Why, Jed, there's ever so much to tell and ask. And we can't stand here in the yard and talk. Look at Selena. There she is, watching us from the kitchen window. She'll watch as long as we stand here."

Jed swung himself around. Over the little valley below the Adams homestead was a steep, treeless hill, and on its crest was perched a bare farmhouse with windows stuck lavishly all over it. At one of them a long, pale face was visible.

"Has Selena been pasted up at that window ever since the last time we stood here and talked, Mattie?" asked Jed, half resentfully, half amusedly. It was characteristic of Mattie to laugh first at the question, and then blush over the memory it revived.

"Most of the time, I guess," she said shortly. "But come—come in. I never could talk under Selena's eyes, even if they were four hundred yards away."

Jed went in and stayed to tea. The old Adams pantry had not failed, nor apparently the Adams skill in cooking. After tea Jed hung around till sunset and drove away with a warm invitation from Mattie to call every time his rounds took him through Amberley. As he went, Selena's face appeared at the window of the house over the valley.

When he had gone Mattie went around to the classical porch and sat herself down under the honeysuckle festoons that dangled above her smooth braids of fawn-coloured hair. She knew Selena would be down posthaste presently, agog with curiosity to find out who the pedlar was whom Mattie had delighted to honour with an invitation to tea. Mattie preferred to meet Selena out of doors. It was easier to thrust and parry there. Meanwhile, she wanted to think over things.

Fifteen years before Jedediah Crane had been Mattie Adams's beau. Jedediah was romantic even then, but, as he was a slim young fellow at the time, with an abundance of fair, curly hair and innocent blue eyes, his romance was rather an attraction than not. At least the then young and pretty Mattie had found it so.

The Adamses looked with no favour on the match. They were a thrifty, well-to-do folk. As for the Cranes—well, they were lazy and shiftless, for the most part. It would be a *mésalliance* for an Adams to marry a Crane. Still, it would doubtless have happened—for Mattie, though a meek-looking damsel, had a mind of her own—had it not been for Selena Ford, Mattie's older sister.

Selena, people said, had married James Ford for no other reason than that his house commanded a view of nearly every dooryard in Amberley. This may or may not have been sheer malice. Certainly nothing that went on in the Adams yard escaped Selena.

She watched Mattie and Jed in the moonlight one night. She saw Jed kiss Mattie. It was the first time he had ever done so—and the last, poor fellow. For Selena swooped down on her parents the next day. Such a storm did she brew up that Mattie was forbidden to speak to Jed again. Selena herself gave Jed a piece of her mind. Jed usually was not afflicted with undue sensitiveness. But he had some slumbering pride at the basis of his character and it was very stubborn when roused. Selena roused it. Jed vowed he would never creep and crawl at the feet of the Adamses, and he went west forthwith, determined, as aforesaid, to make his fortune and hurl Selena's scorn back in her face.

And now he had come home, driving a tin-wagon. Mattie smiled to think of it. She bore Jed no ill will for his failure. She felt sorry for him and inclined to think that fate had used him hardly—fate and Selena together. Mattie had never had another beau. People thought she was engaged to Jed Crane until her time for beaus went by. Mattie did not mind; she had never liked anybody so well as Jed. To be sure, she had not thought of him for years. It was strange he should come back like this—"romantic," as he said himself.

Mattie's reverie was interrupted by Selena. Angular, pale-eyed Mrs. Ford was as unlike the plump, rosy Mattie as a sister could be. Perhaps her chronic curiosity, which would not let her rest, was accountable for her excessive leanness.

"Who was that pedlar that was here this afternoon, Mattie?" she demanded as soon as she arrived.

Mattie smiled. "Jed Crane," she said. "He's home from the West and driving a tin-wagon for the Boones."

Selena gave a little gasp. She sat down on the lowest step and untied her bonnet strings.

"Mattie Adams! And you kept him hanging about the whole afternoon."

"Why not?" said Mattie wickedly. She liked to alarm Selena. "Jed and I were always beaus, you know."

"Mattie Adams! You don't mean to say you're going to make a fool of yourself over Jed Crane again? A woman of your age!"

"Don't get excited, Selena," implored Mattie. In the old days Selena could cow her, but that time was past. "I never saw the like of you for getting stirred up over nothing."

"I'm not excited. I'm perfectly calm. But I might well be excited over your folly, Mattie Adams. The idea of your taking up again with old Jed Crane!"

"He's fifteen years younger than Jim," said Mattie, giving thrust for thrust.

When Selena had come over Mattie had not the slightest idea of resuming her former relationship with the romantic Jedediah. She had merely shown him kindness for old friendship's sake. But so well did the unconscious Selena work in Jed's behalf that when she flounced off home in a pet Mattie was resolved that she would take Jed back if he wanted to come. She wasn't going to put up with Selena's everlasting interference. She would show her that she was independent.

When a week had passed Jed came again. He sold Mattie a stew-pan and he would not go in to tea this time, but they stood and talked in the yard for the best part of an hour, while Selena glared at them from her kitchen window. Their conversation was most innocent and harmless, being mainly gossip about what had come and gone during Jed's exile. But Mattie knew that Selena thought that she and Jed were making love to each other in this shameless, public fashion. When Jed went, Mattie, more for Selena's benefit than his, broke off some sprays of honeysuckle and pinned them on his coat. The fragrance went with Jedediah as he drove through Amberley, and pleasant thoughts were born of it.

"It's romantic," he told the pony. "Blessed if it ain't romantic! Not that Mattie cares anything about me now. I know she don't. But it's just her kind way. She wants to cheer me up and let me know I've a friend still. Get up, my nag, get up. I ain't one to persoom on her kindness neither; I know my place. But still, say what you will, it's romantic—this sitooation. This is it. Here I be, loving the ground she walks on, as I've always done, and I can't let on that I do because I'm a poor ne'er-do-well as ain't fit to look at her, an independent woman with property. And she's a-showing kindness to me for old times' sake, and piercing my heart all the time, not knowing. Why, it's romance with a vengeance, that's what it is. Get up, my nag, get up."

Thereafter Jed called at the Adams place every week. Generally he stayed to tea. Mattie always bought something of him to colour an excuse. Her kitchen fairly glittered with new tinware. She gave Selena the overflow by way of heaping coals of fire.

After every visit Jedediah held stern counsel with himself and decided that he must not call to see Mattie again—at least, not for a long time; then he must not stay to tea. He would struggle with himself all the way down the poplar hill—not without a comforting sense of the romance of the struggle—but it always ended the same way. He turned in under the willows and clinked musically into Mattie's yard. At least, the rattle of the tin-wagon sounded musically to Mattie.

Meanwhile, Selena watched from her window and raged.

Amberley people shrugged their shoulders when gossip noised the matter abroad. But, being good-humoured in the main, they forebore to do more than say that Mattie Adams was free to make a goose of herself if it pleased her, and that Jed Crane wasn't such a fool as he looked. The Adams farm was one of the best in Amberley, and it had not grown any poorer under Mattie's management.

"If Jed walks in there and hangs up his hat he'll have done well for himself after all."

This was Selena's view of it also, barring the good nature. She was furious at the whole affair, and she did her best to make Mattie's life a burden to her with slurs and thrusts. But they all misjudged Jed. He had no intention of "walking in and hanging up his hat"—or trying to. Romantic as he was, it never occurred to him that Mattie might be as romantic as himself. She did not care for him, and anyhow he, Jed, had a little too much pride to ask her, a rich woman, to marry him, a poor man who had lost all caste he ever possessed by taking up tin-peddling. Jed was determined not to "persoom." And, oh, how deliciously romantic it all was! He hugged himself with sorrowful delight over it.

As the summer waned and the long yellow leaves began to fall thickly from the willows in the Adams lane Jed began to talk of going out west again. Tin-peddling was not possible in winter, and he didn't think he would try it another summer. Mattie listened with dismay in her heart. All summer she had made much of Jed, by way of tormenting Selena. But now she realized what he really meant to her. The old love had wakened to life in her heart; she could not let Jed go out of her life again, leaving her to the old loneliness. If Jed went away everything would be flat, stale, and unprofitable.

She knew him to be at heart the kindest, most gentle of human beings, and the mere fact of his having been unsuccessful, even what some of his old neighbours might call stupid, did not change her feelings toward him in the least. He was Jed—that was sufficient for her, and she had business capability enough for both, when it came to that.

Mattie began to drop hints. But Jed would not take them. True, once or twice he thought that perhaps Mattie did care a little for him yet. But it would not do for him to take advantage of that.

"No, I just couldn't do that," he told the pony. "I worship the ground that woman treads on, but it ain't for the likes of me to tell her so, not now. Get up, my nag, get up. This has been a mighty pleasant summer with that visit to look forward to every week. But it's about over now and you must tramp, Jed."

Jed sighed. He remembered that it was more romantic than ever, but all at once this failed to comfort him. Romance up to a certain point was food; beyond that it palled, so to speak. Jed's romance failed him just when he needed it most.

Mattie, meanwhile, was forced to the dismal conclusion that her hints were thrown away. Jed was plainly determined not to speak. Mattie felt half angry with him. She did not choose to make a martyr of herself to romance, and surely the man didn't expect her to ask him to marry her.

"I'm sure and certain he's as fond of me as ever he was," she mused. "I suppose he's got some ridiculous notion about being too poor to aspire to me. Jed always had more pride than a Crane could carry. Well, I've done all I can—all I'm going to do. If Jed's determined to go, he must go, I s'pose."

Mattie would not let herself cry, although she felt like it. She went out and picked apples instead.

Mattie might have remained so and Jedediah's romance might never have reached a better ending, if it had not been for Selena, who came over just then to help Mattie pick the golden russets. Fate had evidently destined her as Jed's best helper. All summer she had been fairly goading Mattie into love with Jedediah and now she was moved to add the last spur.

"Jed Crane's going away, I hear," she said maliciously. "Seems to me you're bound to be jilted again, Mattie."

Mattie had no answer ready. Selena went on undauntedly.

"You've made a nice fool of yourself all summer, I vow. Throwing yourself at Jed's head—and he doesn't want you, even with all your property."

"He does want me," said Mattie calmly. Her lips were very firm and her cheeks scarlet. "He is not going away. We are to be married about Christmas, and Jed will take charge of the farm for me."

"Matilda Adams!" said Selena. It was all she was capable of saying.

The rest of the golden russets were picked in a dead silence, Mattie working with an unusually high colour in her cheeks, while Selena's thin lips were pressed so closely together as to be little else than a hair line.

After Selena had gone home, sulking, Mattie picked on with a very determined face. The die was cast; she could not bear Selena's slurs and she would not. And she had not told a lie either. Her words were true; she would make them true. All the Adams determination—and that was not a little—was roused in her.

"If Jed jilts me, he'll do it to my face, clean and clever," she said viciously.

When Jed came again he was very solemn. He thought it would be his last visit, but Mattie felt differently. She had dressed herself with unusual care and crimped her hair. Her cheeks were scarlet and her eyes bright. Jed thought she looked younger and prettier than ever. The thought that this was the last time he would see her for many a long day to come grew more and more unbearable, yet he firmly determined he would let no presuming word pass his lips. Mattie had been so kind to him. It was only honourable of him in return not to let her throw herself away on a poor failure like himself.

"I suppose this is your last round with the wagon," she said. She had taken him out into the garden to say it. The garden was out of view from the Ford place. Propose she must, but she drew the line at proposing under Selena's eyes.

Jed nodded dully. "Yes, and then I must toddle off and look for something else to do. You see, I haven't much of a gift so to speak for business, Mattie, and it takes me so long to get worked into an understanding of a business or trade that I'm generally asked to quit before you might say I've really commenced. It's been a mighty happy summer for me, though I can't say I've done much in the selling line except to you, Mattie. What with your kindness and these little visits you've been good enough to let me make every week, I feel I may say it's been the happiest summer of my life, and I'm never going to forget it, but as I said, it's time for me to be moving on elsewhere and finding something else to do."

"There is something for you to do right here—if you will do it," said Mattie faintly. For a moment she felt as if she could not go on; Jed and the garden and the scarf of late asters whirled around her dizzily. She held by the sweet-pea trellis to steady herself.

"I—I said a terrible thing to Selena the other day. I—I don't know what I'll do about it if—if—you don't help me out, Jed."

"I'll do anything I can," said Jed, with hearty sympathy. "You know that, Mattie. What is the trouble?"

His kindly voice and the good will and affection beaming in his honest blue eyes gave Mattie renewed courage to go on with her self-imposed and most embarrassing task, although before she ended her voice shook and dwindled away to such a low whisper that Jed had to bend his head close to hers to hear what she was saying.

"I—I said—she goaded me into saying it, Jed—slighting and slurring—jeering at me because you were going away. I just got mad, Jed—and I told her you weren't going—that you and I—that we were to be—married."

"Mattie, did you mean that?" he cried. "If you did, I'm the happiest man alive. I didn't dare persoom—I didn't s'pose you thought anything of me. But if you do—and if you want me—here's all there is of me, heart and soul and body, forever and ever, as I've been all my life."

Thinking over this speech afterwards Jed was dissatisfied with it. He thought he might have made it much more eloquent and romantic than it was. But it served the purpose very well. It was convincing—it came straight from his honest, stupid heart, and Mattie knew it. She held out her hands and Jed gathered her into his arms.

It was certainly a most fortunate circumstance that the garden was well out of the range of Selena's vision, or the sight of her sister and the remaining member of the despised Crane family repeating their foolish performance, which many years previous had resulted in Jed's long banishment, might have caused her to commit almost any unheard-of act of spite as an outlet for her jealous anger. But only the few remaining garden flowers were witness to the lovers' indiscretion, and they kept their own counsel after the manner of flowers, so Selena's feelings were mercifully spared this further outrage.

That evening Jed drove slowly away through the twilight, mounted for the last time on the tin-wagon. He was so happy that he bore no grudge against even Selena Ford. As the pony climbed the poplar hill Jed drew a long breath and freed his mind to the surrounding landscape and to his faithful and slow-plodding steed that had been one of the main factors in this love affair, having patiently carried him to and from the abode of his lady-love throughout the summer just passed. Jedediah was as brimful of happiness as mortal man could be, and his rosy thoughts flowed forth in a kind of triumphant chant which would have driven Selena stark distracted had she been within hearing distance. What he said too was but a poor expression of what he thought, but to the trees and fields and pony he chanted,

"Well, this *is* romance. What else would you call it now? Me, poor, scared to speak—and Mattie ups and does it for me, bless her. Yes, I've been longing for romance all my life, and I've got it at last. None of your commonplace courtships for me, I always said. Them was my very words. And I guess this has been a little uncommon—I guess it has. Anyhow, I'm uncommon happy. I never felt so romantic before. Get up, my nag, get up."

The Tryst of the White Lady

"I wisht ye'd git married, Roger," said Catherine Ames. "I'm gitting too old to work—seventy last April—and who's going to look after ye when I'm gone. Git married, b'y—git married."

Roger Temple winced. His aunt's harsh, disagreeable voice always jarred horribly on his sensitive nerves. He was fond of her after a fashion, but always that voice made him wonder if there could be anything harder to endure.

Then he gave a bitter little laugh.

"Who'd have me, Aunt Catherine?" he asked.

Catherine Ames looked at him critically across the supper table. She loved him in her way, with all her heart, but she was not in the least blind to his defects. She did not mince matters with herself or with other people. Roger was a sallow, plain-featured fellow, small and insignificant looking. And, as if this were not bad enough, he walked with a slight limp and had one thin shoulder a little higher than the other—"Jarback" Temple he had been called in school, and the name still clung to him. To be sure, he had very fine grey eyes, but their dreamy brilliance gave his dull face an uncanny look which girls did not like, and so made matters rather worse than better. Of course looks didn't matter so much in the case of a man; Steve Millar was homely enough, and all marked up with smallpox to boot, yet he had got for wife the prettiest and smartest girl in South Bay. But Steve was rich. Roger was poor and always would be. He worked his stony little farm, from which his father and grandfather had wrested a fair living, after a fashion, but Nature had not cut him out for a successful farmer. He hadn't the strength for it and his heart wasn't in it. He'd rather be hanging over a book. Catherine secretly thought Roger's matrimonial chances very poor, but it would not do to discourage the b'y. What he needed was spurring on.

"Ye'll git someone if ye don't fly too high," she announced loudly and cheerfully. "Thar's always a gal or two here and thar that's glad to marry for a home. 'Tain't no use for *you* to be settin' your thoughts on anyone young and pretty. Ye wouldn't git her and ye'd be worse off if ye did. Your grandfather married for looks, and a nice useless wife he got—sick half her time. Git a good strong girl that ain't afraid of work, that'll hold things together when ye're reading po'try—that's as much as you kin expect. And the sooner the better. I'm done—last winter's rheumatiz has about finished *me*. An' we can't afford hired help."

Roger felt as if his raw, quivering soul were being seared. He looked at his aunt curiously—at her broad, flat face with the mole on the end of her dumpy nose, the bristling hairs on her chin, the wrinkled yellow neck, the pale, protruding eyes, the coarse, good-humoured mouth. She was so extremely ugly—and he had seen her across the table all his life. For twenty-five years he had looked at her so. Must he continue to go on looking at ugliness in the shape of a wife all the rest of his life—he, who worshipped beauty in everything?

"Did my mother look like you, Aunt Catherine?" he asked abruptly.

His aunt stared—and snorted. Her snort was meant to express kindly amusement, but it sounded like derision and contempt.

"Yer ma wasn't so humly as me," she said cheerfully, "but she wan't no beauty either. None of the Temples was ever better lookin' than was necessary. We was *workers*. Yer pa wa'n't bad looking. You're humlier than either of 'em. Some ways ye take after yer grandma—though *she* was counted pretty at one time. She was yaller and spindlin' like you, and you've got her eyes. What yer so int'rested in yer ma's looks all at once fer?"

"I was wondering," said Roger coolly, "if Father ever looked at her across the table and wished she were prettier."

Catherine giggled. Her giggle was ugly and disagreeable like everything else about her—everything except a certain odd, loving, loyal old heart buried deep in her bosom, for the sake of which Roger endured the giggle and all the rest.

"Dessay he did—dessay he did. Men al'ays has a hankerin' for good looks. But ye've got to cut yer coat 'cording to yer cloth. As for yer poor ma, she didn't live long enough to git as ugly as me. When I come here to keep house for yer pa, folks said as it wouldn't be long 'fore he married me. *I* wouldn't a-minded. But yer pa never hinted it. S'pose he'd had enough of ugly women likely."

Catherine snorted amiably again. Roger got up—he couldn't endure any more just then. He must escape.

"Now you think over what I've said," his aunt called after him. "Ye've gotter git a wife soon, however ye manage it. 'Twon't be so hard if ye're reasonable. Don't stay out as late as ye did last night. Ye coughed all night. Where was ye—down at the shore?"

"No," said Roger, who always answered her questions even when he hated to. "I was down at Aunt Isabel's grave."

"Till eleven o'clock! Ye ain't wise! I dunno what hankering ye have after that unchancy place. *I* ain't been near it for twenty year. I wonder ye ain't scairt. What'd ye think ye'd do if ye saw her ghost?"

Catherine looked curiously at Roger. She was very superstitious and she believed firmly in ghosts, and saw no absurdity in her question.

"I wish I *could* see it," said Roger, his great eyes flashing. He believed in ghosts too, at least in Isabel Temple's ghost. His uncle had seen it; his grandfather had seen it; he believed he would see it—the beautiful, bewitching, mocking, luring ghost of lovely Isabel Temple.

"Don't wish such stuff," said Catherine. "Nobody ain't never the same after they've seen her."

"Was Uncle different?" Roger had come back into the kitchen and was looking curiously at his aunt.

"Diff'rent? He was another man. He didn't even *look* the same. Sich eyes! Al'ays looking past ye at something behind ye. They'd give anyone creeps. He never had any notion of flesh-and-blood women after that—said a man wouldn't, after seeing Isabel. His life was plumb ruined. Lucky he died young. I hated to be in the same room with him—he wa'n't canny, that was all there was to it. *You* keep away from that grave—*you* don't want to look odder than ye are by nature. And when ye git married, ye'll have to give up roamin' about half the night in graveyards. A wife wouldn't put up with it, as I've done."

"I'll never get as good a wife as you, Aunt Catherine," said Roger with a little whimsical smile that gave him the look of an amused gnome.

"Dessay you won't. But someone ye have to have. Why'n't ye try 'Liza Adams. She *might* have ye—she's gittin' on."

"'Liza ... Adams!"

"That's what I said. Ye needn't repeat it—'Liza ... Adams—'s if I'd mentioned a hippopotamus. I git out of patience with ye. I b'lieve in my heart ye think ye ought to git a wife that'd look like a picter."

"I do, Aunt Catherine. That's just the kind of wife I want—grace and beauty and charm. Nothing less than that will ever content me."

Roger laughed bitterly again and went out. It was sunset. There was no work to do that night except to milk the cows, and his little home boy could do that. He felt a glad freedom. He put his hand in his pocket to see if his beloved Wordsworth was there and then he took his way across the fields, under a sky of purple and amber, walking quickly despite his limp. He wanted to get to some solitary place where he could forget Aunt Catherine and her abominable suggestions and escape into the world of dreams where he habitually lived and where he found the loveliness he had not found nor could hope to find in his real world.

Roger's mother had died when he was three and his father when he was eight. His little, old, bedridden grandmother had lived until he was twelve. He had loved her passionately. She had not been pretty in his remembrance—a tiny, shrunken, wrinkled thing—but she had beautiful grey eyes that never grew old and a soft, gentle voice—the only woman's voice he had ever heard with pleasure. He was very critical as regards women's voices and very sensitive to them. Nothing hurt him quite so much as an unlovely voice—not even unloveliness of face. Her death had left him desolate. She was the only human being who had ever understood him. He could never, he thought, have got through his tortured school days without her. After she died he would not go to school. He was not in any sense educated. His father and grandfather had been illiterate men and he had inherited their underdeveloped brain cells. But he loved poetry and read all he could get of it. It overlaid his primitive nature with a curious iridescence of fancy and furnished him with ideals and hungers his environment could never satisfy. He loved beauty in everything. Moonrises hurt him with their loveliness and he could sit for hours gazing at a white narcissus—much to his aunt's exasperation. He was solitary by nature. He felt horribly alone in a crowded building but never in the woods or in the wild places along the shore. It was because of this that his aunt could not get him to go to church—which was a horror to her orthodox soul. He told her he would like to go to church if it were empty but he could not bear it when it was full—full of smug, ugly people. Most people, he thought, were ugly—though not so ugly as he was—and ugliness made him sick with repulsion. Now and then he saw a pretty girl at whom he liked to look but he never saw one that wholly pleased him. To him, the homely, crippled, poverty-stricken Roger Temple whom they all would have scorned, there was always a certain subtle something wanting, and the lack of it kept him heartwhole. He knew that this probably saved him from much suffering, but for all that he regretted it. He wanted to love, even vainly; he wanted to experience this passion of which the poets sang so much. Without it he felt he lacked the key to a world of wonder. He even tried to fall in love; he went to church for several Sundays and sat where he could see beautiful Elsa Carey. She was lovely—it gave him pleasure to look at her; the gold of her hair was so bright and living; the pink of her cheek so pure, the curve of her neck so flawless, the lashes of her eyes so dark and silken. But he looked at her as at a picture. When he tried to think and dream of her, it bored him. Besides, he knew she had a rather nasal voice. He used to laugh sarcastically to himself over Elsa's feelings if she had known how desperately he was trying to fall in love with her and failing—Elsa the queen of hearts, who believed she had only to look to reign. He gave up trying at last, but he still longed to love. He knew he would never marry; he could not marry plainness, and beauty would have longed to love. He knew he would never marry; he could not marry plainness, and beauty would have none of him; but he did not want to miss everything and he had moments when he was very bitter and rebellious because he felt he must miss it forever.

He went straight to Isabel Temple's grave in the remote shore field of his farm. Isabel Temple had lived and died eighty years ago. She had been very lovely, very wilful, very fond of playing with the hearts of men. She had married William Temple, the brother of his great-grandfather, and as she stood in her white dress beside her bridegroom, at the conclusion of the wedding ceremony, a jilted lover, crazed by despair, had entered the house and shot her dead. She had been buried in the shore field, where a square space had been dyked off in the centre for a burial lot because the church was then so far away. With the passage of years the lot had grown up so thickly with fir and birch and wild cherry that it looked like a compact grove. A winding path led through it to its heart where Isabel Temple's grave was, thickly overgrown with long, silken, pale green grass. Roger hurried along the path and sat down on the big grey boulder by the grave, looking about him with a long breath of delight. How lovely—and witching—and unearthly it was here. Little ferns were growing in the hollows and cracks of the big boulder where clay had lodged. Over Isabel Temple's crooked, lichened gravestone hung a young wild cherry in its delicate bloom. Above it, in a little space of sky left by the slender tree tops, was a young moon. It was too dark here after all to read Wordsworth, but that did not matter. The place, with its moist air, its tang of fir balsam, was like a perfumed room where a man might dream dreams and see visions. There was a soft murmur of wind in the boughs over him, and the faraway moan of the sea on the bar crept in. Roger surrendered himself utterly to the charm of the place. When he entered that grove, he had left behind the realm of daylight and things known and come into the realm of shadow and mystery and enchantment. Anything might happen—anything might be true.

Eighty long years had come and gone, but Isabel Temple, thus cruelly torn from life at the moment when it had promised her most, did not even yet rest calmly in her grave; such at least was the story, and Roger believed it. It was in his blood to believe it. The Temples were a superstitious family, and there was nothing in Roger's upbringing to correct the tendency. His was not a sceptical or scientific mind. He was ignorant and poetical and credulous. He had always accepted unquestioningly the tale that Isabel Temple had been seen on earth long after the red clay was heaped over her murdered body. Her bridegroom had seen her, when he went to visit her on the eve of his second and unhappy marriage; his grandfather had seen her. His grandmother, who had told him Isabel's story, had told him this too, and believed it. She had added, with a bitterness foreign to his idea of her, that her husband had never been the same to her afterwards; his uncle had seen her—and had lived and died a haunted man. It was only to men the lovely, restless ghost appeared, and her appearance boded no good to him who saw. Roger knew this, but he had a curious longing to see her. He had never avoided her grave as others of his tribe did. He loved the spot, and he believed that some time he would see Isabel Temple there. She came, so the story went, to one in each generation of the family.

He gazed down at her sunken grave; a little wind, that came stealing along the floor of the grove, raised and swayed the long, hair-like grass on it, giving the curious suggestion of something prisoned under it trying to draw a long breath and float upward.

Then, when he lifted his eyes again, he saw her!

She was standing behind the gravestone, under the cherry tree, whose long white branches touched her head; standing there, with her head drooping a little, but looking steadily at him. It was just between dusk and dark now, but he saw her very plainly. She was dressed in white, with some filmy scarf over her head, and her hair hung in a dark heavy braid over her shoulder. Her face was small and ivory-white, and her eyes were very large and dark. Roger looked straight into them and they did something to him—drew something out of him that was never to be his again—his heart? his soul? He did not know. He only knew that lovely Isabel Temple had now come to him and that he was hers forever.

For a few moments that seemed years he looked at her—looked till the lure of her eyes drew him to his feet as a man rises in sleep-walking. As he slowly stood up, the low-hanging bough of a fir tree pushed his cap down over his face and blinded him. When he snatched it off, she was gone.

Roger Temple did not go home that night till the spring dawn was in the sky. Catherine was sleepless with anxiety about him. When she heard him come up the stairs, she opened her door and peeped out. Roger went along the hall without seeing her. His brilliant eyes stared straight before him, and there was something in his face that made Catherine steal back to her bed with a little shiver of fear. He looked like his uncle. She did not ask him, when they met at breakfast, where or how he had spent the night. He had been dreading the question and was relieved beyond measure when it was not asked. But, apart from that, he was hardly conscious of her presence. He ate and drank mechanically and voicelessly. When he had gone out, Catherine wagged her uncomely grey head ominously.

"He's bewitched," she muttered. "I know the signs. He's seen her—drat her! It's time she gave up that kind of work. Well, I dunno what to do—thar ain't anything I can do, I reckon. He'll never marry now—I'm as sure of that as of any mortal thing. He's in love with a ghost."

It had not yet occurred to Roger that he was in love. He thought of nothing but Isabel Temple—her lovely, lovely face, sweeter than any picture he had ever seen or any ideal he had dreamed, her long dark hair, her slim form and, more than all, her compelling eyes. He saw them wherever he looked—they drew him—he would have followed them to the end of the world, heedless of all else.

He longed for night, that he might again steal to the grave in the haunted grove. She might come again—who knew? He felt no fear, nothing but a terrible hunger to see her again. But she did not come that night—nor the next—nor the next. Two weeks went by and he had not seen her. Perhaps he would never see her again—the thought filled him with anguish not to be borne. He knew now that he loved her—Isabel Temple, dead for eighty years. This was love—this searing, torturing, intolerably sweet thing—this possession of body and soul and spirit. The poets had sung but weakly of it. He could tell them better if he could find words. Could other men have loved at all—could any man love those blowzy, common girls of earth? It seemed impossible—absurd. There was only one thing that could be loved—that white spirit. No wonder his uncle had died. He, Roger Temple, would soon die too. That would be well. Only the dead could woo Isabel. Meanwhile he revelled in his torment and his happiness—so madly commingled that he never knew whether he was in heaven or hell. It was beautiful—and dreadful—and wonderful—and exquisite—oh, so exquisite. Mortal love could never be so exquisite. He had never lived before—now he lived in every fibre of his being.

He was glad Aunt Catherine did not worry him with questions. He had feared she would. But she never asked any questions now and she was afraid of Roger, as she had been afraid of his uncle. She dared not ask questions. It was a thing that must not be tampered with. Who knew what she might hear if she asked him questions? She was very unhappy. Something dreadful had happened to her poor boy—he had been bewitched by that hussy—he would die as his uncle had died.

"Mebbe it's best," she muttered. "He's the last of the Temples, so mebbe she'll rest in her grave when she's killed 'em all. I dunno what she's sich a spite at *them* for—there'd be more sense if she'd haunt the Mortons, seein' as a Morton killed her. Well, I'm mighty old and tired and worn out. It don't seem that it's been much use, the way I've slaved and fussed to bring that b'y up and keep things together for him—and now the ghost's got him. I might as well have let him die when he was a sickly baby."

If this had been said to Roger he would have retorted that it was worthwhile to have lived long enough to feel what he was feeling now. He would not have missed it for a score of other men's lives. He had drunk of some immortal wine and was as a god. Even if she never came again, he had seen her once, and she had taught him life's great secret in that one unforgettable exchange of eyes. She was his—his in spite of his ugliness and his crooked shoulder. No man could ever take her from him.

But she did come again. One evening, when the darkening grove was full of magic in the light of the rising yellow moon shining across the level field, Roger sat on the big boulder by the grave. The evening was very still; there was no sound save the echoes of noisy laughter that seemed to come up from the bay shore—drunken fishermen, likely as not. Roger resented the intrusion of such a sound in such a place—it was a sacrilege. When he came here to dream of her, only the loveliest of muted sounds should be heard—the faintest whisper of trees, the half-heard, half-felt moan of surf, the airiest sigh of wind. He never read Wordsworth now or any other book. He only sat there and thought of her, his great eyes alight, his pale face flushed with the wonder of his love.

She slipped through the dark boughs like a moonbeam and stood by the stone. Again he saw her quite plainly—saw and drank her in with his eyes. He did not feel surprise—something in him had known she would come again. He would not move a muscle lest he lose her as he had lost her before. They looked at each other—for how long? He did not know; and then—a horrible thing happened. Into that place of wonder and revelation and mystery reeled a hiccoughing, laughing creature, a drunken sailor from a harbour ship, with a leering face and desecrating breath.

"Oh, you're here, my dear—I thought I'd catch you yet," he said.

He caught hold of her. She screamed. Roger sprang forward and struck him in the face. In his fury of sudden rage the strength of ten seemed to animate his slender body and pass into his blow. The sailor reeled back and put up his hands. He was a coward—and even a brave man might have been daunted by that terrible white face and those blazing eyes. He backed down the path.

"Shorry—shorry," he muttered. "Didn't know she was your girl—shorry I butted in. Shentlemans never butt in—shorry—shir—shorry."

He kept repeating his ridiculous "shorry" until he was out of the grove. Then he turned and ran stumblingly across the field. Roger did not follow; he went back to Isabel Temple's grave. The girl was lying across it; he thought she was unconscious. He stooped and picked her up—she was light and small, but she was warm flesh and blood; she clung uncertainly to him for a moment and he felt her breath on his face. He did not speak—he was too sick at heart. She did not speak either. He did not think this strange until afterwards. He was incapable of thinking just then; he was dazed, wretched, lost. Presently he became aware that she was timidly pulling his arm. It seemed that she wanted him to go with her—she was evidently frightened of that brute—he must take her to safety. And then—

She moved on down the little path and he followed. Out in the moonlit field he saw her clearly. With her drooping head, her flowing dark hair, her great brown eyes, she looked like the nymph of a wood-brook, a haunter of shadows, a creature sprung from the wild. But she was mortal maid, and he—what a fool he had been! Presently he would laugh at himself, when this dazed agony should clear away from his brain. He followed her down the long field to the bay shore. Now and then she paused and looked back to see if he were coming, but she never spoke. When she reached the shore road she turned and went along it until they came to an old grey house fronting the calm grey harbour. At its gate she paused. Roger knew now who she was. Catherine had told him about her a month ago.

She was Lilith Barr, a girl of eighteen, who had come to live with her uncle and aunt. Her father had died some months before. She was absolutely deaf as the result of some accident in childhood, and she was, as his own eyes told him, exquisitely lovely in her white, haunting style. But she was not Isabel Temple; he had tricked himself—he had lived in a fool's paradise—oh, he must get away and laugh at himself. He left her at her gate, disregarding the little hand she put timidly out—but he did not laugh at himself. He went back to Isabel Temple's grave and flung himself down on it and cried like a boy. He wept his stormy, anguished soul out on it; and when he rose and went away, he believed it was forever. He thought he could never, never go there again.

Catherine looked at him curiously the next morning. He looked wretched—haggard and hollow-eyed. She knew he had not come in till the summer dawn. But he had lost the rapt, uncanny look she hated; suddenly she no longer felt afraid of him. With this, she began to ask questions again.

"What kept ye out so late again last night, b'y?" she said reproachfully.

Roger looked at her in her morning ugliness. He had not really seen her for weeks. Now she smote on his tortured senses, so long drugged with beauty, like a physical blow. He suddenly burst into a laughter that frightened her.

"Preserve's, b'y, have ye gone mad? Or," she added, "have ye seen Isabel Temple's ghost?"

"No," said Roger loudly and explosively. "Don't talk any more about that damned ghost. Nobody ever saw it. The whole story is balderdash."

He got up and went violently out, leaving Catherine aghast. Was it possible Roger had sworn? What on earth had come over the b'y? But come what had or come what would, he no longer looked *fey*—there was that much to be thankful for. Even an occasional oath was better than that. Catherine went stiffly about her dish-washing, resolving to have 'Liza Adams to supper some night.

For a week Roger lived in agony—an agony of shame and humiliation and self-contempt. Then, when the edge of his bitter disappointment wore away, he made another dreadful discovery. He still loved her and longed for her just as keenly as before. He wanted madly to see her—her flower-like face, her great, asking eyes, the sleek, braided flow of her hair. Ghost or woman—spirit or flesh—it mattered not. He could not live without her. At last his hunger for her drew him to the old grey house on the bay shore. He knew he was a fool—she would never look at him; he was only feeding the flame that must consume him. But go he must and did, seeking for his lost paradise.

He did not see her when he went in, but Mrs. Barr received him kindly and talked about her in a pleasant garrulous fashion which jarred on Roger, yet he listened greedily. Lilith, her aunt told him, had been made deaf by the accidental explosion of a gun when she was eight years old. She could not hear a sound but she could talk.

"A little, that is—not much, but enough to get along with. But she don't like talking somehow—dunno why. She's shy—and we think maybe she don't like to talk much because she can't hear her own voice. She don't ever speak except just when she has to. But she's been trained to lip-reading something wonderful—she can understand anything that's said when she can see the person that's talking. Still, it's a terrible drawback for the poor child—she's never had any real girl-life and she's dreadful sensitive and retiring. We can't get her to go out anywhere, only for lonely walks along shore by herself. We're much obliged for what you did the other night. It ain't safe for her to wander about alone as she does, but it ain't often anybody from the harbour gets up this far. She was dreadful upset about it—hasn't got over her scare yet."

When Lilith came in, her ivory-white face went scarlet all over at the sight of Roger. She sat down in a shadowy corner. Mrs. Barr got up and went out. Roger was mute; he could find nothing to say. He could have talked glibly enough to Isabel Temple's ghost in some unearthly tryst by her grave, but he could not find a word to say to this slip of flesh and blood. He felt very foolish and absurd, and very conscious of his twisted shoulder. What a fool he had been to come!

Then Lilith looked up at him—and smiled. A little shy, friendly smile. Roger suddenly saw her not as the tantalizing, unreal, mystic thing of the twilit grove, but as a little human creature, exquisitely pretty in her young-moon beauty, longing for companionship. He got up, forgetting his ugliness, and went across the room to her.

"Will you come for a walk," he said eagerly. He held out his hand like a child; as a child she stood up and took it; like two children they went out and down the sunset shore. Roger was again incredibly happy. It was not the same happiness as had been his in that vanished fortnight; it was a homelier happiness with its feet on the earth. The amazing thing was that he felt she was happy too—happy because she was walking with *him*, "Jarback" Temple, whom no girl had even thought about. A certain secret well-spring of fancy that had seemed dry welled up in him sparklingly again.

Through the summer weeks the odd courtship went on. Roger talked to her as he had never talked to anyone. He did not find it in the least hard to talk to her, though her necessity of watching his face so closely while he talked bothered him occasionally. He felt that her intent gaze was reading his soul as well as his lips.

She never talked much herself; what she did say she spoke so low that it was hardly above a whisper, but she had a voice as lovely as her face—sweet, cadenced, haunting. Roger was quite mad about her, and he was horribly afraid that he could never get up enough courage to ask her to marry him. And he was afraid that if he did, she would never consent. In spite of her shy, eager welcomes he could not believe she could care for him—for *him*. She liked him, she was sorry for him, but it was unthinkable that she, white, exquisite Lilith, could marry him and sit at his table and his hearth. He was a fool to dream of it.

To the existence of romance and glamour in which he lived, no gossip of the countryside penetrated. Yet much gossip there was, and at last it came blundering in on Roger to destroy his fairy world a second time. He came downstairs one night in the twilight, ready to go to Lilith. His aunt and an old crony were talking in the kitchen; the crony was old, and Catherine, supposing Roger was out of the house, was talking loudly in that horrible voice of hers with still more horrible zest and satisfaction.

"Yes, I'm guessing it'll be a match as ye say. Oh the b'y's doing well. He ain't for every market, as I'm bound to admit. Ef she wan't deaf she wouldn't look at him, no doubt. But she has scads of money—they won't need to do a tap of work unless they like—and she's a good housekeeper too her aunt tells me. She's pretty enough to suit him—he's as particular as never was—and he wan't crooked and she wan't deaf when they was born, so it's likely their children will be all right. I'm that proud when I think of the match."

Roger fled out of the house, white of face and sick of heart. He went, not to the bay shore, but to Isabel Temple's grave. He had never been there since the night when he had rescued Lilith, but now he rushed to it in his new agony. His aunt's horrible practicalities had filled him with disgust—they dragged his love in the dust of sordid things. And Lilith was rich; he had never known that—never suspected it. He could never ask her to marry him now; he must never see her again. For the second time he had lost her, and this second losing could not be borne.

He sat down on the big boulder by the grave and dropped his poor grey face in his hands, moaning in anguish. Nothing was left him, not even dreams. He hoped he could soon die.

He did not know how long he sat there—he did not know when she came. But when he lifted his miserable eyes, he saw her, sitting just a little way from him on the big stone and looking at him with something in her face that made his heart beat madly. He forgot Aunt Catherine's sacrilege—he forgot that he was a presumptuous fool. He bent forward and kissed her lips for the first time. The wonder of it loosed his bound tongue.

"Lilith," he gasped, "I love you."

She put her hand into his and nestled closer to him.

"I thought you would have told me that long ago," she said.

Uncle Richard's New Year's Dinner

Prissy Baker was in Oscar Miller's store New Year's morning, buying matches—for New Year's was not kept as a business holiday in Quincy—when her uncle, Richard Baker, came in. He did not look at Prissy, nor did she wish him a happy New Year; she would not have dared. Uncle Richard had not been on speaking terms with her or her father, his only brother, for eight years.

He was a big, ruddy, prosperous-looking man—an uncle to be proud of, Prissy thought wistfully, if only he were like other people's uncles, or, indeed, like what he used to be himself. He was the only uncle Prissy had, and when she had been a little girl they had been great friends; but that was before the quarrel, in which Prissy had had no share, to be sure, although Uncle Richard seemed to include her in his rancour.

Richard Baker, so he informed Mr. Miller, was on his way to Navarre with a load of pork.

"I didn't intend going over until the afternoon," he said, "but Joe Hemming sent word yesterday he wouldn't be buying pork after twelve today. So I have to tote my hogs over at once. I don't care about doing business New Year's morning."

"Should think New Year's would be pretty much the same as any other day to you," said Mr. Miller, for Richard Baker was a bachelor, with only old Mrs. Janeway to keep house for him.

"Well, I always like a good dinner on New Year's," said Richard Baker. "It's about the only way I can celebrate. Mrs. Janeway wanted to spend the day with her son's family over at Oriental, so I was laying out to cook my own dinner. I got everything ready in the pantry last night, 'fore I got word about the pork. I won't get back from Navarre before one o'clock, so I reckon I'll have to put up with a cold bite."

After her Uncle Richard had driven away, Prissy walked thoughtfully home. She had planned to spend a nice, lazy holiday with the new book her father had given her at Christmas and a box of candy. She did not even mean to cook a dinner, for her father had had to go to town that morning to meet a friend and would be gone the whole day. There was nobody else to cook dinner for. Prissy's mother had died when Prissy was a baby. She was her father's housekeeper, and they had jolly times together.

But as she walked home, she could not help thinking about Uncle Richard. He would certainly have cold New Year cheer, enough to chill the whole coming year. She felt sorry for him, picturing him returning from Navarre, cold and hungry, to find a fireless house and an uncooked dinner in the pantry.

Suddenly an idea popped into Prissy's head. Dared she? Oh, she never could! But he would never know—there would be plenty of time—she would!

Prissy hurried home, put her matches away, took a regretful peep at her unopened book, then locked the door and started up the road to Uncle Richard's house half a mile away. She meant to go and cook Uncle Richard's dinner for him, get it all beautifully ready, then slip away before he came home. He would never suspect her of it. Prissy would not have him suspect for the world; she thought he would be more likely to throw a dinner of her cooking out of doors than to eat it.

Eight years before this, when Prissy had been nine years old, Richard and Irving Baker had quarrelled over the division of a piece of property. The fault had been mainly on Richard's side, and that very fact made him all the more unrelenting and stubborn. He had never spoken to his brother since, and he declared he never would. Prissy and her father felt very badly over it, but Uncle Richard did not seem to feel badly at all. To all appearance he had completely forgotten that there were such people in the world as his brother Irving and his niece Prissy.

Prissy had no trouble in breaking into Uncle Richard's house, for the woodshed door was unfastened. She tripped into the hostile kitchen with rosy cheeks and mischief sparkling in her eyes. This was an adventure—this was fun! She would tell her father all about it when he came home at night and what a laugh they would have!

There was still a good fire in the stove, and in the pantry Prissy found the dinner in its raw state—a fine roast of fresh pork, potatoes, cabbage, turnips and the ingredients of a raisin pudding, for Richard Baker was fond of raisin puddings, and could make them as well as Mrs. Janeway could, if that was anything to boast of.

In a short time the kitchen was full of bubbling and hissings and appetizing odours. Prissy enjoyed herself hugely, and the raisin pudding, which she rather doubtfully mixed up, behaved itself beautifully.

"Uncle Richard said he'd be home by one," said Prissy to herself, as the clock struck twelve, "so I'll set the table now, dish up the dinner, and leave it where it will keep warm until he gets here. Then I'll slip away home. I'd like to see his face when he steps in. I suppose he'll think one of the Jenner girls across the street has cooked his dinner."

Prissy soon had the table set, and she was just peppering the turnips when a gruff voice behind her said:

"Well, well, what does this mean?"

Prissy whirled around as if she had been shot, and there stood Uncle Richard in the woodshed door!

Poor Prissy! She could not have looked or felt more guilty if Uncle Richard had caught her robbing his desk. She did not drop the turnips for a wonder; but she was too confused to set them down, so she stood there holding them, her face crimson, her heart thumping, and a horrible choking in her throat.

"I—I—came up to cook your dinner for you, Uncle Richard," she stammered. "I heard you say—in the store—that Mrs. Janeway had gone home and that you had nobody to cook your New Year's dinner for you. So I thought I'd come and do it, but I meant to slip away before you came home."

Poor Prissy felt that she would never get to the end of her explanation. Would Uncle Richard be angry? Would he order her from the house?

"It was very kind of you," said Uncle Richard drily. "It's a wonder your father let you come."

"Father was not home, but I am sure he would not have prevented me if he had been. Father has no hard feelings against you, Uncle Richard."

"Humph!" said Uncle Richard. "Well, since you've cooked the dinner you must stop and help me eat it. It smells good, I must say. Mrs. Janeway always burns pork when she roasts it. Sit down, Prissy. I'm hungry."

They sat down. Prissy felt quite giddy and breathless, and could hardly eat for excitement; but Uncle Richard had evidently brought home a good appetite from Navarre, and he did full justice to his New Year's dinner. He talked to Prissy too, quite kindly and politely, and when the meal was over he said slowly:

"I'm much obliged to you, Prissy, and I don't mind owning to you that I'm sorry for my share in the quarrel, and have wanted for a long time to be friends with your father again, but I was too ashamed and proud to make the first advance. You can tell him so for me, if you like. And if he's willing to let bygones be bygones, tell him I'd like him to come up here with you tonight when he gets home and spend the evening with me."

"Oh, he will come, I know!" cried Prissy joyfully. "He has felt so badly about not being friendly with you, Uncle Richard. I'm as glad as can be."

Prissy ran impulsively around the table and kissed Uncle Richard. He looked up at his tall, girlish niece with a smile of pleasure.

"You're a good girl, Prissy, and a kind-hearted one too, or you'd never have come up here to cook a dinner for a crabbed old uncle who deserved to eat cold dinners for his stubbornness. It made me cross today when folks wished me a happy New Year. It seemed like mockery when I hadn't a soul belonging to me to make it happy. But it has brought me happiness already, and I believe it will be a happy year all the way through."

"Indeed it will!" laughed Prissy. "I'm so happy now I could sing. I believe it was an inspiration—my idea of coming up here to cook your dinner for you."

"You must promise to come and cook my New Year's dinner for me every New Year we live near enough together," said Uncle Richard.

And Prissy promised.

White Magic

One September afternoon in the year of grace 1840 Avery and Janet Sparhallow were picking apples in their Uncle Daniel Sparhallow's big orchard. It was an afternoon of mellow sunshine; about them, beyond the orchard, were old harvest fields, mellowly bright and serene, and beyond the fields the sapphire curve of the St. Lawrence Gulf was visible through the groves of spruce and birch. There was a soft whisper of wind in the trees, and the pale purple asters that feathered the orchard grass swayed gently towards each other. Janet Sparhallow, who loved the outdoor world and its beauty, was, for the time being at least, very happy, as her little brown face, with its fine, satiny skin, plainly showed. Avery Sparhallow did not seem so happy. She worked rather abstractedly and frowned oftener than she smiled.

Avery Sparhallow was conceded to be a beauty, and had no rival in Burnley Beach. She was very pretty, with the obvious, indisputable prettiness of rich black hair, vivid, certain colour, and laughing, brilliant eyes. Nobody ever called Janet a beauty, or even thought her pretty. She was only seventeen—five years younger than Avery—and was rather lanky and weedy, with a rope of straight dark-brown hair, long, narrow, shining brown eyes and very black lashes, and a crooked, clever little mouth. She had visitations of beauty when excited, because then she flushed deeply, and colour made all the difference in the world to her; but she had never happened to look in the glass when excited, so that she had never seen herself beautiful; and hardly anybody else had ever seen her so, because she was always too shy and awkward and tongue-tied in company to feel excited over anything. Yet very little could bring that transforming flush to her face: a wind off the gulf, a sudden glimpse of blue upland, a flame-red poppy, a baby's laugh, a certain footstep. As for Avery Sparhallow, she never got excited over anything—not even her wedding dress, which had come from Charlottetown that day, and was incomparably beyond anything that had ever been seen in Burnley Beach before. For it was made of an apple-green silk, sprayed over with tiny rosebuds, which had been specially sent for to England, where Aunt Matilda Sparhallow had a brother in the silk trade. Avery Sparhallow's wedding dress was making far more of a sensation in Burnley Beach than her wedding itself was making. For Randall Burnley had been dangling after her for three years, and everybody knew that there was nobody for a Sparhallow to marry except a Burnley and nobody for a Burnley to marry except a Sparhallow.

"Only one silk dress—and I want a dozen," Avery had said scornfully.

"What would you do with a dozen silk dresses on a farm?" Janet asked wonderingly.

"Oh—what indeed?" agreed Avery, with an impatient laugh.

"Randall will think just as much of you in drugget as in silk," said Janet, meaning to comfort.

Again Avery laughed.

"That is true. Randall never notices what a woman has on. I like a man who does notice—and tells me about it. I like a man who likes me better in silk than in drugget. I will wear this rosebud silk when I'm married, and it will be supposed to last me the rest of my life and be worn on all state occasions, and in time become an heirloom like Aunt Matilda's hideous blue satin. I want a new silk dress every month."

Janet paid little attention to this kind of raving. Avery had always been more or less discontented. She would be contented enough after she was married. Nobody could be discontented who was Randall Burnley's wife. Janet was sure of that.

Janet liked picking apples; Avery did not like it; but Aunt Matilda had decreed that the red apples should be picked that afternoon, and Aunt Matilda's word was law at the Sparhallow farm, even for wilful Avery. So they worked and talked as they worked—of Avery's wedding, which was to be as soon as Bruce Gordon should arrive from Scotland.

"I wonder what Bruce will be like," said Avery. "It is eight years since he went home to Scotland. He was sixteen then—he will be twenty-four now. He went away a boy—he will come back a man."

"I don't remember much about him," said Janet. "I was only nine when he went away. He used to tease me—I do remember that." There was a little resentment in her voice. Janet had never liked being teased. Avery laughed.

"You were so touchy, Janet. Touchy people always get teased. Bruce was very handsome—and as nice as he was handsome. Those two years he was here were the nicest, gayest time I ever had. I wish he had stayed in Canada. But of course he wouldn't do that. His father was a rich man and Bruce was ambitious. Oh, Janet, I wish I could live in the old land. That would be life."

Janet had heard all this before and could not understand it. She had no hankering for either Scotland or England. She loved the new land and its wild, virgin beauty. She yearned to the future, never to the past.

"I'm tired of Burnley Beach," Avery went on passionately, shaking apples wildly off a laden bough by way of emphasis. "I know all the people—what they are—what they can be. It's like reading a book for the twentieth time. I know where I was born and who I'll marry—and where I'll be buried. That's knowing too much. All my days will be alike when I marry Randall. There will never be anything unexpected or surprising about them. I tell you Janet," Avery seized another bough and shook it with a vengeance, "I hate the very thought of it."

"The thought of—what?" said Janet in bewilderment.

"Of marrying Randall Burnley—or marrying anybody down here—and settling down on a farm for life."

Then Avery sat down on the rung of her ladder and laughed at Janet's face.

"You look stunned, Janet. Did you really think I wanted to marry Randall?"

Janet was stunned, and she did think that. How could any girl not want to marry Randall Burnley if she had the chance?

"Don't you love him?" she asked stupidly.

Avery bit into a nut-sweet apple.

"No," she said frankly. "Oh, I don't hate him, of course. I like him well enough. I like him very well. But we'll quarrel all our lives."

"Then what are you marrying him for?" asked Janet.

"Why, I'm getting on—twenty-two—all the girls of my age are married already. I won't be an old maid, and there's nobody but Randall. Nobody good enough for a Sparhallow, that is. You wouldn't want me to marry Ned Adams or John Buchanan, would you?"

"No," said Janet, who had her full share of the Sparhallow pride.

"Well, then, of course I must marry Randall. That's settled and there's no use making faces over the notion. I'm not making faces, but I'm tired of hearing you talk as if you thought I adored him and must be in the seventh heaven because I was going to marry him, you romantic child."

"Does Randall know you feel like this?" asked Janet in a low tone.

"No. Randall is like all men—vain and self-satisfied—and believes I'm crazy about him. It's just as well to let him think so, until we're safely married anyhow. Randall has some romantic notions too, and I'm not sure that he'd marry me if he knew, in spite of his three years' devotion. And I have no intention of being jilted three weeks before my wedding day."

Avery laughed again, and tossed away the core of her apple.

Janet, who had been very pale, went crimson and lovely. She could not endure hearing Randall criticized. "Vain and self-satisfied"—when there was never a man less so! She was horrified to feel that she almost hated Avery—Avery who did not love Randall.

"What a pity Randall didn't take a fancy to you instead of me, Janet," said Avery teasingly. "Wouldn't you like to marry him, Janet? Wouldn't you now?"

"No," cried Janet angrily. "I just like Randall, I've liked him ever since that day when I was a little thing and he came here and saved me from being shut up all day in that dreadful dark closet because I broke Aunt Matilda's blue cup—when I hadn't meant to break it. He wouldn't let her shut me up! He is like that—he understands! I want you to marry him because he wants you, and it isn't fair that you—that you—"

"Nothing is fair in this world, child. Is it fair that I, who am so pretty—you know I am pretty, Janet—and who love life and excitement, should have to be buried on a P.E. Island farm all my days? Or else be an old maid because a Sparhallow mustn't marry beneath her? Come, Janet, don't look so woebegone. I wouldn't have told you if I'd thought you'd take it so much to heart. I'll be a good wife to Randall, never fear, and I'll keep him up to the notch of prosperity much better than if I thought him a little lower than the angels. It doesn't do to think a man perfection, Janet, because he thinks so too, and when he finds someone who agrees with him he is inclined to rest on his oars."

"At any rate, you don't care for anyone else," said Janet hopefully.

"Not I. I like Randall as well as I like anybody."

"Randall won't be satisfied with that," muttered Janet. But Avery did not hear her, having picked up her basket of apples and gone. Janet sat down on the lower rung of the ladder and gave herself up to an unpleasant reverie. Oh, how the world had changed in half an hour! She had never been so worried in her life. She was so fond of Randall—she had always been fond of him—why, he was just like a brother to her! She couldn't possibly love a brother more. And Avery was going to hurt him; it would hurt him horribly when he found out she did not love him. Janet could not bear the thought of Randall being hurt; it made her fairly savage. He must not be hurt—Avery must love him. Janet could not understand why she did not.

Surely everyone must love Randall. It had never occurred to Janet to ask herself, as Avery had asked, if she would like to marry Randall. Randall could never fancy her—a little plain, brown thing, only half grown. Nobody could think of her beside beautiful, rose-faced Avery. Janet accepted this fact unquestioningly. She had never been jealous. She only felt that she wanted Randall to have everything he wanted—to be perfectly happy. Why, it would be dreadful if he did not marry Avery—if he went and married some other girl. She would never see him then, never have any more delightful talks with him about all the things they both loved so much—winds and delicate dawns, mysterious woods in moonlight and starry midnights, silver-white sails going out of the harbour in the magic of morning, and the grey of gulf storms. There would be nothing in life; it would just be one great, unbearable emptiness; for she, herself, would never marry. There was nobody for her to marry—and she didn't care. If she could have Randall for a real brother, she would not mind a bit being an old maid. And there was that beautiful new frame house Randall had built for his bride, which she, Janet, had helped him build, because Avery would not condescend to details of pantry and linen closet and cupboards. Janet and Randall had had such fun over the cupboards. No stranger must ever come to be mistress of that house. Randall must marry Avery, and she must love him. Could anything be done to make her love him?

"I believe I'll go and see Granny Thomas," said Janet desperately.

She thought this was a silly idea, but it still haunted her and would not be shaken off. Granny Thomas was a very old woman who lived at Burnley Cove and was reputed to be something of a witch. That is, people who were not Sparhallows or Burnleys gave her that name. Sparhallows or Burnleys, of course, were above believing in such nonsense. Janet was above believing it; but still—

the sailors along shore were careful to "keep on the good side" of Granny Thomas, lest she brew an unfavourable wind for them, and there was much talk of love potions. Janet knew that people said Peggy Buchanan would never have got Jack McLeod if Granny had not given her a love potion. Jack had never looked at Peggy, though she was after him for years; and then, all at once, he was quite mad about her—and married her—and wore her life out with jealousy. And Peggy, the homeliest of all the Buchanan girls! There must be something in it. Janet made a sudden desperate resolve. She would go to Granny and ask her for a love potion to make Avery love Randall. If Granny couldn't do any good, she couldn't do any harm. Janet was a little afraid of her, and had never been near her house, but what wouldn't she do for Randall?

Janet never lost much time in carrying out any resolution she made. The next afternoon she slipped away to visit Granny Thomas. She put on her longest dress and did her hair up for the first time. Granny must not think her a child. She rowed herself down the long pond to the row of golden-brown sand dunes that parted it from the gulf. It was a wonderful autumn day. There were wild growths and colours and scents in sweet procession all around the pond. Every curve in it revealed some little whim of loveliness. On the left bank, in a grove of birch, was Randall's new house, waiting to be sanctified by love and joy and birth. Janet loved to be alone thus with the delightful day. She was sorry when she had walked over the stretch of windy weedy sea fields and reached Granny's little tumbledown house at the Cove—sorry and a little frightened as well. But only a little; there was good stuff in Janet; she lifted the latch boldly and walked in when Granny bade. Granny was curled up on a stool by her fireplace, and if ever anybody did look like a witch, she did. She waved her pipe at another stool, and Janet sat down, gazing a little curiously at Granny, whom she had never seen at such close quarters before.

Will I look like that when I am very old? she thought, beholding Granny's wizened, marvellously wrinkled face. I wonder if anybody will be sorry when you die.

"Staring wasn't thought good manners in my time," said Granny. Then, as Janet blushed crimson under the rebuke, she added, "Keep red like that instead o' white, and you won't need no love ointment."

Janet felt a little cold thrill. How did Granny know what she had come for? Was she a real witch after all? For a moment she wished she hadn't come. Perhaps it was not right to tamper with the powers of darkness. Peggy Buchanan was notoriously unhappy. If Janet had known how to get herself away, she would have gone without asking for anything.

Then a sound came from the lean-to behind the house.

"S-s-h. I hear the devil grunting like a pig," muttered Granny, looking very impish.

But Janet smiled a little contemptuously. She knew it was a pig and no devil. Granny Thomas was only an old fraud. Her awe passed away and left her cool Sparhallow.

"Can you," she said with her own directness, "make a—a person care for another person—care—very much?"

Granny removed her pipe and chuckled.

"What you want is toad ointment," she said.

Toad ointment! Janet shuddered. That did not sound very nice. Granny noticed the shudder.

"Nothing like it," she said, nodding her crone-like old grey head. "There's other things, but noan so sure. Put a li'l bit—oh, such a li'l bit—on his eyelids, and he's yourn for life. You need something powerful—you're noan so pretty—only when you're blushing."

Janet was blushing again. So Granny thought she wanted the charm for herself! Well, what did it matter? Randall was the only one to be considered.

"Is it very—expensive?" she faltered. She had not much money. Money was no plentiful thing on a P.E.I. farm in 1840.

"Oh, noa—oh, noa," Granny leered. "I don't sell it. I gives it. I like to see young folks happy. You don't need much, as I've said—just a li'l smootch and you'll have your man, and send old Granny a bite o' the wedding cake and fig o' baccy for luck, and a bid to the fir-r-st christening! Doan't forget that, dearie."

Janet was cold again with anger. She hated old Granny Thomas. She would never come near her again.

"I'd rather pay you its worth," she said coldly.

"You couldn't, dearie. What money could be eno' for such a treasure? But that's the Sparhallow pride. Well, go, see if the Sparhallow pride and the Sparhallow money will buy you your lad's love."

Granny looked so angry that Janet hastened to appease her.

"Oh, please forgive me—I meant no offence. Only—it must have cost you much trouble to make it."

Granny chuckled again. She was vastly pleased to see a Sparhallow suing to her—a Sparhallow!

"Toads am cheap," she said. "It's all in the knowing how and the time o' the moon. Here, take this li'l pill box—there's eno' in it—and put a li'l bit on his eyelids when you've getten the chance—and when he looks at you, he'll love you. Mind you, though, that he looks at no other first—it's the first one he sees that he'll love. That's the way it works."

"Thank you." Janet took the little box. She wished she dared to go at once. But perhaps this would anger Granny. Granny looked at her with a twinkle in her little, incredibly old eyes.

"Be off," she said. "You're in a hurry to go—you're as proud as any of the proud Sparhallows. But I bear you no grudge. I likes proud people—when they have to come to me to get help."

Janet found herself outside with a relieved heart in her bosom and her little box in her hand. For a moment she was tempted to throw it away. But no—Randall would be so unhappy if he found out Avery didn't love him! She would try the ointment at least—she would try to forget about the toads and not let herself think how it was made—something might come of it.

Janet hurried home along the shore, where a silvery wave broke in a little lovely silvery curve on the sand. She was so happy that her cheeks burned, and Randall Burnley, who was sitting on the edge of her flat when she reached the pond, looked at her with admiration. Janet dropped her box into her pocket stealthily when she saw him. What with her guilty secret, she hardly knew whether she was glad or not when he said he was going to row her up the pond.

"I saw you go down an hour ago and I've been waiting ever since," he said. "Where have you been?"

"Oh—I just—wanted a walk—this lovely day," said Janet miserably. She felt that she was telling an untruth and this hurt her horribly—especially when it was to Randall. This was what came of truck with witches—you were led into falsehood and deception straightaway. Again Janet was tempted to drop Granny's pill box into the depths of Burnley Pond—and again she decided not to because she saw Randall Burnley's deep-set, blue-grey eyes, that could look tender or sorrowful or passionate or whimsical as he willed, and thought how they would look when he found Avery did not love him.

So Janet drowned the voice of conscience and was brazenly happy—happy because Randall Burnley rowed her up the pond—happy because he walked halfway home with her over the autumnal fields—happy because he talked of the day and the sea and the golden weather, as only Randall could talk. But she thought she was happy because she had in her pocket what might make Avery love him.

Randall went as far as the stile in the birch wood between the Burnley and the Sparhallow land—and he kept her there talking for another half-hour—and though he talked only of a book he had read and a new puppy he was training, Janet listened with her soul in her ears. She talked too—quite freely; she was never in the least shy or tongue-tied or awkward in Randall's company. There she was always at her best, with a delightful feeling of being understood. She wondered if he noticed she had her hair done up. Her eyes shone and her brown face was full of rosy, kissable hues. When he finally turned away homeward, life went flat. Janet decided she was very tired after her long walk and her trying interview. But it did not matter, since she had her love potion. That was so much nicer a name than toad ointment.

That night Janet rubbed mutton tallow on her hands. She had never done that before—she had thought it vain and foolish—though Avery did it every night. But that afternoon on the pond Randall had said something about the beautiful shape of her pretty slender hands. He had never paid her a compliment before. Her hands were brown and a little hard—not soft and white like Avery's. So Janet resorted to the mutton tallow. If one had a scrap of beauty, if only in one's hands, one might as well take care of it.

Having got her ointment, the next thing was to make use of it. This was not so easy—because, in the first place, it must not be done when there was any danger of Avery's seeing some other than Randall first—and it must be done without

Avery's knowing it. The two problems combined were almost too much for Janet. She bided her chance like a watchful cat—but it did not come. Two weeks went by and it had not come. Janet was getting very desperate. The wedding day was only a week away. The bride's cake was made and the turkeys fattened. The invitations were sent out. Janet's own bridesmaid dress was ready. And still the little pill box in the till of Janet's blue chest was unopened. She had never even opened it, lest virtue escape.

Then her chance came at last, unexpectedly. One evening at dusk, when Janet was crossing the little dark upstairs hall, Aunt Matilda called up to her.

"Janet, send Avery down. There is a young man wanting to see her."

Aunt Matilda was laughing a little—as she always did when Randall came. It was a habit with her, hanging over from the early days of Randall's courtship. Janet went on into their room to tell Avery. And lo, Avery was lying asleep on her bed, tired out from her busy day. Janet, after one glance, flew to her chest. She took out her pill box and opened it, a little fearfully. The toad ointment was there, dark and unpleasant enough to view. Janet tiptoed breathlessly to the bed and gingerly scraped the tip of her finger in the ointment.

She said so little would be enough—oh, I hope I'm not doing wrong.

Trembling with excitement, she brushed lightly the white lids of Avery's eyes. Avery stirred and opened them. Janet guiltily thrust her pill box behind her.

"Randall is downstairs asking for you, Avery."

Avery sat up, looking annoyed. She had not expected Randall that evening and would greatly have preferred a continuance of her nap. She went down crossly enough, but looking very lovely, flushed from sleep. Janet stood in their room, clasping her cold hands nervously over her breast. Would the charm work? Oh, she must know—she must know. She could not wait. After a few moments that seemed like years she crept down the stairs and out into the dusk of the June-warm September night. Like a shadow she slipped up to the open parlour window and looked cautiously in between the white muslin curtains. The next minute she had fallen on her knees in the mint bed. She wished she could die then and there.

The young man in the parlour was not Randall Burnley. He was dark and smart and handsome; he was sitting on the sofa by Avery's side, holding her hands in his, smiling into her rosy, delighted, excited face. And he was Bruce Gordon—no doubt of that. Bruce Gordon, the expected cousin from Scotland!

"Oh, what have I done? What have I done?" moaned poor Janet, wringing her hands. She had seen Avery's face quite plainly—had seen the look in her eyes. Avery had never looked at Randall Burnley like that. Granny Thomas' abominable ointment had worked all right—and Avery had fallen in love with the wrong man.

Janet, cold with horror and remorse, dragged herself up to the window again and listened. She must know—she must be sure. She could hear only a word here and there, but that word was enough.

"I thought you promised to wait for me, Avery," Bruce said reproachfully.

"You were so long in coming back—I thought you had forgotten me," cried Avery.

"I think I did forget a little, Avery. I was such a boy. But now—well, thank Heaven, I haven't come too late."

There was a silence, and shameless Janet, peering above the window sill, saw what she saw. It was enough. She crept away upstairs to her room. She was lying there across the bed when Avery swept in—a splendid, transfigured Avery, flushed triumphant. Janet sat up, pallid, tear-stained, and looked at her.

"Janet," said Avery, "I am going to marry Bruce Gordon next Wednesday night instead of Randall Burnley."

Janet sprang forward and caught Avery's hand.

"You must not," she cried wildly. "It's all my fault—oh, if I could only die—I got the love ointment from Granny Thomas to rub on your eyes to make you love the first man you would see. I meant it to be Randall—I thought it was Randall—oh, Avery!"

Avery had been listening, between amazement and anger. Now anger mastered amazement.

"Janet Sparhallow," she cried, "are you crazy? Or do you mean that you went to Granny Thomas—you, a Sparhallow!—and asked her for a love philtre to make me love Randall Burnley?"

"I didn't tell her it was for you—she thought I wanted it for myself," moaned Janet. "Oh, we must undo it—I'll go to her again—no doubt she knows of some way to undo the spell—"

Avery, whose rages never lasted long, threw back her dark head and laughed ringingly.

"Janet Sparhallow, you talk as if you lived in the dark ages! The idea of supposing that horrid old woman could give you love philtres! Why, girl, I've always loved Bruce—always. But I thought he'd forgotten me. And tonight when he came I found he hadn't. There's the whole thing in a nutshell. I'm going to marry him and go home with him to Scotland."

"And what about Randall?" said Janet, corpse-white.

"Oh, Randall—pooh! Do you suppose I'm worrying about Randall? But you must go to him tomorrow and tell him for me, Janet."

"I will not—I will not."

"Then I'll tell him myself—and I'll tell him about you going to Granny," said Avery cruelly. "Janet, don't stand there looking like that. I've no patience with you. I shall be perfectly happy with Bruce—I would have been miserable with Randall. I know I shan't sleep a wink tonight—I'm so excited. Why, Janet, I'll be Mrs. Gordon of Gordon Brae—and I'll have everything heart can desire and the man of my heart to boot. What has lanky Randall Burnley with his little six-roomed house to set against that?"

If Avery did not sleep, neither did Janet. She lay awake till dawn, suffering such misery as she had never endured in her life before. She knew she must go to Randall Burnley tomorrow and break his heart. If she did not, Avery would tell him—tell him what Janet had done. And he must not know that—he must not. Janet could not bear that thought.

It was a pallid, dull-eyed Janet who went through the birch wood to the Burnley farm next afternoon, leaving behind her an excited household where the sudden change of bridegrooms, as announced by Avery, had rather upset everybody. Janet found Randall working in the garden of his new house—setting out rosebushes for Avery—Avery, who was to jilt him at the very altar, so to speak. He came over to open the gate for Janet, smiling his dear smile. It was a dear smile—Janet caught her breath over the dearness of it—and she was going to blot it off his face.

She spoke out, with plainness and directness. When you had to deal a mortal blow, why try to lighten it?

"Avery sent me to tell you that she is going to marry Bruce Gordon instead of you. He came last night—and she says that she has always liked him best."

A very curious change came over Randall's face—but not the change Janet had expected to see. Instead of turning pale Randall flushed; and instead of a sharp cry of pain and incredulity, Randall said in no uncertain tones, "Thank God!"

Janet wondered if she were dreaming. Granny Thomas' love potion seemed to have turned the world upside down. For Randall's arms were about her and Randall was pressing his lean bronzed cheek to hers and Randall was saying:

"Now I can tell you, Janet, how much I love you."

"Me? Me!" choked Janet.

"You. Why, you're in the very core of my heart, girl. Don't tell me you can't love me—you can—you must—why, Janet," for his eyes had caught and locked with hers for a minute, "you do!"

There were five minutes about which nobody can tell anything, for even Randall and Janet never knew clearly just what happened in those five minutes. Then Janet, feeling somehow as if she had died and then come back to life, found her tongue.

"Three years ago you came courting Avery," she said reproachfully.

"Three years ago you were a child. I did not think about you. I wanted a wife—and Avery was pretty. I thought I was in love with her. Then you grew up all at once—and we were such good friends—I never could talk to Avery—she wasn't interested in anything I said—and you have eyes that catch a man—I've always thought of your eyes. But I was honour-bound to Avery—I didn't dream you cared. You must marry me next Wednesday, Janet—we'll have a double wedding. You won't mind—being married—so soon?"

"Oh, no—I won't—mind," said Janet dazedly. "Only—oh, Randall—I must tell you—I didn't mean to tell you—I'd have rather died—but now—I must tell you about it now—because I can't bear anything hidden between us. I went to old Granny Thomas—and got a love ointment from her—to make Avery love you, because I knew she didn't—and I wanted you to be happy—Randall, don't—I can't talk when you do that! Do you think Granny's ointment could have made her care for Bruce?"

Randall laughed—the little, low laugh of the triumphant lover.

"If it did, I'm glad of it. But I need no such ointment on my eyes to make me love you—you carry your philtre in that elfin little face of yours, Janet."

Here and Beyond
Edith Wharton
Benediction Classics, 2011
150 pages
ISBN: 978-1-84902-421-1

Available from www.amazon.com,
www.amazon.co.uk

Edith Wharton (1862 - 1937), was a Pulitzer Prize-winning American novelist and short story writer. She grew up in upper-class pre-WWI society and many of her stories critique this culture, using subtle irony. Here and Beyond was written in 1926 and includes ghost stories, social dramas and character studies set in Brittany, New England, and Morocco.

A Christmas Carol - The original manuscript - with original illustrations
Charles Dickens
Benediction Classics, 2012
166 pages
ISBN: 978-1-78139-068-9

Available from www.amazon.com,
www.amazon.co.uk

Charles Dickens wrote "A Christmas Carol" in six weeks at the end of 1843, during a particularly intense time of creativity. He was having financial difficulties and was determined to have the manuscript ready for publication for the Christmas market. This book contains a clear copy Dickens' one and only manuscript, written by his hand, with his revisions and corrections evident on every page. The revisions show how Dickens made the verbs become more active, the number of words became fewer, achieving greater immediacy and vividness. This manuscript was handed to the printer in this form and was published on 19th December 1843. This edition has each of the 66 pages of the original manuscript copied onto the left hand page and the corresponding words typed on the right hand page. The book also contains the eight original illustrations by John Leech, the four color illustrations are on the cover of the book.

Gomez Arias;
Or The Moors Of The Alpujarras.
A Spanish Historical Romance
Joaquín Telesforo De Trueba Y Cosío
Benediction Classics, 2011
354 pages
ISBN: 978-1-84902-462-4

Available from www.amazon.com, www.amazon.co.uk

This paperback includes all three Volumes of the novel 'Gomez Arias The Moors of the Alpujarras, A Spanish Historical Romance'. It was written in 1826 by the Spaniard Joaquín Telesforo de Trueba y Cosío who wrote in English and belonged to the Romantic movement. It is set in the province of Granada. A censored version was produced in 1831

The Complete Novels of Jane Austen (unabridged): Sense and Sensibility, Pride and Prejudice, Mansfield Park, Emma, Northanger Abbey, Persuasion, Love and Freindship, and Lady Susan
Jane Austen
Benediction Classics, 2012
1118 pages
ISBN: 978-1-78139-211-9

Available from www.amazon.com, www.amazon.co.uk

This edition contains Jane Austen's six novels unabridged: Sense and Sensibility (1811), Pride and Prejudice (1813), Mansfield Park (1814), Emma (1815), Northanger Abbey (1818, posthumous), Persuasion (1818, posthumous). It also contains the short fiction story, Lady Susan (1794, 1805). In addition one of the Juvenilia stories is included, Love and Freindship.

Also from Benediction Books ...
Wandering Between Two Worlds: Essays on Faith and Art
Anita Mathias
Benediction Books, 2007
152 pages
ISBN: 0955373700

Available from www.amazon.com, www.amazon.co.uk

In these wide-ranging lyrical essays, Anita Mathias writes, in lush, lovely prose, of her naughty Catholic childhood in Jamshedpur, India; her large, eccentric family in Mangalore, a sea-coast town converted by the Portuguese in the sixteenth century; her rebellion and atheism as a teenager in her Himalayan boarding school, run by German missionary nuns, St. Mary's Convent, Nainital; and her abrupt religious conversion after which she entered Mother Teresa's convent in Calcutta as a novice. Later rich, elegant essays explore the dualities of her life as a writer, mother, and Christian in the United States-- Domesticity and Art, Writing and Prayer, and the experience of being "an alien and stranger" as an immigrant in America, sensing the need for roots.

About the Author

Anita Mathias is the author of *Wandering Between Two Worlds: Essays on Faith and Art*. She has a B.A. and M.A. in English from Somerville College, Oxford University, and an M.A. in Creative Writing from the Ohio State University, USA. Anita won a National Endowment of the Arts fellowship in Creative Non-fiction in 1997. She lives in Oxford, England with her husband, Roy, and her daughters, Zoe and Irene.

Anita's website:
http://www.anitamathias.com, and
Anita's blog Dreaming Beneath the Spires:
http://dreamingbeneaththespires.blogspot.com

The Church That Had Too Much
Anita Mathias
Benediction Books, 2010
52 pages
ISBN: 9781849026567

Available from www.amazon.com, www.amazon.co.uk

The Church That Had Too Much was very well-intentioned. She wanted to love God, she wanted to love people, but she was both hampered by her muchness and the abundance of her possessions, and beset by ambition, power struggles and snobbery. Read about the surprising way The Church That Had Too Much began to resolve her problems in this deceptively simple and enchanting fable.

About the Author

Anita Mathias is the author of *Wandering Between Two Worlds: Essays on Faith and Art*. She has a B.A. and M.A. in English from Somerville College, Oxford University, and an M.A. in Creative Writing from the Ohio State University, USA. Anita won a National Endowment of the Arts fellowship in Creative Non-fiction in 1997. She lives in Oxford, England with her husband, Roy, and her daughters, Zoe and Irene.

Anita's website:
http://www.anitamathias.com, and
Anita's blog Dreaming Beneath the Spires:
http://dreamingbeneaththespires.blogspot.com

www.ingramcontent.com/pod-product-compliance
Lightning Source LLC
Chambersburg PA
CBHW081129300726
48982CB00005B/894

* 9 7 8 1 7 8 1 3 9 2 3 9 3 *